Zmok Books is an imprint of Winged Hussar Publishing, LLC
1525 Hulse Road Unit 1
Point Pleasant, NJ 08742

www.WingedHussarPu
Twitter: WingHusl

www.Wildwestexc

Cover by Micha

Wild West Exodus, the characters, inventions, and settings were created by Romeo Filip and Outlaw Miniatures, who own all rights, registers, and trademarks. This book is published by Winged Hussar Publishing, LLC under agreement with Wild West Exodus.

ISBN: 978-0-9896926-7-0
EPCN: 2014956951

This is a work of fiction. All the characters and events portrayed in this book, though based in some case on historical figures, are fictional and any resemblance to real people or incidents is purely coincidental.

Zmok Books

Wild West Exodus

The Jesse James Archives

Something Wicked is Coming

Blood drenches the sands of the Wild West as the promise of a new age dies, screaming its last breath into an uncaring night. An ancient evil has arisen in the western territories, calling countless people with a siren song of technology and promises of power and glory the likes of which the world has never known. Forces move into the deserts, some answering the call, others desperate to destroy the evil before it can end all life on Earth.

Legions of reanimated dead rise to serve the greatest scientific minds of the age, while the native tribes of the plains, now united in desperate self-defence, conjure the powers of the Great Spirit to twist their very flesh into ferocious combat forms to match the terrible new technologies. The armies of the victorious Union rumble into these territories heedless of the destruction they may cause in pursuit of their own purposes, while the legendary outlaws of the old west, now armed with stolen weapons and equipment of their own, seek to carve their names into the tortured flesh of the age. Amidst all this conflict, the long-suffering lawmen, outgunned and undermanned, stand alone, fighting to protect the innocent men and women caught in the middle . . . or so it appears.

Within these pages you will find information on wild skirmishes and desperate battles in this alternative Wild West world, now ravaged with futuristic weapons and technology. Choose the methodical Enlightened, the savage Warrior Nation, the brutal Union, the deceitful Outlaws, or the enigmatic Lawmen, and lead them into the Wild West to earn your glory.

As you struggle across the deserts and mountains, through the forests and cities of the wildest frontier in history, a hidden power will whisper in your ear at every move. Will your spirit be strong enough to prevail, or will the insidious forces of the Dark Council eventually bend you to their will? Be prepared, for truly, something wicked is coming!

Learn more about the world of the Jessie James Chronicles at:

www.wildwestexodus.com

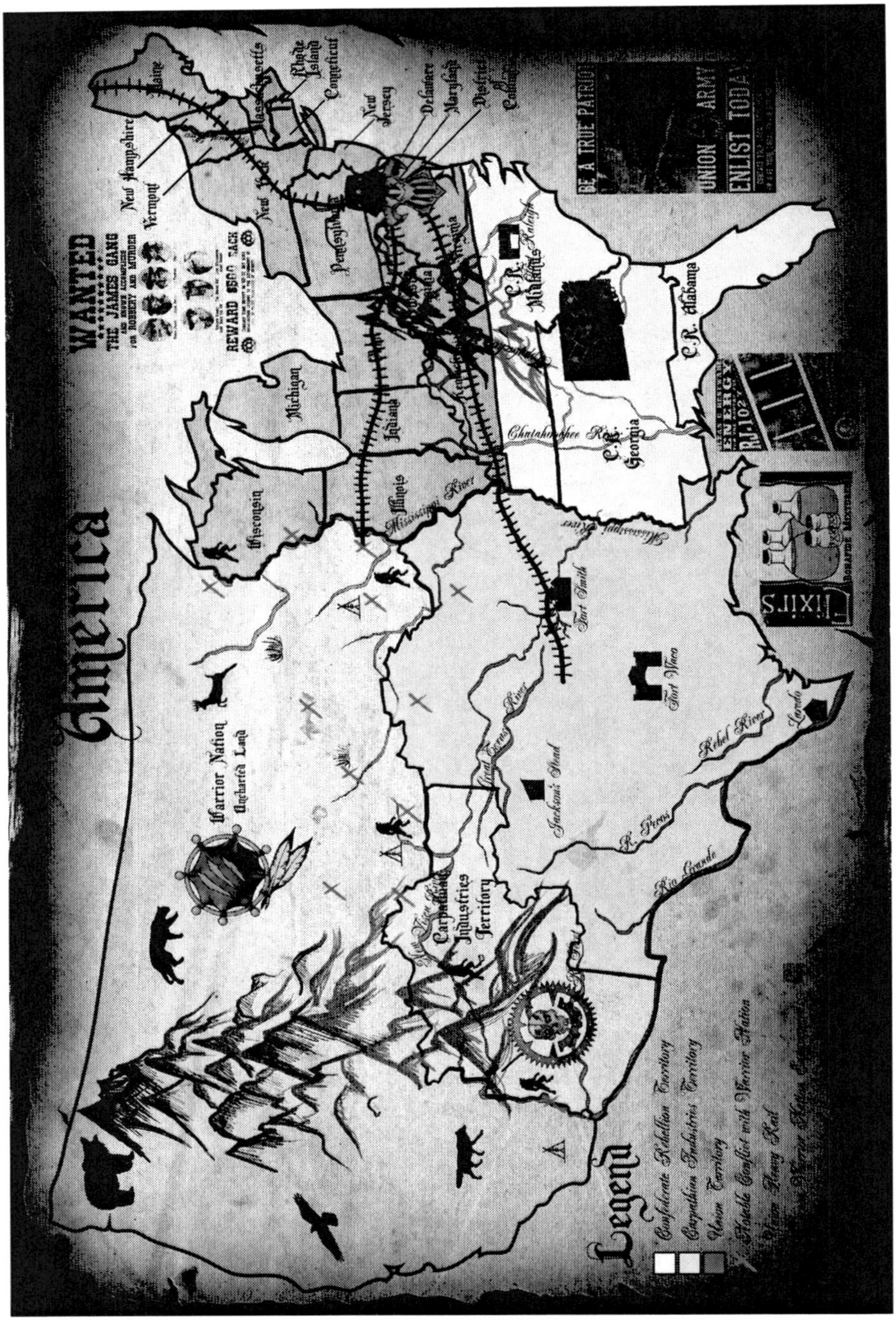
America
WANTED
THE JAMES GANG
REWARD
Warrior Nation
Uncharted Land
Carpathian Industries Territory
Maine
New Hampshire
Vermont
New York
New Jersey
Delaware
Maryland
Pennsylvania
Michigan
Wisconsin
Illinois
Indiana
Mississippi River
Georgia
C.R. Alabama
Fort Smith
Fort Waco
Jackson's Stead
Rebel River
Rio Grande
R. Pecos
BE A TRUE PATRIOT
UNION ARMY
ENLIST TODAY
Lixir's
Legend
Confederate Rebellion Territory
Carpathian Industries Territory
Union Territory
Hostile Conflict with Warrior Nation

Origins

by

Craig Gallant

Life is cheap in the Western Territories, and a man who acknowledges that has a marked advantage over the idealistic and naïve every day the sun rises over the arid, empty region.

In the dark back corner of the Union Star Saloon sat a man in crisp, black attire, with a black-dyed duster draped neatly over a chair opposite. His sable hat rested on the table in front of the empty chair as the man himself lounged back easily, one big, scarred hand held loosely around a glass half-full of a rich, amber whiskey. Beneath full dark eyebrows, eyes scanned the busy saloon, nodding occasionally at the odd sign of respect or homage silently paid to him by someone in the wary crowd.

Various men and women in the saloon cast furtive glances into the dark corner from time to time, trying to catch a glimpse of the man in black. His smile curled up beneath his sleek mustache as he pretended not to notice. It was clear that he fed off their fear and respect, and did not care if they wished to gaze upon him as he sat quietly sharing a drink with his companion.

Sitting beside him was another man, dressed in far more common frontier gear, dusty from the road. The second man was hunkered forward a bit, watching the crowd suspiciously with eyes gleaming red with the reflection of lamps and candles. Occasionally, he would lean toward the man in black and make some whispered comment or observation. The darker man would sometimes smile, often simply nod, but gave no further response.

The attention of the crowd was suddenly drawn to the batwing doors as they were thrown wildly open to admit a rowdy group of men who pushed their way to the bar, heedless of the looks and exclamations tossed at them. At the center of the group was a large redhead; a man known as Skinny Joe O'Reilly, he was the tallest and loudest of the bunch and clearly their leader. Most of the others in his group were laughing with the loud, edgy laughter of men trying to impress. A small, quiet man, not sharing in the laughs and smiles, stood beside the red-haired giant, looking around the room distrustfully.

"Barkeep!" The big man's rough voice slashed through the crowd and brought a sudden hush of stillness. He tossed small bag of rough burlap onto the scarred surface of the bar as he sidled up. "Should be 'nuf there for everyone to have a drink wit me and my friends, here!"

The angry looks and mutterings instantly melted away in favor of great smiles and cheers at these words, and the crowd once again pushed forward trying to get their free drink. The man's companions smiled wider and gave a great cheer even as they moved farther into the press of bodies, clearing a way to the bar for their leader.

"No reason a man can't share the wealth when he's had a bit of success, eh, lads?" He slapped one big hand down on the bar and all the boisterous noise and bustling stopped as the men and women closest saw what he had left there: a dented sheriff's star, bright polish partially hidden beneath an ugly brown stain that could only be blood.

The people in the saloon stared at the symbol of fallen law for a moment, and the stillness that settled upon the room was heavy with fear and disbelief. Then with an upbeat shout, the laughter resumed, as did the press toward the lines of mugs being laid out by the harried bartender.

"Can't fault a man for trying his best, now. Although, gotta keep in mind," the tall man indicated the dented, stained star. "Old Rusty oughta've known better'n to get between us'n that bank teller, eh boys?" The laughter intensified, and everyone hoisted their mugs and glasses in a toast to the fallen lawman.

In the dark corner, the man in black looked sideways at his companion. The red-eyed man nodded in turn, and tilted his head at the crop of Skinny Joe's red hair barely visible over the rest of the crowd.

The dark man stood and began to move slowly toward the bar. He made no move to avoid people in the crowd, barely acknowledging them or slowing his pace, and yet, with just a quick, nervous glance behind them, each person jumped out of his way, their eyes moving away as they saw the intense lines of the man's face. Moving swiftly in his wake, the smaller man slid through the crowd, ignoring the frightened faces that continued to push away.

"So when he said they didn't have no cash, Jonesy here just bashed him one!" The crowd around the bar, oblivious of the dark man's approach, renewed their belly laughs as O'Reilly slapped the bar again in amusement while another man, presumably Jonesy, nodded to them with a gap-toothed smile. The laughter died down, however, as the dark man continued to cut through the crowd, a circle of silent awe and dread moving with him.

The big man, sensing the amusement of his audience wavering, turned slowly to watch the approach of the man in black. Both men stood with less than a foot of humid silence separating them as they stared into each other's eyes. O'Reilly's expression was annoyed, while the calm man in black radiated cold contempt.

"Hey, mister, I don't know who you think you are –" Jonesy moved to intercept the man in black, but with a deceptively slow and fluid move, the dark man caught his outstretched hand and proceeded to whip it around through a quick series of moves that left Jonesy face down in a puddle of warm beer on the bar, groaning. With a slight smile, the dark man twisted one last time and the sharp report of a breaking bone echoed through the bar. Jonesy, whimpering and cradling his released arm, sank slowly to the dirty floor.

"Your friend's had a bad tumble." The man's voice was soft and refined, but carried an edge of authority that could not be denied.

Skinny Joe looked down at his minion and then back up at the dark man. "You didn't have to do that, mister."

The dark man shrugged with a slight sneer. "I needed to get your attention, and your friend's lack of manners seemed to offer just the opportunity."

The tall man looked down at his moaning friend again and then scowled at the dark stranger. "Well, you got my attention." His hand drifted to the well-worn grip of a pistol in a bleached old holster.

The dark stranger looked down at that drifting hand and looked up again with a wide smile on his face. "Excellent. Then it's time to begin your education."

A big hand jerked down for a pistol and the dark man slapped it away without effort. O'Reilly stared incredulously as the dark smile spread even wider.

"You don't know who I am, so I'm going to give you that one for free." The crowd continued to press away from the two men, an ever-widening bubble of tension surrounding them with a hushed silence.

Beside Skinny Joe, his silent companion stared at the dark stranger with barely contained frustration. Behind the dark man, his own companion watched the other silent one with an amused smugness.

"I'm going to let you enjoy the fruits of your labor, here," the dark man gestured with one graceful hand at the drinks scattered across the bar. "And then you and your . . . friends," he gently nudged Jonesy with one polished toe, "will leave town and never be seen again."

The big man bowed his head, his eyes wide with dread, and turned partially away. His gang looked confused, staring from the dark stranger to their cowed leader and back with a growing fear of their own. The dark man, his smug smile growing ever wider, turned to wink at his silent companion's returning grin.

Just then, O'Reilly's offhand lashed across his body with the speed of a snake. The dark stranger spotted the movement and moved to slap a hand away, but his fist swept through empty air, balked by the bigger man's feint. The old pistol hissed out of the holster and whipped up to rest its cold metal against the dark man's forehead where it dimpled the skin slightly as Skinny Joe pressed it in.

The dark man's eyed widened in confused alarm.

"No thanks," O'Reilly sneered, and pulled the trigger.

The dark man's head rocked away from the concussion, blood and solid matter spraying out across the room behind him. A small hole, black bordered by pink and gray, leaked a thin stream of blood from between his wide round eyes. Without a sound, the dark man slowly toppled onto his back.

For a moment, there was stunned silence within the Union Star Saloon. The crowd stared at the dead body, then up to the big redhead looking down at the lifeless corpse. O'Reilly then gave an inhuman roar of triumph that scaled quickly into peels of deep laughter, and the rest of the patrons and gang members started laughing again themselves.

"Another round!" he shouted, producing another ratty purse, and the crowd surged forward and over the dead stranger as if he weren't there.

Only two men stood still and silent in the rowdy celebration that swirled through the saloon. The two silent companions, their eyes glinting a uniform crimson color, stared at each other. The man who had entered with the rowdy posse smiled widely at the dark man's companion. And then the dark man's companion smiled too, nodded a silent two finger salute, and made his way toward the door.

Life is cheap in the Western Territories, and although none of the poor bastards that call it home knew it yet, the price has just dropped much, much lower.

* * * * *

The taste of failure and loss is something that never fully fades from a man's mind after the first bitter bite. The more spectacular the disaster, the more public the humiliation, the harsher that taste will be. The young man riding slowly down the Missouri trail, shoulders slumped and head bowed, was experiencing one of the most historically bloody and rancorous failures in centuries. It was enough to have reduced countless grown men to tears. The weight of it nearly crushed the boy whose broken down nag swayed back and forth across the rutted path.

With each slap of the horse's hooves, the boy's mind churned slowly through his past, tracking the desperate path that had led him to this final humiliation. His family had been ardent supporters of the Confederacy for as long as he could remember, and in fact his mother had been the most vocal proponent of the south in the run-up to open war. When their native Missouri had declared for the damned Union, the entire family had been furious, and the young man had been burning to take up arms against the sneering abolitionists and their eastern allies.

But even his furious mother had declared he was too young, and so he watched at the splintered fence gate before their house as his older brother Frank had ridden off to join a Confederate bushwacker unit fighting farther east. Frank's letters, few and far between as they were, conveyed a world of adventure and honor to the young man's mind that no amount of petty vandalism and sabotage at home could provide. With each passing month, he felt his heart pulled toward battle, and life at home seemed to get more and duller.

The boy had been walking the fence line for his mother one afternoon, about a year after Frank had left for the war, when a stranger had ridden up on a dusty old nag blowing hard and coat crusted in dried lather. The man had looked down at the boy through eyes that glinted like rubies in the reflected sunset from beneath his battered hat, and asked him what he thought he was doing while better men than him were dying for their families against the tyrants of the north.

The boy had not given a thought to how the man had known his name, or his situation. The accusation had burned like scalding water poured over an open wound. He had wanted to explain to the man how much he wanted to fight, how many times he had pleaded with his mother, and how often those conversations had ended in screaming and curses, but the man would listen to none of it. There were thousands of men dying for the freedom of the south, and hundreds of thousands rising up to fight the tyranny of the Union. And here he was, safe in a little town in a backwater Republican state, walking a fence. The angry boy had felt tears of frustration burning in his eyes, and was debating whether he could drag the stranger off his horse before the man could draw on him.

The man looked down one last time, his head shaking in contempt, and before the youth could decide to jump him, the man's horse turned wearily away and continued on down the track. The boy stared after the stranger for several long minutes, his breath heaving and his vision blurry with rage and shame.

That night when his mother returned home from a meeting of Confederate sympathizers, she found her son was gone.

But now, just about a year later, here he was, riding home on a broken horse, with his heart in pieces, his chest aching from a terrible wound he'd taken the summer before, and the cold knowledge in his gut that the Confederacy was doomed.

The year he had spent with the rebels had been glorious. Running rings around the Republicans, attacking out of the night and then fading away before a counterattack could be formed. Several times they had fallen upon isolated supply columns and killed the dirty bastards to the last man. While the Union forces in Clay County were battered time and again, bloody Grant and his army of demons had crushed the Army of Northern Virginia back east, scattered the survivors throughout the south, and driven straight on through to Richmond and burnt it to the ground. No one knew where Jefferson Davis had gotten himself off to, and the Republicans, unsatisfied with decimating the Confederate forces along the borders, had then continued to drive deeper into the south, burning and marauding as they went. Wild rumors had begun to spread of incredibly powerful weapons and fanciful machines of war that could kill a man from over a mile away. Even in Missouri it became clear that the end had come.

Many of the men were not giving up. Many had opted to head west, or to sneak in small groups east, through New Orleans and into Florida where rumor had it there were growing bands of unrepentant rebels plotting the resurrection of the Confederacy in the swamps and pine forests of the central peninsula. But the boy had seen enough of war.

He had seen enough friends die for no good reason, and had felt the pain of a grievous wound himself, that still plagued him when he went to lay down at night, or when a storm was brewing. Word had reached him that Frank had surrendered with most of his unit in Kentucky, and that had been the final blow to his revolutionary passion.

And so his path to glory and renown had landed him on a deserted back road on a half-dead horse. His dull mind was filled with bitterness and frustration, and his plans, beyond heading toward home, were vague at best. There was a garrison near his home, he knew, and he could give his official surrender there. If Emperor Lincoln was half the man he claimed to be, the boy should at least be able to keep his freedom . . . or at least as much freedom as any man could claim, under the iron rule of such a dictator.

These were the harsh thoughts that churned through his mind as he turned a corner and halted abruptly at the sight of a large party of cavalry sitting their horses astride the road ahead. Their blue uniforms were dusty and tattered, but there was no mistaking their Republican allegiance. They seemed to be resting, their horses cropping the grass to either side while the men smoked, drank, or merely sat idly watching the surrounding hills and forest. When they saw the boy in his battered grey, however, they stopped whatever they were doing to stare at him with their strange new rifles clenched tightly in their hands.

After a year of warfare, the boy could not repress the first impulse he had, to drive straight at the troop, drawing his carbine, and blasting away with a vigorous rebel yell, but there were more than twenty men on the road, and God alone knew how many more besides. The caustic thoughts gave way quickly to a resigned exhaustion; he had been planning on surrendering when he made it back, he might as well offer up his weapons to these blue bellies and get it done with.

The boy put both his hands into the air and nudged his horse into a weary walk with his knees.

"I ain't gonna shoot none a ya's," his voice had deepened while he was away, but in his own ears he sounded like a little boy.

The men laughed among themselves, confident in their numbers. Several drew their own weapons and readied them, although no one was aiming directly for the boy.

"You shootin' us ain't somethin' we're worryin' about, kid." The officer prodded his horse with silver spurs and the beast hopped forward with a soft shimmy. "Awfully far north to be wearin' such an ugly color, ain't'cha?" His right hand drifted lazily to the pistol at his side.

The old rage rose in the back of the boy's throat, but he forced it down, took a deep breath, and nodded. "I'm just tryin' to get home, fellas. I don't want no trouble, and I'm looking to offer my official parole, like the posters say."

Another of the troop, a sergeant by his sleeves, snorted. "We're all lookin' to get home, reb. If'n you lot had seen sense, we all coulda been there years ago."

The officer laughed and then looked back at the boy. "Well, if you're willing to give up the irons, son, I reckon we can let you go on your way." He looked the youth up and down with a sneer. "Not like you'll be much trouble one way or the other."

A corporal rode forward, reaching into a saddle bag for a tattered notebook with a pencil tied to it by a string. The man peered through dusty glasses at the boy and made to write in his book.

"What's yer name, boy?"

He cleared his throat and tried to raise his jaw against the dejected feelings of failure and defeat that threatened to force him down. "Name's Jesse James."

The man was writing Jesse's name in the book when another soldier held up a hand. "Hold on one second, you the James kid that was ridin' with Bill Quantrill?"

The boy's chin cranked up another degree. "Yeah, I was. Me an' my brother Frank. What of it?"

The man turned to the officer. "Sir, Quantrill's lot are the ones that killed over a score of unarmed boys an' cut up their bodies like they was savages." The man spit in Jesse's direction. "War criminals and savages ain't covered under no amnesty I ever heard of."

The officer looked coldly back at Jesse again, his eyes now tight. "That true, boy? You rode with William Quantrill? You cut up an' maim Union soldiers like some savage?"

Pride rose in Jesse's chest, forcing down the cold gall of defeat, and before he could stop himself his mouth ran away from him. "Yeah, I did. It was a battle like any other, and your men were the losers. Every battle has one, an' they was real good at it."

"They slaughtered every last man, sir. Even those trying to surrender."

Another angry voice rose out of the troop, and the horses whickered and whinnied uncertainly, scenting the aggression now riding the air.

"Stuff happens in war, soldier-boy." Jesse could not stop now, and the anger and frustration boiled over. "Stuff happens in war every day, and people die, and people get buried in a muddy ditch miles from their home, and that's just the way it is."

The officer nodded once, his eyes dark. "Yup, son. People die in war every day."

Another man smiled a wicked grin, his eyes flashing redly. "That's just the way it is."

Without an order or a warning, the man brought his carbine up to his shoulder and the weapon barked a single, echoing shot. The horses of the troop shied away from the sudden noise, and the officer turned around to see who had fired. The cavalrymen milled around trying to bring order to their horses, shouting and hissing at each other and the animals.

Jesse felt the shot strike him with a sickeningly familiar punching impact. Right in the chest, exactly where he'd been shot last summer! Part of his mind told him the bullet had past clean through again, and that he would live, but it would take painful weeks to heal. It was almost like a bad joke or terrible luck. He felt the wave of warm blood flood down his shirt as his shocked mind struggled to keep his seat while the horse skittered backward and the impact almost drove him over its rump.

Exactly where he'd been shot last summer! The pain was dull and distant now, padded with shock and the adrenaline burning through his body. How could he have been shot, again, in the exact same spot? He tried to bring his horse's head around, to get away from the troop and into the woods. Out of the corner of his eye he could see the men milling around, the officer looking over his shoulder at Jesse as the wilting youth moved off under the trees. There did not seem to be any effort to pursue him, and if he had not just been shot, he'd have the presence of mind to be thankful for small favors.

The exact same spot! The thought kept rolling through his mind. Only incredible luck, or inhuman skill and surgical precision, could have assured that shot. It was painful, it was nearly driving him into unconsciousness with the rising pain, in fact . . . but he knew he'd survive. As long as the wound did not go bad, and he made it to a doctor, he knew he wasn't going to die. But, damn, the pain!

He could tell it would be another case of months of enforced rest before he would be at full strength again. He felt almost as if some higher power was punishing him for something, holding him back from his vengeance while the world went on without him, as he waited for his wound to heal all over again.

And damn the damned Union, too! And the Republicans! Damned Abolitionist blue bellies; shot him while he was trying to surrender! As Jesse pushed his horse deeper into the forest, holding one hand tightly to his chest in an attempt to stop the flow of blood, the other, slick with the same fluid, clenching tightly to his reins, all feelings of defeat and surrender were burned away with a single, growing, glowing, burning thought.

Revenge.

* * * * *

The pine scrub along the ridge line whispered with the cool autumn winds, and Jesse James looked down upon the small town huddled in the valley with a stomach-churning combination of excitement and nerves. Somewhere down in that little burg was the Daviess County Savings Association, and he had it on very good authority that their vaults were brimming over with newly-minted Federal bills. Jesse had every intention to see that a healthy batch of those bills were in his saddle bag by the time the sun set behind them.

Beside Jesse, his older brother Frank stood looking down at the town with an old Confederate spyglass. The elder James had always been more calm and calculating, and he was not about to let the thought of all that money get into his head and cause him to make a mistake. This was Jesse's rodeo, but Frank was not going to skip any steps along the way.

Behind the two brothers, a small gang sat their horses, impatient to begin. Jesse looked over his shoulder at four of them, strangers to him but old friends of his brother's from the war; the Younger boys, they were called. Their eldest, Cole, was a close friend of Frank's, and so here they were. Jesse had wanted to go with a gang of local Clay County boys, but his brother had been a right pain in the ass about it, and so the Youngers were riding with them, and Jesse guessed the coming day would show what they were made of.

Jesse and Frank had been robbing banks and shaking down local Republicans since the war had ended. It had taken nearly a year for him to recover from the wound those blue bellies had inflicted upon him when he'd tried to surrender, and while he was down, the damned Radicals had seized power in Missouri and the next thing you knew, if you'd stood with the Confederacy during the war you couldn't vote, hold any public office, or hell, even preach the bible. Everything he'd feared about the Union had come to pass, and he'd been moaning on his back the whole time. But when he'd been well enough to mount a horse, he'd gone off, and he and Frank had set about making the Republicans pay.

And with every job, for every coin or bill they'd lifted or burned, Jesse was the motivating force. Frank was smart, and he'd always be willing to put in his two cents, but when it came time to slap skin to leather, he knew Jesse was the one with the drive. He knew, too, that Jesse had the patience of a starved wolf and the subtlety of a stampede of buffalo. And when someone had to rein the firebrand in, it would be his older brother. These new folks, though . . . that was something different.

Jesse could understand why Frank was concerned. Word throughout Missouri and beyond had it that some new weapons were making their way into the holsters of some of the local law. They had not talked to anyone yet who had seen the weapons themselves, but you could not have a quiet drink from Clay County down to Kentucky without some drunk going off at length about how he knew a man who had known a man who saw a man who had been killed by these strange inventions. The details were always different, but always bloody.

One thing could be readily counted on, and that was Jesse's reaction to any talk of these new inventions. Jesse would talk for hours on end, proclaiming, "If anyone even looks at me with one of these smoke wagons in hand I'll burn the life clean out of them." The rumors of the speed and deadliness of these weapons aggravated the young outlaw to no end, and he bragged often that no man who had ever doubted his speed and deadliness was above the dirt today.

Jesse was not sure there were any new-fangled weapons, although if there were, he planned on removing them from the cold dead hands of the men that had them.What he did know was that Frank was getting edgy. Frank thought there were weapons out there, and he thought these Youngers watching their backs were going to make a difference. So Jesse had relented, with a sneer, and the strangers were riding with them, and God help the law if they were feeling their oats down in the valley this day.

"Look down at the main street." Frank handed the spyglass to his younger brother without taking his eyes off the town. "Not a lot of people about."

Jesse snatched the tube and thrust it to his eye with poor grace. He did not care who was on the main street. The plan – to ride down hooting and hollering, crash into the bank, take the cash, and run before the lazy lawmen got off their fat, Republican asses – was plenty good enough for him. But he knew that Frank never did anything without a reason, so he carefully moved the field of vision through the spyglass up and down the main street in front of the bank. It did seem to be pretty empty.

"That guy who recommended this to you . . . you trust him?" Frank now looked down at his brother suspiciously with a familiar tightening of his eyes.

"Trust him?" Jesse grinned and handed the glass back to Frank. "Hell, big brother, I don't trust you none, why would I trust him? Just some guy, heard me talkin' with some of the boys. Knew a fair deal about the bank's layout, and the town, and that the new money was comin' in this week."

He reached over and slapped his brother on the back. "Don't worry, Frank, it's a good score, it's a solid hit. We'll be in and out faster'n shit through a goose, and we'll all have plenty of bills to stay warm for the winter." His famous grin peeked out from beneath his mustache.

Frank had gone back to watching the town below through the glass. "Hmmm," he grunted. "Just seems a little too good to be true is all. And an empty town . . . that'd be the first sign to make me think we're walkin' into a trap."

Jesse laughed and brought his horse around to address the rest of the gang. "Frank's got a pretty high opinion of us all, boys. Thinks the Radicals know we're such a band of badasses, they've laid a trap for us!"

The local boys all laughed with Jesse, but Cole and his brothers just watched quietly, and soon the laughter died a slow, sickly death.

Jesse cleared his throat and moved back to look down again. "Well, I ain't seein' no law, and my man tells me they ain't got none right now. So the plan's the same. We charge in, smash and grab, and we're out again."

He gestured with one gloved hand and the gang rode out of the stand of pines and headed down the grassy slope toward the quiet town. Pistols were drawn, carbines and rifles were leveled, and with a raucous rebel scream, Jesse slashed at his horse's barrel and the beast threw itself down the hill with the rest of the shouting band galloping hot behind him.

There were a few men and women in the street as the gang came pounding into town, several men firing shots into the air to frighten and intimidate the civilians. In front of the squat brick building of the Daviess County Savings Association, the men pulled up their horses and jumped off, still yelling and brandishing their weapons menacingly at anyone who showed their face.

Jesse leapt from his horse and strode purposefully toward the front door, his duster billowing behind him like the great cloak of some melodrama villain. Without pausing in his stride, he struck the doors with one boot heel hard enough to splinter the wood around the frame and set them both to swinging drunkenly on warped hinges.

"Alright you sons of bitches, put your dirty faces on the floor!" Jesse hollered into the warm darkness of the bank as his men ran in, fanning off to either side behind him. "We all are the James boys! And –"

"James-Younger boys!" Cole's voice cut Jesse off, and he gave the young James brother a stubborn look. Jesse wanted to punch it off his face, but he was too wrapped up in the moment, and so nodded, still with a single sharp glance at the man to show him this was not over, and then continued.

"We're here for the cash and I just beg you to be the first hero to end up on his back. None of you'll make it out o' here alive if even one of you makes a single move. Now who would be the bank manager, you reckon?"

Two of the Younger brothers, Jim and Bob, fired several shots into the wall behind the clerks, and the men and women in the bank lobby threw themselves down on their faces screaming and crying in a babble of terror.

There were three tellers at the counter and one man whose suit proclaimed him the bank's manager. The manager and two of the clerks were petrified, their eyes white and round as they stood, hands shaking visibly as they hung in the air. The third teller, however, had moved quietly back against the far wall and seemed to be watching the whole event calmly, as if he had been expecting them all along.

Jesse stared into the man's emotionless face for a moment, the crimson reflections in his flat eyes reminding the young outlaw of something just out of reach, and then snapped back into the moment and leveled one of his heavy revolvers at another teller.

"You deaf, son? Start filling bags up! It ain't like we got all day!"

The man stood a little taller as if trying to convince himself of courage that was not there. "You can't do this. The sheriff –"

"Sheriff ain't here, chief!" Jesse rushed forward and whipped his pistol grip into the man's temple. The man's skull cracked beneath the blow and blood dribbled from his nose and ears. He fell, stone dead, and another wave of cries rippled through the patrons on the floor as the manager and the last remaining clerk rushed to fill bags from a safe behind the counter.

"Nice work, there, boys." Jesse grinned at the workers and then over his shoulders at the gang. "Why don't you all see if any of these fine men and women wouldn't like to donate their own cash to the cause?"

With rumbled laughter and more kicks than were probably necessary, the men started to move through the crowd, taking wallets and jewelry held aloft in shaking hands.

Frank stayed by his brother, covering the tellers and the bank manager, while the Youngers stood by the door, two of them keeping a keen eye out the window.

Several sacks bulging with new bills were tossed onto the counter and the manager, again with his hands in the air, gestured toward the door. "That's all we got. Please, just go before the lawmen come."

Jesse felt the ingrained need to argue with anything a Republican said welling up in his throat, but he knew that even if there was no law in town that day, the braver locals would be working themselves up to charge the bank, and the best move now was to get away with the cash before that happened.

Jesse nodded, grabbing two of the heavy bags and gesturing for Frank to take up the others. "Well, thanks for the withdrawal, sir. Mighty obliged, and maybe we'll come in and give you our custom again someday." He moved slowly toward the door, grinning all the while, and could see the rest of his men moving as well, hands full of bills and jewelry.

The whole gang was bunched up by the door when one of the strangers that had come in with the Youngers, Jake was his name, although he kept insisting folks call him 'Blackheart', pointed to the manager. "I think this here's that blue belly, Sam Cox!"

Jesse stopped moving and stared at the manager, noticing the sweat standing out on the man's forehead and lip. He was shaking his head, eyes round again, muttering some sort of incoherent denial.

Jesse took a step forward. "That true? You Captain Cox, that did for Bloody Bill?"

"N-n-n-no . . . I a-a-a-ain't, I s-s-s-s-swear! I d-d-d-d-didn't never –"

"You bastard!" One of the local Clay County boys shouted, fanning his revolver at the manager, who dove behind the counter with a girlish shriek.

Before Jesse knew what was happening, the entire gang was firing; several would-be heroes in the crowd were firing back, many hiding behind the screaming forms of women. Bullets zipped past in both directions as the roar of gunfire in the enclosed space of the bank's lobby was nearly deafening. The manager emerged from the counter making a run for a back door and several bullets struck him in the head and neck, throwing his lifeless body forward like a rag doll. Jesse could not tell if any of the shots were his.

"Go, go! Let's get a move on!" Jesse yelled over the gunfire, waving the men toward the front door. Cole Younger, however, was just turning away from the door, a look of concern on his face.

"The law –" was all he had time for before the door exploded in red-tinged fire behind him, scattering burning splinters across the room.

Several more detonations blasted the front of the bank, throwing bits of wall and flurries of glass across the still, bloody scene. The silence that fell after the last shot seemed to weigh Jesse down with anticipation.

"Okay, dogs, slink back on out here and face what's comin' to ya!" The voice was harsh, and did not offer any hope at all to the men within.

"Ain't no way yer gettin' away alive, so's you might as well make it quick." Another voice, and this time they fired another bolt of crimson force into the gaping holes in front of the bank.

One of the local boys jumped up and ran for the gap, screaming incoherently and firing his carbine again and again into the street. Jesse reached out as if to stop him, commands rising to his lips just as the kid's entire upper body disappeared in a red burst of light and noise. The legs continued running for a few steps before tripping over a screaming woman and toppling over her, blood flooding out over her back.

"Bastards." Jesse thought it was one of the Younger boys who had talked, but he could not tell, and did not care. He agreed, whoever had said it.

"That's one down, Jesse." The voice was clearly amused, and the young outlaw felt a cold hand grip his heart as the man used his name. "Plenty more where that came from, too."

Jesse was hunched down behind the counter and could not remember how he had gotten there. His brother was beside him, and most of the other boys were crouched down behind desks and other bits of furniture scattered around the lobby.

Frank's voice, clear in his ear, was harsh. "We gotta head out the back, Jesse." He nodded toward the crumpled body of the bank manager. "He was runnin', there's gotta be a way out back there."

Jesse was thinking fast, but felt like it wasn't fast enough. "But what if they've got the place surrounded?"

Frank nodded to the front of the bank. "Cole 'n' his brothers'll set up a ruckus out here, they won't expect us, we bust out the back, even if they're waiting, we got a fightin' chance." He looked down at the still twitching legs. "We stay here, we ain't even got that."

Jesse nodded, and then gestured for the gang to gather around him. A few whispered instructions set most of the men moving through the back door while the Youngers, without a hint of bother, moved toward the front of the bank.

"What about the horses?!" It was another of the local kids.

Frank waved one of the heavy bags. "We walk out with these on our own legs, we get new horses. We try to get the horses," he moved his chin toward the twitching remains, "all we got left is legs."

The kid's mouth snapped shut and he nodded once. None of the boys were having any luck in their efforts not to stare at the remains. Quietly, they moved over the dead manager's body and through the back door. Frank and Jesse stood there, between the two rooms, until the Youngers were in position. At a nod from Jesse, Cole and his brothers began firing out the shattered front of the building, screaming bloody murder and hopping from cover to cover. The crowd was screaming again, the law outside firing blindly into the shadows, and Jesse could not suppress a grin as he turned back to leave.

But as he spun, he saw the silent teller again, still standing by the back wall watching him with those weird eyes. The man nodded with a slight smile, almost as in recognition, and Jesse felt a cold chill down his back.He wondered how this man could have managed to survive the gunfire that had ripped the life out of everyone else that had been standing in the bank. It was by pure luck that his own gang was still on their feet.

In front of the strange man a wounded clerk stood up, looking back and forth between Jesse and the Youngers. He took in a breath as if to shout, and Jesse's pistol snapped up and barked once. A black hole appeared between the man's eyes, and he went cross-eyed as he toppled over onto his back. In the chaos and confusion, no one even noticed another man had died.

Behind the bank, Frank had sent most of the boys running up the slope toward the trees. Jesse saw that several of them were carrying the bags his brother had dragged out. Jesse nodded and tossed his bags to two other men. "Run!" he shouted the order, pulling his own weapons and spinning to cover the corner of the building with Frank shouldering the long rifle beside him.

Frank favored the rifle over his six-shooter and Jesse always took the wind out of him for it. Maybe it was Frank's time in the army or his love for the long range kill. Whatever it was, it had been the source of countless debates between the brothers on the subject of looking a dying man in the eyes over the pleasure of a long range bullseye.

"Comin' through!" Cole Younger screamed as he barreled through the door followed closely by his three brothers. "Run!" And the six men took off after the rest of the gang, sprinting breathlessly for the tree line.

Jesse was storming up the hill, arms pumping and pistols flashing at his sides. He could not keep the smile off his face, knowing how much money was running up the slope with him. The smile was still there when the first of the gang holding a bag flew forward with a shout that coincided with a deep-throated boom from the valley below. Jesse could see daylight through the ragged hole in the man's back as the body tumbled to a boneless halt, the bags thumping into the grass beside it.

The smile was replaced by a ferocious snarl. "Run!"

The men moved even faster, pulling from reserves they did not know they had. Another man's head detonated further up the slope, his body flopping down clumsily even as its legs continued running without guidance; more bags fell to the dirt.

"Damn it!" Jesse screamed, spinning around, duster flaring, and his two pistols came up and began hammering shots back down the slope. Behind him, he could see two men on galloping horses, and he shifted his aim for the broad chest of the closest animal. The bullets cratered the sensitive flesh and the horse went down squealing, throwing its rider high into the air. Beside Jesse, Frank had also stopped, taking careful aim at the final rider, a man in dusty trail gear who was taking a bead on another bag carrier. The rifle spat a spear of fire downhill and the man flew off the back of his horse as if he'd been pulled off by a rope. He rolled to a stop in the grass and didn't get up.

"Now run!" Jesse and Frank turned again and pulled for the top of the hill. Ahead of them, most of the men had made it to the trees. Behind them, one of the men was up again, and another Clay County boy fell, throwing his bags down. This time the powerful blast had blown the lower half of his body to bloody rags, leaving the poor kid screaming, scrabbling at the dirt in mindless pain.

As Jesse ran by him, the boy reached up with one bloody hand, pleading not to be left behind. His skin was grey and the light was already dimming from his eyes. It was a look Jesse had seen many times during the war, and he knew there was no hope.

"Sorry, kid, best I can do." He muttered breathlessly as he put one bullet through the man's head and ran on past and into the shadows of the forest.

Under the trees, Jesse stopped and looked down the slope in fury. Nearly all the money they had taken from the bank was now scattered across the hill with the bits and pieces of several of his best boys. But the last lawman was still down there, hunkered down behind his dead horse, and beyond him Jesse could see a band of men from the town, building up their courage now and heading up the slope. This was no safe place to be, and he knew he would have to leave the money behind.

This new breed of lawmen had a strange brand of courage he had not seen before. Those new blasters seemed almost to have brought life to men that in past years would have cowered at the sound of Jesse's name.

"Damnit!" He snorted, pounding a tree trunk with the butt of a pistol.

"That was brisk, heh kid?"

Jesse turned to see 'Blackheart' Jake smiling over at him. Jesse turned away, not wanting to deal with the blowhard from the Younger gang. He grunted quietly, hoping the man would leave him alone. But it seemed today just was not going to be Jesse's day.

"Damned dirty Union tricks, that what that was." Blackheart jerked his chin back down the hill. "Those fancy guns? They're from Washington, back east. Just gonna be more and more of them, too, time goes by."

Jesse hit the tree again, not feeling the bark digging into his flesh. "How the hell . . ."

Blackheart nodded. "How the hell indeed. Once every one horse town's got a couple of those new-fangled irons, won't be a bank this side of the Rockies we can touch."

Jesse snorted while the men down below scrambled around for cover, building up the courage to take the hill.

"'Till we get some of our own."

He could feel the old need building again. The knowledge that those Republicans down there possessed something over him, something that would keep him from what he wanted, or help him achieve it on his own, was bitter in his throat.

The sudden crack of Frank's rifle startled Jesse, although he noticed that 'Blackheart' didn't move a muscle. Down below, a man threw up his hands and tumbled limply backward as the rest dove for cover.

"That'll keep 'em for a few more minutes. Jesse, we gotta get gone before the rest get up here."

Jesse nodded, holstered his guns, and moved back into the woods with his brother, the stranger bringing up the rear.

As Jesse took one last look down into the valley, he caught just the barest crimson gleam.The strange bank teller had been watching from the back door of the bank the whole time. He seemed unfazed by all the death and destruction as he gave Jesse a final odd smile that sent chills down his back.

* * * * *

The dusty road below was empty and had been for hours. The small group of men sitting along the low canyon rim looked down in silence, obviously waiting for something, and obviously with no great desire to talk to one another. Several of the older men were spitting gobs of tobacco down onto the road.

One man shook his head at the display and moved off to talk to another man sitting a bit apart from the rest of the group. "Johnny."

The man did not look up from the road below. His eyes darted from one end of the canyon to the other, restless and alert. "Cole."

Cole Younger crouched down beside him. "How you feelin'?"

"Fine. Just want to get it started is all."

The man was considerably younger than the outlaw, but there was a slight family resemblance. "Johnny, you don't have to do this."

The man laughed. "Cole, what else I gonna do? You want me pickin' up a spade on some Republican's ranch? You been talkin' up this route for years. 'Bout time you brought me in on the action."

Cole grinned. "Well, it is easier than diggin' holes, for sure."

Johnny grunted again, a mix of nerves and suspicion. "Thing I don't get, is why you're back down here. You been runnin' with those James boys down around Clay County, Cole. Why you back this way?"

Cole stared down at the road, his smile slipping from his face. "You can't get anywhere with them boys less'n Jesse trusts you. An' Jesse don' trust me. But there's one thing he wants more'n anythin' else, an' the man who can get him that, well, that man's gonna rise. Better jobs, bigger cut, more back up. So's I'm here, for one quick job, and I thought, why not bring in my cousin Ringo, since he's been itchin' for a chance."

Johnny murmured, "Big on ya, cuz." He looked up at his cousin. "What's he want, anyway?"

Cole stood up and stretched. "Lawmen back in Clay County been showin' up heeled with some new kinda irons, an' Jesse wants one mighty bad."

That got Johnny's attention. "New guns?"

"Yeah. We been callin' 'em blasters, on account they don't leave nuthin' left o' ya when ya get hit."

"And you reckon, this stagecoach . . ."

"Heard tell the guards on this route been given the new cutters, an' I bring one back to Jesse, that's my ticket, Johnny." He looked back at his cousin. "Could be our ticket, cuz."

Johnny's eyes tightened but he did not look up. "So, one of these irons and you're quite the man, then, eh?"

Further down the line a man with wild eyes snorted. "James ain't nothin' much, Ringo. Yer cousin, I'm thinkin', might be in love."

Johnny winced and waved the big man off. "Shut it, Smiley. Now's not the time."

Cole smiled as he turned to the big man. "Smiley, that's quite a name for a man whose mouth runs away like that."

The wild eyed man smiled wider. "Ain't never put a man in the ground an' left him fit for an open casket." His eyes gleamed as he gestured, as if holding a knife, across his face up from either corner of his mouth. "And I ain't afraid of that sissified city boy, James, neither."

Cole looked at the man they called Smiley for a moment, shook his head, and turned back to the road below. "The stagecoach should be coming around soon. We should all get ready."

Smiley pulled his two revolvers and wheeled them both with a flourish. "I hear Jesse likes this one, Younger. He this fast?"

Cole shook his head and stared at the large man with dead eyes. "I never seen him twirl his smoke wagons like that before, no. Seen him kill a couple men who did, but ain't never seen him do it."

Smiley slapped the two weapons back into place and scowled at Cole before turning to Johnny. "I'm here so's you got someone at your back, Ringo. And I get a chance, I'm gonna snag me one of them new irons." He glared a challenge at Younger, who snorted and looked back toward Johnny.

"I need this, Johnny. We're all going to need this. With the law packing these irons, we're all going to be going up to the hill if we get left behind. It ain't fer James, its fer me, and maybe fer you."

Johnny Ringo nodded, again looking down at the road below. "It ain't fer James. It's fer you." He looked up at his cousin. "But I don't need James, and I don't need to run with him, or you. I shoot better'n Smiley here, better'n Jesse James, 'n' better'n you." He jerked his chin toward the road. "Now let's get this fandango movin'."

A sharp whistle from below caught their attention, and all the men lurched upright. One of Younger's men, posted by the road at the head of the canyon, waved his hat in the air and gestured around the bend.

"Right. Everyone scatter." Cole waved his arm and the band dispersed across the ridgeline. "And remember, take whatever cover you can git, cuz these guns, they ain't nothin' to mess about with."

The men nodded as they moved out, pulling pistols and wrapping the shoulder straps of rifles around their forearms.

When the wagon came around the turn, she was making good speed, the four horses blowing hard and hooves pounding the packed dirt of the road. The driver was sitting easily on his bench, while a man in a dark duster, hat low over his eyes, sat in the shotgun seat. It was a heavy vehicle, the kind generally used for mail or cargo, with no windows.

Cole was surprised to see that there was only the one guard, and he knew they were going to have problems when it came time to split the weapons, if they took them.

With a shrug, Younger gave a sharp whistle and fanned his pistol into the valley, sending five shots into the stagecoach. The driver flinched, more in surprise than pain, and the wagon swerved as the horses, confused by the jerked reins, staggered toward the side of the road.

The riflemen, briefed by Younger, took aim at the guard, but before the first bullets tore into the bench, the man had leapt from the top of the wagon. He rolled in the dust of the road, coming up with a massive gun in either hand. The weapons flashed with crimson fire, and blazing lines of force shot up into the rocks. Plumes of dirt and flesh shot up into the air, marking the end of two of his men.

"Damn. Get him!" Younger knelt behind a warm boulder and wheeled his casings into the dust while he grabbed for shells on his belt. The crack of rifles and pistols echoed back and forth down into the canyon, and the sudden roar of a shotgun signaled the entrance of the driver into the fight.

Cole looked up over the rock to take stock of the situation. The coach looked as if it had been chewed on, with bullet holes scattered over the whole thing. One of the horses was down, kicking in the dust and screaming like a tortured woman.

The guard and the driver had gone to ground in the ditch beside the road, and the guard was sending crimson-tailed bullets searing up into the rocks. Several more of his men were down, the dust drinking up their blood.

"Johnny, this's gotta be it!" Cole's cousin was hunkered behind another boulder further down the slope. Smiley, on the other side, grunted and hopped over his own cover without warning and began to sprint down the hill, blazing away with both of his guns.

"Damn," Younger scrambled around his boulder and followed the crazy man down, seeing Johnny Ringo sliding out and running beside him.

The three men raced down the slope, slamming lead down into the ravine that sheltered the guard and the driver. Younger pulled even with Smiley, who staggered over a loose stone trying to pick up his speed. The crazy man was soon rolling painfully down toward the road. Ringo and Younger kept up the steady drumbeat of shots.

The driver, having reloaded his shotgun, took a chance at going for a shot, and two bullets tore into his chest and neck, tossing him back against the hard dirt of the ravine in a spray of blood. The big weapon discharged up into the air as it hit the ground beside him. The guard, hearing the pounding footsteps approach, knew his situation was dire. Rather than stay to be gunned down on his belly, however, the man stood up screaming, both of his glowing weapons leveled up the slope, and unleashed hell. The bolts slapped past Ringo and Younger, detonating on the slope above them. Both men fired their last shots and the guard went back into the ditch, half his head scattered against the opposite slope.

Cole and Johnny stopped on the road, barely able to breathe and leaning down to ease the cramps in their sides. The other men came warily down, covering the wagon and the two still bodies in case there was still some surprise waiting for them.

Cole walked up beside the dead lawman and pushed the man's coat open with his toe. The burnished star gleamed in the sunlight, and he kneeled down to pick the massive gun out of the corpse's stiffening hand. He looked around for the other, but it was nowhere in sight.

"It's up here, cuz." Johnny held up the other gun. "And it's stayin' here."

Cole stared at his cousin for a moment, then nodded. "You earned it."

"Hey!" One of the men by the wagon yelled in an angry voice. "Ain't nothin' in here but mail n' feed! You said there'd be gold."

Cole nodded again, looking down at the heavy, sleek weapon in his hands. There were vents or windows along the six-shooter's cylinders, glowing a baleful red even under the hot sun.

"We got better'n gold . . . We got the future."

* * * * *

Jesse turned the weapon over and over in his hand as if memorizing every smooth line and strange angle. His brother Frank sat across from him with Cole Younger, both watching the young outlaw as he studied their prize.

Clearly it was based upon the standard six-shooter, although it was heavier and its lines were more rounded. Where the cylinders would be in a standard weapon, this pistol held small chambers filled with a glowing red material that shone out from vents or windows, lighting Jesse's face eerily from below. Tubes or pipes led from the chambers down the barrel and into the main housing, where more vents glowed softly with a throbbing light.

Only three of the cylinders were glowing now, the other three showing only a muted crimson shadow. When Cole had handed the weapon over, four of the chambers had been burning. In the excitement and confusion of the stagecoach job, no one had thought to check the lawman for ammunition.

Even if they had thought to look, they would not have known what to look for. It almost seemed that each strange chamber provided the weapon with multiple shots. With this widow maker, the owner would have a huge advantage over any poor son of a bitch with a standard weapon.

Jesse had tested the weapon out behind their house, taking a shot at a scarecrow in a neighbor's field. The thing had detonated as if half a stick of dynamite had been shoved up its ass, setting a ring of small fires scattered throughout the field.

The feeling that had tingled up his arm as he pulled the trigger was indescribable. The rush of pure power had nearly caused him to lose his balance. Then he'd remembered that he only had a few more shots, watching as the red glow died in the next cylinder.

"It's not enough." His voice was barely a mutter as continued to turn the gun in his hands.

Cole's annoyance was clear. "I'm sorry, Jesse, but it's the best—"

Jesse raised a single hand without looking up. "Not talking about you no more, Cole. This one gun, it ain't enough. We go in to do a job with this, we scare the ba-Jesus out of some yokels, and then we're back where we started. From the looks of it, we got ten, twenty more shots at best. You gonna be the one caught with your pants down when this devil runs out of Hell-fury?"

His dark eyes rose to look into his brother's face, and then Younger's. "We need more if we're going to be taken seriously. The world's speedin' up, and we need to run to keep up or we'll be left behind." He sneered as he looked back down at the gun. "Left behind like Dixie.

"I even heard of some crazy metal horse that don't need no feed or water. Some wild story about an 'Iron Horse' or something that the Union Cavalrymen have been seen ridin'. Some folks are even sayin' they fly! We're being left behind I tell you, livin' in the past while these bastards speed by us into the future."

Frank reached over and patted his brother on the shoulder. "We ain't gettin' left behind, Jesse. We're doin' just fine. We use that piece o' jewelry you got there right, that'd be two or three jobs that'd be like a walk in the park. Set us up real good, an' we head south for a while, let the heat die down."

Jesse looked back up at his brother, frustration clear on his young face. "We need more, Frank. You been reading the papers as much as me. Every day there's some new fancy toy being cranked out by those Yankees. Don't matter who we hit or what we take, no one cares a wit, next to the damned super weapons comin' out of Washington."

He slammed his fist on the table, making several of the men sitting at the bar turn toward them for a moment before going back to their own drinks.

The James brothers and their associate settled back into their chairs, staring into their glasses and darkly pondering a destiny dominated by Republicans armed with weapons of the future. Even Frank saw the shadows ahead. A man sitting at the table beside them, however, leaned over a little and cleared his throat to get their attention. Three sets of eyes swiveled to take him in, although none of them moved further.

"Couldn't help overhearin', son. You Jesse James, an' his brother Frank?" The man's voice was quiet, pitched low enough to give the illusion of privacy.

Jesse nodded, turning toward the man, but said nothing.

"Thought so. Son, I want to shake the hand of the man who won't let the Confederacy die in Missouri." He reached his hand across the space between them and after a moment Jesse took it for a quick shake. "There's many a man'd give up tomorrow if you weren't takin' down the Radicals an' keepin' 'em honest, Mr. James."

Jesse smiled a little and nodded. "Well, thanks'e, sir. That's nice to hear."

"Ye'r the man, Mr. James, that we all look up to in these dark times. An' you can't give up, sir. No matter what they bring against you. The Almighty'll surely reward you for the good yer doin'."

Cole snorted and slapped the table. "Easy for you to say, old man. You ain't seen what one o' these can do to a man."

" Oh, but I have, Mr. Younger." Jesse looked annoyed that the man knew who Cole was as well, but he leaned forward all the same.

"Well, everything you say might be true, sir, but ain't no way we can stand against the Republicans when they're all toting these gizmo'd up shootin' irons." He tossed the strange pistol onto the table. Everyone could clearly see the large 'U.S.' stamped into the grip.

"You could if you all had such weapons of your own, though. And more besides." The man's eyes were more intense now, and reflected the light of the saloon's lamps and candles with a ruby gleam.

Cole huffed. "You got any idea what it took to get that one gun, old man?"

"I'm not talkin' one gun, son. I'm talkin' about enough ordnance to change the fate of the entire nation. Maybe the world." There was no deference in his tone or bearing now, and he sat up straight, staring right into Jesse's eyes. "Somethin' you might be interested in, Mr. James?"

Jesse looked suspiciously at the stranger, but nodded once. "I'm listenin'."

The man returned the single nod. "You know those tracks they been layin', straight down through the state and out west? Wider gauge than even the big routes up north?"

Jesse and Frank nodded while Cole sat back, arms crossed sullenly in front of him.

"Well, those're special tracks, meant to carry a special train. Another one of Washington's new-fangled contraptions. Runs on that crimson poison," he gestured toward the pistol on the table. "Covered in armor, loaded with weapons. It's bein' sent out west to establish a depot and outpost for Grant's advance into the western territories. It'll be carryin' everything a whole army'll need. Could even be there might be some flyin' horses on there somewhere."

Jesse's eyes were on fire, barely seeing the room as his mind was filled with visions of all the power of the Washington Republicans at his disposal. Not to mention the polish it would add to his name, taking down a behemoth like this man had just described.

"Old man, we look like we're taking on a military train right about now? With no more'n a dozen shots in our little hold-out here?" Cole sounded bitter and annoyed. Frank, however, just seemed nervous, watching his brother's dreaming face.

"Well, you'd need to put together a big gang, fer sure. But you boys know folks, don'tcha? Gotta be plenty of folks'd raise a shootin' iron if Jesse James put out the call."

Jesse nodded. "We could put a mighty big team together." He looked at Frank. "Just might be, big enough."

Frank shook his head. "We don't need firepower like that, Jesse. Even if we did take somethin' like that off the Union, you think they'd just let us keep it? You don't think that'd put our names on every post office and marshal's wall from here to California? Shit, Jesse, a hit like that would see us on top of the Most Wanted list in a New York minute, and we'd have every lawman around buzzing down on us like flies on shit."

Jesse's smile grew even wider. "Damn straight it would."

Cole leaned forward. "Jesse, you'd need an army to tackle a train like the one this flannel mouth is describin'."

Jesse was staring down at the gun again as if he could not look away. "Yep, we'd need an army . . . an' I might just be able to raise one . . ."

* * * * *

Jesse crouched down in the cool wet undergrowth and looked out at the wide-gauge track that slashed its way through the forest. The man in the saloon had given very specific information on the train's supposed schedule, and there was not much more time to wait. He glanced from side to side, taking note of the men and women arrayed around him, all clutching various weapons and even a stick of dynamite.

There were over forty outlaws from all across the west crouching beside the gleaming tracks, and Jesse could not help the flush of pride that rose in him each time it struck him that they had been brought together to fight the Republicans under his direction. In fact, nearly every hard case that had made a name for himself in the last ten years was sharing that stand of trees with him just then.

One intense thin young thing from Arizona, sporting a sombrero and cheeks smoother than a baby's ass, seemed a little fidgety a couple places down the line. Behind him was a big man known to most of the boys as simply 'The Butcher.' He'd been a butcher once, Jesse knew. But after a band of outlaws had burnt down his home and killed his family, he'd set aside that life and taken up crime himself. Looking into his eyes now you would never have taken him for a family man. Cold, reptilian eyes, like an alligator's, looked out at a world that held little in the way of pleasure for him now. He ran with several different gangs, moving from one to another and all the time welcome because of his massive build, great strength, and complete lack of morals.

Jesse knew that Cole was disappointed that Johnny Ringo had not answered the call. He'd made quite a name for himself down in Cochise County, running with some really rough men. But nobody had heard from him in over a month, and Jesse knew Cole was getting a little concerned.

The men were fidgeting, waiting for a machine most of them had never seen, but each and every one of them had heard the stories. They knew the times were changing, and they knew the Washington forces, armed with these new weapons and machines, would be unstoppable. This new train, if half of what they'd heard was true, was the latest step into the future, and it scared most of them just as much as it lured them in.

There was not a single man among them who had not wondered where these creations had even come from. How could one country go from steam trains and horses to this armored giant bearing down on them, or flying iron mounts, in so little time?

The ground beneath Jesse began to shake. Barely noticeable at first, but soon the leaves around him began to bounce in time to a low, menacing growl that seemed to rise from one breath to the next. When the monster came around the bend, barreling toward them like a bull on a red flag, not even Jesse was prepared for the sight of the Union supply train as it roared on.

The train was massive, like a wall of black iron, fat rivets gleaming in the warm sun. Tubes and pipes woven all over the massive engine, vents and indicators flaring a hellish ruby light across the trees to either side. A huge cowcatcher was attached to the front of the engine, its flanged blades clearly capable of dissecting anything unable to get out of its way. Huge vanes swept up from the cowcatcher and away down the flanks of the train, gleaming like sharpened sword blades. Jesse could not tell if they were decorations, defenses, or served some purpose for the arcane motor that drove the thing along at such frightening speed.

The plates of armor riveted all down the sides of the train were proof against all but the most potent weapons, and at a glance, Jesse knew nothing being carried by his small band was going to even dent the thing. He made a pressing down gesture with both hands and the outlaws were only too happy to crouch lower, watching in awestruck silence as the beast rushed past. Gun turrets and firing ports studded the entire length as it swept on by, and a huge U.S. flag, snapping in the wind of its passage, flew from the last car, a final taunt as it swerved away into the forest.

Jesse stared after the train for several minutes. No one seemed eager to stand up, which turned out to be a good thing as two high-pitched roars came sailing along behind, and Jesse and his men got their first look at the fabled Union Iron Horses. It was only a quick glimpse as the things flashed past. Men sitting in high saddles straddling some sort of metal shape, flame flaring from the back of the things as their riders clung precariously from handles that must have approximated the work of reins.

Between the apparent invulnerability of the train and the terrifying prospect of these newfangled creations roaring along just over the massive tracks, the outlaw army was even slower to stand after the Federal forces had past.

Jesse slowly rose to his feet and stretched, putting on a brave show for the others around him. The questions came fast and thick as the men processed what they had seen, and what he had asked them to do.

"Ain't no way we coulda taken that train on, Jesse!"

"We done now, James? We got killlin' to do down south."

"Jesse, what we gonna do now?"

The babbling crashed upon the outlaw leader like waves on a beach, and for a moment, he felt like taking out his blaster and killing at least one of the bastards in spectacular fashion. But he kept his smile steady, took a deep breath, and began to walk back up toward the path where they had left their horses and supplies.

"No worries, lads. I've got it all sorted out." He moved up the forested slope quickly, forcing the rest of them to jog to keep up.

"Did you see that thing, Jesse? It's huge!"

"And ain't no way we gonna catch it now, Jesse!"

Jesse put up his hands for quiet. He moved out onto the road and up beside a wagon he'd ordered brought along, its cargo covered by several blankets. When the outlaws had gathered around and quieted down sufficiently for him to be heard, Jesse lowered his hands and flashed his famous grin.

"First, we don't have ta catch it. It's gonna be stopped in Kansas City tonight. The train don't move at night. So all we gotta do is ride on down, get ahead of it, and we're good."

"Good to get chopped up and spit out, you mean!" One of the younger men cried out.

"Well, yeah, if we try to shoot it up, yeah, we won't hurt it much. But, ya see, just a bit south o' Kansas City, there's a ravine, and the tracks pass along a shallow bridge . . . ." He pulled the blankets aside and revealed a heaping pile of dynamite in kegs and sticks. "The bridge is far enough south, the train'll be back up to full speed. We blow the bridge just before it hits . . . won't matter how much armor it's carryin'. In fact, the more armor, the more it'll rip itself apart."

Slowly the cries settled down, and the grins spread throughout the mob.

* * * * *

As the sun rose over the plains to the west of Kansas City, Jesse gave one last check over his crews and the dynamite stacked around the standings of the low bridge. Everything seemed to be in order, and The Butcher sat idly by the dynamite, a lit cigarette hanging from his lower lip. Jesse nodded to him and the man nodded back without a momentary change in expression. Jesse moved away, walking back to where Cole Younger, two of his brothers, and Frank were talking quietly.

"Speed it was going yesterday, we might lose a lot of the cargo this way, Jesse." Frank was not finding fault, just making an observation, and Jesse nodded.

"Yeah, I know." He shadowed his eyes with one raised hand and looked down the long stretch of wide track.

"Gang like this, this big, this full of itself . . . you won't get away without handing out a lot of the candy you're about to pick up." Cole took a toothpick out of his mouth and spat into the scrub brush.

Jesse nodded again. “I know.”

He moved toward a large boulder with a couple small scrub trees peeking out from underneath. “Frank, I want you here with your long iron. Those flying bastards make an appearance, they’re your problem. The train’s gonna take care of itself, but those boys . . . we don’t know what they can do . . .”

Frank nodded. “You count on it, Jesse. Just leave some goodies for your old brother, yeah?”

Jesse smiled and patted him on the back. “They make a nice fancy rifle, first one’s yours.”

Again the rumbling sounded beneath the outlaws’ feet, and again all eyes turned to the northeast, along the wide tracks that somehow seemed suddenly menacing in their silence. On either side of the tracks, the outlaws settled down to whatever cover they could find, again readying their weapons. In the gully, at a signal from Jesse, The Butcher touched his cigarette to a long wick and started off down the ravine at a slow walk as if he did not have a care in the world.

The black engine was as monstrous as before. Its riveted steel as intimidating, the low howl of its demonic engine as terrifying. The weapons in the turrets swiveled back and forth as if scenting prey.

The train raced down the track as the men’s hearts pounded louder and louder in their chests. Jesse could barely resist laughing out loud, anticipating the coming events. The enjoyment he always got out of violent conflict was enough to concern even Frank at times.

When the engine reached the bridge, it was suddenly engulfed in an enormous eruption of dirt, wood, and fire. A flaming wall of destruction lashed out in all directions as the wicks were devoured and the sparks disappeared into the TNT.

The explosion flattened every outlaw in the band and tossed the enormous engine up into the air as if it were nothing but a discarded toy. The body of the machine spun in a tight spiral as it flew, twisting the cars behind it off their carriages and onto their sides. Following cars plowed into those fouled by the initial detonation, and pushed the entire mass of twisted and screaming metal over the ruined bridge and into the ravine where they dug an enormous furrow in the dry soil.

When the engine finally succumbed to gravity and plummeted back to earth, the outlaws who had struggled back to their feet were thrown into the dust once again. The plume of dirt and smoke that thrust into the air blotted out the sun; and stone, sand, and twisted debris rained down all across the plains. As the echoes of the detonation and the impact faded, the outlaws began to rise once again, covered in dust and dirt.

Jesse was shaking his head to clear it of the ringing when a sharp crack slapped out from his left. Frank, his long rifle held steadily in grimy hands, had fired a single shot back down the tracks, and his younger brother had the presence of mind to roll to the side and come up with his blaster at the ready. One of the Iron Horses was spiraling unmanned down the tracks, its rider falling limply to the dirt not far away. The thing soared along unattended for several hundred feet until finally coming to a hovering stop just above some bushes.

The second flying machine, roaring past at terrific speed, thundered blaster fire into the rising outlaws. Two massive Gatling cannons mounted on either side sprayed crimson bolts. The gunner’s accuracy was obviously affected by the wild ride, but several outlaws stumbled back, surrounded by clouds of pink mist, and fell to the ground missing an arm or a leg.

“You gotta get that other one!!!!” Jesse screamed over the ringing in his own ears, but Frank either ignored him or did not hear. It was unnecessary, anyway, and even as he screamed, Jesse knew it. Frank was taking careful, steady aim, and when the Iron Horse thundered down to make a second attack, the long rifle bucked, a cloud of smoke erupted from its muzzle, and there was a slight pop behind the ringing in Jesse's ears. A puff of smoke or dust blew up from the rider's headgear, his head was ripped backward, and he tumbled from his saddle. The machine spiraled into the ground and detonated with a red-tinged fire.

Jesse shook his head again, looking around to take stock of the situation. The massive armored train was scattered across the plain like the toy of some spoiled child. Crates, boxes, and bits and pieces of gear were scattered everywhere across the ground, as well as twisted, steaming chunks of the train itself. Scattered through the debris were countless blue-jacketed bodies, many so torn and shattered as to be barely recognizable. Some of those bodies were stirring, though, and Jesse could just make out the sound of desperate moans under the persistent ringing.

At the first pop of a gunshot, Jesse's head snapped around, his pistols in his hands without conscious thought. But it was just an outlaw putting paid to some blue belly piker too stupid to know he was dead. Soon, a ripple of gunfire swept across the fields as other outlaws took up the grisly work. Jesse was a little alarmed to see smiles on many faces as they walked from body to body, putting shots into heads, guts, and groins.

The big bastard the boys from Arizona called 'Smiley' knelt beside each body he came upon and sliced it across the face, widening the mouth of each into a horrible parody of a smile. Jesse was moving toward the freight cars when he heard a scream that told him not all of Smiley's subjects were dead yet.

Jesse saw Frank and Cole moving through the field as well, but they were keeping their eyes down, looking for any of the glowing red tell-tales that would indicate the new Federal technology. The ground was scattered with personal weapons, rifles, and ammunition bandoliers, and the men quickly armed themselves with these new weapons.

Jesse watched with the eyes of a hawk as some of the men unloaded the latest freight car, handing down boxes and crates in a brigade line that ended at his dusty old wagon. There were already several of the 'Horses tied down in back, battered and dented, but otherwise in pretty good shape. The tell-tales were all glowing with their crimson flame, so he assumed they were okay. There were other crates and boxes, containing weapons, ammunition, and several things that looked promising, but that, Jesse could not identify on the fly.

"C'mon, boys. The Republicans out of Kansas City will be here in less'n an hour or so, we want to be long gone when they get here and see what we done to their train."

Several of the men laughed, but there were dark looks as well. Many were strapping bags to their saddles, trying to fit as much as they could into whatever they had to hold it in. Some were walking around like pirates in the old books, several pistols shoved into their belts. Most were grumbling about how much they would have to leave behind.

"Nice o' ya to bring a wagon fer yerself," grumbled Smiley, looking with heated eyes at Jesse. "Woulda been nice to been told to bring our own."

Jesse smiled slightly. Cole had filled him in on the big boy's attitude, but he figured he had the measure of the man. Cold-blooded killer, eager to make his name, but too worried about dying to really matter much.

"Brought the wagon for the TNT, fella, this here's just a lucky chance. Besides, we never woulda been able to get in front of the train if we were dragging a trail o' wagons behind us. You lookin' for any other answers Smiley, I'm afraid you're sniffin' up the wrong tree. I suggest you get what's yours and move on along."

"What you gonna do with that wagon, James?" Another angry voice cried out.

"Wagon's mine, so I'd stop worryin' about it if I were you. But any you lot want more loot, you come up to Clay County, and I'll see that each one of you gets their fair share."

He paused, but there did not seem to be any more objections aside from the continued low-grade growling. He pointed to the smoking wreckage of the train. "You all been inside, I know. You seen what's there, that even I can't take away. There's things in there look like a cross between a stagecoach and an ironclad, guns the size o' yer head. They got cannons, too, not to mention more o' these flyin' 'Horses, if we coulda got 'em to work."

"How you gonna learn?" It was more an honest question than a challenge this time.

"Well, Frank happened to find one of these fine lads here still breathin', barely, had him a nifty little castle surrounded by some feathers 'r somethin' on his collar. We're figurin' he might be able to tell us how to use 'em, and other stuff besides."

One of the older outlaws from up north winced at that. "Kidnappin' a officer? You reckon that's smart?"

Jesse let out a bark of genuine laughter and gestured behind them to the twisted wreckage. "You reckon that's even gonna register, considerin' what a busy day we already had?"

He straightened his face as the mob laughed and shoved the old man back into the crowd. "Now, you gotta know, they're gonna come gunnin' for us all after this." He held up his new blaster. "But they gotta know, the whole game's changed today. We stay in contact with each other, we work together, we come together again, maybe, for another big job like this one, an' ain't tellin' what we can't get done."

* * * * *

Dry Wood Creek was not even a one horse town, it was a one mule town. But it had a bank, in a fancy new brick building, and Jesse did not want to take too big a bite on a day when Frank was feeling peevish, and Cole was off tracking down his cousin Ringo. So Jesse and a small team of greenhorns, loaded for bear but keeping their new blasters hidden, rode into town from opposite ends. They came up on the bank all nice and quiet, and entered as smooth as you please, all smiles and easy courtesy.

Word was the local lawman was packing a blaster of his own, and Jesse had decided that you could never have too many blasters, so grabbing some much-needed gold and then skipping town with another shiny new gun did not sound too bad to him. Jesse knew, however, that as soon as the law knew they were carrying the same kind of heat, all hell would break loose, so his boys were under strict instructions not to show their blasters until he gave the high sign. Until then, they were carrying good old fashioned revolvers, and since they had been good enough for years, they would be good enough today. Unless someone showed up with something better, of course.

Inside the bank, it was the work of mere moments to get the squirrely patrons on the floor and the clerks shoveling bills and coins into sacks. One man, maybe a hero in his own head, maybe just unlucky, sat against a back wall, his own blood drawing a sloppy line down behind him where he slid after one of Jesse's boys had shot him.

Jesse moved to a front door and glanced out into the packed dirt of the street. The gunshot should have the law coming up on them any time now. Truth to tell, he was itching to use the new shooting irons himself, even if they did have the damned 'U.S.' pressed into them, and was hoping things went down as planned.

"You boys been doin' some mischief in there, now?" The voice was high and reedy, but it was not scared or concerned in any way.

Jesse moved around to look down the other end of the street and cursed to see a small group of men sitting their horses, calmly watching the bank. Several of them were holding new pistols or rifles. He turned to give his men their last orders when he saw one of the young kids step up to the window and smashed it out with the butt of his pistol.

"You gonna stop us, you bastards?" Jesse had to give the kid credit for guts, anyway.

"Well, gee . . . Bob, you reckonin' on stoppin' 'em?" The tall man in the middle said with a smile.

The man to his left grinned and shook his head. "Nope. I don't care. Emmett, you gonna stop 'em?"

Another man on the other side spit a dollop of tobacco juice into the street. "Nah. Ain't been paid in over a month. Grat?"

The man in the middle smiled even wider. "Well, I figure we don't do somethin', we ain't never gonna get paid."

Without warning, he fired his Union blaster through the window, through the wall, and through the mouthy kid. The kid's legs, all that was not splattered across the screaming crowd and the back wall, staggered back and flopped over, still kicking.

"Damnit," muttered Jesse.

Bolt after crimson bolt slashed into the bank as Jesse's boys dove for cover. Even though they had seen the new weapons in action, nothing could have prepared them for being on the receiving end of such hellish fury. The back wall had taken fire, and smoke and dust were already filling up the bank.

"Get 'em!" Jesse shouted, and fired his own blaster through the small door window. He saw the bolt hit one the center man's horse through the barrel, and the sheriff was launched into the air as the animal exploded in looping guts and shreds of fur-lined meat. Jesse's next shot caught a deputy in the shoulder and blew a hole that stretched from his armpit to his ear, head flopping nightmarishly as he slumped off his own horse.

Jesse saw two more of the deputies blasted back against the buildings on the far side of the street before the lawmen retreated around the corner, taking up positions in an alley. Soon, ruby beams were lashing back and forth across the street, and buildings on both sides were smoldering. Jesse lashed the bank patrons through a back door and out an alley, not needing to deal with their screams and scrambling anymore. He'd lost two more men, their innards sprayed across the walls and ceiling. This was not going quite according to plan after all.

After a particularly vicious fusillade of fire back and forth, the building opposite slumped in upon itself, sending sparks rising into the clear sky. The law, laying back as the ashes and sparks settled, seemed to talk to one another for a moment, and there was a pause in the firing. After a few minutes a dirty hanky flew out and landed in the street.

"We wanna talk fer a minute!" The high-pitched voice called out.

"You wanna surrender?" Jesse smiled as he said it, fueled by the violence and the adrenaline.

"No, but might be we can make a little deal . . ."

Jesse looked at his boys. They were exhausted, and a little wild around the eyes. Too green for much more of this, that was for sure. "What kind of deal?"

"My brother Emmett ain't lyin'. We ain't been paid in over a month. These bastards have left us out here to hang, and we sure as hell ain't been paid enough to face down Union weapons! You boys work the train job awhile back?"

Jesse grinned wider. "Mighta been some of us were there. Why?"

There was another pause. "You Jesse James?"

The grin was so wide as to split his face. "Who's asking?"

"Name's Grat Dalton. My brothers Emmett and Bob. Cousins with Cole Younger, actually. He in there with you?"

That took a little of the grin off Jesse's face. "Nope, went down south lookin' fer Johnny Ringo. What's it matter, though? You still wearin' that tin star?"

"We followed our brother Frank into the Law, Mr. James. Frank's dead, though, and the pay's been dyin' off, and like I said, ain't no pay enough to get blasted like that. We been talkin', for a while now. Knew the day'd come, we got out of lawin'. Looks like, we work somethin' out here, that day might be today."

Jesse sat with his back against the door for a second thinking. "How much you want?"

"Well, I figure, you give us half, we each ride out in separate directions. We might meet up again, as associates or whatnot, but today'd be done and clear."

The thought of another rival gang toting Union weaponry on the wrong side of the law was not pleasing to Jesse, but he knew the advantage was still on the Dalton's side, and half the money breathing would be better than all the money burning any day of the week. He'd always known you could never trust a lawman, but he'd never figured it would weigh in his favor one day.

"Sounds good, Mr. Dalton." He kicked the door gently open. "Welcome to the side of righteousness."

* * * * *

The Red Dog Saloon was nearly empty, which was how Jesse liked it when he was feeling peckish. Frank was making noises about leaving the gang again, accusing him of greed and envy and every other sin dripping from the Good Book. He did not understand Jesse's all-consuming drive to slap the Union in the face and make them sting for all the wrongs they had done. Jesse was hoping his brother would join him on this latest job, but he was not holding his breath.

Across the dusty street was a mighty two story building of brick and masonry, the word 'Bank' etched into a granite plate over the big double doors. This small burg of Carthage was growing quickly, and the region had been graced with a new savings association to feed that growth. Jesse meant to get a cut of that action today, with or without his brother.

The batwing doors creaked uneasily open and Jesse's eyes flicked in that direction from old habit, not really concerned with who might be coming in. It was an old man, scarred face twisted and bitter, eyes flicking around the room suspiciously from beneath a shock of white hair. The man hobbled in, cane clacking on the wooden slats of the floor. Two hulking men in long shapeless dusters shuffled in behind the old man, faces hidden completely beneath slouch hats over drawn hoods. Jesse's eyes slid right over the old man, but the sight of two men with hats and hoods on in the heat of deep summer was more than enough to catch his attention.

The man limped past Jesse's table and sat nearby at another that offered an equally unobstructed view of the street. The shambling companions did not sit at the table, but rather moved to stand behind the old man without direction or guidance, taking up a guarding position on either side of him. He waved at the bar without looking, grunted something, and for some reason the bartender jumped up and hurried over with a glass and a bottle, as if the old gent was some big swell. Jesse looked more closely, but there was nothing great that he could see. The barman seemed more scared than a long-tailed cat in a room full of rocking chairs, though, as he scurried back behind the counter as quickly as he could. Jesse's eyes flicked back to the old man again, but he was staring out the window, and a growing suspicion began to itch in the back of the outlaw's brain.

"Planning on making a withdrawal, old timer?" Jesse tried to stop himself, but his frustration with Frank and the rest of the ill-tempered outlaws was getting the better of him. No way was this old stick going to rob a bank. He looked so old he was afraid he wouldn't die, but Jesse could not help but poke him.

The old man's eyes rolled slowly from the street to the outlaw, and his face twitched into a leering half-smile. His grizzled mutton chops hid what looked like some type of metal gizmo sunk into one eye socket. "It might be I am, son. Any of that money in there yours? You might want to take it out before this afternoon, if so."

The itch in the back of Jesse's mind got worse. "I reckon it's all mine, old man, and I reckon I'll be getting it whenever I damn well please."

The man's smile grew wider, showing small, pointed teeth in an unsettling, shark-like expression that went well with his dead eye. "Do not mistake age for feebleness, young man. There is always more than one road to Rome."

Jesse's eyebrows came down in confusion and the man laughed a mean little snort that brought them down even lower. “Listen, crow-bait, you have no idea who you’re dealing with, obviously.” And he laid his blaster down on the table, U.S. stamp prominent on the grip.

The old man’s eyes were wide with surprise and a growing impression of rage as he looked at the gun. Jesse braced himself for the old man to do something rash when the last thing he expected happened . . . the old coot started laughing.

The laughter was high and thin, wheezing through ancient lungs and shaking the man’s thin shoulders convulsively. It went on and on as if he could not stop. He heaved himself up away from his table and Jesse’s hand made an involuntary move toward his gun. He forced his arm to stillness and schooled his face to a calm, expressionless mask. The old man shuffled to his feet with a gasp that interrupted the laughter, but a low chuckling continued.

The old man pushed back his duster to reveal a massive weapon that shamed the gun sitting on the table, despite obviously being descended from the same technology. Stamped into the grip of the old man’s weapon was a ‘B’ and a ‘C’ in fancy, intertwined letters. But even more shocking was the old man’s legs, which appeared to be completely encased in sleek, silver-tinged armor sheathed in tubes, cables, and other odd parts. Jesse stared at the legs and had the creeping thought that it might not even be armor. Had the old man’s legs been replaced by these metal constructs? It was easily the most advanced technology Jesse had ever seen.

“Believe me, young man; I know who I am dealing with far better than you ever could. I think it might be time for you to leave.” Behind the man, the two hulking attendants shuffled forward to stand at either side of him, and Jesse looked up, finally able to see beneath their hoods. He felt the heat drain from his body as if someone had pressed snow down his back.

Beneath the hoods and hats, the two men’s faces were pale, twisted wrecks. Massive gaping wounds crisscrossed the pallid flesh, sewn clumsily together with ugly stitching that pulled at the flaccid meat. Jesse looked from the ruin of a face into the eyes and shrank even further into his seat at the cold, dead, blind orbs that seemed to stare right through him. A dim red glow seemed to flicker within the eyes, but beyond that there was no energy or emotion at all. A faint stink of corruption seemed to hang about the figures as they swayed slightly to either side of the old man.

“What . . . what kind of minstrel show you runnin’, old timer?” Jesse stiffed and forced himself to sit up straighter, putting a brave blank expression on his face. “And what’s up with yer legs, tin man?”

The old man lurched forward in rising anger, his laughter forgotten and his face wild with growing rage. “Maybe you will be forced, through the cruel vagaries of humanity, to choose between clumsy prosthetics or no limbs at all, you little villain. And on that day, you will know how it feels for some young wastrel to bait you with such effrontery.”

The man sneered down for a moment more and then lurched clumsily past, and toward the door, followed by his two clumsy minions. Jesse sat quietly and watched them go, eyes narrow and brow furrowed. At the door, the man stopped and allowed his two servants to move past him as he turned to look back into the saloon at Jesse.

“You may survive to learn discretion, young man, and on that day, maybe we will meet again. Perhaps we may even work together, you never can tell.” He gestured with one clawed hand at the gun still sitting on the table. “You might even tell me one day how you came about owning such a fine piece of stolen firepower.”

He sneered and then turned away, calling out over the shoulder. “And who knows? Perhaps you may even learn a thing or two.”

Jesse could only sit, watching as the batwings swung squealing back and forth through the empty doorway.

Jesse once again realized that the world around him was changing faster than even he could comprehend. He would surely cross paths with this man again, and the outcome would be much different.

* * * * *

"Gunned him down in cold blood, is what I've heard." Cole Younger's voice was low, but it was filled with anger. "Scores 'o folks saw the body, saw the hole in his head, an' he was put in the ground without anyone to say the words over him or nuthin'."

Jesse grunted, but his eyes were scanning the forest around them and his mind was far away. The two men were at the head of a small column of rough boys gathered together to hit a Federal supply column moving west. Jesse could not shake the feeling he had been here before, however. It seemed like none of the jobs he'd picked up recently were panning out, and he was hoping this one would be different. The crazy old man, Carpathian, seemed to know what he was about, but still. He could not shake the feeling he had been chasing ghosts for months now; jobs that seemed to promise aces always dried up completely or resulted in weak tea at best.

News had also traveled fast that the reward on their heads had reach the unholy amount of $100,000 dollars dead or alive; more money than many of them had even believed existed.

Cole, on the other hand, could not stop talking about his missing cousin.

"I went out to the grave site, and you know, someone'd dug 'im up?" The indignity in his voice was humorous, coming from a man who had left so many bodies unburied in his wake, but Jesse doubted the older man was in any mood to have this pointed out to him. "Some said it musta been those Earps, or that damned hack, Holliday. You know those boys are twisted, an' would carry a grudge to Hell and back without havin' to ask."

Jesse mumbled something vaguely sympathetic, still not really listening. The woods all around them seemed to press in, and he could not concentrate on Cole's ranting or anything else at the moment. He knew the men following them were getting tired of the constant running monologue also, and knew he would have to do something soon to shut the old hand up before one of the harder men coming up behind decided to take matters upon themselves.

"There were other rumors, though, of some new gang working in the Territories. Some Able, or Abe, or some such, running with a group of city swells packing the latest in Union gear. Some were saying they worked for Pinkerton, or it was Pinkerton, or something, couldn't quite figure it out, myself, but they had somethin' to do with his death, I just know it."

"Cole, you gotta give it a rest." Jesse tried to be gentle, but he knew that his voice was harsh with his own frustration and annoyance. "We needa stay sharp in these woods. Carpathian didn't think there'd be Republicans this far in, but that old coot don't know everythin'."

Jesse looked behind him as he stepped over a fallen tree. Behind him, the huge man known as The Butcher walked, dark eyes scanning the trees around them.

"Smith, you see anything?"

The big man shook his head, eyes still roving restlessly.

Jesse nodded and moved forward again. Visions of Carpathian's legs, and the huge brutes that accompanied him everywhere, had haunted his thoughts for months now. He knew there was strength there, and the embodiment of the future bearing down on all of them. A future he was still determined to seize for himself, despite the fact that merely possessing the advanced weaponry of the Republicans had not granted him the fame and power he knew he deserved.

It was a moment he would remember for the rest of his life, however long that lasted. His mind, far from the dark forest through which he moved, was completely oblivious of the danger until his first man went down screaming, a glowing blue bar sinking into his spurting neck. Jesse's head whipped around to see that the bar was an arrow, hanging with feathers and other savage fetishes. Several more shafts whistled through the trees. They glowed a deep blue, and when they struck a tree, it exploded in blue fire and crawled with azure lightning.

"Down!" Jesse fell heavily to the wet dirt, pulling his blasters and looking for targets, but the woods appeared as dark and empty as they had for their entire journey. The arrows continued to fall, keeping his men's heads down, and the sound of something heavy crashing through the trees behind him caused him to whip back around onto his back in time to see a giant nightmare creature come bursting out of the darkness; massive claws stretched wide and fanged mouth gaping in a roaring scream. It appeared to be some unholy combination of a man and a savage bear, and it fell upon one of his Missouri boys before the kid could even roll over, ripping him in half and tossing the parts deeper into the trees.

More shadows were moving then, weaving through the trees with unnatural speed. And still the arrows rained down upon them. Whatever the monsters were, they were part of a very well executed ambush, and Jesse knew it would require all the luck he hadn't had for months to get out alive.

"Back! Move down trail, now!" Jesse scrambled backward, firing off the cuff at the bear-thing and the other creatures now emerging, more vile hybrids, combining man and various types of wild animals that tore into his boys as they tried to disengage. The outlaws blasted out in all directions with their Union cutters, shattering trees in the distance and occasionally winging one of the howling fiends. Jesse noticed something almost immediately and stopped firing.

Each time one of his men fired their weapon they were soon bracketed by falling arrows, sparks and arcs of lightning flaring out from their point of impact lighting small, smoldering fires in the underbrush. Most of the arrows were missing as his men kept their heads down, but it was clear that firing a blaster caught the attention of the hidden archers. And then he saw the beasts bearing down on the men, and saw that they, too, were targeting the shooters, tearing into them with violent abandon.

All around him, Jesse's men were dying.

"Come on you mud-sills! Get up and run!" He screamed, all of his frustration and anger burning to the surface and driving him to his feet. He felt an arrow strike his shoulder, the lightning and the fire burning into his shirt and flaring in his eyes, but he did not care as he brought up his blasters and started firing into the creatures around him. Searing bolts of red fury sailed back into the shadows as he laid down covering fire for his surviving men. Behind him, Cole did the same, and the Butcher, massive knife in one hand, pistol in the other, was holding his own against one of the warrior creatures.

The bear-shape reared up before Jesse as he fired his last bolts, howling to keep the attackers' attention. He flipped the weapons up into the air, ejected the spent cartridges, and then slapped the weapons down at his opposite wrists where backup cylinders were held in place with leather thongs. The new cartridges snapped into position and he brought the weapons back up, blasting with both guns into the towering creature's chest. The bolts slapped home one after another, but their red energy seemed to be devoured by an aura that flared with blue energy, leaving the creature nearly undamaged. With each lumbering footstep it came closer, and he knew there would be no escape.

"Run, boys, and let 'em know I went down shootin'!" Jesse howled with a sudden burst of energy, feeling the weight of months of disappointment and unrealized dreams fall away in the face of his imminent death.

The monster was so close he could see the yellowed whites of its beady eyes, and he pointed his blasters directly at them, blazing away at the thing's head. Each bolt, again, was intercepted by that sapphire energy, and not a one of them landed with its full impact.

Just before the creature reached him, his weapons fell silent, their firing mechanisms falling on dead, cold chambers as wisps of red haze leaked from their vents.

"Damn . . ." Jesse muttered just before he felt himself lifted bodily up into the air by his arms. The thing's face was inches from his own, and he could feel its hot breath as it stared down at him. A sudden burning pain in his shoulders flared through him as the thing began to pull his arms in different directions, adding to the constant dull ache of the arrow already sunk there. His vision started to feather into blackness as he felt the beast's claws puncturing the flesh of his wrists, slicing through flesh and muscle and entwining in the sinews beneath.

He was struck by the injustice of it all, of the utter futility of all the striving and struggling that had marked his life, as with a savage twist, the world around him went blissfully black.

* * * * *

A dim, foggy light came swimming slowly back into his eyes as he became aware of his surroundings. Smoke hung in the air, a clash of noisome, unpleasant smells flooded his nostrils, and a blurry shape hovered above him. He tried to speak, but his mouth was as dry as a desert, and his tongue felt swollen and heavy as it moved sluggishly against his wishes. All he could manage was a guttural moan.

"Easy, Mr. James." The voice was familiar, although he could still not see the face clearly enough to identify the man. "Your friends, it would seem, have pulled you from the literal jaws of death. Your injuries are most grievous, and I am afraid your arms are in absolute ruin."

He heard the words, but they carried no concrete meaning for him until the end. Suddenly he panicked, his heart began to hammer in his sore chest, and pain flooded back into his mind. Every inch of his body seemed to burn with agony, but all of that was only a sad echo of the torture of his shredded arms. The fight in the forest came rushing back to him, and his head began to whip back and forth, trying desperately to identify where he was. He felt a tight strap across his forehead, and realized with horror that his head was completely restrained.

Other sounds began to infiltrate his fuddled world. Hulking shapes all around him wheezed and hissed, glowing with a malevolent sanguine gleam, attached to him with pipes, hoses, and wires.

Again he tried to speak, and again could only moan.

"Rest easy, Mr. James." The voice was eerily familiar, and Jesse focused on the blurry shape until the face swam slowly into focus. Spectacles shielded old, tight eyes behind their glare. The rest of the face was hidden behind a broad cloth mask, a cloth hat covering the hair above. But he recognized the eye piece, and there was no comfort in the knowledge.

"Ca . . . Car . . . Carpathian . . ." He croaked out at last, and it was more an accusation than a mere name.

"Yes, Mr. James." The mask moved as if the mouth behind it were smiling, but there was no light of amusement in the single human eye. "Your people have brought you to my facility and begged for me to help you."

Other shapes moved around beside Jesse on the other side. He turned as far as the restraints would allow, to look at Frank, Cole, and The Butcher. Frank reached out and patted his shoulder. "Don't worry, Jesse, we can cover it." At a gesture from the doctor they moved back away, Frank giving one last reassuring grip before letting go.

The eyes moved up and away, looking at something behind Jesse's head and out of his field of vision. "Payment has already been agreed to." He looked down again and this time the amusement was clear. "More gold, it would amuse you to learn, than you would have gained had you gone through with your schemes in Carthage."

There was a slight flare of anger, but there was not enough energy to sustain it, and it died a lonely death in the quiet despair of Jesse's heart. The shape moved closer to him, whispering into his still ear.

"Of course, the money is only the beginning, Mr. James. One day you must repay the debt that remains, and the cost will be . . . steep . . ."

The man moved aside and gestured behind him. On a table nearby Jesse could just see, out of the corner of his eye, two gleaming metal arms surrounded by several angry-looking saws and knives, as well as other objects whose purposes his addled mind could not begin to guess.

Jesse tried to swallow, then nodded silently.

"Is that an agreement, Mr. James? It would be a shame for your burgeoning legend to end here, in this dank, out of the way barn. This is your chance to catch up to the advancing world. I promise you, my techniques and abilities have grown by leaps and bounds since my poor attempts to bolster my own ravaged legs."

Jesse worked his mouth, swallowed around his swollen tongue, and then nodded again. "Do it." It sounded distant and ugly in his own ears, but he saw the doctor nod in turn.

Carpathian placed a rawhide strap into the outlaw's mouth and Jesse bit down upon it. It was his turn to grab the future. It would be a part of him, a part of his body, and no one would be able to take that away from him.

As Carpathian leaned closer to him, a massive, ugly knife held in one hand, Jesse was alarmed to see a smile finally lighting up the doctor's eyes.

The future was about to become part of Jesse James, whether he welcomed it or not.

Honor Among Outlaws

by

Craig Gallant

Prologue

The shadows of the tall pines lurched and danced to the silent music of the campfires, giving the scene a strange, dreamlike atmosphere. Around each fire relaxed the members of a Warrior Nation scout party, speaking quietly and laughing behind raised hands. They were young men and women, the best the tribes of the Nation could spare from the ongoing battles in the east, and White Tree smiled at the sense of calm confidence they projected.

It had been many seasons since White Tree had taken to the trails with a war party. Apart from the great migration itself, when Sitting Bull and the assembled chiefs had led the united Warrior Nation into the west, he had not stirred from the comfort of a camp or long hall since before most of these warriors were born. Far more than his arm, his mind had been his weapon of choice in defense of the tribe.

However, the new age dawning over the lands of the People was drenched in crimson, and every man, woman, and child was called upon to serve in any way they could. When the existence of the ancient relics first came to the attention of the council of chiefs, there was a great deal of skepticism. The Nation was flush with the powers of the Great Spirit, resurgent after an age of dormancy, but in a succession of horrors erupting out of the east, the dreaded European and his nightmare legions had established strongholds across the plains and deserts. The soldiers pursuing the mad Doctor Carpathian cared nothing for the land or the People in the prosecution of their war, and warriors were taxed beyond exhaustion trying to defend their newly-taken land. The elder council knew that behind the European, behind his implacable enemies from the north and even the chaotic lawless men of the west, stalked the ruby-eyed minions of an ancient enemy far greater than any other.

White Tree glanced back into the shadows; the scouts crouching out in the darkness should be relieved, but young Chatan was a good war leader despite his age, and White Tree knew the boy would be replacing his sentries soon. The white-haired elder looked back into the leaping flames, his mind once more wandering along dark, familiar paths.

Each generation of medicine men, for ages beyond counting, had lived with the knowledge of the ancient foe. Each had lived in the hope that the next great battle would not take place in his lifetime. White Tree sighed, for that hope, in his case, had proven fruitless. The red-eyed demons, twisting the hearts and lives of men to suit their dark purposes, were moving across the earth once more, and the elders of the Warrior Nation knew the only hope of combating them was to reclaim the ancient relics of the elder days, secreted throughout this western region in the times before living memory. Faith in the old stories was all they had; that these tales were correct, and that the relics, once united, could destroy a rising darkness that had stalked the earth since the dawning of memory.

White Tree pulled his blanket more tightly across his stooped shoulders as a chill swept down his back. Sitting Bull and the other chiefs had pried open the Nation's eyes, and there was no denying the truth any longer. They were living in the final days of this age, with the ancient enemy rising up around them, and they were alone.

"Chatan, do you not think it time to relieve the scouts?" White Tree cursed himself even as he spoke, remembering the resentment of youth. The boy was doing fine and did not need the meddling of stodgy old men. The medicine man knew he was letting the shadows in his mind color his judgment.

Chatan looked up from the largest, central circle, the fire throwing harsh shadows across his proud face. A flash of annoyance flared in his eyes, but he mastered it quickly enough and nodded. Further proof of his strength and maturity, the elder thought.

The young war leader stood and gestured for the men around one of the outlying fires. "Enapay, Gray Horse, gather your warriors. It is your turn to watch the forest."

The young warriors stood without question and moved off among the towering pines. Each disappeared into the shadows in a different direction. When they were gone, Chatan cocked an eyebrow at White Tree and then sank back to the ground, a shared laugh rippling quietly around the central fire.

White Tree smiled and shook his head, bending back to his own flame and the dark thoughts that haunted him. Chatan was a good man; he had listened well. The chiefs could have made a far worse choice to lead the party searching for the lost valley of Teetonka.

The first cry, tearing out of the shadows, brought White Tree's head jerking up. Around him the warriors were rising, reaching for weapons and calling out into the darkness. Chatan gestured for two groups to move into the forest while he drew two long knives already glowing with a faint blue warmth. Fat sparks of spirit energy snapped off the blades and onto the damp earth while a similar gleam erupted deep within the young warrior's eyes as he squinted out into the darkness.

"Enapay! Gray Horse! Red Leaf! What is wrong?" His voice was strong and steady, carrying none of the self-doubt of youth. Around the fires, the weapons of the war party were all glowing a deep turquoise, dripping liquid fire. White Tree had been too old to master the new ways of the spirit warriors when the Great Spirit had reemerged among the People. He was still in awe at this physical proof of the Spirit's power.

The only answer from the darkness was a heavy silence.

"Chatan," White Tree moved slowly toward the boy, eyes ceaselessly roving through the shadows. "If the scouts have been taken, perhaps more than just your blades will be called for . . . "

The young warrior looked quickly at the elder, a momentary fear in his glowing eyes, before he nodded sharply.

"Namid," another warrior sidled near, her eyes fixed on the forest around them. "Keep the clearing secure and defend the elder at all costs."

The other young warrior looked concerned for a moment before nodding. "You will take to the woods?"

Chatan was already placing his weapons beside the fire, his eyes shining like miniature stars. "The Great Spirit will guide and protect me. You protect the elder."

Even watching for the moment, White Tree was startled by how quickly Chatan disappeared into the darkness.

Namid began to deploy the remaining warriors around the outskirts of the clearing while White Tree moved to pick up one of Chatan's fighting knives. The blade was hard and sharp, obsidian polished to a deep shine, but there was no mystical fire in it now. The elder gripped the handle tightly and moved to stand beside the young woman assigned to guard the clearing. Together, they stared into the darkness.

"You boys got any room 'round yer fires? It's pretty cold up here 'n the mountains!" The voice was harsh, seeming to emerge from the shadows all around. It spoke in the English of the invaders rather than any of the languages of the People, and it sent a cold chill racing down White Tree's back. How had they defeated the sentries without a sound?

"Now, boys, you know you ain't in a good position, with or without you all got your eyes all glowy and whatnot." The mocking tones were clear, and the remaining warriors began to bridle beneath their impact.

A dull, muffled detonation sounded in the distance. A cloud of smoke, eerily lit from within by a snap of red flame, erupted off to White Tree's left, followed immediately by an angry streak of crimson light slapping through the leaves toward them. The missile briefly illuminated the forest around the war party in stark red tones, wild, dark-ruby shadows swinging in wild counterpoint as it slashed into the clearing.

The bolt flashed between two warriors, across the clearing, and struck another in the back. The poor boy's body was shattered by the impact, arms flown wide, the ghost of a cry emerging before the ravening fire of the blast consumed the breath from his lungs. The body tumbled into a still heap, streamers of red-tinged smoke rising from the ruin of its back.

"Well, seems you got some room there now, yeah?" The same voice, coming from another direction entirely, mocked them once again. "But you know what?" The voice turned thoughtful. "I do believe we'll just kill the lot of you and then have a seat when there's plenty o' room. What d'you say about that?"

Suddenly the forest was alive with fierce crimson bolts, smacking through the trees and striking warriors down all around. The rattle of demonic gunfire echoed from all directions as the warriors, shaken out of their astonishment, flung themselves into the darkness with ululating war cries.

Namid, Chatan's warnings forgotten, leapt after the others, leaving the elder alone with the gently-snapping camp fires. White Tree knew he would be less than useless trying to follow and so moved slowly to the bole of a giant pine. He crouched into the shadows and followed the battle from his hidden vantage point.

Crimson bolts were answered by the electrical flash of spirit energy as the warriors fired their charged arrows at targets White Tree could not see. Streaks of red and blue passed each other in a chaotic mayhem of light and shadow. Many of the bolts blasted the thick trunks of trees in passing, filling the night with shattered splintering and firefly sparks, illuminating roiling clouds of ash and smoke. Screams echoed among the trees as warriors died. Howls of victory were proof enough that the attackers were not having it all their own way.

As the combat moved deeper into the woods and farther from the clearing, White Tree lost any sense of what was happening. Distant flashes and muffled wails were the only indication that the elder was not completely alone. Carefully, he rose and began to move toward the fighting, the long knife held high and at the ready. He saw the twisted bodies of young Nation warriors who had been blasted by the demonic weapons the European had introduced to the land, their faces contorted with the savage pain of their last moments. A building anger caused the knife blade to tremble as the elder's mind registered the extent of the massacre.

Soon, however, the bodies of strangers were intermixed with the fallen warriors, and White Tree bent down to inspect these new dead as best he could in the shifting shadows. Worn leathers, old gear but well-maintained, and a mix of weapons showing hard use all pointed to one thing: outlaws. If these men had been fighters for the brutal Union they would have been in uniform, their gear more standardized and better-maintained. If they were deputies of the self-proclaimed men of law, there would have been glittering metal stars of office. And only a cursory investigation proved that they were not the abominations of Doctor Carpathian.

White Tree stood and continued to move carefully through the shifting darkness. The battle still raged ahead of him, the blue and crimson flashes like distant heat lightning on the rolling plains of his youth. He began to move faster as his heart perceived a slackening in the azure flames.

"Come on, ya damned savages!" It was the same taunting voice, coming out of the blinding swirl of light and shadow. "Ain't ya got no more fight in ya than that?"

White Tree came slowly out into a wide clearing, a shallow stream flowing away on the far side. Most of the warriors of the war party were scattered across the grassy sward, bodies twisted in violent death. The number of dead outlaws here was nearly equal, but at least the same number, appearing unhurt, were standing along the tree line opposite. In their center stood a young looking scoundrel with a red kerchief tied around his neck, pulled to one side. He wielded two old-style six shooters that bore the obvious marks of upgraded weapons, the tell-tale red gleam from various components announcing the presence of the European's foul technology and the corrupting energy of his unnatural new energy source.

Nearer to White Tree crouched the remnants of the war party, their turquoise flames guttering in the darkness. There were not many left.

"Well, now, I guess we know who the curly wolves are, don' we, boys?" The young man laughed and his friends quickly joined in. "Figure we better clean this up, call it a night?"

A resounding shriek echoed from above and a streaking blur fell from the trees overhead. A creature out of nightmare dropped among the outlaws; a grotesque amalgam of man and some mysterious bird of prey. Hands hooked into brutal claws, glittering talons erupting from fingers, sank into the eyes of an outlaw. The man spun, screaming, down into the dirt. The nightmare vision's head slashed down again. Its vicious, hooked beak tore into another man's head, sending a shower of blood across his companions.

White Tree shrank back for a moment. He had never become accustomed to the changes wrought by the Great Spirit upon its most potent warriors. The familiar form of Chatan was scarcely recognizable within the twisted, violent creature tearing into the outlaws before him. But the elder was a warrior still, in his heart, and he gestured at the rest of the war party.

"Move forward! To Chatan!" And with that, White Tree ran toward the startled outlaw posse, the thrill of battle singing in his veins. Behind him, the remaining men and women rose up, the flames in their eyes and along their weapons roaring back to azure life.

The young outlaw leader grinned to see the renewed attack and waved one of his altered pistols into the shadows behind him.

"Guess you were right, Clem! Let'er rip!" The man's smile turned savage as a quick clattering from the darkness was followed by an explosion as if the world was ending. A seemingly unending spray of crimson bolts flew from the shadows, slashing out with the constant hammer-blows of an automatic weapon.

White Tree felt as if he'd been kicked by a horse and found himself flying sideways through the air. An alarming numbness spread out from his side, but not before he felt burning heat as a wash of blood ran down his ribs. His head was spinning as he landed in the soft grass, the ironic counterpoint to the violence and the pain resonating in his mind. All around him, the few remaining warriors were pounded off their feet, their spirit fires extinguished and their blood spraying across the cool grass.

Through the haze of pain and despair closing down around him, White Tree watched as the spirit creature that was brave Chatan slashed through the outlaws. The young outlaw leader danced among his own men, many standing still in shock, and cracked blast after blast against the young warrior. Chatan leapt into the air, spinning around as he soared over the heads of the outlaws, landing lightly behind one large brute wielding a massive meat cleaver. The talon-hands arced up, blood-spattered claws hooked to strike.

"Watch it, Smiley, somethin' behind ya!" The young man had spun around with the Warrior Nation scout, and as Chatan landed, ready to strike, the outlaw was bringing both of his pistols into line with the warrior's bare chest.

"Fly away, birdie!" The young man sneered, and then fired both pistols. The dual streaks slashed out, striking Chatan in the chest and blowing him backward into the trees. The azure flame in his eyes, wide in surprise in the moment before the outlaw fired, was quenched before his body tumbled to a halt in the dirt.

White Tree slumped down, his vision fading and his mind beginning to wander. Who would recover the artifact . . . if there even was an artifact in Teetonka valley? His people needed him. The chiefs had entrusted the wellbeing of these young warriors to his care . . .

The elder felt the cool grass against his cheek and fought to claw his way back into consciousness. There was so much that needed to be done. But he was so very tired, and the leaden numbness from his side was spreading across his entire body.

"How many's that?" A voice on the edge of his awareness dragged him back. The voice seemed so young.

"Twenty, Billy. We got 'em all." Another voice, harsher and more grating. " W e l l , twenty one if you count the old one, but o' course we ain't got his yet."

The voices drifted back and forth, but seemed to wander closer. White Tree felt the Great Spirit summoning him, and was filled with a sudden desperation to answer the call. Something within him screamed that he needed to flee this life and listen no further to the voices closing in.

"Still," the young voice again. "These folks are pretty far afield. And they're all a lot younger than you'd expect, exceptin' pops, here."

White Tree's spirit tried desperately, but the voices called him back, and he was unable to deny them.

A burning pain flared in the body he had forgotten, dragging him screaming out of the shadow realm between life and death. He could see nothing but a red-tinged blur and the voices speaking above him were distorted and strange, but still he could not sink away.

"So, old man, what brings you so far from the new hunting grounds?"

The voice lowered toward him, circling ever-nearer.

There were things White Tree must not say. Knowledge he dare not pass on to one so clearly tainted by the evil of the ancients. But what were they? He felt the most sacred knowledge slipping from him, and tried desperately to retain it. He felt his dry lips, salty with his own bloody, forming the words, giving shape to the sacred trust. Teetonka. The artifact. He remembered. He remembered, and his lips smiled as he felt a vague tugging across the throat of his body, and his spirit was allowed to drift downward once more, into the Spirit Realm, to continue his journey.

In a blood-drenched clearing far above, a young man's face creased in a very similar smile.

Chapter 1

The Union packet boat, Lincoln's Gift, roared up the wide waters of the Missouri River. It kicked up a frothing wake behind it. The massive RJ-1027-powered engines that took up the rear third of the small craft thundered out across the water as red-tinged flames shot from the exhaust pipes along the boat's flanks. It had the sleek, hard lines of a predator as it slid in an easy back and forth motion that tore the river into foaming waves that were left to pound the distant green banks as it passed.

On the shore to either side, keeping pace with the boat, two outriders hunched over the control consoles of their armored steeds. Heavy iron bodies stretched over eight feet long from scooped nose fairings to flaring exhaust funnels. A pair of long metal skids hung below the trim bodies, skimming a foot over the grass and brush growing along the river's edge. The Iron Horses had made their first appearance nearly twenty years ago, but they were a common sight throughout the western territories in modern times.

Slung high on the front of each vehicle, to either side of the rider's dust fairing, hung a pair of heavy weapons. The lead 'Horse on either bank was armed with rotating Gatling cannons, RJ-1027 telltale lights winking among the boxy firing mechanisms of the weapons. Rocket pods nestled in the weapon mounts of the rearmost vehicles. Their massive bores seemed to scent the air ahead for trouble.

The crew of the Lincoln's Gift was sweating horribly within the armored confines of their crew compartment. The heat of the summer sun blazed down from above. Combined with the furnace bellow of the massive engines, the temperatures inside were barely tolerable whenever the boat was battened down for full thrust. All viewports were closed and sealed; cutting off nearly all circulation of outside air and leaving only the narrow vision slits to navigate by. The crew was out of uniform, wearing only soaked undershirts above their blue trousers. Only the most inhumane officer would hold any crew to standard codes of dress during the very rare Treasury run out to the territories.

The coin to run the territories was almost always transported by Union Heavy Rail; the enormous armored behemoths that growled along the railways of the continent. Occasionally, due to maintenance schedules, military movements, or some other, less-obvious intrusion on the status quo, one of the armored Union packet boats had to make the run instead. On those trips, the crews knew that more than the standard oversight would be in effect.

Each man's mind was never far from the heavy strongbox that sat in the boat's small, locked hold just aft of the crew compartment. Holding the bullion necessary to keep the western territories operating for a month, the gold would have been enough to set up the four men pushing the packet boat westward as petty kings for life. If only it were not marked by the government for easy tracking. And, of course, if only they could spirit it away from the Federal agent that accompanied each shipment.

There were rumors among the men and women of the packet boat that a crew had tried it once. No one could agree on what happened to them, but the details of every version were gruesome enough that no one had turned traitor in living memory.

The man in the dark suit stood calmly at the rear of the crew compartment, despite the horrific heat and the constant shifting of the boat beneath him. His eyes were hidden behind dark, smoky goggles. However, a gleam of crimson occasionally escaped, hinting at advanced augmentation of some kind. He wore a massive Union blaster strapped to one hip, and the weapon did all his talking for him. The agent had not uttered a single word since boarding back in St. Louis. The crew went about their work, casting an occasional daunted look aft.

Otherwise, the group took no notice of the large, dark figure in their midst. Lieutenant Truett kept his gloved hands tight on the helm and his mind focused on the river ahead. Each bump and shudder registered through the old wooden wheel. He read the signals like words in a child's chapter book. He had been aboard packet boats since the War Between the States, and had captained Lincoln's Gift for nearly five years. He never looked forward to his turn at the Treasury run, but his daddy had always told him when he balked at work as a kid that the soonest run was soonest done. He took that advice to heart each time he shut down the hatches and viewports on the old Gift and prepared to the run the gold to the hayseeds running amok out west.

The lieutenant kept his hands on the wheel steady as he peered out the tiny slit to starboard. He could just see the two escorting Iron Horses soaring along on the bank of the river. Even after all these years, it seemed strange to watch such heavy machines floating on cushions of thickened air. The boat crews never knew the men and women who rode herd on these trips. They joined the boats just outside of St. Louis and flew along with her to Kansas City, where they peeled off and presumably made the return trip.

He shrugged; each to his own. When they got to Kansas City, the gold would be the agent's trouble, and Truett would be free to enjoy the barbarian society's entertainments for a night before returning to civilization. If the cavalry boys were alright sucking dust for most of a day and a night, that was their lookout. Mama Truett had not raised such a dummy.

Truett's second in command, Engineer's Mate Hadley, waved a hand in the lieutenant's peripheral vision to get his attention. The only way to communicate in the compartment, when the hatches were all secured and the engine was roaring out at top speed, was with gestures. With a rapid fluttering of hand signals, Hadley indicated that they should be stopping soon. Each packet boat running full out needed to stop every four hours or so; long enough for the engine components and hull seams to be inspected for wear and damage.

The lieutenant nodded and flashed two quick gestures to Seaman Graff, the signalman. He moved to the signals station as Truett gunned the engine into a quick surge of power that sent the boat roaring ahead of the 'Horse escorts. There, the flickering signal lamps would be more easily seen. Graff worked the controls for a moment, slamming the handles back and forth several times, and then rushed to a starboard vision slit. He nodded to Truett as he turned and moved to a port slit, and then straightened up, giving the commander an 'okay' sign with his fingers.

Truett pulled back on the throttle of the boat, easing the power down gently so as not to swamp the small craft with its own surging wake. He nodded to the fourth member of the crew, Gunner's Mate Travis Stint, who immediately moved forward and worked the anchoring controls. A shudder ran beneath their feet as the barbed iron dropped from the bow. The metal bower fell into the debris at the bottom of the river and snagged there. After a moment of gentle drifting, the Lincoln's Gift swung slowly to its anchor against the soft but persistent push of the current.

The commander brought the enormous engines down to a low idle and then cut them completely. The silence within the close metal chamber was heavy, the ringing in the crews' ears pushing in on them uncomfortably. The agent continued to stand, unmoved and unmoving, his face immobile behind the dark lenses.

"Alright, boys, let's get this done so we can get moving again. I don't relish the idea of sitting here with a fortune of gold for ballast." Truett nodded to Hadley and Graff. "See to the inspection, but keep it quick. I don't want us to shake apart before we get to KC, but I don't want to sit here all day either." The older man turned to the gunner. "Stint, stand your watch as usual. Man the cupola cannons and keep those cavalry boys honest. No napping while they're supposed to be babysitting the president's coin."

The men saluted and moved off to their areas. Truett turned to the agent and smiled grimly. "Agent, if you would care to conduct your midday inspection of the cargo and sign off?"

The agent nodded once and turned to a small hatch behind him. Spinning the lock wheel with practiced moves, he knelt down to reach inside the hold and pull out a compact iron box. He grunted slightly at the weight, but the container slid out easily enough. He leaned in to open the lock with a key he pulled from around his neck. Truett tried not to watch over the man's shoulder, but the temptation proved too great. That much gold in one place was enough to make even a loyal man like the lieutenant entertain impure thoughts.

The officer whistled and shook his head. He knew it would never do any thief any good, even if they could take out the escorts, peel open the packet boat, and kill the crew. Each of the heavy coins gleamed in the soft red light of the compartment's RJ bulbs, but he knew they would gleam with a tinge of red no matter what color the lighting was. Each coin was enriched with the mystical substance that had changed the world in the last months of the war. The government was jealous of its wealth, and it tracked these government coins with the greedy obsession of a miser. Without this gold, and the structure and stability it paid for, the western territories would soon devolve into utter chaos, threatening to drag the rest of the republic down with them. It was a sobering thought, and more than enough to quench the impure thoughts of a moment before.

"Are we just about ready?" Truett stood up and glanced around the crew compartment. Hadley was still trapped in the broiling confines of the tiny engine room while Graff had moved through a crawl hatch forward to check the seams below and to the bow. Stint gave an all clear, and the agent, pushing the strongbox back into the hold, nodded over his shoulder as he spun the locking wheel tight.

"Just replacing one of the coolant hoses, sir." Hadley's voice was muffled, buried within the maze of pipes, tubes, and arcane components that made up the enormous engines.

"Got a small leak at junction two, sir." Graff shouted from below. "Giving it a quick splash of sealant and we should be good."

Truett settled against the small pilot's seat. He wiped the sweat beading down his forehead with the back of one hand and tilted toward the vision slit, hoping for a slight breeze. Of course, there was none. The lieutenant rested his forehead against the warm metal anyway in the hopes one may come up before it was time to push forward again.

Hadley was backing out of the engine room and Graff had just scrambled back into the crew compartment, gleaming with sweat, when Stint tapped at the collar of the cupola. "Sir, something strange on the south bank – off to port, I mean."

Truett slid off the jump seat and to a vision slit on the port side of the boat. "A little more information, if you please, Gunner's Mate?"

"Sir, I don't know. The cavalrymen over there seem a bit jumpy. And I thought I saw—"

Truett swung his head back and forth in front of the slit trying to find the Iron Horses in the tight field of vision. He found them after a moment and could see that they were, indeed, moving about. One man had dismounted and was moving away from the river, a large blaster rifle raised in a firing position, but sweeping back and forth as if unsure of a target. The other cavalryman was still mounted, but his 'Horse was operational, hovering on a cushion of blurred, dense air and swaying slightly as he brought it around to face away from the river as well.

"Damnit, what do they think they're doing?" Truett muttered. "Stint, anything from the two on the north bank?"

"No sir!" Stint's voice had ratcheted up slightly with this change in routine. "They're watching those two, opposite, sir."

Truett, still bent to the vision slit, shook his head. "Hadley, prep the engines for restart. Graff, be ready with the anchor. If there's something going on out there, I want to be somewhere else as quick as possible."

The agent had moved to another vision slit and was watching the two cavalrymen as well. The man on foot was moving deeper into the trees along the bank, while the active 'Horse was pushing up after him, Gatling guns swiveling, searching for prey.

A furious detonation erupted on the north bank of the river. A dragon's breath of blast wave pushed out over the water and set the packet boat to rocking in the sudden, vicious swell. Truett rushed to the starboard bulkhead and pressed his eye to a vision slit there.

"Stint, talk to me!" The commander's eye roved over the bank. He could not to see what was happening within the restricting little rectangle. With a violent mutter, he stood up and began to spin the securing wheel to the larger hatch. "Toss this over for a game of soldiers." He rumbled. If he could get the larger hatch open he'd be able to see more clearly, better know what should be done—

The butt of a large pistol cracked against the hatch and snapped it shut under his fingers. Truett spun around, face twisted with anger, but came up short as he found himself staring into the warped reflection of his own angry face in the agent's goggles.

"Opening the hatches is against protocol." The man's voice was devoid of any tone or emotion, but carried with it a strength and authority that could not be denied. "We must move forward."

"Sir!" Stint's voice was ragged with shock and fear. "That blast took out one of the cavalry boys! He's – he's in pieces, sir! In the water! His 'Horse was torn to shreds! What could have—"

The young man's legs, standing on the firing platform below the cupola-mounted gun, gave a sudden, savage jerk and then relaxed. The body slumped back down into the compartment. Its head was a bloody, shredded ruin.

"Hadley, now!" Truett snarled aside at the agent as he jumped back into the pilot's position. The Engineer's Mate was frantically working the controls at the aft of the compartment, bringing the engines back to life. Graff slapped the switch for the anchor mechanism and the small motor growled into life. The deck beneath their feet began to shake slightly to a rattling sound forward.

The agent took Stint's body beneath the arms and hauled him back into a corner, sitting the grotesque figure against the aft bulkhead where it would be out of the way. He resumed his position in front of the cargo hatch, blaster held in one steady hand.

Truett brought the throttle forward and the engines behind him roared back into life. The boat surged ahead just as another explosion tore up the northern bank. Bits of burning wood, twisted metal, and other wreckage arced over the water into the lieutenant's narrow field of vision. He tried not to think about what some of the softer, more irregular pieces flying into the river might be as he concentrated on the course ahead.

"Sir!" Graff's shout could barely be heard over the roaring engines. "The anchor's not—"

The boat was wrenched quickly around, throwing everyone off their feet. The agent fell heavily against Stint's body as the howling of the engines rose several octaves. Truett dove back for the controls, bringing the bow of the boat back up in a wide turn into the current before it could be driven ashore. The engines struggled against the ensnared anchor, digging the boat deeper into the water, before the chain gave way and the Lincoln's Gift was launched forward, sending everyone but the lieutenant staggering back against the bulkhead. Truett, braced against the pilot's jump seat, leaned into the thrust and kept his eyes pressed to the vision slit.

"Get to the gun!" The commander's shout was lost in the deafening roar that shook the compartment, but his pointing finger was all that Graff needed. He jumped up onto the blood-stained firing platform, his head and shoulders thrusting through the cupola. At once, the gun collar spun around, facing back into their wake, and the stuttering concussions of the Gatling guns pouring fire aft growled beneath the heavier sound of the engines tearing away at the water beneath them.

Truett navigated the sleek boat around a lazy bend in the river and then pushed the throttle all the way down as he swept on into a straight section, making for the middle of the flow and away from the rocks along the banks. Above them, the firing stopped, and the commander gestured for Hadley to check on their escorts. The young man stepped to the port vision slit first, and then hopped to the starboard side, before turning to Truett with a serious face, shaking his head.

The commander snarled under his breath as he concentrated on the river ahead. Constant slight corrections swayed the boat first one way and then the other as he wove between tumbled rocks. Behind him, the agent pulled Graff off the firing platform and took his place, scanning their wake for any sign of attackers. The signalman and Hadley stood uneasily behind the firing platform, grasping grip rings with white knuckles. Their eyes twitched from the commander's back to the agent's legs and back again. Time stretched on, no further attacks erupted from the blurring shorelines, and the three navy men began slowly to relax.

The agent continued to stand his watch in the cupola, muscles tense and legs unmoving.

*****

An hour had passed since they had lost Stint and their escorts, but no further assaults had occurred. Graff and Hadley had wrapped the Gunner's Mate's body in a rough blanket and wrestled it into a small unsecured hold forward. The agent had come down off the gun not long ago and was standing once again before the cargo hold, face inscrutable. The signalman had taken his place and was standing on the hastily-wiped platform, keeping watch behind them.

Graff had been on watch for a few minutes when the boat thrashed violently without warning; there was a tortured screeching of metal, and his body was yanked upward and out of the hatch. Any scream he may have uttered was lost in the continuous roar of the

RJ engines.

Hadley crouched down in shock and surprise as his friend was sucked from the boat. The agent lunged for the firing platform and Truett shouted soundlessly over his shoulder, demanding to know what had happened. He was whipping his head back and forth between the forward vision slit and Hadley's pale face when the boat staggered beneath them, the noise from the engines rising in a crescendo of furious howls.

Lincoln's Gift careened around in a stuttering arc as the engines whined and screamed. The deck shook to the rhythm of the tormented engines, then jumped sharply as something crashed against the hull. The boat jumped away from the impact but then lurched the other way as something else crashed against the outer armor. An abrasive, grinding sound shook the entire boat and it came to rest, canted up at an odd angle. The engines screamed as if animals in pain and abruptly sputtered into silence.

The deathly stillness was haunting. Truett and Hadley looked to each other and then up to the cupola. The agent eased himself back into the boat, one arm cradled tightly against his ribs. His face was pale but still impassive.

"The gun is gone, torn away." With his good hand he pulled the heavy pistol from its holster. "You will need to open the arms locker."

"What?" Truett's voice was high with disbelief. "How—"

"A chain strung across the river, secured to boulders on either bank." The agent bent down to check on the cargo hold's lock. "It rode along the top of the boat and took out the gun and the gunner." He looked over his shoulder at Truett. "He's still hanging from it behind us. I'm sorry, but you will need to open the arms locker now. They will be upon us at any moment."

"Who?" The commander knew he need to shake off the confusion of his shock, but his mind would not cooperate.

The agent turned his blank gaze upon Hadley. "Can you open the arms locker?"

"I can do it!" Truett pushed past Hadley and the agent and knelt down beside another hatch on the aft bulkhead. He spun several dials on a large lock and then snapped the bar open, pulling on the hatch. He withdrew a long blaster rifle and handed it to Hadley. Another was handed back for the agent. He pulled an additional pistol for himself, then rose.

"What should we do?" The commander put every effort into keeping his voice steady. "We're in the middle of the run, hours from anywhere, and we've lost our escorts. How can we—"

The agent held up a small black object with a flaring red light embedded in it. "The Treasury offices in St. Louis know we are in difficulty. They will send help immediately."

"What—?" The Engineer's Mate's eyes were wide with awe.

"Never mind." The agent slipped the box back into a pocket and nodded toward the gaping cupola. "We need to secure the area so we can wait for recovery. This has been elaborate and well-executed." He tilted his head toward the secured hold. "We cannot allow that gold to fall into their hands."

Hadley nodded. "Right. Damn corn-husking dirt farmers."

The commander just shook his head. "We're sure the cavalrymen are down?"

The agent moved toward the firing platform, the rifle gripped by the barrel in his good hand. "Someone took out the ones on the north bank with heavy weapons. The southern team was hit with personal weapons." He tucked the rifle under his bad arm and reached for the twisted wreckage along the edge of the cupola. "We're on our own."

"Hey!" Truett rose and slapped the roof of the compartment with an open palm. When the agent ducked back down the commander shook his head.
"You're wounded. I go first."

The agent thought about it for a moment and then simply nodded, easing himself off the platform.

Truett stepped up onto the platform, trying to ignore the dark stains still clinging to the edges of the metal's diamond texturing. He poked his head through the cupola, past the twisted wreckage of the weapon collar, and just high enough to scan the area around his crippled boat.

The Lincoln's Gift had come to rest up against the southern bank of the river at a relatively wide, shallow point. The bow of the boat was tilted upward against the shoreline, smoke pouring from the engines aft of the hatch. Truett noticed the sad figure hanging limply over the water about a hundred yards downstream and quickly looked away. There were areas of relatively thick scrub pine clumped along either side of the river. More than enough cover to conceal any number of ambushers.

The lieutenant lifted himself up out of the wrecked cupola and onto the tilted deck, drawing both pistols as he came to his feet. His weapons were standard-issue Union blasters, heavy weapons powered by clips of RJ-1027 that fired bursts of crimson fire far more devastating than any black powder weapon they had wielded during the War Between the States. With far more accuracy and range than those antiques he had grown up with, Truett knew that if a target presented itself, he would be able to take it down.

Behind the commander, Hadley lifted himself up out of the boat and onto the deck, a blaster rifle cradled in both hands. Truett gestured for the engineer to keep a watch out over the water and the northern bank as he started to sidle toward the bow, scanning the southern bank for danger. The agent threw his blaster rifle up onto the deck from below and began to crawl up out of the boat as well.

Truett moved to the bow of his boat and looked down. It was not a long drop to the shallow water below, but he was not sure he wanted to abandon the Gift quite so soon. Glancing behind him, the commander could see that Hadley was keeping a good watch out over the glistening water while the agent was settling against an intake fairing. The man cast his shrouded gaze all around, assessing their current situation.

The lieutenant looked back down and crouched, preparing to jump.

"That's a mighty fine rowboat you got yerself there, mister!" The voice came out of a cluster of low pines off to Truett's right. He brought his pistols up, arms straight and firm, but he could not see a target within the shifting shadows beneath the trees.

"Now, that's hardly friendly, is it?" The voice was light, and the old lieutenant felt his anger rising at its tone.

"Show yourself, or we're going to come in and drag you out!" Truett's pistols were rock steady. He edged back down the slanting deck toward Hadley and the government agent, both of whom were now watching the small grove.

"Well, I sure don't wanna be dragged nowhere, an' that's a fact!" The voice laughed. "Though, I'm not sure that I'm all that much concerned. You boys look like you've been havin' a bad day." Somewhere in the shadows, the smile widened. "Looks like you got ten or twenty nets caught up in yer little motor, there!"

Nets in the water. Truett's eyes narrowed as he considered the idea. If they were heavy enough, like the metal nets used by some of the fishermen working the Great River back east . . .

"In the name of the federal government, come out or we shall open fire." The agent may have been injured when the boat heeled over and threw him, but his voice was still strong.

"Oh! The federal government now, is it? Well, that there is certainly a hound of another litter, as they say!" The voice was harder now, and for some reason, Truett was suddenly very aware of how much colder it was outside the crew compartment of his little boat.

"You heard me." The agent eased himself to his feet. "Every minute of this inane chatter makes you look more suspicious to me."

"Well, I wouldn't ever wanna look suspicious to a man from the federal gov'mint, sir. An' that's a fact!" The voice was now a dangerous mix of hard edges and amused disdain, and Truett felt himself grow even colder.

The figure that swaggered out of the shadows was sneering through its beard. Heavy goggles, similar to the agent's, but tinted with a bright red shade, gleamed in the sun beneath the tilted brim of a battered stetson. The stub of a hand-rolled cigarillo hung from the corner of the man's mouth, and his thumbs were hooked nonchalantly in an elaborate cross-draw gun belt. His stance was aggressively casual, and Truett felt the heat rising once again in his chest at the man's clear lack of concern. He felt his hand lifting the pistol before he heard Hadley behind him whisper. "Oh, damn."

The lieutenant was brought up short by the fear and awe in his engineer's voice. His eyes tightened as he took a closer look at the stranger. The man was wearing a duster, common enough in the territories, although out of fashion back east for years. However, the arms of this man's coat had been removed, with fancy stitching around the sleeve hems showing that it was intentional and decorative. Truett's eyes widened as he saw why the arms had been cut away from the long coat.

The man's arms, fully revealed by this custom duster, were not flesh and blood. They were sculpted shapes of iron and rubber, armored sheathing protecting delicate-seeming components within that gleamed silver and gold. The telltale ruby-red glow of RJ power glinted from several points along each arm. As the man lowered one arm and raised the other to tip his hat to the men aboard the wrecked riverboat, the tiny parts inside of each whirred and spun in the sunlight, small bursts of smoke or steam flashing out and pulled away on the gentle breeze.

Only one man in the world had mechanical arms like that. Tales said they had been crafted for him special by the mad European: Doctor Burson Carpathian himself. Carpathian had discovered RJ-1027 and its many applications and changed the world, and the course of the American Civil War, in the process. The man who might have been viewed as a hero was a monster to nearly everyone in the Old States, as word of his terrible experiments and devastating inventions continued to spread. It was said that a savage, mysterious vendetta against the Union hero, General Ulysses S. Grant, had driven him to horrible deeds. Now, back east, anything involving Carpathian or his inventions was looked upon with suspicion and dread.

None of the tales were as dark or fearful as the outlaw whose arms, torn from his body by a Warrior Nation chieftain, had been interchanged with metal replacements by the great doctor.

"Jesse James." For a moment, Truett thought he had spoken without thinking, but out of the corner of his eye he saw the agent step up to the edge of the tilted deck, rifle hanging loosely in his one good arm.

The man on the riverbank nodded. "The one and only, gentlemen!" His smile widened. "And now that the mystery is solved, if you might care to hop on down from up there, we can see about securing you all and liberating my gold?"

The agent had only moved a fraction of an inch, the barrel of his rifle swaying slightly, before those horrible metal arms had flashed down and two enormous weapons, gleaming with the crimson glow of RJ-1027, filled both iron fists. Each was pointing directly at the agent.

"Now, old son, I don't think you wanna be doin' that." James nodded.

"You had a rough enough day as it is. Why not relax, make it a little easier on yerself?" But the smile had never faltered, and the first signs of emotion crossed the agent's face as it tightened up behind the thick goggles.

One of James' pistols floated out to his left, in line with the stern of the crippled boat. "Don't be a hero, son." His voice was flat. "There ain't nothin' or no one on that boat worth dyin' fer. Trust me."

Truett looked back to see Hadley lowering his rifle, a look of sheepish apology on his face. The commander looked back down at James.

"There's three of us, and even you only have two arms." The lieutenant's grip tightened on his pistols and he stood up taller. "You going to shoot all three of us at one time, before we can get a shot off on you?"

From the corner of his eye, Truett could see the agent and Hadley standing taller as well. He knew, whatever he did at this point, they were going to back his play.

James' smile just widened. "Three of you. You new in the territories, there, Billy Yank? You heard o' me, but you think three men at once is goin' to pose a challenge?"

Truett wished he could see the eyes behind those red goggles. The sardonic grin in that trim beard, the careless pose, and the curious tilt to the head were all playing havoc on his mind. The gold on the Gift was important. It was to keep men like this in check. It was to make the territories safer for decent folk. One month's loss would not cause the downfall of the west, but it was more than he wanted this nasty little road agent to get his filthy paws on.

"Roll the dice, bas—" Truett brought his pistols to bear on the outlaw's sneering face. He saw Hadley's rifle rise almost at the same time, and the agent's come up as well. All three of them were going to fire within a second of each other. There was no way—

The lieutenant did not hear the shot that hit him. He felt like someone had kicked his leg out from underneath him. He went down hard on the deck of his boat. His head slammed into the armor with a thick clang, and a sickening haze rose up over his vision. He felt himself rebound off the deck and fall.

There was a staccato string of detonations from terribly close by and yet somehow muffled. There was a strobing crimson light that flashed like summer lightning all around him. He heard a dull splash not far behind, and a gentle sizzle in the distance like rain on the surface of a lake. Then he hit.

Truett landed in the sandy shallows and his breath was knocked out of him. He rolled in the warm water, struggling to breathe, and fought desperately when he felt two hard arms wrap around his chest and begin to haul him backward. His entire body was on fire, pain throbbing in almost every muscle and joint. Only his right leg was free from agony; cold and heavy.

The lieutenant coughed up a stream of water and rolled over onto his stomach, wrenching away from the arms that had dragged him clear of the river. He coughed with ragged breath, trying to struggle to his hands and knees only to tip onto his right side as his cold, heavy limb refused to support him.

"Now, now, kid." The voice was hovering over his head and maddening in its friendly openness. "Don't hurt yerself any more'n you already did."

Truett felt a hard hand patting him on the shoulder and tried to shrink away.

"Don't touch me!" He tried to shout, but it came out as a feeble whimper.

"It sure has been a bad day, now, ain't it." The voice spoke in consoling tones and the hand patted him on the shoulder again. Truett forced his eyes open and looked up into the grinning face of Jesse James. He tried to surge to his feet, but his body failed him, and the outlaw reached out and casually pushed him back into the warm sand.

"Now, son, I'd hate fer you to try to stand up and bleed out, now." James stood up and looked down at Truett, mechanical hands on his hips.

A terrible thought rushed into the commander's mind and drowned all the heat that had settled there. He struggled up onto his elbows and looked down at his legs. Or rather, he looked down at his leg. His right leg ended just below the knee. Ragged tatters of flesh and fabric trailed off into the shallow river where a swirling stain of red eddied away into the deeper water.

"Oh my sacred God . . . " The lieutenant's whispered words were not lost on the outlaw standing above him. James smiled down with an even broader grin.

"Well, you're a might better off than yer friends over yonder." One metal arm rose to indicate the boat.

Every element of Truett's mind shouted at him not to look down that articulated mechanical limb, but he could not stop his head from swiveling on his neck. His eyes searched along the side of his boat and out into the river.

Nearby, floating on its back in the shallows was the dark-clothed body of the agent. A massive red crater had been blasted out of his chest, and the water all around him was cloudy with his blood. The goggles had been torn from his head and crude ruby lenses flashed in the bright sun. Further out, beyond the stern of the wrecked boat, there was nothing to mark the passing of Engineer's Mate Hadley but a few bubbles and an ever-widening pink stain that rushed away downriver while the lieutenant watched.

Truett looked back up at Jesse James, hatred rushing through his body and mind. "You bastard . . . "

James crouched down beside the Union officer and all traces of his grin were gone. "Well now, that's hardly a complimentary thing to say, old son. Especially by a man wearing the uniform of the very folks who hanged my old man, and then whipped me in front of him, tryin' to get at the whereabouts of my big brother." The outlaw leaned back a little to look at Truett's gory wound.

"This looks like it's gonna hurt a whole lot more before it might start gettin' to feel a little bit better, boy." A ghost of the grin came back, but it was cruel and cold. "Which means I got some good news for ya."

Jesse James stood again and drew one of his sleek, custom-looking pistols. "You ain't gonna have to worry about sufferin' through the pain."

"Just kill me, you gray-back bastard!" Truett could feel the tears of rage and frustration coursing down his face. He cursed the weakness of his own body that denied him the dignity of facing this moment with a dry eye. He could feel James pacing around him.

"Oh, you were a dead man the day you named your damned boat, Billy Yank." Jesse James took the toe of one boot and gently settled it over the wounded officer's shattered leg. "Who you think you are, comin' into the territories sportin' a boat with a name like that?"

Truett screamed as the outlaw applied gentle pressure with the boot. James crouched down by his head again and the officer tried to muster the strength and coordination to spit. He only managed to dribble bloody liquid down into his own beard.

"You folks back east, you think you won yer war, but yer wrong." Hot breath brushed against Truett's ear. "Out here, that war ain't even close to bein' done yet. And you ain't even come close to winnin' it. Out here, you ain't just fightin' those of us left who remember the Confederacy. You're fightin' the doc and his monsters; you're fightin' the savages of the Warrior Nation an' all their ghost story shenanigans; an' yer fightin' the people, old son."

Truett watched as Jesse James stood up once more. "Because the people out here, they ain't havin' none of it no more, soldier boy. The world's rollin' along, and it's gonna roll over you, an' yer Union, an' yer president too."

The lieutenant found himself looking down the wide muzzle of the outlaw's pistol. "When you see 'im, you thank Lincoln fer his gift now, ya hear?"

A crimson-edged flash was the last thing Lieutenant Joseph Truett ever saw.

*****

Jesse was stretched out on the canted deck of the wrecked Union packet boat. His mechanical arms were crossed casually behind his head, back resting on the twisted metal wreckage of the weapon cupola. The distant grumbling of Iron Horses had been growing for some time, and it was no surprise when his brother Frank rode up, his machine stopping abruptly in a sharp turn that threw sand and dirt across the body of the dead Union officer.

Another 'Horse roared up behind Frank. The youthful face of John Younger, the fledgling of the notorious outlaw family, smiled beneath layers of grit and trail dust. The young man looked up at the ruined Union boat and whistled.

"Damn, if we didn't do a number on this ol' girl! Eh, Frank?" John Younger leaned in over the control panel behind the wind fairing of his 'Horse to get a better look.

"Well, I'm damned glad those old fishing nets you got from St. Louis worked, Frank." Jesse stood up, brushing non-existent dust from his legs. "I wasn't lookin' forward to tryin' to take this thing down with that old rocket launcher you left me."

"Damnit, Jesse, you were supposed to wait for the rest of us before you took on the survivors! There was a damned federal agent aboard this boat!" Frank swung his leg over the saddle and dismounted, pulling an elegant, elaborate long rifle from its boot behind his seat. He careful sidled down the embankment toward the crumpled bow of the boat.

"Yeah, I know." Jesse grinned at his brother. "You wanna meet 'im? He's takin' a swim right over on the other side of the boat."

Frank shook his head. "An' you din't have to kill every livin' soul, neither. You are gonna get yerself killed one of these days, an' there won't be nothin' I nor anyone else can do about it."

John shrugged. "Looks like he did a pretty thorough job of it, Frank." He smiled up at Jesse and gave him a mocking salute.

Frank snorted. "Yeah, he did a great job. Your brothers blew up two of the cavalrymen, you an' I took out the other two, an' I took out the boat gunner with Sophie here." He patted the scoped long rifle. "Then the chain we strung up took out another one, hangin' yonder." He pointed the rifle at the figure hanging over the river not far away. "And the nets we all put out took out the boat's engines and sent it crashing into the dirt here so he could gun down the wounded folks who survived." He spit off into the sand. "But yeah, he did a great job."

Jesse grinned even wider. "Don't be sore, Frank. It's always your plans work out best." He jumped down into the shallow water. "An' now we got more gold'n we'd know what to do with! We'll be havin' ourselves a hog-killin' time fer months now!"

Frank frowned at his brother and shook his head. "You ain't got the brain's God gave a beaver, Jesse. I swear."

Frank tossed Sophie up onto the tilted deck then jumped up, grabbed ahold of the deck edge, and heaved himself up and onto the boat. He was still talking to himself as he jumped down through the wrecked cupola and into the metal chamber within.

"I thought you was awesome, Jesse." John Younger grinned at Jesse as the outlaw chief sloshed ashore.

"Thanks, John. You guys seen any sign of yer brothers as you rushed up here to save my virtue from the terrible Union?" Jesse walked up to the other man and stood with his back to the officer's sprawled body.

"Well, they was supposed to stay behind an' make sure no one was followin' along. Then they was supposed to get here to back us up backin' you up. But no, I ain't seen 'em yet."

Jesse nodded and turned, moving around the body to look out over the water. Over the constant rushing of the shoreline he could just hear a distant rumble, almost like thunder that never ended but instead built slowly over time. He grinned at John.

"Johnny, I think this might be them makin' their heroic arrival already."

The sound grew louder and louder until there was no doubt. Soon after, three Iron Horses burst out of the brush on the far side of the river and rode straight into the water. Huge clouds of vapor boiled up around the three vehicles as they tore across the Missouri River. Jesse smiled to hear Cole's rebel yell as he shouted out, seeing the crumpled ruin of the boat.

The three eldest brothers tore up out of the river in a cloud of moisture that soaked Jesse, John, and the ruined boat. Cole Younger grinned hugely behind his thick goggles and hooted. “Man alive, that is some ride! You remember when we had to worry about bridges an’ the like, Jesse?”

Jesse nodded as Cole and his brothers leapt off their ‘Horses. The machines growled down to idle, hovering just an inch off the ground. “Yeah, I do, Cole. I hear you boys din’t run into too much trouble takin’ out the Yanks.”

Bob Younger, older only than their little brother John, grunted. He was always putting on grave airs, trying to come over the big man on the scene. “Wasn’t nothin’. They weren’t even watchin’ fer us. Jim took out the first one with rocket pods, ‘n’ the other one, we got ‘em with blasters between us.”

“Weren’t no one followin’, neither. So it’s a good thing you lot din’t need no babysittin’.” Cole grinned and leaned over to spit a stream of tobacco juice into the sandy soil.

John shook his head. “Weren’t us t’all, Cole. Jesse took three of ‘em out all on his own afore we ever got here!”

Cole laughed. “I’m sure that set Frank off into a tizzy, eh?”

“You ladies want to stop with yer afternoon tea and help me with this damned strongbox?” Frank called out from inside the boat. Soon the men were on the tilted deck, tossing small, heavy bags of coin up and then handing them along until they could be thrown onto the shore.

When all the gold coin was piled up in the sand, the outlaws stood around admiring their handy work. “This oughta keep us livin’ the life o’ Riley over in Kansas City for a while more, don’t you think?” John’s smile was as wide and open as a child’s, as if there weren’t dead bodies floating just yards away.

“Well, not exactly.” Frank was crouched down on his haunches, frowning down at the pile. He had a small wooden box in one hand, several winking red lights flashing dully in the sun. When he did not offer any further comment, Cole knocked one foot against his leg.

“What you mean, Frank? By ‘not exactly’?”

Frank shook his head and waved a hand over the pile. “The coins‘re all shot with RJ-1027. This level, won’t fade fer months. An’ no way to get rid of the trace no matter what you do.”

Jesse frowned down at his brother. “What?”

Frank tapped the top bag. “There’s always been rumors they zap all gov’mint gold headin’ west.” He waved the wooden cube. “I ain’t never been sure ‘till now.” Frank stood and stretched his back. “Nope, if we want face value on this plunder, we’re gonna have to bury it and wait a few months at least. Probl’y as much as a year.”

Jesse kicked at the sand as his mechanical hands came to rest on his hips. “Well that ain’t all! We din’t just blast this boat outta the water so’s we could live like paupers fer a year!”

Frank gave his brother a tired, irritated look. “We ain’t livin’ like paupers now, Jesse. We got plenty of coin stashed away, we don’t live too high on the hog. But we might not have to wait, neither.”

The outlaw chief’s lip curled in a barely-controlled scowl. “You see a trail clear o’ this bein’ fer nothin’, Frank, you best speak up now.”

Frank shook his head again. “No, I know some folks, back in St. Louis, can unload gold like this, even with the mark.” He shrugged. “They work for the government, but they ain’t too partic’ler about extra business they can pick up.”

Jesse sighed and crossed his mechanical arms. “So, we don’t just go back to KC and whoop it up, but we can get us the payola?”

Cole laughed. "You mean you don't go back to KC and whoop it up, kickin' yer heels with the lovely Miss Mimms, don't you? I ain't noticed the rest of us moonin' over any dancehall girls lately that'd have us rushin' back to Kansas City any time soon."

Jesse shrugged, shooting the firstborn Younger a sharp look. "I mean, we ain't goin' back to KC?"

Frank shook his head. He picked one of the bags up and tossed it in his hand as if weighing it. "No, I don't think we all need to go into St. Louis. Besides," he looked up and gestured with the bag at his brother's arms. "You stick out like a nun in a whore-house wherever you go, dressed like that. No, I think Cole an' me, we can take care of this."

He shot a warning finger up at the other men. "Now, you keep in mind, marked goods like this, we ain't gonna get even a solid part of what normal gold would be worth. We gonna have to settle with a beggar's share. But that's better than nothin'."

Jesse snorted and threw up his arms, spinning to walk away. "We gotta do it this way, Frank? We can't just unload this plunder in Kansas City?"

Frank gave his brother a pitying look. "Where's your brain, Jesse? We rode all the way out here so we wouldn't draw attention to us layin' low in KC. You wanna push queer gold right where we're livin'? That ain't no way to avoid the marshals, an' you know it." Jesse kicked at the sand and swore under his breath.

"Hey, it ain't all bad!" John Younger grinned. "I always wanted to go see St. Louis! Jesse, you get a coat with some sleeves on, the rest of us are good as we are, an' we all go into town and kick us up a good row in the big city!"

Jesse shook his head. "Naw. I wanna get back. I don't need to go into no big Yank city anyhow."

Cole chuckled. "I knows a lot of folks'd take exception to that remark, there Jesse."

"I don't care none. This is all a crock." Jesse moved back toward the trees where his own Iron Horse was hidden. "I'm goin' back to KC, you boys get what you can for the plunder, and I'll meet you back there. Maybe we do another job when you get back."

"Jesse," Frank's tone had a warning edge to it. "We don't need to do another job anytime soon. We got enough coin to set us up right nice for a while. We need to lay low for a bit. Give the marshals some time to find another diversion."

"We'll see." Jesse did not turn around as he moved into the trees. "I'll see you all in Kansas City."

"Say hello to Misty for us!" Cole laughed and his brothers joined in.

"It'll be a few days, maybe a week before you see us." Frank's voice was sharp. "Don't get into any trouble before we get back."

Chapter 2

The sun beat down on the dusty streets of Tombstone, driving most folks indoors despite the close heat they found there. The bulky shape of a rare civilian Iron Horse sat shimmering in the sun outside the dark, quiet saloon. It might have been a Union castoff cobbled back into working order by a local blacksmith, or one of the crude copies that had been making their way out of Burson Carpathian's hidden city of Payson of late. Long landing skids rested on the rubber bed of one of the recharge pads lining the street. Blurring waves of heat rose off the barrel-shaped forward cowling and empty weapon mounts. The leather seat strapped above the powerful RJ-fueled engine had cracked and dried under the punishing sun. Beside each recharge pad, an RJ generator hummed softly, winking crimson lights barely discernible beneath the sun's hot glare.

A single man in shirt sleeves and a tight vest ran from the protected walkway of a small building and into the headquarters of the self-styled Federal Bureau of Lawmen, formerly the Sheriff's office. He ran past an old crow hunched on a rotten hitching post. The bird barely ruffled a feather in acknowledgement.

Virgil Earp pushed through the creaking door of the office with one balled fist, pulling his hat off with the other and fanning himself desperately.

"Damn, it's hotter'n a whorehouse on nickel night out there!" He sat down heavily in a creaky old chair that was already host to the heavy uniform duster of a Federal Lawman. The room held several desks cluttered with chunks of rock, paperwork, and a strange array of mechanical parts including two RJ power cylinders, their glows a dull, pulsing burgundy.

Wyatt Earp, Over-marshal of the western territories and de facto leader of the Federal Bureau of Lawmen, looked up from the report he was reading with an exasperated sigh.

"Did they have anything?" He looked pointedly at the flimsy piece of paper clutched in Virgil's fist.

"Don't get 'em in a bunch, Wyatt, town ain't gonna burn down while I catch my breath." The older man carefully folded the paper flat against the desk top and handed it over to his brother.

"Your friend's been seen in Kansas City. No official reports yet, but I sent out specific inquiries, knowin' you'd want hard info before you stirred from here. The wires ain't that reliable out this far, but we should hear something before too long."

Wyatt sat back in his chair, ignoring the plaintive creak from the ancient wood. "What friend are you talkin' about, Virg? I got an awful lot of friends in that line for you to be playin' coy." He glanced over the wrinkled paper and frowned when he came to a name. "Jesse James?"

Virgil smiled widely beneath his massive mustache. "The same. We been gettin' reports he'd moved out east for a few months now, but nothin' certain. That there's from a local sheriff. Claims the word comes from one of Jesse's own men."

Wyatt snorted. "They all turn on each other if you give 'em enough time." He quickly read through the rest of the message.

"No Frank? No Younger boys?"

Virgil shrugged. "Not in that report. But I couldn't ask for much detail. You know how the connection can get." He looked around slowly, grizzled brows pulled together in mild discomfort. "We got anythin' to drink?"

Wyatt turned his chair around to face his desk and cleared an area for the message. "I think I drank the last of it before you came in." His voice was muffled as he bent down over the sheet of paper. "This says there hasn't been any major activity in Kansas City. You'd think if Jesse was there, he'd've felt the itch by now."

"Don't piss where you drink? There's been some activity within a day or so's ride of Kansas City. One big job, took out the Union packet. O' course, the government boys are claimin' it din't have anything onboard, but those ain't easy to take down. A lot of trouble for someone to take, to sink an empty boat." Virgil stood up with a groan and moved to the window, looking out onto the barren street. "Damn, I don't want to go out there again. You ain't got nothin' to drink in here?"

"Comes to that, Jesse's never been the soul of discretion where it came to pissin' and drinkin'." Wyatt stood up with a shrug and joined Virgil by the window. "The boys have been keepin' a jug out back since the heat got up. Ask nicely, they might let you have a sip."

Virgil gave a quick bark of laughter. "They ask nicely and might be I won't drink the whole damned jug."

Wyatt smiled and shook his head. “Come with me first.” He moved to a small side door and jerked it open with a quick pop. “You checked on ‘em lately?”

Virgil followed his brother down a small hall. “Nah, they put my hair up, an’ that’s a fact.”

Wyatt stopped at the end of the hall where a pair of wide doors stood closed. The raw wood made for a marked contrast next to the old, faded paneling of the hallway. The Over-marshal reached out and slapped down a locking bar. With a quick twist, he pulled one door open. Virgil stepped back, hand resting on the butt of his pistol.

The door opened to reveal a small, closet-like room where four human shapes stood stock still. Flickering red lights winked at several points on each body. Rigid metal armor was visible beneath mundane-looking riding leathers and wide-brimmed hats. Each figure sported a single crimson eye flaring from the center of its head, their light pulsing with an eerily synchronized rhythm. Each form wore a large metal star built into its armored chest.

“Well, they look alright to me.” Wyatt stood, eyes running quickly along each figure, glancing with cool familiarity for the story the flickering lights would tell. Each form was connected to a large, barrel-shaped RJ generator by a series of rubber hoses and metal wires.

“Sittin’ here in the dark, just waitin’ for their next chance to raise hell.” Wyatt’s eyes took on a look that mixed equal parts pride and wary discomfort.

“Wyatt,” Virgil’s tone was casual but curious. “You been leadin’ the charge for years to get one of these into every pissant town too poor for a decent whorehouse. You mind tellin’ me why you keep yours locked in a closet?” His voice had picked up an edge of dark humor.

Wyatt turned to his brother with a grin as he swung the doors closed again. “Simple, Virg. Too many folks have been jawin’ about these things spyin’ for Washington and Grant’s pet European Johnny-Come-Lately. Now, I don’t know if that’s happenin’ for a fact ‘r not. But I figure, we got plenty of real live human marshals and deputies hereabouts, we don’t really need these metal brutes on a regular basis. I figure, we keep ‘em in the closet ‘till we need ‘em, we take ‘em out, shake ‘em down, and set ‘em off. Then, when we don’t need ‘em anymore, we put ‘em back in.”

As the door creaked shut, Wyatt rested one hand upon the rough fresh wood as if feeling for a pulse. “Damn if these ain’t interestin’ times we’re livin’ in, eh, Virg?”

Recognizing his brother’s mood, Virgil spun slightly and rested his back against the hallway wall, kicking one boot heel up against the wood. “What you mean?”

The younger marshal knocked on the door twice as if calling the metal men within to open up, shaking his head with a rueful smile. “You remember what it used to be like, before Carpathian? Before Grant came chargin’ over the hill? Before James and his filthy band of pirates took down that first Heavy Rail?” He turned to rest his own back against the wall. “You remember when none of this damned crimson gold existed? It was a man, standin’ or fallin’ on his own, and the speed of his arm was the difference between a tale worth tellin’ and sloppin’ for hogs on some dude’s ranch?”

Virgil screwed up his mouth as if sucking through his teeth, then spat on the floor in a neat, studied movement. “Wyatt, I followed you out here cuz you’ve always been the man with the plan. Whether you were firing lead or bolts of hellfire from your shootin’ irons, I been able to back your play cuz you always been good to me and ours. Now, we got fearsome weapons, and that’s not mistake. But damn, you gotta have noticed by now, those of us who are packin’ RJ on a regular basis, we ain’t getting’ old nearly as fast as we should? And don’ you forget Doc, Wyatt. Without the Union tech they brought out with ‘em, he’d been dead several times over by now.”

“Yeah, an’ we gotta beg for every power cylinder, every gun, and you remember the dancin’ we had to do to get Doc that fancy get up that breaths for ‘im? Like I been sayin’, I don’t know whose team those Union boys are pullin’ for half the time.”

Virgil pushed off the wall and turned to face his younger brother. "Wyatt, Grant and his eastern pals mightn't have the best manners, and they sure's manure don't care about the little folk out in the territories, but we wouldn't be able to do our jobs without 'em. So, we beg when we gotta, we steal when we can, and we stand between the folks an' everythin' that'd roll over 'em, whether it's Injuns, outlaws, or the damned Union itself. But right now, Wyatt, my throat's gonna burst into flames if I don't pour some water down it soon . . . "

Wyatt grinned at Virgil and nodded, spinning on his heel to walk back down the hall. He stopped at the door to the back room and gestured for his brother to go in ahead of him. "Well, you make a good point as always, Virg. And as far as the UR-30s go, if these reports of Jesse James in Kansas City are true, we're probably going to need to bring all four of those galoots out of hibernation before we're done."

In the back room, several younger lawmen were sitting around a large table rolling dice or playing cards under the disapproving glare of an older man in long, black leather robes. The conversation came to an abrupt halt as the older men walked in. The deputies shot each other several furtive glances. Virgil did not seem to notice, kicking one man's boots off the table as he passed, growling something about manners and pig sties. Wyatt pushed through a moment later and tapped the same man on the shoulder.

"Provencher, watch the front." The small man hopped up seeing the Over-marshal standing there, and Wyatt smoothly slid into his seat.

"Ah, boss!" The young man whined, his dark eyes pleading. "Can't I just—"

"The front, shave tail!" Virgil barked. "Or you want another smack upside of your head you'll feel till next Tuesday?"

Provencher shot the Over-marshal's brother a spiteful glance and skulked out of the room.

"Damn, that man's wearing a ten dollar stetson on a five cent head." Virgil shook his head in disbelief. "This here the lot that's gonna save civilization, Wyatt?"

Wyatt put the wrinkled report paper on the cluttered table, nodded to the man in the robe, and looked up at the rest of the men gathered there. "So," the lead lawman smiled wisely at his charges. "What were ya'll talkin' about when Virg an' I happened on in?"

One of the younger marshals looked at the others before clearing his throat. "Seems the Kid turned up in Yuma, claiming the bounty on twenty Injun scalps. Sounds like they had quite a little shindig up in the mountains."

Wyatt stared the younger man down over the tips of his boots, now propped up on the table. "Might you be a tad clearer, Marshal?"

The man cleared his throat and sat up straighter.

"William Bonney, sir. Billy . . . the Kid."

The man in the robe snorted in contempt.

Wyatt snarled and turned to spit on the floor. "These animals and their pet names. G'damned William Billy the damned Kid Bonney! An' who the hell's paying out bounties for scalps in Yuma, for the Lord's sake? Didn't we announce we were stoppin' that?"

Another of the men nodded. "Yessir, we sent that out over the wire first thing after the meeting at the Cosmopolitan. But some's ain't followin' suit, sir."

"The warden over at the Territorial Prison, sir, he's got some strange notions. An' he's been known to back 'em up with gold he says is from the government. Word is, the Kid—"

"Can we please not call him by that ridiculous nickname?" Wyatt's tone was even, but he was clearly getting annoyed.

The deputy speaking swallowed. "Yessir. Bonney, sir. Word is, Bonney turned his twenty scalps in to the warden at the prison, sir, and got paid in good hard gold."

Wyatt stared off into space for several moments, his left hand playing with the end of his mustache. His eyes flashed as he scanned around the room. Many of the younger men were smiling at the news, some even muttering behind raised hands.

"Has anyone given any thought to what Sitting Bull and the other chiefs may well do when news of this reaches them?" The Over-marshal's voice was cold despite the room's oppressive heat.

The man in the robe shook his head. "You're askin' fer a bit much, Over-marshal. Thinking, and whatnot."

That seemed to put a damper on the men. "Well, sir, they're already savages, killin' innocents wherever they go."

Virgil shook his head and looked down at the younger men with contempt, wiping water from his lips with the hand that held the sweating metal cup. "The Warrior Nation hasn't wandered into civilized areas for over a year now. They're out there in the waste-lands, in the hills, deserts, and mountains, running around bouncing off the army troops, Carpathian's nightmares, and anyone else stupid enough to go seeking them out. They haven't been a danger to normal townsfolk in a coon dog's age."

"Well, they weren't much of a threat to the K- . . . to Bonney, sir." Another of the young men tossed out. "I have a cousin in Yuma, said he and his men just threw twenty bloody scalps on the table, pretty as you please, and then tore the dock district up raisin' hell with the gold the warden gave 'em."

"And that's interestin', Johnson, but it doesn't really address the issue at hand, now, does it." It was not a question, and the men at the other end of the table sat up to hear what Wyatt thought the real issue was.

"What was Bonney and his bunch of misfits doing out in the mountains in the first place? How'd they find a Warrior Nation war party? Those folks aren't the easiest to find when they're out in the boonies, and why'd they even go lookin' for the savages? And what in the name of Sam Hill were the Injuns doing out that far west? Twenty Injuns, that's no walk in the park back east, if you follow me."

"Well, they were talkin' that they took some hits, sir. There was a lot of talk that they were splittin' the take on fewer shares than they'd expected."

Wyatt pinched the bridge of his nose with one rough hand. "But what pushed them out there that far? Either of them, for God's sake?" He looked over at his brother. "We ain't heard the end of this, have we Virg?"

Virgil shook his head. "No, Wyatt. No, we ain't. Somethin' goin' on out there, and that's for sure."

The robed man nodded earnestly. "Going to get worse before it gets any better."

Wyatt looked at the robed man. "What do we have over that way? Are there any of our new-minted marshals out that far?"

"Slaughter ranges out that way, sir, but we ain't heard from him in months." He looked apologetic.

Wyatt pursed his lower lip and shot a gust of breath up into his mustache as he thought. "Any UR-30 units around Yuma?"

Blank stares and vaguely-shaken heads were the only responses, and Wyatt lifted up his boots, letting the chair slam back down onto the wooden floor. "Well, fat load of good those damned machines have been, eh? Anyway, send a wireless out for Slaughter. Tell him to be on the lookout for Bonney or any of the men he's known to run with. That damned Johnny Ringo was running with him for a while, along with that Injun outcast, and the big ugly guy with the teeth . . . what was his name?"

Virgil grinned around a thick toothpick. "Williamson. They call him 'Smiley' . . . " The old marshal grinned even wider at the younger men. "You don't want to know why."

Wyatt gave his brother a look before going on. "Anyway, yeah, send out a mes-sage for Slaughter to be on the lookout for any of these boys. I want to know what they're up to, if we can find out. It's about time we hit some of these larger outfits – Bonney, the James 'n' Younger gang, the real players that have been causin' the most grief in the new order."

"Ah, sir, James ain't so bad, surely?" The youngest man in the room was smiling openly. "I mean, he's sorta like Robin Hood, ain't he?"

Another of the younger men perked up. "Yeah! I mean, I heard he took down banks, stages, and the like, but he's the Simon Pure when it comes to raisin' hell out in the territories!"

The younger men were laughing again, slapping each other and nodding.

"You remember the stories come out of Diablo Canyon? Before the UR-30 automaton got sent that way? Place was like a bandit's paradise, and Jesse James was king!"

"He was! He was! They say, before the metal marshal got turned loose on that burg, Jesse'd come an' go like a lord! Wasn't a workin' bank in the town, cuz'a he and his boys!"

"Bah, hobble your lip!" Another young marshal waved away that whole line of thought. "Jesse's yesterday's dime novel, boys! You heard about the scalps! Jesse don't hold a candle to Bil- . . ." A look at the Wyatt brothers sitting blank-faced at the end of the table, then a quick resumption. "William Bonney, that's how he rides! Why, Jesse James is a coffee boiling flannel-mouth when you put him next to Bonney!"

"You ain't got nuthin' under yer hat but hair!" One of the young men stood up, fist on the table. "You gotta shut your shave tail, corn-cracker mouth! Jesse James'd—"

When the butt of Wyatt's massive pistol cracked against the surface of the table, it sounded like an explosion in the small, close room. The heavy metal of the handle left a gauged scar in the surface, and every man, including Virgil, leapt up and stared at him. There was an array of emotions flaring in the eyes around the room that ran the gamut from angry to terrified. Most of the young men were deep into the terrified band.

"I see one of y'all smiling for Jesse James or any of these other yahoos, it'll be the last fool thing you do wearin' one of my stars. An' the next thing you'll be doin' is sittin' in my calaboose for givin' aid and comfort to a confirmed enemy o' the people. Have I made myself crystal clear?"

The Over-marshal's voice was cold, his eyes blazing with radiant hatred. The younger men in the room could only nod as Virgil shook his head and resumed his seat.

"These men are nothin' but unreconstructed algerines, and they," he gestured out the back door to the rest of the town, "don't need us throwin' fuel on the fire of their so-called 'legends'. And as for Jesse James, the man's a foul little bully, a heartless killer, and an empty-headed blowhard playing to the gallery an' feeding off the gullibility of people too stupid to realize they're as much victims of him and his ego as any bank ever was."

Wyatt Earp's eyes were wild as he scanned the room, nostrils flaring. The young men, cowed back into their seats without a sound, could only nod again, eyes pinned to the Over-marshal in his red-faced fury. The robed man stared severely at the cowed youngsters.

Wyatt looked into each man's eyes before leaning back in his chair with a sharp nod. "I trust I won't have to speak on this again. I don't care how the gullible rubes out there feel about a man. Anyone who don't respect the law gets no respect from us. We've got to start reinin' in these bandits, show the people we mean it when we say we can keep 'em safe. First chance we get, we're gonna hit one of the big boys, and we're gonna hit 'em hard."

The Over-marshal reached out and picked up the wrinkled wireless report with a fist that shook with anger. "Jesse James is still the big bug as far as most folks are concerned, regardless of your little shindig here today, and especially if he was behind that boat job. You just know it was loaded with Treasury gold, too. He's been on the shoot the longest." He was calming down a little, and sat back into his chair, a thoughtful look on his face. "If we can put a spoke in his wheel, we can nail his legend to the counter and convince the rest of them to pull in their horns a bit."

Wyatt looked around the room again. Virgil was grinning around the stick in his mouth, but the younger men looked questioning; one of them even on the verge of speaking. The Over-marshal put up a single finger to forestall a potentially-career-ending gaff.

"Jesse was the mastermind behind the big train job that hit that first Union Heavy coming out of Kansas City for the border forts all those years ago. Before that, we had every bunko artist, four-flusher, hard case, and soaplock on the ropes, heeled with the army's castoffs. Not a one of them could stand against even the underpowered RJ weaponry we were gettin' back then. But that all ended the day one man convinced every last knuck and road agent to band together and hit that supply train."

Wyatt's voice had lowered to a harsh whisper, and every man in the room bent closer to hear. "Ever since that day, every one of these low-lives has come at us armed with the heaviest tech around. They're wearin' the armor, they're packin' the guns, and they're ridin' stolen Iron Horses as free as they please." He waved a hand at the men, one of whom had opened his mouth to speak. "I know, they get a lot of their newest stuff from Carpathian now. But it was the plunder from that first job that gave them the stones to make a stand. Sure, they coppered their bets, they lit a shuck out from under James' shadow first chance they got. But it was him that sent them through the mill, put some iron in their spines, and set this all in motion. And you know and I know, they still come together to kick up a big row every now and then."

Wyatt stood up and stabbed each man there with a fiery glance. "Make no mistake, gentlemen, Jesse James is the root cause of almost every fallen marshal, sheriff, and deputy going on over a decade now. It don't matter if he's laying low now. Hell, he could be movin' to set up a homestead with some grass widow out in the prairie for all I know, an' I don't care. We take him down, we settle the score on hundreds of souls demandin' vengeance, we send a clear signal to the rest of those lawless bastards, and we take a big step toward cleanin' up the territories from this point onward."

He sat back down and held up the paper. "We have it on good authority that James is back in Kansas City. God alone knows how long he's been there. Probably tossin' back some tar water every night with the local mamby-pamby deadbeat sheriffs if they're anything like you lot, and couldn't be bothered to send in a report."

Wyatt cleared his throat and then spoke with the full weight of authority in his voice. "We're goin' down to Kansas City right now." He turned to the man in the leather robes. "Is yer Judgment wagon all set and ready to head out?"

The man nodded solemnly. "Fully fueled and armed. It's even got the new wireless unit packed away."

Wyatt grunted in satisfaction. "Good. We'll also want a full squadron o' Interceptors ready to go as soon as the afternoon takes the curse off out there. We're gonna need everyone we can take along, if we want to bring down Jesse James." He turned to Virgil. "We'll want to bring all four of the UR-30s." A look of discomfort passed over his face as he continued in a lower voice. "And we better let Morgan know as well."

Virgil nodded. "Might be time you rethought your decision not to deploy one or two into KC permanently." Virgil got up and moved to a battered sideboard to pour himself another cup of water. "They made good points when they first argued against it, but if they're failing to call in a report on a sightin' of the James 'n' Younger boys, might be time we sent a metal man their way, watch over their shoulders?" The jug yielded a drop or two of lukewarm water. "Damnit. Provencher, get in here!"

The dark haired young marshal stuck his head in the door. "Sir?"

"Go across the street and get some more water from the Cosmopolitan, will you?" Virgil sat back down, gesturing to the sideboard with one casual hand.

"Sir? But . . . the front office . . . and . . . the heat . . . "

"You're makin' some fierce shirker-like noises there, Provencher." The elder Earp cocked a sardonic eyebrow at the miserable officer.

"Sir." The look Provencher shot the older man was ripe with frustration and resentment. As the front door banged shut with a dull sound, rendered flat beneath the heat, Virgil smiled at his brother.

"I'm tellin' you, Wyatt, that boy's hat's nine dollars and ninety five cents too big."

Chapter 3

The gentle swaying of the old horse, liberated from a republican couple too afraid to fight for it several days back, was lulling him to sleep again. The old wound, lack of food, and the hot sun blazing down all conspired against him, but they were old friends compared to the true enemy that sat behind his eyes, mocking his every breath. Defeat, cackling away at the lofty pride of man, rode with him everywhere now, and leached all the color out of the world.

The boy looked up suddenly. Something was not right. The old nag, the dusty Missouri road, even the heat of the sun beating down upon his high gray hat was all familiar to him. Too familiar, for he had never ridden this way before, and he had only stolen the horse a couple days ago. The taste of defeat, though, that was new. He had forgotten over the years how that had felt, how his heart had ached at every beat, knowing that everything he had loved and stood for was passing from the Earth.

The boy felt his chest, where some strange ghost of a memory told him he should find a still-tender wound, only recently healed. The wound that had put him on the sidelines of the great war's last moments, and stolen him from his brother's side just when he was needed the most. The wound was there, but the pain was dull, as if only half remembered, or much more healed than it should have been.

He looked around, starting to grow wary. The occasional clumps of trees were familiar, although they swayed gently back and forth in a breeze that he did not feel. The split-rail fencing along one side of the road echoed similar images in his mind down to the last splinter or scuff. As the road rose up and curved down into a shallow valley, he somehow knew what he was going to see before the old horse had even topped the rise.

A group of men in faded blue uniforms sat on exhausted horses across the road, but they were all staring straight at him as if they had been waiting for his arrival. An officer was in front of the group, with a sergeant at his side, both smiling wicked smiles. This all seemed wrong, but the boy could not have explained why. He remembered the heartache; he felt the thirst, the exhaustion, the despair. But at the same time, he felt almost as if he were in a dancehall show, acting out a part for the amusement of some unseen audience.

"We've been waiting for you, Jesse," the officer called, lifting his voice to carry over the wind in the trees. "You got something you want to say?"

The boy's eyes tightened. How did they know his name? They had not known his name. That last thought, carried through his mind as a whisper from the shadows, concerned him even more.

Who had not known his name?

Jesse shook his head and tried to think clearly. He was on his way home. The men before him, though hated and despised, representative of everything he loathed in the world, were the very men he was searching for. In a young life full of adventure and pain, he was trying to do the right thing, trying to offer his surrender to the men he hated most, so that he could return home and try to salvage what was left of his life.

"I want to surrender." Jesse tried to shout but his throat was dry and sore, and his chest was hurting worse now, as if the pain of his wound was intensifying with the thinking of it. He cleared his throat and tried again. "I want to surrender, like the flyers say."

The Union cavalrymen laughed among themselves, and the officer nodded over his shoulder to them, sharing in their joke.

"Not sure we're going to let you get away so easily, son." The man's face was twisted with hatred, looking less and less human with each passing moment.

This was all wrong. Jesse knew, on some deep, visceral level that he could not explain, that this was wrong. Those soldiers below were savage; they were fierce, but they were just men. They were tired and hungry, and they just wanted to go back to their own homes. It was not until—

"We know you're one of the savages that rode with Bill Anderson, one of those that killed Major Johnson and his entire command back at Centralia." The officer's face began to writhe, its color burning with rage.

Reality seemed to snap into place around Jesse, and he knew what was about to happen. The brave words that rose naturally to his lips died without breath, and he began to urge the old horse backward up over the hill. He raised his hands, desperate to alter the scene, knowing that it was hopeless.

"Ain't no amnesty for savages like you, son. We only got one thing for you." The man who spoke looked like all the other soldiers, except that there seemed to be a flicker or reflection of red flame deep in his sunken eyes. The moment seemed to freeze in the young man's mind. Those eyes. Those eyes had haunted him for years. Wait . . . what did that mean, for years? He could not remember ever seeing them before! Except . . .
Jesse's head began to spin and he lowered his hands to the reins, desperately clinging to the worn leather, feeling their rough texture in his hands as he sawed them back and forth, trying not to fall. The old horse jerked beneath him.

The soldier with the flaring eyes turned to another and whispered something, his face twisted into a cruel grin.

Jesse, even as he swayed and shook on the horse's back, saw the flare of red pass from the one man to the next. The new man, listening with a harsh smirk of his own nodded once and brought his carbine up to his shoulder.

Something was wrong with the gun. He could see the blued metal, the worn wood, as if he were holding it in his hands. It was old, antique, without any of the gleaming dials or indicator lights of a modern weapon. The boy's brow wrinkled in confusion and fear. What had he meant by modern weapon?

The man with the fire in his eyes turned back to Jesse and nodded as they were old friends, his smile widening. "People die in war every day, Jesse. That's just the way it is."

When the carbine fired, it seemed to catch most of the cavalrymen by surprise. Horses shied and started, sending men pulling at their reins as the formation disintegrated.

But Jesse had no attention to spare on the milling, comedic scene. The bullet struck him right in the chest, as he knew it would. Dull, black . . . not crimson. If it had had the crimson trail of RJ, he would be dead; but instead he was . . . what?

Jesse's world tilted with the impact. The bullet had slapped directly into the old wound, redoubling the pain but reassuring him in one way at least: he had already survived an identical wound. That got his mind to thinking further, what were the chances that the scruffy Union bluebelly, taking a snap shot from the back of a shying horse, would hit that exact same place?

Jesse felt himself lose his seat as the old horse slid sideways and down, frightened by the sudden blast and the smell of blood. The shifting saddle tossed Jesse off, spinning dully into the dust, his world shrinking to the flare of pain in his side. The fall seemed to take an eternity, however, and he began to notice that the world around him was again not behaving the way it should.

The trees behind him, lush and green a moment ago, now presented a kaleidoscope of browns and yellows to his spinning vision, the emerald clarity fading before his shocked eyes, the trees wilting and withering away. The color of the sky deadened, the deep blue of the Missouri summer fading to the stark iron of a hot desert noon. Even the smells were changing, grass, mud, and dust giving way to a sterile, dry suffocating emptiness.

By the time Jesse hit the ground, landing on his wounded side, naturally, the entire world around him had changed. He found himself lying on the desiccated sands of an empty desert. There was no sign of the road he had travelled or the horse he had been riding. The trees were gone, the fence was gone, even the Union cavalrymen were gone; although one figure remained for a moment longer, the strange, smiling corporal with the burning eyes. And then, with a swirl of sand, even he was gone. Jesse was completely alone.

The boy looked down to his side where his hand was clutching at his blood-slick shirt. Something about his hand seemed wrong as well, but the pain flaring from the wound denied him the luxury for further analysis. He looked around, not understanding how he could be where he was, and yet, the pain from his wound, the dust in his eyes and throat, and the sun beating down upon his uncovered head were all undeniably real.

He shielded his eyes from the worst of the sun with one upraised hand, searching the horizon for any sign of help. The desert stretched away all around him, featureless and empty, for as far as he could see. Tears burned tracks through the dust on his cheeks and he tried to sit up, gasping as the wound was once again wrenched open, spilling more blood into the hot, dry air.

At the sound of his ragged breath he heard a harsh, hissing croak from nearby. His searching found an enormous black vulture watching him with beady black eyes that flashed with a reflected crimson whenever it bobbed its head from side to side. The vile bird gave another croaking bark that sounded almost like laughter, and Jesse felt a burning desire to throttle the beast if only he could reach it.

With more effort than he had ever been called upon to make, Jesse first got one leg beneath him, then the other. Kneeling in the sand, he paused to catch his breath, hand once again pressed to the wound. He could feel the slick heat of his own blood on his fingers, and something about that bothered him more than he could have said. He flexed the other hand, looking down at it, trying to force his mind to focus, but there was nothing there but the dirty flesh of his own hand. For some reason, that was not right.

Jesse looked up again, casting his eyes all around for lack of anything else to do. This time, however, where before there had been nothing but the emptiness and the vicious bird staring arrogantly at him, now an enormous structure rose up into the burning sky behind him. With another grunt of effort, he pushed himself to his feet, blinking away the tears and the pain, and looked up at the mighty edifice. Even through the haze of his throbbing agony, Jesse could sense that the thing was ancient. Shaped like some kind of stepped pyramid, its sandstone construction was covered with strange symbols and carvings. It was like nothing he had seen before, and yet something about the place called to him. He could sense there was something inside, something that cried out to him. It was an ancient power that seemed to make his bones vibrate with its immediacy.

Not far away, the vulture hopped away from him, hissing a harsh warning call.

Jesse ignored the bird and took a single step toward the structure, then stopped. The hand clamped to his side had tightened of its own volition, digging painfully into the wound and driving him to his knees with a bright new explosion of agony. The desert, the ancient pyramid, even the sun above disappeared in the blazing pain that drove him down, growing more intense as his hand continued to squeeze the tortured flesh. The boy stared down through fresh tears, desperate to understand what was happening. When he saw his hand, time froze once again. It was not his hand.

Jesse was staring at a sleek metal construct, all wheels and gears and pistons, tubes and cables and brass fittings. It was entirely alien, unknown to him, and with a mind of its own it dug deeper into his wound, driving upward toward his heart. Jesse rushed to grab the alien hand with his other, and screamed in terror to see that this hand, too, was an artifact of steel, rubber, and brass. The second hand heeded his commands, however, and grasped the first, attempting to pull it away from the wound. The two arms struggled, causing even further pain as they mauled the injury, and Jesse howled up into the empty sky, his raw voice rippling out across the barren sands; the only reply, the raucous call of the red-eyed vulture as it launched itself into the sky.

*****

Jesse James was fighting for his life. Something bound his limbs as he struggled, wrapped tightly around his sweat-slick torso as he thrashed in the parched darkness. His mind was a panicking blank, visions of empty deserts, grasping metal arms, and flaring red eyes swirling in his brain as he desperately wrestled with an unknown assailant.

"Jesse!" A voice called out to him, sounding far away. "Jesse, stop!"

The words did not sooth him, but rather drove him to greater effort. Stop? When some damned son of a bitch was trying to kill him? Not likely! He thrashed from side to side, trying to hold his attacker's arms back as he attempted to free his own.

His own arms.

The attacker's arms.

"Jesse, it was a bad dream!" The voice again, but this time it was barely a senseless whisper as he realized where he was, and what must have happened. Suddenly, his tense body relaxed, lungs still heaving from the struggle, but shoulders slumped in a mixture of resignation and relief. He was in his small attic room above the Arcadia Saloon in Kansas City, his body was wrapped in sheets drenched with his own sweat, and each hand firmly gripping the opposite forearm as tightly as the mechanical gears and servos would allow.

Jesse forced his fingers to loosen their death-grip, wincing slightly as the rubber feedback pads on the inside of his grip peeled away from the hard metal of his forearm sheaths and pistons. He would not be surprised to see dents in the metal once he got a chance to inspect them in better light.

"Jesse, are you alright?" The voice was softer now, a mixture of concern and fear. "You were runnin' wild there for a little bit. Growlin', screamin' an' the like. Were you havin' a nightmare?"

Jesse smiled a bit despite his roiling mind. There was nothing like waking up to a woman's tender thoughts to set a man straight. He liked to fancy he knew more than most. He could just make out her shape on the other side of the bed, her skin glowing faintly from the ruby indicator lights along his arms and the spark from the bedside lamp's lowered element. But the fear in the girl's voice bothered him, and he reached out into the darkness in her direction.

"A humdinger of a nightmare, there Misty, an' no mistake." He tried to make his voice light, but even in his own ears he knew he was not entirely successful.

He felt the rubber pads graze the showgirl's bare shoulder; felt her shy away from the touch, and his face tightened in the gloom.

He and Misty had been an item since his posse had come to Kansas City a few months earlier. At first she had been just another girl, a roaring good time in a long line of similar experiences. A very pleasant byproduct of his fame, he found many women were drawn to the rougher crowd, and him in particular. Whether it was some instinct to save a bad man, change him, or more akin the fixation of the moth to the flame, the more a woman knew about his past, the easier it was for him to monopolize her time. And he had certainly been monopolizing Misty's. Women were fascinated by his arms, as well, mesmerized by their alien appearance, their hard metal armor, and the countless moving parts ticking away within. Thinking about his arms Jesse frowned again.

"Could you get a light, darlin'? I'm still a might jumpy." He unwound the sheet and settled it in a more comfortable position. Misty reached up to the lamp and turned the key, bringing the element up to a warm glow.

The illumination revealed a pretty face framed by wild honey brown hair falling in ringlets over her shoulders. She turned back to look at him with wide green eyes, and he tried not to notice the edge of fear that remained there, coloring the concern for him just enough that he could not ignore it.

"Baby, you were makin' the worst noises, an' your hands were smashin' against each other like you was workin' a forge right there in the bed!" Her gaze flickered down to the mechanical arms and the ember of fear burned a little brighter. "You sure you're okay?"

Jesse looked at her a moment, sheet pulled up tight beneath her chin despite the little garret's oppressive heat. He wanted to reach out and pull her into a hug, but he had no idea how she would react, given her fixation on his arms. With a frustrated sigh he spun his legs off the bed and reached down for the pair of denim pants he'd dropped there the night before.

"I'm fine. Just a dream is all. You twitch when you're sleepin', don'cha?" he looked over his shoulder at her while he fastened the pants. When she nodded, he nodded back.

"Well, this was the same thing. 'Cept my arms're tougher than yours, and harder, and make a lot more noise. Wasn't nothin'." He threw a shirt over his head as he rose and moved away from the bed.

"Jesse, I din't mean nothin' by it. I was just scared." She was scuttling down the bed now to sit at the foot, legs dangling over, eyes wide. "I din't mean to say nothin' 'bout your arms—"

Jesse felt the frustration and annoyance rising, and he wanted to cut her off before she had his head spinning too fast for him to stop. He turned and held out the gleaming metal hands for her to get a good look.

"You mean these arms, Misty? Nothin' to worry 'bout, with these arms! Best tech money can buy, from anyone!" He gestured broadly with both arms as he danced toward her, a wide grin blossoming across his sharp features. As he moved, the myriad gears, pistons, and counterweights moved with him, causing the various red lights to flash or dim with each movement.

"You know what these arms are capable of, honey." His smile turned a little sly. "You seen 'em drawin' a gun faster'n lightning, you seen 'em flippin' pasteboards at the gaming tables an' shootin' billiards to beat the band, an' you din't seem to have any complaints about 'em last night, now, did you?"

He folded his arms in front of him, noting the play of pistons and gears beneath the bands of armor. The movement within was smooth and seamless, but he could not forget the sensations of the dream, or the waking nightmare of the two arms fighting against each other.

"Maybe I oughta go visit the doc though . . . " His words were soft, hesitation struggling against concern. "Just in case. Payson's a bit of a trek, but our gear's getting' worn anyway. 'Bout time we headed west for a bit."

"You gotta go to the doctor's baby?" She took a step toward him, and he smiled slightly at her concern. "We got doctors right here in Kansas City, you know."

"Nah. Talkin' about Carpathian; the ghoul who fixed me up with these arms. You ain't got no doctors like him 'round here, trust me. You'd know it from the smell." A shadow passed over his eyes and his nose twitched as if he had sensed something foul. He shook his head quickly and threw the dancer a wide smile.

Jesse swooped Misty up in the powerful arms and swung her around the room in a passable imitation of one of the moves he'd seen her perform with the other showgirls plenty of times before. She whooped in surprise as he picked her up and spun her around, a giggle escaping as her feet left the floor, kicking a little before they came to rest again. She held tightly to him after he had stopped spinning, and he tightened his grip, thankful that the episode seemed to be over.

"You got fine arms, Jesse, and no mistake. Ain't none of the local girls ain't jealous o' me, an' you know that." She spoke into the rough spun fabric of his shirt, arms tightening even further as if afraid he would disappear.

Jesse gently disentangled himself from the girl's arms with a grin and a laugh, but he turned away before she could get a good look at his face. Something about her sudden surrender bothered him, and he could not have said what it was. A moment ago he had been desperate to reinforce her affection for him, to distract her from her doubts and fears. And now that he had done just that, he could not shake a rising feeling of guilt.

Jesse moved to the bed and took his gun belt from the bedpost where he had hung it the night before. With quick, practiced motions he whipped the belt around his waist and fastened the buckle, leaning down to tie the leather thongs that would hold each holster in place. Out of habit, he drew the Hyper-velocity pistol riding on his left hip. His iron hand spun the weapon first forward, then backward, and then around in a flat horizontal spin around his trigger finger. The metal of the trigger guard clicked rhythmically against the metal of his finely articulated fingers.

Jesse stopped the gyrations of the pistol with a sharp clack as the pistol grip slapped into the feedback pad of his armored palm. He inspected the weapon quickly. The dull metal of the long, angular barrel thrust out from the cylinder of the RJ power core, which gleamed with the subdued crimson radiance of its constant standby setting. The enrichment cartridge, feeding from beneath the barrel, was fit snuggly in place, indicator light winking its own ruby reassurance.

Jesse flipped the weapon back into its holster with one studied motion. He would check the other later. He moved to the small window opposite the bed and pulled back a curtain to peer out at the street below.

Misty pouted. "You got yer smile, now yer just ridin' off, are you?" She did not try to hide the frustration rising in her voice.

Jesse kept looking out the window, giving no sign at all that he had heard her until he suddenly turned back into the room, his grin back in place, and shook his head.

"You gotta know, Misty, I ain't one to go givin' up what I taken off anyone." He swooped in for a quick kiss and then moved back to the bed, grabbing his heavy boots and dropping to the old mattress with a grunt.

"Where you goin? She wrapped the sheet tighter about herself and sat beside him. "It ain't barely light out yet! Ain't like no one's gonna be open for business at this hour."

Jesse gave a mighty pull with both of his mechanical hands and his foot slid smoothly into his boot. "Well, firstly, darlin', ain't like I much care what some shopkeeper's posted hours are, is it?" He grinned sideways at her before moving to slide on the other boot. "And secondly, ain't like I can go back to sleep now, that damned nightmare still rattlin' around in my skull. Frank an' Cole an' the gang're supposed to be comin' back in today, and I got an idea fer a job I wanna have lined up fer when they land."

Jesse rose once the other boot was on, planted a quick kiss on Misty's forehead, and moved back to the window.

"Frank don't like me." Her voice took on a sulking tone that set Jesse's eyes to rolling. "He don't!" she repeated, as if she could see through his head.

"That's just Frank. He's quiet, and smarter'n everybody in the room, an' no one knows it better'n him." Jesse bent down to get a good view of the street. Misty was not wrong: it was too early for most civilized men to be up and about. The buildings lining the street were tall for the west, but then again, Kansas City was right on the edges of the territories. Not many lights twinkled in those windows, though, and the street itself would have been heavily shadowed if it were not for the lampposts rising out of the wooden sidewalks at regular intervals. The base of each was wide and fat, the glowing crimson telltales of RJ generators gleaming around them.

"Misty, you ever miss the ol' days?" Jesse's voice was soft for a moment, as his eyes focused on the winking red lights far below.

"What?" Her voice was muffled. "What ol' days?"

"You know," he gestured vaguely with his robotic arm at the street below. "Before Carpathian discovered RJ an' made all this tech stuff. When a man on the road just had a normal gun by his side, and he knew the other guy only carried a gun the same kind. None o' these Gatling cannons, or rocket pods, or Heavy Rails or Carpathian's monsters . . . Just seems sometimes like the world was a lot simpler back then."

"Well, I don' know about none o' them guns, an' I only ever heard o' Carpathian's craziness, but I don't remember ever playin' a house that didn't have RJ-powered lights, or ridden in a horse-drawn cart instead of an auto-wagon run by one of them big motors. I reckon, for most of us, the world's a sight better with RJ-1027 than it used to be."

Jesse grunted. "How old you think I am, Misty?"

"I don't know, 'bout my age, prob'ly?" He gave a single harsh grunt of a laugh and her voice was tart as she continued. "You're changin' the subject. I know Frank's older'n you, an' I know he reckons he's smart, but that ain't it. He don't like me. Thinks I'm trouble." She was moving around behind him, most likely getting her own clothes on now that it was clear he was up for the day.

Jesse smiled and turned enough to watch her admiringly. "Well, you are trouble, ain't you, girl?"

She threw a small shoe at him and turned around to adjust her dress. "You got a lot of girls. I know that, Jesse, I ain't dumb. But your brother, he's thinkin' you been around KC too long, and he's blamin' me. I can tell."

Jesse was looking out the window again. The sky in the east was taking on a rough, almost burlap texture as rays of light reached into the west. The light gleamed off the massive glass and steel dome of the Heavy Rail station rising up above the buildings across the street. He imagined what sorts of technological treasures the trains pulling through that station were carrying west nearly every day and felt the feedback pads on his palms twitch.

"Misty," he turned and looked into her deep green eyes. "Frank and me, and the other guys too, I reckon, we seen a lot of people come and go. We seen a lot of friends die, or move on, or even get sick of our bilk and try to turn us in. This life we're leadin'? It's not always a happy one. Frank ain't tryin' to protect me from you, darlin', he's tryin' to protect you from all of us."

Jesse walked to the girl, now in a tight-fitting blue bodice and flowing yellow skirts, and hugged her to him once again. "An' when I'm not bein' selfish, I gotta say, I agree with him. There's paths that'll end much happier for the both of us, ain't got you an' me together on 'em, Misty." He kissed the top of her hair. "You deserve better'n I can give you, more security, and more o' my time. I just gotta grow up enough to let you go."

He held her out at arms' length, the mechanisms of the limbs whirring and clicking as he moved. His grin was back in full force. "But I ain't grown up yet, and I've had more opportunity than you'd guess from lookin' at me. So I'm thinkin', till I do grow up, you're stuck with me, whatever Frank says, or thinks, or feels."

She smiled up shyly at him and kissed him quickly. He ended the kiss first, pulling away from her before she had begun to loosen her own grip.

"I'm goin' over to the station, see what's comin' through over the next few days, an' see what I can hear 'round town. I reckon I'll be back downstairs in time for dinner." He moved toward the door, pulling his hat and coat off a hook on the wall. "You girls still playin' the Occidental?"

Misty nodded at his retreating back. "Yeah."

Jesse stopped in the doorway and flashed his gleaming teeth one more time. "Well, maybe, if Frank and Cole get back in, we'll swing by there, an' we'll see if we can't get Frank to loosen up a bit, eh?" With one last wink he let the door close behind him.

Jesse's heels snapped down the old, dry wood of the narrow hallway toward the steep stairs leading up from the saloon. As he walked, he looked down at his arms, flexing the fingers and rotating the wrists. They seemed perfectly fine, but he could not throw off the memory of the two limbs struggling against each other in his dream. Or when he had awakened.

Jesse shook his head and tramped down the stairs, one hand lightly sliding along the old splintered rail, the feedback pads registering every nick and gnarl.

*****

Across the street, two figures stood together in the darkness of a cheap room, the only illumination leaking in from the lighted window in the back of the Arcadia Saloon. They peered out at the window, watching carefully for any further sign of movement. A moment ago, they had seen a shape look out the window, but there had been no movement since then, and they waited to see what would happen next.

"It's him?" A harsh voice with a northern accent asked.

"Yes. They were quite explicit. The arms and everything. It's him, and some woman." This voice was much higher than the man's, but still strong and heavy. A dusky contralto that matched well with the surroundings.

"I don't give a rat's ass about that damned gold shipment. They think he can lead us to the doctor?" There was doubt in the harsher voice, and the creaking of wooden furniture as the speaker sat down.

"Nothing else has worked, so they think this is at least worth a chance." The lighter voice moved off into the darkness. "And if it turns out he's got the stamped gold, we can pick him up on that, all the better." There was a pause, then a yawn. "I'm going to try to get a little some sleep. Wake me if anything interesting happens."

The heavy voice snorted. "Yeah, I'll do that. I just hope he doesn't do something stupid before we can see what he knows."

Across the street the light continued to burn softly, but nothing in the room moved.

Chapter 4

Jesse focused on the dusty road as it swept beneath the heavy weight of his Iron Horse. Scrub brush flew past on either side of the narrow track, and occasionally he could see the glittering surface of the Missouri River through the tracery of leaves off to his left. It felt good to be out on the trail again, away from the tall buildings and crowded streets of Kansas City.

The outlaw shot a glance to either side, nodding to the men riding there, their Iron Horses rumbling along beside his. He hid his clinging annoyance at Frank's refusal to participate in this latest job behind his ready grin. Frank had been mad enough to bite and had not bothered to hide the fact from any of the other men. Cole Younger and his brothers had followed Frank's lead, as they usually did; leaving Jesse to ride out for the first time in months without any of the old gang beside him. It bothered him more than he was willing to admit, but he knew he could never show that to the men who had agreed to go with him.

Frank was angry, and Jesse knew he had had a good point. They had enough coin laid up in town; they did not need more right now. They had a good thing going in Kansas City, with most of the local law dogs fawning over them and everything the city had to offer laid out before them every night. Frank was also concerned that one of the damned marshals was eventually going to twig to their presence, and then the whole lot of them would be on the run again. Frank was no slick city man, but he liked his comforts sure enough. He would not want to leave Kansas City until absolutely necessary.

Jesse had never been a creature of the city; he felt the call of no-man's land too strongly. He was most at home in the wild places, where a man defended himself, took what he wanted, and kept what he could. He felt the pull back into Missouri, to their old stomping grounds, and he had known he would not be able to deny himself that satisfaction much longer. And so he found himself roaring down an empty road accompanied by a posse he barely knew, but every one of which was desperate to earn himself a place in the legend of Jesse James. That brought a more natural gleam to the smile, and he settled back in his saddle, comfortable with his position, his decisions, and his life.

Frank had been upset when Jesse told him about the plan to take out the bank in Missouri City, a few miles down the river to the east. Missouri City had been a favorite target of theirs during the war, and most of the folks who had reestablished their businesses and their lives were still the same damned republicans that had been trying to lord over his family since before the first shots were fired. Although the coin would be welcome, this little trip was more about sweet revenge than anything else. When the young local back in Kansas City had mentioned the new bank going in down the river, it had seemed too perfect. When he had offered to lead Jesse James there, it was too good an opportunity to pass up.

Who needed Frank anyway? Or Cole and his damned family? These boys seemed plenty sturdy, and besides, it had been too long since he had tested himself under fire. If a man did not push himself every now and then, he went soft. And if a man went soft, someday someone would be coming up behind him when he least expected it, and that would be the end of that. And besides, since when did he ever need an excuse to take a chunk from some hayseed republican?

"Hey, Jesse!" The local boy, riding a borrowed Iron Horse at the rear of the group, called out over the growl of the engines. "You think we could stop for a bit?"

The boy had been getting steadier on his mount all day, although things had gotten off to a shaky start in the morning when he had almost knocked Harding off his feet. He was still swaying a bit from side to side like most new riders, getting used to balancing on the cushion of thickened air that the vehicles rode on, but he was doing alright.

"You need a piss already?" Harding, just ahead of the local, sneered over his shoulder from behind wide, blue-tinged goggles. "We ain't on some church outin', boy!"

The younger man frowned, glancing quickly between Jesse and the other outlaw while still trying to keep an eye on the road ahead. They had not slowed down during the exchange, and he was obviously not entirely sure in his seat.

"No!" His voice was firm. "I just gotta walk this off for a sec is all. Feel free to piss if you need to, though, Harding!" There was just enough attitude in that to get the rest of the men grinning, and Harding's hands tightened on the control handles of the Iron Horse, revving the engine and tearing off up the road ahead. The reddish flame licking out from the drive nozzle lengthened as he worked the engine, red lights flaring along its flanks.

Jesse smiled and nodded to the young man. "Sure, Ty, we can take a bit of a break. I could stand to get a drink myself, maybe take a few steps."

The rest of the men nodded in agreement, as they always did, and the party pulled off into a small clearing, the wide river rushing by not far away. Each vehicle gave a quick, angry snarl as the engine was cut, and then sank towards the soft ground beneath the trees. The men swung their legs up and away from the saddles with easy grace. Ty nearly mirrored them before the heel of his boot caught on the pummel and almost spilled him into the dirt, but he caught himself, grinning openly at the rest of the men.

"Ty, you're gonna have to get better with that thing if you wanna stick around with us." Another outlaw, Gage, shook his head with a quick laugh. "I wouldn't wanna be seen dead with you in public right now, the way you swing that machine all over the road like the worst kind o' greenhorn."

"Not bad for your first time out, though." Jesse hefted a canteen and took a healthy slug before throwing it to another man. "Although I gotta say, you keep ridin' Harding that way, only gonna be room for one of you in this gang, before long."

Ty shrugged as he stood beside his borrowed mount, clearly unconcerned.

"Harding'll do what Harding'll do, an' I can't worry myself about it either way. 'Sides, I'm not here to ride with Harding."

Jesse laughed and almost missed the canteen being lobbed back to him. "Kid, you sure do have some balls, and no mistake. If you're right about this bank, and you don't embarrass us all when the penny drops, I think we might just have a 'Horse you can call your very own when we get back to KC."

Ty nodded in calm agreement. "That's the plan, Jesse. An' you can trust me about this bank. My cousin lives in Missouri City, and she was just sayin' last week that all the folks there were chipper as hell to be gettin' their own savings and loan. The reserves were supposed to be delivered by yesterday, so we should be all set for a mighty withdrawal today, don't you worry."

One of the older men coughed, and then looked sideways at Jesse. "Jesse, you mind if I ask again, how come Frank and them ain't comin' along?"

Jesse's eyes grew cold and he shook his head. "Frank's tired, Chase. He din't wanna go rushin' out after he just got back from bein' away."

"Um, okay." Chase nodded. "But . . . the Youngers?"

Jesse whirled on the other man, one hand floating by the butt of a Hyper-velocity pistol. "You wanna ride with my brother and the Youngers, Chase? Or you wanna ride with me?"

Chase put his hands up and took a step back. "With you, o' course, Jesse! With you! Those other guys, they're coffee boilers next to you! No joke!"

Most of the other men were nodding fiercely, some glaring at Chase for even bringing the question up. Jesse shrugged, slapped the other man on the shoulder, and moved back toward his 'Horse. "They're tired, boys, an' I ain't. That's what it comes down to."

Most of the men chuckled at that, and everything calmed down. Jesse shook his head and turned around to shove the canteen back into his saddle bag. The rest of the men were leaning against their mounts, smoking quirleys. The blue-tinged coils of smoke from the home-made cigarillos were pungent in the clear country air. Two of the men had wandered back toward the road, watching for Harding's return.

"Jesse, you been doin' this for a while, huh?" Ty rested his hands on the worn leather of his saddle, straight arms supporting him as he leaned across to look at the outlaw leader. "Like, I remember hearin' stories of you back before I was hip-high to a horny toad, an' my daddy, he said there'd been stories goin' for years back to when he was little. I was mighty surprised when I met you. You don't look too much older'n me!"

Jesse shrugged. "A man's as old as he feels, kid. An' I feel pretty damned good." He grinned at the other men.

"Man, Jesse, me an' the other kids when we was growin' up, weren't a one of us didn't dream of ridin' with you someday, and look at me!" He gave the saddle a hard slap. "I'm the one who made it!"

"Well, we'll see, kid. Don't get your hopes up. Ain't no tellin' how you'll act once you've seen the elephant." Jesse tipped his hat back a little bit with one metal finger. "Some folks just ain't cut out for the sharp edge. No way of knowin' till you're there."

Ty shook his head. "Nope, this is for me. You ridin' wherever you want, not havin' to listen to nobody, takin' what you want whenever you want it! And the girls! Man, you guys have all the luck with the womenfolk! A kid like me? I can't even get a girl to so much as look at me by wavin' a greenback in her face!"

One of the other men barked a sharp laugh at that. "Kid, you don't wanna go judgin' how much action the rest of us get by watchin' Jesse here. He sort of has a reputation for that sort of thing that belongs to him all alone."

"Ah, keep a hold o' yer jealousy, Chase, kid don't need to hear that." But Jesse's smile was wide as he continued. "Hell, we all got talents we're born with, right? Besides, just because you lot o' trolls can't get a lady to look at you twice, ain't no reason to make the kid here feel like he'll live a life as empty of a lady's affection as you all."

Chase snorted. "Well, you don't seem to be makin' the rounds as fast as you once did neither, old man." The two men returning from the road laughed at that. "All the time you been spendin' with that new sweetheart dancin' girl, half the ladies of KC are pinin' away every night."

"An' so you'd think that'd make it easier for you boys to sweep 'em off their feet while they're distracted, yeah?" Jesse laughed. "But instead, ya'll just end up cryin' into yer joy juice come closin' time every night."

The men laughed good-naturedly, one of them scuffing at the dirt with a heavy boot. But Ty looked far more intense, watching Jesse's face with a steady eye. "She's a beauty, though, that Misty Mimms. Half Kansas City's been in love with her for years, and they fall all over again every night. But you're the one she comes back to, eh, Jesse?"

Jesse nodded with an open smile. "Reckon she does seem smitten, now that you mention it."

"She must have a soft spot for rough n' ready boys, I guess." Ty smiled, but the expression seemed vaguely predatory.

Jesse's face stilled slightly. "Whataya mean, Ty?" He stood up straighter, and the rest of the men quieted, looking from one to the other.

Ty shook his head as if clearing it, his smile showing genuine again. "Oh, just that she was spendin' a lot of time with Bill Bonney a year or so back. Now, it's almost like she's workin' up a collection."

Jesse looked sour for a moment. "Misty used to walk with the Kid?"

Ty's face loosened in thought for a moment, then tightened with concern. "Um, yeah. I wouldn't guess it was nothin', Jesse. He ain't been near KC in almost a year."

Jesse's eyes grew unfocused for a moment, his mechanical hands tightening as he turned to look out through the trees and over the slowly rolling waters of the Missouri. The men exchanged looks with each other, none sure what they should do.

When Jesse turned back around, he gave the young man a quick glance, then swung back up into his saddle. The Iron Horse gave out a throaty growl as he kicked it to life. It lifted up onto its cushion of thick air, wind tearing at the men still standing around him.

"I'm sure it ain't nothin' either, Ty." He pulled his red-tinged goggles down over his eyes. "Let's head out. Missouri City ain't that far away, and we want to get there before Harding decides to go in without us."

He gunned the 'Horse and sent it spinning in a tight circle back toward the road. The men reached for their hats as they jumped into their own saddles, the roaring of motors rising as each iron beast was thrashed back into life.

Ty was the last to jump onto his borrowed steed, watching as Jesse led the way back to the road. His face was blank as he mounted with casual grace, but his eyes, perhaps reflecting the flaring engine wash from the machines ahead of him, glowed crimson as they tightened slightly in amusement.

*****

Jesse pulled his Iron Horse up to where Harding sat, his machine idling roughly in the middle of the road. They were on the crest of a hill overlooking a bend in the Missouri River, and on the other side of the slowly moving water they could see the quiet collection of buildings that marked the center of Missouri City. Men and women, tiny in the distance, moved among the buildings, going about their daily business blissfully unaware of the gathering on the ridge above them.

Jesse stared down for a moment and then cast around looking for Ty. The young man, swerving slightly as he approached, pulled his 'Horse up beside the outlaw leader with a slight jerk and a quick exclamation of concern.

"Easy, Ty, don' wanna lose you this close to the bank!" Jesse reached out one hand, metal gleaming dully in the flashing sun, and grabbed the boy with a solid, steadying grip. Ty nodded his appreciation with an embarrassed grin.

Once the younger man was steady in his saddle, Jesse rocked back onto his own machine and rested his armored forearms across the control panel. He gestured down the hill with a jerk of his chin. "Which one's the bank, kid? They had to pretty much rebuild the whole town since the last time we was through, so it all looks new to me." His grin was wide and warm.

"Well, Jesse," Ty pointed toward the center of the cluster of buildings. "That there, the white one? That's the Missouri City Savings and Loan."

The men scanned the town, several using stolen Union monoculars bulky with RJ-1027 enhancements. Gage grunted once and passed his heavy piece of equipment to Jesse who immediately raised it to his eye and made some minor adjustments. He wished he had Frank with him once again. Frank's long-scoped rifle, Sophie, had the best optics he had ever seen. If anyone could twig to a law dog ambush from afar it was Frank and that damned gun of his.

Within the view of the monocular, the little burg of Missouri City sprang up at him out of a swirling confusion of colors. He panned the machine from one side of town to the other, trying to decipher from the shaky images what sort of opposition they might encounter if they made a direct run in. Beneath the dull blue of the monocular's bulk, Jesse's smile widened even more.

Not even half the buildings below them were sporting RJ-powered generators, which was unusual for a town this far east. Most of the generators he could see, of course, were the bulky units being produced back in Washington and distributed through the government offices. There were a few of Carpathian's more streamlined pieces, but it was clear, even from the ridge across the river, that Missouri City was nothing but a bunch of mudsills; probably still holding a torch for old Emperor Lincoln, martyred to his unholy cause all those years ago. Jesse's smile widened just a little bit at the thought.

"I'm not seein' any law, Jesse," Chase muttered. "No sign of any o' them UR-30 statue-men, neither."

Ty nodded, looking from one outlaw to the other. "No, it's like I told you, Jesse; ain't no real law in Missouri City right now. They's got a sheriff, but he don't like that new-fangled marshal's gang they put together over in Tombstone. He's an ornery old guy, and might not even be around on a day like today! He spends a lot of time riding between here and KC."

Jesse continued to move the monocular around the town, smiling widely. He was hoping someone was going to put up a fuss. Last time they had ridden through this way, Missouri City had been nothing but filthy turncoat republicans, and the James gang had charged the entire town a heavy price for that lack of loyalty. Today, itching for some action and annoyed by his brother's absence, Jesse was hoping for an excuse to burn the whole damned place to the ground.

One of the men behind Jesse murmured to another while they waited for him to formulate a plan. "D'you hear about Billy down Yuma way? I heard they claimed bounty on over a fifty Injun scalps!"

"Nah, I heard it was more like ahun'erd," Harding, arms crossed, muttered over his shoulder. "He ain't no blowhard, Billy the Kid. I run with him a few times. He ain't no flannel-mouthed city slicker."

"I don't know, Harding." The first man said. "A hundred braves? That seems like it'd be an awful lot, even for the Kid."

"He ain't no blowhard," Harding repeated.

Jesse's grin faded slightly, his teeth grinding together before he realized it. He quickly relaxed his jaw, gave his head a quick shake, and continued to scan the town below.

Beside the outlaw leader, Ty watched, from the corner of his eye, and seemed to take satisfaction in the minute motion.

"Boys," Jesse lowered the instrument and gestured with it at the town. "Ain't time to be shootin' yer mouths off about the Kid with such a ripe peach waitin' to be plucked down yonder. Everybody loosen those holsters an' have the rifles at the ready. I don't much think today's a day for slow 'n' easy." The smile was back and the men responded to it with vicious smirks of their own.

"Now, you boys remember back when we used to have to worry about things like fords and bridges?" He looked around him with a laugh, but most of the men looked blankly back at him. Some shook their heads slightly. It seemed to take the wind out of Jesse's sails a bit, and his shoulders slumped.

"Would you wanna try to cross that river on horseback, without a bridge, you bunch of shavetail croakers?" He flicked the monocular downward again before tossing it to Gage in frustration.

"Forget it, let's just get down there and do some damage, eh?" He revved the mighty engine of his 'Horse, sending crimson flames flaring from the drive nozzle. He stood tall in his saddle, leaned his weight forward, and the machine tilted its nose downward. The rest of the gang followed quickly as he tore down the hill in a plume of choking dust. Even over the roaring of the motors he could hear the rebel yells of the men behind him, and Jesse's smile came back full force.

Jesse was hunched behind the control console of his Iron Horse when he took the machine off the road and aimed it directly at the glittering river ahead. When he hit the bank, a geyser of green water flashed up all around, sparkling in the sun and sending rainbow prisms dancing behind him. Each of the other outlaws crashed through the falling curtain of mist, their own plumes exploding out around them. To the men and women on the waterfront across the way, it appeared as if an enormous cloud had suddenly erupted from the far bank, rushing toward them like a vicious storm front. Ruby flashes from within marked the flickering afterburn of the engines and the pulsing lights of the modules along their flanks.

The townsfolk stood staring numbly as the rushing wall of vapor rolled toward them, and Jesse, soaked to the skin by the roiling moisture, grinned evilly. He crouched down lower, peering ahead through the swirling crimson-stained chaos of his goggles. He could just make out the shapes of the people on the waterfront, and so he tilted his body slightly, bringing his center of balance over and throwing up a high white rooster tail of foam. The roar of his motor rose an octave as he gunned it toward a gap in the crowd.

Jesse's 'Horse threw up a bow-wave of churning water, flashing fish, and shredded vegetation as it erupted out of the river and onto the dry bank. The surge of muddy water broke the spell that held the crowd in thrall, and they began to run inland, shouting and screaming. Jesse laughed as he pulled one of his Hyper-velocity pistols and fired over the heads of the fleeing crowd. The shattering blasts struck against the walls of water-front buildings and set small, vicious fires. The crowd scrambled even faster, covering their heads with desperately up-flung arms.

Jesse took one quick glance over his shoulder and then gunned the 'Horse again, tearing between two buildings and forcing the stragglers in the fleeing mob to dive out of the way. One fat old man was too slow and the outlaw nudged him aside with the nose of the vehicle. Jesse hooted as the poor old muggins fell into the dirt, arms wind milling wildly.

Behind Jesse, the rest of the gang roared down the alley. Two of the boys revved up the Gatling guns on their machines and sent sheets of crimson bolts sleeting out after the fleeing townsfolk. Buildings detonated in red fury, sending burning chunks of wood, masonry, and shingling sailing into the air. A pair of rockets sailed down the street on twinned lines of white exhaust, punching through the front wall of a small two story business and exploding within. Fire and debris crashed back out through every door and window, while the chimney coughed up a column of dark smoke and then collapsed into the building.

Jesse gave an invigorated whoop of his own as he saw the building cave in on itself, sending a plume of dust and smoke into the clear blue sky overhead.

Within the confines of the town center, the roar of the Iron Horses was nearly deafening. The terrified men and women were gone, still fleeing out the other side of town and into the hills, but horror-stricken eyes stared from many darkened windows as the outlaws slashed through town, their thunderous machines throwing up gouts of dirt and dust as they slid to a stop in front a neat, trim building sporting a freshly-painted sign, 'Missouri City Savings and Loan'.

Jesse leapt from the saddle and landed in a slight crouch, pulling his other custom pistol and scanning the surrounding buildings for targets. Most of the outlaws were quick to follow him, but two brought their mounts around to cover the approaches down either side of the street with Gatling guns still glowing from recent use.

"Okay, boys, just like we planned it!" Jesse did not even try to hide his wild grin. The rest of the gang, especially young Ty, were smirking and wild-eyed themselves. Jesse knew the feeling well, and he welcomed it. "Harding, you and Chase watch the street, any sign of one of them metal men, you give the signal and the rest of us'll come runnin'. Any sign of the sheriff, you start shootin', and we'll finish up our business right quick an' join you."

He turned to look at Ty, standing nearby and eagerly shifting his weight from foot to foot. "Ty, you come with me, the rest of you, follow behind and back my play. Ain't no need to end any of these folks today less'n they get ornery, but I'm in no mood to back down neither, so if you see me light one up, you consider it open season on dirty rat mudsills, and we'll start keepin' score."

The men nodded eagerly and Jesse turned back toward the building. He could just make out some movement from within, the windows now coated in the dust from the Iron Horses still rumbling in the street. He leapt up onto the raised walkway, his heels cracking against the fresh wood, and moved toward the doors. His duster flared behind him with the speed of his excitement.

The doors to the bank yielded immediately to the first savage kick, the wood crashing inward as the hinges gave way. Both doors fell off to the side with a clatter that caused the people within to cry out. The sight of the men in the door, brandishing RJ-powered weapons and faces snarling beneath the dust of the road, set the entire crowd surging away. The mob did not stop until they were pressed to the wall, hands in the air. Some glared in anger, but most were terrified, emitting a low moaning sound heavy with fear and despair.

Jesse walked straight into the bank, noting quickly the folks huddled along the walls to either side, and lifted an unlit quirley to his grinning lips.

"Howdy, folks! This ain't gonna take but a second, and I'd be right obliged if you'd just do as I ask, no one playin' hero 'r nothin'." He lifted one heat gun to the end of his cheroot and lit it with a blast that cracked into the ceiling, leaving a scorched ring of shattered plaster and wood.

Jesse and his boys crowded into the room. Jesse lowered his pistols casually, grinning widely at the terrified clerks behind their barred windows. The rest of his men took up positions behind him, covering the small group of customers cowering against the side walls.

"Okay, boys and girls, let me explain real quick how this is goin' to play out. Ya'll know me," Jesse spun his two pistols in quick spirals around his articulated metal hands with smooth, deceptively slow movements. Silvered elements beneath the dull armor glinted in the bright bulbs overhead. Jesse smiled even wider, teeth clenched around the cigarillo.

"Ya'll know you're dealin' with Jesse James, and ya'll know this ain't my first visit to your little burg." He gestured with one Hyper-velocity weapon at a grizzled old man crouched in the corner. "Hell, grandpa here probably remembers it his own self, don'cha, grandpa!"

The old man cringed, his head lowered.

"So," Jesse holstered one of his pistols and gestured vaguely toward the clerks. 'Less'n ya'll are plannin' on hidin' behind those bars all day long, I'm thinkin' we need to start passin' yer cash on through, so's my boys here can help themselves and we can be on our way before any of these nice folks out here start crampin' up."

The clerks stared, only the tops of their heads visible through the barred windows. They did not so much as blink, and Jesse's smile slipped with annoyance as they failed to move.

"Maybe you din't hear me, Billy Yank." He walked quickly toward the window and tapped heavily on the bar with the barrel of a gun. "Less'n you want me to decorate that back wall there with what you spent your life holdin' yer ears apart with, I wanna start seein' greenbacks flyin' through this window."

"Get down, ya little coot!" One of Jesse's boys rushed forward, a modified rifle gripped tightly in both hands, barrel jabbing toward a man staring up from the floor. Jesse's eyes never left the clerk's as his free hand flew to his holster, drew his second pistol, and brought it unerringly up at the face of the man on the floor.

"You gettin' some unhealthy ideas, Lincolnite?" The words were soft, all vestiges of Jesse's smile worn completely away.

The man raised his hands over his head, stammered out an apology, and scuttled backward through the crowd until his back was pressed up against a wall.

"My patience is peter'n' out, folks. Now, if you don't get a wiggle on and start pushin' some coin our way, I'm about to kick up a row the likes o' which this bug hill ain't never seen before." Jesse's voice was low and even, his eyes flat as he stared through the bars.

"Sure thing, sir!" The blonde clerk nodded suddenly. "Sorry, sir." The top of the man's head began to bob as he reached beneath the counter, coming up with sheaves of cash that he pushed through the bars. He jerked his head, eyes wild, at the other clerk, but the man merely stood dumbfounded, unable to move.

"Alrighty, lads," Jesse tossed over his shoulder, eyes and pistol still on the moving clerk. "Why don't you all see what sort of financial support the kind folks of Missouri City would like to donate to the cause while our friend here empties the drawers?"

The gang started to move toward the crowd, stabbing barrels at folks moving too slow for their tastes. Watches, wads of cash, and jewelry were handed over and the outlaws grinned wider and wider as their pockets filled. The clerk, working under Jesse's calm direction, had begun to shove the cash into a bag he had grabbed from behind the counter. Several bags lay nearby, already bulging with money.

"Ty, any sign of the law dog out in the street?"

The young man was standing by one of the doors, a pistol clenched in one hand. He peeked out the small window and shook his head. "Can't see no one, Jesse."

Jesse's smile was slowly coming back and he began to toss stuffed bags at the men who had returned to the door. He spit the soggy cigarette onto the floor and gestured with his chin at a pin on the collar of a sullen man crouching nearby.

"Ty, scoop me that little broach on yonder Zu-Zu, will ya? I seen one o' them before, an' I been meanin' to pick one up."

The young man moved quickly while the man's face went through several painful contortions, blurring from terrified to indignant and back again faster than the naked eye could follow. In the end, he merely sat completely still as the young outlaw reached down and yanked the pin out, tearing the cloth.

Ty looked at the little object quizzically then shrugged. "Some old guy's head?" Jesse nodded, tossed the last bag of cash to one of the waiting men, and crossed the room, one of his mechanical hands outstretched. "You said it, Ty. Some old guy's head." He took the small token and held it up the light. "Howdy, Abe!"

If Jesse had been paying closer attention to the men and women on the floor, he would have noticed the dark looks and shifting glances. His men were no more attentive, laughing as the legendary outlaw made an ironic leg as if bowing to a great man.

"Gentlemen, I give you the original big bug himself, Abraham Lincoln! Of course, in this partic'lar rendition, he's got a bit more head than the esteemed man himself currently sports. . . " With a chuckle, Jesse moved to slip the pin into a watch pocket. As he looked down to the small opening the pin's original owner made his move.

"You southron knuck!" The man was rising from the pile of cowering civilians, a small enhanced pistol appearing in his hand. "Get your freak hands off that pin! You're not fit to lay a finger on—"

Jesse's face hardened as time slowed around him. The pin fell from his hand, tumbling end over end toward the hard wooden floor as the leather duster flared out with the outlaw's spin. The Hyper-velocity pistol, already skinned, came up in a smooth arc as its twin seemed to leap out of its holster into his other hand. Across the small room, eyes widened in horror, mouths dropped down to scream. The man with the holdout shooting iron tried desperately to bring his weapon up, but there was a look in his eye that Jesse had seen many times before; he knew he was dead, but the day just had not caught up to him yet.

As Jesse's muzzles settled on the man's head he snarled, "tell 'im I said 'hi'." With slow deliberation he pulled the triggers.

The crimson flashes from the two pistols snapped out as if reaching for the man's face. For a split second, Jesse's world narrowed to focus solely on the man's eyes. Did they flash red for a brief moment? Was that just a reflection of the muzzle flashes in his terror-wide eyes? Was the man actually smiling?

The dual shots crashed into the man's head simultaneously. His entire upper body splashed backward, showering the cowering townsfolk with gore. The murmurings and cries rose to a fevered pitch.

Time stopped. Jesse felt as if he had eternity to study the scene before him. The cringing men and women now dripping blood and viscera, the tellers diving behind their wall, the outlaws arrayed behind him with weapons half-raised to threaten the room. Blood drops glistened in the artificial light, hanging in the air like tiny balloons. Through it all, Jesse could not shake the memory of red eyes smiling at him before the face disappeared forever.

When time resumed, it did so with the deafening crack of gunfire erupting all around. Bolts of red energy slashed into the wall as the bank's unlucky customers flattened themselves on the floor. The blonde teller rose up behind his window holding a massive hand cannon, its muzzle gaping darkly.

"Die, you bastard!" Jesse's eyes widened as a cloud of crimson-edged smoke billowed out of the giant weapon, reaching out for him like a creature out of a nightmare.

With a grunt, Jesse hit the hard floor, the ravening blast roaring over him. He reached out with both of his pistols, blasting holes in the wall at knee height. A scream rose over the ringing in his ears and a confused jumble of movement flashed from the window as the gun-slinging teller went down.

Jesse leapt up, his anger high, and stalked toward the window, his right arm outstretched, his pistol slapping bolt after bolt through the bars. The far room was a chaotic confusion of debris and smoke, flames spreading out over the wall and across the floor.

"Jesse, we gotta go!" Someone shouted from the door. Jesse glanced back and was shocked to see three of his men down, bodies torn and lying in a spreading pool of blood.

"Damnit." Jesse looked up at the iron frame holding the bars. Teeth flashing in a snarl, he raised both pistols, mechanical thumbs flicking a small switch on each pistol grip. Both weapons flared crimson for a moment and then launched a beam of solid, furious heat through the bars. The metal kissed directly by the light simply ceased to exist, while the remaining bars and the frame itself sagged in place, the molten ends burning with eerie blue flames. The entire metal structure collapsed backward into the teller's room.

Jesse stepped up to the window and leaned inside, one armored limb rising to shield his face from the heat. The two tellers were cowering in a corner, the blonde whimpering as he held a shredded leg with red-stained hands.

"Looks like it ain't my day to die, chiseler." He put one shot into the blond man's head without warning, then swept the pistol over to point at the other man. Just as the targeting blade settled on his forehead, however, the gun bucked beneath his hand and blasted a hole in the wall behind him. Jesse growled, looking down at his hand and the weapon, and shook his head.

"Well, if that don't take the rag off." He shook his head. "Someone up there shinin' on you, Jonah." He looked around at the building, its walls now fully engulfed in red-tinged flames. "You might wanna light a shuck before whoever it is loses interest."

He spit a heavy wad into the furnace heat and turned back toward the door. One of his pistols slid quickly into its holster as he bent down to grab a bag of cash.

"Get the rest of it," Jesse growled under his breath as he swept out the door.

The outlaw jumped onto his rumbling Iron Horse, his face set in grim lines of discontent. The excitement and the joy were gone, drained from him as if someone had burst a water skin. He turned to Ty as he and another man stumbled from the burning building loaded down with heavy bags.

"Ty, you get on Lyndon's machine, he ain't gonna be needin' it no more." Jesse drew one of his custom pistols and riddled the engine on Ty's borrowed mount before the young man could answer. "Chase, take care of the others before we skedaddle. We ain't leavin' nothin' behind these mudsills could get a lick o' use out of."

Jesse gunned his 'Horse in a tight circle, throwing out a wave of dirt and dust that rattled off surrounding walls and windows. He headed back toward the river without looking back, leaving his surviving men standing in the street watching his retreating back. As he leaned into a tight turn and disappeared from view, Chase turned to Ty with a shrug.

"He don't take kind to folks shootin' at him, 'specially in a loser burg like this." The big man cupped one hand around his mouth and yelled into the burning bank. "You folks know what's good for you, you'll sit pretty 'till you can't hear us no more! Believe you me, that fire's a lot less scary than you come out and meet up with an ornery Jesse James!"

Ty smiled with a sharp edge. He hopped up onto his new machine as if he'd been born into its saddle. The Iron Horse slid smoothly beneath him as he pushed it backward into the street, bringing its forward cowling into line with the bank. Behind him, he could hear Chase slapping several bolts into the dead men's vehicles. Ty was not thinking about those rusty old hulks, however. He was bringing his new machine into line with the bank, where shadows were moving against the rising flames inside, the people trapped within gathering up the courage to emerge despite Chase's warning.

When the massive Gatling cannons on Ty's Iron Horse began to fire, Chase and the other outlaws ducked and skittered away, startled by the furious hammering after the fight had long gone out of the men and women trapped in the bank. Chase and Harding looked on in disbelief as the young man pumped bolt after bolt into the building, shattering the front wall, blasting the glass from the windows, and slaughtering the terrified, helpless men and women within.

"What in the name of Heaven are you doin', boy?" Harding raced to Ty and pushed him hard back into his seat, forcing his hands from the weapon controls. "You gone loco?" His eyes were wild as he screamed, gesturing behind him at the devastated building with one clawing hand.

Ty's face was twisted in a savage grin. "Well, somebody's gotta watch out for the big man's name, eh? Jesse's obviously too tired to care, but he's got a reputation, and we can't let him sully that, am I right?" He was breathing heavily as if he had just run a long way.

The rest of the outlaws stared at the bank as the upper floor collapsed into the inferno below, the blasted first floor now unable to support its weight. There were no more screams emerging from within.

Chase looked back at the young man, the light of the blaze reflecting redly in the young man's eyes.

"Damn, son, you are the very devil himself."

Ty erupted in a moment of laughter as if Chase had just said something particularly funny, then gunned his 'Horse around and roared after Jesse James.

Chase looked back to Harding and the other men, all scrambling now for their own mounts, knowing that they needed to escape before the townsfolk realized exactly what had been done. Chase shook his head in disbelief.

"The devil himself!"

Chapter 5

"Jesse, I swear to God." The older man sitting across from him in the Arcadia Saloon looked disgusted, his face twisted with frustration and contempt. "They're sayin' more'n twenty people died in that fire! You have any idea what kind of red flag that'll wave in front of the law? They can't ignore somethin' like that! Even the tame ones round hereabouts can't turn a blind eye to that kind of body count! An' after all that gold went missin'?"

Jesse stared into his whiskey glass with a scowl. "Twenty little coots, Frank. World's better off without 'em. Asides—"

"Asides nothin', Jesse!" Frank slapped the rough table with an open hand. His custom-scoped long rifle, Sophie, shifted slightly where it rested against his chair. At the tables around them, men and women looked up quickly before turning back to their own business.

On either side of Frank sat Cole Younger and his brother Bob. Both men stared hard at Jesse, hands resting loosely on the table in front of them, empty glasses resting forgotten nearby. Cole's jaw worked slowly as he shifted a large wad of chaw from one side to the other and back again.

"Don't matter if they were the entire Lincoln family, Jesse! The law just can't ignore somethin' like that! What were you thinkin'? We got plenty of scratch, I told you we didn't need another job so soon!" Frank leaned back in his chair, gesturing for his brother to speak as if inviting a child to expand on stellar navigation.

"I told you, Frank, I wasn't there." Jesse glared and leaned toward his older brother, mechanical arms folded before him. His voice was a menacing whisper as he continued. "An' you don't dare dress me down like this, Frank. Not in front of the Youngers, 'n' not in front of nobody. I'm still leadin' this gang o' pie-eatin' knucks, and I won't stand for tryin' to dry gulch me here in the middle o' the day."

Frank waved the threat off as if it were an annoying fly. "I don't give half a rat's ass what you are gonna or ain't gonna stand for, Jesse. We all told you, that Missouri City job was a bad one. We had a good thing goin' here! An' we're gonna have to leave sooner rather than later now, 'less you were itchin' to decorate that sweet set o' gallows they got erected down by the waterfront?"

Cole Younger snorted and spat a wad of dark juice near a spittoon not far away. "I'm figurin' the law'll be followin' us as we leave, too, so's my brothers 'n' I, we're not too keen on the whole situation. Jim and John'r gettin' supplies together so we can light out of here quick as you please, soon as you two stop yer dancin'. "

Jesse picked up his whiskey with the faint ring of metal on glass and knocked back the rest of the amber liquid inside. "You an' yer brothers've been lookin' for an excuse to get outta KC since we got here, Cole. Don't play like you ain't been holdin' the same hand since the beginnin'."

"I don' see you rushin' out California-way, eager to hang a hat in that ratty little camp where your father coughed out his last breath, eh, Jesse?" Bob Younger, his face pale, leaned toward the outlaw leader, his elbow resting on his knee. "Our daddy was done for in this very town, not half a mile from where you're sittin' there grinnin'. Gunned down by a rat bastard group o' Billy Yanks as he was walkin' in the street!"

The young man stood and sneered down at Jesse, whose eyes were focused entirely on his own brother. "So yeah, if we're not gonna shed no tears over those uppity Zu-Zus over in Missouri City, don't expect us to be throwin' you a parade, with you getting' all promiscuous with the tech and violence, neither. My brothers 'n' me, we ain't comfortable here in the city where they killed our pa, and no mistake. But we stuck with you, and we won't leave 'till it's time." He reached down for his glass and kicked back the contents with a jerky motion. "An' thanks to you and those shavetails you brought with you, I think I hear a clock tickin' while we sit here bendin' our elbows and catchin' flies."

The glass came down on the table with a crack and the young man stormed off, pushing past several people on his way to the door.

Frank and Jesse were completely still, eyes locked on each other as if there were not another soul for miles. Cole Younger sat back for a few moments pushing the tobacco around his mouth, then stood up, shaking his head.

"You two are a hoot, you know that?" He knocked his own glass over with the slow, deliberate motion of a single finger and then grinned at the two brothers. "When you two're done dancin', we might wanna think about ponying up and headin' west, maybe?" He chuckled once and moved toward the door. As he came up to the doorway he stopped, gesturing grandly for an attractive brunette to enter. As she swept past he looked over to see Jesse James watching out of the corner of his eye. Cole's grin widened, he waggled his eyebrows meaningfully with a jerk of his head toward the newcomer, and slipped out the door, pushing past a large, finely-dressed man trying to enter at the same time.

"I'm sorry, Jesse, but you and those greenhorns have knocked this whole caper into a cocked hat, and no mistake." He leaned toward his brother again, his voice low and earnest. "You gotta see we can't stick around here. We gotta not be here when the law gets around to doin' its job again, Jesse, and there just ain't two ways about that."

Jesse sighed with a mixture of anger and resignation. "I din't mean for any of that to happen down river, Frank, you know that. We was just gonna rough 'em up a bit, ruin their day, you know?" He shook his head. "But those damned yahoos, they never know when to quit! Next thing you know, the bolts 'r flyin', we got folks droppin' on both sides, and everyone's got their blood up somethin' fierce. An' then, Ty let fly with his Gatlings, and I wasn't even there to see."

"Ty, he the young local scrub, convinced you it'd be an easy mark in the first place?"

Jesse nodded, but his eyes were now tracking something across the room, moving behind Frank and into the region of gaming tables in the corner. "Yeah. Nice enough kid, for all that's the freshest fish you ever met in your life."

Frank looked skeptical. "Fresh fish? To hear Chase 'r Harding tell it, he's the coldest soaplock who never sucked an ice chip."

Jesse shook his head, his eyes still looking past his brother's shoulder. "Naw, he's a quiet kid, didn't know what he was gettin' into. Just went a little salty in the moment, is all."

A shadow passed over the younger man's face. Jesse looked back down at his arms for a moment, turning the hands over against the table. "An' Frank . . . my arms . . . "

Frank cocked his head. "Yeah? What about 'em?"

Jesse shook his head as he tapped a rapid staccato rhythm on the table, his eyes drifting back over his brother's shoulder. "Nah, never mind. It was nothin'."

Frank nodded, his expression thoughtful. "Whatever you say, brother. They're your arms, after all. Or at least, they are now." He leaned back a little bit, watching his brother speculatively for a moment before asking, "Jesse, you gonna tell me what you're lookin' at, that's got your eyes just about ready to pop from your skull? I ain't got one of them metal marshals comin' up on me or nothin', have I?"

Jesse shook his head and gestured with his chin as he sat back. "No, just some swell, all dressed up in widow's tackle. Looks like he's got a right pretty friend, though."

Frank shrugged and turned his head just enough to get a glimpse out of the corner of his eye. Sure enough, there was a man in a very expensive-looking suit sitting down to one of the gaming tables. The man's face was hard, the stub of a cigar hanging from one side of his mouth, nodding to the other players as he took a seat at the table.

Behind the man in the fancy gear stood a stunning brunette in a fancy dress that revealed almost as much as it concealed. Her fine features were distant and uncaring as she scanned the room, as if she could not find a single item of interest within sight. Her smile was radiant as she nodded to the men around the table, however, obviously having been introduced by her companion, she leaned down to allow each man to take her hand in turn, and laughed at some remark one of the men must have made.

"Damned dirty dude trick, that," Jesse snarled.

Frank turned back from assessing the newcomers and shot his brother a questioning look. "Trick?"

Jesse nodded and gestured back toward the gaming tables with a flip of one mechanical hand. "Card sharp like that comes in with a looker on his arm, and she's all smiles and light from word one? Yeah. She's there to distract the other players, scoop 'em into throwin' their money away, and the fella cuttin' a swell there, he'll pick it all up." He shook his head again. "Damned dirty trick."

Frank muscled his chair around so he could get a better view, and then settled back as if he were watching a wrestling match or a horseshoe tournament. He stretched out his long legs, crossing them casually at the ankles, and folded his arms across his chest with an appreciative smile.

"Well, if I ain't got no coin ridin' on it, guess I can just enjoy the view, eh?" Frank's grin widened even more.

Jesse watched as the cards were dealt around the table in the corner, the men settling back, fanning their hands and watching their opponents. He noticed the eyes constantly flicking toward the tall beauty standing behind the fancy-pants, and watched as she smiled and winked at each man as if he were the only one in the room.

"Damn, I'd be forkin' over every cent in my pocket before the first hand was up." Jesse shook his head. "Frank, I'm goin' to get a beer before we head on over to the Occidental. You want one?"

Frank's face soured. "The Occidental? What're we doin', headin' over to the Occidental? Your lil' bed warmer dancin' tonight? I seen about enough o' her as I need to see, thank'ee." He grinned again and indicated the woman in the corner with his chin. "'Sides, your poor Misty don't hold a candle to that sweet thing over yonder. And I ain't gettin' any closer to either one o' them, so's I might as well stay right here and enjoy the view."

Jesse scowled as he stood. "You're a right bastard and no mistake. You want a beer, or don'cha?"

Frank smiled benignly up at his younger brother and nodded smoothly. "Why I do believe I would, brother, thank'ee kindly."

Jesse was muttering under his breath as he worked his way through the tables to the bar along the back of the saloon. He flashed two fingers at the harried looking bartender and then set his elbows against the wood with a hard thump. His head sank down toward his crossed wrists and slowly rocked back and forth in vague puzzlement.

"Those are some fancy pieces of jewelry you got there, mister." The voice was a soft contralto that sent a shiver up his spine, and Jesse snapped upright, turning quickly around.

The woman who had come in with the card sharp was standing behind him, her full lips pursed in a mischievous smile. Her deep brown eyes flickered down to his mechanical arms again and then back up into his, one delicate eyebrow arched questioningly.

Jesse felt his old grin sweep across his face without conscious thought and brought his hands up between them, turning them back and forth, looking down as if seeing them for the first time.

"You talkin' about my arms, darlin'?" He smiled even wider as he looked back into her eyes. "Most advanced tech you're goin' to find in the territories, little lady. Ain't nothin' these arms can't do, and that is a verifiable fact."

Jesse plucked a silver dollar from a pocket and held in up in front of the woman. The coin popped up onto his knuckles as if it was alive, and then began to dance back and forth across them as the fingers beneath rippled back and forth like waves on a burnished steel ocean. The coin bounced toward his thumb, which flashed out, sending it springing up into the air where the other hand swooped across, catching it with a faint click.

Jesse cocked an eyebrow at the woman as he slipped the silver dollar back into his pocket. "Did I tell ya? Ain't nothin' these arms can't do."

The woman smiled slyly at him, tilting her head down slightly and pushing her bare shoulder toward him in a faint mockery of self-defense. "Maybe you'll get a chance to show me just what those arms can do sometime?"

Jesse's smile widened immensely, threatening to reach right around and meet on the back of his head. In a moment, however, his look became tinged with doubt. His head moved back a bit, cocked to one side, and the intensity of his smile lowered slightly, but a deeper appreciation dawned in his eyes.

"Damn, you're good, missy." He shook his head at her and leaned back against the bar, his elbows striking with a muffled thump. His entire demeanor was more relaxed, and his smile was easy.

The woman, too, seemed to sense a shift in the mood, and smiled more openly, mischief still glittering in her eyes. "Whatever are you about, Mr. James?"

Genuine pleasure washed over Jesse. "So, you know me, then?"

She reached out with one small hand and rested it on his shoulder. "Oh, please,

Mr. James. As far as I've heard tell, there is only one singular pair of arms in the entire world like your own. And after that bravura performance with the coin, I could, of course, have no doubt!"

Jesse nodded, casting his gaze over the crowded room affecting a vague indifference. "Well, you've got me dead to rights, miss."

The woman gracefully slipped into a bar stool beside the famous outlaw, her hand never moving from his shoulder. "From what I hear, sir, that does not happen very often."

Jesse snorted, turning to face her. "You'd be surprised. Here, you've got me at somethin' of a disadvantage, miss. You know me, but I don't know you at all. Please tell me a girl as pretty as you's got a name just as handsome?"

She smiled again, her eyes never wavering from his. "My friends call me Lucy, Mr. James."

"Lucy . . . Yeah, that'd do it." He nodded to the bartender as the man placed two glasses beside him, and pushed the silver dollar across the bar. "Oh, where are my manners! Would you like something, Miss Lucy?"

She smiled wider, but there was a canny edge, as if she'd caught him at some game. "No, thank you, Mr. James. I've my own means." She leaned across the bar and snapped a quick order that Jesse could not quite make out. When she turned back to him, she was smiling openly again. "Where were we, Mr. James?"

"Please, call me Jesse. Mr. James passed on a long time ago, and I don't have any thoughts o' followin' him for a long time to come."

Lucy looked concerned, her hand drifting from his shoulder to the back of one met al hand. "Oh, I'm sorry . . . Jesse."

He looked down at her hand for a moment, then shrugged. "No, it ain't nothin'. He passed on a long time ago. Plenty of time to recover from that particular heartache."

"There have been others?" She leaned closer to him, giving him her complete, undivided attention.

Jesse retreated slightly from her. "Well, sure. You ain't livin' if you ain't bleedin', as they say."

She frowned slightly. "That strikes me as rather a dark way to live, Mr. James – I mean Jesse. Aren't there any other times you feel alive than when you're bleeding?"

He shook his head. "There's plenty of times I'm happy I'm not bleedin', Miss Lucy, but there been lots of folks through the years taught me real good that those times don't last, an' I'll be bleedin' again soon."

It seemed as if all pretense had fallen from Lucy's face, and she looked at him with clear eyes. "So you live every moment expecting violence to engulf your world? That seems like a very sad way to move through life."

Jesse barked a short laugh, shaking his head. "Lady, if you'd seen half of what I'd seen, you'd know there ain't no other way. I was sixteen when I was wounded in the war—"

She held up one smooth finger. "Wait, you fought in the war? The War Between the States? I would never have thought you were old enough!"

His smile faltered and began to fade as he continued speaking. "Well, I'm aging well, let's say. And I was young. Joined up with the raiders when I was younger'n I was supposed to be. Got myself shot toward the end, spent the last few months of the war laid up in a bed recuperating from the wound. Eventually, I went home. I'd seen the flyers, promises of amnesty and forgiveness if you'd just give your word to the degenerate turncoats that had inherited the late great state of Missouri. On my way to give my parole, the bastards shot me, again, and left me for dead."

A warm concern wrinkled her brow and she leaned toward him again. "Shot you right where you stood? Without a warning?"

"Well, I was sittin' on a horse, but yeah, shot me without a warnin'." His grin came back, causing years to drop from his face. "'Course, I been a right thorn in the Union's side ever since, and no mistake. Next time one of them blue-bellies gets the drop on me, you can be sure they ain't goin' to half ass the job, neither!"

There was venom in his voice as he finished, and a crease appeared between Lucy's beautiful eyes. "You hate them."

"Northerners? Hell, miss, I ain't alone in hating those high-brow Yanks, not even in a burg as ignorant as this one is. There's plenty of folks holdin' a torch for those old northern states, waitin' for the day."

Lucy sat back in her stool, regarding him calmly, but with no warmth. "You truly hate them."

Jesse turned fully around to face her, taking both of her hands in his metallic grasp. "Let's not beat the devil around the stump, miss. I hate them. I hate everythin' the Yanks stand for. I hate what they done to my family, I hate what they done to my friends, and I hate what they done to my home and my way o' life." His voice got lower and lower, more of a growl than a speech, and his eyes bore into her own with an intensity that seemed to rattle her.

"I hate their high-handed way of dealin' with folks they don't agree with, an' I hate the way they'll stomp all over anyone who gets in their way."

Lucy put up a hand to stall his diatribe. "But that's the government, the military. Surely you can't blame the men and women of –"

"They vote up there in the north, Miss Lucy?" His face was twisted with loathing.

"I beg your pardon?" The apparent shift in topic had caught her flat footed.

" They vote up there, in those states we're talkin' about, right? Vote for their mayors, an' for their governors, for their senators an' for their dog catchers? They vote for their president, Miss Lucy?" The anger was building again.

"Well, to answer that last question, no, Mr. James, they do not vote for their presidents. As any school child knows, there hasn't been a presidential election since the assassination of . . . President Lincoln. President Johnson's held the post ever since. Congress declared a state of emergency over a decade ago, imposing martial law and all the rest . . . "

Jesse waved her response away. "I know all that, but you get my point. Those folks that sit in their little log cabins, those folks who you say are innocent? They're the ones voted in the men who sent those other men after me on that road all those years ago, shot me in the chest and left me for dead. Robbed my family of their means of support and left us to fend for ourselves. Gunned down my friends' pa in the streets of this very city. So no, Miss Lucy, I am sorry to say I do not hold out any warm feelin's for the innocent civilians of the northern states."

She stared at him for a moment before responding. "That's why you rob banks and such? For revenge?"

He laughed once more, and again the darkness fled before the humor and good-nature in his eyes, as if the cold killer staring out from them had never been. "Well, I rob banks 'cause I like money, and I got a right nasty aversion to honest work, Miss Lucy, to be honest. But do I take special pleasure in hitting a republican when I can? You better believe it!"

She shook her head sadly. "And does that bring you peace, Jesse? Attacking and stealing from men and women who had nothing to do with what was done to you?"

His own demeanor turned cold. "Ma'am, ain't nothin' brings me peace, but yeah, knockin' a mudsill republican on the head every now and then, yeah, that brings a smile to my face."

"You realize that will never bring any of those people you lost back? The way of life you're talking about, that went away a long time ago, and was fading long before the first shot was fired at Fort Sumter. You can't give your life meaning by striking out at people who had nothing to do with that. Are the men and women you ride with any better than the people you terrorize?"

He stared at her for a moment, blinking as if waking up from a hypnotic state. But when he spoke, his words were calm and clear. "Have you ever tried living off revenge?"

She stared into his eyes, her gaze not wavering at all as she answered without hesitation. "Yes. It brought me nothing but pain."

That brought Jesse up short for a moment. In the end, though, his old familiar smile returned. "Well, I find it suits me just fine. Just because a fine filly can't live off a fresh kill, Miss Lucy, don't mean that it ain't good for a mountain lion."

She looked at him for a long time without speaking. There was an almost imper ceptible shaking of her head, and an almost unnoticeable hint of pity in her eyes. She reached toward him and he leaned away, his smile faltering slightly. But she reached past him, taking up two tall glasses that had been set on the bar beyond.

"I'm being summoned, Mr. James. This was . . . enlightening, to say the least." Her amazing smile flashed once again, and all of the tangled emotions running rampant through his chest eased immediately. But before he could think to make one final statement, she was gone, weaving her way gracefully back through the crowd toward the gaming tables. He could not help but notice every man's eyes following her as she past. He snorted, shook his head, and grabbed his own beers off the bar, moving back toward where his brother still sat, unmoving, an appreciative grin still firmly fixed in place.

"Damn," Frank said as he sat up and grabbed one of the beers. He tilted it toward where Lucy was handing her friend a glass, once again charming the men at his table. "D'you ever notice, the way they move when they put their mind to it?"

Jesse grunted as he sat heavily back into his own chair. "What?"

Frank gave a chuckle. "Women! When they put their minds to it, they move unlike anything you've ever seen before! All the parts moving in so many different direction all at once, and yet it gets them right to where they're going, and you can't take your eyes off 'em!" He made a face as he knocked back a slug of his beer. "Damn, Jesse, you couldn't of taken a second to run this over? Tastes like two week old mule piss and it's flatter'n a cow flap in August!"

Jesse's forehead was furrowed in thought and frustration as he settled back in his seat. He did not spare his brother the briefest glance. His eyes were fixated on the gaming corner, where Lucy was smiling and laughing at the players around the table as her dour companion, all but ignored in the glow of her beauty, proceeded to once again drag handfuls of cash back to his corner of the table.

His voice was vague and without force as he muttered, "shut up and drink your mule piss, you bastard."

*****

The streets of Kansas City were nearly empty as the roaring growl of Iron Horses swept up the waterfront from the west and into the center of town. It was a large gang, and the townsfolk could tell from the poorly-maintained vehicles and the wild variations in clothing, that despite the massive weaponry mounted on the 'Horses, this was no military unit coming in on leave.

William Bonney, known to most folks as Billy the Kid, rode at the head of the gang, his back straight, his smile carefree, and his kerchief whipping along behind him. He nodded mockingly to various men and women as he passed, reveling in the fearful looks and angry glares this earned him. He knew that if he wanted to take the time to circle back around, not a single man who had glared at him would have the sand to back it up. He smiled even more widely.

Billy throttled back his machine to allow the men just behind him to catch up.

"Now, don't forget, we're just here to talk!" He shouted over the reverberant rumble of the engines. "You know Jesse don't like to be baited in his own lair, and word has it he's been here in KC long enough, he's bound to be feelin' like he owns the place."

The men who could hear him nodded. Many of them had ridden with Jesse James in the past. It was inevitable in the fluid structure of loyalties and alliances that connected the various outlaw bands together. But as was often the case with Jesse James, the more a man knew him, who was not riding in his inner circle, the less he trusted him.

"We gotta approach this delicate like, okay? We come up on him like we're on the shoot, that's what we're gonna get." Billy shook a bag he held in his right hand. "And this ain't the time to be stirrin' up trouble amongst our own selves. There's too much ridin' on this, and Jesse'll make it all a whole lot easier if he's ridin' with us . . . for now, anyway." He grinned wickedly to the rest of the men, and they snickered and nodded their heads.

"Okay, so when we go in, I just want Smiley and Garrett with me. All the rest of you, go find somewhere to spend whatever coin you've got left 'till I need you. I don't think Jesse'll want to start any trouble here even if he's of an ornery mind. But just in case, I don't want ya'll too far away, you got me?"

The men nodded, and in twos and threes the Iron Horses began to peel away from the formation in search of their various amusements until called upon. Two men stuck with their outlaw leader, one greasy and obese with the flat, dead eyes of a snake, the other a pleasantly nondescript young man with a mean-looking gun slung over his shoulder.

Billy looked up at the buildings as they slid by on either side. "Word is he's staying up on Independence." He peered up at the signs, noting the wildly diverse types of architecture that helped make Kansas City one of the largest burgs in the west. Brick three story businesses stood beside the rough and ready timber construction of frontier settlements across territories. Everywhere, there was the red glimmer of RJ-powered generators supplying power to nearly every building. He had not been in Kansas City for more years than he could remember, and he knew it was going to take a while for him to find Jesse, wherever he had dug himself into.

*****

Lucinda Loveless, assassin and secret agent for Abraham Lincoln, wove through the crowd in the Arcadia Saloon holding two drinks high and smiling at every man who looked her way. Damn, she hated this role. When her partner, Henry Courtright, had suggested they assume the guise of a gambler and his professional girl, she had argued against it. But the situation in Kansas City was quite fluid. The dynamic energy of a frontier city clung to the place despite its more refined facade and the power and prestige of the Heavy Rail hub station. In the end, although she hated playing to the crowds like this, she had failed to come up with anything with an equal chance of success, and so here she was, smiling until her jaw ached, and carrying drinks to Courtright. It only made it worse, knowing that he loved it.

"Well, gentlemen," Courtright was blurring his accent a bit, hiding its deep northern roots behind a slight twang that seemed to recall the Carolina coast more than anywhere else. He leaned back in his chair, one elbow thrown over the back, raking in the pot with his other hand. "I'm amenable to a cessation of hostilities until you can replenish your funds, if you are willing?" He smiled a rare smile that seemed more of a challenge than a friendly gesture, and the men around the table looked grim and uncertain. Grim and uncertain, that was, until Lucinda came gliding up behind Courtright and gently placed a drink at his elbow. She swirled around to stand beside him, her smile bright and her eyes shining. The men, instantly changing their attitude as she sailed back into the picture, were all smiles as well.

"Well, sir," one older gentlemen said, his eyes never leaving Lucinda's neckline. "It's right neighborly of you to give us the pleasure of a further game." He looked back up to meet Courtright's eyes without any awareness that he'd been staring. "Shall we say a quarter of an hour before we reconvene?"

Courtright smiled again at the rest of the men. Lucinda noticed that several of the smiles her return had solicited faltered slightly at the prospect of continued play.

"It is so nice of ya'll to make us feel welcome, boys." She leaned over slightly to pick up a few coins from Courtright's pile, pretending not to notice the effect it had on the other men. She straightened and then slowly walked around the table. "I wouldn't want you all to go dry while you prepare yourselves for valiant combat once again, and I so do want to watch more of your game! So, please, take back some of Henry's ill-gotten gains for a drink on us, to replenish your strength for the renewed battle." With a smile, she pressed a coin into each man's hands, being sure to maintain the contact with a lingering motion for each. It was as if she were casting a spell, and each and every one of them were following her with their eyes, dumb smiles on their faces, when she returned to stand beside Courtright once again.

The men stared at her, dumbstruck, and nodded slightly to the cadence of her voice. "Now, boys, you go do whatever it is you have to do, so you and Henry can continue this fascinating ritual in, what did you say, Mr. Stanfield? A quarter of an hour?"

The distinguished older man took her hand and bowed low over it. "Indeed, young lady. More than enough time to prepare for another skirmish with your imposing companion, but far too much time to be away from your radiant beauty."

The others nodded rapidly, and then followed Stanfield away, muttering to themselves. Lucinda could not quite make out what they were discussing, but it seemed to involve the source of the capital for their next attempt.

"I hope you're planning on filing a report for that money." Lucinda sat down beside Courtright. Her hand rested teasingly on his shoulder, her face was bright with open admiration and warmth, but her voice was coldly amused.

"For what they pay us?" Courtright leaned closer, his northern accent seeping through. "They can raise taxes, if they need more cash." He flicked his eyes toward the table where the James boys still sat, trying not to stare at Lucinda now that the game had broken up. "That them?"

Lucinda laughed as if her companion had made a hilarious remark, tapping him lightly with the hand on his shoulder. Her voice, however, was still cold, and she leaned in close, pitching her response beneath the room's general chatter. "With those arms? Who the hell else would it be? I swear, Courtright, sometimes it feels like I have to do all the thinking around here."

He smiled wickedly at her and flicked a golden coin up in the air in front of her. She jerked back slightly but caught it readily enough with her off hand. "Buy yourself somethin' pretty, little lady. And you don't worry your lovely little noggin about the deeper thoughts."

She let a bit of her sour response leak through her kept-woman demeanor before smiling brightly at him again. "Keep it up, you'll be waking one night missing a part or two that I know you, anyway, look upon as essential. I know where you sleep."

He snorted and tossed back half his drink. He grimaced at the taste. "Christ, Luce, what'd you do, sit on this for an hour?"

She kissed him fondly on the cheek, eyes twinkling. "You got complaints," she whispered, "get your own damned drink next time. Now, what are we going to do about the James boys?"

Courtright looked over at the back table again with a speculative eye. "Well, we think those were Youngers we bumped into on the way in, right?"

She nodded, easing back into her own chair and taking a delicate sip of her drink. It was clearly an effort for her not to react visibly to the taste.

"Well, if both the James boys are here, and at least two of the Younger brothers, then that means they're probably all here. Did you get anything out of him about Carpathian?"

Lucinda shook her head. "No."

Courtright looked at her sharply. "No? He didn't say anything about the old man?"

She shrugged. "I didn't ask." There was a sharp edge of guilt beneath her response. Usually she was much better at getting the information she needed from a mark, but she had somehow lost her way while talking with Jesse James.

"You didn't ask?" Courtright sat back and stared at her in dismay. Coming back to himself, he looked around and then leaned back toward the table. "You were over there for God knows how long, Luce, and you didn't bring up the one thing that brought us here in the first place?"

She shrugged again, trying to hide her embarrassment. "It didn't come up."

Courtright leaned back in his chair and stared at Lucinda speculatively. "Hmmm," was his only response a moment later.

"What do you mean, 'hmmm'?" Her eyes were now flinty, and she leaned forward in a way that could easily have been seen as threatening.

He waved it off. "Nothing. You're going to have to go back and talk to him again, though, you realize that, right? I mean, we didn't come all this way to stop off for a quick flirtation before getting back to the real job, you know."

The anger in her eyes flared. "I was not flirting. Understanding what makes that man tick could open up the whole outlaw organization to us. I don't have to explain to you what that would mean to all our efforts out here, do I?"

He put his hands up in mock surrender, shaking his head but smiling still. "Hey, hey! I was just having fun with you. You're a professional, I get it. Laying the ground work, it's all standard. No problem." He lowered his hands to pick up his drink, thought better of it, and folded them before him on the table. "That doesn't change the fact that you have to go back over there and talk to him some more, however. We have to find out where the damned doctor is, or Lincoln will have our hides."

She nodded, looking down at her own hands, sneering slightly at the paint and polish that adorned her nails like some common dancehall girl. "I'm giving him a few minutes to miss me, then I'll go back in. Is that damned brother of his still at the table?"

Courtright glanced back and then nodded. "Yeah. Can't keep his eyes off you either." He smiled slyly again. "Looks like you may just have bagged yourself two James boys for the price of one." The smile faltered. "Now go and bag us a doctor."

Lucinda shook her head faintly. With a look her partner could not interpret, she stood again. Anyone who did not know her would have missed the transition from resigned acceptance to graceful playfulness as she rose. She gave Courtright one last look and then turned on one high heel, swaying her way back through the crowded tables toward Jesse James.

As she moved through the crowd, she reflected on why she had been so distracted with the outlaw in their first encounter. It had certainly been a strange path that had brought them together here in this filthy little dive in Kansas City.

She saw Jesse watching her approach. He had been watching her since she rose, she realized, and summoned her most alluring smile. She glided up to the outlaw's table and indicated a chair beside him. "Mind if I have a seat, Mr. James?"

The older brother, Frank, jumped up and pulled back the chair for her. "Certainly, miss! Glad to have you!" He gave her a bright smile of his own as he settled back into his chair. "Might I say, you have certainly brightened the premises of this poor establishment today?"

She caught Jesse giving his brother a dark look and wondered if it was jealousy or just annoyance at his forward older brother.

"Ain't you got someplace you gotta be, Frank?"The sour tone matched the look, and Lucinda smiled a little more genuinely to think that it might just be a tinge of jealousy after all.

Frank looked at his brother, his smile slipping a little, before he shook himself, smiled even wider, this time equal parts charm and amusement, and stood with a nod.

"Certainly do, little brother. Gotta see a man about a horse."

Frank James nodded at Lucinda and took her hand, glancing at his brother with a grin before gently brushing the back of it with his lips. "You don't tucker the lad out now, little lady. He's got work he's gotta do." He stood back up and gave his brother a glance that Lucinda could not interpret, but it had a dark edge. "Don't forget what we were talkin' 'bout, Jesse. We got pressin' business that ain't gonna press any less the longer we hang about KC."

Frank lifted the elegantly-scoped long rifle from where it rested against his chair and began to walk away and then turned, a downright vicious glint in his smile. "Oh, and remember, we're all meetin' up at the Occidental for the show. Wouldn't want to disappoint Misty, right?" With a quick chuckle, he turned again and was gone.

"Misty?" Lucinda pretended to be unaware of the name.

Jesse shot his brother's back a dark look, shaking his own head in disbelief. He looked back at Lucinda. "A girl. Frank's just shootin' his mouth off again. He does that a lot."

Lucinda nodded. For some reason, the fact that he had not identified Misty more clearly annoyed her.

"So, what brings you back to my table, Ms. Lucy?" His smile was back as he leaned into his chair in a relaxed pose. His eyes flicked over to the gaming table where Courtright was organizing his winnings with a slight smile of his own.

"Well, I just wanted to talk some more, and my . . . friend," she nodded over her shoulder to the gaming tables, "won't be needing my help for a while."

Jesse smiled at that. "Friend. That's rich. Tell me, you get a cut of his take? Or does he just pay you a flat fee? Or maybe you do it for true love?" His voice was a little bitter, and she decided she needed to go forward with a little more caution.

"It's purely a business relationship, I assure you, Mr. James." She tried to put a little chill into her words to convince him he had wandered close to a line.

Jesse smiled again. "Well, ain't nothin' stoppin' a lady from conductin' her own business, that's for sure."

Lucinda's shock at his words caught her by surprise. She made a show of lowering herself into a chair, masking the momentary lapse with another smile. Haunting words from her unhappy childhood rang in her ears. It had not been pleasant, after her father was killed at the Petersburg siege. Her mother, bitter and resentful, had tried to fill the gaping hole he had left behind with alcohol and a succession of gentlemen callers who made the house a living hell for little Lucy. She had escaped as soon as she could make her own way, and had struggled against perception and expectation as much as any other obstacles as she established herself in one of the most competitive arenas in the world. She brought herself quickly to the present and shook her head slightly.

"Well, back in Georgia, it's not everyone that shares your view, Mr. James."

He smiled wider. "Georgia! I thought you was a bit of a peach, miss. An' I believe I asked you to call me Jesse?"

Lucinda lowered her eyes demurely, trying to reestablish her equilibrium. "Of course, Jesse."

"So, Georgia. Well, you can't feel none too charitable toward the Union either, then, can you? After what Grant and his pet pyromaniac did to Atlanta?"

Lucinda shrugged. "That was a long time ago. If you want, we can trace every little grudge back to Cain and Abel, and just all kill each other and leave it to the birds and lizards. Does that sound about right?"

Jesse stared at her without responding, then laughed. "Yeah, we could do that. But Cain and Abel, that was a powerful long time ago. Atlanta, that seems a tad closer. When you lost as many folks as I did—"

"You're not the only one who lost folks, Jesse." The facade of easy grace and beauty slid from her face and she stared at him, anger and pain very real in her eyes. "We all lost people. And if there weren't bigger problems in the world, then I'd say sure, let's keep fighting that war until we all felt satisfied. But you can't do that, Jesse, not with all the problems we got nowadays. We all stand together eventually, or they're going to hang us all alone in the end."

Jesse cocked his head to one side. "Who's 'they', sweetheart? Who's got you all scared?"

Lucinda cursed herself for losing focus again. What was it about this man? "The natives are getting restless, Jesse, and they're on the warpath. And everyone has been talking about nightmare creatures, and walking dead, and lights that set fire to the desert sky. What do you think is happening, while you sit here and nurse your cheap beer?"

After she snapped, she pulled back, not sure how he would react. When she saw his smile grow a little wider, it made her even more angry. His words, however, brought her back to the task at hand.

"I don't know about the Injun magic, Lucy, but you don't have to worry about those walkin' corpses. They smell to high heaven, and they ain't much good for much as far as I can see, but there ain't nothin' biblical about 'em, I can tell ya'."

Lucinda schooled her face to casual attention. "Really? You've seen them? I thought they were never far from that Doctor Carpathian?"

Jesse gave a jerk of his head. "Yeah, they're usually around the doc. But they're all over, now, really."

She folded her hands on the table before her. "Why do you say they aren't 'biblical'?"

Jesse waved that question away with an annoying lack of concern. "I don't know the specifics, but they're just like those UR-30 law mechanicals, just made out of flesh and bone instead of metal an' rubber. They aren't like folks comin' back from the dead 'r nothin'. They don't have any recollection of who they were or what they done before. They're just like machines, runnin' on doc's crimson gold, is all."

"But they don't scare you?" It was a question a woman in her supposed position would have asked, so Lucinda forced herself to ask it even though she was fairly certain of the answer.

Sure enough, Jesse laughed. "Scared? Nah. They ain't so fast, an' most of 'em ain't so big, and if I wouldn'ta been scared of 'em when they were alive an' fast an' thinking fer themselves, what'd I be worryin' about now that they're all dead and rottin' and slow?"

He grinned at her broadly. "How 'bout you, darlin'? Do they scare you?"

Lucinda knew what her answer should have been. She began to formulate it in her mind, with the requisite shiver and fetching wide eyed look, but she heard herself respond before she even knew she had taken a breath. "No. They don't frighten me either. I'm just curious."

Jesse seemed pleased by that response, and she felt a genuine answering smile on her own face. She cursed herself in the silence of her own mind. The smile, however, remained professionally in place.

"No, I didn't figure you'd be scared of too much, actually."

They found themselves staring at each other. The silence stretched on. Lucinda could feel Courtright's eyes on her back. She tried desperately to summon up some thought or statement that would break the lull, but all she could do was smile.

All he seemed to want to do was grin back at her.

*****

Henry Courtright watched as Lucinda and James fenced back and forth. Every gesture and look she employed was masterful. He had seen her use it all before. She was deploying her full arsenal on the poor copperhead, and the secret agent had no doubt the rube would not know what hit him.

But at the same time, Courtright felt a touch of nerves. Lucinda was usually focused to a fault and would never let a mark go by without getting the answers she needed. The fact that James seemed to fluster her at all was reason enough to feel concern, despite the fact that she seemed to have marshaled her efforts back to the task at hand.

A whispered doubt crept into his mind, however. She had never acted like this before. How would he know if she was back on her game? If she started to use her talents on him, would he be able to puzzle out her true intentions beneath the layers of falsehood and illusion she had spent a lifetime learning to weave?

Courtright eased back into his chair, elbow once again hooked over the back, and stared openly at a Jesse James too caught up in Lucinda to even notice. The freak's artificial hands were clasped behind his head in an attitude of complete relaxation. The dull metal of the arms contrasted sharply with the brighter metal of their internal components and the flat black of the tubes and wires. And of course the flickering gleam of RJ-1027 cells and indicators winked here and there along their lengths.

What were the chances that any man, no matter how good he had been with the arms God had given him, was as good, never mind better, replacing them with gears and pulleys, wheels and pistons? There were many stories, told and retold across the territories, about Jesse and the speed of his draw. Most of the tales sounded fantastical, painting a picture Courtright found it impossible to fully believe. And yet there seemed to be a path of dead bodies behind the man, and the agent wondered how many of those had thought the same thing.

Courtright patted the blaster pistol riding on his hip and thought fondly of the mini Gatling in his room. He felt a smile tug at the corner of his mouth. Their orders were to find Carpathian wherever he was hiding, and to get that information back to Washington. But everyone knew that Jesse James had ties to the mad inventor. If their paths should cross in the wilds, things might just develop on their own. And maybe, just maybe, Mama Courtright's little boy would get a chance to see what Mrs. James' little pissant was capable of.

Chapter 6

Jesse stared at the cards in his hand without seeing them. There was no forgetting those dark eyes and that wide smile. He could not deny that Lucy had made quite an impression on him. She had left when a few of his posse came in, and even after she had gone back to her card sharp friend, Jesse had been sitting there trying to remember their conversation. He could not recall much, and for some reason that did not bother him. When Harding, Chase, and a couple of the other men asked if he wanted a game, he just nodded and they sat down, oblivious to their leader's lack of focus.

Despite his inattention, however, his stake was still healthy after several hands. His eyes kept drifting back toward Lucy, although he never caught her looking his way. Even though his heart was not in the game, his luck was bearing up better than usual. The same could not be said for Harding.

"Who brought this tainted deck o' pasteboards into this parlor?" Harding threw down his hand and spat off into the corner. "I swear, one more hand goes 'round that way I'll know one of you is bilkin' the table." The other men were not trying hard to conceal their amusement.

"Well, you know what they say, Harding: Unlucky at cards, lucky in . . . what are you lucky in?" A red haired outlaw chuckled as he went back to looking at his cards. Jesse smiled as Harding sputtered.

"Bryce," Harding growled, low in his throat. "You wanna make it out of here to spend any of that coin you're hoardin', you best hobble your lip before I beat you within an inch of the Almighty, and we'll see if your luck'll save you then."

The men laughed as Harding organized the coins and notes in front of him, ignoring the continued banter.

"Hey, isn't that Billy the Kid?" Ty's voice was curious and soft as he whispered into the considering silence of the game. "I think that's Billy the Kid, right?"

Jesse looked at the youngster with a blank face, all of the warm confusion draining from his mind. When he spoke, he did not take his eyes off Ty.

"Gage, William Bonney just step into the establishment?"

In a moment, Jesse's mind had gone from a pleasant, relaxed state to a vicious tension as Ty's words about Bonney and Misty on the trail to Missouri City came back to him. There was no sense of guilt or irony as he shifted from idle speculation concerning one lady to a building jealous rage over another. He had entirely forgotten the beauty sitting not twenty feet away. As the heat began to rise in his chest, he could only think about Misty, and Ty's innocent words.

It had been years since the big train job that had ended the brutal persecution of the men and women living on the edge of society, putting them on an even footing with the soldiers and lawmen who had been trying to exterminate them. Nearly a decade since those seemingly hopeless days when RJ-1027 tech was new, and Carpathian's weapons had suddenly shifted the balance of power forever. Since then, he had worked a couple jobs with Billy the Kid, but it had been a couple years since he had seen the Kid in person. Jesse contemplated all the different ways he could welcome the Kid into Kansas City, from a hug to a handshake to a hole in the head. Instead, he decided to ignore him and continued to look at his cards, waiting for Chase to make his call on the current hand. Conversation around the saloon died down, however, and Jesse could feel William Bonney coming toward him through the room.

"I'll see your whole pot and raise you one of these, Jesse!" The voice was pitched high with excitement and anticipation, but he refused to turn. When an object sailed over his shoulder and landed in the pile of coins and notes in the center of the table, however, he could not ignore the Kid any longer.

Jesse leaned forward a bit to look at the thing in the middle of the pot: a piece of poorly cured leather trailing a tuft of long white hair. Jesse looked over his shoulder to where Billy the Kid stood with a wide grin, and jerked a thumb at the object.

"What is that?" Jesse kept his voice flat, knowing the anger building in his gut could get the better of him at any moment.

"Why, don't you recognize it?" The Kid's voice was mocking. "Well, that there is a bona fide Injun scalp, that is! And ain't no normal brave, neither. That there's the scalp of a gen-u-ine medicine man!"

Jesse looked at the sad, pathetic thing with a curled lip. "Get it outta my pot before I lose my manners."

An enormous fat man beside Billy gave a wet chuckle and reached out with a long, wickedly curved knife, picking the scalp up by its white lock with a neat twist. He swung the thing wide and offered it back to the grinning young outlaw leader.

"Thanks, Smiley." Billy took the scalp and gently put it back in a cloth bag. "You remember Smiley, Jesse? He was in on the train job." Being in on the train job was often a way of dividing the innumerable outlaws throughout the territories between the established and respected and the inexperienced and green. It did not always work like that, however, and Jesse remembered the man most folks called 'Smiley' for a violent lunatic who enjoyed disfiguring the faces of his victims. He grunted without a smile and looked back at Billy.

"Is there a reason you come lookin' for me, Billy?" Jesse's tone indicated that the younger man was beneath him within the obscure outlaw pecking order. "Or am I just lucky today?"

Billy's smile never faltered as he swung an empty chair around, bringing his leg up and over to sit down backward. "No, sir. I came here to find you."

"Ain't exactly like you been hidin' yourself out this way, you know, living like a bunch of city swells." The younger man on Billy's other side muttered.

Billy grinned at the boy and wagged a finger at him, still swinging the bag. "Now, Garrett, we're all friends here, right?" He looked at Jesse. "Right, Jesse? All friends?"

Jesse grunted and put his cards down. "Sure, Billy. We're all friends. Now you care to tell me why you're lookin' for me? I got places I gotta be, and you're seriously queering my luck."

Billy nodded, his pleasant smile still firmly in place. "Sure, Jesse, I get it. You're a busy man." He looked at the cards in front of the other outlaw and his grin widened slightly. "We're all busy men." He gestured broadly toward the bar and then signaled for the man standing there to bring three whiskeys. "You heard what went down out in the mountains, a couple weeks ago?"

Jesse nodded sourly. "Yeah. Heard you ran into some squaws and cut 'em down from behind." He pointed to the bag still swinging in Billy's hand. "That a bit o' one of them poor ladies?"

Billy's smile darkened a bit before coming back full force. "Squaws. You're funny, Jesse. I always said that about you." He turned to the fat man now sitting beside him. "Don't I always say that about Jesse, Smiley? That he's funny?"

The man's small eyes tightened. "Yeah. You say that."

"See? Jesse's funny. I always say that." Billy leaned back, relaxing in his chair as if he owned the Arcadia. "No, they weren't squaws, Jesse. We hit ourselves a Warrior Nation war party, wanderin' around out there in the wilds, way past their usual haunts. An' we dry gulched 'em somethin' fierce. Din't we, Garrett?"

The young man, still standing behind Billy, nodded.

Jesse nodded, mechanical arms folded over his chest. "Okay, so, you got lucky against some Injuns. An' that lands you all the way back here, in Kansas City, sittin' at my table?"

Billy frowned and shook his head. "You're missin' the point, Jesse. What was a war party of braves, led by this white haired bug himself, doin' kickin' around up in the mountains? Almost all of Sittin' Bull's savages are back this way, gettin' fancy with Grant and the Union slugs." He met Jesse's disdainful glare with a steady look. "Why were they that far west, Jesse?"

The older outlaw shook his head. "This ain't my tale, Billy, it's you'rn. So why don't you tell it?"

Before Billy could continue, one of the barkeeps stopped by and dropped three heavy whiskey glasses on the table, standing stubbornly by until Billy nodded to Garrett, who pulled a couple coins out of a pocket and handed them over. The barkeep looked as his palm, sniffed, and turned to walk away.

"Okay," Billy sat back, resuming his nonchalant pose and idly picking up his drink. "They was lookin' fer somethin', Jesse. Somethin' big. Twenty braves, led by one o' their white-hairs hisself?" He waved the bag again for emphasis. "You don't see that kind of weight out that far for nothin'."

Jesse's mouth quirked into a tight grin for the first time since Billy had walked into the saloon. "That's what you got? Injuns don't go that far, so they musta been lookin' fer somethin'?"

Billy's smile dropped completely from his face and he shook his head. "No, Jesse, that ain't all I got. Before we sent Señor White Hair to the happy hunting ground, we got some words outta 'im. He was singin' like a showgirl afore Smiley finally did for him. So yeah, we got a lot more to go on." He smiled again, leaning back in his chair. "Way I figure it, we got a real hog-killin' time comin', and I'm the only one knows where to start lookin'."

Jesse stared at William Bonney for a moment, eyes flat and blank, before he said, "So, what were they lookin' for, Billy? You ain't mentioned that."

Billy's smiled faded again. "Well, we din't get that outta him, but we know where they was headed! An' we know it was real important-like, cuz'a they had a medicine man with 'em!"

Jesse nodded. "So, you don' know what it is you're lookin' for, or why even the savages woulda wanted it, but you're hell-fire sure you wanna go hairing off into the wilds after it? And, since you dropped your sorry ass here on my doorstep, half a country back in the wrong direction, I'm assumin' you wanna drag me in after you?"

Billy nodded, ignoring the sarcasm. "They was good, Jesse. It took everything my posse had to take 'em down, and even then, I lost half my guys. Half of 'em, Jesse, and that was with we had the drop on 'em! Sittin' Bull and the other chiefs, they never woulda sent that many o' their best young braves, led by a white hair, out that far, in the middle of a war where they need every one o' their boys an' girls close to home, lessen there was a damned good reason."

Jesse shook his head. "That ain't necessarily true, Billy. Coulda been they saw a shape in some smoke, or a bird crapped on the wrong man's head, and they thought it was their Great Spirit jawin' at 'em from the Big Beyond, and off they go, gallivantin' into the wilds, to get chewed up by the likes o' you, who then comes runnin' back to civilization with this tall tale an' your eyes all full o' gold, 'r gems, 'r God knows what you think is out there."

It was Billy's turn to shake his head sharply. He leaned over the table; his hands pressed wide to either side, and tried to force belief into the skeptical outlaw across the table. "You weren't there, Jesse. You weren't lookin' into that old man's eyes as he died. He was terrified, man. He was terrified we was gonna find this thing. Whatever it is, it meant enough to them to send some of their best, with one of their elders, an' you know how they guard those old men, Jesse. They sent their best, an' this old man, far away lookin' for this thing when they needed 'em most against Grant. It's big, Jesse, its mighty big, whatever it is."

Jesse stared at the younger man for a long time. When he spoke, he was careful to keep any tone of agreement or warmth out of his voice. "You know where we'd have to go to get it?"

Billy's eyes dropped and his hands started to tap randomly on the back of his chair. "Well, not exactly—"

Jesse barked a laugh. "Not exactly!" He slapped the table and then looked around at his own men. "Not exactly! Well, hell, Billy, what does that mean, exactly?"

Billy's eyes flared at the tone. "I know what the Injuns call the place. I figure, we get closer, out into the desert, we start talkin' around, there's always some folks out that way, half breeds an' whatnot. Probably, someone'll know where it is we're tryin' to get to."

Jesse watched him squirm. "And leavin' aside for a moment the location of this great treasure of yours, you're thinkin', if this is so all-fired important, you're figurin' you'll need extra bodies to go get it?"

Billy shrugged. "They sent twenty of their best braves, Jesse. An' those folks near-wrecked my crew. I'm figurin' they was expectin' a fight, an' we better expect one too, if we take up their trail."

Jesse grinned. "Or coulda been, they were expectin' the fight you gave 'em, Billy, and they lost that one. Maybe all the fightin's done, and you just gotta walk into this fairy-tale place an' grab whatever it is they were headin' for!" Jesse could see that possibility had not occurred to the younger man, and he shook his head. "Course, it's probably two dusty old buffalo hides and a spittoon of squaw piss that you'll be grabbin', blessed by the Great Googely Moogely, or whatever."

Billy brought his hands down on the table, ready to push off with anger, and beside him Smiley and Garrett were frowning as well, hands on their weapons. Jesse raised one finger to stave off a fight.

"But let's assume there is somethin' worth havin' out there, Billy. An' let's assume we're gonna have to fight to get it. That still don't answer my original question: why've you come lookin' fer me? You ain't never lacked for lads to fill up yer posse whenever you were on the shoot."

Billy settled back down, fingers steepled across the back of his chair. "Well, Jesse, first, I'm figurin', for somethin' this big, I really need someone I can ride the river with, you know? Someone I can trust to watch my back, an' everyone knows, that's gotta be you, right?" His smile was as wide as it was false.

Jesse watched him with lidded eyes, knowing full well that there had never been any great trust or faith between them. However, he merely waited, a growing curiosity as to Billy's true destination growing in him. He gestured with one lazy hand for Billy to continue.

Billy was ready to charge right in and continue the flattery, but something stopped him, he paused to take stock, and then with a sharp nod, he said, "I figure, once we find whatever it is, we gotta get rid of it. Find someone to buy it. Ain't nothin' any good to ya if you can't find someone else who wants it." He flipped a hand toward Jesse. "You got a lot more inroads with folks that could pay big, when we gotta unload it."

Jesse watched him fidget for a moment and then said, "You gonna tell me the rest, or you gonna make me guess?"

Billy sighed, but then lurched forward, his eyes glowing with an idea he had kept close to his vest, from even his closest men, until now.

"Well, Jesse, the Warrior Nation is fightin' for its very life against the Union, right? So I figure, they're lookin' for somethin' that desperate like, it's gotta be somethin' they think they can use against the Union, am I right?"

Jesse nodded for him to carry on. He could tell that this was the first Billy's men were hearing of this new wrinkle because all of a sudden Smiley and Garrett were watching their boss with growing interest and confusion.

"Well, I'm thinkin', if they could use it against Grant and his bully boys, what's stoppin' anyone else from usin' it the same way, right?" Billy's mind was racing now, his eyes bouncing around the table, and Jesse could almost taste his excitement. There was doubt there too, however. Billy did not have full confidence in his conclusions; he was following blind impulse, or advice that he did not fully understand, and it was clear that he was riding full tilt without a map.

"Sounds like that might not be completely mad, Billy. But so what, you plannin' on goin' up directly against Grant and the whole Union, now?"

Billy looked around the table, his eyes sly again. "Well, no, not me, exactly." His eyes slid sideways back to Jesse. "But it struck me, we got some mutual friends that might not mind gettin' their hands on somethin' powerful enough, the Nation thinks it'll help against the Union. Strikes me, we know some folks got their own grudge against Grant and the rest of those damned Lincolnites, an' they might be more'n willin' to entertain some generous thoughts for the folks who brought 'em a little treat like that."

Jesse's brow furrowed in confusion for a moment before clearing, and then rising in disbelief. "You mean the Rebellion?" Since Grant's armies had crushed the Confederacy, the remnants had been skulking around in the swamps of Florida and Louisiana, calling themselves the Confederate Rebellion, swilling rotgut and singing Dixie at the moon. Jesse was disgusted with what had become of his former comrades in arms, and he let that distaste show now.

Billy, either because he was more of an idealist or, more likely, because he'd been too young himself to fight in the war, did not share Jesse's disdain. "Yeah, the Rebellion! Those boys're just waitin' for their chance, Jesse, an' we could give it to 'em!"

Jesse looked at Harding and Gage, the only other men at the table who had fought in the war. "This strikin' you boys as a good idea?"

Harding spit a plug onto the floor nearby with a snicker. "Rebellion don't have a pot to piss in, literally. They're down in those swamps, chasin' gators and getting' eat by gallinippers. And besides, they ain't got two copper pennies to rub together, neither."

Billy leaned in again. "But Jesse, if this thing the savages were after, if it's all that, don' you think it could make a difference? Don' you think those ol' graybacks out in the swamps, they're just lookin' for some way they can get their own back?" He leaned even closer. "An' don' you think, they'd jump at the chance to follow whoever it was that showed 'em that way?"

Billy leaned back, his hands grasping the chair back on either side, a smile forming once more on his face. "You see the possibilities now, don'cha? Two gents like you an' me? Showin' up in the swamps with a way to put Grant down, and the south can rise again? Hell, Jesse, we'd be writin' our own ticket at that point!"

Jesse stared at the bag still dangling from Billy's wrist. Although he could not tease it out right now, Billy's whole scheme had a lot to recommend it. It was not like the war leaders of the Warrior Nation to send a party out under the command of an elder on a frivolous mission. There could very well be something out in the desert, and if so, it was something Sitting Bull, Geronimo, and the other chiefs who now led the unified Warrior Nation were keen to collect. It could be some sort of weapon, the way new and alarming things kept popping up ever since Carpathian had arrived toward the end of the war. If someone were to appear down in the swamps with some new super weapon, to rally the shattered forces of the Confederacy, reshape them into a fighting force once again, wielding whatever it was that Sitting Bull seemed so eager to recover . . .

"Most o' those I rode with in the war come up a cropper a long time ago, Billy." Jesse leaned back, the picture of regret. "Those that ain't, most o' them are still ridin' the trails up here with us. I'm not sure who all ended up down in the swamps, but I'm not sure they'd give a lick for me or what I thought, if I was to suddenly appear down there. I wouldn't even know who to ask for."

Billy nodded at this renewed interest. "I get it, Jesse. I do. But you knew a bunch of folks! Gotta be some of 'em 're still down there, an' if we could bring 'em somethin' big, somethin' they could use to get back on top? I'm pretty sure, we follow it through, we could end up big bugs ourselves, one day soon."

Jesse noted the excitement in Billy's eyes. "These are pretty grand plans, Billy. You're thinkin' mighty big all of a sudden, ain't ya?"

"Well, ain't nothin' says we gotta stay in the shadows forever, now, does it?" Billy gestured to the saloon around them. "Kansas City gets 'emselves some decent law, an' they will, we're out in no-man's land again. As long as the Union is in charge out here, we ain't gonna have nowhere to go. We're gonna be stuck on the fringe. But if we can tip that balance? If we can bring back the Rebs? Why, then, Grant's gonna have a whole lot more to worry about than us, eh?"

Jesse nodded slowly. "Might be you're onto somethin', Billy. I'm willin' to give you that. An' you say you got an idea of where we'd be headed?"

Billy's energy dimmed slightly with suspicion. "Yeah, I got a name. I figured, though, we'd share that sort of details when we got a bit closer."

Jesse laughed. "You don't trust me, Billy? That hurts. That really does a number on my insides. Okay, well, that'll come. Can you give me an idea of what types of terrain we'll be lookin' at? If my boys an' I go with you, what're we gonna need?"

Billy shrugged. "Desert, I think, like I said. An' the white hair said it was buried. So we might need to be diggin' it up."

Jesse was blank. "Dig? How deep?"

Billy shrugged again. "I don't know. But the Injuns, they were carryin' an awful lot o' spades, axes, an' things like that. They looked like they were plannin' on some serious excavation."

Jesse tapped the table, his eyes unfocused slightly as he thought. "Well, if we're gonna have to be doin' a lot of diggin', I'm thinking maybe we wanna stop somewhere along the way an' get some serious equipment, do it right."

Billy brightened. "Carpathian? You think he could help us?"

Jesse shook his head. "No, not the doc. I'll go see him anyway on our way west, my boys and I need to see him about a few things." He looked down at one mechanical hand, opening and closing the fingers quickly. "But I was thinkin' we swing through Diablo Canyon. We need heavy equipment, there's enough there, pretty much all we'd have to do would be to throw it in a wagon–"

Billy nodded, smiling, but Garrett and Smiley shared a hooded glance as soon as Jesse mentioned Diablo Canyon, and Jesse stopped.

"What?" The older outlaw's face was blank as suspicion flared again in his heart.

"You ain't heard about Diablo Canyon?" Smiley was not smiling.

The suspicion built. "Yeah," Jesse kept his voice even. "Diablo Canyon. Best place in the territories to kick up a fuss if you're feelin' the need. Ain't been no law down there since those odd sticks ran the railroad tracks right to the edge of the cliff with no ideas on how to get across. Place is a pirate's paradise, with all that equipment just sittin' there, waitin' for someone to shoot or get off the pot."

Jesse twisted to look over at Gage and Ty. "Boys, if we're goin' to Diablo Canyon, you all are in for a right good time."

"They got themselves a 'bot." Garrett's voice was flat as he spoke, and his words brought Jesse's head snapping back around.

"They got a 'bot? You mean a UR-30?" His tone rose incredulously. "How in the name of Hell did one o' them metal marshals get down to Diablo Canyon, for God's sake?"

Billy looked grim and shrugged. "The townsfolk were bein' bled dry. They sent a telegram to Tombstone, an'—"

"Damned Wyatt Earp." Jesse collapsed against the back of his chair. "Damned Earp and his damned fool lawmen, stickin' their noses in where they don't belong." He looked up at Billy. "The thing any good?"

The younger outlaw nodded. "Ringo and the Apache Kid got caught by it, the thing cleaned their plow somethin' fierce, left most of their boys pushin' daisies before they could skedaddle."

Jesse pursed his lips. "Ringo and the Apache, eh?"

"They ain't no slouches, Jesse." Harding muttered. "Johnny Ringo and the Apache Kid ain't no slouches."

Jesse nodded. "So, they got themselves a 'bot . . . "

Billy nodded, and then added, somewhat sheepishly, "that might be another reason I need you to ride along, Jesse. The way Ringo talked, this thing's a killer, and no mistake."

Jesse's smile returned. "Well, now everything makes a lot more sense, Billy! I was worryin' you'd gone all mamby-pamby on me all of a sudden! So, you knew we'd need to go to the Canyon."

Billy shrugged. "Thought it might come up."

Jesse thought for a second and then nodded. "Okay, I think I can work with all this. Tell you what, you an' your posse head on over toward Diablo Canyon. We'll follow you, and we'll meet just above town, where the tracks go through that cut in the hills?"

Billy nodded, a slight smile returning to his own face.

"So, we meet up in the hills, an' we'll come up with a plan on how we're gonna get around the metal man." Jesse paused and then gave Billy a sharp look. "Your boys are all heeled with the latest, right? Crimson gold all around?"

Billy took out one of his modified RJ-1027 six-shooters and gave it a quick twirl around his trigger finger before sliding it back into the holster. "'Course, Jesse."

Jesse nodded again. "'Course. Well, then. You boys be on your way, an' we'll meet you in the hills, bout seven days from now?" They all nodded. "We take care of the UR-30, we go find this mysterious oasis, dig up our treasure, and see if we can't raise the south once again, eh?"

Jesse reached out for his glass and raised it toward the other outlaw boss. "You wanna drink on it?"

Billy smiled and raised his own glass, and the two gave a heavy clunk as they hit over the center of the table. "Seven days from now, just above Diablo Canyon." They shot back the warm remnants of their drinks and nodded to each other.

Jesse held up one gunmetal finger. "An' you don' go rushin' in without us, now, you hear? Or lightin' a shuck ahead of us an' leavin' us seven days from civilization and nothin' to show for it."

Billy waved with both hands, his smile firmly in place. "Jesse, we're in this together, thick or thin. I won't let you down."

They reached over the table again to shake hands, and Jesse gripped tight when Billy expected him to let go. The older man pulled his younger compatriot closer and stated, "I know you won't."

Billy pulled his hand away with a start, and a cloud moved over his face before his smile came swiftly out again. "That's you, Jesse, always funny!" He nodded to the other men and then moved toward the door, Smiley and Garrett following behind, not breaking eye contact with Jesse's boys until they had to, their faces grim.

"So," Harding muttered, playing vaguely with his cards. "We headin' west?"

Jesse smiled and shook his head. "Not necessarily."

The men all leaned forward. The boss held up his mechanical hands, still smiling widely, and gestured with a thumb over his shoulder toward the door. "That little corncracker ain't ever gonna tell me 'r mine what to do, first off. So, if'n I see's fit to let him stew in the hills for a few days, he's gonna grin and take it. He knows it, an' I know it. But if we do wanna throw in with the Kid and his mob of misfits, well then, we're all set to do just that." He wove his hands behind his back with a series of soft whirs and clicks, his grin growing wider. "So, we either got the Kid stuck in the middle of nowhere waitin' for us for God knows how long, or we got us partners in what might or might not be the damned-foolest thing I ever heard of."

Gage chuckled. "Secret Injun weapons, raisin' up the damned Rebs outa their fool swamps, save the world, and damn the Union!" He downed the last of his own drink. "Sounds like a good enough ride to jump on, just to see where it takes us!"

Harding grunted. "I don't trust Bonney. He ain't nobody's baby, and those soap-locks he rides with are all of 'em worse."

Jesse did not disagree. "Well, there's nothin' sayin' we gotta ride with 'em. Plenty of time for us make that call later. Billy'll wait for a few days, anyway, afore he goes chargin' in or runs off with tail tucked. Ain't no rush."

Jesse flipped his cards over, a quick glare daring any of his men to say something. "Well, this game's dead, boys. I'm gonna head up to my room for a sec, then move on over to the Occidental. Who's with me?"

Although most of them had the grace to look sheepish, all of the men around the table muttered something about other plans. Jesse's smile hardened. "Well, that'd be your loss, ya'll. I think I want ya'll with me anyway, in case I need to get a hold of you. Meet you all over yonder?"

He picked up his hat, settled it on his head, and tapped a single mechanical finger to its brim before turning and heading for the door.

It felt as if he'd been hearing William Bonney's damn fool nickname every day for a year. And he knew that his own men were starting to feel that they had spent too much time in Kansas City. The cockup in Missouri City hadn't helped that at all, either.

Harding and the other steady hands had come to him and recommended they lose Ty after the Missouri City job. But there was something about the kid that made Jesse feel more comfortable with things, and he had denied them. He knew Harding had talked with Frank, though, and he knew his older brother would be watching the young kid like a hawk, and there was nothing wrong with that.

Jesse knew that Billy's whole story seemed absurd, and he was trying to convince himself there was nothing to it, and the best he could hope for was a good laugh next time he ran into the Kid, after leaving him with his britches around his ankles out in the badlands above Diablo Canyon. But something about the whole thing would not let Jesse go. He had friends in the swamps far to the south, and although he had played it cool with Billy, he would like nothing better than to see them emerge and confront Grant and his galoots, now that the Union was fighting on a couple different fronts.

He thought back to what Lucy had said, about killing random Yanks not leading to a fulfilling life. What if he could somehow bring the Rebellion something it could use to bring Grant down? And not only Grant, but maybe the whole damned Union?

His eyes were dark and his brow furrowed as he took the steps to the second story rooms two at a time. He was far too preoccupied to notice Lucy and Courtright watching him as he disappeared onto the second floor.

*****

Wyatt stood amidst the wreckage in the center of Missouri City with a blank face, his eyes flicking from detail to detail, absorbing the entire scene. This was worse than anything he had imagined when they followed the column of smoke seen from the road to Kansas City.

In the middle of the street was a double row of bodies covered in sheets and blankets taken from nearby houses. Most of the shapes beneath their coverings were shrunken and contorted; the sign of an excruciating death by fire. These were the casualties of the bank job, as well as two women and a man who had been killed when a building down the street had collapsed. Quite a death toll for a single visit to this poor, sleepy town.

The bank itself was completely gutted. The corner posts and a few charred remnants of support beams were all that remained standing. A thick cloud of greasy smoke continued to rise into the clear warm air, and an oppressive heat still radiated from the wreckage as if, somewhere in the ruins of the once-grand building, there was some sort of portal straight to Hell. Wyatt's mustache twitched at the thought, or maybe at the sickly-sweet smell in the air.

There were three poorly-maintained old Iron Horses in front of the shattered bank. Each had been riddled with bullets, rendering them inoperable. The blasts had been carefully placed and, as far as Wyatt could tell, the machines probably would not be moving again anytime soon. Wyatt's eyes flicked to the row of bodies again, particularly the shriveled bodies from within the bank. He was willing to bet that careful inspection would reveal at least circumstantial evidence indicating that three of those bodies were perpetrators, not victims, in the previous day's events.

Behind Wyatt stood his brother Virgil, silent as the grave, and Doc Holliday, standing unmoving except for the constant whisper and hum of his re-breather. Further behind them, across the street and keeping folks at bay by their mere presence, was a line of figures, menacing in their utter stillness. All four of Tombstone's UR-30 Enforcer units, activated for the hunt, stood in a line like statues from some ancient temple. Their armored forms were visible beneath their standard riding leathers; both clothing and metal skin scorched and soot stained from recovering the bodies from the seething Hell of the bank.

There were five figures in the line, Wyatt knew without looking, and the fifth figure, the hulking form of his brother Morgan, was what truly kept most of the townsfolk of Missouri City back. Wyatt shook his head slightly and continued his methodical examination of the scene. He hated brooding over Morgan's condition, and often hid behind the needs of the moment to avoid doing so.

A little further away from the robots and the massive, armored form of Morgan, sat the brooding hulk of a Judgment support wagon. The enormous vehicles were usually assigned to circuit judges moving through the territories, and made perfect mobile court-houses and jails, as well as fortresses in times of serious trouble. For this foray, Wyatt had grabbed one as a mobile headquarters and a way to transport his brother and the Enforcer units. He also knew bringing the judge along with him might grease some wheels, the deeper into trouble he got. A squadron of marshals and deputies on Interceptors, the lawmens' own unique variant of the Iron Horse, rode along as outriders and scouts, and added gun hands if things got ugly. The Interceptors and their riders were now scattered around the town collecting statements and looking for other witnesses.

"So, there were eight of 'em." Wyatt's drawl was low, and the town officials had to lean forward to hear.

"Yessir," the old sheriff, Casey Stillman, said. The old man had been mortified by the devastation visited upon his town in his absence. He was a broken man, something inside him had died with the folks lined up in the dust behind them.

"Eight, including Jesse James?" Wyatt turned his head to look down at the slope-shouldered sheriff.

"We think so, sir." He shrugged. "They hit the town from over the river, their 'Horses throwing up a terrible fog. Most folks ran. Those that didn't . . . " he gestured weakly behind them, and Wyatt nodded.

"And you were in the big city whoopin' it up." Virgil's voice was low but filled with contempt. The old man could only nod, and the big marshal snorted and looked away.

"Any of the bodies identifiable as the outlaws?" Doc spoke over the hissing of his breathing apparatus, and another man, the town manager, shook his head.

"By the time most of us come back, the bank was completely goin' up. There weren't no way we could stop it at that point. It was lost, an' . . . all those folks that hadn't gotten out."

Doc leaned toward Wyatt and murmured, "Taking another gander into the bank might prove useful. Morgan'd be game."

Wyatt grunted over his shoulder at his friend, one hand smoothing his mustache in a habitual gesture. He hated asking anything of Morgan because of his younger brother's special status. With a quick shake of his head, however, he bowed to necessity. No one else was going to be able to go into that hell except a UR-30 unit or Morgan. And the UR-30s were not known for their delicacy.

"Morgan," Wyatt pitched his voice to be heard over the muttering crowd behind the marshal's line.

The Over-marshal felt, more than heard, the impacts of his brother's footsteps as Morgan approached. There were always moments when Wyatt allowed himself to forget what had happened to his younger brother, but those footsteps always brought it all rushing back.

"Wyatt." The voice was toneless, buzzing with the inhuman resonances of the UR-30 vocal interface.

Wyatt schooled his face to stillness and turned to regard the hulking form of his brother. Morgan had nearly died over a year ago, the victim of an assassination attempt, gunned down while playing pool at Campbell and Hatch's. The bastards had fired right through the back door, catching Morgan in the side and throwing him across the table.

Wyatt's eyes were firm and still as the scenes played again in his mind. The desperate rush for doctors, the bleak diagnosis from all that came, and Virgil's refusal to abandon their little brother. The sharpest memory he had, however, was the bitter disappointment in Morgan's voice as he grabbed Wyatt's collar with failing strength and spat, 'I don't see anything'. Morgan had always shared Wyatt's fascination with life after death, and had often speculated on what he would see as life ebbed away.

They were the last words Morgan ever spoke with his own voice.

Virgil, refusing to stand idly by while Morgan passed, had bundled their brother in a cloak and rushed out the door. No one knew where he had gone, although many had strong suspicions. He returned late the next day, exhausted and travel-stained, but had never spoken of where he had gone or what he had done. Morgan was not with him, but he reported that he believed they would see their brother again. And he had been right. Nearly a month later, Morgan had returned, after a fashion.

Wyatt nodded to Morgan, forcing himself to look into his brother's blood-shot eyes. Morgan's pale face was completely framed by the iron support structure that held his head erect. The supports were affixed to the bulky suit that sustained the young marshal's life and held him upright, bypassing his severed spine and allowing him to walk. The supports and braces incorporated a comprehensive array of armored plates, as well, offering him a great deal of protection from further harm. Wyatt did not know how much of his brother's own body still existed within the armored suit, as Morgan was unable to remove even parts of it and survive. The armor moved with the natural grace and flexibility he had possessed before the attack, however, rather than the more rigid, jerky movements of a UR-30 Enforcer, but its bulk and weight forever set him apart from normal men.

"Morgan," Wyatt's voice betrayed nothing of the guilt that rose in him each time he thought of his brother. "Do you think you might take a look inside there, see if there's anything worth seein', before we continue on to Kansas City?"

"Sure, Wyatt." The pale lips quirked in a slight smile that was not even the ghost of his former jovial self, and he turned toward the smoking pile of rubble. As he walked toward the ruined building, Morgan lifted his helmet to his head and settled it in place, armored fingers deftly securing the latches on either side of his throat. He looked back at Wyatt through the distorting lenses of thick glass and nodded once.

"This really necessary, Wyatt?" Virgil's tone was neutral, but it was obvious by the way his heavy brows lowered that he thought the answer was clear.

"Virg, if there's anything in there that can help us, either link this more firmly to James or, God help us, give us an idea that he might o' gone elsewhere, can we afford not to look?" Wyatt was watching Morgan's heavy bulk push past the wreckage of the bank's front doors and into the terrible heat within.

"What the hell you think would still be in there that might help at all?" Virgil always got protective where Morgan was concerned. "The animal's been stayin' in Kansas City for months. He's in Kansas City. Anything we do that costs us so much as a minute, will be somethin' we regret for the rest of our days, if he gets away."

"Damnit, Virg," Wyatt snapped. "How the hell do I know what we might find in there?"

"If we don't look, and we miss somethin' that would lead us in a different direction, we'll have even longer to regret it." Doc's calm voice, muffled as always by his leather breathing mask, eased through the brothers' frustration.

The three of them watched as Morgan's armored form, obscured by smoke and the intense shimmer of the brutal heat, moved through the wreckage. He walked in an awkward, hunched position as he scanned the floor for any signs or clues. The young marshal was slow and methodical, and for his colleagues, time seemed to crawl as they waited in the street for what seemed like hours.

When Morgan emerged he was covered in soot but otherwise none the worse for wear. He held something clenched in his armored fist, and as he approached his brothers he held up his arm, servos whirring, and opened the fingers.

In his palm was a metal pin of some kind, deformed and partially melted by the intense heat. Wyatt took it carefully, shifting it quickly from one hand to the other. After a moment he held it up to the light, grasping it carefully between thumb and forefinger. He could just make out a familiar silhouette mostly hidden within the smudged metal.

"A mourning pin." Wyatt muttered.

Doc, looking over his friend's shoulder, sniffed. "A Lincoln mourning pin. Damn, you Yankees never get tuckered out from worshipping that man."

Wyatt gave the former Georgian a sour look a then went back to the pin. Sure enough, the familiar nose, the top hat, and the beard were clearly visible despite the damage. He looked back to Morgan.

"Where was it?"

Morgan's emotionless face looked out from its metal cage and spoke with his soft, buzzing voice. "The floor, near the tellers' windows."

"If anything would set that bloody-minded bastard off, Wyatt, it'd be findin' one o' these on somebody." Virgil soft voice was intense.

Wyatt nodded, then looked again at his younger brother. "Nothin' else in there?"

Morgan's head shifted slightly from side to side, all the movement his restrictive supports would allow. "No."

Wyatt looked at the pin for a moment longer and then shrugged. "Okay, gents. Then it's on to Kansas City." He looked up into the sky, noting the position of the sun. "We should be able to pull in not long after nightfall, if we push on through."

"Or it might be better we stay here for the night," Doc Holliday offered. "Leave with the crack of dawn, hit KC early enough in the morning, we got a whole day's worth of light to root 'em outta wherever they're hidin'."

Wyatt looked from Virgil to Doc, then to Morgan. Each man's face was impassive, allowing the Over-marshal to make the call.

Wyatt shook his head after a moment. "Doc's right. We been riding hard already, and now this." He gestured disgustingly at the ruins of the Missouri City Savings and Loan. "We'll bunk down here, get up before dawn, and hit them as soon as we can. Take the Judgment just outside of town, have the deputies and the outriders sleep there. The rest of us will find beds in Missouri City."

Virgil nodded and turned to say something to Morgan, then shouted to one of the deputies standing near the Enforcer units. "Provencher, take first watch, through midnight."

The dark-haired young lawman looked sourly at the robots, then flicked a bitter salute from the brim of his hat.

The Over-marshal turned to Sheriff Stillman and leaned in close. "If any word beats us to Kansas City, I'm comin' back here first thing, and I'll be lookin' fer you."

The diminished man could only nod in numb fear. The townsfolk watched silently as the senior lawmen gathered their equipment and moved toward a tall hotel on the waterfront, speaking quietly among themselves as they moved away.

Chapter 7

The Occidental was the fanciest establishment in Kansas City. Every aspect of the place screamed class at the top of its frontier lungs. The floor was carpeted with an intricate, and ironic, oriental pattern. The tables and chairs were dark, polished wood, and the lights overhead were draped in dark red shades and hoods, giving the entire dance-hall a shadowy, exotic atmosphere.

Jesse sat at a card table toward the back of the room that still afforded him a decent view of the stage. Ty's story about Misty and William Bonney had continued to haunt him, and he had no interest in sitting near the front as he usually did. His men sat around the table, most not trying to hide their resentment at being forced to come to the Occidental. They stared down at their cards or took sips from glittering glasses. Even springing for a bottle of genuine bourbon had not softened anyone's mood, and that just tossed grease onto the cooking fire for Jesse.

"She sure is purty, Jesse." Ty was the only man at the table paying any attention to the show, and he was enjoying it with an openness that underscored the sullen set of the other men. "Any man'd feel like a king, standin' next to her!"

Jesse grunted and tossed two coins into the pot. The cards were not being kind, which had added to his dark mood. He wished Ty would shut up about Misty.

Play moved around the table, with coins arcing into the pot or cards flopping down onto the felt-topped table, but Jesse was not paying particular attention. He looked at the men still holding cards, glanced down at his own sad hand, and shrugged, tossing in another coin to follow the raise. As he moved to lower his cards, however, his thumb gave a slight jerk, and the cards shifted in his grip. He clutched at them, but they slid out and flipped onto the table, revealing his pathetic hand.

The men all stopped playing, staring down at the revealed cards; all low numbers and off-suit, and then up at Jesse's dangerously still face. An awkward silence stretched out as everyone around the table waited to see how the outlaw boss would react.

Jesse looked down at the hand that had betrayed him, turning it over to stare at the palm, each finger curling and relaxing in turn. Everything seemed fine, and Jesse shrugged slightly, his shoulders lifting with a heavy sigh.

"You know, boys, some days it just doesn't pay to get outta bed." He gathered up the money that was still in front of him and jerked his head at the pot. "You boys keep that, it wasn't doin' me any good anyway."

Jesse stood up and grabbed the bourbon by the neck of the bottle. "Sorry to've dragged you boys away from your fun. I do think I'll be takin' this with me, however, to keep me company on the long walk back to the Arcadia." He looked up at the stage where Misty was moving sinuously with the other girls, large feathered fans waving to the swirling piano music. He shook his head and looked down at Gage.

"When she's done, tell her I've gone back to my room, will you?" His voice echoed his flat, empty eyes.

"Sure thing, Jesse. You want me to walk her back over when she's done?" Gage's young face was worried, and Jesse knew he did not look good. His men were already concerned that he was losing his edge, and all this talk of Billy the Kid had them thinking about their own situations, riding with Jesse and the Youngers. The older outlaw summoned up a smile and shook his head, pushing as much bravado into his voice as he could muster.

"No. Anyone who thinks they can mess with Jesse James' girl, any time o' the day 'r night, is gonna have another thing comin' at 'em faster than they can know." He pulled one of his Hyper-velocity pistols and sent it spinning and whirling around his hand before it leapt back into the holster, forcing a grin for moral. "Am I right, boys?"

The men around the table agreed with energy that seemed just a little forced. It struck Jesse that they were putting perhaps a little too much effort into being agreeable, but he decided to let it slide. He tipped his hat to the table, gave one quick glance at the stage where Misty was watching him out of the corner of her eye, and turned toward the door.

Maybe with a little time alone, he'd be able to calm himself down enough to talk some sense.

*****

Jesse stared at the small lamp on the little table in his room. The empty bourbon bottle lay on its side nearby, a glass upside down a little beyond. His dark eyes peered into the depths of the lamp, searching out the swirls of ruby highlights present in all RJ-powered lighting. The flecks of color within the lamp's illumination seemed to dance, suspended in the glow. He had lost track of time, slumping down at the table, mechanical arms folded before him, chin resting on the hard armor of his forearm.

His mind had been running through the same familiar paths all night. He could not remember being as happy as he had been in Kansas City with Misty these past few months. But still the constant need to throw himself into the fire was always overpowering. And now, with the return of Bonney . . . Jesse had gotten so used to being at the top of the pile, he had forgotten what it was like struggling to get up there in the first place. He knew Bonney, Ringo, hell probably even folks like Carpathian and his little stooges, were struggling every day to make names for themselves.

All Jesse had ever wanted, since he was a little boy back in Clay County was for folks to know his name. Sure, he had joined Frank fighting the Union because he believed in the Confederate cause, and because he had hated those treasonous jayhawkers with every fiber of his soul. The filthy bastards had strung up his stepfather trying to get to Frank, and when that failed they had whipped Jesse himself until his back had bled. Those scars were more than enough to drive him into joining his brother's unit as soon as he was able. Even then, however, it was the lure of fame and notoriety that drove him to his wildest exploits.

When he had first thought up the train job, to seize back the initiative from the law, to salvage the position and prominence of the renegades of the western territories in the face of the new weapons and power the European brought with him, he knew he had established his name in the histories for all time.

But time was like a river, as the saying went, and she kept on flowing even after you docked your boat in the big city. With Carpathian, the Injuns, and now Grant flooding into the western territories, his greatest exploit seemed to be disappearing into the mists of history before he could really revel in the victory. Years had passed, he knew, but somehow it still seemed like only yesterday. And it seemed terribly unfair that folks were forgetting so soon. Without him and his train job, every one of them knucks, hard cases, thieves, and road agents would be dead by now, victims of the new law and the new weapons. The fact that most folks had forgotten that was the hardest thing to bear.

That old frustration and the happiness he had found with Misty were crashing together in his mind over and over as he sat in the small, warm room with Ty's words churning over and over again through his sluggish thoughts. The idea of Billy, the boy who had risen among the outlaw elite to be his foremost competition, spending time with Misty, the source of the greatest peace he could remember in many years, was plaguing his mind.

Jesse shook his head and lurched up, pacing back and forth as he tried to focus his thoughts. Misty had been besotted with him since they had first met, and she had been nothing but devoted to him through their months together. They had spoken of his past many times. In all that time, she had never mentioned Billy the Kid, or in fact anyone else within the outlaw brotherhood. Ty was almost certainly mistaken, despite his confident manner.

The outlaw stopped at the window, grabbed the sill with both iron hands, and looked out into the streets. They were almost empty. Still, there were men and women, usually walking in couples or small groups, moving along on whatever business had them out so late. One large cargo wagon, a ghostly crimson glow flaring from beneath as its engine sent fat red sparks sailing through the night, rumbled down the street, pausing for pedestrians trying to cross through its harsh white headlamps.

Nothing in the street offered any insight, however, and Jesse sighed and returned to his pacing. The floor creaked beneath him, the heels of his boots cracking harshly in the silence of the night. Most of the lodgers staying in the other rooms of the Arcadia had gone to bed over an hour ago, and those that were not sleeping were quiet, only faint, muffled mutterings showing that they were awake. Jesse suddenly felt very much alone and wondered where his brother might be. Frank had taken a room at another hotel, smaller than the Arcadia but much closer to the edge of town, right near where the Heavy Rail line ran out into the western plains.

Jesse heard a scraping at the door as a key went into the lock, and without thought one of his pistols was in his hand, pointed rigidly at the door. Whoever was on the other side was having a hard time with the knob, and the outlaw sidled slowly toward the bed in case he found a sudden, overwhelming need for cover. When the door swung open, however, it was only Misty standing there, a look of frustration on her pretty face.

The girl looked up and her deep jade eyes widened as she stared down the bore of Jesse's massive pistol. He immediately lowered the weapon, but the damage to the poor girl's calm had already been done.

"Jesse, are you okay?" She bent down to pick up her key from the floor where she had dropped it, and eased into the room carrying a couple of bags with her. "Were you expectin' someone a little more intimidatin', maybe?"

Jesse was caught on the verge of two reactions. He wanted to scoop her up right then and there; she looked so pretty and so vulnerable, but Ty's words, and the image of Billy the Kid's smug face, kept rising in his mind. He stood there, pistol lowered but still out, arms heavy, hanging at his side. He knew the bourbon had not helped his situation any, but could not, for the life of him, clear his head of its fog.

Misty put the bags down on the little table and turned gracefully, her hands on her slender hips. "Why did you leave the show early, Jesse? To come up here and get full as a tick all on your own?" Her tone was light but her face was pursed in disappointment.

Jesse gaped at her for a moment, his mind running in too many directions at once. He stood there mute, staring at her with dull eyes, swaying slightly as she sat down at the table, pulling pins from her elaborately piled hair. "I swear, Jesse, if you don't put that gun away I'm going to slap you." He could see, in the mirror in front of the table, that annoyance was giving way to anger and disappointment.

Jesse looked down at the pistol in his metal hand as if seeing it for the first time. He looked up at the back of her head, tilted as she washed the makeup from her face. She looked at him through the mirror and her eyes tightened. "Jesse, put the gun away."

Almost without thinking about it, the gun rose, and then softly slid into the holster. After he took his hand off the butt, however, he stopped moving again, staring at Misty's back. The girl was now combing through her honey brown hair with an ivory-handled brush he had given her. He stared at the brush, watching as the crimson-tinged light reflected softly from its curved surface.

Sensing him standing there motionless, Misty eventually stopped brushing and swiveled around daintily in the chair. She stared up at him, one eyebrow quirked, and asked, "Jesse, is there somethin' on your mind?"

He stared at her face: that beautiful face that had captivated him for so long. He could not remember the last time a woman had kept him in thrall this way. The long, wavy hair that swept down her neck, the big green eyes, the soft, clear skin; she was truly a beauty by any measure. Something in his chest seemed to crack slightly, and he blurted what had been plaguing his mind.

"You been with William Bonney?" It came out harsher than he had intended, the tone accusatory, but he straightened his shoulders and raised his chin as if daring her to take offense.

Misty sat staring at him in blank confusion for a moment before her head tilted to one side and she said, "are you drunk, Jesse?"

Jesse shook his head and snapped around on his heel, pacing once again. He had taken that first dreadful step; it was too late now to go back.

"Answer the question, Misty. You been with the Kid?" He could not look at her.

Misty stood slowly, hands on hips, and stared at him incredulously. It was clear she was caught between rage and laughter. "Jesse, are you jealous?"

He continued to pace. "Tell me, Misty. I need to know."

"Jesse, was I the first girl you were ever with?" Her tone was flat and uncompromising, and it stopped his pacing in its tracks.

He turned to her, his look comically confused. "'Course not."

She nodded and gave him an arch look. "An' did I at any time give you the impression I was a pure 'n' pristine unplucked flower when we first met?"

He smirked despite himself. "Ah, no, you didn't . . . "

She nodded firmly. "There you go."

The shadow returned immediately to his face at her tone of dismissal. "Now, hold on, Misty. Billy the damned Kid?"

She put up a hand. "Din't we just agree it don't matter?"

He shook his head. "No, we didn't. The Kid?"

She huffed angrily and turned back to the table. "Forget it, Jesse. I was never with Billy the Kid, I've never even met Billy the Kid. I wouldn't know Billy the Kid if he walked into this room right now and shot you. Satisfied?"

He found himself once again staring at the back of her head, at a total loss for words. "But . . . but you said . . . "

She did not turn around. "I said we weren't neither of us virgins, is what I said, Jesse. An' you agreed. So it don't matter if I was with Billy the Kid or not. I'm just sayin', I wasn't."

His confusion deepened. He felt like a child lost in unfamiliar territory. "But why din't you just say—"

She clapped the brush down on the table. "Because it don't matter none, Jesse! And we both agreed it didn't." She stopped moving for a moment, still and silent, and then spun to meet his searching gaze. "Why're you suddenly so concerned about Billy the Kid, Jesse?"

He shrugged, feeling even more like a boy caught in some foolish act. "Ty was talkin'—"

"Ty?" Her voice rose, an angry note rumbling beneath its usually soft tones. "That little pie eater from Missouri City? That little cretin? What the hell do you care what that little offish tick has to say?"

Jesse struggled to convey to Misty the confused jumble of emotions he was feeling, about his place in the world, his feelings for her, and his fear of sliding into insignificance. The thoughts and images swirled in his foggy brain, but the words would not come. Over all of the images, William Bonney's face rose like a mountain looming over a darkened landscape.

"Jesse, what does it matter what that worm of a boy had to say? Some jailbird-in-waiting mouths off about me, an' your first thought is against me?" She stood up, her back straight and her shoulders back, and looked him directly in the eye. "Jesse, if you don't trust me, why am I even here?"

He shook his head, emotions rising up to engulf him. But now, over everything, was the fear of losing her. He reached out with his mechanical hands, and tried to ignore the slight flinch she gave before making the conscious decision not to pull away. Was it the fight, or was it the damned arms that she was flinching from?

"Babe, you know I trust you." He muttered the words, and even in his own ears they sounded weak. "It's just the boys, you know. An' damned William Bonney always comin' up." He tried to pat her hair, but at that she pulled away.

"No, Jesse. You gotta put Bonney, and Ty, and whoever else has gotten into your head aside, now, before you're touchin' me again." She leaned toward him, her eyes earnest. "I ain't never lied to you, Jesse James, I ain't never jabbed you in the neck over nothin', and I ain't never walked out with anyone behind your back. An' I never would."

He looked into her eyes and everything else seemed to fade away. He felt safe. His head started to shake back and forth. "Baby, baby, I'm so sorry." He held a hand out but did not take hers until she offered it. "You're right, Misty. Completely right. This was all me, babe. It weren't you, it weren't even Billy or Ty or any of the other guys."

She slowly allowed him to pull her into his arms, burying her head in the crook of his neck. "This is real, Misty. I know. I'm sorry. I'm gonna make it up to you, I promise. I'm gonna—"

He held her out at arm's length so he could look at her, drink in her beauty, and the returning warmth of her eyes. There was nothing there now but trust and love. The suspicion, the anger, and the frustration were all gone. He felt answering emotions rising up within him as well.

"Next time, Jesse James, you better just trust me, or —"

When his arm lurched back he did not understand what was happening, but when it slashed across his body, the armored hand taking Misty full in the face, he staggered back in horrified disbelief. She flew backward, spiraling hard into the wooden floor. Jesse stopped, arms out-flung as if to keep his balance. He stared at her in complete shock. He had no recollection of reaching out with his arm. He looked down at the offending limb. There were no feedback pads on the back of his mechanical hands, so he had felt nothing but the jolt up his arm upon contact, but there was a garish splash of blood across the armored plate. Far too much blood, he thought as he stared.

A whimper from the ground brought him back to the stuffy little garret, and he rushed toward the huddled shape in the corner. Misty was crouched down as if expecting another blow, one shaking hand raised up over her head to defend herself. Her face was pressed against the wall, cradled in the other hand, and her shoulders shook with terrified, silent sobs.

"Honey, I'm so sorry!" Jesse reached out toward the cowering woman. "Baby, I don't—"

"Stay away." Her voice was muffled and slurred, but the stone beneath it was unmistakable. She slowly curled around herself to bring her head up and around, her mouth and nose hidden behind her raised hand. Her other hand, still shaking, was brandished before her as if it were a weapon, one finger wagging toward him. "Don't you come near me, you monster."

He stopped, the words twisting in his gut. "But, Misty, please—"

"Get. Away." The fire in her eyes froze him in his tracks. She gingerly pushed herself to her feet, swaying slightly as she rose. Her finger was still raised like a talisman, the only thing holding a ferocious beast at bay. The fear in her eyes was harder to bear than any burning anger.

"I want you to leave. I want you to leave an' I don' want you to come back." She was now standing, her back pressed to the wall, one hand still pushed to her face.

He shook his head, not believing how swiftly things had turned. "Misty, please. It wasn't me, it was –"

"Stop talking!" she screamed the words, closing her eyes to the pain it obviously caused her. "I don' wanna hear another word, Jesse, I jus' want you to leave, and never come back again'. I seen those other girls, let men hit 'em, an' that ain't ever gonna be me." The finger now pointed toward the door. "Leave."

Jesse felt completely empty. He felt exhausted, as if he had gone the full three rounds with a raging bull. He stood there, his arms hanging limp at his sides, staring at the woman he would have done anything for.

He looked more closely and his eyes widened to see the extent of the damage hidden by her upraised hand. That hand was now soaked in blood, and he could see torn flesh behind. Her eyes were blazing even as tears poured from them, fear and fury mingling in their jade depths.

Jesse took a halting step backward, and then another. He could not take his eyes from the wreckage of Misty's cheek. He could see her strength failing her, could see the sick anguish rising in her eyes as the shock began to subside and the pain truly made itself felt.

And his heart took another blow as he realized that, despite his immediate impulse, he was the last man on earth who could comfort her now.

His back came up against the door behind him and he stopped. He had to force himself to move sideways, his hand reaching out behind him for the knob. He searched for some words, something he could say that would make her feel better. He could not salvage this for himself, he could see that now. Whether it had been a bitter remnant of his emotional pique or his damned arms acting all on their own, all of the trust that she had held for him was gone. Between his thoughtless accusations and this last, fateful blow, he could feel any ties between them severing forever. Still, there was a desperate need in him to bring her even a shred of comfort.

But nothing came to his mind.

"I'm sorry, Misty." He shook his head, bitterly feeling failure of his own mind. "I'm so sorry."

She stiffened, standing straighter again, and her hand reached out to jab that finger at him one last time. "Out." She said it in a flat voice that carried a finality he knew he would never forget.

Jesse bowed his head, slipped out the door, and muttered "I loved you," in a broken voice as Misty slammed the door after him.

The sound of her suddenly released sobs made him feel worse than he had ever felt in his life.

*****

Frank sat in the Arcadia, enjoying the peace and quiet. The men around him were all old timers with the James and Younger gang, men he knew he could trust to watch his back, because they had been there too many times to count. Ty and the rest of the shavetails Jesse had been bringing into the group lately were absent. Probably past their bedtimes, he thought with a slight smirk.

The bottle at his elbow leached the smile away again, however, and he grasped it by the black fabric tied around the neck. He and the men with him were drinking to the three old hands that had fallen with Jesse at Missouri City, the bottle bought with coin from that job for this express purpose. Frank shook his head sadly. He knew that Jesse had not so much as said some words for the fallen men, and after waiting all day, Frank had taken it upon himself to arrange for this late night drink. They were chasing some coins around the table too, of course. But then, the boys who would not be coming down for breakfast again would never have begrudged them a little poker at a time like this.

Frank looked through the amber liquid in his glass and thought again of his brother. Jesse had been happier with this new dancehall girl than he had been in a long time, but Frank knew his younger brother would be itching to move on eventually, and when he did that, the closer the two had grown, the harder it would be for him to leave. It would be infinitely harder on the girl, though, to have been left by the legendary Jesse James. He had broken hearts across the western territories, and this girl just seemed too sweet to let his randy little brother wreck her life.

Somewhere upstairs a door closed with a firm bang. Frank could tell that he was the only man at the table who had heard, and as he turned to see who was coming down, he lost the thread of the conversation around the table. As soon as he saw the boots thumping slowly down the stairs he could tell that it was his brother. What was more, however, he could tell that something was wrong.

Jesse walked down the stairs like a man in a fog. As his head came into view, Frank's frown deepened at the pallor of his brother's skin and the empty look in his eyes. Ever since Jesse had slinked back into town after that Missouri City job yesterday, he had not been acting like his old, confident self.

Jesse took the steps slowly as if he were carrying a massive weight on his shoulders. Each step jarred his entire body, sending his listless arms swinging aimlessly.

His face, an empty mask that seemed to radiate a dangerous mix of loss and hatred, was downcast, eyes staring into nothingness.

Frank was shocked to see his brother so diminished. He knew the men saw his brother as an indomitable force of nature; his wry grin and his glinting eyes were known across the territories. He also knew how fragile a legend could be. The wrong person seeing the shuffling wreck moving down the stairs could well damage his reputation for years to come. Frank knew how important his brother's reputation was to him.

The older man looked sharply around the table, saw that the rest of the boys still had not noticed Jesse, and rose to intercept his brother. Jesse was moving faster than it appeared, however, and when Frank stopped him, they were close enough to the table that Jesse could make out the general point of the conversation. Frank turned to look at them, realized what they were saying, and cursed under his breath.

"I'm just sayin', Billy's one hell of a curly wolf and no mistake. That boy shows up on the street, you know he means business." Chase's voice was pitched low, even unaware of Jesse's presence. But not low enough.

"Sure 'nuff. D'you guys hear what he did to those deaders of Carpathians awhile back?" Gage's eyes were alight with the fire of a storyteller with a good tale to tell. "Ripped one of 'em's jaw right off, and rammed a note into its mouth, blamin' the whole thing on ol' Jesse!"

The men snickered, but came up short as they realized that Jesse was standing not far away, his brother's hand on one shoulder. The men stopped laughing and turned in their seats to look at their leader. Frank could tell that they were shocked at what they saw.

Jesse's face was slack with grief and shock. Deep within his eyes, a flicker of the old flame ignited as Gage's words registered. Those eyes snapped from man to man around the table as he ignored his brother's hand. The light within guttered and rose as if his mind were engaged in an intense inner battle. Frank could only imagine what sorts of things had happened upstairs to push his brother so close to the edge. The calm, cold outlaw, with a reputation as wide as the territories and frightening as death, looked like he had been run over by a freight wagon. That fire was coming back again, however, and it was burning hotter than ever.

"That one was a hoot, Gage." The smile twisting Jesse's thin lips did not reach his fiery eyes, and the boys around the table sat back, looking at each other sideways.

"Didn't mean nothin' by it, Jesse." Gage's smile was hesitant.

"Nah, 'course not, Gage." The ghastly smile was still in place, the eyes still flat, as Jesse grabbed a chair by its back, spun it around, and sat down backward with a mocking tilt to his eyebrow. "An' that was a ripper, that note in the ol' animation's brainpan. Had Carpathian lookin' to wind me up but good, 'till I could convince him it wasn't me. I think we lost, what, five guys, cuz o' that note, Frank?" Jesse's eyes stayed firmly on the three men at the table as he addressed Frank, who had walked up behind him.

"Yeah, Jesse. 'Bout that." Frank's voice was cautious.

"Yeah. Five o' my boys, all up the spout cuz o' that little joke. You guys twig to that? Five o' my guys, bleedin' out into the dust, all ripped up with RJ bullets, 'r worse, at the hands of the doc's animations, afore I could convince him it wasn't us had done for that entire column in the woods." His smile widened as his eyes grew flatter. "Guys just like you, Gage . . . 'n' you, Chase."

"Jesse, honest, we was just talkin'. Frank was with us!" Fear had seeped into Gage's voice now, his courage failing him in the continued pressure of Jesse's blank stare.

"Gage, you ain't got nothin' to worry about." Jesse leaned back, one arm still wrapped around the chair back as he took his hat off in a grand gesture. "You was jus' talkin'. I get it."

Jesse stood and turned back to Frank. "Frank, I need you to go get the Youngers. We're headin' out o' town now. We got a meetin' out in Diablo Canyon, an' we better get a wiggle on afore we're late."

All four other men stared at Jesse for a second. "Jesse," Frank leaned in to speak low in his brother's ear. "It's after midnight. Most o' the boys'll be unconscious, this time o' night. Maybe we can wait till first light, anyway—"

Jesse cut his brother off with a chopping motion that set the inner workings of his arm buzzing and purring. "We ain't waitin', Frank, we're leavin'. An' anyone who can't drag their sorry asses out o' their bunks can damn well stay here an' wait for the law."

All three of the other men were standing now as well, and Gage coughed. "Jesse, it's really late, an'—"

Not even Frank, who had been watching for something like this, saw the gun leap from its holster, or any more than a rushing blur as the armored arm snapped out, Hyper-velocity pistol filling the metal fist, and angular barrel pressing up against Gage's forehead.

"Word one, an' it'll be your last, boy." The false smile was gone, and only the hard, dark eyes remained to communicate what was going on in the outlaw's mind. Frank had seen that look once or twice, but not more than that, and it had never ended happily for anyone.

Gage backed away, his hands raised to either side of his head, his mouth slack.

"Jesse, I think maybe," Frank began, his own hands upraised to fend off any aggression thrown his way. Jesse's pistol wavered slightly in his direction, but settled back on Gage's forehead. "Jesse, I think maybe you wanna put the smokewagon down, an' have a seat? This seems to be somethin' we should all be talkin' about, rather than you throwin' yer weight aroun' when somethin's got you all riled up."

Again the hand moved faster than anyone could follow, this time to flip the pistol around so Jesse was holding it by the barrel and then bringing the heavy gun down onto the table with an echoing crack. The sleepy bartender snapped awake, looking around blearily as he reached beneath the bar for a weapon. The rest of the men and women jerked upright at the sound, but Frank noticed that they made no move toward their weapons. They just watched the famous outlaw from the corners of their eyes.

"You dictatin' actions to me, Frank? You wanna be leadin' this gang?" He glared over his shoulder at his older brother. "You sick o' followin' your little brother? Time to reach for the brass ring on your own?"

"'Course not, Jesse." Frank raised his hands a bit higher, trying to find a neutral expression for his worried face. "Gang's yours, Jesse. Always has been, always will be. You make the call, I'll back your play, same as always."

"Same as Missouri City?" Jesse sneered, and Frank felt a pang of guilt, his eyes flickering toward the black-draped bottle.

"Missouri City was a mistake, Jesse. You knew it. I couldn't of—"

"It was a mistake, I know that." Jesse spat at him. "I went off half-cocked, and drug some good boys with me." He nodded at the bottle. "An' yeah, some of 'em didn't come back. An' that's been eatin' at me since we rode back into town. But you know what, Frank? If you had been there, if you'd o' just ridden along anyway? You mighta saved those men, Frank, just by bein' there." His empty hand jerked toward the bottle. "You and that damned rifle Sophie mighta saved 'em, and you mighta saved those people down in Missouri City, too."

The pistol whirled around, almost as if by magic, and he slashed it back into its holster with a slap. "So, when you start thinkin' you're gonna start tellin' me what to do, or where to go, or when, I want you to think about that, okay?"

Frank knew the argument was not a fair one, and knew that Jesse's own guilt was a major source of the anger and frustration being thrown his way, but something had happened upstairs to bring this all to a head, and things did not look like they were going to be easy to defuse, now that he had his dander up.

"There's some fair words there, Jesse, and that's the honest truth." Frank tried to strike a reasonable tone, but he saw that he had lost before he had begun as Jesse's eyes flared again.

"Nothin' you're gonna say is gonna matter, Frank!" Jesse's mouth was twisted into a snarl. "You're right! You wanna hear me scream it? Wake up half this bug hill? You're right! Frank James is right!" A mechanical arm lashed out, latched ahold of Frank's vest, and pulled him close. "You're right, Frank," Jesse whispered. "The law is comin'. They're comin' because we sat on our asses here too long, an' their comin' because of what we did down the river, and when they get here, they'll be loaded for bear."

One metal thumb jerked toward the stairs, and for a moment, Frank thought Jesse was going to choke on his words, but he twisted his neck, never breaking eye contact, and spat, "Ain't nothin' holdin' us here, we got the law bearin' down on us from God knows where, an' we got us an appointment out in the hills we're gonna be hard pressed to meet if we don't leave soon."

Frank looked from his brother to the three men, none of them willing to speak, Gage nearly drowning in his own sweat. Frank looked back to Jesse and lowered his hands. "What is it you want us to do, Jesse? You just say the word, an' we're there."

The tension in Jesse's face eased slightly, although the anger and the pain still burned in his eyes. He nodded. "I – We, need to leave. We need to round up as many as we can, an' we need to leave here tonight." He tapped Frank on the chest with the back of one heavy hand. "You're right. They'll be comin', an' I've had an itch between my shoulder blades since ridin' out o' Missouri City." His eyes flicked up the stairs. "An' I just wanna go, Frank. I just wanna get out of Kansas City, hit the trail again, and leave this damned manure pile behind."

Frank gave an answering nod. "Okay, boys, you heard 'em. Roust up as many as you can, an' have 'em meet us all on the edge of town, where the tracks run out west. I'll get Cole an' them, an' we'll be gone in less than an hour. That sit right with you, Jesse?"

The three men nodded and walked toward the door, casting backward glances at their shaken boss. Gage could not stop rubbing the center of his forehead, a wary look in his eyes.

Jesse collapsed back into another seat, right way around this time, and Frank sat down next to him. "Thank you, Frank. I really gotta get out of this burg, 'r my head feels like it's gonna explode."

Frank nodded. "Um, Jesse," he did not know how to proceed, but knew that he must. "Your plunder . . . is it upstairs still?"

Jesse looked at his older brother, eyes haunted again, face pale but blank. "Yeah, Frank. It is."

Frank looked at the stairs and then back to his brother. "An' you can't go up an' get it?"

Jesse looked down at the table, his hands lifting up to fold before him with studied calm. "No, Frank. I don't think I can."

Frank nodded. "An' it prob'ly wouldn't do for me or one of the boys to go fetch it?"

Jesse shook his head in silence.

Frank looked around, then pushed away from the table. "I'll be right back." He moved toward the bar, casting a couple looks over his shoulder to see his brother still slumped there, exhausted. The rest of the men were gone, and the other folks in the room studiously avoided looking at Jesse.

At the bar, Frank made a quick inquiry about the old lady that worked most nights, and then turned to wait, back resting against the rough wood, while the bartender went to drag the poor woman out of bed. Frank could feel the exhaustion of the day pressing down on him and did not relish the thought of riding out into the dark of the night like common thieves; it did bring a smile to his face, however.

When the old woman dragged herself out from a small back room, Frank apologized and passed her a coin, asking if she would be willing to do him a favor.

Frank waited by the bar while the old woman went upstairs, keeping an eye on his brother's stooped, still form. When she returned, lugging Jesse's worn leather bags, duster draped over one arm, and horrified, accusatory heat burning in her eyes, Frank gave her another coin and a shrug, pulling the things away from her. Something told him he did not want to hear anything she might have said. If there had been a dead body up there she would have already raised a stir, but from the look on her face, what was up there could not have been much better.

The old woman muttered something to the bartender, who turned back to Frank. "There's a broken mirror, cost more'n a dollar to replace."

Frank shook his head and handed over another coin before turning away. He moved through the room holding the heavy bags high. He needed to get Jesse up and moving before he went searching for the Youngers. Another duty he was not much relishing in a night that had really just gone all to hell in a matter of moments.

Chapter 8

"So you're telling me he's gone." Courtright's voice was even, but there was something in his eye that set the bartender back a step.

"Yeah, skedaddled in the night. He'd been paid up through the end o' the month, so weren't no reason' to make 'em stay." The man's voice shook slightly, but his eyes darkened as he continued. "Shame what happened to the girl, though."

Loveless rested on the bar, leaning toward the shaken man. "The girl? What happened to the girl?"

The bartender shook his head. "He roughed her up somethin' fierce, miss. Struck her in the face with one of those arms o' his. There were folks, told me I shouldn't o' let no outlaw freak like him board here. But din't seem too bad to me, you know? And he was so personable. There's folks tell he's like a Robin Hood outta the old stories, right?" The man's face darkened again. "'Cept he was pretty tight with his coin, if you want the truth. And 'course, when he run off, he left that poor girl from the Occidental all beat up. The missus, she had to go up and get his stuff, and she found the girl sobbin' her heart out on the floor."

"He hit her?" Loveless could not believe the urbane man she had spoken with the day before could have beaten a defenseless woman. Then again, talking to him it was easy to forget that he was a known criminal with an impressive trail of bodies behind him. If the army found out she had been within arm's reach of him and not taken him into custody, there could very well be hell to pay.

"I'm not sure what else he could o' done, miss. My missus, she said the girl was bleedin' like a stuck pig all over the floor." His look soured even more. "The mirror was broke into a thousand tiny pieces too. Took my idiot boy most of the day to clean it up."

Courtright turned away from the bar, leaning against it. He rolled his head toward Lucinda with a fixed smile. "So, there goes our only lead in this latrine trench of a town. And he managed to assault an innocent girl on the way out, too. The president will not look kindly upon the results of our latest outing."

Lucinda snorted. "Since when do you care about the wellbeing of some fast trick from the territories? No one in Washington is going to care about Miss Misty Mimms either, so you can quit your carrying on over the poor innocent and her blood and tears."

Courtright smiled and turned back to look out over the saloon's common room. "Well, fair enough. But that doesn't change the fact that James was our only lead on Carpathian, and he's gone."

"He's not the only one who's gone, Henry. His brother left his room, none of the

Youngers are in town, and none of the locals that had been taking up with Jesse have been seen all day. The entire gang's cleared out. And it can't have been because he roughed up some dancehall girl." She was still facing the bar, looking at her hands as her fingers tapped softly on the scarred wood. "There must be a reason they all left in the middle of the night like that."

"They're corn cracking road agents, Luce. Ripping out in the middle of the night is sort of central to who they are." He threw an elbow up on the bar and turned to face his partner. "The real question is what we do next? I don't relish the idea of going back east empty-handed. The president won't like it. And it's not going to make us look like very good agents if we let this country rube hightail it out of town in the night, taking our only leads with him."

She could only nod, her eyes unfocused. "I didn't get any sense yesterday that he was planning on leaving."

Courtright leaned toward his partner, his face wrinkling slightly in concern. "Luce, where's your head? You need to get back in the game before we find ourselves taken out of things completely. Half the towns along the Missouri are sporting Carpathian Industries generators and tech. The lunatic is strengthening his hold over the whole region and stretching eastward every year. If we can't pinpoint his position for a major strike, he'll own the west before Grant can push through with the army and take care of things." He shook his head. "If I didn't know you for the ice cold bruja you are, I'd swear that filthy cowboy got into your head." He sneered slightly, "or someplace lower."

She snapped a dirty look at him and snarled. "My head's right where it should be, chiseler. Worry about your own; I'm fine." She shook her head trying to clear it of the vaguely melancholy fugue that hung behind her eyes. "Anyway, I know what it'll mean, but maybe if we talk with the girl he left behind? Maybe he told her something before he took off."

Courtright's smile was hard and without humor. "Sure, maybe he was keeping up with the light banter between slaps." He shook his head. "A guy who's hard enough to hit a woman and draw blood is not going to be taking the time to pass along his itinerary." His face darkened again. "You don't tell a woman you're hitting where you're going to next."

Lucinda looked sharply at her partner. "You got a lot of experience with that sort of thing, Henry? Roughing up girls?"

Courtright's smile widened. "I haven't ever roughed you up, have I? So don't worry about it."

She snorted. "If you ever tried to rough me up, it'd be days filling out the paperwork explaining to Washington about your tragic and untimely death at the hands of a passel of prairie school girls."

"School girls, would it be now?" He completed his turn and rested his elbows on the bar. "Wouldn't be doing the dirty work yourself?"

"No, that sort of thing is really beneath me at this point in my career." She sniffed primly and then looked at him again. "Seriously, though. Any other ideas, if you don't think Miss Mimms will offer any hope of tracking James down to his next destination?"

Courtright's expression turned grim. "Sadly, no."

"Well, since that's what we've got, I'd say we would be remiss in our duties were we to not, at the very least, check in on the girl and get her statement." Lucinda pushed her way from the bar. "Damn, but this report is going to read like a flipping tragedy."

Courtright nodded and turned toward the door. They were just moving away from the bar when a seedy-looking local stepped in front of Courtright. The man seemed loath to make eye contact, but stood like he meant to stop them, one hand braced as if expecting them to push past.

"You talkin' 'bout Jesse James?" His voice was hoarse, his eyes flitting around like skittish wild animals.

Courtright casually put a hand on the butt of his pistol. "Not sure you were invited into the conversation, friend. Maybe you should see yourself back to your seat, now, before you upset the nice lady here." He indicated Lucinda with a jerk of his chin. "She's not nearly so pleasant when she's upset."

"I's in here last night," the reticent man continued. "I heard 'em talkin'."

Lucinda put one graceful hand on Courtright's, pushing the blaster back into his holster. "Wait a second, Henry. It's quite possible this nice man can help us. Sir, did you happen to hear Mr. James or any of his companions talking about where they might be headed?"

Courtright grudgingly stepped aside, but there was something strange about the man's face that he could not quite put a finger on. He examined him carefully while Lucinda continued speaking.

"We're friends of his, and his sudden departure caught us by surprise." She was employing her most ravishing smile, but she could see it was having little effect on a man that refused to meet her gaze. "We would be ever so thankful if you could give us even an inkling of where to look?"

The man snapped sidelong glances at Lucinda and Courtright. "Well, I'm not sure how much I remember . . . it was late, I mean . . ."

"Would a slap up the side of your head jar your memory at all?" Courtright snarled as he took a step toward the cowering man.

Lucinda put a hand on her partner's shoulder and drew a coin from her purse. "I'm sure a drink would refresh you and restore your memory. Perhaps after we talk you can treat yourself to a bottle of something nice?" She handed him the silver coin and the man smiled a thank you. The coin swiftly disappeared, although neither Lucinda nor Henry would have been able to say where it went.

"They mentioned some canyon out west aways. Devils canyon? Demon canyon?" He muttered as if unsure of his memory.

"Diablo Canyon?" Courtright snapped. Whatever it was about the man, it was getting harder and harder to stop himself from slapping him.

"Yeah, that was it. Diablo Canyon. Means devil, though, in Spanish . . . don't it?" The man's vague bearing was getting worse.

"Yes, it does mean devil in Spanish. Very good." Lucinda tried one more of her smiles, but again the man's flitting eyes rendered her efforts useless. "Thank you, sir. Jesse and his friends will be very happy to see us."

"Who wouldn't be, miss?" For a split second all the fuzziness and jittery energy seemed to settle, and the strange man looked right into Lucinda's eyes. She blinked and drew back away slightly from the sudden directness of his eyes. She was staring straight into them, but she would not have been able to say what color they were.

"Well . . . thank you . . . " Lucinda attempted to regain her bearings.

"Thanks again, folks." The man ducked his head again and turned away from them. "A right pleasure doin' business with ya'll."

Lucinda and Courtright were left standing in the middle of the floor, watching the man push quickly through the doors and out into the morning air. For a moment, they just stared at the doors as they slowed in their swinging. Courtright's head swiveled back to his partner's.

"Was that guy's eyes red?" He said the words hesitantly; as if not sure he wanted to ask.

Lucinda shook her hear. "I'm not sure. There was something . . . I don't know."

Courtright stood up straighter and sniffed loudly. "Anyway, Diablo Canyon. That make any sense?"

Lucinda nodded. "The place was a ruin for years. One of the railroad companies had commissioned a line to go through there, take a bridge over the canyon, and continue on to the west coast. But everyone forgot to plan for the bridge, and so things stalled. All the engineers and workers were staying in tents, waiting for the equipment. When the equipment got there, they started to lay out the foundations for the bridge, and then the government began its Heavy Rail program. All the funding for new civilian lines dried up as the situation out in the west got progressively worse. No one ever cancelled the Diablo Canyon project, but no further work got done, either. The tents gave way to wooden structures, all the various folks went about trying to make a living until the bridge started up again, and then continued on out of habit long after it should have been clear that there wasn't going to be any bridge." She shrugged. "For a long time it was a bandit's paradise. No law at all, since the town didn't officially exist. Outlaws basically made it their own, treating it like one of those pirate's lairs from the old stories."

Courtright was staring at her with puzzled admiration. "How the hell did you know all that?"

She smiled and shrugged. "I did some research years ago, when it was obvious this is where someone with my . . . talents . . . would most likely get sent, in the event that I was hired."

Her partner shook his head. "Damn, but the stuff you've got shoved into that brain pan of yours." He gestured back to the door. "You think there's anything to what the old coot said about Diablo Canyon? What the hell would James need with construction machinery?"

Lucinda shook her head. "It's not just the machinery. The whole town was a chaotic den of thieves and barbarians, and Jesse James fit right in. In fact, there were a few years where he basically ruled Diablo Canyon, before he decided he'd rather be closer to civilization. The place is completely isolated."

"Great, sounds like a lovely place for a holiday. But if it is the machinery they're after . . . why?"

Lucinda pursed her lips. "James has never been famous for an eagerness for hard labor. If they're planning on using machinery, it must be something big."

A dark cloud lowered over Courtright's face. "Like they might be trying to dig something up?"

His partner nodded. "Maybe."

Courtright's brows lowered further. "Would this not fit into the latest bulletin from Washington, requiring immediate report?"

Lucinda's eyes met his. "If this has anything to do with that last bulletin, and the James gang is heading for it, then yes, one of us will need to make an urgent, personal report."

"Well, we can draw matchsticks on that. You really think we should split up?" He gestured toward the door and she nodded her thanks, moving toward it.

"I think we should probably complete an interim report here and get it sent off to Washington over the wire. We should check on Miss Mimms, see if there are any other leads, and then both set off tomorrow when we'll be fresh." She pushed her way through the doors and then stood on the other side waiting for him on the rough wooden boardwalk.

He followed her out into the shade of the saloon's overhang, his eyes dazzled by the brightness of the sun in the street. "Well, hell. I was thinking, this lead's hot enough, maybe we had to rush off before we got a chance to complete any written . . . bloody hell."

She looked back at his sudden shift in tone. He was staring out at the street, shielding his eyes from the glare of the sun. A massive freight wagon had pulled up across the street accompanied by a formation of low-slung one man vehicles. The entire entourage glided to a stop nearby, their engines roaring with the full-throated fury of an RJ-1027 power plant in hard labor. The smaller machines had two wheels and were ridden like ground-bound Iron Horses. The men were dismounting, long tan dusters flaring out as legs came up and over. Most of the men wore shining silver stars on their chests or hats, and she shook her head in disbelief at the bad luck. Realizing she was seeing a large band of federal marshals, she looked more closely at the larger vehicle and her mouth fell open in disbelief.

Lucinda had heard of the big circuit court support vehicles that been sent out west, but she had never seen one. She understood now, given the reputation of the circuit court judges, why most folks had taken to calling the vehicles 'Lynch Wagons' despite the official

government designation, 'Federal Judgment'.
The vehicle was massive, a wall of riveted armor carried along on three enormous iron wheels on each side. It cast a long shadow across the dusty street. Small firing ports dotted the flanks, while two long slits perched at the front provided the driver with visibility from within his armored protection. On the roof of the monster was a socket large enough for a man, housing an imposing Gatling gun. Obviously this was for supporting fire during particularly salty legal debates. The strangest feature of the vehicle, however, was the armored box built into the rear. Barred windows looked out over the street. The thing had its own jail cell built directly into its armored bulk for transporting prisoners who had not suffered the ultimate sanction. And for that, the government had provided as well.
The mechanisms of the retractable gallows were stowed for transportation, but Lucinda had heard rumors, and could see the armatures, hydraulic pistons, and winch system that would deploy to provide immediate and irrevocable judgment should the circuit judges and marshals deem it appropriate.
It was nothing if not dramatic.

The smaller vehicles, however, must have been the Interceptors the marshals were always complaining about. They seemed quite sleek and vicious to her. They looked less bulky than the Iron Horses, carrying less armor, but they made up for that with their understated, low-slung lethality. They were a perfect match for the methodical men who were now gathered around the side of the support wagon.

One of the men in the small group pointed at the Arcadia. From Lucinda's vantage point on the long porch, it appeared that the men turning in her direction were focused on only on the building. She quickly pulled Henry aside, catching him off balance and having to steady him before he toppled them both into the dust.

"What the—" Courtright growled as he pushed off Lucinda and gave her a hard look.

She gestured with her head toward the Federal Judgment. "That's no standard circuit court."

Courtright looked back at the vehicle and saw two of the new UR-30 Enforcer units moving smoothly down the hull ladder from the access hatch. Two more moved around from the far side. "Four of those chiseling automatons?"

Lucinda gripped Courtright's arm with painful intensity. "That's not all." Her eyes were riveted to the back of the vehicle, where a massive armored door was unfolding to provide a ramp up into the cell compartment. A rumbling hiss escaped from within the wagon, and then a loud clank echoed across the street. Another metallic clang sounded, and then another. The vehicle shook slightly with each sound, despite its size. A huge hand reached out and gripped the side of the doorway in grinding metal fingers. Another emerged on the far side, and then a hulking form pulled its way out of the hatch. It stalked out onto the ramp and down to the street. Each footstep resounded with a metallic clash, shaking the Judgment.

"What the—" Courtright repeated, but this time his voice was soft with awe.

"It's Morgan Earp. Gotta be." Lucinda's eyes would not move from the enormous figure now standing in the street. A pale face, tiny amidst the armor and iron, blinked in the sunlight. It was a colossal form, armored plates and support braces melding together like a bulky statue come to life. The only flesh visible from her vantage point was the man's face, peeking out from an elaborate framework that almost completely enclosed his head.

"They reported an attempted assassination a year or two ago, and then a couple weeks later reported that it had failed, and that was it for official reports." She flicked a finger surreptitiously toward the armored man, her voice still hushed. "There's been a lot of speculation, and unconfirmed reports that Carpathian was somehow brought in to repair the damage, but no one knew for sure."

"Are you telling me that the Federal Bureau of Marshals has known where Carpathian is for years?" Courtright's voice rose, his eyes widened and his color darkened. It was clear from his tone what he thought of the self-styled Federal Bureau of Marshals. Lucinda agreed with him, as did most federal agents working in the western territories. The federal government continued to deal with the marshals, providing them with material support and the damned robot Enforcers. Although there was no officially sanctioned Federal Bureau of Lawmen, the very fact that they were allowed to continue to function without any legal sanction from the federal government made them the de facto law in the west until someone in Washington did something about it.

"I swear, if we've been kicking around out here in the sand and the scorpions for months, and Earp and his damned merry band of hooligans knew where the mad European has been all this time—" His growl was rising to a roar, and Lucinda's fingers tightened painfully around his arm.

"Earp doesn't know, and neither do most of the other marshals. Word is that Wyatt's oldest brother, Virgil, grabbed Morgan on his death bed, threw him in a wagon, and disappeared with him." Her mouth stopped moving, assuming a vapid smile as the lawmen approached, but she continued to speak in a husky whisper. "Two weeks later, he's completely encased in steel, breathing, folks think; alive, apparently; and back in the saddle, so to speak."

Lucinda pushed Courtright farther into the shadows with an empty smile and nodded toward the group of lawmen clumping onto the boardwalk. Courtright grunted in offended surprise but tipped his hat toward the group.

Most of the marshals moved past the pair without a second glance. One of the men, wearing an elaborate set of black leather robes, eyes completely obscured behind dark, smoky goggles, looked them up and down with an impassive face and continued on into the saloon behind his companions.

"What the hell was that sand head supposed to be dressed like?" Courtright straightened his gambler's clothes, mustering what dignity he could.

"Circuit Judge. Sort of a liaison between the Federal Bureau of Marshals and Washington." She shook her head. "Pretty odd sticks, from the reports I've been reading. Some have even taken to wearing wigs like the judges back in merry old England like to sport."

"Well, damn. That fella ain't gonna be standin' long in this heat, he keeps traipsin' around in all that leather." He shrugged. "What you think's brought Earp and his traveling circus into Kansas City?"

Lucinda rested against the warm wall of the saloon and produced a lacey fan. She began to work it back and forth in front of her face while smiling at one of the marshals that had been left behind. The man tipped his hat to her and then turned back to the UR-30 units and the hulking Morgan Earp. Behind the fan she continued. "Well, pretty much what brought us here, Henry, if I had to venture a guess."

"They're after Carpathian as well? Well then, why they hell wouldn't they just hold down that gray-haired old sod and force 'em—"

"Not Carpathian. Our ultimate goal is Carpathian, but we did not come here to Kansas City thinking to find the great man here walking the streets, did we?" Her face was still empty and smiling, but her tone was cold behind the fluttering fan. "His animations haven't been seen within a hundred miles of KC, and he never goes anywhere without them, as you know. Why, oh Henry dearest, were we submitting ourselves to the provincial mercies of Kansas City in the first place?"

Courtright turned to face the wall, pretending to check his boots by kicking them against the worn wood. "So they're here looking for Jesse James?"

"Or for his gang, or someone in the gang, would be my best speculation, yes."

Courtright grunted around a cruel grin. "Well, looks like we won't be the only ones who had their whole day ruined by their late night withdrawal." He spit a solid plug out into the sunlight. "At least we didn't drag a freak show into town in our wake. They really aren't going to be happy when they—"

"What!?!" The shout from within the saloon was harsh, and several folks walking along the street were distracted from their fascination with the Judgment wagon. They cast cautious glances at the saloon before hurrying along on their way.

Courtright smiled tightly at Lucinda as the shouting continued inside, muffled just enough to mask the words. It looked as if they could add the bartender to the list of folks who were not having a good day.

Earp and his gang pushed through the doors with enough force to send them crashing into the wall with a resounding crack. Lucinda and Courtright once again assumed their roles, empty smiles in place, and nodded to the retreating lawmen. Henry could not quite keep the edge from his smile, however, and he realized he may have overplayed his hand when one of the marshals hesitated in his stride, looking right at him. But the man shook his head slightly and continued after the Over-marshal and the judge.

The two agents watched as the lawmen conferred by the flank of their massive wagon. Almost immediately, the four UR-30 units snapped into motion, moving off in four different directions, bodies moving smoothly down the street while heads began to swivel continuously, scanning everything in sight. One unit moved down the street past the Arcadia, and Lucinda and Henry watched as it strode by, head swiveling with every step. It was past them already, moving down to the east, when its pivoting head stopped suddenly, followed almost immediately by its entire body.

The body of the Enforcer was still for a moment, standing in the shining sun, staring into their shadowed retreat. When it began to move toward them, a ruby beam lashed out from its single eye, scanning them up and down several times before winking away again. When the metal man was about ten feet away it stopped, and in a buzzing, unnatural voice, began to speak.

"Federal agents Lucinda Loveless and Henry Courtright, currently on assignment for the president in the western territories. Please accompany me to the Over-marshal."

Courtright looked at Lucinda with an upraised eyebrow, but she was staring at the machine, real anger flaring alight in her brown eyes.

Lucinda snapped her fan closed and stalked off the boardwalk and into the blazing sun, not flinching for a moment under the brilliant heat. She walked past the automaton and directly into the circle of lawmen standing beside the looming wagon. The men all turned to watch her approach with faces that ranged from expectant to appreciative to surly. One of the men was wearing a bulky rebreather mask that covered the lower half of his face, but his eyes seemed to crinkle with amusement. The man at the center of the circle, however, with long flowing mustaches and hard, flat eyes, merely stared at her with cold calculation.

"Over-marshal Earp, I assume?" Lucinda's voice was harsh. With a jerk of her head she indicated the robot that had followed her back toward the lawmen. Henry, following a little way behind the robot, watched the proceedings calmly with a hand casually hooked into his belt near his blaster. When Earp nodded once in recognition, she snapped, "and who do you think you are, endangering federal agents like this?"

Earp's head tilted slightly at the attack, but otherwise registered no reaction. "I'm sure I don't know what you're talkin' about, young lady."

She pivoted slightly to stab a finger at the robot. Now her voice was harsh but low, hissing with anger. "Your creature, here, just called my partner and me out in the middle of the street! We are currently working in the territories under cover for the president himself, Over-marshal! If our work here has been jeopardized, the president will—"

"Which one?" The mild tone of the question caught her off guard and Lucinda stuttered to a temporary pause.

"What?" Her anger was still boiling, and it was clear she did not like being forestalled this way.

Earp shook his head with a slight smile. "Never mind. I apologize for the actions of the robot, however." His eyes flicked to the machine now standing behind the agent. "They ain't known for their subtlety, and half the time, I don't know what they know. They sure as Sam Hill weren't supposed to go pulling you out of your lair, though, miss. So again, I apologize."

The apology took much of the steam out of her approach and she paused again, attempting to rally her thoughts. While she struggled, however, Henry stepped up, hand still near his weapon, eyes tight with suspicion.

"Well, an apology is all nice and good, Over-marshal, but it doesn't do us any good now if our cover has been blown."

Earp smiled even more broadly, hooking his thumbs into his vest pockets and rocking back on his heels. "Well, folks, you do have my sympathies, but if your real concern was maintaining some sort of fictional cover, it don't strike me as you're doin' yourselves any good, comin' at me guns a'blazin' in the middle of the street. Am I wrong in that, though? Is this some sort of secret agent trick, maybe an honest lawman wouldn't know about?"

Lucinda's anger blazed anew, and her own hands balled into fists as she leaned closer to the Over-marshal. "Why you bastard pissant! How dare you lecture us—"

Earp raised a hand, head cocked to one side. "Now, don't get your bloomers in a bunch, there, miss. I'm just makin' a point. But maybe it ain't the best time nor place to make it, as the milk's already been spilled."

An older marshal standing by Wyatt Earp's shoulder snorted. "Don't make his point any less relevant, miss. Weren't more'n a soul or two could o' heard the mechanical man's words, but you rushin' this way . . . that weren't none too smart."

A muffled laugh quickly followed. "Virg, always makin' friends with the ladies." The man in the breathing mask shook his head. "Anyone else curious as to why the metal man called 'em out in the first place?"

Earp nodded. "Unit AZ-21, why did you stop the agents here?"

"And how the hell did it know they were agents?" One of the marshals muttered under his breath, shying away from a dark look from the Over-marshal's brother as soon as the words were out of his mouth.

"Federal information indicated agents Loveless and Courtright are currently on assignment in Kansas City region." The machine's voice, with its unpleasant buzzing, was at the same time hard to hear and hard to ignore. "Recent reports indicated the agents were currently searching for Jesse Woodson James in the same region. Federal asset requisition protocols indicate immediate contact with agents authorized and advantageous under current circumstances."

Lucinda scowled at the inhuman metal face with its single eye and round, grill-like mouth. She looked back at Earp without changing her expression. "What circumstances?"

Wyatt Earp coughed apologetically, looking down for a moment and kicking a small stone aside with his boot. "Well, miss, there was an incident down the river aways, in Missouri City. A bank job, saw over twenty people killed, more'n that injured. Don't know how much money they made off with, as there weren't no one left to ask."

Lucinda looked confused, her hands falling at her sides. "Over twenty dead? Was it a battle? Did they fight back?"

Virgil Earp snorted. "Did they fight? No, miss, they didn't fight. What they did, mostly, was die. James and his gang burnt the bank down when they were done, most of the customers trapped inside to burn like animals."

The circle of faces turned bleak and angry. "Miss, if you'd a seen what we seen down Missouri City, you'd be angry, for sure, but it wouldn't be us you'd be cussin' at."

Lucinda was still distracted, turning to look at Courtright with a questioning tilt to her head. "Over twenty people?"

Courtright stepped up and made a big show of offering his hand to Earp and then the other marshals in the circle. "Over-marshal Earp, sir, my name is Agent Courtright, sure enough. Sorry for the earlier misunderstanding. We have been, in fact, seeking contact with James, but not as a direct part of our investigation. He was a source of intelligence in our current assignment, is all."

Earp stared at him, the smile gone from his face. "By that flannel-mouthed response, Agent, I'm going to assume you met Jesse James, but did not apprehend him or his men?"

Courtright's own eyes flared. "Sir, it is not our job to apprehend petty criminals. If we had been aware of the events down in Missouri City, then we may well have taken a different tack. But we had not heard anything about it, and we are in the middle of our own assignment."

"You know for a fact it was Jesse James that killed those people, Over-marshal?" Lucinda's voice broke in on their conversation and both men turned to look at her. "It couldn't have been some other gang? Perhaps one of the unaffiliated groups working out of the badlands?"

Earp shook his head. "No. We had several folks down there who recognized him. It's been awhile since he's been active, but there wasn't any doubt, this was his job."

Lucinda's thoughtful gaze passed beyond the circle of men and robots, focusing on some distant object. "But Frank James and the Youngers were all in Kansas City the whole day." She turned to Courtright. "He almost never does a major job without his brother and one or two Youngers with him. And he's never put up numbers like that before. Twenty civilians?"

Earp shook his head sharply. "Sorry, miss, but that just ain't so. During the war, Jesse James and his brother took part in more than one massacre, killing scores of unarmed soldiers. He's capable, and he's done it in the past. And we know he was in Missouri City, in the bank, with a force of men on their damned Iron Horses." He gave her a closer look, and she could feel his eyes boring their way beneath the facade of her role. "And what I'm wonderin' right now, if you don't mind my speculatin' out loud, is why it is that a Federal agent seems to be lookin' for excuses that this atrocity can't have been perpetrated by a man who's been known to commit worse crimes." His eyes flicked to Courtright. "Am I wrong, Agent Courtright? Or is your agency, perhaps, working along a different set of assumptions than us lawmen, scratchin' along on the sharp edge out here?"

"I'm not looking for excuses for anything." Lucinda snapped, and she tried to reign herself in, knowing she would not be doing herself any good if she let this Podunk yahoo get under her skin here in the middle of the street. "Jesse James puts on a good act, Over-marshal, and he's got quite a reputation. But you're going to see, as you continue to track him, that he's a lot smarter than you'd think. You'll also see, I believe, that he's done a lot of growing up since the war. I have no doubt this atrocity you're speaking of took place, and that those poor people were killed. I have no doubt that Jesse James was there." She shifted her gaze to take in all of the men around the circle. "What I am saying, however, is that there is more here than what you are reporting. Something about the events in Missouri City does not add up, and you'd do well to take that into consideration before rushing off into the wilderness after them all."

The men were momentarily taken aback by her harsh words, but even as she allowed herself to think that maybe she had gotten through to them, that they were looking at the evidence before them with clearer vision, Virgil Earp leaned forward and muttered through his mustache. "No, look here, miss. That was a nice little speech you just gave, but it sounded a lot more like a wife arguin' for a guilty husband than a Federal agent giving a concise field report."

Wyatt Earp's eyes tightened at his brother's words, and his gaze remained steady on Lucinda. "Gotta admit, miss. Virg's got a point. Is there any chance you ain't lookin' at this whole thing with a complete lack of bias?"

There was no warning as Loveless' hand suddenly plunged into the slit of her dress and whipped up, holding a long, slim knife. Even the UR-30 unit was only beginning to react when her arm hurtled back down again, sending the knife tumbling through the air.

The knife glittered as it spun through the harsh sunlight, and when it smacked into the packed dirt of the street directly between Wyatt Earp's dusty boots, it was as if a brief electrical current had run through the entire group. Every marshal around the circle tensed at the exact moment, hands on gun butts or reaching for knives of their own. Doc Holliday already had his weapon out and pointing straight at Lucinda's head at the end of an arm as steady as bedrock. Virgil Earp was crouching down, a hand on either pistol grip at his waist. Only Wyatt had not moved.

"Well, that was mighty fine knife work, miss." Wyatt lobbed a gobbet of spit out of the circle and into the dust. "Don't really address the issue at hand, however."

Courtright grabbed Lucinda by the shoulder and forced her behind him, his other hand raised in a placating gesture that took in all the marshals but focused primarily on Holliday and the bore of his pistol.

"Now, Over-marshal, to be fair, I think Luce meant that for being in the way of addressing that very issue." His voice was steady and calm, but Holliday and the robot were particularly unnerving, neither moving but both focusing hard on the two agents. "We been together a long time, and we've been together on this assignment the whole time. No one's been compromised. She just took exception to your tone, I think. Isn't that right, Lucinda?"

The snarl was still firmly on her face, but she thawed it through a force of will and gave a bright smile to the Over-marshal and his brothers. "Absolutely."

Earp nodded with a grin. "Well that's good. I'd hate to think that we were all workin' at cross-purposes on something this important." He scuffed the street with his boot again, then looked up with a purposefully vague expression. "Now, did you folks already mention where James and his gang had scarpered off to?"

Courtright looked to Lucinda to respond and the weight of his gaze was crushing. She flicked her eyes from her partner to Earp and back again, and was hurt and irritated to see the sudden doubt in Henry's eyes. She sighed, shook her head, and looked back to the Over-marshal. "An old man in the bar told us he'd overheard them talking about Diablo Canyon."

"Makes sense, go back to hide in his old stomping grounds." Doc Holliday nodded.

Virgil looked puzzled, however. "Don't they still have AZ-20 in Diablo Canyon? Ain't gonna be like nothin' he'd be expectin', he heads back there right about now."

Wyatt nodded. "First UR-30 we sent out from Tombstone went down that way, been keepin' the place quiet as a crypt ever since. That oughta be a nice surprise to tide them over till we come ridin' down their backtrail, eh boys?"

The other marshals had already begun to mount their Interceptors while Morgan Earp and the robots were making their way back into the Lynch Wagon. As Wyatt was climbing up the access ladder to the high hatch, he stopped and tipped his hat to Lucinda. "Now, miss, if you're assignment should happen to bring you up toward Diablo Canyon, I trust you'll have the professional courtesy to let us know we're all playin' in the same sandbox again, okay?"

Lucinda said nothing, her jaw clenched tight, but forced herself to give a single jerky nod.

With low, growling roars, the Interceptors moved out, taking up an arrowhead formation and roaring down the street into the west. The Judgment support vehicle, its tone a much lower, subterranean bellow, rocked into motion and followed behind at a more dignified pace.

Lucinda and Courtright stood alone in the middle of the street, watching the monstrous vehicle disappear around a corner. Lucinda reached down to retrieve her throwing knife, wiped the dust and dirt off the blade, and then slid it back into her dress.

"Well, that could have gone better." Courtright looked at his partner with a lop-sided grin. "It's a good thing Washington doesn't care much for the marshals service's opinion, or we'd be getting our hides tanned over this." He nodded to the disappearing knife. "Now, am I remembering correctly, or did you just throw one of your little party favors directly at the Over-marshal of the western territories?"

Lucinda was still in no mood for joking. "If I had thrown it at him, he'd be dead, instead of making foolish accusations and riding off into the sunset."

"Well, setting aside the immaterial article of evidence that it's hardly past noon, I agree with your assessment of the situation, anyway. I don't think I've ever seen you miss something you meant to hit, so, excellent bit of inter-office relations, there, then." His smile was wide, but his eyes were serious as he assessed his partner.

"His words did seem to strike a nerve, though." He leaned in toward her. "Enough to make some folks who might not know you as well as I do wonder some things we'd rather not have them wondering, no?"

She forced herself to snap out of the fugue state and shot him a look. "I just didn't want to be giving too much away, was all. Do you think Grant or the president would thank us for letting the Earps in on all this drama swirling around the good doctor?"

Courtright went back to looking down the road. "Well, one thing's for sure. Dragging that enormous contraption with them wherever they go, there ain't no way they're going to be able to get to Diablo Canyon before whatever James and his boys have in mind has already gone down." He let a moment's silence stretch on for a while before looking at her out of the corner of his eye and whispering. "He's an outlaw, Luce, ain't no two ways about that."

Lucinda nodded silently. Jesse James was an outlaw, and the body count he had racked up throughout his extended life was enough to make any peace officer blanch. And yet, while they talked the other day, she knew, against all reason and right-mindedness, she had seen something in his eyes that mirrored something in her own mind. He was a man hounded by his past, doomed to make the wrong decisions until he found the strength to break the cycle. It had taken a great man, who also happened to be a good man, to help her break the cycle in her own life. Was there any hope for Jesse, out in the middle of the badlands, hunted down by an army of lawmen itching to make a point?

Lucinda sniffed, shook her head, and gestured for Courtright to follow her back to their room. "We better get going. I think our best bet will be to split up at this point. I know some folks might be able to get me to Diablo Canyon quick as a wink, and you've always been better with those office types back east."

He grunted in reply, not looking up. Lucinda continued, "We've got too much ground to cover, and not much time, if we want to get useful information from James before the Earps and their traveling Wild West show catch up to him."

Chapter 9

The town was tucked into the dark forests in the northern edges of the territories, and no one left there remembered what its original name was. The place had been called Payson for decades, named by the world-renowned Doctor Burson Carpathian. It was a dirty town in the middle of a once-beautiful country. Filthy brick buildings of almost entirely utilitarian aspect lined the streets, granting no decoration or ornamentation of any type. Factories, mostly, spewed red-tinged smog into the crystal blue sky, giving everything for miles around a sickly, pink pallor.

Jesse and his gang rode into town along the single dirt road connecting it to the rest of civilization to the far south. Everyone was exhausted from days of hard riding, but this would be no place for them to recoup their strength. There were no signs on any of the buildings, and the streets seemed all but deserted. Jesse raised a single fist into the air, and the Iron Horses of his posse drifted forward on their roaring engines, settling down around him.

Most of Jesse's men had never been to Payson before, and these were in some danger of damaging their necks as they swiveled from side to side trying to take it all in. The sickly-sweet smell that was always Jesse's strongest memory of the place had made itself known nearly a half hour before. It was even stronger than he remembered as they sat in the middle of the main street, wondering what they should do next.

"Jesse, you reckon there's anyplace we can get a drink, recharge the 'Horses, maybe, while you talk to the doc about new equipment and weapons?" Frank was leaning against the control panel of his machine, his hat in one hand. "I don't relish the idea of going into the lion's den myself, an' I'm wonderin' if it ain't best for the rest of these boys to be keepin' a bit of distance as well?"

Jesse did not stop scanning the street, but nodded. "The saloon used to be down that alley to the left. It's as far from the main row of factories as the folks who have to live here could get the doc to put it. Every now and then they move everything around, though, so it might not be. I better get a move on or we're gonna miss Billy at Diablo Canyon."

"I hope this side trip was really worth it, Jesse." Harding's voice was grim, his tone frustrated. "We went straight past the turn off for the Canyon more'n a day back. The way you was pushin' us, we woulda beaten the Kid there by a few days at least. Now, we'll be lucky if we get there on time."

"You got any pressin' need to see Billy the Kid, Harding?" Jesse turned a severe glare on the older man. The look was rendered more effective, however, by the ruby lenses of his goggles, reflecting shards of light back into Harding's face.

"Just don't wanna have to ride any further than we gotta, is all," grumbled Harding.

"Jesse, you go on down and see the doc. I'll let these dirt farmers in on the great and mysterious secrets of Payson while you're gone. Who knows, maybe they'll see an animation close up. Bryce's been havin' a bit of trouble moving his bowels. That oughta set you right as rain, eh, Bryce?"

The young kid snorted and flipped a middle finger in Frank's direction, causing Frank to chuckle, shaking his head.

"You keep those foul Eye-talian gestures out of my face, Bryce, you hear? Or Sophie'll have somethin' to say to ya." He reached around for his gun, as if threatening to pull it on the boy.

Jesse shook his head. "You lot of numbskulls go find the damned saloon while I go see what I can't pry out of the doc's warehouses for this little shindig."

"What's it called, Jesse?" Ty had been quieter since leaving Kansas City, mirroring Jesse's own dark silence.

"What's what called?" Jesse goosed his machine forward a bit, drifting off down the street.

"The saloon?" Ty yelled after him.

Jesse called over his shoulder as he gunned the rumbling vehicle forward. "They call it the saloon, ya silly cracker. Payson ain't got but one."

As Jesse moved further down the main street he could hear Bryce say, "town this size only has one waterin' hole?" It made him smile.

The main street of Payson wound its way down a moderate incline in a slow turn that eventually left even the echo of his men's Iron Horses behind. The echo of his own, bouncing off the plain brick buildings, was familiar enough but offered no comfort. He knew they had been under observation for days, and he knew that if Carpathian had wanted to keep him away, they would know it by now.

The fact that there were no animations present was a pleasant surprise. Every time Jesse had visited Payson before, he had seen many of the disgusting things shambling about on one errand or another. He knew the town was lousy with them; that they were, in fact, the source of the smell that troubled his dreams for days after every visit. Their absence, however, was almost as troublesome as their appearance would have been.

The main road continued down, side streets reaching away on either side almost at random. Eventually, the road leveled out to a wide, straight boulevard, and the first buildings with some style made their appearance. Along either side of the broad street, intricate building fronts featuring dizzying arches, shaded promenades, large windows, and even gargoyles made out of some substance the color of the ubiquitous red brick rose into the sky. Large buildings marched down toward an edifice that looked like it had been dropped right out of a fairytale, except that rather than the smoothly polished, dressed marble of a castle, this one was built, once again, out of fired red brick. Flying buttresses, crenellations, turrets, and other archaic features completed the appearance. The presence of the bricks just made it all seem as bizarre as the rest of the town.

Jesse gunned his 'Horse forward, watching, with his peripheral vision, all of the shadowed nooks and crannies in each building that he passed. He kept his head rigidly forward, however, and his chin up. It would never do for any of Carpathian's creatures to read weakness or hesitation in his manner. He took a deep breath and banished the heartache, confusion, and anger of the last few days to a corner of his mind. He would be able to deal with all of that later. Right now, he needed to have all his wits about him, dealing with the doctor.

The Iron Horse rumbled to a halt in a grand parade ground before the castle-like main house. Jesse allowed the machine to rumble into silence and slowly swung his leg up and over the saddle, standing in an assured and easy pose beside it. The heat from the exhaust pipes radiated through his riding leathers and warmed the backs of his legs. He stood completely still, mechanical hands confidently on hips, and looked up at the big house, waiting for a sign.

The sign was not long in coming, as the large double doors in the center of the massive, intricate facade opened with a slow, dramatic movement. A large man in dark clothes and a grim face hiding behind a massive black beard stepped out and gestured with an abrupt wave of his hand for Jesse to approach.

Jesse forced the cocky, self-sure grin onto his face and began to saunter forward. He raised one arm and gave a quick wave to the figure at the top of the steps. "Howdy, Ursul. How's things goin' behind that awful thatch of brush you call a beard?"

The man scowled but made a slight bow. "Domnule James." His accent was so thick that Jesse could never be entirely sure he understood every word. There was a grudging respect there, however, and Jesse had found himself in desperate need of that lately. One of the many reasons he had been hesitant to make this journey was a very real fear of his own reaction, should Carpathian be in a foul, sharp-tongued mood. He had no doubt, if it ever came to it, he could shoot the old man ten times before the body fell and the old coot would never know what happened. He also knew he would never make it out of Payson alive if he did it.

"Ze Doctor iz busy now. Eef you vill come vith me, I vill zee that you are provided vith refreshments unt somevere to zit down." The big man gestured with one hand into the cool interior of the castle.

Jesse nodded his thanks and moved past the imposing guardian. "Thanks, Ursul. Mighty kind of you an' your boss. You have any idea when he'll be free, though? I'm in a bit of a hurry, with an appointment I gotta make back east. I really need to talk to him 'bout some stuff afore I feel comfortable makin' the trip."

Ursul led the way deeper into the castle. He answered with a tone completely devoid of pity or concern. "Ven zee Doctor iz busy, he brooks no disturbance. Zis you know, Domnule James, yah?" The man did not turn around, but Jesse could hear the shrewd smile in his voice.

"Yeah, whatever you say, Ursul." Jesse looked around at the wide hall with its dark wood paneling and gothic decorations. There was even an old suit of armor standing on a pedestal in one waiting area they moved through. They were almost past when Jesse noticed the two men lounging in the shadows. They both sported dark goggles, considering they were indoors, and both wore sleek black leather dusters of a strange design. Their hair, too, was strange; long like a woman's hair, and blacker than a mineshaft at midnight.

One of the men looked up at Jesse and smiled, nodding slightly and raising a glittering knife to tap at his own forehead in a salute Jesse could only interpret as ironic.

"Couple o' new pets, Ursul?" Jesse followed the large man down the hall and away from the strange pair. He forced his body, against every impulse, to move straight and not turn to look over his shoulder.

"A couple uv young men from zee old country, Domnule James. Zee Doctor prefers, ven possible, to provide assistance and guidance to such as they." It was even harder to understand him as he powered down the hallway, heels clacking on the wooden floor.

"Ah, Europeans then?" Jesse called out for lack of anything better to say.
Ursul paused for a heartbeat in his stride, casting an astounded look over his shoulder. "Ah, yes, yes. Europe." He nodded, then turned away, shaking his head, and hurried on at a greater pace.

*****

Frank led the men into the building they assumed was the saloon of Payson. A nondescript brick building like all the others, this at least had the look of constant use, and the windows along the front of the building were at least slightly larger than the rest that looked out onto the street. The door had a knob rather than the freely-swinging batwing doors favored by most establishments that might require the speedy eviction of a patron in the heat of battle. Frank had tested the knob, felt it give, and then nodded to the rest of the men, pushing the door warily open.

Inside, the room was much more in keeping with saloons across the west. There were tables, a long bar running across the back, with a wall of bottles and glasses behind it. One thing they all noted with some relief was the fresher air within as the door closed behind them. Probably another reason to avoid the batwings, Frank thought as he surveyed the darkened room. A barkeep stood behind the bar polishing a mug with a clean white towel; however, he gave it one last brush and then placed it on the counter behind him when he saw the small crowd enter.

He stared at Frank and the other outlaws guardedly, taking in their dusty, trail-stained clothing and weary gaits. He nodded to Frank, who nodded back, and then gestured with one hand to any of the unoccupied tables.

Frank had been to Payson before, and as the saloon had not been moved since last time, he had even been in this very bar. He was not surprised to see that most of the tables were empty. In fact, he was moderately surprised to see any patrons at all. Only a couple of the tables were occupied, and the men sitting around them were sullen and quiet as they slouched in their chairs in the semi-darkness.

Frank gestured to the men to take a couple large round tables in the corner and then waved at the bartender, although the man was still staring at them as they moved through the room. "Barkeep, send over a couple bottles and enough glasses for the lot, will you? And good bottles, real whiskey, now, none of that ole Red Eye you push off on the locals, you hear?"

The man sneered slightly but reached under the bar and produced two dusty old bottles. He put them on a tray and loaded it up with enough glasses for the whole band. He pushed his way around the bar and to their tables, depositing the lot with a rattling crash. He held out a palm. "That'll be ten dollars." The man's voice was harsh, as if he was not used to speaking.

Frank's eyebrow shot up. "Ten? You gonna kiss us each afore you go back to settin' there, doin' nothin'?"

The large man's hands balled into fists that he rested on his hips. "You want the Simon Pure, you pay for it, son. You want the same tar water the locals here suffer through, you can save yourself some coin."

Frank smiled at the men with a shrug. "Well, nothin' but the best for these boys, I guess." He dug a few coins out of his pocket and made to hand them over, dropping them to the floor just as the bartender was about to grab them. "Oops. Sorry, barkeep. Guess I slipped."

The smile Frank gave the bartender was lethal, and after a single glance, the man quickly looked away, ducked down to grab the money, and backed off with a nod and a mutter of thanks.

"Damn hayseeds." Frank sat down heavily. "Don't know who the hell they think they are, way out here in the middle of nowhere, puttin' on airs."

The men nodded while Bryce opened the bottle and began to pour generous glasses for his table. "Hey, Frank, how come Jesse calls this place, 'The Town That Death Built'? I ain't seen anythin' too scary here 'bouts."

Cole Younger snorted from the other table and lobbed a healthy gobbet of tobacco juice onto the floor. "You ever face any animations on the trail, kid? Ever stared into the dead eyes of one of those walking corpses the doc uses for all his dirty work?"

Chase nodded. "Doc's animations ain't nothin' to shake a stick at, Bryce. If you'da seen a bunch of 'em in action, you wouldn't be havin' any doubts now. You'd be just as happy they don't seem to be hangin' around today."

Frank snickered as he took a sip of his whiskey, sighing harshly with satisfaction. "Now that is the good stuff. But yeah, what these old hands'r sayin', kid. Folks say, once the doc scared those who used to live here off the land – or convinced 'em to join him – or killed 'em all, depending on who's tellin' the story, he raised up a whole army of the dead with his RJ tech, an' they went straight to work rebuildin' the town. First thing he had 'em build was a bunch o' kilns, an' then, digging up clay from the canyon up thata way, they just started churnin' out bricks to beat the band, an' the buildings just kept goin' higher and higher, day 'n' night. Pretty soon, faster'n any living men could o' built it, Payson was as big as you're seein' it now. Some say he went through a thousand Boot Hills full o' the dead before he was done, and ain't a grave with a body in it for miles in any direction. Folks round these parts, they've taken to burnin' their dead when they pass." He took another sip. "Well, those that don't up and sell 'em to the doc, that is."

Gage looked around at the quiet men, and put his own glass down. "Well, if these dead folks are so good at workin', how come there's any live folks at all shufflin' around?"

Frank shrugged. "God alone knows what the doc needs these folks that ain't done breathin' yet for. There ain't a lot of 'em, but there's enough. Jesse once tried to explain to me, the animations don't have any brains o' their own. They're like idiot dogs, gotta be led around nonstop. They're not as smart as those crazy metal marshals. So, could be, you need live folks to tell 'em what to do."

The outlaws focused on their drinks, occasionally shooting sidelong glances at the other men in the room. Most of the younger men had heard the stories but never seen an animation. Frank knew from personal experience that those creepy bastards were hard to believe in until you had seen one for yourself. He shrugged. They would see some soon enough, he had no doubt.

The men were muttering quietly, speculating on how long they would have to wait, when the door banged open and a smell worse than a charnel house wafted through the saloon. The outlaws all turned as one and stared as a figure shambled quickly in through the door, closing it clumsily behind.

As soon as Frank saw, he turned to look at his companions' faces, especially the young ones. He watched for their reactions at the animation that had shuffled into the room, carrying with it the unmistakable stench of death.

The men stared as the thing moved slowly toward the bar. The bartender, looking slightly paler than he had, stood up straighter to receive the thing.

The walking corpse was dressed in ratty working clothes that would have been common on any unskilled laborer throughout the western territories. Beneath the clothing, the body seemed as if it must have been a very robust figure in life, with muscles straining at the ragged shirt. The flesh of its face hung loosely, its mouth gaping partly open, its filmed, milky eyes staring fixedly ahead. A collection of metal supports and leather straps served to hold the thing upright, and a dark metal collar was fitted around the back of the corpse's neck and head. A small cylinder, glowing with the crimson light of RJ-1027, was rammed into a socket in the contraption and into the thing's skull.

The animated body moved to the bar where it raised one desiccated hand, a wrinkled piece of parchment grasped loosely by the lax fingers. The bartender took the paper and unfolded it, read it with a jerky nod, and then reached under the bar for another dusty bottle. He wrapped some sort of netting around the bottle, looking sourly at the table of outlaws, and then draped the netting, now snagged around the bottle of premium alcohol, over the corpse's head.

The bartender said something to the corpse, again with a sheepish glance at the newcomers, and then had to repeat it several times before the animation nodded once, turned ponderously around, and shuffled back out the door. The stench of the thing lingered for quite a while before it faded into the general background stink of the town outside.

The outlaws stared at the door for a moment before they turned back toward each other, the younger men with faces pale with disbelief.

"He weren't that fast, though . . . " Gage muttered. "Fightin' 'em can't be that hard, can it?"

Frank snorted and picked up his drink. "That was a laborer, boys. Not made for speed 'r fightin', just fer liftin' and carryin'." He nodded at the door. "The fighters the doc makes, they're sometimes even bigger than that boy, an' fast as you can think, some of 'em. An' they have all sorts of 'emselves cut off, replaced with blades 'n' guns 'n' other weapons. The doc's a pretty odd stick, but he's a cracker when it comes to makin' up ways to kill folks from a distance."

"But . . . how come the thing was fetchin' and carryin' for a bottle o' rotgut?" Harding muttered to Frank. "I ain't never seen 'em doin' stuff like that before."

Frank smiled knowingly. "Well, boys, unless I miss my mark, I'm thinkin' that poor galoot was sent traipsin' through here strictly for our benefit." He looked at each man in turn. "Well? Everyone feel special now?"

Gage cleared his throat. "When you reckon Jesse'll be comin' back? I'm not eager to be here if that thing has to come back in lookin' fer seconds."

*****

The room to which Ursul had led Jesse was very comfortable, but he had already developed an itch to leave. The walls were darkly paneled, the furniture covered in luxurious supple leather, and the window looked out over the canyon behind Payson. The outlaw chief paced back and forth in the small room, occasionally stopping to puzzle out the titles on the spines of books in the various shelves, or to look out the window at the wide-spread mining and refining works built up all throughout the canyon.

Jesse knew the Payson canyon works had been under development for decades.

Nevertheless, he was surprised at how extensive they were. He knew originally the work had been for clay along the riverbed that meandered below. Since then, far more elaborate works had been sunk into the canyon walls. He thought most of it looked like gold or silver mining, but the massive silos of glowing crimson fluid at the far end were clear indications that whatever they were pulling out of the ground, it was being converted, somehow, within the long low brick buildings, into RJ-1027.

Jesse knew that the secret of the mysterious 'Crimson Gold' was one of the primary sources of Carpathian's power. Speculation abounded throughout the territories on what the substance could possibly be. Theories ranged from some fetid, naturally occurring mixture like the oil bubbling up across the arid plains of Texas, to the captured souls of innocents, trapped by the doctor's arcane machines. Jesse did not think they were souls, or spirits, or whatever, but he did not pretend to know what it was, either. He knew, however, that what he was watching through that high window was a good hint toward where the stuff came from.

The outlaw stared out the window at the bustling industry rushing from one end of the canyon to the other. It sent a creeping sensation up his spine to realize that nearly all the figures moving around down there were the corpses of men and women who had once moved around just like him. He looked down at one mechanical hand, flexing the fingers, and realized that in one way, at least, he was even less human than most of the workers down below.

"Zee doctor vill see you now, Domnule James." The large door had opened without a sound, and Ursul was standing there, glaring at Jesse as if he was convinced the outlaw had somehow managed to steal every coin in the doctor's vaults while he had been waiting.

"Thanks, Ursul." Jesse tipped his hat with a jaunty metal finger toward the massive, hairy man, and walked past him into the hallway again.

"Vee vill be moving up to zee doctor's receiving room. Vee vill be taking the lift. This way." He moved smoothly in front of Jesse again and led the way down a side-hall and into a large chamber that featured several sets of double doors. Each set of doors had a fan-shaped arrangement above it, with elaborate, wrought iron arrows pointing to numbers or symbols arrayed across the top of the arch. The arrow over one set of doors was moving steadily downward from the far right-hand symbol, what looked like a very ornate 'A', to an equally elaborate 'P' at the far left.

"Wait, lift?" Jesse's eyes widened as his mind finally reshuffled the muffled syllables into an order that made sense. "We're gonna get lifted all the way . . . up there?" He pointed at the 'A'. "Wherever that is?"

Ursul nodded without looking at the outlaw. The arrow finished its journey to the 'P', and there was a series of cracks and hisses behind the doors. They suddenly flashed open without warning or obvious assistance, revealing a chamber far smaller than Jesse would have guessed from the size of the doors themselves. The room was paneled in more dark wood, and Ursul moved quickly inside, gesturing for Jesse to follow.

Jesse looked at the other sets of doors, down the hallway, and then back into the small chamber. Ursul looked at him with a snide grin and gestured for the outlaw to enter and stand beside him.

After taking one more look around, Jesse stepped gingerly into the room, eyes roving over the paneling. A cluster of glowing red knobs was arranged in a double column to the right of the doors, and Jesse saw that one of the buttons, toward the bottom of the left-hand column, had the same 'P' symbol, while the bottom-most right-hand button was decorated with the same 'A' character. As soon as Jesse was completely in the room, Ursul reached out and pressed the 'A' button with one blunt finger.

"Da." Ursul's voice rumbled with amusement as he straightened, shooting Jesse a look out of the corner of his eye.

The doors to the tiny room slid closed, again without any apparent reason. The floor beneath Jesse jerked. A grinding sound seemed to reverberate all around him. The outlaw reached out with one mechanical arm, slapping the wall and digging metal fingers into the woodwork for stability as the room began to shake and rattle. Something within Jesse's ears told him he was rising. Without windows, however, there was no way to tell what was going on outside the little room. Jesse's stomach gave a lurch.

"Zee doctor vill not be pleased that you damaged the paneling." Ursul gestured toward Jesse's death grip with another nasty smirk.

Almost before Jesse could process what was happening, the floor shuddered again, lurched once more, and then the doors slid open. The dark-paneled corridor was no longer there, replaced by what looked like the stone walls of an ancient castle or palace. The floor was polished wood, and Ursul gestured for the shaken outlaw to precede him out into the new hallway.

Jesse was in no mood for further verbal knife fighting, so he just nodded and moved out. They soon reached an intersection and turned right. The hall was flooded with bright sunlight from windows along either side, showing a soaring view of the valley far below. Ahead of them stood another pair of double doors, this time thick, old wood, intricately carved, with an ornate 'C' in the middle of each.

"He eez in there."Ursul pointed at the door and then pivoted on one foot, moving back down the gleaming hall.

Jesse rallied himself for a quick, "thanks a bunch, Ursul!" before the large man was gone around the corner and the outlaw leader was alone, staring at the elaborate doors at the end of the corridor.

Jesse moved up to the doors and looked for a place that would be safe enough to knock. He had settled on a small flat area in the center of the left 'C' when the door creaked open without warning.

"Come in, Mr. James." The voice was cultured, with rich tones that hinted at a foreign land without drowning the ear in strange sounds that robbed the meaning from the words.

Jesse stood by the open door for a moment before walking in, leaving the brightly-lit hallway with its panoramic views behind.

The room he entered was a large round chamber, with tall, wide windows stretching almost entirely around the circumference. A great fireplace dominated one side of the room, the only area that was not graced with the large, clear windows. The walls were the same stone as the rest of this level, and adorned with a staggering collection of weapons, old and new, as well as tattered flags and pennons that seemed to be ancient. The furniture, like in the parlor far below, was covered in supple leather, interspersed with dark wood tables. Opposite the fireplace was a long desk cluttered with a mess of mechanical bits and pieces, RJ cylinders, and a small collection of shapes covered with a shiny black cloth. The persistent sweet undertone of Payson hung over everything, as it always did. Although Jesse remembered, from his last visit, that the smell was usually less offensive in Carpathian's castle.

In the center of the room stood a man Jesse had not seen in several years. He was taller than the outlaw remembered, standing straighter. His face, a mask any grandfather would be happy to have, was still framed with billowing white hair, glorious muttonchops reaching down toward a smiling mouth. The entire effect was only slightly ruined by the ungainly metal prosthetic that clasped around his left cheek, housing a large glowing ruby of an artificial eye, and the flexible black tubing that entered a similar mechanical housing at his right jawline. Relics of the doctor's first moments in the New World, Jesse knew that the facial augmentations were the mildest of the surgical scars the old man bore.

Although Jesse was never sure how much of the doctor was reconstructed or supported with metal parts or replaced completely, he knew that Carpathian's legs and at least one of his arms were heavily modified. No one knew exactly how the doctor had come by his extensive injuries, but they must have been nearly fatal. Only one thing was known for sure throughout the territories: Carpathian blamed the famous Union general, Ulysses S. Grant, for all of them.

"I trust my brother-in-law was more polite this time around, Mr. James?" Carpathian moved around the furniture and reached out with a hand that seemed equal parts flesh and metal reinforcement.

James looked back to the doors, which had closed silently behind him, and then nodded. "Ursul? Yeah, I can stand Ursul's gaff. In small doses, anyway."

The doctor nodded. "You have to forgive him, of course. Veronica's death hit him hard, and he came all this way for vengeance, as is our cultural obligation. But he feels that I do not move fast enough, of course, and so, much like an over-eager thoroughbred, things appear to be moving far too slowly for his tastes."

Jesse walked around the room, looking at the various objects on the tables or hanging from the walls. "Yeah, I get it, Doc. If anyone ever tried to off Susan, you better believe Frank and I'd be out to beef 'em by hook 'r by crook!"

"Please don't call me that." The older man's voice was flat, his hands firmly grasping the back of one of the high chairs.

Jesse looked around, his eyes slightly surprised. "Eh? Oh, sorry, D- . . . sorry, Doctor Carpathian. No disrespect intended."

The doctor nodded and gestured to one of the chairs by the cold fireplace. "Now, Mr. James. Care to have a seat? I'm sure you've got plenty you'd like to discuss?"

Jesse looked at one of the wide windows, the desk with all of its technological clutter, and then the offered chair. A small table beside the chair had a dusty bottle of amber liquid and two glasses. With a smile he sat down and popped open the bottle. He looked at the faded label and his smile grew even wider.

"Real Kentucky bourbon, sir! That's not easy to come by!" He poured himself a healthy dose and then settled back in the seat, holding the glass up to the light.

"It is not. I had that particular bottle brought up especially for you, however. I hope you enjoy it." The doctor lowered himself into the large seat opposite. He sat stiffly, back rigid, hands folded on his knees, looking expectantly at the famous outlaw.

Jessse crossed his legs, dangling one dirty boot off the beautifully carpeted floor, swinging it back and forth as if to some music only he could hear. "That's a pretty fancy magic room you've got there, Doctor Carpathian, that 'lift' of Ursul's? I can see how that'll save you some walkin', over time!"

Carpathian smiled politely but did not speak.

Jesse looked at the doctor for a few minutes, nodded, and then sat forward, both feet firmly on the carpet. "Okay, sir, I can see you're busy, so we'll jump straight to the point. I've got a notion of headin' out into the badlands, an' I've got an idea that we're gonna be meetin' up with some stiff resistance. Might be Injuns, might be Union, might be God knows all. But I'm thinkin' we might need some more heavy firepower to copper our bets, just in case."

Carpathian nodded, pursing his lips thoughtfully. "Interesting, Mr. James. Tell me, before we spend too much time and energy on such discussion . . . do I perchance have an outstanding balance toward you and your energetic little band?"

Jesse looked confused but tried to hide it behind a sip of bourbon. "Not sure I follow, Doctor."

Carpathian smiled thinly. "Well, it sounds to me as if you are asking for equipment, weapons, power, perhaps even upgrades? Such things do not come cheaply, Mr. James. Am I indebted to you in a way I was unaware? Do I owe you, say, enough to justify you coming to my home and asking for such dear gifts?"

Jesse's answering smile was as open as he could make it. "Well, no, Doctor, o' course you don't owe me nothin'. I was thinkin' I'd pay you, maybe half now, half in services down the road, once we agreed to a figure?"

Carpathian's smile widened. "Ah, now we are talking, as you say. Well, Mr. James, what exactly would you be looking for?"

Jesse's smile darkened slightly as he thought. "Well, we're heading into the wastes, an' our Iron Horses haven't seen a repair dock in a good long while. Most of 'em have developed some mighty queer habits lately. An' of course, we always need RJ fuel." He jerked a thumb toward one of the windows. "An' I couldn't help but notice you got plenty o' that, just lyin' around."

Carpathian's eyes were flat as he responded. "Plenty is a subjective term, Mr. James. And I assure you, it is not merely 'lying around,' as you say. What else do you envision needing on this expedition?"

Jesse pushed his feet out in front of him, cradling his glass in both hands on his belly and looking up at the ceiling, lost in thought.

"Well, not knowin' what we're gettin' ourselves into out there, I guess whatever you could spare that you'd think might be useful. Weapons, o' course. And anything you think might be of help." He raised one hand to look at the back of it, working the fingers and watching the pistons and wheels move beneath the armor. "Might be good for my piece o' mind if you'd take a gander at my arms, actually, while I'm here. It's been awhile."

Carpathian shifted his weight forward slightly, peering at Jesse's arms from a distance. "Is there something wrong with the arms, Mr. James?"

Jesse's confidence slipped a little as he continued looking at the arm, then over at the doctor. "No, not really. Just curious. You've done a lot of work like this, rebuilding bodies and
such . . . have any of the parts ever failed completely? Or begun to move on their own notions?"

Carpathian sat back in his chair and gave the outlaw chief an appraising look. "Not that I know of, Mr. James. Why, have your arms begun to take on a . . . life of their own?"

"No!" Jesse raised both hands up as if to prove their power. "Not at all." The guilt rose in his chest as an image of Misty's face peered at him from the back of his mind. "Nothing like that. Just curious, is all. Just wonderin' if somethin' like that could happen."

Carpathian's smile was predatory. "Not that I know of, Mr. James, no." Jesse nodded. "But would you still like me to look at the arms? It has been quite a while since I first replaced your own shattered limbs with these priceless augmetics, after all."

Jesse nodded, lowering the arms back into his lap. He could not forget the wrenching jar to his shoulder as the metal hand connected with the poor girl's face. The other instances where his arms seemed to have failed him, or acted on their own, paraded past his inner eye. In a more subdue voice he muttered, "yeah, I think maybe that'd be good."

"Excellent, then." The doctor stood and gestured for Jesse to follow him over to the desk. As the outlaw moved toward the windows, he was shocked again to see how high they were. The workers down below seemed smaller than ants. A chair sat next to the desk, and the doctor pointed him toward it. Soon the armored shrouding of his left arm was lying on the table while the doctor tinkered with the intricate mechanical workings with long, silver tools.

"So tell me, Mr. James, what is pulling you so inexorably out into the wastelands so precipitously?" The tool moved deftly from component to component, causing the fingers to jerk rhythmically in response.

"Not much, Doc . . . tor." Jesse looked quickly at the doctor out of the corner of his eye. He was not afraid of any man, including the mad European, but with the doc up to his wrists into Jesse's arms, it did not seem like the time to push the man. "Just felt like it was maybe time to see somethin' new, push out into the unknown for a while. See if there weren't some shots to take out that way."

The doctor nodded while continuing to work in the arm. "William Bonney chomping on your heels, is it, Mr. James?"

Jesse's head jerked around to look at the doctor, but the old man was entirely focused on the components of the mechanical arm. From the slight smile twinkling from between the imposing muttonchops, Jesse could see that he had noticed the outlaw's reaction. "Don't know what you're talkin' about, Doctor."

Carpathian chuckled. "That's alright, Mr. James, nothing to worry about. Every now and then the leader of the pack must prove his dominance. It is nature's way." He tapped on the armored side of Jesse's arm with a musical chiming sound, then gestured for him to spin the chair and present the other arm.

As Jesse moved, he shook his head. "Still don't know what you're gettin' at, Doctor. Me an' the Kid, we ain't got no unpleasantness between us."

Carpathian's smile was so condescending, it was everything Jesse could do not to slap it off of him. "I understand. Well, your arms look to be in tip-top shape." He lifted the sleeves of Jesse's shirt and prodded at the flesh where the metal was connected to his body. "Connection points seem healthy and robust. I would not imagine you should have any further troubles." He looked up quickly with a look of apology whose sincerity was entirely suspect. "I mean, I do not think you should have any troubles at all."

Jesse could feel the guilt burn behind his face while the feeling of loss and anger he had been living with for days threatened to engulf him all over again. While he struggled with these feelings, however, Doctor Carpathian was already moving on.

"Now, Mr. James, let us further discuss this adventure you are planning. You are wishing for me to look into your transportation, and I think I have just the thing for you. As for weapons and power, again, I think I can do more than you might have wished. But as for any additional assistance, I would need to know what type of work you are contemplating. I am guessing you are not just looking to stir up mischief. Your demeanor suggests there is something . . . extraordinary about this expedition."

Jesse shook his head trying to clear it of the guilt, fear, and confusion. "Well, we reckon we might be havin' to dig. If you've got anythin' fer diggin'—"

"You have looked out the window, I know, Mr. James?" Carpathian sat back with a wry smile.

Jesse was even more flustered. "Sure. 'Course. You got a huge mine back there. You got any diggin' tools we might be able to . . . borrow?"

Carpathian shook his head, smile firmly in place. "Sadly, no. As much as I would love to let you . . . borrow, expensive excavating equipment, I'm afraid nothing I have would be portable enough for you to take with you. All of my workings are designed and built on-sight. Unless you would like to take some of my modified animations, to save you some manual labor?"

Jesse answered quickly. "No, no, that's okay. We'll just pick up some shovels and picks along the way."

Carpathian's eyes drifted toward the window and he pushed himself back up out of his chair, moving around the desk. "I must admit, however, that you have piqued my interest, Mr. James. Buried treasure not being among your usual repertoire, not to mention the tantalizing mention of the Warrior Nation, the hated Union, and so on. What, if I might make so bold, is it exactly that you are designing to dig up?"

Jesse stared down at his right hand, opening and closing the fingers into a hard metallic fist. Everything seemed to be moving smoothly, but then, everything had been moving smoothly, for the most part, before his arrival. He looked up as the expectant silence registered in his distracted brain.

"Hmm? Oh, I don't even know, Doctor." He shrugged. "Someone got a line on somethin' big, maybe, buried out in the desert. We're thinkin', maybe if someone else thinks it's big, maybe it's somethin' we might want to look into." He shot the Doctor a grin. "See what the market will bear, you know?"

Carpathian smiled and nodded, but he seemed distracted as he sat down behind the desk. "Yes, well, excavation, still, does not strike me as being strongly placed within your bailiwick, if you do not mind my saying, Mr. James." He folded his hands in front of him and gave the outlaw boss a warm smile. "Whereas, I was thinking, perhaps another train job? I have been tinkering with a new weapon system that I think is about ready to test on a major target, and I cannot think of a better subject than a Union Heavy Rail train. What would you say to another joint venture, Mr. James?"

Jesse shook his head. "'Fraid not, sir. I've got an appointment in Diablo Canyon that I better not miss." Carpathian's reaction to the buried object, and Jesse's interest in it, was ringing false to him, and he suddenly realized he needed to tread carefully with this man who was not a friend. The doctor was a sometime-ally, and a sometime-adversary, and unfortunately necessary to keep sweet in case anything ever happened to his arms, but he was no friend.

"Are you quite certain? I believe my ion energy net device will be capable of catching all manner of vehicles and technology in its web, and there could be no better test than the Heavy Rail. We could choose almost any target. Some of them are coming down from Washington absolutely laden with gold and notes, I hear." The smile grew wider.

Jesse gave the doctor a look he hoped seemed speculative. "Well, Doctor, I have to admit, you're makin' a pretty good case. If we do go after a Heavy, though, we're still gonna need this new gear. What say, you give me a price on the new plunder, I talk to my boys, an' we make the call later. I still may need to make a quick stop if we're headin' back east."

The doctor's smile widened slightly. Jesse marked this sudden release of tension for further thought. He wanted to hear what Frank might have to say about the doc's reactions. "That sounds excellent, Mr. James. Now, let me see." He looked down at a sheaf of papers on his desk. "Judging from reports, you rode into town with roughly twenty companions?" Jesse nodded, no longer surprised at the information the doc always seemed to have at his fingertips.

"Excellent. Well, refurbishing weapons and vehicles, providing replacements and energy cylinders for the lot." His finger moved down a column of numbers on one piece of paper. "Let us say, twenty thousand, for the entire group?" His smile was predatory again, and Jesse tried not to let the shock show in his face.

"Twenty." He kept his voice flat. "That would leave us with a tad less than we were hopin' to walk away with, to tell you the truth, Doctor."

The smile widened. "Well, remember, that we have said, half now, half in services at some later date? And of course, if you should choose to assist with the ion energy net test, that would certainly go a long way toward equaling this particular debt." The grin grew downright smug as the doctor's eyes flicked down to Jesse's arms and back up again.

Jesse thought for a moment. He knew they could pay half immediately, although Frank would howl to the heavens about it. But they had the coins and the notes to do it. The last bit, about paying for the second half in services in the future . . . exactly what would Carpathian think would be equal, in the services of Jesse's gang, to ten thousand dollars in hard currency?

Jesse knew there was no way they could face down Billy's gang with the equipment they had available. If Billy was right, and somewhere along the trail there was going to be someone mean enough that Billy really did need Jesse and his boys . . . Well, it was not going to go well for Jesse if he decided to go it alone and they did not have the latest the doctor could provide. Yet, twenty thousand was a lot of dinero to be throwing around.

"I don't know, Doctor. That's a hefty bill, to be honest." He watched Carpathian for his reaction, and was happy when the old man leaned forward, eagerness to strike the deal flaring in his eyes.

"Well, Mr. James, let me see if I can entice you perhaps a little bit further. I have been designing a new transportation, something perhaps more robust than the Iron Horses so graciously provided by the Union and your first train job. I have not yet decided what to call it, but it can cover difficult terrain more easily, is faster in overgrown areas, carries more armor, and has a greater carrying capacity." His smile broadened and he gestured widely with both arms. "Not to mention that it is the latest technology I have to offer."

Jesse looked at the old man for a moment. It never failed. Carpathian always knew what a rube he was for new tech, and even knowing that, Jesse was always scooped in by the latest shiny. "I wouldn't mind seein' somethin' like that for myself, Doc . . . tor . . . if you've got one layin' about."

Carpathian smiled even more broadly. "Excellent! And let me show you something we have just put into production today." He pulled the small sheet from the objects on the desk, revealing several small, sleek-looking pistols, each of similar design.

The doctor picked one of the weapons up and held it out to Jesse. The thing looked almost like a child's toy. Its sleek lines were clearly made of some light metal from the weight and feel, and yet there were no cylinders for the RJ-1027 cartridges. He flipped the small pistol easily in his hand to look sideways down the barrel, only to see that there was no real bore. The barrel ended in a clear chunk of crystal or glass. He looked up at the doctor with a questioning eyebrow.

The doctor's responding smile was almost childlike. "Is it not fantastic? It is something that Thomas has been working on nearly since his arrival. We call it an ion pistol. Fairly short range, I'm afraid, but any RJ-1027 technology you shoot with this pretty little thing will immediately cease to function. It fires an agitated stream of ions . . . but never mind, you do not care for the technical minutia, I know." The smile took on a slightly patronizing edge. "Anyway, suffice it to say, you fire this weapon at anything carried by the Union, or anyone else bearing modern weaponry, and you will swiftly have them at a severe disadvantage!"

Jesse looked quickly down at his own arms and up again, not trying to hide the dismay. Carpathian immediately reached out to pat the outlaw's armored forearm reassuringly. "Do not worry, Mr. James. Your arms are only moderately powered by the RJ-1027 within them. Most of their power comes from your own body's electrical field. Even should the unthinkable happen, and someone fire one of these weapons at you, your arms would still function. You would not be helpless."

Jesse tried to imagine what it would be like, in the middle of a fight, if his arms suddenly stopped working. Many of his hidden fears came surging up at the thought. To be helpless before the enemy, to be at the mercy of anyone, never mind someone actively seeking to do him harm?

The outlaw came back to himself when the doctor patted his forearm again with a dull thud. "Please, Mr. James, do not fret. There are only four of these weapons extant throughout the wide world, and I am giving you two of them. The other two remain here, where myself and Mr. Edison will continue to perfect the technology. For now, look upon them as nothing more than a great advantage being proffered to you and you alone."

Jesse nodded vaguely, unable to completely shake the terror that had been rushing through his mind. "How much would these add to my tab, Doctor?"

Again the old man's arms were thrown magnanimously wide. "Why, included in the original fee, of course, Mr. James! I am not trying to render you destitute! In fact, for field testing these new weapons for me, I will reduce the balance somewhat. Shall we say, upon receipt of ten thousand dollars, you will only owe me eight thousand more in services? And the return of the ion pistols, of course. And, should you decide to keep the new vehicle, I would make that a gift, for loyal service in the past, and continued friendship in the future?"

Jesse found his brain starting to tie up in all the numbers and conditions, and nodded before he could work himself into a paralyzing bout of self-doubt. He reached out across the desk and Carpathian took his hand, shaking it vigorously. "I think you have yourself a deal, Doctor Carpathian. Our cash is with my brother right now, so let me head down to the saloon, meet back up with the boys, and I'll get you your money."

Carpathian rose from behind the desk with a broad smile. "Excellent, Mr. James! I shall walk you to the lift and see you on your way. Ursul should be at the bottom to guide you out."

"Thanks. I'm not sure I could make it on my own. These new digs are pretty impressive, Doctor." Jesse allowed himself to be led out of the turret room and across the bridge hallway, bright sunlight still streaming through the long windows.

"Thank you. Yes, it was designed as homage to my ancestral home, abandoned under duress many, many years ago. Its halls and rooms provide great solace when my work threatens to overwhelm me with its scope and weight." They walked down the corridor and stopped before the strange double doors. "Will you need assistance with the lift controls, Mr. James, or do you feel capable of finding your way down to the ground level?"

Jesse forced himself to give a smile that could, charitably, be considered friendly. "No, Doctor, I reckon I'm good. I just press the button with the 'P' on it, right?"

The old man nodded with a gracious smile. "Indeed, Mr. James. The button with the 'P' will bring you safely down to the ground level. Good day, to you. Ursul will arrange for a way you can communicate with us, when you decide the time has come for another great train heist to enter into the Jesse James legend. I hope to be hearing from you very soon."

Jesse shook the extended hand again and walked cautiously into the tiny room behind the double doors. He turned around, forcing his back to remain straight, and gave a sidelong smile to the doctor before reaching out and gently pushing the correct button. The door slid shut on Carpathian's smiling face, and Jesse signed with relief.

He looked at the array of buttons, wondering what all these disks above the 'P' might mean. He had puzzled out the basic structure of the control pad, and so he was fairly confident that the buttons between the 'P' and the 'A' were the levels from the ground floor to the tower room he had just left. But what were all of the other buttons? Basement levels? He counted them. Ten? He did not want to even contemplate what Carpathian might have going on ten levels below ground.

As the floor rumbled away and the walls creaked and hissed, Jesse tried to recall everything that had happened while he had been speaking with Carpathian concerning Billy's mysterious object. The doctor had seemed most eager to change the subject, trying to divert Jesse from this particular job. Was there a reason? Did he know something about more about the whole affair than Jesse or Billy?

Jesse felt a smile spread over his face at the thought. If Carpathian knew, or thought he knew, what was out there, it could very well be that Billy was right, and it was something important after all. If it was something important after all, it was possible that this caper could do everything he wanted and more.

Now he just needed to convince Frank the price was right, stick around for the repairs and refitting, and get out of Payson without tipping his hand.

The smile faltered slightly before flaring back full force. Well, what was life without some challenges?

Chapter 10

Jesse hunched over the controls of his new mount and was thrilled at the growling roar. He had been calling it a trike after the three wheeled vehicles city swells had tried to introduce into Kansas City. His men, however, following the lead of damned Cole Younger, had taken to calling it a Blackjack, because, as Cole was swift to point out, the twenty other men riding in the posse were moseying along on the same old Iron Horses that had been seeing them through for well over a decade now. However, for Jesse, the twenty first of their number, it was nothing but the absolute best. There may have been a small touch of frustrated bitterness behind it, as there often was when Cole got clever about something Jesse had going, but it was plenty rich for the rest of the boys, and at this point even Frank was calling the big armored brute a Blackjack. Jesse had stopped trying to fight it.

With two large drive wheels in front and a smaller stabilizer wheel behind the driver, the Blackjack was far steadier in high-speed maneuvers than the top-heavy Iron Horses. The big craft was locked to the ground by its heavy wheels as opposed to riding on the blasts of heated air that suspended the 'Horses, but the Blackjack was actually faster on the straightaway. The broad armored nose provided more protection from a wider arc to the front in battle, as well. The four blaster muzzles that thrust from fairings in the front promised that it could rack up the pain when it had to as well.

Jesse cranked the power higher and gloried in the change in pitch from the engine beneath him. The thing vibrated like there was a demon from Hell trapped inside, and the image pleased the outlaw to no end. Behind him, his men struggled to keep up, their own machines grinding out an even louder, thunderous bellow that echoed off the low hills and scrub pines around them. Each of those machines had been completely refurbished by the best engineers the doctor had on hand, but still they were no match for the Blackjack.

Blackjack. Lucky 21. Jesse grinned savagely behind his red-tinted goggles and gunned the engine again, reveling in the feeling of freedom that only such a burst of power along an empty open road could offer. Maybe he would let them call it a Blackjack after all.

They had been riding nonstop since Payson, and he knew the relentless pace was once again taking its toll. After riding all last night, the blazing sunset was a stark reminder of the exhaustion that plagued them all at this point. Still, they needed to get to Diablo Canyon if Jesse was going to have any chance of getting the lay of the land. He wanted to prepare something clever for the Kid. Most of the men still believed they would be joining Billy and his gang at the canyon, but Frank and the Youngers knew better. They knew Jesse had no intention of sharing whatever was at the end of the trail Billy had stumbled upon up in the mountains, and he certainly had no intention of sharing the glory and the influence, if any was to be had, with the no account little sand lizard.

Jesse had not formulated any concrete plans for Billy yet, but the wheels of his mind spun nearly every minute of the day, looking at every angle and trying to decide the best way to set events. It had been years since he had been to Diablo Canyon, and he had heard some nasty rumors about the metal man that had been lawing it up in the town recently. At the same time, his last couple of days in Kansas City still haunted him. The knowledge of how wrong things had gone in Missouri City, along with those terrible last moments with Misty, were never far from his thoughts. Every time he closed his eyes, he knew the image of her, face torn and bleeding, hatred and fear blazing in her red-rimmed eyes, would be waiting for him.

Frank and Cole had been trying to jolly him out of his dark depression, but even his brother's efforts had slackened over the last day as Jesse's mind refused to give ground. He was either thinking about Diablo Canyon and how he could euchre Billy the Kid, or he was obsessing upon those last moments in the little garret apartment above the Arcadia Saloon. He schooled his face to an impassive mask, smiled when the boys joked around during stops, and nodded as if he were listening whenever Frank or the Youngers had something to say. Yet, within the silence of his own mind there was only the whirlwind of images from Missouri City, the Arcadia, and the desperate hope that whatever was buried out in the badlands could somehow make it all better. He needed to believe that whatever it was, it was big enough to put the polish back on his name, heavy enough to convince himself that he was still on top.

None of this was fully formed in his conscious mind. He knew only that he felt the terrible guilty weight over what happened with Misty, and a ravenous, driving hunger to be the man with his boot on the treasure chest when this latest adventure reached its conclusion. He knew there was no line he would not cross to see himself on top. A part of himself was obscenely happy it was Billy the Kid who would be left holding the bag when all was said and done.

As Jesse's mind had rumbled along these familiar tracks, the rest of the posse caught up to him. He was only aware of this as Frank waved a gloved hand toward his unresponsive face, shouting something that was drowned out by the Blackjack's demonic roar. That was another thing Jesse liked about his new vehicle: it was nearly impossible for anyone to speak to him on the road, so they tended to leave him alone until it was time to stop.

Jesse nodded to his brother and looked up ahead to the trail that stretched out before them. A small stream had been running parallel to the track for several hours now. A nice flat meadow ahead seemed as good a place as any to walk some of the stiffness out of their legs and replenish their water. He pointed to the meadow with two metal fingers and Frank nodded in turn, raising one hand in the air to get the attention of the men behind him. They thundered onto the field, the Iron Horses blasting dust and yellow grass into the air as the Blackjack rolled to a halt beside a couple of low trees that offered what meager shade there was to be had.

As the others cut the power to their engines, allowing the Iron Horses to settle into the brittle grass of the field, Jesse pulled his goggles down under his chin and took a quick look around. There were clumps of low bushes and stunted trees dotting the entire region, but not much else that afforded any kind of cover. The shallow depression that channeled the stream would never hide a force large enough to challenge the outlaw gang with all of their overhauled firepower. The men were swinging down off their vehicles, many moving toward the stream or off to find a bush of convenience. Frank and Cole spoke together briefly, Frank nodded, and the two men approached Jesse. The outlaw chief braced himself. It was never good news when Frank and Cole came at him paired up this way.

"Hey, Jesse, we been thinkin'." Frank's voice was casual, but Jesse rolled his eyes at the opening salvo.

"Yeah? Must o' missed the smell, on account of the vehicles." Jesse stretched his arms out, noting the clicks and whirs as the machinery within slid smoothly from one position to another without a hitch. Whatever the doc had done, it seemed to have worked.

Frank smiled thinly at Jesse's retort and then continued. "We been ridin' for almost a day and a half now without much of a break. The boys are all dragged out, an' we should be back on schedule, after the way you rode us all to get to Payson in the first place." Cole stood off Frank's shoulder, nodding. His mouth worked around a solid plug of chaw.

Jesse looked at his brother for a moment and then flung his arms wide to indicate the barren landscape. "So, you wanna throw a roll down and take forty here in the scrub, Frank? You so tuckered out you wanna sleep on the ground for a bit?"

Frank shot a sour look at Cole, who shrugged. "Jesse, you don't have to come over the tartar with us. I'm just thinkin', you want the boys ready for a shindig when we get to Diablo Canyon, you might wanna think about givin' 'em a chance to take a least a little rest afore we get there."

Jesse turned away from his brother and spat trail dust off to the side of his Blackjack. He looked back at Frank with an annoyed expression. "You might have missed it when I said we needed to get to the Canyon as fast as we possibly can?"

Frank shook his head, with Cole behind him echoing the motion. "No I did not, Jesse, an' you know it. But if we pull into the Canyon half shagged and dull-minded, it ain't gonna matter that we made it in time, is it? Now, Garland over yonder says there's a small town, 'bout a couple more hours ride from here. Place called Sacred Lake, even has a small lodge for travelers. We roll into town, get some shut eye, we're up at the crack of dawn, an' gone faster'n a milkmaid's virtue."

"Boys could really use some shut eye in a real bed, Jesse." Cole's voice was respectful, but his gaze was steady, almost challenging the outlaw boss to contradict him.

Jesse thought about it for a second. "Sacred Lake, eh?" He made a show of looking all around them at the rolling fields as far as the eye could see. "You figure there's a lake out here somewhere?"

Cole said, "it ain't always there, Jesse. It sometimes is and it sometimes ain't, accordin' to the seasons. Like a lot of things out here. But some religious folks, awhile back, came in and set themselves up some dairy farms." He spat into the dirt. "There's some as see it's sometimes bein' there sometimes not as a bit of a miracle. They been there a few years now. They got a nice little village an' everythin'."

"Garland says it ain't fancy, Jesse, but it don't need to be. We don't lose much time for stoppin', and it would mean an awful lot to the boys. They're ridin' as hard as they can, brother, but you'll be drivin' 'em into an early grave you keep this up. When you need 'em the most, they ain't gonna be worth a tinker's fart."

Jesse scowled, but he considered what his brother and Cole had said. He still could not figure out Billy's angle. It was unlike the younger outlaw to share in any major score like this. Billy was either scared of what he was apt to find out in the badlands, or he was working at something Jesse had not been able to figure yet. The last thing Jesse wanted was to get it in the neck from Billy, though. Knowing as little as he knew, the best way to get the bulge on the Kid would be to get to Diablo Canyon as early as possible and see what could be seen.

But Frank made a good point, also, that no matter what Billy's scheme was, he would need his boys in the best shape possible if he was going to have any chance of turning the cards on him.

"This lake is a couple hours ahead?" He knew he sounded angry, and he did not much care.

"We just take the Lake Mary trail, up ahead aways, an' we should be there before full dark." Frank looked to Cole for confirmation and the other man nodded.

Jesse looked back over the men as they moved about, taking water from the stream or resting against their 'Horses. They were clearly all exhausted beneath their forced bravado, but they were all also clearly watching the exchange between their boss and his brother as closely as they could without being obvious.

Jesse nodded. "Okay, if you boys think we need it, we'll take the time," he scowled at his brother. "But I swear, Frank, if things get knocked into a cocked hat in Diablo Canyon because I didn't have enough time to scope the lay of the land —"

Frank held up a hand to stop his brother's words. "Jesse, you push on through now and ain't none of us, including you, who will be able to catch a case o' scabies in a bawdy house at the end of the ride."

That brought Jesse up short and he could not keep a grin from twisting his lip. "Well, I don't know about that, Frank. Cole ain't never had a hard time catchin' scabies."

Cole snorted and hooked his thumbs beneath his holster belt. "Just cuz you boys don't like to live on the edge o' danger ain't no reason I ever seen I should settle for the tame fillies."

Jesse shook his head, one hand raised in surrender. "Okay Frank, you win. " He pitched his voice to be heard by the rest of the men. "Alright, you coffee boilers, listen up. Frank here has convinced me you rough 'n' ready algerines need your beauty sleep afore we ride down on Diablo Canyon. Appears some gospel sharps have set up shop on some magical lake just north of here, and they got themselves a lodge. You boys wanna sleep in some beds afore we brace whatever we find in Diablo Canyon?"

There were many smiles and nods, most weary, and Jesse could not stop a pang of frustration. If even a few of the men had put on a brave front he could have faced down Frank's suggestion and pushed the men through. Still, if every one of them was ready to settle down for a night, maybe it was for the best.

"Alright, then. We'll ride on up to Sacred Lake and see what's there. But don't you lot be thinkin' of sleepin' in, now!" He scowled at them and they grinned back, some raising their hands in mock surrender. "First yahoo among you don't get up, we'll be draggin' him the rest of the way to Diablo Canyon, see if that don't wake 'im up!"

As Jesse and his gang rode down the dusty trail, the grassy fields along the left hand side slowly gave way to the tall, dark Ponderosa pines of the Coconino Forest. Majestic peaks reared up out of the west, blocking the last rays of the sun and providing dramatic silhouettes for the final shimmering colors of sunset. The muted rumble of their mounts bounced from the trees, and as they pulled into the township of Sacred Lake, lights were already appearing in many of the houses. Jesse noticed something strange about the nature of the lights without really thinking about it. It was soon clear that something was very different about Sacred Lake.

"There ain't no RJ." Jim Younger, the second oldest of the four brothers, muttered as the posse pulled up on the edge of town. "No generators 'r nothin'." Jesse realized the lights lacked the reddish tinge of RJ-1027 lighting, and there were no winking tell-tales anywhere to be seen. Sacred Lake, in fact, looked exactly like a town out of his distant youth, without any of the technology or equipment Carpathian's Red Renaissance had introduced to the western territories.

A two story building, larger than any other in the town center, had a shingle-sign hanging from a post in front, and as the roaring machines came close, their road lights flaring, Jesse saw the name 'Sacred Lake Lodge' emblazoned on it. There was a rough image of a lake in the middle of the sign, and floating above it a strange symbol he had never seen before.

"No recharge stations, Jesse." Frank pulled up beside his brother and leaned over to shout into his ear. "Some of the boys'll be coastin' into Diablo Canyon at his rate."

Jesse nodded to his brother and pulled the Blackjack nose first against the hitching post in front of the lodge. The others slotted themselves into position as well, and soon, the last Iron Horse stuttered into silence. The silence was oppressive, and he realized it had been a very long time since he had been in a town with no generators at all.

The tall door of the lodge opened, throwing a soft yellow fan of light onto the front lawn and its flagstone walkway. A man in an apron and a wide smile stepped out onto the stoop and waved to the group gathering at the gate.

"Welcome to Sacred Lake, strangers!" He stumped down the steps and as he came closer, Jesse saw that the man had the heavy, muscular build of a farmer. His hair was cut in a strange fashion that left the sides long, hanging down past his ears, but the top was a rough bristle. "You boys need some vittles? I'm afraid we don't have any alcohol, but we've got good honest food, milk and cool water, and clean beds a plenty for the lot of you."

The man stopped a couple paces from Jesse and a vague look of recognition came over his face before smoothing away. Jesse wondered if he had imagined it.

Cole stepped up to the fence, one hand on the rough wood. "You ain't got no generators or recharge stations hereabouts?"

The man smiled warmly and shook his head. "No, I'm afraid not. We aspire to a simpler lifestyle here in Sacred Lake. We do not allow any of the newest technologies to come between us and the soil."

One of the younger men, Bryce, grunted. Jim Younger stepped up to his brother's side. "You got a problem with what we're packin'?"

The man shook his head again. "Of course not. Travelers cannot be expected to adopt the deeper philosophies of every small town at which they sojourn. Might I entice you all to come in and lay down your loads, however? It is pleasant inside, and our prices are fair."

"Fair." Another of the boys snorted. "Old man don't know from fair yet." Jesse stepped from the pack and put out his hand. "We'd be most obliged to you, Mr. . . . ?"

The man's hand came up automatically. "You can call me Elijah, son." He raised a finger with another of his honest smiles. "And don't feel you have to pass along your name. I'm no stranger to the wider world, and I can tell by your clothing and your transportation that you all are travelers on the verges of life. We of Sacred Lake will not pry."

Jesse tilted his head at this forward statement, but looked around at his men, reading nothing but hunger, thirst, and exhaustion there, and nodded. "Thank you, sir. We'd be much obliged, as I said."

Jesse followed the grey haired man up the steps, looking back to give his men a stern glance. If the folks of Sacred Lake were not going to give them any trouble, then it was best to play along. They could decide in the morning if they wanted to pay or not.

A flicker of movement across the street caught the outlaw's eye as he was about to turn to go into the lodge. A curtain or drape over a window had been dropped, muting the soft glow of a lamp within. The fabric still shifted slowly back and forth as he watched, settling into stillness. Jesse shrugged. Just a local, curious at the crowd of vehicles. It was surprising there were not more gawkers, really, considering this little burg did not have so much as an RJ-warmed outhouse.

Jesse shrugged and went into the lodge. His band tramped in after him, quickly filling the small common room inside.

"Feel free to have a seat, gentlemen," Elijah waved to the empty room, full of mismatched tables and chairs. "Let me speak to my wife, see what rooms would be best for ya'll." He disappeared through a small door, going deeper into the building.

Frank looked around as the men settled down at tables all around. Some were rolling worn dice, others dealing tattered cards, but most were just sitting wearily, little more on their minds than the promised beds.

"This is a pretty nifty joint, eh, Jesse?" Frank nodded to the fireplace across the room. "That's quite a pigsticker for a bunch of doxologists, wouldn't you say?"

Jesse picked his way through the tables to get a better look at the weapon. The blade was a shining silver sweep of steel, nothing like the dark metals used by the Union in its charged blades. The handle of the thing continued the graceful curve, with supple black leather wrapped around two different sections, suggesting it was to be used two handed. All the metal work on the handle, including the butt end, the cross piece, and a fancy, fluted bit that divided the two areas of leather, were all done in gleaming silver. Jesse did not know much about swords, but he could see that the silver alone on that weapon would probably buy an Iron Horse if the owner was willing to part with it.

Jesse grunted at Frank. "Mighty fancy."

The outlaw chief was reaching out to touch the soft leather of the handle when Elijah came back in through the heavy door. His voice stopped Jesse's hand in mid-motion despite its casual tone.

"Ah, you've noticed Isten, I see." The man's smile was still in place, still open and honest as it had been since he had opened his door to the outlaws.
Jesse looked at the older man with a quirked eyebrow. "What now?"

The innkeeper gestured to the sword. "The scimitar on the wall. A family heirloom my father called Isten Kardja. No idea what it means, I'm afraid. It's been on one wall or another since before I was born."

Jesse turned back to look more closely at the sword. Frank was still staring and gave his younger brother a quick look before purposefully moving away from the wall. With a small shrug, Jesse did likewise.

"It's a lovely piece, and no mistake, Mr. Elijah." Jesse moved back toward the innkeeper.

"Please, just call me Elijah. My wife and sons have gone upstairs to get the rooms there ready. We've plenty, as we don't often receive guests. There is only one man upstairs now, a victim of an unfortunate accident on the road, I'm afraid. We've been taking care of him since some friends of his left him behind yesterday."

Cole and Jim exchanged looks and then Cole shot a glance at Jesse, who nodded before turning back to the innkeeper. "Well, that's great, Elijah, thank you kindly. My friend here," he gestured to another of the Younger clan, Bob, giving the man a quick glare. "He's a bit of a frontier sawbones, if you think it might help to get something of a professional opinion on the situation?"

The man's smile did not fluctuate at all. "Oh, I'm certain he's in as good hands as will be possible, never fear. Nothing to worry about. His friends had dressed his wounds quite well, and left plenty of money for his care and lodgings."

The man's smile did not shift. Jesse noticed, as did Frank and Cole, and their eyes grew suspicious. "They had plenty of money, these friends of his?" The outlaw chief's voice was casual.

"Well, I can't speak to one man's definition of plenty, son, but they had enough for me and mine to offer what help we can." Elijah's smile widened. "Now, would you boys like me to show you to those rooms before some of you peter out right here in the common room?"

The stairway was narrow, the stairs steep. The upper level of the building was stifling, but cozy. A small chair on the upper landing held a well-made afghan that sported the same symbol as the sign out front, and the walls of the upper hallway were decorated with paintings of far-off exotic locations that featured many strange trees and animals. Jesse was a little startled to realize that the strangest things of all, however, were the mundane oil lamps hanging from the ceiling.

"My wife made the last ten rooms at the end of the hall ready. I'm afraid the five at the far end are none too big, we don't usually get more than a couple visitors at a time here at the lodge." The innkeeper's voice was apologetic as he spoke over his shoulder, gesturing down the long hallway.

"No problem, Elijah, thank you very much for your kindness." Jesse was about to move around the man and down toward the rooms when a thought occurred to him and he turned back. "Which room is the wounded man in, sir, so that we might not disturb him?"

Elijah smiled and nodded. "That's right kind of you, son. The young man is in the room at the top of the stairs, so as far from you and your friends as possible. But judging from their demeanor, I'd venture to guess that your friends won't be kicking up too much of a fracas tonight."

Jesse shook his head. "No, probably not. Thanks, sir. We'll see you in the morning?"

"Indeed, young man. G'night. Feel free to lower the lamps when you're ready to retire." Elijah nodded once more and turned back down the hallway.

Jesse waited until the old man was gone before he gestured for Frank and the Youngers to join him in the nearest room. They went in to find a single bed, nicely made, and a small bedside table. A small desk with a pitcher of water and a basin was against the far wall. A well-made chair sat before the desk. Jesse gestured for the men to relax as he looked out the door and made sure his men were settling into their rooms. There was a quick, whispered commotion over who would be sleeping where, and then things settled down. Jesse carefully closed the door and turned back to the five other men.

"This place strikin' anyone else as strange?" He scanned their faces and found in every one a disquiet matching his own.

"What kinda hotel has this many rooms, this far out into the middle o' nowhere?" John Younger, the youngest of the brothers, had leaned against the wall behind the desk.

"An' I'm not buyin' the soft solder the old man's givin' us, neither." Cole, as the eldest, was usually the most outspoken, although his vicious sense of humor also meant he was probably taken the least seriously.

This time, however, Jesse could only nod. "Yeah, an' I'm not sure about this yahoo down the hall, but I'm thinkin' we need to at least peek in on him before we vamanos in the morning."

Frank nodded, but his face was worried. "I don't think we want to raise a fuss here, Jesse. Somethin' about this little burg don't add up, an' I'm not thinkin' things go in our favor if they go south."

Jesse rested a boot on the chair, articulated wrists crossed over one knee, as he stared out the small window at the silent street below. "I'm feelin' exactly what you're feelin', Frank. We gotta flow smoothly through this little bug hill, settle quietly, and move on. We still don't know what's waitin' for us out at Diablo Canyon, an' we can't get wrapped up in this no whorehouse town and its peculiarities." He looked over at his brother and the Youngers. "I'd say we bunk down, get up with the cows, visit our friend down the hall, and leave a nice pile o' notes for old Elijah before we skedaddle."

The men nodded and began to file out of the room. Jesse's arm struck out to snag Frank's sleeve before he left, and Cole, in the back of the pack of Youngers, nodded and closed the door behind them.

"There's somethin' more than strange about this whole place, Frank. Go back 'round to the boys and set up a watch through the night. I need you and Cole and the boys sharp, so keep the watches two men, by room, and keep it to the younger men." Frank nodded and turned toward the door, but Jesse jerked gently on the sleeve to turn him again. "The younger boys we can trust, though, Frank. None o' the shavetails."

Frank shook his head. "You mean like young Ty? Why we got boys we can't count on to watch our sleepin' backs at all, I don't know, Jesse. But you're the boss." He turned to go, then looked back at his younger brother. "See you in the mornin'?"

Jesse gave one sharp snap of his chin. "No doubt. See you in the mornin'." After the other men had left, Jesse shrugged off his duster and draped it over the chair, moving toward the small window. Below, the street was still and dark. Most of the houses around them still had the odd window lit, but there was no movement to be seen.

Despite his exhaustion, Jesse spent a long time at the window before settling into the bed with his boots still on.

*****

The interior of the Judgment wagon was not conducive to clear thinking, and as Wyatt braced himself against the constant rolling motion by grabbing an iron rung near his jump seat, he shook his head in frustration. The passenger compartment was small, and when you took into account the four UR-30 units that usually sat immobile in their harnesses along the walls, alongside Virgil and Doc, and the emotional crowding of Morgan's immense form taking up the cramped jail cell, he did not think the conditions could have been much different from those suffered by the slaves brought over packed ass to teakettle in the slaver ships from Africa.

The fact that two of the UR-30s were currently pacing along in front of the Judgment made the crowded situation slightly more tolerable, but the sound still pounded in his ears, the nearly unbearable heat churning up from the engine beneath them still steamed up through the air, and the placid look on his younger brother's pale face behind the heavy iron bars drew his constant and distressing attention. One good thing about the infernal machine, however: it was so loud inside, there was no way anyone could try to engage him in casual conversation.

They had been dragging the heavy machine across the trails for more than four days now. Wyatt knew any band riding Iron Horses would be making far better time, and so the chances of the lawmen getting to Diablo Canyon in time to stop whatever was going to happen there was slim. But he also knew something he believed the outlaw scum did not know about their own agile vehicles: all RJ-powered machinery left behind a trail when it was used at high power. Not a trail visible to the human eye, and not even something that a normal person could smell, or feel, or track on their own. It turned out there was something that could track that trail, though, and that was the UR-30 Enforcer units.

Right then, two of the units were ranging ahead of the Judgment and its flanking Hogs. Their cyclopean eyes had been adjusted to see the faint RJ-1027 trail, slashing bright columns of visible red light out in front of them like the lighthouses of his childhood on foggy nights. Wherever the red beam made contact with an RJ-1027 trail, the trail suddenly became visible as a glittering ruby path hovering eerily about a foot off the ground.

Wyatt pulled himself up to peer out one of the forward observation ports and checked the Enforcer units at work. Sure enough, the trail ahead of them was still glowing with heavy red tracks left behind by a large band riding RJ-powered vehicles. He grunted in satisfaction and sat back down on the wooden seat. He flashed a quick grin at Virgil, who was keeping busy cleaning a large hand cannon he had acquired from a Union officer a while back. Doc was sitting upright against the iron wall of the compartment, swaying with the motion of the vehicle, and gave Wyatt a slight, tired smile from above his breathing mask. Wyatt nodded and then settled back to his own meditations.

It seemed like it was only a few minute further down the trail before the

Judgment rolled to a halt and the driver let the engine idle down to a dull rumble. Wyatt leapt up to thrust his head onto the driver's deck and shouted, "Why the hell've we stopped? Don't you boys know nothin' 'bout the concept of hurryin'?" "Sir, the UR-30s have stopped. I . . . I don't think they're sure what to do." The driver shouted down at the Over-marshal, his thick goggles giving him an alien look.

Wyatt cursed under his breath and threw his weight against the closest side hatch, throwing it open to crash against the armored flank. He swung himself through the hatch, grabbed the access ladder half way down, and leapt the rest of the way, landing lightly on his feet with his duster flaring around his legs.

"What in the Sam Hill is going on out here?" Wyatt stalked forward to where the two robots had stopped moving nearly altogether. Only a slight swaying from side to side differentiated them from strange ancient statues set to guard the road from otherworldly threats. At the Over-marshal's voice, both metal heads swiveled to home in on his approaching figure, their bodies pivoting to follow the alignment.

"Current trail has deviated from expected parameters," the buzzing voice of one of the units said. Wyatt felt his shoulders rise slightly. He could never abide those strange voices, or the uncomfortable harmonics they seemed to set up in his chest.

"What does that mean?" Speaking with the Enforcer units often took more patience that dealing with Virgil's least gifted deputies.

"It means these wily coyotes are slippin' north instead of continuing up the straight trail toward Diablo Canyon." Virgil leapt down off the access ladder, catching himself with slightly less grace than his younger brother. Virgil pointed to where the trail diverged just ahead of them. "Point your damned headlamps back that way."

Wyatt watched as the lamp beams switched back on and tracked across the intersection. It was clearly visible where one trail, the heavier of the two, moved off onto the overgrown trail to the left. Another trail, weaker or more faded, continued up toward Diablo Canyon.

"Damn," Wyatt stared at the revealed trails, hands on hips. "Well what the hell does that mean?"

"We knew there was something odd with the trail for the last couple of days, Wyatt." Virgil turned to his brother. "You remember, there was a clear trail moving out of Kansas City toward Diablo Canyon, but then, two days ago, a trail came up out of the west and joined this one?" He nodded toward the intersection. "Looks like some of them took a sharp left here."

"But which is which, damnit, Virg?" Wyatt flung one arm toward the enigmatic trails. "And where the hell does this left hand fork go?"

Doc emerged from the side hatch to sit on it, one leg dangling out, while he unfolded a faded old map. "Well, Wyatt, that there looks to be Mary Lake Trail. Nothin' up thata way but a little settlement o' religious folks, calls itself Sacred Lake."

Wyatt scuffed his heel against the dust of the trail. "Goddamn whoreson sumbitch! So, whoever it is, they're headed straight for a bunch of gospel slingers?"

Doc folded the map swiftly and jumped down to the ground. "Looks it. And from the trail, looks like it was either more recent than the other group of tracks, or much, much larger."

All of the men were completely still as they all stared at the Over-marshal, waiting for him to process the situation and make the call. Would they be continuing on after Jesse James, or would they be taking the left fork, and face whatever unknown threat had headed down that way so recently? Wyatt cursed again as he realized there was only one real choice.

"Damnit!" Wyatt ripped his hat from his head and smacked it against his hip. He stood still for a moment, bringing his breath back under control, and gestured to the left hand trail. "Well, we can't leave those folks to whoever left those trails. Virgil, get five of your deputies into the Lynch Wagon. We'll be takin' their Interceptors and go on ahead at top speed. Two of the UR-30s will come with us. We need to try to get as much force there as possible, as quickly as possible."

Virgil rattled off five names and four deputies dismounted. The old lawman sensed something was amiss and turned back to find the fifth man looking at him stubbornly, refusing to release the steering handles of his Interceptor.

"Provencher, get down off your vehicle as ordered," Virgil's voice was hard, his eyes steady.

The deputy shook his head. "No, sir! This here's my vehicle! I ain't getting' off it, an' you can't make me! I earned my place on this mission, an'—"

Provencher hit the dirt before the blow that put him there had even registered. He scrambled up onto his backside, dragging the back of his hand across his mouth. It came away bloody. He looked at the crimson smear in disbelief.

"You hit me! You can't—"

"Provencher, you are the worst excuse for an officer of the law I have ever seen." Virgil towered over the whining man, hands on hips. "You will go where you are ordered to go, you will do what you are ordered to do, and we will not be sharing these words again. Have I made myself clear?"

The young man looked up at the legendary lawman and sputtered. He pointed at the other deputies still mounted on their vehicles. "But how come they don't—"

Virgil crouched down beside the cringing figure so fast the man cowered back, fearing another blow. "You wanna know why they ain't givin' up their rides, son? You wanna know why I'm puttin' you in the big iron box? Because if things go south when we hit this little town up ahead, there ain't a single one of them that I wouldn't trust at my back. An' you? You're no better than a player piano at a round up when it comes to thirsty work." He looked up at the four men who had moved toward the Judgment without comment. "And before you think about sowing dissent among the other four men that'll be joinin' you, they're there to keep an eye on your sorry behind, an' make sure you don't cock anything up in the big iron box. You got all that, deputy?"

Provencher nodded, his eyes dark with resentment.

"Good. Now, you go on back, mount up, and follow behind. Maybe we can forget this little unpleasantness ever happened, eh?" Virgil stood and walked away without offering a hand up.

Provencher watched the old man, his head shaking slightly. He pushed himself up out of the dust and moved sullenly toward the wagon.

The deputies shuffled themselves quickly, with Wyatt, Virgil, and Doc joining the two lamp-eyed UR-30s on the newly-dismounted Interceptors while the deputies clambered up the access ladder, a sullen Provencher pulling up the ladder last.

"Man that fire hose, boys," Wyatt gestured at the massive Gatling gun mounted on the copula of the vehicle. "Anything other than us comes down this road as you're followin', you light 'em up. You got that?"

One of the deputies thrust his body up through the top hatch and gave the Over-marshal a thumbs-up as he did a quick check of the weapon's mechanisms and feeds.

"Okay, boys, no restin' till we fetch up on Sacred Lake, right?" Wyatt pulled a pair of goggles from a wide pocket in his duster, slipped them over his head, then returned his hat to its customary place. "We can't go slow enough for the UR-30s to be on the lookout for the trail, so we gotta use our old fashioned eyes till we get to town. Let's go."

The Hogs rolled out, the roar of their engines rebounding off the low hills as Wyatt and his men opened them up, tearing down the trail at full speed.

Behind them, the Judgment rolled back into motion, its own engine setting the entire landscape to rumbling with its power.

Chapter 11

The pocket watch in Jesse's vest beeped gently, dragging him out of the abused torpor of exhausted, haunted sleep. He snapped awake, staring blankly at the cold white ceiling before he rolled off the bed. He rested his forearms on his knees, reorienting himself with his strange surroundings. The window showed nothing but black emptiness; the distant sound of crickets the only noise he heard. Moving as quietly as he could, Jesse gathered his things and crossed the hall, knocking gently. The door opened silently on the second knock and Cole and Frank stepped out, nodding as Jesse raised a single finger to his lips.

The three men moved carefully down the hall. The air was still warm, but much cooler than when they had arrived. They came to the door at the top of the stairs and the intricate metalwork of Jesse's hand wrapped softly around the knob, testing it. The knob turned with a soft click, and the outlaw boss looked back at the other two men, nodded, and turned it the rest of the way.

Inside, the room was much the same as the others, with a single bed and a few small pieces of furniture. There was an elaborate cross on the wall that re-called the symbol from the Lodge's sign again, but Jesse had no time to spare for the oddity of the decorations as his eyes settled on the man asleep in the bed.

"I'll be damned . . . " Frank's whisper was harsh. "Bennett Vaughn."

"The rat bastard." Jesse moved up to the wounded man's bedside and glared down at him.

"Well, you warned him what'd happen if you ran into him again, Jesse." Cole's voice was soft but his eyes were alight with anticipation.

Jesse shook his head. "Bastard's been riding with Billy the Kid for more'n a year now, Cole." His eyes flicked up to the other two men. "'N' no one else. How much you wanna wager, these friends Elijah was talkin' 'bout last night was Billy an' his boys?"

"Well, you was wonderin' what to do next, Jesse." Frank tipped his chin toward the wounded man. "Ask and ye shall receive, as I don't doubt Elijah would say."

Jesse grinned at his brother and took a knee beside the bed. He reached out with one mechanical hand and clapped it suddenly and firmly over the wounded man's mouth. Above the armor the eyes popped open, a cry stifled by the metal and rubber shoved against his face.

"G'mornin', sunshine." Jesse's smile was fierce as he leaned down over the wounded man. "Fancy meetin' you out here in the middle o' nowhere, eh?"

There was a sudden sharp click and a buzz as Frank activated his blaster pistol, its red tell-tales flaring in the dark room. Over the skeletal hand, the man's panicked eyes darted from Jesse's face, to the pistol, and back again.

"Now, Bennett, my friend, this can go one of several ways," Jesse's voice was reasonable and steady, still pitched too low to carry into the hall outside. "But I'm only goin' to give you one option. You're gonna talk, an' we're gonna listen, and then we're gonna leave you here with these nice Biblical folks, cuz we don't want no trouble with them, right?"

Bennett's eyes were wide with terror, the whites visible all around. Still they flicked occasionally back to the pistol in Frank's hands, but mostly they stayed fixed on Jesse's grinning face.

"That's good, Bennett. We're gonna start with a couple yes or no questions, alright? Ease you into the whole process?"

The man tried to say 'yes' but his efforts were foiled by the ironwork clamping his mouth shut. Cole slapped him across the top of the head contemptuously. "You nod or shake your damned fool head, you idjit." The growled words were loud enough to raise Jesse's eyebrow, and Cole nodded in apology. "Sorry, Jesse."

Jesse shook his head and looked back down at Bennett. "Okay, Bennet. Let's try this again. You understand?"

Bennett nodded with desperate energy, moving roughly against the metal hand.

"Good. Now, you come through here with Billy yesterday?" A nod. "Nice. I knew you weren't as dumb as Frank says you were. Billy goin' to Diablo Canyon?"Another nod. "Good boy. I'm proud o' you. It's like you got the hang o' this. Billy got his whole gang with 'im?" A nod, with a desperate flick of the eyes toward the unwavering pistol. "Good, good. And that would be what, after his little shindy in the mountains, about twenty fellas?" The eyes flicked back to Jesse, there was a pause, and then a slight shake of the head.

"How many boys he got ridin' with 'im, Bennett?" Jesse's tone was flat and left no room for discussion or debate.

"Fifteen, Jesse." The man's voice was high with terror, and he scrambled up with his back against the headboard, as far from Jesse as he could get, as soon as the metal hand released him. "Well, twelve, now. Twenty two, I guess, not countin' me."

Cole rolled his eyes. "Oh, Lord preserve us. Billy had to leave his idiot step child behind."

Jesse ignored the comment and leaned back in to Bennett, pushing the man farther up the wall with the force of his own fear. "So you all ran into some difficulties on the trail, then?"

Bennett nodded. "Ran into a Union advanced patrol coming out of the Coconinos. We fought 'em off, but we lost three men, and they got me pretty bad." His eyes flicked down to the bandages wrapped around his chest.

"You're just shootin' your mouth off," there was more hope in Jesse's voice than certainty. "What the hell would a Union advanced patrol be doin' out in the middle o' nowhere?"

Bennett shook his head. "I don' know, Jesse, honest! Billy, he was totally caught flat footed. They came out of the woods, guns blazin', and we just went right at 'em, Billy in the lead."

Frank spoke up, his voice gruff. "What'd the Union have on the ground, deadbeat?"

Bennett's eyes flashed again from Jesse to his brother and back. "Don't know that either. I'm sorry, Jesse, I really am! I got hit right at the beginnin'! Some-thin' blew up nearby, took out my 'Horse, and I was out!"

Jesse sat back on the bed and stared at the cowering man without seeing him. When he spoke, the change in topic was enough to catch all three other men in the room off balance.

"Where's Billy goin' after Diablo Canyon, Bennett?"

Bennett's face paled even further in the ruby light of the pistol's tell-tales. "I—I don't know." This time his terrified eyes flicked all over room, looking any-where but at Jesse.

"I don't believe you." Jesse's voice was flat, his entire body still.

"What d'ya mean, Jesse? I don't know! We was goin' to meet you in Diablo Canyon! I don't know more'n that." His head shook back and forth slowly as if it had a mind of its own. "I don't, I swear."

Jesse nodded, then looked down again at the bandage. "Your wound opened up again."

Bennett looked down in surprise and fear, then relaxed. "No it didn't, its—" The man's scream tore through the room like a banshee wail, echoing off the clean walls, the cross glowing dull red. Jesse's face was impassive, but one mechani-cal finger pressed against Bennett's dressings, a dark crimson circle beginning to seep through the fabric.

"Where's Billy goin' after Diablo Canyon, Bennett?" The words were the same, the tone was the same, but the man panting on the bed was now shaking in pain as well as fear.

"I told ya! I don't—" Again the scream. This time, there were muffled shouts from other parts of the house. Jesse's men were being roused from their sleep, flooding into the upper hall to see what was wrong. Cole went to the door to calm things down and get everyone ready to leave.

"Bennett?" Jesse's voice was calm and reasonable.

"I don't know! No, no!" Bennett scrambled to escape the clutching metal hand, pressing himself against the headboard with all his failing strength. "I swear! Billy don't even know! Just what that damned medicine man let slip afore Smiley slashed him! Some canyon out west! Billy don't know where it is! He's hopin', after he gets out closer, he'll find folks who recognize the name!"

The metal finger began to move toward Bennett's side again and the man's sobs became desperate and ragged. "I don't know, I told ya! I don't know. He never said!"

Jesse rested his hand in his lap, regarding Bennett with flat, dull eyes. "I believe you, Bennett. It's okay."

The man's gasping breath, half relief, half disbelieving fear, escaped him in a shuddering wave. However, he came up short when Jesse raised the finger again.

"But you gotta remember, that last time we saw each other, what I said?" Jesse's eyes were hard now, drilling into the terrified man's mind. Bennett shook his head violently back and forth.

"I didn't mean nothin' by it, Jesse, honest! I was just movin' on! I just don't know . . . " His hands rose in a futile attempt to defend himself.

Jesse sat back on the bed, his hands raised in a gesture of peace and acceptance. "I know that, Bennett. Folks move on. I get it." Bennett relaxed slightly on the bed. "But I did say—"

The metal arm sailed across Jesse's body and connected with Bennett's face in a vicious open-handed slap that sent the man sprawling out of the bed and onto the floor. His screams ended abruptly as he landed badly, one arm twisted beneath him. Low sobs shook his shoulders and he remained on the floor, hunched there as if waiting for the final blow.

Jesse stood up and stared down at the pathetic form. "We'll start the countdown over again now, shall we, Bennett? The next time our paths cross, this time, I'm not gonna leave you enough breath left to cry like a little baby."

Jesse swept past the huddled form and Frank followed. He stopped by Bennett and leaned down. "I hope you realize how lucky you been today. My brother's in a righteous mood. If I see you before he does next time, you Jonah, your own sweet momma ain't gonna be able to recognize you."

They left the man sobbing on the floor of his room in total darkness.

In the hallway, the gang was gathered, gear in hand and ready to return to the trail. At a nod from Jesse, they moved out and down the stairs. At the bottom of the stairs the outlaw chief was surprised to see Elijah sitting at one of the tables, Bob and John Younger standing over him with blaster rifles at the ready.

"Boys, I'm sure you can let our host up." Jesse took a wad of notes from a back pocket and deftly thumbed several of them flat, pulling them away and tossing them onto Elijah's table. "I'm sorry for our premature departure, sir, and for the untoward disturbance." He pulled another note and dropped it. "I hope that will cover any cleaning required."

Elijah stood as Jesse moved toward the door after his men. "I won't be trying to stop you. From the continued sounds of distress upstairs I can see that you left the young man alive. But there will come a time in your life when you need the compassion of a stranger, and you might want to think to your behavior today, regarding your expectations for tomorrow."

Jesse stopped in the doorway for a moment and then looked back. "Sir, if anything had ever led me to expect anythin' comin' close to compassion from any stranger, I might not o' turned out to be quite the hard case I assure you I am." He tipped his hat brusquely and closed the door behind him.

In the street, several men were moving around, going about the business of the day. All of them were strong-looking, and each wore the same strange hair-style that had caught Jesse's attention last night.

"Okay, boys, I hope you enjoyed our little stay, but we gotta pick up the pace now." Jesse shouted to his men as he jogged down the walkway toward the Blackjack. "Seems we're not the only ones in this race now. Union's got a pony runnin' too."

The men muttered to themselves but Jesse put up a hand to forestall the grumbling. "Now, it's just an advanced patrol, and as long as we know they're out here with us, we ain't got a thing to worry about. But I'll tell you what I am worried about, and that's Billy havin' time to prepare a surprise for us before we get where we're goin'. So we gotta ride hard, and we gotta ride fast."

He gestured at the sweeping plains off to the north and east. "I'm sure ya'll have noticed the local terrain. Ty made a good suggestion, sayin' we go overland, down around the south end of the lake, and shoot north over the plains. Frank and I agree. It should cut some serious time off our travels. You boys think you can take your sorry ass machines off the trail?"

Cole grunted as he pushed a bushel of tobacco into his mouth for the trail. "You think you can take your shiny new toy off the trail, Jesse? I'm pretty sure our flyin' 'Horses'll be able to make it without a hitch."

"We're still goin' to Diablo Canyon though, right Jesse?" Ty's high voice was clear in the morning air.

Jesse turned sharply to stare at the young kid in disbelief. Many of the townsmen around them had stopped to watch the outlaws depart. "Ty, I swear, you are hell-bent on makin' me regret takin' you in on this."

The boy raised his hands. "Sorry, boss! I didn't know . . . we still . . . yeah, okay, Jesse!"

The outlaw leader shook his head in disbelief and swung his leg over the barrel of the Blackjack.

"C'mon, boys, before I decide I'm better off leavin' half of ya behind."

Jesse gunned his machine back down the main road the way they had come, back toward Mary Lake Trail. They were behind schedule even more now, with even more need to hurry. It was bad enough, knowing that he was up against Billy, not even knowing quite what for. Now, with the Union in the region, and Carpathian's acting strange, even for that strange old man, Jesse was starting to feel a might crowded. If you included the Warrior Nation that Billy had run into that put the whole kit and caboodle in motion, there were not many players in the territories that were not somehow tied in now.

Jesse snarled, echoing the sound of his rumbling Blackjack, as he tore out of Sacred Lake heading south. The growling thunder of twenty Iron Horses leaping into the air and rushing after him bounced off the houses and buildings all around. Still, another benefit of going overland that he had not told his men was the fact that the trail they'd laid down up to Sacred Lake would now take anyone tracking them far off course. If anyone was tracking them, that was. He could feel the phantoms drawing in from all around him, and he knew that there was every chance most of them did not even pose a real danger. Still, better to take care now and not need the extra slack than to need it and not have it.

In the street, the men all stood and watched as the outlaw band sped down south, leaving the town once again silent except for the disconsolate sobs from the upper hall of the lodge.

*****

Wyatt knew, as they pulled into Sacred Lake, that something was not quite right. He also knew that whatever it was, it was not anything he had been expecting.

The marshals looked at the small collection of buildings. Groups of men worked the fields or stood silently in the road, watching the approaching lawmen. Wyatt brought his Interceptor rumbling down the center of the packed-earth street and pulled up in front of the largest building, a long two story structure with a sign proclaiming it Sacred Lake Lodge. The building was set apart from the street by a split rail fence, with hitching posts for real-live horses spaced along it. Wyatt shook his head. He could not remember the last time he had seen real hitching posts in a town.

With a practiced flick, the Over-marshal shut off the engine of his vehicle, and soon the rest of the Interceptors grumbled into stillness.

"Damned if this ain't the quietest burg I've ever seen." Virgil muttered to his brother. The other marshals were standing in a wide circle around their leaders, watching the townsfolk with calm, professional faces. Wyatt nodded and looked around, surprised to see that there were no recharge stations in front of the tavern. In fact, as he took a more careful look around him, he saw that there was no sign of any RJ-tech to be seen, anywhere.

The UR-30 units stalked into the street, playing their crimson beams across the area in front of the lodge and revealing many interwoven Crimson Gold trails hovering above the dust of the street. They had been moving far too quickly for the robots to track the residue on their way to Sacred Lake, but clearly, the men they were following had been here, and judging from the intensity of the trails, not too long ago.

Wyatt pulled his gloves off and stuck them into his holster belt as he stood at the gate looking up at the lodge. The door swung silently open and a large man with iron-gray hair stepped out, an honest smile on his broad face. The man's hair was cut in a strange pattern, nearly shaved on top with long locks down the sides and back. Looking around, Wyatt noticed that the rest of the men he could see wore similar haircuts. He filed the curiosity away for later scrutiny as he moved toward the large man, hand outstretched.

"Welcome, gentlemen, to Sacred Lake Lodge!" The man's handshake was firm without being overbearing. He looked over Wyatt's shoulder at the lawmen standing behind him, the deputies fanning out across the street, and the UR-30s walking the perimeter of the parking area, heads tilted down and coherent beams sweeping back and forth over the ground. Wyatt was curious to see a look he could not quite decipher cross over the tall man's face at the sight of the robots.

The man did not miss a beat, however, and his smile never slipped, as he focused back again on Wyatt's face. "My name is Elijah, proprietor of the

Sacred Lake Lodge. Can I get you and your men refreshment, sir? It seems a little early to be stopping for lodgings for the night."

Wyatt nodded, turning slightly to scan the streets again. He assumed a consciously casual pose. "Yeah, no, we're right as rain, sir." He looked at the gray-haired man out of the corner of his eye. "That accent of yours, ain't from around here, no?"

The man's smile widened even further. "Very perceptive,
Mr. . . . ?"

Wyatt smiled. "Marshal, actually. Over-marshal, in fact, if we're getting' technical. But you can call me Marshal. Marshal Wyatt Earp."

"Ah!" Elijah's smile grew even warmer. "We have heard good things of you, sir, and the work you have done. It is truly an honor to welcome you to our little enclave!"

Wyatt could not have said why the man's words made him uncomfortable, but for a moment he had a hard time meeting Elijah's gaze. "Yes, well, thank you very much. Actually, we're following a band of wanted criminals, headed by Jesse James. Maybe you've heard of him as well?"

That saw the smile fade from Elijah's face, but even in its new, neutral configuration, there was a pleasant openness to it. "Well, no, Marshal, I can't say that I have. We do take in travelers, of course, and we never turn folks away who aim to behave. But once they're gone, they are no longer our concern here. We cannot allow ourselves to be sucked into the conflicts and struggles of the world outside."

Wyatt nodded, looking back at Virgil and Doc by the gate. "But a group was here." He looked back at Elijah. "We know they were, so please, think carefully before answering."

Elijah nodded. "You will find no duplicity here, Marshal. Those questions we answer, we answer honestly."

Wyatt grimaced, looking down at his boots for a moment. "Would there happen to be any other guests here currently, Elijah?"

Elijah smiled. "There is one sojourning wayfarer currently with us, yes. A poor man who seems to be the very personification of ill luck. Jonah returned, if you will."

Wyatt looked quizzically back at his brother. It was Doc who answered, his eyes smiling over the mask. "This boy must have powerful bad luck indeed, Wyatt."

Wyatt nodded thoughtfully again, then looked back at the man standing on the stoop beside him. "I'm going to have to see your guest, Elijah. I believe he may well be helpful in following our current trail."

"I'm afraid I can't let you do that, Over-marshal." Elijah's stance was casual and relaxed, but something about the man's demeanor registered as a threat in the lawman's mind. He also noticed the gray-haired man look out into the street, giving a minute shake of his head.

Wyatt turned to see several strong-looking men approaching from various angles. The deputies were pulling back slightly, pistols and rifles rising in warding gestures. The UR-30s had abandoned their lamp sight, crouching slightly in gunfighter's poses, metal hands hovering over the butts of their massive pistols.

"Boys, stand down!" Wyatt barked to his men, and they reluctantly lowered their weapons. "AZ-24, you're with me." One of the UR-30s immediately pivoted and approached the front of the lodge. Wyatt turned back to Elijah.

"My metal deputy and I will be going into the lodge, and we'll be in there for a few minutes, and then my men and I will be leaving." For the first time since the front door opened, Elijah's face assumed a dark aspect. "Now, if you or your people are feelin' uppity, sir, I'm afraid things won't be goin' that smoothly. We will be questioning this man. Other than that, there is all sorts of unpleasantness we can avoid."

Elijah stared at Wyatt for a moment, then looked out again at the street. He nodded slightly to his people. The large men all faded back, standing like trained soldiers ready for a fight despite the gray-haired man's signal.

"Thank ya kindly, Elijah." Wyatt tipped his hat and then pushed through into the lodge. The robot followed close behind.

As the door swung shut, Elijah was left standing alone on the top step. The man slowly put his hands on his hips and looked out at the marshals, his face schooled to an empty coldness.

Time seemed to have frozen, and when the door banged open again the lawmen in the street jumped at the sound. Elijah and his men, however, did not so much as twitch. Wyatt hurried out, taking the stone steps two at a time, the UR-30 hurrying along behind him. The Over-marshal flipped a silver coin into the air over his shoulder and Elijah deftly caught it.

"I'd recommend a pauper's funeral on the edge of town. That ought to pay for the necessaries." Wyatt's voice was cold as he called over his shoulder, his eyes fixed on his Hog. "Anything more you want to spring for, you can pay for it yourself."

Wyatt hopped onto his Interceptor, the rest of the marshals and deputies jumping on their own vehicles.

"It was James, and Billy the Kid too, apparently." Wyatt shot his brother a sour look. "And it looks like Grant's got some boys in the area as well, so things just got even more interestin'."

"Back to the Judgment, we'll turn it around as soon as we can and get back on the main trail. This is all goin' down in Diablo Canyon, and we've wasted too much time here already."

The lawmen roared off down the road, leaving a pall of dust and smoke in the air. As the grit settled, the sound was swiftly replaced once again with the village's peaceful silence.

Elijah was still standing on the top step of the Sacred Lake Lodge, eyes fixed on the road to the south where a dark plume of dust marked the lawmen's retreat. Another of the village men stepped up, turning to watch the road with a dark scowl.

"Three times in two days. Events are threatening to overtake us, Elijah. And every one of them tainted with the foul stain of the Great Enemy." The man's voice was soft but insistent.

Elijah shook his head. "The time is not yet ready. The Holy Council is not prepared to make themselves known, and many of these men know not what path they walk. Many will choose otherwise when the time comes. Have the men take care of the body upstairs, and then go about their business." He looked down at the other man and put a comradely hand on his shoulder. "We will be farmers and innkeepers for a bit longer, my friend, before we may once again take up the sword of our lord."

*****

The Judgment wagon had not quite travelled half the distance to Sacred Lake by the time Wyatt and the outriders returned. He waved for the giant vehicle to stop and then rolled up beside it, the other Hogs rumbling to a halt nearby.

Wyatt pulled down his goggles and took his hat off, wiping the dust and grime from his face. He looked up to the access hatch as it opened, the judge poking his head through, and waved him down.

"We need to set up the wireless. This is getting ridiculous." Wyatt dismounted his vehicle and strode toward the Judgment. Behind him Doc Holliday hurried after, while Virgil followed at a more sedate pace. The rest of the marshals and deputies stayed with their Interceptors.

"Wyatt, you sure you want to bring the feds in on this? They'll hogtie us sure as sure, and we'll be left with nothin'." Doc's voice was low but intense.

"We've now got two damned outlaw gangs running through the same stretch o' dirt, and on top of that, we've got the damned army running through here shootin' eveyrthin' up!" Wyatt's anger was barely contained. "You saw the trailhead overland clear as the rest of us did. At least one of the gangs isn't even takin' the trails no more. We need to get in touch with someone, and we're out in the middle o'nowhere. Somewhere out east there are people who know more than we do, damnit! And we need as much information as we can get before we go ridin' into Diablo Canyon guns a'blazin'!"

Virgil nodded as he came up to his brother. "Wyatt's right, Doc. We need to know what we're ridin' into. The James and Younger gang, that's bad enough. But we gotta deal with Billy the Kid and his boys too? If there are Union troops around here, we should know why, and we should know if they can help us."

Wyatt shook his head. "That ain't it, Virg. They know somethin's goin' on out here, those blue-belly bastards. Why else would they have an advanced force out this far, when they're facing down Sitting Bull and the Warrior Nation off east?" He rested up against the leather seat of his Interceptor and wiped his forehead again. "No, this is bigger than we thought. An' those damned Union agents in Kansas City? They weren't just there whippin' up biscuits, you can bet."

The judge and several deputies were wrestling a large canvas bag from one of the storage compartments along the rear of the vehicle. Clearly it was heavy, and it jangled when they dropped it as if it were filled with pots and pans.

"Careful with that damned equipment!" Wyatt barked. "God alone knows how much that would cost to replace. And He also knows that General His-High-and-Mightiness Grant the First would order us to replace it if we broke it." He finished in a mutter.

The bag was dragged away from the trail into an area of flat grass. A confusion of metal struts, beams, and tubing were dumped out onto the brittle grass. A large black iron box was taken out and placed beside the jumbled mess, a single red light twinkling on its side.

"Alright, get that set up pronto, and we'll see what we have to see. I don't wanna waste any more time than absolutely necessary, you hear me?" Wyatt pushed himself away from the Interceptor and moved into the shade of the Judgment's flank. Holliday and Virgil followed, and one of the marshals standing there offered them a canteen.

"Thanks." Wyatt took a quick swig and wiped his mouth with the back of his hand, tossing the canteen to Virgil. "You know, there's gotta be an easier way to contact Washington than this."

Virgil nodded before taking a sip. "You know we ain't gonna be able to hear half of what they say. An' we're gonna be lucky if we can understand every other word, the way those things work. An' you also know, half the time they don't work at all."

Doc, who had declined a sip of water, nodded toward one of the UR-30 units standing guard nearby. "Folks whisper as how your little tin soldiers, there, can sneak reports back to Washington without anyone knowin', spreadin' their secrets far an' wide. Maybe they can contact 'em for us?"

Wyatt snorted, shaking his head. "We been tryin', Doc, you been there." He turned toward the robot. "Hey, metal man, get over here." The head of the machine tracked to the sound of the Over-marshal's voice, then the rest of the body revolved to orient on the men in the shade. With regulated precision it stalked over to them.

"AZ-21, reporting as ordered." The robot stood stiffly in front of the lawmen, its single, baleful eye staring straight at the iron flank of the wagon.

Wyatt stood up and addressed the robot in a loud voice, as if speaking to a deaf person. "Okay, 21, can you communicate with Washington?"

There was a momentary pause before the eerily still figure spoke through its vibrating voice grill. "Query cannot be processed."

Wyatt's face twisted slightly in bitter amusement. "See? Hell, I don't even think they're speakin' English half the time." He turned back to the robot. "21, tell Washington we need to know what's goin' on out here."

Again a pause, before, "Directive cannot be processed."

"Send us some girls from Washington!" Doc's voice was quite loud despite the leather mask, and his eyes crinkled with amusement.

"Hell, send that little piece from Kansas City, she was a stunner." Virgil chuckled along with Holliday as Wyatt shook his head.

"Directives cannot be processed," the still figure replied.

"Go back to sentry duty, await further instructions." Wyatt did not try to keep the disgust from his voice. As the thing turned away, he sighed. "An' you just know they're a heck of a lot smarter than they let on, too."

"Well, they can't be a heck of a lot dumber than they seem, 'r they wouldn't be much use." Virgil was still smirking, but he shook his head in bemusement.

The men working on the communications assembly were just about finished as the UR-30 returned to its position. Three tall legs, articulated like the limbs of a giant insect, were affixed to a much taller pole that stabbed up into the sky, a strange ball glowing faintly red at the very top. Tubes and wires were spiraled around the pole to the box at the bottom. Another of the deputies came back from the wagon holding a wooden package the size of a small valise.

"Sir, we're ready for you." Another of the deputies opened the package and took out another black box, and something that looked like a thick wand, a black ball at one end and a tangle of cables and wires connecting it to the smaller black box by the other. This new contraption was held by one deputy while another handed the wand to Wyatt.

"You just speak into the ball, there, sir, and anything we get back will appear here, in this window." The young man indicated the smaller box. A square about the size of a dime novel had begun to glow faintly red when it had been plugged into the larger case on the ground.

Wyatt took the wand and shot his brother a quizzical look. Virgil just shrugged his shoulders. Wyatt cleared his throat and spoke, loudly, into the ball. "This is Over-marshal Wyatt Earp, is anyone attendin' the network?"

Doc gave Wyatt a wry look. "Ain't gonna follow procedure?"

Wyatt snorted. "You mean all that stoppin' an' rogerin' an' such? No. They can figure out what I'm sayin' just fine with me talkin' straight."

The ball at the top of the staff glowed more strongly, the box buzzed in the deputy's hand, and a series of red characters began to burn deep within the box's frame.

"THIS IXXXARSHALXXXXLER IN TOMXXXXXE
STOXXXXESTION WXXX DO YOXXXEED OVEXXXXRSHAL STXX"

Wyatt stared at the glowing characters with rising frustration. "Now you see that? What in the Sam Hill is that even supposed to mean?"

Holliday looked over Wyatt's shoulder at the box. "Marshal Miller back in Tombstone, mannin' the board, Wyatt. He's asking you what you need."

"Don't see that that's so tough, Wyatt." Virgil smirked beneath his sweeping mustache.

Wyatt gave them both a sour look and then addressed the wand again. "Miller, go up the network and get me someone from Army HQ."

A pause, and then the earlier message disappeared, replaced with another.

"SORXXXXIR I COXXX NOT UNDEXXXXXD
THXXXUESTION PLEASXXXXPEAT STXX"

"God damn this contraption straight to Hades!" Wyatt took a turn and kicked at the unoffending grass underfoot, then turned back to the machine, holding the wand in both hands.

"Get me Army HQ now." He said the words slowly and loudly, every muscle in his body tense with annoyance.

The men waited a moment for the box's message to change.

"YEXXXIR ARMXXHQ PLEASXXXXXT A MINUXXXXTOP"

"I swear, I'd rather be using smoke signals at this point." Wyatt paced back and forth while the rest of the men watched him from the corners of their eyes. Most of the deputies had never seen the far speaking machine used before, but all knew that the Over-marshal got downright ornery whenever he had to resort to it. There was a reason most communication still went over the wires.

"Sir, I think it's Army HQ." The deputy holding the box jiggled it slightly to get his attention.

Wyatt walked back to the box and looked into the window where, indeed, the letters had changed again. He looked up at Virgil and Doc. "Well, trust the Army to have a stronger machine than the one they sent to Tombstone." The letters were much clearer.

"THIXXIS UNION AXMY HQ STOXXPLEASEIDENXXFY YOUXSELF STOP"

Wyatt sighed with frustration and yelled into the wand. "This is Over-marshal Earp. I need to speak to someone in authority of Arizona Territory Operations!"
The letters almost immediately faded out and were replaced in a new configuration.

"OVEXXMARSHXL PLEXXE STAXD BY STOP"

"Hmmm," Virgil straightened up from reading the words. "Looks like you mighta hooked a big bug with that one, Over-marshal, sir."

Wyatt growled wordlessly and waited for the reply. When the letters rearranged themselves again the three men all bent down. Doc whistled low and muttererd. "Damn . . . "

"THIX IS GENXXAL GRAXT WHAXXSEEMS TO
BE TXE PROBXXM OVERXXARSHAL"

"He don't much cotton to the procedures himself, looks like." Doc was smiling.

"He's a blue-belly, they don't much cotton to anythin' if you think about." Wyatt jabbed an elbow into his brother's ribs. "This thing ain't half bad when you got the power of the whole Union Army behind you."

Once again, Wyatt spoke into the wand.

"Good afternoon, sir. I was wondering if you could tell me if you have any operations currently active in the north eastern quadrant of the territory, around the Coconinos?"

This time there seemed to be a very long pause before the words in the box changed.

"THE SITUXTION IN ANXXAROUND THE COCXNINXS IS UNDER
COXTROL OVER MARSHAX PLEAXX STAND DOWX AND
RETUXX TO TOMBSXONE FOR FURXHER INSTRXXTIONS"

The men straightened and glared at each other in disbelief.

"Did that bastard just order me to stand down?" Wyatt's voice was high and incredulous. The flare of disbelief in his eyes was matched by every other man watching.

"Damned if he didn't do just that." Doc seemed more amused than disbelieving. "Never trust authority, Wyatt. Isn't that what I always tell you? Especially when you are authority." It was clear that his smile was enormous behind the ornate leather mask.

"Well, he can just take his orders an' drown 'em in a spittoon! I ain't in his damned outfit, and he can't tell me nor my men what to do!"

Wyatt was grasping the wand with white knuckles as he shouted into the black ball. "Listen, Grant, my men and I are conducting our own operation, and we will continue—"

"Sir, the box is . . . General Grant must still be talking . . . "

Sure enough, the words continued to form.

"CEAXE AND DXXIST ALLXOPERATIXNS IN THE DIXBLO CANYXN AREA XNDER PXESIDENXIAL AXTHORXZATION"

"Damn," Doc repeated.

Wyatt looked down at the words as they swam in their crimson-tinged darkness. Presidential authorization meant something truly momentous was occurring. Or Grant thought there was, anyway.

"You think he's really got President Johnson on the hook for this?" Virgil looked at his brother, then to Holliday, then out to the deputies and marshals watching from a distance. He could not keep his gaze from lingering on the robots as they stood motionless at their posts.

Wyatt was still staring at the words. "Damned if I know, Virg. Still an' all . . . are we plannin' on backin' off, even if it is the president his own self tellin' us we're done?"

Virgil looked down the road, then back up toward Sacred Lake, and then over to his brother again. "Well, Wyatt, if there's anyone can tell us to stand down, it's Johnson."

"But it's not Johnson." The buzzing voice brought them all up short. They had all been so wrapped up in the conversation over the far speaker that they had not noticed the rear ramp being lowered, or Morgan coming down to join them. That said something for their depth of focus, anyway.

Wyatt nodded, forcing himself to look into Morgan's placid face. "Hey, Morg, thanks for joining us. What're you sayin', now?"

The enormous metal arm rose to point at the far speaker's window. "That is not President Johnson." There was a little more emotion in the voice than in a UR-30, but not much. "That is General Grant claiming the president's authority."

"Still, sir," one of the deputies looked pale. "The man's a general. If he tells us to back down—"

"Provencher," Virgil's voice was gravelly with anger. "You wanna add coward to the list of words that pop into my mind when I see you?"

The man backed down, but he was looking at Wyatt with grey determination.

"No, Virg, the little shavetail's right. Grant's a general, hell, he's the General of the United States Army." Wyatt took a few steps away from the box until the cords brought him up short, then turned and paced a few steps back the other way. "He can't have got that much out here to stop us, but at the same time, if we go against his word, he's got plenty he can send after us after the fact."

"Easier to ask forgiveness than beg permission, Wyatt." Doc's smile was still there behind the leather.

Wyatt's look at his old friend was sour. "That ain't no way for a grown man to live his life, Doc." He gave the robots a speculative look. "But still, that don't mean it ain't true. And I'll tell you what else is true, the Army ain't been there to help with the outlaw problem much at all either way. So, if they come farther into the territories, thinkin' their comin' after us, maybe that ain't such a bad thing neither. "

Wyatt smiled and went back to the box. The window was shifting as he looked into it.

"OVXR MARSXAL EARPXPLEAXE ACKNXWLEXGE STAND XOWN OXDER"

Wyatt cleared his throat and then raised the wand to his mouth again. "Sorry, General. Your last messages have been garbled. We will try to communicate with you again at a later date."

The Over-marshal tossed the wand to one of the waiting deputies and started walking back toward the Judgment wagon.

"Alright boys, let's pack up and move out! We've got us an appointment in Diablo Canyon we ain't about to miss. I want all the Interceptors topped off from the wagon so we're all goin' in on full burn. We gotta take the roads, so we're gonna be late to the party anyway, but that don't mean we ain't gonna be bringin' the real entertainment!"

The marshals snapped back to life and began to gather the equipment. Wyatt noticed the robots standing hesitant for a moment longer than usual before following the orders, but he just shrugged it off.

The men working to take down the far speaker all stopped and the deputy holding the small box called out. "Sir, it's the general again! He's askin' you to confirm the orders!"

Wyatt smiled and called over his shoulder. "Just take it down, son. He got the message."

Chapter 12

Through the monocular, the town of Diablo Canyon looked much like any other town in the western territories. It had not changed much, in fact, since the last time he had visited, almost ten years ago. Sure, it was in better repair, many of the buildings were sporting big, new RJ generators, and there was even some new construction toward the center of town, but it still looked fairly normal.

The gang had parked near a set of railroad tracks that looked frail in comparison to the modern Heavy Rail tracks the Union was dropping down all over the place, but Jesse remembered when they marked the cutting edge of transportation technology. The tracks ran down a gentle slope toward the town, right through the middle, and then, of course, stopped abruptly at the dark scar of the canyon on the other side. Jesse did not know what the plans had been, all those years ago, to complete the rail line. He knew there was supposed to be a bridge, of course, and over time a great deal of equipment had been brought in to assist with constructing, but for some reason it never had completed. From his vantage up on the hill Jesse could see the shrouded forms of construction equipment parked up against the cliff, tarps billowing in the warm winds coming out of the canyon.

Somewhere in that maze of giant machines would be tools to dig, he knew. The plans to sink the massive iron suspension pylons deep into the canyon floor would have required more than just dynamite or whatever RJ-1027 equivalent construction crews were using these days. They would have digging gear for sure. And more importantly, due to the strange nature of the town, they would have folks who could operate it.

Many engineers and skilled workers had followed the high tech equipment out to the construction site. For years, they had been kept on retainer in the small camp that had grown up around the equipment and the rough barracks. Home had sprung up while they waited, and then a tavern, and then stores. Other people came to the area to provide food, entertainment, and willing company. Soon a thriving town had formed around the camp. When finally the retainer checks had petered out, many had felt right at home and stayed. Most of them had developed other businesses or skills over the years in an effort to stave off boredom.

Because it had developed organically, with no plan or engineering, civil or social, there had not been any law, either. The place had become an outlaw's paradise, where the only rule was the commandment of strength. The place had been a playground for Jesse and folks like him. He had lived here for several years, in fact, during the little burg's heyday.

And so there it was: Diablo Canyon, where a man looking for the best excavating machinery from ten years ago could find it in abundance, along with the men and women to run it. It now only remained to liberate some of the machines and persuade some of the workers to accompany him.

Jesse's lips frowned in the shadow of the raised monocular as he remembered that this was not, in fact, all that remained. He had heard the rumors about the UR-30 unit that had been sent to Diablo Canyon. He had heard the story of Johnny Ringo and the Injun runaway that usually rode with Billy, The Apache Kid. They had apparently come rolling into town to break some heads and collect some coin, like in the good old days. The stories of what happened next differed; some said they had only been riding with a few friends, others said they rode in with twenty men beside them. All the versions agreed on one thing though: Ringo and the Apache Kid had been the only ones to make it out alive. Apparently it had been a slaughter, and every dead outlaw had been credited to the metal marshal.

There was no sign of the robot lawman now, however. As Jesse and Cole Younger looked through Union monoculars at the sleepy town, Frank sweeping the place with his rifle Sophie's high-tech scope, it looked as if folks were going about their business like folks did in most towns. The place looked like an idyllic little community, and something about that aggravated Jesse more than he could say. The damned Union, once again swooping in and taking his home away from him. Never mind that he had left years ago. What sat before him now was nothing less than the rape of his memories, again, before his very eyes.

Jesse spat into the dirt at his feet. "An' no sign of damned Billy, neither."

Jesse lowered the blocky monocular, his face set as a grim mask. "Well, it looks all peaceful-like, but you've all heard what Ringo and the Apache Kid had to say about their last visit here. There's a metal marshal down there that's really acquired a taste for the blood of us folks who like to live on the fringes." His mouth twisted with contempt as he spat out the words. "Way I heard it, Ringo and his boys rode in free and clear and only saw the thing when it pounced on 'em."

"Sounds like we need some bait, Jesse." Cole smiled brightly as he said the words, spitting juice into the dust. "We gots plenty of new blood needs testin', eh?"

Most of the younger men shared nervous glances, and some giggled in a high-pitched nervous reaction, hoping the outlaw was joking. The giggling stopped abruptly as Jesse spoke.

"Yeah. Can't be wastin' proven hands on somethin' like this." He looked back over his shoulder at the men standing around him. He pointed to two. "Gage, Randall, you two got enough RJ to get into the center of town down yonder?"

The two young men swallowed hard, glancing down at the indicator panels on their Iron Horses. Gage spoke in a voice he was obviously struggling to keep steady.

"Just enough, Jesse."

The other new man, Randall, nodded. It appeared his mouth was too dry to speak. He kept working it but no sound came out.

Jesse nodded and gave both of the men a brief smile. "Nice. Don't worry, boys, we'll be right behind you. You'll have the best shot in the west watchin' yer back, as Frank'll be takin' Sophie fer high ground." He looked around to where his brother was bringing his storied rifle out of its holster. "Frank, 'bout time the ol' girl saw some action, you reckon?"

Frank nodded to his brother, then to the pale young men. He patted his massive rifle affectionately. "You bet. Boys, don't you worry none. Once I got that thing in my sights, it won't be but a moment before I clean its plow but good."

The young men nodded, but they did not seem overly comforted.

"Alright, here's the real deal," Jesse gestured with his whirring arms to gather his men closer to him. "Gage and Randall will drive down to the center of town. Just havin' the guns on their 'Horses should be enough, illegal weaponry 'r some such. But just in case, I want you guys to go in, smoke wagons in hand, and launch some shots up at the sky like you was celebratin' at some wild shindig. That ought to get the metal man to come runnin'."

He then addressed the rest of the men, pointing with one hand at several negligently holding rifles over their shoulders. "Before you go in, though, the rest of us'll get into position. I want you rifle boys with Frank. He'll put you in the best positions to take advantage of the terrain. The rest of us'll approach on foot from the front and sides, weapons hidden from view and actin' like civilized folks." He gave a sly wink, and added, "Cole, you an' yer brothers'll have to just watch the rest of us an' follow along best you can."

Cole snorted with indifferent amusement, although his younger brothers all looked mildly annoyed.

Randall finally found his voice, speaking in a hoarse croak. "Why ya'll gonna need to be backin' us up if Frank's all we need?"

The chatter among the men died away as they all looked at Randall and then quickly looked away. Jesse gave them a short glare and moved to the young man, resting one metal arm across his shoulders. "Randall, you'll be glad we're there. Ain't nothin' to worry about, right? Soon as the metal marshal shows his eye, Frank's gonna put it out for him, and that'll be it. But what if other folks start gettin' ideas? Or what if the thing goes haywire when Frank takes its head off?"

Jesse raised his voice to speak to the whole group again. "Don't forget, boys, this thing ain't no man. It might have the right number o' arms an' legs an' such, but it's metal, not flesh 'n' bone, and it prob'ly ain't built like a man inside. We gotta be ready for anythin' when we go down there."

The men nodded at the words and Jesse could sense they were as ready as they would ever be. "Alright then boys. Frank, take your long-shooters off first. The rest of us'll filter down in a few minutes." He turned to Gage and Randall, both mounting back up onto their 'Horses. "You boys wait 'till I give you the signal, then you come down directly, right?"

"We twig, Jesse." Gage had his chin lifted higher than normal, but the outlaw chief just nodded and patted him on the back, then did the same to Randall.
"You boys'll be right as rain, don't you worry none." He put all of the confidence and assurance he could into his smile. He immediately felt a twinge of guilt as he saw how well it worked on the two greenhorns.

It took a bit more than fifteen minutes for Frank to infiltrate the riflemen through the edges of town, walking casually with their rifles flat against one leg beneath their dusters. Once Jesse, following their movements through the monocular, saw them in place, he nodded to Cole who returned the gesture and started down the tracks toward town. Jim Younger had another group that moved out to the right, and their brother Bob, often rumored to be the toughest of the four, led a small group out to the left. Jesse waited for the groups to get about halfway to town before he turned back to the two young men who had been chosen, tipped one metal finger to the brim of his hat with another confident grin, and then turned to make his own slow, casual approach.

Jesse watched the last of his men disappear behind the outermost buildings of Diablo Canyon and was glad he had not yet heard any disturbances. There was no telling where the metal marshal was in the town, and he had been half-sure that one of his flankers would roust the thing from its hiding place long before Gage or Randall ever had time to leave their starting positions. He had figured, even if that happened, that Frank and his riflemen would be able to nail the thing anyway, so the plan had seemed pretty sound coming and going. That did not make his slow, lazy walk any more bearable.

Everything was peaceful, and so he turned slightly, raised one arm straight up to heaven, gave two quick shakes, and then dropped it again. He heard the sudden roar of the 'Horse engines as his two young greenhorns gunned them to life. Jesse casually moved to the side of the trail as the sound got louder behind him.

Jesse made sure he was even with the first buildings on the main street when Gage and Randall burst past. He grinned with honest affection as he heard their rebel yells over the howling of the engines. It was nice to see they had some fire in their bellies, even after hearing the stories.

Gage and Randall tore down the street, a ragged wake of dust and grit flaring out behind them. They were each brandishing a pistol in the air as if they were posing for the cover of a penny dreadful novel, launching bursts of ruby fire up into the clear sky. The few folks who had been out and about in the heat of midday jerked crazily at the sound of the shots, covered their heads, and ran, crab-fashion, for the cover of the surrounding buildings. Jesse could swear he heard Gage shout out as he entered the center of town, "we're here fer yer whisky an' yer women!"

The outlaw boss smiled under the shadow of his hat brim, shaking his head. Had he ever been that young?

The smile faded quickly as a shape walked calmly from the darkness of an alley across the center of town. Despite the vest and riding leathers, Jesse knew from the angular lines and the unnatural shape of the head beneath the straight-brimmed hat that he was looking at one of the UR-30 Enforcers. The same one, he knew, that had almost killed two of the most formidable men in the territories, and had managed to kill all their companions. It looked like a man as it sauntered out of the darkness, but Jesse knew it was nothing of the sort.

Gage saw the thing first, and deliberately put a bolt into the building behind it, just above its head. "C'mon over here, you tin can! Let's see what kinda beans they loaded you up with!" He fired again.

A strange, buzzing, inhuman voice echoed through the street. "Discharge of contraband military hardware and weaponry excessive to personal protection. Summary provisional sentencing."

Time slowed to a crawl. Jesse knew he had men sown all through the town by now, but for a moment he felt completely and utterly alone as that alien voice droned through the streets.

The robot's arm blurred and rose with a massive hand cannon clenched in its metal fist. "Relinquish your weapons and dismount. Prepare for summary provisional sen—"

A vicious crack exploded from above, like thunder from a clear summer sky, and the robot was sent reeling backward, arms flailing for balance, weapon flying wide. It had happened so quickly, that Jesse could not be sure of the shot. The thing's hat was certainly shredded, fluttering into the street like a rag. The structure of the hat was gone, and for a moment, Jesse was sure his brother had leveled the thing with a single shot. He raised his arm in triumph, ready to give a resounding rebel yell, when the machine steadied itself, stopped the wild milling of its arms, and stood tall once more.

There was a huge dent in the UR-30's temple, and several of the elements of its face were clearly misaligned, knocked out of place by the shot. The skull itself was intact, however, and the eye still glowed a menacing red. A second pistol lashed upward in its left hand.

The robot did not move like a man, there was no apparent processing or thought connecting one motion to the next. It flowed through a series of positions, the gun rising, blasting as it came in line with one of the mounted boys, continuing to float upward with the movement of the entire body, and then fired again when it was aligned with something high and away on Jesse's right. The outlaw chief was not paying attention to that second shot, however, as he stared in horrified fascination at the results of the first shot.

The gunshot was like nothing Jesse had ever heard before, a sharp, humming sound that lasted only a moment, but seemed to echo eerily in the air for a spell after the shot had been fired. The muzzle blast was a hellish eruption of crimson fury, rich with traces of RJ-1027 swirling within it. The shot took Randall in the chest, blasting most of his innards out across the street behind him. A grisly framework of glistening bone and gristle remained to connect the poor kid's arms and head to the rest of his body. Not enough to support him, however, and the whole disgusting mess collapsed back into the saddle. As he fell forward, the boy twisted, his face just becoming visible to Jesse's horrified eyes. The mouth was working frantically as if screaming for help or vengeance or death, but all that emerged was a faint red mist. The kid's pistol dropped from his jerking fingers and clanked off the footpad of his vehicle, floating slowly forward with no one at the controls.

And then Jesse realized where the second blast from that demonic Hell cannon must have been aimed. "Frank!"

Jesse jerked out both Hyper-velocity pistols, his arms swinging seamlessly through the motions. His face was twisted into a mask of fear and rage as he began to fire un-aimed shots at the thing standing before him. Part of his brain knew there was no way he was going to score a hit at this range, not while running. But he could not bring himself to care.

The UR-30 was swinging back into line with Gage, the poor kid staring gape-mouthed at the gory remains of his friend. The giant weapon was sliding into firing position and Jesse knew there was no way he would be able to stop it in time.

From another roof farther to the right, another thunder crack echoed off the buildings. This time the robot was thrown off its feet and into the dust, its head deformed from a blast that had hit it directly above its single eye. Even then, on its back in the dirt, the thing was not finished. It began to rise, once again bringing its pistol to bear up and to the right. Another shot rang out from overhead, and then another. Each struck the robot in the center of its metal face, driving it back time and time again into the dirt. The limbs began to jerk spasmodically as the twisted iron ruin took impact after impact.

Eventually, the gunshots from above stopped. The thing was still in the dirt, its head completely blasted away, a collar of springs, tubes, and wires erupting from its savaged neck.

The entire event had taken only moments, and Jesse slowed to a stunned walk, and then stopped completely, looking at the still-twitching metal man in the dust. He looked off to the right and saw Frank rising up from his firing position, nodding in satisfaction and propping Sophie on his hip. Frank jerked his chin toward his younger brother and then tilted his head toward the smoking hole in a sign that had once said 'Dry Goods' one building over.

"Garland couldn't hold his water, shot before I tol' 'him to." The voice was harsh, but Jesse knew his brother was troubled by Garland's death. He nodded back at Frank, smiling despite his heaving breath, and then started to walk again toward the downed robot.

"Damn, d'you see what it did to Randall?" One of the outlaws emerging from the surrounding alleys muttered to another.

"I'll venture a guess Garland ain't much better, up there on that rooftop yonder." Another pointed up at the smoking sign.

Their reactions were familiar to Jesse. He had felt them countless times himself. There was a savage thrill at being alive when others had failed to survive. There was a guilty twinge knowing those that fell had been friends and comrades. There was also an unspoken feeling of relief that the violence was over. He smiled and shook his head. No matter how many times he faced violence, it was always the same.

As each man processed what had happened, staring at the terrible proof of their own mortality slumped in the saddle of Randall's Iron Horse, none of them were watching the UR-30 unit, thinking that it had been completely destroyed by Frank's well-placed shots.

Every one of them had forgotten Jesse's words. Jesse had forgotten his own words. They were not facing a man.

The robot jerked upright without warning, ghoulish as it cast around without a head. Its movements were jerky, no longer smooth or choreographed. The massive gun was still gripped in its hand, and despite the utter destruction of its eye, the weapon slid smoothly into line with its next target – Gage. The young outlaw was numbly wiping blood from his face, breathing in shallow gasps as he tried to cope with everything that had just happened.

The robot may have been able to move again, and it may have been able to wield a weapon, but whatever drove it, whatever lent it the deadly accuracy it had shown earlier, that power was gone. The blast from the thing's weapon took Gage's Iron Horse in the flank, ravening crimson energy devouring the metal and unleashing the RJ-1027 stored in the vehicle's fuel tanks. The boy's leg, brushed by the devastating beam, was splashed away before the explosion, throwing him away like a limp rag just before his mount erupted in a ball of dazzling fire. He was dashed against the side of a building over ten feet away. The bike's destruction threw ragged bits of metal and bone in a wide circle that caused most of the approaching outlaws to dive for cover, some screaming as the bits and pieces struck home.

"Kill it!" Jesse's pistols rose again, almost of their own volition, and this time his shots were deadly accurate. The Hyper-velocity pistols ripped off a double stream of red bolts into the rising robot's chest. The metal man was sent flying back into the dirt, but the headless creation was not finished yet. It began to fire its terrible weapon in a wide fan of destruction, clearly lacking any rational direction. The blasts struck surrounding buildings, punching glowing holes in some, clearly starting fires inside. One collapsed in upon itself as soon as the blast struck, the roof slumping in to fan the fires within as it fell.

The outlaws were not standing motionless now, however. They were running for cover, directing a withering rain of red darts at the writhing metal machine in the middle of the street. Most of the shots were striking the thing, on its arm or leg or body. Some, however, were sailing right over the flailing target to slap into buildings on the other side, starting more fires.

"C'mon, you deadbeats! Beef this thing!" Two more of his men were down, their bodies twisted and torn, smoke rising from their smoldering clothes. Jesse spat again and ran across the street, keeping at an angle, both of his pistol's tracking with the robot's aimless movements. Each shot struck home, his arms guiding the devastation masterfully. The blasts tore through the thing's torso, shoulders, arms, and legs, but it continued to fire, flailing around with the force of its battering.

"Gotta be the chest, Jesse!" Frank shouted from a rooftop. The angle was too severe now for the older brother, and he could not get a shot at the monster's body.

Jesse nodded. He had figured as much himself. He stopped, digging the heels of his boot into the dry dirt of the street, and brought both of his arms together with a sharp clap. The pistols cracked together, the energy in their power cells reaching out toward each other with ghostly crimson tendrils. Jesse gritted his teeth, flipped the switches on each gun with his thumbs, and then sighted down the gap between the two barrels directly at the robot's battered and dented chest. He took a slow breath and pulled the triggers as one.

The catastrophic wave of heat and force that blasted from the two pistols was unlike anything either of them could have achieved on their own. It struck the staggered robot in the chest and lifted it bodily up into the air. The blast wave pushed a storm of dust and dirt before it, driving the robot and the collected filth of the road against the side of a building ten feet away. Every window shattered as the wall bowed beneath the pressure and the heat, then collapsed backward into shadow.

As the tidal wave pushed the robot into the building, it seemed to disintegrate beneath the ravaging heat of the joined pistols. The tatters of its clothing burned away in the blink of an eye, the remaining color bleached from the metal. Wires and hoses melted to black liquid streams that steamed away into the furnace heat. By the time the UR-30 disappeared into the building, the headless body was falling apart, limbs dropping from the shattered torso with a din that was lost in the raucous destruction of the wall.

Jesse stood in the ensuing silence, breath coming in ragged gasps. His pistols were still gripped in rigid arms, pointing at the smoldering hole. The wood all around the hole was scorched and blistered, and an alarming amount of smoke was pouring back out, rising in a dark column into the sky.

The outlaw chief shook his head to clear it, keeping his weapons at the ready but casting his eyes from side to side while he assessed the situation. The devastation that had been wrought upon the center of Diablo Canyon was staggering. The rain of fire the outlaws had called down upon the robot had shattered several buildings on the far side of the street. Each sent a gyrating column of smoke and ash up into the sky. And despite having had its head removed, the Enforcer's blind shots had torn through the buildings on the other side of the street. Hardly a building in the center of town, in fact, appeared to have escaped unharmed.

There were three more bodies in the street as well, boys from Jesse's gang who had been unable to reach cover or were unlucky enough to avoid the random shots. Jesse slowly became aware of the looks he was getting from the rest of his men, and he lowered his gun to stare back into the smoldering hole. He knew what had his men spooked, and he did not want to think about it.

He had stood in the middle of the chaos, actually running toward the rabid metal man, while everyone else was hell-bent on running away. He had stood in the middle of the firestorm and had walked out the other side without a scratch. It had happened so often before that he almost took it for granted now. Often at night, staring into a campfire, he wondered if a person who felt no fear could even be considered to have courage anymore. He had never even spoken to Frank about these dark thoughts, and he knew that he probably never would. Shaking himself again, the street came back into focus, and with it, the sound of muffled sobs coming from behind the wreckage of Gage's 'Horse.

By the time Jesse fetched up beside the overturned vehicle, a circle of his men was already standing there. Pushing through the crowd, Jesse crouched down beside Gage's head, resting on a rolled-up coat Frank had put beneath him. The kid was a nauseating pale green color, and a growing pool of blood beneath the ragged stump of his left leg was all the evidence the outlaw chief needed to know that Gage would not be leaving Diablo Canyon alive.

"It's okay, kid." Jesse grabbed a canteen from one of the other men and twisted off the cap, offering to pour a little water into Gage's blood-rimmed mouth. "It's not that bad. This burg's gotta have a decent sawbones. We'll get you looked at, set you up with a nice shiny replacement like mine." He flourished his empty hand back and forth in front of the fluttering yes. Those eyes were fading fast, and Jesse knew it would not be much longer.

"Randall . . . " The voice was thin and whispered, pulsing strangely with the heart that labored to keep him alive.

"That was bad, Gage, real bad." Frank pushed a lank sweep of dirty hair from Gage's face. "That ain't you, though, son. You're gonna be ridin' again in no time."

"Randall . . . " Gage coughed weakly, his breath speeding up, each one more shallow than the one before.

"Gage, hobble that lip o' yours, kid. Randall caught it, an' he's gone. But you're still with us." Jesse was at a complete loss for what to do. Most injuries in the territories were either immediately fatal, or with some good medicine, you could make it. Especially with the arrival of RJ-powered weaponry. No one survived a gut shot long enough to suffer much anymore, not when a gut shot looked like the one that had taken Randall out.

Frank gave Jesse a look over the dying boy's head, a question in his eyes. Jesse felt a rising surge of anger at his brother for even looking at him that way, as if there was any question, with the kid's leg splashed ten feet across the street and him turning the color of winter grass. He gave a jerky shake of his head and offered Gage some more water.

"Take a sip, kid, it'll make you feel better. Ease that throat o' yours." Gage opened his mouth weakly, but the water that Jesse poured into it pooled there and ran down his cheek and chin. The outlaw stopped, afraid he might drown the boy, and noticed the glazed, distant cast to his eyes. Gage was gone.

Jesse stood up in the street, offering the canteen up behind him without looking. Someone took it with a mumbled thanks and he nodded. His eyes were stuck on Gage's face. This kid had ridden into this bug nest on a brass set, full of life and his own immortality. An immortality Jesse knew he had in part instilled. Now, because of that damned metal terror, here he was, leaking his life's blood all over the parched main street of a town not worth a name.

"We still don't know what Billy's got planned, Jesse." Frank was standing beside him. He did not notice his brother rising from the corpse's side. "And the townsfolk are startin' to take notice of our little fuss out here."

Jesse looked up to see several faces watching the outlaws from different windows and doorways around town. They were pale and shocked at the devastation that had been visited upon their little town. He called out to a knot of his men standing by the shattered wall that marked the UR-30's last stand.

"You all, get some rope and truss that thing up. I want it out here faster'n a tick." He turned back to Frank. "I want you and the Youngers to round up the brains, and then take them down to the park 'n' get whatever we need."

He was turning away when Frank's hand landed on his shoulder. "What do we need, Jesse? If we're rushin' off half-cocked without Billy, do we even know how far down we're gonna have to be diggin'?"

Jesse took a deep breath, focusing with some effort. He nodded. "Okay, assume we gotta dig, through dirt not rock, and assume we gotta go down pretty deep, like maybe the height of a wagon or two, stacked atop each other, but not down to China, okay?"

Frank nodded. "You got it, Jesse." He walked away, calling for Cole and his brothers. The men came running from various groups scattered along the street, disappearing deeper into town.

Jesse looked around again. "Harding, get our boys that didn't make it and line 'em up here in the street. Get me a count, an' see if anyone else is hurt. I need to know if it's just these five, or if we're gonna be down more afore our next little shindig."

Harding nodded and started pointing to the men around him. The groups started to drag the dead bodies into the center of the street. Those that had worn dusters were wrapped in them, those that had not were laid bare, hats over their faces. Only Gage and Randall had their Iron Horses, and so, their kit bags. Gage was wrapped up in his duster, while two white-faced boys did their level best to gather up what was left of Randall on a blanket, rolling it up into a sodden, misshapen tube of coarse wool.

Jesse scanned the townsfolk watching from the windows and singled out an older looking gent with iron-grey hair and spectacles. He started walking toward the man, who began to fade back into the shadows of the building.

"No, no, hey!" A Hyper-velocity pistol leapt into Jesse's hand, pointing steadily at the retreating man. "You ain't goin' nowhere, son! You get your flannel-mouth out here on the pronto 'r I end you and find someone more punctual to talk to!"

The man's arms flew up, head shaking from side to side in denial, as he walked toward the window. "We don' want no trouble!" The man began. "You just—"

"Case you ain't been payin' attention, grandpa, what you want ain't of much concern today. And what we just, is only the beginning." He gestured toward the front door of the building. Two scorched holes marked where crimson bolts had slapped into it during the gunfight. "Come on out this door here so's we can talk like civilized folks, without this wall here between us."

The door creaked open almost immediately and the man came shuffling out. He was hushing someone behind him, making gestures for them to stay back inside the building.

"'S okay," Jesse said, lowering the gun. "The lady folk can stay inside for now. I just got some questions, and I'll ask 'em, and you'll answer 'em like a good little burger, an' my friend's and I'll be on our way in no time, and you lot not much the worse for wear." The pistol spun once around his metal finger, slapping back up to point into the old man's face. "You lead me a dance, though, husker, an' this goes down a whole different trail. Comprende?"

The man nodded, hands still in the air, eyes still wide with fear.

"Alrighty then." Jesse turned and gestured across the street to where a group of his men were dragging the remains of the UR-30 Enforcer through the shattered hole with a great deal of difficulty. "Now, that thing there yer only law 'round here?"

The man nodded again, slowly.

"Great. You seem like a man who knows what's goin' on. You a big bug here 'bouts?"

The man shook his head. "I – I just help the mayor –"

Jesse wagged the barrel of his weapon in the man's face. "No, no, no. Helpin' the mayor, that's pretty big, you ask me. So, you know stuff, 'bout what's goin' on in town?"

The man looked confused, but nodded again.

"Right as rain. Then tell me, Billy the Kid been through here lately?" Jesse's playful tone dropped away without warning, his entire body still and dangerous, his eyes boring into the man's.

"N-n-no! 'Cept for that one time with Ringo an' the Injun, we ain't seen anyone like him 'r . . . 'r you . . . fer years!"

Jesse leaned closer, the barrel drifting toward the man's nose. "You sure?"

The nodding was so vigorous this time Jesse was afraid the man's head was going to drop off. He raised the pistol away from the frightened townsman and rested what he meant to be a reassuring hand on his shoulder. Whether it was the touch itself or the nature of the limb that made it, the man squeaked and jumped sideways slightly to escape the hand. Jesse shrugged.

"Okay, I believe ya. So, no Billy, no more law." The outlaw chief turned back in the direction of the distant canyon cliff. "My brother and his friends 'r lookin' fer some engineers. They gonna find any?"

The man nodded again. "Most of those folks who still know anythin' stay near the park. There's a couple saloons and a hotel still over that way."

Jesse nodded again and rested the pistol casually against his shoulder, giving the shaken man a grin. "Well, that oughta cover it, old son. Go ahead back inside with the ladies."

Jesse holstered his gun and stepped lightly back out into the street. Five pathetic bundles lay there in a row, boots to the sky. Except for Randall's, of course. God alone knew which direction his boots were pointing, inside the dark-stained blanket.

"Who'd we lose?" He lit a quirley with one hand and flicked the match behind him into the street.

Harding stood over the bodies with his hat in his hands, his gruff face troubled.

"Well, Randall and Gage, 'o course." Then he nodded to the three men at the end, two thin men with hats over their faces and one much larger body wrapped in its duster. "An' Boyd, Clay, an' Sisco Pete."

Jesse spat the end of the quirley down by his boot and shook his head. "Damn, Sisco Pete, eh? That boy never could dodge worth a tinker's promise."

Harding put his hat back on, nodding in reply. "No sir, Jesse."

Jesse took a long drag on his quirley and moved toward the group of men standing nervously around the battered wreckage of the robot. The thing was wrapped in coil after coil of rope, as if the men were still afraid it might spring back to life despite its having been reduced to so many tangled pieces. Jesse rolled what looked like a forearm back and forth beneath his boot as he looked down thoughtfully.

"What you boys say to seein' how well our friend here flies down by the canyon rim?"

Several of the outlaws nearby chuckled nervously or muttered their approval, and Jesse nodded. "Okay, then, let's see what we shall see, eh?" The men hoisted the bundle of metal parts over their heads and began to walk down the street. He looked over to Harding.

"You mind watchin' the store while I take out the trash?" He grinned around the smoldering hand-rolled cigarillo.

"No, you go right ahead, boss. I don't feel no need to get any closer to that thing or a cliff than I have to." Harding jerked his chin in the direction of the retreating mob.

"Okay, then. You just watch the locals, you got that? I don't want any of 'em gettin' funny ideas while I'm gone." He started to follow the mob but then turned. "An' keep an eye out for Billy. I still don' know what his game is, but he's gonna pull somethin' fer sure. When he does, we ain't gonna have a lot of time to adjust." Jesse began to walk and then turned around. "Have the men start relaying the 'Horses down here to the recharge pads in town, we should get enough of a charge to make a clean getaway. 'N' bury Gage an' the rest out in the flats a bit. Hurry, though, we won't be gone long."

Harding nodded and Jesse followed the rest of his men. As they left the devastated center of town behind, he paid more attention to the buildings, noting again how well-maintained they were. Back when he was riding out of Diablo Canyon, the place was a pit; half the buildings in no condition to house a dog, and the folks sporting a strange mix of squirrelly fear and wild aggression. Now, even after the big fight downtown, the folks who started coming to their doors and windows looked afraid, yes, but they were also clearly angry and outraged.

Jesse made a big show of tipping his hat to the ladies with a wide grin and nodding to the men who stood staring back with steely eyes. There was no way any of these folks could mistake what his boys were carrying down the street, or what it meant. Getting out of town before the realities started to settle on these folks was going to be important. Jesse hoped Frank was having some luck with the brains across town.

The rim of Diablo Canyon was crumbling rock and twisted scrub brush. The canyon wall fell away in a series of abrupt steps that continued, jutting out farther and farther, until it gave away to a small stream glittering in the distance. Jesse frowned. Throwing the metal man off this cliff was not going to be as dramatic as he had thought.

As Jesse looked to either side, he saw the struts of the aborted bridge sticking out into thin air a ways off to his left, and smiled. "C'mon, boys. We're gonna go make use of the local facilities."

They walked along the lip of the canyon, the weathered back walls of the town on their left. Hauling the metal body was starting to take a toll on many of the boys' spirits, and the talk had died down. But there were still wolfish smiles, especially as they stared at the metal rails springing out from the buildings ahead.

The tracks that came down the center of Diablo Canyon and continued for ten or twenty feet out into midair cut through the impromptu equipment yard that had developed over the years. Jesse paused to admire the piles of material and machines, most covered with shrouds of stained, flapping canvas. In the center of the yard Frank was talking with Cole Younger, gesturing toward a truly impressive vehicle whose canvas covering was now piled loosely up on the ground.

The thing looked like an enormous scorpion or ant, standing tall on six metal legs that arced up and then back down in wide, splayed metal feet. The body was a boxy shape that looked a lot like most wagons did in the post-RJ-1027 age, but the nose of the beast was truly awe-inspiring. An array of drills, each articulated on its own extended arm, thrust out from the cab of the wagon. Jesse could see how they were built to be able to direct their attention in a wide arc in front of the crawler, for digging large, deep holes in almost any terrain. His smile widened around his smoke.

"Well don't that just beat all, eh?" He nodded to Frank and Cole as they turned at his voice. "We got anybody hereabouts that'll be able to drive the thing?"

Frank nodded. "We found a few guys in the saloon over yonder, eager enough for a fresh perspective, they were willin' to sign on." Jesse looked over his brother's shoulder at a small group of five men standing beside the drilling machine. Frank gave him a meaningful look. "I told 'em they'd be gettin' equal shares o' the treasure."

Jesse smiled even wider and raised his voice so the men could hear clearly. "Well ain't that grand! Ain't nothin' goin' on here ain't everybody gonna take home some nice coin on!" He looked back at his brother. "They got anythin' else that could help us? I'm thinkin' you didn't sign on five galoots to be drivin' this one rig, eh?"

Frank frowned. "No, I didn't. There's a bunch of equipment we're loadin' in the driller. Stuff you wouldn't believe, Jesse. They got a thing that can see through rock! An' another that can listen to the ground and tell you what you'd be lookin' at if you dug down there! You find us where to dig, we'll find this thing for you." His look grew more sober. "It'll be easier once we know what we're lookin' for, o'course."

Jesse took the cigarillo out of his mouth and spit a bit of tobacco away to the side. "Easy, Frank. Now that we got the equipment, Billy'll have to be square with us, if we can't get the info out of one of his boys. Ideal situation, we hide this stuff away a bit down south, then come findin' Billy. We either snatch one of his boys and get the name o' this canyon the Kid's been holdin' so close to his vest out of 'im, or we just talk to Billy directly, but this time with a much stronger hand, as we got the tools he's gonna need!"

Jesse looked over to where his men were waiting impatiently to toss the UR-30 into the canyon. "Ain't like we didn't pay the full ante, now was it."

Frank nodded. "We did that, Jesse. You want comp'ny? 'R you want me to get this stuff up onto the main road?

Jesse looked back toward the center of town, clearly identifiable from the columns of dark smoke rising into the air in that direction. "Yeah, get this back, and get the boys ready to go. We'll just leave the two 'Horses. Randall had one o' the slowest anyway, and Gage's ain't fit fer parts no more. I'll be done here in a jiff, 'n be followin' you directly."

Frank nodded and turned back to the giant drilling machine. "Let's get her up'n runnin' boys!"

Jesse returned to the men carrying the dismantled Enforcer. "Okay, lads, what're you thinkin'? We dump the whole thing over at once, or one piece at a time?"

*****

After disposing of the robot, Jesse and his gang gathered back in the center of town. The enormous drilling machine was snorting softly, its fuel tanks and engine core glowing red from many ports and dials. The thing had left a trail of deep divots in the street, and Jesse knew sneaking it out of town was going to cause some problems.

The bodies of his men had been buried by a detail of the younger gang members, and the two Iron Horses they would no longer need were dumped back in the equipment yard, covered in the tarp that had once shrouded the driller.

Frank and the Youngers stood in the center of the street, ignoring the growing group of townsfolk that gathered along the boardwalks.

"Well, boys, think we're about ready to move out?" Jesse took the stump of the quirley out of his mouth and flicked it toward the smoldering building where the UR-30 had come to rest. "I'm thinkin' we take all this stuff south a few hours, find a nice little niche to stow it, an' wait for Billy to show himself." He tapped on the metal legs of the crawler with one metal forearm. "Think this thing can go overland, Frank? I'd rather not bump into any-body on the trail."

Frank nodded. "What it was built for, Jesse. Or so they tell me."

"Alright then, let's move out." He moved to his big Blackjack and swung his leg up and over, settling into the saddle. He raised his voice to be heard over the cacophony of sixteen engines roaring to life. "Now, you folks done yourself proud, keepin' to yourselves. But I swear, I hear you disturbed my boys so's you could lynch their bodies, I'mma gonna come back, and I ain't gonna be happy."

The only response was a universally sullen, flat glare, and Jesse smiled at their cowardice. "Alrighty then. See ya'll!"

The column of Iron Horses moved out, the Blackjack in the lead, and the lumber-ing drilling machine sliding along in a strange, swinging gait behind. It had been surprising, how quickly the thing could move with a full burst of power behind it. They had had to steal batteries from half the machines in the lot to top off the thing's power cells, but two of the men Frank had found were old hands at that sort of thing, and it had not taken long. They had also been able to hot-charge the 'Horses and the Blackjack, so everything was heading out fully charged. The driller was never going to keep up with an Iron Horse at full throttle, but they were making excellent time out into the brittle grasses of the badlands, and Jesse could feel everything coming together for him.

He could not quite see what Billy's plan had been, but he knew the younger man would be coming this way eventually, and when they ran into each other again, the world was going to see that Jesse was still the curly wolf in the wild west.

He was leaning back in his saddle, smiling at these heart-warming thoughts as they ran through his head, when a shattering detonation erupted just in front of him. The entire plain seemed to lift into the sky as a sheet of red fire flashed out from underneath. Dirt, dust, and clumps of grass began to rain down all around, covering the gang in a layer of grit and coating the 'Horses and the drilling rig in fine reddish dust.

Men behind Jesse were yelling and screaming, demanding to know what was hap-pening. Jesse thought he knew. When that familiar old voice, high pitched like a young boy's, shouted at him from out of the curtain of dust, he was not surprised in the slightest.

"Howdy do, Jesse!" Billy the Kid sauntered out of the floating smoke and grit, a titanic grin across his face. "You made it!"

Chapter 13

Jesse James was plenty familiar with the feeling of a smug, self-satisfied smile. He did not, however, enjoy being on the receiving end of one.

Billy spit a stream of tobacco juice off to the side, his thumbs hooked nonchalantly behind his pistol belt. "'Course, you're not quite where I thought you'd be. Took a bit o' scramblin' to get ahead of ya, once you decided to head out across the flats." The grin grew even wider. "But wasn't much trouble, was it boys?"

A series of hoots and laughs sounded from out in the stunted clumps of yellowed grass. The great plume of dust had begun to settle, but there was still an acrid-tasting gritty fog hanging over the entire area. Jesse thought he could see a glint of light here or there reflecting off a piece of equipment or a weapon lens, but he could not be sure.

"Where ya been, Billy?" Jesse's voice was calm and relaxed. "Thought we were gonna meet up in the Canyon, no?"

"Oh, c'mon, Jesse! That jig is up, friend. When you decided to go in after the equipment on your own and not wait for me an' mine!" Billy spit again, his grin reddish with the tobacco. "You think I'm some sort of mooncalf, do ya?"

Jesse made a great show of thinking for a second, then shook his head. "No, I figured you more for a chiselin' coffee boiler, who'd rather let someone else do their work for 'em, is what I figured."

Billy's grin slipped, but then shone brighter than before despite the pall of smoke and dirt. "Well, there may well be somethin' to that, Jesse, there sure is." He lazily flicked a hand toward the column of 'Horses behind the older outlaw chief. "Fer instance, I'd much ruther let you run into that mill blade metal man they had shepherdin' the fine folks o' Diablo Canyon for me. An' I knew, if I set it up for ya, you'd be more than happy to oblige. How'd that work out for ya?"

Jesse felt his own smile tighten. "Lost five o' my men goin' in alone, Billy. One o' my best." He pulled his goggles down around his neck. "That ain't likely somethin' I'm gonna forget."

Billy laughed. "That's a grand yarn yer spinnin' there, but I don't think yer foolin' anyone within earshot. Ain't no one forced your hand on that one, my friend. We was supposed to go in t'gether, an' you rushed out here an' raced in on yer own. I'm right sorry fer yer boys, Jesse, but that ain't on me, an' it ain't on none o' my boys."

Jesse ground his teeth, working his jaw in frustration. He shifted to the side and spit bitterly into the dirt. "Well, one thing 'r another, we're all here now. What'aya wanna do?"

Billy's smile cranked a little bit wider. "Well, I figured, we'd take that fine contraption an' all the gear off of ya, an' yer fuel, an' you all can ride shank's mare back to Diablo Canyon, 'r Kansas City, 'r wherever, where the dice might start rollin' a bit better for ya!" Another stream of tobacco spit spattered into the dirt.

Jesse adjusted himself slightly in his saddle, his features shifting angrily. "The hell you say, Billy. I ain't gonna—"

Billy raised one hand casually into the air and a loud detonation sounded from out of the dust. A blaster shot streaked through the gritty haze and impacted into the grass by Jesse's foot. The little clump of yellow vegetation exploded in a geyser of dirt, smoke, and burning strands.

"Now, Jesse, I don't wanna gloat, but what we got here is a great example of a dry gulch. I got you pinned to the counter, Jesse, and there ain't no way yer gettin' out. I ain't got as many men as you, but I got plenty, and all mine got rifles, an' they got all you in their sights already." He called over his shoulder. "Kid, you ready?" There was a gruff bark from back in the shifting shadows of the dust cloud, and Billy nodded. "Why don't you let slide, then?"

A blue bolt streaked out of the shadows, flashing through the dust like heat lightning, and came down on the nose of an Iron Horse in the middle of the formation. The bolt sank right through the metal without a pause, and with a wheezing crack the vehicle collapsed to the dirt, throwing the rider into the grass and dust.

"Now, you see? I even got the Apache Kid back there, summonin' the spirit mumbo jumbo of his people down on yer head." The grin now threatened to split Billy's face in two. "What say you all just turn off your machines, dismount, and mosey on back the way you come? You can leave the Canyon-folks in that fine contraption. They'll be stayin' with me."

Jesse stared at the younger outlaw for moments that stretched on into minutes. Every man in the column gripped his controls tightly, wondering how it was going to go down. Far off in the distance, Jesse thought he heard a familiar sound, and he cocked his head to try to catch it better. It seemed to fade in and out, the surrounding cloud of thick dust playing games with his hearing.

As he thought about the cloud, his head snapped upright. He looked up to where the vast column that had been thrown into the air by the explosives was still reaching for the clouds. He turned in his saddle to look back the way they had come. The smoke rising from the center of town was dying down now, but there were still faint lines of white in the sky, fading downward toward the earth. He turned back to Billy and this time his own face wore a grin far more genuine than it had been.

"Billy, you think a'tall about your little plan when you decided to launch half the badlands up into the sky like that?" His tone was light and casual, but there was iron beneath it.

Billy's smile faltered slightly. "I'm not gettin' yer meanin', Jesse."

"Bumped into Bennett Vaughn back down in Sacred Lake." Behind Billy the pulsing sounds rose a notch, bolstering Jesse's confidence. "He had a right interestin' tale to tell. 'Bout you havin' a bit of a run in on yer way north?"

Billy's eyes widened slightly, and he looked to the left and right. He muttered something over his shoulder and one of the shadows in the shifting dust moved and disappeared deeper into the cloud.

"I'm surprised, you already knowin' you weren't alone out here, that you'd send up a smoke signal quite this big." He nodded his head up at the column towering above them. "Apache!" Jesse shouted, a smile growing wider and wider on his face. "You din't tell Billy sendin' smoke signals that high was a bad idea?"

Billy's eyes were less certain. He began to walk slowly backward into the settling dust cloud. "If this ain't a trick, Jesse, it's gonna go poorly fer both of us, y'know."

Jesse's grin was back in full force. "Well, that's a sight better than it just goin' inta the johnny fer me an' mine, Billy!"

A series of sharp blasts diffused through the dust cloud. One large blast flashed up on his right. Incoherent screams echoed through the grit, and Jesse settled back on his saddle with a laugh as the first clear word rang out of the chaos.

"Union!"

"Okay, boys, you c'n hear it with yer own ears," Jesse called over his shoulder to his men. "Billy's done dropped it in the crapper, but he knows he ain't gettin' out of this without our help, so we face down these blue-belly mudsills side by side!" He gunned the Blackjack into motion, crouching down behind the control console. One of his fingers flicked out for the weapons toggle, setting the little light winking red. He looked back over his shoulder with a smirk and called out, "If you get a clean shot at one of his bastards, though, you go ahead and take it."

Inside the spreading haze, it was absolute madness. The grit was dispersing, and visibility was better than it had been. Still, everything beyond a stone's throw was shadowy and indistinct. The crimson bolts of blaster weapons streaking back and forth ignited the floating particles, leaving streaks of sparkling red stars swirling in their wakes.

Jesse could make out shapes running away to the left and right. He knew those must be Billy's men, fleeing from their ambush positions and running for their 'Horses. Farther ahead he could see the low sleek shapes of light vehicles, the source of most of the incoming fire.

Jesse hugged the controls, hunched low over his seat, and gunned the throttle of the Blackjack straight down the throat of the incoming shapes. The vehicle bounced and staggered over the uneven ground and thick clumps of desert grass, but the heavy wheels dug deep, throwing plumes of dusty earth behind him. He squeezed the firing handles with both hands and ruby darts spat out into the eddying dust ahead. Behind him, he could hear the roaring of the Iron Horses as they rushed to follow, and streaks of crimson gunfire flashed past him on both sides, slapping into distant targets.

Jesse's charge carried him through the dust cloud, amid the rushing enemy, and out the other side. He had seen one hulking shadow in there, nearly as fast as the others. That brute had given him pause, but he was too caught up in the moment to give it another thought. He knew he had scored at least two direct hits as he watched the bulky shapes of Iron Horses caught by his blasts flip up into the air. The dust got immediately thicker around them, and a familiar, satisfied surge kicked in his gut as he heard them come crashing heavily back to earth. He smiled, feeling the caked dust and dirt crack on his face, and brought the Blackjack whipping around to face the confrontation again.

Most of his men tore out of the dust cloud behind him. The Youngers were all grinning and hollering, except for Bob, but he was always a sour one. Frank looked grim, hunkered behind his own controls, and Jesse knew that he was wishing he could head for higher ground with Sophie to offer more direct protection to his brother.

"Okay," Jesse shouted to be heard over the grumbling engines. "We gotta get back in there and clean up right quick! Billy's gang'll be on either side of 'em, if they can rally, we'll get 'em between us all, take 'em down, an' then we can have our words with Billy in a much more pleasant setting. Anybody seen the driller?"

"They were backin' up as we rushed in, Jesse." Frank hawked up some dust-laden spit and launched it into the grass. "It ain't that fast, though. We gotta get in there if we're gonna have a chance o' savin' it."

Jesse shook his head. "They ain't gonna touch the driller. They might have sharp words for those that were drivin' it, but these blue-belly bastards'll see it as their duty to get the driller back under its tarp where they fancy it belongs." He pulled one of his pistols out and checked its charge. "But yeah, we gotta get back in there anyway. Afore Billy's gone and done all the killin' without us!"

Ahead of them, the cloud had continued to dissipate. However, many smaller clouds were now rising into the sky and expanding across the desert where the battle was raging the hottest, marking the death sites of vehicles or men. There were shapes staggering through the fading haze as well, so more than a few fighters had been knocked from their mounts. Jesse squinted into the settling dust, trying to judge from the flashing lines of blaster fire and the red-cored detonations of impacts where the best insertion point would be for his gang.

Jesse once again gunned the engine and raced back into the battle, heading for a point where one of Billy's groups seemed to have gotten itself organized into a coherent attack on the Union right flank. Jesse hunkered down, squinting behind his red-tinted goggles into the rushing wind and the harsh dust, and aimed himself at that contact point.

The battle seemed to narrow itself down to two indistinct shapes leaping closer as he accelerated, and three of Billy's Iron Horses rushed in from the right. Jesse knew that the Blackjack lacked the heavier weaponry of some of the 'Horses, but he also knew what four blasters firing in unison could do, even to an armored transport, especially from behind. He lined up on the left-most target and pressed down on the firing handles. Streams of crimson fire lashed out, his Blackjack shuddering with the blasts. He watched the four streams crash into the rear of a Union Iron Horse. It exploded, the bolts coring the engine and detonated the fuel. Burning wreckage, roiling black smoke, and swirling dust flew in all directions as the driver was thrown roughly out into the desert, trailing a streamer of dust, arms and legs flapping without control. He hit the sand and rolled loosely to a stop, unmoving.

Jesse swung his head toward the other target, but it slewed away from its spectacularly deceased compatriot. Unfortunately for the luckless soldier, he veered right into the sights of Billy's gang, who shattered his 'Horse with two blasts from their mini cannons. The vehicle came apart, scattering its parts and the parts of its rider across a long streak of devastation carved into the desert surface. Jesse nodded to the two outlaws and swept around toward the center of the battle, looking for more targets.

There were wrecked Iron Horses scattered across the desert, smoke and dust rising into the sky on all sides. Jesse could tell the Union boys were getting pounded. He could not see more than ten of them still fighting. There were plenty of outlaws to finish this easily between the two gangs.

Jesse looked around him, trying to find Billy to coordinate the last attack, when he realized that the men around him now were his own. He could see the Youngers and Frank. He thought he saw a knot of men, most dismounted, fighting from behind disabled 'Horses. Harding was there for sure, and Chase crouching beside him. Two men were prone, firing around the corners of their machines on their bellies, and he thought it was Bryce and Ty. A few others were still driving, either with the Youngers or on their own.

A quick count revealed that they were nearly evenly-matched with the Union, even now regrouping atop a low hill nearby. Jesse scanned the desert for Billy's gang and found them exactly where his gut told him he should look: they were high tailing it back toward Diablo Canyon, pursuing the driller as it scuttled toward safety.

"You yellow dog!" Jesse screamed at the top of his lungs, feeling his dry throat tear with the strain. "You bastard, come back here!" Over the sounds of the battle and the roaring vehicles, there was no way Billy could have heard him. Jesse knew it would not have mattered if he could. He watched the 'Horses disappear toward the distant town, trailing plumes of dust into the sky as they chased the tiny scrambling shape of the driller.

"Damn." Jesse shook his head and looked back to the battle. The Union had regrouped and were swinging wide of the main battle zone with its columns of smoke and dust, its litter of shattered transports and human bodies. One of the Union riders suddenly toppled over from his saddle, his 'Horse dropping out of formation and gliding to a halt. Looking over his shoulder, Jesse felt a sudden surge of excitement and energy at the sight of Frank once again wielding Sophie. His brother gave him a quick nod and then aimed for his next victim.

"Okay, boys, this'll be tough, but nothin' we ain't done afore!" Jesse gunned his machine toward the clump of dismounted men, gesturing for the Youngers and their group to join him. "They're gonna come in on you all, cuz you ain't got any way to skedaddle. We'll swing back, like we're runnin' away, then we'll hit 'em in the side. Make sense?"

Harding looked up at the boss with a frown. "What keeps you from runnin', leavin' us to pay the bill?"

Jesse looked down at him. "I ain't gonna leave no one behind. I'm gonna need all of ya'll when we catch back up with that chiseling rat bastard, Bonney, ain't I?"

Harding nodded and turned back toward the regrouping Union force. "Just our luck, eh? To run into a forward patrol like this?" Chase muttered.

"I ain't sure this was luck, boys." Jesse watched as the Union troops gunned their engines and began to accelerate toward the outlaws. "But we'll have plenty of time to look into that later." He turned his head to the other mounted men. "Let's go!"

The 'Horses and the Blackjack slewed around, throwing up dirt and rocks as they spun. They made a great showing of their sudden retreat, flying off toward the far off town. The men now on foot began to fire at the approaching soldiers, shouting defiant insults and obscene suggestions at the advancing men.

Coming around wide, Jesse saw the larger, bulkier shape that he had caught a glimpse of in the dust. It was coming up behind the Iron Horses leading the charge. It looked like an Iron Horse, but instead of an open saddle there was a massive armored box. Instead of a single linked weapon system riding high on the forward body, the thing seemed to sprout a terrifying number of barrels from out of its armored bulk, thrusting out from its iron flanks.

The Union formation spread out, leaving the beast in the center with a free line of fire to the men Jesse had left behind as bait. Crimson bolts began to crisscross the air between the outlaws and their charging attackers. Most of the outlaws' fire was being absorbed the armored fairings of the Union 'Horses, or glancing harmlessly off the daunting shape of the thing holding the center of their line. The Union fire was slapping into the downed 'Horses, keeping the men cowering behind them, rendering their fire less effective.

Jesse saw the inevitable result before the first man at the impromptu barricade even went down. A series of images flashed before his mind. He saw the burning wreckage of Missouri City. He saw Billy the Kid standing tall and proud in the Arcadia. He saw a line of ragged Union cavalry with outdated equipment blocking the path of a small, wounded boy. Lastly, he saw the tiny garret above the Arcadia, a light spray of ruby droplets on the wall.

"No!" Jesse viciously wrenched at the accelerators, sending the Blackjack hurtling toward the impending disaster even though he knew he would be too late. He saw an errant Union bolt strike Chase in the leg. The poor kid, suffering pain beyond reason from the wound, leapt into the air in an effort to escape. Several bolts struck him in the chest and thigh, spinning him over and spraying blood into the sand. Bryce rose, fear getting the better of him in the last moments, and tried to run. A rocket caught him in the back, lifting him off his feet, and then detonated, spreading thin strips of the poor boy out over the sand. Harding pushed away from the burning wreckage of his 'Horse, taking potshots over its saddle, shouting defiance right up to the moment a glancing bolt struck him in the temple. His head spun around, his neck clearly snapping, as blood and grey matter foamed out of the wound, steaming as it hit the burning metal of his 'Horse.

The last survivor of the little band rose up to face his death. But Ty was not looking at the onrushing horde, nor was his expression the least concerned. He turned to look directly at Jesse and his lips stretched into a wide, friendly smile. He waved once, gave a jaunty salute, and winked. Jesse knew it must have been a trick of the light that made the kid's eye gleam that unnatural color, or it might have been the crimson bolt that was even then blasting through his head. The body took several more hits as it danced and staggered away from its cover, finally sinking slowly into the grass.

Jesse shook his head in disbelief. He desperately scanned the area for survivors. He could hear the Youngers and the last remaining mounted members of the gang behind him. Off in the distance behind the burning wrecks that marked his men's last stand, however, he found who he was looking for. Frank was crouched down behind his 'Horse taking careful, measured shots at the incoming Union forces. Every time he fired, a vehicle would fall out of formation, either damaged or abandoned by its dead driver. Jesse was not the only person on the field to notice Frank's effectiveness, and the giant monster 'Horse slewed toward him, all of its weapons roaring back into life.

The heavy weaponry chewed the ground up ahead of Frank's position and then tore, like invisible buzz saws, into the 'Horse. Dust, grass, and metal, RJ-1027 fuel and fabric scattered up into the air. Jesse saw his brother, arms thrown wide, sail back away from the detonating vehicle, a look of vague dismay on his face before he disappeared down into the growing explosion.

Jesse's eyes went wide for a moment, and then a furious, tight, pressure filled his mind, pushing at his eyes and roaring in his ears. Without conscious thought, the Blackjack swerved around and headed straight for the heavy, armored shape that had blasted his brother. The lighter weaponry of his new vehicle rained down upon the beast, but the shots glanced off like a burning fan in all directions. He was doing no damage that he could see. The pressure built even greater and Jesse pulled one of his Hyper-velocity pistols, firing bolt after hopeless bolt as the range closed. Then the monster opened up with its weapons again.

Jesse did not know where the enemy shots caught up with him. He felt himself launched into the air, flying through the dust and the grit. He knew he had been thrown from his vehicle in a violent rush of fire, smoke, and swirling sand. He heard a terrific crash behind him, the wrenching of metal and the screams of components bent past their best tolerances, all over-powered by the hammering thunder of the Union weapons and their ceaseless detonations.

Jesse hit the ground hard, rolling several times before coming to a stop against a hard clump of desert grass. He could not breath, he could not hear a thing, and his mind was lost in a buzzing daze of blurred images and dull, distant pain. A curtain of red washed over his vision and then everything went black. The bright world snapped back into focus again for a moment, but when he tried to raise his head, the red leaked back in, the black followed, and his head fell back into the gritty sand.

When light leaked back into his world, the roar of engines was still heavy in the air, bolts of crimson force still crashed back and forth in the distance. His vision faded in and out, and each time he tried to move, there was a crushing moment of intense pain and then nothingness.

Words, screamed over engine-noise, seemed to echo in his ears from a far way off. He thought he heard a deep, voice screaming "Grab one!" There were detonations, screams, more shouting, this time in words that would not make sense in his shaken mind.

As even these noises faded into the far distance, Jesse could think of nothing but the look on his brother's face as he fell back into the flames.

Chapter 14

The rasping sensation of sand blown across his face recalled Jesse to the waking world. It was a slow journey, with pain a constant companion and confusion hovering overhead. He felt the sand, and the scratch of the grit, first on his face, hot and stretched by the beating sun. Then he felt it in his throat, as each attempt to swallow drove jagged shards of glass across the sensitive flesh. Each of his legs made the same slow progression as his body: dull, distant ache to furious, vague itching, to pulsing, shocking pain. As the pain retreated to a manageable, steady throbbing, he felt his legs move, slowly drawing up, the heels of his boots digging furrows into the sand.

He knew a short jolt of terror when he realized he could not sense his arms. However, he soon began to register the odd alien impulses that more than a decade of familiarization had taught him to expect from the artificial limbs. He focused on one hand and then the other, clenching them into tight fists. Feedback pads dragged across dirt and grass as fingers flexed with growing strength. Finally, his gummed, sensitive eyes peeled open, the sunlight stabbing right though to his brain. He muttered in pain, bringing further agony to his torn throat. With the combination of pain and surprise, he lurched over onto his hands and knees, gasping for breath. Each one scratched further at his tormented gullet.

Coherent thought came back much more slowly. He could make no sense of his situation. He could see, through squinted eyes shaded by one mechanical hand, that he was in the high desert. He was surrounded by desiccated soil and clumped up scrub grass. There were shattered wrecks all around, some still leaking black smoke up into the sky. Bodies lay amongst the wreckage, men in the mismatched clothing of the outlaws mixed with the forever-damned blue uniform of the Union Army. He stumbled over to a couple of the bodies. As was true in most modern gunfights, there was not much left to help with identification.

He found several bodies lying amidst what looked like a hasty defensive position made out of battered Iron Horses. He could not tell who the men had been, their features blasted or burnt. He recognized Harding's 'Horse among the machines, though, and knew that one of the bodies must have belonged to that tough old dog.

The thought brought his head sharply up. As last moments of the battle came flashing back, his neck wrenched around to look for his brother's final position. He saw the wreckage, far more devastated than any of the others, on a low rise. With a rising groan he stumbled toward the smoking ruin. That big monster of a Union 'Horse had unleashed an avalanche of fire on this vehicle, and there was almost nothing left but its twisted frame. The blasted remains of its bodywork, the equipment, and his brother's belongings were scattered all around, covered in a liberal coating of dust, ash, and ragged grass.

Jesse staggered up the slight slope, stumbling to his hands and knees more than once. Each time he slipped and fell, his entire body was wracked with agony, but still he drove himself upward. The wreckage was still smoking, sending several different trails of black soot spiraling up into the sky. The grass all around was charred and churned, a devastation for yards in all directions. Jesse dragged himself around the ruins of the 'Horse, collapsing to his knees on the other side. There were tattered strips of his brother's duster and the crumpled remains of his hat, but that was all. There were two deep trenches, parallel, through the blackened sand, marking where a person had been dragged from the area of burnt waste. Of his actual brother, however, there was no sign.

Jesse swayed to his feet once again, looking all around. Nothing moved on the battlefield, aside from the smoke, as far as he could see. A quick check of the remaining bodies assured him that none of the Youngers had fallen, but that was all he could tell. Maybe they had dragged Frank to safety? Or maybe the Union had gotten him . . . or maybe Frank was dead, and whoever it was had just taken the body. Jesse lowered himself to the ground again, weeping in enraged impotence.

When the moment had passed, Jesse stood up unsteadily and retraced his path through the ruin to the overturned wreckage of the Blackjack. The vehicle had definitely seen better days. Most of the protruding details and equipment had been blasted away. The shiny paint had all been blasted off, and many of the intricate spokes within each wheel were torn, twisted, or simply gone. But clearly the barrage that had descended upon him had not struck directly, but rather torn up the desert all around, tossing his vehicle and himself into the dust like toys.

With grunting, heaving effort, Jesse pushed the heavy beast upright once more. It rocked unsteadily, shedding dust in dry, whispering showers that spread out as they hit the ground. Jesse checked the telltales, looking to see if there was any way the engine could be brought back to life. Most of the power cells had ruptured, but the actual engine itself seemed to be in good enough shape to operate. He looked around again at the wreckage. If he could not find spare parts on this prairie, he would be in big trouble.

He sighed, pushed himself back up to his feet, and stumbled toward the most intact wreck.

*****

As the Blackjack stuttered its way back into town, Jesse tried to ignore the looks of the townsfolk of Diablo Canyon who had come out onto the street to watch him drive past. He kept his back as straight as he could despite the pain. He had found some unruptured canteens among the dead, enough that he was not dying of thirst, and he had found a little jerky, but he had been in no danger of developing a hunger for the tough meat, surrounded by the dead and the inevitable vultures who had circled down to feast.

There had been no sign of the Youngers or any of his other survivors. There had been nothing to show if Billy had returned, or if the battle had ended with everyone running in a different direction. He had looked at his reflection in one of the Iron Horses' side mirrors, and knew that if he had seen that blood- and dust-stained visage tumbled into the dirt, he would have assumed the person was a goner as well. So he had been left, by friend and foe alike, for dead.

Jesse drove slowly, the only speed the damaged Blackjack would allow, and only stopped when he pulled up in front of a saloon that abutted the equipment lot on the cliff edge of town. He looked up at the sign; a simple, white painted marquee with the word 'Saloon' painted on it in black. He shook his head. Whether at the sign or his own sorry lot in life, he would have been hard-pressed to say.

He was alone. Not just without Frank or the Youngers, but his whole gang, dead or scattered to the dusty winds in one afternoon. He could not remember the last time he was this isolated, this lost. Never mind turning the tables on Billy. Never mind proving, once and for all, his own prominence in the hierarchy of western legends. He could very well fade into obscurity right here in this dingy little burg at the arse end of nowhere.

Jesse shook his head and dismounted. He pushed the Blackjack up onto a recharging pad and jury-rigged a connection between the built-in generator and his battered ride. He then pulled the two saddle bags from their armored compartment, and pushed his way into the darkening interior of the saloon.

Inside, the place looked much like any other frontier watering hole. With a few words to the leery bartender, he was able to discover that Billy had, indeed, intercepted the driller during the battle and had made off with it back south, the way Jesse himself had intended to go. The remnants of the Union advanced patrol had fled back east. He felt bitter amusement at the thought that Billy must have driven right past him.

Did the Kid think he was dead? Did he even care? Jesse was troubled by the fact that the Youngers had not returned for him. Most upsetting of all, though, was the lack of any sign concerning his brother. Had Billy dragged him out of the wreckage? Had the Youngers? Had the damned Union? Jesse was shocked by how much he did not know.

The outlaw found a table in a darkened corner and carried a small bottle and glass from the bar into the shadows. The red-tinted lighting here was spotty, it seemed to waver gently, brighter and then softer, brighter and then softer. It was nearly enough to make him sick.

Jesse stared into the liquid in his glass. Part of him wanted that drink very badly, but another part of him was absolutely sure the pain it would cause his tortured throat would knock him out for sure. He straightened his shoulders, steeled himself, schooled his face to stillness, and tossed the shot back. He needed the alcohol more than he needed to avoid a little more pain.

He nearly screamed as the drink hit his gullet. After a moment, though, he shook himself and settled back. He could feel his body starting to relax, and knew he was going to be okay.

As he had entered, most of the folks inside had looked at him with hooded, resentful eyes. They knew who he was and what he had done, but their fear kept them cowed. He felt a slight grin twist one side of his face as he thought about how much harder his life would be if people were not such gutless sheep.

Jesse poured himself another shot and was preparing himself to toss it back when a lithe shape glided up beside him and immediately drifted down into the seat opposite without asking for permission.

"Look, kid, I don't wanna—" His voice cut short as he looked up into the eyes of the woman from Kansas City; Lucy.

She looked concerned, but also angry, and a little frightened. "Fancy meeting you here, stranger." She gave him the full force of her smile, and his heart nearly stopped.

"Hey, Lucy." He pummeled his mind desperately for a witty remark. "You followin' me?" It was the best his mind could provide, and he cringed as he heard his own voice.

Her smile widened. "Sort of, yeah." She took the drink from him and tossed it back, gasping slightly as the heat hit her stomach. She seemed to be struggling with something herself, and Jesse wondered what it could be. He could not look at her without seeing that cringing form in the garret back in Kansas City, though, even though he knew Misty had never been any kind of a match for Lucy in any way. The guilt and the anger and the confusion were still very much there, and conjured every time he looked into Lucy's eyes.

So why, then, was it so hard to look away?

"You look like death warmed over, Jesse." Her words were playful, but there was real concern in her eyes. "Did you get in a fight with a mountain lion or something?"

He shrugged, putting a brave face on his injuries and his appearance. "You know what they say, Lucy: if yer bleedin', yer still breathin'." He grinned as much as his tight, torn face would allow.

She nodded, clearly not convinced that he was alright, but shrugged in return. "So," she continued, ignoring the conflict in his eyes. "I would love to hear the tale that ends with you sitting alone in a saloon in Diablo Canyon, a wrecked battlefield nearly within walking distance to the south, and a heap of machinery reported stolen from the equipment yard just yonder . . . all with a UR-30 Enforcer stalking the premises."

He stared at her for a moment, confusion and the brutal force of recent memory driving the phantoms away. Again his brain failed him. "What?"

She smiled, but generously toned it down to a more manageable radiance. "I'm just saying, the last time I saw you, you were holding court in that little dive on the back end of Kansas City, surrounded by the knights and jesters of your merry band." She gave him a brief inspection, her beautiful dark eyes running quickly up and down. "Now, I would hardly recognize you."

He shook his head and then realized that the image of the two of them sitting in a saloon in Diablo Canyon was strange on more than one level. He peered at her, taking his glass back. "Mind telling me how you ended up here? I'm sure there's an exciting tale to tell there as well."

She leaned back, one elbow thrown casually over the chair back. "Not really. Got a hankerin' for a different vantage, so came on over this way."

Jesse nodded and then made a show of looking around. "And your partner? Hank, was it?"

She laughed. "Henry. Business called him in a different direction."

Jesse shook his head. "So now you're wanderin' around the territories on your own, brazen as you please, and just happened to turn up in Diablo Canyon?"

It was her turn to shake her head. "Not just turn up, no. And not wandering, either." Her smile turned sly. "As for brazen, well, you'll have to make your own judgment on that call. You were going to tell me about the robot?"

His old grin began to return, and he settled back against his own chair, ignoring the pangs of torn muscles and bruises. "Well, why d'you assume I'd know anythin' about that?"

Lucy looked around the room. "I'm not seeing anyone else that could have handled one."

He perked up a bit, wincing at the pain but ignoring it. "So, you admit you think I could handle one."

"I'm not saying you could, either." She smirked and jerked her chin toward the rest of the room. "But the rest of these boys? No, there's no way they could have handled it."

Jesse's grin was wider as he made a great show of relaxing. "Well, to tell you the truth, the way I heard it, the thing went for a walk across the bridge."

Her smile slipped a little. "The bridge that isn't finished?"

His grin grew wider still. "Isn't it? Then yeah, I guess that one."

She stared at him, either impressed or angry, he could not tell. "You destroyed a UR-30 Enforcer."

Jesse shrugged. "Don't much matter to me, now." He poured himself another drink and tossed it back without thinking. Frank's face kept rising into his mind, followed by Harding, and Gage, and Chase. Lastly the ghostly image of the kid, Ty's, face rose up in his mind, the eyes glowing a hellish red.

"You destroyed the most advanced tool of law enforcement in the world, and it doesn't matter?" It was definitely anger in her eyes now.

Jesse leaned over the table toward the woman, his mechanical hands folding together before him. "Listen, lady. You obviously know about the battle, you mentioned it. Any thought to what I might have lost out there? My brother's gone. My friends are gone, either dead or fled. I'm alone, and the last thing I'm gonna worry about is that damned metal man. Did we blast 'em? Yeah, we blasted him to Hell! And yeah, we tossed the bits down into the canyon. So what?"

"Your brother is dead?" Every other emotion or thought had drained from her eyes as he'd said Frank's name, and now she reached out to lay one delicate hand over his mechanical claw. For the first time in his life, he wished there were feedback pads on the backs of his hands, but he could not have said why.

He shook his head, not wanting to meet her gaze. "Don't know. His body ain't back there, but that don't mean much. His 'Horse got blown to kingdom come, 'n' I woulda sworn I saw him burnin' up. When I came to, he was gone, dragged away, maybe. But whether he was alive or dead? That I couldn't say."

She said nothing for several minutes, but then she took his metal hands in both of hers, and he could tell from the feedback mechanisms that she was squeezing hard. "Maybe it's time to put all this behind you."

He barked a cruel laugh and moved to pull his hands away, but she held them tighter with surprising strength. "No, listen to me. Maybe now is the time to turn your back on all of this. Break the cycle and make a new choice? You don't have to chase the blood forever, Jesse. You could walk away."

He snorted and shook his head, but the dire urgency in her eyes trapped him and he could not look away.

He stared into her eyes and muttered, "you goin' to walk with me?"

Lucy pulled back abruptly, releasing his hands and looking at him as if she were shocked at the suggestion. There was a blush there too, however, and a confusion that she could not completely hide. "Me? No! I mean, why would I . . . What do I have to walk away from?"

He laughed at her discomfort and relaxed back into his chair. "Life? Eh, you know what they say, you can't cash in your chips till yer done, an' even then, no one knows what they'll be good fer. The Gospel sharpes, they'd like us to all 'walk away', eh?" He shrugged. "There's only one life I know, an' only one thing I'm good at, but I'm the best. I ain't gonna walk away 'till I can't play no more."

She watched him, then said, "do you know what you and your gang have done, destroying the UR-30? What's going to happen now to Diablo Canyon?"

He shrugged. "Be a bit more like home?" His grin was bitter.

"This town will tear itself apart, Jesse, it will be a pit of vipers again in a matter of weeks at most. All of the people here who have spent years trying to build something of their lives will once again be at the mercy of men and women who don't care about such effort, and don't think past their next swill of whiskey, or their next bed."

"Folks like me, you mean." He shrugged again, clearly not finding the idea troublesome.

He watched her react to his words, and would have put money on her leaving right then and there. He could tell what he had said troubled her more than he would have expected. Could she really care about the sheep mewing around Diablo Canyon or any of these other two bit towns? He shook his head, the anger returning, and spit on the floor beside him.

"Don't matter one way or t'other." He put his hands on the table, but he could feel the red-tinged darkness rising behind his eyes. His brother, Billy, all the dead men who had followed him out here, every fear that had driven him, and every mistake he had made along the way, built up inside him. Now this belle wanted to know how he felt about the cattle?

Jesse's hand snapped closed, shattering the bottle and sending the rest of the whiskey washing over the dry wood of the table. He forced his hand to slowly open and looked at his palm. Several splinters of glass were embedded in the rubber pads. He quirked an eyebrow as the pain registered, then carefully pulled the long shards out. He watched as the black liquid inside spurted out into the pool of whiskey, quickly clouding it up. The fluid stopped almost immediately. He looked back up into Lucy's face. She was staring at him in a mix of concern and frustration.

"There's more you don't understand than you do, Lucy." Jesse shook his head and looked back down at his hands. All signs of damage had smoothed away. "William Bonney is convinced there's something out there in the dust and the grass that'll be worth an awful lot to the right people. Whoever gets it, though? They'll be writing their own ticket, and when everything shakes out, their name'll be written so big in the history of the territories, ain't no one ever gonna be able to erase it."

She shook her head in response. "I don't care. Whatever this thing is, how many lives have you destroyed already, just following its trail? You're better than that, Jesse. You've got real power, you've got real strength. You could be a force out here in the territories. You could help make them safe for these people, as everyone tries to build a better tomorrow than the sad today they were born into."

He snorted again. "The sheep? Who gives a tinker's fart what the sheep want? Not that it matters. I don't even know where to go next. My brother –"

"Is out there somewhere, Jesse, and finding him would make perfect sense. I could help you with that. I want to help you with that. Frank's smart, I know. He might even agree with me." One of her hands was on his again, and it was as if neither of them even thought twice about it.

He looked at her, stunned. "You want to help me?"

She nodded. "I do."

He swallowed, looked away, then forced his eyes to return to her face. "Why?"

It was her turn to look away. "Jesse, that's about enough heavy thinking today, without quite enough heavy drinking." She stood up. "I'm going to secure myself a room upstairs. It's almost dark, anyway."

Lucy turned away, but quickly turned back. "You can join me upstairs. Plenty of time to think tomorrow."

He could see she was not completely comfortable with the advance, but of all the offers he had ever received, this one was the only one to hit him this hard. His mind, once again, failed him. "What?"

She looked exasperated, shaking her head and almost walking away. With a careful breath she calmed herself enough to look down, putting her hands carefully back on the table as she leaned over. "I'm getting a room. You may come up and join me if you wish." Their eyes were locked on each other, and he felt an unfamiliar, warm burn rising in his chest. She stood abruptly and turned away, leaving him to fall back into his own mind.

"But I don't want you to make the right decision for the wrong reason, Jesse. I want you to have all the information in front of you before you make a call. Billy took the drilling machine south, wide of the battle, following the railroad a bit first to hide its tracks. And although I doubt Billy knew it, there's enough old RJ residue on the rail bed that it should mask them from anyone using tracking tech as well. You should be able to pick up their trail just south of the battle site."

His face twisted in confusion. "How could you—"

She saw a myriad of questions in his eyes, and chose to answer one. "I saw the tracks from . . . my transportation. You'll have to trust me, that's where they went." She did not look down at him again but moved toward the front of the saloon. "I'm going to get that room now. I'll see you when I see you."

*****

Lucinda made her way up to the small room and put her things in a corner. She sat on the bed, a torrent of thoughts running through her mind. What had she done? She had never been so hopelessly entangled before. She looked down at the small pistol in her hand. The barrel was not the bleak hole of a normal gun's snout, but a fork-like two-pronged affair. Tesla promised it would discharge a bolt of RJ-1027 into a target from a few feet away and knock them painlessly into a deep, instant sleep.

Did she have the nerve to shoot Jesse when he came through the door? For a woman disused to ever questioning herself, she had already shown quite a bit of nerve already that day, so who knew? She had made sure he knew what room she was in, so there was really no question he would come. But would she shoot him, or . . . ?

The agent paced up and down along the wall of the small room, the pistol in her hand. Her nerves kept her moving around the room, and soon she put the weapon on a small side table and continued to pace. Her hands writhed nervously against each other. What was keeping him?

Soon she was too tired to pace. The energy and emotion of the past few days caught up with her. She sat on the edge of the bed and meditated for a while, bringing her heart and her mind into cold alignment. The sudden exhaustion hit by surprise, and she lay back on the bed to stop her head from spinning.

Lucinda awoke to warm light streaming through the chinks in her window's slats. Warm morning light.

She sat bolt upright and reached for the weapon. A quick survey of the room showed that none of her things had been tampered with. No one had entered the room.

"Son of a . . . " She rushed to the window and threw it open, thrusting her body out into open air, hanging by one hand and her knees on the sill.

Below the window was the reason she had chosen this room; she could see the recharging platforms in front of the saloon. Most of them were occupied. All but one, in fact.

A single recharging station was empty, its pad stained with puddles of oil and other liquid, as if the vehicle that had rested most recently there had been in very poor repair.

Or severely damaged.

Lucinda Loveless slumped back against the window frame, unable to untangle her own complex emotions. "Damn."

Chapter 15

The machine struggled through the rutted, reddish dust of the desert. It had bulled its way through gullies and across vast stretches of open, rocky ground for hours. Its rider, slumped in the saddle and barely conscious, watched the land drift by through slit eyes, focused on the regular pattern of massive divots and impact craters that lined his path. He had learned early on in the chase that his goggles made spotting the tracks difficult in the shifting sands. The glare and grit were small prices to pay for staying latched to his prey.

Jesse's mind kept slipping back to the previous night. He had almost taken those stairs. In fact, he had stood with every intention of following Lucy right up to the room before she had even disappeared up to the next level. As he turned, however, he had a sudden flash back to Kansas City. A flickering image of Misty crashed into his mind with force enough to drive him back into his seat. A ghostly figure of his brother loomed up before him as well, and he knew his path lay elsewhere.

Had it really only been a few short days since Kansas City? Not time enough for the memory to fade. He had struck her, or his arm had struck her, and he had left her alone; bleeding and sobbing, in that tiny little furnace of a room. And now, his brother, lost or dead or taken, disappeared into wastes while he lay unconscious. He knew, no matter how alluring he found this strange woman who had followed him into the desert, his path that night led him in a different direction.

There had been a little whiskey left in his glass, and he had downed it with a single tip. He looked back to the stairs with a mixture of regret, frustration, and determination. He had stalked out of the saloon and toward the battered shape of the Blackjack, taking the first steps toward Billy the Kid, vengeance, and, he hoped, finding his brother.

And so for hours he had nursed the damaged vehicle across the desert. He had left the scrub grass and the pine forests far behind and was now deep in the wastes, surrounded by nothing but rock, sand, and the occasional stubborn bush or tree. He had stopped at the battle scene to pick over the remaining vehicles for canteens and power cells, and strapped it all to the back of the Blackjack. He had driven along the railroad tracks at an agonizing pace, watching for the telltale marks of the driller. When he found them, he turned without pause and followed them into the wastes.

He drove the first day until nightfall, having been in the saddle all night and day. He was parched despite the water he had salvaged, and his stomach was a distant rumbling insistence that he found it all too easy to ignore. As the miles reeled out beneath him, his mind leapt from image to image, replaying everything he had lost since that morning he had decided to hit the bank in Missouri City without his brother. The two images that constantly churned to the surface were his brother's face and a face he knew was Misty's, although it seemed to melt from the beautiful, smooth, young face of the dancing girl to the twisted, angry, torn face of the victim he had cruelly left on the floor of the tiny room.

Where was Frank? Was he even alive? Jesse's mind was tormented with fear and worry, but he knew he could never have tracked down the survivors of the Union advanced patrol. Even if he could have, what could he have done then? Billy's gang was almost completely intact, and they had to have been nearby, in Diablo Canyon, when the Union must have fled. Maybe they had seen something? It was Jesse's best hope that the Youngers had taken his brother away after the battle. The fact that they had left him but taken his brother, he thought, was a good argument that his brother still lived, while they had been convinced that he had died. Cole had always been Frank's friend and war buddy first, and Jesse's friend and loyal follower a distant second. The rest of the Youngers followed their oldest brother's lead without question. The scenario was not so far-fetched that it failed to offer at least slight comfort.

Still, if Cole and his brothers had managed to spirit Frank away, where would they have taken him? Not back to Kansas City, not after the run in against the Union. So as Billy's was the only trail he had to follow, he chose to see this as a gift from fate. Following this path, he might learn more about his brother. At the very least, he should be able to learn where to start looking. He would definitely be able to seize this moment from Billy and make sure he could not enjoy the benefits of his backstabbing scheme. If anyone was going to emerge from this whole mess as an outlaw of the first water, it was going to be Jesse.

As the sun set on his first full day in the desert, he felt the first hints of despair. There was every possibility that his damaged Blackjack would not be able to outpace the driller. He would be no match for Billy's 'Horses, he knew. He figured he could at least catch the driller, but there was no way to tell how old the tracks were as he raced along the desert. There was plenty of room for his mind to torment him, amidst all the other torturous images, with fears that he would never catch his rival.

When the flaring reds and oranges of the glorious desert sunset finally faded from the sky ahead; he triggered the Blackjack's running lamps. The frantically jumping shadows made it nearly impossible to see the driller tracks unless he slowed his movement to a crawl, however. He continued for a time, but he felt his vision blurring, his attention wavering from one moment to the next. The second time he lost the trail completely, jerking awake to realize he was staring at smooth, featureless sand, he circled back, found the trail once more, and then stopped for the night.

He took a strip of the jerky from his saddlebags, a sip of water from his last canteen, and then huddled up against the warmth of his machine, wrapped in a duster, and succumbed to an uncomfortable, fitful sleep.

His dreams were a blurred moving picture array of faces. Frank was there, then Cole, smiling his cruel, open smile. He saw Billy, forever trapped between boy and man, and he saw Lucy, looking over one smooth shoulder as she moved through a crowded room toward a steep set of stairs. Each time, the faces melted into the next, however, there was a flash of Misty's face, twisted in hatred or soft in sleep, smooth as the day he met her or torn as the day he had left. The only thing that never changed were her green eyes, always boring into his, never letting him go.

Jesse came awake slowly, eyes blinking in the harsh glare of sunrise, mouth working to generate any moisture it could. He threw off the duster, took another quick swig of water, and mounted up once more. Hanging over the saddle to get a better view of the tracks, he continued on his way.

The Blackjack had sputtered along well past midday before Jesse saw, in one of his quick glances ahead, a confused jumble a little ways off from the driller's track. He found a narrow trail intersecting with Billy's path. The remains of a wrecked wagon were piled up in the sand and rock a couple hundred feet away from the driller tracks. Jesse looked up the digger trail. It took a sharp left turn and then continued on into the distance. Off the trail, the tumble of wood, canvas, and metal gleamed dully in the rising sun, a silent pivot point for Billy's change of direction.

He nursed the Blackjack down into silence and then swung off, pulling a Hyper-velocity pistol as he moved toward the wreckage, weapon down and to the side.

"Hey, anybody there?" Jesse shouted more to make himself feel better than in the honest thought that there might be people nearby. The wreckage looked totaled. Anyone left alive probably would have retreated long ago. He was not surprised when there was no answer.

"Hey, you okay?" He repeated, not knowing what else to do.

As Jesse came up on the wreckage he noted the charred blast marks of RJ weaponry across the sideboards of the wagon, and the blasted wheels, spokes scattered across the sand. The small generator that had been jury-rigged beneath the body of the wagon to drive the rear wheels was dead, none of its vents or telltale lights winking at all in the shadow of the cart.

Jesse moved around the wagon, his gun still held level. The canvas cover of the main compartment was collapsed, more blackened holes blown through it. Much of it had burned away. The wagon was canted to one side, resting on the remains of one shattered wheel. Pots, pans, and clothing were scattered across the desert all around, mixed in with a muddle of booted prints. He had nearly completed his circuit around the devastation when he saw the bodies.

There were two of them, slumped to the side and tied back to back. They both looked like half-Injun outcasts judging from their skin, hair, and clothing. Middle-aged, they looked similar enough to have been brothers. There were flint knives and a bow nearby, a quiver of arrows half emptied into the sand. Both of the men had had their throats slashed. Their faces had been further brutalized with a sharp knife.

"Smiley," Jesse muttered under his breath as he crouched down beside them.

Their clothing, mostly leathers, were decorated with the bone and feather fetishes he had seen many folks of mixed heritage wear in an attempt to identify with a culture that had denied them as surely as 'White society'. Jesse wondered if the Apache Kid was traveling with Billy, and if so, what he must have thought of this work. He shook his head again.

Jesse reached out with one hand, laying the feedback pads against one corpse's arm. Information compelled its way into his mind. The body was cold. The newly-risen sun had not had time to warm it again. They had been dead for some time.

Jesse stood up and stretched his back. Whatever had happened here, Billy had learned something that had changed his course. Could these two outcasts have known something about the artifact Bonney had been hunting? Or at least, knew of this mysterious valley the dead medicine man had mentioned?

Something about the torture, about the way the bodies had been left, filled Jesse with a new sense of urgency. He ran back to the Blackjack. He muttered a quick prayer to a God he barely thought of anymore as he turned the key and closed his eyes with a quick nod of thanks as it stuttered back to life. He leaned down to quickly check the indicator lights along the charge cells. Not strong, but no need to replace them yet. He opened the throttle on his machine and roared off after the tracks turning south, deeper into the wastes.

The new trail moved straight as a Warrior Nation arrow for the rest of the day. When the light faded off to his right again, he did not even try to push himself; he simply slowed to a stop in the middle of the track and huddling down for the night.

The newfound sense of urgency woke Jesse before the sun and he resumed his travel, going as slow as necessary to keep the tracks clear in the murky dark of pre-dawn. He did not mark the rising of the sun except to slowly bring up the speed of the Blackjack as the divots became clearer.

Jesse sipped down the last of his water on the morning of the fourth day. He had eaten the last of his jerky the night before. Voices of defeat and a sad, pathetic death alone in the middle of the desert had been whispering in his ear all night. His sleep had been restless and broken. He was too far gone now, though. He would never make it back to civilization now, not without water or food. If he could not catch up to Billy in the next couple of days, the voices would be proven correct. He would die, alone, in the desert.

As he rode along, Jesse thought of all the people who would be affected by his death. Most folks would think he really had died in the shootout with the advanced patrol. Lucy would know better, but maybe she should think he had just lit out. She would think he cared nothing for her proposal, and forgotten about her. For some reason, that thought bothered him more than he felt it should. The most driving fear he felt at the idea of dying, however, was that Frank, if he still lived, would never know he had survived the battle.

Thoughts of his brother distracted his mind so that he did not know how long he had been staring at the tall streaks of smoke in the sky. He slowed to a crawl over the sand and then stopped. Somewhere, not too far ahead, someone had lit several fires. The smoke rose up into the clear blue sky overhead. Jesse squinted up at the smoke, trying to judge how far away it was. He did not hear machinery or engines of any type, but if it was Billy, he did not want to give away his position until he was good and ready to face the puling chiseler on his terms.

Jesse killed the Blackjack's engine and slipped off the saddle. He opened up the cargo compartments and dug through the plunder there. He pulled out an ammo belt of RJ-1027 cartridges and slung that over his shoulder, pulled a holdout pistol and shoved that into the back of his belt, and was about to close the hatch when he saw the sleek shape of Carpathian's new weapons lying in the bottom of the hold. He reached in and looked again at the mysterious ion pistols. With a shrug, he shoved one into a pocket, closed the hatch, and began the hike toward the distant smoke.

He heard the machinery long before he reached the lip of the shallow canyon. He heard a vicious, grinding whine, strangely muffled, beneath the dragon-roar of an

RJ-powered engine running at full power. A column of white dust or smoke rose into the sky over the canyon. He slowly lowered himself to his belly and began to crawl to the edge, moving toward a gnarled, spidery tree that might offer a little cover. He moved up behind the tree and peeked over, his heart suddenly thundering in his chest as he realized that he had actually made it.

The valley was not deep, possibly the bed of a long-dead river tangled up with countless others forming a maze in the middle of the lifeless land. Billy's men had parked their Iron Horses all along the bottom and were lounging around, taking their ease. They obviously trusted the remote location in the middle of nowhere to provide their security. Jesse could see Billy standing near a large hole that had been blasted into the side of the canyon. The driller was backing out, accompanied by the plume of dust and grit. The men of Diablo Canyon were standing nearby, directing the drill or holding a mixture of strange equipment. Off to one side was a framework of metal struts that had been built to support another machine that seemed to be pointed at the wall.

Two of the Canyon men were arguing, one pointing to the shadowy hole, the other back at the framework with its machine. Billy walked to them, bringing them together, and listened carefully to what they said. He nodded once, patted one man on the back, and then pointed to the hole. Both of the men shrugged, and one yelled something to the driver of the drilling machine. The thing reversed course and crawled slowly back into the hole, the many drills reaching out in front of it spinning back up, creating the terrible, echoing roar that had led him to the location.

Jesse scanned the crowd of men below. He saw Smiley resting against the canyon wall a bit away, taking advantage of what shade there was. He saw Johnny Ringo and the Apache Kid standing together off to one side. They did not look amused, and they cast constant looks along the rim of the canyon. Several times Jesse had to duck back behind his scrubby little tree to avoid their notice.

A man walked from behind a small pinnacle of rock toward Ringo and Apache Kid, and for a moment Jesse would have sworn it was John Younger. A surge of anger and hatred filled his mind. It was everything he could do to stop himself from leaping down into the canyon, both guns blazing. The anger caught him by surprise even as he realized the man was not Cole's youngest brother. Could he be harboring so much animosity toward Cole and his brothers? Jesse shook his head and forced himself back into the moment. His time had come, and his opportunity to stick Billy in the neck and grab the brass ring for himself had arrived. All he needed was a plan.

Below, the drill continued its grinding work. Choking dust blasted back out of the hole and swirled through the canyon, up into the sky. The men stopped their talking whenever the drill began to work, continuing their conversations only after the hellish noise trailed off. Most of the men turned to Billy and the cave during these lulls. The few remaining watched the sky, or the lip of the canyon, or the dirt at their feet as their own individual impulse dictated. He saw that Ringo and Apache Kid usually watched the cave mouth whenever the machine was working, their expressions unreadable from this distance.

The driller stopped and backed out of the shadows again, and again the Diablo Canyon men argued about what was happening inside. Most likely the driller would head back into the darkness again, and Jesse knew he should be ready when it did. The drill's noise would present him with the best opportunity to make it into the canyon unopposed. Get the drop on Billy, bring him under the weight of the Hyper-velocity guns, and the jig would be up; Jesse would be back on top. Most of the men in the canyon were men he had ridden with in the past, and they would take their share of whatever the driller found from his hand just as readily as from Billy's. Ringo would be tough, and so would Apache Kid. Smiley was a monster, but he did not much care who he was killing for, as long as he had the opportunity to kill.

No, the entire thing came down to Billy. It was always going to be between Jesse and Billy when the penny finally dropped. And here it was, tumbling toward the sand.

Frank's face floated up into Jesse's mind again. Frank was always the one he could bounce an idea off of. Frank would know which parts of his plans were good and solid, and which ones were harebrained notions that could not possibly survive the light of day. Without Frank there to listen, it almost felt as if any plan could not hope to succeed. He did not even want to think about jumping into that canyon without Frank's Sophie to watch his back.

For a moment, he thought about going in brazenly calling for his brother's support, pretending he was up in the hills waiting to slap down any mudsill yahoo that got ornery. Then he remembered that there was every chance Billy and his gang knew more about Frank's whereabouts than he did. He could almost hear his brother's voice mocking him for the very thought. A chill ran down his back as he thought about what else he might have missed as he made his simple little plan.

Without Frank, this was going to be even harder than he wanted to admit. Yet, he told himself that this was his best chance to learn more about his brother's fate.

And besides, Billy really needed a good spoke in his wheel. And Jesse James was just the man to do it. For the first time in days, the old familiar grin came easing back.

*****

Hanging from the flank of his wagon, Wyatt looked out at the center of Diablo Canyon and shook his head at the devastation. It had looked bad through the vision slits of the Judgment wagon, but without the solid iron frame limiting his view, he could fully appreciate the impact. Two buildings seemed to have completely burned down, and many others showed the unmistakable blast damage of countless shots. Something monumental had occurred in the center of town, dwarfed only by the scatter of wreckage and bodies marking the sight of the battle a stone's throw to the south.

"Wyatt, you gonna keep movin', or you gonna trap the rest of us in here for the rest of the day?" Virgil's voice muttered from behind him. The Over-marshal nodded an apology and leapt down onto the street.

The marshals and deputies riding their Interceptors had spread out through the center of town at the first sign of trouble. As they had ridden in, several suspicious figures fled before them. They had seen at least three bodies lying at various points along their journey that had been left to rot in the sun. Smoke was also rising from a couple points farther back in town. Wyatt had set his men to create a perimeter and move no further until they learned what had happened, but a dark thought moved in the back of his mind . . . he was afraid he already knew.

The UR-30 units with the Over-marshal had been unable to establish contact with the unit assigned to Diablo Canyon, and that could mean nothing good. An Enforcer unit, even after it was rendered non-operational through damage or malfunction, should still be able to relate its position to another unit unless catastrophic damage to its reporter beacons had occurred. They were getting absolutely nothing from the Diablo Canyon unit.

The people of the town slowly came out from hiding as they realized who the lawmen were. They seemed shy, as if expecting violence to erupt around them at any time. Wyatt tried to reassure them, but they were unable or unwilling to believe him when he said that the worst was over. He had his men interview as many folks as he could track down and it quickly became clear what had happened.

Wyatt called Virgil, Doc, and Morgan to him while he left the judge to push the cordon of lawmen wider into the city to look for some of the local perpetrators.

"Well, this ain't good." Wyatt spat into the dust of the street. "Looks like we got road agents ridin' into town, blowin' the center of the burg down to get at the UR-30, and then clearin' out with some equipment. They then run into some Army boys down south, kick up a terrible ruckus, and then . . . no one seems to know." He shook his head. "You boys get anything better than that?"

"No one's talkin', Wyatt." Virgil gave a sour look at a knot of townsfolk standing in the shade of an overhang across the street. "Since the Enforcer got taken down, things have gone to hell in a hand basket here. Folks that'd been clingin' to grudges for over a decade came outta the woodwork. There's been a lot of dyin' ever since."

Morgan's eyes moved from face to face from within the iron framework of his support suit. It was clear he would have nodded if he could. "Someone took out the robot, then fought a major battle with the Army. They ain't here anymore, and neither is the Army. None of that makes any sense."

"Why take out the robot if they weren't plannin' on stayin'?" Doc was staring at a massive hole that had been blown in a building down the street. "It's not like it's an easy trick."

"An' our own units haven't had any luck trackin' anyone leavin'." Wyatt nodded. "A lot of trails out to the battle site, from a bunch of different directions, and then runnin' away. But nothin' clear. An' with the ol' railroad messin' with their head lamps, there ain't no way we're gonna be able to track 'em out o' town this time."

"I don't see what else we can do, Wyatt." Virgil's face was long, his slow voice full of anger and regret. "He'll turn up again soon, his kind always does. That is, if he didn't get beefed by the Army boys over there so bad we couldn't even recognize the body." He shrugged. "Might be Jesse James is dead, Wyatt."

The Over-marshal barked a sharp laugh. "I ain't never been that lucky, Virg, and I ain't likely gonna start bein' now." He looked back at the heavy wagon. "No, someone come in here a day 'r so ago and did all this, and there ain't no way we're gonna pin it on anyone without some of these local yokels bein' willin' to talk more than they are."

"Maybe if you leave them a UR-30 unit?" Morgan's buzzing voice was nearly devoid of all human emotion, but it managed to convey a sense of dismay at his brother's resignation.

"'Course we will, Morg. We ain't gonna leave these folks high and dry." Wyatt forced himself to pat the hulking form of his brother on one broad shoulder, trying not to wonder if he could feel it. "Problem's more long range than that, though. We nearly had Jesse James, boys. We were closin' in on him, and it looked like we might even hook William Bonney into the bargain. Now . . . this?" He gestured at the shattered town.

"You reckon we move back to Tombstone, then, Wyatt?" Virgil's voice was bitter.

Wyatt shook his head. "I don't know what else we can do, Virg."

"Unless we suddenly run into an old friend that might be willing to help . . . " Doc's muffled voice was amused, and everyone turned to look at him. Without moving his eyes, Holliday nodded the brim of his hat in that direction. They all turned to stare at the distant telegraph office and the woman who had just emerged, blinking, into the sunshine.

"Well, I'll be damned," Wyatt whispered.

"Most assuredly." Doc muttered, casting him a sidelong glance. "But hopefully not for a while yet. You reckon she might know somethin' about all this?"

"I ain't got a better idea. Boys, you stay with the wagon. Keep an eye out for that yahoo partner of hers. Morgan, why don't you come on over with me. Let's go have a chat with the lovely agent, shall we?"

Wyatt crossed the street at a brisk pace, his brother's heavy footsteps thundering along behind him. He saw the woman turn toward the edge of town and called out in a sharp voice, "A word, Agent Loveless, if you don't mind?"

Lucinda Loveless turned quickly, her hand flashing down and back to her bustle. She stopped as she recognized the Over-marshal. A professional smile pursed her full lips as he jogged up beside her. She nodded politely, then without missing a beat nodded to Morgan as well. "Gentlemen. Fancy meeting you all the way out here."

"Miss, if you don't mind me askin', how in the Sam Hill did you manage to beat us out here?" Wyatt's hands were on his hips as if berating a schoolgirl.

"Well, let's just say the kindness of new friends in . . . high places . . . and leave it at that, shall we?" Her smile turned slightly mischievous.

"Friends?" The word was so flat as it left the Over-marshal's mouth it could have been his brother who had spoken.

"Well, perhaps 'friends' is a strong word." She shrugged. "Let's say happy acquaintances. Or at least, our sudden acquaintance was happy for me, anyway." Again she flashed them the perfect smile.

Wyatt waved the smile and the non-explanation off. "Never mind, then. Do you have any idea what happened here? Where is everyone?"

Lucinda looked surprised. "Why, whomever do you mean, Over-marshal? Are there stalwart townsfolk missing?"

"There's a field of corpses just outside of town, miss." Morgan's voice caught her off-guard, Wyatt could tell. "And innocent civilians are dyin' in Diablo Canyon itself. Your jokes ain't proper at a time like this. You work fer the president, you might wanna start helpin' his people, 'stead of laughin' at their expense."

That seemed to trouble her, and the smile faded. "I'm sorry. It's been terrible since . . . since the whole thing began."

Wyatt smiled with the flat eyes of a serpent. "Well, why don't we start there, then. What is the whole thing that began?"

Loveless looked into Wyatt's eyes for a moment and he could tell she was weighing something in her mind. When her smile returned, he knew whatever she said next was going to be suspect.

"Well, it was Billy the Kid and his gang, Over-marshal. Came in here, shooting up the town, and took out the UR-30 Enforcer." Her gaze was steady, her smile firm, and her tone even. He sighed, knowing the truth would be permanently locked behind that professional facade.

"That what you just reported to the president?" Wyatt nodded toward the telegraph office behind her.

Loveless nodded. "Yes, as a matter of fact it is." She injected some iron into her tone with the artful skill of a professional actress. "I'm not in the habit of including anything beyond the truth in my reports, Over-marshal."

Wyatt shook his head. "Well of course not, miss. I'd expect nothing less from Washington's finest." He made no attempt to hide the frustration in his tone. "You wouldn't happen to know what . . . Billy . . . did to the robot, would you?"

She smiled again. "Well, Over-marshal, some of the boys in the saloon were saying as how they watched Billy and his gang bring it to where the tracks lift off into the canyon and toss it down. I didn't go over to see for myself, not having a head for heights, you know. I don't see why they would have lied." Her smile grew coy. "It's not like it's a very interesting story, anyway, is it?"

Wyatt shook his head again. "Of course not. I'll have some of my men check it out, see if the remains are retrievable." He looked back at the wagon where the lawmen were gathering, coming back from combing the town. He started to walk back but then stopped and turned.

"You didn't happen to see Billy, or anyone else suspicious, leavin' town, did you?"

Again her gaze was steady, looking him right in the eye. "I'm sorry, Over-marshal. I arrived after the whole uproar was long over. I did not see anyone leave town at all. When I got here, all the major characters had already fled."

He nodded, not breaking eye contact for a moment. "So, there is no way you can assist my men and me in following these animals and stopping their violent attacks on decent folks." His voice, again, was flat.

She looked into his eyes and he could tell there was something more churning just beneath the surface. There were choices being made, and he would not be privy to them or their consequences. She blinked once, the only concession to an expression she made, and then her beautiful face pivoted on her perfect neck in the most graceful negation he had ever seen.

"No, Over-marshal. I'm afraid I can't think of any way I could help."

Chapter 16

From the northern edge of the canyon, Jesse had a perfect view of the cave and the men standing around nearby. Most of Billy's gang were scattered toward the eastern end to avoid the worst of the dust and noise. Johnny Ringo and the Apache Kid, however, had not moved. They were almost directly below Jesse, with no way to avoid them. Still, they were probably the greatest threats in the entire canyon, after Billy himself, so it only made sense that he take care of them first.

The problem, as Jesse saw it, was that he did not want to kill Johnny Ringo. He knew Ringo was some kind of distant cousin to the Youngers. No matter what happened out in no-man's land, no matter where Frank was, Jesse would need to put together a new gang if he was going to take Lucy's advice and brace a more meaningful challenge. That would be a lot easier with the Youngers riding with him.

There was a pyramid of blaster rifles standing against each other about ten feet past Ringo and Apache Kid, and Jesse knew that if he could get there, he would be able to lay down enough fire to keep the rest of the gang at bay until he could get to Billy. He had to figure the engineers from Diablo Canyon would not a threat. As soon as he could take care of Billy, he would not have to worry about the rest of the gang.

Across the canyon, the driller stalked back into the shadows, and Jesse knew that at any moment, the horrific noise and billowing dust would begin again. They would find what they were looking for soon, and after that, there would be no chance for him to take anyone by surprise. He was going to have to strike soon or lose his chance forever.

Jesse shuffled around the lip of the canyon, shifting his weight beneath him as he prepared to leap. He had a moment's doubt. What if his arms acted up again? He was about to jump into the middle of a hostile gang. If his arms were not at their absolute best, he was going to buy a nice six foot stretch of sand for sure. But there was nothing else he could do. Alone, without food or water or enough fuel to get out of the desert, his back was well and truly against the wall.

The thought of water sent a sharp pang through his throat, which set the rest of his injuries to throbbing as well. Rather than frighten him, however, it only made him smile. He was worried about his arms being at their best? There was not a single part of his body that was currently working in tip top shape. His arms, very probably, were the least of his concerns. At the same time he reached this conclusion, the howling roar of the driller machine echoed out of the cavern. Without another thought, Jesse dropped.

He landed on Ringo's back, planting the heels of his boots on the other man's shoulder blades and pushing down with all his strength. Ringo was launched down onto his face into the sharp rocks on the valley floor. Without pausing to regain his balance, Jesse used his momentum off Ringo's back to fly up and over the Injun outcast they called the Apache Kid. He flipped his orientation over the other man's back, landing on his feet behind him.

The Kid spun in place, his hands flashing to the knives at his waist. As the ebony blades left their sheathes, they blazed an intense bluish white, spirit fire igniting up their entire lengths. The light guttered and failed as Jesse brought first one pistol butt and then the other down on the Apache Kid's head. The man staggered backward into the sun, legs unsteady and face slack behind the war paint. Jesse jumped back up into the air, planted one boot on the man's chest, and shoved him backward into the pile of rifles. Following up mercilessly, one final blow to the back of the head sent the renegade warrior slumping into the rock and sand.

Jesse looked up quickly, but the other men in the canyon had noticed nothing. They were either absorbed in the raucous drilling, or looking down or away, trying to ignore the sound. Jesse moved toward the scattered rifles, picking one up and moving toward a pile of broken rock for cover. He felt a near-constant itching between his shoulder blades as his mind constantly reminded him that he was alone. Frank was not above, watching through Sophie's scope to take out any threat Jesse had missed. Cole was not nearby, ready to lend the weight of his guns to the battle. Jesse was completely alone.

He was surrounded by enemies that had once been his friends. Nearly everyone in this canyon had ridden at his side at one time or another. He had trusted most of him with his life, and they had trusted him. Even if he had been planning on euchering Billy over this latest find, Jesse would have made sure he got his cut! He was not going to cut him off completely, let alone leave him in the middle of a battle to die!

Whether Jesse believed his own thoughts would be something for a deeper man to contemplate, but in that instant, grasping the butt of a stolen blaster rifle to his chest and preparing to brace an entire gang on his own, he believed it wholeheartedly. The righteous indignation fueled his anger to new, boiling heights.

Jesse was so tense, so wrapped up with his own thoughts, that he did not at first register when the drilling machine suddenly stopped. A shout from deep within the tunnel snapped him back into the moment at the same time that most of the men he was aiming toward all turned to look into the shadows as well. A strange smell tainted the air, but Jesse was so aggravated he could not be bothered to notice. In front of him, the men began to move toward the cave. He could tell, although they were not visible from his current position, that Billy must have disappeared inside.

He was too late. They had found what they were looking for, they would take it out, and he had lost his only chance to strike from surprise. His anger, towering a moment ago, reached even new, impressive heights. There were no more distracting thoughts of Lucy or Misty, no more worrying about Frank or the Youngers. He had had everything taken from him. He was alone in the middle of the desert. He had followed what he felt was his destiny laid clearly before him. And now he had nothing.

Without a thought, Jesse stood up with the blaster and started to fire into the small group of Billy's remaining men as they moved toward the cave. The first blasts caught them completely unawares. Two outlaws were struck in the chest, their bodies shuddering with the impact as dust flashed off them in a halo, knocked clear with the impact. They flew backward into the rest, the light fading from their eyes before they even knew they were in danger. The rest of the men stopped walking, cringing backward in surprise and reaching for their own guns.

Jesse screamed, his wounded throat opening blood frothing from his mouth as he charged forward. He fired the rifle over and over again, bracing it against his hip as he ran. There was no way the Hyper-velocity pistols would have had range to reach his targets, so it was a good thing he had grabbed the rifle. There was no room in his frantic mind for rational thought now, and he would have fired with any weapon he had to hand. More of his shots blasted into the tightly packed enemy, knocking two more men down. Blood sprayed into the dust-covered canyon.

By the time Jesse had crossed half the distance between himself and Billy's gang, the survivors had begun to return fire. They blasted bolts of crimson light back at the figure running toward them as if it were a vengeful ghost roaring up out of Hell. Jesse's extensive injuries, the dust covering him from head to toe, and the hoarse, hollow cry that was escaping his wide, cracked lips all combined to reinforce the image. Fear had a terrible effect on the men's aim.

Jesse rushed through the oncoming wave of blaster fire with no thought at all to his own safety or survival. He had lost everything. Now, he would take everything. Suddenly the blaster rifle was ran dry, its charge light dull. He tossed the weapon aside and his custom pistol leapt into his hands. The sheer number of shots he poured downrange was staggering. The three survivors, faced with that hurricane of ruby light, dropped their own pistols and fled down the canyon in their efforts to escape.

Jesse had just enough presence of mind to stop himself from rushing into the desert after the fleeing shapes. He paused for a moment, breath heaving in tortured lungs, and searched around for something else to destroy. The madness of the moment clouded his eyes, but eventually his fevered gaze fell upon the cavern entrance. He pivoted on the spot to rush headlong into the darkness.

Inside, the new smell was far more intense, but he was even less inclined to stop and consider it now. The floor of the cavern was irregular, and the bulk of the driller loomed up ahead, lighting the cavern with red-tinged beams slung from the thing's flanks and belly. The engine was on but idling low, giving out a constant, low-grade buzzing sound to reverberate in the darkness.

Jesse was gasping like an angry animal as he hunted through the tunnel for his next victims. There had been a world full of promise, and now there was nothing. The only thing his fevered mind could grasp upon, as a talisman against the emptiness, was this strange thing Billy had tracked across the length and breadth of the territories. Something with the power to pull Jesse so far, to make him go through so much, would have the strength and power to rise him up again. He would bring it to the Rebellion himself. Wielding that much power, he could begin to pursue the only vengeance that would satisfy him now.

And so, toward that end, no one in the tunnel could be allowed to stand in his way.

Jesse readied his Hyper-velocity pistols, one held high, one held low. No matter where a threat emerged, it would be met with brutal force. But no attacks came. Instead he heard, echoing from ahead in the thick, reeking air, voices arguing petulantly. He growled under his heaving breath and inched his way forward. He had taken down Ringo and the Apache Kid, but he knew there were several more men with Billy still, and he had not seen Smiley since that first survey of the canyon.

Jesse's mind was slowly returning, but none of the anger, despair, or determination was draining away with the madness. Somewhere up ahead was Billy. If Billy had been honest from the beginning, Jesse would never have been forced into this situation. Whatever else was about to happen, Billy would answer for his part in Jesse's troubles.

Jesse eased his way along the flank of the driller, gingerly picking his way past each insectile leg. The voices echoing from up ahead became clearer with each step, and he paused to listen, in case any tactical advantage could be gained.

"I told you I heard something!" The voice was high pitched and peevish. No one Jesse recognized.

"You never said anything like this! Digging? You didn't hear digging?" It was another voice that he did not know. "How about gagging? Do you hear me gagging now?"

Jesse shook his head. It had to be the Diabló Canyon men. Something had gone wrong, and under Billy's cold eyes they were arguing over whose fault it was. Jesse smiled at the thought. Usually it took Frank to come up with conclusions like that, while Jesse was far more the man of action in the family. The thought of Frank swept the smile from his face, and the rage threatened once again to boil up. It did not matter what was going on ahead of him. It was time for someone to answer for Jesse's current predicament.

He moved forward again and came around the front of the driller, looking past the enormous array of blades and bits mounted on the armatures at the front. They were hot, releasing wisps of smoke or steam up into the fetid air. The rough, churned walls and uneven floor ended abruptly in a concave area. A soft, reddish light was pouring through a hole in the stone, about waist-high, just wide enough for a man to crawl through. The voices, still grumbling and muttering, were coming from that hole. Jesse moved toward the gap, pistols at the ready.

"I tol' 'em you'd be comin'." The thick, heavy voice emerged from the shadows. "Billy, he said nope, said you were outta the pichure. But I said yup. An' here you are." Deeper in the darkness something stirred, moving toward him, and Jesse cursed under his breath as Jake Williamson sauntered forward, the weak light glinting off his greasy, bald head.

"Smiley." Jesse nodded to him. "This ain't between you an' me. I'm just after Billy. You can walk away."

Smiley's grin widened beneath its thick mustache. "You an' Billy, always thinkin' everythin' came down ta you two." The grin disappeared, collapsing into a vicious glower. "You an' Billy ain't no more special than anyone else, Jesse James. An' I'll be proud ta prove it to ya. Cuz today, you're story's gonna end. Time to make room for some new stories now."

Jesse tried not to react. He knew the worst thing he could do at that moment was to provoke Smiley even further. Unfortunately, he could not keep the grin from sweeping across his face. It had been too much, and Smiley was just another laugh line in a dance-hall show.

Jesse snickered. "You couldn't lead a pack o' cowboys fresh off the trail to a whorehouse on nickel night, Smiley. You just ain't got the smarts." Jesse moved to turn away. "Also, you don't smell so good."

Smiley charged at Jesse, as the outlaw boss knew he would. The bigger man could not get up much speed in the confining spaces of the cave. Jesse had no trouble stepping back behind the drill to avoid his ungainly rush. The Hyper-velocity pistols in Jesse's hands spun around, barrels slapping into his palms. Before Smiley could turn around, Jesse brought both weapons down, like clubs, on the back of his broad bald head. Two heavy cracking sounds echoed through the tight space, and the giant man collapsed without a sound.

Jesse watched the body for a moment. Aside from the rapid rise and fall of labored breathing, however, there was no other sign of life. With a wide grin, Jesse moved to the small, broken hole and dove through.

Jesse figured that, warned by the sound of the tussle in the tunnel, the men on the other side would be waiting for him, weapons raised. Not only were they not waiting for him, they were not even looking at him as he rolled up out of his lunge with both pistols raised and ready to fire. As Jesse took in a breath to shout an order, he fell back against smooth stonework, gasping at the smell. The scene in front of him disappeared behind a curtain of blurring tears.

Jesse quickly holstered one of his guns and pulled out a handkerchief with the freed hand, wiping at his eyes with the rough fabric.

"What in the hell is that stench!" Jesse barked, pushing himself back up to his feet and looking around owlishly as he tried to clear his eyes.

The room slowly swam back into focus. Billy stood across a large stone chamber from him, two lanterns resting at his feet. Four men were standing nearby, their argument cut short by Jesse's sudden appearance. All of them were holding handkerchiefs over their mouths. None of them looked like they had any intention of drawing a weapon. Even Billy, eyes haunted and empty, was only staring at him in mild surprise.

Seeing that he was not in immediate danger, Jesse took a moment to look at the room. It was dressed stone, with designs or sculptures that looked eerily familiar carved into every wall. Angular, unnatural animals walked among strange, abstract, curlicue designs. Everything in the room seemed to focus in on a central plinth that rose out of the mosaic floor. A plinth that was completely empty, although the patterns of dust atop it suggested that, until very recently, something about the size of a small beer keg had rested there.

There were no doors in the chamber, as if it had been built to hold the plinth, its occupant, and nothing else. The hole Jesse had leapt through had been knocked in by the driller, but it was not the only hole. In about the same place on the opposite wall was another hole, a black, empty eye staring at them from across the room. And it was from this hole that the stench came pouring.

With another quick look at Billy and the engineers, Jesse moved slowly toward this second hole, his kerchief still held to his face. It was not doing any good, however, as the reek just kept building with each step he took. Looking sideways through the hole, avoiding approaching it from the front, Jesse could not see anything but the fitful shadows thrown by Billy's lanterns.

"Get me a damned light," Jesse snapped, holding out the hand with the useless cloth. One of the engineers looked at Billy, who nodded, and then scuttled to get Jesse one of the lanterns. Jesse took it carefully, turned back toward the hole, and eased his mechanical arm through it and into the darkness.

The smell was like a wall pushing back at him as he moved his head in after the lantern. He was almost certain now what he would see, but he needed to check for himself. Sure enough, the rough cavern on the other side was strewn with desiccated, ravaged bodies. They were encased in metal and wire frameworks, built specifically to hold up dead bodies incapable of providing their own balance and support.

Some of the bodies had had mining tools surgically implanted where their hands had been, but most of them had arms ending in nothing but shattered stubs of bone sheathed in tatters of rancid flesh. They had been worked quite literally until their tools and hands were worn away, and then they had been discarded. Jesse could see the cranial battery sockets, where the cylinders would be inserted to animate the ghoulish creations. Each body completely dead, the RJ machinery dark and silent, and each socket empty, their batteries removed.

Jesse tried to get a quick count of the bodies in the tunnel, but his eyes were tearing up again and he could not keep his head through the hole any longer. He withdrew, pulling the lantern with him, and the shadows of the caves swallowed the sad remnants of the abandoned animations.

"Damned foreign bastard." Jesse spit on the mosaic floor over and over again, ignoring Billy and his three companions as they stared at him in dull confusion.

"You damned daffy European bastard." He spat again. He knew exactly what had happened. He remembered Carpathian's welcome, back in Payson, with a bitter laugh. Offering to help Jesse take on another Heavy Rail. The blatant attempt to distract him seemed clear now, looking back. But at the time, Jesse had been so sure of his own superiority. And the old man had been a step ahead the whole time.

Jesse shook his head, the anger now aimed inwardly as much as at the rest of the world. He glared at Billy for a moment. The Hyper-velocity pistol wavered in his hand and slowly rose. The other outlaw's eyes went round as his hands rose up in a warding gesture. Jesse shook his head again, muttered a dismissive curse under his breath and moved toward the hole in the chamber wall.

"Hey, wait!" Billy snapped out of his fugue. "You're alive!"

Jesse stopped, and spat an answer over his shoulder. "Guess it wasn't my day to die, Billy."

The younger man's hand drifted toward his pistol. "Where you think you're goin'?"

Jesse spun around so quick, the three Diablo Canyon men flinched away, their empty hands raised in placating gestures. The older outlaw boss rushed across the dusty old chamber, his sleek custom pistol leading the way. The barrel jammed up beneath Billy's jaw and slammed him up against the crumbling wall. Billy's face contorted in pain as the sculptures in the wall behind him dug into his back.

"Whoa!" Billy's hands were raised high, his voice contorted by the barrel pressing into the soft flesh under his jaw. "Jesse, ease up!"

Jesse's face pressed in close to Billy's, his brows drawn down in barely-contained rage, his eyes wild. "I got a couple quick questions for ya, Billy, before I light outta here on my way."

Billy tried to nod, but choked as the barrel pressed harder against his skin. "Ya," he gasped, minimizing the movement of his head.

Jesse nodded once, his face a mask half way between confused and furious. "Okay. First, where's Frank?"

Billy looked down at the barrel with an exaggerated roll of his eyes, and Jesse relaxed the tension in his metal arm, drawing the weapon down slightly.

Billy rubbed at the spot left behind by the muzzle, an exaggerated look of hurt innocence in his eyes. "Jeez, Jesse, you feel alright? You din't have to bury the damned muzzle in my craw, you know!"

Jesse's flat eyes grew harder and his pistol rose slightly. "Frank."

Billy's hands rose quickly again. "Whoa, Jesse! Pull in yer horns, fer Pete's sake!" He swallowed, and it looked painful enough to spark a pang of sympathetic pain in Jesse's own torn throat. "Honest, Jesse, before I talk, you gotta put the shootin' iron down, okay? I'll be straight, I promise, but it's a might hard to think with that fancy blaster warmin' my jaw."

Jesse blinked, then lowered the weapon further. "Where's my brother?"

Billy lowered his own hands a bit, sure to keep them wide, far from the butts of his own pistols. "Well, see, an' this here's the Gospel truth, Jesse." He swallowed again. "I don't know."

The Hyper-velocity pistol jammed back up under Billy's jaw as Jesse's eyes burned with frustrated anger. The younger man scrambled against the wall to avoid the gun. "I swear! I swear! We lit out of there as soon as the blue-bellies showed up! You all were tearin' it up like the Kilkenny cats out there, an' we just ran! I din't see nothin'!"

Jesse lowered the gun, his shoulders sagging. "You din't come back fer 'im?"

Billy's head shook back and forth with furious, nervous energy. "No, we din't. We grabbed the driller machine with these galoots, looped through town up onto the tracks, and headed back down after the dust had settled. Wasn't none of you movin', an' we figured you'd all either run with the others 'r you was all up the flume." Billy's eyes were clear, his voice as even as he could make it. "Honest, Jesse. I thought you was dead or fled. I was hopin' you'd run'd off."

Jesse turned away, his unseeing eyes scanning across the ancient carvings on the walls. "You really ain't got 'im."

Billy shook his head furiously. "If I'da grabbed 'im, Jesse, I'd tell ya."

Jesse started walking toward the shattered hole in the wall again, but his steps were hesitant, his eyes seeing nothing, his mind a swirling darkness circling a black, empty hole. "Then they got 'im. Alive 'r dead, they got 'im."

Billy started to cautiously follow Jesse as he crossed the room. "Who got 'im, Jesse? Those Union bastards? You think they grabbed 'im." Billy hesitated before continuing in a softer voice. "You sure he ain't beefed, Jesse? I saw that thing ridin' up on 'im. That thing was a beast, packin' more hardware than I seen on anythin' short of those wagons that're poppin' up all over."

The older outlaw's head shook in vague negation. "Naw, I picked over the bodies but good. He weren't there."

"But maybe he's okay, then!" Billy tried to sound hopeful. "If he's alive, maybe we can go get 'im!"

A light flickered deep in Jesse's eyes for the first time since he had drawn on Billy. He turned back to look at the younger man, and Billy shied away from the growing heat there. "Go get 'im from the Union?"

Billy shrugged. "Sure! We put a nice gang together, like that first train job, an' there ain't no place they can stash 'im that we can't get 'im out!" More and more energy seemed to bubble into Billy's voice. "An' you know, there ain't no outlaw in the territories, wouldn't come if you put out the call!"

Jesse tilted his head as if processing Billy's words, then shook it again. "Naw. If they took 'im, they'd mean to keep 'im. An' if they mean to keep 'im, they'll stash 'im someplace, you'd need an army to get 'im out."

A glum silence settled over the ancient room again. Jesse's eyes snapped up after a moment, looking back at the second hole breaking into the room. "An' I know some folks that got an' army they ain't doin' much with."

"Jesse," Billy inched his way around into the other man's line of vision. "You got an idea on how to make this right?" He jerked a thumb at the empty plinth.

The older outlaw was not paying attention, but he muttered aloud as he thought, and Billy nodded with the words. "Carpathian can't be far away, those animations ain't been dead again long. Should be able to catch up with 'em without too much trouble."

Billy nodded vigorously. "Yeah, Jesse, that's it! We'll catch up with the old bastard, an' take back what's ours!"

Jesse turned to take notice of the younger man again. Looking at him as if he had forgotten he was not alone in the chamber. He spoke as if he had not understood the words. "We?"

Billy gave Jesse a hard look. "Yeah, we, Jesse. This plunder's mine by rights. I found the Injuns, I got the info, I tracked it down an' dug it up. It's mine more'n it's anyone else's. So yeah, if anyone's ridin' out after it, it ain't you, it's we."

A smile tugged at Jesse's lips, the first since he had leapt into the stench-filled room. "We."

Billy nodded. "Yeah, we! Jesse, you can't take him on alone, an' you know it! He sure as Hades ain't gonna be alone, you know that! You need me!"

For a moment Jesse stood completely still, staring at the younger outlaw boss with a blank expression. Then he started to laugh, and Billy's expression snapped from eager to angry without a pause. "What's so all-fired funny, Jesse? I got out here without you, din't I? I got into this here buried room without you, din't I? You don't think you'll need me when you catch up to the old man?"

The laughter continued, bouncing off the surrounding yellow stone, absurd in the foul atmosphere. Billy's face hardened further, his right hand floating toward his gun belt.

"We made a deal, Jesse!" The hand slid over the butt of the modified six-shooter. "We were gonna ride together on this!"

The laughter cranked up another notch, but rather than fanning Billy's anger, the young outlaw backed up a pace. A manic edge had entered Jesse's mirth, a frantic energy that had not been there before. The fire was back in his eyes.

"We made a deal, Billy, you're right." Jesse nodded and took a step toward the retreating boss. "We were gonna ride this trail together, right as rain." He took another step.

Billy nodded, but there was a hesitant doubt in his eyes. "We were, Jesse. We were gonna work together, like the old days."

Jesse stopped advancing and looked down at his clenched fists, the metalwork of his arms gleaming redly in the RJ-1027 lantern light. He forced the fingers to relax, watching as the mechanisms beneath the armor moved smoothly and flawlessly. When he looked back up at Billy, the grin was back, but it was feral, and Billy tried to back up again only to find himself up against the rough wall once more.

"We were gonna ride together, Billy, 'till you let my boys die takin' down the damned robot for your gear." The broad shoulders flexed, the arms wide, and Billy's eyes flicked down to the hands and back up to Jesse's frenetic eyes.

"That was business, Jesse!" He forced himself to speak in an even tone. "That was just the way we all been workin' since long before you or me picked up a slingshot fer the first time!"

Jesse nodded, lowering his hands a bit and turning away slightly. "That's true, Billy. That's true. We ain't always been straight, an' that's business."

Billy relaxed slightly, a smile starting to cross his lips.

Jesse's right arm swung up faster than a rattler striking from the shadows. Power moved through rubber conduits, clockwork gears ran their teeth smoothly through each other and pistons pulled and released with tiny puffs of smoke. The armored back of Jesse's mechanical hand caught Billy squarely on the cheekbone with all the power of the steel and rubber machinery backed up by the hulking human muscles of his shoulder and back, and the younger man, stepping forward when the blow struck, was hurled back up against the wall with a muffled snap.

A pained gasp escaped Billy's torn lips before he hit the uneven wall with a grunt. He bounced away from the ancient carvings and fell forward as his legs collapsed beneath him. He slumped down to the dirty floor where he rolled half over, his shoulder resting against the wall and his face, twisted in pain and torn from the blow, rocked back and forth in the dust.

"You – you – you killed him!" One of the engineers screeched, staring down at Billy in horror.

Another man pointed at Jesse. "Now who's gonna pay us!"

Jesse watched Billy for a second then shook his head. "He ain't dead. He's bleedin'. If yer bleedin', yer breathin'." He smiled slightly as he looked at the second engineer. "An' in case you missed it, flannel mouth, there ain't nothin' here. You was gonna get a cut o' what we all dug up." He pointed to the empty plinth. "Yer welcome to one hunnerd percent o' what you dug up."

"But, what about us?" The third man whined, following Jesse as the older outlaw stalked back toward the hole.

Jesse shook his head. "Ain't my problem, boys. Head on back to the Canyon, would be my best advice. Ain't nothin' out here for ya, or fer anyone, when you get right down to it."

"But they won't let us back to town! Not after we came out with you! You killed the metal marshal! The place is gonna be a mad house now, and everyone will blame us, because we rode out with you!" The second engineer was near tears.

Jesse turned at the hole and gave the three men a grin. In the vague red light and the swirling fetor he looked like a demon peering out of Hell. "Sounds to me like you boys've made some bad choices, then, don't it?"

As Jesse eased backward through the hole he looked back at the three men standing lost and alone in the foul-smelling semi-dark. "Good luck, boys. I got an old man to catch."

Even after the outlaw chief had gone, the three men from Diablo Canyon stood uncertain, their eyes flickering from the still form of Billy the Kid, to one blasted hole, to the other, to the empty plinth, and back to Billy.

After a moment the first engineer muttered, "You reckon the driller'd be any good at fishin'?"

Chapter 17

Jesse rushed across the desert on the half-wrecked Blackjack. He had almost taken an Iron Horse from the canyon, but they were all too low on fuel. None of them would be good for a long chase. The new vehicle was running rough, but with the salvaged batteries, he knew he would be okay. He grumbled in annoyance as he ran back to the Blackjack. Trust Billy to let his boys lounge about while their transports sat around dry.

Frank never would have let Jesse's boys do that. The thought was true enough, but it hurt as soon as it occurred to him. Knowing the Union had Frank was eating at his mind even when he forced himself to focus on his immediate concerns. There was no telling what the blue-bellied bastards were doing to his brother while he was dancing around in the desert. Despite Billy's bravado, there was no way a band of shabby outlaws was going to assault an armed Union camp without help.

Jesse was convinced that the only prayer he had of helping his brother was at the head of an army, and the only army he could hope to win over to his cause was languishing in the swamps far to the south. He would need to have something special to convince the Confederate Rebellion to join him. Something big enough, for instance, to bring Carpathian out of his brick castle and into the desert wastes.

The Blackjack bounced and leaped over the rough terrain as Jesse nursed more speed out of the tortured engine. He had been chasing a fading plume of dust and grit for over an hour, and was finally able to make out a dot at the bottom of the plume: a large vehicle, racing away to the south. Out here in the middle of nowhere, there was no one else it could be but Carpathian. The doctor was rushing back to Payson, prize in hand.

Jesse hunched low over the control console of the vehicle, muscles straining as he willed the machine to go faster. With each violent bump over dry ridges or clumps of desert grass, he would leap into the air before slamming back down into the saddle. Aside from an occasional grimace of discomfort, he continued on without pause.

Jesse's crimson goggles were caked with dust and grime, but he could not take the time to clean them. The dark shadow ahead grew moment by moment, and with his quarry in sight, his fear, anger, and instincts all argued against any further delay. In that vehicle was the object that would bring the Rebellion back from the dead. In that vehicle was a man he had not viewed as an enemy in many years, but who had betrayed him in his moment of greatest need. In that vehicle was an old man that needed to be reminded of his place in the western territories.

The shadow ahead resolved itself into a boxy shape that could only be some kind of RJ-powered wagon. There was a door high up on the rear panel and a ladder of sorts sweeping down toward the ground. The whole thing looked more decorative than utilitarian, just Carpathian's style. Atop the tall machine was a low wall or parapet, and he hoped whoever might be up there was not keeping a close lookout.

The thought had barely formed in Jesse's mind before a ragged shape, locks of thin hair waving in the wind, rose up over the parapet. The Blackjack was too far away to make out much detail. The rough, unfinished look about the face, with hollow, shadowed sockets and a flashing rictus-wide grin, however, were enough to show him it was an animation. The thing brought an arm up and pointed it at him. Its hand had been replaced with a jury-rigged blaster rifle: a red-lined muzzle-flash lashed out, the recoil pushing the thing's shoulder backward and away.

Jesse ducked as low as he could and gunned the engine. The howling of the vehicle rose another octave, but it was running with a dirty cough now. He knew he would not be able to nurse much more speed out of the tortured machine.

The animation on the wagon fired again and again. The blasts were disconcerting, but none of the shots landed anywhere nearby. Jesse thanked his stars, figuring that a stinking corpse firing from a rattling platform high atop a moving vehicle backward at a moving target . . . the chances of a hit were probably slim enough he could afford to ignore the—

A bolt struck the forward fairing of the Blackjack with a hollow ring. The blast deflected off into the desert, but it drove Jesse even further back into his saddle. A grim snarl twisted his features below the red goggles. He wrenched the hand controls of the vehicle and dragged them backward. The four blaster muzzles in the sloping armor ratcheted up into the sky.

Jesse stabbed his thumbs down on the firing mechanisms and grunted in satisfaction as the guns began to blaze away, the red-tinged fire lipping off their muzzles and back along the Blackjack's flanks. He marched the blaster impacts up the wagon's rear armor, unsurprised that the shots were ricocheting off into the distance without visible effect, but as he brought the stream into line with the animation up top, the blasts had a most satisfactory result. Several bolts slapped the ungainly shape upright as they impacted across its chest.

Rotted fabric and dried, dead flesh blasted away in tatters that fluttered into the wind as the bolts battered their way through the body and flew out the other side and into the sky. The energy stood the animation up and knocked it over. The creature disappeared as it flew off the front of the wagon, then reappeared a moment later from beneath. The ruins of the corpse tumbled out from under the wide, thick-treaded rear wheels.

Jesse's grin was short-lived, however, as two strange shapes swept off to either side from in front of the wagon. Strange, ungainly vehicles, they seemed almost like mechanical pillars, each seated upon a small, furiously spinning wheel. Atop each was the desiccated body of an animation, permanently fixed to their strange, top-heavy mounts with bolts and straps. Heads lashed from side to side looking for their prey and the outlaw boss was shocked to see that they were completely encased in iron helmets and masks. What looked like weapon barrels thrust out from beneath the swaying bodies, and Jesse knew he could not let them get behind him.

He took out the left-hand abomination with a sharp burst of his lowered blasters. Mechanical parts scattered across the desert, sand thrown up into the air as the single wheel spun away as if eager to escape. He brought the Blackjack in line with the other vehicle, and his shots struck the pilot in the back and head, spraying rotting flesh and the twisted wreckage of its helmet into the sand. The machine, now without guidance, bounced over the uneven terrain and went down, cartwheeling in a furious explosion of sand and grit.

Jesse grinned before two more of the things swept into view. He looked back at the wagon to see that it was pulling ahead again. The primary weaponry on the Blackjack made short work of these new threats, but they forced him to follow an irregular course as he had to aim with the body of the vehicle, allowing the wagon to pull away. He shook his head and drew one of his Hyper-velocity pistols, knowing that it would be less than ideal against an armored target at this range.

The Blackjack surged ahead again, pulling to within an easy stone's throw of the sloped ladder.

As Jesse tried to maneuver up behind the wagon, two more animations rose to take the place of the original shooter on the roof. Soon, he was weaving back and forth in the wake of the wagon, doing his best to close the gap while avoiding the stuttering shots from above. Another bolt panged off his front armor and the tone of his engine changed again. Something inside the body of the Blackjack must have been damaged from the hit. As the vehicle started to shake madly, Jesse knew his mount was living on borrowed time.

The Blackjack leapt forward in response to Jesse's desperate urgings. He sent streams of crimson bolts up at the animations above to keep their heads down, and then to one side and the other, aiming at the drivers of the top-heavy vehicles rather than the armored transports themselves. One stream of shots stitched across the torso of the creature on the left and the tall vehicle canted over, caught a high clump of red rock, and rolled away into the desert shedding mechanical parts and tatters of ragged meat as it went. Jesse's other shots, however, glanced off armored components, leaving the remaining outrider unharmed. Out of the corner of his eye he saw two more sweeping out from the left.

Jesse cursed, looking at the ladder as it bounced along ahead of him, then at the riders closing in. A sudden thought struck him and he holstered the pistol and made a desperate grab for the small shape pressing against his back. Carpathian's ion pistol felt strange against his feedback pads, but if there was ever a time to test a weapon that might shut down RJ-1027 technology, it seemed like now.

The pistol gave off a strange vibration as he fired it at the closest rider, and a snapping reddish flash zapped out and wrapped around the outlandish vehicle. Instantly, all the telltales winked out, the ruby glow of the vents and power sources faded. The entire thing slowed down, toppled over, and rolled to a gentle stop in the sand.

Jesse grinned as he watched over his shoulder as its journey ended. He turned back to point his mechanical arm rigidly at the next animation. Again the flash and buzz, and another animation tumbled into an awkward heap. But when he tried to shoot the last target as it flashed past, the small pistol made a plaintive beep and died.

Shaking the pistol had no effect, and Jesse growled as he shoved it into a side pocket. He pulled his own pistol again and fired backward under his steering arm. A sleet of shots slapped into the animation's armored vehicle as two simultaneous bolts from above struck the Blackjack, knocking more of the vehicle's internal parts out of line.

Jesse's wild, desperate shots managed to hit something vital within the creature blasting away behind him. The tall thing began to sway back and forth as it fell away. He continued shooting, striking the body of the animation several times. When it detonated in a furious ball of red-tinged fire, he spent no time celebrating. He spun around as fast as possible, eyes fixed on the ladder swaying back and forth nearby, and holstered his pistol. He took the extra moment necessary to snap the strap securely over the butt. He reached across his stomach to secure the other pistol and then rose up out of his saddle.

His eyes flicked from the heavy ladder to the wide front tires of the Blackjack, to the ornate cowcatcher between his two wheels. Each time he tried to imagined the leap across, he could see that the bulk of the Blackjack would keep him from closing the distance enough to give a jump even the slimmest chance of success.

He brought his mount over and craned his neck, trying to get a glimpse along the side of the wagon. Two enormous wheels churned away, but between them he could just make out an access ladder leading up to an armored side door. With one more glance up at the firing animations and over at the wide rear ladder, Jesse shrugged and crouched down again, urging the Blackjack into one last burst of speed.

The two gargantuan wheels ground along beside him as he inched up on the wagon, dust and smoke and strings of dry, crushed desert grass swirling all around him. Between his own front tires and the wide wheels of the wagon, he could not get as close as he would have liked to the access ladder. However, he thought he could make a jump with a little luck. His eyes moved from the ladder to the heavy rear wheel that would crush the life from him, leaving his flattened and torn body crushed into the desert for the buzzards. He was due for a little luck.

Jesse swallowed and looked up for the annoying animations that had been firing clumsily from above. They seemed to have lost him for the moment. Silently, he promised them their time would come. He crouched low in the saddle, making ready for the leap.

Jesse's legs uncoiled beneath him as he launched himself into the gritty air. The enormous wheels roared up on either side as he sailed between them, hitting the armored flank of the wagon with more force than he had intended. He scrambled desperately, his metal arms clanging loudly on the armored wall. He clawed for the rungs of the access ladder as he stared at the blurring pattern of metal treads spinning past less than a foot away. He felt the feedback pads press against a textured iron crossbar and gripped with all the strength of his unnatural arms. He swung back and forth for an alarming moment until he could bring his legs up out of the torrent of dust and onto the ladder beneath him.

The Blackjack, without direction, began to drift away to the left. As he climbed, it fell farther and farther behind. It hit a rocky lip that abruptly ended its journey, however, sending it flipping high into the air, trailed by a plume of dust and sand. It tumbled across the desert behind him, exploding as the jury-rigged power cells finally ruptured, scattering the remains in a wide, burning circle in the sand.

Jesse climbed up the ladder to the access door, hugging the metal for what little cover he could find from the animations still searching for him from above. He was hardly surprised when the hatch was locked, but a quick glance showed him that there were plenty of handholds above leading up to the firing platform on the roof. He began to make his way past the hatch, eyes fixed on the parapet, waiting for the animations above to realize his location.

Just as the outlaw boss came up to the low wall, the dull, empty face of an animation rose before him. The thing brought up its blaster arm with a clumsy jerk. Jesse held onto a bolted cargo ring and reached up, grabbing hold of the rifle with one mechanical hand. His metal fingers closed over the barrel and pulled with all his strength. A human would have released the rifle and lived to fight on. The animation, however, did not have that option. It followed the weapon up and over the edge, tumbling down into the swirling sand of the wagon's wake.

Jesse surged up onto the roof before the other animation could take its partner's place. He snaked a leg over the railing and swung onto the platform, not allowing himself to hesitate as he saw that there were two rotting corpse-shapes awaiting him instead of one. He brought one heel up and planted it on the closer animation's chest, pushing with a quick thrust that sent the unsteady creature up and over the far side of the parapet. It disappeared down between the two growling wheels on that side.

Before his foot even came down on the metal grating, his hands flashed down to his holsters. His metal fists came up with both pistols, clapping them together for their conjoined heat blast. He was angry, he was tired and sore, and he had had enough of these stinking abominations. He flicked the switches with his thumbs, pulled the triggers, and grinned wildly as the animation was blasted into splinters and shreds that flew off into the wind, nothing left larger than a whiskey bottle.

Jesse holstered one pistol and stripped off his begrimed goggles. He reached down for the locking wheel in the middle of the hatch at the center of the firing platform. Beneath him, the wagon churned along, and the outlaw felt a moment's flush of triumph as he realized he was only steps away from confronting Carpathian. Soon, he would seize the ancient artifact that would unlock his future.

Before Jesse could pull open the hatch, it came open on its own, pushed by the bulging muscles of a misshapen animation much larger than the others he had already taken care of. With a disgusted grunt, Jesse dropped his pistol and clapped his hands to either side of the malformed head. Within their armored casings his arms' mechanisms whirred, driving his hands together, crushing the slack-jawed visage. There was a moment's hesitation as the reinforced skull resisted, and then with a wet crunching sound, the face deformed and his hands met in the middle of the thing's gelid brain. A quick snap and spark marked the shorting of the RJ battery cylinder. The light faded from the thing's empty eyes.

Jesse screamed in annoyance. He grasped the loose body by the shoulders and pulled it up through the hatch, heaving it off the roof. His hands were covered in gore, further fueling his rage as he recovered his pistol.

"Hey, Doc!" Jesse grinned as he spat out the title he knew Carpathian hated. "Don't get your back up, but I think you're outta hired hands!" He jumped down into the darkened interior of the wagon.

Jesse bent his legs to take his weight as he plummeted to the iron deck of the compartment beneath. There was a loud, surprised shout as someone fell away, but a dry hiss clearly announced the presence of another animation. Jesse brought the pistol up and fired into the corpse's face, splashing the entire head against the bulkhead beyond. The body slumped back onto the floor and Jesse brought the pistol around toward the muffled shout.

The muzzle of the Hyper-velocity pistol came to rest pointing at its creator as he lay on his back on the iron floor, legs bunched up before him. Before Jesse could say anything, however, Carpathian's augmented legs came pistoning up, catching the outlaw in the arm and chest. The pistol went spinning away and Jesse was driven against the forward wall. His arms flailed wildly to keep his balance as he stumbled over the headless corpse.

Jesse brought his fists up before him, nose wrinkling once again at the familiar smell. He pushed off the wall with his elbows. Carpathian had risen and had assumed a fighting stance of his own, fists floating back and forth before him in a practiced formal boxer's form. Jesse was annoyed to see the old man was smiling.

"I'll never be out of hired hands, Mr. James. Something you might want to consider as you move forward in this brave new phase of independence you've embarked upon." One fist lashed out and wove past Jesse's defenses to strike the outlaw in the jaw. His head snapped back and then came down quickly as he moved around trying to put some space between his adversary and himself.

"As you can see, Mr. James, I may not be the helpless old man you expected when you dropped in unannounced." He moved forward, sending a rapid series of jabs flashing out to test Jesse's reactions. "Another rudeness I intend to take up with you, I might add." Another jab snapped out, followed quickly by a flashing hook that caught Jesse's mechanical arm on the elbow, knocking it aside. Feedback buzzed in Jesse's mind as internal damage was reported.

The outlaw came around again, still trying to keep his distance. His own jabs were repeatedly beaten aside with a negligence that would have been frightening if it was not for Carpathian's goading smile. Jesse reminded himself that Carpathian's arms and legs were at least as advanced as his own augmented arms. Probably more so, given it was the doctor who had invented the technology.

Jesse watched his opponent's fists warily, their speed and strength distracting him from the basic rules of fighting. And so, when the doctor shifted back and brought his foot up again, mechanisms whining and hissing, Jesse was out of position to block or avoid the kick. The heavy boot caught him in the side and battered him against the wall where he staggered, his hands tangling up with equipment hanging there, a knee fetching up painfully against a metal bench.

"I do apologize for the confining space, of course." Carpathian remarked calmly as he lashed out with two jabs and a cross that sent Jesse reeling back onto the bench as he tried to rise. "But then, mendicants must not be discriminating, as they say." His weighted foot came crashing cruelly down onto Jesse's instep.

Blood was dribbling from Jesse's mouth as he looked up at the doctor standing over him, a youthful smile out of place amidst the wrinkles and white whiskers. Jesse knew, with an infuriating twist in his gut, that Carpathian was letting him catch his breath before going at him again. It was that condescension, more than the pain or the fear or the frustration, which drove Jesse back to his feet. He roared at the doctor as his arms lashed in one after the other, landing body blow after body blow as the doctor tried to bring his elbows down to defend himself.

Jesse was beyond words, and so he merely grunted as he lashed out, his arms moving with cold strength and mechanical precision. Carpathian staggered back into the equipment on the other side of the compartment, his arms pulled close as he tried to protect himself from the enraged attacks. Finally, Carpathian managed to get a foot up, planted on Jesse's thigh, and pushed him back for just a moment. In that temporary reprieve, the doctor reached down for a small dark box that was lying abandoned on the floor.

A fist lashed out and caught the doctor on the chin, sending him back against the wall. If Carpathian wanted the box, Jesse did not want him to have it. He brought a metal elbow down on the back of the old man's head and stepped aside to avoid the falling body. The mechanical hands reached down and pulled both Hyper-velocity pistols from their holsters. As he lifted them up to brandish in the doctor's face, however, his eyes went round to realize that Carpathian was smiling gleefully, one hand wrapped around the little box.

"Drop the box, Doc, and I might leave you with your head." Jesse flicked the switches on his pistols with his thumbs and the power chambers burst into crimson life, glowing with a bloody illumination as a lacework of energy arced between them.

"Oh, Mr. James, I do find you so amusing. I hope we can continue to do business together in the future." And Carpathian's thumb came down on a small button in the middle of the box.

Jesse was about to open his arms and bring the pistol butts down on either side of Carpathian's head. Instead, his arms gave a sharp, painful jerk. A sudden snap of agony scorched down the feedback pathways to his brain. He gasped despite himself. A brutal, excruciating weight began to pull his shoulders down and he realized he could no longer feel anything from the feedback pads. The arms dropped like iron weights and he staggered back. His eyes rose in horror to Carpathian's vicious grin.

"Oh, Mr. James. As I said, you amuse me so." He slowly and methodically placed one boot on Jesse's chest and pushed him backward onto the bench. "Have a seat, do?"

Jesse tried to rise but could do nothing against the weight of the old man's boot. Tears of frustrated rage streaked his dirty cheeks.

"I can only assume you are coming after that little artifact your youthful compatriot stumbled upon in the wastelands?" The doctor shook his head. "Amusing as it might be to allow you primitives to run around the world for a time with such power, it does not, unfortunately, coincide with my long term plans. I would let you see it, however, I would hate for you to have gone through such exertions for nothing." He pursed his lips in a sad, disappointed frown. "Except I have already had my minions secure it for travel." He nodded to a niche in one armored wall where a wooden strongbox was secured to the bulkhead.

Jesse shook his head, barely able to form words around the storm of anger and frustration raging in his mind. "My friends—"

Carpathian threw back his head with a genuine laugh. "Your friends, Mr. James! Was it not trust in your friends that led you here? Was it not you friend William Bonney that left you for dead on that battlefield in the north, lying amongst your vilest enemies? Was it not your friends the Youngers that abandoned you in the very midst of that selfsame battle? You have singularly bad luck with friends, Mr. James. But then, what might one expect, when one entrusts themselves to the honor of outlaws?" He leaned in close to Jesse, a look of pity in his eyes. "Among you who disparage the very concept of honor, what honor can there truly be?"

"You – won't – I will come for you." Jesse's voice sounded plaintive, even to himself, but his pride demanded he speak in the face of those words.

"Oh, please, Mr. James. Don't you realize yet that we're all puppets, dancing to a tune we can't even begin to understand? Well. . . at least, that is what our fiery-eyed friends would like to think." He pulled a small pistol from his belt and casually pointed it at Jesse as he sat back against the far wall. "But only one man can ever be the smartest man in the room, is that not right, Mr. James?" He gestured with the pistol, smiling at Jesse's impotent rage. "And what, please tell me, are the chances that that man is you?"

Carpathian reached back and rapped twice against the forward bulkhead. Jesse could feel the rumbling movement of the wagon slow down and then subside as they came to a stop.

"Unfortunately, Mr. James, I have pressing business elsewhere, and I will have to now cut our pleasant discourse short." Carpathian stood and stepped aside as a large hatch swung open. Jesse could not keep his eyes from widening at the appearance of the animation that came crouching into the chamber. The thing was enormous, dead muscles bulging, rough stitching marking where large pieces had been added, bulking the creature up even further. Its face was nearly blank, as most animations, but a strange, hungry light illuminated its foggy eyes. A slight snarl twisted its slack features.

"Please see our guest out the back door, could you?" Carpathian gestured with his pistol toward the hatch in the rear bulkhead.

The animation lumbered ahead, crouching in the confines of the compartment, and grabbed Jesse by the shoulders.

"Carpathian, you best kill me if you don't mean for me to come back and end you!" Jesse's voice was shrill as he felt himself lifted off the seat and dragged backward. "If you leave me alive, I swear, you'll never survive my return!"

"Mr. James, I fully expect you to return." The doctor looked kindly as he peered around the shoulder of the giant animated corpse. "And I trust that your time in the desert will provide ample opportunity to reflect upon your place in the world, and your attitude toward your betters."

With a final nod from Carpathian, the monsters unlatched the rear hatch, swung it wide, and heaved the outlaw into the heat of the open desert.

Jesse grunted with the impact as he landed on his back in the burning sand, rocks digging through his jacket.

"Oh, have some water, my boy, in case you ventured out here unprepared!" Something struck the sand by Jesse's head and the metallic slosh of water in a canteen was audible over the growl of the great wagon.

"I trust we will meet again, Mr. James, in the not so distant future." Carpathian was resting an arm against the combing of the hatch as if chatting with a neighbor through a kitchen window. He waved the little black box in a gesture of farewell. "Good luck with the vultures!"

The old man's cruel laughter echoed from within the chamber as the hatch clanged shut. The wagon rumbled into motion once again. It began to crawl away, picking up speed with each passing moment.

Jesse rolled onto his stomach and struggled to rise to his knees. All coherent thought had fled from the rage rising within the hollow of his chest. A mad hatred surged through his burning throat and flared behind his burning eyes. Words failed him as he screamed formless curses at the retreating wagon, tilting his head farther and farther back until he was howling his fury up into the empty sky.

*****

Jesse would never be able to say how much time had passed as he lay on his back in the desert. His mind wandered along sharp and jagged paths of isolation and despair as his body succumbed to exhaustion, dehydration, and the loss of hope. Slumped into the dust and sand of the deep desert, Jesse James lapsed into unconsciousness, his pain the last tangible connection to the world around him as everything faded from a flashing bright heat into blackness.

Jesse's eyes fluttered open at the sound of a raucous barking sound not far away. He could see nothing.

He knew he must have fallen off his horse. The wound must have opened while he was riding. God alone knew how much blood he must have lost, slumped in his saddle, before losing his seat. He could not hear the horse nearby, and his sightless eyes rolled at the realization that he had to add a lost mount to his list of current difficulties.

Images rose up out of the darkness to swim before his twitching eyes, then went sinking once more from sight. He could make no sense of them. He saw his brother Frank, but as an old man, face wrinkled and eyes cold. He saw a woman he did not recognize in a dancehall costume, honey-brown hair flaring out around a sweet face as she flashed through the moves of a kick line dance, green eyes smiling at him the whole time. He saw a mysterious beauty, another woman, dark eyes flashing in a smile that threatened to stop his heart. He could feel, as if far away, a smile tugging at the flesh of his face.

Jesse tried to push himself upright in the darkness, but his body refused to respond. A dull, throbbing ache pulsated through his being. It was a pain that was not isolated to one part of his body, but rather radiated out through ever limb and nerve. His breath shortened, coming in shallow gasps, but everything still seemed terribly distant and vague. He felt himself easing back against the cool ground.

Another image rose before him, an old man, strange ironmongery attached to his face in some sort of nightmare combination of man and machine. He had long, white cheek whiskers and one eye was covered in a block of metal, a wide red lens flashing in the socket. Jesse's distant body tingled with cold sweat, but he could not have said why. He did not remember the strange old man.

The hoarse call sounded again, a hissing noise moving closer, but still Jesse's mind refused to focus upon it. He was lost in the swirl of images that raced around him. Cole Younger's face rose up, and a dull, brooding anger and vague sense of betrayal accompanied the image. Cole, too, seemed to have aged more than he should have, and an unpleasant pressure began to build within Jesse's mind.

With the anger, the images began to flash faster. A stranger's face swam up before him, distorted as if staring blankly at him from shallow water. The face blurred and was gone. He saw Frank, fear widening his eyes; the pretty dancehall girl, tears and blood mingling on her pale cheeks; the old man, laughing a silent laugh; a strange young man whose eyes flashed with an unnatural crimson glow. As this last face disappeared, disintegrating into the darkness with a cruel, savage smile, Jesse felt his eyes snap open again, but still only blackness met his gaze.

A face emerged then from the darkness that he did not know, although he felt he should. Another young man, about his own age, with a mischievous gleam in his laughing eyes. Despite his confusion, Jesse felt another surge of anger bubble up within him. His tortured mind refused to sit idly for further blows, and he heaved up, reaching for the unseen sky . . . with arms that did not move.

Jesse collapsed back to the gritty earth with a hoarse groan of pain that was answered by an indignant hissing grunt. What was wrong with him? Had he hurt himself further when he fell off the horse? He had a sudden image of a line of Union cavalrymen watching him fall. The blue-belly bastards! Had they done something to him? Tied him up, or worse, shot him again?

The young man's head jerked from side to side, fearing now that he had been blindfolded and hogtied by the hated traitors that had stood between him and his home. The parade of faces behind his eyes was forgotten as he wrenched at his body, trying to free himself from bonds he could not feel.

Finally, Jesse stopped struggling, his breath continuing to shake his body with its short, convulsive heaves. The angry hissing grunt sounded farther away, but his mind was completely submerged in a surge of fear and confusion that threatened to drown his distant body.

With a desperate heave, Jesse sat up, his arms awkward, useless weight. The first vague hint of movement came into focus nearby, and soon a sky full of stars swam into clarity above him. It was night, the cool of the nocturnal desert caressing his heated flesh. An outraged flutter nearby caught his attention and he whipped his head around to find an enormous black vulture sidling closer. Its head bobbed as it stalked toward him, staring at him from the corner of its vicious little eye.

With a cry, Jesse tried to scuttle away, only to fall abruptly onto his side as his arms refused to move. He hit the cold sand hard, squinting against the abrasive spray. He opened his eyes wide to stare at the inert hand lying before him, as unfeeling as if it belonged to another man. It was strange, that hand so close to his face. It was as if he could see through the flesh to the bones beneath, except there was no flesh, only the hard lines of dull iron, and the bones beneath seemed to be made of the same material. Where veins, tendons, and muscles should have been were strange dark tubes, wires, small, sleek barrels holding gleaming silver rods that slid in and out, and countless tiny wheels whose teeth fit together, spinning each other in a tiny, coordinated dance as the hand rocked slightly from his fall.

A cold spike of certainty and despair plunged into Jesse's mind. The wounded boy on that far away road in the distant past was instantly replaced by the seasoned, lawless rebel whose name had risen to dark prominence throughout the Wild West. In that moment, the memory of his traitorous arms came slashing back as well. His face twisted into a snarl of maddened rage as his sanity tottered once more on the brink.

Jesse grunted and growled like an animal as he tried to rise. His throat was raw, a pink foam flecking his lips as the memory of Carpathian's laughter squeezed the breath from his lungs. Jesse struggled back to his knees, warning the vulture away with a savage bark. He stared down at his motionless arms. He laughed with a bitter, twisted croaking. He was the big bug of the Wild West; the curly wolf every man envied and ever woman wanted. And he was reduced to a helpless, disfigured, pathetic wretch left to die alone in the middle of the desert wastes.

A long line of victims and dead companions rose up around him. Mute, haunted eyes stared down accusingly, mocking his helplessness with their cold, lifeless glares. He could not meet their illusory faces and bowed his head in defeat. When he looked up, the images were gone. He was truly alone, with the single, strange bird crouching nearby. All the visions and apparitions vanished in the cool desert night.

He remembered his confidence and ability with an empty, desolate chuckle. Everything he had done, everything he had accomplished, all the lives he had touched for good and for ill, and it all came to this, a lonely death in the middle of nowhere. The end of a line of betrayals any mooncalf idiot should have seen coming a mile away. He tried to think of the last time he had made a move on his own instead of reacting to others. Of working on his own initiative instead of racing to beat Billy to the next big caper, or taking Carpathian's advice on a job or score, or rushing off to prove himself to Frank, or Cole, or anyone else.

Jesse shook his lowered head. Carpathian was a foreign rat and a chiseler, but he had gotten one thing right: Jesse had spent too long dancing to someone else's tune. Without his arms, there was nothing he could do about it. He would die out here, and everyone in the wider world would know he had been a fraud all along. Worst of all, he was helpless to change that now.

He sat in the cold darkness, the wary vulture waddling back and forth nearby. Jesse was at first unaware of the twitching that sent the bird flapping back with a quick squawk. He looked dully puzzled down at the trailing fingers of his foreign hands only to see the metal digits twitch spasmodically. Each finger flexed much faster than a flesh and bone finger could have ever moved. Then the digits closed into two iron-hard fists.

When a violent pulse of pain ran up the metal arms and into his shoulders, he gasped again, falling backward. He reached back, out of a lifetime of reflex. To his surprise, the arms flashed back to catch him. A torment of rippling sensations roared up and down the limbs, but they responded when he pushed himself back onto his knees, and then steadied himself. Slowly he rose to his feet. The prickling feeling quickly faded, leaving Jesse standing tall on the sands, his arms crooked slightly at his sides, hands hovering over his gun belt. He turned his head slightly to glare at the vulture who had retreated further away as he stood.

"Looks like it's not my day to die, croaker." He gave the bird a twisted, bitter grin that faded quickly as it laughed a very human laugh, its eyes flashing with a crimson gleam. The ugly bird heaved itself heavily upward, wide wings pounding at the cold air. It sailed over his head and off into the dark sky, trailing the eerie laugh into the distance.

Jesse watched the bird fade into the darkness. A nearly overwhelming urge to draw and blast the filthy creature out of the sky set him to shaking, but somehow he knew it would not have done any good. He was half-sure it only existed in his mind.

Jesse looked back north to where clusters of wreckage still smoldered in the dry scrub grass, scattered over a mile behind him in the wake of Carpathian's giant wagon. Back that way, he would find Billy's camp, he knew. Thinking of the camp reminded him that the doctor had heaved a canteen out into the sand with him, and a quick search nearby turned it up. Jesse dove for it and had to use all of his power of will not to guzzle the cool liquid, letting it wash down his chest. He took a quick sip, sloshed it around his dry and scratchy mouth, and then spit it out to the side. Next he took a small sip and eased it down his tortured throat, wincing slightly as the water slid over the damaged flesh. He shook his head at the sweet pain and then tossed a little more back. Shaking the container, he knew he would just have enough to make it back to Billy's encampment.

The massive wagon's grinding wheels had left wide tracks across the desert and Jesse knew he could follow those as well. He looked down at one hand and tightened it into a metal fist. He could not face Carpathian now, knowing the old man could rob him of his arms at a whim. He looked back up at the stars overhead and sneered. Somewhere, he would find a way to deny Carpathian that ability. When that day came, he would come back for the old man and there would be a reckoning. No one would be playing a tune for Jesse James again.

But for now, he was still alone. Jesse's face sagged into a hopeless mask once more. Frank was gone. Without Carpathian's artifact, how could he persuade the Rebellion to stir itself from the swampy camps that had protected them for over a decade?

Jesse sank back to the sand, the canteen grasped in his mechanical arms, and stared down at his treasonous metal hands. The emptiness within rose up to devour him. It was more than Frank's absence, more than Billy's betrayal, beyond even whatever had happened with Misty. He was alone. Even the furious anger that had ridden beside him since he was a small boy had betrayed him. That rage, fixated upon the tyrannous north, had eaten away at his spirit and left a gaping hole behind. A hole that mocked the losses he had suffered since.

Lucy was right. Without a purpose, his life was a pointless dance of violence and petty revenge, not enough to justify an existence that threatened to go on forever.

He looked back at the wagon's trail, stretching down out of the north and into the distant south. The emptiness within called to him, and he rose once again to his feet, grinning as he decided at last to embrace it. He would carve his name across the flesh of the western territories in his quest for vengeance. He would exact the blood price from every opponent that had wronged him.

His mechanical hands flexed angrily, metal components sliding smoothly against each other, leather feedback pads creaking with the pressure.

He grabbed the straps of the canteen that had dropped at his feet. With a single look to the south, he turned around and began the long trek down his back trail. Somewhere over the rolling, dusty hills ahead, William Bonney and his hired hands were waiting. His face twisted into a death's head grin at the thought.

An Outlaw's Wrath

by

C. L. Werner

Prologue

Heat shimmered from the clay floor of the canyon. Weeds, withered and yellowed by the merciless sun, trembled in the desert wind. Buzzards circled in the cloudless sky, casting their sinister shadows across the rocky ridge rising at the back of the canyon.

Below the rise, nestled against its base, was a ramshackle bunkhouse, planks stripped from its roof by wind and rain, boards torn from the walls by the violence of beasts and men. A stone-lined well, its mouth covered with a piece of lumber, faced toward the building. Across from it was a simple corral with mud-brick walls and a small lean-to cobbled together from branches and thatch. A system of wood fences had once broken up the corral, separating an area for horses and a larger area for cattle. A jumble of iron rods rested against one of the walls, a collection of branding irons with complex and ponderous emblems: the sort of insignia that was condemned across the west as 'robber brands' for their ability to cover and obliterate legitimate marks of ownership.

No cattle milled about in the corral now. It had been several years since the market for steers had been lucrative enough to support large-scale rustling. The advent of RJ-1027 transformed the west, shifting the reins of power from the cattle-men and land barons to those who could provide the wonder-fuel and the mechanical marvels it could power. Where a string of fast horses and a herd of stolen cattle once stood, there were now just the cold steel bulk of machines glimmering in the sun. Iron Horses and Interceptors, vehicles that depended upon only the fabulous crimson ichor that had become the new life blood of the nation to power them.

"Polecats must have stolen them off a patrol somewhere," growled a low, gravelly voice. The speaker was a tall, spindly man. He was sprawled along the top of a shallow draw, lying on his belly as he studied the corral through a set of oversized field glasses. A soft hum and red glow emanated from the RJ cell fitted to the top of the glasses in order to provide the enhanced magnification properties of the lenses. "They haven't even bothered to melt off the Union insignia! Like the peckerwoods were proud of murder and theft!" The disgusted words came from a man whose somber black clothing almost lent him the air of a preacher. The effect was somewhat ruined by the silk cravat around his neck, the gilded electriwork hatband with its RJ-powered automations, and the double-holstered gun belt around his waist.

"Well, Billy's known for being the boastful type." The words came from a man in a grey felt hat; the gaudy carbine in his hands made a jarring contrast to the dull brown that dominated the rest of his attire. Richly engraved barrel, a stock fashioned from pearl, a scope that shone with the red glow of an RJ-powered amplifier, these were the signs of an ostentatious weapon only a renowned gunman would carry. There was scorn in the gunman's eyes as he watched the brown-garbed man. "You are familiar with how he gunned down Sheriff Brady? Just walked up to him in the middle of El Paso, in front of God and everyone, and cut the man in half with his blaster? I mean, you do know who it is you're after?"

The man wearing the cravat rolled over and scowled at the accusation. "Washington is quite aware of William Bonney's history, Garrett. You might not believe it, but we aren't so fool-all as to ride across half a continent without full knowledge of who it is we're looking for."

"And who is that, Charlie?" Garrett wondered. He jabbed a finger at the slope in the direction of the bunkhouse. "Because I'm betting Pinkerton didn't send you all this way just to tangle with a varmint like Billy. Who else do you think he's got in there, Charlie?"

"That's Agent Siringo to you, Pat," the detective snarled.

Garrett turned away, pacing past the pair of deputies and UR-30 Enforcers. The grimly silent automatons shifted their cyclopean heads to track the sheriff as he walked toward the group of operatives dispatched by Washington. "Who the hell do you think recommended you for that job, Charlie?" Garrett growled over his shoulder, not bothering to look back at Siringo. His attention was focused on one of the agents the Pinkerton-man had brought with him.

Garrett adopted his most ingratiating smile and tipped the brim of his hat as he approached the agents. He ignored the two men, concentrating on the woman who was with them. The sheriff had seen his share of femininity in his time, from governors' wives to barhall strumpets, but he didn't think he'd ever seen anyone so splendid as this girl from Washington. Even the mannish style of her outfit, from canvas breeches to waxed cotton overcoat, couldn't smother the appeal of her figure. The cold glint in her eyes and the Navy-pattern blaster holstered at her hip, however, could stifle any man's ardor.

"Miss Loveless, it seems the cat's made off with Charlie's tongue," Garrett stated. "Maybe you might like to tell me what I'm doing out here."

Lucinda Loveless returned Garrett's stare with an unflinching gaze. "Sheriff, you've been told all you need to be told," she said, her tone making it clear there would be no further discussion. "Whoever's down there, just know that your government wants them."

Garrett ripped his hat from his head, slapping it against his leg in disgust. "If that don't beat all!" he cursed. "What the hell do you think I am? Some hired hand?"

"If you don't like it, Sheriff, you could always turn in that badge," Loveless told him. "Or would that mean being taken off the Murphy-Dolan payroll?" A flicker of a smile crossed her face as she saw Garrett wince at the implication of corruption. "Just do your job."

Charlie Siringo crawled down from the top of the draw, brushing dust from his clothes. "The Kid's in there alright. Saw him at the window."

"Did you see him?" Loveless asked.

"Nope," Siringo answered, shaking his head. "But we know he was riding with the Kid."

Loveless pondered that for a moment, almost laughing at the idea of their quarry taking orders from an impetuous gunslinger like William Bonney. It was far more likely that the Kid had been the one following orders. "We'll have to act accordingly."

"How is that exactly?" Garrett demanded. He waved his hat at the deputies and robots, and then gestured to the corral. "Whoever's in there, they outnumber us almost two to one. And that's if nobody was riding double on them Iron Horses." He pointed at the cliff above the bunkhouse. "Don't forget they've got a lookout up there too. If it's the Kid in there, he'll have posted a good man too. We so much as raise our heads from this draw, they'll know we're coming. You need more men for this hoe-down."

Loveless snapped her fingers at the Pinkerton-men with her. One of the detectives marched over to her, removing the scabbard from a long-barreled energy rifle as he approached. The woman's gloved hand caressed the deadly instrument with an almost loving touch. Raising the gun, she pressed her eye to the telescopic sight. "The lookout won't be a problem."

"Your part, Pat, is to get one of these through that front door," Siringo said. A smooth black bomb was in the hand he held out toward Garrett. "It's an incendiary, something new cooked up by Tesla and his boys. Bonney will have the choice of surrendering or burning alive. Either way, he's out of your hair."

Garrett mulled that prospect for a second, imagining the bonus Murphy would pay him for eliminating the troublesome outlaw. "Bob, I have a job for you," he called over to one of his deputies.

Bob Olinger was a stocky, brutish man; his face looking as though a buffalo had trampled it. For all his roughness, there was a shrewd gleam in his piggish eyes. "Not for what you're paying, Garrett," Olinger replied, punctuating his statement with a hawk of spit.

The sheriff glowered at his defiant deputy, then turned to his other man. "Zeke, how about you? Or are you yellow like Bob here?"

The other deputy, a short, wiry thug with broad features and stringy hair, smiled at his boss. The gleam in his eyes wasn't one of cunning, but of greed. "Fifty dollars," he cackled. "Fifty dollars and I'll do it."

"Of all the low-down, conniving, feckless... It's your bomb, pay the man, Charlie." He grinned at the incredulous expression on the detective's face. "Or maybe get one of your expensive Washington boys to do it."

Grudgingly, Siringo reached into his vest and removed his billfold.

*****

Lucinda Loveless crawled into position at the top of the ridge. The long, lethal length of her rifle was wrapped in the dull material of her coat to hide the telltale gleam of metal. Her eyes roved across the top of the cliff, keen for the least suggestion of the Kid's sentinel. She'd only have one shot, but the prospect didn't bother her. There was a reason both Garrett and Siringo left this part of it to her – it was without question that she was the best shot in the posse. The rifle she carried was a specialized weapon designed for sharpshooters in the Union cavalry. It traded the brutal force of the typical blaster for extra range and precision, an exchange that Loveless preferred for this kind of work.

Garrett's deputy made his dash from the bottom of the draw, sprinting across the open ground toward the bunkhouse. As soon as he was clear, Loveless saw motion at the top of the cliff. Quickly, she whipped the rifle to her shoulder and squeezed the trigger. There was a sharp crack as the hot beam of energy leapt from the gun, stabbing upwards. The lookout pitched over as her shot slammed into him, searing through his throat. Soundlessly, the smoking body hurtled to the earth far below.

Zeke reached the wooden porch at a bound. In a final rush, he charged the front door, kicking it open with his boot and flinging the bomb inside. The deputy turned to make his retreat, but it was there that his luck finally ran out. A fusillade of fire erupted from the dark interior behind him, beams of scorching energy that shredded the lawman before he was more than a few yards. Bloody, smoking ribbons of humanity collapsed to the earth in a puddle of steaming entrails and shredded flesh.

An instant later, one of the outlaws appeared in the doorway, the bomb in his hand. Before the bandit could throw it, the incendiary detonated, saturating the porch and the wall with burning jelly. The outlaw himself was transformed into a shrieking torch, stumbling about in a paroxysm of agony.

"Billy!" Garrett shouted from the top of the draw. "This is Pat Garrett! You boys have got about five ticks to come out of that stove with your holsters down and your hands up!" The sheriff ducked as the face of the draw was peppered with shots from the bunkhouse. He looked over at Loveless. "Doesn't seem they're of a mind to surrender, does it?"

Loveless sighted down the scope of her rifle. A second beam of energy dropped the living torch, silencing the outlaw's screams. "Did you really think they would?"

Charlie Siringo and the other Pinkerton agents peeked over the top of the draw, smashing the facade of the bunkhouse with a withering barrage. Wood exploded and rock melted as the blasters delivered their lethal discharge. The agonized shrieks of an outlaw caught in the salvo rang out. The bandit's fate didn't stop the other men inside the hideout from returning fire. Molten flecks of dirt erupted from the rise as the outlaw guns scorched the ground into something closer to glass than sand.

"Sheriff, you'd better send the 'bots to keep them busy," Loveless called out to Garrett. The lawman looked ready to argue, but the icy gleam in her eyes advised him such an approach wouldn't benefit him.

Garrett reached inside his coat, removing the bulky Vocal Reiterator, a control mechanism used to maintain command over the robots from a distance. The UR-30 Enforcers were attuned to the timbre of his voice, and when he spoke into the electrical box, it rotated a different set of waxen command cylinders into activation inside the mechanism that served as the brain of each automaton. Garrett turned the hand-crank fitted to the side of the box, stirring its energy cell into full power. He flipped open the shutter-like grill that protected the bronze speaking tube fitted into the face of the box. A tug of his fingers brought the horn-like tube from the recessed cavity, a string of wires connecting it to the relay buried inside the Vocal Reiterator. Garrett blew into the tube, then tested its transmission by turning his back to the Enforcers and whispering into the control box. "Flank the target. Engage hostiles," the sheriff ordered. He watched as the two machines marched out from the shelter of the draw.

Near the top of the ridge, Loveless saw the outlaws react to the advance of the robots. One ruffian, with the dusky cast of a Mexican and the scruffy gear of a buffalo hunter, appeared in the burning doorway, snapping off shots from the hip with a cut-down carbine. The energy blasts seared the ground but the Mexican's aim was slovenly, missing the robots by a wide margin. With his homebrew customization of his weapon, the outlaw had increased its devastating power but at the expense of accuracy. In close quarters, the carbine could have melted straight through the armored core of each Enforcer, but at a distance he couldn't even hit the mark.

Loveless didn't give the Mexican the chance to close the gap. While he was still pumping shots from the hip, she sent a bolt from her rifle burning through his skull. The twitching carcass toppled backwards into the bunkhouse, eliciting fresh cries of alarm from the men inside.

The Mexican bandit wasn't the only gunman interested in the Enforcers. From a pair of windows on the side of the hideout, other blasters blazed away at the robots. Most of the shots failed to do more than set fire to the woolen uniforms draped about the automatons in a sorry effort to humanize their appearance. One shot, however, blazed through a robot's knee. The crippled Enforcer slammed to the ground, sparks crackling about its damaged leg. Pressing one steel hand against the ground, the 'bot hefted itself upright, shrugging off a blast that slammed into its chest, and a third that crackled across its shoulder and ignited the linen vest draped about the automaton's torso. Before further injury could be dealt to the robot, the concentrated fire from Garrett and his remaining deputy turned the offending window into a burning mass of splinters.

The other Enforcer reached its flanking position. Drawing its own pistols, the robot began raking the side of the hideout with a merciless flow of fire. More agonized wails from inside were testimony to the rapidly diminishing security afforded by the shattered, burning walls.

There was a crash from the side of the bunkhouse nearest the corral, followed by an outlaw leaping through a window, scurrying toward the array of vehicles. Siringo's men opened up on the bandit, but their nimble foe kept a pace ahead of the shots scorching the ground.

Loveless hesitated as she sighted down her rifle's scope. She felt a tremor of doubt tug at her. Only when she saw the man's pinched, pock-marked face, saw that the outlaw wasn't someone else, did she fire. Her shot sheared through the runner's leg, tumbling him into the dust.

"Go to Hell, Garrett!" a venomous voice shouted from within the bunkhouse. The next instant, the burning facade exploded outward as an Iron Horse came roaring through the front of the building. Loveless swung around, but again she felt herself hesitate. Only when she recognized the battered bowler with gold hatband of Billy the Kid did she fire. By then it was too late, the outlaw's mechanized mount was already speeding past the draw and out of the canyon. Her shot blackened the armored plate bolted to the front of the machine, shearing away a fist-sized blob of steel. The outlaw hunkered low in the saddle, juking his mount from side to side before vanishing beyond a bend in the canyon.

Garrett and Siringo were too busy cutting down the pack of robbers streaming toward the corral. Thinking to use the Kid's escape to cover their own bid for freedom, the outlaws were scrambling to reach their own Iron Horses. The fire from sheriff and operatives alike took a withering toll, turning the area between bunkhouse and corral into a bloody abattoir. In less than a minute, nearly a dozen men were splattered over the parched earth.

Loveless was the first to break cover. Discarding her rifle and drawing her pistol, she hurried down to the killing field. In rapid precision, she went from one savaged body to another, turning each onto its back. She knew the face she was looking for. She felt a strange sense of relief each time she failed to find it.

"Don't seem right," Garrett snarled as he came marching over to join her. The sheriff scowled down at a shapeless mass of burned flesh that had lately been a man. "Some of Billy's crowd had posters on them. I figure even without the Kid there was around two thousand dollars holed up inside there."

"I guess doing your civic duty is all the reward you can expect," Loveless said, flipping over another body with the toe of her boot.

"Any sign of our man?" Siringo asked as he came striding down from the ridge. Uneasiness had replaced arrogance in the agent's expression. For the first time since setting up the ambush, it seemed he was worried he'd made a mistake.

Garrett exploded at the question, spinning around and gesturing angrily at the Pinkerton-man. "If you mean Billy, he's already lit out! Just like that sidewinder to keep his Horse inside with him! I've lost a deputy and have a damaged 'bot and all I have to show for it is a bunch of carrion their own mothers wouldn't recognize!"

"Your government will make good your losses," Loveless told the sheriff as she started toward the burning hideout itself. She didn't have any worries about lurking gunmen. If anybody was still alive in there, the UR-30 Enforcer wouldn't have holstered its weapons.

"It sure will," Siringo agreed. A smile worked itself through his worry. "Just as soon as you dispatch all the proper forms to Washington. In triplicate."

Garrett's reply was both vicious and incoherent, involving Siringo's parentage and several feats of physical impossibility.

Loveless sighed at Siringo's attempt at humor. She could almost hear Henry Courtright, the agent she'd usually been paired with, saying something to that effect, only he'd have said it with more panache than Siringo. Overall, next to the brash Siringo, Henry was cultured and refined, positively cosmopolitan. He also had a better knack for getting his job done without upsetting the local law. She didn't know what secretive affair Henry had been detached to investigate, but she hoped it wouldn't be a lengthy diversion. Partnering with Siringo made her miss Henry's stolid presence.

Peering through the flames crackling about the hideout, Loveless tried to see the bodies strewn about the place. She counted eight men in the carnage, bringing the total to just under a score. By rights, it should be a resounding feat for the forces of law, order, and federal government. Instead it represented wasted time and resources. The man they wanted wasn't there, if he ever had been.

She didn't need to see the faces of the men inside the bunkhouse to know it either. In the shadowy gloom of the shack, his presence even in death would have been betrayed by the dull crimson glow of his augmetics, of the mechanical arms grafted to his body; the 'quick-devil' arms developed by the renegade Dr. Carpathian for the notorious Jesse James.

"He's not here," Loveless reported as she stalked away from the burning hideout. Siringo nodded grimly. He'd made some big promises to Washington. It'd been a big gamble, one that he'd lost. If he didn't find himself reassigned to the Alaska Territory he'd count himself lucky.

Garrett glowered at Siringo. "Last time, Charlie, who were you really up here gunning for?"

Loveless waved a warning finger in the sheriff's face. "For the last time, that's information the Sheriff of Presidio County doesn't need to know." The gunmetal chill in her gaze was such that Garrett quickly looked away, hurrying to chastise Bob Olinger as the callous deputy pawed through Zeke's remains in search of Siringo's fifty dollars.

"We'll find him," Siringo swore in a low whisper after Garrett was out of earshot.

The statement sent a quiver through Loveless. The certainty of that fact was beyond doubt. The Union had resources to ferret out a hundred needles in a thousand haystacks. It wasn't a question of if they found Jesse James, simply a matter of when.

What happened then, that was the real question. One that Loveless no longer felt comfortable trying to answer.

Chapter 1

With chiseled features, broad shoulders, and a smooth smile, Jim Younger was accustomed to the attentions of the fairer sex. Whether he was sitting in a church pew or striding through the batwing doors of a saloon, he was sure to turn a few feminine heads. Even those twenty some odd years ago during the war when he rode with Colonel Quantrill, Jim'd always been able to whistle up a companion to while away a lonely night. Since then, there was hardly a town west of Kentucky that was without a woman he'd been friendly with. More than a few of those liaisons had ended with Jim skedaddling out a back window or dueling some outraged husband. Such complications were simply part of life, the spice of danger that made the encounters all the more thrilling.

Enforced isolation was something that came much harder to Jim. It made his body subject to nervous tics, his attitude to become surly, and his temper to be somewhere between that of a badger and a rabid wolverine. Most men stepped lightly around him when he was in such ill humor, warned off by the malignant curl of his lip and the ugly gleam of light in his eye.

"You're going to wear them cards out if you keep staring at them." The lean man sitting across the table affected an indulgent grin as he baited the discomfited outlaw. It wasn't ignorance of Jim's smoldering temper that made him prod the bushwhacker, but rather contempt for the man's ire born of long familiarity.

Jim Younger pounded his palm against the table.

"Now I know those cards you're holding ain't worth a spit in Hell," his adversary quipped, running a thumb across his moustache. "Guess you didn't find any ladies in the deck either?"

"Leave it be, Cole," the admonition came from a spare young man straddling a bench across the room. He set down the bit of wood he'd been whittling at with a large Bowie knife, favoring the two card players with his full attention. "I don't understand why in tarnation you always have to needle him like that."

Cole Younger leaned back in his chair, careful to keep his cards facing inward as he waved his hands in a helpless gesture. "Brotherly devotion. I can't stand to see any of my little brothers being led into distraction." He leaned forward again, letting his elbows rap against the edge of the table and rattle the gold eagles sitting in the pot. "Shoot, Luke, or give up the gun," he told Jim. The other bushwhacker glared daggers at his eldest brother.

"Women are a distraction, but robbing banks is respectable?" the whittler asked. His eyes darted from Cole to the fourth man in the room, a youth who was little more than a boy. Seated on a stool behind the shack's only window, he was keeping his young, sharp eyes trained on the trail leading up to the building. It was little more than a dirt track, a goat path that even an Indian would think twice about using, but Cole had given him orders to keep a steady watch.

Cole scowled over his cards. "Bob's grousing about us robbing banks, Jim. What do you make of that?"

"We're robbin' Yankee banks," Jim snapped. "Ain't like we were takin' money from decent folk!"

Bob Younger sighed. He slid the knife he'd been whittling with back into its sheath. "I know." Again his eyes strayed to the youth sitting at the window. "Somehow it just don't seem right no more."

Jim slammed down his cards and came to his feet. "Devil hang what's right! Yankees killed Pa and them blue-belly bastards are gonna pay for that, so long's there's a Younger with a lick of life left in him!"

Color rushed into Bob's face. "You think you have more cause to hate them blue-bellies than me? While you were out raising Cain with Quantrill, I was in Kansas City when they gunned down Pa like a sick dog. I was the one who brung him home to be buried only to have Jayhawkers pitch his body into a ditch and burn down our farm!"

Cole rose from his seat, interposing himself between his two brothers. "Hell, wasn't much of a hand anyway," he observed with disgust as he tossed his cards on the table. Sternly, he eased Jim back into his chair, then turned and faced Bob. "He didn't mean that. You know he's on the prod when he's put out to pasture this long. We're all a bit on edge since the split. A nice, juicy mine payroll and things won't look so bleak."

"You have the next job all laid out, Cole?" The exuberance of the question brought an indulgent smile to the man in question's face.

"I told you to keep your eyes on that window," Cole said, taking it for granted that the youngest member of their band had allowed his excitement to entice him away from his post.

Bob pointed to the enthusiastic youth. "That's what I'm talking about. You, me, Jim, we're used to this. It don't seem right to bring John into it."

"He's just as much stake in this as any of us. It was his father they murdered. His farm they burned. His state they stole." There was reproach in Cole's tone as he spoke. "The few years you've got on him don't make it right he should tuck tail and crawl back to Missouri. Feed pigs and mend fences for some carpetbagger on land that should be his."

Bob gripped his eldest brother's arm. "He's the last chance for us, Cole. Last chance for the Youngers to be respectable. He hasn't killed nobody yet. Let him get out before he does." Bob could see his words weren't having any impact, so he tried a different tact. "You know he's started favoring a cross-belly draw? Started calling himself 'Kid' Younger?"

Cole frowned. "He can call himself what he likes, just so long as he minds himself who's 'Boss' Younger."

"Cole!" John cried out suddenly. The youth leapt up from his stool, half-raising his rifle. "Somebody comin' up the trail!"

"Kid makes a good lookout," Cole smiled at Bob before turning toward the excited John. "Don't put a hole in him until you know what he is. It ain't respectable."

John pressed close to the glass, peering intently at the figure he saw approaching. "One man riding an Iron Horse. Looks like somebody knocked the stuffing out of it. Ain't moving so good."

Jim Younger pushed away from the table, fingering the guns he wore. "Sounds like a star-packer. I told you I should have gone with Potts and Danby for the supplies."

Cole shook his head. "I want to eat, not wait around a few days until you dry up your credit with the box herders." He smiled coldly. "If Potts and Danby did get in some trouble, obviously they didn't tell nobody who it was holed up in here."

"How do you figure that?" Jim growled.

Cole stared back, wondering if Jim's wits had become addled by isolation. He rose to his feet and patted the leather of his gun holster. "Who in their right mind sends one man to bring in the Younger Gang?"

At the window, John gave vent to a Rebel yell, whooping as he danced away toward the door. "The James-Younger Gang!" he hollered as he flung open the door and dashed outside. Cursing, Bob and Jim hurried after him, blasters clenched in their fists.

Calmly, unhurried, Cole went to the window and looked out. "So much for a good thing," he grumbled as his eyes focused on the lone rider. Scooping up the gold coins from the table, he stepped outside to join his brothers.

The rest of the Youngers were fanned out between the cabin and the trail. Jim's arms were crossed, a pistol gripped in each leathery fist. Bob kept a hand close to his holster, his attitude one of wary attentiveness as his eyes scanned the craggy hills to either side of the trail. John was anything but cautious, his entire body quivering with excitement.

The Iron Horse slowed and stopped a good dozen yards from the men. The machine's hull was battered, its left side disfigured by an enormous dent. Red phosphorescent liquid drooled from its undercarriage, mute evidence that its fuel system was compromised. A smell of ozone crackled from its engine and as it powered down, a sputtering wail rattled through the vehicle.

Cole appeared on the cabin's porch just as the Iron Horse shuddered to a stop. He nodded toward the conveyance. "If that thing had legs, it'd be on the last of 'em."

The rider dismounted from his damaged vehicle. He was a tall, broadly built man, his body draped in the somber folds of a brown linen duster. A wide-brimmed leather hat covered his head, casting his face in shadow. It wasn't necessary to see his face to know who he was, however. The sleek metal arms fixed to his shoulders proclaimed his identity louder than any face. Those arms had become infamous throughout the west, the widow-makers that could snatch a blaster from its holster faster than lightning. A string of corpses from Missouri to California could attest to the lethal precision that guided those mechanical killers, the unerring marksmanship that had been honed on the bloody battlefields of Kansas.

Jesse James, the most wanted man in the Union, the most ruthless robber and bandit in the whole of the west.

"It got me where I need to be," Jesse said as he looked up toward the cabin.

There were a lot of things that ran through Cole's mind as he met Jesse's stare. They'd served together in Quantrill's Raiders throughout the war. They'd ridden with Archie Clement together, robbing Yankee banks in Kansas and Missouri. After that gang broke up, Jesse had been the center of a new gang and Cole was among his very first recruits. From the bayous of the south to the plains of the north, they'd earned themselves the reputation as the most notorious outlaws in the country. They'd been in more gunfights than he could remember, killed more sheriffs than small pox. Pottersonville, Fidelity, Franklin, all those towns had earned their part in the lore of the west when Jesse James and his men descended upon them. The double-bank heist in Dodge was still the subject of dime novels. Two banks at the same time, and with twenty regulators guarding the vault that held the season's proceeds of the Stockton Cattleman's Society and Trust. Not to mention, Cole counted Jesse's brother Frank as his best friend in the world. He knew there wasn't a braver, bolder man to have as a comrade in arms. At the same time, Jesse was headstrong, impulsive, and prideful; qualities that Cole had tried his best to restrain himself after taking on the mantle of leadership and the responsibility of taking care of his brothers. A leader needed to be careful and calculating, not rambunctious and flighty. Since the accident that had removed his real arms, Jesse'd also developed an ugly vein of temper, a propensity toward violence that bordered on sadism at times. All things told, Cole had more reason to resent than welcome the notorious gunslinger.

Reason, however, wasn't something that applied once a man felt Jesse's eyes on him. There was an innate charisma, a natural magnetism about Jesse James that compelled a man regardless of careful planning and common sense. Jesse was like a force of nature, terrible and irresistible - even when your name was Cole Younger.

"You can stop eyeballin' them hills for hidden marshals," Cole told Bob and Jim. "Any lawdog who got his hands on Jesse James would hardly risk his blood money bringing in the likes of us."

Bob nodded and strode toward Jesse. Still nursing his distemper, Jim merely stood his ground and watched.

John dashed ahead of Bob, wearing a wide smile and uttering another celebratory whoop. "Jesse James!" he crowed. "The Jesse James!"

Jesse stared past the boy, removing his crimson-tinted goggles and directing his attention to Bob. "Who's this one?"

"You remember our little brother? Once we set up here, John came out from Missouri to join up." Bob laughed and wagged a finger at his brother. "Calls himself 'Kid Younger' these days. Wants to be the terror of the territories."

Jesse cast an appraising eye over John. "Find a new moniker. I'm not too fond of 'Kids' at the moment." He turned away and started marching toward the cabin.

"Things go sour in Diablo Canyon?" Cole called out.

Jesse glowered up at the bushwhacker. "Might have gone less sour if'n the Youngers had stuck around. Law showed up the day after you lit out."

"I didn't know there was any law around Diablo Canyon," Cole snarled back. "You think I'd have left compadres in trouble like that and just moseyed off on my own? Hell, if'n you think that, we'll slap leather right now. Don't matter none if'n those arms of yourn are fast as quicksilver. I ain't gonna stand fer that kind of insult." Cole's face twisted into a sneer when he saw the fire in Jesse's eyes. "If'n you're so fool-all stupid to believe that of me, then maybe I'd better talk to Frank. He was always the smart one anyway."

Mention of Frank James caused Jesse to stand stock-still. Cole could see the gunman's shoulders sag as though some great weight was pressing down upon them. The fire he'd seen in Jesse's eyes drained away, all the angry strength of a moment before evaporating in the desert sun.

Jesse was close enough that Cole could see the pinched, drawn visage hiding in his hat's shadow. He could see the lines of pain etched into those lean features, the wince of agony that pulled at his mouth every time he had taken a step. More, he could see the hollow emptiness in the outlaw's eyes, the haunted look of a man whose suffering goes far deeper than flesh and bone.

"Things went bad," Jesse said, his voice hollow and empty. "Leave it at that."

"That's a tall order," Cole said. "When you and Frank lit out, you were full of talk about a big payout. You want to waltz back in here and build back the gang, might be some of that loot should be ours."

In a blur, Jesse's arm came whipping up, snatching at Cole. Halfway to the bushwhacker's throat, the metal limb froze, the fingers flexing like the talons of a buzzard. "There weren't no payout," Jesse growled. "Just a pack of lies and liars." He glanced away from Cole, staring instead at his extended arm. A look of cold fury blazed in his eyes as he stared at the mechanical limb. His face contorted in pain as he rolled his shoulder and brought the arm slowly down to his side.

"I need to rest," Jesse said, brushing past Cole. "I'm gonna hole up here for awhile. I'm sure you don't mind." He paused as he opened the door. "Frank's dead," he said, his voice a low, anguished whisper. Without giving Cole a chance to say one word, Jesse started into the gloom of the cabin.

"What do you mean 'Frank's dead'?" Cole demanded. He caught Jesse by the shoulder, cringing at the cold feel of the steel augmetics beneath his hand. "How?"

"Blue-bellies got him after you lit out," Jesse said, his voice as cold and hollow as the steel shoulder under Cole's hand. "A Yankee patrol just outside Diablo Canyon. They got Frank. Didn't even leave me enough chance to fetch back his body." He slipped free from Cole's grip, not by brushing him off, but simply by shrugging clear. His eyes, as they stared at Cole, were absolutely empty. "I had to leave him there, with them damn blue-bellies."

Words caught in Cole's throat. He didn't know what to say. Except for John, they'd all ridden the outlaw trail long enough to know what became of a dead gunfighter like Frank James. The body would be put on display somewhere so that yokels could gawk at it and the law could crow about how mighty powerful it was and how nobody was beyond its reach. Depending on how much hate there was in the sheriff or marshal, they might even let some of the locals take bits of clothing as souvenirs. The more sadistic might even let them cut bits off the body. Archie Clement's trigger finger was said to be in a bottle of preserves in Kansas City and there was still a cantina out California way exhibiting the mangled hand of Three Finger Jack, old Joaquin Murrieta's lieutenant.

The idea of Frank ending up like that was something to make the blood boil. Feeling that rage building up inside him, Cole recognized the magnitude of Jesse's hurt. Losing his brother had drained everything out of Jesse, leaving him as cold and lifeless as Carpathian's arms. He was too empty to hate, too filled with pain to think about revenge. He might be back among friends, but he was still as alone as though he were the last man in the world.

"Anything you need, Jesse?" Cole asked.

The barest flicker of a smile was the only show of emotion Jesse made. "Just a place to hole up for a time, and the time to clear my head." He stared into Cole's eyes, acknowledging the concern he saw there. "Just let me lie for a bit," he said, turning to withdraw into the cabin.

Cole stared after the departed outlaw, digesting everything he'd seen and heard. He wondered if the shot that had killed Frank James hadn't done for Jesse as well.

"In all my born days, I ain't never seen no man so big!" The statement came from John as the boy scrambled up onto the porch. Cole directed a sour look at the youth's enthusiasm.

"Boy, you sure go whole-hog, don't you?" Cole scowled. "You're supposed to be my kid brother, not Jesse James'!"

John stepped down from the porch, a sheepish expression of apology on his face. "I didn't mean nothin'. It's just, well, that's Jesse James!"

Sighing in disgust, Cole turned his attention to his other brothers as they returned to the cabin. The germ of an idea was starting to form. The best thing for Jesse right now was to heal up, let the hurt settle a bit. After that, he'd need to be busy, keep his mind from dwelling on Frank and leaving him behind. Cole knew exactly how to keep Jesse busy and at the same time make the Youngers a lot richer. "Have a look at his 'Horse?" he asked Jim. "Does it look like it can be salvaged?"

"Might be we could fix 'er up," Jim said, "but I wouldn't like to bet my stake on it."

Cole frowned. Getting new equipment of that sort would mean tangling with lawmen or Union troops, circumstances that always involved high risk. "Keep a good watch on ours then," he told Jim. "Jesse's welcome to stay a spell, but if he gets the notion to rustle one of our 'Horses, he's gonna find out in a hurry that the Youngers ain't nobody's boot-licker!" He jabbed a finger at John. "That includes you. I didn't shoot no regulator just so's you can give your 'Horse away."

"Jesse won't like that," Bob pointed out.

"Jesse be damned," Cole growled back. "I'm runnin' this outfit." His expression darkened. He was remembering all the good times he'd had with Frank James. Frank had been a man cut from the same cloth as Cole, a careful planner and shrewd thinker. Whatever trouble had put him in a boot orchard, he was certain that it was Jesse's impetuousness that brought it about. Frank'd never been able to shrug off his little brother's charisma, even as a kid he'd allowed Jesse to talk him into the most fool-all ventures.

"We ain't been doing so good, Cole," Jim stated. "Might be Jesse's got some ideas to turn that around."

Cole slapped his hand against one of the beams supporting the awning above the porch. "Sure he's got ideas. One of his ideas put Frank in the ground. Bad enough he got his brother killt, I ain't gonna see one of mine dropped into a grave patch. He wants to stick around; he'll start listenin' to me."

"Jesse'll have something to say about that," John declared, squaring his shoulders in a brazen show of defiance. "He's too big to be takin' orders from a two-bit border ruffian..."

Again Cole's hand slammed against the post, this time with enough force to knock little streams of dust from the awning. "Gettin' a lot of sass, boy. Keep it up and big brother'll be fetching a switch to your hide." The threat brought John a pace nearer, one hand closing about the grip of his pistol. Cole arched an eyebrow when he saw the menacing gesture. "Us Youngers done a lot of bad things, but we ain't yet drawed on kin." The anger drained out of the youth, replaced with a crimson flush of shame. Cole grinned and clapped his little brother on the shoulder. "I said it afore, you got brass, kid."

Bob breathed a sigh of relief as he watched his brothers reconcile. Still, there was a nagging worry in his expression. "John's right, Cole. What'll we do about Jesse?"

"There's a fire gone out of him," Jim said, shaking his head sadly. "Don't even seem like the same man. Like somebody just went and scooped out his innards."

John rounded on his brother. "You callin' Jesse yeller?" he demanded, one hand clenched into a fist.

"He's sayin' the heart's gone out of Jesse," Bob said, trying to keep tempers from flaring up again. "Frank's death is bound to have tore him up inside. Imagine what'd be like for us if Cole was gone."

The three brothers looked to the eldest Younger. Cole had a pensive expression. He was thinking about this reunion with Jesse, pondering it like a preacher might ponder a passage of scripture. He was careful about putting what he thought into words until he was certain there was some veracity behind them.

"There's somethin' wrong with them quick-devil arms of his. I could see it in the way he moved." Cole nodded his chin toward the Iron Horse. "Maybe his 'Horse weren't the only thing got shot up."

"You thinkin' Jesse needs doctorin'?" Bob wondered.

"Nope," Cole stated. There was a cunning gleam in his eye. "I think he's just fine way he is. If them arms of his are givin' him problems, he'll be easier to handle. More apt to listen to reason."

John grabbed Cole's arm. "But if he's hurt, we gotta help him."

"Hardly," Cole answered, pulling away. "When Jesse started focusin' on chasin' tall tales, he cut his string with us. We ain't under no obligation to him now." He nodded pensively. "We do right by the Youngers first."

"What you got in mind, Cole?" Bob asked.

Cole glanced over his shoulder at the darkened cabin behind him. "I've got a few jobs in mind, but we'll need more men. Good men, not buckaroos like Potts and Danby." A foxlike smile spread across his face. "Right people hear we've got Jesse James behind us, we'll get all the guns we could ask for." He jabbed a thumb at the cabin. "See Jesse stays put," he ordered as he stepped down from the porch.

"Where are you goin'?" Jim demanded.

Cole paused in his march to the barn where the gang's Iron Horses were stashed. "Tombstone. I'm gonna look up Ringo. He's been runnin' with the Clantons last I heard. I'll see if him and his pals might be interested in doing some work with the Younger

Gang."

"The James-Younger Gang," John corrected him.

"Yeah," Cole grumbled as he swung open the barn door. "The James-Younger Gang." It hurt his pride to admit it, but he needed the bandit's fame to work things the way he wanted. For most of the outlaws of the west, the name of Jesse James was like a sacred banner waving up on high. Ringo might balk due to his loathing of Jesse, but he was kin to the Youngers, and Cole knew he'd never be turned away by his cousin. For the rest, he'd use Jesse's notoriety, play it out to the last card to bring them onboard. It might be a gamble, but the rewards were too big to pass up.

His Iron Horse growling beneath him, Cole Younger emerged from the barn and set out on the long ride to Tombstone and his cousin, the notorious Johnny Ringo.

*****

John Younger stood in the doorway to the back room Jesse James had taken for his own. It had been Cole's room, but any amusement John might have felt at his eldest brother's expense was stifled by his concern for the man now lying sprawled across the bed.

Despite the assurances of Cole, John wasn't so certain about the severity of Jesse's wounds. The outlaw's flesh had a ghastly pallor and perspiration beaded his brow. Jesse's breathing came in ragged gasps and several times an inarticulate cry rattled past his lips. Jim and Bob both claimed that this was usual for Jesse, that the mechanical arms Dr. Carpathian had fitted him with often provoked bad dreams and fitful sleep. It was the price, they claimed, for his supernatural speed and reflexes. Nothing came without a cost; not even the medical miracles of the so-called Enlightened.

John wasn't convinced. As he watched his idol sleeping, he felt a growing sense of anxiety and frustration. The callousness of his older brothers toward this man they'd rode with and fought beside made him feel guilty. Standing by while this man he admired, this unrepentant rebel who'd become a hero to the Secesh of Missouri, suffered, was a thing that made him ashamed.

Hang what Cole said! His older brothers were a damn sight too cautious. They were too afraid that if they went someplace to fetch a doctor for Jesse that they'd be recognized! Well, the Devil could take their timidity! The faces of Cole, Bob, and Jim Younger might be well known, posted to marshals and sheriffs across the territories, but John hadn't earned the same notoriety. He could slip into a town without drawing any notice; do what his brothers were afraid to do.

The boy nodded his head as he made his decision. He'd heard Potts talk about a sawbones in San Diablo who was a wonder-worker when it came to knife wounds and blaster burns. Well, then Doctor Fletcher would have his chance to show off his skill! John would ride out and fetch him, bring him back to work on Jesse!

John stared at the unconscious Jesse, his eyes drinking in the image of the prostrate outlaw, letting the picture of his infirm hero sink into his mind. Whatever lay ahead of him, the knowledge that Jesse was depending on him would spur him on. He wouldn't let him down.

Quietly, wary lest the slightest sound alert Bob and Jim to his intentions, John crept out of the cabin and made his way to the barn. It took him the better part of an hour to accomplish the arduous task of pushing the dead bulk of his inert Iron Horse far enough down the trail as to be out of sight of the cabin. It was a Herculean task. Before he had gone more than a couple of yards, the boy's shirt was soaked in sweat, his face scarlet with the strain of his exertions, his palms blistered where they pushed against the dead bulk of the machine. Soon, the muscles in his arms began to feel as though they were on fire, shivers of pain pulsing from them to infect every inch of his body. Fatigue dragged at him, the breath that he sucked down into his gasping lungs burned and tormented, perspiration dripped into his eyes and cascaded down his neck. The outlaw's body begged him to relent, to abandon this impossible task he had set himself. He resisted the pleas of his abused body, forced himself onward with imperious resilience. Jesse was depending on him, and the boy wasn't going to let his hero suffer because of his own weakness. Only when he was certain his brothers couldn't see him did John activate the machine. In that moment, the thrill of prevailing at the end of his ordeal washed away his exhaustion, the raw exhilaration of victory energizing him even more fiercely than the RJ fuel in his 'Horse.

Shouting a Rebel yell, the young bandit rode off into the darkening night.

*****

Lucinda Loveless presented a far more comely appearance sitting in the Territorial Governor's office than she had crawling in the rocks outside Billy the Kid's hideout. Her long tresses were plaited and piled atop her head, vibrant ribbons of lace holding the complex arrangement of hair in place. A flowing gown of silks and satins clung to her shapely frame, accentuating each curve with the most lascivious detail. Powder hid the dark tan her skin had acquired on the long trail while expensive Parisian perfume blotted out the acrid stink of RJ.

Behind the sprawling mahogany desk, Governor Lew Wallace smiled at his attractive guest, extending a teakwood cigarette case toward her. A graceful twist of her hand retrieved one of them from the velvet-lined box. The governor leaned forward with a pearl-inlaid lighter, its tiny RJ-1027 furnace glowing with an infernal crimson light as it ignited the cylinder of tobacco.

"There was one thing the Secessionists knew how to do: they knew a proper blend of tobacco," the bearded governor proclaimed as he returned the lighter to the brass holder sitting on the desk. "This weed from Hispanola simply doesn't have a civilized flavor. It smells of swamp and malaria and the old tyrannies of the Spanish Dons. " He drew a breath from his own cigarette, frowning at the taste of the smoke. "It is keenly to be desired that the Midlands be restored to the Union and we can see about cultivating a decent tobacco leaf again. If Grant would only consider dispatching a division or two to install a territorial governor in the old Carolinas, the matter would be quickly rectified."

"The Secessionists still pose a problem, governor," Loveless observed. "There are still considerable..."

"Rabble, nothing more," Wallace declared with a wave of his hand. "But for the outrages of the Warrior Nation, General Grant would have cleansed this Union of all rebel elements. Instead we must be content with containing the remnants while we attend to these savages."

"And these marauding outlaws, governor. Do not forget them." The speaker was a middle-aged man with a thin moustache, his trim suit screaming of New York and its expensive clothiers. He didn't wear any weapons openly, but the bulge under his coat betrayed the presence of at least one shoulder holster. "Day by day they grow more bold and ruthless. Frankly, Washington is finding them an embarrassment. Their crimes make the whole country look barbaric and uncivilized. We will never impress the crowned heads of Europe while their newspapers recount gunfights in the streets of El Paso and hold-ups on the Union-Pacific."

Lew Wallace darted a venomous look at the man. The barb about Europe coupled with a reminder about the lawlessness in El Paso had been thrust at the governor with all the cruelty of a Bowie knife. Wallace had risen to his posting as Governor of Texas Territory especially because it was felt the former general could reign in the outlaw elements and lingering Secesh attitudes until such time as the region could be partitioned off into smaller, more manageable states and territories. His true aspirations, however, were to achieve a position as American ambassador to one of the European courts.

Wallace appreciated exactly how precarious his posting really was. When he'd accepted the position as Governor of Texas Territory, he'd been led to believe the land was firmly in Union hands. Nothing could be farther from the truth. Bands of Warrior Nation marauders were a constant threat, massacring entire communities before vanishing back into the trackless wilds from which they emerged. The forces of the Confederate Rebellion were a persistent menace, slipping across the Mississippi to raid for supplies and assassinate Union soldiers. Close to the frontier between the borders of Texas and the region claimed by Dr. Carpathian and his Enlightened, there had been numerous incidents involving bio-mechanical abominations that had either escaped from or been loosed by the sinister cabal of scientists and inventors. The southern border was always menaced by the Golden Army of Mexico and the potential for further violence with those fierce legions.

To all of these threats, Wallace had to add the depredations of the outlaws. Texas Territory played host to the most infamous criminals in the nation. The Wild Bunch and the Daltons, the Rufus Buck Gang and the Burrow Brothers, all of them had chosen the wide expanses of Texas for their hunting ground. To their numbers had to be added the James-Younger Gang and, more recently, the murderous Billy the Kid. The other malcontents menacing the area were forces of such magnitude that the solution to dispatching them would require federal resources. The outlaw bands, however, were something his superiors in Washington expected Wallace to resolve with the assets already at his disposal. If some progress wasn't forthcoming, some example that would impress upon the still-rebellious population of Texas that the Union was firmly in control of their country, the governor's political career would crash in flames.

"Your agents, Mr. Pinkerton, had their chance to bring down Billy the Kid," the governor declared. He'd long ago decided that of the two, Billy was the target to focus upon. His was a name that would carry weight in Washington, but at the same time he didn't have the experience and resources of the more established outlaws. Wallace tapped his fingers against a stack of papers. "I have Sheriff Garrett's full report right here. He places the blame for the Kid's escape on your man, Charlie Siringo." Wallace bowed his head apologetically to the woman seated across from him. "I fear he also mentions you, Miss Loveless."

Loveless took a long draw from her cigarette. "Billy is only a symptom. Jesse James is the disease. Once he... once he is apprehended this wave of outlawry will come to an end."

"You will forgive me, Miss Loveless, but my constituents are more worried about Billy the Kid. Removing the menace this crazed gunfighter poses the people of Texas will impress upon them far more keenly that the Union is here to help and protect them from these lawless elements."

Pinkerton smiled at the governor. "I was unaware your sense of civic responsibility ran so deeply. Perhaps I should inform Washington that General Longstreet should assume the position of Minister Plenipotentiary to the Ottoman Empire?"

Wallace leaned back, stubbing out his cigarette in a marble ashtray. One glance at Pinkerton told the governor that the agent was fully aware of his fears regarding the precarious state of his political future, should one of the many threats hanging over Texas Territory suddenly explode into full-blown warfare. "What is it that Washington would like me to do?"

"Post a reward for Jesse James," Loveless stated.

"That's been done before. I believe the reward currently stands at $5,000."

"Yes," she agreed, "but this time in addition to the reward, you will offer amnesty. Complete exoneration for all past crimes."

The governor shook his head. "That would be condoning murder. The people would never stand for it."

"The people will stand for what Washington tells them they will stand for," Pinkerton retorted. "The only way we're going to catch this man is by getting the scum he associates with to turn on him. That won't happen if they think there's a necktie party waiting for them if they come in."

Wallace drummed his fingers against the desk, still shaking his head. "It's an affront to law and decency," he declared.

Loveless stared into the governor's eyes. When she spoke, her tone was sympathetic yet firm. "Think of all the havoc these men will do if Jesse isn't brought in. We can't think of past crimes. We have to prevent new ones."

"Yes," Pinkerton agreed. "Don't dwell on the past. Think of the future. Think of Istanbul and the Sultan's court."

It was a visibly shaken governor who made his apologies a few minutes later, claiming a sudden illness prohibited him from attending his guests further. There was certainly a drain of color about the man as he bowed himself out and retired to his quarters.

"He'll do it," Pinkerton predicted as he escorted Loveless from the governor's palace. "Grant knew exactly who they were putting in charge down here. A man bold enough to follow orders but not brave enough to stand on his own. It might take his conscience a few days to come around, but in the end we'll get what we want. When he does, every paper in the country will carry notice of the amnesty offer."

Loveless shuddered under the heavy wrap she'd adopted against the chill night air. The darkening twilight was broken by the sputter of automated lamps. Much of San Antonio remained an isolated backwater, a confusion of narrow dirt streets that hadn't been improved since the days of Mexican rule, but the immediate vicinity of the palace of the governor sported the latest in the way of eastern technology and improvement. As the lamps burst into brilliance, bats swooped down to attack the congregating swarms of moths.

"How long do you think before somebody turns him in?" Loveless's question came in a flat, emotionless tone, giving no hint to the strange flutter that twisted her stomach into a knot.

Pinkerton paused, scratching his chin as he contemplated the answer. "If he's keeping to the company of Missouri border trash, we might be in for a long wait. But if he's playing around with malcontents like Bonney, we could hear something within a few days of the announcement. There's no honor among thieves, you know, and most of these outlaws don't even feign the justification of being Secesh for doing what they do."

"They'll want to get him alive," Loveless stated. "Find out how closely he's working with Lee."

"I don't think so," Pinkerton said. "Alive would be nice, but James has grown too dangerous. At this point, however we get him, so long as we get him." He smiled as he withdrew an envelope from the breast of his coat. "That won't be your problem, though. You've been reassigned."

A quiver of alarm ran through the agent. "Reassigned?" she wondered as she took the envelope from Pinkerton and started to read its contents.

Pinkerton laughed. "Don't worry, you're not joining Siringo in Alaska. Washington thinks you'd be better employed doing the same sort of thing Courtright's working on. Seems there's some Indian holy relic the Army's gotten wind of. They're worried about the Warrior Nation getting ahold of it and using it to whip the savages into an even worse frenzy. They've asked us to slip some of our top people into Carpathian's kingdom to find it." His smile broadened. "Naturally, you are on the list of our top people."

Loveless shook her head and tried to return the document to her superior. "My assignment here isn't done."

Pinkerton's expression hardened and he thrust the envelope back into her hand. "I apologize if I made that sound like a request, Agent Loveless. I assure you it wasn't." He reached into his vest and examined his watch. "There's a stage to Lawry in two hours. From Lawry you can catch a train to El Paso down near the border. Get this hoodoo for the Army and then we'll discuss Jesse James. That is, if he isn't already swinging from a noose by then."

Chapter 2

An old kerosene lamp sputtered on a clapboard table, casting long shadows through the room. The mangy head of a buffalo hanging over the stone fireplace was transformed into a demonic goblin by the flickering shadows. The iron framework of an old bed standing in one corner became a skeletal slashwork of wire. Most of all, the men gathered around the table were twisted into ghoulish apparitions, their eyes glittering wickedly from the darkness.

Cole Younger shrugged. Where the men were concerned, more light would hardly make them more appealing. When he'd ridden up to the dilapidated ranch house, he'd seen some of the ruffians in broad daylight. 'Cowboys' they styled themselves, but Cole doubted any of these desperados had ever punched an honest steer in their lives. They might have rustled their share, but men with faces like these didn't take to hard work and regular hours.

They'd rather steal.

The Missouri bushwhacker kept a ready hand on his pistol. He felt like a wolf that had plunked itself down in a coyote den. It didn't matter that he could whip any five of these contemptible backshooters, not when they had the guns at hand to make up the difference. Of course, if they didn't have the numbers, he'd never have made the trip to Tombstone. The Cowboys hadn't taken part in the train heist that had brought arms and gear to so many of the west's badmen. They'd been raiding in Mexico during the heist and their absence from the train attack had left the gang at a distinct disadvantage, one that no amount of terror and brutality could overcome. They needed blasters and Iron Horses, needed those the way a starving wolf needed meat.

The only real gunman among them was Johnny Ringo, the only one who'd taken part in the great train heist that had enriched the arsenals of most of the badmen in the west. Where the others would plug a man through a window or from behind a door, Ringo had too much brazen conceit. It wasn't any sense of decency or fair play that made him prefer an open fight. It was a sick sort of pride, a sense of accomplishment he simply couldn't get any other way. Ringo'd once told his cousin that he never really felt alive until that second when he looked into the eyes of a man he was about to kill. It was that moment, that instant, when he could feel Death standing at his shoulder that made everything else worthwhile.

He cut a sinister figure, Johnny Ringo. He sported a long duster and a gaudy crimson vest with gold embroidery. The grips on the brace of blasters that hung from his belt were ivory, engraved with writhing dragons by Chinese artisans of Tombstone's Hoptown. The gunfighter wore them butt-forwards, favoring a cross-draw that he always claimed caught his adversaries off-guard. Cole thought it more likely was that it was Ringo's way of giving his opponent an edge, of making the duel more interesting for himself. Among pistoleros, Johnny Ringo was held in a class all his own, feared because when he stepped out in the street to square off, it seemed he really didn't care who it was who ended up on Boot Hill.

The other men in the ranch house had reputations far more unsavory. 'Curly Bill' Brocius was a horse thief, stage robber, and rustler. His trim beard and heavy features, the scruffy and soiled garb he wore, everything about him screamed aloud his savage and untamed disposition. He'd earned a reputation for viciousness after the grisly Skeleton Canyon Massacre when he'd personally tortured six vaqueros to death with the heated induction coil from the engine of a ranger's Interceptor. He was also a vicious drunkard, having shot off a preacher's feet with a blaster when he'd tried to make the man dance during a sermon. He'd narrowly escaped a lynching after blasting Marshal Fred White in half during a drunken escapade outside the Birdcage Theater.

Frank Stilwell was a weasel-faced Texan with mean little eyes and the morality of a rattlesnake. He'd been a deputy sheriff in Tombstone until Wyatt Earp discovered Stilwell's rampant extortion and embezzlement. In his time, he'd been both stage robber and claim-jumper. He was a human rat to whom life was cheap, having once murdered a man for serving him tea instead of coffee.

'Indian' Charlie was a half-breed Mexican, reputed to be a deserter from the feared Golden Army. More than half-deranged, he was given to psychotic fits and bizarre mood swings. During one raid on a fuel station, he'd insisted the stationmaster and his family dance naked until the outlaws were out of sight, blasting the hand off one man who tried to quit early with a buffalo gun. Another incident had involved him wandering into a saloon and smashing every bottle behind the bar over his own head, utterly oblivious to the blood streaming from his slashed scalp.

Pete Spence, Tom and Frank McLaury, Pony Deal, Frank Patterson, 'Rattlesnake' Bill, Jim Hughes, Jack Gauge – all of them robbers and rustlers. However, the guiding force behind this confederation of desperados and renegades were the Clantons. Ike Clanton was a spruced-up scoundrel who styled himself like a gentrified landowner; the sombrero on his head offset by the sleeves of his shirt adorned with gilded elctriwork garters with tiny RJ-powered horses prancing around his arms. His younger brother, Billy, was a hulking brute with a penchant for opium. The oldest brother, Phin, was a reclusive and submissive personality always ready to follow the rest of the gang.

Though Ike and Curly Bill acted in the capacity of captains or foremen of the Cowboys, the leader was Ike's father, the bearded patriarch of the Clanton family, Newman Hayes Clanton, commonly referred to as simply 'Old Man' Clanton. He was a tough, grizzled veteran of the Missouri border wars, a man upon whose face was etched all the cruelty of a hard and unforgiving life. Skin like boiled leather, eyes like chips of lead, he was the despotic chieftain of crime in Arizona's Cochise County and whatever regions of Mexico were unfortunate enough to attract his savage attention. He was a throwback, an atavism from a more brutal time. Like Curly Bill, Clanton was fighting tooth and nail to keep the complexities of this modern age at bay. The avarice in Old Man Clanton's eyes, however, was unmistakable as he listened to Cole describe the benefits of joining up with the James-Younger Gang.

"Some of your boys are packing some slapdash shooters and I saw a mighty sorry bunch of blackhoofs in that corral outside." Many of the Cowboys carried old-fashioned blasters that looked like they might have come from a US cavalry scrapyard. The corral had only a few Iron Horses and Interceptors in it, the bulk of the gang riding a motley array of blackhoofs; mechanical horse-like automatons that were fabricated by blacksmiths and horse-traders throughout the west. The robot stallions were immensely varied; no two machinists constructed them in exactly the same pattern. The ones in the Cowboy corral, despite bearing the magnetized stamp of a Clantonville workshop, exhibited a range of styles that encompassed the handiwork of at least a dozen different manufacturers. Slower and more fidgety than the vehicles built by the Union, blackhoofs weren't the sort of thing any outlaw wanted to rely on. The fact that the Cowboys had so many of them told Cole all he needed to know about how their fortunes had been faring. Cole swept his gaze across the Cowboys. "Guess you boys missed out not bein' around for the big train heist. You fellas have been bushwhacking prospectors and raiding sodbusters when you could have been layin' siege to ranches and bustin' banks. You been hidin' from the law when you could have been spittin' in its eye. How many men'd you lose that time Wyatt Earp sicced his Enforcers on you down in Gila Crossing? Seven, was it? And what about when that range detective Horn came nosin' around lookin' for Chisum's cattle? Think he accounted for nine men with that long-distance blaster of his afore you paid Chisum for the cattle you stole.

"I also hear tell it was only six who got themselves planted in a bone orchard when you tried tacklin' that refueling station in Apache Creek. I imagine Ringo's told you all about the difference modern arms and modern mounts will make until he was blue in the face. Behind the times, runnin' round Old Mex, rustlin' when you could have been gettin' yerselves dandied up with proper shootin' irons. Well, I'm sayin' we can fix all that. Get you enough blasters and Iron Horses to arm a whole company."

"We ain't doing so bad now," Ike stated, scowling at the seated Cole. "Indian Charlie gutted two marshals just last month, brought us their blasters and their hosses. What do we need you and James for?"

The Old Man turned a withering glare on his son. "Set your backside down and shut yer gob. Can't you see big folks is havin' a palaver?" He turned his snake-like gaze on Cole. "Say yer piece son, but make it good."

Cole smiled indulgently at the assembled Cowboys. "Well, I mean Ike's already said it for me. You can just keep moseying on out and kill star-packers. 'Course I imagine it won't take 'em long to reckon just who it is planting marshals and rangers in the ground. What do you think'll happen then? My way, we rush in and everybody gets what they need in one go. Then you can meet the lawdogs on their own terms."

"That the way Jesse figures it?" Curly Bill asked.

"That's the way Cole Younger figures it," Cole scowled back. He noticed the flicker of uncertainty that crept into Curly Bill's eyes. "The scheme's good enough for Jesse," he told the Cowboy.

From the corner of the room, Johnny Ringo's cold voice rang out. "I hear tell Billy the Kid split off from Jesse. Musta been a good reason fer him to do that. Maybe Billy figured Jesse ain't such a sharp blade to be around. Maybe him and his boys decided to find themselves friendlier company. Company who ain't so full of themselves like Jesse. Ask me, it sounds like the James-Younger Gang's on the skids. Why should we hitch our wagon to a train that's going downhill?"

Old Man Clanton rounded on the gunfighter. "Because there's damn good money to be had. Enough sugar to keep you coyotes in booze and women for a good long spell." The outlaw patriarch frowned when he saw his words made little impact on the baleful Ringo. He turned his tyrannical oratory on the rest of the Cowboys. "Cole's promisin' us blasters, armor, and Iron Horses. Enough so's we don't need to fret over Neri or the damn Earps!"

"I still don't like it," Ike grumbled. He flinched as the back of his father's hand cracked across his matted beard of a cheek.

"I telled you once afore to shut yer gob!" Old Man Clanton snarled. He turned back toward Cole. "You can set yer war bag over in the bunkhouse. Might take us a day or two to get things situated here, but I speak for all the Cowboys when I say we'd be right proud to ride with Jesse James."

Cole hid his annoyance at that last statement as he rose from the table. "Fair enough. But don't keep me waitin' too long. Jesse's the impatient type. He might decide he wants different partners if'n you dilly-dally."

As soon as Cole Younger had withdrawn from the room, the assembled Cowboys erupted into a babble of argument, some excited by the proposal Cole had brought them, others clearly angry that they'd be giving up their autonomy and taking orders from Jesse James. Old Man Clanton silenced the discord by slamming the butt of his blaster against the table. The weapon discharged in a violent blaze of energy, the shot searing through the shoulder of Rattlesnake Bill and throwing the outlaw to the floor. The maimed man writhed in agony, shrieking as blood spurted from his ravaged body. The other Cowboys stared down at their stricken comrade in mute horror, then back at their glowering boss.

Old Man Clanton was careful not to let on that shooting Rattlesnake Bill had been accidental. Assuming an imperious scowl, he glared at his underlings. Stepping around the table, he gave the bleeding rustler a savage kick.

"Quit yer hollerin'!" he snapped. "I said we're gonna ride with Jesse an' that's what we're gonna do!"

Still caressing his cheek, Ike turned toward his father. "It don't make no sense, Pa! We get mixed up with James and it won't be marshals and rangers dogging us, it'll be Pinkertons and the damn Union Army!"

An ugly chuckle bubbled up from behind the Old Man's beard. "Don't think I knowed that? Just 'cause we sign on with 'em don't mean we stay signed on!"

The statement had the outlaws eyeing their boss uneasily. Curly Bill was the first to vocalize why the plan seemed so appalling. "You're fixin' to cross up Jesse James?" With the exception of Johnny Ringo, every Cowboy in the room looked like he'd rather arm-wrestle an Enforcer robot than cross the infamous outlaw.

"Jesse'll have bigger problems than us to occupy himself," Old Man Clanton said. His malignant eyes roved across the faces of his followers. "Biggest nuisance we've got are those damn carpetbagger Earps. Well, we'll kill two buzzards with the same rock! We'll fix it so's the Earps take up Jesse's trail. He'll be so busy tryin' to stay ahead of them, that he ain't gonna have time to think about us. And while the Earps are busy hounding Jesse, we'll have a free hand here."

The Old Man waved his hand, drawing his followers closer. "Now just you listen to how I figure we'll fix it..."

*****

The town of San Diablo stretched along the barren, rocky slope of a large hill. In better days, a string of rich gold mines had burrowed down into the hillside above the town. Indiscriminate blasting, spurred by the Union's frenzy for the particular breed of gold the San Diablo mines offered, had led to catastrophe. Trying to sink shafts on the reverse side of the hill, miners had instead collapsed many of the existing workings. Hundreds of men had been buried alive in the blink of an eye and the richest gold veins sealed off by tons of solid rock.

The hunger of the Union, however, wouldn't let the gold slip away so easily. A private firm from Chicago had been contracted to examine the feasibility of reopening the mines. A small army of surveyors and engineers had descended on San Diablo, bringing with them all manner of strange technological inventions from the east. Henry Irons, bulky automatons cast in the vague semblance of men, were lowered into the few shafts remaining. Day and night the robots toiled away, striving to unearth what human sweat and muscle claimed to be impossible. Some of the old miners who had lingered on resented the robots, but most of San Diablo welcomed their advent. Without the men from Chicago and their machines, they knew their town would have dried up and blown away like so many other boom towns before them.

Like the eye of the Devil himself, the hot West Texas sun scorched the winding main street of San Diablo. Many of the structures perched upon the jagged hillside were simple canvas tents with wooden facades. Only a few were proper buildings, chiefly the offices of the various mining companies that had once headquartered in the town. One of these had been repurposed into a replacement for the crumbling adobe hovel that had served as combination courthouse and jail for the community.

John Younger kept a wary eye on San Diablo's new bastion of law and order. There was some commotion there with people dashing to and fro. He could see the menacing metal chassis of an Enforcer standing on the walkway just beside the entrance, its cyclopean optic glowing menacingly each time someone rushed past it. Sometimes, one of the men would pause to yell something at the robot as he ran past, but the machine was indifferent to whatever abuse was being thrown at it. The Enforcers would only listen to those they'd been programmed to obey.

Still keeping one eye on the jail, John looked down the street. He could make out the smoky lean-to of a blacksmith, the lumber-strewn workyard of a cooper, even the tent where the local undertaker must have established himself, judging by the profusion of coffins lying stacked outside. Of anything that might resemble a doctor's office, however, he could see no trace.

The young outlaw let his Iron Horse drift slowly toward the sprawling structure that seemed to be the center of town, a gigantic mass of logs and adobe that bore the title of Blackheart's Hotel and Saloon. Judging by the charred ground outside the building, it seemed to be frequented by men who had access to Iron Horses and Interceptors. The thought gave John a moment's pause – lawmen and soldiers were the sort of folk who had easiest access to the vehicles, most civilians making do with blackhoofs. A careful look at the single machine currently parked outside made him feel a little easier. A big brass plate was bolted to its hull, proclaiming it the property of the Illinois Mining and Assay Company.

Powering down his vehicle, John dismounted and stepped through the bat-wing doors. After the harsh light of the sun, the interior of the saloon seemed black as a cave. The young outlaw stayed in the doorway until his eyes had adjusted to the gloom.

"Don't dawdle there, boy," a sharp voice with a Texan twang called out. "With the sun at yer back, you make a damn fine target."

John's cheeks turned red at the reprimand, but he shifted to one side just the same, putting the saloon wall between himself and the street outside. Now that his eyes had started to adjust to the darkness, he could see the extent of the saloon. A long timber bar stretched across the back of the room, a series of glass mirrors mounted to the wall behind it. A few mechanized lanterns swung from the ceiling, but in the middle of the day none of these had been activated. A motley collection of tables and chairs were scattered about the main floor, and in one corner a small stage had been erected. He could see a narrow set of stairs climbing up to the second floor where he imagined the private rooms for hotel guests were situated. Flattened against the wall, just beside the stairway, was the splayed hide of some strange animal the likes of which John had never even heard tell of before.

"That would be Blackheart," the same Texan drawl announced. "Warrior Nation medicine man. The proprietor of this establishment was with Kit Carson when they brought down his warband. They say Blackheart changed himself into some horrible devil-buff when they caught up with him. Killed seven men before Carson's bullet punched through an eye and into its brain." The speaker laughed. "They have the heart pickled in a bottle behind the bar, but it'll cost you ten cents to see it."

John's gaze strayed back to the bar, for the first time really noticing the man standing behind it. He was a middle-aged, brawny-looking man, his hair just starting to abandon his head. He was wiping glasses with the apron he wore, but there was a nervous intensity to his chore that at once struck John as far from normal. When the bartender happened to look up, he didn't look John's way, but instead toward the right-hand side of the room. There was an unmistakable look of fear in his eyes, the terrified expression of a rabbit who sees a coyote.

John followed the direction of the bartender's gaze. Seated at one of the tables was a lone man dressed all in black, from boots to hat, offset only by the ruby-encrusted electriwork armbands he wore and the crimson vest peeking out from beneath his frock coat. There was a strange-looking blaster in his hand, its cylinder looked to be a single octagonal piece with a long hose snaking away from it to what looked like a ring of metal bottles fastened to the man's gun belt. There was a look of grim determination and almost sardonic amusement on the man's face. When he saw he had John's attention, he waved the barrel of his pistol at the outlaw. "Sit a spell," he ordered, kicking one of the chairs opposite him away from the table. One look into the man's cold eyes told John all he needed to know about his intentions. They were utterly without empathy, the eyes of a practiced killer.

So much as a threatening twitch on his part, and John knew this man would gun him down like a dog.

Keeping his arms raised and well away from his own blasters, John marched over to the stranger's table and sank down into the chair. Inwardly, he chided himself for walking into such a predicament. He wondered if any of his brothers would have been so foolish as to let someone get the drop on them so easily. Most of all, he felt guilty. He had come to San Diablo to get help for Jesse, and he knew deep inside that his hero was depending on him. Failing himself, he could accept, but failing Jesse James was too bitter a pill to swallow.

"You a bounty hunter?" John asked as he lowered his arms and set his hands palm-down on the table.

The question seemed to pique the stranger's curiosity. "What an interesting thing to ask," he observed. He leaned back in his chair, his free hand twisting the end of the thin moustache he wore. "Why on earth would you ask such a thing? Is it maybe you're a wanted man?"

John just stared back at the stranger. The man could shoot him, but he wouldn't tell him anything that would lead him back to Jesse and Cole.

"Better answer him, kid," the bartender warned. "That's John Wesley Hardin and he'd as soon shoot you as spit."

Hardin shifted around in his seat, glaring at the interruption. "Mind your bottles and mind your mouth. I was having a discussion with this gentleman." He turned back to the outlaw. "Now you know who I am. Maybe you've heard of me."

John nodded slowly. There were few men who hadn't heard of John Wesley Hardin, a name that blazed large in dime novels and newspapers. He was an unrepentant Rebel who'd started on the outlaw trail in the days immediately after the Union claimed victory over the Confederacy. Hardin had celebrated the end of the war by killing an emancipated slave with an old shovel. He'd been twelve years old then. It was the start of a long and bloody career. Throughout the west, Hardin was infamous for burning down a man with his blaster just because he'd been snoring too loud.

"I'm John," the boy outlaw declared. He hesitated, then added "John Fletcher from Missouri."

Hardin smiled. It was the cheerless smile that might belong to a snake. "A fellow John and a Southerner to boot? Tell me, John, you Secesh or a Yankee bootlicker?"

The mocking scorn in Hardin's tone stirred John's pride. Defiantly, he glared back at the gunman. "I ain't got no cause to love them blue bellies," he snarled. "Drove me and my brothers off our land. Burned our farm and killed my Pa!"

Hardin nodded his head, appreciating the fire in the outlaw's voice. "Too young to fight in the war," he said. "Just like me," he added, tapping his chest. "But we'll learn them tyrants just the same, won't we John?" he shifted around, snapping his fingers at the bartender. "Whiskey for me and my new friend. If you're fast about it, I won't shoot off one of your feet."

John watched as the bartender scrambled to obey Hardin. "I thank you for the drink, but it'll have to be just one pull. I came into town lookin' for the doctor."

The statement brought a gasp from the bartender. The man dropped the bottle of whiskey on the floor, shattering it into a puddle of booze and glass. Hardin rolled his eyes and sighed. "Get another one and try again," he ordered with a wave of his gun. The bartender scurried off to do as he'd been told.

"Fetchin' the doctor might be a sight difficult," Hardin explained. "You see, I shot him last night. The way folks are carryin' on, I suspect he died sometime this morning."

John sat back, his face going pale. "You killed the doctor?"

"Well, what else could I do?" Hardin laughed. "I burned the sheriff and the galoot was tryin' to patch him back together! Don't cotton to folks who meddle in things ain't none of their affair!" The gunfighter looked up as the bartender set the whiskey down on the table. He tapped the bottle with his finger. "You may add that to my account," he declared before waving the man away. When he saw the bartender glance toward the door, Hardin sprang to his feet.

A man was framed in the entranceway, much as John had been. There was a rifle clenched in his hands. Before his eyes could adjust to the dark, Hardin fired. It wasn't a beam of energy that left the gunman's strange blaster but something that looked more like a little ball of red clay. When it struck the rifleman, the ball exploded into flame, bathing the man in molten fire. The man shrieked, swatting desperately at the flames as they quickly spread and engulfed him. He pawed in agony at the wall, leaving little slivers of fire crackling down its length before he crashed to the floor in a blazing heap.

"Be happy I heard your Iron Horse and knew you weren't a local," Hardin told John. The gunman reached down and bolted a last glass of whiskey before dashing toward the front of the saloon. "If you're a stranger to San Diablo, you might want to light out. Don't think they'll be too particular who they lynch!"

From outside, a barrage of energy beams came sizzling through the front of the saloon, scorching holes through the timber facade. Displaying reckless bravado and incredible luck, Hardin dodged the murderous fire. Rolling across the floor, he aimed under the sweep of the batwing doors and opened up on the vigilantes. A shrill scream told that at least one of his shots struck home.

"Never thought they'd have the spine!" Hardin laughed. "Guess they got tired tryin' to coax some action out of the sheriff's 'bot and figured they could do it themselves!" He flattened himself against the floor as another vengeful barrage raked the building. He looked back at John. "I'm gonna make a play for my 'Horse afore some wiseacre gets a mind to start shootin' at it. If'n your of a mind to leave, I suggest you join me."

Shaking his head at the stream of fire pouring into the saloon, John unholstered his pistol. He didn't have a personal grievance against the people of San Diablo, but at the same time he wasn't going to take a chance that Hardin was right. 'Ride with outlaws, hang with outlaws' was a truism many men lived by in the Territories. Shot down by vigilantes was far better than dancing from a rope.

Checking the charge on his blaster, John scrambled to where Hardin was stretched along the floor. Nearby, flames were starting to spread from the body of the first man Hardin had killed. "What's the plan?"

Spinning around like a striking sidewinder, Hardin fired on the bartender, burning the man's head from his shoulders. A sawed-off shotgun tumbled from beneath the slaughtered man's apron. "Was wonderin' when he'd find the sand to use that," Hardin said as he turned his attention back to the vigilantes in the street. He squinted down the barrel of his gun, calmly squeezing off a shot. An agonized shriek answered the blast.

"How do we get out of here?" John demanded as he added his own fire to that of the gunfighter.

"We rush out of here, hop on our 'Horses and ride away, shootin' anything that moves while we're doin' it," Hardin answered. He winked at the young outlaw, and then ducked his head as another fusillade slammed through the saloon.

"It's always worked for me before," Hardin assured him.

*****

Jesse James rolled onto his back, twisting the sheets tighter about his body. Every coil impressed itself upon his slumbering mind, conjuring up a hempen noose that drew close around his neck. He could feel his feet mounting the thirteen steps to the gallows, he could smell the blood of executed men that had soaked into the old rope. The crowds were there, mocking and jeering, resplendent in their uniforms of blue and their garish three-piece suits. There was Pinkerton himself, waving at him with the severed arm of Jesse's mother, an arm blasted from her body when the detectives had thrown a bomb into her house thinking Frank and Jesse were there. He could see Captain Laine, his Union uniform caked in the blood of murdered men, his red leggings filthy with the gore of slaughter. Laine smiled up at him and fondled the bullhide whip in his hands, the same whip he had used to stripe Jesse's back when his band of Jayhawkers had come raiding into Missouri before the war. Just behind him was Starkweather, the abolitionist fanatic who'd marched with John Brown at Harper's Ferry and who had later served with murderous glee in the Kansas Red Legs.

The crowd of soldiers and carpetbaggers parted, allowing a troop of painted savages to march toward the scaffold. With every step, the Indians seemed to discard a little more of their humanity, their eyes glowing with an eerie blue luminance, their bodies becoming more and more beastlike until they were nothing but a pack of snarling animals gnashing their fangs at him. He saw one of them, a great bearlike horror, rear up on its hind legs. Its roar echoed the jeers of the Yankees, filled with scorn and mockery. Dangling from the necklace it wore, Jesse could see the gnawed debris of human arms. He knew they were his own.

"We declare that this Union is indivisible, with tyranny and oppression for all." The words growled through Jesse's mind. The executioner was stalking toward him now, but with each step, like the Indians, he was changing. The black hood lengthened into a beaverskin hat, the uniform thickened and darkened into a long frock coat. A pale, leprous face grinned at him, diabolic in its malevolent expression. Eyes like pits of hellfire bore into his own as the fiendish visage leered at him. There was a bright flash, the familiar blaze of a blaster shot. The ogre-like head vanished in a burst of fire, smoke billowing away from a charred stump of neck and exposed spine. Despite the obliteration of the deadman's head, his hateful voice roared in Jesse's ears. "There can be no Secession from this Union."

The rope around Jesse's neck drew tight and he was jerked up into the air. His breath was choked off, his lungs turned to fire. He tried to grab at the rope, to ease its strangling pressure, but his mechanical arms refused to obey. They remained frozen at his sides, unhearing of his desperate demands.

In the crowd, he could see an old man in a white suit smile up at him. Dr. Carpathian shook his head and a strange brace appeared in his hands, a metal funnel sporting a riotous confusion of wires and pipes. "Don't worry. We can fix anything. Even a stretched neck. Just as long as you are willing to pay the price."

Screaming, Jesse tried to lunge at the scientist. He felt the rope saw into his flesh, felt the last wisp of breath ripped from his body. Still he persisted, persisted until he felt the rope snap, felt his body hurtle down from the scaffold. The fire of rage throbbed through his veins, through his nerves. Under the intensity of his fury, his arms rose, his fingers tightened into claws. There was a gratifying look of terror on Dr. Carpathian's face as Jesse brought his hands closing about the old man's throat.

Tighter and tighter Jesse clenched his grip. He felt the scientist's neck crumpling beneath the pressure, groaning with a shriek of tortured metal...

With a start, Jesse emerged from his nightmare. He discovered himself crouched on his knees, his hands wrapped about the bedstead. The brass frame was twisted out of any semblance of shape, the marks of his steel fingers stamped into the metal. He blinked in surprise at the display of raw strength. Since his confrontation with Dr. Carpathian, since the scientist used one of his infernal inventions to shut down Jesse's arms, the outlaw had believed such strength beyond him. It had been pain beyond compare simply to move them.

Yet they had responded before, acted almost of their own accord when he'd reacted to Cole's taunting. There was some secret there, something maybe even Carpathian didn't understand. Some link between the mechanics that had been fused to his body and the mind that controlled that body. Not the rational thought, the deliberate exertion of control. It was something stronger than that, something more primal. Something that didn't fit into Carpathian's books and experiments.

Jesse turned away from the crumpled bedstead. Sitting on the mattress, he stared down at the arms Carpathian had given him after the beasts of the Warrior Nation left him mutilated and crippled. He'd been so proud of these arms, so vain of what they could do. Yet in the end, they had betrayed him.

"Feeling better, Jesse?" The outlaw raised his head to see Bob Younger standing nearby. The way his eyes kept straying to the bedstead, it was easy to guess the reason for his uneasiness.

Without concentration, allowing only the slightest thought, Jesse reached out and grabbed the brass ball at the foot of the bed. His hand tightened, crushing the ball into a tangle of brass.

"Not yet," Jesse told Bob. "But I'm getting there."

Chapter 3

John Younger idled his Iron Horse at the top of the rise overlooking the isolated cabin. He knew at least one of his brothers would be on guard, allowing that Potts and Danby hadn't returned with the supplies yet. Cole might even have returned with Ringo and the desperados from Tombstone. Not knowing who might be keeping an eye out, the young outlaw was especially wary. The hideout had been chosen not only for its isolation but also for the view it commanded. He had no great desire to be gunned down by a friend who didn't recognize him.

"You sure this is the place, Kid?" Hardin asked. He leaned from the saddle of his 'Horse and spit a plug of tobacco into a patch of dry weeds.

John nodded and cupped a hand against his mouth. A shrill noise vibrated through the bowl of his hand, a sound that was part bird-call and part savage war-whoop. He waited a few seconds and then repeated the strange cry.

"Don't seem to be anybody home," Hardin commented. Even as the words left his mouth, a man appeared on the porch. A moment later, John's signal was repeated by the man below.

"That's my brother Jim," John said, a note of pride in his voice. "He's tellin' us we can come on down and we won't get shot doin' it."

Hardin slapped the holster on his hip. "Folk find I don't get shot none too easy," he declared.

John smiled back at the notorious gunman. They'd traveled together a fair distance, Hardin content to follow the young outlaw back to whatever hideout he'd been holed up in. The boy had told him that much, and the gunfighter hadn't pressed for more details. It was one thing every man respected in the Territories, the decency not to pry into another man's past. If someone wanted to talk about who they were or where they had been, that was something they would do in their own way and their own time.

John decided now was the time to let Hardin know exactly who it was he'd been riding with - to knock the gunman's arrogance down a couple of notches. "My brother Bob's probably inside still. Don't think my brother Cole's back from Tombstone yet."

Hardin laughed. "Bob, Cole, and Jim. Who do you fellas think you are, the James-Younger Gang?"

The youth bristled under Hardin's laughter. "That's exactly who we are!" he snapped, gunning his Iron Horse down the rise and toward the cabin. Still laughing, Hardin opened up his own machine and followed John down.

Jim glared at the two riders. Only when John was close enough to recognize did he wave a hand toward the barn. Potts scrambled out from the loft, an energy rifle slung over his shoulder. Danby emerged a moment later from behind the fuel shed, a carbine in his hands.

"Who's the dude?" Jim demanded as the riders parked their 'Horses in front of the cabin. His surly temper had only blackened since John's unannounced departure three days before.

Hardin glared down at Jim. "I been called lots of things. Smart folks call me 'sir', but you don't look so smart, so I'm inclined to let you slide this once."

John dismounted and hurried to put himself between his brother and the gunman. "This here's John Wesley Hardin of Texas," he said, hoping Hardin's name and reputation would get Jim to back down. One look at his older brother told him it wouldn't matter if it was King Fisher sitting there, Jim was spoiling for a fight."I went to San Diablo looking for a doctor."

"That explains why you left," Jim growled. "Doesn't tell me why you brought this buzzard back with you."

Hardin favored Jim with a thin smile. "That lip's gonna get you in trouble," he said.

Potts and Danby circled around at the edges of the conflict. The two men wore anxious expressions on their faces, clearly unhappy with the prospect of going up against the infamous Hardin. At the same time, they'd been with the Youngers long enough that Jim could depend on them to back any play he made.

"Trouble's one thing we Youngers make plenty of," Jim said. "Be sure you don't pick off more than you can handle."

Hardin leaned back in the saddle. His eyes darted from one side to the other, judging where the other outlaws were. He nodded to John. "Well, kid, you stayin' out of this or do I carve four notches instead of three?"

The sharp crack of a blaster exploded the tension in the air. Hardin watched in shock as his hat went flying into the air. Before it could fall, it was struck again, the energy bolt setting the felt of the brim on fire.

"Before somebody goes puttin' holes in members of the James Gang, they better ask my permission."

Stalking out from the cabin, a blaster gripped in each of his metal hands, was Jesse James. Jim and the other outlaws gazed in open wonder at their leader's approach. All of them had assumed Jesse would be laid up for weeks yet. To see him up and around, much less spry enough to shoot the hat off a man's head, filled them with awe.

Hardin raised his hands, keeping them well away from his holster. Quick-tempered and violent as he was, a fool he was not. He'd heard enough about Jesse's mechanical arms to know a man would have to be an idiot to think he could outdraw the bandit. With pistols already in Jesse's fists, a man would have as much chance as a three-legged mule in a horse race.

"I'll bear that in mind," Hardin said. He went to tip his hat in apology, and then remembered it was lying on the ground burning. "I didn't half believe the boy when he said his compadres were the Younger Brothers."

"You know better now," Jesse told him. "Matter of fact, only reason I don't burn you off that 'Horse right now is because of your reputation." The outlaw paused in his advance. His metal arms slowly lowered, sliding his blasters back into their holsters. Jesse frowned when one of the trigger guards got hung up for a moment. Not too long ago, it would have been the easiest thing in the world to holster the weapons faster than the eye could follow. Damn that traitor, Carpathian!

"I'm obliged for the courtesy," Hardin said, doing his best to watch Jesse and the other outlaws at the same time.

"Don't be," Jesse told him. "Frankly, I can use a man like you. I've got a job in mind for a nice juicy bank. A few extra hands would make it a plumb prospect."

The statement brought an excited whoop from John Younger. Jesse smiled at the boy's enthusiasm, and then fixed Hardin with a steely gaze. "Being new to the gang, you'll understand getting the small end of the split."

Hardin bristled at the remark, then uttered a bitter laugh, staring down at the blasters Jesse'd returned to their holsters. The outlaw was making a point, reminding him that he was the boss, whether his guns were in hand or not. After a moment, Hardin shrugged. "So long's you buy me a new hat outta your share, I'll oblige you." He jabbed a thumb at the smoldering ruin of his old hat.

"What's the job you got picked out for us, Jesse?" John Younger wondered.

Appearing in the doorway behind Jesse, it was Bob who answered the boy's question. Unlike Jesse, the look on Bob's face made it clear he didn't approve of John's excitement. "A bank in a town called Charity. Jesse says it'll be a push-over."

Jim snorted derisively. "Sure it will," he agreed. "That's because there ain't nothin' in it. I used to cowboy out that way. Big horse ranches back then, only nowadays, with the Yankees using Iron Horses and everybody else 'spected to use blackhoofs, there ain't a plugged nickel to be had bustin' broncs. Land up there ain't no good for cattle..."

The icy glower in Jesse's eyes silenced Jim's protest. "Some money is better than none," Jesse told him. He glanced over at John, then fixed his gaze on Hardin. "Besides, I don't cotton to draggin' new blood on a big job when it's their first dance."

*****

Cole Younger scowled at the lack of progress they'd made since leaving the Clantonville ranch. He longed for the thrill of opening up his 'Horse and speeding across the desert, the throb of the RJ engine rattling through his bones and the feel of the wind whipping through his hair. Instead, he had his Iron Horse throttled down to its lowest pace, something between the waddle of an overstuffed duck and the lumber of a pregnant bear.

The reason for such delay rode beside him. Old Man Clanton and his gang didn't have Iron Horses; at least those of his men now riding out across the desert. Instead, they were mounted on blackhoofs, mechanical stallions patented by Tesla and assembled by blacksmiths across most of the west from whatever parts they could barter, scavenge or hammer out on their own. Some of the Cowboys sported extravagant steeds, their metal frames adorned with silver conchos and gaudy spangles. Curly Bill had even gone so far as to display the scorched stars he'd plucked from the chests of dead lawmen to the saddle of his blackhoof.

On its best day, a blackhoof would be eating the dust of an Iron Horse or an Interceptor. The machines gave the Union speed and mobility far in excess of what any outlaw gangs who hadn't taken part in the great train robbery could manage. It allowed them greater facility to react to the depredations of the Warrior Nation and the intrusions of Carpathian's Enlightened.

The Old Man and Curly Bill were too locked in the past to readily accept the advantages of the new devices and inventions that streamed out of the east, but even they had to grudgingly allow the necessity of progress. One glance at either of the Cowboy leaders was enough to hammer that point home. The men were throwbacks to the days of highwaymen and road agents – Old Man Clanton even had a black powder pistol stuffed into the waist of his pants to compliment the blaster holstered at his side. Curly Bill, with his grizzled garb, was like some wild beast. He had a gigantic knife strapped to his leg, some Mexican contraption called a machete. Dangling from his gun belt by little leather cords was the handiwork of that brutal-looking blade, a collection of shriveled objects that closer inspection revealed to be trigger fingers hacked from the hands of those unfortunate enough to cross Curly Bill. Cole was reminded of Colonel Quantrill's right-hand man during the War, Captain William T. Anderson, known to friend and foe alike as 'Bloody Bill' Anderson had a penchant for collecting the scalps of the men he killed, festooning the tack and harness of his horse with them until the animal resembled a Mongolian pony. But that had been war. Curly Bill was just unabashed meanness.

"See somebody you know?" Curly Bill laughed when he noticed the direction of Cole's gaze.

Cole smiled coldly at the bandit. "Nope, just marveling that there are so many slow gunmen hereabouts. Must be the heat sucks all the quickness out of a fella."

Curly Bill surprised Cole by laughing at the taunt. "Never did cotton to standin' in the street like some fool-all idiot waitin' for the galoot you come to plug to call the dance. I decide to kill a man, I kill him. Simple as that, and I don't make no particulars about how it's done." He brushed his hand across his gruesome collection, setting the fingers wiggling against his gun belt.

"The Devil takes pride in his work too," Cole said, shaking his head.

Old Man Clanton grinned at the bushwhacker. "Never would have figured you for the sensitive type, Cole. Guess you fellas ridin' with Jesse, gets used to livin' high on the hog. You start to ferget the things what need doin'. Get all squeamish inside."

Cole glared at the old outlaw. "Maybe we just remember there's a difference between killin' and murder."

"Dead's dead," Curly Bill stated coldly. "Every finger here came off'n a lawdog or a Unionist or some damn fool who didn't hear so good." The Cowboy's smile broadened. "Some Mex and Indians too, but it don't seem right to go countin' that sort."

Cole turned away from Curly Bill and his sadistic smile. In that moment, he looked just a little too much like Archie Clement, Bloody Bill's chief scalper and torturer. Cole'd seen Little Arch do things to a man that would make the Devil sick. Somehow, he felt that Curly Bill could have taught even Little Arch a thing or two about viciousness.

A fine band he was bringing back to Jesse, Cole reflected bitterly. Robbers and gunmen he'd expected, but a lot of the men who called themselves "Cowboys" were just murdering marauders; only difference between them and with the Nations on the warpath was a lick of paint on their faces. He wondered why his cousin Johnny Ringo had taken up with such a brutal outfit. He also wondered if Jesse's name and reputation would be enough to keep the Cowboys in line. Cole knew it was more than he could do, unless he gunned a few of the leaders like Curly Bill.

"Let's talk again about the split," Old Man Clanton said, turning the subject away from the macabre collection of his lieutenant. "I have a mighty big gang to keep comfortable. I think maybe our cut of the take should reflect that."

"All I'll promise is a third," Cole said. "You want more than that; you'll have to talk it over with Jesse. Might be he'll see things your way. Might be he'll figure a third is too generous and whittle it down a bit." He slapped his hand against the Iron Horse he was riding. "What I will say is that any man rides with us is gonna get one of these under him and sooner rather than later. Jesse likes his gang to be fast and mobile. Can't really be trotting around on a four-legged chunk of pig-iron."

"They done good by us this far," Old Man Clanton said.

"If that's so, then why are you still hidin' out from the Earps?" Cole asked.

Old Man Clanton's eyes took on a steely glint. "Who says we're hidin'?" he asked as turned away.

Something about the Cowboy's tone made Cole look back over his shoulder, to stare out across the desert. Johnny Ringo, Ike Clanton, and several of the other Cowboys had lingered behind in Clantonville to 'attend to business' as Old Man Clanton put it. The outlaws each had one of the Iron Horses the Cowboys had acquired from dead lawmen, so there was no question that the men would catch up to the slow moving blackhoofs. What disturbed Cole, what he'd wondered about ever since they rode out from the Clanton ranch, was what sort of business was so important as to delay Ringo and the rest.

*****

Dust billowed up from the parched dirt of Fifth Street as three Iron Horses came rumbling through Tombstone. Townsfolk scrambled into shops and saloons after one look at the three riders. At first, with the speeds in which the vehicles moved in, it could be thought that these men were lawmen. Upon closer inspection, there was no mistaking these men for anything associated with the law. The darkbrown linen dusters the three men wore were infamous throughout the west. They were the 'uniform' adopted by the Archie Clement gang after the War, when the vicious bushwhacker led embittered Rebel guerrillas in robberies across Kansas and Missouri. After the death of Little Arch, the same style of duster had become the recognized mark of his even more notorious successor: Jesse James and the James-Younger Gang.

The men sitting on the benches outside the Tombstone Cattlemen and Miners' Trust scattered when the three machines swung toward the brick-faced bank. A leathery-faced guard stepped out onto the plank walkway that ran down past the front of the bank. Even behind the brick wall, there was no mistaking the growl of an Iron Horse's engine, much less three of them. He'd come out to investigate, his hand already closed upon the grip of the blaster holstered at his hip. He visibly paled when he saw the brown dusters and the bandanas pulled up over the riders' faces. Any doubt about their intentions was gone when they dismounted and started toward the bank.

The guard started to back away, but then his eyes fixed on the elegant blaster resting across the belly of one of the men. He'd seen that ivory grip with its Oriental dragons before. There couldn't be another pair of guns like them in the whole Territory. He looked up into the gunman's eyes. The words that left his mouth came in a quivering whisper. "I know you..."

"Well ain't that unfortunate," the gunman hissed back. Before the guard could even start to raise his blaster from its holster, the man in the duster had ripped the ivory-gripped gun from his belt and loosed an energy bolt into his breast. The guard didn't even scream, his burned body simply folded in on itself and crumpled to the street, the bricks behind him scorched black by the heat of the beam that cut him down.

Screams rang down Fifth as those still abroad saw the brutal murder. Alarm accompanied the frenzied cries as they spread along the street.

"That tears it," one of the masked outlaws snarled. He pushed past the gunman, brought a silver-toed boot crashing against the bank's iron-banded door. The portal crashed inwards, bowling over the teller who had dashed forward to bar it against the men in the street. The outlaw stormed onwards, pausing just long enough to kick the fallen teller's face as he started to pick himself off the floor. The blow sent the man sprawling.

"This here's a robbery!" the outlaw declared, brandishing his blaster and sending a bolt searing into the ceiling overhead. With his other hand, he pulled a pair of canvas bags from the pocket of his duster and threw them at the teller who'd remained behind the steel bars of the banker cage. "I'd like to withdraw my money," the bandit laughed, "and everybody else's too. Be quick about it and don't get any fool ideas," he wagged the smoking barrel of his blaster at the man. "This'll cut clean through them bars and I won't be none too happy if I have to waste my time doing it." The warning took, and the teller began to stuff the bags with handfuls of bills and coins.

The other two robbers brought their weapons to bear on the few customers standing in the bank's lobby. One of them shook his head when he saw that one of their captives was a woman. "This don't seem right, Ike," the outlaw said. Immediately he cried out in pain as the gunman with the ivory-gripped blaster clubbed his ear with the butt of his gun.

"Seeing you done mentioned Ike by name, it sort of settles matters, don't it?" Johnny Ringo snarled down at Pete Spence.

The teller inside the cage froze. He stared in terror at the outlaw on the other side of the bars. "Ike Clanton?" he gasped. His shivering grew so bad that he started to drop gold coins onto the floor. "Honest, Mr. Clanton, I won't give you no trouble."

"Glad to hear it," Ike snarled back. "Maybe you get to live awhile longer." He turned his head and glared over at Ringo. "You'd better hope Stilwell and Indian Charlie are where they need to be. We weren't countin' on any shootin' this soon."

"Then we'll just have to improvise," Ringo said. "I told you I'm your huckleberry for that job."

"Old Man wants them ornery, not dead," Ike said. "I can trust Stilwell to do that, which is more'n I can say for you."

Ringo spun around, loosing another blast from his gun. One of the customers in the lobby crashed to the floor, a gory hole drilled through his midsection. "Don't anybody else get the notion of inchin' toward that door," Ringo warned.

Ike reached through the gap in the bars of the cage and snatched the filled sacks from the teller. For an instant, his eyes drifted toward the huge safe at the back of the building. He shook his head sadly. "Too bad we don't have more time," he grumbled. A quick lift of his gun and he turned the teller's head into a smoldering husk.

The brutal murder of the man in the cage was Ringo's signal to let loose. Without hesitation, the gunfighter swept his gun across the customers, burning them down where they stood. One of the terrified victims made it as far as the door before Ringo's blast caught him in the back. The impact of the blaster flung the man's body out into the street where he lay like a bundle of burning rags.

Money bag in hand, Ike motioned for the other Cowboys to quit the bank. They'd accomplished what they needed to do here. The rest would depend on Stilwell and Indian Charlie on the roof of the Bloody Bucket Saloon.

*****

Virgil Earp rushed down Allen Street, hurrying toward the sounds of gunfire and screaming. He'd been dining with his wife in the restaurant in the Cosmopolitan Hotel when the shooting started. Dashing from his interrupted breakfast, the marshal had hesitated for an instant, debating if he should race down the street and get the Enforcers. Turning as he heard more gunfire, he decided he didn't have time to race down to the marshal's office and fetch the 'bots.Every moment he wasted might mean someone's life.

The direction of the gunfire told Virgil what was happening. Somebody had taken it into their head to rob the Cattlemen and Miners' Trust. He glanced down Fifth Street, watching people fleeing the area of the bank. Longingly, he looked back down Allen Street toward the building where the marshal's office was situated. Wyatt wouldn't be there this early, but Morgan should be. It wasn't like he had anywhere else to be.

Virgil shook his head. Yeah, Morgan was probably there, but ever since he'd been gunned by outlaws and had most of his body replaced with machinery by Dr. Carpathian, he'd been distant and apathetic. The cyborg was dependable enough in a fight, but he lacked the initiative to investigate trouble on his own. Sometimes, Virgil was tempted to agree with Wyatt. In moments of anger, Wyatt would berate his eldest brother, saying they'd given Carpathian their brother and what they'd gotten back was little more than a 'bot.

More gunfire erupted from within the bank. Virgil watched in disgust as a man's body was flung through the doors to crash in a heap in the middle of the road. His hands tightened about the blasters he gripped in both hands. If these murdering varmints were to be stopped, the job was one he'd have to do all on his own.

Rounding the façade of the Crystal Palace, Virgil ducked down behind a balustrade and drew a bead on the bank's doorway. The moment the bandits made their break for the Iron Horses parked outside the building, he'd cut them down as ruthlessly as the man they'd left burning in the street and the guard slumped on the walkway with his chest turned into a blackened crater.

A masked man wearing a brown duster was just starting to poke his head out the door when a fresh burst of gunfire sizzled through the air. Virgil screamed as he felt searing agony race down his side. The balustrade exploded into splinters, the planks of the walkway were scorched by the withering energy of a blaster fired from above and behind the marshal.

Rolling among the cinders, clutching at the charred flesh of his arm, Virgil blinked through the flames of his pain to see two men in brown dusters drop down from the roof of the saloon on the corner opposite the Crystal Palace. The back-shooting assassins went running off toward Toughnut Street, smoke rising from the red-hot barrels of their carbines. The sound of Iron Horses roaring into life turned the marshal's gaze back toward the bank in time to see three more men in brown dusters leap into the saddles of their 'Horses and tear off toward Fremont Street. As they sped away from the bank, each of the robbers vented a fierce Rebel yell.

Virgil wriggled across the charred walkway, propping himself against the wall of the Crystal Palace. Now that the shooting was over, he could hear people rushing back into the streets, babbling about the attack, bemoaning the carnage that had erupted on Fifth Street. Through his agony, Virgil heard horrified citizens describing the massacre inside the bank. More than one voice gave a name to the perpetrators of this atrocity: the James Gang.

The anguished shriek of Virgil's wife Allie sent a fresh spasm of pain rushing through the lawman. Mustering what strength he had left, Virgil propped himself against the wall of the saloon and pulled himself up onto his feet. He embraced her with his remaining good arm, holding her tight.

"For God's sake!" Allie raged at the gawking people around them. "Someone get the doctor!"

Virgil shook his head. "Somebody get Wyatt," he groaned. "Tell him it was Jesse James. Jesse James shot up his town and bushwhacked his brother."

Fighting to stay conscious, Virgil let Allie lead him into the Crystal Palace to await the doctor. As the barman cleared away one of the poker tables and helped Allie lay him down on it, he kept picturing the night Morgan was shot and what had happened afterwards. In a sudden burst of panic, he reached for the arm the assassins had shot, his fingers sinking into the burned flesh down to the bone within.

With a moan of agony, the crippled lawman fled into the mercy of unconsciousness.

Chapter 4

The dusty main street of Charity was bustling with activity, farmers and ranchers streaming into the town in hopes of securing contracts to provide food for the workers at the new RJ refueling station that was set to be constructed on the trailhead leading back to Abilene. Along with the inhabitants of the outlying homesteads, a number of itinerant tradesmen had descended on Charity, intending to peddle their wares to the citizenry. The overall atmosphere was that of a market day, complete with a snake oil salesman loudly extolling the virtues of his medicinal elixir in a breathless harangue.

Such a climate of distraction suited the seven men who started to drift into town just after the clock tower above the assay office began to toll away high noon. In a less congested and confused time, the people of Charity might have paid closer attention to the Iron Horses the men rode or the brown dusters they removed from their saddlebags when they parked the vehicles and threw across the crook of their left arms. They might have wondered about the blasters the strangers had holstered at their sides or the carbines they carried with them.

Just now, however, Charity was too involved in its own business to be vigilant. The farmers and ranchers were worried about getting their deals with the RJ station, contracts that might mean the difference between survival and ruin for men who'd been hard hit by the collapsed demand for horseflesh. The shops in town were trying to lure customers off the street and exploit the sudden boom in potential profit. Wives and children scurried about the stalls and wagons of the traveling traders, trying to secure anything that seemed exotic or unusual, particularly the mechanical devices brought out from the east. Powered by a little button of RJ, these came in almost every shape and size, from little automated toys, to elegant armbands and hatbands, watches, and even rings.

The people of Charity had no idea that the grim-faced men who slowly made their way through the crowd were anybody special, much less that they were the notorious James-Younger Gang.

Jesse had been careful to pick this day for their raid on Charity. The crowd was effective camouflage for the outlaws as they advanced upon the bank. Later, they'd provide the gang with a smokescreen of confusion when it came time to stage their escape. Nothing was quite as chaotic as a mob of terrified civilians. That was a lesson Jesse had learned well from his years as one of Quantrill's Raiders.

Individually and in pairs, the outlaws moved on the Central Union Bank of Charity. The first men through the doors of the adobe building were Bob and Jim Younger. Once they were inside, the two men made a pretense of gawking at the rich appointments inside the bank, running their hands along the mahogany runners along the walls and extolling the exquisite etching on the glass hood of the RJ lamp hanging from the ceiling.

Hardin came in next, scowling as he strolled toward the tellers' cage. He paused before reaching the bars, fishing in the pocket of his vest and removing a little leather pay book which he made a great show of consulting. Though his eyes seemed to be focused on the pay book, the gunfighter's gaze roved across the faces of the other occupants of the bank. He didn't like the scrutiny with which the armed guard was studying him, much less the scattergun in the man's hands.

Jesse James and John Younger were the next inside, Jesse's metal arms hidden in the sleeves of a bulky cattleman's coat. As they came in, Jesse was explaining how banking worked to the boy, telling him all about deposits and interest in such a simplified fashion that it brought chuckles from the tellers inside the cage and a smile from the elderly rancher who was just making his own deposit.

"First time inside a bank, son?" the rancher asked, turning around to address John.

"Nearabouts," Jesse answered. "I can't seem to convince him his money'll be safe. He's all worried Billy the Kid or somebody's gonna ride right in and steal it."

The rancher laughed. "They got a safe back there that'd take an elephant to break open," he said. "Operates on a time-lock too. Some new gewgaw from back east. Can't be opened 'cept at particular times of the day."

The rancher's eyes went round as saucers when Jesse suddenly pulled both his blasters from their holsters. "Unfortunately we don't have the time to wait," he said, pushing the man aside and leveling his guns at the tellers inside the cage.

Across the lobby, the guard was startled when he suddenly found one of Bob's Bowie knives at his throat. The man was so suspicious of Hardin, he neglected to keep an eye on the older Younger brothers, who he'd dismissed as country bumpkins. Hardin replaced the pay book in his vest and came strolling over toward the frightened guard. The gunfighter's gloved hands drummed ominously against the grips of the smokers he carried.

"Seen something funny?" Hardin challenged the guard. The gunfighter's eyes gleamed like those of a snake as he glared at the man. "Maybe you'd like to cut loose with that hog-shredder of yourn?"

"Settle yourself, Hardin!" Jesse's voice cracked across the gunfight like a whip. "I'll tell you who to shoot and when." He nodded to the windows at the front of the bank. Jim Younger had drawn down the shades and was now peering out from behind one corner to keep an eye on the street. "Help Jim keep watch," Jesse advised the gunman. Sullenly, Hardin turned away from the guard and stalked over to the window.

Jesse turned back toward the tellers. Neither man had dared to twitch a muscle even with the robber's attention focused on Hardin. In drawing his blasters, Jesse's coat had slid back, exposing the metal sheen of his mechanical arms. Those arms told the bankmen exactly who was robbing them. Neither man was suicidal enough to oppose Jesse James.

"I suspect you fellas know what I want, so get to it," Jesse told the tellers. He glanced aside as the men behind the cage began emptying their tills into a canvas mail bag. The outlaw smiled when he saw that John had the barrel of his blaster planted in the belly of the old rancher.

"Step back a pace," Jesse told the boy. "Close like that, if you have to shoot you'll foul up the exhaust when all the fat in his belly turns to grease and goes splashing across the gun. Never stick iron up against a man, hang back a bit and give you both a little space to think. You about why you should shoot, him to think about why you shouldn't. Man don't think clear when he feels a gun prodding into his gut."

As Jesse spoke, John slowly backed away, color rushing into his face. He kept both his blaster and his eyes fixed on the rancher.

"Thank you, Mr. James, sir," the rancher said, drawing a deep breath now that the gun wasn't pressing into him.

"You a Yankee?" Jesse asked him, studying the rancher's expression as the man reacted to the question.

"If'n I were a Yankee, I coulda stayed back in Virginia," the rancher grumbled. "Wouldn't been drove out by them damn carpetbaggers."

Jesse nodded. Turning back to the cage and the tellers he snapped his fingers, relieving one of the men of a bundle of bills. "How much of your money's in here?" he asked.

"Jesse, we ain't got time for this!" Jim complained from his post at the window. Every minute that passed increased the chance that somebody would come into the bank or maybe start to wonder about the seven Iron Horses parked out in the street. Potts and Danby were keeping watch over the vehicles, but even with them providing cover, it would go hard on the outlaws if they had to fight their way back to the Horses.

The rancher was pensive a moment. "I reckon there's two hunert fifty four dollars and two bits of mine in here."

Jesse counted out the bills and then fished a twenty five cent piece from his own pocket. Sternly, he placed the money in the rancher's hands. "We rob banks, we rob trains, but we don't rob good folks," Jesse said. "Next time, bury your money in a coffee can before you go handin' it over to a Yankee bank."

The outlaw turned back to the cage. "You fellas just about done in there?"

"Yes, sir, Mr. James," one of the tellers said, hurriedly relieving his co-workers of the bags they'd filled and pushed them one after the other out the cage. "I'm sorry it's not more, but most of it's in the safe and as Mr. Parker explained, there's a time-lock."

Jesse took the bags, handing them off to John. He glared back at the teller in the cage. "Where's the banker?" he asked.

Bob rolled his eyes. "Jesse, Jim's right, we don't have the time. Forget about the safe!"

Jesse ignored Bob's protest and continued to train his threatening gaze on the teller. "Where's your boss?"

"Mr. Temple isn't here," the teller stammered. "He... he always dines... takes lunch... at the Palace Hotel..."

"Satisfied, Jesse?" Jim asked. "Can we light out now?"

Jesse looked around the office behind the cage. He pointed at a tintype in a gilded frame hanging on the wall, motioning for the teller to give it to him. Snatching the picture from the man's hands, he tossed it across the lobby. It landed on the floor and slid almost to Jim's feet.

"Have a gander and tell me if'n he's not worth the wait," Jesse told Jim.

Confused, Jim reached down and picked up the tintype. He squinted at the picture a moment, but then went livid. Spinning around, he shook the picture at Jesse. "This is why we came here!" he shouted. "It warn't the money! It was him!"

"Him who?" Bob wondered, craning his head to try and get a look at the picture while still keeping his knife against the guard's throat.

"Captain Thomas Archibald Temple," Jesse hissed. "Late of the Kansas Redlegs, now a respectable bank president." A murderous glint crept into Jesse's eyes. "He's gonna be the first notch in payin' the Yankees back for Frank."

Hardin rounded on Jesse. "You drug us out here knowin' there waren't any money?" the gunfighter roared.

"Yeah. Yeah, I did," Jesse said. He punctuated the statement by firing both of his blasters. The shots sizzled past Hardin, striking the windows behind him. Glass exploded across the boardwalk. Townsfolk screeched as blobs of liquefied window spattered across them.

"Now you're all elected," Jesse told his horrified gang. "You can break for the Horses like a pack of coyotes or you can stand with me and make these curs pay for what they done to Frank!"

"Dammit, Jesse!" Hardin raged. The gunfighter darted for the door, but no sooner had he poked his head outside than he was ducking back. Energy bolts sizzled through the front of the building. "Must be fifty rifles out there! How're we supposed to get out of here now!"

"Calm down, Texas," Bob growled. "Can't be more'n six out there."

Jim shook his head. Hardin might be overreacting, but that didn't mean he was entirely wrong. The plan, as Jesse had explained it to them in the hideout, was to hit the bank quietly and then slip out the same way they had come into town, using the crowd as camouflage. Now, Jesse's shots had scattered that crowd and stirred up the town. The only way out now was to shoot their way out.

"You... you have a plan... right, Jesse?" John asked, shocked by the duplicity exhibited by his hero.

Jesse smiled coldly at the boy and nodded. "Hardin, keep them farmers busy with your smokers," he said. "Don't matter if you hit nothin', just so's you make lots of noise. Bob, you start them prisoners out the door when I give the high sign." He spun around to the cage, burning open the door with a shot from his blaster. "Gentlemen," he told the tellers. "You'll oblige me by getting over there by Bob Younger."

"Please, Mr. James," one of the bank-men pleaded. "They'll shoot us if we go out there."

The outlaw's eyes were as sympathetic as two slivers of steel.

"Then you'd best squawk real loud like and make damn sure they know it's you," he advised. Jesse turned to the rancher. "You can try and light out with them or stick around in here," he told the man. "Either way you're apt to be duckin' a fair parcel of gunfire." The rancher swallowed the knot that had grown in his throat and ambled off to join the bank-men, reasoning his chances would be better with them than alone.

"Jim, John," Jesse called to the last men in his gang. He swung around toward the far wall of the lobby. "You're gonna help me blast a door over here. With all them Yankees watchin' the front, we'll see how they favor a flank attack."

John barked out a Rebel yell, aiming his blaster at the wall. Jim was more cautious in his enthusiasm, impressed by Jesse's reasoning but also mindful that once they'd burned their hole in the wall they'd still have a town full of riled up farmers to deal with.

Jesse raised one of his metal arms, then brought it flashing down. At his sign, Bob rushed the prisoners out the front while Jesse, Jim, and John opened up on the wall.

*****

The captives from the bank were screaming as they scrambled through the door, shouting and wailing to their friends and neighbors to hold their fire. A few shots sizzled down at them from across the street, but the aim was hasty and the fire uncoordinated. Moreover, the men firing at the prisoners were themselves rattled by the tumultuous explosion that shook the town as the sidewall of the bank burst outward in a cloud of smoke and dust. The gritty fog of pulverized adobe went billowing out into the street, blinding the men arrayed around the bank and forcing them to retreat back behind whatever cover as was near at hand.

Through the murk, the outlaws scrambled out into the street. Bob and Jim dove behind a wagon that Hardin's smokers had set on fire, tipping it onto its side. Hardin himself slithered behind the iron bulk of a blackhoof dropped by the barrage the townsmen had fired at the bank. Jesse and John rushed the carriage of the snake oil salesman, knocking over the table on which he'd set his noxious wares. Crouching down by the steel steps leading up into the charlatan's wagon, Jesse stared into the cloud of dust, his sharp eyes picking out the silhouette of a rifleman creeping out from the boardwalk. A bolt from his blaster ripped across the street and splashed the man against the wall of a tobacconist's shop.

"This here's Jesse James," the outlaw barked out. "Anybody don't want to get shot better clear out now. Anybody sticks around best be warned the James Gang fights under the black flag!"

Silence held the town as men trembled at the threat in Jesse's words. The black flag; the warning that no quarter would be shown to the enemy, no mercy given. It was under such warning that Confederate guerrillas had burned Lawrence, had massacred Union soldiers in Centralia. It took some men a few moments of hesitation for the words to sink in. Even though it had been a very long time ago,the image of such wartime atrocities cast a long shadow and it fell squarely upon the defenders of Charity.

One of the riflemen across the street emerged from behind the sacks of feed where he had taken shelter. Whether to take aim at the outlaws or to flee to safety was a question never to be answered. From where he lay,concealed by the chassis of the mechanical horse, John Wesley Hardin peeled off a shot from one of his smokers. The rifleman shrieked as the blob of jellied fire splashed against him, and his body erupted in flame. A living torch, the stricken man stumbled and screamed, flailing about as the flesh melted off his bones.

The sickening display sent many of the townsmen throwing down their weapons and running off in total retreat. Others, those with more courage or a sharper sense of justice, held their positions and began to direct a vindictive fusillade against the robbers.

The outlaws returned fire, blasting holes in walls and shattering windows and doors as they tried to roust the townsmen from their cover. Jesse, exhibiting the almost preternatural speed of his mechanical arms and the unerring accuracy that had been honed during the War, caught two of the defenders on the run as they tried to dash from the cover afforded by a stack of wooden crates for the more promising shelter of a water wagon. A third man he picked off from the roof of a saloon, sending his mutilated remains dripping from the overhang onto the boardwalk below.

"Jim! Bob! Help Potts and Danby!" Jesse shouted to the two Younger brothers. With the set of their wagon, the two bushwhackers were the closest of the gang to the livery stable where the buckaroos were being hard-pressed by a mob of a dozen men. It didn't need to be impressed on any of the outlaws what would happen should they lose their Iron Horses.

"Give your brothers some cover," Jesse told John. Both of them dashed across the street, blazing away at the cluster of buildings around the hotel where the defenders seemed most firmly entrenched. Their rush to the far side of the street brought a withering stream of fire sizzling after them, but it served to keep those same rifles from menacing Bob and Jim as they rushed toward the livery stable and attacked the rear of the townsmen who had Danby and Potts bottled up inside.

John threw himself behind the stack of long wooden boxes piled up in the work yardon the other side of the street. As he leaned up to fire at the townsmen, the boy shouted in alarm, recoiling from what he now realized was a pile of coffins.

Jesse glanced over at him and shook his head. "You don't believe in that kind of thing," he told the boy. "I ain't never seen no omen could stand up to one of these," he added, spinning back around and tapping off shots from each of his blasters in turn.

More than a little ashamed by his display of superstitious fright in the presence of his hero, John leaned back over the coffins and started to take aim. What he saw had him throwing himself flat into the dirt. An instant later, the coffins exploded into splinters.

Marching down the middle of the street was a UR-30 Enforcer. The robot bore a pair of military pattern blasters; ugly snub-nosed weapons that traded accuracy for destructive power. It was a fair trade where a 'bot was concerned, as its mechanized brain couldn't match the speed and marksmanship of an experienced gunfighter. At the same time, the 'bot was absolutely fearless and hideously tough to bring down. That was proved when Hardin opened up on the thing, striking it with one of his incendiary pellets. Fire splashed across the Enforcer, burning away the vest and pants that had been fitted to it in a crude attempt to make the thing seem more human. The robot itself was utterly unfazed, oblivious to the licking flames as it continued its march down the street.

Hardin rolled away from the fallen blackhoof, squirming underneath the boardwalk like some overgrown lizard, only seconds before a concentrated barrage from the Enforcer slammed into the iron chassis. It broke apart in a burst of flame and shrapnel, twisted limbs scything through the air and embedding themselves in the facades of nearby buildings.

In the undertaker's yard, John Younger writhed in agony, splinters of burning coffin embedded in his flesh. The boy tried to maintain a brave front as he tried to pluck the slivers from his skin, but the pain of each piece of pinewood imbedded in his flesh was excruciating. Lost in the oblivion of his own pain, he was shocked when a metal hand closed about his shoulder and pulled him back against a pile of boxes. Jesse glanced over John's injuries, deciding that even though they might be painful, they weren't serious. Not as serious as a necktie party, anyway.

"John," Jesse called to the boy as they both crouched amongst the coffin splinters. "I need you to keep these farmers anxious. Don't care if you hit nobody, just so they keep their heads down."

'What're you gonna do?" John asked as they both crawled over to a stack of marble slabs.

"I'm going to take all the fight out of them yellow-livered townies," Jesse swore. Before John fully understood the man's meaning, Jesse threw himself out into the street in a long dive. The Enforcer, starting to shoot up the boardwalk Hardin was sheltered under, turned back around to address this new threat.

The bolts from the robot's guns went wide, gouging craters in the street around Jesse but missing the outlaw himself. Dirt from the explosions covered Jesse's duster and hung in clumps from his hat. Tiny rocks thrown up by the blasts had cut his cheeks and dug a little furrow across one side of his neck. He paid the hurt as little notice as the

Enforcer would have. Displaying the steely nerve for which he was famous, Jesse took deliberate aim before opening up on the 'bot.

In deploying the UR-30's throughout the west, entrusting them to sheriffs and marshals in hundreds of towns and camps, the Union had thought to make a quick end of the outlawry that threatened the stability of the region. Impressed with the capabilities of their machines, the government had paid little attention to training the men who would be called upon to use them. The sheriff of Charity was one such example. Believing the scuttlebutt that the machines were impervious to gunfire, that they would boldly walk through blasters to get their target, that no man had the stomach to trade shots with the things, he deployed his Enforcer with all the subtlety of a bull in a china shop. Instead of using cover, instead of having the 'bot working in tandem with the armed citizens, he sent the machine lumbering down the middle of the street, thinking to use the mere threat of the Enforcer to force the outlaws to surrender.

Jesse tapped off two blasts from his pistols. With the enhanced speed of his quick-devil arms, the shots struck almost simultaneously. Sparks and flame erupted from the Enforcer's chest as the robot staggered back under the double impact. Pivoting at the waist, the machine returned Jesse's fire, sending him scurrying across the street as the 'bot's fire scarred the earth.

Jesse thought back to the UR-30 Enforcer his gang had faced in Diablo Canyon. Destroying that machine had taken the entire gang and even then there had been moments when the outcome looked to favor the 'bot. He'd made the mistake, then, of thinking the thing would go down like a man. Now, he prayed that Charity's sheriff had made the mistake of expecting the Enforcer to fight like a man.

"Bob! Jim! Try an' get its attention!" Jesse shouted, lunging across the boardwalk just as the Enforcer's guns reduced the façade of a dentist's office into a charred wreck. From their vantage, the Younger brothers opened fire on the robot. Jim's aim was more accurate than that of his brother, but all the shots did when they struck was scorch the machine's hull and cause its ponderous march into a leftward lurch as a lucky hit fused some of the gears together just below its hip.

The Enforcer reacted just as Jesse had hoped. The fresh assault from the Youngers brought a speedy reprisal. The 'bot swung around and started pumping shots into the livery stable, blasting chunks from its loft and sending a spent fuel cell skittering down the street.

In Diablo canyon, the Enforcer the James Gang had fought had been almost loquacious in its mechanized demands for surrender and capitulation. This 'bot was utterly silent, the only sound rising from it was the whizzing of gears and the tromp of its steel feet. Jesse suspected its silence was because, unlike the Enforcer in Diablo Canyon, this 'bot wasn't acting with independence of its own. It was operating under a far less flexible liveliness, enslaved by the commands given to it by the sheriff. It could react to the situation, but it wasn't allowed to interpret the stimuli. It wasn't given the freedom to think and act for itself.

"Hardin!" Jesse yelled. "Try yer smokers again!"

The Texan poked his nose out from under the boardwalk. "Hell with that," he snarled.

Jesse glared at the black-clad gunslinger. "Do it, Johnny, or the 'bot will be the least of your worries."

Hardin blanched at the threat. Screwing up his courage, the gunfighter scrambled out from under the walkway. Shots from some of the townsfolk peppered the street as he dashed across. As he drew parallel to the Enforcer, he peeled off a shot from his smoker. The incendiary pellet splashed across the robot's side, turning it into a walking torch. The machine swung around, tracking Hardin as he ran to the opposite side of the road. The Texan gunned down a townsman who rose up from behind a heap of grain sacks, and then threw himself through the window of an assay office. The next instant, the front of the building was hammered by the Enforcer's shots.

"Jim! Hold off on shootin' the 'bot!" Jesse hollered. For what he had in mind, he needed the UR-30 focused on the assay office, its back to him. Any stray shot from the livery stable might bring the machine turning back around and spoil his plan.

Rising up from the burning dental office, Jesse ran toward the middle of the street. A few farmers fired at him, but his bold dash toward the Enforcer threw off their aim. The last thing anybody expected was that the outlaw would run toward the murderous robot. Jesse rushed to within a few yards of the machine before it reacted to him. As it swung around, the left side of its body still wrapped in flame, the outlaw chief brought both of his blasters to bear. The double shot struck the Enforcer in the neck. Jesse thought of the 'bot back in Diablo Canyon and how it had gone wild when its head had been blasted from its shoulders. He intended to use that to his advantage. As the head was ripped from its shoulders, the 'bot's body froze, its automation seizing up. Jesse ran past it, rushing at the head and kicking it down the street like an old tin can.

"What'll you do now, you mutton-punchers!" Jesse shouted at the horrified townsfolk. He rushed to cover as vindictive fire pursued him across the street. The outlaw felt a cold satisfaction at the violence his jeers had provoked. The farmers had acted exactly the way he wanted them to.

The decapitated Enforcer turned around once more. Loss of its head had removed much of its cognitive ability and reduced its sensory input, but the machine was still capable of functioning. The 'bot swung around and began firing at the shooters its reduced senses could detect. Oblivious that it was now firing on the very people it had been dispatched to protect, the Enforcer limped through Charity, both its blasters blazing away. The sheriff appeared on the balcony overlooking a saloon, shrieking orders to the robot, trying to end its mindless rampage. A quick shot from Jesse put an end to the lawman's effort.

The savage destruction wrought by their own Enforcer broke the back of Charity's resistance. Crying out in horror, men threw down their weapons and fled. Jesse spun around at the glint of bronze on the chest of one of the refugees, a blast from his pistol throwing a retreating deputy through the enormous window at the front of the hotel. The Enforcer staggered on, pursuing a group of farmers who kept stopping to take shots at the thing, oblivious to the fact that it was their constant attacks that kept the machine on their tail. Already, the Enforcer had been hit upwards of thirty times, so what the farmers expected to do was a mystery to Jesse. He suspected it was a mystery to them as well. The outlaw almost felt sorry for them as he watched them flee town with the robot still dogging their heels.

Then Jesse saw something of far greater interest. Leaning across the banister on the balcony which fronted the hotel's upper floor was Temple. The banker was dressed in a fine suit of powder-blue, a derby squashed down about his ears, its extravagant metal band shining like gold in the noon sun. Temple had a heavy-bore rifle in his hands, but looked more apt to toss it aside than try to draw a bead on Jesse now that the Enforcer was down.

Jesse didn't give Temple the time to make his choice. Peeling off a shot from each blaster, he blew apart the floor beneath the banker's feet. The blast threw Temple through the air and plummeting to the ground in front of the hotel. The terrified man started up onto his feet, cradling a broken arm against his chest. He made a frantic dash for the open doorway of a mercantile.

He didn't make it.

"Redlegs don't run," Jesse roared at Temple, firing his blasters at the man. The banker's anguished howl thundered across Charity as Jesse's shots tore off both of his legs. "They crawl."

The vengeful outlaw watched Temple flopping about in the street. Jesse didn't see the banker, but instead the murderous Union captain who'd led his barbaric border ruffians in terror raids up and down Missouri. They'd hung any guerrillas or suspected guerrillas they caught, at least once they tired of whittling away at their hides with knives and branding irons. Many times during the War, Jesse had seen the handiwork of Temple and his Redlegs dancing from a tree, birds pecking at what were left of their faces.

The roar of Iron Horses shook the street. The metal steeds of Bob and Jim Younger hurtled down past the ruined hotel toward Jesse. "Potts and Danby are holding the stable," Bob called down to the gang leader. "Better get down there afore these farmers get their second wind."

The advice didn't need to be given a second time for Hardin; squirming out from under the boardwalk, he set off down the street toward the livery stable. John Younger started to follow the black-clad gunfighter, but froze when he noticed that Jesse hadn't moved an inch from where he stood. The long rider was just staring down at Temple screaming in the dirt.

"I'd be obliged for yer rope, Jim," Jesse said, eyes never leaving the mutilated man writhing in the street. "We ain't quite done here yet."

The same vengeful light was in Jim's eyes as he pulled a coil of old hemp from his saddle bag and threw it over to Jesse. In a blur, Jesse holstered one of his pistols and caught the rope. He glanced up at the smoldering balustrade along the balcony, and then returned his hateful gaze to Temple.

"You might'nt have a leg to stand on, Captain Redlegs," Jesse snarled at the man, shaking the rope at him. "But by thunder, yer gonna dance just the same!"

*****

They met in the office on Allen Street, the noise of the traffic outside drifting in through the open door. Wyatt Earp, ever a stickler for observing propriety, always a staunch exponent of law and order, couldn't bring himself to use the Over-marshal's office for this meeting. What he had in mind was less about law and more about vengeance.

Pacing across the hardwood floor, Wyatt presented an imposing sight. He was tall, dressed in a long leather lawman's coat with steel plates reinforcing its shoulders to afford some degree of protection against back-shooters. The metal cleats in his boots grating across the boards, his broad-brimmed hat casting most of his face into shadow, Wyatt presented the image of an enraged lion prowling in its den. When his face did emerge into the light, there was stamped upon it such an expression of fury that even close friends and kin hesitated to look on him.

"First Morg, now Virg!" the Over-marshal roared, slamming his fist against the cherrywood top of the desk that dominated one corner of the room. "Them mongrels think they can go gunning the law and then skedaddle back to their hidey holes and brag about it!" He tapped his finger against the emblazoned bronze pectoral he wore, setting his finger against the star engraved at the center of the metal plate, causing it to jounce on the chain that held it across his chest. "Not anymore! They're gonna learn this means somethin'!"

"And how do you aim to learn them?" The question was distorted; the voice was rendered into an almost metallic quality as the words were forced through the silvered grill of an ornate mask. The speaker leaned against one of the book cases lining the walls of the office. Neither so tall nor solidly built as Wyatt, the metal casing that covered the lower half of his face leant the man a menacing aspect unmatched even by Wyatt's fury. Thin, almost shriveled in build, the man's eyes seemed the only thing vibrant about him, glistening with a callous, sardonic intensity that was at once mocking and threatening. The ruffled front of his Spanish-style shirt, the rich embroidery on his vest, the golden filigree of the garters that circled his arms, all of these stood out in stark contrast to the bulky gun harness he wore and the lethal blasters hanging from the shoulder holsters underneath each of his arms.

"You figurin' to ride out with Bob Paul? Take the county sheriff up on his gracious offer to include you in his posse?" The last word was almost distorted beyond recognition by the shallow cough that rattled through the silver grill. The mask was a wonder of science and medicine, tiny bars of RJ acting as a filter to burn away the impurities in the air and provided relief from what many called the White Plague. It could suppress the affliction and its grisly symptoms, but it was a remedy rather than a cure. His coughing might not have John Holiday lying on a hotel floor spitting up blood as it had so often before, but it still made certain to remind the gambler that whatever relief the mask provided, the rot was still down there in his lungs.

"I wouldn't bet a Boston dollar on Bob being able to catch a cold," Wyatt snarled. "No, Doc, we do this, we do this on our own."

Doc Holiday nodded. "Just one question, Wyatt. Are we doin' this for the law, or for your brothers?" The gambler's gaze shifted from the Over-marshal to the spot where Morgan Earp was standing. Throughout Wyatt's tirade, the hulking cyborg had been silent, his expression as impassive as the Sphinx. They might have been talking about the weather for all the effect the discussion had on Morgan. It wasn't that Morgan was daft or dull in his mind, he understood what had happened well enough. It had been Morgan who'd carried Virgil to his home, had watched him through that first night as the maimed lawman kept asking why he couldn't move his right arm. No, Morgan understood everything perfectly, it was simply that the cyborg didn't seem to feel anything about his brother's crippling. Doc had often been accused of being a cold-hearted sidewinder, but on his worst day he'd never become as devoid of compassion as Morgan seemed to be.

Wyatt scowled up at Morgan, pain clouding his eyes as he looked upon the cyborg Dr. Carpathian had sent back to Tombstone after Virgil brought their dying brother to the wonder-worker's enclave. Losing Morgan had been the hardest thing he'd gone through in his life, far more painful than even the death of his wife had been. What Virgil had done was worse. There were moments, times like now, when Wyatt wondered if what had been brought back from Carpathian was still their brother. Certainly it was Morgan's face, sometimes even acted like Morgan, but something important appeared missing. It pained him to think like this, but it was like a 'bot playing at being Morgan, a machine with oil where it should have blood and pistons where it should have a heart. Just looking up at Morgan was a reminder of what the family had lost. At his lowest, Wyatt wondered whatif Virgil had only let him die; they'd have been able to bury the memory of their brother and move on. Instead, everyday, they were forced to watch that memory walking around, a steel echo of their brother.

Wyatt could almost hate Virgil for what he'd done. Now, it was Virgil lying in bed, waiting for the doctors to decide if he would live or die. Their older brother, James, was with him now, standing vigil over him. Unlike the younger Earps, James wasn't a fighter; he was instead content to tend bar in the saloon the brothers owned. He didn't have the ability or the drive for what Wyatt was planning. It was just as well. The Earps had too many enemies in Tombstone between the Clantons and the rest of the Cowboys. He'd already deputized 'Texas' Jack Vermillion and seven other men, but he'd feel better knowing there was somebody who was family keeping an eye on Virgil.

"This is all about family, lunger!" the growl came from a gruff, bull-necked man leaning back in a cowhide chair. He wore the same leather lawman's coat as Wyatt, even copied the cut of the Over-marshal's broad-brimmed hat. The same curled handle-bar moustache spread across his lip. To a casual observer, he might have been a reflection of Wyatt that had climbed down from its mirror to sit a spell. A closer look would have revealed the absence of the fierce sense of duty and obligation that framed the Over-marshal's features even in a time like this. This man's face was harsher, his eyes gleaming with a streak of viciousness that didn't need the excuse of vengeance to rise to the fore. For all the youth in that face, Warren Earp had already packed a lifetime of brutality behind it.

"Your puppy's barkin' again," Doc complained to Wyatt.

A simple glance from his older brother had Warren sinking down in his chair. Wyatt turned back to Doc. "He's right. This isn't about the law. This is about family." He turned and addressed the other men he'd chosen to form his posse. "'I'll understand if the rest of you boys want to sit this out."

A few of the men glanced anxiously at one another, but it was Doc who broke the tense silence. "That's mighty considerate of you, Wyatt, but I've got nothin' more important on my dance card." He nodded at the other men. "I rather suspect none of us does. And there is that nice fat reward to take into consideration," he added, raising his voice so that he was certain the other men heard every word despite the distortion of his mask. "Split nine ways," Doc added, then glanced over at Morgan. "Or are marshals excluded from taking bounty money? That'd make a seven way divvy, six if you'll pin a star on Warren before we ride out."

"Why you brayin', lowdown..." Warren had barely started to climb out of his chair before another glower from Wyatt made him choke down the rest of his outburst.

Wyatt looked across the men he'd gathered together. He waited for each man to give his nod, feeling pride deep inside him as Sherman McMaster, 'Turkey Creek' Johnson, and the others each gave him their nod. Last of all, he turned toward Doc.

"You know better than to even ask," Doc said. "But before we light out after them, you'd better give me one of them stars."

The Over-marshal reached into his vest and drew out a simple tin badge. "Getting superstitious, Doc?" he asked as he handed it over.

The gambler shook his head. "Nope. I just feel there's things you do for money and things you do for friendship. Wearin' this'll remind me why I'm tradin' shots with Jesse James."

Chapter 5

It was an impressive pack of outlaws that Cole Younger led back to the old hide-out. Even after he gave the signal, he was certain that Potts or Danby were going to open up on them, convinced that such a big mob could only mean a posse. It took the familiar cadence of Cole's Rebel yell to get the lookouts to be uncertain enough to dash back to the bunkhouse and fetch one of the senior members of the gang.

Even from a distance, Cole recognized the refined coachman's top hat that was his little brother Jim's prized affectation. It always amazed Cole that Jim spent so much time trying to dandify himself for the ladies, when he'd invariably just take up with the first wag-tail who gave him the squiny. Jim had another of his prized possessions in his hands – the nickel-plated carbine he'd stripped off a Pinkerton-man down near Centralia. Cole gave out a second Rebel yell to make sure Jim didn't snap the weapon up to his shoulder and peel off a shot. His brother wasn't an especially fast gun, but he could pick a coon out of a tree at five hundred yards. Cole figured he wouldn't tempt fate.

Jim waved his carbine overhead when he heard the second yell. Cole waved the men following him forward. The threat of being shot by their new allies having diminished, the Cowboys reverted to the grumbling and complaining that had characterized the long ride from Clantonville.

"Don't look like much," Ike Clanton observed, spitting a plug of tobacco into the dirt. "I'd have figured the James-Younger Gang would be keeping themselves in style. This sorry set-up wouldn't impress a bean-eater."

Cole growled under his breath. He'd crossed half the territory listening to the Cowboys grouse about everything from saddle sores, to fleas in their bedrolls, to the severity of the weather. Most of it was just the sort of venting you'd expect from men on the trail. The big exception was Ike. If it wasn't something that already had a Clanton brand on it, the slicked-up saddle tramp went out of his way to find fault in it. If it wasn't in his pocket, he could make a gold eagle sound rowdy-dow. Cole figured he must have offended the Almighty at some point, since it was Ike who had to be the most loquacious of the Tombstone bunch.

"We like to keep on the move," Cole snapped back at Ike, not appreciating the rustler's high-handed tone. "Old habit we picked up ridin' with Quantrill a long, long time ago. You keep movin' and any folks lookin' fer you have a plum difficult time trackin' you down. Beats havin' the law knockin' on the door every time a steer goes missin'."

Ike scowled back at Cole. "Might's well be livin' like a pack of Indians," he sneered. "You fellas take up with squaws too? Oww!" He clapped a hand to his ear, massaging the enflamed skin where his father had slapped him with a cow-hide cattleman's gauntlet. The metal ribbing lining the fingers had split the skin in a few spots, bringing blood oozing up from the shallow cuts.

"I warned yeh afore!" Old Man Clanton yelled at Ike. "Shut yer gob and mind yer manners!" He looked apologetically at Cole. "Don't mind Ike's bark. He's either half way to makin' hisself a ringster or a half-wit, and the jury's still deliberatin' on which."

"Just see he remembers who's big auger of this outfit," Cole said.

Old Man Clanton leaned across the saddle of his blackhoof. "And just who is tall hog at the trough? That be you or would that be Jesse?"

"Far as you Cowboys are concerned, it's both of us," Cole answered. The rustler had a way of getting under his skin just like his son Ike, only the Old Man was better at it. Ike just made himself obnoxious; but the Old Man would needle a man where he lived, dig around in his skull, and figure out what made him tick before stinging him with his tongue. Cole was constantly fighting to keep either from getting to him, or at least letting them know that they were. Maybe it was just sheer cussedness on the Old Man's part, but Cole couldn't shake the impression that he was scouting out the terrain for reasons of his own.

As the outlaws came riding close to the hideout, Jim ambled toward the newcomers. He waved at his cousin Johnny Ringo, and then turned toward Cole. "You said you was gettin' more guns. Didn't 'spect you to come ridin' back with a whole damn regiment."

Cole smiled, looked over his shoulder at the Cowboys following him. All told, there were twenty five men who'd mustered up with the Clantons. Even though it was a relic of a memory, Cole recalled that during the war, Quantrill and Bloody Bill had put whole towns to the torch with fewer men.

"You know me, Jim. When I do something, I like to do it big." Cole smiled and waved his hand at the men around him. "You already know Cousin Johnny. The mean fellow who looks like a twenty-card speeler is Ike Clanton, the curly wolf sittin' on that tin crowbait there is Bill Brocius, and the head honcho beside me here is Old Man Clanton, Ike's pa."

Jim nodded to each of the outlaws as they were introduced, and then turned back to his older brother. "Cole, Jesse's up and about. Took the whole gang out to tackle the bank at Charity."

Cole felt a cold shiver rush down his spine. "He take John too?" was the first thing that leapt off his tongue. He knew Jesse's penchant for just bulling into a place and trusting to luck and brass to carry him through. Without the restraining influence of Frank James at hand, Cole didn't like to think about how the raid on Charity might have gone.

"John's fine," Jim assured him. "Everybody came out in one piece, though Hardin'll be picking splinters from his prat for a few weeks and John's got a few along his forearm."

Ringo straightened up in his saddle when he heard that name. "Hardin? You mean John Wesley Hardin?" An ugly light crept into Ringo's eyes. "I heard of him. Folks say he's fast."

"Not sure about fast, but he'd win a contest for plum meanness," Jim said. "He favors a brace of ugly-looking irons that don't just shoot a man, but light him up with fire. Watched him laugh when he done it, too."

"What was the take from Charity?" Ike asked.

"Near on two thousand dollars," Jim said.

Ike laughed. "Two thousand? Jesse'd make more turnin' himself in for the bounty!"

"He didn't ride us in there for the money," Jim growled at Ike, resenting the rustler's mockery.

"What did he ride you in there for?" Cole wondered, feeling as though he already knew.

"We rode in there to hang a banker," Jim said. "Man named Temple who'd been a captain in the Redlegs."

"And did Jesse hang him?"

Jim shuddered. "Yeah. We hung him, or what Jesse left for us to hang."

Cole felt an icy cold creep into his veins. That first day when Jesse'd come back, when he'd talked of Frank's getting killed, Cole had seen the look in the outlaw's eyes. The same look he knew had filled his own eyes when his father had been murdered during the war. The look of a hurt, pained animal that only wants to ride out and kill, to kill and kill again until the empty hole inside was all filled up.

*****

"You promised us blasters and Iron Horses!" The words exploded from Ike's mouth like a volley from a cannon. He pushed his chair away from the table and glowered down at the outlaw seated across from him. "We didn't ride out all this way just to divvy up some chicken feed cash box or penny-ante payroll!"

"Then maybe you Arizona boys have wasted your time," Jesse James snarled back, metal fingers drumming against the raw wood surface of the table, leaving little dents in the soft pine.

The air within the bunkhouse was tense. The two groups of outlaws eyed each other suspiciously, keeping among themselves while their leaders discussed their next job. The Cowboys were spread out across the left side of the room, the Youngers to the right with Hardin keeping off on his own near the stone fireplace. Danby and Potts, along with two Cowboys, were outside keeping watch.

Old Man Clanton wagged a finger at Cole Younger. "My boy's got the right of it. It was a lot of fine talk about newfangled guns and hosses that brung us all this way. You'll understand our displeasure to hear it ain't so."

Cole turned toward Jesse. "I've had a plan drawn up for a while now. The Union's got a nice cache of gear over at Fort Concho and they've been pullin' troops out for months to send out with Grant and his expedition against the Warrior Nation."

Jesse's expression darkened at mention of the Indians. He folded his metal arms across each other, working his fingers along the shoulders, feeling along the join where flesh gave way to steel.

"I didn't try tacklin' it afore," Cole explained, "since we didn't have enough hands to do the job. But with Ringo and the Clantons along, takin' the fort'll be screamin' simple. We can just waltz right in and take whatever we like."

Jesse shook his head and glowered at the Cowboys. "I don't cotton to ridin' with men I don't know. I like to see how they handle themselves in a scrap. Find out who's a dabster and who's a spooney."

"And how you figurin' on findin' that out, Mr. Bushwhacker?" Ike growled.

"We could throw down," Jesse suggested, "but that wouldn't do none of us any good. Bunch a folks'd be restin' in a grave patch with a sin-buster prayin' over 'em."

"You have somethin' better in mind?" Old Man Clanton asked.

"I figure'd we mosey on out a ways and slap leather where it'd do some good," Jesse said, fingers still feeling along his scarred shoulders.

Beside Jesse, Cole noted the ugly light in the outlaw's eyes. Killing the banker hadn't even started to fill that hole inside the outlaw chief. It hadn't even made much of a start.

*****

Old Man Clanton squinted through the telescopic lens, frowning as he felt the heat from the optical intensifier's power cell against his cheek. He didn't like all these modern contraptions, far less when he was reminded of the weird ways in which they worked. He liked them still less when they told him things that weren't to his favor. Just now, he felt like taking the telescopic glass and smashing it on the ground.

"You teched in the head, Jesse?" the rustler asked. "Ain't nothin' down there but a bunch of Indians!"

Ike snatched the glass from his father and peered down the lens. "Don't that beat all!" he cursed. "What're we supposed to do, steal their beads?!"

The outlaws had ridden hard for most of the day to reach this spot. Jesse had insisted they hit an easier target before tackling Fort Concho, a plan that Cole had finally endorsed and which Old Man Clanton had eventually come around to. When Jesse'd led them up into the foothills, they'd thought it was a mining camp or a refueling station that they were striking.

Now, they found themselves lying on their bellies on the top of a ridge, staring down at a cluster of domed shaped huts known as "wickiups" and a dozen or so young warriors. A few elk hung from wooden frames and several of the natives were busy cutting steams from the animals. A couple of the other Indians were tending the fire that was smoldering in the stone-lined pit between the huts.

"Looks like a hunting party," Curly Bill suggested, using his own set of field glasses to study the encampment. "Mostly young bucks. Don't see any women or children. If I were pressed, I'd make 'em out as a hunting party."

"They wearin' paint?" Bob Younger asked the Cowboy.

The rustler shook his head. "Nope. These bucks are just hunting, not a war band." He waved a hand toward the rugged mountains rising above the foothills. "Probably got themselves a village somewhere yonder."

"I don't care what they got or where they got it," Ike grumbled. He turned onto his side and fixed Jesse with a scowl. "I want to know what business we got with a bunch of scruffy Indians."

Jesse returned Ike's scowl with a cold stare. "Better change that look on your face afore I change it for you."

Cole was familiar enough with Jesse's moods to know that Ike was within a hairsbreadth of opening up more trouble than he'd ever want. He also knew that if things came to that pass, the gang would bust up in a blaze of violence. Ideas about hitting Fort Concho would go up in that same blaze. They needed the Clantons if they were going to steal supplies from the Union garrison.

"Think about it, Ike," Cole interjected himself into the standoff before it could boil over. "Jesse wants to see how we operate together, wants to see for himself how good you Cowboys are and show you how good the James-Younger Gang is. We go hittin' a ranch or a town and folks'll notice, start spreadin' the word." He smiled and waved a hand down at the camp below. "Who'll notice or care if we attack a parcel of scruffy Indians?"

Cole could tell his words had little impact on Ike, but they took root with his father. Old Man Clanton scratched the stubble on his chin as he mulled them over.

"Makes a right bit of sense at that," he decided. "I still don't like it, but I kin see the sense of it."

Cole looked back at Jesse, watching with dismay as the outlaw glared down at the camp, as one hand reached to the scarred shoulder beneath his coat. Cole didn't know what it must be like, having your arms torn to shreds. He didn't know what something like that would do to a man's mind, the kind of hate it would kindle in a man's heart.

What was about to happen here wouldn't be over the loss of Frank. It would be for Jesse and the arms he'd lost. The outlaw had purposefully brought the gang here knowing there'd be Indians around. It wasn't for some tactical purpose as Cole'd managed to sell Old Man Clanton. Jesse hadn't had anything so pragmatic in mind. For him, this attack was about nothing except revenge.

This was almost to be expected. Jesse was always the emotional type, living in the moment, acting on his desires and impulses without first scoping out the trail ahead. It was always left to Frank to work out the details. With Frank dead, Cole was the most obvious choice to fill that role. Jesse was not about to change who he was to fill that void; so it fell to Cole, the only other person that knew best how Frank's mind worked.

"We'll spread out from here," Cole told the Cowboy leaders. "We leave five men back with the mounts. You don't have to worry about an Indian stealin' one of 'em, but he'll damn sure try to wreck it if'n he gets half a chance." The bushwhacker paused a moment. "Two men from our outfit, three from yours. We'll leave Potts and my brother, John. Whoever you like from your end." He knew his youngest brother would object to being left behind, but Cole's mind would rest easier knowing he was out of the way. Just now, he needed his wits as sharp as they'd ever been if he was expected to juggle Jesse's thirst for revenge and appease the Cowboys.

"We can circle around from the left," Curly Bill pointed a finger at a dried-out creek bed. Thick clumps of brush lined either bank of the creek, ample cover for the outlaws until they got within a couple hundred yards of the camp.

Cole nodded. "There's a gulley down along the back that'll keep us hid until we get within spittin' distance." He pulled his watch from his vest. "I reckon three quarters of the hour and everybody can be in place."

"Just mind everyone stays downwind of that camp," Jesse said, his steely gaze sweeping from Cole to the Cowboy leaders. "They can smell a man coming long afore they can see or hear him." He slapped a metal hand against a steel forearm to emphasize the point. Even Ike lost some of his bravado as he thought about how Jesse had lost those arms.

"Hit 'em hard and hit 'em fast," Jesse told the outlaws. "Shoot to kill and be sure what you shoot stays dead. Remember that and you might see yourself through with all your parts still attached."

*****

From the gulley, Jesse watched as the Indian warriors prowled about their camp, skinning the elk they had taken. It was hard for him to focus on the young natives; his mind kept drifting, conjuring up visions of the Warrior Nation. He could see half-human monsters rearing up from the dark, fangs and claws flashing in the moonlight. He could hear the crunch of bone as it twisted and remolded itself into new shapes, the shredding of skin as it split apart and the flesh beneath shifted and flowed into the foundation of a monstrous form. He could see the shimmer of spectral arrows as they rained down from the sky, granted unholy powers by the medicine men. He could smell the sharp tang as the ghostly arrows came hurtling down. He could feel again the phantom chill as they dropped down toward him in a shower of death.

Jesse's hands dropped to the blasters at his sides. He almost tore them from their holsters; he almost rose up from the gulley and charged into the camp, not so much to gun down the warriors but to vanquish the gruesome images swarming inside his head. Action, the imperative of battle; that would drive down the nightmares, force them back into the shadows where they belonged.

Grimly, Jesse fought to restrain himself. He had to wait, had to hold back until everyone was in place. Attack now and some of the Indians would almost certainly escape. And that was something the hate inside him just wouldn't allow. The savages had taken his arms and the Union had taken his brother. One and all he would pay them back. He would teach them all what it meant to trifle with Jesse James.

Beside him, Cole Younger was keeping one eye on his watch. Jesse could hear the soft buzz of the RJ button inside as the chronometer slowly ticked off the minutes. How many minutes had passed during their crawl along the bottom of the gulley? How many more were left until they would spring their ambush? Jesse held back from asking. It would be an exhibition of weakness to ask Cole, a confession of the anxiety he felt inside, an admission of the bloodlust thundering through his veins. He had to be bigger than that. He was the leader of this gang and he had to have the respect of every man who followed him. He couldn't have that if they thought he was weak, if they stopped thinking for even one minute that he was bigger than they were.

Jesse glanced away from Cole, studying the other men in the gulley. Jim Younger had his carbine already aimed at the camp beside him; Bob had his hands filled with both a blaster and one of his Bowie knives. The buckaroo Danby, much like Jim, had his rifle trained on the camp, but he kept looking away to wipe at the nervous sweat that beaded across his forehead and threatened to drip down into his eyes. Hardin's attitude was more eager, his fingers fondling the grips of his smokers as though impatient to draw them from their holsters and burn down the Indians and their brush-wood shelters.

Time slowly ticked away. Every moment, Jesse expected one of the Indians to turn and stare directly at him, warned of his presence by some preternatural sense unknown to any white man. He expected any one of the warriors to suddenly collapse, for his body to undulate and spasm while his flesh reshaped itself into something obscene and monstrous. He could almost hear the half-human howl of an abomination that was neither man nor beast echoing across the darkening sky.

Then, with an abruptness that startled him, the agony of waiting was over. Cole stuffed his watch back in his pocket, peered down the sight of his carbine, and shouting a fierce Rebel yell sent a blistering bolt of energy slamming into one of the natives butchering the elk. The Indian was lifted off his feet, shot straight into the hanging animal. Corpse, carcass, and frame all came crashing earthward in a smoking mess.

Cole's shot was the signal that caused the entire gang to open up. From the creek bed, the Cowboys sent a withering fusillade pouring down, blasting apart stunned warriors who had just turned away from their chores. The men in the gulley added their fire to the barrage and the Indians were locked in a murderous crossfire.

Jesse peeled off shots at the natives, scowling when his first shot went wide, roaring with dismay when the second fell short. He glared at his metal arms; those fantastic contraptions Carpathian had so graciously endowed him with, the miraculous remedy for his horrific mutilation. They'd betrayed him once, when Carpathian had treacherously shut them down. Now, they were doing so again, refusing to coordinate with the demands made of them by his eyes.

The twilight exploded into light as one of the wickiups caught fire. Soon, a second hut erupted into flame, and then there came a piercing shriek as one of the warriors was turned into a living torch. Jesse spun around to see Hardin laughing like some devil from hell. The gunman had broken cover, risen up from the gulley to slowly walk toward the Indian camp. With each step, he squeezed off a shot from his smokers, immolating either a hut or a man with each shot. Watching the sadist's brazen attack poured fire into more than the camp, it set a fire inside Jesse too. Angrily, Jesse shoved his blasters back into their holsters. He didn't need the guns to do what needed doing.

Lunging up from the gulley, Jesse rushed toward the burning camp. He heard Cole curse loudly behind him, listened with half an ear as the bushwhacker started shouting at his brothers to give Jesse cover. A few of the warriors had managed to reach their wickiups and fetch their rifles, the mystic blue aura of the natives' spirit energy flowing through the air as they were channeled into their weapons. Jesse ignored the fitful shots, too fixed on the hate boiling inside him to worry about insignificant things like keeping his own hide intact.

As he came into the burning camp, what Jesse thought had been a dead native lying on the ground, suddenly leapt to his feet and rushed at him with a tomahawk that was wreathed in blue flame. Jesse met the warrior's charge, catching the downward sweep of the hatchet with his metal forearm. The scrape of steel against steel shrieked out across the camp for a second, but Jesse brought his other hand flashing for the Indian's wrist. His steel fingers tightened, and with a twist he snapped the warrior's arm, sending the tomahawk tumbling from the Indian's grip, at which point the fire went out. Jesse pulled back, dragging the foe with him, shaking him like he was a child's rag doll. The outlaw brought his fist slamming down on his opponent's arm, snapping it like a twig. The crippled Indian collapsed to the ground, shrieking in pain.

In the next instant, Jesse found himself bowled over by a tremendous force. He could hear his coat being shredded by vicious claws, could feel sharp talons raking across his armored vest. A heavy, animal smell was in his nose, a musky stench so overpowering that he could taste it in his mouth. Rolling across the earth, it took every speck of power Carpathian had endowed his mechanized arms with to push the bestial bulk of his attacker off of him. Grunting with the effort, Jesse was just able to thrust his attacker back, pushing it toward one of the burning wickiups.

By the flickering firelight, Jesse could see that the thing was an Indian shapechanger, one of the ghastly and rare monsters that were sacred within the Warrior Nation. This one had the brawny build of a grizzly bear, a kindred beast to the one that had torn Jesse's arms to shreds. The thing's massive body hunched forward, a great hump of fat rising between its broad, almost manlike, shoulders. Manlike too were the powerful hind legs of the beast, taller and straighter than the bandy legs of a natural bear. The muscular forelegs weren't quite like human arms, but the clawed paws at the end of those legs were uncomfortably like human hands. The head and face, however, were utterly devoid of anything human, the low brow and broad snout of a bruin jutting from the merest stump of neck. The beady black eyes that stared out from the bear's face shone with intelligence beyond any animal, yet they glowed in the light like those of any beast.

Jesse stood frozen for a moment, staring in horror at the monstrosity. His body trembled, every nerve afire with the remembered agony of when a beast such as this had torn him apart and left his mangled body helpless on the ground. The bear snuffled, lips peeling back from its fangs in a grisly smile. It could smell the outlaw's fear.

A blaster cracked from either the creek or the gulley, glancing across the bear's back, burning a bloody furrow along its side. The sudden discharge broke the spell of fear that gripped Jesse. Terror became hate in the outlaw's heart, a blazing fury that enflamed every fiber of his being. Throwing up his arms, Jesse shouted at his gang. "This one's mine!" he cried, ordering his men to hold their fire. The bear glared back at him, opening its fanged muzzle in a rumbling roar, as though accepting Jesse's challenge. The next instant, the enormous brute was marching toward Jesse on its hind legs.

"Jesse! Are you loco?!" Cole's cry rang out across the night. Jesse heard similar cries of disbelief from the other outlaws when, instead of drawing down on the bear, he charged straight at it.

The beast swiped at him with one of its claws, a powerful blow that would have split Jesse in two had it connected. The bear was built for strength and power, it couldn't match the infernal speed of Jesse's quick-devil arms. Catching the bear's forepaws as it swatted at him, Jesse wrenched the beast around, using the trapped limb to shield him from the other claw with brutal jerks and tugs that kept forcing the trapped leg into the path of the other paw.

For a moment, the bear roared and raged, trying to break free from Jesse's clutch. Again, Jesse mustered every last ounce of power in his mechanized arms, taxing their superhuman strength to the limit. By degrees, the bear's roars became less furious and more anguished. It flailed desperately in Jesse's grip, trying to pull itself free. Finally, there came a sickening sound of tearing meat and cracking bone. Blood jetted into the twilight as with a howl of triumph, Jesse tore the bear's leg from its shoulder.

Some of the Cowboys, less concerned with Jesse's longevity than the Youngers, had been whooping and hollering from the creek bed, relishing the spectacle of the infamous Jesse James wrestling a bear-changer. The most callous of the Clanton crowd had even wagered on the outcome. Now, even these ruffians fell into a stunned silence, awed by the Herculean feat of the outlaw leader.

Panting from the strain of his fight, Jesse staggered away from the maimed bear. He braced his legs wide and defiantly waited for the monster to come at him again. All the fight had gone out of the bear, however, draining away with the blood spurting from its ripped shoulder. The brute stood there for a moment, glowering at Jesse, then slumped to its knees.

Tossing aside the leg he'd ripped free, Jesse lunged at the dying monster. His metal arms closed about the bear's remaining foreleg. Sweat streamed down Jesse's face, soaked his torn vest, and dripped across his slashed pants as he bent himself to a repeat of the awesome feat that had so stunned his gang. Wrenching the bear's leg backwards, using the beast's own body as a fulcrum, the outlaw pulled until he'd ripped the limb clean from its socket.

Brandishing the gory limb overhead, waving it like a captured flag, Jesse screamed his rage into the night. It had been a beast like this which had cost him his arms, now he would do the same to every skin-changer unlucky enough to cross his path.

"Jesse!" a panicked voice cried out from almost beside the outlaw. He spun around in time to see the young man, whose arm he'd broken, rushing at him. The Indian was holding his tomahawk in his offhand now, the metal glowing with eerie blue energies as he charged. But it wasn't that which gave Jesse pause. It was the anguished look in the native's face, the tears spilling from his eyes as he gazed past Jesse at the dying bear.

Before the warrior could close with Jesse, he was struck down, sent spinning into the dirt by the impact of a Bowie knife slamming into his back. For a moment, the Indian tried to pick himself up, for an instant, the young warrior glared up at Jesse with eyes completely consumed by hate. The outlaw found himself transfixed by that dying gaze, unable to look away until the boy's dead face slumped back down into the dust.

"That would'a been plum tragic," Bob Younger declared as he came stalking over to the dead boy and ripped his knife from the Indian's back. "You go and kill that bear-walker with your bare hands and then this little sidewinder gets you."

Jesse barely heard Bob's words. He was still looking down at the dead warrior, thinking about the ghastly look that had been in his dying eyes, the look that Jesse saw staring back at him whenever he gazed in a mirror. It was the look of love twisted in upon itself until it became a burning knot of hate. What, Jesse wondered, had the bear-changer been to this boy. Uncle? Father?

Brother?

"They'll all be eating out of your hand after this," Bob said, nodding toward the creek where the Cowboys had emerged from cover and were now waving their hats and firing their guns into the air, celebrating Jesse's astounding victory. "Right now, I think those boys will follow you to the gates of Hell."

Jesse turned away from the dead warrior. "Good," he growled as he walked away. "Because that's just where all of us are headed."

Chapter 6

Fort Concho was nestled at the convergence of the North and Middle Concho Rivers, surrounded by miles of treeless prairie. The Union had started construction of the fort immediately after the war, intending to protect the trailheads that passed near to it from the lingering pockets of Secesh in West Texas, while at the same time suppressing Warrior Nation bands. Border violations by Mexico's Golden Army and the criminal activities of Mexican and American Comancheros had, for a time, increased the importance of Fort Concho to a degree where the whole of the 3rd and 10th Cavalry were based there.

The very importance of Fort Concho, the grand ambitions of the generals and politicians who lobbied for its establishment, had played against the post almost from the start. The original site selected for the fort had been abandoned after being flattened and cleared for construction when it was deemed too constrained for the immense compound the generals had envisioned. Part of a perimeter wall had been built from pecan wood before the hard, rough timber was determined to be too difficult to work with. Ugly mounds of earth scattered outside the walls gave evidence to another failed construction material – nearly one hundred yards of wall had been constructed from adobe brick before a demonstration of the penetrating power of an RJ blaster convinced General Grant to order all adobe fortifications dismantled and replaced.

The new construction was sandstone, drawn from local quarries. Thick enough to obstruct light arms and even small cannon, the sandstone brought with it a different problem – the expense of importing stone masons from the east to work it. The added expenditure, in the face of the rising threat posed by the Warrior Nation in the north, finally forced a budget conscious War Department to suspend construction of Fort Concho.

The end result was a fully garrisoned and operational outpost with large gaps in its stockade, guarded by nothing more substantial than wooden posts and steel wire. The size of the garrison and the commanding position of Fort Concho were felt, in a show of insincere optimism by those in Washington, to be sufficient to discourage any attack by hostile elements.

One of those hostile elements now gazed on Fort Concho through an optical intensifier, a broad smile on his face. When he'd first seen the fort, Cole Younger saw it as a ripe plum just waiting to be plucked. That opinion hadn't changed in the months since. If anything, Fort Concho had only become more attractive to the outlaw. The 3rd Cavalry had been withdrawn to the north to address the Warrior Nation's depredations, and whole troops of the 10th Cavalry had been sent to other posts in the area like Fort Clark and Fort Richardson. This left only a hodge-podge of units from other Infantry divisions and Cavalry companies manning the fort, each with their own array of commanders and officers over them.

Cole had seen enough during the war to recognize, whether Union or Confederate, the more brass there was hovering over any group of soldiers, the less effective and slower to react they became. The situation was bound to be made still worse by the commander that Grant had put in charge of Fort Concho; Colonel Ranald S. Mackenzie, a bold cavalry officer but a strict and exacting disciplinarian who tolerated no initiative in the officers under his command. His men were there to follow orders, not discuss them. Since 'Perpetual Punisher' had taken command of Fort Concho, many soldiers had deserted the post, several of them just bitter enough to air the fort's dirty laundry in the cantinas and saloons they drifted through on their way west.

"It looks good, Cole," Jesse observed, peering through his own scope at the fort. "The big stone building at the end of the parade ground is the storehouse?"

"Just to the left of the headquarters' building. There's two of 'em. First one's the commissary, second one is the quartermaster," Cole explained, drawing a rough map of the fort in the dirt. "I figure we set fire to the commissary and at the same time we hit the quartermaster. Them blue-bellies will have to waste time roundin' up vittles in San Angelo if'n we burn up all their hardtack before we skedaddle."

Jesse stared in surprise for a moment at Cole. He was impressed, these were the sorts of military tactics he'd expect to hear from Frank, not a gunman like Cole. "Seems a might of Frank musta rubbed off on you."

"Might be," Cole replied. Despite himself, he relished the fact that he'd managed to impress Jesse. "You're the boss, Jesse. Who'd you like where?"

"Hardin, Stilwell, and Spence can take care of the commissary storehouse," Jesse said. "I want you, Jim, and any decent shots in Clanton's crowd pinning down them blue-bellies in their barracks buildings."

"Ringo and Indian Charlie," Cole said. "Maybe Curly Bill too," he added after a moment's consideration.

"The Old Man and the rest of his crowd can hit the stock yard," Jesse said, pointing at the long stone building where the Union troops kept their Iron Horses. He smiled at Cole. "They want to ride 'em, then they can fetch 'em themselves." He gestured to the stockade wall and in particular the watch towers at each corner of the forty acre base. "We can forget about the towers out to the east, but we'll need to take care of the ones up close." He laughed grimly. "Bob's still damn handy with a knife. He can take out the guard in the tower close to where we slip in. Once hell breaks loose, somebody'll have to settle the guard in the other tower."

"I'll give that job to Ringo. He'll enjoy the challenge and it'll keep him away from you. You ain't exactly his favorite person, you know." Cole pulled at his moustache, hesitating before broaching the subject that had been nagging at him. "What job do you reckon for John?"

"He'll come in with me," Jesse said. "John and those two buckaroos of yourn. We'll bust into the quartermaster storehouse and swipe anything not nailed down."

Cole's expression remained worried. "John ain't exactly used to all this."

"He did just fine in Charity," Jesse said, a hard edge in his voice. "Don't worry about John, he'll make out." The outlaw chief fixed Cole with a steely gaze, almost daring him to flout his decision.

Cole clenched his teeth, biting down on the angry retort that was on the tip of his tongue. Challenging Jesse now wouldn't do him or his brothers any good. He couldn't explain that it wasn't John who had him worried, but Jesse himself. The man who'd used the attack on Charity as a pretext, an excuse to kill a Yankee officer, wasn't about to listen to reason now. There was a whole headquarters full of Union officers right next to the storehouse. He knew Jesse's penchant for taking risks, his impulsiveness once the shooting started. This was the same man who only three days before had waltzed out and wrestled an Indian bear-changer. Cole still wasn't sure if the word for that was brave or crazy.

What he was certain of was he didn't like the idea of his youngest brother taking the kind of chances Jesse James accepted as just part of the job. That sort of recklessness might be fine for Cole Younger, but not for John.

*****

The dull crunch of vertebrae being crushed told Jesse he could release his grip on the sentry's neck. The man in the dark blue shell jacket collapsed to the ground, a look of surprise frozen on his face. The first the soldier was aware of Jesse James lurking in the shadows near the brick guardhouse was when the outlaw's metal fingers closed around his throat. Except for a strangled gasp, the trooper hadn't even made a sound.

Danby crept forward, snatching up the dead trooper's rifle and dragging the corpse back into the shadowy alley between the guardhouse and the nearest of the stone buildings where the enlisted men were bunked. Potts and John Younger eased their way forward to join Jesse against the guardhouse wall. When Jesse tapped Potts on the shoulder and pointed to the guard patrolling in front of the two storehouses, the buckaroo drew his knife from his boot and nodded. Unless Hardin or one of the Cowboys caught the soldier when he came to the corner of the commissary storehouse, it would be left to Potts to eliminate the man when he passed them to make his circuit around the quartermaster storehouse.

"How's your shootin' iron?" Jesse whispered to John, gesturing toward the massive headquarters building beside the storehouse. There were two more sentries patrolling the front of the building, a soldier on the ground and a second making a circuit of the roofed belvedere rising above the headquarters. He was especially worried about that man. There were outlaws creeping all over the fort at this point. The men in the watchtowers had their view of the base obstructed by the buildings; the guards on the ground were a bit too comfortable with the routine of their patrol to be vigilant enough to spot anyone unless they walked up and shook their hand. The trooper up in the belvedere though, with its commanding view of the parade ground, wouldn't have to be particularly on the ball to notice furtive activity below. That one soldier could sound an alarm that would turn out the whole fort against them before they were ready.

"Bob reckons I'm a damn good shot," John said with pride.

"Is that brag or fact?" Jesse demanded, fixing the boy with a commanding gaze. "It'll be all our hides if you can't do what I need you to do." He pointed at the headquarters. "I've got to knock out the blue-belly up top there. I can't risk gettin' tripped up settlin' the fella down below and maybe warning his pal. So I need you to watch him. If it looks like he's got wise that I'm around, there won't be any more need to play sneaky, so you just let him have it."

John's face spread in an exuberant smile, thrilled that his hero trusted him, him, to guard his back. "You can count on me, Jesse."

Jesse nodded once, then slipped away from the guardhouse. He had three different men to keep tabs on as he dashed across the front of the parade ground: the two men outside the headquarters and the sentry patrolling around the storehouses. His thoughts strayed back to similar times many, many moons ago when he'd ridden with Quantrill during the war, hiding out from Redlegs and Jayhawkers.

He'd been fighting for his country then, trying to push back the Unionist tyranny. Now, Jesse had far less lofty ambitions. All he was fighting for was himself.

Darting across the parade ground, Jesse pressed close against the side of the storehouse, feeling a bit safer with the building's shadow wrapped around him. He watched the guards in front of the headquarters building and tried to listen for the man making the circuit of the storehouses, unable to see the soldier now that he was around the corner. He gritted his teeth as he saw both of the sentries outside the headquarters turn their backs to him, stalking off in the other direction as they paced back and forth. Unable to hear the sound of footfalls at the front of the storehouses, Jesse decided that Potts or one of Hardin's men had settled the man. He had to, because with every passing second the chances of the man in the belvedere spotting one of the raiders grew.

In a bold dash, Jesse raced toward the headquarters and leapt at the wall. His metal fingers dug into the sandstone and he pulled himself partway up onto the belvedere. Wrapping his legs around the base of one of the columns supporting the Spanish-style roof, he drew himself up against the side of the building. He felt like a raccoon slinking around in someone's attic as he shifted his position, squirming along the outside of the belvedere toward the footsteps of the sentry.

When he drew parallel with the marching steps of the guard, Jesse lunged up and over the side of the belvedere. He hurled himself full on the man, crushing him down beneath the impetus of his lunge. The outlaw's steel hand closed across the soldier's windpipe, crushing it beneath his vice-like grip before the man could even think to shout.

It was then that things started to go wrong. The boom of a blaster sounded from the area of the guardhouse, and Jesse felt the air turn hot at his back as an energy beam went sizzling past. A Yankee officer, just climbing out onto the belvedere, crumpled against the wall, his head reduced to a steaming ruin. Almost immediately, Jesse heard another shot sizzle away from the guardhouse. Shooting the intruding officer had forced John to shift his attention away from the sentry on the ground. Now, the soldier was scrambling for cover, avoiding John's shots as the boy tried to burn him down.

The nimble soldier ducked behind the steps leading up to the headquarters, using it for cover as he tried to draw a bead on John. The protection offered by the steps, however, wasn't any obstacle for Jesse up in the belvedere. The Union trooper had made the mistake of not realizing there was an enemy already above him. Taking careful aim, Jesse sent a bolt searing straight down into the top of the soldier's head. The trooper pitched across the steps, his carcass flung back when one of John's shots slammed into the twitching corpse.

From his vantage in the belvedere, Jesse watched as chaos erupted throughout Fort Concho. Hardin and the men with him blasted open the door to the commissary storehouse while Danby and Potts did the same to the quartermaster storehouse. Cole and his shooters, however, weren't in position yet, nor were the Clantons and their rustlers. Both groups of outlaws were still crossing the parade ground when soldiers began swarming out from the barracks. The troopers might have been half-dressed, but not a man-jack of them had failed to snatch up his rifle. Caught in the open, the outlaws would swiftly be massacred.

Jesse's vision went red. He thought of Frank, he thought of their home in Missouri, their old mother with her arm blown off by a Union bomb. Between the beats of his heart, his quick-devil arms snapped down to his holsters and ripped his blasters free. Before he even realized what he was doing, Jesse began pumping shot after shot down into the soldiers scrambling from the barracks, mowing them down with the remorseless intensity of a gatling gun. Shocked by the intensity of this one-man fusillade, most of the soldiers scrambled back into the safety of the buildings. The few still exposed out on the parade ground were quickly settled by the vengeful fire from Cole and his sharpshooters.

Jesse could see that Cole and Ringo were slowly falling back toward the stockyard, snapping off shots at the barracks to keep the soldiers penned inside. The original plan had been for Cole's outfit to provide cover from the roof of the fort's chapel, but the early alarm now forced them to support the rustlers more directly, Jim and Curly Bill helping the Cowboys force their way into the stockyard.

Flames crackled from the commissary storehouse as Hardin's men set fire to the Union supplies. As the outlaws dashed away from the burning building, a group of black cavalrymen came rushing out from behind one of the barracks to intercept them. From the top of the belvedere, Jesse could hear Hardin's sadistic laugh as he opened up on the soldiers with his smokers, splashing the entire group with liquid fire.

The roar of engines rumbled from the stockyard. Ike Clanton came barreling out of the building on a shiny new Iron Horse with 'US Cavalry' embossed on its hull. He was followed an instant later by Indian Charlie. The two outlaws made a half circuit of the parade ground, peppering the front of the barracks with shots from the blasters of their Iron Horses before racing away toward the unfinished stockade wall. In short order, other

Iron Horses came whipping out from the stockyard. Curly Bill slowed his steed just long enough for Johnny Ringo to clamber aboard. Jim Younger began to brake in order to pick up his elder brother. Cole waved him on toward the guardhouse, ordering Jim to pick up John instead. As Jim sped off, Cole turned about and dashed into the stockyard to secure a mount for himself, almost getting plowed over by Old Man Clanton as the grizzled rustler bolted out from the building on his Iron Horse.

Jesse did his best to keep the soldiers pinned down inside the buildings. The more care he seemed to take with his shots, the more accuracy he seemed to lose; Carpathian's cursed arms refused to adjust to the demands of his mind. Perversely, when he didn't really think about what he was shooting at, when he just snapped off a shot more or less from sheer instinct, the bolts struck true. For an accomplished gunman, it was an infuriating vexation, another reason – if he needed one – to squeeze the life out of the treacherous doctor.

Accuracy, however, wasn't a tall order to keep the soldiers penned up. With almost a dozen of their comrades scattered about the parade ground, it didn't need much to make them keep their heads down. The buildings themselves were large enough that even with his mechanical arms defying him, Jesse couldn't help but hit something each time he squeezed off a shot.

"Jesse!" John's voice shouted up to the outlaw. "We gotta git!" Jesse looked down to see John slung up behind Jim. Fire from the porch in front of the headquarters sent Jim speeding off around the side of the fort. Jesse smiled when he heard John shouting in protest, insisting Jim wait until Jesse could join them.

The outlaw shook his head. The boy would have to learn that, in a fight, worrying about anybody but yourself was the best way to get yourself killed. That was a wisdom that had seen him through many decades of outlawry. You just didn't stick your neck out for anybody.

Not unless they were family.

The hairs on the back of Jesse's neck suddenly prickled, causing him to spin around. He snapped off a shot at the Union major who was creeping up over the body of the officer John had dropped. The major shrieked as Jesse's blast caught him in the chest, but even as he started to fall, a second officer was rushing up after him, thrusting the body before him like a shield.

Jesse threw himself flat as the second officer started shooting at him. He'd wondered how long it was going to take before the men in the headquarters realized there was somebody up on the belvedere and decided to do something about it. From the floor, the outlaw sent a shot shearing through the officer's forearm. The soldier screamed and clutched at the spurting stump. Jesse silenced his shrieks with a second, mortal shot to his gut.

The distraction presented by the officers gave the soldiers in the barracks the opportunity to come rushing from the buildings. Cole, the last man to come riding out from the stockyard, had to dodge a gauntlet of fire as he tore across the parade ground and hurtled into the night. Before he vanished into the darkness, the bushwhacker shouted a defiant Rebel yell at the enraged Yankees he left behind.

With all the other members of his gang fled, Jesse considered it was time he made himself scarce too. As he rose from the floor, however, he was nearly cut down by a blaster. Hastily he snapped off a shot at yet another officer climbing up onto the belvedere. There was a dull, metallic clang followed by the sound of splintering wood and a body crashing to the ground.

Leaping to his feet, Jesse dashed across the belvedere; throwing himself out over the balustrade before any other officers could come climbing up from below. He flung himself into the open air, hurtling across the span between the headquarters and the quartermaster storehouse. He slammed into the tile roof, feeling it crack and crumble beneath his impact. Before he could consider if the roof would bear his weight, shots came sizzling up at him from both the parade ground and the headquarters. Flakes of terracotta slashed across his face as the soldiers did their best to pick him off the roof.

Jesse didn't give them the chance, sliding off the back of the building to the earth below. Almost the instant his feet touched the ground he heard a shout of alarm, and the wall beside his ear exploded as a shot barely missed taking his head off his shoulders. The outlaw swung around, blasting the black cavalry trooper trying to burn him down with a rifle. He could hear more soldiers rushing around the side of the storehouse, their officers bellowing at them to cut Jesse off before he could reach the perimeter wall.

The prospect of being surrounded seemed a certainty until Jesse heard the roar of an Iron Horse. Speeding out from the smoke boiling up from the blazing commissary storehouse, was Cole. The bushwhacker fired at the advancing blue-bellies, driving them back as he sped toward Jesse. The outlaw leaped up into the saddle behind Cole as he brought his machine roaring around the building.

"You know better than this," Jesse growled at Cole as he brought the Iron Horse whipping around. Shots from Union rifles pursued them as they raced off into the night.

"Somebody has to watch out fer yer neck," Cole said. "Frank's not here, so I figured that means I'm elected."

Jesse was quiet as Cole's steed punched through a gap in the stockade wall and went racing across the dusty prairie. It had been a long time since anything had made Jesse James feel humble, but Cole's gesture and the sentiment behind it came close.

*****

Colonel Mackenzie was sprawled across the divan in his drawing room, his shirt torn away so that Fort Concho's surgeon could pull slivers of wood from the commander's flesh. One side of the colonel's face was an angry welt, the skin blistered by the heat of a near-miss from Jesse's pistol. The eye that stared from that side of Mackenzie's face was like a pool of blood, the white turned red by all the little blood vessels that had boiled and burst.

Mackenzie glared up at his subordinates while the doctor worked on him. "That makes eight," he snarled, rapping his hand against the metal plates bolted into the left side of his body. "Six times I was wounded by Secessionists during the war. A damned spirit arrow nearly took my leg off last time I rode against the Warrior Nation." His hand clenched into a fist, a grotesque gesture with half his fingers replaced by steel talons and a steel plate bolted to his forearm. The Indians called Mackenzie 'Bad Hand' because of that mechanical claw, a memento from injury number three during the siege of Petersburg. Tonight, Mackenzie's metal hand had saved his life, deflecting the shot Jesse James had fired at him, earning him his eighth injury in the line of duty.

"Death reached out for me this night, gentlemen," Mackenzie snapped. "I want to know how such a thing was possible. I want to know how a bunch of outlaw vermin snuck onto my post, fired my buildings, killed my men, and stole my supplies."

"Colonel, sir, the stockade wall..." A glower from the wounded Mackenzie caused the infantry captain to choke down the rest of his speech.

"Put yourself on report, Hawkins," Mackenzie growled. He swept his gaze across the other officers. "The stockade wall's condition is one you've all known about. I expect it to have been taken into account when posting sentries and assigning duties. Men secure perimeters, not fences!"

"It's them colored troops, sir," a cavalry officer declared. "You can't expect them to obey like regular soldiers."

"You're on report too, Lutherlyn," Mackenzie said. "Discipline and training don't recognize the color of a man's skin. If you can't get an African to fight like any other soldier then you need new officers, not new men!"

"Sir, we weren't attacked by just any border trash," a young lieutenant said. "It was the James-Younger Gang that raided us."

Mackenzie waved aside the surgeon and leaned up from the divan. "Jesse James," he mused. "He rode with Quantrill and Bloody Bill. He used guerrilla tactics on us."

"Yes, sir," agreed Captain Hawkins. "No disgrace being tricked by Rebel raiders. Some of the best generals have been..."

Mackenzie fixed the captain with an angry stare. "Failure is always a disgrace. Whatever James might have been before, he's an outlaw now. Nothing more. He isn't owed the dignity of military consideration." His sullen gaze swept across his officers. "Governor Wallace already has a $5,000 reward on Jesse James. We're going to double that, even if it has to come out of the pay of every man in this command. I want every bounty killer and scalp hunter in the territory after that man's hide!"

*****

The smell of smoke was what drew the warband down into the foothills. Even in his human shape, Broken Fang could smell smoke from seven miles away. The scent of a fire had guided the medicine man and his warriors across the prairie in the dead of night to strike a lonely homestead or a settler's camp many times.

This time, the smell guided them to a very different scene. The warriors prowled among the ruin of the hunting camp, poking about among the ashes of the wickiups. Only a generation ago, Broken Fang's warriors would have looked on the slaughtered young men as so many dead enemies. That was before the great chief Sitting Bull had started his big talk about all red men being brothers, about how they must all come together if they would keep the white man from ravaging the land and poisoning the earth. That was before the Warrior Nation and the spread of the great secret.

Broken Fang stared down at the butchered carcass of the slain elder. In death, the bear-like shape had started to slip away from his corpse, reverting back into a semblance of human form as decay began to rot the skin-changing magic. By the time the body was reduced to bones, there'd be no sign that he'd been anything other than just another man.

If not for the smell of metal and the taint of devil's blood lingering around the corpse, Broken Fang might have thought another skin-changer had killed the bear. The spirits of beast and man weren't always in harmony, and a skin-changer had to be very wary of how much of the beast he let into his mind.

Broken Fang shook his head. The lowest beast was a clean thing beside these crazed white men and their unclean inventions. They could never be content, never be satisfied, until there was nothing left for them to destroy. The dead warriors had been mere boys. Their faces didn't have war paint; they'd been on a spirit walk with their elder, seeking the isolation of the wild in order to commune with the Great Spirit.

Broken Fang's lips pulled back in a vicious grin, exposing the long sharp canine tooth, the wolf-tooth that never turned back when he changed from man into animal. The massacre wasn't old, the scent of the men who had done this would be easy to follow.

As the white men had shown no mercy, as they had spared no one, Broken Tooth and his warriors would do the same.

No mercy. No pity. Only the fury of tooth and claw.

Chapter 7

The James-Younger Gang doubled back upon their own trail several times as they sped across the prairie, putting ground between themselves and whatever pursuit Fort Concho would send after them. Cole didn't think there'd be much to worry about from the Union soldiers. He'd shot up a fair number of the Iron Horses the gang hadn't been able to steal. The danger, as he saw it, was more likely to come from Concho's sister forts, Clark and Richardson. Those garrisons would have full compliments of equipment and regiments that hadn't already been shot up by outlaw raiders.

Jesse's thoughts echoed those of Cole. As they crisscrossed the area, they were careful to give the two forts a wide berth, avoiding them as keenly as they did the cache where they'd stashed the Clantons' blackhoofs and the extra Iron Horses they'd stolen from Fort Concho. After going to all the trouble of stealing the vehicles, there was no sense in leading the Union right to where they were stashed.

They'd have to pick their next target carefully. Jesse's mind wavered between picking something quick and easy like a mine payroll or intercepting a stage and going after something that would set the Yankees quaking in their boots. Rob one of the Texas-Pacific trains or maybe head down to San Antonio and burn down the governor's mansion. Something that would send a clear message to the rattlesnakes in Washington that they didn't have everything their way; that there were still people who weren't just going to lie down and let themselves be walked over by carpet-baggers and ringsters.

Making his escape from Fort Concho on the back of Cole's 'Horse, rather than speeding away on a mount he'd stolen on his own, stuck in Jesse's craw. It irritated his pride to know that ruffians like Ike and Curly Bill were riding fresh mounts while he had been forced to take up his old steed at the cache. The continuing vexation made him irritable and short-tempered to a degree where even the Youngers were giving him a wide berth. All except the imperturbable John. The boy's worshipful regard for the outlaw chief blinded him to Jesse's black mood.

"We're gonna be the terror of the territory now!" John crowed, a grin on his face as his 'Horse raced across the prairie. The outlaws had entered the vastness of West Texas, travelling through a seemingly endless swathe of rolling grass. The inland sea of blue grama stretched to the distant horizon, swaying like ocean waves in the crisp breeze. Cole had chosen this route deliberately; reckoning that with such an unlimited view there could be no chance of any pursuit from the Union forts catching them by surprise.

It took a moment for Jesse to react to John's enthusiasm. He'd been watching Johnny Ringo off to his right, casting more than a little envy on the gilded molding around the engine casing of his 'Horse and the electriwork ornaments fitted to its saddle, their internal RJ-cells making the ornaments whirl in intricate spirals. The steed Ringo had taken must have been that of an officer – probably the commandant himself – to heighten his grandeur when on parade. Whatever its purpose, Jesse coveted the machine. It was too fine by a damn sight for a scoundrel like Ringo. By hook or crook, he intended to get the gunfighter into a hand of poker and take the gilded vehicle from him.

With a bit of reluctance, Jesse glanced away from Ringo's machine. "We're already the terror of the territory."

"Them Yankees ain't gonna forget it, either!" John declared, his hand slapping against the blaster holstered on his hip.

Jesse started to echo the boy's sentiment, but in that instant his sharp eyes spotted a disturbance in the long grass. Years spent as a guerrilla fighter under Quantrill and Bloody Bill, many decades plying the outlaw trail first under Little Arch and then as the leader of the James-Younger Gang, had honed his senses to an almost preternatural keenness. Even from the saddle of his speeding 'Horse, he noticed the disturbance in the swaying grass. For an instant, a brief blink of time, part of that rolling vista had been upset. A clump of grass had shuddered more violently than the greenery around it, the tall stalks moving against the breeze.

The outlaw's hand flew to one of his holsters. Every nerve in his body bristled with instinctive alarm. A sense beyond the ordinary thundered in his ears, warning him that danger was near.

The senses of those lying in wait for the outlaws were even sharper than Jesse's. Knowing that their presence had been betrayed to the metal-armed gunman, the lurkers sprang up from the tall grass. Before Jesse could shout a warning to his comrades, dozens of savage warriors materialized before them. Savage, primal cries of wrath and fury howled across the prairie as the Warrior Nation attacked the mounted badmen.

Arrows whistled through the air, their heads ablaze with the ghostly blue fire that so often empowered the weapons of the Warrior Nation. One of the Cowboys was pierced by a glowing arrow, the shaft catching him in the breastbone and rocketing him from the saddle of his 'Horse. The stricken outlaw's body tumbled through the grass, forcing the others following behind to juke and brake to avoid the cadaverous obstruction that had been thrown into their path.

The Indians whooped and howled as they continued to launch flights of glowing arrows into the speeding outlaws. Grotesque in their grisly warpaint, savage in their dress of buffalo hides and bone talismans, the fighters of the Warrior Nation seemed more like inhuman devils than anything born of woman. As each archer loosed his arrow, the warrior would drop down into the grass, hiding beneath the greenery only to pop up again some distance away and loose another deadly shaft of spectral malignance.

For Jesse and the other outlaws, the tactics of the savage warriors were infuriating. The steady volleys of arrows forced them to constantly shift and weave, never presenting the Warrior Nation with a steady target. At the same time, the frustrating habit their foes had of ducking back down into the grass every time they fired an arrow made it all but impossible to draw a bead on them and try to strike back.

Except for their first casualty, the outlaws had good fortune in eluding the attack of their enemy. It was Cole who sickeningly realized why. He shouted in alarm to Jesse and the others. "They ain't fightin' us! They're herdin' us!"

Jesse appreciated the dire import of Cole's warning. The volleys of arrows were driving the outlaws toward the left and it didn't take long to figure out why. Ike Clanton was ahead of the other Cowboys when the grass suddenly disgorged a howling, shrieking savage. The Indian warrior was stripped to the waist, his chest daubed in primitive designs that echoed the warpaint spread across his face. In his hands he gripped a tomahawk, its head blazing with the same phantom luminance as the arrows. The half-naked warrior lunged at Ike, and the speed of the outlaw's 'Horse thwarted the blow directed at his head. Instead of smashing into Ike's skull, the tomahawk scraped across the side of his machine, gouging the metal and sending sparks dancing.

Before the Indian could turn and leap at Ike's back, he was ripped in half by the murderous fire of Curly Bill's blaster. The gory fragments of the warrior were thrown asunder by the brutal discharge, further mutilated an instant later as the trim rustler drove his 'Horse over the mangled carrion.

The slaughtered warrior wasn't the only savage lying in wait for the desperados, however. As they drove their 'Horses further away from the archers, every clump of grass seemed to disclose a hidden Indian. Whooping their primitive war cries, the warriors threw themselves at the mounted badmen with glowing knives and tomahawks, with brutal clubs and vicious spears. A scene of pandemonium ensued as outlaws tried to dodge the screaming Indians who threw themselves at the speeding 'Horses. Jesse saw three of the Cowboys pulled from their saddles by the attacking warriors, the men shrieking as glowing knives and blazing axes bit into their scalps.

Jesse snapped off a shot from one of his blasters, scoring a hit against the flank of an Indian with a tomahawk as he leapt at John's 'Horse. The savage was sent rolling through the grass, one leg nearly torn from his body. The startled John recovered his wits enough to gun his 'Horse forwards and smash down a second warrior as he came charging out from hiding.

There was no chance for Jesse to render aid to any of his other men. Squeezing off that shot at the Indian threatening John had caused him to neglect his own defense.

Screeching a long, low howl, a warrior festooned in a long headdress of eagle feathers leapt up onto the crumpled hood of Jesse's steed. Before he could even think to fire at the man, the Indian's glowing club cracked into the outlaw's gun hand, forcing his arm sideways. Jesse braked his 'Horse hard and without a lick of warning.

It was as though the Iron Horse had struck a stone wall. With the weight of the warrior on its hood, the abrupt arrest of the machine's motion set it spinning end over end. Jesse was thrown from his saddle, but the Indian, in a panic, tightened his hold on the hood of the machine. He was still holding fast as the 'Horse spun forward to crash down upon its back.

Jesse ripped his other pistol from its holster as he slammed against the ground. Even as sparks flashed through his vision and his teeth rattled in his jaw, the outlaw brought his blasters sweeping toward his crumpled steed. A blaze of energy, the smell of vaporized flesh, and Jesse's attacker was reduced to a smoking tangle of meat.

"You wrecked my ride," Jesse snarled down at the smoldering corpse. "You shouldn't mess with a man's ride."

A low snarl to his left brought Jesse spinning around just in time to see a grisly figure turn away from the wreck of another Iron Horse. It was an Indian warrior, his body spattered with blood. In his gory hands he brandished a dripping human scalp. At the warrior's feet, Jesse recognized the tortured ruin of the buckaroo Potts.

Jesse took aim at Potts's killer just as the savage came charging toward him, murder shining in the warrior's eyes, eerie blue flame pulsating about the blade of the Indian's knife.

Again, Jesse's arms betrayed him. Aiming directly at the man, his shot instead went wide, scorching the grass just to its left. The Indian didn't give him time for a second shot, leaping on him in a long, low tackle that bounced the back of his head against the sun-baked earth. The knife slashed at Jesse's face, only a last second roll keeping the blade from raking across his flesh.

The Indian's savagery intensified. There was vengeance in the warrior's eyes as he reared back and brought his glowing blade stabbing down at the outlaw's throat.

*****

Old Man Clanton peeled off a shot from his blaster, sending another warrior hurtling back as though fired from a cannon. The rustler sent another shot chasing after the savage. "Dry-gulchin' cur!" Clanton roared at the Indian, spitting in contempt in the direction of the corpse.

"They don't seem in any mind to call it quits!" Curly Bill declared. The marauder's shirt was torn and bloodied, his trim beard matted with blood from a wound across his cheek.

"Be that as it may," Old Man Clanton said, a greedy light creeping into his eyes. "These ornery galoots 're gonna help us."

Curly Bill frowned, dabbing a handkerchief at his torn cheek. "How's that?"

The Old Man chuckled darkly. "We got the rides and the shooters Cole promised. I don't see where's we exactly need Jesse James no more." There was an agonized screech from nearby as Johnny Ringo blasted the arm off a spear-wielding warrior, then finished the cripple with a shot that splashed his skull across the grass.

"You fixin' to turn on Jesse?" Ike asked, a trace of horror in his tone.

"I'm sayin' we light out of here and let nature take its course," the Old Man laughed, waving his hand at the ongoing fray. Most of the Cowboys had won their way clear of the fighting. It was Jesse and the Youngers who were still surrounded.

"Don't seem right, leavin' men to die like that," Ike said.

The Old Man glared at his son. "That's a strange sentiment for a man that done what he's already done to that outfit," the rustler snarled. "Or maybe yer forgetin' that little job you done in Tombstone to set the Earps on Jesse's tail? This ain't cowardice, it's just good business." The Old Man laughed again when he saw Ike's embarrassed expression. "You just keep playin' at respectability and leave the strategizin' to me." He made a quick count of the Cowboys around him, scowling at the result. "We've got six men lying around here someplace. That's all we're givin' Jesse James. It was his damn fool idea to attack that huntin' party," he added, ignoring his own endorsement of Jesse's plan. "He called the tune, now he can pay the fiddler." Waving his arm, the rustler pointed westwards and threw his Iron Horse into full gear. The other Cowboys followed after their boss, speeding out over the prairie without a backwards glance at the men they were abandoning.

*****

Pinned beneath the warrior, Jesse brought one cyborg arm up to catch the descending knife. For an instant, the spectral blade bit into the cold steel of his hand. Then the glowing blade was snapped by the mechanized might of the outlaw's hand as he twisted it to one side. Taking hold of his attacker's neck, Jesse quickly ended the man's life, squeezing until he felt the Indian's bones pulverized by his steel fingers. Grimly, the outlaw tossed aside the warrior's twitching corpse.

Jesse was back on his feet in a flash. Nearby, he could see Bob Younger trying to hold off an Indian armed with a glowing spear with his Bowie knives. The longer reach of the spear was keeping Bob on the defensive, denying him any chance to slip in and strike his foe. Off to Bob's right, Jim was struggling with a hulking warrior gripping tomahawks in each hand. It seemed the two brothers had crashed their Iron Horses together in the confusion of the initial ambush. Cole and John were still mounted, making a wide circuit of the shortgrass as they tried to drive more lurking warriors from hiding. John Wesley Hardin's strategy was both more direct and more brutal, using his smokers to set the grass alight and burn the men right where they lurked. As the fires caught the Indians, the eerie blue glow of their weapons flared brighter, expanded into a purplish aura before fizzling into a wispy gray smoke. The fires caused by the Texan seemed to be poison to the enchantments of the Warrior Nation's spiritual powers.

Those same fires, however, would settle for white men as well as red. Jesse watched the spreading flames with alarm. A shift in the wind, and Hardin's fire would be blown straight back at the outlaws. Indeed, the way the flames were spreading, it might eat up thousands of acres before it spent itself out.

More troubling than Hardin's psychotic pyromania, however, was the desertion of the Cowboys. Jesse could see the Clantons and their followers speeding off across the prairie, turning their backs on the rest of the outfit. Such base treachery made the blood rush hot in Jesse's veins. This was the second time Ringo had deserted him. He was reminded of how Billy the Kid had run out on him and Frank when the Union had come down on them outside of Diablo Canyon, leaving them for dead while he skedaddled off to safety." Ugly visions of what he'd like to do to such traitors blazed before the outlaw's eyes.

Viciously, Jesse snapped off shots from his blasters. Seemingly awed by the rage boiling inside him, his metal arms didn't stray from the demands imposed upon them by his brain. His aim was precision itself when he blasted the leg off Jim's foe and tore the head off Bob's enemy. The same withering stream of shots cut down a squat axeman and pulped the chest of a lanky bowman.

Then, Jesse himself was knocked flat, bowled over by the hurtling bulk of his ruined vehicle. Something inhumanly strong and powerful had tossed it through the air, deliberately throwing it at him. Another inch and Jesse would have been pulverized by the wreckage; as it was, the glancing blow left him sprawled across the ground, his blasters flying from his hands.

A fierce howl rolled across the prairie, and Jesse could see his attacker loping toward him at a run. This creature was more lupine than human in shape, covered in short gray hairs. Its body was lean and powerful, great cords of muscle rippling as it moved. The head was stretched into the elongated muzzle of a wolf, long and sharp teeth gleaming in its fanged smile. One of those fangs, longer and thicker than the others, protruded over the beast's lower lip like the blade of a dagger.

Before the monster could charge him, the deafening roar of an Iron Horse powering forward at full throttle rumbled over the shortgrass. John's steed was just a steely blur as it hurtled toward the huge skin-changer. The boy was trying to ride down the beast. However, he'd underestimated his enemy.

Broken Fang sprang upward just as John's 'Horse came streaking toward him. The great wolf threw its body forward, over and across the speeding machine. Its immense claw raked out at the boy, catching in his brown duster and tearing him from the saddle. John was flung across the ground in a violent tumble, pitching and rolling across the grass. Broken Fang growled at the stunned youth, the animalistic impulse to rend this helpless prey driving the wolf-beast into a fierce leap.

As Broken Fang started to lunge, the metal hood from Jesse's Iron Horse swatted across the monster's face, breaking its dagger-like tooth and ripping the ear from the side of its head. The wolf-beast's leap became a slide, its paws digging at the ground as it spun to face its original enemy. Jesse flung the crumpled hood he'd torn from his steed at the creature; forcing it to duck as the crude missile went sailing over the skin-changer's head.

Then it was Jesse who was charging Broken Fang. He hadn't wasted any time looking for his blasters when he saw John's peril. Much as he had against the bear-beast, the outlaw had only his bare hands to fight the monster.

But they were hands fixed to the mechanical devilry of Dr. Carpathian's perverted science, the wondrous miracle that merged man and machine. Broken Fang's speed was inhuman, but the speed of Jesse's arms, the power behind them, was superhuman.

A bloody cough erupted from Broken Fang's jaws as it reeled back from Jesse's assault. For only an instant, the huge wolf-beast stood there, towering over its enemy. Then the cold glaze of death settled across Broken Fang's eyes and the skin-changer fell to the ground, blood jetting from the hole Jesse's fist had punched into its chest and the ruptured heart behind the wolf's shattered ribs.

Jesse turned away from the dead wolf-man. He could hear the yips and yelps of alarm as the surviving savages fled across the prairie, their appetite for battle lost with the death of their leader. Behind them, the Warrior Nation's warriors left a landscape of mangled bodies and ruined machines. He could see Bob and Cole crouching beside a prostrate Jim, trying to peel away their brother's vest and coat to tend the wounds the enemy had inflicted on him. Danby tried to help by tearing off bandages from an old shirt he removed from his saddlebag. Hardin's contribution was the sadistic execution of every wounded Indian he could find.

Jesse hurried over to where John Younger had been thrown. Reaching down with a bloodied hand, he helped the boy back onto his feet.

"Thanks," John panted, the terror of his ordeal still pounding in his veins. "I... I... thought I was a... goner."

"Just returning the favor, kid," Jesse said, clapping John on the shoulder. He spun the boy around, pushing him in the direction of his brothers. John gave a cry of alarm and ran off to see if he could help the injured Jim. Jesse didn't follow after him. Instead he turned away and stared out across the prairie, not at the fleeing Warrior Nation, but at the distant cloud of dust thrown up by the Cowboys and their stolen vehicles.

"They're some other favors I'll be returning afore long," Jesse snarled under his breath, his steel hands tightening into fists at his sides. He knew it wouldn't be straight away; Cole would want to see that their wounded were tended to first, that they had time to strategize and make careful plans. He knew it might be weeks, even months before everything fell into place. But he knew somehow, somewhere, he'd be paying Old Man Clanton a visit, and only one of them would be walking away from that reckoning.

*****

The atmosphere in Colonel Mackenzie's office was heavy enough to cut with a knife. Fort Concho's commanding officer still had half his face swathed in bandages and was forced to employ a cane to amble about the base. Despite the assurances of Governor Lew Wallace and the War Office, little had been done by way of sending fresh troops and supplies to the fort, the attitude of both politicians and military appearing to be along the lines of seeing no point in pouring resources into a place that had already been hit by the outlaws. Lightning had already struck, what sense was there in worrying about its striking twice?

Seated in a leather-backed chair, Over-marshal Wyatt Earp had listened with mounting annoyance to Mackenzie's tirade against his superiors tying his hands and making it impossible for him to do his job. The colonel seemed to take great pains to blame his subordinates for what had happened, but didn't seem to find any fault in his own leadership.

"Colonel," Wyatt addressed the officer. "What you're telling me is that these outlaws absconded with fifteen Iron Horses and enough military-grade weaponry to start a range war. If that don't amount to dereliction of duty, I don't know what does."

Mackenzie lurched up from his chair, shaking the metal talons of his maimed hand at the lawman. "I was fighting to defend this Union when you were still swindling chuckleheads at a faro table! I been shot eight times protecting this nation..."

The metallic rasp of Doc Holiday's laugh scratched across the office. "Sounds to me like maybe you should practice gettin' out of the way sometime."

Mackenzie's eyes narrowed. "You can tell the sort of man you got by the company he keeps," he snarled. "What're you palling around with, Earp? Card-artists, lead-bellied 'bots, and cow-town copperheads!"

Wyatt returned the colonel's hostile glare. "You call me what you like," he warned, "but watch how you talk about my friends and my kin."

Standing behind Wyatt's chair, Warren Earp pointed an accusing finger at the officer. "And I ain't no damn copperhead!" he growled. "Just 'cause I said Jesse James must know a thing or three to pull off a raid like this don't mean I hold no Secesh sympathies!"

"Gentlemen, this arguing gets us nowhere." Stepping away from where she'd been standing against the wall, Lucinda Loveless had shucked fine gowns and fancy dresses for riding breeches and a corduroy shirt. She moved stiffly, her body still sore from the injuries she had taken during her recent trip into Carpathian's Kingdom and the ancient Anasazi cliff ruins nestled within the territory's canyons. She had been promised a vacation after successfully bringing to Washington the eldritch Indian relic she'd been sent to find. Any notion of rest had evaporated when news of Jesse's raid on Fort Concho came across the wire. Pinkerton knew, of all his agents, Loveless had developed some sort of connection with the outlaw. She would be the most likely to have some insight into how his mind worked, and what he might be expected to do next.

The problem right now was getting Wyatt Earp to understand that. "We're all on the same side," she reminded the lawmen. "We want the same thing. We want to bring Jesse James to justice."

The smile Wyatt turned toward Loveless was thin and cold. He knew she was a special operative connected with Mackenzie and ultimately his superiors. That didn't impress him any. Not when it was a question of avenging his brother. "I want Jessie," he said. "Washington can have what's left when I'm done with him."

Loveless arched her eyebrow. "That sounds like revenge talking, Over-marshal," she said. "What we want is justice. You swore an oath to uphold the law, remember?"

"Ride out to Tombstone and take a gander at my brother Virg, allowing he's not already planted in a bone orchard," Wyatt advised her. "Or better yet, just look over yonder at Morg," he added, jabbing a thumb at the hulking cyborg. "There's some things the law'll just have to settle for second helpings."

"Hell, leave the tin-badge be," Mackenzie told Loveless. "Maybe him and James'll shoot each other and do the nation a big favor." The unmarred side of the colonel's face pulled back in a snide grin. He stabbed a finger against the electric bell set into the side of his desk. The door at the back of his office swung open and a young adjutant poked his head in. "Send the bounty hunter up," Mackenzie ordered. As the adjutant withdrew, the colonel returned his attention to Wyatt. "I'm going to get you some help."

Wyatt shook his head. "I don't need any bounty killers."

"My mistake," Mackenzie said. "I thought you wanted Jesse James." He turned and waved his clawed hand as the door swung open again.

Framed in the doorway was a tall, lean man, a wide slouch hat shading a thin, sharp-featured face. It was the face of a ferret or a weasel, the face of a hunting creature that relies on cunning to wear down its prey. The eyes in that face were like flattened bullets, leaden and lifeless. A long leather slicker, its collar padded with wolf fur, framed the man's body. An armored breastplate, still retaining the glimmer of brass beneath its patina of dust and grime, protected the man's chest, serpentine shapes in the stylized patterns of Meso-America etched across its surface. The heavy gun belt that circled his waist was reinforced with steel ribbing, chains securing the holster against his right leg. At the left side, the grisly spectacle of three shriveled human heads, shrunk and mummified by some obscene process, grinned at the marshal.

"Thomas Tate Tobin," Mackenzie introduced the bounty killer. "Finest tracker and man-hunter in the Territory. Man who single-handedly brought in the Sanchez brothers."

"And where would they be now?" Doc asked.

"Shakin' hands with Old Scratch down in the infernal fires, I reckon," Tobin answered in a voice that sounded like a snake shedding its skin. His hand brushed across the scalps of the shrunken heads on his belt. "Leastwise, those bits that wasn't worth a payday."

"We don't need no damn headhunter!" Warren growled, echoing Wyatt's earlier position.

Tobin sneered at Warren. "You two shop at the same chandler, or are you just wearin' your older brother's hand-me-downs?"

Warren bristled at the bounty hunter's mockery. He started to reach for the long-barreled buntline holstered at his hip, but Wyatt slapped his hand away before his fingers could even start to ease around the grip.

"I want Jesse bad," Wyatt said. "But not bad enough to partner up with a bounty-sniffin' buzzard."

"Then you don't want Jesse at all," Tobin hissed back. "Because I'm the man who can show you right where he is." The bounty hunter jerked the chain he held in one hand, dragging into the office the man shackled at the other end. Wyatt leapt up from his chair in surprise, shocked to find that he recognized Tobin's captive.

The bounty hunter's catch was Ike Clanton.

Chapter 8

Jim Younger's jaws clamped tight against the wooden block in his mouth, his teeth digging into it as pain lanced through his body. A muffled scream dribbled from his throat as raw, searing agony pulsed down every nerve. The stink of his own burning flesh was heavy in his nose, causing him to clench his eyes tight and try to crush the tears of agony streaming down his face.

Bob's face was almost as agonized as Jim's. Standing over the table where his brother lay, the knife fighter pulled his smoking blade away from Jim's exposed chest. He squinted down at the scorched flesh, studying it to see if the heated blade had sealed the outlaw's cut. Grimly, he nodded to the men holding Jim down. Cole and Hardin maintained their unyielding grip on the wounded man's arms and legs while Bob stepped away from the table and approached the iron stove.

"Has to be done," Cole reminded Jim, more too soothe his own conscience than to succor his brother. In his current state, Jim was beyond reasoning, beyond being placated. All that mattered to him right now was pain and making it stop. The necessity of his suffering wasn't even a thought. "That Injun cut you good," Cole said, frowning at the hideous string of slashes running across Jim's chest. "We don't stop the bleeding, you'll end up in a bone orchard."

"Hold him tight," Bob warned as he came toward the table. He'd removed the Bowie knife that had been nestled in the belly of the stove; its tip glowing like it had an RJ fuel-cell fixed to it. He waited a moment for Cole and Hardin to secure their grip, and then he leaned over Jim again. "I'm sure sorry about this," he said as he brought the red-hot blade against Jim's chest. The outlaw's body thrashed wildly as pain shot through him, his back arching as he struggled to free himself.

Cole cursed lividly as Jim slipped one of his arms free. Before he could try to grab him, Jim's hand was clawing at Bob's arm, trying to pull him away and stop the burning pain of the knife he was using to cauterize the wound.

"John, get over here!" Cole shouted, his eyes still fixed on Jim.

John Younger came limping across the cabin. After being pulled from his 'Horse by an Indian warrior, the boy's whole body seemed to be one big bruise. Nothing had been broken though, and such cuts as he'd taken weren't serious enough to warrant the agony Jim was going through. John reached out and pried Jim's hand away from Bob's arm. Slowly, he forced the clawing hand back against the table, holding it flat against it while Bob continued his torturous work.

"Take over for me," Cole told John. "I can't do it by a long chalk." As John grabbed hold of Jim's other arm, Cole stepped away from the table. Immediately after he was relieved of holding Jim down, Cole was clutching at his side, poking his hand under his shirt. He smiled when he failed to see any blood on his fingers. He'd worried that the strain of pinning Jim down had opened his own wound, but it seemed the bandage was holding tight.

Cole turned away from the table and the agony on Jim's face. More than the physical strain, the ordeal of watching his brother suffer was taking an onerous toll on him. He hadn't seen Jim so bad off since the war when they'd ridden into a Yankee ambush. That time, they'd at least been able to fetch a surgeon for him from a Confederate encampment. Now, they'd have to tend him on their own until they could figure out where and how to smuggle him into a doctor.

Cole walked back across the cabin, taking up John's position at the window. Jesse was already standing there, his steely gaze roving the landscape. He didn't look up when Cole approached, just kept his eyes staring out over the rocks.

"How's Jim?" Jesse asked.

"Above snakes," Cole answered. "He's not ready for a boot yard yet, but we need to get him to a doctor to make sure he stays that way. All Bob's doing is makin' sure he don't bleed out before hand."

Jesse nodded, a grimace coming across his features. "That'll be a damn sight dangerous," he said. "Lawdogs will be sniffin' around for us. Blue-coats too, more than like."

"We'll lose too much time sendin' someone out to fetch a sawbones back," Cole said. "Jim don't have any to spare. The Indian that cut him didn't do him no favors. We have to take him out soon's Bob gets the drippin' stopped."

"Hardin burned the doc in San Diablo," Jesse said. "That means our best bet is Tucumcari. Sheriff there's a copperhead. Long's we don't cause him a ruckus, he's liable to play dumb about who we might be."

"Damn those Clantons anyway!" Cole snarled, smacking his fist against the wall. "Yellow-backed polecats! Never expected them to cut dirt like that, leave us danglin' in the wind!"

The wood frame of the window splintered under Jesse's metal fingers as they tightened. It was the only physical sign of the anger boiling inside him. "
"They cut and run, but I don't think it's because they got funkified by them Indians. The Old Man and that barber's clerk son of his probably reckoned they'd got all they needed from stringin' along with us. Lightin' out while them Indians were tryin' to cut us down must have been mighty appealin' to a low-down four-flusher like Clanton."

"You lie down with snakes, yer apt to get bit."Cole looked back at the table, at Jim's agonized form;he looked at John's bruised face, and thought of his own hurts. It was bad enough to think that all of this had come down to the Younger Brothers because of cowardice, but to think it stemmed from treachery, from callous opportunism, it was almost too much to bear. "Well, I figure once we get Jim settled, we go and pay Clanton's brood a visit. It was a long ride from Tombstone and Johnny Ringo told me a fair deal about how the Cowboys operate." The outlaw spat a cold laugh. "And whatever he didn't tell me that brayin' ass Ike did with his brag and boast show."

Jesse turned away from the window, fixed his hard stare on Cole. "We'll have to talk a spell, Cole. Because I'm tired of wearin' other people's dirt. Clanton thinks he can play Jesse James like a fiddle, then he's gonna find out he has to pay the band."

*****

"That's the place," Ike Clanton said, waving his hand at the lonely hideout. "Jesse James and the Younger Brothers are all holed up in there. Just like I said."

Lying against the side of a boulder, Wyatt Earp kept his eye pressed against the lens of the optical-magnifier, studying the bleak terrain, checking for any sign of ambush. "You also said we'd find the whole gang lying butchered by Indians on the prairie."

The Cowboy cringed at the snarl in Wyatt's tone. "Listen, I don't know how he got hisself out of there," Ike protested. "He should have been strewed across half an acre by them braves."

"I believe you, Ike," the Over-marshal said. "Not because I trust you, but because I figure you're just the sort of coyote who would leave a fella in a heap of trouble like that." He looked away from the scope, fixing the shackled outlaw with a contemptuous gaze. "What happen, Ike, you get to worryin' that the Warrior Nation didn't finish the job? It start botherin' your insides that Jesse might still be alive and maybe lookin' for the varmint that left him to die?"

Ike yelped as he was struck in the side by the long barrel of Warren Earp's pistol. The thuggish lawman glowered at Ike as he pulled back and swatted him against the ribs a second time with his Buntline Special. The pistol had a barrel over twelve inches long with a large bore and at close range would do maximum damage. "Answer my brother, crow bait."

"You ain't got no cause to treat me poor!" Ike whined, clutching at his side. "Alls I was doin' was sellin' some beef to this here outfit and soon's I realized who they was, I lit out and tried to do my duty as a respectable citizen."

The outlaw's statement brought a raspy, metallic chuckle from further back among the rocks. "If'n a buzzard could sing, it'd call itself a canary," Doc Holiday proclaimed. The gambler's eyes were like chips of ice as they stared from above his breathing mask. "Whatever the song, it's still a buzzard. Mighty fair trail to ride to sell beeves, don't you think? Unless maybe you don't have a good brand artist down there in Clantonville and were afraid somebody'd recognize their stock if you sold them closer to home?"

Ike scowled back at the gambler. "Nobody asked you nothin' lunger," he hissed. "I come in of my own accord. Least I would've if that rattlesnake Tobin hadn't bushwhacked me!" He looked back over at Wyatt, more than a tinge of fear on his face. "You can't let that headhunter keep me," he said, making the statement half demand and half plea. "The governor's promised full pardon to anybody brings in Jesse!"

Warren brought the barrel of his gun slamming into Ike's ribs again. The finely etched design in the metalwork glinted off the light. The length of the barrel put a great deal of space between the two men, so Ike could see it better than he would have liked "You figure you earned that?"

Wyatt waved his brother off. Warren was a good, dependable man in a fight, but he had a mean streak in him as wide as the Missouri. Let him off the leash too long and he'd push his authority to the limit and then some. The last town he'd been sheriff in had voted him out of office because of his brutality; even Bat Masterson over in Dodge had been obligated to ask him to hit the trail after only a few weeks serving as his deputy. Of course, Wyatt had an edge over Warren that his friend Bat would never have. His little brother looked up to him like he was Hercules, King Arthur, and George Washington all rolled into one. The bully had never grown out of his childhood hero worship of Wyatt.

The Over-marshal looked out across the rocks to where the rest of his posse was arrayed, their numbers augmented by a dozen cavalry troopers from Fort Concho. The black cavalry troopers and their lieutenant had proven a mixed blessing; they gave Wyatt the firepower he felt he needed to ensure a fight with the James-Younger gang wouldn't go sour. At the same time, the troopers had been forced to ride blackhoofs commandeered from the inhabitants of San Angelo. The plodding metal horses had slowed the posse's progress to a crawl compared to what they could have managed on Interceptors.

At least the lethargic advance had produced one satisfactory result. Thomas Tate Tobin had parted company with the posse a day out from the gang's hideout, turning Ike over to Wyatt and declaring that he could fare better on his own. Wyatt wasn't deceived. The bounty hunter didn't want to share the reward with anybody. Like a blood-sniffing weasel, he'd gone to try to get Jesse all on his own.

Studying the hideout, Wyatt couldn't help but smile. Whatever had become of Tobin, it was clear that the bounty killer had failed to get Jesse James. Through his RJ-powered glass, Wyatt could see Jesse appear at the window of the cabin. There was no mistaking those metal arms of his. Other men who had appeared at the same window could have been some of the Youngers. There was a man prowling around outside who matched Ike's description of one of the buckaroos who rode with the Youngers. There was no sign of the other brothers or John Wesley Hardin, but Wyatt reasoned they might just be lying low inside either the cabin or the barn-like stables.

Wyatt tried to control the eagerness that burned inside him; the same eagerness that he knew was making Warren even more ornery than usual. Jesse James and his gang, the scum who'd bushwhacked Virgil, were so near he could just about smell them! It took all of his will power to keep from rushing in there with guns blazing. That'd be too easy and a damn sight better than Jesse warranted. Wyatt wanted the outlaw alive, wanted to drag him back through the streets of Tombstone on the end of a lasso. He wanted to lead Jesse up the courthouse steps and then up the steps of the gallows. Virg deserved that. He only prayed that his older brother was still alive to see justice brought crashing down about Jesse's ears.

"Better settle for the pardon and the colonel's handshake," Wyatt advised Ike in a low snarl. "I'll gun you here if you so much as ask about the reward money. That's for men who rode out to help the law, not exploit it."

"You listenin' to him, cur?" Warren snapped, cracking Ike's ribs with the barrel of his Buntline.

"Yes, you damn tin-badge pimps!" Ike growled back. "You just go ahead and keep all the money!"

Wyatt scowled, but didn't bother to correct the rustler's allegation of corruption. It would be wasted breath on his sort. Ike'd never believe the Over-marshal if he said the money would go to Turkey Creek Johnson, Sherman McMaster, and the other men in the posse.

"Doc, I'll be leavin' you up here with Ike," Wyatt said. He turned his cold gaze on the would-be ringster. "We get down there and it looks like they're waitin' for us, you'll know what to do. Unless, of course, there's something Mr. Clanton would like to say first."

Ike turned his head, blanching when he saw Doc Holiday checking the charges on his blasters. Of all the men in his posse, Wyatt could not have picked a more threatening presence. Wyatt, Morgan, even the bullying Warren might have shown some restraint, might have hesitated to sink so low as to shoot down an unarmed prisoner, even if saidcaptive had led them into an ambush. With Doc there wasn't any such question. The gambler had few scruples and even less charity. If he thought Ike'd led the posse into an ambush, he'd shoot the rustler down like a sick dog and not blink an eye while doing it.

"If you hear a loud noise from these parts, that'll be Mr. Clanton shaking hands with the Devil." Doc stuffed one of his pistols back into its holster.

"It's all on the line!" Ike swore, panic in his voice. "Jesse don't know yer comin', I swear it on..."

Ike's oath ended in another yelp of pain. "Don't blaspheme," Warren growled at him.

Wyatt picked up a stone from the ground and tossed it over to where the cavalry lieutenant had concealed himself. The officer turned toward him, nodding when he saw Wyatt give him the high sign. Following the marshal's example, the lieutenant passed word along to the rest of his men. Wyatt turned and repeated the procedure, getting the notice of Turkey Creek and the other men of his posse. The best long-distance shot among them, Turkey Creek raised his rifle and drew a bead on the man patrolling outside. It would be his job to drop the outlaw the moment the ruckus started. All the other men had to do was keep the gang pinned down inside the cabin.

The heavy work was going to fall to Wyatt and his brothers. He wouldn't have it any other way. As he scrambled back down from the rocks, he tapped Warren on the shoulder. "Let's to it," he told his brother. With a last vindictive swat of his Buntline against Ike's back, Warren followed the marshal down the slope.

The posse and their cavalry allies had parked their steeds below, but it wasn't toward these that the two lawmen made their way. Beyond the Interceptors and Blackhoofs was a gigantic steel behemoth, an armored carriage supported on three enormous wheel sets that looked as though they might have been stripped from a locomotive. Similar to a train engine in overall appearance, the machine boasted a huge blade-like cattle-catcher at the front of its chassis and an elevated turret of armor plate from which projected the menacing barrel of an energy cannon. A mobile fortress, the vehicle was designated as a 'Judgement' by its manufacturers in the East, but for the inhabitants of the west and the still-contested hinterlands of Texas Territory; it was more commonly referred to as a 'lynch-wagon'.

The sight of a posse riding out with the support of one of these armored RJ-engines had killed the fight in many an outlaw band. Only the most reckless or determined would try to hold out against such an imposing machine. A part of Wyatt hoped Jesse would be one or the other. He hoped the outlaw would try to make a fight of it. It would make the bushwhacker's defeat all the more satisfying.

As he approached the rear of the Judgement, Wyatt climbed up into the bed of the carriage. A trio of UR-30 Enforcers sat against the walls, still as statues, blasters holstered at their sides. Standing between the unmoving 'bots, displaying the same stony silence,

was Morgan Earp. The cyborg nodded his head when he saw Wyatt.
"Everything is ready," Morgan told the Over-marshal.
Wyatt winced at the steely lack of emotion in his brother's voice or on the cyborg's face. The fact that they were about to attack the lair of the most notorious outlaw in the west didn't seem to concern Morgan whatsoever. Wyatt shook his head.
"When we get up to the cabin, I want you to deploy the 'bots," Wyatt told Morgan. Perhaps because the cyborg was more machine than man, he had an incredible facility with the Enforcers, able to coax them to an efficiency nobody else seemed able to match. Morgan accepted his assignment with the same emotionless nod. Wyatt turned toward Warren, who was just climbing up into the carriage. "I want you in the cab, driving. Get us as close to the hideout as you can and turn the Judgement to its side to give Morg and the 'bots some cover." The Over-marshal glanced over at the steel ladder suspended below the turret. "I'll be up there manning the cannon."
"We'll do for those skunks," Warren vowed.
Wyatt nodded. "Jesse's gonna learn right fast that he's played out his string this time." An ugly light shone in the Over-marshal's eyes. "Nobody bushwhacks an Earp and lives to brag about it."

*****

Jesse James had been uneasy for most of the day. Years as a guerrilla fighting for the Confederacy and the years of crime afterward had honed his instincts almost to an animal keenness. There were times when he didn't need any trace of danger to be visible for him to know it was there. He could feel when someone was hunting him; when somebody was lying in wait just around the next bend or stalking his trail just over the horizon.

The uneasiness Jesse felt now was no different than the impulses that had kept him one step ahead of the Pinkertons in Missouri after the war. Throughout the morning, he'd kept close to the window, watching and waiting for whatever was coming. He was waiting for the threat hanging over him to show itself, thenhe would know how to react. Maybe it was the betrayal of his mechanical arms, maybe it was Cole's new facility for strategy rubbing off on him, or maybe it was the death of Frank. Whatever the cause, he was trying to be less impulsive and more cautious. Work out a plan rather than leaping headfirst into trouble.

Beside him, Cole was going into detail about how the Clantons and the Cowboys operated. He was fixated on the idea of getting revenge on the gang from Tombstone; maybe that was why Cole didn't have any premonition of danger until the desert solitude was broken by the sharp crack of a rifle shot.

Reflexively, without conscious thought, Jesse's quick-devil arms had his hyper-velocity blasters drawn from their holsters. Through the window, he could see Danby lying in the dirt near the stables, smoke rising from the ugly hole in his chest. The way the dead buckaroo was strewn on the ground drew Jesse's gaze toward the rocks along the eastward rise. He cursed when he saw about a dozen men up there, more than half of them dusky Africans wearing blue shell jackets.

"Down!" Jesse snapped at Cole as the other outlaw turned toward the window. Both men dropped low an instant before energy beams came crashing against the cabin's exterior. At such range, the rifles the men on the ridge were using didn't have the strength to penetrate timber, but as Danby gave mute testament, they still had more than enough punch to put a man in a grave patch.

"Posse?" Cole snarled, drawing his own blasters.

Jesse nodded, peaking up from below the base of the window frame to fire a pair of shots up at the ridge. "Buffalo soldiers from Fort Concho and some civilians," he said.

"Might be a posse from San Angelo paired up with them," Cole suggested. As

Jesse dropped down, Cole popped up at the other corner of the window and sent a bolt sizzling up toward the rocks. "Could be vigilantes or bounty hunters. Maybe even them damn Pinkertons!" He glanced over at the table where Bob and John were carefully lifting their brother down to the floor. Hardin was dashing over to the door, one of his smokers in his gloved hand. Cole yelled in warning at the gunfighter before he could pull open the door. "They're up on the ridge!"

Hardin glared at the smoker and thrust it back into its holster. The incendiary bullets that the gun fired weren't made for anything resembling accuracy at more than a hundred yards. Scowling, the gunfighter rushed to where Jim's gear had been stowed, rummaging about until he could find the man's blaster.

"Whoever they are," Jesse said as he snapped off two more shots, driving two of the black cavalry troopers into cover, "they've got us cold. They can sit up there and wait us out until the Jubilee."

As Jesse dropped back down, Cole popped up to fire again. He spat a curse and ducked down again as soon as his head peaked above the sill. "They ain't of a mind to sit anything out! They've got a lynch-wagon rolling up on us!"

Cole's shout froze Hardin just as he was about to pull open the door and add his fire to the barrage against the men on the ridge. "That about tears it," he hissed. "Ain't no way we can fight one of them steel armadillos. Can't even put up a decent fight without a damn sight more iron than we've got."

Jesse kept his head low as another fusillade from the rocks crackled against the frame of the cabin, a few beams even flashing through the open window to scorch the back wall. When he judged the worst of the barrage was spent, he peaked over the sill. What he saw confirmed Cole's grim report. A Judgement rumbled at full steam toward the cabin, dust billowing about it as it charged toward them. He could see the cannon mounted in its turret. It didn't take any stretch of imagination to know that weapon would tear through the cabin destroying anything in its path.

"What'll we do, Jesse?" John Younger asked as he came rushing over to the window with his hands wrapped around an energy rifle.

Jesse frowned as he slid back down to the floor. "Ain't too much choice left. The deck's stacked and them fellas out there are doing the dealing."

*****

Wyatt peered through the narrow viewport in the Judgement's turret, watching as the outlaw's hideout rapidly drew closer. He was coming within range now. If he was so inclined, he could use the cannon to blast the cabin into splinters along with everyone in it.

That wasn't appealing to the Over-marshal. He was determined to see Jesse hang for bushwhacking Virgil. That meant dialing down the power of the cannon and using it with far more discretion. It would make a powerful threat, might even persuade the James-Younger Gang to throw down their guns and surrender. If it came to ferreting the outlaw from his lair, then the heavy lifting would fall to Morgan and the Enforcer 'bots.

As the Judgement rumbled closer to the cabin, Wyatt opened fire. Crimson streams of crackling light exploded from the barrel, scything into the roof of the structure, blasting planks and timbers into the sky. Whatever wasn't obliterated outright by the cannon began to burn, crackling and popping as flames licked across them. Ugly black smoke billowed into the air. The Over-marshal turned and barked down to Morgan in the Judgement's cargo bed below. "Get the Enforcers movin', Morg!" he shouted. There was little of Wyatt left to worry about family at this point. He was focused on his objective. Blasting the roof off the hideout would give the outlaws an incentive to keep their heads down while the Enforcers deployed.

The Judgement slowed to a stop a dozen yards from the cabin as Warren cut the impetus of the wheels and brought the armored machine into a leftward slide. Even before the wagon came to a complete stop, Morgan had the back door open and was jumping down to the ground. The cyborg hefted his blaster and sent a shot burning through the cabin wall. Instantly, he was in motion again, his mechanical legs propelling him at superhuman speed to the cover afforded by the corner of the cabin itself.

After Morgan came the robots. Lacking a human brain to guide them, the Enforcers moved with less speed and precision than the cyborg. They clomped down from the bed of the Judgement with the steely resolve only an unliving automaton could exhibit, indifferent to the threat of gunfire from the enemies holed up inside the building.

"Ten-Nine, cover the rest of the troop," Morgan ordered one of the 'bots. At his shout, one of the machines dropped to one knee and began to pump shots from its carbine into the door of the cabin, a steady fusillade to hold back any rush from inside the building. The other Enforcers fanned out, using the armored hull of the Judgement to block their deployment from the attention of the outlaws.

Wyatt glowered through the viewport. He pressed his mouth to the speaking tube set into the side of the turret. When he spoke, his words were transmitted and amplified by the metal horn fixed to the top of the Judgement's hull. "Jesse James! This is US Over-marshal, Wyatt Earp! You are under arrest for the crimes of murder, bank robbery, horse stealing, treason, firing upon a law officer in the performance of his duties, and a dozen other outrages against decency! I have you surrounded! Lay down your guns and come out grabbing sky!"

The Over-marshal waited a few seconds for any sort of response. He expected at least some jeers and catcalls from the outlaws; maybe even a futile sally against the armored Judgement. He wasn't so naïve to think Jesse James would surrender without a fight, but what he didn't expect was to be greeted with stark, stony silence. Wyatt fingered the energy cannon's actuation lever, dialing it to the next intensity. Maybe taking the roof off hadn't impressed upon the outlaws the severity of their situation. Vaporizing one side of their hideout might be the next step to hammering home the hopelessness of their position.

Before Wyatt could fire, the wooden doors of the stables exploded outward. As he brought the turret swinging around, he saw a number of Iron Horses leap out from the building. A half dozen of the machines charged out at full throttle, speeding away across the broken ground. Three of the machines sped northward, two headed south. The last came hurtling straight at the Judgement.

Wyatt tried to train the energy cannon on the 'Horse as it came streaking toward him, but the angle was too steep and he couldn't bring the gun to bear against a target so near to the wagon. The marshal cursed and called down a warning to Warren. "Grab somethin' and hold tight!"

In his effort to shoot down the 'Horse, Wyatt had seen that it didn't have a rider. Its throttle had been tied back with a loop of barbed wire. Aimed by the outlaws while they were inside the stables, the Iron Horse had been launched at the Judgement like a steel thunderbolt.

The Judgement rocked on its chassis as the unmanned machine smashed into it. For an instant, Wyatt thought the wagon would roll over onto its side, but the tremendous impact failed to provide the collision with that much force. Even so, he was thrown about in the turret, his head cracking against the metal hatch, a stream of blood gushing from his torn scalp. His right arm, looped about the top rung of the ladder, felt like it had been all but wrenched from his shoulder. There was a salty taste in his mouth from where his clamping teeth had bit down on his lip.

Dust and smoke drifted before the turret, obstructing Wyatt's view. Angrily, the Over-marshal threw back the armored hatch and peaked up, spitting a mouthful of blood into the dirt. He could see the smoking wreck of the Iron Horsethrown twenty yards away by the collision, its frame reduced to a tangle of tortured metal. Further off, he could see the outlaws making their retreat. There were three Iron Horses speeding to the north, one of them lagging with the double-weight of two riders. To the south there were only two riders. While he watched, he saw them divert slightly, angling toward the ridge and trading shots with the posse up in the rocks.

"Warren, get this buzzard-box moving!" Wyatt roared down at his brother. Warren grunted back an inarticulate reply, but the Judgement's engine soon rumbled into life. The armored wagon started to lurch into motion, but then shuddered to a stop. The grisly shriek of metal grinding against metal assailed Wyatt's ears. Looking down, he saw the crumpled side of the Judgement where the Iron Horse had crashed into it. One of the wheels was pushed up against the hull; Warren's efforts to get it moving only serving to dig the wheel still deeper into the armor.

Cursing, Wyatt dropped down from the roof of the Judgement. He watched in impotent fury as the two bands of outlaws made good their escape. He didn't have to go inside the cabin to know that he'd find some sort of tunnel connecting it to the stables. While he'd been closing the noose around the cabin, Jesse and his men had simply slipped out to their rides.

"Morg, get the 'bots together and see if you can't get the wagon fixed," Wyatt called out to the cyborg. "Warren, hop over to the stables and see if these coyotes left any transportation behind."

The posse up on the rocks broke from cover, the soldiers galloping off on their blackhoofs, the rest of the men speeding down to the hideout on their Interceptors. Wyatt waited until the men drew close, his fury mounting with each passing breath. By rights, they should be splitting off and taking up the outlaws' trail, not stopping for anything. Even for him.

When the riders pulled up beside the crippled Judgement, Wyatt glowered at his men. "I suppose you've got a good reason for dilly-dallying when you should be riding down Jesse James?"

Doc Holiday met his friend's anger with a rasping chuckle. "The cavalry boys have called it quits and are riding back to Fort Concho. McMaster was wounded, so they're taking him along to get patched up." The gambler shook his head. "Long odds if we split up, Wyatt. Unless that lynch-wagon gets rollin' again, we'll have to leave Morg and the 'bots. We just don't have enough mounts for everybody and if we leave the Enforcers behind there won't be enough of us to light out after both packs and still have the advantage."

Wyatt glared up at Doc. "What're you sayin'? We just up and let Jesse slip through our fingers? After what he did to Virg, you have the gall to ask me to do that?"

Doc's voice was an angry hiss when he answered. "What I'm sayin' is we can only chase one pack of them critters. I felt it was your call to make, your choice which one we mosey after."

The Over-marshal nodded in apology to Doc. Being old friends, the gesture was enough to smooth over any ill feeling his harsh words had engendered. He realized Doc was right, chasing after both bands of outlaws would only split their strength, especially with Morg and the Enforcers out of the picture and with McMaster wounded. They had to try for one or the other. Wyatt mulled that over, considering what he knew about Jesse and balancing it against the way the two groups had made their escape. The bravado displayed by the two riders who'd traded shots with the men in the rocks seemed like just the sort of thing Jesse would do.

"We run down those varmints who headed south," Wyatt said. He turned his head as Warren came running back from the stables. "Any luck?"

Warren shook his head and cursed lividly. "They left one 'Horse, but the polecats trashed it afore lightin' out! Won't be doin' anybody any good for quite a spell!"

The report brought a gruff laugh from Ike Clanton. "Gonna be a long walk, marshal," he cackled. "You bein' without a ride now and all. Gotta say you lawdogs really made a mess of things! I hand you Jesse James on a silver plate and you let him get away!"

"Over-marshal to you, Ike!" Wyatt rounded on the smirking rustler. Seizing him by his vest, he dragged Ike from the saddle of his 'Horse and threw him into the dirt. "I ain't the one who's walkin'."

Ike rolled onto his back, his face black with dust and dirt. "You damn star-packer! You can't treat me like this! I got a pardon! I'm a reg'lar citizen now!"

Wyatt scowled at the rustler. "I should burn you down right here, Ike," the lawman hissed. "Do the territory a favor and save some respectable folk a spell of trouble down the road. But, like you say, you got a pardon." He reached into the pocket of his vest and drew out the keys to Ike's shackles. The rustler reached up to take them, but before the keys were in his hands, Wyatt pulled back and threw them into the rocks.

"Work for it," Wyatt told the rustler, leaving the cursing Ike to scramble in the brush. He mounted the outlaw's Iron Horse and turned back to Doc and the rest of his diminished posse. "Turkey Creek, you figure you can pick up their trail?"

Turkey Creek Johnson nodded. "Lessn' they sprout wings or turn Indian," he answered.

Wyatt turned back to his brothers. "Warren, Morg, stick here and see if you can get the lynch-wagon up and rollin'. One way or the other, we'll swing back around for you in a few days."

The lawman stared out across the desolate horizon, picturing in his mind the two outlaws who had sped off toward the south. Jesse James would answer for his crimes. That was a promise Wyatt intended to keep. Come hell or high water, he'd see the bushwhacker swinging from a rope.

Chapter 9

Jesse's Iron Horse sped across the rocky wastes, letting the miles stretch between him and the abandoned hideout. He'd done his best to antagonize Earp and his posse, hoping to goad the lawmen into pursuing him instead of Cole and the others. With Jim wounded, Jesse wanted to give the others as much advantage as he could. If Cole's trick with the spare Iron Horse had played out right, then Earp's lynch-wagon would be immobilized. Unless the lawmancould find enough vehicles for the 'bots,Earp would be forced to abandon a good chunk of his posse with the armored wagon.

Riding beside Jesse, John Younger let loose with a Rebel yell. "Damnation! That was Wyatt Earp and you done made him look ten kinds a fool!"

Jesse couldn't help but smile at the boy's fawning admiration. Still, it was a smile that quickly turned sour. The Earps were the most renowned lawmen in the west. An outlaw with any sense would rather have the whole Pinkerton agency on his tail than the Earps. What had set Wyatt riding out from Tombstone into Texas, Jesse didn't know, but he had an idea it must have had something to do with the Cowboys. Yet another debt he had to take up with Old Man Clanton.

"Don't reckon Wyatt down," Jesse cautioned John. "Man like that'll eat dust a long time if'n he thinks he's got a trail he can follow."

John laughed, his eyes beaming as he met Jesse's gaze. "He catches up to us, then he'll have real trouble! I'd like to see him lock horns with Jesse James!"

Jesse matched John's laugh. It was hard not to feel prideful with John's boisterous faith in his prowess riding right at his elbow. When they'd separated, John had volunteered to ride out with Jesse, leaving his brothers to follow after his hero. It was a testimony to the regard in which John held his hero.

"We'll riddle that star-packer so full of holes, that he'll look like he fell in a briar patch," Jesse agreed. "But let's give him a good chase first," he added with a wink.

John started to say something in reply when his 'Horse juked violently to the side. Smoke belched from the machine's engine. As the boy tried to wrestle with his machine, he cried out in pain, smoke rising from his hands and little slivers of electricity crackling from his teeth. The Iron Horse skewed downwards, plowing nose-first into the earth and launching John into the air.

Jesse didn't have time to swing back around and come to the boy's aid before his own steed was struck. The outlaw saw the flash from a stony butte, even fancied he could see the crackling finger of lightning that came streaking down to sizzle across the Iron Horse. Unlike John, he didn't try to wrestle for control of the machine. Twisting the control neck one direction, he threw himself in the other. The 'Horse veered off, mimicking a half-circle before it dipped its nose and slammed into the ground.

The outlaw landed hard, feeling all the wind kicked out of him as he rolled in the dirt. Before he could rise, he was smashed flat by the explosion of his crippled machine. Shrapnel from the machine scythed overhead, gouging the earth around him. He bit down on a cry of pain as a red-hot sliver of steel sliced across his leg. Pain was something he didn't have the luxury to feel. Not with a sniper lurking somewhere up on the butte.

Picking himself up as best he could, Jesse drew his blasters and fired. He didn't have a target that he could see up on the butte, so instead he fired at the ground between himself and the ambusher. The shots kicked up a screen of dirt and rock, a veil to hide Jesse from the sniper.

The trick worked. When the sniper's electric blasts came crackling down at Jesse, they lacked the precision of the shots that had disabled both of the Iron Horses. The outlaw dashed along, favoring his injured leg as he made for a cluster of boulders. The blind fire of the sniper crackled all around him, sizzling against the ground and leaving ugly craters with each blast. Unable to draw a bead on Jesse, the ambusher was trying instead to lead his prey, following the outlaw's shots and trying to predict his position.

Jesse nearly reached the boulders before one of the ambusher's shots caught him a glancing blow. The entire side of his body tightened like a tense muscle, his metal arm falling limp at his side, fingers clamped so tight that the grip of his hyper-velocity blaster was crushed out of any semblance of shape. He crashed to the ground, shivering as though seized by an epileptic fit. Through the screen of dust, he could see a figure in a long coat and sporting a strange shirt of gold step out from a crevice in the side of the butte, a massive rifle clenched in his hands.

Jesse could guess the sort of trash that had sprung the ambush. Not one of Earp's men, but a scavenging bounty hunter. He'd probably watched the whole fracas at the hideout from a distance and then hurried off to intercept whoever slipped through Wyatt's trap. Jesse only hoped there weren't more of the vultures lying in wait for Cole's group.

Any moment, Jesse expected another blast from the bounty killer's rifle to finish him off. When the shot never came, he realized the scum either thought he was dead or wanted to take him alive. Either way, it gave him a slight edge over his adversary. It was an edge he'd have to exploit to the fullest if he was going to win out over the hunter.

Straining his ears, Jesse listened for the sound that would tell him it was time for action. With his left side still quivering, he didn't know if he'd be able to make it to the rocks. He also knew that if he didn't try, he was as good as a dead man. John would be as well, if the boy had survived the wreck of his vehicle. With the big reward on Jesse, a bounty killer wouldn't look twice at John Younger; he'd be more apt to simply gun him down and save himself any trouble.

The noise Jesse's ears strained so desperately to hear finally reached him. It was the clatter of loose rocks rolling down the slope. The bounty hunter was starting his descent. On such treacherous ground, the ambusher would be paying more attention to his footing than he would the men he'd shot down. That would give Jesse a small lead, perhaps just the briefest instant when the bounty killer would be distracted. It'd take brass and a fair bit of luck to make it to the rocks, but the outlaw had been in tougher spots with nothing more than high hopes and recklessness to see him clear. He just had to trust that his string hadn't run out yet.

Mustering all the strength in his body, clenching his teeth tight against the pain in his side, Jesse lunged up from the ground. Half falling, half jumping, he propelled himself toward the rocks. Up on the slope, there was an instant of confused violence as the bounty hunter rushed downward, seeking a spot of even ground from which to take another shot at the outlaw. Jesse didn't give him the chance. With another bone-wracking effort he threw himself forwards again, slamming down hard into the packed earth at the base of the nearest boulder. The rock just above his head exploded in a burst of crackling energy, splinters of stone peppering his face. He felt his brain pounding against the inside of his skull from the concussion of the blast. It took more strength than he thought he had to reach out with his right arm and claw his way back behind the boulder. If not for the enhanced power of his mechanical arm, he doubted he could have managed to drag himself to safety before another shot from the bounty man's rifle cracked against the boulder.

"Give yerself up!" the bounty hunter shouted. "You ain't got food and you ain't got water! I can sit you out, so you might as well save us both the inconvenience!"

Breathing hard, Jesse pried the crumpled pistol from his frozen left hand and transferred it to his right. His other blaster was lying out there on the ground where he'd fallen. In fact, it had been a bit of a blessing that his left hand had locked itself so tight about the other gun. The grip might be ruined, but the gun was still functional. Accuracy might be a problem, but there was no way the bounty hunter could know that.

Groaning with the effort, Jesse leaned around the boulder and peeled off a shot in the direction of his ambusher. The shot went wide, but it did send the ambusher scrambling down the slope, rushing to get himself some sort of cover. More importantly, it impressed on the man that he was still up and able.

The bounty hunter started to dash toward a stand of cactus, but changed direction abruptly, diving toward John's Iron Horse. Jesse snapped off another shot at the ambusher, but again the blast went wide of the mark. Before he could fire again, Jesse saw the man pick John off the ground, holding the boy before him like a shield.

"I've got your partner here, James!" the bounty man shouted. "If'n you don't want to see me excavate his head, throw down yer iron and come out!"

"Don't do it, Jesse!" John shouted back. "Don't mind me, just plug this buzzard!" The boy's outburst ended in a moan of pain as the bounty killer smashed the butt of his rifle into the outlaw's back.

"Come out or the kid dies."

Jesse could tell it was no bluff. The scavenger would gun John down the instant he didn't have any use for him, whatever Jesse did. There were a few cards left in the outlaw's hand, however. The bounty hunter was after reward money and it was pretty obvious he didn't favor the notion of sharing it with anyone.

"Better settle for the reward on him," Jesse shouted from the rocks. "That's one of the Youngers you got there!"

The hunter's voice was a thin snarl. "Yeah, and its Jesse James I got pinned down in them rocks."

"Settle for what ya got, buzzard," John hissed in his captor's ear. He'd caught the turn of Jesse's taunting. "Wyatt Earp and his whole posse are gonna be comin' this way any minute."

The bounty killer cast an anxious gaze over his shoulder. He cursed when he saw a distant cloud of dust. Swinging back around, he sent a stream of invective at Jesse.

"Real simple, buzzard," Jesse called out. "Stay here and wait me out, you can share out the whole reward with Wyatt's posse. Or you can take my partner in by yerself and keep the whole poke. Better make up yer mind quick."

The scavenger glared at John, studying him with an avaricious eye. "Which one are you? Bob?" he asked, almost visibly appraising the value of his catch.

"Guess," John spat at his captor.

The bounty man took a step back, and then brought John low by smacking his rifle against the boy's head. Before the outlaw could fall, the killer sprang forward and caught him. "I'll be takin' the boy!" he yelled up at Jesse's refuge. "You can give the Over-marshal my apologies that I didn't wait around fer him."

Jesse watched as the hunter carried John to the crippled Iron Horse and slung him across the saddle. If he'd been able to trust his aim, Jesse might have picked the man off in that moment of vulnerability, but with his arm acting up and the grip of his blaster twisted, he didn't risk shooting. He could only play the part of an observer as the bounty man sat behind John's sprawled body and spurred the 'Horse into action. The damaged machine started off. It was obvious to Jesse that the machine couldn't get far, but it was equally obvious that the bounty hunter didn't need it to. He had his own steed somewhere up behind the butte.

As the assassin started off, he made a final strike against Jesse's refuge, snapping off a string of shots, not from his rifle, but from the pistol holstered at his side. The outlaw was forced to crouch down as splinters of rock exploded from the face of the boulder. He made one halfhearted attempt to return fire, his shot again being thrown wide. It was just as well. With John slung across the saddle ahead of him, any shot that took the bounty hunter was just as likely to claim the boy too.

Snarling in frustration, the scavenger sped away with his prisoner, resigned to leave Jesse behind in the rocks. The last the outlaw saw of him, the ambusher was swinging around the far end of the butte.

The bounty man's retreat seemed to drain Jesse's body of the desperate vitality that had forced him to the Herculean efforts needed to get him into the rocks. The outlaw all but collapsed as the strain of his recent exertions came flooding through his body. Every hurt, every speck of fatigue, seemed magnified by those long minutes of denying them. Like a weary moth, Jesse wilted against the rocks. His last conscious thought was the image of a rabbit hole, then darkness swallowed his senses and he knew nothing more.

*****

The sound of angry voices roused Jesse from the clutch of black oblivion. Except for a thin sliver of light, everything around the outlaw was darkness. Dimly, he remembered collapsing to the ground and sliding into a declivity beneath one of the boulders – the rabbit hole that figured so prominently in the confused muddle of his recent thoughts. Without moving his head, without twitching a muscle, he rolled his eyes toward the little sliver of light, the narrow gap that yawned beneath the edge of the boulder. It was through that gap that the voices drifted down to him.

"Has to have been Tobin and that Fancy Dan rifle of his," one of the voices cursed. "He must have laid up somewhere in the rocks and waited for 'em to ride by. Probably hit 'em before they knew he was there."

The exclamation was answered by a voice Jesse recognized as belonging to Wyatt Earp. The Over-marshal's tone was as murderous as a ten-button sidewinder. "I should have shot that bounty-sniffing coyote when he decided to light out and try a lone hand! Well, if he was here, then we know where he's taking Jesse. He'll be riding back to Fort Concho for the reward. He'll have taken him alive; too, otherwise he'd just have hacked off the head and left the rest for the vultures."

A raspy, metallic voice urged Wyatt to caution. "If Tobin's taken him to Concho, then that's an end of it."

"The hell it is, Doc!" Wyatt snarled back. "We'll ride back there and demand Mackenzie turn Jesse over to us!"

"You can't buck the Union," Doc warned. "I know you're upset about what he done to Virg…"

Jesse's brow knotted in confusion. It had bothered him that Wyatt Earp had taken up his trail, but now the discussion between the lawmen put things in a clearer light. For some reason, Wyatt thought the James-Younger Gang was responsible for holding up a bank in Tombstone and shooting his brother Virgil. It didn't take any imagination at all to see the treacherous hand of Old Man Clanton behind such a play. It seemed blasters and Iron Horses weren't the only things the Cowboys had hoped to get from their alliance with Jesse James. They'd also planned things so that they'd have a free hand back home while the Earps were busy pursuing a vendetta against Jesse James.

Well, the Clantons would have a few things coming back to them as soon as Jesse got himself clear of Wyatt and his posse. Nobody made a fool of Jesse James! He'd taken dirt from too many people; from the filthy Union and from the savage Indians and from that lying Carpathian. The Cowboys weren't going to pass this one over on him. He'd settle this treachery and pay the varmints back in their own coin.

"We're going back to Concho," Wyatt declared. "That's the end of it. If Mackenzie has Jesse, he'll have to cough him over. The Union can have him after he stands trial in Tombstone."

Doc's laugh was like the hiss of escaping steam. "After you try him or after you hang him?" the gambler asked.

Wyatt's answer was uttered in a hiss every bit as grisly as Doc's laugh. "That depends on how Virg is when we get back to Tombstone. If I have to plant him in Boot Hill, he won't be going there alone. I'll see the man responsible dead, if it means bucking the army, the Pinkertons, and the whole damn government!"

Down in the hole, Jesse carefully squirmed his arm out from beneath his body, pointing his blaster up at the opening. So far, the lawmen hadn't found him; but if they did, he was going to make sure a few of them rode along with him on the trail to Hell.

"Here I was thinkin' you had some respect for that bit of tin you wear," Doc said. "Imagined you were after more'n just revenge. I thought you were seekin' justice. Ain't that what you say Virg deserves?"

Jesse tensed as he heard footsteps starting to circle around the boulder. Whoever was prowling around the rocks was near enough that he could hear the creak of their leather holsters as they moved and smell the grease in their hair. Shutting one eye, he squinted down the barrel of his blaster and waited for a face to peak down at him. He felt like a rattler, all coiled up and waiting to strike. And just like a rattler, he knew he wasn't apt to get the chance for a second attack, so he'd have to make it count. The little sliver of light shining down into the hole flickered as a shadow passed across it.

"I won't be talked out of seein' Mackenzie," Wyatt said in firm, unyielding voice. "You can ride back to Tombstone if it makes you uncomfortable, but I'm goin' to Concho and I'm tellin' that eagle-button I want custody of Jesse."

Doc sighed, a sound that bubbled like boiling coffee in the filter of his mask. "They say never stand betwixt a fool and his folly," he rasped. "But that don't hold when the fool's your friend. If your dead set on this, I'm plumb dumb enough to stick to you."

A few pebbles trickled down into the hole as one of Wyatt's posse walked past the boulder. Jesse could almost picture the man staring down at the ground, studying the marks he'd left behind. Slowly, his finger tightened around the trigger of his blaster.

"Doc's ridin' with me to Fort Concho," Wyatt's voice was raised to a shout, carrying to the scattered members of his posse. "The rest of you light back and see if you can help

Warren and Morg get the Judgement runnin' again. We'll head back for Tombstone after I palaver with Mackenzie."

The man near the boulder called out to the Over-marshal. "We'll string along with you Wyatt. We come this far."

"Thanks, Turkey Creek, but two's enough for this job. If Mackenzie won't hand over Jesse, it won't do any good getting' the rest of you involved."

"What he's tryin' to say is there's no use in everybody goin' against the law," Doc elaborated. "My reputation's already blighted enough that another black spot won't make no nevermind, but the rest of you have your respectability to take into consideration."

"I ain't of a mind to jaw over this all day," Wyatt said. "Me and Doc are goin' and the rest of you ain't. That's an end to the discussion."

Jesse relaxed as he heard Turkey Creek walking away from the boulder. He listened as the lawmen returned to their Interceptors and spurred them into action. The racket of their firing engines soon faded off in the distance, four of the machines heading northward, two of them rocketing eastward in pursuit of Tobin and the outlaw they were certain he'd captured.

It never occurred to Wyatt Earp that the man he wanted so badly had been practically under his very feet.

Sometimes the turn of Jesse's luck astonished even him.

*****

Jesse waited the better part of an hour before he finally crawled out from under the rock. His left arm still felt like a lump of dead iron dragging on his shoulder, but at least most of the numbness had left his leg. He was able to move with at least a semblance of normality, though he still felt a shot of pain rush through him whenever he planted the sole of his foot against the ground. The same pain struck at him whenever he bent his knee at too sharp an angle.

The outlaw scowled as he contemplated the bleak, inhospitable terrain around him. His infirmity would have been just an inconvenience in more settled surroundings, but out here in the wild, where the odds were already weighted against him, his debility could prove fatal.

One glance at the wreck of his Iron Horse was enough to tell him there'd be no salvaging the machine. A quick examination of the ground showed him that the blaster he'd dropped was gone. Purloined by one of Wyatt's lawdogs, Jesse was certain. He shook his head as he stared down at the crumpled, twisted weapon in his hand. That abused gun was the only tool he had, the only weapon available to see him safely across the hostile west Texan desert.

Squinting up at the sun, Jesse tried to figure out where he was and where he should be going. The frantic ride away from the hideout hadn't left him much opportunity to consider his bearings, and he wasn't as familiar with the area as Cole and the Youngers were. Bitterly, he once again wished Frank was with him. His brother would have made it his first priority to study the lay of the land and pick out the spots where they could secure supplies and remounts. Frank was always the strategist; he was always the one who figured out how something could be done. All Jesse did was tell the gang what it was they were going to do. The details had always been left to Frank.

The Yankees had taken so much from Jesse; it still seemed unreal to him that they'd taken Frank too. His older brother had seemed indestructible to him, able to wade through a shootout without batting an eye, able to brain his way into any bank or supply depot. It chafed his pride to admit it, even to himself, but Frank had been a better man than he was. Left on his own, Frank would have settled down after Little Arch got himself gunned by the law. It had been Jesse's vindictive streak, his refusal to accept the carpet-baggers and the glad-handing Yankees, that had Frank follow him when he formed the James-Younger Gang. Devotion to his brother, more than anything, had kept Frank riding the outlaw trail.

Jesse choked down on the regret and guilt that welled up inside him, and he tried to turn it into something else. Shame wouldn't give him the sand to see his way back to civilization. Thinking about Frank, he turned his mind to the men who had taken him away. He thought about John Younger, the boy who idolized the great Jesse James, and how he'd been bushwhacked and abducted by that bounty killer.

Feeling the fire of determination coursing through his veins, Jesse turned eastward. Wyatt claimed Tobin would be taking John back to Fort Concho. Following the Over-marshal's trail would be Jesse's first step in helping the boy. Grimly, the outlaw started out across the desert.

All through the day and long into the night, Jesse continued to plod along. The pain in his left leg had eased somewhat, or else become so persistent that he became so accustomed to it, that it stopped vexing him. His left arm still hung limp at his side, but in those brief moments when he allowed himself to stop and rest, Jesse found he could force the fingers of his hand to twitch, allowing he concentrated hard enough. Like his body, the shock from Tobin's glancing shot seemed to be wearing off from the mechanisms in his metal arm. However treacherous he had proved, Jesse had to confess that Carpathian knew his business when it came to designing machinery.

As darkness settled over the wastes and night cast its cloak over the sky, Jesse pressed on. The chill of the desert darkness cut at him like a thousand icy knives, yet still he continued his long march through the desolation. Eyes focused on the trail left by the Interceptors of Wyatt and Doc, Jesse didn't appreciate the crumbling edge of the arroyo until it gave out beneath his feet.

The outlaw slid down into the declivity, crashing into a tangle of mesquite. Lying on his back in the dirt, the fatigue he had resisted for so long closed about him. The tyrannical call of sleep drowned all other thoughts, smothered all other intentions. One effort to raise himself off the ground, and then Jesse's head slumped back in the dirt. For a minute, he blinked up at the stars. Then all was darkness.

It was the feel of steel against his throat that awakened Jesse. The outlaw didn't move, didn't twitch a muscle. The only sign of life was when he opened his eyes. When he did, he found himself staring up into the lean, hawk-like face of an Indian. The man's coppery skin was daubed with paint, the white slashes and whorls of the Warrior Nation.

More than the man, however, Jesse noticed the long cavalry saber clenched in his fist, its point pressed against Jesse's throat. A single thrust and the Indian would skewer him like a pig.

"Iron Knife," a sharp voice called from the darkness. "Do not kill. This man must not die."

The Indian with the saber scowled, his face contorting into an inhuman expression of viciousness. "The stink of abomination is on him, Two Wolves!" He pressed the sword just a little closer, drawing a bead of blood as the tip cut Jesse's skin. "He is part devil already."

"He is Metal Hands," Two Wolves declared. Jesse could see the other Indian emerge from the darkness. Like Iron Knife, he had the squat build of the desert and his face was painted for war. "He is the one from the medicine vision. You must not kill."

"I do not believe the medicine," Iron Knife snapped at the other warrior. "I do not believe anything that says I must not kill the white man."

The expression on Two Wolves' face became grim. "Then you do not trust the Great Spirit. You do not trust those to whom He speaks."

The accusation took some of the fire out of Iron Knife. With an inarticulate snarl, the Indian drew the sword away from Jesse's throat. "I will kill you," he glared down at the outlaw. "But first I will take you to see Geronimo."

Chapter 10

Thomas Tate Tobin stalked across Colonel Mackenzie's office, the bounty hunter's fist clenched around the handful of greenbacks he'd been issued by Fort Concho's purser. "Fifty dollars?" he growled. "You're tellin' me I traded shots with Jesse James and crossed up Wyatt Earp for fifty dollars?"

Mackenzie leaned back in his chair, his metal fingers drumming against the top of his desk. "That's the standard reward for any member of the James-Younger Gang. Now if you'd managed to bring in Cole or Jim, you'd have the individual rewards being offered for them. Hell, you didn't even bring in Bob Younger."

Tobin spun around, slamming his hands against the desk and leaning over the colonel. "You suggestin' maybe I should fetch that boy out of your guardhouse and let him run about a spell so's he gets as notorious as his brothers?"

"Maybe you should have tried harder to get Jesse James if you wanted a big pay day." The stern words came from Lucinda Loveless. The Pinkerton operative strolled across the office, her lovely face curled in contempt, her eyes flashing angrily at Tobin. As far as she was concerned, the bounty hunter was no different than an assassin or a range detective; a hired killer devoid of decency and honor. The idea of paying out any blood money to this human vulture was repugnant to her. "If you decide to play it safe and settle for an easy catch, don't go bawling to your government when you don't strike the mother lode."

Tobin leaned away from the desk, glaring at Loveless. "I was head-huntin' Mex for Colonel Tappan when you weren't even a gleam in your daddy's eye. I was one of two men to escape the Battle of Turley's Mill during the Taos Revolt. I was the man who brought back the heads of the Espinosas when every posse and cavalry troop in the territory couldn't."

Loveless turned a cold smile on the bounty hunter. "It sounds to me like you've been at your job too long. Like an old wolf whose fangs are getting too weak to hang onto prey."

"You ten-penny painted cat," Tobin growled back. "Waddle back to yer hog ranch!"

The bounty hunter's crass insult brought Mackenzie up from his chair. The colonel's steel fingers clenched tight as he shook his fist at Tobin. "You ain't got no call to speak to a lady like that, you flea-ridden dog."

Tobin sneered at the outraged officer. "You blacksmithin' for this horse-poker?" he snarled. Before he could say anything more, Tobin felt the cold press of a gun barrel against his side. He turned his eyes toward Loveless, surprised to see a snub-nosed derringer in her slender hand. "Never figured you for a pocket advantage," he said, raising his arms from his sides.

"Take your blood money and get," Loveless told him. "You can be grateful I'm a forgiving sort and didn't take any offense to what you said… this time."

The bounty hunter slowly backed away, bowing his head ever so slightly toward Loveless. "My apologies, ma'm," he said, waving the bills in his hand. "I forgot myself in my excitement. I promise I'll be more mindful of my company when I bring in Jesse James." He looked back to Mackenzie. "You'll have the reward ready, I trust."

"Ten thousand, but I want him alive," Mackenzie reminded the killer. "I've got a hemp party all planned for that bushwhacker."

Tobin smiled as he turned toward the door. "Start makin' out yer invite list, Bad

Hand, because Jesse's on borrowed time."

Loveless waited until the bounty hunter was gone before she returned her derringer to the sleeve of her blouse. She was sorely tempted to have Mackenzie arrest Tobin, throw the bounty killer in the guard house along with John Younger. She, however, resisted that temptation. She knew it wasn't Tobin's lack of respect for her or the law that fired her resentment, but rather the thought of the back-shooting killer being at liberty to track down Jesse. She understood that Jesse was the enemy of everything she'd sworn to protect and uphold; he was an unreconstructed rebel, a man still living like a Secesh guerrilla. This strange fascination she held for him, this attachment she had formed; it was a toxic, poisonous thing. By rights, she should be happy an accomplished assassin like Tobin was out on Jesse's trail. Anything that would bring an end to the outlaw's campaign of robbery and murder was something she should support.

Maybe it was naïve of her, but Loveless couldn't bring herself to accept the mantra of the ends justifying the means that Pinkerton and the officials in Washington seemed so ready to adopt. She knew Jesse had to be brought in, but when it happened, she wanted it to be clean and above board. When the outlaw was apprehended, it should be lawmen who brought him in, not some bounty hunter sniping him from half a mile away.

"You ever hear how a Chinaman gets rid of a snake?" Mackenzie asked. "He sends a bigger snake down into the hole. That's what I feel like I'm doin' right now."

"The only way that prairie tenor will get Jesse is by pluggin' him in the back," Loveless said.

Mackenzie shook his head and laughed. "I'm sure he'd favor that approach, but he's too greedy to give up on the bonus fer bringin' Jesse back alive."

"Maybe, but I don't relish the idea of relying on a bounty hunter." Loveless fixed the colonel with a questioning look. "Have you considered my idea?"

Mackenzie frowned. He reached into his desk and produced a sheaf of papers. "I decided against it, ma'am. I'm not keen on the risk involved."

"It's my risk to take," Loveless reminded him.

"Not entirely," Mackenzie smiled. "If anything went wrong, you can bet the War Office would make me the goat. John Younger might not be a big noise, but he is one of the Youngers. This idea to turn him loose so's you can trail him back to Jesse... I'm sorry, but I'm not gonna stake my career on it. Been shot too many times defending this country to give it up on a cracked scheme like that."

Loveless came around the corner of the desk and brushed her hand across the colonel's cheek. "He's the best chance I have of finding Jesse. You know that."

Mackenzie pulled away from the woman's caress. "I've already arranged for his transfer. It's out of my hands." He laughed and flexed the metal talons of his maimed hand. "Or what's left of 'em anyway."

"Then I'll take it up with the warden at the territorial prison," Loveless said, stepping away from the colonel's chair.

"I'm not sending him to the territorial prison," Mackenzie's voice fell cold. "I'm sending that ringy to Andersonville."

Loveless stared in disbelief at the seated colonel. Andersonville housed the most notorious Confederate prison camp of the conflict; it had been renamed as Camp Lincoln and employed for the reeducation and rehabilitation of 'recidivist Secesh.' Most of those sent to the prison to be reconstructed never left. Loveless had never been there herself, but she'd heard it described by other Pinkerton agents as the worst hell-hole in America.

"You can't do that," Loveless protested. "John's too young to have fought in the war. He's not a Secessionist."

"He's a Younger, and that's good enough," Mackenzie countered. "That little mongrel helped shoot up my fort. Now, he can rot in Camp Lincoln." The colonel perked up when he saw Loveless head toward the door of his office. "Leaving so soon, Agent Loveless?"

"I have a job to do," Loveless reminded him. "I came to Fort Concho trying to get a lead on Jesse James. Now you're shipping my only resource to Camp Lincoln."

"So what are you going to do?" Mackenzie asked.

"That isn't your problem," Loveless told him. "If I were you, I'd be more worried about what Jesse James and Cole Younger are going to do if they find out you've shipped John off to Camp Lincoln. Somehow I think they might prove a sight more debilitating to your career than Washington or the War Office."

*****

Sweat dripped from every pore in the medicine man's body, streaming into a puddle on the dirt floor of the lodge. Hot vapor filled the tiny room, a stifling mist that transformed the whole lodge into an indistinct gray cloud.

Within that cloud, the medicine man could see two great serpents writhing. They were as pale as snow, their rattles flecked with gold like slivers torn from the sun. A shrill, whistling sound rose from the rattles as they shivered at the end of each serpent's tail. It was the voice of the great iron snake that crawled across the land,leaving a metal trail behind in its wake. As the sound of the whistling rattles grew louder and rose to a frenzied wail, the serpents balled themselves into tight coils. Their flattened heads arched toward each other, their forked tongues flickering as they tasted the air.

When it seemed the whistle of their rattles could grow no louder, the two snakes struck at each other. Their fanged jaws clamped tight about the other's scaly neck. An ugly purple stain spread through each reptile, discoloring the snowy scales. The fangs of each snake pumped poison into its enemy, unrelenting and merciless. Only when both serpents were turned completely purple, only when their rattles lost strength and fell silent, did the reptiles relent. Bloated with poison, their fangs still sunk into each other's neck, the two vipers fell dead.

The gray clouds swept in, blotting out the spirit vision. The medicine man rose from his crouch and flicked the sweat off his fingers before he drew back the buffalo-hide flap that closed off the sweat lodge. He stood for a moment at the entrance, letting his body adjust from the sweltering miasma within, to the comparative cold without. Then, with a firm step, he descended the sandy slope to the camp below.

Young warriors and veteran raiders alike bowed their heads respectfully as he strode past them, many of them touching the iron of their knives or guns as a sign of devotion to him. For he was more than just a medicine man and spiritual leader to these men, he was also their war-chief. Short, stocky of build, his face so weathered the skin seemed more leather than flesh, the Indian was the most notorious marauder in the whole of the American southwest. His name was the terror of a thousand communities from Texas to Arizona and from Utah to Mexico.

He was Geronimo.

As he walked among his followers, Geronimo pondered the vision he had seen. It was a vision that the spirits had shown him many times; always two pale snakes, striking at one another, and killing each other with their poison. After the first time he had seen the vision, he had known its meaning. Each time the vision reappeared, it only reinforced his belief that the way of Sitting Bull was not the way to victory. The war-chief was the great voice of the Warrior Nation; he had forged an alliance between all of the great tribes, overcoming the entrenched animosity of generations. But Geronimo was more than just another chieftain. He had the sight; he had the gifts and knowledge of the medicine man. He had seen that there was another way to stop the white man.

Sitting Bull urged all the tribes to unite and drive the white man's poison from their lands. Geronimo saw another way. The two snakes. Not so long ago, two great white tribes had fought. If their war had persisted, they would have destroyed one another. The vision he had seen seemed to urge him to help the whites make war again.

Geronimo marched through the camp, past the clusters of wooden wickiups. At the very center of the camp, he found what he was seeking. Lashed to a wooden frame by rawhide thongs was the outlaw the Warrior Nation called 'Metal Hands,' and who the white man knew as Jesse James. Many times the medicine man had seen this face in his spirit visions and heard the outlaw's name whispered on the wind. He had an important part to play in bringing the white tribes to war again. It was for that reason he had warned his warriors that they must never harm Metal Hands if they should see him, but must instead bring him to stand before their war-chief.

A large band of warriors stood guard around the prisoner, knives and hatchets at the ready. It was more the threat of the warriors than the restraint imposed upon him by the rawhide bindings that kept the outlaw confined. The Warrior Nation knew the strength in Jesse's mechanical arms and the infernal power of the devil's blood that gave them that strength. It was the great poison which had polluted the spirits of the white men and driven them to ravage the land in search of the red gold. Only evil could come from such poison, an evil that had to be exterminated before it destroyed the balance set in place by the Great Spirit.

Many of Geronimo's warriors held with the teaching of Sitting Bull that, anything touched by the red gold had to be destroyed immediately. This was mostly because they couldn't understand their own leader's talk of turning the white men against each other, letting them destroy themselves. Sometimes, even Geronimo questioned his visions, wondering if they were true wisdom or lies sent by demons to deceive him.

As he stared at his captive, as he felt the outlaw's hateful gaze stare back at him, Geronimo wondered if it wouldn't be better to kill Metal Hands now. There would be none in his war band who would question such an act, none who would doubt the rightness of such a thing. Only he would have doubt, only he would wonder if what he had done was for the good of his people. If his visions were true, then he couldn't kill this man.

"We have brought Metal Hands to stand before the great Geronimo," the hulking warrior Iron Knife announced, waving his captured cavalry saber at the prisoner. "Now we wait for Geronimo's word to kill."

Geronimo was silent for a moment, studying the mood of his warriors. Iron Knife spoke the truth; many of them were expecting, even eager for the war-chiefto give them the signal so that they might butcher Metal Hands. He could understand their attitude. With his mechanical arms, Jesse was a living manifestation of the perversion the white men were practicing, their defilement of nature and the land. He could appreciate their hate, even share in it, but he also knew that they had to strive for things more important than hate if they were to help their people.

Patiently, Geronimo explained his visions to his warriors. He told them of the two serpents and how they killed one another with their poison. He spoke to them of the war he had seen, the war between the white tribes that would destroy them both.

Most of the warriors attended Geronimo's words, listening to his talk about spirit visions with gravity. A few, however, remained unmoved. Even those warriors kept silent, their respect for Geronimo as medicine man and war-chief too great for them to question him openly. Only Iron Knife remained defiant, only he raised his voice in protest.

"The poison of Geronimo's vision already pulses through this man's heart," Iron Knife said, pointing his sword at the outlaw. "He is already a dying thing. Let him die then and bring great power to the Warrior Nation!"

Iron Knife was a vicious fighter, a man who reveled in killing. He had ripped the sword that had given him his name from the belly of its former owner. Around his neck he wore a string of bullets and animal claws on a band of wire, each talisman a memento of some foe he'd killed in combat.

"It is not the Warrior Nation you think of," Geronimo accused. "It is the glory of Iron Knife that fills your heart. What power can our people have if the land cries out with pain? What greatness can we keep in our hearts if the red poison pollutes our hogans? We do not have the strength to stop the white man. Only by turning the white tribes against each other can we find victory."

Iron Knife folded his brawny arms across his chest and glowered down at the stocky medicine man. "Geronimo speaks with the tongue of a sick woman, afraid to fight the white man." He wagged the tip of the cavalry saber in the air. "I am not afraid. Metal Hands is my captive, he is mine to do what I want with! The word of Geronimo said he would see Metal Hands, so I have brought him. Now Geronimo has seen! Now let all the Warrior Nation see the power of Iron Knife!"

The Indian's arrogant taunting was an open challenge to Geronimo, but it was not the war-chief who answered it. Since his guards were distracted by the confrontation among their leaders, Jesse James seized the slim opportunity he'd been given. Rawhide thongs snapped like string as he pulled his mechanical limbs free, the infirmity left by Tobin's glancing shot having dissipated over the long journey to Geronimo's camp. The outlaw roared a fierce Rebel yell as he reached a hand to his neck and ripped away the thong binding his head to the framework.

As Jesse bent down to tear the thongs binding his legs, the startled Indians started to rush in with their spears and knives. It was a sharp cry from Geronimo that stopped them from descending on the only partially freed outlaw in a flurry of stabbing blades. At their war-chief's bellowed command, the warriors backed away. Geronimo nodded to Jesse as the outlaw used the reprieve to break the bonds around his legs.

"Now let all see the power of Iron Knife," Geronimo tossed Iron Knife's words back in his face.

Letting loose a brutal war-whoop, Iron Knife charged at Jesse, his saber held before him like a buffalo spear. It was more than hate of the white outlaw that drove Iron Knife; it was the mockery of Geronimo that sent fire rushing through his veins. The brave's always volatile temper now held complete sway over him, making him forget all strategy and caution in his lust to kill and destroy. Goading Iron Knife into mindless fury was the last gift Geronimo could give Jesse -.the rest would be up to him; it would be up to the outlaw to prove whether the vision of the two snakes was truth or lie. The other question was whether the future of the Warrior Nation lay with Geronimo or Iron Knife.

As the Indian came rushing in, trying to spit Jesse on the end of his sword, now sheathed in a flash of blue flame, the outlaw swung sideways, letting the enraged warrior charge past him. In passing, the outlaw's metal fist smashed into Iron Knife's shoulder with a brutal, meaty impact that bespoke of torn muscle and shattered bone.

Iron Knife reeled away, twisting about and lunging back to the attack. He tossed the glowing cavalry saber from his injured right arm to his left, and then waved it through the air in a savage flourish. The warrior's face twisted into a ghoulish mask of hate; the war-paint staining his features, enhancing their natural harshness. In his eyes were gleaming with azure fire and filled with the malevolence of the hunter who delights in the kill and the suffering of his prey.

Jesse's metal hand closed about one of the poles which formed the frame he had been tied to. When Iron Knife came charging at him again, the outlaw pulled on that pole, ripping it away from the rest of the frame. He cracked the heavy shaft of wood like a whip, swatting the charging Indian as though he were a stampeding steer. Teeth flew from Iron Knife's jaw as the pole crashed against his face, the impact sending him sprawling in the dust. Jesse brought the tip of the pole slamming down, narrowly missing his foe as he scrambled through the dirt on all fours. Warriors scattered as Iron Knife's retreat brought the fight close to them.

His face rendered demonic by the intensity of the rage boiling inside him, Iron Knife leapt up from the ground. He lashed out with the flame-wreathed saber, knocking aside the pole and rushing at Jesse before the outlaw could recover.

The burning cold steel of the sword came hurtling toward Jesse's head, but before the blade could cleave into his skull, the outlaw caught it in a metal hand. Iron Knife strained to free the blade, but the mechanical strength of Jesse's grip held it like a vise as fat blue sparks dripped from between his metal fingers. Scowling at the enraged warrior, Jesse dropped the pole and brought his other hand slapping against the imprisoned blade. The tang of the sword snapped like a twig and the cerulean energy fled, leaving an overbalanced Iron Knife to stumble into his enemy. Jesse's fist crashed into the Indian, throwing him into the air as though he'd been kicked by a mule.

Wiping blood from his mouth, Iron Knife rose to his feet. The blue feral gleam of his eyes sent the circle of watching warriors back a pace, a few nervous murmurs spreading among the braves. The Indian grabbed his dislocated jaw and pushed it back into place. A grisly popping sound then rose from his shattered shoulder, a sharp cracking sound shuddered from his legs, his spine groaning as it began to bulge outward. Before the shocked eyes of his enemy, Iron Knife's body began to change.

"You have lost. Accept this with dignity," Geronimo ordered the warrior.

Iron Knife's reply was barely intelligible, forced from a throat that was already thickening and swelling into bestial shape. "I accept nothing from the white man except his death," the shape-changer growled. His head began to elongate, flesh cracking and sloughing away as mottled fur pushed itself upwards. Hands lengthened into feline claws, each finger tipped by a wicked crescent razor-like tip. Sharp fangs jutted from cat-like jaws.

Once, the animal whose shape Iron Knife wore had ranged throughout the west, but the encroachment of the white man had steadily depleted its numbers, pushing them steadily southward until the cry of the jaguar was barely even a memory in the lodges of the Warrior Nation. Perhaps it was a manifestation of the hate inside Iron Knife's heart that the animal whose form he should adopt was one that had been exterminated by the white men. Perhaps it was simply that no beast except the jaguar could emulate the warrior's vicious brutality and the thrilling feeling of slaughter.

Uttering a low, rumbling snarl, the transformed Iron Knife lunged at Jesse. The jaguar's claws raked the outlaw's side, sheering through his leather coat and slashing across the ribs beneath. The outlaw was sent sprawling into the dust. Roaring with delight, Iron Knife paused to lick the blood from his claws before turning to pounce upon his fallen prey.

As Iron Knife tensed his powerful muscles and made ready to leap on the outlaw, Jesse's hand clawed across the ground, his fingers gouged into the dirt, and he flung a cloud of dust into the jaguar's eyes. The blinded shape-changer cringed back, rubbing at the grit in his eyes with his paw-like hands. While his foe was blinded, Jesse came charging up, flinging himself upon the monster.

Iron Knife flailed and raged as Jesse's metal arm coiled around the jaguar's chest, holding the brute fast. The outlaw's other hand grabbed the necklace hanging around the shape-changer's neck. The chain hung loosely about the Indian's neck when he'd been in human form, but it was as tight as a choker now that he had transformed. Working his finger beneath the chain, Jesse twisted it tighter.

The jaguar thrashed and struggled, throwing himself to the ground and rolling through the dirt in his effort to dislodge the outlaw. Jesse clung fast, his metal finger steadily tightening the necklace. The chain began to dig into Iron Knife's throat, bright blood streaming as the necklace bit into his skin. The fierce roars of the jaguar were reduced to ragged, choking coughs.

A last twitch of the improvised garrote, and Jesse's bestial enemy went limp. A grisly rattle wheezed from the jaguar's body as its head lolled to one side. Carefully, Jesse loosened his grip and rose from the carcass of Iron Knife. Defiantly, he glared at the surrounding Indians.

Geronimo made a slashing motion of his arms, dismissing his warriors, sending them off to break down the camp. The war-chief stared at the bloodied, panting outlaw. Slowly, he paced over to the body of Iron Knife. Reaching down, he ripped free one of the totems from the dead shape-changer's neck. "You fight," he told Jesse in broken English.

"You fight, you kill." Carefully, he handed the totem, the gray feather of an owl adorned in gold and turquoise, to the outlaw.

Jesse replied with a simple nod as he cautiously accepted the grim totem, Iron Knife's blood staining the edges of the feather. "The day I stop fighting is the day they plant me in the ground."

The war-chief smiled. "We go our way," he said, pointing to the north. "Metal Hands goes his way," he added, pointing west. "Keep the feather of Iron Knife. All the Warrior Nation will know what you have done. They will know that it is Geronimo who has allowed you to live. If they believe the vision of Geronimo, they will not seek the life of Metal Hands."

Geronimo reached under the calico sash circling his waist and removed the crumpled blaster that had been taken when Jesse was captured by Iron Knife and Two Wolves. To the Nations, such a weapon was repugnant, a tool of the white man's poison. He tossed the blaster into the dirt at Jesse's feet.

Geronimo watched as Jesse recovered his gun. He saw the brief temptation flicker across the outlaw's face. The idea was there, the thought that with one shot he could eliminate the most feared Indian in the southwest. The idea quickly died, as quickly as Jesse knew he would die if anything happened to Geronimo. It was only the medicine man's protection that kept the rest of the war band from killing him.

"Much obliged," Jesse said as he stuffed the weapon back into its holster.

"Kill much Blue Shirts, Metal Hands," Geronimo told him. Again, he pointed to the west. He stood and watched as Jesse cautiously descended the slope and stole away into the brush. In his mind, however, he didn't see a man striking out across the badlands. What he saw was a great snake, a snake that would soon sink his fangs into the other great serpent and kill it with its own poison. In giving the outlaw the token of the owl, Geronimo had marked him as a man already belonging to the realm of the dead.

*****

It was well after midnight when the commotion rising from the corral outside drew the old miner from his bed. Catching up the shotgun from where it hung on a hook beside the door, he stepped out into the darkness. The chill of the desert night bit through the threadbare long johns he wore, lending a shiver to his voice as he called out into the dark.

"Who's there? What're you doin'?"

The miner's questions were answered by in a stern snarl. "I'm Jesse James and I'm stealin' your horse." The miner's eyes went as wide as saucers as he spotted the red glow of the outlaw's RJ-powered arms in the darkness. By that crimson glow, he could see the blaster pointed at him.

"Yes sir, Mr. James," the miner said, letting the shotgun fall to the ground and hurriedly reaching his hands into the air. "I'm sorry I ain't got anything better to offer you, but my claim ain't panned out so good. Can't even afford a blackhoof."

Jesse kept his gun trained on the miner as he moved along the corral and began to gather up tack and harness for the grizzled old nag standing behind the fence. "What's the nearest town and how much law's it got?"

"Tombstone, Mr. James, sir," the miner said. "Wyatt Earp's the law there."

Jesse froze as he was reaching to pull down bit and bridle from the fencepost. "I understood Earp was away east somewhere."

"He was," the miner agreed. "Came back a few days ago. Went lookin' for you, matter of fact. Understandable, allowin' how you robbed the bank and shot up his brother and all."

Jesse waved the miner over to the fence. Reluctantly, keeping his eyes on the blaster, the man complied. “Listen, old timer, I done a lot of bad in my time. Some of it I take pride in, some of it I don’t, but whatever I done I own up to. So when I tell you I didn’t shoot no Earp or rob no bank in Tombstone, you can believe me.”

The miner smiled nervously, still looking at Jesse’s blaster rather than the man who held it. Deciding the old man wasn’t a threat, Jesse holstered the weapon with a quick twirl and flourish.

“I ain’t the one you gotta convince, Mr. James. It’s the Over-marshal you need to talk to.” The old man laughed, a chuckle as dry and cheerless as the Arizona desert. “Only I don’t think he’ll oblige you. More’n like he’ll hang you first and talk about it later.”

Jesse nodded his head, as though giving the miner’s joke serious consideration. “It’s all about how you talk to somebody. Now I’d be beholden if’n you’d help me saddle that nag of yourn.”

The miner frowned. “Mr. James, please don’t steal my horse. She ain’t much, but she’s all I got.”

The outlaw reached into his pocket and set a gold eagle on the fence post. “I rob banks, not honest folk. Consider I’m just hirin’ your horse. You mosey into town and she’ll be there wait’n.”

“Town?” the miner asked. “Which town?”

Jesse smiled back at him. “Tombstone. I have to have a bit of a palaver with the marshal.”

Chapter 11

Wyatt Earp left Allen Street’s Alhambra Saloon with a belly full of whiskey and a pocket full of money. That night’s round of faro had been particularly lucky, but he took little pleasure in ‘bucking the tiger.’ His thoughts were with his brother Virgil. The doctors had managed to save the lawman’s life, but his right arm was crippled and useless. It was a hard blow for someone like Virgil to accept. Wyatt had tried to talk sense to his older brother and get him to at least come to terms with what had happened to him. Every time he looked at Morgan, however, Wyatt felt a shiver of fear run down his spine. If Virgil had gone to such lengths to try to save their brother, what might he do now?

The idea that Virgil would go seeking more of Dr. Carpathian’s infernal ‘curatives’ was something Wyatt didn’t want to face. He’d lost one brother that way; he didn’t want to think about losing another in the same manner.

Marching alongside the Over-marshal as he made his way down the boardwalk, Doc Holiday muttered something under his breath, the words turned even more indistinct by his breathing apparatus. Wyatt stopped and stared at his companion. “How is that?”

“I said, a man running ace high like you are should playing at the Crystal Palace,” Doc replied. “That’s where all the real money’s going to be on a Friday night.”

Wyatt stared down the street. The damage inflicted on the side of the saloon by the men who’d ambushed Virgil was still evident, only the blood had been cleaned away. There was a bit of disagreement between the county and the city about who should pay for the damages. In all likelihood, it would keep getting pushed back and forth until the proprietor of the Crystal Palace took things into his own hands and replaced the scorched woodwork and broken column himself.

“The Crystal Palace ain’t been so lucky for my people of late,” Wyatt shook his head dejectedly.

Doc shrugged his shoulders. “You won’t mind if I take a turn, then?” The gambler held his hand toward Wyatt. "That is if you'll oblige me. I seem to be a bit embarrassed."

Wyatt frowned. "I always thought you kept the advantage." He reached into his vest and brought out a stack of bills. He didn't count it, but just handed it over to his friend. "If anything's left in the morning, you can bring it by. I'm headed over to the hotel to get some shut eye."

Doc tapped the brim of his hat. "You are a credit to your profession, Wyatt. Don't let anyone tell you otherwise." The gambler peeled off as the two men passed the intersection of Fifth and Allen, striding over to the Crystal Palace while Wyatt continued on to the Cosmopolitan Hotel further down the street.

The gambler's parting words recalled to Wyatt the ugly scene when they'd gone to confront Colonel Mackenzie at Fort Concho. He'd been less than cooperative with the lawmen, complaining rather loudly about the troopers who'd been shot up at the James-Younger Gang hideout, and he was exceedingly abusive in his opinion of the Over-marshal's failure to bring in Jesse James. The fact that Wyatt thought he could find Jesse in Fort Concho's guardhouse had made an already hostile encounter even worse. If not for the restraining influence of Doc Holiday on the one side and Lucinda Loveless on the other, it was entirely probable that Fort Concho would be looking for a new commander and Tombstone a new Over-marshal.

Wyatt cursed under his breath as he thought about what Mackenzie had told him, which Loveless confirmed as truth. Thomas Tate Tobin had indeed been lying in wait for Jesse James after Wyatt's posse flushed him from his hideout. But the bounty hunter had been unsuccessful, returning to Fort Concho, not with Jesse, but only John Younger. The killer had gone out to try again, but it was Loveless's opinion that the outlaw was long gone.

Loud, boisterous laughter from the porch in front of the Grand Hotel drew Wyatt's attention. He scowled when he saw Ike Clanton and several of the Cowboys sitting in front of the hotel, drinking and swapping ribald jokes. Curly Bill Brocius was feting Clanton's return, presenting him in grand style to his comrades. The bearded rustler was bedecked in extravagant new duds, electriwork filigree sewn to the front of his vest and around the brim of the beaverskin hat he wore. With the promise of new wealth that their recent acquisition of arms and machines promised the Cowboys, Curly Bill had cast aside the rough savagery of his old stylings for the gaudy ostentation of a would-be ringster like Ike.

Ike might not have received any part of the reward posted for Jesse, but the varmint had exploited Governor Wallace's pardon to the full. It galled Wyatt to think that if Ike played things careful and kept himself from taking a direct hand in the criminal enterprises of the Cowboys, that he'd be outside the Over-marshal's reach. He didn't believe Ike would go honest for a second, any more than he thought a leopard could change its spots. The outlaw brand was imprinted on Ike's very soul, put there by the Old Man. Where the Clantons were concerned, the apple hadn't fallen far from the tree.

By some irony, the Cosmopolitan Hotel where the Earps had their headquarters was directly across the street from the Grand Hotel, which served as rallying point for the Cowboys when they were in town. As Wyatt marched down the boardwalk, a few of the more intoxicated Cowboys whistled and tossed catcalls his way.

"Next time, lawdog, maybe you should treat me respectable!" Ike Clanton shouted, swaggering out into the street.

"Next time I'll let you walk, instead of letting you ride on a 'bot's lap," Wyatt said, regretting now the twinge of sympathy that had moved him to let Ike ride in the back of the repaired Judgement when the posse made its return to Tombstone. A few weeks without Ike around had not made him miss the Cowboy any more than he had before.

Ike puffed out his chest, poking his thumbs into the pockets of his vest. "You got some nerve jawin' at me like that, star-packer!" He turned and smirked back at the other

Cowboys on the porch. "I'm the big bug around here. You'll be workin' for me one of these days."

"The way I see it, Old Man Clanton calls the shots in your outfit. He just lets you off the leash when he gets tired of your yappin'."

Wyatt didn't bother to listen to the tirade of abuse Ike hurled at his back. If it was Indian Charlie or Johnny Ringo or especially Curly Bill, Wyatt would have taken the insults with far more severity. Those men were killers just looking for an excuse. Ike wasn't; he was the sort who got others to do his killing for him. When he barked, it wasn't a challenge, it was just hot air.

The Over-marshal tipped his hat to the clerk at the desk in the Cosmopolitan's lobby, and then made his way upstairs to his room. The instant he turned the key and stepped into the room, he knew something was wrong. When he'd left that morning, the shade over the window had been up. Now, it was down. The maids at the Cosmopolitan had standing orders to leave his room alone unless he was there to watch them. There'd been an incident where somebody had put a Gila monster in his pillow case while he was out. Ever since, he'd been careful about any repeat of that experience.

He just started to ease his blaster from its holster when a cold voice from the darkened room warned him against such action. Wyatt turned slowly. In the blackness, the crimson glow of two cybernetic arms shone with hellish brilliance. The marshal didn't need two guesses to know who those arms belonged to.

"At this range, I can hardly miss," Jesse said. "Take your left hand and unbuckle that belt, then kick it over this way. We're gonna have a little palaver, you and I."

"This is very obliging of you," Wyatt said as he unbuckled his gun belt. "I thought I was going to have to ride all the way back to Texas to track you down."

"You must need that feather in your cap awful bad." Jesse reached down and plucked Wyatt's gun belt from the floor. He holstered the damaged Hyper-velocity blaster he had crushed in Tobin's ambush and armed himself with the Over-marshal's guns. "Never did believe the stories that Wyatt Earp was a glory hound. Lowdown, Free-Soil, copperhead, maybe, but not a braggart chasin' laurels."

Wyatt turned away from the door, taking a step into the room. The glow from Jesse's arms was just enough for him to make out the outlaw's features. He glared at Jesse's disapproving expression. "You want to shoot, then you shoot, you Secesh trash," Wyatt sneered. "But know I ain't interested in money or glory or even the law! I want to see your neck stretch on account of you bushwhacking my brother!"

Jesse shook his head at Wyatt's outrage. "Fair enough, marshal, but how would it strike you if I told you tonight's the first time I've been anywhere near this town? What if I told you it wasn't me or any of my people had anything to do with gunnin' your brother?"

"I'd likely call you a liar. Everybody saw the men who robbed the bank and shot Virg from ambush. They were wearin' your brown dusters, the sort of thing nobody outside the James-Younger Gang has the guts to wear."

"Unless maybe they wanted somebody to think they was the James Gang," Jesse mused with a glint in his eye. "We can't be the only people in the county with brown dusters? I understand you've caused Old Man Clanton and the Cowboys a fair heap of trouble. Enough trouble that they'd be mighty keen to see you out of their hair for a spell. Chasin' after me would be one way of removin' you from the vicinity. Wyatt Earp huntin' high and low for the James Gang, while the Cowboys are free to rob and steal to their hearts' content."

"Don't you mean the James-Younger Gang?" Wyatt taunted.

Jesse waved the blasters at Wyatt, motioning him to seat himself on the bed and away from the door. Walking across the room, the outlaw put himself between his prisoner and his only avenue of escape. "Just now it ain't my concern whether you believe me or not. I was in the rocks listenin' when your posse rode up. I know you followed after the bounty man who ambushed me. What I want to know is where that polecat took John Younger."

"You're going to shoot me either way," Wyatt spat. "Why should I give you the satisfaction?"

"Shoot you?" Jesse scoffed. "That ain't my notion at all. Did it occur to you, Wyatt, that if my gang went to all the trouble to rob your bank and shoot your brother that we'd just light out for Texas Territory? A man in your position must know somethin' about what we've done and how we operate. When we pick an area, we pick it clean, stick around until there's Pinkertons behind every tree and in every stage. We don't just hit willy-nilly and move on."

Wyatt sat forward on the bed and made a slashing motion with his hand. "Then you really are saying somebody else gunned Virg and tried to frame you?" If anything, the lawman's expression became even grimmer. "Tell me, Jesse, if it was one of the Cowboys, which of Clanton's scum did it?"

Jesse smiled coldly. "We bargain for that answer. First, I want to know what happened to John and if he's alive or not."

"Answer the Over-marshal's question, Jesse," the rasping voice of Doc Holiday sounded from the doorway behind the outlaw. The gambler had eased it open just the slightest crack. The lethal barrels of a chopped-down shotgun protruded from the opening, aimed squarely at Jesse's back.

"Come on in, Doc," Wyatt called to his friend. "The conversation was just turning interesting." He smiled at Jesse. "Drop the irons. There's no way you could know this, but anytime Doc asks me for money it means he thinks I'm being followed. I think he'd rather stake his breather than ask a friend for a loan."

"Only this time I figured it wrong," Doc admitted as he slipped into the room. "I thought somebody was following you on the street. It didn't occur to me he'd already be up here waitin' for you." The gambler's voice trailed off into a mechanical cough.

Despite Wyatt's command and the menace of Doc's shotgun, Jesse kept his blaster aimed at the Over-marshal. "Seems what we have here is a Mexican standoff," the outlaw declared. "The lunger can drill me sure as hell, but not before I burn myself a star-packer."

"So how do we fix things so we both don't end up on Boot Hill?" Wyatt asked.

"We deal," Jesse said. "I take you to the coyotes who gunned your brother, you tell me where John is."

Wyatt shook his head. "Why should I trust you?"

Jesse smiled. "Because you should be askin' yourself a question right now. And that question is, where are the rest of the Younger Brothers? You see, I didn't come here alone. Cole and the rest are keepin' tabs on your kin right now. We didn't come in here gunnin' for any Earps before, but the Youngers feel just as concerned about their brother as you do about yourn." The outlaw's smile broadened when he saw the flicker of concern that crept into Wyatt's eyes. He knew his bluff had been taken as gospel by the lawman.

"Damn you, Jesse," Wyatt growled. "Anything happens to my brothers, I'll stretch your neck from hell to Kansas!"

"Nothin' will happen if you deal square," Jesse said. "Do I have your word of honor that we have ourselves a deal?"

The Over-marshal nodded. "Fine, but you ante-up first. Who do you claim shot Virg?"

"I don't rightly know, but I have my suspicions," Jesse admitted. "What I can tell you is who ordered it done. I also happen to know where he'd be just about now."

Wyatt glared coldly at the outlaw. "Then you take me to him. I get this sidewinder, I'll tell you what you want to know and maybe a little more besides. I'll raise up a posse and we can head out..."

"No posse," Jesse nodded his head toward Doc Holiday. "Just you, me, and the lunger. Call me scared, but I have a notion that if'n you brought more men, you might just take it to mind to have your cake and eat it too. The Youngers wouldn't like it much if you took me into custody. Might give them some funny ideas."

Wyatt rose from the bed. "Alright, we play it your way. Just you, me, and Doc."

A cough wheezed from Doc's breathing mask. "Play a straight hand, Jesse," the gambler warned. "Because whatever else happens, I can promise you'll be cut in half if anything untoward befalls Wyatt." His eyes glittered menacingly as he stared at the outlaw. "You can bet your bottom dollar on that."

*****

Mounted on Interceptors drawn from the stockyard, the strange trio sped across the dark, bleak desert. The Interceptors were the top of the line – fully capable of running down blackhoofs, but not as fast as the Iron Horses used by the Union and many outlaw bands. Their major handicap was range, depleting their RJ cells at a far quicker rate than either of the other machines.

As the broken terrain of gulches and wind-etched plateaus receded into the distance, the three riders found themselves on a flat plain. By the moonlight, they could clearly see the mass of cattle being herded along the plain. The guide-lights on the Iron Horses that zipped about the periphery of the herd were dulled, appearing only as the faintest pinpricks against the shadowy terrain. Far more distinct were the whine of their engines and the rumble of their exhausts.

Wyatt activated the brakes on his Interceptor, slowing the machine as he glared down at the herd. It was blatantly obvious that this was no legitimate drive. The closest market for beef would be out toward Yuma, yet these animals were being moved north in the direction of Tombstone... and Clantonville. The Over-marshal didn't need to see the red sashes around their waists to know that the rustlers below were Cowboys.

"Old Man Clanton," Wyatt spat the name like it was the vilest obscenity.

"Give a coyote the best tools in the world and he still thinks like a coyote," Jesse said. He focused on the Cowboys through the crimson lenses of his goggles, analyzing their layout. "Big money these days is in hitting trains and stages or knocking down a refueling station, but Clanton still clings to rustlin' like it's his religion."

"A man behind the times," Doc coughed. "Heard he gunned down one of them two-bit stealin' chance machines over in Campbell and Hatch's Billiard Parlor on account of the noise it made." He chuckled into his mask. "Not that I blame him none, them one-armed road agents is an affront to respectable gamblin'."

Wyatt continued to glare down at the rustlers. "The Cowboys," he said, rolling the word over on his tongue. It made sense, of course. With the Earps out of the way and no effective lawmen in the area, the Cowboys would have the run of the county, free to pillage and maraud without any real threat of reprisal. The closest law would be the soldiers in Fort Yuma and the Mexicans across the river. "I always figured they were behind Morg's ambush, I should have reckoned they'd be behind hitting Virg too." His eyes narrowed as he reflected on his earlier brush with Ike Clanton outside the Grand Hotel. He was trying to remember all the faces he had seen hanging around on the porch. Curly Bill and Pete Spence for certain; Indian Charlie and Frank Stilwell, possibly the McLaureys as well. A lot of the Cowboys' big guns were in town. That put things into a different perspective. Reaching to his holster, Wyatt checked the cylinder of his blaster.

"How do you reckon we handle this?" Doc asked in his metallic rasp.

Looking up from his inspection of his guns, Wyatt frowned. "What I'd like to do is charge down there and burn those curs out of the saddle, but that scum needs to be brought to trial."

Jesse shook his head. "I'm more particular to the first idea," he said, opening the throttle on his Interceptor and launching the machine full bore down toward the rustled herd.

He could hear Wyatt and Doc cursing behind him. An instant later they had their own Interceptors charging across the plain in tow.

It wasn't bravado that spurred Jesse into immediate action. Seeing the rustlers in action, knowing the treacherous Old Man Clanton was so near, these things had set the outlaw's belly boiling with the lust for revenge. Just like Clanton had set the law after Jesse and his gang, so the bushwhacker was going to return the favor. Even the deal he'd made with Wyatt and his concern about John Younger were secondary to that almost primal need to exact retribution.

Speeding toward the rustled herd, Jesse's ears rang with the alarmed shouts of Clanton's outriders. One of the men stood up in the saddle of his vehicle, snapping a rifle to his shoulder since the blasters in the Interceptor had been disabled by Wyatt. Before the Cowboy could fire, the blaster in Jesse's good hand barked. The impact of the energy bolt ripped the rustler out of the saddle and sent him flying back to crash among the herd. The loud noise, the bright flash, and the stench of burnt meat were all too much for the cattle. Bellowing in panic, the herd rushed away from the scorched carcass of the Cowboy.

More shots sounded around Jesse. Some were the hastily loosed gunfire of the rustlers; others were the coldly precise and lethal marksmanship of Doc Holiday and Wyatt Earp, opening up with the high-powered blasters in their mounts. The screams of Cowboys as they were struck down rang out above the roar of engines and the trumpeting cries of the frightened cattle.

"Stop that shootin'! You'll stampede the herd!" the shout came from somewhere at the back of the herd, but Jesse couldn't mistake that gravelly voice. It was Old Man Clanton himself trying to restrain his men and save his plundered livestock. Vindictively, Jesse spun about in the saddle and stabbed a blast right into the middle of the herd. The agonized cry of the steer he hit was all it took to send the cattle into absolute chaos.

An Iron Horse came speeding out of the darkness, swatting aside a steer with the cattle-catcher bolted to the front of its frame. Energy bolts crashed all around Jesse as the rider fired the Gatling blasters built into the 'Horse's faring. The momentary glimpse Jesse had of the outlaw showed him the hateful glower of Johnny Ringo. Jesse snapped off a shot at the gunfighter, the bolt passing so near to him that it scorched a line across the gunman's coat and set the material smoking. Ringo ducked low over the side of his ride, drawing his blaster and firing blind as he rocketed past Jesse.

Jesse sent a few more shots chasing after Ringo as he went speeding off into the darkness, but he didn't pursue the fleeing outlaw. As badly as he'd like to deal with Johnny Ringo, he wanted Old Man Clanton more. Weaving his Interceptor around the edges of the stampeding herd, he tried to work his way past the panicked cattle to reach the outlaw chief.

The ground was a scarred mush of earth that was gouged by hundreds of pounding hooves. Here and there, the carcass of a dead steer lay heaped, crushed beneath the hooves of the herd. Twice, Jesse sped past the grim remains of an Iron Horse and its rider, flattened by the stampede they had tried in vain to turn. He slowed briefly when he passed these macabre markers, lingering long enough to ensure that none of the dead men were Clanton.

When he sped past the back of the herd, Jesse could hear renewed blaster fire ahead. The roar of Doc's shotgun and the shriek of a crippled 'Horse told him that the shots were more than just Cowboys trying to turn the cattle. Driving onwards, Jesse came upon a violent tableau. Old Man Clanton's 'Horse had been shot down. In crashing, the grizzled outlaw had been unable to clear the stricken steed, and he was now pinned underneath it.

Nearby, Phin Clanton, the Old Man's eldest son, had braked his 'Horse and was using it for cover as he tried to fend off Wyatt and Doc. The speed of the modified Interceptors made a mockery of Phin's efforts to bring them down.

In a sudden burst of speed, Wyatt drove his Interceptor full into Phin's parked 'Horse. The rustler was driven from cover as the Iron Horse was knocked back by the impact. As he scurried away, Wyatt sent an energy bolt slamming into his side. Phin screamed, and then crashed into the dirt, ribs standing stark against the ghastly burn inflicted upon his body. He made one last, sorry effort to aim his pistol at the Over-marshal, then sprawled limp in the dust.

There were no other Cowboys in evidence. The rest of the gang had either fled like Ringo or were still trying to stem the tide of the stampeding cattle. It didn't matter to the two lawmen who now dismounted from their Interceptors and approached the Old Man trapped under his own crippled vehicle.

"Damn you Wyatt!" Old Man Clanton raged. "You killed my boy!"

"And you tried to kill my brother," Wyatt said, fingers tightening about the grip of his blaster.

The Old Man struggled to reach his own guns, but the Iron Horse pressing down on his chest made such an effort impossible. "It was Jesse James, you damn fool! Everybody knows that!"

"Everybody except Jesse James," Jesse snapped as he brought his Interceptor prowling out from the darkness. He brought the machine to a slow crawl, advancing until its nose just touched the edge of Clanton's overturned 'Horse. "Why don't you tell the marshal the truth?" Jesse punctuated the suggestion by nudging the 'Horse. The Old Man screamed as more of the machine's weight pressed down on his chest.

"Alright! It was me! I had it done!" the Old Man shrieked, flecks of blood flying from his mouth, his arms pushing frantically against the ponderous weight of his metal steed.

Wyatt Earp crouched down close to the pinned rustler. "Who did it? Who'd you send?" When the Old Man didn't answer quick enough, Jesse gave his wreck another nudge.

"Johnny Ringo!" the Old Man screamed. "Him and Stilwell and Indian Charlie!" The rustler's face contorted with pain as the 'Horse continued to press on him. "Pete Spence too. He was there with Ike..." The outlaw's face contorted with pain of a different sort when he realized that he'd just indicted one of his other sons. He knew enough about Wyatt Earp's ways to know that nothing would stop the Over-marshal from exacting justice from Ike's hide, either from the barrel of a gun or the end of a rope.

"Ike Clanton," Wyatt said as he stood up. "Looks like somebody's pardon ain't gonna be worth a hill of beans."

"It weren't Ike!" the Old Man shouted. "Curly Bill, it was Curly Bill who was there!"

"A man shouldn't lie when he's so close to meetin' the Almighty," Doc said, slamming fresh RJ charges into his shotgun.

Jesse eased his Interceptor back from Clanton. "Well?" he asked Wyatt. "You find out everything you wanted?"

The Over-marshal stared down at the Old Man. Slowly, he nodded his head. "The Old Man tried to do a frame up. Doesn't make you any less a polecat, but at least you're not the polecat I'm lookin' for."

"Glad to hear it," Jesse said with a sardonic smirk. He opened up the Interceptor and slammed into the underside of the Old Man's Iron Horse. The trapped rustler shrieked once as the machine rolled over and crushed him.

"What the hell, Jesse?!" Wyatt roared, looking down in horror at the Old Man's splattered remains. He froze when he looked up and found himself staring into the barrel of Jesse's blaster.

"Lose the hardware," Jesse told the Over-marshal. He waved a pistol at Doc Holiday. "You too, Doc. I don't have time for another Mexican standoff." He smiled as he watched the gambler discard the shotgun and the pistol at his waist. "Better lose your pocket advantage too," Jesse told him, waiting patiently as Doc removed the derringer from his sleeve. "Old Man Clanton owed me for betrayin' me and leavin' my gang to die," Jesse said, spitting at the bloody ooze streaming from under the Iron Horse. He fixed his gaze on Wyatt. "That just leaves the balance between you and me to be settled. What happened to John?"

Wyatt matched Jesse's icy gaze. Still bristling from the outlaw's sudden murder of the Old Man, he took a cruel pleasure in telling Jesse what he wanted to know. He knew the impact it would have on him. "John Younger was handed over to Colonel Mackenzie by Thomas Tate Tobin, same bounty hunter that ambushed you. He was alive when I saw him, shackled in the guardhouse and looking a bit peeked, but alive. Mackenzie didn't keep John in Fort Concho long though. He had him shipped out first chance he had."

"Where'd that blue-belly ship him off to?" Jesse snarled through clinched teeth.

Wyatt's answer was like a sneer of defiance. "Andersonville. They sent him to Camp Lincoln."

A cold chill swept through Jesse's body. Andersonville was home to one of the most infamous Union prison camps in the country; Camp Lincoln! It was a place where recidivist secessionists were sent to be 'reconstructed' and turned into 'loyal' members of society. At least such was the official explanation for its existence. In truth, any man who went there never came out again. Alive or dead, once a man entered Camp Lincoln he never left. It was a fate supposedly reserved for men who'd fought in the war and had never embraced the Union afterwards. For John, a boy who'd been too young to fight for the South, to be sent there was an act of such injustice it made Jesse feel sick inside. A surge of guilt welled up inside him. He should have taken the risk and gotten the answers he wanted from the commander at Fort Concho when he'd first heard it mentioned. His lust for revenge on the Clantons had sent him off in the wrong direction.

"I guess I'll have to let you lawdogs live. You'll oblige me, marshal, by dealing with Ike and the rest," Jesse growled. "Much as I'd like to do it myself, it appears I've got bigger things to worry about."

Wyatt scowled up at the mounted outlaw. "You know I'll have to come after you."

Jesse spun around, firing a bolt from each of his pistols. The shots slammed into the engines of the Interceptors, blasting them into shrapnel. Turning his right-hand blaster to keep Wyatt and Doc covered, he sent another shot into Phin Clanton's Iron Horse, disabling it as effectively as he had the two Interceptors. "Walkin' back to Tombstone should slow you down."

"What about the Youngers?" Doc coughed. "You swore to call them off if Wyatt helped you."

Jesse laughed. "Call them off? I'm not even sure I know where they are! I do know they ain't nowhere near Tombstone!"

Uttering a sharp Rebel yell, Jesse sent his Interceptor speeding away into the darkness, leaving behind him two fuming lawmen.

Chapter 12

Jesse James rode into the winding canyon, feeling the jagged cliffs pressing in around him. The chill within the shadowy ravine was remarkable in its contrast to the heat of the west Texas desert he'd been traveling across for days. Except at noon, when the sun was directly overhead, the canyon was always in shadow, allowing it to retain much of the night's cold throughout the day.

The narrow pass channeled Jesse down a familiar path and made him appreciate what a formidable defense the canyon presented. It was a natural choke-point, one well-armed man could hold off an army in this winding ravine. That consideration and the remoteness of the location had been the key reasons the James Gang had employed this place as one of their hideouts. Riding into the canyon now, however, Jesse fully appreciated the uneasiness a posse or cavalry troop would experience trying to root outlaws from this lair. He had no way of knowing if the Youngers had returned to this refuge or if some other party had taken it over – no way at all of knowing who might be watching him from behind the rocks. With his stolen Interceptor loaded down with canisters of extra fuel to feed its powerful but rapacious engine, he felt like he was sitting on a stick of dynamite as he made his way deeper into the ravine.

He was about halfway through the chasm before he was challenged. A sharp voice barked at him from behind a boulder that had fallen into the canyon and partially blocked the fissure. It was as Jesse slowed to maneuver around the rock that he caught the gleam of a rifle barrel and heard the order to power down his steed. Despite the threat of both rifle and voice, Jesse smiled.

"Hell, Bob, you mean to tell me I come all this way just to get shot?" Jesse called out as he pulled the handkerchief down from his face.

An excited yell and the clatter of stones being kicked loose answered the outlaw. Only a moment later, Bob Younger came running out from behind the boulder, his brown duster looking just a bit more worn for all the dirt and sand covering it. Somehow, he'd contrived to keep his bowler clean and even managed to pick up a striking leatherwork hatband for it that depicted a bear hunter stalking a grizzly. Or perhaps it was the other way around, given that the two little silver figures rotated in an endless circle around the hat.

"Jesse!" Bob shouted. "We'd just about given you up! You've been gone near-on a month! Cole's been sendin' Hardin out once a week to snatch a gander at the news sheets over in Wolf Bend, hopin' and dreadin' to read that you and John were caught!" The knife-fighter hesitated, turning away from Jesse and staring down the canyon. It was easy to figure out who he was looking for.

"They got John," Jesse confessed, his heart going sick with guilt. "When we lit out, there was a bounty hunter lying in wait for us. Just luck of the draw he got John instead of me."

The excitement of a moment before vanished from Bob's face, turning into a dour expression. "Them's the breaks," Bob tried to choke back the emotion threatening to overwhelm him.

"He took John alive," Jesse did his best to assure Bob. After what he'd gone through when Frank had been shot, he knew only too well the anguish Bob was feeling. He also knew how dearly he had prayed someone would say those words to him and change all that grief and despair into hope.

When Bob looked at Jesse again, he could see the hope glistening in the man's eyes. "Alive? You know where they took him?"

"Yeah, but it's somethin' I'd rather not tell twice. Take me up to Cole and I'll tell you all about it."

Returning to the Youngers without John was hard enough for Jesse. He felt like a coward and a traitor, the guilt of escaping when John was captured was like a knife twisting around in his gut. Telling them that their little brother was rotting away inside Camp Lincoln was going to be much worse.

*****

Midway along the ravine, the canyon widened out for a mile or so. It was here that some enterprising wag had tried to make a go of a mining operation. Silver, gold, whatever they'd tried to make their fortune on hadn't paid out. Given the remoteness of the area and the difficulty of navigating the ravine, it was likely that the labor of extracting and transporting the ore simply hadn't been worth the effort. Then again, it could have been the attentions of Indians and Comancheros that had driven off the miners. This part of Texas allowed for only the most Spartan law enforcement and the last significant military presence had been during the Mexican War.

Whatever the cause, the abandonment of the mine came as a boon to outlaws like Jesse James. The tunnels and mine shafts presented a hidden warren of bolt holes and hiding places, while the old sheds and storehouses made convenient shelters for their Iron Horses and other equipment, such as an extra pair of Jesse's Hyper-velocity blasters.

For the sake of sparing Jim the long climb up into the cliff and the numbing cold of the mine shafts themselves, Cole had established the gang in the old foreman's office. A few blankets thrown over the broken windows kept out the worst of the wind and dust, while a little RJ-powered heater fended off the chill of the canyon. As hideouts went, they'd all been in far more primitive conditions.

Jim Younger was pale and in pain, lying on a pallet when the group entered the shack. His whole chest was wrapped about in plaster and he was obviously uncomfortable. Little buttons of RJ were embedded in the plaster strips the doctor had banded about his body, each button connected to a wire that was woven into the strips. The end of the wire was fitted to a little iron box with a crank attached to it. Turning the crank sent a little charge running through the wire and heated the RJ buttons. The doctor who'd attended Jim claimed the heat would speed his body's natural healing, selling the whole apparatus as the latest medical marvel from back east. Jesse wasn't sure about that, but he had to admit that for a man who'd been at Death's door the last time he'd seen him, Jim was acting mighty spry.

At that moment, spry meant slowly trying to stuff himself into a shirt too small to accommodate the plaster bands bulking out his body, while at the same time trying to squeeze his feet back into his boots. It was obvious that he should have been staying put, but Jim Younger was not one to sit still when there was work to be done. There was a furious cast to Jim's features, an almost frantic need to leap into action.

"Settle yourself," Cole leaned across the table and pointed a finger at his headstrong brother. "We rush into this, we don't do any good for anybody except them blue-bellies. We have to take our time, think things through."

Bob whittled away at a stick with one of his Bowie knives, angrily slashing strips from the wood. "Thinkin' won't do no good, Cole. They took John to Camp Lincoln! Worst hellhole in the Union!"

"That's why we plan this careful," Cole snapped at Bob. "We think it through, leave nothing to chance." He turned his eyes to Jesse seated across from him. "That's how you figure it, right Jesse?"

Slowly, Jesse nodded. "We can't leave John in there, that's for damn sure. At the same time, this isn't going to be like knocking over some adobe-walled jail in a one-dog town. We have to think this out, plan every move. We don't make a move until Cole's satisfied we've got a chance of gettin' John out of there."

"Then you'll back our play?" Cole asked with a note of eagerness in his voice.

"I can't help but feel that I got John into this," Jesse's voice grew heavy, somber. "I know what it's like to lose a brother. I don't want you to go through that."

Cole rose and set his hand on Jesse's shoulder. There were no words he could use to express his appreciation for Jesse's friendship in that moment. There wasn't any need to. Cole turned away, looking toward the window of the shack and the black-garbed man standing there. "How about you, Hardin? Are you in?"

The gunfighter laughed. "Deal me out, Cole. If you have any sense you'll deal yourselves out too. The Yankees have that place guarded better'n the Washington Mint.

Ain't but one man ever escaped from that place."

Hardin's statement brought Jesse spinning around. "I never heard of anybody breakin' out of Camp Lincoln."

The gunfighter bristled at the challenge in Jesse's tone. For a second, it seemed his hand was going to dip toward the smokers hanging from his belt. "You callin' me a liar?"

"I'm sayin' maybe you heard things wrong," Jesse said, shifting around in his chair so that if it came to it he'd be able to draw his own guns without the obstruction of the table. "Or maybe you were a little quick to credit somebody's tall tale."

Hardin scowled back at the outlaw. "I met the man himself. Saw with my own eyes what Camp Lincoln done to him. Man named Kelso Warfield used to ride with Mosby. Said he spent nigh on six years in Andersonville's hellhole after the war."

Jesse turned and looked over at Cole. "What do you think?"

Cole tugged at his moustache as he mulled the question over in his mind. "I think, allowin' for a moment that this Kelso Warfield isn't the biggest liar since Lincoln, that before we make any plans we should look this fella up."

"That's exactly what I was thinkin'," Jesse said as he turned back toward Hardin. "Where'd you meet up with this Kelso Warfield?"

*****

Robbers Roost was a hideaway so notorious that even the Texas Rangers gave the place a wide berth. Situated at the extreme edge of the territory, nestled in the contested region on the periphery of what the Union derisively called 'Carpathian's Kingdom' and the almost completely depopulated wilderness left behind by Sitting Bull's Warrior Nation, the old mining town had become a veritable outlaw community. Smugglers, gun runners, Indian traders, Comancheros, criminals of every stripe and brand, all made their way to the security of Robbers Roost when they felt no place else could afford them shelter. A lawless outpost on the very frontier of civilization, there was only one rule in the town: might makes right. It was the kind of place Diablo Canyon had been before Wyatt Earp had assigned an Enforcer to maintain the law there. It was perhaps only a matter of time before the same happened to Robbers Roost, before a lawman like Pat Garrett or Bass Reeves came along and forced the town to become civilized. Until then, it existed as a way station on the road to hell. The strong could prosper in Robbers Roost, the weak would be chewed up and spit out.

Brazenly, the James-Younger Gang marched down the dirt street, openly displaying their weapons in a show of force that would impress any onlookers too ignorant to recognize the quick-devil arms of Jesse James. Power was the only thing that was respected among these outlaws. By such a bold show, Jesse hoped to keep these renegades and rustlers in their place. It was something of an irony that he could thank Dr. Carpathian for enhancing Jesse's reputation as a gunfighter to a degree where even the most arrogant hot-head wouldn't challenge him now. To face another man was one thing, but these would-be gunslingers balked at the idea of going up against the sinister technology of the Enlightened. Even for men out to steal a reputation off a living legend, there was a reluctance to play against a stacked deck.

"Looks like we have some friends here," Cole said as they made their way into the town. He pointed to several rebel flags fluttering from the facades of the buildings.

Hardin laughed. "Yeah, they'll whistle Dixie while they cut your throat and clean your pockets. Don't make any mistake, the only friends you have here are the ones you bring in with you."

"Comin' from a guy who'd place second to Yellow Fever in a popularity contest, you'll forgive me if I take that with a grain of salt," Jim told the gunfighter, wincing as his own laughter sent shivers of pain coursing through him. He'd improved enough over the last week to sit on a 'Horse, but beneath his shirt his body was still swaddled in bandages and

RJ heating pads. He was cagey about letting the others know how much pain he was actually in, fearing they'd leave him behind when they made their play to rescue John.

"Suit yourself," Hardin smiled at Jim with all the friendliness of a rattler. "It's your neck."

Studying the men they passed lounging in front of the saloons and brothels that lined the street, Jesse was more inclined to back Hardin's opinion. The inhabitants of Robbers Roost were the scruffiest, meanest bunch he'd ever seen; a polyglot mix of whites, blacks, Mexicans, and half-breeds. Whatever their background, there was the scurvy cast of a hungry coyote in every face, a predatory gleam that made Jesse grateful for the blasters hanging on his hips.

"How do we even start lookin' for Warfield?" Bob asked.

"Hell, if he's been here any length of time he's probably already been knifed and buried," Cole said, keeping a wary eye on a pack of Comancheros as they prowled past them.

"Sometimes you've got to play the long hand," Jesse said. "Press your luck and hope for the best."

Cole shook his head. "Sometimes I think I used up all my luck in the war. That's why I stick around with you, Jesse. Your run never seems to dry out."

A sharp whistle from Hardin brought the rest of the gang turning around. The Texan pointed across the street at a man leaning against the hitching post in front of a gambling hall. "Would you look at that," he hissed through clenched teeth.

The man Hardin indicated was wearing the grey shell jacket of a Confederate soldier over a buckskin shirt and a cowhide vest. The pants he wore were tucked into a set of cavalry boots with the flared tops favored by rebel horsemen. Among the arsenal of weapons draped about the man's body, the grips of several rebel-pattern blasters were evident. The big brass buckle on his gun belt bore the initials 'CSA.'

What galled Hardin was the fact that the man wearing all this Confederate regalia was black.

"That darkie has some nerve," Hardin growled.

"Yeah," Cole agreed, following the Texan's pointing finger. "I don't see how a man can move around wearing that much iron." The veteran guerrilla made a quick study of his arsenal. "Looks to be two in shoulder holsters, two on the hips, one across the belly and another in his left boot."

"The one on his right hip is a chopped down carbine," Jesse chimed in. "Way his jacket bulges I think he's got another pistol behind him too."

"Shouldn't be surprised if he doesn't have a pocket advantage too," Jim said.

Bob chuckled. "That's a damn big knife he's carryin'. One of them Mexican things they call a machete. Chop a man's boots right off with one of them."

Hardin rounded on the rest of the gang. "You don't see what that darkie's wearin'?" he snapped. "That don't rile you none? It's like he's laughin' at the South just by standin' there!"

"Leave it be," Jesse told Hardin. "We ain't lookin' for trouble."

Hardin sneered at Jesse. "Well that darkie is," he spat as he turned away from Jesse and the Youngers, proceeding to prowl across the street.

"Hey boy!" Hardin shouted at the black man. "Your master know you're wearin' his duds?"

The outlaw flashed a cheerless smile at Hardin. "Givin' he's rottin' in the ground somewhere nears Appomattox, I doubt he knows nothin' just about now."

The gunfighter sneered at the black man's retort. "I'm tellin' you to get out of them clothes, boy."

"Mister, I don't know what your problem is, but if you'd like to settle it, I'm your huckleberry." The outlaw stepped away from the hitching post and ambled out into the street. He nodded his chin at Hardin. "Let's keep this between the two of us. Your friends can wait their turn."

Hardin didn't look around. He could hear the footsteps behind him. Thinking one of the others was coming over to back his play, he simply growled a warning. "I killed one of these baboons when I was barely off my momma's tit. I don't need no help now…"

The Texan's growl ended in a gasp as a metal fist smacked into the back of his head. For Jesse, it was barely a tap, but to Hardin it was like being hit by a sledgehammer. The gunfighter dropped into the street and his eyes rolled back as all sensation abandoned him.

"Bob, Jim!" Jesse called to his gang. "Find someplace where Hardin can sleep things off for a spell. Maybe when he wakes up he'll feel a might less ornery."

"Yeah, and pigs'll fly," Jim said as he helped Bob lift Hardin from the street and carry him off toward a hotel a few blocks away.

The black man watched as his unconscious antagonist was carried away. "I could have handled that myself, Mr. James."

Jesse wasn't surprised that the outlaw recognized him. There were only so many men prowling the west with a set of mechanical arms bolted to their shoulders. "My apologies, friend, but there's a chance I'm going to need that curly wolf later. I couldn't take the gamble." He waved his hand at the departed gunfighter. "Besides, that's John Wesley Hardin. He ain't exactly a slouch when it comes to a fast draw."

The outlaw smiled and slowly eased back the front of his shell jacket, exposing a brace of derringers sewn into the lining. "I ain't so quick, but when you cheat you don't have to be. Just as happy not to have to tangle with you, Mr. James."

"Jesse," the bushwhacker said. "This old guerrilla behind me is Cole Younger and the fellas carting off your would-be playmate are his brothers Jim and Bob."

"Will Shaft," the black man introduced himself. "Virginia by way of Kansas, in case you was wonderin'."

"An Exoduster?" Cole asked. A great many freed slaves had struck out to make new lives for themselves in the plains of Kansas, terming themselves 'Exodusters' after the Exodus of Moses and the Israelites from Egypt and the dusty climate of the Kansas prairie. Finding themselves isolated by their white neighbors in their new land, the blacks had maintained their identity as Exodusters, feeling they'd yet to reach their 'promised land.'

"Yes, sir," Will said. "They told me I was a free man and I should try to make my own way in the world. Only thing those Free Soilers and abolitionists didn't bother to say was that they didn't want me bein' free anywhere they was. Man gets kicked around from town to town he gets a might riled."

"Riled enough to wear rebel gray?" Jesse asked.

"Blue was never my color," Will grinned. "Besides, that ain't such a good thing to wear hereabouts. Anybody spots a speck of Union uniform on a fella, he starts thinkin' maybe he's found himself a deserter. Army pays fifty dollars for a deserter." His eyes narrowed as he asked his own question. "What is it brings the great Jesse James to a hole like Robbers Roost?"

"I'm lookin' for someone. Though it seems like now I'll have to wait for Hardin to finish his nap before I can try to find him."

Will shook his head. "Most folks drift in and out of here all the time, but maybe I've seen this man you're lookin' for."

"This varmint supposedly escaped from Camp Lincoln," Cole said. He would have said more, but he saw that he'd already said enough. There was an uneasy, almost haunted expression on Will's face.

"You're lookin' for Kelso Warfield," he said. Will closed his hand tight about the rabbit-skin gris-gris bag hanging about his neck. "I don't suppose I can talk sense to you and get you to leave him be. Warfield's… Well, he ain't right. Even in a place like this, he…

Well, you feel dirty just bein' around him. Almost like you brushed up against somethin' unclean." His hand closed tighter about the Voodoo bag.

"He's been inside Camp Lincoln," Jesse said. "We need to talk to him about how the prison is laid out."

"I wouldn't trust anythin' Warfield told me," Will said.

Cole scowled and clenched his fist. "I knew the coyote had to be a liar."

"I didn't say he was a liar," Will corrected Cole. "I just said I wouldn't trust nothin' Warfield told me. Still, if you all are determined to see him, I'll take you to where he's holed up."

*****

Will Shaft led the outlaws to the edge of Robbers Roost. The crumbling remains of a Spanish mission squatted on the periphery of a disused stockyard. The entire area had a forsaken atmosphere, an uncanny air of desolation that seemed to stifle the very breath the outlaws drew as they walked toward the collapsed chapel. Stepping inside the rubble, they approached the old bell tower, the only part of the structure that was still mostly intact. The man they were looking for, Will had told them, lived on the middle floor of the tower.

A simple wooden ladder led up from the base of the tower. Before starting their ascent, Jesse called out in a loud voice, "Warfield! Kelso Warfield! We're coming in and we don't mean no harm." There was silence. Only the wind whistling through the crumbling walls answered him. After a few moments, Jesse started his climb. Cole covered him from the ground, keeping his blaster trained on the hole leading up into the tower. Only when Jesse reached the platform above did Cole start his climb.

The room was small, furnished only with a rickety table and chair. A crude pallet of straw was just visible in the gloom. Jesse prowled about in the dimness of the room, but he couldn't see any trace of an occupant.

"Where is he?" Cole asked as he joined Jesse.

Jesse shrugged, knowing that the gesture would be visible even in the weird shadows thanks to the glow of his cybernetics. "Not here, anyway. Not unless..." He remembered what Will had said about this being the middle tier of the tower. That meant there was a room above it. He raised his eyes toward the ceiling.

Instantly, he froze. Just visible by the faint daylight drifting through the broken roof of the tower was the silhouette of a man, poised in the gap leading up to the next level. Although it was just a vague, dark shape, Jesse could feel hostile eyes glaring down at him. Not knowing if there was a gun in the shadowy figure's hand, he was careful to keep his own away from his blasters.

"Kelso Warfield?" Jesse called up to the figure. Cole spun around, following the direction of Jesse's gaze even as he darted behind the ramshackle table.

"Some folks call me that," a dry, somehow desiccated voice drifted down from the ceiling. "Other folks call me other things."

"We only came here to talk," Jesse said. "We wanted to ask you about Camp Lincoln."

A grisly chuckle rose from the shadowy phantom. "Then have Cole light the lantern on that table he's crouching behind. I can see you fine as things are, but you'll no doubt feel more at ease if you can see me too."

"He's got us dead to rights already, Cole," Jesse told his friend. "Might as well light the lamp."

As the lantern slowly sputtered into life, Jesse saw a wooden ladder being lowered from the ceiling. A tall, gaunt figure started climbing down, a heavy black cloak draped about his shoulders. Black boots, black pants, black gloves; the only spot of brightness in Warfield's raiment was the hat he wore. Like the scraps of uniform Will affected, it was rebel gray, the floppy hat of a Confederate cavalry officer, one side of the brim curled back. A black plume was pinned to its side by a silver button.

It wasn't until Warfield reached the bottom of the ladder and turned around that Jesse and Cole had a good look at the man's face; and when they did, both gasped in shock. They knew that face, even if it was much more lean and more pallid than they remembered it, even with tinted glasses covering the eyes.

"Some folks call me Kelso Warfield," the recluse said again, bowing with exaggerated military courtesy as if they were children playing adults. "Some folks know me as Allen Henderson." He said the name slowly, lading on the last syllable for emphasis.

"Henderson," Cole echoed in a whisper. Here was the adjutant of their old commander, Colonel Quantrill. Both of them were supposedly killed decades ago in the last years of the war.

"I ain't no ghost," Henderson assured his former compatriots. "The Yankees shot down others and claimed it was us. A band of Red Legs caught us down in Louisiana, but they didn't have no clue who we were. I gave 'em the name Kelso Warfield and that's who I was while the blue-bellies had me. They kept the boss in Camp Davis, but he escaped shortly afterward. Killed a guard, put on his uniform, and walked out. They had already shipped me off to Andersonville when they reopened the camp, renaming it Lincoln." The leather of Henderson's glove creaked as he clenched his hand into a fist. "Wouldn't grovel afore them none, no matter what name I carried. They tried everything they could to break me, make me submit. They beat me and they starved me, and when that didn't work they threw me in the hole."

Henderson raised a hand to the glasses he wore, tapping the side of one darkened frame. "They kept me down in that pit for months on end. Kept me down there without a speck of light so long my eyes got so I can see as clearly in the blackest night as you can in broad daylight." He laughed bitterly. "Of course there was a trade-off. I can't handle the light very well anymore."

"But you escaped, Henderson," Cole shook his head, still in disbelief. "Nobody else has ever done that."

Henderson nodded. "I escaped. After fifteen years in that hellhole. Made my way out west, nearly dead when Captain Quantrill somehow found me. He kept me hid until I could heal up good enough to strike out. The Captain was heading back into Rebellion territory, but I'd had a bellyful. Weren't so many places a man as wanted as me could go, and I ended up in this little Algerine's paradise.

"While I was in Camp Lincoln, the Union didn't particularly care about Kelso Warfield, but now that I've escaped their impenetrable prison, they're as keen to get Kelso Warfield as they would be Allen Henderson or William Quantrill."

"Well, that escape was the whole reason we came to see you," Jesse said with a nod toward Cole. "John Younger's been sent there and we're going to get him out."

"John Younger?" Henderson asked.

"You wouldn't know him, sir. He was too young to fight in the war," Cole said.

"Too young to go through Camp Lincoln then," Henderson said, and then paused to look at each of the outlaws in turn, his expression and tone both etched with stern sympathy. "Believe me when I say it, but if they've sent John to Camp Lincoln, then he'd be better off dead."

*****

The timber stockade stood almost thirty feet high, running in an unbroken ring about the acres set aside for Camp Lincoln. At each corner, a guard tower rose above the wall, the sinister frames of Gatling guns projecting over the parapets, soldiers manning the weapons day and night. Spotlights, humming with crimson RJ power, yawned from the face of each tower, able to bath large swathes of the prison in a brilliance to match that of the noonday sun. Decking stretched across the inner face of the stockade, set twenty-five feet above the ground. Along this walkway, marching in ceaseless cadence, were robot sentries, Army models designated as UR-25 Warders. They were slightly bigger and bulkier than the UR-30 Enforcers; less agile and versatile than the 'bots issued to lawmen in the west. One arm of each Warder was replaced by the bulky barrel of an energy rifle, the weapon built into the 'bot's very frame, making it impossible for a prisoner to disarm it and use its weapon against his captors.

The prison itself was a squalid morass of mud, across which a miserable expanse of canvas tents had been pitched. Here and there, small fields were tended by the inmates; patches of rice, beans, and potatoes that the prisoners desperately tried to cultivate in a hopeless effort to supplement the trifling rations their captors issued to them. Along the eastern wall of the camp, a vast graveyard stretched; simple wooden crosses marking the final resting place of men who weren't allowed to escape captivity even in death.

At the center of the camp, surrounded by a stone wall, were the administration buildings and medical facilities. With most of the guards taking the form of robotic Warders, a large machine shop dominated one of the structures, acting to repair and refit the 'bots as they wore down. A contingent of Rolling Thunder assault wagons were parked against the high wall to one side, insurance against the unlikely event of an attempted prisoner riot. The 'bots were the key to the economy of the prison camp. Although there were better than ten thousand prisoners interned in the prison of Andersonville, only a little more than fifty human soldiers watched over them; the rest of the guard duties fell to the untiring, pitiless Warders.

When John Younger was processed by the prison administrator, the official didn't even raise an eyebrow at the youthfulness of his latest captive. The boy was pushed through channels like any other Secesh. His photo was taken, his name and vital statistics recorded. He was dumped into a vat of chemical powders to remove any lice from his body, and then given a hasty shower where a blue-belly sergeant scrubbed him with a hog-hair broom. Finally, he was brought before the prison doctor, a ridiculous-looking man wearing a gaudy, somehow European-looking military uniform and sporting an enormous walrus-like moustache. The doctor gave him a cursory examination, made a few notes in a leather-bound ledger, and then curtly ordered him removed.

It was when John was led away from the medical building and shoved out the gates and into the camp itself that he understood the full level of misery he had been condemned to. The prisoners gathered about the stone walls were a wretched, ragged sight. Many of them had blotchy, diseased complexions; others were missing hands and feet, arms or legs. Men already reduced to a near skeletal appearance were further tortured by wracking coughs and the sweating shivers of malaria. These were the desperate and the forsaken, those whose dignity and composure had ebbed to such a degree that they gathered around the walls of the inner compound to beg their captors for even the slightest consideration or expression of mercy.

In their despair, these wretches turned their ire against John. As he was pushed out the gate, the prisoners jeered at him, mocking him for his youth. They wondered how a boy so young could have fought the Yankees in the war. Several made lewd suggestions about John's mother and her activities during the war. When John reacted to the catcalls and jeers, a crude wooden crutch cracked against his back, spilling him into the mud. Kicks and punches soon followed as the prisoners vented their frustration and dejection against the outsider who had been thrust into their midst.

The strength behind those kicks and punches was too feeble to deal John any real physical harm; the pain was emotional. It was the humiliation, the sense of utter isolation and loneliness, that truly beat him down. Such was his inner turmoil that he didn't realize his tormentors had withdrawn until he felt a hand reach down and lift him out of the mud.

As he regained his feet, John gazed in shock at his rescuer. He would have collapsed back into the mud if the man hadn't helped him to stay standing. He couldn't believe who was in front of him.

His rescuer was Frank James.

Chapter 13

There was an unseasonable chill in the darkened ruin of the mission's old sanctuary. The outline of a cross, long ago stolen and melted down by impious bandits, was etched high upon the inner wall, the adobe brick behind it discolored by the long years when this had been a place of worship. Now, it was just a dilapidated hall; one wall completely caved outward in a jumble of broken bricks, many of the wooden support beams stabbing down from the roof into the floor below. The pews had been broken down long ago to use as firewood, the top of the altar looted so that its granite surface might serve for a hearthstone in some plunderer's home. Except for the dust and tumbleweeds, skittering horny toads and scurrying armadillos, the old chapel was empty.

The outlaws of Robbers Roost gave the crumbling mission a wide berth, uncomfortable with any reminder that they might be answerable to a Higher Power for their sins. For someone wanting to conduct a clandestine meeting, no place in the town could offer better seclusion.

Such, at least, had been Henderson's advice. With strange shadows trickling down through the shattered tile roof, the men of the James-Younger Gang gathered in the forsaken sanctuary, perching on piles of broken brick, sitting on the splintered remains of fallen beams, leaning against the stone columns that reached up toward the decayed roof. John Wesley Hardin, the Younger Brothers, even the Exoduster renegade Will Shaft all watched as Henderson climbed up into the iron-railed pulpit. He adjusted the cloudy glasses he wore, pushing them closer to his eyes when a stray beam of sunlight shot across the pulpit and illuminated the defiled altar.

When he spoke, Henderson addressed his words to the metal-armed bushwhacker sitting on the toppled mass of some defaced plaster saint. Jesse James listened with such an enthralled ear that he didn't even notice when a lizard scrambled over his pant leg on its way across the fallen statue.

"You all know the bold plan Jesse proposes. You all know he's come here to ask me how you can break into Camp Lincoln and liberate John Younger from the vengeful grasp of the Yankees." Henderson shook his head, his hardened voice taking on a note of regret. "I admire your pluck and the nobility of your purpose, but I have to tell you here and now that gettin' somebody out of that pit is above one's bend. The blue-bellies have got walls thirty feet high all around the place, with 'bots prowlin' about 'em day and night. They got seven towers, each with an automatic repeating gun that can splatter two score rebs in the wink of an eye. That ain't to mention the vocal reiterator. Make a move on them and they'll have every Yankee soldier from Virginia to Christmas prowling the roads looking for you."

"You got out," Jesse said. "If'n a man can get out, it means other men can too." He looked around at the rest of his gang. "We figure out how it was done afore, and we see how it can be done again."

Henderson leaned heavily on the pulpit railing. "I don't think you'd much favor the way I got out of there." The shadowy man shook his head and there was a sick curl of his lip as he recounted to the outlaws how he'd escaped from the prison. "There'd been another outbreak of cholera. I'd been there when it happened before and I knew upwards of a quarter of us wouldn't make it through the winter. And sure enough, I took sick. The blue-bellies let me out of the hole when they saw that. They didn't see no sense keeping a man who was more'n half dead down there. Once I was back circulating among the rest of the rebs, I watched and I waited.

"The chief medical officer at Camp Lincoln is a human devil who took full advantage of the outbreak to experiment on the prisoners. He had the camp commandant wrapped about his finger and could pretty well do as he liked. Anyway, he'd send his orderlies out to gather up the sickest men, drag them off to the hospital shed and, well, ain't but a few fellas ever came back from there. Sometimes wagons would leave, always loaded down with big wooden casks."

Henderson's smile projected a wickedness that lingered below the surface and he again pressed his glasses close to his eyes, as though trying to blot out the image he saw in his mind. "A few of us managed to sneak around and crack open one of them casks late at night while the wagon was being loaded. What we found inside was all that was left of a captain from the Texas Cavalry. I can't even describe half what the doctor did to 'im, but what was left he'd stuffed into the cask, leaving it to float in something like a brine mixed with grain alcohol.

"The other prisoners weren't so ornery then. Once they saw that corpse floating about in there, they was done. I was too sick to be squeamish, though I knew if I didn't get out of Camp Lincoln, I'd be a dead man. So I hunkered down in that there cask, down in that briny alcohol, with the bits of that captain floating around me, and I waited. Weren't long before the wagon got moving and the Yankees drove me straight out of the camp. Never did learn where they was taking the pickled bodies they was hauling. A few miles out of Andersonville, I crawled up out of that cask and I kilt both them ghouls driving up front. Afore I left, I set the whole corpse-coach on fire. Burning, I figured, was a damn sight better'n whatever the Yankees were gonna do to them bodies, wherever they was going."

Cole rose slowly to his feet. "Murderin', thievin' coyotes!" he shouted. "Won't even let a man be buried decent and Christian!" He ripped his hat off his head and shook it at the pulpit. "Hang what you say Allen, but I ain't leavin' my little brother in the hands of such low-down grunters. By hook or by crook, we're gettin' him out of there!"

"Ease off, Cole," Hardin said. "You heard what Henderson done told us. That dog won't hunt. Ain't no way nobody is gonna bust somebody out of that pit."

Jim and Bob glared at the black-clad Texan. Cole looked irate enough to go for his guns. Jesse distracted the outlaws before their tempers could get worked into a worse state. He'd seen both Cole and Hardin in action, knew that if it came to a standoff then Hardin would handily outdraw Cole. Then Jesse would be obliged to avenge his friend. That'd diminish his gang considerably right when he needed every gun he could get.

"It ain't open for discussion," he told the outlaws. Jesse held each man's gaze with a steely stare. "We're gettin' John out of there, whatever it takes. Any man feels otherwise can light out now. I won't call him a coward." The way Jesse said the last bit made it clear that while he might not say it, he would most certainly think it.

Up on the pulpit, Henderson smiled down at Jesse. "You were always a bold one, saw that when we rode in and burned Lawrence. But I wonder if you really are bold enough to tackle Camp Lincoln."

"Ride with us and see for yourself, Henderson," Jesse said.

"I might do that," Henderson nodded. "If I thought you were doing it for something right. For something bigger than just rescuing your own." The shadowy figure pointed his finger accusingly at Jesse. "You used to fight for more'n just one man. You used to fight for a cause."

"We lost the war, Allen," Jesse said. "Only a fool can't see that. The cause is over."

"Is Yankee tyranny over?" Henderson asked. "The Union still imposing its word and its will on folks who don't want any part of it? President Johnson sittin' there nigh-on twenty years without any election? This freedom they're so quick to impose, how many people are they really willing to let share in it? They let our folks down in Missouri live their lives, try to prosper, or are they busy sending copperheads and carpet-baggers down there to steal every speck of land and every yellow hammer they can pick out of man's pocket? Are the courts upholding laws or just rubber-stamping whoever pays them the most? We have representation now, or just whatever skunk Washington thinks will do and say what they expect him to do?"

Jesse brought one of his metal hands crashing down against the fallen saint, sending a jagged crack running the length of the statue. "It don't change facts. The cause is lost."

"It's only lost if you let it be," Henderson told him. "You want to break into Camp Lincoln, I say you go big figure. Don't just do it for yourself, do it so you strike a blow against the whole damn Union! Send a message loud and clear to all those who still keep the Confederacy in their hearts, that the time of tyrants isn't gonna last!"

Henderson lifted his arms, his coat spreading about him like the wings of some black angel. "Be more than just Jesse James the bandit and robber. Set that aside! Be Jesse James the rebel! Jesse James the revolutionary! Jesse James the hero!" The man, who seemed like a prophet at this point, shook his head. "You want to rescue only John from that camp? I say that's selfish and petty! I say what you should really be thinking about is how to liberate Andersonville and rescue every man-jack in Camp Lincoln!"

Henderson's shout reverberated through the ruined sanctuary, but nowhere did it echo louder than in Jesse's heart. The prophetic speech was like lightning searing through him, forcing him to confront the pettiness of his ambitions since the end of the war, making him face the hedonistic materialism that had become his only purpose in life. Even rescuing John – even that had selfishness about it, a personal drive to ease the guilt he felt over the boy's capture. Henderson was right; he didn't think about others, he didn't appreciate anything bigger than himself. He'd allowed everything he'd ever believed in to die inside him; he had accepted that the victorious Union had taken hope from him. What Henderson was saying was that it stayed dead only as long as he allowed it.

Slowly, Jesse walked over to the pulpit. He reached out, laying one of his hands against the base of the platform near Henderson's boot, and looked up at him. "You really think it's possible? You really think everyone can be rescued?"

"If anybody else asked me, the answer would be no. But with the legendary Jesse James leading the charge, I think the chances are good. A lot better than those men have if they stay there under the doubtful mercies of the blue-bellies."

Jesse nodded. "Then we'd better make our plans. Because if it's possible, I'm gonna empty that prison right down to the bury patch."

*****

John Younger sat at the opening of the miserable canvas tent, staring at the man sprawled on the thin layer of straw that was the closest thing to a bed most of the prisoners of Andersonville would ever know again. The cotton blanket was pulled tight about the man's body, but it was too thin to effectively fend off the cold; especially for a man wracked by fever.

"I want his boots, boy." The words came in a low hiss from just outside the tent. From the corner of his eye, John could see the speaker; a snaggletoothed villain who still had the remnants of a Georgian insignia on his decayed shell jacket. The human vulture had been perched outside for most of the previous night and all through the morning. "He ain't got no use for 'em, nohow. Give 'em to me."

John looked over at his sick tent-mate, at the bare stockings sticking out from the edge of the blanket, and at the boots standing neatly beside the man's head. Leaning forward, he retrieved the footwear, trying his best not to disturb his companion.

"That's it!" the vulture cackled, but his laughter ended in a pained yelp as John spun around and smacked the heel of the boot across his jaw. The scavenger was knocked onto his rear, sputtering and cursing at the young outlaw.

"You made a mistake boy!" the vulture snarled. "Your pal ain't never gonna get off'n his sick bed! We'll be plantin' him in the bone orchard afore long. Then where'll you be?"

John glared back at the Georgian, a vicious smile on his face. "Where'll you be if his brother ever hears about this?"

The question made the color drain out of the scavenger's face. His curses faded off in a frightened sputter. John's suggestion was more than an empty threat. Every day, the Union was investing more resources in the hunt for Jesse James. When they caught him, there was only one place they'd send him to. The same place they'd sent his brother Frank. The vulture knew this and lost interest in a new pair of boots, instead scurrying off to lose himself in the maze of tents all around them.

The man disgusted John, but at the same time it was hard not to pity him. The inmates of Camp Lincoln had suffered so much for so long that they'd lost most of their humanity. They couldn't afford anything more than whatever would keep them alive, no matter how callous their actions. Before he'd taken sick, Frank James had told John about how he'd seen food stolen from sick men on a regular basis, their fellow prisoners reasoning that it was wasted on men who were going to die anyway.

Maybe it was naïve of John, but he refused to view Frank in that light – he was, after all, Jesse's brother. He was made of sterner stuff. He kept thinking of the wonderment and jubilation Jesse would have when he found out his brother had survived the battle outside of Diablo Canyon. He kept thinking of all the raids Frank had ridden alongside his brothers Cole and Jim. Frank was still the man who had pulled him out from under that sad mob when he first arrived in Camp Lincoln, a thought that kept running through John's mind. He owed Frank for that, if nothing more, that alone would make John beholden to him.

Disease was an omnipresent threat in the squalid, unsanitary confines of Camp Lincoln. Still weak from the wounds he had received when he was captured, Frank had succumbed to the latest round of illness sweeping through the camp. From what Frank had told him, John knew how slim the chances of recovery were. Without the assistance of the camp doctors, few who took sick in Andersonville's prison ever recovered.

Though it rested heavy on his conscience, John realized the only way for him to help Frank was to leave him alone and try to beg help from the camp doctors. The notion of joining that same desperate throng that had nearly mobbed him on his arrival to the prison was revolting to him, but what else could he do?

"I'll be back," John promised the man shivering on the ground. Before he left the tent, he tucked Frank's boots under his arm. The desperate inmates all around them might not stoop to murder, but theft was almost a certainty. The boots would be just too much of a temptation, as the Georgian vulture had so vividly displayed.

Quitting the tent, John looked across the morass of muddy earth and filthy canvas shelters. Many of the prisoners still wore the gray tatters of their uniforms, the garments tied crudely about their starved bodies by bootlaces and strips torn from tents and blankets. Everywhere there was the haunted, empty look of broken men; faces so oppressed by the misery of existence that not only hope, but even fear, had been beaten out of their eyes. What was left was only a terrible blankness, the unfocused stare of men trying to lose themselves in a landscape of memory.

Very few things could spark an ember of interest or excitement in such men, but one of those things was the appearance among them of what the prisoners called 'rebel angels.' These were volunteer nurses, southern ladies who offered to administer aid to the inmates of Camp Lincoln. There were never many of them, but their presence was the only bright spot in the dreary ordeal these men endured day upon day. It was the strictest rule that these female Samaritans never be harassed or offended; the prisoners were quick about policing any of their own who broke this rule. More than the meager medical aid that the nurses provided, it was the lifting up of their spirits that the mere presence of a woman provoked, that the prisoners held sacrosanct.

As he looked across the camp, John noted some of the inmates displaying the excitement that characterized the proximity of a nurse. Jogging down the muddy path between the tents, John soon saw a figure dressed in white, kneeling down in the mud and changing the bandages wrapped about the foot of a scarecrow-like Virginian. There was no small crowd around the nurse, but John was only recently arrived in Camp Lincoln and he was still hale and hearty, while the men around him were half-starved and sickly. It was moral repugnance rather than physical impediment that delayed John's thrust to the front of the crowd.

"Nurse!" John cried. "My friend, he's taken sorely sick! I wish you'd come and look at him."

The nurse looked up and John couldn't help but marvel at the loveliness of her face, the admixture of natural beauty colored by sympathy and utmost concern. She finished binding the man's foot and then turned toward John. "You're new to this camp, aren't you?" she asked. It was a question he thought fairly obvious by the condition of his clothes, much less the fact that he was at least a decade younger than any other man in the camp. His youth made him stand out like the spots on a playing card.

"Yes, ma'm," John said. "My friend's been here a sight longer. Long enough to catch the fever. Please, you've got to come help him." He injected the last of his words with that desperate, boyish smile that Jim always resented because of its effect on women. The nurse wasn't any exception. Finishing with the man she was ministering to, she made her apologies to the other sickly men begging her for help. John felt pangs of guilt as he led her away from them, but there was nothing else to be done if he was going to help Frank. That was the blunt, brutal truth, as unsavory as it might be to swallow.

Outlaw and nurse hurried through the labyrinth of tents, both of them forcing themselves to be deaf to the weak voices that called out to her as her white uniform was noticed by men too sick to leave their shelters. The guilt John felt turned into a smoldering anger. Rage built toward the Union fiends who would inflict such misery on these men; to abandon them to such slow, lingering torture. It was with a relief more profound than anything he'd felt before that they reached Frank's tent and he pulled aside the flap to admit the nurse.

"Frank," he called to the man lying on the ground. "I've brought you help. This here's Miss... ah... Miss..."

"Lucy," the nurse finished for him, crouching down beside Frank. Frank looked at her through his fever. She looked familiar, but his eyes kept going in and out of focus. She laid her hand across his forehead, feeling the sweat beading his brow and the fever burning inside his head. She frowned and looked up at John. "Has he been like this long?"

John nodded. "It might have been settin' in even afore I was brought here two months ago, but it really struck him down last night. Is there anythin' you can do?"

"It looks like malaria." She reached into the pocket of her coat, drawing out a small leather pouch. Carefully, she counted out a handful of tiny pills. John handed her the battered canteen that the two men were forced to share. "Hold up his head," Lucy ordered. As John complied, she tugged open Frank's mouth with her thumb and forced one of the pills onto his tongue. A swallow of water sent the medicine down his throat.

"Quinine," Lucy explained. "It will help to break the fever, though it should have been more effective if he'd been given it before the disease was ever allowed to settle into him. Now, I'm afraid, he'll have the potential for relapse the rest of his life."

"But, he'll live?" John asked eagerly.

"If the fever breaks," Lucy said, worry straining at her voice and turning her expression grim. She turned her head, wincing when she found Frank's eyes fixed upon her. She could almost feel the outlaw's mind struggling to pierce the confusion of fever to understand why she looked familiar to him. To remember the woman who had been introduced to him as Lucinda Loveless. How he would react when his mind made that connection was a problem that troubled her almost as much as the fever itself.

Despite the hundreds of other men needing her attentions, the nurse remained to watch over Frank for several hours. Only when the fever lessened, and Frank was able to not only open his eyes, but actually focus on those around him, and frame a coherent request for more water, did she accept that her vigil had ended. Handing John a half dozen pills, she gave him instructions for Frank's continued treatment.

"Bless you, Miss Lucy," John said, bowing with that same gentlemanly mannerism with which his brother Cole always favored a lady.

"Yes... thank you," Frank said, lifting his head from the pallet. For a moment, his eyes held the woman's. There was no mistaking the recognition in that look. "Thank you... nurse," the outlaw said before sliding back against the pillow.

Loveless rose and made her way to the tent's opening, relieved that the outlaw hadn't revealed her secret. "See that you give him the pills," she cautioned. "If you want him to recover, you need to promise that you'll remember that." She nodded toward Frank. "It would be awful for the brother of Jesse James to die such a useless death."

John gave a start, his eyes narrowing as he looked at the nurse. "You... you know who he is?"

"There's no mistaking Frank James," she said. "They've plastered his picture on wanted posters across the entire Union. It'd take someone far less observant than a nurse to forget a face they've seen every time they wanted to post a letter."

The young outlaw looked back at Frank. "Don't let anybody know he's sick," his voice was pleading. "Frank's big fear was that the commandant would take him back to the doctors. I don't know what they done to him when he first came here, but he'd rather die than go through it again."

Smiling sympathetically, the nurse nodded. "I'll check back on you tomorrow. And I won't tell the doctors." Slipping through the flap, the nurse returned to the maze of tents and the hundreds of sick prisoners clamoring for her help.

"That's... that's a fine... woman," Frank muttered, his voice a harsh croak.

John hurried over to his friend's side. "She gave me medicine. She broke your fever."

Frank managed a weak nod and sank back onto the bed of straw. "Then I'm obliged. I always feel uncomfortable being obliged to women."

"She's tryin' to help," John said. In his fever, it seemed Frank was becoming paranoid, imagining that Lucy was some spy or agent of the camp commandant. When the old bushwhacker spoke, however, he revealed that his fears weren't about spies.

"She can help us," Frank said, "but how can we help... her?"

"I don't understand," John said. "She's got reg'lar meals and a real roof over her head. She's better off'n we are."

Frank's eyes focused on John, becoming fierce in their intensity. "She ain't," he said. "Not by a long shot. Them rebel angels don't tend to last too long." He pointed at the flap of the tent. "You watch for her. If'n you ever see her sent at night to that big wooden ward building on the north side of the compound, you won't never see her again."

John kneeled beside Frank, grasping his shoulder, a sudden surge of panic sweeping through him. "Why? What're the Yankees doin' there? What kinda danger would they pose to a woman?"

John could feel the shudder that passed through Frank's body. Even in the misery of Camp Lincoln, there were some horrors too terrible for the prisoners to speak of. The building in question was one of them. "She goes there, she's goin' into Dr. Tumblety's surgery," Frank said. "Ain't no woman goes in there and comes back again."

*****

The surgery had the stinging pungency of antiseptics in the air, a chemical stink that was restrained and magnified by the closed confines of the building. The many windows were kept bolted and shuttered day and night, many of them nailed closed permanently. The doors were similarly kept locked, a UR-25 Warder standing before each one in perpetual vigil. A regular rotation of the 'bots patrolled the flattened roof of the building, the steady tromp of their steel feet creating a dull throb that pervaded every corner of the ward.

The building was one of the few survivors of the original Confederate prison that had stood there. Defying the flames of the vengeful conflagration that had consumed the rest of the camp, the old hospital had assumed a haunted reputation among the staff of Camp Lincoln. The outrages and atrocities inflicted upon the Union prisoners who had once been confined there seemed to resonate through the grim halls of the hospital. There were few in Andersonville who would willingly venture near the shunned and blighted place.

It was that pungent atmosphere of offense and wrongness that had drawn Dr. Francis Tumblety to select the old hospital for his surgery and recovery ward. He wanted seclusion and isolation, two commodities that were in short supply within the cramped confines of a prison camp. Selecting the one spot which prisoners, guards, and townspeople alike regarded with natural aversion was simply the logical decision.

Tumblety prided himself on his logical, keenly analytical mind. He was a man of pure reason, guided by the principles of rational science rather than emotional urges and the stubbornness of tradition. As he'd taken great pains to illustrate in his self-published volume, Dr. Francis Tumblety – Sketch of the Life of the Gifted, Eccentric, and World Famed Physician, he was a man of humble mien and selfless devotion to science and medical advancement. Let self-aggrandizing cretins like Tesla and Carpathian court the press and seek the laurels of an overly credulous public; he would lay before the people of the world a new science that would shake the very pillars of convention! His name would stand above the scions of reason, greater than Galileo, Newton, and Copernicus!

Tumblety leaned back in his chair and smoothed the luxuriant mass of his walrus-like moustache. His eyes roved about the immaculate tile floors, the unblemished plaster walls of his surgery. He frowned slightly at the huge electric lamps arrayed about the various vivisection stations; a concession to Tesla's inventions and the practicality of avoiding the soot from oil lamps. The galvanic batteries that were arrayed around each station were a far more clever creation, derived from Tumblety's own experiments with electrical stimulation of living tissues. It was a magnificent derivation of applied reason, extrapolating such stimulation from the semi-occult researches of Johann Konrad Dippel, the notorious 18th century German alchemist. Only a man of Tumblety's vision could have stripped away the arcane nomenclature of Dippel's writings to recover the anatomical and physiological theories that lay hidden beneath the trappings of soul-transference and the Elixir of Life.

He had, of course, gone far beyond Dippel. The German simply never had the resources available to him that Tumblety had acquired. He had known Lincoln when he was in office and enjoyed the favor of the War Secretary Stimson. He was so renowned that at the snap of his fingers, he could get any consideration his experiments required from the government – the obfuscations of that foreign ass Tesla notwithstanding. It grated on Tumblety's sensibilities that a barely civilized Serbian should be afforded an American citizenship of the same caliber as an Irishman like himself. He was minded to take the matter up with Secretary of War Upton the next time he was in Washington, to impress again on him the erratic temperament of people like Tesla.

Tumblety gave his moustache an anxious twist, his eyes roving over to the rack of bottled surgical specimens that formed his own personal collection. Perhaps it would be better not to broach the subject to the Secretary. He might – irrational though it was – draw a comparison between Tesla's eccentricities and the recent unpleasantness that had accumulated around Tumblety's last visit to London. There was nothing to it of course, nothing but lies and innuendo, but he couldn't quite forget the unseemly haste with which Pinkerton agents had collected him in New York and spirited him away. It was, naturally, preposterous that Scotland Yard had actually sent detectives looking for him, but that was the story they'd used to ensure his cooperation.

The door into Tumblety's surgery slowly creaked open. He swung around in his chair, his eyes focusing on the white-uniformed figure that came creeping into the ward. The nurse was timidity itself, so demure and shy in her manner that he was reminded of a scared rabbit stealing across a meadow. Her face was comely, her hair descending in a dark cascade about her shoulders. He could see the swell of her body beneath her uniform as she moved; the inviting sway of her hips as she walked toward him. Yet, there was a slatternly wantonness in the curve of her lips. Her scent was intoxicating, overpowering the clean antiseptic smell of the surgery. He could feel it seeping down into his body, threatening to overwhelm his senses, to drown his intellect beneath a patina of primitive emotion.

"You... you sent for me?" the nurse asked.

Tumbletey was not deceived by the faltering words and the tremulous voice. He knew every inflection was calculated to entice and entrap. His eyes strayed again to the collection of surgical specimens lining the shelves. He'd built that collection himself, piece by piece and bit by bit. Every organ floating in its solution of alcohol had a memory associated with it, a moment in time when he'd struck back at the irrational tyranny of instinct and nature.

"You sent for me... Doctor?" the woman asked again.

Tumblety's face spread in a cold, reptilian smile. He rose slowly from his chair. Without saying a word, without even looking at the nurse, he stalked across the surgery toward one of the vivisection theatres. He could feel the nurse's eyes watching him, could sense the uneasiness throbbing through her veins. She was perplexed, discomfited that her feminine wiles were ineffective on him. The first flickers of fear were running through her veins, the fear of a man she couldn't control and bend to her will. Fear of a man she couldn't seduce and betray.

Picking up a bone-handled surgical knife, Tumblety turned back toward the nurse, his eyes glittering with undisguised malignance. There was no need for pretense, not here. Let her know what was coming, let her appreciate the magnitude of her defeat. There was no escape. Not from this place.

"My colleagues call me 'doctor,'" Tumblety said as he advanced toward the nurse, the knife gleaming in his hand.

"Whores call me Jack."

Chapter 14

Jesse James sat in the old mission's bell tower, leaning over the table in Henderson's reclusive quarters and studying the map arrayed before him. The former raider had drawn the map from memory and Jesse was impressed by the sharpness of his recollections. Every tent and grave seemed to be picked out, much less the buildings and fortifications that the outlaws would need to overcome if a raid against Andersonville's prison was to be any kind of success.

In many ways, Jesse still found the prospect of such a raid staggering in its audacity. This wasn't going to be a simple attack on a train or bank. This was going to be altogether different than anything he had been involved in since RJ technology had been invented. This was going to be a direct attack against the hated Union itself; he would be spitting in the face of Grant and all of the other reprobates in Washington. It would be no different than the battles they'd fought during the war.

That wasn't quite right either, Jesse reflected. In the war, even for a loose outfit like Quantrill's Raiders, there had been rules and obligations, a chain of command to answer to, a country to support and defend. None of that applied now. This was just Jesse James, answerable only to his own conscience. The decisions were his to make. The risks were his to decide.

"It'll take at least a hundred men to hit that camp," Jesse said, one of his metal fingers sliding along the demarcation of the perimeter wall. "I'll need five for each of the towers, enough to keep the guards pinned down if they can't kill 'em outright. No less than thirty to hit the main gate. We'll need a good cadre of sharpshooters with heavy-hittin' blasters to pick off them Warders as well. Stuff with enough kick to put a bot down for good." The outlaw sighed as he ran his finger into the sprawl of the camp itself and the confusion of tents strewn about the grounds. "Breakin' in will be a damn sight easier than gettin' the men back out."

Henderson sat in the corner of the room, little more than a shadow in the darkness. "You'll do it, Jesse," he assured the outlaw. "You'll do it because it's what needs doing. Those men are depending on you, not just John but all them thousands of rebs in there with him. You won't let them down."

Jesse shook his head. "When we hit that camp, sure as shootin', somebody's gonna call out the troops against us across the whole state. Every garrison between there and Texas will be mobilized. Our only chance is to have enough firepower that there won't be a fort or cavalry troop that'd dare tangle with us. Make the Yankees turn out a whole army to put us down. And while they're gatherin' up such a force, we skedaddle into parts they won't be too keen to follow."

"That'll take resources," Henderson observed. "More men and equipment than you're going to find in Robbers Roost or a dozen places like it."

"We can pick up gear off'n the blue-bellies. Just like we always done." Jesse paused for a moment, picturing the other possibility. Dr. Carpathian would sell guns and mounts for such an adventure, but given his recent encounter with the scientist, Jesse knew that such a price would be paid in more than gold alone.

Henderson seemed to be considering the same option. "We go hitting all these forts and trains like you want, even the Yankees will get wise to what we're up to. They'll start pouring more troops into Andersonville, then turn the prison into a stronghold that we'll never be able to break." The shade's voice dropped to a grisly hiss. "I wouldn't put it past them to start shooting the prisoners just to make sure we couldn't free them."

Jesse's eyes blazed as he mulled over that possibility. Anyone who'd seen what was left after Sherman's March knew there were no limits to what the Union was capable of. Still, if they turned to Carpathian to outfit them, they'd just be trading one Devil for another. "What do you suggest, Allen? We go with hat in hand to beg supplies off'n Carpathian and his Enlightened?"

"I wasn't thinking of Carpathian," Henderson said. "I was thinking that a venture such as this would be of interest down south to President Lee."

Jesse almost laughed at that. The continuing Confederate Rebellion had been isolated and cordoned off in the extreme southeast of the country. Some disparagingly referred to it as the 'Remnant,' and even for the Confederacy's staunchest supporters, there was no denying the diminished, impoverished state of the territory Robert E. Lee and his troops continued to hold. If not for the more immediate threat posed by the Warrior Nation and Carpathian's Enlightened, the Union Army would have smashed Lee's forces years ago. As it stood, the blue-bellies were content to simply contain the secessionist forces and leave them to wither on the vine.

"I don't see how Lee's in any position to help himself, much less anybody else," Jesse said.

Henderson stepped out of the darkness, his face drawn and grave. "Lee doesn't have the resources to fight a prolonged campaign. He can't capture territory or go toe-to-toe with the Yankees. Mustering the troops and providing provisions for a raid on Andersonville – that would be within his capability. The key will be to impress on him the feasibility of such an assault. You'll have to sell him on the idea, Jesse."

"I'm a fighter, not a diplomat," Jesse said with a scowl.

"A leader has to be whatever the situation calls for," Henderson told him. "He has to stop thinking only about himself and start considering the bigger picture. He has to think about all those things that are bigger than himself."

"Is that how Quantrill led us in the war?"

Henderson pushed his tinted spectacles closer to his eyes. "That was war. Things were different. What you're planning isn't war, it's liberation. You aren't leading men to death; you're leading them to life and freedom. That calls for an entirely different sort of man; the kind of man who not only destroys but who can rebuild."

Jesse tapped his metal fingers against the table. What his old commander's adjutant told him was simply the echo of what he already felt inside. He could free these men, of that he was certain. It was what happened after they were liberated, that was the problem which both tantalized and troubled him. On the one hand, it was an onerous burden to be responsible for so many lives. At the same time, the possibilities having an army behind him would open up were all too enticing. He could carve out a new land away from Yankee oppression, a land where those who rejected the tyranny of Washington could be free.

It was a captivating vision. Freeing the men trapped in Camp Lincoln would be the first step toward making that dream a reality.

*****

It wasn't long before word of Jesse's presence in Robbers Roost made the rounds, spread along that phantom network that lawmen sometimes termed the 'outlaw telegraph.' It caused a steady stream of road agents, rustlers, and bandits to come trooping into the lawless town. They were all drawn by the same thing: the fame and reputation of the notorious bank robber. The same nebulous network that told them Jesse was in Robbers Roost also claimed he was looking to expand the James-Younger Gang. A position in the infamous outlaw band was something to be coveted by hardened gunslingers and criminals. Around the Laughing Wolf Saloon, where the gang had established its temporary headquarters, a mob of desperados gathered each morning, keen to extol their virtues to Jesse James and Cole Younger. Each man spared no effort as he tried to inveigle himself into the gang's ranks.

The three riders who slowly made their way into town this particular morning had a very different objective in mind. Two of the men, scruffy-looking ruffians, were dressed in sorely weathered oilcloth slickers and sporting the battered remnants of broad-brimmed cowboy sombreros, the felt stained and weathered by the dust of the trail. They had broad, boyish faces with close-set eyes and only the slightest trace of chin. It was clear from a glance that the two were branches from the same tree, brothers or cousins of some close affinity.

The third rider, draped in a black duster to conceal the brass armor beneath that had been bought with blood money, had the predatory cast of a wild beast about him. While his companions rode blackhoofs, he was mounted on a sleek Iron Horse, its hood adorned with the ossified remains of a cattle skull. The eyes of the balding man with a thick beard roved from side to side, watching the outlaw denizens they passed on their slow ride down the street with keen wariness. The brain behind those eyes was putting names to some of those faces, and affixing prices to many of those names.

"I still don't like it," the older of the two brothers hissed at the man in black. "Our part in your plan is the riskier one. We should be gettin' a bigger share of the reward."

Thomas Tate Tobin fixed a withering glare on the boyish rider. "A quarter of the reward is already generous," he said in a low growl. "Don't forget the pardon waitin' for both of you when we turn him in. Or maybe I should have just turned you two over for the bounty on your heads and tried a lone hand?"

The younger brother eased across his saddle, his eyes glittering like those of a snake. "If you'd thought you could pull this on your own, you'd never have offered us a deal."

"A deal you accepted," the bounty hunter reminded him. "You were quite happy to agree to my proposal when I made it."

The older outlaw scowled. "You don't exactly negotiate with a man who has the drop on you and says if you don't do as he tells you he's a goin' to shoot you like a dog and turn your head in for two hundred dollars."

"One hundred dollars," Tobin corrected him. His smile was as cold as ice. "Two hundred is for the set."

"However that might be, Mr. Bounty Man," the younger of the outlaws said. "We still figure we're runnin' most of the risk. We should get more of the reward."

Tobin nodded, seeming to take the question under consideration. He patted the rifle scabbard bolted to the side of his steed. "Well, I reckon if'n we trim my share it might interfere with my marksmanship. Don't forget, I only need one of you to get Jesse's head."

The expressions on the faces of the two outlaws grew vicious. "You do that and you'd better watch your back," the older one warned.

Tobin chuckled at the threat. "I've never seen a rat yet that went out huntin' a wolf. More like whichever of you makes it will forget about the other and start thinkin' about how his own share just got bigger." Tobin laughed again when he saw the brothers cast suspicious glares at each other. Scavenging vermin, they knew each other well enough to appreciate the truth in his assessment of them.

They also knew what the opportunist expected of them. As Tobin's eyes roved the dusty main street of Robbers Roost, his gaze focused upon the old mission and the bell tower rising above the ruins. He pointed a gloved finger at the structure. "That's where I'll be. You'll bring Jesse out into the street, lead him off toward the stables. He gets to about this point, and I'll gun him."

"And what if you miss?" the younger outlaw asked.

"In that unlikely particular, you two will be right beside Jesse," Tobin said. "He'll be payin' attention to me up in the tower. He won't be keepin' his eyes on you. I don't reckon shootin' somebody in the back'll bother you none."

The outlaw brothers glowered at Tobin, but they didn't say anything about his contemptuous remark. There was too much truth behind it to challenge.

*****

The bounty hunter climbed up toward the old mission, using the block of crude cabins ranged behind the town's main street to conceal his approach for most of the distance. His hand tightened around the neck of the rifle he carried at his side. Not for the first time, he thought of the reward being offered for Jesse. After leaving Fort Concho, he'd reached the decision that trying to collect the bonus for bringing the outlaw back alive wasn't practical. It was better to settle for a sure thing than play the long odds. Besides, his pride still stung from the way Jesse had slipped through his fingers before. He wasn't going to take any chances of that happening again.

The two desperados he'd recruited would do their job. They'd lead Jesse out into the ambush Tobin was preparing. The story they were to give was that their partner had a number of Iron Horses to sell. The way Jesse was recruiting men into his gang, the outlaw was certain to be in need of mounts. Tobin was relying on that. Necessity was the quickest way to penetrate someone's caution.

They'd lead Jesse off to the stables to examine the 'Horse that Tobin had rode in on, a 'sample' of the steeds they had to sell. As he crossed from the saloon to the stables, Jesse would come in range of Tobin's rifle. The bounty hunter's first shot would settle the outlaw; after that, he would maintain a steady fusillade to drive the inhabitants of the town from the streets. In the confusion, his two desperados would snatch up Jesse's body and make their escape.

Tobin could count on the scum to do that much. The reward was big enough that their greed would pour some iron into their yellow spines. He wasn't fool enough to think they'd stick to the rest of their agreement. They'd try to cut him out of the bounty and claim it for themselves. Well and good. Let them try. It was a long trail back to Fort Concho.

Stealing toward the ruinous mission, Tobin glanced back at the town below. He'd always resisted making a catch in Robbers Roost before, judging the risks to be unequal to the rewards. The outlaw town had been more useful to him as a place to pick up the trail of a bandit or gunslinger, to track his quarry and run them down miles away. After this, those days would be through. There'd be too much chance somebody would recognize him and remember him as the 'man who shot Jesse James.'

The bounty hunter crept into the dim chamber at the base of the tower. He lingered in the darkened setting, letting his eyes adjust to the change in light, listening for any sound from the rooms above. When he was satisfied that he was alone and his eyes were as accustomed to the shadows as they were going to get, Tobin started his climb up the wooden ladder.

He emerged through the trap door into the center level of the tower. At once, Tobin took stock of the sparse furnishings and the clear evidence that someone had been holed up here. Reaching down, he eased the knife out from his boot.

While the bounty hunter's body was bending down to retrieve the knife, a figure sprang at him from the gloom. Tobin was knocked back as arms coiled around him, obviously having had practice at fighting in the shadows as Tobin was locked in a bear hug. Driven against the wall by his attacker, he wrenched the knife from his boot and drove upwards. The tight grip around his abdomen faltered as the knife stabbed into his adversary's body. In the next instant, Tobin was free and his foe was staggering back in the shadows. He could hear his assailant's body crash to the floor.

Tobin leaned against the wall a moment, drawing breath into his gasping lungs. Though they had been around him for only a moment, the awful strength in those arms had come close to throttling him. Warily, he watched the dim shape of the body sprawled on the floor. When he'd recovered his breath, Tobin approached it. Keeping his knife poised to deliver a stabbing thrust, he reached out and seized a wrist. A moment passed and then another. A cold smile formed on Tobin's face. He could feel no pulse under his fingers. The enemy he'd knifed was dead.

Tobin didn't trouble himself about who his late adversary had been. Comanchero, rustler, or madman, it mattered nothing to the bounty hunter. The attacker had been an obstacle, an inconvenience standing between himself and Jesse James. No, he was nothing but carrion, unable to obstruct Tobin further.

Moving away from the body, Tobin started toward the ladder leading up to the bell itself and the parapet overlooking the main street of Robbers Roost. It was from here he would watch his 'partners' bring Jesse out into the open. The first the outlaw would be aware of Tobin's ambush was when a bolt of electricity came crackling down from the bounty hunter's rifle. So much cleaner than the destructive charge of a regular blaster, the electrical ammunition would kill the target, but leave him intact enough to be identified when it came time to collect the reward.

As he climbed up into the tower, Tobin didn't notice the body on the floor stir, watch it raise its head, or see the pallid face gazing up at him with its red, glowing eyes.

*****

Jesse followed the two horse-traders out from the saloon. Their arrival had been opportune. Many of the recruits the gang had taken on had ridden into Robbers Roost on blackhoofs; a few were even in such dire straits that they'd made the trip on live horseflesh and mules. Without proper mounts for his men, Jesse knew it would be a long trek to the Confederate Rebellion and any meeting with President Lee. After coming around to Henderson's way of thinking, he was once again reconsidering that position. A solid raid against a Union outpost or two would get his men mobile, and it would drastically cut down the time they'd waste making contact with Lee.

Every day they spent in preparation was like a knife twisting in Jesse's gut. The image of John Younger rotting in Camp Lincoln was sickeningly omnipresent. After hearing firsthand from Henderson the horrors of the prison camp, Jesse couldn't abide the thought of leaving John there any longer than he had to. His sentiments were vociferously echoed by Bob and Jim Younger. It was rather ironic that Cole was the voice of caution. Even with his little brother languishing in captivity, Cole considered himself the shrewd strategist and tactician. He wanted to free John just as badly as any of the others, but thoughts of the loss of his best friend, Frank James, also urged him to make sure that when they made their raid they would be successful.

It was for that reason Jesse brought Cole along with him as he followed the two rustlers out to the big stable yard. As eager as he was for action, Jesse was apt to take anything that was offered. Cole would appraise the quality of the stock with a far more critical eye. The outlaw knew that such discrimination was exactly what they needed right now. Anxious men made mistakes. It was a lesson Jesse had been slow to understand.

Iron Horses. Jesse cast a wary glance at the two horse thieves. He didn't care for them at all. There was a rat-like meanness about them that set him on edge. Their story didn't sit easy on Jesse's mind; they didn't strike him as the kind of men with the grit to go stealing anything from the Union. Unless this third partner of theirs had a good deal more sand than these two displayed, he had misgivings about where exactly they might have come by their stock. That was why he was thankful to have Cole along. Cole would be able to pick apart the quality of their 'Horses. If they hadn't been stolen then they'd likely been scavenged, picked off some battlefield up north. The Warrior Nation had settled for more than a few troops of cavalry in their war against the white man, and the Indians had a religious repugnance for anything powered by RJ. Blasters, Iron Horses, even fob-watches and electriwork garters would be left to rot if the victorious Indians didn't have a medicine man around to destroy them more thoroughly in a ceremonial fire. Some human buzzards would follow troops of cavalry, hoping to pick up any technology that might be left lying around if the 'Horse soldiers were massacred. Sometimes these jackals would even go so far as to give the Indians warning so that they could prepare an ambush.

Jesse had no love for the Union, but such murderous treachery was beyond the pale. It was the lowest thing a man could sink to. Looking over the two horse thieves, he considered that they'd be perfectly capable of that kind of villainy. Cole swore that the older of the men had ridden with the James-Younger Gang many years before, down in Missouri just after the war. The man had been with them on a few train robberies Cole thought, but it had been so long ago that even he could not be certain. Usually Jesse's memory for names was excellent, but he just couldn't place Charley Ford and he was certain he'd never seen that baby-faced weasel Robert Ford before.

"You sure this ain't wampum you're tryin' to sell?" Jesse asked as they walked down the street. It was a question he'd asked the brothers before, but he still wasn't satisfied with their answers.

The Ford brothers scowled at the question. "Wampum" was tantamount to the vilest slur a man could invoke, indicating something that was either bartered or otherwise acquired from Indians. Before the vicious rise of the Warrior Nation, Indian traders had been held in the lowest repute, the bottom rung on the hierarchy of criminal society, lower than horse thieves and slavers. Now, they were considered traitors; even worse than Comancheros. A Comanchero might sell Indians guns and liquor, he might take whatever loot the braves had in trade, but he'd draw the line at scavenging massacred soldiers for plunder.

"As I said, Mr. James," Charley whined. "Me and my brother are just agents, facilitators if you would. Our partner, Mr. Howard, is the one who actually takes in the stock. I can't say for sure where he gets it."

Robert shook his head. "It ain't wampum," he declared, the fire in his tone reminding Jesse of a rat backed into a corner. "Howard's been a good deal evasive on where he gets his rides, but they look too good to be wampum." He waved his hand toward the stables. "You'll see for yerself when you look over the one he brung as a sample."

Jesse frowned at Robert, the intensity of his gaze wiping the smirk off the 'Horse thief's face. "Yeah, I'll see. And I'd better like what I see. Because, if I don't, it's going to go hard on you fellas and your friend Howard."

"Where is this Howard?" Cole asked. Because Charley had ridden with the gang in the past, he was less dubious about the Ford brothers, but their unknown partner was what kept his guard up.

"He's in the stable yard," Charley said quickly.

"A place with a reputation like Robbers Roost, Howard felt he'd stay close to his stock," Robert explained. "He didn't want some coyote ridin' off with the sample before he had a chance to show it to you."

Jesse nodded. It was a reasonable precaution to take. There was a certain rough code of honor among the outlaws of Robbers Roost. They didn't steal from one another; that was one of the things that could see a man lynched by his fellow bandits. However, that rule didn't apply to any outsiders who came into town, such as the mysterious Howard. "Well, let's mosey over and meet your partner and take a gander at what he's got to sell," Jesse said as he stepped down from the boardwalk and out into the street.

The four men had only started to walk across the dusty road when a voice shouted in warning to Jesse. The outlaw spun around, startled to see Allen Henderson rushing toward him. From Will Shaft's description of the habits of his old colonel's aide, the old guerrilla was pretty much a hermit and kept to the ruined mission. Even in his meetings with Jesse, Henderson insisted they have their talks in the ruins. To see the recluse running down the street, his black clothes and pallid face jarringly incongruous with the bright noonday sun overhead, made even more of an impact on the outlaw than the words he was shouting.

"The tower!" Henderson yelled. "There's a rifle in the tower!"

Jesse didn't need to ask which tower. If Henderson had been rousted from the ruins, he could only mean the bell tower. He also didn't need to ask what a rifle would be doing there. The instant he heard the man's warning, Jesse was throwing himself to the ground. Almost in the same instant, a bolt of electricity went crackling past his ear to scorch the dirt beside him.

There was a terrible familiarity about that crackling blast and the acrid smell its discharge left behind. It wasn't the usual explosive burst of a blaster or even the incendiary flare of Hardin's smokers. It was the sizzling electrical shock that had struck at Jesse when he'd escaped Wyatt Earp's posse. Without so much as a glance at the sharpshooter in the bell tower, Jesse knew in his bones that he was once again in the sights of Thomas Tate Tobin.

Jesse rolled along the ground, a second blast searing into the earth as he shifted position. There was no question that the shot came from the bell tower, and the outlaw didn't give the bounty hunter any opportunity for a third chance. The quick-devil arms Dr. Carpathian had grafted to his body leapt to his holsters, his guns clearing leather in less than a heartbeat. Two bursts of energized annihilation leapt from the pistols.

Unable to sight Tobin up in the darkened bell tower, Jesse instead fired his Hyper-velocity blasters at the base of the structure, shattering it in a staccato series of savage blows. The crumbling brick shattered as though struck by a mechanized hammer. With a groaning roar, the base of the tower exploded outward, the upper floors telescoping downwards in a catastrophic collapse. Dust and debris billowed from the jumble of cracked beams and smashed adobe, the tarnished bronze bell tolling dolefully as it crashed atop the rubble.

Somewhere under the mound of destruction, the body of Thomas Tate Tobin was buried. There'd be no more electrified blasts fired at Jesse James from ambush. Not from him. The entire incident, from the first attack to Jesse's dramatic demolition of the tower, took less than half a minute. As he picked himself off the ground, Jesse found that both Cole and Charley were still standing in shocked silence. Only Robert Ford had made any action, his own pistol half-clear of its holster. Jesse smiled and waved one of his smoking blasters at the young 'Horse thief. "You can leave that where it is. I've settled with the polecat."

Robert hesitated, and then slowly slid his gun back into the holster. "Thought you might need help, Mr. James."

Jesse nodded. "Damn quick reflexes," he said. "It might be I didn't remember your brother Charley, but it's damn certain I won't go forgetin' you, Bobbie." He looked over at the crowd that had come rushing out from the saloon and several of the other buildings. A wave of his metal hands reassured Bob, Jim, and the other members of his gang that their leader was alright.

"Any idea who that back-shooter was?" Cole's voice was full of fury, not least at his own lack of action in those critical seconds when the first shot had been fired. He glowered over at Henderson. "How is it you knew this fella was up there?"

Henderson chose to ignore the suspicion in Cole's tone. "He snuck up on me when he was climbing up. Threw me down the ladder and left me for dead." He continued with a description of the ambusher. With every word, the faces of the Ford brothers grew paler and sweat began to bead across Charley's forehead.

It was Robert who spoke first. "Damnation!" he cursed. "That's Tom Howard!" he glanced over at his shaken brother, then back at Jesse. "That's the man who wanted us to help him sell 'Horses to you!"

"His name was Thomas," Jesse said, turning his head and staring at the dust still rising from the pile of rubble. "But it weren't Howard, it was Tobin."

"The bounty man?" Robert gasped.

"He's the one who caught John," Cole spat. "He must have picked up your trail again, Jesse."

"I reckon," Jesse turned his gaze on the Ford brothers. "He must have figured to use you two for camouflage. Nobody'd pay too particular attention if'n he rode in here with known outlaws."

Robert nodded his head. "We didn't think he was anythin' more'n he told us he was," he declared, eliciting a quivering affirmation from the still shaken Charley. "Hell, if'n we'd know'd he was a bounty killer, I don't know how we'd have made it this far. There's posters out on the two of us, you know."

"That's right," Charley said. "Two hundred dollars."

"We'll have to see if we can't make you more valuable," Jesse said before he started toward the stable yard. "For now, let's see about puttin' Tobin's 'Horse to good use."

Henderson stepped into Jesse's path. "There isn't the time to dawdle anymore," the guerrilla cautioned. "If Tobin could track you here, other bounty hunters can do the same. We'll have to fit out what men we can and leave the rest." He raised his hand to deflect the protest he saw forming on Cole's tongue. "When Jesse explains his plan to President Lee, he'll get all the men and gear he needs to raid Andersonville."

Henderson's words evoked Jesse's own irritation at further delay. "Allen's right, Cole. We stay here and who can say how many more of these buzzards will come swoopin' in." He turned toward the Ford brothers. "I'm sorry boys. The furtherin' of your reward posters will have to wait. Rest assured, I'll remember you if'n you want to sign on once my business in Andersonville is done."

Robert nodded. "Well, Mr. James, if it's guns you need, my brother and I will be glad to sign up!"

"W-We will?" Charlie stammered, but a glare from his brother shot the nerve back into his spine. "I mean, w-we will! Of course we will!"

"We got no more business here, so if'n you'll let us, we'd be glad to ride with the famous Jesse James!"

Jesse stared at the brothers for a few moments, as if contemplating their offer. He eventually nodded and gave them a grim smirk. "Normally, I wouldn't be so sure, but since we're needin' more hands, it's you boys' lucky day." With that, Jesse turned back toward the stable yard. "Come on, Cole! Least we can do is check out Tobin's 'Horse. Will Shaft ain't got one and I reckon it'd be a mighty fittin' present for him."

"That'll really make Hardin hot," Cole warned.

A boyish grin formed on Jesse's face. "All the more reason," he said.

The two outlaws headed across the street. The Ford brothers watched them for a moment and then gradually drifted back to the saloon and the crowd that had gathered in front of it. Nobody paid any particular attention to Henderson as he studied the ruins of the mission before following Jesse and Cole into the stock yard.

Nobody noticed the tear in Henderson's shirt just above his belly or the pale, unblemished flesh beneath. His gaze lingered on the dust-shrouded ruins, a crimson glint sparkling behind the thick glasses.

*****

Colonel George Armstrong Custer stalked into the laboratory-surgery of Dr. Francis Tumblety with a face that could have sent a lion cringing into the back corner of its cage. A bold, reckless general during the war, Custer had been effectually put out to pasture by the War Department. Demoted after the official cessation of hostilities, he'd been bounced from one desk job to another until he'd finally ended up here, as commandant of Camp Lincoln. A dirtier job in the whole Union Army was something Custer didn't believe existed. His posting was all the more onerous for the very vivid memory of the fate that had befallen Captain Wirz, the Confederate commandant of Camp Sumter during the war. For the mistreatment and torture of the Union prisoners under his charge, Wirz had been executed, hung by the neck in Washington.

Custer was a tall, strongly built man. Partially out of pride, partly out of protest for his unglamorous posting, he wore his blonde hair long, well past the military custom of being cropped above the collar. His moustache was broad and thick, curling across his cheeks. Over his regulation uniform, he wore a buckskin jacket with a long leather fringe across the shoulders. He was a commanding presence, his every motion overlaid with a quality of energy that quickly affected the men he led. It was more his personal vitality and drive, his ability to inspire and lead, rather than any tactical acumen that had won him his victories in the war.

As he stepped into the sanitized sprawl of Tumblety's surgery, Custer reflected bitterly on how little those victories had won him. He was a man who longed for the glory and acclaim afforded to a hero. Instead, he found himself a mere jailor and custodian of a degenerate monster.

The costume Tumblety had adopted for this meeting with the commandant was still more infuriating to Custer. So far as he was aware, exempting some especially dubious claims that he'd done some espionage work for the Union during the height of the war, Tumblety had never served in the United States military, or the military of any other country for that matter. Yet here he was, bustling about his laboratory in a starched uniform of such ostentation that it would have shamed the extravagances of a Napoleon. Royal blue tunic over purple trousers adorned with a single stripe of crimson down the leg. Gilded shoulder boards struggled beneath coils of jade-colored brocade. Across his breast was a menagerie of medals and honors simulating everything from the Congressional Medal of Honor to the German Iron Cross and the French Pour le Merit. Custer noticed with extreme revulsion what looked to be Tumblety's own profile etched into an ivory cameo that served as the centerpiece for an enormous sunburst of bronze and silver – a decoration that its Latin inscription indicated was an award for 'excellence in the fields of science and humanity.'

Tumblety was fussing over one of the contraptions that had caused him to award himself such an honor. Resting on a steel table, the device looked like nothing Custer had ever seen. It was a bulky armature of steel and wire, pipes and hoses running away from it to a small RJ engine that had straps fastened to it so that it might be worn across the back like a mountaineer's rucksack. Protruding from the side of the armature was a hopper of some sort, a platter-like feeder that dropped serrated metal disks into a slot fitted to the top of the armature.

"My dear Commandant," Tumblety beamed as he looked up and saw Custer walking toward him. "It is so good of you to accept my invitation."

Custer frowned at the experimenter. "I've told you before, my rank is colonel. You will address me as such."

Tumblety stroked a finger across his walrus-like moustache. "Of course, yes. Forgive my lack of propriety. I sometimes forget myself. The weight of my indignation for the War Department's lack of foresight sometimes is too onerous to bear! They squander so much time and resources on that foreign charlatan, Tesla! Do you know what that crackpot has them believing he can do now? He actually has them convinced that he can translocate physical material! Imagine! The audacity! To suggest it is possible to transmit an object or a person from one place to another in the same way a sound is transmitted by the vocal reiterators! Have you ever heard anything so absurd?!"

The colonel barely heard Tumblety's tirade. He was more interested in the scrawny prisoner pinned to the wall of the surgery by a set of steel staples. For a moment, he wondered if the wretch was a more reasonably formulated specimen of Tumblety's research, the creations he sardonically termed his 'Reconstructed.' A brief study, however, didn't reveal any of the surgical scars that would have indicated the man had been subjected to one of the ward's vivisection theatres. This prisoner, it seemed, was there to indulge one of the experimenter's side projects.

"The Secretary of War expects results from you," Custer warned the scientist. "Don't worry about Tesla, worry about your own work. The War Department has invested a lot of money on you. They've put all the resources you need at your disposal, turned a blind eye to a lot of things just so you can further your work."

Tumblety started to strap himself into the device he'd constructed. "My work proceeds apace," he assured Custer. "There's no fear on that count. The process just needs a little more refinement and then you will have a weapon that will make those painted savages in the Nation only too eager to sign every treaty and smoke every peace pipe Washington sees fit to send their way!" He stroked the steel armature, closing his eyes and giggling as he savored the feeling of his fingers running down the framework of his creation. "Genius doesn't limit itself. If I were a boastful man I might describe myself as a prodigy. A scientific virtuoso." He nodded his head, endorsing his own statement. "You have seen my facility with surgery, but now let me exhibit my expertise with mechanical engineering."

Custer stepped aside as Tumblety walked toward the exposed section of wall, the metal armature supported by the straps across his back and a broad belt around his waist. The experimenter wound the tiny crank set into the contraption's side, generating the spark that set the entire armature aglow with crimson lines of energy. One of the saw-edged disks came sliding down from the hopper and into the slotted top of the armature.

"This will revolutionize warfare," Tumblety promised. Swinging around, he aimed the device at the man shackled to the wall. The prisoner flailed under the steel staples, opening his mouth in a grisly croak of terror. Custer could see the jagged stump where the captive's tongue had been.

With a ghastly screech, the saw-blade was launched from Tumblety's weapon. It whirled across the lab to slice into the wall... easily missing the prisoner by a dozen feet. The scientist glared at the shivering metal embedded in the wall. "I fear my aim isn't what could be expected of a trained soldier," he apologized. Taking a few steps closer, he fired a second disk at his prisoner. This time, the blade went sweeping high above the man, slamming into the wall a good two feet over his head. The mute screams of the wretch increased in their frantic violence.

"A few bugs still," Tumblety said, coughing loudly to clear the knot in his throat. Again, he took a few steps closer to the prisoner. When he launched a third disk at the captive, it glanced off the floor and went spinning into the wall. Deflecting off a support beam, the deadly missile careened across the lab to shatter several of the biological specimen jars before it sliced into the opposite wall.

"Leave the technology to Tesla," Custer growled. Casting a withering gaze at the experimenter, he started to storm from the lab. "Just concentrate on the research covered in the War Department's orders."

Tumblety shrugged out of the armature and hurried after the withdrawing officer. "Give me time!" he pleaded. "I will work out all the problems! It is this tension, this foolishness with Tesla! I am not in a proper mood to perform at my best."

Custer spun around at that last statement. His expression was one of complete disgust. "No."

"I need another one! My nervous disposition requires recalibrating."

"No!" Custer snarled. "I'll not be a party to your outrages. What you do to these Rebs is despicable enough!"

An unctuous smile formed on the experimenter's face. "Shall I wire the Secretary and tell him you won't give me what I need?" he challenged.

Custer shook his head. He knew that the murderous scientist had him at a disadvantage. When he'd protested to the War Department before about Tumblety's activities, he'd been told in no uncertain terms that they were both aware of and indifferent to the bloodthirsty peccadilloes of the experimenter. "It'll take a few days. Try to control yourself until then."

Tumblety clapped his hands, rubbing his palms together like a little boy anticipating Christmas. "Pick a nice one. Soft and pretty with nice white skin. The sort of skin just made for a knife."

Custer didn't answer the madman's request, instead hurrying from the surgery and back into the comparative wholesomeness of the squalid prison camp. Tumblety laughed at the officer's agitation and then turned back to his malfunctioning device. Lifting it back onto the table, he started to attack its workings with screwdriver and wrench.

"Don't worry," Tumblety told the captive bolted to the wall. "I'll have everything set to rights soon. Then we can try again."

Tumblety reached under the table and retrieved a new supply of saw-edged disks. He smiled as he started to stack them on the platter inside the weapon's hopper. "We have all night to get things right, after all."

Chapter 15

Jesse was able to outfit eighteen men by the time his gang left Robbers Roost. Grudgingly, he'd been forced to leave the Interceptor behind. It was simply too fuel hungry for the long trek across the Texas Territory, and at any event, it would draw too much notice from lawmen. They might be able to buffalo sheriffs and rangers into thinking they were an outfit from one of the big eastern companies, but if a lawman spotted an Interceptor among the Iron Horses, he'd need to be a half-wit not to appreciate that something untoward was going on.

Keeping to old Indian trails and back roads known only to Hardin and other Texan desperados, the gang was able to avoid any contact with the law until they were well past the panhandle region. It was there, in the desolated region south of the old Indian Territory, that the James-Younger Gang found themselves confronted by a Union patrol.

The outlaws were just clearing a stand of scruffy pine trees, heading into the grassy plain beyond, when the sound of whirring motors brought them whipping around in their saddles. From both sides, blue-uniformed soldiers came streaking toward them, blasters firing from their vehicles as they charged. For an instant, Jesse considered trying to outrun the Yankees, but a warning hiss from Henderson brought his attention to a rocky hill at their left. Jesse could see the gleam of metal reflecting among the rocks. The soldiers hadn't left much to chance, positioning sharpshooters up in the rocks. Any move to try to speed away would simply draw the outlaws into the killing ground the Yankees had prepared.

"Ease off, boys," Jesse warned his men, powering down his 'Horse and bringing it to a stop.

A yowl of pain sounded from Jesse's left. He glanced aside to see Hardin rubbing at his hand and glaring daggers at Cole Younger. "The man said leave your smokers alone," Cole growled at the gunfighter.

"We're just out surveyin' for the Texas-Union Railroad," Jesse reminded his men. They'd been fortunate enough to buy some stolen surveying equipment off a claim-jumper in Robbers Roost, and Will Shaft had provided the gang with two fellow Exoduster outlaws who'd previously worked as laborers for a surveying crew out in the Dakotas. "We ain't got no cause to be afeared of the law."

"And if they don't buy that?" Bob Younger asked.

Jesse nodded his head toward the hill and the glint of gun metal shining among the rocks. "We try to give as good as we get. Might be a few of us can win our way clear."

"Won't come to that, Mr. James," Will Shaft assured the outlaw. He gestured with his thumb to the other Exodusters. "Freddy and Moses know what to say if'n the blue-bellies get inquisitive."

"See that they do," Hardin snarled. "Or it won't need any Yankee gun to settle things where you darkies are concerned."

Jesse rounded on the gunfighter, but before he could reprimand Hardin, he saw the Union patrol closing in. "Everybody play nice," he reminded his men, adopting a broad smile as he removed his hat and waved it in greeting to the uniformed cavalry troopers. "Mornin' gents!" he called out.

The Union captain commanding the patrol didn't respond to Jesse's greeting. Keeping one hand on his blaster, the officer studied the well-armed gang of riders, his gaze lingering on the faces of John Wesley Hardin and Cole Younger. Then he turned his attention directly at Jesse. "You folks are mighty well-heeled and a damn fair sight off the beaten path," he said.

"We're surveyors for the Union-Texas," Jesse told the officer, then laughed. "That is, some of us are. The rest of us're engaged as guards to see their hair stays in place. Word is this region's crawlin' with dog-soldiers."

"Did you say, 'dog-soldiers?'" There was the slightest crack of a smile from the otherwise gravel-faced sergeant at the naivety of the phrase. "The Nation's on the war-path alright, but that's away over in the northern part of the territory. These parts it's the Hole-in-the-Wall Gang causin' all the ruckus."

The captain shot his subordinate a warning glance, immediately producing a sullen silence. The officer turned back around, staring suspiciously at Jesse. "Surveyors?" he asked, craning his head to one side as he looked over the equipment strapped to the Iron Horses.

"Yes, sir," Will Shaft said. "We's been sent out to figure a new route up into Tulsa." He lowered his voice to a confidential whisper. "I don't think the company has any intent of layin' track, they just want to secure the rights to the land so's nobody else can do it. Have to make sure they keep their monopolies."

The captain scowled at all the Confederate regalia adorning Will's body. "Where'd you pick up all that Secesh trash?" he asked, pointing at the hat and belt buckle.

"War trophies," Will said, adding a wide grin. The comment brought some laughs from the surrounding troopers. The captain allowed himself a faint semblance of a smile before turning toward Jesse.

"How about you?" the officer asked. "You have any trophies off'n the rebs? Seems to me I've seen you somewheres."

"I don't see how that's possible," Jesse said. His metal arms were hidden beneath the long sleeves of his duster and a set of cow-hide gauntlets, but even so, it would only take a fraction of a second to rip his blasters from their holsters and hurl the inquisitive officer into eternity.

Will Shaft hurried to explain to the officer. "We weren't in the reg'lar army during the war, sir. We was in a raider outfit. Chased Bloody Bill all across Missouri and Kansas we did."

The captain turned back around. "You two rode together in the War?" he asked.

"Come on, Cap'n," the sergeant grumbled. "These fellas don't look like the Wild Bunch and if'n they're ridin' with the Emancipated, it's damn sure they ain't any o' Lee's scum."

The captain whipped his head back around at the sergeant. "You tellin' me my job?"

"No, sir," the sergeant said, straightening up in his saddle.

The captain held his subordinate's gaze for a moment, and then addressed Jesse. "The Butch Cassidy bunch has been on the prod lately. With them 'Horses, your outfit would make a temptin' target for them. I suggest you forget all about scoutin' the terrain hereabouts."

Jesse shook his head. "Railroad wouldn't like that much. Some of us got wives and children to feed. Can't go offendin' the big bugs back east. 'Sides, like you said, we're well-heeled. I don't think any outlaw'd be fool-all enough to tangle with us."

The captain nodded. "You might be right about that," he conceded. Reaching into the breast of his coat, the captain pulled out a crumpled wanted poster. "Been puttin' these out at every stage stop and fuel depot. Cassidy's gang was brazen enough to have their picture took." He handed the poster over to Jesse. The officer gave him a moment to glance at the faces in the picture. "You boys keep that one. If'n you see one of them, get yerself to the nearest telegraph and signal the closest fort. Worth a two thousand dollar reward if'n your information lands us the whole gang."

Jesse smiled and slowly folded the poster, tucking it into a pocket of his duster. "We'll be sure to keep our eyes open, Cap'n."

The captain gave a last lingering look at Jesse, some familiarity about him nagging at the officer's memory. Finally, he gave up the elusive connection he was trying to make. Raising his arm, he waved Jesse's outfit onward. The outlaw wasn't fooled; the gesture wasn't for his benefit, but a signal to the men in the rocks to let the 'surveyors' pass.

Opening up their Iron Horses, the outlaws sped off across the plain. In a few minutes, they'd put the Union patrol and their lurking sharpshooters far behind.

"Damn lucky back there," Jim Younger winced from the lingering pain of his wounds as he spoke. Soon, the Yankees were a distant memory over the horizon.

"I thought for certain that eagle-button officer recognized me," Cole said. "Would have had a bad fracas with them shooters up ahead and Yankee 'Horses to either side."

Jesse slowed his steed, dropping back until he was riding beside Will Shaft. "You're the one got us out of that spot, Will," he told the Exoduster. "If not for you, I don't think them Yankees would have believed a word we told them."

"Darkie camouflage," Hardin sneered. "Now that we can't have 'em pickin' cotton, it's nice to know they're good for somethin'."

Will glared at the Texan, a cold glint in his eyes. "Any time you'd like to dance, buckra, you jus' say the word." He noticed Hardin start to reach for his smoker. Before the gunfighter could finish the move, Will whipped one of his own blasters from a shoulder holster.

Before either man could bring a weapon to bear, he found himself looking into the barrel of one of Jesse's guns. While gently guiding the Iron Horse with his knees, the quick-devil arms Carpathian had given the bushwhacker made a mockery of both Hardin's speed and Shaft's cunning.

"I happen to need both of you right now," Jesse warned the outlaws. "So if I'm goaded into shootin', I'll just have to oblige both of you." The warning didn't need to be repeated. Hardin scowled and shoved his smoker back into its holster. Will nodded and put away his blaster. "Hardin, seein' you know this country, why don't you light out ahead and play scout for a time. Give you a chance to act civilized when you get back." Hardin glared at the guerrilla and then cast a murderous look at Will. Without saying a word, he opened the throttle on his 'Horse and sped off down the trail.

"He's gonna be trouble, Mr. James," Will said.

Jesse holstered his weapons. "He'll bide his time a spell yet. He's ornery as a curly wolf, but he's still a damn good hand in a fight. I'm hopin' he doesn't push things too far until after we get John and the others out of Camp Lincoln."

Will looked dubious. "As you say, Mr. James, but I wouldn't turn my back on that sidewinder for nothin'."

"Call me Jesse," the outlaw said. "Damn if you didn't earn that much and more back there." A distant look crept into his eyes. He might not have been as belligerent as Hardin, but he'd been brought up in the same culture. He'd been taught that black men were only partly human, that they couldn't think or act for themselves. He'd been raised to think of them as property, like a horse or a dog, not as people. Certainly not as equals.

He repented that attitude. Listening to Will speaking up for them, trying to ease off the Yankee officer's suspicions, had made him confront his old prejudices and beliefs. It was a hard thing to set aside everything you'd been taught, even more to grow past everything you'd believed. It was worse to think that maybe the Confederacy's defeat had been necessary, that the Union tyranny which followed had in some ways done some good. At least for Jesse, the Union oppression made him understand what it was to not have freedom. It made him experience what it was like to have men standing over you telling you what you could do and where you could go. It gave him a taste, however slight, of what it must have meant to be a slave.

The blacks, they were people too. It was a realization that came hard to Jesse. He could feel all the things he'd been reared on resisting that idea, but something far deeper and more profound within him knew it was the truth. He knew it was the right and decent thing. He'd taken up arms because the Union thought it could glad-hand the South; to rob and steal without conscience, and bring low the pride of those who'd been beaten in the war. Yet, what about the pride of men like Will? If he was so set on deposing the tyranny of the blue-bellies for his people, shouldn't he feel it only right to do the same for anybody who'd share his cause?

"Why're you ridin' with us?" Jesse asked Will at last.

Will was quiet a moment, considering how exactly he would answer that question. "You know, Jesse, I asked myself that too. I reckon in the end, I just decided we had the same enemy. Fightin' back on my own just wasn't good enough. Fightin' back with Jesse James, maybe I could make the Yankees hurt some afore I was done." A wistful look came upon the Exoduster's face. "All them years as a slave, I clung to the idea of freedom. Then the war come along and the Yankees made me free. Then there was peace and they show'd me how much my freedom was worth. I wasn't allowed in the front door of a saloon, had to sit in the back of white folk's churches, couldn't even sell my crops for the same as white sodbusters could. The same folks that went to war because I was a slave didn't care two-bits now that I wasn't." He turned and spat into the dust of the trail. "I was obliged to watch my son starve, had to bury my misses after her grief got too bad and she hung herself. All that 'cause the fort wouldn't buy supplies off'n an Exoduster – not for anythin' reasonable."

"They done a lot of bad to a lot of folk," Jesse said. "But I give you my word, Will, they're gonna answer for it. Maybe we can't get Lee to see things our way, maybe we can, but however it goes, I want you to know that I'm proud to share my revenge with you."

Will nodded and smiled. "Ain't nothin' more personal a man can offer to share than his revenge."

*****

Some weeks later, the James-Younger Gang had put the prairies and forests of Texas Territory behind them. Slipping past the cordon of Union outposts, they entered the region claimed by the Confederate Rebellion. A grizzled ferryman smuggled them across the Mississippi for one of their blasters and the surveying equipment. Jesse'd been more than willing to hand over the surveyor's instruments, but he regretted the loss of even one blaster. If their plan to liberate the inmates of Camp Lincoln panned out, there'd be a lot of men in need of guns after the raid.

On the other side of the Mississippi, the gang found themselves following a narrow road winding its way through a vast stretch of bottomland. The half-sunken cypress trees rose grotesquely from winding creeks, the brown water carrying a stagnant smell as it flowed sluggishly through the swamp. Veils of Spanish moss swayed in the humid breeze, the droning buzz of cicadas filled the air and drowned out even the hum of the outlaws' RJ-powered vehicles.

Though they'd crossed beyond the Union frontier, the gang still kept a wary eye for blue-coat patrols. Infiltrators and raiders of both sides were constantly making forays across the demarcation, stealing supplies or gathering intelligence from the other side. The full weight of the Union Army might have been drawn away from the lingering Rebel presence by the double threats of the Warrior Nation and the Enlightened, but Washington had by no means forgotten about the Secessionists, and had no intention of allowing the rebellion to spread. Now that the outlaws were over the border, there'd be no discussion with any Yankee troops they stumbled upon. The blue-bellies would shoot without question and the outlaws had to be ready to oblige them in kind.

When Jesse's men were finally challenged, it wasn't by Union troops. For several miles, Jesse had felt a menace growing around them. Henderson whispered a quiet warning to him as they passed a stand of willows that the gang was no longer alone. Though they couldn't see them, they had acquired a shadow as they passed through the swamps. Henderson couldn't offer any clue as to who was following them or how many they might be, only that they were there.

Jesse passed the warning along to his men. He advised them to keep a ready hand near their blasters, but not to shoot until they were dead certain who or what it was they were shooting at. There was just a chance that the unseen lurkers might prove to be friend rather than foe.

The swamp unexpectedly flattened out, the ground becoming much more solid and substantial. Jesse could see the great sprawl of what must once have been a cotton field, but which had now been given over to more essential crops like corn and potatoes. The remnants of the Confederacy needed food more than cotton.

"Jus' y'all turn off them motors and ease away fra' yourn shootin' irons," a gruff voice challenged the outlaws as they emerged from the swamp. "Y'all got ten rifles on yeh an' don't take but the tick o' a hound's ear ter turn the lot o' yeh inta fert'lizer."

The whine of energy rifles cycling somewhere behind the cornstalks and among the willows convinced even Hardin that the unseen speaker wasn't making an empty threat. As the outlaws powered down their vehicles and raised their hands, Jesse glanced over at Cole.

"Gettin' a bit tired of folks getting' the drop on us," he remarked to his friend.

Cole scowled at the cornfield. "Well, Jesse, you wanted to be the leader." He winked at his chief and smiled. The twang in their ambusher's voice made it clear he wasn't anybody from up north. It was possible, of course, that they'd run into some Cajuns hired out as scouts to the Union or maybe a band of opportunistic bounty hunters, but both Cole and Jesse felt it was more likely they were being challenged by Confederate pickets.

Jesse flexed his arms, ripping open the seams on the sleeves of his coat. As the torn linen flopped against his side, his metal arms glistened in the sunlight. A few startled gasps sounded from behind the willows. "Lord above!" a shocked voice cried from the cornfield. "That thar's Jesse James!"

In the Union, Jesse was a feared gunfighter and robber, but to the folks of the Confederate Rebellion, he was something far different. He was a hero, a freedom fighter, a Rebel version of Robin Hood.

From out of the cornfield stepped a grizzled-looking man wearing a battered felt hat and the grubby remains of a gray shell jacket. Double bandoliers of ammunition crossed his chest and about his waist hung a massive hatchet with an ugly alligator-hide handle. The rebel's face was grimy with mud and dirt, strands of grass and weed poking out from his bristly black beard. One of his eyes was lazy, vacantly staring away to the left. The other squinted at Jesse, looking him over from head to toe.

"Thet gospel, mista?" the swampy asked, displaying a mouth of blackened teeth. "You'n heem, true an' true?"

Jesse returned the scout's stare. "I'm him," he told the sentry. Before the rebel could react, the outlaw's metal arms whipped to his holster and had both blasters drawn and pointed at his face.

Far from being terrified, the scout grinned and shouted in delight. "Tarnashun! We's got us the Jesse James!" The scout's excited cry was taken up by the other hidden rebels. In a mass they emerged from their hiding places, streaming toward Jesse, reaching trembling hands to shake his metal fingers. Cole watched the display of worshipful adoration with an expression that suggested he'd swallowed something foul. He made an effort to impress on the pickets that he was Cole Younger, but no one seemed interested.

It was Henderson who interrupted Jesse's moment with the rebels. "We've ridden a fair piece to get this far. Jesse wants to see President Lee. Wants to offer his services to the rebellion."

The grizzled swamp-rat seemed to be the man in charge. He squinted his good eye at Henderson, studying him with an almost open hostility. Jesse noticed the scout had a weird fetish hanging about his neck when the man reached up to it and crossed two fingers over it. Pressing the charm into his breast, the man turned his head and spat three times on the ground.

"Can't take ya'll nowheres," the swamp-rat said, stepping back a pace.

Even with his eyes covered by his tinted glasses, the severity of Henderson's gaze could be felt by the scout as the guerrilla leaned forward in his saddle. "Then you can take us to a higher authority who can conduct us where Jesse needs to go."

For a moment, it seemed the scout might offer up some protest. Many of the other rebels were looking at their commander with a puzzled expression, unable to account for his sudden fright. Jesse thought of Will Shaft and the gris-gris bag he sometimes held when he was around Henderson. As he glanced over at the Exoduster, he found that this was another of those times. The uneasiness in Will's face might be less, but it was certainly kindred to what gripped the swamp-rat.

When the tension in the air was almost tangible, the swamp-rat finally nodded. "Can take ya'll ter see the general," he decided. "He's the one in charge o' these here parts. It's rightly General Mosby's decision ter let ya'll pass through."

A flicker of amusement played on Henderson's gaunt visage. "So they made the 'Gray Ghost' a general, did they?" His words had just a trace of bitterness in them.

Jesse could appreciate Henderson's sentiment. During the war, his raiders had been regarded as nothing more than marauders by both sides. They were criminals that were useful to the Confederacy, but criminals just the same. Mosby had commanded a similar unit in Virginia, but his men had been esteemed as partisans and irregular cavalry by the Confederate generals. Colonel John S. Mosby had commanded rangers. Colonel William Quantrill was chief of a gang of raiders. It was a scornful distinction that still stung the Missourians who had ridden beneath the black flag.

"Take us to Mosby," Jesse told the scout. "When he hears what I aim to do, he'll make sure I see Lee."

*****

"Frank's much better thanks to you, Miss Lucy." There was a boyish, almost shy smile on John Younger's face as he spoke, his eyes not quite able to maintain contact with those of the nurse.

Lucinda Loveless felt embarrassed by the boy's display of gratitude and emotion. She'd taken on the mantle of a 'rebel angel,' and infiltrated the organization of Camp Lincoln with the intention of gaining a lead on Jesse James. It was in many ways a scheme hatched from her own ingenuity, something outside the provenance of the Pinkerton Agency. Her intention had been to pump Frank for any information that might give her an insight into his brother's future plans, hints as to his hideouts, details into how he operated; anything that might give her an edge in tracking down the outlaw. Helping Frank to recover from his illness had simply been a part of that plan.

As Loveless looked over at John, however, she knew that things had changed. By slow and insidious degrees, all the things she had seen in stark black and white, right and wrong, had become distorted and muddied into a great morass of gray. The quagmire of gray that rotted away within the palisades of Camp Lincoln had dissolved many of the beliefs and ideals she had held. If a place like this could be allowed to exist on the behest of the Union, if such suffering could be inflicted solely to prosecute vengeance upon the

Secessionists, then what moral justification did her government truly possess? She was reminded of the philosophical warning that maintained revenge was a disease that destroyed the perpetrator as much as the victim.

Loveless glanced across the rows of tattered tents and the muddy ground between them, at the bedraggled men who trudged through the muck to toil away in their miserable little fields. This was the fate that Pinkerton would have Jesse condemned to. She knew if they ever got their hands on Jesse alive, Pinkerton wouldn't be content for mere hanging. Jesse's numerous escapes, the brazen bravado of his escapades; these had become deeply personal to the chief of the Secret Service. The hate that had been building up inside him wouldn't be content merely to visit justice on Jesse. He'd need his revenge, just as the men who permitted Andersonville's prison to exist needed to slake their own thirst for blood.

It could only be a matter of time before Pinkerton or some other lawman decided to announce Frank's incarceration to the country. When they did that, they'd bait a trap Jesse was certain to ride into. Loveless didn't think the outlaw would risk trying to break into Camp Lincoln for John, but she knew nothing on earth could stop him if he knew his brother was here.

Motioning to John, Loveless made a quick withdrawal from the miserable file of sickly rebels she'd been ministering to. John followed her down a muddy track running between two rows of tents in a winding, circuitous route. Only when she felt certain nobody had followed them did she stop and address the boy.

"We have to get Frank out of here," Loveless told him. "He's not out of danger unless he's someplace more healthful than this place."

John almost laughed. "That'd sure be a nice trick, if'n you could pull it. Somehow I think them blue-bellies might take poorly to such a suggestion. In any case, the 'bots on them walls certainly wouldn't listen."

"I'll figure out a way," Loveless promised. Since deciding that Frank needed to be removed from Camp Lincoln, she'd been making a careful study of the camp's routine. Sooner or later, she'd figure out the most practicable way of getting him out. In the meantime, it was essential that Frank and John had the strength to make good any escape when it came. Reaching into her white blouse, she removed a small wooden box and handed it to John.

The boy outlaw flipped the box open, staring in bewilderment at the little pellets inside. They looked like little sausages made from sawdust. Loveless noted his confusion.

"Marchtack," she said, providing the pellets with their name. "The latest in industrial convenience. Each of those pellets has enough nutrition to provide a grown man with all the rations he needs for an entire day. It's the same as what the sentries posted here are issued."

John continued to stare at the unappetizing pellets. "Look like horse-pills," he declared.

"Just take them," Loveless said. "One for yourself and one for Frank. I'll steal more from the commissary as soon as I get a chance."

"You'd better steal some extra," a scratchy voice suddenly rose from between the tents. Loveless and John both spun around, startled by the interruption. They found themselves staring into the ugly face of a scraggly prisoner. Clenched in the man's fist was a jagged piece of wood, the end filed down into a crude point.

John glowered as he recognized the rogue. "Shouldn't you be somewheres tryin' to steal boots?"

The scavenger sneered. "Can't get much nourishment off'n boots. These here pellets though, they sound like they'd turn the trick." As the rogue moved to reach for Loveless, John stepped into his path. The scavenger scrambled back, glaring hatefully at the outlaw.

"Nobody harms an angel," John reminded the vulture.

A ratty gleam crept into the scraggly rebel's eyes. He glanced from Loveless to John. "Maybe I'll just have to forget the rules," he said. He made a feint for Loveless, then whipped around and brought his stick stabbing up at John's gut. "Or maybe I'll just take 'em from you."

John caught the scavenger's hand before he could stab him. A vicious twist snapped the rogue's wrist. The vulture flailed about, howling in agony. The scream rang out over the maze of tents. The satisfied expression on John's face collapsed as he looked out across the tents and saw the immense bulk of a Warder looming above them. The 'bot was turning about, doubtlessly ordered by whoever was commanding it to investigate the scream. He could see the machine's claw reaching out and pulling down tents as it forced a path through the camp.

"Get out of here!" John yelled at Loveless, thrusting the box of marchtack back into her hands.

Loveless hesitated. It offended her to leave John to the dubious mercy of the Union guards, but at the same time she knew there was nothing she could do. Revealing herself as a Pinkerton agent might defuse the immediate situation, but it would scuttle any plans for helping Frank and John escape.

The boy's next words decided her. "Go," he said. "Help Frank."

Resisting the urge to rush to John's aid, Loveless turned and retreated down the narrow track between the tents. Behind her, she could hear the harsh voice of a soldier demanding the submission of John and his foe. She could hear the angry growl of the Warder as its mechanized brawn forced the two combatants apart. A stab of pain shot through her heart as she heard screams and recognized one of them belonging to John.

When she gained the main path between the tents, Loveless crouched down and waited. After a few minutes, she saw a pair of Union soldiers step out onto the track, the gigantic Warder lumbering behind them. In their wake came a group of prisoners, the rebels laboring under the weight of two bloodied bodies: John and the scavenger he'd been fighting. At first glance, she thought the men must be dead, but then she heard a soft groan rise from the scavenger and saw John move one of his arms.

"What'll we do with 'em?" one of the guards asked his comrade.

"The dispensary is already full," the other said. "Besides, the way the 'bot handled them, they won't be fit to work for quite a spell."

"So what do we do with 'em?" the first soldier persisted.

Even from a distance, Loveless couldn't mistake the grim humor underlying the response from the other soldier. "They're still breathin'," he said. "So why don't we take 'em to the surgery. Tumblety is always need'n fresh materials."

Loveless suppressed a shudder as she watched the soldiers march off toward the compound, the entourage of prisoners they'd impressed to carry the wounded men following after them. Tumblety? Since coming to Andersonville she'd heard too many ugly rumors about what went on behind the locked doors and closed windows of his surgery. John Younger was little more than a boy. To think of him being subjected to the mad doctor's experiments was too awful to contemplate.

She waited until the soldiers were out of sight before making her way back through the tents. Loveless knew she'd have to tell Frank what had happened. Someone had to know where John had gone. After that, she'd have to turn her energies to two important tasks: finding a way out of Camp Lincoln and finding a way into Tumblety's lab.

Chapter 16

General Mosby's headquarters was situated in the partially burnt-out ruin of a plantation house. The old antebellum finery had been defiled by the filth of war. Gabled roofs had been torn by artillery shells, marble floors cracked and irreparably scarred by tromping boots and heavy machinery, Greek columns scorched and blackened by the heat of blaster beams, and the white facade smirched and made dingy by the dust of marching men and the smoke of battle.

The Gray Ghost remained a dashingly handsome figure, his looks as fine and remarkable as they had been during the War through the strange, preservative power of the RJ. His gray uniform was immaculate, tailored to accommodate a lean frame just beginning to trade the musculature of youth for the fat of middle-age. Several medals gleamed on his chest, and about his neck dangled the diamond Dixie Sun, the highest honor the Confederate Rebellion could bestow upon one of its soldiers. The bright feathers of a peacock protruded from the side of Mosby's hat as he entered the old ballroom that now served him as a command center, and a wide-bladed sword with a curious mechanical hilt was scabbarded at his side. When he saw his visitors, Mosby smiled and doffed his hat in a sweeping bow.

"The renowned Jesse James," Mosby said. "If something isn't done, your legend is going to eclipse my own." The general laughed and unbuckled his sword belt. A gray-uniformed aide scrambled forward to relieve his commander of both the weapon and the hat. Mosby glanced over the other men with Jesse. Most of the gang had remained outside, but both Cole Younger and Allen Henderson had insisted on accompanying their leader to this meeting. Mosby's gaze didn't linger on Cole, but when he stared at Henderson, his smile faltered. "I heard you died in the war, Henderson."

Henderson's voice was as cheery as a breeze blowing across an open grave. "Did you hear that, or hope it?" He shook his head. "Doesn't matter. What does is that I'm back."

Mosby nodded. "There's some that would celebrate your return. And there's a damn sight more who'd like to hear that I hanged you."

"That'd inconvenience me considerable, General," Jesse said. "Mr. Henderson used to represent an old friend and what's more, he has crucial information. Information that could be of great benefit to the Confederacy."

"The man has no recognized military rank," Mosby continued to scowl at Henderson's pallid face and darkened glasses. "He didn't earn any rank in the war and he damn sure hasn't earned any since."

The shadowy figure's face spread in a menacing grin. "I've earned more than anyone you know, General."

"He's spent the years since the war in Camp Lincoln," Cole explained, trying to cut the mounting tension emanating from the two officers. "Henderson's the only man to ever break out of that place."

The news seemed to shock Mosby even more than the ghastly resurrection of Henderson had. "Impossible. We've been trying for years to slip spies into Camp Lincoln, trying every trick in the book to sabotage that place and free our men. The place is an impregnable fortress.

Mosby turned and gestured to the sprawl of his command center. The old ballroom had been transformed by the demands of military intelligence into a tangle of desks and tables, each lorded over by a clerical-looking officer and littered with a chaotic profusion of reports. The walls were papered over in immense maps depicting not only the contested banks of the Mississippi, but also the rest of the Confederate Rebellion's frontier. A few harried-looking soldiers repositioned markers indicating both friendly and enemy units on the maps as reports came in, employing curious mechanized claws fitted to steel poles to move those markers too high to reach by hand.

The most arresting feature, at least to Jesse and Cole, was the corner of the command center given over to a vast array of machinery. Carpets of wire dripped away from the machines, snaking along the floor before vanishing into a trapdoor. More wire crawled up to the ceiling and then arched its way through a hole gouged into the wall to affix themselves into the base of what looked like a copper flagpole bolted to the side of the mansion. Each of the machines was fronted by a crazed array of glass tubes and crystal spheres. A soldier was seated before each machine, connected to it by a strange helmet that fitted down over his ears and which had wires slithering back into the face of the machine. A secondary apparatus, like a curved length of bull's horn, was clenched in each soldier's hand. Jesse could see them frequently raise the devices to their mouths and shout into them. A small mob of pages waited behind the banks of machines, hurrying to relay written messages from the helmeted soldiers to the officers behind the desks.

"An invention of a man named Bell," Mosby explained to Jesse when he noted the outlaw's fascination. "With these machines we can instantly communicate with stations all across the Confederacy. Something like the vocal reiterators our enemies use, but far quicker and more efficient. It isn't muddled written messages that we receive or transmit. This is even more advanced than the vocal reiterators. We send and hear the voices of the men at each end of the line clear as a bell."

Cole smiled and shook his head. "A fancy contraption, but you'll understand if'n I'm none too keen on seein' it passed along. Invention like that'd be pure murder on our profession. Sheriff in one town tells the law around him to be 'spectin' us in their area after we pull a job..."

"Where'd you get these machines?" Jesse interrupted. His metal hands clenched into fists at his sides. Before he even heard it, he felt he knew what the general was going to say.

"Carpathian," Mosby said. "The Enlightened have been most sympathetic with the aims of the Confederacy. They've supplied us with a lot of weapons and material, much of it on credit to be paid after cessation of hostilities. It's the same exact thing that Washington is using to keep tabs on the rest of the Union. This system is so rare, that we believe to have the only other one like this in existence. What more, from what Carpathian told us, it was very time consuming and expensive to create."

Jesse turned away from the machines, fixing Mosby with a reproachful look. "You should be careful about taking things on credit," he said as he again flexed his steel hands. "There's always a price to pay and sometimes it's more than you reckoned."

"The South doesn't have the luxury of picking her friends," Mosby answered, a hint of annoyance in his voice. "Carpathian, the Indians, the Europeans, we'll take whatever help we can get from wherever we can get it! The Yankee factories turn out more guns and vehicles in three days than ours can in a month. If they weren't too busy worrying about the Warrior Nation and the Enlightened, they could come down here and squash us like a bug! We're fighting for our survival, Jesse, and we'll do anything – anything – for that right to live and be let alone."

Henderson's dry chuckle hissed through the command center. "As you said, General, the South needs help and can't afford to be choosy about picking her friends. We've come here to offer you help." He pointed a gloved finger at Jesse. "He's got a plan to bust into Camp Lincoln and free all the prisoners. It's a good plan. It's a plan that will work. But he needs the resources to pull it off. He needs men, weapons, and transport."

"I've seen that place," Mosby said, shaking his head.

"I've been in that place," Henderson countered. "I say Jesse's plan can work. Certainly it's a gamble, but the stakes are ten thousand rebel soldiers." Again, the black-clad guerrilla laughed. "A couple of thousand rebs and the chance to jab a finger in the Yankee eagle's eye."

Jesse stepped toward one of the big maps on the wall. He waved one of his hands toward the region depicting Andersonville and Camp Lincoln. The Yankees had chosen the camp not only for its notoriety during the war but also for its proximity to fresh supplies of unrepentant Secessionists. That meant, however, that they were also close to the ever-shifting Confederate frontier. "A quick, bold strike, General," he jabbed a steel finger at the map. "A raid just like the old days. We strike, do what we need to do, and then fade back across the border."

Mosby pointed at the marks on the map indicating Union forts and outposts. "The Yankees have an entire army scattered about that area. Any effort against Andersonville and they'll turn out every one of their soldiers. They'll lock down that border so tight a coon couldn't sneak across it."

"If the Yankees had something else to occupy them, a distraction to tie them down while we were liberating the prison, it could be done," Jesse said.

"You mean a general advance? Make a feint toward their lines and hope it keeps them pinned down." Mosby frowned. "Not sure if that would turn the trick. What I do know is that it'll need authorization bigger than anything I've got to make an attack happen."

"We came here to speak with President Lee in any event," Henderson said. "Having this palaver with you has just been whistling in the wind."

"What our associate means is we're anxious to lay this plan out before President Lee," Cole said, again trying to break the tension Henderson's lack of civility threatened to cultivate.

"I know what Henderson's meaning is," Mosby said. "It doesn't change things. In good conscience I can't send notorious outlaws – even if they have been attacking our enemy – deeper into Confederate territory with a pass to see our president."

Jesse slammed one of his hands against a desk, splintering the wood. "General, them men in Camp Lincoln need help! They can't just be abandoned!"

Mosby sighed and started toward the communication machines. "I can't send you along to President Lee, but I can fix it so you can talk to him," he said, his expression became grim. "I can't promise what he'll say. All I can do is arrange so you can ask him yourselves."

"That's fine, General," Henderson said. "Once Lee has heard Jesse's plan, there's no question that he'll know it's the right thing to do."

*****

General Mosby turned away from the advanced reiterator, as he called it, removing the wired helmet from his head and replacing the horn-like vocalizer into its cradle at the top of the machine. He faced the waiting Jesse, nodding to the outlaw. "I've been placed into contact with President Lee. I'll allow you to make your case to him personally."

With some hesitation, Jesse approached the bulky machine. He could see the crimson glow of the RJ disks behind the grill-work vents at the front of the machine. It was a stark reminder that this 'telephone', like the mechanical arms fixed to his body, was an invention of Dr. Carpathian's enclave of scientists. He was anxious about speaking into the device. After the experience with his arms, he wondered what other treachery Carpathian might have installed in his other inventions. Would the machine somehow recognize the voice of an enemy and explode? Would it transmit some electrical shock into his body?

Jesse shook his head. With John rotting away in that Union hell-hole, his own fears and anxieties weren't something he could afford. He had to get him out, had to get all of the imprisoned rebels out. If he had to die in doing it, well, that was just a risk he had to accept.

Removing his hat, Jesse took the helmet from Mosby and lowered it over his head. A Confederate technician helped him adjust the leather straps that would secure the helmet. He could feel the cold metal funnels fitted on the inside of the helmet slip over his ears.

The next instant, Jesse's eyes went wide with surprise. He wasn't sure what he'd expected from the telephone. Some acoustic clicking and buzzing that vaguely sounded like words, maybe a buzzing drone like the whine of an Iron Horse, perhaps even the mechanistic growl of a recharging blaster. The last thing he expected was to hear a distinct voice, much less the precise inflections of a deep and cultured speaker.

"Hello, Mr. James," the voice said. "Are you receiving me? This is President Robert E. Lee of the Confederate Rebellion."

Jesse's hand closed around the speaking horn when Mosby passed it over to him. It took the outlaw a moment to overcome his surprise and lift the tube to his mouth. "It is an honor to speak with you, Mr. President," he said.

"I fear that honor is of less consequence than necessity," Lee replied. "General Mosby has told me something about your intention to strike the Union prison camp at Andersonville."

"We intend to raid it in the same manner as we did Lawrence during the war," Jesse said. "I've Cole and Jim Younger along with a few other raiders to ensure the attack goes like it should. More, I've got Mr. Henderson to smooth out the plan and work out the logistics. All we need is some men, weapons, and transport. If you can give us that, then I can free every man-jack the Yankees have got locked up in there."

Even over the electrical apparatus, the gravity of Lee's voice was conveyed to Jesse. "I sympathize with your ambition and your enthusiasm, son, but we just can't afford such a scheme right now. It's too reckless and too antagonistic. The Confederate Rebellion is a fragile thing, still reeling from losing the War. The Warrior Nation uprisings out west and the territorial expansion of Carpathian's Enlightened have forced the Yankees to deal with other enemies, but don't make the mistake of thinking they've forgotten about us. Don't think that Washington is prepared to 'live and let live.' No, what they want is complete restoration of the Union and the Devil take what anybody else says about it. We've been given a reprieve, a stay of execution, but they haven't torn down the gallows. If we give them enough reason, the Union will turn its troops loose on us."

Jesse's hand tightened about the speaking tube, his metal fingers denting the device. "Mr. President, there's upwards of ten thousand of our people starvin' and dyin' in that place. You can't tell me you'd sit aside and let 'em suffer."

"What I am saying, Mr. James, is that the Confederacy can't afford to start a fight just now." A ragged sigh came across the wire as the rebel president weighed his conscience against the reality of his movement's situation. "We're just now starting to pick ourselves up. Carpathian's men have helped us build great factories to turn out the armaments and machines we'll need to fight the Yankees. The Europeans are sending us supplies through hidden harbors along the old Florida coast. We've formed compacts with the natives, and there are bands of Warrior Nation members that stand with us." Lee's voice became strained. "We're gathering our strength. Five more years and we might be able to match the Yankees, but we can't do it now."

"Then you won't help us?" Jesse demanded.

"What I'm saying is that I can't help you," Lee answered. "My political responsibilities won't allow me to condone such an attack, however much I sympathize with its aims."

Jesse's hand clenched tighter, cracking the casing of the speaking horn. "I'm glad I don't have any responsibilities to make me a coward," he growled in disgust. He didn't wait to hear whatever response Lee might make. Reaching up, he snapped the straps holding the helmet to his head. Frustrated, he threw both the speaking tube and the helmet to the floor.

"I warned you what to expect," Mosby said as Jesse stormed away from the telephone banks.

Jesse paused, turning around slowly. His eyes fairly blazed with outraged fury. "Yes, you did," he said. "I just didn't believe the South was so yellow as you made it out to be." Without another word, Jesse marched from Mosby's headquarters, brushing past the startled sentries who moved to intercept him. A gesture from Mosby sent the guards back.

"There goes a most unhappy man," Henderson said as he turned to Cole. "You might want to rein him in a bit. We're already fighting the Yankees, we don't need to be fighting the rebels too." Cole didn't need to be told twice. Pausing only to recover Jesse's hat from the telephone technician, the bushwhacker hurried after his departed leader.

"Jesse has no reason to worry," Mosby told Henderson. "I might not be able to help him, but I'm not going to stop him."

Henderson's raspy chuckle wheezed across his bloodless lips. "Stop him? After this, nothing will stop him! You and Lee have lit a fire in Jesse James today. You told him that something he knows is right can't be done. That's a challenge he won't let alone. He's going to bust up that prison without your help."

Mosby shook his head. "That's insane," he declared. "He'll just get himself killed and everyone who follows him."

Henderson adjusted his glasses as he turned away from his old rival. "He might at that," the guerrilla conceded. "But at least he'll die on his feet, not crawling around a swamp on his belly. Good day, General."

*****

Jesse marched away from the mansion, making straight for the orchard where his gang had parked their 'Horses and were now lounging in the shade waiting for their leader's return. He didn't know how he was going to break the news to them. After building up their hopes so high, after encouraging them with grand plans of getting the support of the Confederate Rebellion, Jesse didn't know how he was going to tell them it wasn't going to happen. He didn't know how he could tell them that the rebels were too timid to strike back at the Yankees in a meaningful way. He didn't know how he could tell them that the Confederacy was willing to sit aside and let all those men rot away in Andersonville's prison.

Cole hurried down the broad stairway at the front of the mansion, trying to catch up with his leader. "Jesse," he hissed in a low tone as he reached out to catch the outlaw's shoulder. Jesse spun around at the first touch of Cole's fingers, his eyes just as intense and enraged as when he'd thrown down the telephone equipment. "Don't do anything crazy, Jesse. Even if'n they got a yellow streak, these're still our people."

"They ain't our people," Jesse admonished Cole, his eyes staring past the bushwhacker and up at the red and blue battle flag flying above the mansion. "Anybody'd let good soldiers rot in a place like Camp Lincoln ain't folk I'm keen to claim kinship with."

"Damnation, Jesse!" Cole cursed. "Don't you think this has me riled too? It's my brother the blue-bellies got in there. Don't you think I'm even hotter'n you are to bust him out?"

The pain in Cole's tone touched Jesse and defused some of the rage he was feeling. The responsibility and obligation that drove Jesse so hard could be distilled into his guilt over John Younger's capture. For all the lofty ideas Henderson had stirred up in his mind, at the very core it was still the plight of John that made the raid so vital and imperative to Jesse. How much worse it must be for Cole and the other Youngers, he couldn't even begin to imagine. If it was Frank in there, Jesse knew the worry and fear for his brother would drive him crazy.

"We'll get him out," Jesse vowed. He shook his metal fist at the Confederate battle flag hanging over the mansion. "We'll get them all out and to the Devil with what Lee wants."

Cole shook his head. "Fine words, Jesse, but how're we gonna turn it?"

"I'll think of somethin'," Jesse said as he turned and stalked off toward the orchard and his men. He was eager to be quit of Mosby's encampment. He wasn't afraid the rebels would try to hold the gang; it was more the feelings of despair and betrayal that he felt growing in his heart. Once he was away from the rebel headquarters, Jesse would be able to think more clearly. He'd be able to plan out his next move better.

As they approached the orchard, Jesse was met by John Wesley Hardin. The Texan gunfight caressed the grips of his smokers as he stepped out from the trees, an oily smile shaping on his face as he saw Jesse's metal hands drop to his own holsters.

"I didn't mean to scare you, chief," Hardin apologized, though the smirk on his face said otherwise. He nodded his head back toward the orchard. "No need to tell the boys that the rebs ain't gonna help us none. They've already heard."

Jesse glowered at Hardin. "Who told 'em?"

Hardin bristled at the demanding tone, but a glance at Jesse's mechanical arms convinced him not to press the issue. "One of them darkies of yourn went pokin' his nose around. Tryin' to steal supplies most like. Anyway, he was caught and frog-marched back to us. The soldiers who brought him back laughed when they heard about yer plans." The gunfighter nodded his head back at the trees. "They sent back their officer to talk some sense to you when you got back from yer palaver with the president."

Jesse stalked past Hardin, marching quickly through the orchard to where his gang was gathered. He felt a sudden rush of fury when he saw Will Shaft tending one of the other Exodusters. The black outlaw had been badly beaten, his face swollen until it looked like one big bruise. It took him a moment to understand why the sight upset him so. After all, he'd seen slaves beaten far worse when he was a child. The difference, he realized, was that he knew better now. The Exoduster wasn't some slave, some piece of property to be pampered or abused as the owner saw fit. He was a free man and he'd followed Jesse by his own choice, not because somebody had ordered him to do so.

The outlaw chief rounded on a gray-uniformed man leaning against an orange tree and talking with Jim Younger. By the shoulder boards and the braiding, Jesse knew the officer was a Confederate captain.

"Your men do that?" Jesse growled at the officer, pointing a steel finger at the injured Exoduster.

Jim turned toward his leader. "This is Captain Rufus Henry Ingram of the California Rangers," he said, introducing the officer.

"I don't care a damn who he is," Jesse snapped. "What I want to know is have his men been beatin' one of mine?"

Ingram was a stocky, heavyset man, a thick beard covering much of his face. He bore the burn-mark of a blaster across his forehead, leaving a deep furrow between brow and scalp. He had a bulky saber, the same design as Mosby's, dangling from his belt, and keeping it company were a brace of blasters with alligator-hide grips. Each of the pistols had ugly tally-marks etched across the scaly hide. The captain's face had a villainous, thuggish quality about it, reminding Jesse of Mexican bandits he'd seen in Robbers Roost. As he stepped forward, Ingram removed the wide-brimmed cavalry hat he wore, sketching the briefest bow to the outlaw.

"Weren't my boys. We plucked your man out from a tangle of swamp-rats all set to string 'im up." The ranger smiled, an expression that only served to make his face even more cruel and murderous. "Some of these Southerners ain't got so good a sense of perspective. Think it's still like the old days of Mason-Dixon and all that." He shrugged his broad shoulders. "Me an' most of mine are Californians. We ain't got so many notions about where a man's color puts him on the totem pole."

"What do you care about?" Cole wondered.

Ingram laughed. "Gold and glory," he said. "That's what moved us to take up the cause during the war. That's what keeps us fightin' now." He shifted his gaze back to Jesse, his voice dropping into a whisper. "Only there ain't been much of neither. Not with the way Lee wants everybody to pussy-foot around the blue-bellies. I reckon we've about hit the point where we need to be movin' on."

"You're offerin' to ride with us?" Jesse asked. "You'd join the raid on Andersonville?"

"Help free ten thousand rebels?" Ingram laughed again. "Tarnation, can you even dream o' greater glory than that?! Hellfire, we'll be laid out in the history books after that, like old King Henry strickin' it to the froggies!"

"How many are you?" Jesse asked.

"Twenty seven," Ingram said. "Born bastards, each of them. We fought our way across a continent to help the cause. You won't find harder fighters than my rangers. What's more, every man in my command has his own arms and his own 'Horse."

Cole scowled. "We'd still be too few to make it work," he cautioned Jesse.

"We'll make it work," Jesse said. He took a step toward Ingram. "Shakin' hands with me ain't so pleasant since I got these," he said, waving his mechanical arms, "but I'd be obliged if'n you'd give me your word that you'll abide by my decisions an' take orders from Cole and Mr. Henderson."

Ingram nodded, replacing his hat on his head. "I'm lookin' to make my name and my fortune, not saddle myself with the obligations of command. You can keep that if you want it and be welcome to it. My rangers are all the men I can handle."

Jesse smiled at the Californian. "Let's just hope they're more than the Yankees can handle."

*****

Lucinda Loveless shook her head as she listened to the muffled groans coming from the gagged woman lying on the floor of the nurses' barracks. Rummaging about in the bottom of the wardrobe, she produced another stocking and started winding it around the bound nurse's face. The fashion in which she'd been hogtied allowed the woman only the feeblest movement as she tried to struggle against the Pinkerton operative.

"Trust me, this is for your own good," Loveless told her. She cocked her head, listening for any noise. To ensure her captive wasn't playing it smart, she reached down and tweaked her ear. While the nurse's body quivered in pain, no undue noise escaped her gag. Satisfied, Loveless dragged her prisoner across the room and stuffed her into one of the closets. Almost as soon as the captive was hidden away, the sound of tromping boots reached her. Hurriedly, she moved back across the room, sitting herself at the edge of her prisoner's bed and adopting the anxious expression befitting the role she had chosen to appropriate for herself.

The nurse she'd ambushed had been selected by the camp commandant to attend Dr. Tumblety in his surgery. It was common knowledge in the camp that the assignment was a demanding one and that any nurse who failed to measure up was quickly dismissed and summarily removed from Andersonville, removed with such dispatch that their belongings were bundled up and shipped out days after the women had been sent away.

Loveless felt a cold determination course through her. The enigmatic and reclusive Tumblety would have a different experience when it came to her. She was determined on that point.

Once the guards came into the barracks, the sergeant sent to escort her to the surgery began to address her. Loveless, playing the role of an agitated nurse fearful for her position, shook her head and slowly rose from the bed. She smoothed the front of her white uniform, and then followed the sergeant out.

Tumblety's surgery was on the far side of the fenced compound at the center of Camp Lincoln. Loveless had been impressed by the amount of security that had been afforded to the building. It was guarded better than the armory and the supply shed, better even than the commandant's house. As the sergeant led her toward the entrance, the metallic bulk of a UR-25 Warder lumbered out from the doorway, its optics glowing in the thickening darkness. The robot started to raise the blaster built into its arm. Only the magnetized identity disk the sergeant carried stemmed the automaton's aggression. The Warder shuffled aside, making way for the sergeant and his charge.

"The doctor's waiting for you," the soldier said as he thrust a pair of keys into the mechanical locks barring the door. Loveless noticed with both surprise and alarm that the steel beams that held the door fast were bolted on the outside of the door. For the first time she wondered if all the security around Tumblety's surgery was in place to keep people out or to keep something in.

The guard didn't follow her inside. Once Loveless was across the threshold, he hurriedly closed the door. She could hear the bolts locking fast behind her as the sergeant turned his keys. Getting John out of the surgery, it seemed, wasn't going to be as easy as she'd imagined.

Loveless took in the white, sterile dimensions of the ward at a glance. She could see the marks of recent damage, the ugly stains marring the specimen shelves across the room and the vacancies among those same shelves. Plaster patches had been slapped across several of the walls and there was a strange steel disc embedded in the ceiling.

At the sound of her shoes clattering across the tile floor, a tall man dressed in evening clothes rose from behind a desk. He squinted at her from behind a pair of spectacles, then smiled and brushed his fingers across the enormous moustache he wore. Setting down the anatomy book he had been perusing, Dr. Tumblety approached Loveless.

"Colonel Custer said that you required an assistant to help you in your work," Loveless told the experimenter.

Tumblety hesitated, stroking his moustache for a moment as he considered Loveless's words. Finally, he nodded. "Yes," he said. "You will be able to help me in my work. I've been under terrible stress. You will be able to relieve that affliction."

Loveless felt her skin crawl as Tumblety's eyes roved up and down her body. She must have betrayed some sign of her revulsion because the scientist was quick to make a placating gesture with his left hand.

"Oh, no. No, you mustn't misunderstand me," Tumblety said. "I have no lascivious designs upon your body. Such base vileness is beneath a man of my genius. Science is my passion! Knowledge is my lust! Invention is my purpose!"

With each exclamation, Tumblety drew closer to Loveless. She found herself backing away from him, something instinctive deep inside her recoiling before this ridiculous-looking man. When the doctor's right hand came whipping out from behind his back, the gleam of steel shone in the electric glow of the ward's lights. Like a striking cobra, Tumblety drove his blade at Loveless's throat.

Fast as the murderer was, Loveless was faster. She caught Tumblety's hand by the wrist, giving it such a savage wrench that the knife was sent flying from his numbed fingers. The twist forced the scientist's entire body into a downward sprawl, spilling him onto the floor. All the civility and pretense of a moment before was gone now. The prostrate experimenter cursed and howled, a continuous stream of profanity spilling across his lips. Keeping his arm in a firm hold, Loveless planted her foot between Tumblety's shoulders and pressed him firmly against the floor.

"You're strong enough to slip my hold," Loveless told Tumblety, "but you must know anatomy well enough to realize you'll break your own arm doing it. Now, quiet down and be a good boy."

The reprimand only incensed Tumblety further. Despite the threat, he started to force his body up from the floor. Grabbing hold of his finger, Loveless gave it a vicious twist, breaking it like an old chicken bone. The scientist wailed in pain, his effort to break free collapsing into a fit of sobbing moans.

Feeling she was safe from immediate attack, Loveless released Tumblety's arm and quickly lifted the hem of her skirt. Sight of her exposed legs drove the pain from the experimenter's mind. Snarling like an animal, Tumblety lunged at her, tackling her to the floor. All humanity was gone from the scientist's face as he glared down at her.

"Jack'll do for you, whore," Tumblety hissed, spittle flying from his gnashing teeth.

"Whore's charge for it," Loveless snarled back. "This one's free." She brought her hand swinging up, the hand that had drawn the derringer from the holster fastened to her garter belt. The gun cracked against the side of Tumblety's head, gashing his scalp and sending the madman sprawling. Loveless kicked the stunned experimenter's body away, freeing herself of his noxious weight. Scrambling back to her feet, she aimed her derringer at the lunatic.

"Two choices, Doctor," she told him. "You can take me to John Younger or I can blast your brains out." She put the toe of her shoe into his ribs, knocking him onto his back. Tumblety's face turned pale when he saw the large-bore derringer in her fist. It was a compact model designed expressly for the Pinkerton agency, capable of the same destructive power as a full-sized blaster, though limited to a two shot capacity and severely reduced range. Either consideration wouldn't be a problem for Loveless to make good her threat. If she opened fire, all that would be left of Tumblety's head would be a plume of smoke.

"Don't shoot," Tumblety begged, raising his hands and holding them out to his sides. "I'll take you to him. He's only been here a few days."

"Where is he?" Loveless demanded, aiming the derringer at Tumblety's face.

The experimenter craned his head, glancing toward the vivisection theaters. Each station was separated by a white curtain, concealing whatever lay behind them.

Loveless kicked Tumblety again. "Get up," she ordered. "And no tricks."

Awkwardly, Tumblety picked himself off the floor. He dabbed a handkerchief at his bleeding scalp, grimacing at the sight of his own blood. "You've cut me, you filthy strumpet!"

"I'll do worse," Loveless promised. 'Take me to John."

Grumbling, Tumblety led his captor across the ward to the furthest of the vivisection theaters. With a showman-like flourish, he drew back the curtain.

Loveless blanched at what she saw lying on the operating table. It took her a moment to recognize the features of the rebel scavenger who'd attacked them. What had been done to his body was beyond description, flesh peeled away to expose the raw musculature and organs, limbs amputated and weird copper plugs stapled into the stumps. An array of bottles was suspended above the carcass on a spider-web framework, little tubes conveying a constant drip of chemicals into the body.

"I fear I was unable to help that one," Tumblety said. "But I was much more successful with your friend." He gestured toward a curtained alcove at the back of the theater.

Keeping her gun trained on Tumblety, Loveless walked over to the alcove. She ripped down the curtain in a single tug. Instantly she wished she hadn't.

True to Tumblety's words, John was there. What had been done to him was more obscene than the dead scavenger the experimenter had termed one of his failures. John's body was swollen with muscle, patches of skin and flesh stitched to his body to accommodate the extra mass. A third arm protruded from the middle of his chest, sutures and staples surrounding the place where the shoulder merged with breastbone. New legs were sewn to his pelvis, again without any concession to symmetry or conformity, one leg appreciably longer than its opposite. Hoses and pipes ran from bottles of chemicals into the monstrosity and about the whole there was a foul stink not unlike that of an embalmer's studio.

While she gawked in horror at this thing, this obscenity that had been John Younger, Loveless momentarily forgot Tumblety. The scientist scurried behind a cart of surgical tools and then shouted at the creature his madness had made. "Disarm her!"

Distracted by the madman's cry, Loveless didn't react quickly enough when John's misshapen bulk lurched into life. The ghastly arm protruding from his chest smashed down with tremendous force, nearly breaking her hand as the derringer was knocked from her grip. The monster's other arms caught her at waist and shoulder, holding her fast as Tumblety emerged from his refuge.

"What do you think of my lovely Reconstructed?" Tumblety asked, grinning as he stalked toward the captive woman. "A marvelous discovery that will advance medicine by an order of magnitude not seen since... well... since forever."

"It's monstrous!" Loveless snarled at him, struggling to pull free from John's iron-like grip. "It's insane!"

Tumblety shook his head. "All genius is called 'insane' by those too stupid to understand. But I am too magnanimous to hold a grudge. I shall help the world, even if they don't want my help." He leaned down and recovered Loveless's gun from the floor.

"I'm a Pinkerton agent," Loveless warned him as she watched him study the weapon.

Tumblety stuffed the derringer into his pocket. "That might be true," he said. "But who knows you are? Just you and me and John. And none of us are going to say anything." He shook his head. "Things would have been so much simpler if you had co-operated. Now, I fear, it will go harder on you. So very much harder. I'll have to take my time with you now. Nothing quick. Nothing simple."

Tumblety pointed to the specimen racks across the ward. "As you may have noticed, I had an accident and part of my collection was ruined. We'll have to see how much of what I'm missing you will be able to replace."

Chapter 17

The Richmond Terminal Company had gained control over the old railways in what had been Georgia, an aspect of the Union's reconstruction efforts to consolidate the infrastructure of the vanquished South into the hands of a few Northern companies and 'right-minded' Southern establishments. At great expense, the Richmond Terminal Company, imported hundreds of miles of new rail to repair pathways that had been willfully heated and twisted by the invading army as part of Sherman's scorched earth policy. In many places, the malformed knots of iron, grimly termed 'Sherman's neckties,' still lay beside the fresh track, slowly rusting in the humid Georgian climate.

Sherman's intention had been to wreck the track and make it completely unusable to the Confederacy. The neckties of iron were an almost total loss to a mineral-poor nation. It was bitterly ironic that these mementos of the Confederate defeat should now repose beside the newly-constructed symbol of Yankee occupation.

It was still more ironic that these mangled knots should now be put to good purpose by a new breed of rebel. Jesse James admired the scheme Cole Younger and Captain Ingram had hatched between them. Chaining Sherman's neckties to the backs of their Iron Horses, the outlaws could speedily drag the things onto the fresh track. One or two of the knots might be easily brushed aside by a train, but with each 'Horse able to drag a pair of the twisted rails up onto the track, the combined mass would stop the RJ-powered locomotive cold.

It was like the first big heist all over again. Jesse felt a wave of nostalgia wash over him as he thought about the effect that the neckties would have. Well over fifteen years ago, he had sat with an agitated Cole and his brother Frank, as they blew-up the Union train carrying Yankee technology. That heist gave the outlaw parties the technology that they all desperately needed to keep up with the Yankee bastards. Now, here they were again, without Frank, and a lot less of their gang, but it still sent shivers down Jesse's back as he remembered the feel of success from all those years ago.

From the shadows of a stand of willows, Jesse and Allen Henderson looked over the site they had chosen for their ambush. The old guerrilla was particularly happy with the way the track turned at a sharp angle to avoid a rocky slope. The railway company had been lax in allowing the trees to grow so close to the tracks; Jesse thought they would have learned to be more careful with their trains after what he had done. When the train came to the turn, the engineers would have no warning of what lay around the bend until they were right on top of it. The location seemed purposely made for an ambush.

"You'll have to move fast," Henderson reminded Jesse. "I'm sure you remember that the Yankees make it a habit to send a stalking horse ahead of the main engine. You have to let the bait slip through before making any move to catch the real prize."

Jesse frowned, shaking his head. "Yeah, I remember. Still disgusts me that they let the boys in the front stick their head in the noose while the train is left free to skedaddle." He turned and posed a question to Captain Ingram. The Californian's rangers had scouted this area many times on behalf of General Mosby and had more than a passing familiarity with how the Yankees moved supplies through the region. "You're certain about the disposition of guards?"

Captain Ingram ran a finger along the scar across his forehead. "I've been close enough to hear 'em holler," he said. "You can expect ten troopers and a half-dozen 'bots in the Malediction they have running out front. That engine'll have ten inch armor plate all about and enough repeatin' blasters to cut down a forest. If the blue-bellies get that thing rollin' back on us, we're through."

"They won't," Jesse promised with a smile. "You can say that I'm familiar with how to get this part of the job done." He looked over at Will Shaft. Of all the men with him, the Exoduster was the man most familiar with deploying explosives. It was only natural for a man who'd once been a slave in a rock quarry and 'entrusted' with the hazardous job of setting demolition charges to become an expert at handling the stuff.

"I won't let you down, Jesse," Will promised. "That stalking horse won't be comin' back after it passes by."

The Exoduster's vow brought a sneer onto John Wesley Hardin's face. The gunfighter slapped his hand against one of his smokers. "See to it, boy, or I'll tell you right now you'll burn like a pig if'n you betray us."

It took Jesse only six steps to be standing in front of Hardin. His mechanical arm whipped out, cracking across Hardin's face and knocking him from the saddle of his 'Horse. The gunfighter landed in a sprawl. He spit out a broken tooth and then drew his smoker from its holster. Before he could take aim, Cole kicked the weapon out of his hand.

"Damn Free-Soiler!" Hardin cursed at Jesse. "Takin' up for that no good horse thief!"

"Hardin, right now you should be thankful I showed some restraint," Jesse growled down at the Texan. "Otherwise we'd be kicking the bushes lookin' for your head. Will's here to fight the Union, same as any of us. You can't appreciate that, it's all the same to me. But you damn sure are gonna keep them notions to yerself." He turned his eyes across the rest of his gang and the rangers. "Same applies to everyone else. Don't make no nevermind what a man was afore, you're all ridin' with the James Gang now. Pull your weight, and I don't give a hoot in hell what color yer skin is. All that matters is you do yer job."

Wiping the blood from his lip, a sullen Hardin recovered his smoker and stuffed it back into its holster. He glared at Jesse, but his temper had cooled enough to appreciate that there was no way he'd be able to outdraw those quick-devil arms. Chastened, he climbed back into the saddle of his 'Horse.

The distant toot of a steam whistle roused the gang back to the present. One of the Exodusters had staged himself further down the line with a few head of cattle that the rangers had rustled. Positioning the animals on the tracks, he'd wait for the Malediction to come right up to him and blast its whistle to scare the animals out of its way. That would be the signal to the waiting outlaws that their prey was drawing near.

Jesse hurried back to his own steed. He glanced to his left, watching as Ingram's rangers formed up with a precision and discipline that belied their commander's claims about them being merely marauding brigands. Jesse's gang mustered with commendable speed but with a deal less polish. It was something that nagged at his pride and he resolved that once the Andersonville raid was over, he'd be making some changes about what it took to become a member of the James Gang and what was expected of a man once he was in.

Meeting Henderson again had impressed on Jesse the difference between acting like a military unit, even a company of irregulars, and behaving like robbers and road agents. If he was going to aspire toward something greater than simple outlawry, then he'd have to change a lot of things.

"Keep to the willows," Henderson hissed to the men, rangers and outlaws alike. Ingram, commanding the rangers, set about ensuring his men were well within the cover of the trees, as Cole did the same with the outlaws. The screen of the willows would hide them from the men on the train, but the drooping branches would provide no obstacle at all once the time came to gun their Iron Horses and speed down across the tracks.

Jesse smiled at the appropriateness of the old term 'going among the willows,' which meant a man had turned outlaw. They were certainly among the willows now, and quite soon they'd impress on the Yankees the veracity of the old slang.

The Malediction came rumbling past, playing its role as scout for the train behind it. The armored engine looked like some prehistoric behemoth, its dull steel plates layered atop one another like the interlocking scales of a snake's belly. Cupolas jutted from the sides of the single car following behind the engine, a murderous scatter-blaster array fixed into each of the basket-like projections, and a blue-uniformed gunner was poised behind each weapon. A much larger turret rose above the car. A massive blast-cannon scented the air, with two more scatter-blasters situated above it on the sloping armor; an array of weaponry designed to deal with large targets at a distance and smaller ones at closer range. The car was armored like the engine, and along its sides was a covered walkway upon which the steel frames of robots could be seen, rifles clenched in their metal claws. Magnetic clamps built into their feet kept each 'bot in place, defying the momentum of the Malediction as it roared through the countryside.

The outlaws watched the armored train pass, each of them feeling a sensation of dread well up inside him. More than a few turned a worried glance at Will Shaft, praying that the Exoduster's explosives would knock out the Malediction before its vicious armaments could be brought into play against them.

Jesse was one of the few who didn't doubt Will's capability. He kept his eyes on the Malediction, not on the man he was trusting to eliminate it. When the armored train rumbled around the bend, he lifted his mechanical arm and brought it chopping down. At his signal, the outlaws spurred their Iron Horses into motion. Like a horde of wolves, they howled out from the willows and across the tracks. Behind each vehicle, the ambushers dragged a pair of Sherman's neckties. The twisted rails smashed their way through bushes, tore chunks of bark from the willows, gouged furrows in the ground, but the impetus of the Iron Horses pulled them onto the tracks just the same. As each outlaw brought his burden onto the tracks, he leaned back and released the chains holding it. In short order, what had been a section of clear railway was now cluttered with over a hundred heavy lumps of twisted metal.

The Ford brothers were the last of the outlaws to clear the tracks when the Union train came into view. The engine's whistle blared as the crew saw the obstruction on the tracks ahead. Frantically, the engineer tried to brake the locomotive, but the momentum of the speeding train and the over laden cars behind it was too great to be arrested.

The locomotive slammed into the mass of twisted iron with a thunderous screech. The debris was thrust forward by the force of the hurtling train, pushed along the track in a rolling, grinding mass of tortured metal. The track was ripped apart by the knots of iron, ties reduced to splinters and rails ripped clean from their fastenings. As the train neared the turn, its wheels left the track. The entire engine was propelled onward into the rocks, slamming into it with such violence that the front of the locomotive crumpled and was pushed back into the control cabin. The crew vanished, crushed into bloody pulp by the fury of the wreck.

The cars behind the engine slammed into one another, some of them flung dozens of yards into the trees, others leaping upward and hurling themselves atop the cars ahead of them. One flat-car, its length taken up by a dozen Iron Horses, was sent whipping around crosswise across the rails only to be cut in half by the plowing momentum of the car behind it.

The outlaws waited until every car had come to a stop, then with a mighty Rebel yell, they shot out from where they lurked in the trees. Like a flock of buzzards, the ambushers swarmed about the train. Blasters barked out as the attackers fired on blue-coated soldiers crawling out from the wreckage.

Jesse held back, waiting and listening for the explosion that would alert him that the Malediction had been eliminated. The ruination of the train had been achieved, but if its escort returned, then the outlaws' success would be eradicated in a frenzy of vengeance.

From his place among the rocks, Jesse watched his gang and Ingram's rangers rove across the smashed train. He saw Jim Younger shoot a Yankee sergeant as the man stumbled out from the shattered window of a passenger car. He watched as Bob Younger cut down an enraged rail man who came at him with an axe, the seasoned knife-fighter ducking beneath the cleaving blade to open his enemy's belly. He shook his head as he observed John Wesley Hardin immolate a pair of blue-bellies who came crawling out from an upturned supply wagon, the incendiary ammunition of his smokers turning the two soldiers into shrieking pillars of flame.

Most sickening to Jesse, however, was the sight of the man that used to represent his old commander, and supposedly everything he stood for, Allen Henderson. The black-garbed guerrilla had dismounted and was stalking among the cars, dragging injured men from the wreckage. However mangled by the crash the wretch might be, Henderson showed them no mercy. Pressing his blaster against each forehead, he murdered the wounded with icy callousness. Jesse felt a shiver crawl down his spine as he wondered at the cruelty he witnessed, the inhuman monstrousness exhibited by the guerrilla. There seemed no emotion, no rage in the man as he killed his victims. They might have been ants for all the feeling Henderson expressed. That feeling of deja-vu overcame him in a sickening way, as it reminded him of Jake 'Smiley' Williamson and the way he brutalized the victims from the first train robbery.

The deafening bellow of Will Shaft's explosives boomed across the landscape. Jesse could see the fingers of flame and smoke that shot hundreds of feet into the sky as the Malediction was obliterated. The armored gun-car's turret went spinning through the air, smashing down among the trees. Human forms, like tiny motes, went sailing through the heavens. Speeding back to help the train, the escort had tripped the Exoduster's trap perfectly.

Jesse didn't wait, now that he knew the Malediction wasn't coming back. He gunned his Iron Horse and sped down from his lookout post. The outlaw zipped around the smashed and burning coaches and cars. Everywhere, he could see outlaws and rangers plundering supplies from the wreck. Professional railroad wrecking crews couldn't have pillaged the cars more thoroughly. Jesse could see Cole guiding a pair of outlaws as they tried to drive a hulking transport wagon off one of the flat-cars. The bushwhacker waved his arms excitedly when he saw Jesse.

"There's five of 'em!" Cole shouted. "Big ore-cars for some mine outfit down the pike! Each of these lummoxes could haul a hundred men in their beds, maybe even more!"

"We'll make salvagin' those a priority," Jesse said. "We'll need 'em to get our boys away from Andersonville."

Cole's expression grew grave. "Henderson says they're in a bad way. Sick and starvin' and all." He studied the big ore wagon as it rumbled down from the smashed flat-car, the glow of RJ shining from a gash in its engine casing. "If'n we rigged up some sort of tiers inside, like bunks, we'd maybe carry off three times as many men."

"Fix it up, then," Jesse ordered. "Just do it quick." The outlaw chief was already speeding away. He passed Captain Ingram, noticing the way the Californian and his rangers were dragging crates of blasters from a burning supply car. Again, Jesse was struck by the military discipline and efficiency Ingram had drilled into his followers. Not without a twinge of envy, Jesse left the Californians to their work.

He had a different sort of confrontation to address. Speeding around the mangled wreck of a passenger car that had been transfixed by a box car, Jesse found Henderson still pulling men from the wreck and shooting them in the coldest blood. Jesse glared at the guerrilla, and then revved his 'Horse so that the noise of the engine would draw Allen Henderson's attention away from his vicious labor.

"Allen!" Jesse shouted. "What in Hell are you doin'?"

Henderson didn't look up until he'd turned the face of the man he'd pulled from the wreck into a steaming hole. When he did turn to face Jesse, the shadowy man's eyes were inscrutable behind his glasses. "I'm doing what needs to be done," Henderson said. He waved his hand at the smashed train. "You've taken the whole pot with a full house. Now you have to be careful that you don't give away the bigger game. It'll take the Yankees days to figure out what happened here. Their first guess will be Mosby's men, and then they might start wondering about Warrior Nation war parties sneaking around the countryside. They won't think somebody has designs on Andersonville. Not unless you leave somebody around to tell what happened." Henderson pointed at Jesse's mechanical arms. "There aren't too many men with arms like that. The Yankees realize that you're here, it won't take them too long to reckon why you're here."

Jesse felt sick at the bottom of his stomach. What Henderson said made sense. Brutal, horrific, even obscene, but sense just the same. Any witness they left behind, anyone who could even hint that they'd seen Jesse or one of the Younger brothers and they could alert the Yankees, cause them to bolster the guards at Camp Lincoln. Their chances were long already, any significant enlargement of the defenses at Camp Lincoln could spoil them entirely.

"We can take 'em with us," Jesse said, pointing toward the wagons Cole was salvaging. "We can ride into Andersonville with a load of Yankees and leave with a load of rebs."

Henderson stood up, loading a fresh cartridge into his blaster. "And what if something happened? What if one of the Yankees got loose? This is safer, Jesse, and you know it. We didn't put the fear of God into the Jayhawkers during the war by being squeamish."

"Maybe we didn't fight the war the right way," Jesse said. He thrust a steel finger at the armed man. "No more killin'. I want prisoners. Things can go wrong at the other end, too. If'n they do, it might be convenient to have hostages for bargainin'. Don't you go forgettin' who's the one in charge here. You mighta been second to Quantrill once, but he ain't here."

The shadowy figure kept his eyes trained on Jesse for a few moments before he shrugged. "My apologies, Jesse. I'll pass the word along," he said. There was no resentment or hostility in his expression, only a suggestion of disappointment, and an almost fatherly sense of disapproval at the outlaw's compassion. Jesse wasn't sure what made him more uneasy, the thought that this man represented his old commander's ideas, or that Camp Lincoln had changed him so much to act like a savage on the warpath.

The return of Will Shaft turned Jesse's attention away from Henderson. The Exoduster's Iron Horse was coated in soot, as was the outlaw himself. It was obvious that he'd been close when the Malediction had struck the explosives. Jesse'd given him the job of making certain the escort engine was knocked out, but he hadn't expected the man to linger so close to his work.

Beneath his mantle of soot, Will's face was grim. It wasn't the demolition of the armored train that upset him however. "If I'd knowed this was the sort of thing you was goin' to do Mr. James, I'd stayed put in Robbers Roost."

Jesse shook his head. "Henderson was tryin' to make sure the Yankees weren't warned. I've already told him I want prisoners, not a massacre."

Will glowered at the bodies left by Henderson. "I didn't know nothin' about Henderson murderin' nobody. Seein' you've put a stop to him, maybe you'd put a stop to Hardin too."

The Exoduster didn't wait to explain further, he just turned his 'Horse around and sped away. Jesse bit back an outburst and hurried to follow Will. Together, the outlaws rode around the periphery of the wreck to where a flat-car had lodged itself among the trees. Still strapped down to the car's bed were two immense steel juggernauts, mammoth machines that made the Judgement Wyatt Earp had brought against the gang look feeble by comparison. They were the mechanized artillery designated 'Rolling Thunder' by the Union Army and they looked to be perfectly intact.

Less intact were the men cowering on the ground around the flat-car. Crouched down on their knees, their hands folded behind their necks, the men wore the soiled tatters of their Union uniforms. They'd been badly bruised and battered by the wreck, but the ordeal of the crash was the least of the horrors the night held in store for them. Standing before them, smokers gripped in each hand, was John Wesley Hardin. An ugly, sick expression was on the gunslinger's face as he glared at the cowering soldiers. Picking one at random, he lashed out with his boot and knocked the man sprawling.

"Get up, blue-belly. Run fer it! Maybe you'll get further than yer friends!" Hardin laughed as the soldier started to run. Keeping one smoker trained on the other prisoners, he aimed the other at the fleeing man. Before he'd gone a dozen paces, the soldier was struck down by a shot from Hardin's gun. The incendiary struck him square in the back, the chemical splashing over the man's body and turning him into a blazing bonfire. The screaming figure raced on for several yards, then collapsed to the ground in a smoldering heap. The scorched bodies of three other soldiers gave mute testament to how long Hardin had been indulging in his sadistic sport.

Jesse had been appalled by Henderson's cold, calculated murder of the Yankees; he had expected something like that by Smiley back in the day, but not from Henderson. Seeing Hardin's vicious enjoyment of slaughtering helpless men brought raw fury flowing through his veins. Opening the throttle of his Iron Horse, Jesse swooped down toward the Texan. "Hardin!" he shouted. "Stop it, you murderin' cur!"

Hardin swung around at Jesse's yell. For an instant there was a twinge of panic when he saw the outlaw chief, but then he spotted Will riding alongside Jesse. The black gunman's presence enflamed the hate already boiling inside him.

"I'm fixin' these Yankees so's they won't be bringin' their high-falutin' ideas no place 'cept Hell!" Hardin said. He kicked out with his boot, knocking another soldier to the ground.

"Please!" the man howled, reaching his hands imploringly toward Jesse. "I ain't no Yankee! I'm from Virginia! I'm jus' tryin' to make some money for my family back home!"

Hardin kicked the man again. "Then yer a damn galvanized Yankee! Get on yer feet an' start runnin'!"

"Leave him alone," Jesse told the gunfighter. "Leave all of 'em alone. You've murdered enough men tonight."

"Murder hell!" Hardin cursed. "I'm avengin' the indignities heaped up on the South by these blue-belly tyrants!" He glared at Will, then back to Jesse. "Maybe if'n yer head weren't so took up with miscegenation, you'd appreciate that."

"I appreciate I jus' told you to do somethin' and you ain't doin' it," Jesse warned.

Hardin turned away, back toward the prisoners. Suddenly, the Texan swung back around. Will shouted in alarm, but Jesse's reaction was still quicker. His mechanical hands flew to his holsters, ripped the Hyper-velocity blasters free and fired at the Texan before Hardin could pull the triggers of his already drawn smokers. Jesse's blasters picked off the guns in Hardin's hands. The left smoker went spinning off into the coming night, but the one in the Texan's right hand exploded under the impact of Jesse's shot. The incendiary charge contained inside the gun's chamber splashed across Hardin's body.

The gunfighter screamed as the chemical burned his flesh. Hardin threw himself to the ground, rolling in the dirt in a desperate attempt to smother the fires engulfing him. Will raised one of his pistols, pointing it at the Texan to administer a coup de grace and end his suffering.

"Leave him be," Jesse said, waving his hand at Will. "Leave him burn." He glared down at the writhing shape of the Texan. "He should get used to it. He'll find it a might hotter when he gets to Hell."

Will shuddered at the cruelty of Jesse's decision. Hardin was a monster and Jesse'd paid him back in his own coin. Will didn't want to think about what that made the outlaw chief. Instead he nodded to the still cowering Union soldiers. The duel had happened so quickly none of the men had been given the chance to even think about running. "What'll we do with them?"

Jesse turned in his saddle and stared down at the soldiers. He noticed the cannon patch of artillerymen on the jackets a few of them wore. "You're responsible for those?" he asked, gesturing to the Rolling Thunder wagons strapped to the flat-car.

The galvanized Yankee from Virginia was the first to answer Jesse. "Yes sir, we're engineers, 21st Ohio Mobile Artillery Brigade."

Jesse smiled at the statement. He pointed at Hardin's agonized figure rolling in the dust. "You've been given a reprieve, so now yer gonna earn it. Yer gonna show my boys how to operate them juggernauts." A hard edge crept into the outlaw's tone. "If'n you don't, then you'll be prayin' I'd left you to Hardin."

*****

Frank James tried to maintain just the right mix of timidity and uneasiness that the Yankees would expect from one of their turnkeys. Walking down the halls of the Union barracks, he was careful to keep his eyes averted any time a soldier in blue marched past him. When an officer approached, he was quick to snap to attention and salute, a performance that always brought a sneering smile to the face of the Union commanders. He remembered all the little details he'd been told that would help him blend in and allay any hint of suspicion on the part of Camp Lincoln's administrators.

It had been an entire day since he'd seen Lucy the nurse escorted into Tumblety's surgery. Frank had expected he might see her ejected from the place, but since she'd gone in, no one had either visited or left the old hospital building. That simple fact had done more to exacerbate his worry than anything else. If she'd been successful, he would have seen her and John leaving. If she'd failed, then Colonel Custer's troops should have collected her and dragged her off to their guardhouse. Neither had occurred, and that had set his mind to pondering other, darker possibilities.

Even more, Frank wondered why the girl that he had seen all that time ago in the saloon, at the start of the big to-do with Billy the Kid, had suddenly appeared here and now?

Eventually, Frank's worry grew to the point where he couldn't just sit idle and maintain his vigil. Using the marchtack Lucy had given him, he was able to bribe one of the turnkeys. The Union administrators employed trusted prisoners to clean up the buildings inside their compound and handle all the drudgery of day-to-day life. Prisoners represented the cheapest labor, working for only a meager increase in their food ration. For the budget-conscious Custer, they were a boon to his economy.

The turnkey had given Frank the special armbands that would mark him out for admittance into the compound and the magnetized disk that would keep the Warders from firing on him if he was inside the fence – though he warned that the 'bots on the walls and around Tumblety's surgery would still shoot if he got too close. Frank remembered both warnings. The story he'd given the turnkey was one that elicited the man's cooperation to the fullest – a promise that he knew where more marchtack was hidden and that he would share with the turnkey if he recovered it – so Frank was certain the man had left out no detail that would ensure the outlaw's safe return.

If the prisoner had known Frank's objective was the surgery, he'd probably have been a good deal less cooperative. Frank, however, had a good idea about how he'd get inside the old hospital without the man's help. All he needed was the identity disk of the sergeant who'd taken Lucy to Tumblety. For two hours he prowled the halls of the barracks sweeping up and cleaning, his eyes ever on the lookout for the man he wanted. At last he found him.

The sergeant was sitting at a poker game in one of the guardrooms off the main gallery. Frank leaned into the room, watching as the off-duty soldiers made wagers and drew cards. He waited until the sergeant looked up, and then waved his hand in a subtle, beckoning gesture. The sergeant didn't pay attention the first time, but when he looked up and saw Frank repeat the motion, it aroused the soldier's interest. When he lost the next hand, he excused himself and walked out into the corridor. He didn't look at Frank, but he made certain to brush against him as he walked past, his arm nudging the supposed turnkey. Frank waited a few seconds, and then followed after the sergeant.

The sergeant was waiting for him in the darkened doorway of a linen closet. "Well, Johnny Reb, what's so all-fired important?" the soldier growled.

Frank glanced down the hallway, an apprehensive look on his face. "There's a Texas boy who had himself a fine-looking gold ring. It's been took."

The sergeant's eyes gleamed with the glint of greed. It wasn't the ring that excited the soldier's avarice, but rather the prospect of catching the thief. "Who took it? One of us?" Custer had an unbending mania for discipline in his command. It wasn't the crime itself that upset the commandant but rather the breech of discipline the theft represented. He'd deal out harsh punishment to any soldier caught stealing. At the same time, he'd reward any soldier who uncovered such an indiscretion.

"Yeah," Frank said, lowering his voice to a whisper. He glanced around again, smiling at the dearth of potential witnesses. The sergeant had found an admirably isolated spot for their conversation. One that suited Frank's purposes exceedingly well. When the outlaw continued to whisper, the sergeant leaned forward to hear him. Frank brought both hands smashing down into the back of the soldier's neck, flattening him against the floor. Before anyone could come along, he picked up the stunned sergeant and shuffled him back into the linen closet.

It was only a matter of minutes before Frank was wearing the sergeant's uniform and carrying his identity disk. He discarded the turnkey's disk as he walked from the barracks. Two disks had the potential to confuse the mechanical brain of a 'bot. A confused Warder tended to shoot at whatever was confusing it. As he approached the surgery, the hulking Warder on guard outside the door watched him with its glowing optics, the omnipresent threat of its rifle-arm all too prominent. Frank felt as though his legs were jelly. The sergeant had been unarmed when he'd waylaid the man. If the Warder decided to start shooting, there was nothing he could use to defend himself.

The 'bot, however, paid no notice to Frank's anxiety. The only thing that mattered to it was the disk he carried. Holding the stolen disk, Frank was able to walk past the Warder and to the door. It took him a moment to work the keys and slide back the bolts, but the 'bot didn't pay attention to his fumbling uncertainty with the locks.

Slipping inside the door, Frank at once was struck by the size of the surgery and the sterile white walls. For a man engaged in so furtive an enterprise as a rescue, the surgery offered an appalling lack of shadows and clutter to conceal his movements. At the same time, the well-lit conditions made it easy to spy at a glance the whole of the ward room. Almost at once, Frank saw one of his objectives. The sight made him rush across the surgery, outraged by the implications of what he'd seen.

Lucy was lying strapped to a steel table in one of the vivisection stations. Arms and legs bound at her sides, her uniform had been slashed and cut to expose the trunk of her body. Frank noticed that her bare flesh had been marked up with paint, different spots circled or X-marked, often with a number written beside them. Stretched upon a stand beside her was an anatomical chart with the organs designated in similar fashion. A gurney was lying at the opposite end of the table, a motley collection of jars filled with chemical preservatives strewn across it. Beside the jars was a gruesome array of knives and hooks.

The nurse was alive, her captor had gathered the instruments for her butchery, but he hadn't started the operation yet. Lucy stared at Frank, a desperate appeal in her gaze. She struggled to push words through the gag that had been tied across her face. Frank hurried to remove it.

"Hold up," the outlaw told her. "I can't understand you."

"I believe the whore's trying to warn you about me," a mocking voice chuckled from behind Frank.

The outlaw spun around, his hands clenched into fists. With what he'd seen, Frank would happily beat Lucy's captor to death with his bare hands.

Unfortunately, Dr. Tumblety wasn't unarmed. Wearing an ostentatious military uniform, a Prussian-style spiked helmet on his head, the experimenter strode out from behind the shelves holding his anatomical collection. Each of the madman's hands was closed inside a strange metal gauntlet. Upon each forearm there was a little hopper into which tiny steel disks were fed. At the front of each gauntlet was the menacing darkness of a slit-edged barrel.

"I don't know who you are, or how you got here," Tumblety said. "But you've come at an opportune time. One of my subjects is rejecting the last enhancements I endowed him with. I'm afraid I'll need to borrow some of your organs to fix him up again."

Frank took a pace back. He turned his head and started to reach for one of the knives on the gurney.

Tumblety laughed and pointed one of his gauntlets at Frank. "I'll give you a choice," he said. "You can help me with one experiment or you can help me with another." The gauntlet on his arm screeched as one of the saw-edged disks left the hopper and dropped into the magazine below. "I've just been dying to try out my Rippers on a free and unfettered target."

Chapter 18

The lieutenant commanding the gates of Camp Lincoln scowled down at the group of men gathered before the wrought-iron portals. He didn't appreciate being called away from his poker game in the middle of the night. The sergeant on duty should have handled these men on his own. Simply because they clamored for an officer didn't mean the guards had to acknowledge such demands. He almost wished they could get away with posting Warders throughout the prison and do away with soldiers entirely. A 'bot simply obeyed orders; it didn't suffer any failures of initiative. With a little more versatility, 'bots would replace human troops entirely. The lieutenant was convinced of that fact and he was certain that Tesla was already working on the improvements to the robot brain that would make such implementation practical. It would be a happy day when every soldier under his command simply did as they were told.

There were seven men below standing just beyond the stakes that demarked the dead line, the point beyond which any trespass would provoke the Warders patrolling the walls to open fire. The group was gathered around one of the electric lamps lining the approach to Camp Lincoln. By the lamp's light, the lieutenant could see that four of the men were dressed in Union uniforms and that three of them had the dusky color of Africans. A third man was, standing nearby. His pale features standing out stark against the somber color of his clothes and the shadow cast by his wide-brimmed hat. There was a glint of brass armor under his duster. The other two men were wearing gray linen dusters and stood between the others. Their stance was stiff and tense, but they had their faces averted from the prison so the officer wasn't able to form a more distinct impression of their attitude. He could tell that the soldiers were in a state of heightened agitation, their eyes never leaving the two men in the dusters.

"What's all this ballyhoo about?" the lieutenant called down.

The only white soldier among the group muttered a command to the black troopers and then stepped forward. "I'm Sergeant Iverson, 23rd Pennsylvania, detached from Fort Stimson to render aid to Mr. Thomas Tate Tobin." The sergeant nodded toward the man in black.

The lieutenant tapped his chin thoughtfully as he tried to recall where he had heard that name before. He'd read it somewhere, he was certain of that. After a moment, the connection came to him. "Tobin? The bounty hunter?"

"The same, sir," Iverson said. The man in black simply brushed the brim of his hat in a mocking semblance of a salute when the lieutenant looked at him. "We've been helping him track down the James-Younger Gang."

The lieutenant was taken aback by that news. If the James-Younger Gang was in the area, then it was likely the outlaws had learned that Frank James had been confined in Camp Lincoln. The officer blanched at the idea of facing the vengeful outlaws. Jesse James was infamous for the murderous speed of his mechanical arms. What a garrison of some second-string infantry and second rank 'bots of Camp Lincoln could do against the rage of the James-Younger Gang was a question that brought him to the edge of panic. He was just turning to order a message relayed back to Colonel Custer when Sergeant Iverson called up to him again.

"It's been a hard day and we'd like to get our prisoners put away."

"Prisoners?" the lieutenant looked again at the two men in the linen dusters. While he stared at them, one of the black soldiers stepped over to them and pulled back the dusters. The officer could see now that the older of the two men had his hands tied in front of him with rope. He didn't study the captive long, however, for when the duster was pulled off the other prisoner, that man commanded the lieutenant's full attention. He wasn't bound with rope but with chain; chains that were wrapped around his body and pinned his arms at his sides. They weren't natural arms, but powerful steel mechanisms.

"Cole Younger and Jesse James," Sergeant Iverson said, gesturing from one to the other. "We managed to take them alive. The other Younger brothers weren't so fortunate." He gestured to a burlap sack which the black-clad bounty hunter had tied to his belt.

The mere suggestion of what was inside Tobin's bag made the lieutenant shudder. The idea of a white man behaving in such savage, bestial fashion was offensive to him. Just because he was a paid killer didn't mean he had to comport himself like a jungle heathen. "We'll take your prisoners, but that killer and his trophies can stay right where he is."

"Then so do my prisoners," the man in black declared. "Jesse's worth $10,000 to me. I'm not letting him out of my sight." His gloved hand tapped the bag hanging from his belt. "These are worth a thousand each, so they're coming along too."

The lieutenant bristled at the imperious tone and frowned at the faint trace of Southern twang in Tobin's voice. He was tempted to tell the psychopath and his escort to leave, but the idea of Jesse and Cole somehow escaping custody made him hold his tongue. "Turn your weapons over to Sergeant Iverson. I'll be hanged if I let you come in armed."

The bounty hunter shrugged and began turning over his blasters and rifle to the sergeant. He hesitated when he drew the knife from his boot, staring at it a moment before handing it over. "That's the whole caboodle."

"Open up," the lieutenant told the troopers manning the gate. While his men set the machinery in motion, the officer snapped orders to Iverson. "Make sure your darkies keep their guns trained on them outlaws. I don't want any slip ups."

Iverson turned around and snapped a string of orders to the black soldiers. The men kept their rifles at the ready, prodding their prisoners forward with the muzzles when the gates swung open.

The lieutenant met them in the assembly area just past the gate. Like the perimeter outside, there was a series of stakes set into the ground to mark off the forbidden region where the Warders would open fire on trespassers. Beyond the open ground meant for assembly, the squalid sprawl of the prisoner tents stretched across the enclosure. Beyond the tents, rising above them like a distant range of mountains, were the buildings of the command compound.

"Come along," the lieutenant said. "I'll take you to see Colonel Custer. He's commandant here. He'll know what to do with your prisoners." He glanced over at Tobin. "He'll make the arrangements to see that you get paid," he added with disgust.

*****

As they were escorted through the prison camp, Jesse heard his name shouted many times. Prisoners rushed toward the small procession, lining the sides of the pathway the lieutenant was leading them down. In addition to Iverson and his black soldiers, the lieutenant had brought three men from the gate and one of the Warders from the wall. The menace of so many blasters combined with the mechanical strength of the 'bot kept the rebels back.

The prisoners weren't so cowed, however, that they kept silent. Few were the voices not raised in some call of encouragement to Jesse or lowered to spit some derisive curse against the Yankees. The tumult made the lieutenant more uneasy with each step. It wasn't long before he had his pistol drawn. He barked at the prisoners, ordering them back to their tents. The rebels just jeered at his demands.

A motion to his right brought the lieutenant's head turning around. He scowled when he saw Iverson returning one of Tobin's blasters to the bounty hunter. "I don't want that civilian armed!"

Sergeant Iverson nodded at the crowd of angry rebels. "My apologies, sir, but I thought we might need him armed afore long."

The lieutenant shouted at the crowd of prisoners, again enjoining them to disperse. On his command, the Warder swung around and raised its weapon-arm, aiming the built-in blaster at the ragged mob. Snarling, the officer gave the 'bot the command to fire. A bolt of energy slammed into one of the rebels, hurling his charred body back into the crowd. The prisoners fell silent, stunned by the sudden barbarity.

They found their voices again a moment later, screeching a defiant cheer. The Union officer moaned in horror when he looked at Jesse James. The outlaw was straining against the chains binding him. His mechanical arms snapped the steel links before the lieutenant knew what was going on. Terrified, the lieutenant snapped an order to the Warder. Before the 'bot could spin around, a shot rang out and its head was torn from its shoulders. Smoke rose from the barrel of the bounty hunter's gun.

Other shots quickly followed as each of the black troopers gunned down one of the camp guards. The lieutenant didn't have time to process this act of treachery before he felt something sharp punching into his back.

"The name ain't Iverson," the blue-coated sergeant said as he dug the big Bowie-knife deeper into the officer's flesh. "When yer get ta Hell, tell 'em it were Bob Younger sent you there, yer murderin' Yankee bastard!" Bob let the dying lieutenant sink to the ground, freeing his knife with a savage twist of the blade.

Will Shaft threw away his blue-coat and kepi, and then hurried to Jesse James. He handed the freed outlaw the blasters he'd been holding for him. The Exoduster wore a broad grin. "I believe these are yourn," he said.

Cole snatched his own weapons from one of the other Exodusters, the loosened ropes still hanging from his left wrist. The bushwhacker cursed lividly. "We should have been inside the compound afore startin' the shootin'."

As if to confirm Cole's statement, a loud roar boomed through the air. One of the watchtowers vanished in a ball of flame as the artillery from one of the Rolling Thunders slammed into it. The destruction was so swift that the Yankee guards inside didn't even have time to scream. A moment later, the second Rolling Thunder obliterated another of the towers. Soon after, the bark of small arms and the rumble of Iron Horses echoed from outside the palisade walls.

Captain Ingram, Jim Younger, and the Ford brothers had been waiting outside with the rest of the men, waiting for the sound of gunfire inside the prison. That was their signal to attack, to assault the sections of wall Henderson had declared were the most vulnerable.

Jesse shook his head. "Ain't nothin' can be done about it now. That Yankee forced the hand."

Henderson had already tossed aside the black hat he had worn in his bounty hunter disguise and retrieved his rebel-gray cavalry hat from beneath his coat. Straightening it back into some semblance of shape, he set it on his head and began bellowing orders to the stunned, confused throng of prisoners around them. "This here's Jesse James and he's come to fetch you luckless ruffians out of this Yankee hellhole. I need twenty men who haven't gone yellow to step forward and get themselves armed! You want to go free again; you'll have to earn it!"

The former prisoner's raspy snarl electrified the captives surrounding the outlaws. Almost to a man, they forgot their alarm at the carnage they had witnessed and the turmoil unfolding around the palisade. Surging forward with an animalistic bellow of rage, the rebels snatched up the guns of the dead guards. Will and the other Exodusters handed out spare pistols they had smuggled in beneath their coats. True to Henderson's request, there were soon another twenty armed men waiting for Jesse to tell them what to do. Hundreds more crowded close, watching with the keenness of hungry dogs as the notorious outlaw stepped up onto the wreck of the Warder.

"I'm intendin' to get every man in Andersonville out of here!" Jesse told the prisoners. He swung his steel arm down, pointing his hand at the fenced compound. "To do that, we've gotta take the headquarters. Stop the Yankees from tracking us from Hell to Christmas. I need them that've been given guns to help take the compound. The rest of yer go an' spread the word. Get everybody set to charge them gates the moment the men outside have busted through!"

Jesse felt strangely empty when the raucous cheer of affirmation rose from the prisoners. His eyes were roving over every face, seeking out any trace of John Younger. He knew that Cole and Bob were likewise hoping for some glimpse of their brother, listening desperately for the sound of his voice. Jesse's anxiety was the more onerous, however, rooted not in filial devotion and the love of family, but from the pangs of guilt and responsibility. As the crowd began to disperse, as the prisoners started to rush back into the maze of tents to carry Jesse's orders to every corner of the camp, the outlaw kept praying for some trace of John.

Finally, Jesse grabbed one of the armed rebels. "The Yankees brought a new prisoner a few weeks back. A boy named John Younger. Do you know where he is?" The prisoner shook his head regretfully. When Jesse turned his attention on a second man, he also could only shake his head.

"I ain't see any John Younger," a third rebel told Jesse, "but I have seen yourn brother, Frank. He borrowed my badge ter get inter the compound." The prisoner pointed his hand at the fenced area, thrusting a finger at one building in particular. "Saw Frank gussied up liken a Yankee sergeant waltz'n straight inter the doctor's surgery. Never did see him come out."

Jesse couldn't believe his ears. Frank? Frank James, alive and in Andersonville! It was too miraculous to believe, but when they saw the incredulity on his face, several of the other armed prisoners told Jesse that his brother had been imprisoned in Camp Lincoln, though only the turnkey had seen him go into the old hospital building.

Alive! His brother, alive! A warmth Jesse hadn't felt in months rushed through him. He turned toward the compound. It took all the restraint he possessed to keep from running straight to the fence and tearing it down with his bare hands. Frank was in there, somewhere, and he was alive.

Or at least he had been. Jesse's eyes narrowed to pinpoints as he glared at the menacing hospital building.

"Jesse, we've still got to capture their headquarters. That vocal reiterator has to be knocked out afore we start movin' men out of here," Cole shouted at the outlaw. He laid his hand on Jesse's shoulder when his friend failed to respond. "I know what yer thinkin', I'm thinkin' it too, about John, but we can't set aside the plan."

"And they got some o' them heavy wagons in there, too, boys!" A scarred and battered prisoner pushed himself to the front of the crowd. "You gotta get in there fast afore those crews can get all buttoned up!"

Jesse watched the Union troopers scrambling around inside the compound, hurrying to defensive points they'd dug into the ground or quickly created from upturned carts and sledges. Several were running for a darkened corner where heavy, menacing shapes hulked in the shadows: Rolling Thunder Assault Wagons. Will's grenades would make short work of the Yankee positions. The real trouble would come from the soldiers taking shelter inside the big stone buildings, and the heavy wagons, if their crews could get them up and running in time.

Even recognizing that fact, Jesse couldn't set aside the image of his brother languishing inside the old hospital. "You and Henderson will have to see the plan through," he growled through clenched teeth. "Ain't nothin' comin' between me an' what I need to do."

*****

Jesse rushed toward the old hospital, dodging around the smoldering craters left behind by Will's explosives, sometimes forced to leap over the smoking husk of a Yankee guard who had been caught in one of the blasts. He ignored the grisly remains with the same cold determination that kept him from worrying about how the fight for the administration building was faring. That was a conflict that Cole, Henderson, and the men under their command would have to settle on their own; all Jesse needed them to do was keep the guards pinned down while he charged the old hospital.

Only one man was crazy enough to follow Jesse. Bob hurried behind Jesse, supporting his advance with his blaster. Fixated upon the hospital, Jesse directed his fire against the Warders on the building's roof. Trading shots with the hulking robots had been an uneven contest. The mechanical brains in the 'bots weren't capable of the kind of accuracy an Enforcer could muster. There was a reason the Warders weren't considered suitable for front-line deployment. Perfect for guarding unarmed prisoners, they simply weren't equal to the challenge posed by a determined man with a gun. Steel plate designed to withstand early model weapons wasn't equal to the searing heat of a blaster. Each time Jesse fired, he saw the spot he struck turn red hot, the armor of the 'bot become a molten wound that dripped down its body. Arms and legs would seize and lock in place when the molten metal flowed across joints, blasts to the head would cripple the optics and blind the machines. It took several shots to bring down a Warder, for the automatons fought on without regard to their injuries, but Jesse's attack was too remorseless to be denied.

Every time a Warder showed itself, they were brought down by Jesse but he only needed one to end his life. Bob threw himself into the battle trying to protect his chief as they assaulted the hospital. He watched the scarred ground within the compound and picked off lurking Union troops who thought to attack the outlaws by ambush. By the time they neared the steel door of the hospital, Bob had accounted for four lurking soldiers. He was thankful for Jesse's visibility and notoriety; the Yankees had been so intent on the infamous robber that they'd completely ignored Bob, which left them easy targets for his blaster.

A final Warder stood guard before the door. The robot leveled its rifle-arm at Jesse as the outlaw came charging toward it. From each of his blasters, a bolt of energy blazed into the automaton. The first shot slammed into the muzzle of its rifle, reducing it to a blob of smoldering slag. The second blast scored against the Warder's chest, opening a fist-sized gap in its armor. Before Jesse could fire again, the Warder tried to gun him down. Oblivious to the damage inflicted to its arm, the 'bot sent a pulse of energy hurtling down the chamber. Unable to leave the melted barrel of the weapon, the energy blast redoubled against itself. The resultant detonation exploded through the Warder's arm and turned it into a cloud of metal splinters, in turn, throwing the 'bot to the ground by the force of the explosion. It crashed to earth like an overturned turtle, flailing at the dirt as it tried to right itself.

Jesse didn't give it the chance. Aiming at the wound in its chest, he sent a shot searing through the 'bot's internal machinery. With a final shudder, the Warder froze, all animation burned from its frame by Jesse's shot.

The outlaw chief stepped over the inert Warder. He scowled for an instant at the steel door and then brought both pistols to bear against it. In a shriek of tortured metal, the locks and bolts securing the door were blasted apart. A kick from Jesse's boot sent the massive portal crashing inwards.

Smoke from the savaged door billowed about Jesse as he stepped into the old hospital, into the great ward that had become the surgery and laboratory of Dr. Tumblety. It took several steps before he was clear of the smoke, before he could see with his own eyes the place where the Yankees were holding his brother.

What Jesse saw sent a rage of emotions flowing through him. Lucinda Loveless, the beautiful young woman he'd encountered months before, lay shackled and prone on the operating table in the tattered remains of her clothes, her flesh stained with marks that reminded him of a butcher's chart. Looming over her, a knife gleaming in his hand, was a tall man dressed in an ostentatious military uniform. He had a crazed look in his eyes when he spun around and glared at Jesse. Briefly, the surgeon's gaze darted to a nearby table where a pair of strange-looking gauntlets lay.

"Jesse! Don't let that maniac get near them fancy gloves!"

Jesse felt his heart quicken when he heard that cry. He spun around, staring in amazement at the man shackled to the wall of the surgery. It was Frank! It was his brother! Alive! Despite everything he'd been told by the prisoners of Andersonville, Jesse was still stunned to find Frank alive after the long months he'd thought his brother dead.

Tumblety seized upon Jesse's moment of distraction. Like the outlaw, he'd heard Frank's cry of warning. The experimenter made no move to regain the Rippers he'd removed to conduct his vivisection of Loveless. Instead, he dashed across the surgery and threw back one of the curtains. The madman grinned triumphantly at Jesse as the outlaw realized his mistake and swung back around to cover him with his blasters.

"Jesse James!" Dr Tumblety crowed. "You've seen your brother, now let me reunite you with another old friend!"

Before Jesse could fire, a hulking shape emerged from behind the curtain. Recognition of the brute's twisted face froze Jesse as utterly as the Warder he'd disabled outside. The creature that came lumbering out from the darkness was almost twice the size of a normal man, its flesh a patchwork of stitches and scars, its body swollen with immense knots of muscle. The limbs were mismatched, one leg longer and bulkier than the other, and one arm bifurcated near the elbow to allow a second forearm to protrude from its side. An arm dangled from the center of the thing's breastbone, its fingers clenching and unclenching with each step. Yet above this travesty, this abomination of surgery and madness, there sat the recognizable countenance of John Younger – the boy Jesse had traveled across the country to save.

"My God! It's John!" Bob cried out as he entered the surgery and saw the monster lumbering out from the shadows.

The monster's face twisted into a pained grimace as he heard his brother's shout. For a moment, the Reconstructed hesitated in his menacing advance.

Tumblety held his hand toward John, displaying for the creature the vial of cloudy liquid gripped in his fingers. "You're mine! That menagerie of organs and tissues I sewed up inside your carcass is screaming in pain right now! You want the hurt to go away? You obey me! I'm in control; I have the drugs that can hold your pain in check. Only I can make the pain go away."

His face assuming an almost regretful expression, John turned back toward Jesse and resumed his lumbering march.

"Don't damage them too badly," Tumblety warned his creature. "I'll need unharmed parts if I'm to build you some new friends."

*****

Colonel Custer leaned over the terminal, using the vocal reiterators as he tapped the alert signal on the key. It grated on his sensibilities to be down here in the communications center instead of out with his men leading them in battle. Only the vital importance of ensuring the message was relayed as far and wide as possible made him linger in the room. The fact that rebels had somehow broken into Camp Lincoln and smuggled weapons to the prisoners was disastrous enough, but if Custer allowed any of them to escape through negligence, he was apt to see his military career come to an abrupt and ignominious end.

"Ain't you sent that alert yet?" Custer growled at the operator.

The anxious soldier looked up at his commander and shook his head. "Fort Stimson wants to know numbers and their armaments before dispatching any cavalry our way."

"Just tell them to head for the frontier," Custer snapped. The offer of sending a troop of cavalry to relieve the prison was something that stung his pride. The situation might be slipping beyond his control, but he had no intention of letting anybody else see it for themselves. "If they can stop the rebs from linking up with the rest of the Secesh, we can stop 'em cold." The strategy was a sound one; there were enough troops and forts between Camp Lincoln and the Confederate Rebellion to intercept the prisoners as soon as they started south. By suggesting such a course to the other commands, Custer would be able to salvage something from this disaster. His plan was to claim responsibility for the recapture of the prisoners. If he got enough newspapers to print that line, the War Department wouldn't be able to dismiss him out of hand for allowing the escape in the first place.

"I've told them, Colonel," the soldier at the console said. "They still feel..."

Before the man could finish, sounds of violence erupted in the corridor outside the room. Custer drew his pistols and started to step around the terminal. As he began to draw a bead on the door, the portal was kicked inward by a powerful blow. The Union officer fired at the rebel prisoners who started to surge through the doorway. Two men pitched and fell, their chests ripped to shreds by his shots. Custer fired again, driving the rest of the prisoners back.

"Surrender, Colonel," a voice snarled from the corridor outside. "You don't have a chance."

"Then I'll die with my boots on," Custer growled back. He lunged toward the doorway, intending to make good his vow. Just as he started to move, however, a burst of eerily precise marksmanship stabbed at him, and his pistols were ripped from his hands. He could only gape in astonishment as his guns went clattering across the room.

A second mob of prisoners appeared at the doorway. Leading them was a pale man dressed in black, his eyes hidden behind a set of tinted goggles. The man's lean face curled into a sneer as he studied Custer.

"Did you already send out the alarm?" the man asked, pointing one of the blasters gripped in his hand at the vocal reiterator.

Custer nodded, a triumphant smile on his face. "Every fort from here to the border knows about the breakout."

"Much obliged," Henderson said. He wagged his pistol from side to side. The men behind him opened fire on the operator and his equipment. The fusillade blasted both man and machine into a heap of twisted wreckage.

"Now we settle with the commandant," one of the prisoners said, rushing into the room. Before he could close upon Custer, the rebel was struck from behind by the butt of Henderson's pistol. The man staggered, clutching at his bloodied scalp.

"I tell you who dies and when," Henderson warned the prisoners.

The rebels glared daggers at him. "What we've been through, this cur needs to hang!"

Henderson reached up to his face, pulling away the tinted glasses. The rebels cringed in fright when they saw his unveiled eyes. In the darkness of the signal room, Henderson's eyes burned like two crimson fires.

The prisoners didn't get the chance to recover from their fright. Mercilessly, Henderson blasted the four men in the hall with his pistols. The betrayed rebels were splashed across the corridor, dismembered by the murderous salvo. The mysterious man turned back toward Custer, a mocking smile on his face as he regarded the Union officer's bewilderment.

"There's some that feel you're worth more alive than dead," Henderson said. Without hesitation, he put an energy bolt into the head of the prisoner he'd struck with the butt of his pistol. The shot all but decapitated the reeling rebel and dropped his twitching body to the floor. "My friends expect big things from you, General," the gaunt man continued, his red eyes still blazing with an inhuman vibrancy.

"Who… who are you?" Custer stammered.

Henderson shook his head. "A question for another time." He backed through the doorway, keeping the threat of his guns on Custer as he retreated from the room. He pulled the door shut behind him. Custer could hear the bark of Henderson's pistol as the rebel melted the lock and sealed him inside the room.

Looking at the carnage around him, Custer was unable to fathom the stranger's ruthless betrayal of his own men. Destroying the reiterator relays was something he could understand, but killing his followers to spare the life of an enemy was madness!

As he reflected on that insanity, and thought about Henderson's crimson eyes, Custer realized that who the villain was wasn't the important question. It was what he was – that was the bigger question.

A question that Custer knew he might never find an answer for.

*****

Jesse aimed his blasters at John as the hideous beast came lumbering across the ward. He closed his eyes, tried to tell himself that the Reconstructed wasn't really John Younger, that it had no connection to the boy who'd followed him with such worshipful adoration. This wasn't the boy he'd led into ambush and capture.

"Don't shoot!" Bob cried out. "It's still John!"

Jesse shook his head. He wanted to shout down Bob's cry, to tell the outlaw that the Reconstructed wasn't his brother anymore. When he opened his eyes and saw John's face staring at him from atop the gigantic brute, he found the effort impossible.

"Get Frank out of here!" Jesse snarled at Bob. He turned and grabbed the outlaw by the shoulder, shoving him toward the wall where Frank was shackled.

"That thing's not John!" Frank shouted, thrashing against his chains in impotent fury. "Tumblety's destroyed his brain with torture and chemicals! There ain't nothin' left of him!"

"Get Frank out of here!" Jesse repeated. He again tried to train his guns on John, but his determination faltered when he saw the Reconstructed's face twist into the familiar, exuberant smile he'd seen so often. Holstering one of his pistols, Jesse made a soothing gesture to the advancing monster. "John, it's me. Jesse James."

The beast hesitated, blinking in confusion at the metal-armed outlaw. Despite Frank's claims, to the contrary there was still something of John Younger buried inside the grotesque giant. Jesse had to appeal to that, draw it out from whatever foulness Tumblety had inflicted on the boy with his insidious experiments.

Tumblety noticed his monster's hesitation. Some of the crazed light faded from his eyes, replaced with a hunted, rat-like cunning. He could see his triumph collapsing before his eyes. Failure was something the experimenter couldn't allow, not when he was so close to the success that would set his name above Tesla and all the others who'd scoffed at his theories.

Tumblety dashed back across the vivisection theater, dodging around the table upon which Loveless had been strapped down, intent upon seizing the Rippers lying on the wheeled instrument tray. He froze as Jesse noticed him, as the outlaw swung around and trained the blaster he still held on the madman. A nervous twitch flickered across Tumblety's face as he felt the gun aimed at him. Only his proximity to Loveless and Jesse's fear of striking her made the gunman hold his fire. Tumblety noticed the restraint and ducked down behind the edge of the surgery table.

Before Jesse could move, before he could find some fresh angle from which to draw a bead on Tumblety without threatening Loveless, an inarticulate bellow rose from John's mutilated body. Bob and Frank, close to the door of the surgery, shouted a warning to Jesse. Jesse did not react quickly enough when he swung around to meet the Reconstructed. Like a crazed bull, John charged into Jesse, slamming into him headfirst and throwing him back. The outlaw's free hand closed on John's arm, clinging to the monster as it drove him across the room.

"Get away!" Jesse shouted to Bob and Frank. "Find Cole! Find help!" Frank looked as though he would argue, but Bob shoved him through the door and spurred him on in a desperate rush to find the manpower they'd need to subdue the monstrous John.

John's charge ended in a clamorous crash as he drove Jesse against one of the wooden walls acting as a partition between the vivisection theaters. The wall splintered beneath the impact, Jesse felt his bones shiver with the violence of the blow. Still, he retained his grip on the Reconstructed's arm. Pivoting his body, the mechanical strength in his arm pulled John around and slammed the brute into the partition. Beneath John's muscled bulk, the wall more than splintered; it disintegrated, reduced to splinters by the beast's weight.

Jesse loosed his hold on John as the monster crashed to the floor. The pistol he'd still been holding had been knocked from his hand by the impact, but its companion was still holstered at his side. In a flash, Jesse drew the blaster and took aim. From the ground, the creature stared up at him with a bloodied, battered face. Jesse hesitated, once again frozen by the thought that somewhere inside this thing there endured the mind of John Younger.

Even as he hesitated, a whirring noise sliced through the air. The partition a few inches from Jesse's face was suddenly gouged by a razor-sharp disk of steel. The outlaw threw himself into a dive, sprawling across the floor as another saw-blade came streaking across the surgery toward him. This blade struck the floor, skipping as it went whirling through the ward. He took aim at his attacker, and then felt raw horror pulse through his body.

Tumblety had regained his Rippers, but the crafty fiend hadn't depended entirely on his skill with the experimental weapons to finish Jesse quickly. He'd taken the precaution of upending the table Loveless was strapped to, employing it as a bulwark against Jesse's marksmanship. As the experimenter ducked down, all Jesse could see was Loveless tied to the front of his refuge. Gagged by her captor, all she could do was stare at him with hard determined eyes, struggling to escape even though she knew it was useless. He knew the message she was trying to convey. Whatever it took, she wanted him to finish Tumblety.

Jesse's reluctance to fire on John was nothing compared to how repugnant the idea of jeopardizing Loveless was. "Come out of there, yeh yellow dog!" he shouted at Tumblety.

The madman kept himself low behind the table. "Come now, Jesse," he called. "I expect fools to think me insane, but I find it insulting when they think I am stupid. Throw down your blaster and perhaps we can talk things over."

"In a pig's eye!" Jesse spat. He started to make a dash toward the racks of specimen jars, thinking to use Tumblety's morbid collection as cover while he crept up on the lunatic's flank. Just as he began his run, he was struck from behind. Jesse was spun around as John's brawny arms closed about him, the limb stitched to his chest reaching out and locking its fingers around his throat. Jesse pounded at the brute with his steel hands, trying to force the Reconstructed to let him go.

"It seems the situation has changed," Tumblety smirked, stepping out from behind Loveless. He pointed one of his Rippers at Jesse. "Know that your death will advance the cause of science, Mr. James."

Exerting the full power of his mechanical arms, Jesse swung John's immense bulk around just as Tumblety fired. The saw-edged blade from the Ripper went scything through the arm holding Jesse by the neck, slicing clean through flesh and bone, severing the limb just behind the elbow. John bellowed in pain, releasing Jesse and staggering back as black chemicals spurted from the stump sewn to his chest. Frantic, Tumblety aimed the other Ripper and tried to drop Jesse in his tracks. The blade went whirring through the air, but instead of striking vulnerable flesh, it hit the unyielding steel of Jesse's arm. The blade was deflected by the metal and sent ricocheting off through the surgery. Tumblety wailed in dismay as the blade smashed through specimen jars before burying itself in the RJ generator that powered the laboratory equipment and supplemented Tesla's electric lights.

The madman rushed across the operation room, kneeling amid the rancid organs that had spilled from the shattered bottles. Mewing like a panicked child, he tried to salvage the mangled specimens, oblivious both to the enemy at his back and the flames spurting from the side of the damaged generator.

Only one thing granted Tumblety a reprieve. In his struggle with the Reconstructed, Jesse's remaining blaster had been knocked from his hand. The outlaw might have spared a moment to look for it, but sight of the flames billowing from the generator and the vision of the fire spreading along the spilled alcohol from the doctor's shattered jars, decided him upon a different course. Removing the knife tucked into his boot, the outlaw rushed over to the vivisection theater. "Sorry about all the distractions," Jesse apologized as he crouched beside the overturned table and began sawing away at the straps holding Loveless down.

A loud explosion rocked the surgery before Jesse had Loveless free. He glanced up from his work to see the generator engulfed in flames. The fire was rapidly spreading through the spilled alcohol, sending fiery streamers running up the curtains and along the shelves. Several of the intact bottles began to burst as the heat set their contents to a boil. Amid the havoc, the deranged Tumblety still scrambled to preserve the scraps of his collection.

"We've gotta get," Jesse swore as he slashed through the final binding. Loveless slumped to the floor and pulled the gag free from her mouth. Gratefully, she accepted the duster Jesse handed her to cover herself.

Any words of gratitude that might have found purchase on her tongue evaporated when Loveless saw the hulking figure of John come rushing at the outlaw. The Reconstructed held one hand against the set the whole in his chest, but the other reached toward Jesse with all the malignance of the Devil's own claw. Jesse pushed Loveless aside, and in the same motion he caught the edge of the table and flipped it toward the monster. John caught it in his outstretched hand, crumpling it beneath his fingers as though it were an old tin can.

"You have to kill him!" Loveless shouted to Jesse. "Any sympathy you have for John should find solace in the knowledge that death is a mercy after what Tumblety has done to the boy".

Jesse recoiled as the Reconstructed reached for him again. "Good idea. How do I do it without a blaster?" Even as he asked the question, John lunged at him and caught him by the wrist. The brute lifted Jesse from the floor and shook him like a rag doll. The knife in Jesse's hand raked across John's flesh, but the monster didn't seem to notice. What flowed from the slashes and cuts wasn't blood, but more of the black ichor.

Loveless glanced about, searching for any weapon that might stop the Reconstructed and save Jesse. The outlaw had risked his life to save her, it was only fitting she should do the same for him. Tumblety's surgical instruments, for all their horror, wouldn't be much use against John. If she was going to help Jesse, she needed something far more effective.

The spreading flames gave Loveless an idea. Running across the theater, she snatched up a strip Tumblety had cut from her uniform. Passing the cloth through the flame, she soon set it alight. Loveless turned about and ran back to the embattled outlaw and the monster that held him. Holding the burning cloth high, she thrust it full into John's face, scorching the creature's enraged eyes.

A demonic screech echoed through the surgery. John flung Jesse away and clamped both hands about his burnt eyes. Screaming in pain, the monster lurched across the surgery.

From where the beast had thrown him, Jesse cried out a warning to John. If the Reconstructed heard him, the creature didn't show any sign of understanding. He continued to shamble blindly across the theater until he crashed full into one of the specimen racks. Shelves, jars, and monster came toppling to the floor in a calamitous collapse. The alcohol from the jars splashed through the surgery, forming a great morass that quickly took light.

Jesse lurched to his feet, even now intent on trying to help John. Loveless caught him before he could make such a suicidal gesture. "You can't help him," she scolded the outlaw. "It's too late!" Sternly she turned Jesse around, hurrying him along as they dashed for the doorway.

They paused only once, glancing back at the conflagration that was consuming the laboratory. Tumblety was still dashing about among the burning racks, trying to salvage his grisly collection. John's misshapen body lay sprawled among the shelves, thrashing and flailing as the fire began to consume it. With a groaning rumble, one of the roof beams came crashing down, spilling the upper floor into the surgery and obliterating any trace of Tumblety and his creation.

Grimly, Jesse James and Lucinda Loveless retreated out into the comparatively wholesome bedlam of the compound.

*****

Cole Younger and a dozen other men were rushing toward Tumblety's laboratory when Jesse and Lucinda came stumbling out of the burning building. The outlaws and rebels were taken aback when they saw the people they had come to rescue advancing toward them. Frank James ran to his brother, catching Jesse in a fierce embrace. Bob Younger looked past the two bank robbers, staring hopefully at the dark doorway leading into the burning hospital.

Jesse noted Bob's agitation. Pulling away from Frank, he turned to face the two Younger brothers. "I... I couldn't save John. It was too late. Whatever that Yankee devil did to him, there weren't enough left of John to help." He locked eyes with Cole, wincing when he saw the deep hurt in the elder Younger's gaze. Jesse'd recovered his brother, but Cole had lost his. "I'm sorry," Jesse said, appreciating how hollow those words were. "But it's better this way. Better John's dead than walkin' around as some Yankee monster."

Bob dropped to his knees, pounding his fists against the ground. "They're all gonna pay! Every damn blue-belly!"

Cole closed a hand on Bob's shoulder and lifted him to his feet. "They'll pay," he assured his brother. "But not today. Today we've gotta get all these prisoners somewheres safe. After that, then we can talk about revenge."

"The guards been taken care of?" Jesse asked.

It was Robert Ford who answered the outlaw chief. "There's a few blue-bellies in the barracks, but they've barricaded themselves into a few isolated rooms. Trapped themselves in their own cages. Jim and Captain Ingram took care of the guard towers and the 'bots on the walls. Some of the boys got learned on the Rolling Thunders've got the new wagons runnin', and they're guardin' the main gate". Robert's expression turned grim. "With you gone, Mr. Henderson took it on himself to gather all the prisoners and start leadin' them out the main gate."

Jesse was struck by Will's tone. There was something about Henderson's assumption of command that had disturbed the gunman and which, in turn, now aroused Jesse's own suspicions. "Let's head for the gate," Jesse told the outlaws around him. "It might be that Allen needs to be reminded that he ain't in command of this outfit."

Despite the beating he had endured at the hands of John, Jesse hurried through the now abandoned prison camp. Even with the magnitude of their victory over the Yankees and the liberation of not only his brother Frank, but the thousands of captives, he felt a sense of panic welling up inside him: a feeling that this great triumph was going to be snatched away from him in the final instant.

When he neared the gates of Camp Lincoln, Jesse knew his unease was well founded. Allen Henderson stood at the top of the gate, barking out orders to the liberated prisoners, whipping them up into a vengeful fury. Around him, the bodies of lynched guards twitched and squirmed. The revenge Henderson called for, however, wasn't against the guards or other Union soldiers. He was calling upon the rebels to sack the camp itself, to put the nearby town of Andersonville to the torch and slaughter the inhabitants. Jesse felt himself go sick inside when he heard the vitriol spewed by the bespectacled warmonger, remembering another time he had whipped up his troops to a murderous frenzy. Lawrence had been the town to suffer that time under Quantrill. Now, Henderson wanted to unleash the same rage against Andersonville.

Loveless clutched at Jesse's arm. "You can't let him do this," she said, entreaty in her voice.

"I don't intend to," Jesse told her. Leaving Loveless with Frank and Cole, Jesse marched straight toward the gate. Without his duster, the outlaw chief's mechanical arms were fully exposed and visible. The rebels parted in awe and respect before the man who had won them their freedom. He stepped through the ranks of prisoners until he was standing before the gate and looking straight up at Henderson. "What're yeh doin', Allen?" Jesse demanded.

Henderson adjusted his goggles and looked down at the outraged outlaw. "We're going to teach the Yankees a lesson. Pay them back in kind."

Jesse shook his head. He turned and faced the rest of the rebels. "Not like this we ain't. Fightin' soldiers, lawmen, carpet baggers, and robber barons is one thing. This, this ain't any of that! This ain't fightin' at all. It's killin', killin' for the sake of plum meanness." He pointed his hand in the direction of Andersonville. "That ain't even a Yankee town. Them people there are Southerners. They're the same folk as you fought a war to defend. Now you want to kill 'em because they've been conquered? Them are the ones we should be fightin' for, not agin!"

"We need supplies, Jesse," impatience was etched into Henderson's face. "Wagons to transport all these men. Food to feed them. Clothes to replace the rags they're wearing. Guns..."

"Did the guards get off their alarm on the Reiterator?" Jesse asked him.

Henderson nodded. "They sent the alarm. The blue-bellies will be waiting for us if we move toward the Confederate Rebellion."

Jesse grimiced. "Then we gotta put a wiggle on," he said, raising his voice so the prisoners could hear him. "Because we ain't goin' south. We're headin' west, out to where there's open land we can make our own. Land where we can lick our wounds and make our plans without havin' a Yankee boot on our necks. We ain't got enough time to bundle ya'll up. So, those that can, make for the big wagons just this side of town. Spread the word in the camp: the rest of ya'll, scatter. Union'll be down on us shortly, but they won't be able to get you all. We'll take as many north with us as we can."

"We still need supplies," Henderson reminded him.

"We'll get 'em," Jesse answered. "We'll take 'em from Andersonville as we ride through. We'll steal if we have to, but there ain't to be any killin'." He glared up at Henderson. "This ain't gonna be Lawrence all over agin." The shadowy man sketched a slight nod and climbed down from the gate.

Jesse rejoined Loveless and the members of his gang. Will Shaft clapped him on the back as he came close.

"You got more sand'n I have," the Exoduster said. "I don't think I'd ever have the gumption to talk down that man."

Frank's expression was even graver. "I never expected to see you again, Jesse. I damn sure never expected to see him again."

Loveless suppressed a shudder. The murderous intensity she'd felt exuding from the black-clad warmonger during his harangue had been, in its way, even more terrifying than the madness of Tumblety. "Who is he?" she asked Jesse. She was proud that Jesse had stood up to the strange man and could even find it in her to be sympathetic to Jesse's ambition to lead these men away from the reach of the Union. But both pride and sympathy were suborned to the feeling of alarm hammering inside her. This man calling for violence, she felt, was a menace to the safety of not just the government and military of the Union, but to every man, woman, and child who lived in it.

Jesse watched Henderson stalk out through the gates and into the growing night. It was some time before he answered Loveless's question. Who was Allen Henderson?

"I'm not sure I know who he is anymore," Jesse said. "I'm not sure it's somethin' I want to know."

Epilogue

"I ain't goin' for it, Virg. Yer a plum fool to even be thinkin' that way!" Wyatt Earp's voice was livid in its tone; the imperious, unyielding bellow that had tamed towns across the west.

"Take a good damn look at me," Virgil snarled back, weakness and pain underlying the emotion in his words. "Them sawbones mightn't have cut it off, but this arm's useless as a lump of lead! How in Hell am I supposed to help you when I've only got one arm?"

"Who said anythin' about needin' yer help, Virg?" Wyatt retorted. "Me, Warren, and Doc can handle things ourselves."

Virgil laughed, a hollow and cheerless sound. "Yer fergettin' Morg," he said. "Or don't you count him as yer brother anymore?"

"I do, but damnit, Virg, look at him!" Wyatt swung his arm out pointing to his brother. "He's just standing there likea 'bot, starin' down at his crippled brother with all the emotion of a brick wall. I loved Morg, and I don't want you to end up like that!"

Morgan Earp's cold eyes shifted from their wounded brother to the livid Over-marshal without a hint of emotion. When they slid back to Virgil's broken form, something akin to sympathy may have resided in their dark depths, but the face remained impassive and immobile.

"It's only my arm," Virgil retorted. "It's not like I need him to do what he did for Morg. And you'll need my help if'n yer goin' after Ike Clanton and the rest of the Cowboys."

"I've already settled with the Old Man and Phin," Wyatt snapped back. "I'll get the others too. And I'll get 'em without any more help from Carpathian."

Back in his lab, the scientist smiled as he heard the remark transmitted across the audiophonic transposer. The voices of the marshal and his elder brother had a distorted, tinny quality as they left the elaborately funneled transmission horn fitted to the side of the bulky, boxy machine, but the words were distinct enough for Carpathian's purposes. He rose from the claw-footed chair he'd been sitting in for the last hour as he listened to Wyatt and Virgil Earp arguing about the medical miracles only Dr. Carpathian could bestow.

"My invention is remarkable, is it not?" The question came from a bespectacled young man wearing a long white coat and sporting a many-pocketed work belt around his waist. He stepped around from behind the machine, a proud smile on his face.

Carpathian always felt that Thomas Edison's smile belonged to something from the fox family rather than any product of human evolution. The inventor was brilliant, naturally, that was why he'd been recruited into the Enlightened. That brilliance, however, was married to a personality utterly devoid of ethics or conscience. Edison was proud of his inventions – both those of his own creation and those which could more justly be credited to engineers and scientists working under him. Carpathian happened to know that the credit for the audiophonic transposer could be equally divided between the Scotsman, Alexander Graham Bell, and the Italian, Guglielmo Marconi. Edison's contribution had come in the area of miniaturization, a crucial development for the purpose to which Carpathian wanted to put the invention.

Nestled inside the cyborg body of Morgan Earp was a cylindrical audiophone that, when actuated by Hertzian waves emanating from an electromagnetic key, would transmit the sounds of whatever was unfolding around it to a receiver hundreds of miles away. By such means, Carpathian could gain access to the most intimate secrets, the most candid of conversations. There would be no confusion about what was overheard, for wax cylinders fitted to the receiver would record every word and preserve them for later consultation.

"It is a remarkable achievement, Thomas," Carpathian conceded as he set his hand atop the receiver. "Be certain to make a record of the rest of their talk in case one of them should divulge anything useful."

Edison stared in puzzlement as his mentor turned and started from the room. "Where are you going?"

Carpathian turned and pointed at the audiophonic transposer. "You heard the lawmen, Thomas. Virgil Earp is in the market for a new arm, so I think I might make some modifications to existing devices. It would be a shame to disappoint him, after all. I do so have such plans for the west and I'd rather have the Earps beholden to us than working against us." The old scientist shook his head. "Violence is so terribly distressing when it isn't necessary."

*****

The blackened heap of timbers that had once been the old hospital continued to send up streamers of greasy smoke into the overcast sky. Buzzards and crows circled the ruin, squawking hungrily at each other as though complaining about the lingering heat which prevented them from scavenging among the rubble.

Heat didn't keep a very different sort of scavenger from sniffing around the ruin. From where he stood at the edge of the rubble, Colonel George Armstrong Custer could see the hunched figure scurrying about the wreckage like some gigantic spider black from soot. Sometimes the shape would pounce on some bit of twisted metal with a happy yelp, at other times the ghoul would pull an unrecognizable lump of charred refuse out from under a timber and utter a despairing wail.

Custer shook his head. Any sane man would count it a miracle that he'd escaped such a conflagration with his life. Dr. Tumblety, however, was very far from sane. He capered about the smoldering rubble bewailing the loss of his equipment and the destruction of his test subjects. Most of all, he cursed the obliteration of his prize collection, that menagerie of pickled organs he had exhibited with such pride to anyone with stomach enough to gaze upon them and listen to the experimenter's grisly lecturing.

The vivisectionist was insane and so was the ghastly chain of experimentation he had sought to perfect. Custer wasn't sure who it was in the War Department that was crazed or desperate enough to put any stock in Tumblety, but he knew they must have been both powerful and ruthless. Only power could protect a murderous fiend like Tumblety – especially after what he had done in London. Only absolute ruthlessness would try to harness the demonic madness of Jack the Ripper.

"He's here! He's here!" Tumblety suddenly cried out, waving his arms and gesticulating wildly at something lying partially buried under the rubble.

Custer looked worriedly at the soldiers arrayed about the compound. Most of them were reinforcements from Fort Stimson, busy forcing the crowd of prisoners that had been left behind - those too sick or injured to make the trek out to the massive ore-haulers the rebels had brought to the edge of town.. Few of them had any idea what sort of grisly work Tumblety had been engaged in. The commandant hoped that whatever Tumblety had turned up, it wouldn't draw too much attention from the men. He was almost thankful that the experimenter was carrying on in so audacious a fashion. Such was the contempt the troops held Tumblety in, that the louder he carried on, the more the soldiers tried to ignore him.

Keeping a ready grip on the sword sheathed at his side, Custer walked across the jumbled debris and joined Tumblety amid the rubble. He looked down at the thing that had so excited the madman. It looked like the charred body of a twisted giant, a boyish face still visible amid the burnt flesh. He removed a scented handkerchief from his pocket and held it across his face as the stench wafting from the corpse struck his nose.

"Whatever it is, it's dead now."

Tumblety scowled at the commandant. "Do not speak to me of death. That is a technical definition that has no place in my experiments!" He pointed back at the charred body of John Younger. "Perhaps he is without the spark of life, but I was the one who put it there to begin with. It will be a comparatively easy thing to revive him again."

Custer blanched at the very thought. "To what purpose? Look around you! The prisoners are all gone, the camp is a shambles, most of my men are dead. Your experiment is over!"

The madman clucked his tongue in disapproval. "You fail to understand the im-

portance of my work. They appreciate my genius in Wash
is only a setback. A rut in the road to discovery. Discovery
Tumblety tugged at his thick mustache and looked across th
however. The camp was a desolate ruin. All but the least-hearty
north with the outlaws or scattering far and wide across the surrou
those barely clinging to death had remained, and they had been mo
put down, whichever had seemed easiest to the troopers who found th
move the facilities to someplace more conducive to research. I mentione
that it would be interesting to see how efficient my procedures might be whe
aboriginal subjects. There's a certain recalcitrance when it comes to exper
civilized men, even when they are rebels. But to use savages! No one would
experiments then."

The image of Tumblety working his insane science upon entire Indian villages so vile that Custer nearly drew his saber from its scabbard. He was too pragmatic, howev to let his loathing of the experimenter carry him toward an act that would see the end of his career. "I imagine you've already formed an idea about where you want to set up shop?"

Tumblety smiled. "I think the Black Hills would prove ideal. The Nations have some quaint notions about that place being sacred. There have always been savages guarding the hills, and the Warrior Nation can be counted on to maintain a presence there." A cunning twinkle shone in his eye. "I'll need a full facility there. Troops to collect subjects for me and a fort to garrison them in. Naturally, a fort will need a commander."

"You mean me?" Custer said, both shocked and disgusted by the suggestion that he continue his relationship with Tumblety.

"Of course," the madman said. "Who better to help me in my work than an officer who already appreciates what I am trying to accomplish." Tumblety pointed again at the gigantic carcass of John Younger. "That is but the beginning. They will make you a general when I show them what my Reconstructed are capable of!"

Custer listened to the madman rant and plot, but his ears only half heard what Tumblety said. He was thinking about the possibility that the experimenter was right, that by sticking with him he'd be able to aggrandize his own career and reclaim the rank of general once more. It was a temptation too great to resist.

In the back of his mind, however, Custer recalled a red-eyed rebel dressed in black, a sinister enigma who had unaccountably spared his life. The rebel had called him 'general,' almost a prophetic declaration. It was a coincidence that Custer found uncanny. Almost as though some dark force was guiding him and propelling him to some terrible doom.

t Riches

Craig Gallant

Prologue

Shadows stretched over the northern plains as the sun sank into the west. Gently rolling hills swept away to the south, fading to a dull brown in the distance. Lush grass and full trees dominated this border region; a last bastion of quiet, serene greenery. As far as the eye could see, all was at peace.

As darkness settled in, a spray of sparkling lights sprang up across the plains, echoing the stars appearing overhead. Guttering campfires stretched for nearly a mile in every direction. Iron Hawk settled into the grass and eased one hand, palm flat, behind him. Unseen in the growing shadows, a band of Warrior Nation scouts lowered themselves to the ground.

The large force of easterners had moved into Warrior Nation territory several days ago. Armed, they rode a mismatched variety of loud, loathsome vehicles that defiled the land with their foul vapors. Dispatched by the united chiefs of the Warrior Nation, Iron Hawk had stalked into the prairie with his most experienced fighters, shadowing these outsiders as a larger war party followed along behind. The invaders spread across the plains in disorderly camps each night, easy to spot and track. When Iron Hawk's scouts caught up to them, they were settled around a shallow dale, many camping in a series of limestone caves beneath the hills.

There was no real pattern to the mongrel exodus. They had violated the territory of the People, fleeing from the south east. Moving at a slow crawl, they had advanced across the plains in an arch that brought them gradually back around toward the south. Behind them they left a foul trail of discarded equipment, empty containers, and shallow graves.

Iron Hawk touched the medallion at his neck. The stylized bird of prey had been painstakingly carved from a plate of Union armor; its chain had once held a plain gold band and had been snapped from the neck of the armor's previous owner. The rough feel of the iron on his fingers always served to remind the war leader of the new world that had risen up to overtake his people. The men spread across the plains ahead had violated an immutable law of that new world. He had been sent to see that they were punished.

Iron Hawk looked back into the lengthening shadows. He could just make out the shapes of his scouting party crouching in the darkness. He nodded to himself and then made a quick series of gestures. Each warrior raised two fingers in silent acknowledgment and settled deeper into the grass. The sun was nearly gone now, the western sky washed with warm, muted colors that did little to illuminate the dell below.

The war leader lowered his head and began a low, sonorous chant. He felt the power of the Great Spirit rising from the earth, answering his call. Although he had not yet mastered the ability to surrender his body to the shapes of his spirit guides, he had inherited vast reserves of power from his father, the renowned medicine man, White Tree. His father and an entire scouting party had disappeared over a year ago, and Iron Hawk knew in his soul that he would never see him again. He had been eager, ever since, for every opportunity for vengeance.

The shaman stood as the colors and shadows around him began to swirl together, answering his call. Like a massive, impenetrable cloak, the powers of the Earth rose up to conceal him from the eyes of his enemies. He looked back to his warriors, each seeing with clear eyes through the illusion, and nodded once. With calm, measured steps he strode toward the haphazard encampment of his enemies.

The sentries posted by the invaders were nothing to fear. The scent of their unwashed bodies carried for hundreds of paces downwind, further tainted with the acrid trace of tobacco and the sour smell of alcohol. The inescapable stench of their unnatural energy hung over everything. Iron Hawk was certain that, even without the power of the Great Spirit, he could have walked through the camp unnoticed.

The shaman paced among the enemy, his dark gaze passing unseen over the invaders. These poor apparitions radiated wary, brutalized exhaustion. They clung to their ragged belongings as if the horrible conditions of the encampment were a paradise they feared could be stripped away at any moment. The warrior snorted softly in contempt.

Even shadowing the enormous mob for days, he was not fully prepared him for the number of dispossessed. There were thousands, most dressed in tattered rags, their feet bare; their bodies shrunken by starvation. As darkness descended, most of the men were lying down upon the grass without any sense of order, merely falling asleep where they had come to rest. Here or there the massive shadows of vehicles loomed over him, most unarmed and unarmored; rusting wrecks, their twinkling crimson lights dim and dying. Men stood atop some, watching everyone who passed with a suspicious glare, ill-kept weapons clutched in shaking hands.

Moving through the camp, he caught bits and pieces of conversation in their harsh, alien tongue. They crouched in fear; pathetic, flickering fires all the comfort they could claim. Most were silent. Those that spoke did so in dull, stunned tones. Iron Hawk was passingly familiar with the language of his foes, and the conversations all seemed to revolve around a deep sense of betrayal and disappointment.

A sense of disbelief made them numb to their current state and to the world around them. It was as if the changes that had wracked the world for a generation had finally, in their darkest moment, been made manifest. Their reality consisted of their immediate, pathetic surroundings; huddled around ramshackle vehicles in the middle of hostile territory, watching each man that passed as if the whole, shifting world were their enemy.

Iron Hawk shook his head as he passed among them. The trucks likely contained what food and supplies that remained to these outcasts, and yet he was not surprised to see that no unified organization had been made for their defense. Each mob acted on its own, huddled around a decrepit vehicle, or glaring jealously at the vehicles of others. It became more and more apparent that this was not a single army, or even a single united mob. It was, rather, countless smaller bodies of tired, frightened wretches determined to hold their own against the wider world. There was no unity or trust here among his enemies.

Rather than take heart from their obvious weakness, he found it sad.

Iron Hawk moved through the camp, making his way toward the sunken valley at its center. As he came upon the lip of the depression, he wrapped the concealing shadows more closely around himself, peering down into the dell. A series of caves were visible around the bottom of the small valley. Some were no larger than a rabbit warren, but others could hold entire parties of the enemy. More of the defiling vehicles were parked all along the floor of the dell. These seemed to be in better repair and included several heavily armored monsters bristling with weaponry. Scattered among the larger machines were over a hundred of the smaller, horse-sized contraptions capable of carrying men gliding over the ground like low-flying birds.

There was more organization here than with the rest of the rabble above: the leaders of this ragtag band must be camped within. He wanted to get as close as he could, to learn more about these men, before unleashing the full might of the Warrior Nation with the rising sun. His chest reverberated with a low hum, and the shadows grew even darker around him. A ring of more alert sentries watched the valley, but hidden by the power of the Great Spirit, he stalked right through them.

As Iron Hawk moved further into the hollow, he saw that tattered sheets of rough fabric had been hung across the mouths of the largest caves. Dancing firelight or the muted, crimson-edged illumination of their foul lanterns flickered weakly around the edges. One of the curtains sheltering a cave nearby was suddenly pulled back. Light washed out into the clearing as a man emerged, a rifle held in one hand. With his free hand he pulled the cloth shut behind him, killing the wash of light.

The shaman stopped, trusting to his spectral cloak, and the man walked past, oblivious. He found himself wondering at the man's story. Iron Hawk shrugged. It mattered little. Soon enough, they would all be dead. He eased his way closer to the cave mouth and settled in the shadows of a rocky fracture, craning his head toward the opening.

"—left the place standin' at all!" An angry voice muttered from the cave.

"Well, I blame that fast trick he's been ridin' with since the breakout; you want to know what I think. Ain't no way she was a normal nurse, no how." Another voice, bitter but resigned. Both spoke in soft, conspiratorial tones.

"Loveless? She's a bitch Union spy an' you can take that to the bank." The first voice, speaking again, quavered with barely-suppressed emotion. "How else would she have gotten out of there alive? That burg was a nest of whores' sons, and deserved to be burned out after everythin' they done! Weren't gonna be nothin' but pure justice, plain an' simple!"

"Henderson had it right, an' that's true enough." A third voice now, stoking the fires of resentment in the other two. There was an edge to this one that set Iron Hawk's skin crawling. "Burn a place like that to the ground, you send a message that the damned blue-bellies'll get loud an' clear!"

"Shut yer, mouth!" The second voice spoke. "You want 'im to gut us an' leave us behind fer the savages to pick over? Jesse done made up his mind, and it's over. That woman might o' got in his head, might o' turned him around, but that don't matter none now. We been duckin' and runnin' through Injun territory like we was the ones that got whooped, an' that's Gospel." Someone spat. "But Jesse hears you bad mouthin' that Rebel angel or second guessin' his call? We're gonna be staked out fer the scorpions faster'n you can say Billy Yank."

"Ain't no scorpions out there, Galen." The first voice again. "Not in all that grass."

Iron Hawk heard the sharp rip of another spit, then a grunt. "Then snakes, 'r gophers, 'r whatever in the name o' Hades it is up here eats folks that're staked out – It don't' matter none, Colton, fer the sake 'o the Lord! Just hobble yer lip, will ya?"

"I was just sayin'," that angry voice, Colton, again. "We shoulda burnt down that town when we had the chance. Hell. We'd a been better off stayin' in Robbers Roosts for all the boodle we're comin' outta this little adventure with."

Iron Hawk eased away from the cave and scanned the bottom of the dell. There were others, and he could hear the low mutterings of other conversations. Most of the caverns connected farther back beneath the hills. He doubted that the men hiding within them had taken the time to investigate, however. They probably thought they were safe talking about each other as long as they were huddled within different mouths. The warrior smirked. If this Jesse was the bad medicine these cowards were making him out to be, he hoped he was listening. Watching easterners kill each other was always good sport.

He spotted a larger cavern nearby, several strips of cloth obscuring the light within. Iron Hawk slid down next to the opening and settled in to listen once again.

"—would have wanted someone to come after me, that's for sure." This voice carried no anger or resentment. It was calm and relaxed; louder than the other voices. There was no fear of being overheard here. Iron Hawk was sure that would change before long.

"Nah, I get it. And if my brother was being held by those rat bastards, I would have gone in all guns a-blazin' too." There was a crunch and hiss as someone stirred a large fire. When this voice continued, it was pitched lower than before. "Just not sure I would have wanted to be dragged in myself, is all. We could have stayed back with General Mosby and been none the worse for wear. We lost a lot of good men goin' in there."

The first voice muttered grudging agreement. "We did. But Frank James seems like a good man. Captain Ingram says Jesse needs him, if we're gonna be able to turn any of this around."

"He seems like a good man, right enough." Another voice spoke. "But is he better than any of the men who fell fetching him out? Better than Shady Joe, or Johnny Fu, or any of the other guys we lost?"

"You best keep words like that to yourself, Cord." All of the voices around the fire quieted down. "Don't you be in any doubt: Frank's more important to him than any of us he picked up along the way. You know he's been on the shoot since long before Captain Ingram offered up our services. Only safe place to be when he's like that, seems to me, is behind him or beside him, and that's a fact."

"I'm just sayin'," continued Cord in a softer voice. "Something to keep in mind, as touching on the man's loyalties, is all."

"And your loyalties wouldn't lie with your own brother?" This voice was edged with contempt.

"I ain't got a brother." There was a sullen tone to the second voice now. "And I'm not sure I would have traded a bunch of good men for him if I did."

"Well, if he was your brother, he wouldn't have been worth trading good men for in the first place." The contemptuous voice deepened. "If you're so concerned, go back to Cali. It's just about three thousand miles that way, is all. Now shut your trap. I'm trying to enjoy the fire."

Iron Hawk ignored the muttered response as he pivoted on his heel to survey the bowl around him. The man with the rifle had not yet returned. Whether he was heading out to water the grass or to relieve a sentry, someone would be coming back toward the caves soon. He passed several of the larger vehicles as he moved toward another cave. He summoned the Great Spirit's energy, his hands warm as the familiar sensation of ghostly knife handles filled them. But he held the burning fire in check, the radiance of the spirit power the merest aquamarine lightning skittering around his fists and deep within his eyes.

A man surged out of the cave he was approaching, and Iron Hawk lurched back into the deepest shadows, hiding behind an armored brute on metal wheels. The man was careless with the hanging fabric and left it askew as he stomped into the central clearing.

"I don't wanna talk about it no more!" The man gestured behind him, one hand filled with a vicious-looking fighting knife. It was a comment that made no sense to Iron Hawk until another man rushed out into the night after him.

The second man's voice was hushed but urgent as he grabbed the first's arm. "Well, you gotta talk about it some more. He was our brother!"

Iron Hawk looked more closely. He could just make out the family resemblance between the two men in the light from the cavern. The first man spun around to confront his older brother, knife glittering as he spread his hands wide in a dismissive gesture.

The older man ignored the gesture. "He weren't our brother when Jesse did for him. They changed 'im in that Union camp, an' that thing in that building? That weren't Johnny." There was pleading in the man's eyes, and Iron Hawk could tell that it did not sit easily there. "C'mon, Bobbie. I heard what both you and Jesse said. It weren't John. John was gone."

The younger man shook his head, the knife quivering. "An' Jesse couldn't o' saved 'im? He saved Frank, though, din't he. An' that woman from KC." It was a statement, not a question, and the older man shrank from it.

"Bobbie, there weren't none of John left to rescue, you told me yourself. He was like one o' Carpathian's monsters, only worse! Ya'll din't have no choice!"

The younger man, Bobbie, grabbed the other by the shoulder. "Cole, he was our brother, an' we left 'im to die in a hole like an animal, put down by Jesse damned James!"

Iron Hawk did not hear the response, whatever it might have been. As soon as he heard that name his heart surged in his chest and he lurched backward, fetching up against the iron tire.

Jesse James? The man was known by all the Warrior Nation as an avatar of the darkest powers that had come to grip the land. Those unnatural arms of his, monstrous creations of the vile outsider, marked him as a demon of the first order.

If this band was running at the command of Jesse James, then a tribute truly worth of White Tree was near at hand. In the morning, the Warrior Nation would claim a major victory against the darkness and remove the blight of this infamous monster from the sun's sight.

Iron Hawk rose and moved back toward the gently-sloping wall of the vale. When he turned, however, the man with the rifle was there.

"Hey, who—" The sentry tried to bring the weapon up across his body to defend himself. He took in a lungful of cool night air, preparing to sound the alarm.

The shaman did not hesitate. His eyes flared with a burning hatred. His empty hand floated up and past the startled sentry's face, sliding around his jaw and head, grabbing a filthy hank of hair at the base of the man's neck. The white man's eyes went wide.

Iron Hawk pulled with all his might as he brought the other hand, a sliver of burning azure shadow appearing in a reversed, knife-fighter's hold, up and across. The phantom blade dripped with blue flame as the warrior's eyes ignited in an answering surge of power.

The outlaw twisted around, his head yanked in a disorienting spin. He clutched the rifle more tightly to his chest, helpless. As the man's face came back around, pulled by the native warrior's off hand, the burning blade slid across his throat, opening his veins and spraying a fan of burgundy into the grass at their feet. The blue flames flickered into darkness, reflecting once in the depths of the dying man's eyes as he stared, disbelieving, into the face of his killer.

Iron Hawk lowered the body to the grass and glanced around to be sure the scuffle had not been heard. There were no shouts of alarm, only the muffled voices of the two men still arguing over their brother's fate.

With a grim smile, Iron Hawk sneered down at the quivering body. The first blow in retribution for his father's death had been dealt, and with the rising sun, countless more would follow. His father's spirit would rise upon their cries of pain and despair, with the howls of one truly worthy of such sacrifice the last and loudest of all. He made his way casually back up the slope. The other war leaders needed to know who led this tattered army of derelicts.

It was a new world, with new laws and new punishments. And Jesse James, the man whose very body defied the Great Spirit, the wretch who symbolized everything the Warrior Nation fought against, must die.

Chapter 1

Jesse James looked into the depths of the fire and let his mind wander. The landscape that stretched out before his mind's eye was bleak and empty. Nearby, his brother Frank lay curled beneath a heavy blanket. His brother was in rough shape after his ordeal in the prison camp near Andersonville. He was alive though, and he was free. Jesse's face twisted into a vague snarl. For, although he had succeeded in breaking Frank out of Camp Lincoln, nothing much had gone according to plan since then.

Loading up the enormous ore-haulers with the quickest of the prisoners, they had struck north, deeper into Union territory, just as he had planned. Charging up behind them had been an army of prisoners who had not made it onto the massive wagons, but had stolen transportation from the town of Andersonville itself. Jesse knew that once the prisoners had passed through, there could not have been a hand cart left behind. The best he could tell, nearly half of the ten thousand prisoners had joined them as they all fled north and west, visions of a glorious free society alight in their minds.

But the ore-haulers were energy hogs, they sucked down the RJ at a prodigious rate; and most of the wagons freed from Andersonville were rusted out rattle-traps. They had been shedding dead vehicles behind them like a Union cur sheds fleas. The enormous wagons from the Union train, traveling cross-country, had been so slow that only the weakest or worst injured prisoners had been unable to keep up, even after they had been reduced to walking along beside the towering behemoths.

The Union had wasted no time in chasing after the pathetic band, either. Outriders had begun to harry the ragged tail of their scattered column only days out of Camp Lincoln. They lost men every day, traveling under both sun and moon to maintain as much distance as they could from the main force of their pursuers. What food they had taken with them quickly ran low. Their fuel began to run out. First one ore-hauler had to be abandoned, then another; what fuel remained was divvied up among the other vehicles.

As each day ground them down and pushed them onward, Jesse's glorious dreams faded like a washed out photograph. More and more of the freed prisoners were vanishing, losing themselves in the countryside, their faith in Jesse's vision failing. He held no anger toward the men who left, having felt the urge more than once himself as they continued on their way. He would be damned if he was going to let the Union taint this victory like they had soiled so much in his life already.

They had been forced to abandon the last ore-hauler on the banks of the Mississippi. None of them could figure out how to ferry the huge wagons across the mighty river. That had been a blessing in disguise, really, as their company had been able to pick up speed almost immediately. Those who could not keep up were encouraged to scatter and hope for the best.

The Union had been preparing to meet the escaping column in the borderlands leading into the Contested Territory. Jesse knew that, and so, at the last minute, under cover of darkness, he had forced his group to turn directly north, heading straight up into the plains: Warrior Nation lands. It had worked, and it had been days now since any Union forces had been sighted.

Now, Jesse just had to hope he could stay away from the savages long enough to loop back down south into the Contested Territories, and home. His stomach was an aching void, and he knew the sorry souls following him could only feel worse. There might even be a chance to think about establishing that town that had haunted his dreams immediately after the prison break, if God was kind.

If God was not kind, they would all end up scalped, or worse, before they ever saw civilization again.

He reached out with one metal arm and stirred the dying embers of the fire, breathing yellow life into the sullen crimson glow within the charred pile of wood. If ever there was a time to strike out on his own, to make his impression in the world, this was it. The Union was still wrapped up in the east, most of its strength spent against the Warrior Nation. But those creatures of that mad doctor from Camp Lincoln would still be out there, and they seemed like they could well be more than a match for Carpathian and his disgusting menagerie. If he could only bring President Lee around, breathe some life into the old coward, there might be hope for the Confederate Rebellion yet.

Camp Lincoln. His lip curled with disgust as he settled back on his haunches. The man had been twenty years in his grave, and still the very thought of the vile monster filled Jesse's mouth with acid. No one man had every surpassed Emperor Lincoln as the symbol of everything that was wrong and evil and despicable about the Union, and even death had not unseated him in this regard.

Jesse looked across the fire to where Lucinda Loveless sat, legs curled beneath her. She was wearing mismatched men's clothing in place of the tattered nurse's uniform that she had been left with after her ordeal in the foul camp laboratory. The ragged clothing served to enhance her beauty, somehow, rather than diminish it. Every time he looked at her like this, however, his mind threw the memory of a green-eyed dancehall girl back at him. Misty's red, weeping eyes stared accusingly down through the intervening months, causing him to look away from Lucinda with a guilty jerk of his head.

In front of her, on a soft white cloth, were all of the parts to her two over-sized derringers. The RJ-1027 power packs had been removed while she cleaned and serviced the weapons, sitting off to the side and pulsing like tiny ruby hearts. Nothing could have differentiated Lucy more from any other woman than the calm, contented look on her sweet face as she took care of her lethal weapons. The woman's flawless features were at peace as she reassembled one of the pistols, unaware of Jesse's gaze.

He shook his head. What was he doing, mooning over this woman? He knew now that she was a servant of the Union. He knew she had lied to him, allowed him to believe things that were not true. But for the first time in his life, such things did not seem to matter. And if they did not matter, then why bother the ghost of an abandoned dancing girl? The thought of leaving Lucy behind had never crossed his mind. Besides, she had left with him, right? How could she carry one shred of loyalty for the Union after what they had all seen at Camp Lincoln? After what that monster, Tumblety, had very nearly done to her?

Jesse knew that no one in the Union army cared a whit for Lucinda. She was a pawn to be moved around the board and sacrificed at the proper moment. Yet, somehow he knew, even now, that a part of her still clung to her loyalty to the Union. In a way, that loyalty was even attractive. But it was going to cause them trouble if things did not shake out the way he hoped.

"Sir, a group of freed prisoners is outside. They want to speak to you about the food." The voice was hoarse and soft. Jesse had to shake off his thoughts and drag his eyes up to the stoop-shouldered man standing over him.

"What?"

The man stood up a little straighter and forged onward despite the vague animosity in the outlaw chief's tone. "There's a group of prisoners asking to see you."

Jesse's eyes narrowed. He did not know him, but the man was obviously one of the less-damaged prisoners they had pulled from the ruins of Camp Lincoln. As they had journeyed north, he had paid less and less attention to the ragged mob that trailed along behind him. He knew that men such as this, healthier and stronger than their fellows, had risen to lead small groups of fellow escapees. They were starting to act like savage tribes, each man ruling his shabby little empire like an Injun chief.

Many of the men from the prison had been near dead of starvation, and Jesse honestly had no idea where they were getting whatever food they did have. Things were desperate for everyone, and he knew that every day saw several pass away. Those that left friends or kin behind were covered with a loose layer of earth. The friendless and the weak were left sprawled where they fell. Each day more and more were left where they dropped.

What did this man, or his little gang, want from him? Jesse surged to his feet and toward the cave mouth. Lucinda looked up from her work with hooded eyes, but schooled her features to a calm passivity and looked back down. Frank, under his blankets, snorted and sat up, glaring blearily around. By that time, Jesse was gone.

The floor of his little valley was crowded with vehicles. The sun was just rising in the east, the sky stippled with the first rays of dawn. Standing near one of the Union Rolling Thunder assault wagons was a ragged group of men struggling to maintain eye contact with the outlaw leader. Jesse felt his old anger rising. He always hated men who could not look him in the eye.

"What d'you lot want?" He snapped, sneering as he watched them cringe.

One of the men, crushing a soft gray cap in his hands, stepped forward. "Mr. James, sir, we was just hopin' . . . well, there's folks starvin' up yonder, and—"

Jesse stopped the speech with one raised metal hand. “You think we ain’t all hankerin’ after somethin’ we can cram down our gullets?”

The man pulled up short, still struggling to maintain eye contact. “Well, sir, we followed you out of the prison, an’ we thought—”

“You thought I was goin’ to hold yer hands an’ lead you to the Promised Land, did you?” The contempt in his voice was like a lash, snapping down on the shoulders of the cringing men before him.

“Well, you said we were gonna be gettin’ a fresh start.” Now even their leader was looking at the dirt. “But we’re starvin’—”

Jesse stomped toward the man, taking his tattered lapels in both hard, metallic hands. “I ain’t your momma, coffee boiler! It ain’t my lookout to keep you and yours fed and clothed.” He pushed the man back into his friends and a sullen anger kindled in their dull eyes. Jesse could not have cared less.

“Didn’t we just lick the Union for ya’ll at Camp Lincoln?” He demanded. The men nodded slowly.

“Did we free every last mother’s son trapped inside?” His teeth ground together between each word. The resentment in the former prisoners’ eyes started to give way to fear. They nodded silently.

“An’ now, just when we’re on the verge o’ somethin’ great here, you lot are whinin’ about food!” Jesse’s mechanical hand lashed down to his holster and he drew one of his sleek, custom-made Hyper-velocity pistols. He leveled it at the spokesman of the scruffy crew.

“Say, what if I shoot you, an’ let the rest o’ them animals eat yer carcass?”

A thin flap over another nearby cave was torn aside by a strong-looking young man, his sharp, rodent-like face twisted with anger. The man lashed out with a long pistol, gesturing toward the huddled prisoners. “You lot back off!” He stepped in front of Jesse, empty hand splayed out before him as if the cowed men had been an angry mob ready to surge. “Ain’t you got no sense? We gotta get back down outta the grasslands to get food, you idjits! An’ it ain’t Jesse’s job ta feed ya!”

“We’re starvin’!” One of the men in the back of the group barked. The newcomer laughed.

“Damn straight yer starvin’, you dumb knuck! You’re too stupid to live! There’s food up yonder, ya’ll were just too slow to grab it! An’ now you want Jesse to step in and keep the weakest fed? Why for? What good you gonna be when time comes for gun play?”

The disdain in the man’s voice was even harsher than Jesse’s. The prisoners cringed before him, their hands half raised as if fearing a beating. Another man in a trim mustache stepped out of the cave. He bore a close resemblance to the first, and moved toward him, his own hand raised.

“Robert, settle down. They’re just hungry, is all.” He made a soft gesture, his face relaxed, his eyes pleading. “There ain’t no need to draw on ‘em.”

Jesse slid his own weapon back into its holster and nodded, taking a deep breath of the cool morning air. He had known his patience was wearing thin, but to lose his cool like this in front of the men who had followed him out of hell, that was no way for a leader to behave. “No, Robert, Charlie’s right. We ain’t got nothin’ to feed these bummers, but we don’t need to get all out of sorts our own selves neither.”

The newcomer nodded. “Just send ‘em back up to the rest. They’ll stand or fall on their own, up there.”

Robert looked at his brother as he holstered his pistol. “I might be a hothead, Charlie, but that’s cold.”

His brother shrugged, and Jesse nodded. The outlaw chief hooked one metal thumb behind his gun belt. “True all the same, though. We ain’t runnin’ no charity kitchen.”

He turned back to the huddled men. "You lot, you either gotta get yer own food, or make your peace. We ain't got space fer shirkers no more. Until we get back down south, it's every man for hisself. There's food up yonder with the others. You want it? You take it."

The men muttered among themselves for a moment, hope dying in their eyes. As Jesse and the two brothers continued to stare at them in silence, the men began to back away. Some shook their heads, some muttered under their breaths. Jesse noted that some of them had tightened their hands into fists; preparing for the confrontation they knew must come if they were going to eat.

As the small clump of prisoners moved up the slope, Jesse turned to the two men and smiled. "Well, boys, you sure do know how to make an entrance."

"Yeah," the younger man stood up straighter with a smile. "We're reg'lar dancehall swells."

Jesse's eyes darkened for a moment before returning a shadow of the younger man's smile and patting him on the back. "You sure are. Can't wait to see your name up in lights, Robert." He turned to the older brother. The man's face pensive. "You care to jump onto the boards with your brother, Charlie? The two of you could put on a show, call yourselves the Ford Brothers?"

Charlie shook his head. "That's always been more Robert's inclination. I'm more in the way of just wantin' folks to leave me alone." Even now, he seemed uneasy.

Jesse smiled grimly at that, even though he was not entirely sure the elder brother was joking.

"Seriously, Jesse," Robert Ford hooked his thumbs behind his gun belt and rocked back on his heels.

"If any good's to come from all of this, we're gonna need to keep the hale folks healthy."

"We're behind you one hun'erd percent, Jesse, but Robert's right. Even if we had the food to feed those folks, they ain't no real army."

A strong contralto voice emerged from one of the larger cave and Lucinda stepped into the brightening day.

"You won't have any army, soon, if you tell them to fight each other over the food that's left."

Jesse looked a little sheepish and raised both hands to ward off further criticism. "Now, Lucy, you know how things sit! Those folks ran out of Andersonville with us, an' that was all well an' good. An' we outpaced the Union boys sent to chase after us, an' that was swell. But we only got so much food, an' only a few of the prisoners were smart enough to grab what they could."

He tilted his head and raised one hand higher as she started to speak, hands balled on hips. "I know this ain't the best, but it's all we can do fer now. I need my men in fightin' trim, an' that ain't negotiable. We don't know when we're next gonna have a fight, an' we gotta be ready. We're in Warrior Nation territory, an' last time I was here, they weren't none too friendly. We gotta turn around soon. There'll be more food south. Until then, though, we only got what we got, an' we gotta be smart with that."

"Men are dying every day." Her voice was flat, her eyes bleak. "Every day we spend up here, more of them die."

Jesse nodded. "An' that's a shame. It really is. But we're headin' down again, and when we get there, there'll be more food for them that hung on."

Lucy shook her head, her full lips pursed in frustration. "Never mind. I'm going to go up and see what I can do. Cole and his brothers are ready for you inside with that Confederate officer and the odd stick in black, the one from the Butcher of Lawrence?"

Jesse shook his head. "I wish you wouldn't call Colonel Quantrill that, Lucy. An' Henderson is a good man. He's been a big help. Without him, we wouldn't a gotten into Camp Lincoln." Jesse softened his voice, his eyes asking her for patience. "We wouldn't a gotten you an' Frank out without him."

She shook her head again, however, and moved to follow the prisoners. "The man's a butcher, like his boss. Nevertheless, they're waiting for you."

Jesse watched Lucinda walk up the hill and out into the wider camp. "Boys, that woman drives me to madness on a daily basis."

The Fords both nodded but said nothing. Jesse stared up to where she had disappeared over the rise, and then shook his head. "Well, fellas, we gotta figure our next move." He led them back into the cave.

*****

Cole Younger lounged beside a small camp table he had set up. A map sat there, weighed down at the corners by several power cartridges and a small knife. It showed the region that was coming to be known as the Contested Territories, where Carpathian, the Warrior Nation, and the Union continued to clash, turning the land into a tortured, poisoned wasteland.

Cole stood on the other side of the table, his arms folded. To either side of him were his surviving brothers, Bob and Jim. Bob, of course, had one of his huge fighting knives held negligently in one hand, a whetstone in the other. Near them stood Captain Ingram, his cavalry hat spinning slowly atop one long finger. Standing across from them with his legs spread, his hands clasped behind his back, was the slouched figure of Allen Henderson, former adjutant of Jesse and Frank's old commander during the War of Northern Aggression, William Quantrill.

Henderson looked up as Jesse entered with the Ford brothers flanking him. The gaunt figure nodded quickly, shards of reflected fire glinting in his thick spectacles, as he tapped the map with one long finger.

"As I've been saying, we need to strike while we have the force and the Union's on their back foot, Jesse." His voice was cold, his eyes indifferent.

Jesse looked down at the map. Henderson was tapping the region between the Union and the Contested Territories. The outlaw chief could just read the names of several towns straddling the border. He shook his head.

"Hitting those towns don't make much sense. They might not be Confederate sympathizers, but that sure ain't Union territory, neither. Those folks're just tryin' to make a livin'. You want to hit some juicy towns, we gotta move further east, past the Big River." He pulled at his chin with one metal hand. "But I ain't sure we wanna spend this little army here hittin' one-horse towns. I'm still thinkin' we might want to head west, set up shop for ourselves, somewhere away from all this trouble."

One corner of Ingram's mouth turned down, and the Californian shook his head slightly. "I've gotta say, Jesse, this ain't really the hoedown my men and me signed up for. We're looking to pick up some treasure, maybe stick it to the Union. We're not really in the burg-building business, and it's getting harder and harder to keep my men in line."

Henderson nodded. "How many men do you think you have, Jesse?" He picked the knife up and started to flip it between the fingers of one hand. The map, freed from the knife's weight, curled up at the corner. "How many rode out of Andersonville with us, five thousand? O' those, how many are left? How many can fight today, if they had to?"

Jesse shrugged stiffly. "That don' matter if we ain't gonna fight today. Most o' those men'll stand with us when the time comes. You saw Camp Lincoln. You know what they did there. Ain't no man can call himself a man would go through that, come out the other side, and not give his last breath to burn down the bastards that done it to him."

The outlaw boss shot a sidelong look at the Younger brothers, all of whom were staring at Henderson with blank faces.

Henderson looked from Jesse to the Youngers, and then to the Fords. He forced a smile onto his face and gave the hand holding the knife a casual flip of dismissal.

"'Course, Jesse. I just thought, striking along the border, you'd keep both President Johnson AND President Lee guessin'."

That was enough to twist Jesse's mouth into a bitter snarl. "PRESIDENT Lee my old granny's behind. If it weren't for Lee an' his pack of ole biddies, we wouldn't be hidin' up here now."

Ingram's thin lips stretched into a predatory smile. Henderson nodded, his own smile tightening. "Exactly. Hit these towns, towns whose loyalties waver, and neither will know where you stand. It will be the perfect way to keep Lee off balance until you're ready to overthrow him."

Cole raised his hands in a quick warding gesture. "Whoa! What's this talk of overthrowin', eh?" He looked at Jesse. "We're still lookin' at goin' west, right? Where there ain't nobody that'd need overthrowin'?"

Jesse was staring into Henderson's foggy lenses, but he nodded. "I think that's the way to go. We'll head south, cut through the territories, an' see what we shall see. If we find us a juicy Union target, we hit it. Otherwise, we find us some food, look to those that need our help, and see which way the wind thinks to blow us."

Robert Ford coughed. "We never got too far south, Jesse. There's folks down along the gulf I know, feel more'r less the way you do."

Bob Younger laughed. "Yeah, more'r less, 'cept that little bit about the black folks an' all."

Ford glared at him. "An' when they hear Jesse talkin' about how things are, an' how they gotta be, most folks've come around, no?"

Bob shrugged coldly, pointing at Jesse with the knife. "The folks he talked to, sure."

Cole put a hand on his brother's arm. "Bobbie, now ain't the time."

Jesse looked questioningly at the Youngers. Bob's face was cold, Cole's concerned, and Jim's usually dapper face looked torn. There was only one thing that could be pulling them apart like this. Jesse sighed.

"I know there ain't nothin' I can say to bring John back, Bob. Your brother's dead, an' that's that." Jesse tried to speak in even tones. He still felt the edge of guilt, but he also knew there had been no other choice. Cole agreed, primarily because Frank had corroborated the story, had seen the thing that had once been John Younger, and had known there was nothing of the young man left in that hulking, mindless brute. Cole's brothers, however, were harder to convince, even though Bob had seen the beast for himself. Hell, Bob had been there when the beast attacked them. Whether he wanted to admit it or not, he knew what Jesse had had to do.

"I know the story, Jesse." Bob nodded. "An' I know Cole backs it." He looked right into Jesse's eyes without flinching. "But I ain't ready to let it go yet. We went in, we lost a lot of good men, an' we pulled Frank and that Loveless woman out." He nodded to Frank. "I'm glad we got Frank. He's been a friend o' my brothers' for longer'n I can say, an' he's a man I can hold with. But you left MY brother behind, Jesse. No matter the story, that's the fact. It's not somethin' we can't wink at."

Jesse nodded. "Yeah, we left John behind, Bob, because he was dead before we ever got there. What that Union doctor left behind din't have nothin' of John in it. I put a monster out of its misery, an' I did a passed friend a kindness." Jesse stood up taller, metal thumbs behind pistols, and looked straight back at Bob. "It was what needed doin', an' I did it. You gotta be able to drop that an' leave it behind, 'r we're gonna have trouble neither of us wants."

"He's gonna drop it, Jesse, never mind." Jim tried to pull his brother back but Bob shrugged off his grip.

Frank stepped up then, still pale and haggard from his ordeal. He grabbed Bob Younger by the shoulder and pushed his hollow-eyed face into the younger man's.

"You saw him, Bob. That weren't John. He was a goner the minute they dragged him out of his cell."

Bob looked at Frank for a moment longer, nodded slowly, and then looked at Jesse over his shoulder. “I’m goin’ walkin’.”

Jesse nodded and watched him go. Then he turned back to the rest of the men. “So, any other objections? We head south, find those croakers been followin’ us some food, and see what we can see, once our bellies are full?”

“Whatever your lady love prefers, Jesse.” Henderson reached down and pulled the map from beneath the cylinders. He rolled it up with quick, easy motions, a cold smile on his face.

Jesse stared at the skeletal figure in the dusty black for a moment before speaking. “It’s what I prefer, Allen.” He walked toward the man, his own face cold. “You been with us long enough, you best never make the mistake of assumin’ I don’t do my own thinkin’. You got that?”

Henderson’s expression never changed. “Oh, I got it, Jesse. Never fear.”
“Jesse knows what he’s doing, Mr. Henderson. You should believe that if nothing else.”

The men turned to watch Loveless sweep gracefully past the fabric blind and into the cave. “Jesse knows that power grows from a free people, united behind a common cause, regardless of color or creed. Your plan to attack innocent civilians will do nothing but damage his cause, and the cause of the Rebellion.” She moved to stand behind the outlaw chief. “Like Jesse’s said, true power doesn’t come from gold, or fear, or even the barrel of a gun.” She turned a little to grin at Jesse. “Although I have to say I’m not sure I believe that last one completely.”

Jesse watched the woman with admiration. He did not remember saying half of those things, and he was not sure he believed them entirely himself. He knew that the men around him gave him power – more power than he had ever wielded before – and he knew that, if used correctly, they would open up a future for him that he could never achieve on his own. What exactly that future might be, he could not yet say. The grueling journey north had been trying, and the attraction of civil leadership had waned with each punishing step. He found a certain amount of reassurance in the thought that his natural talents were leading him to battle, rather than becoming a burgermeister.

The trail before him might lead all the way to a resurrected south, and maybe even beyond. With the strongest and orneriest former prisoners, outlaws, and bushwhackers behind him, he knew he had the beginning of the Union’s defeat within his grasp. What was he supposed to do now, return to the territories? Throw a barn-raising? Take up his old feud with Billy the Kid, and scrabble in the dust for a few gold coins and a mention in the local paper?

“We’re headin’ south, like I said.” Jesse nodded to Lucy. “As we go, we keep our eyes open. We take what we need, we lick at any blue-bellies we find along the way, and we look for our main chance. Maybe we make contact with folks in the Rebellion that might not agree with Lee and his grannies.”

Henderson’s smile slipped just a bit as he noted the resolve in Jesse’s eyes, then he shrugged and slipped the map into a small leather case beneath his flowing coat.

“Of course, Jesse.”

Jesse smiled and gave the tall man a stiff shot in the arm. “We’ll burn some buildings down yet, don’t you worry. We just need to –”

A shout from outside the cave brought Jesse up short and he stepped to the mouth to look out. Several of his men ran past. Bob Younger was jogging back toward them, his face bleak. He held up one hand slick with blood.

Cole muttered something and stepped forward but Bob shook his head. “It ain’t mine. Dustin Fletcher had the last watch. He’s over yonder, past that Thunder.”

Jesse began to walk in that direction, Frank following slowly along behind, the rest of his party rushing to keep up. Bob Younger fell into step beside him.

Jesse’s words were clipped. “He dead?”

Bob nodded. "Throat slit; all the way back to his spine."

Jesse felt a cold itch down his back. "Cold steel?" He knew the answer, but had to ask.

"Not likely." Bob was breathing heavily, trying to keep up. "The edges were all charred, and there weren't nearly as much blood as there shoulda been. I think you'll recognize it when you see it."

Jesse nodded as he turned around the large vehicle and stopped to stare down at one of his men, a blaster rifle discarded beside him. The man's eyes were wide, staring blankly up into the bright blue sky. The wound gaped sickeningly, and Jesse saw that Bob had been right. Only a small stream of blood was leaking out of the dark slit. The edges were black, small branches of char reaching out like the roots of a vine.

Behind Jesse, Lucinda came up short. One look at the body was enough for her to confirm the suspicions of the others.

"Warrior Nation." The woman's voice was cold. The men all looked from her back down to the terrible wound, the flesh scorched with the furious energy of the Great Spirit.

They had been found.

Chapter 2

Jesse was halfway up the hill, legs pumping furiously and pistols clutched in metal fists, when the screaming began. Barreling up over the lip of the small valley, he was nearly pushed back down by the flood of emaciated prisoners charging toward him. Behind them, columns of smoke rose in the distance. As the terrified mob flowed past, meaning emerged from their panicked noise.

"Savages!"

There was no coordinated resistance. Most of the folks were still in shock from their ordeal in Camp Lincoln and the subsequent retreat through the wilderness. Faced with the full fury of a Warrior Nation assault, their courage had abandoned them. Jesse knew there were only moments to turn the tide before even his seasoned fighters caught the panic and turned tail.

Jesse turned to his posse. "Cole, you and your brothers head out and try to stiffen up the Andersonville boys as close to the front as you can. I'm goin' to have some of the heavy stuff come up behind you. If you can't stop the Injuns short of the vehicles, we're lost."

Cole nodded and jerked his head toward the rising smoke. Jim followed his older brother directly, but Bob gave Jesse one last, dark look before running after.

"Henderson, you go back down and rally some of the boys that've been workin' with the Union armor. See if you can't get those Thunders up and runnin'. That oughta give the savages somethin' to worry about. Ingram, rally up your Rangers and see if you can't set up some firin' positions to fall back on, up here on this lip." Jesse was still moving toward the front, pushing through the frightened men that flowed past. Only the Fords and Lucy were still with him.

"Lucy," Jesse shouted over his shoulder. The roar and echo of the terrified mob was surging around them. "Head south and try to stop this stampede the best you can!"

She nodded. "I had Will Shaft and his Exodusters collect the food wagons down that way. There should be some order there!" She spun around and moved with the flow, away from the onrushing combat.

One terrified man, eyes white with thoughtless panic, tried to push Jesse down in his flight. The outlaw boss had had enough. He cracked the man in the throat with one cold, iron forearm. As the ragged prisoner halted, coughing around his bruised gullet, Jesse brought his knee up into the man's crotch. He dropped like a stone, curled around his pain, all terror forgotten.

"Alright!" He turned his head toward the Fords. "Enough o' this! There ain't no way any of us're makin' it out if these bummers start runnin' down the fighters! I need you two to keep 'em outta the valley while Henderson and Ingram rally the boys an' get the vehicles movin'!"

Charlie nodded, pulling his massive weapon from its sheath. A custom shotgun, barrel sawn-down to a menacing snub-nosed bore, the thing demanded respect, and Charlie knew how to use it. Robert, however, hesitated.

"Jesse, I think I oughta stay with you." He nodded toward the sounds of slaughter and screaming to the north. "It's gettin' hairy out there, an' I'd rather you din't wade into it with no one to watch yer back."

Jesse almost laughed, but stopped himself. "Kid, where I'm goin', ain't no bodyguardin' gonna help." He held up one articulated fist, the lethal beauty of the Hyper-velocity pistol shining in the risen sun. "When you get into the heat of it, only thing that can keep a man alive is himself an' his luck." The familiar grin flashed in the hat brim's shadow. "An' if there's one thing I got in spades, Robert, it's faith in myself an' a heap o' luck!"

Robert Ford nodded and Jesse moved away, shoving a path through the thinning crowd of terrified prisoners. As he pushed his way toward the fighting, he could hear the Fords behind him, shouting for the attention of the mob. Several sharp gunshots sounded, and the tenor of the screams changed again as the flood of panicked men split like a river, flowing to the east and west around the shallow valley.

Jesse moved through the churned ruins of the camp, stepping over discarded clothing, boxes and bags of God knew what. He moved quickly past the bodies of those who had been trampled by their friends. Ahead he could hear the crack of RJ gunshots, detonations as munitions exploded, and the shouts of his men forming up a decent defensive line under the direction of the Younger boys. With each step that Jesse took, the lyrical chanting and harsh war cries of the savages grew louder.

The line of contact was clear as he moved up. At first, he was surprised there were not more dead prisoners scattered about. A line of outlaws and rebels hunkered down behind hasty fortifications built around the rusted-out bodies of the worst Ironhide wagons they had taken from Andersonville. Many had been overturned to provide better cover. Men were crouched down behind them, taking careful shots with rifles and pistols into a massive swirling wall of bodies that pushed ever-closer.

The surging wall consisted of more Warrior Nation savages than he had ever seen in one place before, spinning and dancing through an undisciplined mob of prisoners who had been too stunned or too stupid to run. These men clutched ancient, makeshift weapons; they stumbled around, slashing blindly or firing wild shots, trying to stagger back toward the line Cole and his brothers had been building around the abandoned vehicles.

Jesse dismissed the tangled free-for-all, more concerned with what might be hidden on the other side. He could see flares of blue spirit energy on the warriors' primitive weapons as they slaughtered the prisoners, but there were none of the nightmare man-beasts dancing among them. The strongest warriors, he knew, would be coming up behind. There was also no sign of the twisted horses the natives rode into battle. With a mob the size of this one, they had to be out there somewhere.

"What's happenin'?" Jesse shouted to be heard over the clamor of battle. Cole Younger leaned down with his rifle braced across the back of an old flat-bed wagon, taking careful aim on the press of bodies that crawled ever closer. He held up a hand, settling behind the sight of his short weapon. The thing barked, spitting crimson-edged smoke out toward the line, and then he stood up.

"The braves're all tied up with the prisoners who din't run." He gestured toward the fighting with his chin. "But those sad bastards ain't gonna last long." He grinned.

"We'll be dancin' soon enough."

Jesse scowled and shook his head. "We don't wanna be dancin' here, Cole. We wanna be savin' our strength for the damned blue-bellies." He scanned the line of combat. It was rushing forward now, the last of the prisoners disappearing beneath the wave of doeskin and tanned flesh. Behind the furious line of attackers he could see looming shadows: the true horrors of the Warrior Nation, held back for this final assault.

"We gotta hold 'em off long enough fer Henderson to get up here with the armor. Give 'em a taste o' the ole' Union Thunder. That oughta give 'em pause." Jesse took careful aim with one pistol and dropped a war leader with a tall crest of hair and feathers wagging over his head.

"I'm not sure that's gonna work." Frank, gasping for breath and pale as death, came stumping up beside Jesse, his long rifle, Sophie, clutched in white knuckles. That massive gun had been wrapped in a pack on the back of Jesse's 'Horse for months. He had never been happier for following one of his strange impulses.

Jesse took a shot, watched another savage fall, and then turned to his brother. "What?"

Frank sighted along his rifle, pointing with bladed hand down the barrel. "Those things comin' up? Their some kinda beast we ain't seen before. An' they're nearly big as the Thunders."

Jesse peered through the smoke and rising dust. He could see massive shifting shadows shuffling behind the Warrior line, but could not tell if they were shapeshifters or something worse.

He shrugged. "Well, that's what we got. We take our chances, play the hand we been dealt, an' maybe the draw falls our way."

A deafening roar behind them announced the arrival of the first of the Union armored wagons. The thing was a wall of studded iron, its main cannon sitting in a squat turret that crouched behind a sweeping cowcatcher. It rolled up beside the Ironhide Jesse and his men crouched behind and unleashed a blast of ruby light that ravaged across the field which cut down a swath of natives in the distance.

A heartened cheer rose up all along Jesse's line, redoubling as two more Rolling Thunders came up to rest beside the first. These added their hellish roars to the battle, and soon the Warrior Nation advance was crumbling, falling back across piles of discarded equipment and dead prisoners. The rotating Gatling cannons nestled beneath each turret spat torrents of red fire into the fleeing warriors. Jesse's teeth flashed in a vicious grin. He leapt atop the broken-down vehicle in front of him, sending blasts of crimson energy into the sky.

"Yeah! You rock-worshipin' heathens!"

From the back of the wagon, Jesse got his first good look at the beasts moving up behind the savages' front line. Five enormous monsters, still strolling forward, were splitting the retreating natives into tight streams between them. Their eyes glowed the haunting blue of spirit energy, and an enormous rack of edged antlers swept out from each beast's head, swaying with their shambling gait.

"Well jumped up . . ." Jesse's mouth hung open. The things were at least twice the height of a Rolling Thunder, the ground shaking with each step. As he watched, their pace quickened, thick legs rising and falling faster and faster, and soon they were charging across the churned field. Their plate-sized hooves crushed bodies or sent them spinning up into the air behind them.

"Fire! For the love of –" Jesse screamed, lashing down with one pistol to stab it at the oncoming beasts.

The three Rolling Thunders spat crimson flame at the creatures, the grass before them flattening with the concussion of their blasts. The victorious shouts of the tattered army staggered into silence as the ruby bolts glanced off the surging mounds of muscle and matted fur, blasting into the dirt or scattering up into the sky. One of the animals was struck squarely, the bolt caving in its shoulder and erupting out its back in a geyser of blood and entrails. It staggered as its forelegs collapsed, bellowing as it sank slowly onto its side. The rest, however, did not slow in their ponderous charge.

"Get ba—" Jesse started to shout, jumping off the wagon. His duster was flying behind him like a cape, legs churning the air, when one of the enormous beasts struck the vehicle a glancing blow with one bone-spurred shoulder before crashing into a Rolling Thunder with a deafening clangor.

The rusted wagon cartwheeled away from the impact, crushing several fighters and scattering the rest. The monster's gargantuan antlers caught the Rolling Thunder beneath the turret and tangled with the ironwork of its cowcatcher. With a furious roar, the thing twisted the thick muscles of its neck and sent the vehicle crashing onto its side.

The other animals slammed into the Thunders, silencing their guns. One reared up onto its hind legs and brought the heavy weight of its fore-hooves crashing down, caving in the sloping front armor and pushing the weighty vehicle backward in the grass.

Jesse came rolling up to his feet and glanced around. More and more of his steady hands were rushing toward the front, but most had stopped as the giant, twisted elk made their appearance. He looked back at the mountain of fur and flesh that continued to pound at the overturned wagon, snorting blue-tinged steam.

Gritting his teeth, Jesse clapped his two pistols together, thumbed the switches beneath each barrel, and aimed them at the thing's lashing head. Ribbons of crimson energy reached out from each pistol, tying them together and glowing with a fierce light before he pulled the triggers and sent a single wave of destructive, roiling flame up at the beast. The fireball struck the monster in the head and detonated, sending blood, bone, and curves of antler splashing out in every direction. The beast's body shivered convulsively as it collapsed into the dirt.

The men around him cheered as the beast fell and began to fire into the surviving elk, even though their standard blasters seemed to be having little effect. Jesse took two steps back, surveying the battle around him, and came to a grim decision just as Frank shouted at him.

"They're comin' again!" Frank's voice was muffled by the battle-din. He pointed to the north. The outlaw chief looked back to see the Warrior Nation rallying behind their beasts, once more working themselves up to charge, chanting and waving their weapons in the air.

"Skedaddle, boys!" Jesse started to wave at the men around him, gesturing back toward the valley. "We need to get outta here, get around behind the camp. Go!"

The men tried to follow his direction, firing as they moved backward, but the surviving great elk, turning from the twisted wrecks of the Thunders, snorted fiercely and began to stomp toward the nearest clusters of men, their muscles bunching for another charge. In moments, the most capable fighters his crew could boat were fleeing, running back toward their encampment and the remaining Union armor.

Jesse grabbed Frank by the back of his vest and pulled him away. Cole and his brothers were falling back as well, shooting as they went. The assaulting savages pushed forward in a wave, engulfing the abandoned vehicles and screeching their unholy challenges to the sky. The outlaws and escaped prisoners moved back in good order, though. Jesse was certain that if they could take up positions around the caves with the last few Thunders, and Loveless and Shaft could rally the prisoners capable of fighting, they would be able to hold back the warriors and their twisted beasts indefinitely.

The blast, when it came, took the entire motley army by surprise. A howling like a thousand desert storms fell upon them, the crackling of heat lightning snapping beneath. Sheets of silvery-blue energy came sleeting in from either side, riddling retreating fighters and blasting them off their feet. Jesse had never heard anything like the hellish noises that accompanied this fresh attack. His head whipped around, looking for the source.

Low-slung wagons had been pushed into position along the encampment's flanks while the fighting had distracted the shabby mob. Most seemed to hold antique Gatling cannons, but the savages manning them were chanting and swaying to their own music rather than crouching behind the weapons like a traditional crew. From the spinning barrels of the guns blazed not the grey smoke of black-powder weapons, or the crimson-tinged fury of RJ-1027, but the clear blue fury of the natives' spirit energy.

Jesse shielded his eyes from the glittering brightness as the firing continued. Somehow, he knew, the warriors were channeling their Great Spirit's force through the old cannons, focusing and aiming it like gunfire. The streams of blue bolts blasted men from their feet, sent huge, sparkling geysers up into the sky, and churned the disciplined retreat into a full rout.

For a moment, the fleeing men staggered to a halt as three more Rolling Thunder wagons came up over the lip of the valley, their own Gatling cannons lashing with red flame back at the Warrior Nation platforms. The reprieve was short lived, however, as other platforms, hidden by a dip in the hills, were pushed into place.

These new carts each held massive cannon, their ancient brass barrels darkened and pitted with age. Again, the crews danced and chanted. This time Jesse watched the entire process. Deep within the shadows of each cannon's mouth a blue ghostlight began to form, pulsing with the rhythm of its crews' chant. The glow burned brighter and brighter as phantom lightning began to play along the barrel, crawling from the muzzle and melding with the ancient metal. When the crews' dance reached a frenetic peak, energy tore from the mouth of each weapon with the wrath of a devastating lightning strike. The blasts struck the emerging Union wagons with a thunder crash.

Each vehicle was rocked back on its massive iron wheels. The armor held under the onslaught, but molten steel dripped into the burning grass and smoke began to pour from the vision slits of each wagon. The munitions in one vehicle detonated in the heat and the entire thing disappeared in an eruption of twisted metal and burning fuel.

Jesse looked down at his pistols in helpless rage. There was no way he could range in on these new weapons. There was no way he could close the distance in the face of their power. Beside him, Frank was taking slow, methodical shots at the weapon crews. Each time Sophie barked her sharp report, a warrior was thrown into the smoldering grass. No matter how many he took down, however, it was not enough, as others came to take the place of the fallen.

Jesse's army was paralyzed by the incoming fire and the approaching wave of beasts and warriors. From behind, he saw a small group come up out of the valley, Lucinda and Will Shaft in their midst. The agent's eyes were haunted as she rushed to Jesse, her head shaking.

"Their cavalry was waiting to the south." The anger burning in her eyes was a match for his own. "Ingram's Rangers charged in and saw the braves off, but they took heavy casualties. The runners didn't have a prayer."

Jesse shook his head. "I'm not sure any of us have a prayer, darlin'." He holstered one pistol and bent down to pick up a discarded blaster rifle. "But they sure are gonna know they been kissed."

"Jesse!" Frank's voice was sharp.

The outlaw boss looked quickly to where his brother was pointing. The crews of the strange spirit weapons were silent, watching the huddled remnants of the refugee mob with dark, hooded eyes.

"Well, why don't that make me feel any better . . . " Jesse murmured. He turned around again to where the mass of the Warrior Nation was still approaching, although with a slow, terrible pace now. The warriors in front of the mob were clearly eager to get to grips with their enemy, but something held them back.

All along the rolling hills, the savages began to close in on Jesse's exhausted, ragged force. At a glance, the outlaw would have sworn he had less than a few hundred fighting men left. He did not know how many might still be in the valley, nor what vehicles might remain. But he did not think it was going to matter, as the natives in their thousands stalked in for the kill.

A large warrior with glowing azure eyes emerged from the press of bodies moving toward Jesse. The man was at least a head taller, his muscles bulging beneath ceremonial armor of bone and leather. He held a long slashing blade low, the entire length of the weapon glowing with blue energy and dripping sparks of force into the grass.

With his free hand the warrior pointed to Jesse with an animal snarl on his smooth face.

Jesse stepped forward with a slight nod. He grinned at the approaching warrior and then casually raised his pistol and shot the man in the head. The body fell heavily backward into the torn mud. Jesse looked down at his hand in uneasy admiration. The arms had been giving him so much trouble lately, it was almost a surprise to have them answer the call so readily.

A howl arose from the surrounding warriors and they crouched down at the sharp blast of the pistol.

"Ya'll ain't gonna fool me into some dancehall show, you savages!" Jesse barked out, and the natives slowed their advance. "You got plenty of bodies, you're gonna take me down eventually." He grinned even wider and spat into the grass at his feet. "But I reckon I can take twenty, maybe thirty of ya'll with me afore you do. So, if those folks wantin' to die'll step forward, I say let's start this little dance, no?"

Both of his pistols were drawn, held casually to either side. Behind him, Frank, the Younger brothers, and Loveless stepped up to stand with him. Will Shaft and his two dark friends stood warily by the lip of the canyon. The Fords, nearby, were the only people moving on the plain as they paced carefully toward their boss.

The warriors watched the outlaw with blank, glowing eyes, their mouths a uniform snarl of rage. Every muscle tensed for a final charge.

"Wotaka!" The voice was strong but fluid, like the water of a slow but powerful river.

"Eenahzee Keezay." The wall of braves parted and a man stepped gracefully through. He was younger than Jesse might have expected, but his body was thick with muscle and he walked with the grace of a giant cat. The man's hands were empty, held wide in a gesture of pacification. His eyes were dark and cold, with just the slightest azure flame burning within their depths. He was wearing elaborate ceremonial armor beneath a beaded vest. Around his throat flashed a silver chain holding some sort of strange bird-shaped medallion. He stared at Jesse with a deep loathing.

"I am Maza Chaydan, leader of this band. You are the outcast known as Jesse James?" The man's voice was still soft, but there was a contempt in it that almost convinced Jesse to charge him then and there and damn the consequences.

Instead, he merely nodded.

Maza Chaydan nodded in turn. "Then I commend your ghost to the Great Spirit, demon. And I cleanse the world of your poison."

Without further warning, the savage war leader barked a thunderous chant, his hands flying up in a rapid series of gestures. Bolts of cerulean lightning leapt from his fingers, crashing down around Jesse and slapping him into the churned earth. There was a buzzing in his ears that he tried to shake out as he leapt back to his feet, his clothing steaming and his trembling arms sparking.

"Why, you ten bit savage bastard." Jesse's hands still clenched his Hyper-velocity blasters, and he slashed them both up at the snarling brave. Dual streams of crimson fire lashed out at the undefended target, and Jesse snarled in frustration as half his shots sailed wide, his left arm twitching aside.

Jesse's eyes widened as the savage, a grim smile playing about his thin lips, brought one hand up in a warding gesture. A shimmering curve of blue energy intercepted the barrage of ruby bolts and sent them streaking up into the clear sky.

The outlaw chief's brows came down, his eyes hardened, and he muttered, "Alright then, dog-boy. Let's dance." He jerked his entire body to the right, then dove to the left, sprinting around the brave, his custom pistols stabbing out and crimson bolts flashing between them, only to bounce away over the silent, gaping crowd.

Outlaws, rebels, and savages all watched the cataclysmic battle as legendary outlaw boss and mystical Warrior Nation shaman clashed across the muddy earth. Bolts of nature's own lightning crashed down upon Jesse like a lash of fire, while his answering attacks were turned aside by Maza Chaydan's glowing shield of flickering, ghostly blades that shimmered into and out of existence at need.

Jesse's mouth was twisted in desperate hatred now. His clothing was scorched, his arms slow and clumsy, and yet he had not managed to land a single bolt on his proud foe. With a grunt of effort Jesse brought both of his pistols together and stroked the small buttons that would combine their power cells. He laughed with grim triumph as he brought the twinned weapons to bear on the shaman, a wispy red power-bridge forming between them.

Before Jesse could launch the most devastating attack, the brave dove toward him, rolling on one shoulder and standing quickly within the outlaw chief's defenses. His left hand swung wide, a glowing blade appearing in his clenched fist and burying itself in Jesse's thigh.

The enormous wave of crimson fire billowed up into the air as Jesse collapsed to one knee with a furious cry. He punched out with one fist, still filled with a custom pistol, and drove the savage's hand away from his wounded leg. Maza Chaydan danced away before he could do more, however, and the outlaw chief was left panting in impotent fury, looking up at the calm face of his enemy. What he saw there, however, gave him cold pause.

The powerful young medicine man gestured toward the outlaw chief's battered Stetson. "You bear a token from our people." One hand gracefully rose to indicate something hanging from the back of Jesse's hat. The outlaw was discomfited to see tears of frustrated rage standing out in the war leader's glittering eyes. Jesse grasped the hat and looked at the leather thong fastened around its base. Geronimo's feather hung there, limp and forgotten. The thing had flapped along behind him throughout his adventures in the south.

Jesse sucked in gasping breaths of air, looking up at the war leader standing before him, and nodded again. "It was given to me by Chief Geronimo." He tried to grin through his confusion and exhaustion. "He seemed impressed."

The war leader's eyes turned hard. "Do not speak the name of Goyahkla in this place again. Do you know the significance of the token you hold in your cursed hands?"

Jesse looked down at the feather. It was pretty ratty. He had dragged it through hell and back, it seemed, since that day the Injuns had handed it to him and let him walk away. He shook his head, pushing himself back to his feet. "It's an owl feather. They gave it to me and let me go."

Maza Chaydan nodded again. "It is an owl feather. I do not know why Goyahkla released you, but with this feather, it was not as a friend, nor for you to return to our lands with a ragged band of wastrels at your heels."

The men behind Jesse bristled at that, but he quieted them with a raised hand, never taking his eyes off the Injun. "Well, they weren't talkin' much after I got it."

The war leader raised his voice so that all of the men and women nearby, rebels, outlaws, and natives, could hear him. "Jesse James bears a token of the People. An osniko wiyaka rests in his hands."

As he said the words, a hushed murmur rose up among the surrounding warriors.

Maza Chaydan turned back to Jesse. "You must leave the lands of the People at once. And you must not return. The osniko wiyaka is not the badge of a friend, nor will it save you again."

Relief warred with disbelief in Jesse's chest as he struggled to bring his breathing under control. "Hold on one cotton pickin' second," he holstered a pistol and raised a hand. "You killed all these folks, and now you're just gonna let us go?"

Maza Chaydan shrugged. "We knew nothing of the osniko wiyaka. Had you been killed before we realized it, it would merely have been the wishes of the Great Spirit. But once I recognized the token for what it is, I had no choice."

Jesse sneered. "An' if I shoot you right now?" The free pistol rose to point directly at the tall warrior.

Again, the man shrugged. "If you try to kill me now, there will be no saving you or your people. Every last one will be killed, dying in excruciating pain before your despairing eyes. And only then, when your mind is broken and your body wracked with agony, when every hope and dream you ever held dear has been stolen from you and scattered to the wind, will we throw you down into the dust." Maza Chaydan straightened, hands on hips, and looked down his proud nose at the outlaw chief. "The intentions of Goyahkla, whatever they may be, will have been thwarted by your own stupidity."

The pistol dropped slightly at this, and Jesse's grin slipped to match it. He nodded slowly, his shoulders slumping in exhaustion, and he looked down at one treacherous, gun-filled hand. "Okay, sounds fair."

Maza Chaydan folded his arms before his broad chest. "You will leave the land of the People now."

Jesse looked down at the wreckage and scattered bodies that covered the ground. The smell was already starting to remind him of Payson; reason enough to leave as quickly as possible. "What about our gear?"

The warrior gave a casual flip of his hand. "You may take with you whatever you can carry. Your dead we will see to. You will not be allowed to stay long enough to care for them."

Jesse took a step back and turned to his brother. "South?"

Frank nodded. "As fast as we can."

Jesse scanned the faces around him. Even Henderson, watching from the rim of the valley, nodded.

The outlaw turned back to face the war leader. "We'll take yer offer and head south."

The shaman's head dipped once, but he said nothing.

Jesse looked into the dark eyes for a minute longer before giving his own sharp nod. "Alright then."

The remaining Ironhide wagons and Iron Horses were more than enough to transport the survivors of the attack back into the Contested Territories, escorted by three remaining Rolling Thunder armored wagons. Of the thousands of escaped prisoners, outlaws, and rebel Rangers who had fled Andersonville onto Warrior Nation land, only a few hundred emerged.

Chapter 3

Colonel George Armstrong Custer made sure never to miss the sun rising over the rolling hills to the east. From the high stone watchtower of Fort Frederick, pushed up against the very roots of the western mountains, the sunrise was always beautiful. Unless the savages were attacking that day, of course. Then there were more important things to focus on than the splendor of the morning.

Custer rested his hands against the warm metal guard rail of the tower's outer walkway. Far below, the main gates of the squat fortress were closed to potential infiltrators, despite the apparent emptiness of the land all around. Sentries walked their rounds in squad strength, and an entire troop of his newly-reestablished 7th Cavalry Regiment was somewhere out there, riding the circuit set the day they had arrived, over a month ago.

Custer took in a deep lungful of the fresh mountain air and braced himself for another unpleasant day. Aside from the natural unhappiness of any cavalry officer tasked with the defense of a fixed position, Custer had even greater burdens to bear. Fort Frederick, named after one of General Grant's slaughtered sons, had been purpose-built, here in the middle of God's country, but far from anything remotely resembling the important events of the modern age, to house extensive laboratories and storage facilities for the Union's greatest scientific minds.

The cavalry colonel found those minds to be the most onerous burden of his new, seemingly prestigious, posting. It galled him, every day, to know that he owed the worst of their ill-feathered flock for the meteoric upturn in his professional fate. He cursed the ironic luck that had turned his first full military command in nearly a decade into a prison of the soul.

When Doctor Tumblety had tempted him with the chance to command a mysterious post out west, he had balked. He knew in his heart how much a debt of such magnitude, owed to a creature of such foul character, would weigh upon his conscience. Yet, before being sent to Camp Lincoln, his career had languished in the doldrums of mediocrity for more years than he cared to think.

Of course, that offer was made before the colonel or his patron even realized that just such a post already existed, and that it had already been staffed by none other than Tumblety's chief rival for the War Department's attention, affection, and coin: Nikola Tesla. In the harsh light of reality, Custer was not the only one to find their new posting less than he had hoped.

"Sir." His adjutant, Lieutenant Willa Shaw, broke into his thoughts. Her cavalry boots cracked smartly on the stone floor as she stopped behind him.
Custer looked around, hands still on the railing. He quirked one eyebrow in inquiry.

"Mister Tesla is making ready to open those crates from Washington, sir." The young woman coughed. "You wanted to be notified?"

Custer gave a slow nod, cast one last look out over the rolling hills, and turned from the view. He settled his battered hat over his curly hair and moved around the walkway, back into the tower. The heels of his adjutant's riding boots clicked along on the stone behind him. Even after all these years, he still found it difficult to reconcile himself with serving beside women. Even a woman as competent as Shaw.

He entered a wide room designed to keep watch over all possible approaches toward Fort Frederick. A large seat, almost like a throne, had been built in the middle of the chamber for the officer of the watch. Wide windows of thick, bubbled glass gave a slightly distorted view of the hills below. It all seemed modern and invincible; an appearance he would have more faith in had he not known that, during an overwhelming attack last year, with the fort barely completed, the commander of the watch had been plucked from that very chair, thrown through the window, and fell screaming to his death in the courtyard far below.

The tower was now named Carter's Keep, although the men still called it the high seat. Or the launching pad, if they were feeling spirited.

Fort Frederick had very nearly been abandoned after that attack. General Grant, however, had refused to abandon the fortress to the savages. The Warrior Nation had torn up the fortress's Heavy Rail spur line after the attack. The relief columns sent to retake the fort had stretched for miles, guarding enormous pack wagons built specifically for the purpose. They had travelled for months through hostile territory, fighting a running battle all the way.

But that had been over a year ago. Now, Fort Frederick was one of the most well-defended strongholds of the Republic, even if few in the Republic knew it existed. Given how strange most of the communication with Washington had been since his arrival, Colonel Custer was not entirely sure even President Johnson knew about the place. Grant did, that was for sure. He watched over everything that happened here like an eagle from afar.

The spiral stairs leading down from Carter's Keep were steep, opening out into cramped firing positions every half-turn. The place reflected the very latest in defensive engineering. Custer's mouth twisted in a slight, bitter sneer that curled his mustache back from his lip. He wondered if Captain Carter had thought the same thing, before the twisted half-man, half-bird savage had yanked him from his chair and tossed him through the window.

The courtyard at the base of the tower was extensive, but the massive pack wagons, their RJ engines cold and dark, dominated the space. The heavy iron gates had been rebuilt and reinforced since the attack. Heavy cannons were interspersed with Gatling positions all along the parapet of the thick outer wall. The local natives were now aware of the weapons' maximum range, always stopping to taunt their crews from just out of reach. Custer had been forced to assign an officer to watch over each battery, lest they be in danger of wasting their precious power cells. Here, trapped at the ass-end of the longest land-supply line the Union had ever tried to maintain, there was no room for waste.

The heavy metal doors into the squat fortress itself were open, the unmistakable burning smell of RJ-1027 thick in the air. The recharge stalls for the Regiment's nearly one thousand Iron Horses and Locust support vehicles were dug into the walls of a long bunker sunk into the bedrock beneath the fortress. The bunker was wide enough for five 'Horses to ride abreast during deployment, which made for quite a sight when a troop was heading out or returning from a patrol. Twenty ranks roaring out was a brave show of force; but it was nearly as disconcerting when they disappeared into the surrounding hills almost at once.

Custer continued to move deeper into the fortress, waving a cursory salute at troopers and soldiers that snapped to attention as he stormed past. If Tesla was opening the damned crates, they better still be isolated in Deep Storage D, where the colonel had put them. Grant's pet scientist had a way of making free with orders, and the thought of whatever monsters might be contained in those coffin-like crates made Custer's blood run chill after the things he had seen at Camp Lincoln.

"Are they still in the same storage room?" Custer snapped the question over his shoulder without slowing down. Shaw, skip-stepping to keep up, responded in a level voice.

"Yessir. D, sir." The answer echoed away down the wide corridor.

"Well, let's hope he doesn't smell up the room the way that damned sawbones soils his area, eh?" Custer's muttered question did not call for a response, so Shaw merely nodded in the semi-darkness.

Down several wide flights of stairs, the dressed stone walls gave way to carved bedrock. The bones of the mountains had been hollowed out to make way for the Union's greatest minds and stockpiles of their inventions. Banded wooden doors came up and receded into the shadows on either side as they stalked down the narrower hall. Most of these massive chambers were empty, waiting to be filled with mechanical marvels from Washington, stores from the border forts, or the products of the advanced manufactories being planned for deeper underground.

Each set of doors was labeled with a double letter painted in hurried splashes. They stopped at two messy 'D's dashed across one set. The doors were partly ajar, a dusky light spilling out in a wedge over the packed earth of the floor and slashing up the opposite wall in a ruddy bar. Low, muttering voices could be heard from within. Without waiting to listen, Custer rapped twice and pushed the door wide.

The room was large, more than fifty feet to a side, with low, vaulted ceilings looming overhead. Several piles of large crates bearing stenciled military-style labels stood near the center of the room. Three men stood over a box that had been set close to the door. Illumination was provided by RJ-powered wall sconces, but two stand-alone electric lamps of Tesla's own design had been set up to provide further lighting near the crate.

In the shadowed recesses of the large room were tables of equipment that the colonel could not identify. Coils of metal rose toward the low ceiling while twists and loops of glass and rubber connected a collection of boiling containers in tangled snarls. Throughout the confusing mess were an array of black boxes attached with wires and coils of tubing.

"Mr. Tesla." Custer's voice rang out in the stone room. "I believe I asked you to inform me before you began to access your new cargo?" The colonel forced his voice to remain calm. Tesla had never quite recovered from his weeks of hiding in these very tunnels after the savages sacked the fortress above.

The youngest man in the group, standing beside the box and wedging an iron crowbar beneath the lid, shrugged. "Is that Shaw there beside you?"

Custer looked at his adjutant, who gave a shrug of her own, and then back down to the scientist many were claiming would be the Savior of the Republic. "Yes."

"Well, then somehow, word got to you." The man tilted his smooth, mustachioed face up into the light with an unkind smile. "And so any further effort I spent on the task would have been wasted, would it not?"

Custer stared into the snide face for a moment, fighting the urge to slap it. When he had tamped down his reaction, he sniffed slightly and nodded to the box. "You have not yet opened one?"

Tesla shook his head and bent back to his task. "I have not. The boys back at the Pipetown Works in Washington were most diligent in their application of nails and hammers."

Shaw cleared her throat, glanced at Custer to make sure it was okay for her to speak, and then continued at a nod from her superior. "Should we have more troopers here, just in case something goes wrong, Mr. Tesla?"

"We should be perfectly safe, Lieutenant Shaw. I had not intended to activate the unit at any rate. We are merely inspecting today." The two older men, wearing long, thin white coats identical to Tesla's, cast quick glances up at the colonel and his assistant, and then looked just as quickly away.

Custer grunted softly and gestured for them to continue. The three men soon had the box open. One of the assistants carried the heavy pine lid away, dropping it behind them with a startling crash, and the men leaned down into the box. The colonel, almost against his own wishes, moved forward to look inside. He was relieved when the ruddy light revealed only metal, rubber, and sawdust; no flesh was in evidence.

Tesla pushed the wood chips away from the metal shape. It shared the basic form of a man: two arms, two legs, and a boxy shape sitting on its trunk where a head would be. It was gigantic, however; easily twice the size of an average trooper. It reminded the colonel of the metal marshals deployed into the territories to bolster the lawmen still willing to clash with the vicious criminal caste. Those machines were sleek, with a smooth, rounded look that softened their alien appearance. The manikin shape in the box was crude by comparison. Armored plates were bolted directly to the hulking chassis, giving it a heavy, threatening appearance. Each arm ended not in a hand, but rather in the bulk of a large Gatling blaster. They were clearly a more advanced version of the UR-10s that had guarded Camp Lincoln.

Tesla and his men tried to get their arms beneath the robot to leverage it into a sitting position. They grunted and strained for several minutes, coming at it from several different directions, but it refused to budge. The scientist shot a quick look over his shoulder at Custer, watching with an amused sneer, then reached into the box, around the back of the thing's neck, and flipped a switch.

"Hey!" The colonel's weapon was out of the holster moments before the metal man in the crate sat up, shedding wood chips in a dull cascade.

"Immediate Operational Parameters?" The voice was an unpleasant, insectile buzz emanating from a crude grate beneath its cyclopean eye.

Tesla, with another look at Custer, snapped, "Inspection protocols only." His hand was held toward the colonel as if trying to pacify him while he spoke.

The automaton was still for a moment and then buzzed. "Acknowledged. Inspection protocols." As it spoke, it stood up, rising to an imposing height.

The robot towered over the men in the room, intimidating in its silent, heavy stillness.

Custer whistled softly. "Mr. Tesla, I think you got yourself a winner here."

The younger man nodded slightly. "If we can manufacture them at a quick enough pace, pretty soon there will be no need for conventional soldiers."

Shaw snorted at that, and Custer rocked back on his heels, hands hooked into his belt. "You're serious? You think these tin soldiers are going to replace real fighting men?"

Tesla shook his head quickly. "No, of course not! Nothing will replace the initiative and skill of the modern soldier." He waved a hand dismissively. "Well, not right now, at any rate. However, these automatons will be more than equal to the task of holding a line or standing a post. They will bolster our numbers in the face of growing threats until we can produce something better."

"Growing threats?" Custer paced around the metal man. "We seem to be holding our own well enough for the time being."

Tesla shook his head. "We are holding our own against the savages, somewhat. And through the efforts of the UR-30 Enforcers, the lawmen are holding their own against the lawless ruffians who stalk the Territories. You must remember that Carpathian's forces will not suffer from the vagaries of time and entropy like the rest of us. With each man and woman that falls on the frontier, his armies potentially grow. His prospective strength is no less than every person living, and who ever lived, in the western territories, under the worst case scenario."

Custer shook his head. It was sometimes hard to understand the little man behind his thick accent. "Those walking corpses aren't worth much, if you ask me."

Tesla looked back at the colonel. "As a single soldier? No, you're right. But imagine one hundred of them coming at you at once. Or a thousand? Or ten thousand? The reports I've seen talk about Carpathian's influence stretching throughout the west. Should he suddenly decide to turn every man, woman, and child in those towns and villages into one of his stumbling soldiers, how many do you think he could field?"

The young scientist settled his back against one of the crate stacks, arms folded, and shook his head. "No, colonel. We will need something to help us meet those numbers when he finally decides to make his move. We cannot hope to do that with standard soldiers alone. The race is on for the future of our world, and we can only hope that we win. Because trust me, you do not want to live in a world of Doctor Carpathian's imagining."

Custer nodded. He had fought the animations while serving down in the territories, and he had no doubts the little European was speaking the truth. "So the race is on, between his corpse soldiers and your metal ones?"

"Well, it is a little more complicated than that." Tesla gestured toward the back of the room where his equipment was bubbling away. "The race is between dead flesh powered by RJ-1027, and metal powered by electricity." He shrugged. "I'm afraid my advances with all things electric are not progressing as quickly as I would like. For now, I am using the devil's blood nearly as much as my nemesis. But I have no doubt a breakthrough is near at hand!"

Custer shook his head, but did not seem to be paying too close attention.

"Where's Tumblety fit into this race of yours?"

He grimaced with distaste. "I try not to pay too close attention to that fraudulent butcher, truth be told, colonel."

One of the older men snorted, his eyes flashing in the crimson lighting. "The man's a dangerous quacksalver, not fit to inhabit the same facility as Mr. Tesla!"

The colonel smiled at that. "Really? I would've thought you scientific types would stick together. Especially out here on the edge of civilization, surrounded by us straight-laced military men – I mean personnel." He shot a quick look at Shaw, but she was staring at the assistant who had spoken.

Tesla shook his head. "Dr. Tumblety is following a line of inquiry that posits that the human body, through augmentation and artificial enhancement, can be a match for the animations of the Romanian fiend. The things he is doing crash through the limits of sane scientific inquiry and break every convention of civilized research. We each have our supporters back in Washington, I assure you, but I would rather put my faith in good old fashioned iron and technical innovation, rather than the twisted gothic romance stories fashionable with the wealthy ladies of leisure."

Custer nodded again with a frown. "Can't say I blame you, if it comes to that. Are there any other little inventions you'll be springing on us, just so I can keep an eye out?"

Tesla straightened, a boyish grin on his face. "Oh, I'm following countless avenues of research that have been most promising, colonel! The soldier robots should be ready to stand posts in the next few days at most, and I have several prototypes of larger, assault-oriented automata on the way. But they are honestly the least of my concerns now, their development all but complete. We will be designing and creating construction facilities for them down the hall when I've perfected the design, but for now, I am focusing on a whole new area of research."

The young man gestured for the officers to accompany him deeper into the room. The shadows were darker toward the rear, and the constant babbling of the boiling liquids made for a disconcerting, sibilant backdrop. Tesla's excitement drove his voice into louder, higher octaves, and it was not difficult to hear him.

"You see, I was able to isolate several wavelengths of light while studying the raw RJ-1027 we have been able to obtain from our operations in the west." He was rubbing his hands together gleefully. "The light seems to ebb and flow in a standard RJ generator, yes?"

Custer and Shaw nodded.

"Well, many of us assumed this was an indication of the instability of the material itself. We have yet to create the refined substance ourselves, and are forced to rely on raids into the territories and the open market for our supplies." He gestured to one of the glass containers holding a roiling red substance pulsing like a human heart. "But as it turns out, the light does not ebb and flow due to any inherent instability, but rather the very nature of the element itself! You see, apparently, it exists both within AND without our space/time completely!"

Custer looked into the excited face of the young scientist with an utter lack of understanding. "Space time? What's space time?"

Tesla shook his head in frustration. "No, not 'space time', space AND time! RJ-1027 somehow fluctuates between the here and now, and some other place and time!"

Shaw snorted slightly, and Custer cocked his curly head to one side. "I'm fairly certain you've lost us both, Mr. Tesla."

Tesla's shoulders sagged. "Never mind. Suffice it to say that, manipulating this property, I am toying with an invention that will allow a person to travel from one place to another without having to move through the space between."

Both officers were now staring blankly. Tesla took a deep breath and forged ahead. "If you take one of these gauntlets," he pulled a white sheet from a table and revealed several ancient-looking metal gloves. Each was shimmering slightly with a red glow as if reflecting a bloody sunset. "With a little more work, you will be able to point at a person with one of these and pull them toward you. They will cease to exist where they are and appear before you."

Shaw barked a cruel laugh. "I've seen that done a hundred times in dancehalls and barker's tents across the country, sir! There's nothing new about that!"

Custer nodded. "What you are describing is a fairly common trick, Mr. Tesla."

Tesla balled his fists in irritation and tilted his head toward the ceiling above. When he looked back at the officers, his eyes were flat and cold. "Someday your forces will be able to jump across the battlefield to come to grips with the enemy without having to cross through their fields of fire. Injured will be evacuated without risk. Someday, walls, moats, and even mountains will be as nothing as you assault the enemy." He tilted toward them both, his dark eyes flashing from one to the other. "And when that day comes, I want you to remember that it was in this dank cave that you first heard the idea."

Custer put his hands up to calm to the scientist down. "I'm sure you're right, Mr. Tesla. I'm sure. They look right impressive and no mistake."

"The wealth of the world will be ours one day, colonel, because of science. There will be nothing we do not know, nothing we cannot do, and it will all come to us through the investigation of the world around us and our own powers of creation."

The colonel took a step back, nodding. "I have no doubt." He turned with a casual tap of his finger to the brim of his hat. "Shaw, you're with me."

"Yessir." The young woman hurried to catch up.

Over his shoulder, Custer called out. "Mr. Tesla, I have to meet with Dr. Tumblety now. I'm planning a foray into the surrounding territory in the next month or so to teach the savages a sharp lesson. I would be greatly obliged if as many of your metal soldiers as possible would be ready to take the field with us as you think prudent."

As the colonel walked from the room he could hear the eagerness in the scientist's voice. "I will do that, colonel! And thank you for this chance to prove the efficacy of my work!"

"Shaw, I swear." Custer muttered under his breath as they moved deeper beneath Fort Frederick. "I'm going to go barking mad by the time they get us out of here."

*****

The lowest levels beneath Fort Frederick were damp and poorly lit. As Custer and Shaw moved down the final corridor, their footsteps echoing hollowly around them, the two officers found themselves closing ranks without conscious thought.

Custer shook his head and turned to his young adjutant. "I hate these visits, Shaw. You weren't at Camp Lincoln, but God, if you'd of seen what sorts of things he did there . . . The man's no surgeon. He's a butcher, and a madman." The colonel knew he was babbling, but could not help himself. He had been able to keep ahead of Tumblety's demand for test subjects, barely, with the captured savages his outriders occasionally dragged back to Fort Frederick. He had refused to provide the poor, innocent victims that had kept the maniac's more violent rampages in check. So far, there had been no serious repercussions, but the Colonel knew that time would come.

Shaw nodded as they marched down the hall but said nothing. As disquieting as it surely was for the colonel to visit Doctor Tumblety's dungeons, she found it more disturbing by far.

A scream bubbled up from ahead of them, drowning the fading sounds of their footsteps and opening a ringing cacophony as echoing screams bounced back all around, filling the narrow hallway. Dazed, directionless moaning and animal growls rose up as if in answer to the squeals of pain. Shaw started to take more careful notice of the doors that passed to either side. Most of the windows were barred.

The scream faded into quiet sobbing, and then silence. Custer and Shaw shared a dark look as they stopped in front of a pair of doors set into the rough wall at the end of the hallway. The colonel frowned, Shaw cocked one eyebrow, and Custer turned to knock.

"Doctor, we've come to inspect your work." The colonel pushed the door open without waiting for a reply. Whether his mind had actually banished all memory of Camp Lincoln, or it had only been a moment's lapse, he would spend the rest of his life wishing he had allowed Tumblety time to cover up his current subject.

What was left of a once-proud native was fastened to a slab of shiny metal by leather straps slick with blood. The savage's hands had been removed at the forearm, his legs removed just above the knee. Wires connected the stumps to various metallic items on the table that rattled or scratched as the man's body flailed against its bonds.

Custer was chivalrous enough to hope the subject had been a man. The flesh of the subject's chest had been stripped down to the meat-enclosed ribcage, the bones flashing wetly in the dim, crimson light. The skin had been pulled down like a blanket and was draped, glistening, over the lower abdomen and upper thighs.

The face had also been stripped of several layers of flesh. Lumps of meat floated in various glass containers on a smaller cart, noxious fumes adding to the slaughterhouse stench. Custer saw long, ivory teeth or claws projecting from some of the lumps, lank hair or fur floated around still others. The doctor was working over the pool of blood that had once been the unfortunate victim's eye socket, a pale orb rotating wildly within the crimson fluid. Two strong orderlies, their white aprons splashed with blood, held the wretched creature down.

The self-styled Doctor Tumblety looked up from his work and smiled as he saw Colonel Custer. Beneath the stained apron, the doctor wore a ridiculous costume based upon some fanciful notion of a military uniform. The smile vanished, however, when Lieutenant Shaw walked into view.

"The woman must leave at once, colonel. I do not allow members of the distaff sex to be present while I work." His face, behind the ludicrously elaborate mustache, had hardened into a mask of barely-contained fury. "Their energy is disruptive to the process and distracting to my assistants."

Custer had expected something like this. He had seen for himself the man's downright allergy to women, but he had not expected him to be quite so direct and insulting. He felt his own anger rising in defense of his adjutant.

"Doctor, I'm afraid I'm not going to be able to let you –"

The doctor held up one hand, dripping with blood, and stopped the colonel in his tracks. "I thought we had an understanding, colonel. Further, I was informed by General Grant himself that my work would receive every possible assistance from the command staff of Fort Frederick. Was that assurance somehow in error?" The haughty manner and exaggerated upper-class accent were horribly incongruous with the blood-drenched apron and gore-encrusted hands.

When Custer failed to respond, Tumblety leaned forward. "I'm afraid I did not hear your response, colonel. I would hate to think that I had made an error in selecting my chosen champion. Am I not to receive every possible assistance with my work?"

Custer nodded. The blunt reminder of Tumblety's patronage, and the man's legendary caprice, stung deeply. The anger was still there, but the damned charlatan was right. He waved Shaw back toward the door without turning around. "Go get a drink, Lieutenant. God knows I wish I could join you."

"Sir." The colonel could hear the anger and resentment in the young woman's voice, but she pivoted on one heel and snapped out, closing the door with dull finality behind her.

The moment the door closed, the doctor completely relaxed. His shoulders sagged, his face thawed, and a smile emerged from beneath the mustache. "Thank you, Colonel. I do find the presence of a woman can be so distressing when conducting serious work, don't you?"

Custer shook his head and forced himself to approach the shining table. One assistant moved away to give him a better view. "Lieutenant Shaw is an exemplary officer. Women have been serving beside men for years now, ever since the casualty lists of the war became unsustainable. I guess we just got used to it."

Tumblety nodded. "Indeed, Colonel. The ability of the human mind to adapt to even the most uncomfortable, outrageous situations has always fascinated me. I intend, when time permits, to look deeper into the phenomenon. Perhaps publish a paper on my findings." He waved one crimson-stained hand over the body before them. "But, happily, there is one hardship, I think, that may soon cease to vex us. With my current line of research, our difficulties with recruitment and retention may soon be a thing of the past!"

The body on the table between them shuddered with continued, moaning sobs. Tumblety rolled his eyes and gestured for one of his assistants to wheel the table further into the shadows of the long, low room.

"Honestly, colonel, life can often be quite lonely here on the edge of scientific advancement." His face was curled into a cartoonish mask of sadness. "So few understand the inevitable benefits of my work. For instance, sir, are you aware of the revitalizing blessings of RJ-1027?"

Custer nodded. "There aren't many fighting men today that don't notice we tend to last longer than those who aren't." He grimaced. "Those of us who aren't burned down, of course."

"Of course!" The doctor wagged a finger in the colonel's direction. "And yet, almost no research is being conducted upon this phenomenon! In Zeus's name, sir, we do not even truly understand what RJ-1027 is, entirely!"

"No, I'm aware." Custer's sour tone was lost on the doctor. Most non-military government workers failed to understand the inherent weakness in depending upon the enemy for their only true source of power. The world had been turned upside down by Carpathian's appearance; more than most people realized.

"Exactly." Tumblety nodded. "Thankfully, there are those in Washington who want nothing more than to understand this fascinating world around us and how it can be bent more to our will. By the time I am done here, Colonel Custer, that Romanian charlatan will have no hold over us. His legions of the stumbling dead will hold no terror for a people who have mastered the human body itself."

Custer nodded, eager only to escape. But the doctor continued.

"I was just telling the Secretary of War himself before coming out here, sir. The secret is within us, and we only need to open our eyes to see it!" The man's smile was ghastly. "He agreed wholeheartedly." He made a shooing gesturing with one hand, his face twisted in dismissal. "Let Tesla run around lighting fires and making metal men. The true victory will be here, sir, in this lab, with these all-too human creatures, in elevating them to godhead!"

One orderly stopped to spit on the floor, his eyes glowing with reflected lamplight in the shadows. "Tesla's not fit to polish your medals, sir."

A low moan escaped from the shape on the table, as the doctor glowed in the praise of his minion. He looked to the colonel with sad eyes. "I apologize, colonel." He shrugged. "Sometimes my subjects are less focused upon the work than I would like."

Custer watched the masked attendant pull the mutilated body deeper into the shadows. He nodded vaguely. "I can . . . imagine, doctor." He shook his head and cleared his throat. "Washington would like to know what kind of progress you are making, and if you require any further supplies."

"You are in communication with Washington?" This seemed to perk the doctor up again, his smile wider than ever.

Custer found himself retreating into the stiff parade rest stance of his rocky time at the Academy. "The latest supply run included a command-grade vocal reiterator suite.

If there is anything you require from the War Office or the White House, we are in constant communication as of last evening."

Tumblety dried his hands on a dirty cloth and tossed it onto another table. "Excellent! That will be ideal when I have reached the next phase of my research. Currently, however, I believe I have everything I need . . . That is, as long as you intend to follow General Grant's orders to provide me with my pick of all prisoners taken?"

Custer could not stop his eyes from flicking back into the shadows. The wretch back there moaned softly. He swallowed and clenched his hands tighter behind his back.

"Those are my orders, doctor. I intend to follow them."

"Excellent!" Tumblety came to stand beside the colonel and rested one hand on his shoulder. It was everything Custer could do not to flinch away. "And tell me, Colonel, when might we be finding another opportunity to acquire further prisoners? I am nearly finished with this latest batch, but the next phase will require many more."

There was nothing Custer wanted more at that moment than to escape from this fusty, dark, foul-smelling room. He took a deep breath through his mouth. "I'm inclined to launch a punitive expedition against the local savages in the next couple of weeks, doctor. They are initiating most of their attacks from a nearby village. We will have a strong enough force to ensure overwhelming victory." He swallowed sharply. "There should be plenty of prisoners."

"Excellent!" Tumblety repeated. "And women too, I expect? Then I will await this glorious day."

"Washington is hoping you will have some of your experiments advanced enough to provide the strike force with samples, so they can be evaluated in the field?"

Custer kept his eyes focused on the middle distance.

"Absolutely!" The foul man sounded like a child on the morning of his birthday. "I have some excellent examples prepared!"

"Well and good, doctor." The colonel nodded sharply and stood to attention. "With your permission, I have a great deal that requires my attention."

"Of course, colonel. I will continue with my work here." Tumblety turned, gesturing into the shadows for his assistants to draw the whimpering subject back into the light. As Custer pushed the door open, however, the doctor called back to him. "Colonel, where is this savage village? Is it close?"

Custer nodded without turning around. "Not far. On a small tributary a few miles away. Little Big Horn, the Injuns call it."

Chapter 4

Lucinda held the tin cup of diluted coffee tightly to her chest, absorbing as much of the warmth as she could. Most of the men in the camp could not even claim this much to nurse along, and so she tried not to let the fresh disappointment of each sip affect her. The fires were mere piled embers this late at night, and most of the army was rolling up into their blankets and bedrolls to get what sleep they could. She envied them.

Jesse's ragtag army of survivors, once outlaws, rebel guerillas, or former prisoners, still had faith in the man that led them. Lucinda was not so sure.

"I'm telling you, Jesse," Henderson began again. "You're fighting a two-front war, and you need to use every weapon at your disposal!" The gaunt, black-clad man jabbed the fire with a long stick. "I know you've been shyin' away from it, but that includes the power of fear."

Around the central fire, Jesse and his closest friends and advisors were talking deep into the night. They had been running through the same arguments for the better part of two weeks with no real shift in the battle lines. Stumbling upon a major border trail had brought it all to a head. Frank and Lucinda were adamantly opposed to attacking the border towns, while Jim and Bob Younger, still bitter at John's loss, did not share their restraint. Caught in the middle, either through lack of interest or conviction, Captain Ingram, Will Shaft, the Ford Brothers, and a few of the more prominent prisoners sat back, watching things unfold. As for Cole Younger, he was keeping his own council, for now.

Lucinda's fiercest competition for Jesse's ear was the mysterious Allen Henderson. An advisor and assistant to a man Jesse very nearly worshiped, William Quantrill, Henderson carried far more weight than she thought he should have. The influence he had over Jesse was maddening. So far, Frank and Lucinda had been able to balance the late-night arguments, but eventually Henderson was going to catch Jesse's ear. She had nightmares imagining what sorts of chaos that would cause.

"Ain't the common man's doin', anythin' that happened to us." Frank's voice had been a raw shadow of his old booming tones since being pulled from the hellish laboratory at Camp Lincoln. Somehow, though, the soft words carried even greater weight.

Jesse, gazing down at his arms as if lost in thought, nodded slightly. "Frank talks a lot of sense."

"Well, I can sympathize with your emotional reaction, Jesse." Henderson's voice resonated with reason. "But we're talking about a much larger picture than any of ya'll are focused on presently. You know what we would have done in the old days: the border region has to burn. We have to send a message. Not only to our foes, but, even more importantly, to those who might side with us, should their consciences fall in the right direction."

Lucinda shook her head. There was no way she could let this man coax Jesse down this path. Despite her own freshly-ambiguous feelings toward her lords and masters, she could not let Jesse take his frustration and rage out on the innocents of the border lands, no matter their allegiance.

"Jesse, just think before you do anything rash." She poured every tone and nuance from a lifetime of training in deceit and performance into her voice, infusing it with pure, naked conviction. "Think about your next move. If you kill women and children in their homes . . . That's no easy thing to walk back from. You need to keep that firmly in mind. Whether you want to carve out your own place or you're looking to go around Lee and his cronies and see the south rise again, you don't want that kind of stain on your story."

"It's no stain if they're the very people keeping the south down!" Henderson's poise slipped as his eyes, eclipsed behind their thick lenses, glared at her over the fire. "The Union army does not feed itself, it doesn't give itself orders, it doesn't spontaneously create soldiers from the ribs of the ones that have gone before. The Union army exists on the backs and at the tacit complicity of the people. And that includes those border towns supporting Johnson and his cabal."

"Not the women and children, Henderson." Frank spoke again, taking up the thread. Considering his run-in with the Union at Camp Lincoln, his opinion could not help but carry weight. "Most of the men and all of the women and children of those towns deserve a hell of a lot better from the world than they got. And that means the Union army as much as it means us. The last thing they need is us comin' at 'em from one side, while Grant's grindin' over 'em from the other."

The Youngers maintained their silence, but they watched everything through hooded eyes. Bob, in particular, was staring at Jesse, one of his broad-bladed fighting knives glittering in his hand as he oiled it.

A hard edge had entered Jesse's eyes at Henderson's, and Lucinda knew there was still hope.

"Well, this is a new world, Henderson." Jesse was still staring into the fire, but

Lucinda could see, as Frank relaxed and the Youngers tensed up, that everyone had felt the change. "I don't believe we'll be doin' ourselves any favors, hittin' towns that we ain't sure are standin' with Grant."

That was too much for Bob Younger, who surged to his feet, pointing with the gleaming knife at the outlaw boss. "You got a lot of nerve talkin' about favors, James! Your brother walked out of Camp Lincoln! Ours died there, no matter the why's and wherefores. The Youngers owe those blue-bellied bastards, Jesse, and we mean to make 'em pay!"

Cole sat unmoving. In the old days, he would have reined his hot-tempered brother in with a clever joke or a biting observation. But like all of them, he had changed. He had been far less vocal in his opinions and much less prone to laughter since they had emerged from the prison camp. The fact that he let Bob's comment stand was telling, and Lucinda feared again for the civilians that lay in their path.

Jesse, however, was unmoved by either of the Youngers' speech or silence. He stared into Bob's eyes and spoke in slow, even tones. "John Younger followed me of his own free will. He was followin' me when he was taken. The man who . . . did that, to John, will pay. You have my word on that. But these towns ahead of us now? They ain't never heard of Andersonville, or Camp Lincoln. Killin' 'em for that wouldn't make no more sense than killin' 'em fer the cold weather."

"We also need to think about food." Lucinda pushed forward. "It will be much easier to buy supplies from friendly towns than it will from hostiles. And when you burn your first border town, Jesse, every other town right down to the Gulf will be your enemy."

"You don't do business with the enemy, missy!" Henderson scoffed. "You take what you want. Hell, we got enough food, now that the Injuns separated the wheat from the chaff. We ain't heard no whinin' about it since we headed south!"

Lucinda stared at the old rebel and shook her head, then turned back to Jesse. "The decision has to be yours, Jesse. There's no one else to make it. But if rising to true power and influence, either back in the Territories or down south is your goal, please think about the reputation you'll carry with you if you leave a trail of dead women and children in your wake."

For a moment, the only sound was the soft popping of the fire. When Jesse spoke, he was still staring into the embers. "I'm hearin' everyone's words, an' I ain't made up my mind yet. We'll come up on the first border town in the next couple of days: Moberly, if I've figured our position right. I ain't never been there, so I don't know much about it."

He looked up, first at Lucy, then at Frank, then to Henderson. "I say we leave it up to them. If I walk into Moberly an' I see Union flags flyin' in the town square, 'r any soldiers, 'r any other sign o' twisted loyalties, we'll take up this conversation again." His dark eyes settled on the Youngers. "But if they ain't got no truck with the Union, 'r if they're hidin' the stars 'n bars in their hearts, then we ain't gonna do nuthin' but maybe trade fer some beef 'n whiskey an' be on our way. Is that clear as moonshine fer you boys?"

The Youngers all nodded, their eyes ranging from flat to hostile. After a moment, Jesse nodded in return and rose to his feet. "Well, that's just rosy. Happy to hear it." He turned toward the nearest supply wagon, its RJ engine glowing softly. "I'm gonna saw some logs. I'll talk to ya'll in the mornin'."

The group around the fire sat for several moments in silence and then drifted off to their own blankets. Lucinda was the last to move away, pushing the glowing embers around in the heart of the fire until they muted to a dull, glowing orange. Henderson, settled back against the wheel of one of their remaining Rolling Thunders, watched her through lenses that reflected that light back in crimson gleams. They nodded to each other, faces cold and still. Loveless turned without a word and went to find her own bedroll.

*****

There was nothing to set Moberly apart from any other border town in the war-torn region the big bugs on all sides had taken to calling the Contested Territories. There were twenty or so buildings huddled around the intersection of two major trails. The side streets were little more than packed dirt paths branching off between the rickety structures. Farmland was visible off to the east, small herds of cattle milling in the middle distance. Off south, a low range of hills probably promised silver to any fool willing to put in the back-breaking work. That promise was what most likely kept this little scrub-town alive.

The buildings Jesse could see, as he and his small gang rumbled into town, sported an intriguing mix of RJ generators. He saw both the heavy-framed Union models and the more elegant Carpathian jobs, but neither seemed more prevalent than the other. Clearly, Moberly was a town that had not yet taken sides between the Union or the European. That was good for Jesse and his battered crew, anyway. Not that it meant that his people would be welcome, but at least this little burg was not already taking up with an enemy.

Jesse's eyes tightened behind the rose-colored goggles. Although they had not come down for Grant or Carpathian, that did not mean they might not take up the Union cause against any sons of the south who happened to ride on in.

The outlaw boss raised one metallic fist and the riders with him slowed. The Iron Horses dropped into an idling rumble and glided to a stop in the middle of the packed dirt trail. The Ford brothers scanned the scrub brush to either side. They had hardly left him a moment's peace once they had taken up their self-appointed roles as his protectors. The much larger, dark-skinned man at the back of their little group sat his 'Horse impassively, looking straight ahead with calm, dark eyes. A bandana hid the lower portions of his face, while a tight hood was draped over his head. A strange bulge pressed against the fabric on one side.

Jesse smiled at Marcus Cunningham. They had found Cunningham in one of the deepest, darkest pits in Fort Lincoln. Due in no small part to his strange deformity, he had been a favorite subject of Tumblety's. The big black man had never ridden with the Confederacy; he had been much too young. The mad doctor must have requested his presence, special. One thing was for sure: Camp Lincoln had been no safe place for a man of Marcus's skin tone.

Lucy had been dead-set against it when he told her he was bringing the big black man, but Jesse had been unyielding. He had thought about having Will Shaft join him, but the young man's rebel gear might confuse the issue Jesse was trying to establish. Riding into a border town with a man whose skin was as black as pitch was very likely to cause trouble no matter what flag they flew behind their eyes. Lucy was right about that. If Jesse could not get a bunch of hayseeds in a no-account border town like Moberly to see his new vision, there would be little reason to continue south.

Within the frame of his trimmed beard, Jesse's mouth quirked in a crooked smile. His arms had not twitched once on him since riding out of camp, almost as if they approved of this mission. Besides, he was in the mood to bust some heads, and if there were a few folks in town that would take exception to a black man riding with white folks, well, then, so be it. Jesse knew something about forging a reputation. Making a public display of violence on behalf of a dark-skinned friend would set just the right tone for what had to come after.

Jesse nodded to the big man, who nodded back without a change in his expression. Marcus Cunningham was no man's fool. He knew why he had been chosen to ride into Moberly, and he did not care.

Marcus was the son of escaped slaves. His parents, having crossed the Mississippi looking for a fresh start, had been captured by a Warrior Nation raiding party. His father was killed by the warriors, but his mother, large with child, had been spared and brought into the small tribal village, adopted as one of their own. Marcus had been given his father's name, but he had been raised by the Warrior Nation.

While still a boy, he had been eager to follow the path of the warrior, but had lacked the patience and the serenity to follow the slow pace set by the medicine men. Something had gone wrong, resulting in the misshapen crest of bone that emerged from the side of his head, hidden by the cowl. That horn had landed Marcus in Camp Lincoln, and Jesse knew he was sensitive about it. The big man saw the horn as, not only the cause of his most recent suffering, but also as a reminder of his failure as a boy. He had been known to kill men just for looking at it.

He had just the temperament Jesse wanted for this little detour.

"Looks like the joint's dyin' a slow death, Jesse." Robert Ford spat into the dust. "Not sure they're gonna be any good for much of anythin', you ask me."

Jesse's grin widened as he turned back to survey the cluster of buildings. "Nonsense, Robert. Everythin's good for somethin'. Worse comes to worst, this little burg'll make a great bad example."

The four men brought their mounts back up to a growling roar and rumbled into Moberly in a cloud of dust. The streets were nearly empty. Only a few folks stood around, gaping as the outlaws rode in. A couple of horse shaped blackhoofs, cast iron frames showing no great artistry, were standing still as statues a few buildings down. A large, battered passenger wagon was parked a little ways down the street, probably stopped for supplies and food on a regular passage along the major trail.

Jesse tipped his hat to a pair of ladies standing in front of a row of businesses that shared a boardwalk and wooden sunshade. The women stared as the four vehicles growled past, moving toward a low, two-story corner structure. A sign hanging kitty-corner to the street announced this to be The Pavilion saloon and eatery. Jesse's first thought was that it was a rather grandiose title for the unassuming little shack. His second, as three scowling men emerged blinking into the sunlight, was here we go.

Jesse brought his 'Horse around in a tight turn, nose-in toward the saloon's porch. There were only two recharge pads there, and he settled down on the closest. Cunningham brought his machine rumbling up onto the other, and the Ford brothers settled for grounding theirs in the dirt to either side. Jesse pulled his goggles down off his face and nodded to the three men standing there.

"Howdy, folks!" The outlaw's voice boomed with easy confidence. White teeth flashed in a predatory grin.

The lead man on the porch gave him a grudging nod while his companions stared coldly at the big black man in the strange headgear.

Jesse took clear note of the men staring at Marcus and his grin disappeared. He looked down without a care, pulling the makings of a quirley from a pouch in his front pocket. Casually, he began to roll up a cigarillo. His eyes remained focused on his blurring hands as he shrugged and muttered, "You boys havin' a problem?"

The two men jerked and looked back over to the outlaw chief. The lead man, a healthy gut pushing at his fancy vest, put his hands on his hips. The right hand settled in close to the silvered grip of a custom blaster.

"Folks round these parts don' want no trouble." He jerked his head toward Marcus. "But we ain't likely to cower down when it shows up at our door, neither." The men behind him nodded.

Jesse tossed the quirley into his mouth and caught it with pursed lips, lighting it with a match he swiped across the palm of one hand. He grinned, and smoke began to rise from the corners of his mouth. "Marcus?" He tilted his head in the direction of the big black man. "He don't mean no trouble. You mean trouble, Marcus?"

The large body was completely still, the eyes glittering in the shadow of the hood. "Nossir, Jesse. I don't mean trouble."

Jesse flicked the match in a smoky arc out into the street. "You see?" He folded his mechanical arms across his broad chest. "Marcus don't mean no trouble. I don't mean no trouble. I KNOW these boys don't mean no trouble, do you boys?"

The Fords shook their heads, but their eyes were cold and flat. Each man sat in his saddle with an easy grace, hands not far from weapons.

"You see now, fellas?" Jesse's grin returned full force. "There ain't no reason for things to get ugly. Me an' my friends here, we're just passin' through. Thought we'd get us a drink and a little time in the shade before movin' on. Maybe chat you folks up over current events?" He took out the cigarillo and spit a fleck of tobacco off to the side.

"Current events?" The lead man was still suspicious. The two men behind him looked more confused than anything else.

"Well, fer starters, how're the mines playin' out? How's the crop lookin'? Seen any Injuns hereabouts?" His smile was fixed but his voice became chill. "Any Union soldiers been through lately?"

All three faces on the porch turned sour at the mention of the Union. The man in front spit over the railing and into the dirt. "Don't think much o' the Union 'round here, boys."

"They's like locusts, comin' through on their way west." One of the men in the back of the group snarled. "Take whatever they want: food, water, whatnot; rough up the hands, play lewd with the womenfolk."

"You're not goin' to find many folks carryin' water fer the Union in Moberly, stranger." The lead man's voice was low as he shifted his gaze back to Marcus. "But that don't make them the worst sorts there is, neither."

Jesse swung down off his 'Horse and took a casual turn around the street. The windows of the nearby buildings were filling up with curious onlookers. It was just about time to play to the gallery.

He looked back up at the man on the porch, hooking his thumbs behind his gun belt and pushing back his duster. "Well, that weren't too friendly."

The man on the porch shifted slightly, his own hand creeping toward his gun. The two men behind him moved off to either side, clearing their own firing lanes.

"Marcus!" Jesse pitched his voice to carry out over the street. "You offended by that last remark?"

The big black man nodded slowly. "Yeah, Jesse," he rumbled. "I was."

As Marcus stood up, his size became more apparent. Rather than swing his leg up and over to dismount, he just stood up and stepped over the saddle. He was a huge man, muscles bulging from his doeskin vest. Heavy lengths of chain were draped around his neck and under his arms: the same chains that had held him down in Camp Lincoln, now worn with defiant pride. With slow and easy movements he reached down to a boot behind his saddle and slid out a smooth wooden shaft wrapped in cured leather.

When Marcus turned back to the porch he was holding a massive hammer with a heavy stone head. His brows curled down toward each other as he looked directly into the eyes of the men on the porch. His voice was a low, subterranean growl. "I ain't liked the way you folks been lookin' at me since we rode up."

Jesse smiled even wider and patted the air with one down-turned hand. "Now, now, Marcus." He turned to the locals. "We don't need to resort to violence, do we boys?"

The lead man on the porch had rested his hand on the butt of his pistol. He moved forward and rested his other hand on the railing and sneered down at Jesse and his men. "We don't if you an' yer friend turn those hellish machines around an' get the hell outta town, flannel mouth."

The Fords eased themselves off their 'Horses, eyes watching the men on the porch, hands resting on their weapons. The last words fell into the silence like a lead weight into a stagnant pond. The six men paused as if waiting for the ripples to reach them.

The moment stretched on, the pressure of the silence building. The people of Moberly crept backward, as if afraid they would disturb the tableau. An almost-visible line of tension connected the speaker on the porch with Jesse standing calmly in the street.

When the outlaw chief finally spoke, his voice was light, belaying the tightness that had settled over the scene.

"He just call me a flannel mouth, Marcus?" The quirley shifted from one side of Jesse's mouth to the other with a flash of teeth.

"He did that, Jesse." The large man twisted his hands on the shaft of the massive hammer. The leather creaked with subtle menace.

"That's what I thought." Without warning, one of Jesse's Hyper-velocity pistols was in his hand with reassuring speed, metallic arm rigid as the bore of the weapon settled on the local man's face. "That just ain't gonna stand."

The man had just enough time to dodge to the side before the bolt from Jesse's gun flashed past him and slapped into the front of the saloon, blowing in a window and scorching a wide circle in the dry wood. Rather than snarling in anger at his inaccuracy, Jesse's smile grew wider, as if this had been his intention all along.

The two men who had come out onto the boardwalk with the pie eater crouched down in place, their hands raised momentarily in shock at the detonation. The Ford brothers, on the other hand, had been ready. Their weapons were in their hands and sending shot after shot into the shade of the overhang. Jesse fanned a stream of shots, straight and true, into the flickering shadows as well. His exultant Rebel yell echoed off the saloon's wall.

One of the locals was struck several times in the body and arm, spinning back against the wall in a spray of blood and cooked flesh as his clothing fluttered away from the stunning impacts. Another window shattered as the hapless man crashed through it to hang there, suspended on the broken glass, a sheet of blood cascading down from his torn belly.

The last man on the porch got several wild shots off as he dove for a rain barrel at the corner of the building. The bolts snapped past the outlaws and into the sunny street, hitting buildings across the way and setting several small fires. The Fords ran slant-wise along the railing, their weapons steady, to get a clean shot around the big wooden barrel.

The leader of the local men had hit the wooden planks and rolled on his shoulder to slam up against a thick support beam that held the sunshade steady overhead. His back to the polished wood, he had his weapon held tightly to his chest. He cocked his head to the side, trying to catch a glimpse of Jesse from the corner of his eye.

"Now, I did take exception to the unkind words you sent in my direction, sir." Jesse's tone was still light. He knew that any story spreading outward from Moberly would feature his attitude as an important element. He chose his next words with special care. "But it was the way you treated my friend, Marcus here, that really set me off."

"I'm sorry!" The man squeaked from behind the pillar. His eyes were now fixed on the body of his friend, leaking life down onto the worn wood of the boardwalk. "I din't mean nothin' by it!"

"I give up!" The man behind the rain barrel threw his gun out into the dust, his hands raised, shaking, over his head. He did not stand, but he was clearly out of the fight. The Fords came around and gestured for him to back away down the side of the building while Marcus and Jesse settled the true conflict.

"Marcus, you reckon our local yokel here is sorry?" Jesse sauntered to the side, his pistol pointed, unwavering, at the large post.

The big man stalked toward the porch, hammer hefted easily before him. "He ain't sorry enough."

The outlaw boss nodded, again pitching his voice for the general audience. "No, he ain't. Folks gotta learn, it's a new world, 'specially here in the borderlands. It can't be about color no more, if'n we wanna live to see another day. It's stand together against the savages, the Union, an' the nightmares comin' out o' the west, 'r their gonna drag us down, one lonely fool at a time."

Jesse could see the round eyes of the townsfolk as they heard his words. Most folks on the frontier were too busy surviving to hold too tightly to the old prejudices anyway, but he was glad to see that not many of these folks looked too outraged at his little speech.

"It's fools like this that are as much the enemy as any blue-belly, brave, or walkin' corpse." He gave a theatrical shrug, stretching both metal arms out wide and taking his gun off the cowering man on the porch for the first time since he fired. "An' there's folks who won't understand that 'till they see some blood on the street. Don't you think, Marcus?"

"True words, Jesse." Marcus had reached the pillar on feet far too quiet for a man his size. On the other side, the local man, having found the courage of his convictions, raised his pistol, a snarl wiping the fear from his face as he turned to jump back up into the fight. The muscles beneath Marcus's vest bunched and stretched as he brought the enormous stone hammer back with only a slight snarl of exertion, and then his entire body wrenched with the effort to swing it around.

The hammer head struck the solid wooden post at head height on the man rising up behind it. The wood shattered, sending splinters showering in all directions. The weapon did not slow at all in its arc of destruction. The broad stone struck the cowering man in the side of the head, preceded by a blast wave of sharp wooden shards. Gobbets of wet matter splattered across the opposite wall and windows, and the headless body cartwheeled limply into a still heap in front of the batwing doors.

"Whewee, doggie!" Jesse holstered his pistol with a casual flourish, flexing his metal fingers in surprised satisfaction, and stepped up onto the porch, looking down at the horrific mess. "Marcus, when you make a point, you really make a point!"

The Fords brought the last would-be attacker around the corner, still held at gunpoint. The man's face was as pale as death, his breathing ragged, and he could not take his eyes from the slumped and mangled body of his friend hanging from the window. The headless corpse on the ground in front of him, though, was too much. The man sagged into the dust, nearly losing consciousness.

Jesse grinned at the slumped form and then spun around to cast his gaze among the men and women standing in shocked silence on the street and in the surrounding windows.

"Ya'll saw how that went down, an' I don't want no one missin' the point!" He gestured to the body at his feet with a gentle push of one heel. "We just rode up into town. It was your boys here who decided they wanted a fight, casting unfriendly words at my friend." He jerked his chin at Marcus, standing calmly by his side. Blood dripped gently from the head of the hammer.

"What I said to your man here holds true." Jesse hooked his thumbs behind his gun belt again. "These are dark times we're livin' in, and good folks gotta stand together, regardless of the color of our skin, or we're all goin' down before our time."

Jesse gestured for Robert Ford to bring him the last local man. "An' we ain't here to keep old hate fires burnin', neither." He pulled the limp man roughly forward and draped one solid metal arm over his shoulders. "Grudges won't keep us alive, an' so we ain't lookin' to settle any scores with folks we ain't got no feud with." He patted the man heavily and then gave him a gentle push down the stairs and into the street.

"Now, me and my friends are gonna mosey on inside and get ourselves a drink." Jesse's grin widened again. "I'm hopin' ya'll are comin' around to my way of thinkin' on this, cuz this little dance here," he gestured around himself at the blood and destruction. "This was thirsty work. I'm not lookin' to repeat it, at least till I get around a slug o' whiskey 'r two."

Jesse backed up the stairs to The Pavilion's main doors. His grin was still in place, his thumbs resting easily on his gun belt. Before he could make a dramatic turn,

duster swirling in the warm shadows, a voice stopped him cold.
"Jesse James, as I live and breathe."

Chapter 5

James Campbell awoke to the soft sound of rain on canvas. Diffuse light filtered through the tan fabric, confusing the time of day. With a sour grunt, he rolled over, pushed himself out of his bedroll, and snatched his uniform pants off the end of his cot. Dressing in his tent had been one of the earliest indications that his new post would not live up to expectations. Nowadays, it was barely a footnote in a growing list of disappointments and distractions.

Campbell pushed his way out of the low tent and stood up, arching his back to a chorus of grinding cracks. The camp was coming alive around him, so he must not have slept too late. Taut, buff tents stretched away in all directions. Trails of red-tinged smoke curled into the grey sky from hundreds of powered cooking units. The men moving around him were downcast, their uniforms and gear sodden in the early-morning rain.

"Bill!" Campbell raised his voice, knowing his batman could not be far away. "Blodgett, where the hell are you?"

The former sniper appeared without fanfare or ceremony, standing directly behind his commander. Campbell gave a startled jump before spinning around and giving the larger man a quick shove.

"What have I told you about doing that?" He knew his tone spoke more to his own lack of confidence than his aide's transgressions, but he could not help it. He had to be able to pick on someone in this damned camp, and God Himself knew that none of the other engineers or soldiers paid any more attention to him than protocol demanded.

Blodgett nodded, his face impassive. "Sorry, sir. It certainly was not my intention to startle you."

Campbell snarled, looking around the camp with his hands on his hips. "Right then. I would like some breakfast, Bill. Can we do something about that before going up to view the progress on the outer walls?"

"Hardtack and dried beef is the best I can offer, sir." Blodgett stood at attention and kept his eyes focused just off Campbell's left shoulder.

The commander scowled and gestured to the camp all around them. "I'd rather not suffer through another meal of camp biscuit and shoe leather, Blodgett. These men appear to be cooking their breakfast . . . What are they having?"

The adjutant scanned the clusters of men nearby and shrugged. "At a guess, sir, they are cooking hardtack and jerky with water to soften it up."

Campbell sighed. He was never going to accustom himself to working in the field. "Well, fix me up some of that, then." He looked south, where his command sat just out of sight on the other side of a rise. His face twisted into a disgruntled frown. "I suppose I should go survey the construction while you get to it." He started to move away and then stopped, turning with what he hoped was a forceful energy. "And Bill?" When the adjutant turned back to him with a quirked eyebrow, the commander continued. "See if you can't find something better than camp provisions for lunch, will you? I know this whole mission has been rushing headlong without proper logistics, but much more leather and I might just up and head back to Boston."

Campbell felt a little better as he spun on his heel and headed up the muddy track. As he walked, men tossed him perfunctory salutes, huddled beneath heavy, sodden capes or blankets. The rain had been near-continuous for almost a week, adding to his long list of challenges. He knew there must be a terribly pressing reason for his men to be toiling away like this, but no one had yet seen fit to tell him what it was.

Coming up over the rise, he stopped as the project came into view. A man-made mountain of stone and steel rose before him, glossy with rain. Wooden scaffolds surrounded the edifice, providing steady perches for the men and machines that were climbing up to their day's work in the downpour. Figures swarmed all over the structure, most of them far larger than the human men overseeing the work. UR-10s, mechanical workers from the Pipetown Works in Washington, were lumbering up the steep wooden ramps with heavy slabs of stone balanced on their backs, or fixing those blocks into place with massive metal arms. Fat red sparks scattered down into the puddles below.

Situated a few hundred yards from the construction site was an awning of the ubiquitous tan fabric. Several men and women in the blue uniforms of the Union stood around a drafting table, surveying one of the many large building plans Campbell had brought south with him. When he stepped into the dry space beneath the awning, the officers at the table all popped to attention. His second in command, Major Thomas Dalton, saluted for the detachment.

"Good morning, sir." Dalton's voice was deep and powerful, just the voice Campbell would have liked to possess.

"Carry on." Campbell gestured with his hand for the engineers to turn back to their work. "What are we looking at this morning?"

"Sir," Dalton stepped aside to make room for his commander while pointing with one gloved hand down at a section of the plan scrolled out on the table. Campbell could see that it was the layout of one of the lower levels. "We were discussing the nature of the inner chamber again, sir. There's still a lot of disagreement over its intent."

Campbell leaned over the sheet and looked more closely, although he knew what he was going to see. Within the thick walls of the fortress, honeycombed with fighting positions, rally points, and defenses, the center of the massive edifice was to be entirely hollow, housing a smaller keep in the center. Campbell had never voiced his doubts aloud, but to him, the entire thing reminded him of a vermin trap, with that smaller blockhouse sitting as the bait.

The commander flipped one hand dismissively over the plans. "I'm sure General Grant has his reasons. It might make guarding the lower levels easier should there be a breach, though, don't you think?"

A female officer shook her head. "It doesn't make any sense at all, sir. And then, there are these chambers built into the lower levels. They're just as baffling."

Campbell gave her a weary look and then peered down at the plans again. "Ah, yes. Those were specifically designed by that Euro chap, Tesla? I believe they were also worked to General Grant's specifications."

The officer cleared her throat. "Colonel, what would we need two prison cells in the middle of the armory level for?"

Campbell felt a familiar pressure building in him. He hated being questioned by his subordinates. He particularly hated being questioned by his subordinates when he did not know the answers himself. He felt his lip curl and gave in to the surge of frustration rather than fight the losing battle yet again.

"Captain Baine, where in these plans do you see the words prison?" He tapped the table with more force than he had intended and the thin paper bunched beneath the pressure, threatening to rip. "For that matter, do you see any designation for an armory anywhere here?"

She looked taken aback, but rallied gamely. "Sir, these reinforced bunkers only make sense if they were containing magazines for the fort, or other weapons and ordnance. These two rooms, with only single entryways, heavy locks, and no provision for storage? We've been assuming they were cells for days now."

"Looks more like a trap to me." One of the younger officers, a lieutenant from Maine with more experience in the back woods than on the front line, peered owlishly down at the map from behind thick glasses.

Campbell hid his shock at the younger man's guess and shook his head. "Or guards' barracks? Or communication centers? Or vaults for the storage of General Grant's personal tea set collection?" He was snarling now, and forced himself to bring his temper under control. "I do not know what function those two rooms will serve, captain, and I designed this enormous pile of bricks myself. The entire fortress will be riddled with rooms, passages, and other mysteries whose purposes I cannot even begin to guess at." His voice was rising again, the command staff shying away from his tirade, but he could not stop himself.

"We have been sent down here, deep into what all but the most optimistic fool would consider enemy territory, to construct the most formidable fortification built east of the Mississippi since the war ended. When we are finished, we will have placed a nearly-unassailable fortress on the very edge of Rebellion territory, and we have no idea at all WHY we are doing it!"

"Sir, I thought we had been led to believe this was going to be an advanced base for –" Dalton's mouth snapped shut at the Colonel's sharp tone.

"Based on the plans, Thomas? This will be an advanced base. But it is also appears to be designed as a depository for something that has yet to be identified." He felt his shoulders slump and the men and women sheltering beneath the overhang relaxed slightly, moving forward again as the commander continued in a softer voice.

"They mean to bring something here, and I can't even tell you what it might be." He shook his head and pointed again at the wrinkled section of the plans. "These two rooms? I have referred to them, in my private notes, as the vaults. As you can see, everything around these two chambers is reinforced." He waved a hand with a defeated cast to his face. "Whatever they mean to put down there, it's got to be very important."

For several minutes the command staff stood quiet and still. Some were looking down at the plans, others were looking up at the growing structure before them. Already it was taking shape: long, high walls forming an enormous square, crenellations rising up around the edges. Behind the outer wall rose the beginnings of another, shorter level of wall with a fighting parapet between. When they were finished, if the damned Rebellion let them finish, this place was going to be one of the strongest points on the continent.

"Sir, if they're going through all this trouble to guard something," Baine gestured up at the fortress. "Why put it so close to the enemy?"

The other men around the table nodded or muttered agreement. Campbell could only wish he had an answer for them. Instead, he shrugged. "I don't know, captain. I know we had a small fort here during the war. We kept it garrisoned to stop raiders from striking up into our supply lines. But the site's been abandoned for years." He shook his head. "Now we're rushed down here, put to work with the worst supply situation I've ever seen, and worked under intolerable conditions in hostile territory. All with almost no warning. . ." He shrugged again. "I tell myself ours is not to reason why . . . but believe me, I share your frustration."

"Sir," Dalton's voice was more subdued than it had been. "Has there been any word yet as to what they're thinking of naming the fortress?"

Campbell shook his head. "The name was chosen before I was even brought in." He turned to look out at the pile of glossy stone and the men and machines swarming around it. "They're going to call it Fort Knox, after some artillerist friend of George Washington's."

"Artillerist?" Another of the officers spoke up. "Do you think, maybe, they're planning on putting in some big guns? Something big enough to reach Lee and his cronies?"

Campbell shook his head. "No. You've seen the plans. No big guns. Just the support weapons on the walls."

"But maybe there's some new tech that will give those weapons greater reach?" Baine lifted one of her narrow shoulders. "God knows, they've been coming up with all sorts of strangeness in recent years."

Campbell, his eyes fixed on the hulking form of the fort, shook his head. "I just can't see that. Most of the set defenses are Gatling cannons. Knox also orchestrated Washington's surprise attack over the Delaware River . . . I think the significance of the fort's name is more likely to be found there than in his specialty."

*****

The officers stood watching the construction. Blogdett arrived with Campbell's breakfast in a tin bowl, and the colonel ate absentmindedly. The front wall was nearly done, giant UR-10s hammering locking stones into place and buffing the surface into a single, seamless facade. Clouds of white rock billowed out around the machines smoothing the stone, only to be pounded into grey mud by the rain. Overhead, smaller metal constructs and human workers were moving over the scaffolding, finishing up the forward crenellations and working to extend the corner regions into watch towers. The central bastion, rising above the fortified core, was still little more than a steel framework with just a few courses of large stone laid down.

"Well, whatever it's for . . ." Campbell stood, a tin cup of coffee held tightly in his hands, and stared up at the flagpole rising over the tall framework. "It will be as strong as mortal man can make it."

"Colonel Campbell, a communication over the vocal reiterator." A signals corporal Campbell did not recognize was standing at rigid attention just outside the awning. "It's General Grant, sir."

The colonel exchanged quick glances with the rest of his staff. "Well, we might learn a thing or two sooner rather than later." He nodded for the corporal to proceed, and then followed him to the signals shack.

The small building set aside for the mission's vocal reiterator was one of the few semi-permanent structures on the site. Rough wood with a tarpaper roof, it protected the precious technology that allowed Campbell and his officers to communicate directly with Washington or other military commands. In the center of the shack's single room was a chair seated before a table. On the table was a dark, metallic box connected to other components by tubes and wires. A tall metal mast thrusting up out of the room and into the sky over the hut held aloft a glowing crimson orb.

Campbell swept into the room and the soldier vacated the seat. The commander sat down and crouched low over the table. The black box contained a dark pane of glass that swam with swirling black and red mist. He took up a wand resting beside the machine and pulled to release a length of coiled tubing from the box. Deep within the pane a series of letters floated, shimmering in and out of focus.

"THIS IS ARXXXXQ REQUEXXING IMMEXXXTE COMXXNICATION WITXX-COLONEL XAMPBELLXXTOP"

"Damn, I hate these things." Campbell puzzled out the meaning of the words and then brought the wand to his lips. Forcing himself to speak slowly and clearly, he began. "This is Colonel Campbell reporting, stop."

The machine gurgled and hissed, then the letters vanished, replaced with a new message.

"COLOXXL CAMPXELL THIS ISXXENERAL GRXXT STOX I NEXD A STXXUS

REPORT XXMEDIATELY STXP"

Campbell forced down the chill rising in his stomach and straightened in the camp chair. He gripped the wand with both hands and leaned into it as he responded. "Sir, construction is on schedule, the first level should be finished within the week, stop."

Again the machine rumbled, the words disappeared, and new ones emerged from the fog.

"EXCELXXNT STOXXQUERY THX VXULTS WIXL BE COMXXETED ATXXHE SAME XIME ENXXQUERY"

Campbell nodded but then cursed himself for his foolishness. He coughed and then responded into the wand.

"Yessir. All subterranean levels will be completed with the core structure, including the vaults, stop." Campbell felt a slight twinge of guilt, as that was more reflective of his fondest wish than any realistic assessment. He would rather not get into a deep discussion over the questionable medium of this infernal machine.

"VERY GOOX STOP PREXXRE FOR THE AXRIVAL OXXXREEMINENT WARXMATERIAL XO BE IMXXDIATELY PLACEXXWITXIN VAUXT AXXXOON AS FXXT KNOXXXS COXPLETE AXX ACTIVX XTOP"

The cold in the colonel's gut churned into icy heat. Whatever those vaults were for, they would be needed immediately. Still, there was no clue forthcoming as to what they were intended to protect . . . or contain, if looked at from another point of view.

"Sir," Campbell bent back into the wand. "Query: please advise as to the nature of the material in route, end query."

This time there was a long pause as the black metal box shivered and buzzed. The words within fractured into a thousand vague splinters of light, but nothing rose up to replace them. The chill spread through the colonel's entire body and he was suffering visions of summary executions and familial disgrace before new words appeared.

"MATEXXAL ESSENXIAL TXXFINAX VICXXRY STXP"

Campbell stared at the words as they floated before him. Final victory? Before he could ask for any sort of clarification the words swam away and were replaced once more.

"CONTIXXE THE GXOD WOXX COXXNEL STOX PREXXRE YOXR CXXMAND FOXXTHE ARRXXAL OF MXTERIALXXT OUR EARXIEST CONVXXIENCE STOXXCARRXXON SXOP"

Campbell shook his head at the blunt dismissal. Of course, communicating over the vocal reiterator, conversations almost always ended in such a fashion. The complete lack of emotional context to the communications tended to shade every exchange to pass over the new technology with just a vague hint of mistrust. At least, it seemed that way to Campbell.

The colonel went back to the command pavilion in a foul mood. He was barely aware that the rain had stopped as he walked along the rutted, muddy path. The command staff waited patiently to hear what the general had had to say, but he was not at all sure he wanted to share his ominous forebodings with them.

"Well, we can just start calling those two rooms vaults, now, anyway." He began. He knew he lacked the ability he had witnessed in many other officers, including Major Dalton, to set subordinates at ease with a quick dose of humor. Whenever he tried, he met with just the blank stares he was receiving at that moment. He shook his head and continued before anyone could embarrass him further by asking for a clarification.

"General Grant refers to the two reinforced chambers being built in the center of the armory level as vaults, and informs me that as soon as the fort is complete, we will be in receipt of some extremely important war material that may well be central to final victory."

The other officers all frowned. Baine shook her head, her brows dipped in question. "Final victory against whom?"

Another of the officers shook his head as well. "Never mind that, what are they sending us that they needed to build a whole fort to keep safe?"

Campbell looked into the eyes of each officer before giving words to the fear that had gripped him in the communications shack. "You don't just build vaults to keep things safe inside. You might also build a vault to keep things from escaping."

Dalton's eyes were fixed on his commander's. "He didn't tell you what to expect."

Campbell shook his head again and sat heavily in a camp chair near one of the drafting tables. "No, major, he did not."

"So it could well be weapons of some kind." An adjutant said.

"Or some other tech from the big brains at the Pipetown Works?" Another young man added.

Campbell shrugged. "Or anything else, really. Could be prisoners that need to be isolated. Could be essential personnel needed for the war effort. Damnation, could very well be gold, or jewels, or bank notes. Can't win a war without money, now, can you?"

"I think Baine's point is still a good one." Dalton's voice was low. "Who is this fortress emplaced to win final victory over? The Rebellion? Lee's a cowering dog afraid to come out of his hovel. We're too far away to have much impact on the Warrior Nation, and Carpathian and his creatures are clear across on the other side of the country." He looked back down at Campbell. "Could we really be here just to finish off the Confederates?"

Campbell eased back in the rickety chair and stared up at the fort taking form in the distance. He shook his head again. "Damned if I know, major. I don't have any more information than you have, and damned less insight, I'd have to say."

Campbell would never know if it was a shared sense of helplessness, or the dejected tone of his voice, or the oppressive weather. He felt a loosening of the tension in the officers around him and was only mildly surprised when Captain Baine produced a small silver flask. "Sir, I think you might feel better after taking a quick nip of this."

Everyone became still beneath the awning. Campbell had always avoided fraternizing with subordinates. Of course, fraternization had hardly been a danger in the small office beneath the Capitol Building where he had spent the majority of his career, designing fortifications, supply lines, and the like. He had been the only Army officer present, and the promotions had rolled in regularly as rewards for good designs and innovative thinking rather than stellar leadership or selfless bravery.

The colonel stared at the offered flask as it flashed in the watery sunlight, held stiffly in the hand of a fellow officer. He took the vessel before he could change his mind and dashed a swig down his throat, despite the early hour. The liquid burned as it hit, and he tried valiantly, to no avail, to stop the resultant hacking cough.

Campbell was suddenly aware of someone pounding on his back. His breath came in shallow gasps. His vision was blurred by tears streaming from his eyes. The heat rising from the back of his throat threatened to start him coughing all over again. When he regained sufficient command of his faculties, he gestured for everyone to move away, looking up at the young captain.

"Thanks, Baine." He was barely able to choke the words out, but he managed. The officers standing around him smiled. "That's good stuff. I hardly think it's regulation, though."

She blushed and shook her head. “No, sir. It’s shine one of the patrols in my sector took off some locals a couple nights ago.”

Campbell nodded at Blaine’s admission, and then grinned. “Well, it would be the height of hypocrisy for me to cite you for it now, wouldn’t it?”

The other officers laughed, the tension ratcheting down yet again, and the flask was passed around the circle. Their commander carefully pushed himself back to his feet and moved to the edge of the awning, looking out over his command. After decades in that small office, he still found it hard to believe that he was here, in full command of such a major operation.

Campbell shook his head as he followed the smooth movements of an enormous construction automaton trundling from the supply depot to the fort in the distance. The UR-10s were alien, their blank metal heads housing a single eye that flared redly with RJ energy. Their metal bodies with their dark, shadowed interiors and coils of hose and tubing, were only nominally humanoid, many replacing standard arms or legs with purpose-built elements designed to better perform their construction responsibilities. Most of those arms and legs were interchangeable. It was quite an advancement, and coming to grips with it was quite a struggle for a man who had spent so many years alone in a basement.

So much had changed over the last twenty years, and when he was brutally honest with himself, Colonel James Campbell knew that it was these changes, many of which had occurred seemingly overnight, that made it so hard for him to function out of his little office. Hell and damnation, when even the man who signed your orders was a creature of this new world, where was a man of yesteryear to turn?

Campbell was aware of General Grant’s troubles, of course. The tales were well known throughout the nation and beyond. The slaughter of his family by Confederate insurgents was a tale used to set the heart of every new recruit to burning. The injuries that the general himself had sustained in the attack were also legendary. Terrible, disfiguring burns condemned him to a grotesque iron mask that not only hid the nightmarish injuries, but also sustained his life. General Grant was a legend among the men he commanded.

Campbell sighed, knowing he would never be able to command the fear or respect men like Grant seemed to wield with such ease. His scowl deepened and he shook his head. No wonder he saw contempt in the eyes of so many of his men each day.

Another robot lurched past the command tent and the colonel watched as it carried tools toward the construction. This was a lighter model, almost a walking skeleton, and the sight of the machine brought his mind to the object of Grant’s personal hatred and quest for vengeance: Doctor Carpathian. Hidden away in the War Department’s basement, Campbell had never faced the resurrected constructs of the mad doctor, but he had heard stories and seen the evidence.

The colonel knew the basic theory behind RJ-1027 reanimation, and had even studied the invigorating properties of the substances for the Department. But he had yet to see the dead walk, rods of Crimson Gold jammed into their brains. Army scuttlebutt claimed that Carpathian was raising entire armies of the dead to enforce his will upon the Contested Territories. It was said they worked his factories and served his food, as well as bearing his banner into battle. The thought sent a shiver down Campbell’s spine. Of the many changes that had shaken the world since he had emerged from his little warren, the dead rising from their slumber was one of the most shocking.

Campbell grinned sourly as he caught his train of thought. He was watching animated metal men do the work of thousands, at the order of a maimed, masked, mad genius, while thinking about walking corpses. The world had become entirely unhinged, and he was trying to account for each change as if it even mattered. The savage tribes of the west had united under a council of chiefs and elders for the first time in living memory. By all reports, they wielded weapons that burst into actinic blue flame in battle, rode twisted and metamorphosed parodies of horses to war, and some even said they could twist their own flesh into abhorrent, horrific shapes to practice violence upon their enemies.

The world was nothing like it had been when he had first been assigned to the War Department's Office of Planning and Logistics. It was as if he had awakened from a safe, boring dream into a waking nightmare; and there was no escape.

"Doesn't look real, does it, sir." The deep voice was making a statement, not asking a question. Dalton was a good man, Campbell knew. When the colonel was able to control his raging jealousy, he knew his second in command was a very good man indeed. Apparently, given this last statement, he was a mind-reader as well.

Campbell nodded. "Just what I was thinking, major. We spent so many years fighting the damned Secesh dogs; a generation of blood and treasure spent in a few short years trying to keep the Republic together. And now . . ." He turned and gestured down the southern slope of the hill. "Not only are we still fighting the grey-backs, we've got the Warrior Nation, the lawless vermin of the Territories, and Carpathian's nightmare constructs fighting over the scraps."

After a few minutes had passed, the colonel shrugged. "Well, of all our problems, at least the Confederacy's all but dead. With Lee fighting yesterday's war, they're not much threat at all compared to everything else we're dealing with."

"True, sir." Dalton agreed. "This fort'll be the last nail in their coffin, and then we can focus out west where the true fighting's going to be."

They watched as men and robots continued to raise the walls of Fort Knox, each confident in the security of their new construction.

Chapter 6

The lilting, Ohioan accent was eerily familiar. Jesse James turned slowly around, brows furrowed and left hand drifting toward the butt of a pistol.

Behind Jesse was an older gentleman in the clothing of a man of business. The duds were fine if worn, much like the man himself. The hair was graying, the once-smooth face wrinkled in lines of pain and care, but the broad mustache was still in place, and a twinkle that declared, as hard as the intervening years had been, there was a spirit there that had not been beaten yet.

Jesse staggered back. His usual, sardonic grin gave way to a wide, honest smile that took years off his own face. "I'll be damned! Colonel Bill!"

William Quantrill smiled in return and reached out to shake hands. Jesse stopped cold and stared down at the offered appendage. It was a mechanical replacement, far more crude than the outlaw chief's own. The dull iron structures of the hand and forearm were joined to a rounded stump, shiny with scar tissue, about halfway to his elbow. Iron support rods, with connecting bolts sunk into his flesh, continued up his arm, jointed at the elbow, and formed a thick cuff around his shoulder.

Quantrill shook his head and reached out to grab Jesse's sleek metal hand in his own. "It's been too long to get squeamish now, James." The older man's grin was fierce, and after a moment, Jesse's face smoothed, the smile returned, and he pumped the hand vigorously.

"Sir, is it good to see you!" The smile faltered slightly. "What're you doin' way out here? Were you comin' north to meet us?"

The older man tilted his head at the words and then smiled wider. "Not sure what you mean, Jesse, but I do think maybe we should head in and have that drink you were talkin' about?" He nodded his head toward the locals. "I'm not sure, given the weight of recent events, that we want to spend any more time out here in the sunshine than necessary at the moment."

The men and women in the street stood dumbly, staring at them. Jesse saw that many could not take their eyes off his arms, and he held them up again so everyone could get a good look. "Alrighty, then!" Jesse stepped back toward the door. "We'll see ya'll on our way back outta town!"

The Fords and Cunningham were waiting by the door when Jesse turned, and the four outlaws pushed their way past the louvered wood and into the darkness of the saloon, Colonel Quantrill preceding them at a measured gait. The outlaw chief saw that his old commander walked stiffly, an elegant cane grasped in his natural hand. The cane was of intricately-worked metal, with pipes and wires woven through its center. A red telltale pulsed slowly, deep in the thing's core, as if measuring out the beats of a heart.

Inside The Pavilion, small groups of men stood at the windows or sat at their tables; glasses, cards, and dice lay forgotten behind them. Jesse gave everyone a wide smile and fished out a single gold coin with nimble metal fingers. "I'd like to buy everyone a glass, if you don't mind."

Most folks loosened up a bit at the sight of the gold and the mention of a drink. Some stayed near the windows, more than a few staring at the head and torso of the man who had shattered the glass with his fatal entrance. Almost everyone was quick to take the glasses the bartender and his serving girls began to distribute, though. Soon enough, Jesse and the others were sitting at a corner table, sipping on half-decent whiskey.

Jesse poured Quantrill a generous drop, off-hand resting on the smooth wood of the table top. "Did Henderson get word to you? Are you here to meet us?"

Quantrill tossed the whiskey back with a single powerful motion of his metal hand and then looked across the table. "Who, now? No, I din't have any idea you were hereabouts. I'm heading back west after. . ." He gestured vaguely with the claw-like hand. "Headin' back west to recuperate."

Jesse shook his head, a glass forgotten in his hand. "Henderson din't get word to you?"

The older man leaned back in his chair and quirked an eyebrow at the outlaw. "Son, I don't know who you're talkin' about. Only Henderson I can recall was old Allen Henderson, but he got put down years and years ago, before the war even ended. Can't recall any other Henderson. Certainly there ain't no one I'm in constant communication with, by any name. Now, why don't you slow down and let's chat?" He smiled again. "I can't help but notice you got a sleeker set o' replacements than mine, eh?"

Jesse looked at the dark iron hand again, then down at his own shiny metallic limbs, and shrugged with a smile. "Well, they may be purty, but they seem to have a mind of their own at times, colonel. Seems, though, might be they're comin' around. But I got some good news for you, sir. Henderson ain't dead! He's with me! Well, out on the plains aways, with my folks."

A darkness crept into Quantrill's eyes, and he leaned over the table. "Son, I assure you, Allen Henderson's dead. He died in my arms over twenty years gone. Yer startin' to undo all the good yer kind offer o' whiskey had started inroads on."

Jesse shook his head again. "I'm sorry, colonel. But that can't be. I've been ridin' with Henderson for months now!"

"Jesse," Quantrill leaned into the words. "Allen Henderson died, cut down by blue-bellies out Virginia-way. I din't know you were anywhere around here, an' I don't know what the Sam Hill yer talkin' 'bout. That just about settle things on that score?"

The outlaw chief leaned back in his chair, his eyes dark. He could only shake his head.

Robert Ford leaned over his steepled fingers. "It don't fer me, Jesse. If Henderson's been callin' shots, playin' of this swell's name, but the real Henderson's been worm food since the war . . . what in the name of Hell does that mean?"

A dark suspicion kindled in the back of Jesse's mind as he recalled words Carpathian had spoken during their last encounter. "Our red-eyed friends . . ."

Jesse shook himself and forced a smile through the doubt and suspicion. There would be plenty of time to deal with Henderson, whoever he was, when they got back to camp. "Never you mind, Robert. We'll sort that out later. Boys, let me introduce you to a good friend from back in the war, Colonel William Quantrill."

Quantrill nodded to the men, his eyes settling for a moment longer on Marcus than on the others, before he looked back at Jesse with a sly grin of his own.

"You made quite an entrance into town just now, Jesse." He gestured with his empty glass at Marcus. "Folks here abouts'll be thinkin' twice afore they front yer buck, here. Least, 'till yer gone."

Marcus bridled at the term, and Jesse stiffened a bit as well. "Sir, I wasn't tryin' to make a mash. I meant ever' word I said—"

Quantrill laughed and eased back into his chair. "Son, don't try to teach your ole' grandma how to suck eggs, now, you hear?" He pointed with one iron finger back at the younger man. "Who was it, you reckon, first taught you how to lay a legend down? Couldn't o' been ole' Billy Quantrill, now, could it?"

Jesse started to respond, but was silenced by that wagging metal digit. "Now, son, don't try to bilk an ole' huckster, alright? I recognize speechifying when I hears it, and that was some fine talkin' you were doin' out on the porch."

Jesse opened his mouth again, but the older man rode over him. "Jesse, I'm not questionin' the strength of yer convictions. I don't doubt you an' this big man here is friends of the first water. But I remember a young little coot followed his big brother into my outfit when he was too young to piss straight, an' that young'un din't cotton too much to . . . dark complexions, if I remember well enough?"

"Folks change, colonel, an' that was a long time ago—" Jesse's face was clouded again as he leaned forward on crossed iron forearms.

"No doubt, son. I'm just sayin', time was, you woulda reacted the same way as ole Herschel Brown there, that you left bleedin' out of his neck hole on the porch." Quantrill shook his head slightly as if disappointed. "An' you din't give much thought to the local law, either, did you?"

Jesse sat up straighter at that, an annoyed look on his face. Before he could speak, Quantrill raised his metal hand in a reassuring gesture. "Don't worry, none. Moberly ain't got no law to speak of as yet. Folks here mostly take care o' their own troubles. 'Course, that din't help Herschel none, now did it . . ."

Jesse did not relax. "I ain't much afraid of some Podunk border law, neither way, colonel." But he forced himself back into his chair, sharing a sidelong glance with his men.

Quantrill continued, making a quick, calming gesture with his natural hand. "Way I reckon it, most folks here abouts have you pegged now, James. They're gonna know you're the celebrated outlaw with the famous arms and the imposing body count, and that'll give us a little time afore anyone decides to act on the umbrage they all must be feelin' right about now." He picked up his cane with his flesh-and-blood hand and tapped it absentmindedly against the rim of the table. "Now, where were you boys headin' next, after your fine display of street theatre?"

Jesse's men shared another guarded look and then watched their leader to see where he went with the question. The outlaw boss watched his old commander for a moment before speaking in a lower voice. "Well, funny you should ask that, sir, as we're currently at odds as to our exact next step."

Quantrill made a rolling gesture with his metal hand, indicating that the younger man should continue.

"Well, we're of a few minds, currently." Jesse looked at his men, then shrugged and continued. "Allen Henderson has been urging me to burn out all the border towns to send a message to the Union and the Rebellion alike."

The old colonel stared at Jesse in silence. When he spoke, his voice was dripping with contempt. "Burn out the border towns? You eager to kill everyone in the Contested Territories? And yourself crushed in the middle?"

The tone brought Jesse back more than twenty years and he sat up straighter in his chair. "No, sir. I was doubtful—"

"Doubtful that anyone suggesting such a strategy had half the brain God gave 'em?" Quantrill leaned forward, all tension and disbelief. "Leave off how this yahoo convinced you he was Allen Henderson, didn't that entire plan strike you as hare-brained? Attack in all directions, leave yourself no path of retreat or sanctuary?" He shook his head. "I thought I'd taught you better, James. What happened to Frank? Is he dead? He'd never let you keep something this ignorant in your head long enough to leave an impression!"

Jesse nodded, shook his head, and then nodded again so quickly it looked as if he had suffered some sort of apoplexy. "No, sir. I mean, yes sir. Frank's still alive. He was against that plan."

Quantrill nodded and leaned back a little. "Good. Then you're not completely lost yet. You said you were torn between courses. I hope the next isn't nearly as empty-headed?"

Jesse leaned back, his eyes drifting away and refusing to meet Quantrill's steady gaze. "I got a bunch of men with me, sir. We busted 'em out of Camp Lincoln a month or so back, and I was thinkin' I might head out west, past Carpathian, and the Nation, and all them, and maybe set up on our own. Someplace we can call our own, an' where folks can just leave us be."

Quantrill's brows came down slightly, and his eyes drifted to the table where he gingerly interlaced fleshly fingers with black iron. "You were goin' to found your own town."

Jesse forced his eyes up into his old mentor's, and sat up straighter. "Yessir."

The old man's eyes flattened. "And how were you goin' to live?"

The outlaw's face lost its proud strength as he cocked his head slightly to the side. "Sir?"

Quantrill shook his head, bowing down over his entangled fingers. "God bless you, Jesse. You got such a benighted mix of brains and confusion in that head of yours." He looked up again. "Were you gonna mine? Get your hands all dirty? Were you gonna farm? Herd cattle? Any of these old war hounds you got waitin' on you any good at blacksmithing? Carpentry? Any of the other hundred things you're gonna need, if you're gonna build your own town up from the dust?"

Jesse's eyes flared defensively. "No, but I figured—"

"And who's gonna lead this grand scheme, Jesse? You?" Quantrill leaned in toward the outlaw chief. "You gonna hang up your blasters, there? You gonna spend all day decidin' who owns what square foot o' dirt? Who which cow belongs to?"

Jesse sat back, eyes losing focus as all of his fears and insecurities came crashing in upon him.

"That ain't you, kid. Leastways, it weren't you twenty years ago." Quantrill nodded toward the broken window and the leaking corpse, the crowd still watching him from the corner of their fear-tinged eyes. "And your friend over there in the window, and his friend on the porch, would seem to agree with me."

Jesse stared at the body in the window frame. He could still remember the burning rush of his blood as the locals had sealed their fates with their own mouths. The outlaw chief's head shook slightly back and forth.

"No, that ain't you, Jesse. And I know, somewhere in that head of yours, you knew all along that weren't you." Quantrill tapped briskly on the table, setting all four of the other men jumping, and he smiled. "Now, knowin' you, you got another plan, and I'm willin' to bet it's the Jim Dandy of the lot."

"Yessir." A new, bright smile just touched Jesse's face. "At least, I think so." Jesse swallowed before continuing. "I were thinkin' of maybe headin' down toward the gulf." He sat up straighter, the conviction of this new course lending him strength before his old mentor's contempt. "The Union's goin' to crush the Rebellion as soon as it gets its house in order out west. There's nothin' the southern states can do to stop it, the way they're goin' now. Lee's fightin' a war that ended twenty years ago, and don't even realize that Grant and the rest changed the rules on him. He's goin' to lead the southern states to a defeat they won't ever come back from."

Quantrill settled back into his seat and nodded. "Can't argue with you there, son. Lee ain't the man we all thought he would be. That last runnin' defeat beat the sand out of him, an' he's been runnin' in his head ever since."

Jesse sat forward, fire igniting in his eyes. "Exactly! If we keep fightin' the old war, we're gonna keep losin'! But we don't have to! We got a huge advantage, if only we can take ahold of it while we can!"

Quantrill nodded again, then his eyes slowly shifted to Marcus' still face, and then back to Jesse. "I'll be damned. You're talkin' about black folks."

Jesse nodded. "Honest folks know all that hogwash 'bout black folks bein' less'n white folks is nothin' but tripe. Honest folks who know black folks, anyway. Folks is folks, with some of 'em dumb as a stump, an' others smart as cats. And there's thousands an' thousands of black folks down south, as eager to defend their homes as any white man."

Quantrill put up his metal hand again to stall Jesse's excited speech. "Son, you know, ain't many white men in the south'd be eager to hand a black man a gun, now, don't you?"

Jesse nodded, but the fire was still there. "There ain't, I know. But they gotta wake up. The Union don't care what color a man is if he's in their way. An' anyone who's faced 'em, black or white or brown or yella, knows it. We gotta convince the rest, before we're all crushed beneath Grant's boot."

Quantrill sat back again and stared at Jesse with calculating eyes. The Fords and Marcus stared back at the old commander while Jesse, having wound down, watched for any reaction at all.

The moment stretched on, and Jesse's men shot him glances to see if he was going to speak. But before he could continue, Quantrill cleared his throat, smiled a small, secret smile, and nodded.

"Jesse, you ever been to New Orleans?"

The question caught the outlaw chief by surprise, and he shook his head.

Quantrill's smile widened a little. "Well, I'm just comin' from down that way." He waved the metal hand. "Where I was bein' seen to by a most strange lady of a particularly . . . dusky visage. I think you would be very surprised to experience the difference in opinion most white folks down there have compared to many of the folks you're used to."

Jesse nodded slowly, but his face was a mask of confusion. "Okay . . . ?"

Quantrill settled back. "You see, New Orleans is at least as much a European city as it ever was American, and they've always had . . . a more lenient way with the black folks livin' there. Since the war ended, it's been a free city, not declarin' allegiance to either the north or the south. At the very edge of the Contested Territory, it was quite a bustlin' neutral port for years. Most folks there have been judgin' other folks on their actions an' their history more'n the color of their skin fer a long time, now." He pointed at Jesse with two joined iron fingers. "You gonna find anyone willin' to listen to your line of argument, you're gonna find 'em in New Orleans."

Jesse nodded. "That makes sense, I guess."

Quantrill tapped his cane against the table again. "While I was down there, I made some friends, Jesse. Friends that I think might be very interested to hear your ideas themselves. In fact, I might just turn around myself and head back down there with ya'll, if yer of a mind to go."

Jesse looked down at the dark iron hand and tapped the table with his own metal fingers. "You said they did . . . that . . . down there? Who was it? Last I heard, there's only one man can do that sort of work . . ." His eyes darkened slightly with memory, and he shook his head. "Well, two, I guess, if you're counting that butcher back in Camp Lincoln.

But ain't neither of 'em in New Orleans that I heard."

Quantrill looked down at his own crude hand, flexing the thick fingers. "Well, remember, New Orleans ain't beholden to any of the folks been tearin' the country apart, but they all got people down there one way or 'nother. The Union Army's actually been swarmin' down there, fortifyin' the waterfront an' the harbor for months now, but they don't bother much with the rest of the city. An' there's one lovely lady, a special friend of YOUR friend the good doctor, I believe," he reached across and tapped his iron finger against Jesse's metal forearm. "An' that lady is the one who . . . healed me, so to speak." Again he looked down at the roughly formed hand.

"A lady done that to you?" Jesse's voice was low.

"Well, lady, now, that's a sort of fluid term, is what I learned." Quantrill looked down, the portrait of an embarrassed southern gentleman. "I got caught just outside of Louisville, an' one o' those damned blue-bellies winged me as I rode out. All but tore my fool hand clean off. I was dyin', James. I was bleedin' out an' nothin' the boys I had with me did was doin' any good. So, one of 'em, he'd heard about a black woman livin' in the swamps around New Orleans, could work miracles on folks were injured on farms and in factories and whatnot. Me, I was all but unconscious, so didn't have much say in the matter. The boys dragged me across the country down to New Orleans, and brought me to this medicine woman.

"Her name is Marie Laveau. An . . . older . . . lady." He shot a look at Marcus before continuing. "Dark of skin, with wild hair and burning dark eyes. The black folks of the bayou surrounding the city call her the Voodoo Queen, and say she is attended by a court of the dead. I never did see them, but I don't doubt, having spent so much time around her old mansion while she did this to me," he waved the metal hand listlessly in the air. "I don't doubt it could be true."

Robert Ford scoffed and kicked back in his chair, but Jesse held up one metal hand. "Now, hold on there, Robert. Ain't much to separate those old Voodoo zombie stories from Carpathian's creatures, now, is there? And the colonel did mention as they might be affiliated somehow . . . ?"

Quantrill nodded, looking up at Jesse again. "She's some sort o' ally, or apprentice, is what I come to understand. Their dead, in New Orleans, they hold a lot of sway over the livin'. An' from what I heard, that sort o' thing is just what might draw Carpathian's attention."

Jesse held his eyes for a moment and then gave a shallow nod of agreement. "It might, at that. Truth to tell, though, colonel, I ain't on great terms with Carpathian. Might be this Queen o' yers, she might not take a likin' to me."

Quantrill shook his head. "No, she ain't his creature. She's her own person, fer sure. But might be, she could help us. Also, she's the one we'd have to go through to get to the man I think you need to see."

Jesse's eyes sharpened a bit. "The man I need to see?"

Quantrill jerked his head sharply. "Colonel Warley; Alexander to his friends. Led a platoon of engineers from Louisiana during the war, and as things began to wind down, he returned home. Grew up on a big plantation right up against the bayou. A lot of his boys stayed with him after the war, working his land, his ships, and whatnot." A small smile crept back onto the old commander's face. "And I happen to know he shares your . . . soft spot for . . . well, let's say former slaves and leave it at that?"

Jesse sat back. "A commander from the war?"

"Yeah. And he's still got a lot of his boys with him, an' their families. Fiercely loyal. Had a lot to do with seein' the carpetbaggers off around thereabouts after the war. He's also got connections with the rebel bands still in the swamps and coastal regions that haven't taken to Lee's tender ministrations. If there's anyone can set you up with what you're lookin' fer, it's Colonel Warley."

Jesse stared down at his hands. Another Carpathian . . . ? Or, rather, someone who could do similar work, but was not entirely attached to the madman? That might be someone he needed to meet. This Warley, as well, struck him as a potentially useful person.

All thoughts of destroying Moberly were gone; all designs against the border towns forgotten. The last tattered shreds of an imaginary new town floated away on the rising tide of his chosen profession: violence. There would not be a better chance at raising the south effectively than an ally such as Quantrill described. And it sounded like there would never be a better place to begin than in the free port of New Orleans. It all gave solid form to the fantasies that had plagued his dreams since Billy the Kid had sat down at his table in Kansas City what seemed like a lifetime ago.

"Now, since your original plan was to destroy the entire border region . . ." Quantrill tilted his head toward Jesse's hands. "How big is this little band of yours, out on the plains?"

The responding shrug was eloquent. "A few hundred. And some Union armored vehicles, and the like."

For the first time since he had appeared behind Jesse, Quantrill seemed impressed. "Really? A small army already, and with the armor to support it? I imagine there's a tale worth the tellin' behind that brief comment?"

"Not one I'd care to tell at the moment, sir, no." Jesse was still haunted by the stink of bodies left behind in the rolling northern hills. A few hundred might impress his old commander, but it was a sad number when expressed as the remainder of the thousands who had followed him out of Camp Lincoln.

"No, well, I'm sure we both have our shadowed vales, Jesse." Quantrill lapsed into thought for a moment and then looked up again. "Well, I was going to suggest we head east and pick up a riverboat down to New Orleans, but I'm not sure we could sneak a few of those Rolling Thunders aboard even the biggest."

"Well, sir, the pace of the column I've got now, we won't see the coast for more'n a week. I have folks I can leave in charge of the rest, and we can head down by river with a few chosen hands. I've also got some folks with me, might be able to rustle up some more strength, out back west, in Robbers Roost, Diablo Canyon, an' like that."

Quantrill nodded with a smile. "That sounds fine, Jesse. Mighty fine." He stood up stiffly, bringing the cane back underneath him, and looked down at the younger man. "I would suggest, however, that we take to the trail soon, before someone in town decides to face the infamous Jesse James on behalf of the late, currently unlamented, Herschel Brown?"

Jesse stood up as well, followed by the Fords and Marcus. "Yeah. I do want to head back, and we'd love to have you, too, colonel. We'll just have to borrow that wagon outside, maybe. I can't wait to introduce you to Allen Henderson an' maybe have a little talk 'bout some things."

Jesse was not very surprised when, as they pulled up to the camp a couple hours later, Frank stumped out to tell him that Henderson was gone.

Chapter 7

The low growl of the Interceptor echoed from the surrounding pines, the long, sleek vehicle crawling over the packed dirt of the trail. The rider crouched low over the control bars, his duster fluttering out behind him, blending with the cloud of trail dirt stirred up by his passage. He had been alone on the trail for days, with no sign of other travelers ahead or behind. Well, save for a strange, freakishly tall man, half-glimpsed in the shadows of the pine forest, who had looked out at him from beneath a strange, tall hat. He had left the man behind over a day ago, and seen no one since. The rider still cast nervous glances to either side as he eased his machine along, however. The occasional furtive look cast over his shoulder revealed his fear of pursuit. Such emotion did not sit well with the rider.

Virgil Earp, brother of Over-marshal Wyatt Earp and renowned lawman in his own right, was not used to skulking through his business. Resentment burned behind his eyes, and he was not used to that either. The Interceptor swerved drunkenly, Virgil's control hampered by his injuries. His useless arm was secured tightly to his body with worn leather straps.

Through thick amber goggles, the old law dog could just make out a decrepit sign looming out of the shadows ahead, hanging askew on a dried old signpost.

Green Valley: Five Miles.

Virgil shook his head. He could not believe he was on this road again. This time, though, he was alone. No dying brother to spur him onward, obscuring doubts and fears in the focused light of immediate need. It seemed like forever since those thrice-damned Clantons had shattered his arm, leaving him worse than a hopeless cripple. The injury had not only robbed him of his confidence and his humor: it had taken away his sense of self.

He had been fighting ever since; fighting the Feds for medical help, fighting Wyatt when it became clear that the chiseling government was going to deny their responsibility. Virgil knew that Carpathian was the only hope he had of regaining the use of his arm, but his brother refused to see the truth. And Wyatt had refused, over and over, to let him ride out after the doctor.

And then Wyatt had forged his unlikely alliance with that soaplock, Jesse James, to burn down the Clantons. It has all been to avenge Virgil, but he had been less than useless. It was that day that he had decided: Wyatt had no right to keep him from the help he needed. It was becoming more and more clear, even to the slowest deputy, that anyone working with the Crimson Gold was going to live a long, long time unless he got shot down. Virgil had no intention of living out such a span without the full use of both his arms.

Carpathian was Public Enemy Number One to any and all Federal Lawmen. It would be a dark day if anyone ever found Wyatt Earp's own brother dealing with the madman. Things were deteriorating quickly in the territories. In fact, even in official dispatches they were referring to the entire region west of Kansas City as the Contested Territories now. Although the Warrior Nation savages sweeping down off the plains had a lot to do with that, Carpathian was the man pushing most of the violence in the Union's direction. Very little occurred anywhere within the scorched deserts, rolling, rocky hills, or deep pine forests that did not have Carpathian's fingerprints all over it.

Virgil wobbled his Interceptor to a halt beside the battered sign. The wheels came to a crunching stop and the lawman dropped his feet into the dirt. He would not know when he passed the point of no return. Once Carpathian's guardians noticed him, they would never let him turn around. They would be somewhere nearby, and he knew that once he crossed that profound, invisible line, his life would never be the same. He would be a fugitive, even if only in his own heart.

The old lawman looked down at the twisted claw of his useless hand. The blast had charred flesh and shattered bones. One of the local sawbones had even spoken of amputation for fear of infection. Wyatt had backed his play on that, at least, and they had told the old butcher to walk away before Virgil decided to take HIS arm in trade. So the limb lay still, throbbing with dull pain, but otherwise dead meat hanging in a sling.

Virgil's eyes hardened behind the goggles. He would be damned before he would spend an hour more than necessary as a cripple, dependent upon the charity and assistance of others. He spit into the dust beside his machine and grasped the throttle tightly in his one good hand. There would be no more delays. He was going to do this thing. Further hesitation would not help anyone.

The Interceptor began to roll forward, he brought his boots up onto the footrests, and was about to flood the engine with power when a high-pitched voice snapped out of the silence behind him.

"Why don't you just stay right there, Virgil Earp, or I might satisfy myself with bringin' just yer head back for the law." A short, squat man moved out of the shadows of the forest in front of Virgil. An oversized blaster was clenched in both hands, the muzzle locked on Virgil's forehead. The old lawman let his vehicle's engine idle down to a quite gurgle, and then killed it completely. His eyes did not waver from the slick-haired youngster with the gun as he kicked the support prop down into the dirt, swinging his leg up and over the saddle.

"Provencher." Virgil nodded minutely, his face blank. Before the smaller deputy could reply, however, he continued. "You little pin prick."

The olive-skinned Provencher grunted a quick laugh and then shook the big pistol at Virgil. "Pin prick, is it, VIRG?" The older man's eyes tightened at the familiar nickname. "I'd rather be a pin prick than a dirty rotten traitor. Or a common criminal."

Virgil reached up to pull his goggles down off his face with slow movements. His expression was impassive as he stared at the kid with the gun. "Hmmm," he muttered. "Traitors and criminals, is it, now, son? How you figure?"

Provencher grunted. "Don't think I don't know where you're goin', Virgil. Ain't no one left in Tombstone don't know where you're goin, if they had the sand to stop you!" He gestured with the pistol again, back down the road the way Virgil had come. "Now, I got me a little wagon back yonder, an' yer gonna get in it without kickin' up a fuss, an' yer gonna go with me back to Tombstone, an' yer gonna tell yer brother just what it is you were fixin' to do."

Virgil raised his good hand up to head height. "Well, kid, I'm not sure exactly what yer talkin' about. What is it you think I'm doin' up here?"

"You don't think I know where we are, old man?" The smirk gave way to a dark scowl as the bitter anger surged to the surface. "I've known where you had to be goin' fer days now! Last night, whiles you was sleepin', I left the wagon behind and crossed wide around to lay in wait ahead of you. You ain't nearly so clever as you think you are, Virgil Earp. You ain't so clever by half!"

Virgil nodded. "I was wonderin' how you'd a gotten in front of me." He smiled. "You know, just the information you got would be enough for quite a nice shiny medal from Washington if you left right now."

Provencher laughed again. "Yeah? An' just think how shiny the medal'll be when I bring you in, prove what a bunch o' lowlife four-flushers you an' yer whole family are, AND lead Grant right to Carpathian!"

Virgil's face lost all expression, his eyes flat and dark. "My family don't have nothin' to do with this."

The younger man barked again. "Oh, please! You take me fer a pale fish, Virg? With that metal nightmare of a brother, an' Wyatt supposedly watchin' over all the territories, you think they're gonna believe he had nuthin' to do with you showin' up sportin' a metal arm as well? When the whole Union's lookin' fer Carpathian's hideout?" He shook his head with fevered energy, a cruel grin spreading over his face. "No, this is gonna bring yer whole family down, Virgil. We'll see who's been wearin' a hat too big fer his head when they slip yers through a noose!"

Virgil stood still for a moment and then asked. "My hat?"

That brought Provencher up short. "What?"

"They gonna slip my hat through a noose?" The older man's face was as still as stone.

Provencher looked confused for a moment and then the anger boiled up again. "No, not yer hat, you daft cripple! Yer head!"

Virgil nodded, his good hand resting on his gun belt, just behind the pistol grip. "Din't think it made too much sense, but you did say we'd see who's hat was too big when they slip it through a noose . . . I guess I was just confused, is all."

Provencher stared at Virgil in disbelief. He shook his head, his voice low and menacing. "I got you dead to rights, Virgil Earp." He shook the heavy pistol. "I got you on point, an' yer still shovin' dust my way?"

Virgil shrugged. "It's always been a weakness o' mine. I see a little pisspot, I gotta piss."

The younger man's eyes went wide and round, all color draining from his face, and the massive blaster came back up, every muscle rigid with lethal intent.

The sharp detonation of a blaster shot echoed off the trees. Provencher's weapon lowered with a jerk, his mouth round in a startled 'O' of pain and confusion. He staggered back and looked down to see a dark stain spreading out from his side. The fabric of his shirt was smoldering, tendrils of smoke snaking up into his face. Before he could make any kind of response through the shock and pain, Virgil stepped forward and brought the butt of his own pistol down on the boy's forearms. The deputy made a harsh, clicking noise in the back of his throat as his heavy pistol fell into the dust.

"You think I ever needed both hands to deal with a shavetail Jonah like you?" Virgil gave a gentle push against the boy's chest and he fell over into the dirt of the trail. "Kid, you musta been born under one hell of an unlucky star to have run into me so early in life."

Virgil watched the reactions play out on the deputy's pale face. Pain and confusion were swiftly giving way to anger and frustration with a healthy leavening of fear. "You ain't no man o' the law, Virgil." He snarled from the dirt. "You ain't no good man, an' neither are your brothers. You're all goin' to burn before this is done!"

Virgil shrugged, a thoughtful expression settling over his face. "Well, I ain't sure you're wrong, kid. And that ain't no good thing, given that we're as good as the folks in the territories got. An' you may even be right 'bout us burnin'. Plenty o' folks will, afore this is over. But I don't think that's anythin' you gotta worry yerself about now."

Provencher grunted, one hand clasped to his bleeding side. "I'm gonna see you all burn, you rat bastard! And that monster doctor as well!"

Virgil crouched down close to the deputy's sweating face. "Kid, I promise you, that doctor is gonna burn. But he ain't gonna burn afore I get what I need, an' you ain't gonna be there to see it."

Virgil pushed himself back up to his feet. "Now, I'm gonna continue on my way, son. I'm goin' to finish my business here, an' I'll be comin' back this way sometime soon. If you're here, I'll shoot you, an' this time I won't be aimin' to miss. If I find you back in Tombstone, I'll shoot you. If I ever run into you again, no matter where or when, I'll shoot you." He worked some of the dust in his mouth and then spat off to the side. "That clear enough for ya, big fella?"

Provencher stared up in disbelief, and then found his courage again, spitting weakly back at the tall lawman. "You don't scare me, old man! You an' me, we got a meetin' set, an' we're gonna have it afore too long!"

Virgil nodded as he turned to stride back to his Interceptor. "Whatever it takes to let you sleep at night, you little kit weasel."

In the dust of the trail, Provencher reached down with a blood-slick hand and drew a small hold-out pistol glowing with dull red energy. The gun snapped off two quick bursts of crimson fire, both passing directly through the space Virgil had occupied a moment before. The old lawman had spun to the side, his good hand coming up, and his pistol barked again, slapping several shots into the deputy's chest, sending fans of charred flesh flying into the surrounding forest. The body jerked a couple times before settling into a final stillness.

"Forgot to mention," Virgil holstered his weapon and swung awkwardly back into the saddle. "You draw on me, an' I'll shoot you."

The Interceptor roared back into life, swung wide around the smoking body, and headed off deeper into the trees.

*****

Virgil's mind was clouded as he emerged from the forest into the outskirts of Payson. He had never liked that kid, and he had never thought much of him . . . but he had never wanted to kill him. When Provencher had drawn the hold-out, something had snapped in the old lawman's mind, and that had been the end of the deputy. A quiet voice insisted that Virgil had not had a choice when that second weapon began to fire. But another, darker voice whispered that he had had a choice, and he had made it.

The dirt trail gave way to cobblestones at the edge of Payson, brick buildings rising up before him. Entering the quiet town presented him with more than enough to keep his mind off the dead boy miles behind. The last time he had visited this strange town, the streets had been empty, as if the people had been warned away. Once again, he was presented with an unnatural quiet. A familiar, sweet stink permeated the region, and had been causing his lip to curl in disgust long before he came out of the woods.

Virgil sent the Interceptor growling slowly forward in its uneven path, heading down toward the cliff- edge palace that was Carpathian's seat of power. The smell seemed to be getting stronger, the oppressive air pushing in around him. He slowed down and reached back to loosen his new blunderbuss, Justice, in its boot. The weapon had been a gift from his brothers after the bank heist that had seen him maimed. It was Wyatt who had named the gun. It could sweep a street clean with a single shot, and when it came time to pull the trigger, it was as blind, regarding friend and foe, as the old goddess Justice was said to have been.

Justice was still in the boot when some sense warned him of danger. Whether it was the smell, or a sound only partially heard, or something else entirely, he could not have said. Virgil sat up straight, whipping his head around, and was just in time to dodge aside as a rusty scythe blade swept at him from his left. Virgil felt a moment of startled fear before a lifetime's instincts took over. The thing that had stumbled out of an alleyway to attack him had been a man, once. It was a dried-out old corpse now, tattered rags hanging off in strips while a dirt-encrusted metal frame seemed to be all that held the rotten flesh upright.

Virgil slid off the back of his saddle and drew his pistol. As he lined the aiming blade up with the shambling corpse's forehead, he noticed several others coming up behind it. Their hands had all been replaced with vicious-looking, bladed weapons. Raw scars marked the point where metal and wood had been joined with the meat.

"Doctor, I'm here to trade!" The old marshal waited a moment, and then fired off three quick bursts. The three approaching animations each halted in their tracks, their heads disappearing in ghastly clouds of pink, red, and green. Each one staggered a step or two forward and then collapsed sideways onto the cobbles. Two more were behind them, and as Virgil raised his pistol again he noticed more coming in from the side. "I'd rather we negotiate over a whiskey or a bourbon, to be honest!"

He took several firm steps, punctuating each with a burst of crimson force that blew a body down the street. When he was back beside the Interceptor, he holstered the pistol and drew Justice from the boot. With a practiced, forceful spin, Virgil ratcheted an RJ cylinder into the firing chamber one-handed and turned to his left. A small mob of animations shuffled toward him, their rusty weapons raised listlessly over swaying heads.

Virgil braced his good arm, holding Justice out straight, and steadied his legs against what he knew was coming. With gritted teeth, he pulled the trigger. Justice gave a kick like a frightened mule and roared like an enraged dragon. An enormous cloud of crimson-tinted smoke bellowed out to engulf the unsteady mob. As the old lawman straightened up, he watched through the swirling smoke as shattered bodies collapsed onto the street. Some of them were scrambling limply with ragged stumps, trying to stand or reach out to him with their mangled weapons. Most, however, had suffered damage severe enough to put them down for good.

"Doctor Carpathian," Virgil cast a look around to assess his position. "This don't make much sense—"

Virgil turned Justice on the mob approaching from his right. Again he twirled the gun around his good hand, the mechanisms cracking a new cartridge into place.

"Hope you boys miss hell," Virgil brought Justice back up again, leveling the snout down the street. "Cuz you're headin' back."

Again, the bone-shaking detonation of the massive cannon echoed back off the surrounding buildings, and an entire street of animations was reduced to harmless scrap and putrefied meat.

Virgil impassively watched the feeble, aimless movements of the few corpses left capable of motion. The rest were pressing in, and he knew he would run out of ammo before long. He saw a raised brick landing in front of a building off to the left. He skipped and sidestepped through the shredded remnants of the first group and leapt up onto the platform. He nearly lost his balance as he landed, hindered by his useless arm. He felt himself going over, saw the street rushing up to meet him, and dropped Justice onto the bricks. He made a desperate grasp for the edge of the landing and just stopped himself from falling. Justice struck the street below and he cursed. Over his shoulder, he saw the animations, now joined into a single pressing crowd, moving toward him.

Virgil stood up, brushed off his knees, and drew his pistol. He checked the charge, dropped the current cartridge with a single flip of his thumb and then reloaded a fresh one with a grim glance at the oncoming horde. A fresh cartridge might be worth 30 or 40 shots, but never enough to stop the endless tide of lumbering corpses moving his way.

"Okay, doctor, I'll be here as long as I can!" Virgil pitched his voice as loudly as he could. "The next move's yours!"

Virgil snapped shot after shot down into the swarming mob. He lost count of the animations he had put down. His arm was aching and his body was growing stiff. His grin had slipped a while ago, his face a blank mask of concentration. He would last as long as he could.

The pistol barked in a slow, steady pace. The corpses were close enough, now, that he could see the rubbery texture of their skin and the clouded orbs of their eyes.

Virgil punched the blaster at a large animation staggering up the stairs. He pulled the trigger and the weapon coughed out a weak bolt of crimson that merely slapped the creature back. The thing lost its balance but was pushed back up by the animations pressing in behind it. It shook its head and then fixed its sightless gaze upon him, moving back up the stairs.

"Damnation . . ." He backed up, pressing against the locked door at the top of the landing and brandishing the pistol like a club. "If this is how you want it, doctor!" he shouted. He was startled to realize that his throat was dry, his voice hoarse. "I guess the consideration of the Federal Bureau of Marshals ain't worth what it once was!"

The corpses continued to lurch toward him, their blades glinting dully. The marshal's eyes tightened as he thought about the choices that had led him to that moment, when a shouted order brought the animations to a swaying halt.

"Back avay!" The voice was low and grumbling, but carried more than enough authority to force the nightmare constructs back down the stairs. There was no hostility or frustration on their slack faces, their eyes as wide and dead as ever. For some reason, this gave Virgil more of a pause than anything that he had seen since entering the little town.

"You are Virgil Earp, Marshal of zee United States?" The voice asked. Virgil could see the bodies in the back of the crowd being shoved out of the way as a large man wearing an archaic suit of heavy armor pushed his way through the putrescent crowd.

"You know I am, Ursul." The lawman moved to the edge of the landing and tried to stand easy.

The dark man stopped at the foot of the stairs. Peering from beneath bushy black eyebrows, Vladimir Ursul, majordomo of Doctor Burson Carpathian, regarded Virgil with a slight smile. "You made quite a showing of yourself, Marshal Earp. Vee ver most impressed."

Virgil spat into the crowd. "Hope you were." He gestured at the pile of stilled animations. "You're gonna need some more bodies."

Ursul laughed. "Zese? Zay are but verker drones, my friend. Tools near zee end of zere usefulness, sent here to test your mettle."

The lawman shrugged. "How'd I do?" He sauntered down the steps and retrieved Justice from the pile of dead.

It was Ursul's turn to lift his shoulders phlegmatically. "Vell enough. Come." He turned and started to walk away through the eerily-still crowd. "Zee Doctor eez vaiting."

Virgil watched Ursul push his way through the swaying corpses and then moved to catch up.

"I see you have injured yourself." The hairy man muttered through his tangle of beard. "Not serious, I hope."

The lawman could imagine the man's cruel smile. He decided not to take offense, yet. Carpathian did nothing without a reason. The countless dead scattered across the nearby streets was as nothing to him. Sending this offensive minion could only be another test.

"I've seen better days." It was the best he could come up with while managing his anger and frustration.

"Hmmm." Ursul grunted. "As has zees country of yours, I sink vee can agree? Perhaps a few more of you Union NELEGITIM lacking for better days, and vee vill all see our fortunes restored, no?"

Virgil decided to ignore the foreign insult. Even if he had understood correctly, that was not his fight. "I'm not a Union soldier, Ursul. You know that, and so does your boss."

The majordomo frowned. "Perhaps, for zose of us from more civilized lands, zee difference is not so easy to discern, pricepe?"

"I'm a marshal. I'm only concerned with the law, not the politics of the government or the plots of Grant and his gang of mudsills." Virgil suddenly felt it was important to impress this upon the large man stalking along beside him. "My job is to keep as many folks safe as I can, so they can make their own way in this world."

Ursul grunted. "And yet, still so many die. It vould seem this eez just not a very safe country you have all made for yourselves, from my point of view."

"We do our best." The old lawman felt unsatisfied, unable to give a better answer. "We all do our best."

The stalky man stopped in his tracks and swung ominously toward him, the armor shining in the sunlight. "Your best was not good enough for my sister, though, Marshal Earp. And so vee seek out our own justice here, if you don't mind."

Ursul continued on again, leaving Virgil standing there alone for a moment before hurrying stiffly to catch up. "I'm sorry. I had no idea. How . . . ?"

The big man shook his head. "No, Marshal Earp. You do not deserve zee intimate details of my family tragedies. My sister eez gone; one among countless victims of zee corrupt military of a debased government. Zee price for zat death vill come due, in time. For now, leave your vehicle. An animation will follow along with it later. Vee are late to speak vis zee Doctor."

*****

Virgil had last been in Payson almost two years ago, bearing the broken and bleeding body of his brother Morgan. They had whisked his brother away and he had been summoned up to the tallest tower of the strange, gothic pile of bricks Carpathian called his manor house. He had been half-mad with grief and agitated at the abrupt separation, but even then he had known, once he had decided to come, he had to play the cards the doctor dealt.

And here he was again, playing with a marked deck. As Ursul led him through the big double doors and into the winding hallways of the main house, Virgil knew where they were going. The palace was not nearly as desolate as the city streets had been. There were servants moving quietly, both living and dead. In one salon he saw two sleek young men in black dusters talking quietly with two other young men wearing thin white coats over slick widow's tackle. He did not care for their fancy duds, but somehow their gear blended well with the castle around them.

Finally, Ursul led the marshal to the elevator chamber. One set of double doors slid open onto the tiny room beyond. Ursul urged the lawman inside. "I have too many duties zees time to accompany you. Just remember, go to your right, and you vill find your way." He held out one massive paw, a look bordering on regret crossing his face. "But first, I'm afraid you must surrender your sidearm."

Virgil knew it was coming. There was no way they were going to let him carry a gun into the great man's presence. He nodded, slipped the blaster pistol from the holster, and handed it over, butt-first.

Without a word, Ursul turned and clanked off down the hall, leaving Virgil alone. He went into the room, surveyed the buttons, and pushed one from memory. At once the doors slid shut, a series of clanks and grinding sounds emerged from the floor, and the room began to shake slightly. The marshal's head swam for a moment as if he was dizzy. He had hated this trip the first time he came to Payson, and it had not gotten any better this time around. As suddenly as it had begun, the sensation ended, the sounds ceased, and the doors opened on the familiar upper hallway.

Virgil moved to his right, along the hall, and came to the last, window-lined stretch leading to the heavy, ornate doors. He looked out the tall windows once again, down at the valley and the bustling activity of the mines and factories of Payson far below. He had not enjoyed the views on his first visit, and enjoyed them no better now. He shook the queasy feeling off and moved to the door, knocking sharply on the flat plane within one of the elaborately carved 'C's.

"Come in, please." The urbane voice from inside echoed slightly. Virgil pushed the panel and the door swung silently open. Doctor Carpathian stood nearby, speaking quietly to a tall, elegant woman who hid the lower half of her face behind a crimson fan. Cold, bright green eyes watched him from over the fan, and he felt an unnerving chill.

"Ah, Marshal Earp!" The Doctor smiled warmly without moving from the lady's side. His accent was not as thick as Ursul's; smoother and easier on the ears. "I'm just finishing up here, if you don't mind." He turned back to the woman and took her hand gently in both of his. "Miss Mimms, I think we can help each other a great deal, and I am so very glad we were able to come to this accommodation."

The woman nodded her head gracefully and then turned to go. She shifted the fan so that Virgil never got a glimpse of her face as she passed; only sparing him a last look before walking away. Carpathian followed her to the door and then closed it behind her. He smiled apologetically and gestured for Virgil to have a seat in one of the elegant, high-backed chairs.

As the lawman settled stiffly down, Carpathian sat himself, smiling behind steepled fingers, his elbows resting on the arms of the chair. "Now, marshal. To what do I owe the distinct pleasure?"

Virgil's eyes flitted around the room, only settling upon the doctor for a moment before moving away again. Nothing here offered him the slightest comfort. This man was a ruthless adversary to almost everything the Earps had fought for their entire lives. But with the Union unwilling to help him, there was nowhere else to turn.

Still, he was reluctant to speak of his needs and desires. Instead, he muttered, "You spent an awful lot of your fodder welcomin' me to town, doctor."

Carpathian shrugged, his arms wide. "Now, marshal." The warm smile grew even brighter. "You can hardly fault me measuring your resolve, no?"

Virgil's eyes settled at last on the doctor, and one eyebrow rose in question. "How'd I measure up?"

The doctor smiled. "Quite well! Now, please, marshal. To what do I owe the honor?"

The lawman stared into Carpathian's eyes for a moment more and then brought his shoulder forward, indicating the ravaged arm with a jerk of his chin. He muttered, "I've been wounded." He took a deep breath before continuing. "It's bad. Really bad. No one else can help."

Carpathian glanced down at the arm, his face a mask of sympathy. "Terrible." He leaned forward in the chair. "In the line of duty, I presume? And yet the beneficent Republic cannot help you?"

Virgil grunted. "Can't move it. Can't hardly feel it, except it burns all the time."

The doctor nodded and sat back in his chair. "And, as I said, your government cannot help you?"

The marshal squirmed in his chair as if trying to escape. "My requests were denied."

Again, Carpathian nodded. "Which is good for you, but you know that. You know that their so-called scientists are no match for what I have accomplished here." Before Virgil could respond, the doctor held up a hand. "Of course you do. You have seen the value of my work first hand. See it every day that you spend with that delightful younger brother of yours, in fact."

Virgil looked sharply at the smiling doctor and then away. He jerked a single nod but stared out one of the broad windows at the sky beyond.

"There is literally nothing I can not accomplish where the human body is concerned, Marshal Earp, let me assure you." Again the fingers steepled, the smile replaced with a look of supreme self-satisfaction. "I have worked at the tumblers of life's lock for over half a century, although you would not know it to look at me. There is very little I cannot do."

A light, friendly laugh brought Virgil's eyes snapping back to Carpathian's open face. "Now, President Johnson, General Grant and the rest, they push piles of money and resources toward Tesla and his ilk in the hopes of narrowing the gap before I crush them completely. It's hopeless, of course. I mean, Tesla and his electricity? It's to laugh!" The doctor chuckled again. "There is no way electricity will ever rival RJ-1027 in potency or cost. But you must appreciate their scrambling efforts in the depth of desperation."

Virgil said nothing, sinking further back in his chair and looking out the window. All Carpathian's talk about the Union was making him feel worse for being there at all.

"Have you nothing to say about these efforts, marshal?" The doctor's eyebrow quirked. "What of this Francis Tumblety, ostensible doctor and butcher of Camp Lincoln, as they say? He works for your allies, as I hear it."

The marshal shook his head. "I don't much care about any of that. I just want my arm back."

The contempt Carpathian displayed for the Union was painful. Even though the Earps were not fervent supporters of Grant and all he was doing in the western territories, they still very much viewed themselves as loyal sons of the Republic. Coming to this nightmare sawbones in the middle of this accursed valley of the dead was bad enough. Listening to him mock the very government Virgil upheld twisted the knife.

And the guilt was all the worse, most likely, because feeling abandoned by that same government, he could not help but doubt his own loyalties. Still, it made listening to Carpathian no easier to bear for all that.

"I just want my arm back." Virgil repeated, trying to hide the shame behind a firm voice and a steady gaze.

Carpthian nodded and pushed himself out of his chair with a grunt. "Of course you do, marshal. Of course you do." He moved across the room and kneeled down beside the lawman's chair to get a better look at the arm. "There is no movement at all? No sensation beyond the dull pain you have described?"

Virgil shook his head. "Can't do anythin' with it at all. And yeah, it just sorta hurts all the time."

"May I?" The doctor undid the straps that held the arm immobile and then proceeded to move the limb this way and that, peeling back the sleeve to look at the puckered, mottled flesh beneath. "Hmm." He rocked back on his heels. "The damage is catastrophic. Right through from the hand up into the biceps and beyond." He stood up, looking down at Virgil, and then moved back to his own chair.

Several moments passed as the two men locked gazes, and then with a slight smile, Carpathian looked away, shaking his head. "I'm afraid there is no saving your arm, Marshal Earp."

A cold sensation washed down the marshal's back at the same time a dangerous heat rose in reaction to the doctor's smirk. "You can't do anything?" His voice was heavy with disbelief. He had surrendered his personal honor coming here . . . all for nothing? He was working himself up into a rage when the doctor raised a calming hand.

"I did not say there was nothing I could do, marshal. There is quite a bit I can do, in fact." The smirk blossomed into a fully-grown smile. "You have heard of Jesse James, I believe?"

Hope and suspicion exploded into his chest together. "Heard of him. I met him once."

The smile grew even broader. "Excellent! Then you've seen those wonderful arms of his, yes?"

A greasy taste of dread slid down his throat as Virgil nodded. "I have."

The doctor answered with his own smile. "Very good. And would you be satisfied with just such an arm for yourself?"

Ever since he had been shot, Virgil had hoped that, somehow, his arm could be saved. Despite the constant pain, the total lack of recovery, he had wanted to believe his life could return to normal again.

But the doctor's words pushed him into a reality he knew he had been denying. There was no saving his arm. He would either be forever maimed, or he would be a monster creation, like his brother or that damned Jesse James.

"How much?" He forced himself to ask the question before he responded.

"Well, that is the question, is it not?" Carpathian's smile took on a predatory gleam. "Such technology, such opportunities as I alone in the world can offer. This cannot come cheaply. You agree?"

Virgil shook his head. "I don't have a lot of money—"

The doctor raised a single hand. "I do not require money, Marshal Earp." Now the smile was that of a wolf approaching its prey. "Certain considerations of the Federal Bureau, now . . . And from a brother of the Over-marshal himself, no less . . ."

The marshal shook his head. "It's bad enough me bein' here. I won't betray the law for—"

Carpathian shook his head and raised both hands in denial. "No, no, no, marshal! Perish the thought! I am not asking you to betray the law, or the good people you protect!" He leaned in closer. "No, all I will ask of you, from time to time, is information about the federal forces. I already know a great deal, so please do not believe you are the only person willing to work with me against the Union. For instance, I know all about what happened with the Clantons in Tombstone . . ."

Virgil's eyes tightened. "How –?"

Carpathian leaned back in his chair, smiling warmly again. "I have many sources, marshal. Some in the Bureau itself. Do not concern yourself, aside from knowing that you will not be alone. For the vast majority of your time, your life will continue as it has always been, except that instead of being a pathetic cripple, unable to hold your own in the struggle that slouches toward us all, you will be fit, and strong, and more than worthy of standing by your brother's side when the dark day dawns."

Virgil nodded slowly, unsure of what half of that meant, but desperately focused on the half that made sense. "Alright."

"Excellent!" Carpathian's smile glowed. "I do truly enjoy helping people, marshal. And the more people I assist, the more people will know they can come to me for assistance!"

The marshal shook his head at that. "I won't be spreading no Gospel Accordin' to Carpathian or anything like that . . ."

The doctor smiled more gently and shook his head. "Of course not. But everyone will know where it came from, nonetheless. And they will come to me in their own hour of need, and I will help them as well. For such bonds of goodwill are the only riches with real value in this world, marshal."

And those folks would owe the doctor just as Virgil owed him. And as his reach and his influence spread through these obligations, he would bring people from all walks of life into his control. For everyone is in danger of getting injured, or sick, or old. A chill gripped the marshal's gut as he realized that he was sinking deeper and deeper into a web that would someday spread all across the Contested Territories and beyond.

"Now, we'll need to get you down to my surgical assistant, Kyle. He will prepare you for the procedure. The soonest begun, the soonest done, as they say." The smile was again predatory with anticipation.

All Virgil could think about was what Wyatt would say when he found out.

Chapter 8

Jesse James rested his metal forearms against the railing of the NATCHEZ IX as the distant shores of the Mississippi drifted past. For five days they had been travelling aboard the enormous riverboat, and Jesse was still not accustomed to the daunting scale of the vessel. Aside from the colossal Heavy Rail terminal the Union had dropped into the middle of Kansas City, this boat was the largest man-made construction he had ever seen. The idea that such an enormous edifice was moving bothered him more than he would admit.

Watching the waves thrown up by the bow of the enormous ship slap at the shore reminded him of the Union packet boat he had taken down with Frank and the Youngers back on the old Missouri River. That little war-boat would have fit into the dining hall of the Natchez IX several times over, but back nearly a year ago, he remembered with a smile, it had been more than enough boat for him.

I n fact, Jesse was more than a little suspicious that it was memories of that long-ago heist that had convinced Frank that he would be better off healing on the slow, steady journey south on land, rather than on the mighty steamboat. Remembering his past glories, however, reminded him of his more recent setbacks, and his face settled back into its brooding lines.

Leaving his tattered little army had not been easy, even with Frank and the Youngers in charge. Moberly had yielded up just enough food and RJ to keep the people and machines moving southward toward the planned rendezvous north of New Orleans. The plan, using one of Colonel Quantrill's river contacts to ferry the army across the river at Baton Rouge, would have been nerve-wracking even if Jesse had gone with them. Knowing that it would be up to Frank and the Youngers to pull it off was enough to give him the cold sweats each night.

He had sent Will Shaft and his Exodusters back west to Robbers Roost to collect any desperadoes that might be willing to assist in Jesse's grand new adventure. He had ultimately decided to tell them to avoid Diablo Canyon, where rumor said Billy the Kid had come to rest. No matter how daunting the thought of raising an entire army might be, there were just some bummers he was not ready to ride with again.

If there was one place designed to keep your mind off your worries, however, it was the Natchez IX. Quantrill had somehow finagled passage for himself, Jesse, Lucinda, and Marcus Cunningham, who Quantrill thought would be an invaluable asset once they reached the city. Lucy had spent the first day aboard in the enormous copper bathtub reserved for first class passengers. The Ford brothers had somehow wangled their way aboard as well, but with accommodations much more unassuming than the suites given to the old Confederate officer and his guests.

The river boat was easily the largest plying the wide Mississippi. Its enormous RJ engines drove a single huge paddle wheel, churning the muddy waters of the river into a tan froth that trailed along in the vessel's wake, shimmering with the glow of crimson power conduits and vents. The dining room was the largest chamber Jesse had ever seen. The gaming rooms were the poshest, most brightly lit he had ever lost a hand in. The suites themselves were a level of luxury and excess that he could not have even imagined before boarding the boat at Festus, a dinky little town south of St. Louis.

It had gotten to the point that Jesse had to forcefully remind himself each day that this was only a brief respite along the rough trail. Still . . . He tilted the brim of his hat back to catch the glowing sun. He might just be able to picture himself giving up the dust and the sand for one of these suites and a seat at those gaming tables each night. Maybe, if he could convince Lucy to join him –

"Quite a sight, ain't it?" A voice broke into his reverie. Jesse turned, ready to snap out a harsh response, when he recognized the sharp, rodent-like face of Charlie Ford. Although older by several years, Charlie was by far the tamer and more timid of the two brothers. He followed Robert's lead, staying in the background and letting him do all the talking. In fact, Jesse could not remember the last time Charlie Ford had spoken to him directly.

"Sorry?" Still clearing his head from its wanderings, he had missed what the quiet man had said.

"The shore. It's quite a sight. Ain't it?" It was obvious Charlie was making an enormous effort. His eyes, having established brief contact with Jesse's, flitted out over the glistening water.

Jesse smiled at the kid and went back to resting against the smooth wood. "Yeah, it's quite somethin', that's for sure. Robert still enjoyin' his run of the faro table?"

Charlie shuffled up to the railing and gripped it tightly in one hand, looking down at the water sluicing along the boat's side. "Yeah. The tiger ain't bucked 'im yet."

Jesse grunted and went back to watching the shoreline. He had no idea what Charlie wanted from him, and was in no mood to tease it out. If the kid wanted to talk, he would find the sand. Otherwise, it was too nice a day to waste holding his hand.

"Jesse, I got somethin' I wanna ask ya." Charlie was gripping the railing with both hands now, his eyes fixed fiercely on the rolling water.

The outlaw felt an itch between his shoulder blades. In his experience, there was no good conversation that had ever started with those words. He started to review all of his dealings with Charlie and his brother. Was there some way they might have bilked him? He kept his pose relaxed, his eyes focused on the distant shore, and muttered, "Yeah?"

The young man cringed a bit, but stayed where he was, eyes unmoving. He nodded quickly, and then said. "I ain't brave."

Jesse stared at the boy for a minute, trying to process what it was he had said and what it might mean. He had seen the kid in the thick of things several times. He was never a tomcat in battle, but he had never seemed shy, neither.

The outlaw chief waited for the kid to comment further, but when nothing else seemed forthcoming, he said, "That all?"

Charlie's head snapped around, his face a mixture of shame and anger. "Ain't that enough?" He spat over the railing, his eyes burning. "Hell, you're on the shoot to start a whole damned war, Jesse. You, and Frank, and the Youngers, and Robert, even; you're all of you right tartars in a fight." His shoulders slumped. "Me? It's all I can do not to piss myself when the first shot's fired."

Jesse nodded and rested one elbow back on the rail. He took his hat off with the other hand and let the river breeze cool his head for a moment before he responded. "Kid, that ain't nothin'. You ain't pissed yourself, right?"

Charlie shook his head so fast his hat almost went over the side. "'Course not! I'm just sayin! I . . ."

The silence hung there, heavy with whatever it was Charlie had been about to say. Jesse came to his rescue with a brisk pat on the back that almost cost him his hat all over again. "Charlie, you got not to worry so much. You seen the elephant, and you been fine. There ain't nobody can complain about your worth in a fight."

"But I ain't brave!" The pain in the man's voice was clear even to Jesse. "Robert's brave, he don't care none when the bullets start flyin'! And you don't, nor Frank, nor any of those others neither! Hell, that woman that follows you all over? She don't so much as flinch when the shootin' starts!"

Jesse looked at the pale face for a moment. When he spoke, he tried to inject every ounce of his life's experience into the words. "Kid, let me tell you somethin' about bein' brave."

Charlie turned slowly around at the tone in Jesse's voice, looking into his face with a pitiful hope in his eyes.

"Bein' brave ain't about not bein' scared, Charlie. Bein' brave's about bein' scared and doin' what needs doin' anyway." He shrugged. "Hell, ever'body's scared when the dust is flyin', kid."

The hope flared even brighter, and Charlie stood up a little straighter. "Everybody? Even you?"

Jesse tried to contain his reaction, but the laugh burst out anyway, echoing off the bulkhead behind them. "Hell no, kid! I'm Jesse James!" He saw the hope start to collapse in Charlie's eyes, but after a moment, the outlaw's laughter, rolling over the surrounding water, tipped the balance and he smiled in response.

Jesse slapped Charlie Ford on the back again and they both turned to watch the shoreline slide past, smiling as wide as the river.

*****

As the NATCHEZ IX churned its way through the outskirts of New Orleans, Jesse and his party stood along the railing, watching the city grow before them. Even this far out, the buildings were like nothing most of them had ever seen before. Colonel Quantrill watched their reactions with a wide grin, as if unveiling a masterpiece of his own creation to new eyes.

Most of the buildings were brick and stone with beautifully ornate facades. Most had elaborate gardens that stretched down toward the water in green spills dotted with vibrant color. Small private docks and boat houses held sleek, RJ-powered speedsters. As they approached the main waterfront on the east side of the river, men in the uniform of the riverboat company came running out onto the pale wood. They caught heavy ropes heaved to them by the crew and wrapped them around heavy metal bollards that shone dully in the sun.

Beneath Jesse's feet, the engines surged with a rumbling growl, forcing the vast paddles backward, slowing the boat and bringing it up against the pier.

The wharf was connected to the land by several high wooden bridges. On the shore, a parade of ornate street lamps marched off into the distance up and down the bank. Each had a small RJ generator built into the base, nearly hidden behind decorative iron-work. Jesse could see a broad walkway beneath the lights.

The city, beginning just on the other side of a cobblestone street, struck him once again with its ornate, decorative architecture. Off to the right he could see a broad square where even larger, more impressive stone buildings presided over several monuments and gazebos. There were trees everywhere, along the streets, in cultivated gardens along the public square, and rising up from behind low walls attached to many of the buildings. Crowds of men and women in fancy clothing meandered down the lanes and beneath the gently-drooping trees.

Jesse was about to say something about the beauty and strangeness of the city when the first hot whiff of this new world reached across the cool water and slapped him in the face. As the NATCHEZ IX came to a halt, bumping gently against the docks, the breeze of her passage died away, and the outlaws got their first hint of life in New Orleans.

The foul smell that hit them was accompanied by an oppressive heat, laden with all the moisture of the river. The combination of smells, heat, and humidity was like nothing the men from the western territories had experienced outside the hell of Camp Lincoln itself. Lucinda and Quantrill seemed entirely unaffected, and Marcus's face was as impassive as always behind his kerchief and hood. Jesse looked at Lucy and Quantrill suspiciously; as if there were some secret to their composure they were keeping from him.

In fact, Lucy was never looking better, bedecked in a glittering gown she had picked up in the riverboat's shop. Her shopping spree, and the enormous copper tub, had gone a long way toward washing the stink of Camp Lincoln and the subsequent flight out of her hair.

"Is it always like this?" Robert Ford gasped out. "I'm soaking through my coat! How do those Dapper Dans stand it?"

Quantrill smiled. "It's not always like this." The smile turned downright evil. "I mean, we're hitting the tail end of autumn. Sometimes it's hotter. As for those boys walking the waterfront? Most of them are wearin' linen, or somethin' similar. A man can still cut a fine figure and not drown in his own sweat."

"What's that smell!" Charlie's face was pale.

The Confederate officer smiled as if apologizing. "Well, that there's the smell of the big city, boys. A European city dropped into the middle of a New World swamp, at any rate."

Lucinda smiled and put her hand on Jesse's shoulder. "Don't worry. You'll get used to it."

"Not damned likely!" Jesse scowled out over the city, watching it change from an object of wonder and curiosity, to a foul test of endurance before his eyes.

As Jesse was glowering out over the rail, he saw a detachment of soldiers march past, blaster rifles sloped over their shoulders. Their familiar blue uniforms sent a chill down his back, despite the stifling heat.

"You didn't say nothin' 'bout no blue-bellies, sir." Jesse jerked his head carefully in the direction of the unit as it disappeared down a side street to the south.

Quantrill frowned at Jesse. "I sure did, son. Told you there was a big mess of 'em down by the naval yards off Lake Borgne. They bed down hereabouts in town, but don't kick up too much of a fuss. Like I said, most of 'em's down by the small lake." He reached over and pulled at the sleeve of Jesse's duster. "That's why you're wearing these, remember?"

Jesse jerked the fabric out of the grinning man's hands. "What are they doin' here? Ain't New Orleans supposed to be a free city, you said?"

Quantrill shrugged and rested his elbows against the railing, watching out over the city. "No one knows for sure. They don't much trouble the folks here, so that ain't it. They got the waterfront along the lake shore sewed up to a fare-thee-well, though, almost as if they're expectin' trouble to come in on 'em by sea."

"But if we're hundreds of miles from Union territory, what the hell do those mudsills care what happens to the city?" Robert Ford was annoyed. "Don't make no damned sense!"

Quantrill shook his head. "It don't, but they're here. They do march around like they own the place, but they don't usually get into local goings on too deep." He tilted his head a bit. "No more than they have to, to keep their forces down by the lake."

"It's also the closest port to the Contested Territories." Lucinda had not spoken much for the past day, and her voice was distracted even now. "If someone were to try to get a large force into the territories, they could find a worse way to do it than pushing it up the Mississippi from here."

Jesse watched the street that had swallowed up the Union detachment for a few minutes more. "Well, not much we can do about it. Colonel, you say they don't queer the deal, I guess we gotta believe you."

Most of the passengers were making their way off the boat, crowding onto the docks and moving into the city. A line of wagons rumbled idly nearby, taking up the more lavishly-dressed passengers and whisking them away in clouds of crimson smoke.

Quantrill stood up, hands on hips, and turned to the little group. "Well, shall we? I can speak to the purser, have the Iron Horses brought up?"

Jesse shook his head. "I ain't seen any 'Horses out there. Have they come this far south?"

The colonel shook his head. "To be honest, no. The blue-bellies have them, of course. But the only other source for them would be your good doctor, or those who steal them from the authorities." He smiled as he gestured at Jesse and his companions. "So no, you won't find many, if any, in the city."

Jesse looked back down at the wagons in the street. The sun was starting to set, casting a ghostly reddish hue over the scene. "What's the plan, colonel? I don't think we wanna catch any sort of official attention, but I'm not sure how much territory we gotta cover . . ."

Quantrill nodded. "Well, Colonel Warley's not the easiest man to get ahold of, to be honest. An' if we try to head out toward his plantation without an invitation, the chances of us makin' it aren't gold-plated."

The outlaw chief bridled at the challenge, but his old colonel silenced him with a raised hand. "You'd be goin' up against a small army, Jesse. Until we get yours out of the swamp, I'm thinkin' you don't wanna try those odds." He smiled up at his young friend. "Besides, that's an army you mean to sweet talk over to your side, so killin' 'em all might not be the best notion you've had."

"So what would you suggest?" Lucinda's full lips were quirked in skeptical regard. "We're going to have to get off the boat eventually, and the Iron Horses will be coming off at some point as well."

Quantrill nodded quickly. "Of course. Well, we can have the 'Horses placed in a holding warehouse downriver for a few days without too many questions. I would recommend we take up rooms at one of the local establishments and see if we can't find one of my contacts, or Mistress Laveau, who may also be able to extend to us an invitation to Warley's place."

"Laveau, Carpathian's friend? The one that fixed up your arm?" Jesse's brows came down suspiciously. “Like I said, sir, I ain’t super keen on meetin’ up with a friend o’ Carpathian.”

“And like I said, James,” Quantrill’s voice was firm. “Mistress Laveau uses Carpathian’s technology and techniques, but she is very much her own creature.”

“A creature that uses dead bodies. And ain’t none of those type folks ain’t sick.” Robert Ford’s voice was cold, and his brother grunted in agreement.

“An’ that freak from Camp Lincoln that the Union was usin’, too. That ain’t no kinda shindy we need to be gettin’ caught up in.” His lips were thin and tight as he shot a sidelong glance at Jesse.

The outlaw boss nodded. “We’ll try to find one o’ these ol’ grey-backs first, boys. See if we can’t skip meetin’ the local medicine woman, if it’s all the same to you, colonel.”

Quantrill shook his head. “I’m just interested in bringin’ you and Warley together, James. You know that. Marie Laveau did well enough by me, but I don’t feel the need to drop in an’ say hi, neither.”

The group disembarked from the Natchez IX, the last passengers to step onto the dock as the crewmen and dockworkers began to unload cargo through massive iron doors in the boat’s flank. Quantrill led the group across the cobbled border street and into the tight confines of the French Quarter. The fancy brick and stone buildings, their wrought-iron detailing and elaborate balconies, were like nothing that Jesse had ever seen before. Even the fanciest cathouses back in the territories were no match for the meanest building on the poorest street in this city.

Quantrill led them to a particularly fancy building painted a bright, warm pink with cream detailing. An impressive iron sign painted with delicate letters and the image of a woman’s eyes proclaimed the building to house an establishment named Hotel Ses Beaux Yeux. Judging from the women lounging on the balconies overlooking the street, Jesse thought he recognized the kind of business they were running, alien architecture and jibber-jabber name or not.

“I’m as ready to take a filly for a ride as the next man, colonel.” Jesse’s grin was forced as he glanced around the group standing in front of the building. “But you think this is the best use of our time?”

He had expected Lucy to rise to the bait, but instead she was looking thoughtfully up at the ladies above them. He shook his head at the wasted opportunity.

“Josie’s got some rooms out back she lets friends rent without the usual . . . adornments?” Quantrill took the marble stairs at a jaunty pace, leaving the rest of them to hurry after. Jesse was the last to enter the building, cursing the sodden heat once again.

Inside the hotel, everything was soft and pink, with ladies sauntering through a dimly-lit salon in costumes that would have seen them arrested in most places Jesse had ever frequented. He could hardly keep his eyes focused on the handsome older lady Quantrill was speaking with at a polished wooden desk in the back of the room. He felt exceedingly awkward with Lucy nearby; for some reason, he did not want her to catch him ogling the local talent. Even so, he could not restrain his customary grin, and he took his hat off, nodding to several lovely ladies as he stepped up beside Quantrill.

“We’d be very much obliged, Madamoiselle Reneu, thank you.” Quantrill held his hat tight to his chest as he bowed to the lady. Jesse nodded as well, his grin wider still.

“It is my pleasure, monsieur.” There was only the faintest hint of an exotic accent in her voice. She turned her gaze upon Jesse and he found himself suddenly uncomfortable, as if he might be unworthy. Her eyes were a disconcerting pale gold, only slightly lighter than the caramel shade of her hair. Although she was older, her face was easily the match of any woman in the room, with the possible exception of Lucinda, who was staring at her with open admiration.

“And this must be the famous Jesse James of the Wild West.” Madamoiselle Reneu extended her delicate hand toward Jesse and in a panic he grabbed it, shaking it quickly and releasing it.

"It's a pleasure, ma'am." Suddenly, Jesse could not find a safe place to settle his eyes.

She smiled in warm satisfaction and turned back to the grinning Quantrill. "I assume you'll be out and about till the wee hours, as usual, William?"

Quantrill shrugged. "Well, now, miss, I don't know precisely what the evening holds."

"Well," the lady pouted. "If it does not hold at least a fleeting moment for me, I will be terribly disappointed."

He laughed and nodded. "Me too, mistress, me too." She smiled in answer and gestured for him to lead the group through a glittering beaded curtain and down a dark hall.

Jesse, walking beside Lucy, was increasingly aware of their elbows brushing. He was very happy when Quantrill led them down a narrow stair and into a small suite of rooms. These were not nearly so well-appointed as the upper level, but comfortable nevertheless.

"So, that was Madamoiselle Josie Reneu." Quantrill smiled broadly to the group. "A friend of the cause, let us say." He gestured for everyone to take a seat in the various chairs and sofas in the suite's common room. "I think things would go best if we split up at this point, each take a section of the Quarter, and seek out someone who might be able to make the appropriate introductions? I can give you the proper words and phrases that should open the doors we need opened."

Jesse settled back into the soft cushions of a faded pink loveseat and stretched out his legs. "Well, colonel, you know best. I figure we can make our way 'round here without too much trouble. But someone's gotta head out into the swamps and watch for Frank an' them. They should be crossin' the river in the next couple of days if they pressed things, and they'll get lost in the Mourepas without someone to guide 'em in. I'll wanna know if they're okay before I join us up with any new outfit."

Charlie raised a hand. "I can do that, Jesse. I'll rustle me up one o' those local wagons and head on out later tonight. Shouldn't be too hard."

Jesse nodded and turned to Robert. "You wanna go with yer brother?"

Robert shook his head with a smirk. "No, I'm gonna stick with you. This many blue-bellies runnin' around, don't want you gettin' frisky. Frank'd never forgive me."

"Lucy, you okay movin' about on yer own?" Jesse looked around to find Lucinda moving around the walls of the small room, scrutinizing the fading wallpaper and the shiny metal lighting fixtures. When she heard her name, she looked up, preoccupied.

"Hmm?" When his question registered, she looked at him coldly. "I have been taking care of myself all my life, Jesse. Just because I ride with you for a spell, don't think I'm a helpless maiden."

The outlaw chief raised his hands in mock defense. "No! 'Course not!" He grinned and turned back to his old commander. "So, divvy us up, colonel!"

Quantrill set Lucinda toward the waterfront district, while he went south toward the port. Jesse volunteered to go westward, deeper into the Quarter. There was a moment's trouble as Marcus refused to be separated from Jesse, but the outlaw waved it away.

"So, I'm tramping around with a couple o' thugs followin' me, one in a hood . . . I'm sure we'll blend right in!" He laughed it off, and the five of them moved out into the hall toward the stairs.

"Now, you remember you got a job to do, Charlie!" Robert yelled back to his brother before closing the door.

"Don't worry, little brother." Charlie came to the door and rested his back against the jam. "I don't tucker that easily." His smile would have done a tomcat proud.

*****

Jesse, Marcus, and Robert Ford started to doubt the plan after checking their tenth café. They had found plenty of saloons and taverns, but none of them felt remotely like the watering holes back west. Even at the lower establishments, the furnishings were nice, the folks well-dressed, and the lighting bright. There was plenty of gaming going on, but Jesse refused to indulge. They had a job to do, and they were not going to stop with it still before them.

The phrases they had learned from Quantrill earned them only vague looks, shaking heads, and closed mouths. Jesse was starting to think maybe this Warley was a phantom. That thought led to an image of Henderson floating up in his mind, and he snarled as he forced it down into the shadows.

He had expected to have more trouble with Marcus following him through the streets. Other than an occasional shouted proposal from a woman of the evening, it was as if there was nothing special about the hulking, dark-skinned man. Something about that made Jesse feel better about the place, say what you would about the smell.

Coming out of a café with the wildly improbable name of the Café Joyau du Mississippi, Jesse noticed the skyline drop off ahead of them, a void that seemed strange in a city so dense.

"What you reckon that is over there, boys?" Jesse pointed with a metal hand at the emptiness. He had taken the gloves off a while ago. He was stifling in his coat, despite the drop in temperature with sunset, and any relief, even the phantom sensation of fresh air moving across the feedback pads of his metal limbs, was welcome.

"Hang this for a lark." Jesse looked around at the street signs overhanging their current position. Toulouse and Rampart . . . He felt like he had left his entire world behind. "Let's check out what that might be over yonder, an' then maybe swing back around to sweep the northern streets to the waterfront."

The two other men nodded silently. They were tired, neither of them particularly eager to spend any more time in the oppressive heat and stink of the city.

Crossing the quiet Rampart Street, they swung around to the left and found themselves facing a long, high wall of old stone. It looked like a small fortress, and Jesse thought, for a moment, they had stumbled upon one of the Union garrisons. A small gate in the center of the wall was open, nothing but darkness within. If it had been an active fort, there would have been sentries and weapon emplacements. This place looked deserted and decrepit.

"What you reckon—" Jesse began, but the sharp, grinding sound of many boots slapping against the wet cobbles stopped him. He dragged Robert back into the shadows of a small clump of trees while Marcus disappeared on his own.

A detachment of Union soldiers marched briskly past, looking neither right nor left as they stalked by the wall and its gaping entrance.

"Damn chiselers!" Jesse growled. "Give me half a chance—"

"Jesse!" Robert clipped him on the shoulder. "Look!"

A small figure had broken off from the shadows further down the street and was crossing the road toward the shadowed entrance. It paused to look after the Union soldiers, then ducked into the darkness and disappeared.

"Well, that ain't half queer, eh boys?" Jesse moved to the corner of the building across the street and peered into the gate. He could see nothing. "I say we check this out, and then head back." His voice was light and unconcerned. "What do you say, fellas?"

Robert looked to Marcus, but the big man's eyes were flat, fixed on the gate across the street. Ford turned back to Jesse. "We're with you, boss."

Jesse grinned, nodded, and then gave a quick look back and forth across the street. The wall was not quite twice the height of a man, the stone a white, crumbling rock with dark, meandering cracks that looked diseased in the harsh light of their RJ hand lamps. The gate was an opening flanked by two plain, square pillars, and beyond they could only see a confusion of hard, solid shapes.

Somewhere in the distance, a soft sound scratched at the very edges of Jesse's mind; a clicking, slithering sound that he could not quite place.

Jesse drew a Hyper-velocity blaster, holding it high and leading with his hand-lamp as he walked sideways through the arch. The beam fell on a stone box directly behind the gate and forcing him to the left. He waved his companions after him with his pistol, eyes sweeping the dimly-lit avenue. He turned the first corner and saw what seemed to be a miniature city, small stone houses placed close beside each other, flanking a street that disappeared into the darkness.

The structures came in a dizzying array of shapes and sizes. Many were plain slabs of stone with flat roofs. Others were elaborately carved affairs that reached with towers and columns into the warm night air. Eerie statuary gazed down upon them with cold blank stares as they moved through the twisting streets.

"What in the Sam Hill is this?" Robert's voice was harsh as he clutched his massive blaster with one hand, a knife and his hand-lamp in the other. "Jesse, half these here statues is skeletons!" The clicking sound came again. "And what the hell is that?"

Jesse cocked his head, but the sound was gone. He looked more closely at one of the images hovering overhead. It was, in fact, a skeleton. Its empty eye sockets glared down at him, its skeletal smile unnerving in its welcome. "I don't know, Robert."

Marcus's eyes, reflecting the light from their lamps, burned brightly. "It's a liche yard." He shrugged. "I don't know what that sound was."

Jesse stood up at that, casting an incredulous look at the miniature buildings that now surrounded them. "Ain't no way . . ." He tapped on the side of one tomb with the butt of his pistol. It gave a hollow sound. "I'll be damned. This here's a New Orleans Boot Hill?"

Marcus nodded once. "Ground's too soft, can't bury their dead. They gotta put 'em in these crypts or they'll never stay down."

"You ain't sayin' . . ." Robert Ford's voice was quavering. He had not yet faced Carpathian's animations, but he had heard plenty of the stories from Jesse and the men who rode with him. "They come back?"

Marcus cast a withering gaze toward the smaller man but did not respond.

"Marcus, how the hell you know so much 'bout how they bury folks in New Orleans?" Jesse stood up from his worried crouch to confront the larger man.

"Because Marcus Cunningham has returned home." A soft, melodious voice said from somewhere overhead. "Welcome home, Marcus. We've been waiting for you."

Two enormous men, bigger even than Marcus, with skin the color of midnight, moved out from behind a large tomb directly across from the three outlaws. The tomb was marked with countless scrawled crosses scratched in sets of three into its marble surface. The newcomers moved with an unsteady gait, arms hanging limply at their sides. Upon each man's face had been painted the shape of a human skull in thick, cracking grease-paint. The effect was distracting enough that at first, Jesse did not notice the men's eyes. Eyes that were cold, blank, and clouded in death.

"Damn. Animations." Jesse's gun came up and pointed unerringly at the head of the corpse on the left.

"I would prefer if you would leave my GAD PALÈ intact, MSYE James." Again the voice came from directly overhead, and Jesse dropped his hand-lamp to draw his other pistol, waving it uncertainly at the roof line on either side of the street.

"Come on out, now, where we can see ya!" Jesse was trying very hard to control his annoyance. "I know animations when I see 'em, an' I'm not too worried 'bout takin' down these two rips right here, if'n you feel like staying hid!"

A slim figure rose up on the roof across the cramped street. Robert's lamp beam flashed up to illuminate a beautiful, coffee-colored face. Her dark brown hair floated about her head like a halo; bright white teeth shone down upon them in a wide, welcoming smile. At her feet, looking down from the edge of the roof, was what looked like an enormous half-rotted serpent, its eyes clouded and empty. A framework of articulated metal struts and joints was sunk into the creature's flesh to provide the support its dead muscles could no longer convey.

"There is nothing to fear here, my friends. We are fellow travelers upon the same road." She gestured gracefully at the two enormous animations. "Now, please lower your weapon, Msye James. Although I can make more gad palè, finding the raw materials for such specimens can often present its own . . . challenges."

The woman dropped lightly from the roof and landed with just the slightest of sounds upon the packed dirt of the street. At the same time, a small girl emerged from the shadows behind the tomb with unnerving grace: the figure they had followed into the graveyard. She moved to stand beside the giant animations with a queer smile on her lips. The dead snake stayed on the roof, its white-eyed head swaying back and forth, while the woman rose from her landing, nearly as tall as Jesse himself. Standing proud in an ornate white dress, she nodded calmly to the outlaw chief.

"Marie Laveau welcomes you to New Orleans, Jesse James." He nodded jerkily, not sure what else to do. She grinned and gestured with one graceful hand back up at the roof. "And please excuse my pet, Nzambi. He can be shy around newcomers." The snake stared down and opened its mouth in what probably would have been a hiss if it had had a tongue.

She continued, turning away from the serpent. "You are correct, of course. My guardian gad palè are, indeed animations of a sort." Her smile vanished, and her eyes burned cold. "However, do not, therefore, believe you understand what you see here. There are realities, truths, and powers far older than the clever Doctor Carpathian." She glided toward him, sweeping around the still outlaw as if she were floating on air. "You will meet others, if you sojourn long within the limits of my city."

Jesse's gaze was fixated upon the woman's tawny eyes. He nodded again and holstered a weapon. He used his free hand to tip his hat. "Ma'am."

She smiled at him and moved toward Marcus. He had been staring at her with eyes so wide they accentuated the darkness of his flesh. When she reached up to his hood he shied back, but she persisted, pulling the fabric away.

Jesse looked at the twisted horn, shining redly in Robert's lamplight, protruding from the center of the man's forehead and curling back along the side of his skull. Marie Laveau made a sympathetic sound and drew one finger down the length of the horn. "So, it is true, my Marcus."

The big man continued to stare. His expression was frozen between despair and rage.

The strange woman walked around him, looking at the horn from every angle.

"Marcus . . . it's alright . . ." Jesse patted the air with one hand. Nothing good could come from killing this strange woman before they learned more.

"Marcus was raised among the savage northern tribes . . . Were you not, Marcus?" The woman's tone was soothing, almost hypnotic. "You wanted only to belong. You wanted only to be one with the warriors whose fires you shared. But you lacked their control, their knowledge, their heritage." She reached out again and touched the horn. "And you were marked for your failure."

Marcus only nodded again, his eyes fixed on the shadows between the monuments. He was shaking slightly, as if from cold or exertion. When he swept his gaze back around to stare at the woman, however, his body had become fixed and rigid. "My momma told me stories. It was you who told them to go west. It was you who sent my pa up there to die, an' me to . . . to . . . this!" One big hand wrenched at the horn as if wishing he could pull it out. There were tears of rage in his eyes as he stopped and looked down at her again. "Why . . . ?"

"But, Marcus, that is hardly the right question to beg, certainly? I am the Voodoo Queen of New Orleans! What a creature of power such as myself will always ask herself is not why . . . but why not?" She laughed again.

The big man grasped the haft of his hammer with both hands and began to raise it. "You bitch!" He roared, the animal sound echoing off the surrounding stone structures. The two gigantic animations moved forward and the undead snake reared up to strike as Marie Laveau stepped back lightly, the smile never wavering from her face.

She pursed her lips in mock sadness and shook her head. "Oh, Marcus."
The big man heaved the hammer up over his head, roaring again. Before he could bring it down, however, a booming voice from the cemetery gate bellowed, "In the name of the rightful government of the Republic of the United States of America, come out of there now, with your hands over your heads!"

Jesse's head snapped around to glare in the direction of the gate, then back at Marcus and Robert. Marie Laveau was already gone, disappeared into the shadows with the little girl. Her hulking gad palè were lumbering into the darkness after them. The horrible clicking, slithering sound drifted into the distance, and the roof of the tomb opposite was bare. The last thing they saw of the Voodoo Queen of New Orleans was the dazzling smile disappearing into the shadows as a soft, "Oh, dear!" floated after her.

Marcus shook his head, looking all around, the hammer shaking as its weight bore down upon him.

Robert Ford held his pistol in the air, looking from the distant gate to Jesse and back again.

Jesse stared at the maze of narrow streets that had swallowed Marie Laveau and her entourage. He stood up, the tension leaving his body and his shoulders slumping.

"Damnit."

Chapter 9

"Covert's the third agent we've lost this month, sir." Robert Pinkerton rested his elbows on his knees and tossed the scrap of parchment onto the low camp table. All around them, tall dark trees rose into the general shadows overhead where a thick canopy blotted out the night sky.

"And we're no closer to the bastard than when we first came out." The voice was slow and measured, slightly higher in pitch than one might expect, but still possessing a great deal of power and authority.

Pinkerton shook his head sadly. "No, sir. Each time we believe an agent has infiltrated his supply chain, they disappear. These were all good men and women, sir. And Curt was one of our best. I wouldn't want to be throwing more of my people into the fire for no good reason."

Robert Pinkerton, as the master of the Federal Pinkerton Secret Service, was one of the most powerful men in the country. He preferred to be out in the field, working directly with his agents, than staying in the rat's nest of political intrigue and petty empire-building that Washington had become. This would have hurt the career of any regular civil servant. Pinkerton, however, had friends in very high places, and those friends wanted him right where he was; right where he could do the most good.

The shadowy figure on the other side of the fire leaned back against a chair and pushed his heavy boots out in front of him, stretching with a gusting sigh. "I know, Robert. I agree. I just don't understand how a man can be so successful spreading his influence over such a wide territory, and yet we can't slip a single agent in."

"Well, sir." One of Pinkerton's lead agents, Levenson Wade, shrugged noncommittally. "The truth is, the more territory Carpathian takes from us, the more he can arrange his defense in depth. Those folks that have gone over to him won't talk. Some for fear, yeah. But most know, if they talk to anyone in the other camp, Carpathian'll stop the flow of Crimson Gold and they'll be back to . . . well, back to crouching around fire pits in the cold of the night." He grinned somewhat cruelly as he tossed a stick into the fire.

"It's true, sir." Pinkerton hated to admit weakness. In the nearly twenty years he had been running the organization, very few solutions had eluded him for this long. "We keep trying to get into his supply line and failing. We haven't been able to shadow them, either. That Interceptor heading down his trail looked promising, but then that poor young deputy . . . Once they get into the Tonto, there's no following them. You've seen it. It would take an army to fight down that road."

The tall man across the fire sighed and nodded sadly. Their small team had tried to penetrate the depths of the Tonto Forests several times. Each time, they had been set upon by roving bands of animations, barely able to escape back out into the bordering deserts. The horrific guardians, the irregular terrain, and the thick pine conspired to protect the old European from any attempts to discover the whereabouts of his hidden city.

"Are we even sure it's Green Valley?" The tall man muttered. "Half the folks hereabouts, they claim they've never even heard of Green Valley."

Wade shook his head. "We're not sure of anything, sir. The maps we have, courtesy of Agent Loveless, can't penetrate the pine forests, so there are literally thousands of square miles for us to cover." His mouth quirked in a sour frown and he threw another stick into the fire. "If we could cover it at all."

The man nodded and then turned to Pinkerton, one long hand gesturing to another paper on the camp table. "Speaking of Agent Loveless, do we know yet how she was even able to procure these maps?" There was a smile in the voice now, but it was not a pleasant one. "They're better than anything I ever saw at the War Department, and that's got me feeling a mite bitter, I don't mind saying."

Pinkerton shook his head. "We don't. She drew them herself, we know that. But as to how she was able to put together such a complete picture of the region? No, sir. All we have is speculation."

The tall man nodded again and then turned to Henry Courtright, another of Pinkerton's top agents. He was standing nearby, braced against the thick trunk of a tree and looking out into the impenetrable darkness. "Agent Courtright, could you shed any insight into how Agent Loveless was able to provide us with such faithful reproductions of such forsaken territory?"

Courtright looked down at the man, over to Pinkerton, and then back out into the surrounding forest. "There's no telling, sir; could be anything with Luce. To be honest, I wouldn't be surprised if she flew up there on a bird and sketched them while she floated along."

The tall man's impressive height unfolded beneath him as he stood up with a grunt. He began to pace around the small encampment. There were two or three other agents within view of the campfire, keeping watch over the surrounding forest. They looked up quickly as the man stood, and then went back to their own vigils.

"We've been out here too long to have nothing to show for it but a series of funerals for empty coffins." His hands worked nervously into each other as his mind teased at their situation. "We've been away from things back east too long as well. The Almighty alone knows what they've all gotten themselves into while we've been away. The Republic was tearing itself apart when we abandoned the front with the Warrior Nation to come haring off into the western territories after Carpathian, and we're no closer to solving either situation."

"Sir, to be fair, the Carpathian issue seemed far more manageable when we left the savages to Grant." Pinkerton knew the dark self-doubt that hunched in the tall man's heart, unseen by all but his closest friends and advisors. He knew how that shadow could torture the man when things were not following their prescribed course, and he hated watching him suffer. "None of our information indicated he was as entrenched as he was."

"Indeed, Robert." There was no agreement in the tall man's voice, however. "And despite not knowing, he was, in fact, entrenched. And now the madman owns just about every town and village in the western-most territories. By God, the entire region between here and Kansas City is now being called the Contested Territories, even in the official dispatches!" The man stopped and turned his heel in the deep loam to stare at the agents around the fire. "And nothing we have done for over a year has penetrated his hiding place or given us the least ability to curtail his efforts in any way."

"Well," Courtright looked sour. "Who knows where the stinking corpse soldiers would have been sent if he didn't have to guard the entire Tonto from us?" He stood, looking to Pinkerton for some support. "I mean, even forcing the enemy to reallocate resources can be seen as a partial victory in war, if it wreaks havoc with his intentions."

Pinkerton nodded, eager for the slightest hint of success. "And we have come close several times, sir. I believe, with Agents Courtright and Wade applying their more . . . rigorous . . . questioning techniques to the right individuals, we may yet be able to find a way to track him, or his men, anyway, back to wherever it is he's hiding."

The tall man was less than satisfied. "Robert," his voice was flat. "Why would you think the idea of torturing my own people could POSSIBLY make me feel better about our current situation?"

Pinkerton cursed himself silently. After serving this man for so many years, he should have seen the trap he was setting for himself. He raised his hands in a placating gesture. "Sir, that's not what I meant to say. I meant—"

"You meant exactly what you said, Robert. We have been fighting a losing battle here while the rest of the Republic falls apart behind us. Carpathian will be coming out of this forest someday, and he will have an army behind him. The savages, united beneath that bloodthirsty animal, Sitting Bull, tears our people apart and terrifies them off their lands. And Grant continues to spin his ugly metal wheels, driving first at the Warrior Nation, and then into the south after Lee's pathetic remnants, and then out into the so-called Contested Territories, unable to unite his forces against one threat at a time." One big hand, balled into a tight fist, slapped into the flat palm of the other. "We are worse than Nero, playing the fiddle of vain pursuit while the Republic burns down around us."

Pinkerton knew the man's assessment of many of the threats was not entirely accurate. Early misfortunes with the Warrior Nation, for instance, had forever colored his perception of them and their leadership structure. However, now hardly seemed the time to push him on the subject. "Sir, do you wish to return east? There's no denying that there is plenty we could be doing back home. And I know I would be far more effective running the Service a little closer to civilization."

The tall man seemed to deflate, sinking back down in his seat against the tree. "And yet, if we leave here, what do we have to show for our comrades' deaths?" He shook his head, sadness darkening his deep eyes. "We've all given up so much, and yet things just continue to fall apart. I believe Grant's pet scientists and Carpathian would agree: entropy, not humanity, will win this battle in the end."

"Bullshit." They all looked up sharply to where Courtright stood in the shadows, hands on hips.

"Excuse me, agent?" Pinkerton stood, concerned that he was about to lose one of his best men.

"You heard me, sir." The agent tipped his hat to the tall man by the fire. "With all due respect, of course. But entropy, as you call it, can't win as long as good men are willing to fight for what they know is right." He flung one hand out at the darkness as he continued. "Sure, we're gonna lose some fights. Hell, don't think this doesn't irk me something fierce. I've been out here longer than any of you. But if leaving Carpathian is what we need to do to get our house in order back home, and to assure that we're ready for the sick puttock when he comes out of his hidey hole at last, then that's what we've got to do!"

The tall man stared at Courtright for several tense moments, and Pinkerton was almost sure he was going to have to arrest his own agent. The firelight soon gleamed off a small smile in the shadows, and the tall man nodded, once.

"You speak the truth, Agent Courtright. And you rightfully put me in my place. Hope truly springs eternal in the hearts of lovers, fools, and civil servants." The men around the fire grinned, but he continued. "I fear you are all correct. We must prepare ourselves for a swift journey back east, to set things to rights and see that the Republic is in a position to repulse Carpathian when he emerges from his lair."

A sense of relief swept around the fire, but was swiftly dispelled as another agent stepped up, standing at stiff attention and looking uncomfortable. "Sir, the vocal reiterator." Pinkerton sighed and stood. "Alright, Billy. I'll-.

The agent shook his head. "No, sir. Sorry, sir. They want to speak with . . ." His eyes flicked to the tall man sitting against the tree. "They want to speak with you, sir."

"Well, tarnation." The man unfolded himself once again, a scowl on his face. "I hate that thrice-damned contraption."

The agent brought the man over to a small console on another low camp table on the other side of the camp. A rubber cord led from the back of a large box and up into a nearby tree. The cord was fixed to the bark by spikes, disappearing up into the shadows. At the very top of the tree, far out of sight, the cord ended in a large silvery sphere held in place by a rough scaffold of wood and metal.

The tall man took up a ball-tipped wand attached to the box with a thin wire and looked through the pane of dark glass at the letters that floated in the vermillion fog.

"PLEXXE ADXISEXXXEN REAXX FOXXGEXERAL XXANT STXP."

"This is ludicrous!" The man flung one long hand at the box. "Who can possibly understand this gibberish? It's bad enough with the full power backing it up. Out here in the boondocks? It's all but useless!"

"Sir," Pinkerton tried to sound reasonable. "It's the best way we have to communicate right now. And it's far more effective than anything you or my father had when you first started out. I think sometimes it's easy to lose sight of how far we've come, when we hit the limitations of these new techs."

The tall man shook his head. "No, Robert. It's not that. It's that I can't stand tryin' to communicate with a man if I can't see his face." He jerked his sharp, bearded chin at the vocal reiterator. "And this contrivance is the worst example of that there could possibly be. No artistry, no finely crafted verbiage, no eloquent facial expressions or revealing cast of body or eyes." He shook his head. "No, this machine is almost worse than not being able to communicate at all!"

"Sir," Pinkerton held his hands up in surrender. "I can't deny that everything you've just said is the Gospel truth. But General Grant's on the other end of this line, nevertheless, and he's expecting to talk to you without delay."

The tall man grunted and turned back to the machine, holding the wand loosely as if still entertaining thoughts of flinging it away. "Go ahead, General."

Pinkerton stepped forward with one hand raised. The tall man glowered at him, raising a finger of his own. "Don't you so much as even mention the word 'protocol', Robert." The leader of the Secret Service backed away, shaking his head slightly.

Within the small window, the words had changed.

"SIXXREPOXXING ON XORT KXXCKS SIXX SXXP."

The man shot back up to his full height, his eyes shining with indignant frustration. "Now what in the name of all that's holy is that supposed to mean?"

Pinkerton bent around the other man to look into the box and then stood up. "He's reporting on the Fort Knox site, sir. The machine heard him say 'knocks' . . . It's not too bright."

The tall man muttered under his breath before grasping the wand in an offended huff and nearly shouting into it. "Very well, general. What is your report?"
Pinkerton looked uncomfortable but said nothing.

"I swear, Robert. I'm still not even sure why he wanted this pile of rocks of his built in the first place!" A deep suspicion glittered in the man's eyes and he looked out at the woods, speaking as if to himself. "Not a single one of his briefings on the subject made the slightest bit of sense. And why we need heavy fortifications anywhere near where he's suggesting . . ?" He worked his mouth almost as if he were about to spit.

"Well, maybe that's what this report is about?" Levenson Wade sauntered out of the dark and crouched down next to the camp table. "Maybe we're about to hear just what the great man plans to do with his new castle."

"Remember," Courtright grumbled. "This is his second one in as many years. He had that God-forsaken pile built out in the wilds first. Fort Frederick, did he call it?"

The tall man nodded. "Yes. After his son. But at least I understood his excuses then!" Somehow, the tall man managed to convey an iron, echoing tone with his voice as he assumed a theatrical stance. "A fortress to guard the best scientific minds of the age, safely away from the conflicts of our time."

"The best scientific minds willing to take Republic coin, you mean." Courtright spat into the leaves in the darkness. "And tell all the good men who died during that last big Warrior Nation attack on the place that they were safely away from conflict." His sneer spoke volumes.

"Yes, well, perhaps not as safe as anyone would have wished," the tall man shrugged. "But I understood the concept. This new fort back east? I have not the first notion of what he intends to do with it."

"Well, here we go." Pinkerton indicated the window in the black box, and the men settled down to watch and read.

"SECXXCY REXXINS INTACXXSTOPX FACILIXY IS NXW IXXA
STXTE XX XEADIXESS STOX."

"I'm going to assume he's reporting that secrecy is intact and that the fort is ready . . ." The tall man pursed his lips and turned to Pinkerton. "Ready for what, do you think?"

Pinkerton pointed to the box.

"THE OBJXXT MUXT BX BRXUGXT CLOXER TO THE FROXT STXXXI FULXX EXX-
ECT TXE PRXXXDENT TO BX BXXIND TXXS DECISXXN XXOP."

The tall man stared incredulously into the swirling mists as the letters faded away. "Fully expect the president to be behind this decision? Why, that rat, scalawag bastard."

Pinkerton stepped away to stare up at the tall man. "Sir?"

Leaning over, the man had grabbed the low table with both hands, knuckles white with tension, and his voice shook as he spoke in low, coldly-measured tones. "Easier to beg forgiveness than to ask for permission, hmm, Lyss?"

"Sir," Wade moved beside Pinkerton and spoke in low tones. "What object?"

Courtright moved forward as well, his voice not nearly so low. "And come to that, what front?"

Pinkerton shook his head, staring into the eddying crimson mist. The letters had long since sunk from visibility. "I don't know, but if he's talking about Fort Knox, then he can only mean the Confederate Rebellion. There really isn't anyone else nearby to fight."

Courtright grunted in dark amusement. "You can't really call the border with Lee's pathetic little city state a battle front, though, can you?"

Pinkerton looked at him, his eyes hooded. "Apparently you can." He turned back to the vocal reiterator. "If you're trying to justify something."

"The bit about expecting the president's approval was a little heavy-handed, I thought." Wade folded his arms across his chest and rocked back on his heels. "I mean, no one really thinks he's talking about President Johnson, do they?"

The tall man, still crouched down before the console, spat the words over his shoulder. "That man never uttered a word without careful consideration in his life." He stood, the wand gripped tightly in one hand. He frowned out into the surrounding shadows and spoke slowly into the machine. "I want you to double garrison Fort Knox at once, and hold position until further notice. I swear to you, general, if you move out before you hear from me, you will be removed from command."

The agents standing to the side exchanged alarmed glances. Their leader's legal status was about as gray as you could get, but that threat had been spoken in ringing tones they had not heard in many, many years.

Words began to swirl and form within the window on the box console, but the tall man purposefully turned away. A sneer played across his lips as he spoke one final time into the wand. "All communication will cease until further notice." The sneer grew into a cruel smile. "Stop."

He reached behind him and flipped two metal switches. The red indicator lights and vent glow all died away at once. The words within the window were torn apart, half-formed, as the colors within the display dissolved.

"Well, that was not entirely well-thought out, but it certainly felt good." He dropped the wand behind him and moved back to the tree that had supported his back most of the night. "We need to prepare to break camp."

"Sir?" Pinkerton knew this was coming, but he wanted to make sure before he passed along any orders.

"We're heading back east. We can't do anything more here, obviously." The man threw an open hand out into the surrounding darkness. "As long as we're stumbling around in enemy territory, it's only a matter of time before Carpathian is hunting us instead of the other way around." He shook his head. "This was ill-conceived from the start. We should never have tried to sneak our way into the man's house like common footpads while the might of the Union Army was incapable of supporting us."

The man's long face was sad in the flickering firelight. "We have lost good men and women to no avail. Machinations are beginning to turn back in the Old States that, if left unchecked, could well spell the fall of the Republic. Carpathian and his cabal of characters out of a dark romantic horror novel are potential future threats, but no larger danger for the present."

"There's no denying, sometimes it seems things would be much easier if we could turn back the clock a couple decades." Pinkerton wiped one forearm across his face. "It'd be nice if we could dispense with all these scientists and their damn fool gadgets."

"All of them?" Wade's gave him a lopsided smile. "You want to get rid of Tesla and his crew as well?"

The tall man responded, "I see Nikola Tesla as just another side of the coin of progress represented by Carpathian." A wry grin twisted his face. "Hell, I don't trust anything I can't understand. And I sure as Hades do not understand anything that comes out of that man's mouth." His look darkened. "I have half a mind to stop the spread of his damned metal men now, before they get shipped all over the continent. Something itches in the back of my mind at the very thought."

Pinkerton nodded. "There's something about them that sets my teeth on edge as well."

"Ain't got eyes to look into." Courtright spat into the night. "When push comes to shove, I'm not going to trust anything with a gun, I can't look into its eyes."

The tall man speared Pinkerton with an intense gaze. "Regardless of Tesla and his machines, and even Carpathian and all his schemes, we must see to this Fort Knox, and we need to be there as soon as humanly possible."

Pinkerton nodded again. "Yes, sir."

Wade took the lead and began to snap out orders. The agents were well-trained and had been anticipating a swift departure, in one direction or another, for days. After a quick check with their leader, one of the men scrambled up the tree to dismantle the vocal reiterator and reel the cabling up while others packed weapons and the rest of the equipment.

"We will move out at first light." The tall man took a massive, ornate axe from a supple leather boot and checked some intricate mechanisms around the blade. "Make for the rendezvous at Diablo Canyon, hold tight there for a day, and then make for Kansas City." He turned toward Pinkerton as he returned the axe to its holder. "Make sure your men activate all the dead drops as we head east. I do not want anyone left behind unsupported."

"And who knows what we'll need when we get to where we're going." Wade's mouth was twisted in annoyance.

The tall man stared into the fire for a moment and then turned to Pinkerton with a sigh. "I think, given our current situation, I want to call in those two butchers, Sasha Tanner and the Wraith. If this turns as ugly as I think it might, men of such character might be a key ace in the hole."

Every man around the fire looked surprised at the words. Pinkerton looked at the others, then back to the tall man, his head down. "Sir, we don't need their kind. They're poison."

"They're worse than criminals, sir." Wade's voice was hard. "They're traitorous scum, not worth the bullet it would take to put them down."

The tall man nodded sadly. "And yet I stand by my statement. Grant knows something we do not. And his machinations focus upon this Fort Knox. Having two such men with us, unbeknownst to him, might be advantageous in the end. I want them summoned."

Pinkerton nodded, his arms crossed and his back stiff. He turned to Courtright and growled. "Speaking of needing every man, where the hell is Loveless?"

The agent shrugged. "I haven't seen her since we parted ways back in Texas. I saw the report from that Andersonville fiasco." He frowned. "If I had to guess, I'd say she's still back east."

Pinkerton shook his head. "Is she still shadowing that bastard, James?"

Courtright nodded. "As far as her reports have indicated, yes sir. But we have no idea where they went after Camp . . . Andersonville." For a moment he looked uncomfortable, then continued. "It got pretty ugly there, if you'll remember from the stories."

The tall man glanced over to them. "There have got to be ways to contact her, yes?"

Pinkerton nodded, frowning. "I can activate the deep cover network with a recall order. The army throws fits whenever we have to do that, but it usually works." He grinned. "But, knowing Agent Loveless, I wouldn't give that more than an even chance of working."

Courtright snorted, leaning against a tree without unfolding his arms. "I think an even chance might be giving her more credit than she deserves."

The tall man smiled. "Well, there's no denying the girl's got spirit, gentlemen. She certainly has her own means and methods. However, she cannot be off the table when we brace whatever we will be finding at General Grant's new castle."

"I'm sure she's fine, sir." Courtright 's voice was light. "No one can take care of themselves like our Luce."

Pinkerton nodded solemnly. "She's always been one of our best."

"When she's ours." Courtright's face had darkened.

"I'm not sure I know what you mean by that, son." The tall man raised a single eyebrow more eloquent than the loudest ultimatum.

Courtright met the tall man's eyes. "Nothin' much, sir. Just that Luce has always been her own person. His High and Mightiness, the Over-marshal, has filed several reports questioning her loyalty. The same reports in which he mentions that Ironclad lawdog, that's set up in Diablo Canyon. It's true, though, that Luce can sometimes disappear a bit deep into her cover when it brushes up against her past."

The tall man looked at the agent a moment longer before nodding and turning away. "Well, we all have our pasts, Agent Courtright, and that's the truth." He bent down to fetch the sheathed axe and hefted it in both hands. "And sometimes a fight with that is worse than a life or death struggle with a hundred dead men."

Chapter 10

For a handful of heartbeats, Marcus stood, hammer shaking over his head. Then he bellowed again, all restraint gone. "Noooooooooooo!"

The echoes from the surrounding tombs were unholy. The large man brought the weapon down against his chest and ran into the darkness. He screamed an anguished animal cry as he disappeared.

Robert looked to Jesse, standing in sudden indecision. Then, with a flick of his eyes, he nodded once and gestured for the outlaw to follow after the big black man. As they skittered around the first corner, they came up against a solid stone wall. There was no sign anywhere of Marcus or the strange woman and her posse.

"If you do not come out immediately, we will come in after you, drag you from the shadows, and beat you until you bleed!" The voice from the gate sounded eager. Robert Ford looked from the direction of the gate back to Jesse again.

"Jesse," his voice was harsh as he attempted to whisper against the rush of adrenaline washing through his body. "What we gonna do?"

For a moment longer, the outlaw chief stood in the darkness, shoulders slumped and head bowed. Then, his teeth flashed in the lamplight as his old grin peeked out through the beard once again. "Well, Robert, it's like this. I never met me a stinkin' blue-belly I could stomach . . . I don't see no reason we gotta give these Billy Yanks a pass tonight . . . You?"

The strength in Jesse's voice calmed Robert's racing heart, and he returned the grin with a nod. "I reckon we ain't dead yet, Jesse, might as well kick up a ruckus while we got the breath."

Jesse grinned at him and then jerked his head deeper into the graveyard. Robert followed, and the two men were soon slipping through the shadows, majestic houses of the dead sliding past on either side. Near the center of the cemetery was an enormous tomb. It rose above them in tiers like a huge, waterless fountain, each adorned with ghastly statues of cavorting demons and weeping angels. A flagstone courtyard surrounded the gaudy monument, offering the perfect spot to stop during a casual stroll and reflect upon the tragedies of mortality . . . or at the very least, the questionable tastes of the sculptor. Also, however, it presented the perfect spot for dry gulching an ornery pack of four-flushing Union bastards.

Jesse waved Robert to the right of the giant pile of stone while he scooted toward the deep shadows on the left. They both spun in the darkness, waiting for the soldiers to come. It might have been that Jesse had been too long from an honest fight, or the Yanks he had faced recently had been of a particularly low caliber, but Jesse's little plot to add to the liche yard's body count went wrong almost immediately.

The outlaw chief was crouched in the shadows, wondering what was taking the northern galoots so long, when a flash of red flame erupted on the far side of the tall monument and he heard Robert grunt in surprise and pain. A series of blaster shots echoed off the surrounding tombs. A confusion of shouts, cries, and stomping boots burst from the shadows. Suddenly, the monolithically ugly statuary was lit in strobing red flares.

Jesse scuttled backward, around the monument, and swept up the other side. Both of his Hyper-velocity pistols were out and scenting for targets. They were not disappointed.

A surging mob of figures shuffled around in the dark where Robert had been hiding. Occasional blaster shots cracked out of the group in all directions. Some sailed harmlessly up in ruler-straight courses toward the lowering clouds. Others slapped into stone structures near at hand, sending ruby sparks flashing into the sky. Each illuminated the courtyard and the surrounding mausoleums in crimson-edged flares. The Union soldiers shouldered through the scene with jerky, stop-start movements as they searched for Robert. He was nowhere to be seen.

Jesse prepared to jump up on the first tier of the ugly monument to rain fire down upon the Yanks when a howled warning rang out from his left. He looked just in time to see Robert Ford, blaster streaming crimson flame, throw himself off the roof of a low tomb into the fringe of the crowded soldiers. The bolts struck several of the blue-uniformed men, throwing them into their brothers where they swayed limply, unable to fall in death due to the close-packed bodies. A wavering pistol, its owner's head missing from the nose up, dropped away from its bead on Jesse's back.

Jesse wasted no time running back behind the big monument. Bolts flashed in among the statues, sending sparks, rock chips, and dust billowing out. The outlaw came around the other side, both pistols up and ready, and his robotic arms, shrouded in unfamiliar sleeves, began to whir and scream. The Hyper-velocity pistols spun up and began to fling a glowing double stream of red death into the close-packed Union soldiers. The bolts tore through the men's torsos. They tore arms off in sprays of gore. They splashed heads away into the crowd. Less than a third of the soldiers were killed by the attack, but the rest panicked, the scent of death and the tacky feeling of their comrades' blood warm on their faces. They ran, streaming through the narrow gaps in monuments and mausoleums, and soon Jesse was the only man standing.

Robert jumped down from his perch. He rose, wiping a splash of blood from his face, and grinned with wild-eyed abandon at his boss.

"Damn, Jesse!" He screamed, his ears still ringing from the concussive blasts. "Damn!"

Jesse grinned back at him and then nodded in the direction of the fleeing Union men. "They're gonna come back!" He shouted, knowing Robert would be hard of hearing after the terrific detonations, as well. "We gotta get goin' while the gettin's good!"

A voice rang out through the night. Jesse thought it was the same voice that had hailed them from the gate, but the echoes made it impossible to be sure. The words were unclear, but the panic seemed to subside, the shouts and screams from the retreating blue-bellies tapered off, and a cold tightness twisted in the outlaw's stomach.

"They're comin' back 'round." Jesse gestured with one pistol in the direction the enemy had run. "They ain't gonna all come back that way, neither. They'll surround us again, cut us off from the gate, an' make an end."

Robert nodded, his face set in a grim frown. "Gotcha, Jesse." He cast an overly-casual glance into the darkness. "Where you think Marcus got off to?"

Jesse shrugged, moving a little to place his back against a tall monument of smooth, polished marble. "The way he run off? He's probl'y still runnin' that witch down."

Robert gave a shudder. "I don't much like his chances, Jesse, if he catches her."

The outlaw boss gave the younger man a look and then patted him on the shoulder with a metal fist still wrapped around a pistol. "I wouldn't worry none 'bout Marcus,

Robert." He pointed the pistol out into the now-silent cemetery. "You worry about these poor northern boys, ain't gonna see their mommas no more cuz they picked the wrong fight."

Robert smiled, nodded, and then squatted down beside Jesse. The outlaw stared out into the darkness. Robert had doused his lamp before the Union soldiers had come upon them, so the only illumination was the softly gleaming moss draping some of the oldest tombs, and the eerie crimson glow of the outlaw chief's powered arms. Jesse opened his eyes wide, trying to concentrate on his peripheral vision, sharper in the gloom than staring straight ahead. He was stock-still, tensed to catch any sound or hint of movement in the swimming darkness.

A sound that could have been the scrape of a boot off to the left had Jesse's head jerking that way. But a flash of light that might have been silver-sharp edged steel, glimpsed out of the corner of his right eye, sent him swinging his gaze back in the other direction. Both times, he saw nothing.

"Jesse, I don't know how much longer I can do this." Robert's voice shook with suppressed tension, and the outlaw chief knew just how he felt. Waiting was always the worst part. Once the guns started blasting, there was almost nothing he liked better. He could dance through the sprays of fire and death with seeming-impunity. He never feared for his safety, least of all in the heat of a firefight. But crouching down like this, waiting for the Union to come down on him? That was no fit way for a man to pass his time.

Jesse was standing tall before he even realized he had moved. If he was going to meet his fate, he was not about to meet it on his haunches. Whether it was the sudden appearance of the standing outlaw, or just luck, two Union soldiers appeared right on their left flank, their blasters rising.

"Robert!" Jesse's guns came up at the same time he heard the other outlaw shout in his ear.

"Jesse!" The voice was steady but harsh with surprise. There was no fear at all.

Union troopers had come up on either side of their marble shelter as the rest of their force pushed deeper into the cemetery. Jesse saw the pair coming up on their left, and in a moment of grim anger, slapped his two pistols together, flicking the thumb switches to free the power cells. The vapors of the ruddy brew lashed out, tangling together and binding the two weapons together with a bridge that quickly began to glow an intense crimson. When Jesse pulled the triggers in unison, a blast was unleashed that was so hot, it melted the torso of the man on his right, sending his arms flipping backward, his legs flopping onto the flags, and his head, eyes wide in horrified surprise, tumbling backward into the super-heated backwash. The man's companion flew sideways, hair and clothing ablaze, his mouth wrenched wide in a gasp of pain and surprise.

At the same time, hunkered down beside Jesse, Robert Ford unleashed a fusillade of shots in a steady two-handed grip. The bolts slapped into the chests of the two soldiers coming around from that side, knocking them back into the flagstones, dead before they struck the ground.

The outlaws took a moment to glance at the other's handiwork, nodded, and then began to move side-by-side toward the edge of the cemetery and the small gate. The tombs all around them blocked any view of the remaining soldiers. Both men felt like hunted animals as they eased their way toward escape.

The Union officer, clearly tiring of the cat and mouse game, sent four groups of his men toward the fugitives from four different directions. Jesse was the first to sense their danger as a dark shadow leapt overhead from one crypt to the next. He spun, his duster flaring out, and sent a stream of ruby blasts sleeting up into the sky. The bolts intercepted first one shadow and then another in mid-leap, igniting their uniforms, shattering their bodies, and tossing them down onto the crushed stone of the walkway.

Robert turned at the sound of gunfire, catching sight of two men approaching down a tight alley between two basalt structures, underlit by Jesse's pistol fire. Robert saw their eyes go wide as he registered their presence. Both men, rifles already raised into firing positions, shattered the night with the thunder of their shots. Solid bars of hellish energy flashed out, cracking the stone of the tomb Robert crouched beside. He ducked, shying away from the blast of dust and rock chips, and then placed two carefully-aimed shots back down the alley, taking each man neatly in the head. Their decapitated bodies continued to move forward in an eerie parody of a run until they slumped gracelessly to the ground.

Two more soldiers came pounding down their back trail. Jesse heard the crunching of boots on gravel and continued his spin, sliding down and firing beneath Robert's outstretched arms. Each Hyper-velocity pistol centered in on the chest of a different target, and when Jesse pulled the triggers, both men were stopped as if they had hit a brick wall. They looked like insects pinned in place with massive ruby spikes, then the ravening energy ate through their torsos and blasted out their backs, sending vivid crimson streaks off into the shadows. The tombs all around leapt and shivered in the shattering, irregular light.

The two soldiers fell backward, their hollowed bodies slapping into the gravel. Silence filled the cemetery again, and Jesse and Robert stood up, looking all around for the next threat. Robert had a long scratch down one side of his face where a sharp chip of stone had caught him during the last attack. They were both covered in dust, but otherwise seemed unharmed. Jesse's grin returned full-force, and he shrugged impishly at his young friend. "Ain't so tough, are they."

The remaining soldiers, taking advantage of the momentary lull, rushed the two outlaws from up and down the little street at the same time. Blaster rifles were raised as bludgeoning weapons in the heaving crowd; pistols cracked and spat crimson bolts more to keep the prey's head down than in the hope of doing serious damage in the chaos. Jesse's eyes widened as he watched the wall of blue uniforms storm over their fallen comrades toward him. Behind him, he could hear the other contingent. Robert uttered a single, stark blasphemy under his breath in response. There was no more time for thought.

The world resolved itself into a flaring nightmare sequence of images, targets, and puzzles. The heavy butt of a blaster rifle came sailing in from overhead, a snarling pale face behind it. Jesse could not swing his pistol up in time to shoot, so he simply jammed the entire weapon into the enraged mouth, pulling the trigger several times after it stove in the man's teeth. A knife flashed in from the side and glanced off his left arm, slashing up his sleeve and lodging in the workings of his elbow. Jesse reached across the lowered arm with his right, pressed the smoking muzzle of his pistol up against the man's chest where it sizzled against the sweat-soaked uniform, and pulled the trigger, blasting the man's heart out his back. The fat now sizzling across the barrel's vents might cause him trouble in the next few minutes, but no more trouble than that coot's knife would have caused in the here and now.

Behind Jesse, Robert had drawn a knife in one hand and flipped his depleted pistol over, catching it by the steaming barrel in one gloved hand. He was brandishing the weapon like a blunt tomahawk. He crushed the jaw of the first man to reach him, and then reached out and slashed his knife across the next man's face. The soldier fell back into the surging crowd, his agonized screams and flailing arms causing more disarray to the formation than a collapsing body. Bringing the knife back into a guard position, Robert immediately punched it out again, stabbing another soldier through the neck. Hot blood geysered out over the melee as the gurgling victim slumped against a cold stone tomb and sank into a limp pile at the base of the wall.

Jesse tried to bring his left arm up and across to shoot at another soldier closing in on him, but the limb was too slow, the metal finger spasming against the trigger and sending several ill-timed shots low into the threatening mob. Legs and kneecaps burst and shattered under the impact. The fight was knocked out of the men before him, but he cursed under his breath at the messy manner in which it had happened.

Robert's fight was going extremely well, a low rampart of bodies forming at his feet, when a heavy knife, nearly an Arkansas toothpick, was thrown from the back ranks. It flashed between the bobbing heads of his assailants and took him in the shoulder. It was not a clean hit, glancing off the armored shoulder pad sewn into his duster. The heavy blade bit as it past, sending a jolt of icy fire down his arm, tingling into the hand, and then burning back up again.

Jesse stepped back when he heard Robert's cry. His boot heel crunched down on a limp hand and he almost lost his footing. He cast a quick look over his shoulder, steadied himself, and then started to turn, reaching out with his one good arm.

If the Union soldier had been able to make his charge without screaming in triumph, Jesse may well have died there in that cemetery. But the man was overcome with anticipation of his own victory. Or perhaps his rage had gotten the better of him. Afterward, as he tried to reconstruct the events in his mind, Jesse was unable to shake the feeling that the man's eyes had flared a worryingly familiar shade of red before he had died.

The man wielded a cavalry saber with an RJ charging cell built into the hilt. Jesse had seen weapons like that before, but they were rare in the lower ranks. The blade was long, its metal infused with the shifting, smoky energy of Carpathian's Devil's Blood. It was cocked back, already slicing through the air toward his neck, ready to take his head. The face behind the blade was beyond madness, and its inhuman shriek echoed off the stone tombs around them.

Jesse ducked down. He reached out to steady himself with his left hand, only to have the arm buckle beneath his weight. He curled his body as he fell, losing his bead on his attacker. He hit hard, sooner than expected, and barely got his right arm up in time to block the descending blade.

Fat red sparks spat out into the night, bouncing off bodies, tombs, and the struggling combatants. The smell of hot metal shot through the air as the burning weapon scorched away the sleeve and ground against the mechanical limb beneath. The soldier leaned into his cut, trying to force the powered blade right through the arm and into the body behind. The madness faded from his eyes for just a moment and the soldier sneered, "Henderson sends his regards."

Jesse started at the name, then pushed his left arm up beneath the right. The limb responded slowly, and he was only able to pump two shots into the man's foot. The soldier's scream became a shriek as he fell over backward, the blade wrenching free.

Jesse surged to his feet, fear and anger tangling in his mind. He put three more bolts into the shrieking man, his mouth twisted in furious vindication, when he took a glancing blow to the back of his head that drove him back down to his knees.

Robert had been fending off the larger contingent of Union soldiers. However, he was being ground down by the sheer force of their numbers. Each man he killed was closer than the last, and a series of blows and kicks had been landed, each taking its toll. Dizzy with fatigue, each kill wore him down. The last soldier surged toward him, skittering over the smoking bodies of his comrades. If the man had meant to kill him, Robert Ford would have been dead. Instead, the soldier had seen Jesse James, sleeves torn, guns blazing, rising from the shadows over Robert's shoulder, and he had changed his target. He rushed past the stunned outlaw, blaster rifle raised, and had brought the weapon down in what should have been a crushing blow. But his ankle came down on the cold limb of a dead comrade, twisting and spoiling his aim. The solid wood of the weapon, when it struck, still came down with terrific force. It glanced across the side of the outlaw chief's head, sending him down into the gravel.

Robert was horrified as the man ran past, spinning to follow the movements, bringing up his pistol. It was reloaded and back in a proper grip again, and he stabbed the barrel at the soldier's back as he pulled the trigger. The bolts struck the man low, then walked up his spine and took off his head in a fountain of gory steam. The body collapsed, life's blood pumping from the smoking wreckage.

A silence settled over the cemetery, mocking the solemn tombs and their eternal guardians with mortal finality. Blue uniformed bodies, many mangled by close-quarters violence, were strewn about the narrow street. Blood was splashed across many of the surrounding crypts. Robert collapsed beside his boss. Jesse slid down against a crypt, gasping for breath and covered in blood.

"Damn!" He coughed, spitting blood into the pile of bodies that surrounded him. "Damn!"

Robert smiled through the grit and the bloody slime coating his own face. "Hot damn, Jesse! I thought, when that damned blue-belly rushed past me, you was a goner fer sure!"

"Damn!" Jesse glared around, wild eyed, at the scene around them. There was no way he could get a quick count of the bodies, but it sure looked like they had accounted for the remainder of the platoon. "We gotta get out'a here, Robert." Jesse shook his head, trying to clear it of the ringing and the glaring spots that haunted his vision. He looked up at the younger man and started again. "We both need a sawbones somethin' wicked."

Robert nodded, looking around as he helped Jesse to his feet. "I wish I knew where that damned Marcus went off to."

"Don't worry about him now, Robert." Jesse was standing on his own two feet, barely, but he was looking down at his arms. A steady flow of black fluid with glowing crimson rivulets within it was leaking down his forearms. The left arm was shaking slightly as if in the grips of a palsy. "We really need to get out o' here."

"Well, I hope he caught the damned witch, after this. She coulda warned us." Robert reached out and eased Jesse out of the pile of bodies and separated limbs. He was in little better shape himself. As they dragged themselves down the crunching gravel, a passerby would have been hard-pressed to say who was supporting whom.

The twin columns of the gate swam out of the darkness and Robert put on a surge of energy.

"Well, what have we here?"

The voice was cold. It chilled them to the bone, coming as it did from directly behind. Robert stopped in his tracks, Jesse swaying slightly at his side. Neither looked at the other, neither turned. Both stared out into the emptiness of Basin Street.

The outlaw chief did not turn around. "Some might say lettin' me go tonight'd be the smartest thing a man mighta done in his life." Keeping his voice even took all the energy that remained in his battered body.

A gust of nerve-tinged laughter echoed off the stone. When the man behind them spoke again, his tone was dripping with self-congratulation. "Reward notices have been pretty clear, James. Alive or dead. I reckon I'll be paying for my next big promotion with your head, hayseed."

There was no prearranged signal. They did not speak, sign, or make eye contact. They simply moved.

Jesse spun to his left, away from Robert, spinning to the right. Both men brought up their pistols. Neither of them had holstered their weapons.

A tall Union officer, a lieutenant by the gold bars on his epaulets, stood before them, an enormous blaster pistol in one hand and another glowing, smoking sword in the other. But as the two men before him turned in place, the cruel, gloating look slid into confusion, then concern, then fear. He brought his pistol up, but by then it was too late.

Each of the outlaws fired a single bolt. Both shots took the man in the center of his chest, blowing him back into the shadows. His spasming nerves caused his pistol to flare off once, sending a dart of crimson light flashing off into the tombs. Then he was still.

"That's a Yankee for ya." Jesse muttered, his breath coming in shallow gasps as he looked down at his arm. Even with the damage that had thrown off his earlier shots, both his mechanical limbs seemed to be operating smoother with each step he took down his new, chosen path. He turned back to take Robert's proffered arm. "Never know when they've won."

Robert murmured agreement, and the two men limped out of the cemetery, across the empty street, and back toward the French Quarter. Behind them settled over thirty dead bodies for someone else to answer for.

Robert remembered that Loveless had been sent to the waterfront, and so he made his way in that direction. His head was swimming, and he could barely marshal the focus to put one foot in front of the other, dragging Jesse along behind him. He knew he would never be able to find the damn whorehouse on his own. Jesse was barely conscious and would have been no help at all.

The streets were nearly deserted around the old cemetery, but the deeper the men moved into the French Quarter, the more folks they met, strolling along in their finery, taking the night air, or carousing from one hotel or café to the next. Eventually, several of the men, usually at the instigation of their fair companions, asked if they could be of any assistance. Robert just grunted at them, shook his head, and kept moving toward the river, his eyes fixed on the spires of the large cathedral in the distance.

Each step was torture. Robert started to wonder if he was going to reach the waterfront without help after all. Jesse was nearly unconscious, and the younger man's arm was going numb from supporting the steadily-growing weight. The glowing street lamps beckoned him on, and the cathedral grew larger in imperceptible stages, and he was soon too tired to acknowledge or care about the looks they were getting as they moved down the delicate, gilded avenue.

*****

Lucinda glanced nervously behind her, even though she knew no one had followed from the whorehouse. Her lip twitched at that. This city seemed so sophisticated on so many levels, and yet they avoided certain honest terms as if they were tainted by the touch of the devil himself. She shook her head, dusted her fingers with a delicate sweep of a linen napkin, and moved on down the thoroughfare of the waterfront. Saint Louis Cathedral loomed up behind her, dominating Jackson Square and giving ironic counterpoint to her last thought. Her mind was troubled, and could only dawdle on such trivial curiosities for so long before she found it curving back around to her chief concern.

From the moment the city had slid into view, Lucinda knew her little idyll with the outlaws was coming to an end. There had been a certain drape to the Union flag hanging from the guard station at the port. There were slight alterations in the order of the unit citations flown from the platoon guidons that marched through the city. There were even certain signs along the dock itself that screamed for urgent action . . . if a person knew the codes.

Something important was occurring, and the president was recalling all Pinkerton Agents. She knew she was being ordered to report to the new depot in Kansas City. Not her personally, of course, but every agent currently acting independent of central command. Something big was brewing out there somewhere.

Lucy knew Jesse's plans for the Confederacy would have easily justified such a drastic, universal response, had they been known. But she had not reported those plans. In fact, she was far from certain she would be reporting those plans. After everything that had happened at Fort Lincoln, her once-steadfast loyalties had been severely torn. She felt no certainty at all as to where her allegiance would fall when the dust settled.

As she saw the coded signs, she knew she was not yet ready to make that final decision, one way or the other. She would not high-tail it back to Kansas City just now, abandoning Jesse to his fate and returning to the indomitable will of the Union. Likewise, she was not ready to turn her back on the nation that had taken in her in, given her purpose, and sheltered her for all her adult life.

There were contingency procedures for field agents in the middle of sensitive operations when a recall order went out. When everyone had left the Hotel Ses Beaux Yeux on Quantrill's mysterious quest, she had taken a circuitous route to the waterfront, using all of her tradecraft to ensure she was not being followed. She had taken a small back table in the Café du Monde, ordered herself a plate of beignets and a thick café au lait, and had tried to enjoy the little pastries while carefully composing her response to the men who believed they pulled her strings.

The pastries were as delicious as she remembered, and the message as difficult to write as she had feared. She wrote of Jesse's plans in the broadest possible terms. She was vague where she could be, specific where she felt she had to be, and yet still knew she would be betraying Jesse by sending anything to her superiors.

She folded the brief note, putting it within a small pocket sewn into her sleeve, and then sat quietly, staring into the swirling colors of her coffee. She took the paper out, smoothed it down on the table, careful to avoid the powdered sugar, and read it again. Every word was a betrayal. But to ignore the coded signs and send nothing would have been a betrayal as well. She re-folded the note, returned it to its place, and left the café to walk the waterfront.

And so she found herself pacing the area around Jackson Square, making sure none of her current companions had wandered into her personal tragedy. When a command platoon marched into the square, she hurried toward them. Their guidon flapped limply on its staff, and by the order of the citations hanging beneath, she knew their commander would be able to see her report on its way. She skip-stepped, drawing up her skirts so she could move a little quicker, and made as if to trip just as the young-looking lieutenant, marching along beside his charges, came even with her.

Lucinda cast her arms wide as she fell, and the man's natural reaction to reach out to help her brought them into rough contact. She smiled apologetically up at him and muttered, "These Parisian heels . . ." She thought she heard a voice from around the cathedral call out her name.

At the code phrase the lieutenant's vaguely-concerned face sharpened and he replied, "They do seem high this season." But suspicion almost immediately descended as Lucinda, distracted by the call of her name, failed to give the correct final response. She was, in fact, whipping her eyes back and forth, trying not to look suspicious. She knew she had to complete the ritual.

"They're taller every season." She gave the boy a quick smile, palmed the note into his hand, and then pushed off, a look of indignant fury rising on her face. "How dare you, sir!" She shouted the question in a thick Creole accent, and at once the people wandering the waterfront, a substantial crowd even at that late hour, started to mutter, casting dark looks toward the Union soldiers.

A hard edge settled just behind the young officer's apologetic mask as he tipped his hat to her in a shallow bow. "My apologies, ma'am." He muttered, and then shouted for his men to carry on.

Lucinda watched the unit march away, furtively watching the waterfront crowd. The soldiers were not very far at all when a figure staggered out of the shadows beside the cathedral, moving toward her.

Robert's eyes twitched uneasily between Lucinda and the Union column and back again, and she cursed whatever coincidence had brought him into Jackson Square at that moment. She pushed that down and assumed one of her more attractive expressions, intending to stun him with a frontal assault and then demand how he had come to such a bloody state, and—

"Where's Jesse?" An edge of panic entered her voice as she asked the question before even realizing she had lost her focus.

Robert cast one last look at the Union column, then turned back to her. There was an undeniable suspicion in his eyes, but suddenly she did not care. She grabbed him by his lapels and gave him a single, sharp, jolt.

"Where's Jesse?" She repeated, staring into his eyes.

Robert shook himself, his eyes softening slightly. He jerked his head back in the direction he had come. "I sat him in a café back that way. I'm hopin' no one notices. He ain't much awake—"

"What?" Lucinda was moving in the indicated direction before Robert could even respond. He hurried after her, limping from his injuries.

"Hey!" He called. "What was all that with the blue-bellies?"

She stopped. She knew she needed to address it here, or it would fester in Robert's mind and cause untold trouble later on. She turned around, putting on a pretty but exasperated look, and shrugged. "That oaf of an officer tripped into me, and then had the nerve to proposition me in the middle of the public square!"

He looked into her face for a moment, suspicion struggling with fatigue, concern for Jesse, and the undeniable impact of her beauty. When he spoke, his voice was soft and vague, still floating between distrust and reserve. "Oh . . ." He started to soften. "The chiseling bastards."

She hid her relief, nodded, and asked in a slow, measured voice. "Now, Robert, please tell me where Jesse is and what happened?"

He shook his head. "Sorry. We got in a shindy with some blue-bellies. Didn't mean to, but they jumped us in a cemetery. And we lost Marcus. And there was this witch woman." Once he had started to talk, it flooded out of him. "Jesse and I, all on our lonesome, took on the whole platoon. We won, o'course, but we got beat up pretty bad. Jesse's real bad, but he'll be fine." Now Robert's face turned red and he dropped his gaze. "Truth to tell, Miss Lucinda, I knew I couldn't find that cathouse without you. I knew you was headin' to the riverfront, so's I thought I'd look for you here."

"Well, you did good, Robert." She patted his shoulder, noting with further relief the reaction that caused. "Now, we have to get you both back to the hotel. Do either of you need a doctor?"

He shrugged, suddenly bashful. "I don't think a sawbones would hurt, miss." She always found it oddly disconcerting when hardened killers like Robert Ford could be so easily manipulated by her most basic ploys.

She nodded again. "Alright, we'll have the madam send for one as soon as we get back to the hotel." She started to move back down the street, gesturing behind her for him to follow.

Robert did follow, but his eyes were fixated upon her as she moved away down the street. There was undeniably a stunned appreciation in his eyes. But there was also just a touch of unrelieved suspicion.

It sure had looked like Lucinda had been the one who tripped . . .

Chapter 11

As they entered the salon of the Hotel Ses Beaux Yeux, Madamoiselle Reneu rushed out from behind her small table and met them in the middle of the room.

"Get him to the back at once!" The woman's voice was brusque. She spun and preceded them across the carpeted floor, holding the beaded curtain open for them. "Mon Dieu! When will I ever learn that no good deed goes unpunished?"

Jesse was nearly unconscious, supported between Lucinda and a battered Robert Ford. In the soft light of the brothel's common room, their injuries appeared much worse.

There were cuts, scratches, and bruises over every exposed surface. The fluids leaking from Jesse's mechanical arms had slowed to a trickle, but his duster was spattered with the black and crimson mess.

The salon was almost empty as they staggered through. Most of the girls were either working or had turned in for the night. However, a few night-owls were still lounging among the pillows and elaborate old furniture. They leapt up as they saw the condition of the newcomers. One offered to help, but the others just watched with mild curiosity. Madamoiselle Reneu ushered them all back to their places with a graceful flip of her hand.

As the trio moved past the madam and deeper into the house, she muttered to them. "Your guests are with Colonel Quantrill in your suite. Please keep things civil. I don't want any trouble."

Lucinda cast a confused glance at the madam, but the woman was already turning away, shooing her girls back to their places. Guests? She did not like the sound of that. Jesse was the only one here who really knew or trusted Quantrill. She was not at all sure she wanted to have to deal with the man herself.

The agent paused in the hallway. Could she turn around? Maybe find a cheap hotel on the outskirts of town, bring in a local doctor, and contact Quantrill after the boys were seen to? She looked down at the limp metal arm she held. Her dress was ruined with black and red stains. Jesse's face was pale beneath the dust and the blood. A local sawbones might be able to deal with the scratches and the bruising, but they would never be able to address Jesse's damaged arms. She shrugged. Quantrill would not be able to do much either, but given his own replacement limb, he would know better than she. Besides, she realized, how would she know who to trust, trying to find a doctor in this city? She cursed under her breath. Things were getting out of hand.

Lucinda guided the stunned men through the maze of textured wallpaper and dim light until they came to the short flight of stairs. Robert nearly tumbled over the edge. She had to reach across Jesse's bowed shoulders, grabbing the man and jerking him back to awareness by his collar.

"Uh . . . Sorry." Robert muttered, looking down at the stairs and then across at her. "Thanks."

She nodded. "Do you think you can help with the stairs? Or should I go fetch the colonel?"

Robert shook his head. "No, no. I can do it. Let me just . . ." He readjusted his grip on Jesse's arm and took a first, tentative step down the stairs. It took longer than it should have, but Jesse was safely at the bottom soon enough. The noise they had made, however, had aroused suspicion, and as they began the short trek down the hallway, the door to their suite opened and Quantrill's head appeared from around the door frame.

The old officer took one look at Jesse and Robert and then turned to put his heavy cane down. He rushed out to help, his limp pronounced. "Good God, what happened?" He swept in between Robert and Jesse and tried to support both of them at the same time.

Lucinda shook her head, her voice labored. "Robert said something about a Union patrol, but I didn't get much more out of him." She jerked her head at the outlaw boss. "Jesse had even less to say."

Quantrill guided them toward the door. After a bit of shuffling, they eased into the common room. Lucinda was focused on getting Jesse to one of the overstuffed chairs when she realized that the chamber felt far more crowded than it should have.

Charlie Ford rushed forward with a start. "Robert?" He took his brother from Quantrill and eased him into a chair. "Damn, what happened?"

Quantrill helped Lucinda set Jesse down in another chair as she looked up at the strangers before her. She fought hard not to go for one of her replacement blasters.

They were such a strange group, her mind did not know where to focus first. There was a man seated comfortably in one of the more formal chairs. He was dressed in the fashion of a local swell, his cream-colored suit offset by the deep burgundy of his cravat. The texturing of his rich waistcoat was a warm contrast to the light jacket. On one knee rested a pristine hat that matched the rest of the outfit. He smiled warmly at her as he gracefully rose to his feet with a nod.

In a chair near the man was seated an elegant woman whose café au lait complexion hinted at a mixed heritage that would have been a curse almost anywhere else on the continent. She was wearing an ornate white dress and sat like a queen ready to receive visitors. Her expression was painfully aloof.

In stark contrast to these sophisticated figures, however, were the dark-skinned, hulking brutes standing near the wall. Their black clothing was rough but serviceable. Their faces were decorated with elaborate skull masks painted right onto their flesh. A vaguely unpleasant smell lingered about the room, and Lucinda wrinkled her delicate nose. The smell triggered something in the back of her mind, and she looked more closely at their faces. She was not surprised when she realized that their eyes were cloudy and blank. Dead eyes.

Finishing up the tableau before her, Marcus Cunningham sat in a straight-backed cane chair against the wall between the two hulking animations. His eyes were open, but without expression. He sat loosely in the chair and took no notice of anything going on around him.

Lucinda stood up, one hand resting near her hidden pistol, and turned toward Quantrill. "It's not like you to be so remiss in your manners, colonel." She gracefully nodded her head toward the strangers, a wide, winsome smile professionally applied. "Are you not going to introduce us all?" Her eye flickered over to Marcus as well. Whatever was going on here, it could not be good.

Quantrill knelt down beside Jesse's chair, checking the outlaw's face and eyes. "Well, of course, miss. Sorry. I just thought maybe we'd like to see our boys looked after first?"

Lucinda smiled. She tried to mitigate her tone, but with only partial success. "They'll be fine for a few more minutes, colonel. They made it this far."

Quantrill stared at her for a moment, then looked back at the newcomers and shrugged. "Of course."

The old officer stood with a grunt of effort and indicated the gentleman with the hat. "Miss Loveless, may I introduce the inestimable Colonel Alexander F. Warley."

The man took her hand before she could avoid him. He brushed his lips quickly across her knuckles and then released the hand. "Please, miss, call me Alex, if you will do me the honor." His eyes wrinkled along lines familiar with an easy smile. "And if I may take the onerous duty from my old friend's hands?" He looked a question at Quantrill, who shrugged and leaned back down to Jesse.

"Miss Loveless, I have the unalloyed pleasure and honor of introducing you to one of the most eminent personages of our entire city." He held out one hand and the woman in the white dress nodded regally and stood in one fluid motion, taking the proffered hand. "This is the lovely Marie Laveau; a physician and student of the sciences, both natural and . . . otherwise. She has already made the acquaintance of the messieurs James and Ford." He indicated the wounded men with a tip of his head.

The woman nodded, taking Lucinda's hand in her own. "It is truly a pleasure to meet you at last, Miss Loveless." Her accent was refined, with just a hint of the bayou to give it spice. Her eyes bore directly into the agent's, and Lucinda was suddenly very concerned that Robert Ford might not be the most serious threat to her cover in this room.

"Well, it is a pleasure to meet you as well, Madam Laveau." Lucinda kept her voice even.

"Madamoiselle, actually." The woman smiled warmly, but the warmth never reached her eyes. "Now, let us look to these stalwart heroes, shall we?"

Marie Laveau joined Quantrill beside Jesse, reaching out gently to poke and prod his face and neck, noting the outlaw boss's sluggish reactions. She pushed his eyelids up to look at the unresponsive dark orbs behind, and then stood. "If you will please, I will have my gad palè take Mr. James into one of the side rooms?"

"Hey, what about my brother?" Charlie was indignant as he stood up from Robert's side.

Marie Laveau turned smoothly to regard the other wounded outlaw and then nodded. "He will be fine. Water with a little wine, I think. And clean his wounds." She turned away dismissively and Charlie was left sputtering behind her.

The giant animations moved forward, although the strange woman had not said anything. As they moved past Lucinda to ease Jesse from his chair, she could see the metal mechanisms on the backs of their heads that housed small, delicate-looking RJ cylinders. She could also just make out, beneath their clothing, the support frameworks that Carpathian seldom bothered to hide beneath his own creations' clothes.

She watched the animations take Jesse into one of the bedrooms, Marie Laveau following with a bag she had picked up from beside her chair. When they were gone, she turned back to Quantrill. "Well, I think you might owe us some words."

Quantrill eased himself into a chair and peered up at her. "What words might you be lookin' for, sweet thing?"

Lucinda breathed deeply through flaring nostrils. She sauntered across the room, putting a little extra effort into the sway of her hips, and grinned to herself as she noted the effect it had on both of the old Confederate war dogs. She settled herself into a settee a little apart from the central group and smiled.

"Well, colonel, while we're waiting to hear from the next room, why don't you tell me what's wrong with Marcus?" Her tone was light but her eyes were cold and lethal.

"I might be able to shed some light on that, Miss." Warley raised a finger. "The way I understand it, there was a little . . . misunderstanding, over in old Saint Louise Cemetery Number One. The big man in the hood became distraught, and Madamoiselle Laveau gave him a little something to calm his nerves. Sadly, after being separated, it appears that Mister James and his compatriot were attacked by the Union patrol."

Lucinda turned in her chair, one arm resting against its back, and regarded the slack-faced Marcus. "He looks somewhat more than calmed."

Warley frowned. "As I hear tell, he was extremely distraught."

"Bullshite." The word snapped across the room and they all looked to where Charlie was administering to his brother with water from a shallow porcelain bowl. Robert's eyes were on fire as he glared at the man in the fancy suit. "She had words with Marcus, riled 'im all up, an' then laughed at 'im. He chased off after her at the same time those blue-bellies came rushin' in." He turned back to Lucinda, concern plain on his face. "That woman ain't natural, miss. She knows Carpathian, an' she's done somethin' with Marcus. An' now she's in there alone, with her two monsters, with Jesse." He was struggling to rise, but Charlie pushed him back into the chair.

"O'course she knows Doctor Carpathian." Quantrill muttered. "I told you that already, you silly corn-cracker. And I couldn't help but notice that his arms are all messed up too." The old officer sneered at Robert. "Who you think can fix those, if you don't want to travel all the way back to the Contested Territories?"

"Will Marcus be alright?" Lucinda felt a growing urge to rise and burst into the bedroom, to defend Jesse from God knew what. She forced herself into an unnatural stillness instead.

Warley nodded, one hand flipping up nonchalantly. "I have to assume so." He turned in his own seat, saving his hat from tipping onto the floor at the last minute. "He's a big strong galoot. I'm sure he's going to be fine."

Lucinda turned back to the room and looked first at Quantrill, then at Warley.

She watched Charlie clean up his brother's face, Robert trying to push him weakly away, then turned back to the man in the white suit. "So, you're the man we've come to see. You dress pretty enough, at least." There was just a touch of acid in her voice, and she shot him a smile that artfully combined poison and allure in equal measure.

Her tone did not register with him at all, and from the smile he returned to her, he was either overcome with the allure or ignoring the poison. She suspected the latter. "I believe I am, Miss."

Lucinda nodded. "And you can help Jesse with this big plan of his?"

"Well, now, I'm not sure I can commit myself to anything just yet." He smiled broadly and continued. "But, I must admit I'm intrigued."

"So," the agent forced herself to sit back and give every evidence of relaxing. "What now?"

Quantrill leaned forward, his elbows on his knees. "We still need to get word to Frank and them. We can't move on without them knowin' where we're goin'."

Warley was arranging his hat on his knee, holding it in delicate fingers by the brim. He smiled. "My people can go fetch your boys, William. There isn't anywhere in the great bayou I can't reach."

"They ain't his boys, you flannel-mouth. They're Jesse James'." Robert spat. He was leaning around his brother to glare at Quantrill and Warley.

Quantrill grimaced and waved away the distinction. "They can't be left behind, is what I'm sayin'."

"And they won't be, is what I'm sayin'." Warley's voice was warm. "As soon as we head back to Belle Je, I'll send some of my best men out to fetch them."

"Bell what?" Robert snarled, Charlie trying to get him to settle back down.

"I have a small plantation buried in the bayou off to the east. Belle Je is my seat of power, if you will." He gestured at the closed door through which Jesse had disappeared. "If Mister James is willing to return with us to Belle Je, we can discuss his grand schemes and how they may be brought into line with my own."

Robert pushed his attentive brother aside and leaned forward. "We ain't interested in your schemes, chiseler. Jesse don't need—"

"If Jesse didn't need help, Robert, we'd never have come here in the first place." Lucinda tried to sound reasonable, but before she had finished speaking, the wounded outlaw was glaring at her as well.

Robert looked at Lucinda in a way he never had before. She thought back to the square, and the Union officer. How much had he seen? He spoke in a harsh tone. "We ain't goin' nowhere until Jesse—"

"We're goin'." The voice was weak but unmistakable. The door had opened, and Jesse was braced against the doorframe. Marie Laveau glided past him and moved to examine Marcus. Jesse was pale, with countless cuts and bruises marring his face and his bare chest. His left arm was caught up in a heavy sling tied behind his head, but his right arm seemed to be okay.

Lucinda began to surge to her feet but forced herself to stop. She settled back and turned slowly, her face schooled to calm detachment. "Nice to see you up and about." She kept her tone light.

He grinned at her, although the expression was a little strained. "Thanks. Same to you."

"We're what now?" Robert struggled to his feet, his brother offering unwanted support. "We're gonna rush off to this Zu-zu's fancy house just like that?"

Jesse nodded. "We need to get movin', Robert. If we stay here, we're just gonna keep runnin' into trouble, and we won't be movin' forward. We came here to talk to Colonel Warley, we're gonna talk to Colonel Warley."

"Besides," Marie Laveau stood up beside Marcus, her face still calm and superior.

"I cannot fully repair Msye James' arm here. I will need the facilities of a full smithy. Which they have, at Belle Je."

The colonel rose to his feet and placed his hat back on his chair. Moving around the furniture, he approached Jesse with his arm extended. "It will surely be a pleasure, Mr. James, to have you and your people as my guests."

Jesse's face darkened slightly. He looked over to where Marcus sat, still and immobile. "We'll see, colonel."

*****

BELLE JE was an hour's ride beyond the last buildings of New Orleans. They had made the journey in two powered wagons, both in Colonel Warley's white and burgundy colors. The final approach was a mile long causeway, the old trees reaching up into the darkness on all sides while cascades of pale green moss tumbled earthward from out of the shadows. The bayou lurked just outside the wagon lamps, the sounds of the creatures there a constant buzzing accentuated with occasional shrieks, hoots, and growls.

Jesse rested his head against the smooth glass of a side window and stared into the darkness. The pain of his injuries and the exhaustion of his running battle were still sharp, but he was already feeling better. Whatever that witch woman had done to him while he was out, it was having an effect. Beyond the wagon windows, ramshackle old buildings were just visible between the trees. Vines and grasses surrounded them, engulfing the rotten old shapes and dragging them back into the swamps. Jesse recognized slave quarters when he saw them, and he shook his head.

He had not spoken with Colonel Warley since Laveau had revived him. The old colonel rode with Quantrill, Mademoiselle Laveau, and her minions, in the lead wagon. Marcus, now sleeping comfortably, was with them. In the rear wagon, Lucy and Jesse sat facing the direction of travel while the Ford brothers slouched opposite them. Robert had been asleep since they had sat down, while Charlie was also staring out the windows at the passing view.

"They used to have slaves, anyway." Lucy kept her voice low to keep from waking Robert. She nodded out her own window. There were long, decaying buildings on that side as well.

"Every plantation used to have slaves, Lucy." He frowned. "These quarters haven't been used in a dog's age."

"Any slaves in his past might make this harder for you to do, Jesse." She stared into the darkness. She was exhausted. They all were. Charlie had caught a little sleep about an hour out of the French Quarter, and Jesse had been in and out of sleep for most of the trip, probably as a result of whatever the woman in the white dress had given him.

Above them, the driver of the wagon tapped twice on the roof and then leaned down to call through the window. "We're gettin' close, folks. You might want to start getherin' your things."

Charlie turned to the open window and muttered their thanks while Jesse and Lucy sat up straighter, looking around for anything they might have left behind. Robert grunted as he came awake, looking around blearily at the worn decorations of the wagon's interior.

"Oh, hell. It weren't a dream." He groaned and worked his arms back and forth to drive the stiffness away.

Ahead of them, oozing out of the darkness, an enormous, ancient building appeared. Its columned front porch shadowed the first floor, where many windows were glowing brightly, despite the hour. The upper floor was easier to see in the dim moonlight. Windows were lit there, as well. Elaborate woodwork and decorative dormers of the upper windows made the large house seem more like a palace than a home.

There were several figures standing in the shadows of the porch. As the two wagons pulled up around the long looping drive, they came forward. All were men. None of them were wearing uniforms, but they all had the bearing of experienced veterans. Long-barreled blaster pistols rode on their hips, but none of them seemed concerned about security as they moved to greet the lead wagon. Jesse's nerves rose slightly as he realized all the men gathered around Warley's wagon were white.

Jesse reached over and opened the door to their vehicle with his right arm. His muscles rebelled at the movement, twinging in pain. As Lucy, Charlie, and Robert got out behind him, they all moved toward Warley, Quantrill, and the strange woman in white. The colonel turned at their approach and smiled wanly.

"Your friend is still sleeping, and I'd recommend we leave him that way. Madamoiselle Laveau's . . . guards, can bring him into the house and see that he's placed in one of the rooms upstairs."

Jesse frowned but nodded. "Alright. How about the rest of us?"

Warley made a show of looking his guests over. "Well, you all look like you've had a rough night, and that's the truth. If you'd rather, we can leave off talking over business until you've all had the night to rest?"

Jesse felt his chest tighten and his shoulders sag at the thought of making his case without rest or time to prepare. Then his old grin returned. "Well, I'll tell you what, colonel. You throw down a half-decent spread, and I say we bull right on through!"

Warley's soldiers moved off into the house while Marie Laveau's minions carried a still-sleeping Marcus up the wide stairs with worryingly little effort. Jesse, Lucy, and the Fords followed Warley and his other guests into a tall-ceilinged dining room. A long, polished table dominated the chamber, with ornately-carved chairs flanking the table, each sporting a lush cushion of deep burgundy. High overhead, a glittering crystal chandelier lit the room with sparkling, ruby-tinged light.

Jesse noticed that Quantrill stayed with Warley and the witch-woman. He tried not to let it bother him.

A series of platters had been placed upon the table's snowy central runner. Jesse saw sliced meats, heaps of steaming vegetables, and a tureen of thick gravy. Glasses of sweet tea sat beside each plate. His mouth began to water and he moved for the table, not waiting for an invitation. He threw himself into a chair about halfway down and began to shovel food onto a fine china plate. Before the rest were even sitting, he was pushing food into his mouth with his hands, utensils ignored on the table.

"Well, at least I can assume the food is satisfactory?" Warley smiled warmly as he pulled a chair out for Marie Laveau and then sat down beside her, across from Jesse. The outlaw grinned around a mouthful of meat.

The rest of the party gathered food with a little more patience and grace, and soon they were all eating to the silent accompaniment of metal tapping on china and the clink of glass. Warley and Quantrill ate sparingly, clearly only partaking to be social. Lucy placed a single helping of vegetables on her own plate, but was moving it around with her fork rather than eating. Marie Laveau's was the only empty plate at the table, and she drank from a small silver flask she had produced from somewhere within her dress. The tall glass remained untouched.

As Jesse and his companions finished their food, Warley smiled across at them and then raised his glass. "Shall we make a toast before we begin? Bewilderment to the foe!" Everyone raised their glasses to the sentiment except for Mademoiselle Laveau, who tilted her head with an uncaring curl to her full lips.

"Amen to that, colonel. Although this is the first time I've ever made a toast with anything this soft." Jesse downed the rest of his tea. Without asking, he reached across the table and took the Voodoo Queen's.

"Indeed." Warley's smile slipped just slightly at the breach of etiquette, but he continued. "Now, Mr. James. Why don't you tell me about this grand design I have been hearing so much about?" The smile took on a slight edge. "It sounds quite ambitious, for a man so far from home."

Jesse scowled, wiped his mouth with one ragged sleeve, and pushed his plate away.

"Right." He put his metal hand on the table, arm outstretched, and looked back up at Warley. "How much you know about Lee and his plans for the Rebellion?"

Warley's face was impassive, his hands folded on the table before him, and he gave a miniscule shrug. "I know that he is the rightfully elected leader of the Confederacy. Is there more to know?"

Jesse paused, his eyebrows raising at this apparent show of support for the Confederate president. "Well . . . How much you know about how he plans on fightin' the Union?"

Warley shook his head. "Do we need to be fightin' the Union? It appears to me, they have too much on their plate now to worry about us. A perfect time to shore up our position, lay low, and watch what happens next."

Jesse slapped the table with his mechanical hand. "Exactly! That's EXACTLY what Lee said! But that's ignorin' the fact that it's also the PERFECT time to take the fight back to them!"

"So, you would have us, in our shattered and diminished state, leap once more into the fires of open war?" Warley's face was still blank, his voice calm. The words felt like stinging nettles to Jesse, and he wanted to shout at the man, to wake him up.

"Lee is still fightin' the old war. The world's changed! We're not fightin' for slavery, or state's rights, or any of that now. We're fightin' to defend ourselves from madmen, drunk on power, who want to crush us into the mud for no better reason now than they can!"

Quantrill smiled at Warley. "I told you the boy had fire. Could see that years ago durin' the war."

Warley did not return the smile. "The fact remains, however, that the south is a defeated nation. Has it ever occurred to you that President Lee might not still be fightin' the last war, but rather the only war he CAN fight, given our current situation?"

"That's hogwash, colonel, and you know it!" Jesse felt his anger rising, but he could not stop it. "Out in the territories, we've fought them almost to a standstill with stolen weapons an' clear heads. An' that's without numbers! If we had the numbers over them? They wouldn't be callin' those territories contested, now, they'd be callin' 'em Jesse James Country!"

That got a small smile out of the colonel. "Well, that might be true up in the deserts, but the Old States—"

"No!" Jesse slapped the table again, and this time his heavy hand left a cracked dent in the wood. Men ran in through several doors, but Warley held up a hand to stop them. The guards backed warily away, watching from a distance.

"Colonel, it has NOTHIN' to do with the terrain, or how far from their supplies they are out in the territories! The Union is surrounded by enemies! They're fightin' the Warrior Nation to the north, they've got Carpathian causin' problems off west, and they've got bands like mine wreakin' havoc all through the old western territories. To say nothin' of the Golden Army! The time is perfect, while they're distracted and off-balance, for the Confederate Rebellion to rise up an' push 'em back up north where they belong!"

"And yet," Warley's smile was gone again. "We keep comin' back to the same problem: with what do we fight? And with whom? We lost the cream of our fighting soldiery for a generation when that Devil's Blood swept through and changed the world forever. Our armies are diminished, defeated in spirit, and those that have not already joined Lee are unwilling to rise again."

"There are those who'd fight, if we gave them the chance." Jesse's face was hard, his eyes penetrating as he stared at Warley.

"Is there an army we may have overlooked, Mr. James?" The colonel's eyebrow rose in doubt.

Jesse's hand pressed against the table. "There is an entire nation, living within the borders of the Confederacy, that would fight beside us if we let them."

Warley's face was impassive, his eyes flat. And then a bit of warmth seeped in, and a slight tick erupted at the corner of his mouth. "You are, of course, referring to our former slaves?"

Jesse nodded, ignoring the possessive and waving the other word away with his hand. "That damned Emancipation Proclamation ended that, and you know it. The black folks have been kept down for decades since, on both sides of the border, but there ain't no one been keepin' slaves in all that time."

"And you think the word is what will make the difference?" Warley's eyebrow rose again, and Marie Laveau's face curled into an evil smile of her own. "You think, because they have not been called slaves, that they will rise up and join hands with us now, despite the way they have been treated?"

"No!" Jesse lowered his head, trying to organize his thoughts. "I mean—"

"Mr. James, the majority of black folks, through no fault of their own, lack any sort of training in the art of war." It was Warley, now, whose voice was intense. "Through no fault of their own, most lack education of any sophistication. They have been kept down, slavery or no, for longer than either of us would care to contemplate. And the fear with which many whites regard their black-skinned neighbors is inextricably entwined in that imbalance. Do you honestly believe that most of the white folks you know would agree to arm the colored folks? And furthermore, could you fault a man who had spent his entire life treated as an animal, for looking greedily at any chance he might have to redress that wrong, or generations of worse wrongs that had gone before?"

Jesse stared at Warley for so long the rest of the people in the room started to look toward each other, wondering what might be coming next. The colonel's speech summed up the fears that had been running around in his own head since the idea had first formed. He tried to remember the counter-arguments that Lucy, Frank, and the others had made to him in his moments of doubt.

With a shake of his head, Jesse changed his tack. "Colonel, do you think we're fightin' the same Union that held Fort Sumter all those years ago?"

The man in the white suit blinked at the change of course, his brow furrowed. "What do you mean?"

Jesse leaned forward, his good hand spread on the table. "The first three years of the war, if you can remember back that far, were brutal, weren't they?" He waited a moment for Warley to nod slowly, then continued. "Thousands upon thousands of men died on both sides, and there were some vicious acts of savagery by both north and south. Right?"

Warley sat back, his head shaking in denial. "Mr. James, I don't see how this—"

"There were, and you know it. I was even there for some of 'em." He sat up taller. "Now, do you remember Petersburg?"

The colonel nodded. "I sat out most of the war after New Orleans was taken, but I remember Petersburg."

"Both sides had set up for a major battle for the city. But the Union looked like it had lost its taste for savagery in favor of a long, drawn out siege. I remember. I was on the run down south with the colonel here." He gestured to Quantrill, who nodded, his face intense as he listened to Jesse put all of this together for the first time.

"And then somethin' happened to General Grant. He was up in Washington, and then we din't hear nothin' else for months." The outlaw chief's face looked gaunt by the light of the RJ lamps. "When he turned up at Petersburg, his head was wrapped in bandages, and he ordered the complete destruction of the city."

"He was tired of the war like everyone else." There was doubt in Warley's eyes now. "Except he had the power to end it, where no one else did."

"No." Jesse shook his head, his eyes never leaving the colonel's. "Somethin' happened to him. Everyone knows his entire family was killed, and he nearly died as well. And when he came back from that, he was a bloodthirsty madman, and he's been drivin' the Union war machine ever since."

Warley watched Jesse's face. "You're saying—"

"That the Union's army's bein' driven forward by a savage, murderous lunatic with no regard for human life? Yeah. The attack on Petersburg cost the Union more men than any other battle. They ran right at the city's fixed defenses, floodin' the streets with bodies until we just ran out o' bullets. And then, when Lee was forced to retreat, Grant pursued him, shootin' his men down wherever they were caught, until that bastard Lincoln, of all people, had to call him back."

"But that was war . . ." Warley did not sound convinced by his own argument.

"That was butchery, is what it was, colonel." Jesse leaned forward again. "And then he went on to smash Richmond, slaughtering men, women, and children to get to Jefferson Davis and any other Confederate politician he could find. And then Atlanta . . . The man was like a scourge from God, grinding every last Confederate stronghold into the bloody mud." He sat back, his dark eyes calm. "Now, I ask you, colonel . . . How many black folks died in those cities? How many have died in the years since, as Grant pursued his insane feuds?"

Warley's head slowly pivoted back and forth, his face pale. "I don't . . ."

"Hundreds of thousands, sir. Hundreds of thousands. And they know it. They ain't dumb. You give the black folks in this country an equal stake in their future, and they'll fight for it. Horrible things been done on this soil, an' that ain't gonna change. But you give a man, any man, a chance to fight for the future of his family? He's gonna take that chance, an' he ain't gonna be too worried 'bout the past. Havin' a wolf at yer door tends to make you forget what mudsills your neighbors are, sir."

He sat back, arm resting still on the table before him, and scanned the faces opposite. Warley looked thoughtful; Quantrill's face was troubled. Marie Laveau's beautiful features were transformed by a righteous smile that was cruelly offset by the vengeful gleam in her eyes.

"Damn." Warley muttered to himself.

Jesse nodded. "Don't try to make sense of the actions of a drunk or a madman, colonel. They'll surprise you every time. And Grant's madder than a mountain lion on a hot griddle, and he's drunk on the power Johnson won't take away."

Warley's eyes refocused on Jesse and he nodded slowly. "Well, sir. It seems we had something to learn from you after all."

Lucy and the Fords shifted uncomfortably on his side of the table as Jesse sat back against the curved chair. "Sorry?"

Warley's expression softened. "Well, we hadn't seen the whole situation as nearly so dire as you've painted it, son, but we in New Orleans, at least, had reached the same general conclusion long ago."

Quantrill looked sideways at the colonel, eyebrows drawn down. Warley turned back to Jesse.

"Many folks in New Orleans have always had a . . . different view of race than elsewhere in the south. Some say it's because of our closer ties to Europe, others that things are just softer here. But either way, when we realized we didn't have the numbers to defend ourselves, when the Union started to funnel troops down here and to the navy yards, we knew we needed to do something." He looked at Marie Laveau out of the corner of his eye. "Making an alliance with our dark-skinned neighbors was the only choice we found that made any sense."

The witch nodded, her smile radiant. "My people have answered the call, Msye James. An' with the colonel's help, we've got quite a little army forming, back behind Belle Je."

Warley spread his hands as if in apology. "We don't have much, but we're trainin' anyone who comes to us with whatever we have, regardless of the color of their skin. We've found exactly what you've said, Mr. James. When their homes are bein' threatened, folks around here have answered the call, with no regard to skin color. We've had a few incidents among the men and women who've come, of course, but isolated, and far fewer than I would have expected."

Jesse looked at him with eyes that began to glow with anger. "You mean to tell me you agreed with me this whole time, an' made me jump through yer damned hoops . . ." Jesse knew that this was one of those times Frank or Cole would have tried to rein him in, but even that knowledge was not enough to impose any sort of self-control.

Warley nodded, but his head was cocked to one side, robbing the gesture of wholehearted agreement. "I did. And it worked . . . here. Will it work elsewhere in the Confederacy? I don't know. But I wanted to hear your case, to see if YOU believed, and if what you had to say might seem like it could sway folks more set in their ways than we are here."

Jesse tilted his head up, looking down his nose at the colonel. "And?"

Warley shook his head, his eyes tight. "You scared the hades right out of me, Mr. James. We here in New Orleans have always believed that true riches come from the spirit. And the strongest power obviously comes from the united spirit of a free and dedicated people. But can even that power answer for a madman commanding the most powerful weapons in the world?"

Jesse looked down at his decimated plate. He had not eaten this well in months and suddenly realized he had not tasted a bite. The fatigue of the battle and the drain from his injuries was starting to tell as well. He was not going to be able to stay awake much longer, end of the world or no.

"Well, there ain't anythin' else we can do, colonel." He looked up again, his exhausted face strong with conviction. "But we gotta do what we can. I believe that down to my very core."

Everyone was watching Jesse; the old Confederate officers across the table, the witch-woman, the men around the edges of the room. Lucy was watching him with eyes that looked suspiciously glassy, while the Fords were staring at him like he was the savior come again. He looked at each of them. The weight of their gazes drove him even further toward exhausted collapse.

At last, Warley nodded. "I do, too, Mr. James." He reached across the table, his open hand held firmly before the outlaw. After only a moment's hesitation, Jesse reached out and gripped the hand. "And despite the darkness of your message, you bring hope with you as well. You're not alone in believing that President Lee has grown too timid. In fact, there is a network of us throughout the south. Lee's advisors have been replaced by a new group of men. None of the old guard have even heard of them before. They're a fiery-eyed lot, making grand, blistering speeches, but always seeming to council for prudence and accommodation in the end. We have been agonizing over what to do for a long time now." He shrugged as he sat back. "We have contemplated everything from a vote of no confidence to assassination, but could agree on nothing."

Jesse shook his head. "You can't run a fight by committee, sir. When the bullets fly, the strongest lead, and the weak follow or fall away. I learned that from Colonel Quantrill."

Quantrill smiled vaguely, still lost in thought.

"I happen to agree with you, Mr. James. But until now, I feared there might not be enough of the strong, as you say, to keep the weak moving forward." His smile turned predatory. "I'm very much convinced now, that there may well be."

Jesse gave a single, sharp nod back. "Now, we've got the makings of an army, you and I. And I've got more folks comin' in from the territories, and even a troop of California

Rangers, if they haven't run off yet. But what do we do with them all?"

Warley sat back, threw one arm across the back of his chair, and speared Jesse with his most intense look. "We have identified a possible target, but we didn't think we'd have enough power to give us a realistic chance, until now."

Jesse's look managed to mix suspicion and excitement in equal measure. "What?"

Warley waved a hand. "We've gotten reports that the Union is building a massive fortress along the stabilizing border between the north and the south. Somethin' huge, far larger than a border fort or even a forward base. Somethin' very nearly a castle in proportions and design."

Jesse shook his head. "What the hell'd they need a castle for? It's not Lee's been a threat to them in years."

Warley agreed. "No. And yet, there they are. Now, if we were able to attack this fortress, destroy it utterly and completely . . . Why, that might just be the perfect catalyst for getting all those fence-sitters throughout the Confederacy to fall down on our side."

"Prove we can take down something that big, and we prove that the Union can be beaten." Jesse nodded. "Makes sense. That was sort of my thinking behind burning down Camp Lincoln, but I ain't heard a peep. How many men you got hidden in the swamps back there? Even if Will Shaft and his boys bring all of Robbers Roost back, and Captain Ingram's boys stick close, I only got a few hundred, and a handful of Rolling Thunder wagons."

Warley shook his head ruefully. "Not enough, I'm afraid. But, with you going on ahead, giving your speech about madmen, and wolves at the door . . . I think you might be able to raise us an army large enough, by the time we get there. General Mosby may even—"

Jesse shook his head. "Mosby's not going to take a piss without Lee tellin' him he's gotta go."

Jesse's eyes took on a far-off look as his head moved back to rest against the chair back. He was a long way from the territories, leading a posse and looking forward to the next bank or train. There was a large part of him that yearned for the simplicity of those days, without all these people looking to him for answers.

Everyone sat completely still, waiting for what he would say next. He suddenly snapped his head back down and looked wide-eyed at Warley.

"I think you might be right . . . but right now, I think I need to sleep for about two days straight."

He got up and made his unsteady way back out into the entry hall. One of the soldiers there directed him up the stairs and to an empty bed chamber. A moment later he was gone.

The dining room was silent for quite some time after he left. Each person stared at the door, lost in their own thoughts.

Chapter 12

The camp, hidden beyond the fields and outbuildings of Belle Je, was extensive. It stretched away among the moss-hung trees. Gaps in the tents and lean-tos marked areas of black water where the bayou reached its oily fingers onto the property. Although warm and very humid, it was not nearly as scorching as the city had been. Colonel Warley led Jesse, his arms repaired after a day of extensive work by Madamoiselle Laveau, toward a large tent in the center of the camp. The outlaw chief was still sore from his escapades in the city. Glorious bruises and shallow cuts had made getting dressed that morning interesting.

The colonel waved a hand around them. "What we've done here would never have been possible without Captain Carney." The old officer nodded to several colored soldiers as they passed. "He fought under the Union in the War, but I don't want you to hold that against him, Mr. James. He'll be essential if this is to work."

Warley pushed the flap back on the dun-colored tent and peered into the shadows. "Captain Carney? A word, if you'd please?"

The tent was neat and tidy. A small table and chairs dominated the center. An old uniform coat, blue faded nearly to gray, was draped over one chair, accompanied by a torn and faded Union flag gathered up like a sash. Three men and a woman, all black, stood around the table, speaking in quiet tones. When the colonel spoke, they snapped to attention and turned, smiles on their dark faces. The oldest man, in white shirtsleeves and faded pants that matched the coat, grinned through a thick goatee and mustache.

"Colonel, sir. Always time for our gracious host." The man's voice carried the flat tones of the north, and Jesse had to tamp down his initial reaction. The man nodded to the other fighters, who left, saluting Warley with casual flips as they passed. "What can I do for you, sir?"

The colonel stepped into the tent with a friendly smile, gesturing Jesse to follow. "Someone I'd like you to meet, Bill."

Bill Carney sized Jesse up with a quick glance, his eyes lingering on the sleek mechanical arms. After a moment's hesitation, he reached out with an open hand. Jesse forced himself to take it without pause.

"Good to meet you, Cap'n." Jesse met the man's eyes levelly. There was a terrible scar across his left temple. The puckered flesh disappeared into a curly widow's peak, a streak of white hair continuing the trajectory of the old wound. The man's grip was firm against the feedback pads of Jesse's hand.

"Good to meet you as well, Mister . . . James?" Carney's voice was deep, the question polite.

"Never try to slip one past Bill, Mr. James!" Warley slapped the black officer on the back. "So, captain, I was really hopin' you could fill Mr. James in on the local situation." His face took on a slightly sheepish cast. "I was also hopin' you might tell him a bit about your own story, at least as to how it relates. I think you two, workin' together, are goin' to be quite formidable."

Carney looked at Jesse for a moment and then stepped aside, gesturing toward the empty chairs. Jesse eased his aching body down, but Warley stepped back toward the entrance. "I've heard all this before." He smiled, holding up a placating hand. "You boys have fun." And he was gone.

The black northerner sat lightly down in a chair opposite and folded scarred hands on the table. "So. Jesse James."

Jesse nodded. "Yup."

The other man smiled a sad smile. "A stranger, far from home." He turned in his seat to reach for a metal canteen. He offered a drink to his guest before swigging down a quick slug of his own. "Very far from home."

Jesse nodded again. "Colonel Warley said as how you'd fought for the Union in the war."

Carney's smile faded. "I did, Mr. James. Is that going to be a problem between us?"

Jesse looked into the other man's eyes. They were dark, of course, but they burned with sincerity rare in a man of any color. And here, in the middle of this camp, the man could be no raging blue-belly. He shook his head. "I reckon it won't be."

Carney's smile returned. "Excellent." He leaned back, draping one arm across his chair's back, across the Union flag. "So that might as well be where we start."

The man splayed one dark hand over the table top. "I was one of the first black men to enlist in the Colored Regiments. Back then, the war seemed to make a lot more sense. I was born a slave, you see, in Virginia. My daddy escaped, worked up a stake up north, and bought us our freedom. Seemed like fighting was the only way I could really repay a debt like that, when the call came."

Jesse squirmed a little in his chair. The small wooden seat chafed at his injuries, just as this quiet man's story scraped at his conscience. Jesse's family had owned slaves of their own at one time. The pang of guilt that past reality caused now cast his memories of the war itself into an uncomfortable light.

"I fought through more than my share of battles, some big ones." Carney's eyes were distant as he continued his story. "Got winged a few times." One hand drifted over his chest. "I even won me some shiny medals. And then every man I called a friend, every officer I admired, was killed in a single day. I picked up the colors when the bearer fell." He absently patted the flag draped across the back of his chair. "Took more wounds returning the flag to our lines, and then I collapsed."

Carney's eyes were unfocused, lost in another time. "It took years for me to fully recover. And in that time, the world changed."

"RJ-1027." Jesse muttered under his breath.

The colored officer looked up and nodded. "RJ-1027. And the Confederacy crushed in the last bloody push of the war." He smiled sadly. "It seemed like everything I'd ever wanted was coming true. But things didn't change much. Grant turned the new weapons westward, against Carpathian and his walking dead, and ran straight into the Warrior Nation coming south. There was hardly a month of peace before the entire country was plunged back into war, even bloodier than before." He shrugged. "The plight of my brothers and sisters in the remnants of the Confederacy was little better than before the Proclamation. But this time, the Union, with bigger fish to fry, had turned its back."

Carney's eyes were haunted. "I still had friends and relatives south of the line. I heard terrible stories. The south was in total chaos and disarray, and it took its toll on everyone. But my folks were the hardest hit. It didn't help that Grant wouldn't accept surrender under any circumstances. He wanted the old Confederacy to suffer, and so it let them rot on the vine. I knew I couldn't sit back and let it stand. I took my gear and some extra weapons from a quartermaster friend from the 54th, and I headed south."

Jesse leaned forward. "You were gonna keep the war goin' all on your lonesome?"

Carney shook his head. "No, I weren't gonna be fightin' no war. I came down to try to help my people, is all. I wandered around a bit, put down some dogs, collected a few more scars along the way." He sat back and gestured to the camp around them. "I ended up coming down toward New Orleans. Heard things were different here, and I was tired. I was very tired."

Jesse nodded. "And were they? Different, I mean?"

Carney's smile turned cold. "Not as different as I would have liked. The place was a mess. Different coalitions claimed to rule the city as the state of Louisiana dissolved around us into the lawless western territories and the chaotic Rebellion. One group was a hard-line pack of old-timers from the war. Tried to take control and push the colored folks back into the bayous. The locals wouldn't stand for it, but didn't have much in the way of weaponry themselves."

Carney rose slowly, wincing at a pain in his side, and moved to a low bench in the corner of the tent. He pulled a cloth back to reveal a massive Gatling blaster with a harness and support straps. He turned back to the outlaw chief with a savage grin. "My friend Joseph, the quartermaster? This was his last gift to me, after the war."

Jesse whistled and moved toward the weapon. It was a beautiful example of its type. Six hexagonal barrels were fit into the dull black body of the gun, crimson telltales winking brightly. "A man could do some serious damage with a gun like that." Jesse tapped the barrel with one metal finger.

"Yessir." The black officer nodded and moved back to his seat. "And I did.

Worked with Colonel Warley and a few other locals, black and white, and we set those old bastards an' their carpetbagger friends a-runnin'. New Orleans' been one of the most integrated places on the continent ever since."

Jesse sat back, but he could not keep his eyes off the massive weapon. "So, you an' yer boys'll be fightin' fer the Rebellion now?" One eyebrow quirked upward. "How's that sit with you?"

Carney leaned forward, his dark eyes glittering in the dim light. "I've talked with Colonel Warley. I've heard your plan. My boys and girls won't be fightin' fer a Rebellion that don't recognize us as humans. But you wrench them in the right direction?" The smile was back, warmer than ever. "Then we'll fight next to anyone that'll have us. You just gotta go out there an' make 'em see that what we've done here in New Orleans, it's workin'. And it'll work for the rest of the country too."

Jesse met his gaze. "But what about the Union? Your loyalties must still be strongly inclined up north—"

Carney shook his head. "The Union I fought for, that sheltered my family and provided us with a home?" Once again he patted the flag behind him. "That don't exist no more. And it won't come back until Grant and his bloody-minded cronies fall."

Jesse sat back and nodded. "Well, we might just have more to talk about on the way north, captain, if this all works out. And I think you might just like to meet a friend of mine . . . name of Will Shaft."

*****

Jesse looked around the little hut, trying manfully to keep the disgust and disdain from his face. He could feel Frank standing behind him, his custom long rifle cradled in his arm, and knew that his brother was giving away nothing. Across the ratty little table, paint peeling and wood soft with rot, were three men that he needed to bring over to his cause before he could move out of the bayou and into the higher coastal reaches to the east.

Buford Nash, commander of the St. Tammany Parish Confederate Militia, sat in the center across the table. Bordering the north east shoreline of Lake Pontchartrain, St. Tammany was the gateway to the rest of the south. On the far side, in the true Confederacy, Jesse's real mission would begin.

Nash was a big man. His clothing was rough but clean. The lines on his face were deep, indicating a life far more familiar with frowns than laughter. A close-cropped gray mustache and small chin beard offset the smooth expanse of his scalp above. His watery-blue eyes stared at Jesse without emotion, but the men to either side had more than enough of that to spare.

Deacon Nash, the head man's son, was almost as big as his father. Flaming red hair matched the anger blazing in the young man's eyes as he flicked his attention from Jesse to Frank, and then, always, to Will Shaft standing silently beside Frank. Deacon Nash wore his facial hair wild. His chin had probably not made the acquaintance of a razor in years. His hand toyed with an old RJ power cell that looked like it might be older than he was.

On the other side of the commander sat Jeremiah Longway, by far the oldest person in the shack. The old man's skin was as parched and wrinkled as poorly-cured leather, but it still held the color of mixed parentage. That was something Jesse had become far more accustomed to as he moved through the area around New Orleans. There were more folks of mixed race down here than he had ever seen, and despite his current crusade, he found he still had a way to go to adapt himself.

Jeremiah Longway's beard put young Deacon's to shame. There was almost no way to tell what the color of the old man's vest was beneath the tangled white hair. Unlike Buford Nash, however, his head, too, was covered in an unruly white halo. He stared unblinkingly at Jesse with brown eyes flecked with gold that reflected the RJ lamps with a russet sparkle.

Jesse had finished his speachifying. He had quickly learned to pause here, watching the locals for any sign of which way he should jump next. This was the eighth local militia group he had approached since leaving Warley's estate nearly two weeks ago. His small army, following Warley's scouts through the bayous and the small towns, had managed to join him only a few days after his fight in the cemetery. Shaft and a fairly large contingent from the Territories had ridden into town a few days later, collected by some of Warley's boys, and brought back to Belle Je.

Frank had had no sympathy for Jesse's injuries, nothing but a disappointed look and a shaken head. Bob and Jim Younger had said nothing. Cole, some of his old humor perhaps returning, had made a comment about any man daft enough to go walking around a cemetery when he was hanging his hat in a brothel.

It had taken them a few more days to iron out exactly what the plan was going to be. Warley's sources said this mysterious fort Grant was establishing in old Tennessee would be up and running soon, but there was some wiggle room before the final troop deployments would see the place fully manned. Maps had been drawn, teams chosen, and Jesse, as the point man of the whole endeavor, had been heading east ever since. The further he got from New Orleans, the harder time he was having selling the idea of black folks and white folks standing together against the Union. Something told him Warley had planned it this way, easing him into the whole process.

Of course, now, sitting across from the Nashes and their old advisor, he was wishing he were back in Orleans Parish. He could not read these three for the life of him.

Jesse was about to ask if there was anything he could clarify for them, when old Jeremiah coughed, and then spoke. "I'm still not sure why 'tis ya'll want us heah to join yez, Msye James. What you t'ink Tammany Parish got to offer you an' you boys, when you takin' on bad Msye Grant? An why you t'ink we be wantin' to send our youngin's wit' you dere?"

The elder Nash gave no sign of hearing the comment, but Deacon nodded vigorously. "Yeah, now. Why's we want ta go runnin' after ya'll an' dyin' so far from our homes? We gots Union sojer-boys right heah we can be killin'!"

Jesse took a breath and turned slightly in his seat to look back at Frank. His brother gave the shortest of shrugs beneath his immobile face. Jesse felt his shoulders slumping and turned back to the locals with a sigh.

"Well," Jesse spread both of his hands out on the table in front of him. He had been hesitant to let Marie Laveau near him, knowing the crude work she had done on Quantrill, but the arms were working better than they had in months. Despite her haughty, aloof behavior, she had proven herself quite capable. He had not yet broached the subject of a possible alliance against Carpathian, but he was thinking that she might be just the person he needed by his side when the time came for a return engagement.

Jesse shook his head. He knew his mind was wandering in the face of this crew's blank response. Nonetheless, if he could not count on the militia of St. Tammany Parish, he was not going to get too far.

With another sigh, he replied. "You spend yer blood fightin' the Union troops they're sendin' around down this way, you're wastin' yer time an' yer blood." He jerked a metal thumb over his shoulder at his brother. "We've seen 'em in action up close. They ain't gonna be satisfied, crushin' Lee's little honor guard, when they finally get around to turnin' our way again. An' on some level, you folks know it. We gotta face them down, on their own land, an' show the rest of the south that we ain't beat yet. An' we can't do that, lessen' we dig deep and come together."

The three strangers across the table stared at him again in silence. The older and the younger looked angry. Buford did not move.

Jesse felt his own anger building in his gut. "They're gonna be comin' down here with enough force, they ain't gonna be happy 'till they've killed every man, woman, an' child who ever had a bad thought about 'em. They're gonna crush us, chew us up, an' spit us out lookin' just like 'em."

"An' you gonna stop all dat by rilin' up all the folks here 'bouts and drivin' 'em north?" Jeremiah's unsettling eyes bore into Jesse's. The old man turned to Buford, resting an old elbow on the table. "I say we see 'em on their way, Bue." He stabbed a large-jointed thumb at the thin, moss-covered door. "Let 'em go, an' happy be their goin'."

Buford Nash rested his hands on the table, fingers intertwined, and leaned back. The old chair creaked ominously beneath him. His shining head cocked to one side and his eyes squinted slightly. "You 'tink they's goin' ta be comin' down heah, by an' by?"

Jesse straightened. Buford had not spoken since they had all sat down together. He was getting ready to make his choice. It was up to the outlaw chief to convince him of the correct path. "I know they will. They won't stop until the damned Union flag is flyin' over every town and village from Atlanta to the Colorado and beyond."

Jesse took a deep breath and once again indicated Frank, standing behind him. "They took my brother. They threw him in a camp with thousands of others. The things they were doin' in that camp, sir?" He shuddered. "It don't bear thinkin' on. An' they're gonna be doin' that to everyone that don't bow down to 'em 'till they own it all." He pointed to Deacon, whose face had not relaxed as Jesse spoke. "Sure as sure, they're gonna do it to you an' yours, gatherin' here in the bayou, flyin' the old flags and singin' the old songs. Ain't no way your folks come out of this breathin', Buford."

Jeremiah sneered at this, obviously not convinced. "Ain't no way we can stand against 'em now, boy. Where you gettin' the rifles? Where you gettin' the hands to hold the rifles?"

Jesse stared at the old man, breathing deeply and focusing every ounce of effort on not jumping across the table and throttling him. "I tole' ya. Black folks and white folks, standin' together—"

"Ain't gonna happen." The old man sat back as if he had won the argument, his hands raised as if revealing the final piece of a magic trick. "Here in the bayou, things're different. But out there?" He waved one hand vaguely toward the east. "Out there, it's bad. Black folks is angrier. White folks is more set in their ways, more frightened. Ain't gonna happen. And without it happenin', this scheme o' your'n ain't never happenin' neither."

"It don't have to be that way." Will's voice was deep, almost like distant thunder or the rumble of artillery. "There's white folks and black folks get along fine, here, out west, an' other places. An' when it's a question o' standin' with a man you don't like, or dyin' alone . . . ain't most folks'd be takin' the second choice."

Deacon slammed his hand on the table. "But that ain't all, is it?" His face was twisted with anger and fear. "The Union freed 'em all, din't they! Black folks, they don't hate the Union, most of 'em. They'd ruther move up that way, many of 'em, if they had the chance!"

"That ain't so." Will Shaft spoke with a soft tone, but his dark eyes were intense as he stared at the young man. "Most folks, no matter their color, want to stay in their homes an' live their lives. And maybe the Union once freed my people, yeah. But that was a long time ago. Since then? Since Grant took over? They got nothin' but contempt for anyone livin' in the south, no matter the color of their skin. My folks? We went west after the Proclamation, tryin' to make a new life on the frontier. The same old hates and jibes followed us clear across the country, despite we was in Union Territory. Ain't no one up there cares any more for colored folks than the folks down this way."

"And they ain't gonna care none what color anyone is when they come rollin' down here, neither." Jesse nodded. "And that's the reality we gotta face, and that's why folks've gotta come together now. We come together, or we all die."

"But what is it you want, Jesse James?" The old man leaned forward now, his face intense. "Why're you, a famous villain o' the Wild West, down heah leadin' this chahge?" A fire seemed to light in his eyes as he finished, almost in a whisper. "What're YOU aftah,

Msye James?"

Jesse shook his head. "I never made no secret of the way I feel fer the Union. They ain't never been nothin' but ugly to me an' mine. An' fer years now, they been gettin' worse. We gotta take 'em on here, when and where we choose, if we wanna stop 'em anywhere." He sat back with a slight shrug. "An' I can't do it alone. Folks who love their freedom, they gotta rise up with me, 'r it's all gonna burn away."

The old man seemed dissatisfied by the answer. "I don't believe you, Msye James. What you REALLY after?"

"Buford," Jesse's voice was tight with barely-controlled tension. "Your folks in or not? I don't wanna have to go the long way 'round east, an' we don't wanna go in without you. But we'll do both if we have to."

Jeremiah sat up sharply, his mouth open to protest, but Buford Nash stopped him with a single hand. Deacon looked like he was angry enough to spit, but he remained silent.

"You can move through St. Tammany Parish."

"But Daddy! You can't—" Deacon's voice was high with anger and surprise. He stuttered to a halt as his father slapped his calloused hand onto the table hard enough to buckle the old wood.

"Shut it, Deak!" He glared at his son. "I ain't led Tammany Parish fer as long as I done to get lip from my own son, right?" Deacon glowered back at him, but his eyes were tight with doubt. When he did not immediately respond, his father growled. "I ain't right?"

Deacon looked down into his lap, folding his hands there. "You's right, Daddy."

Buford turned to glare at the old man. "An' I get you, Jeremiah, but you livin' inna past. It gone, and we gotta look for'ard." He turned back to Jesse.

"You can move through St. Tammany Parish." He put up a hand to forestall Jesse's thanks. "But we ain't joinin' you till I see the quality of those that's already with you when you get here. I ain't sending none of my boys 'n girls off to die for some fancy talkin' flannel-mouth from out west, less'n I see there's other believes in you first."

Jesse nodded. Buford Nash was not the first man to make such a statement. Most of these folks remembered the crushing defeats at the end of the last war. Many of them had even been there at the very end, as everything burned behind them and the desperate flight became a thing of nightmare. The Union, little seen since then, was an object of legend more than anything else: a horror story used to terrify small children into obedience.

Jesse looked around the cabin. Hell, most of these folks barely had enough RJ tech to cook their food and keep themselves warm. He had even seen piles of wood stacked behind some of the cabins in the village. Most were not living in the past of twenty years ago; they were living in the past of a hundred years ago, and they did not much seem to care.

Jesse stood and reached out with one metal hand. Buford Nash stood but hesitated before taking the hand in his own firm grasp. "That seems more than fair, sir." Jesse nodded. "I'll have Colonel Warley and the rest of the local officers with me when we come through. I have no doubt they'll be able to give you every assurance."

Nash nodded. "I was surprised he sent you foreigners out without him, truth to tell. I woulda thought he'd of at least sent Captain Carney."

Jesse shrugged as he moved around the rickety old chair, holding onto the frail back with both hands. "He's smoothin' the way for those that're livin' closer to the city, so's they can sneak through without alertin' the Union outfit down near the navy docks."

The big bald man settled back in his chair. "Well, you best be on your way, son. You gotta lot o' work ahead of ya', before yer done."

Jesse nodded, spared Deacon and Jeremiah a sharp jerk of his chin, and turned to leave. Behind him, Frank was already holding the door while Will stared indifferently at the three men at the table. As he passed his brother, Jesse gave him a look. Frank only shrugged, but Jesse knew he would get more once they left the little huddle of huts.

Outside, in the center of the little town, Lucy waited with Robert Ford and their Iron Horses. Each machine sat in its own shallow puddle where it had pushed the soggy turf down into the water. The 'Horses were perfect for travelling through the bayous . . . until they grounded.

Lucy looked at him and he lifted one shoulder noncommittally. He swung his leg up and over the saddle on his machine and said, "No recruits to send back, but we can move through. They may join when they hear from some other locals."

Lucy rolled her eyes. "That's nearly half so far that won't commit without hearing from their neighbors. What do they think is going to happen? They're going to sink or swim together, they might as well get used to that idea."

"Right," Frank stepped up to his own vehicle and slid Sophie back into her boot along the saddle. "'Cept they don't see it that way. 'Till someone makes this real for 'em, it's just a game. Been a game to those that survived since Grant turned westward."

Robert shook his head. "I don't like it, havin' to toady up to these lowlife swamp-grubbers." He spoke softly, his eyes darting among the men and women in their worn clothing, standing around and watching the strangers prepare to depart.

"That old man had an evil in him," Will Shaft said as he slid onto his 'Horse.

Jesse nodded. "I got that. But he din't do much, other than try to get Buford to say 'no.'"

"He was mighty interested in you, though, brother." Frank fired up his 'Horse and the rumbling thunder of the engines rose up to blanket the little village. His brother shouted to finish his thought. "Diggin' after your where's and why-for's!"

Jesse pulled his red-tinged goggles up over his face and shrugged. "Let 'im stew!" He saw that the others had their own goggles on, and he waved a hand for Robert to lead the way. "Take us out, Robert! Get us across the Pearl and we'll make camp in good ole Dixie!"

Robert nodded, grinning, and gunned his machine around in a tight turn that scattered mud in a glistening crescent that sent him between two squat buildings and out over the inky waters of the bayou. A glittering curtain of mist flashed out in his wake. Will and Frank followed close behind, while Lucy waited, watching Jesse. He turned to look at the little hovel where they had just had their meeting. There was no sign of Buford or the others. Jesse waved to the people watching, and then jerked his chin after his brother. Lucy nodded and gunned her own 'Horse after them.

Jesse gave a grin and one last wave at the concerned villagers as he roared out of town.

*****

Lucinda sat as far from the fire as she could while still benefitting somewhat from its light. The heat had been oppressive since they'd arrived in New Orleans, and riding through the country rabble-rousing had not made things any cooler. Nearer to the fire, possibly more used to the blasting temperatures of the western deserts, the men sat discussing their latest victory, of sorts, and their next challenge.

Jesse stirred the fire with a stick. "So, we're lookin' fer some fella named Tinker Thane, head o' the militia for C.R. Georgia, or whatever Lee has taken to naming the place. Why they couldn't o' kept with the old names, I don' know."

Frank looked up from cleaning Sophie. The swamps had played merry hell with her delicate internal workings. "Defeat has a funny effect on folks, Jesse. Some folks, after they get beat, they wanna change everythin', as if that means it was someone else got beat that last time, an' wasn't them."

Jesse shrugged. "Anyway, this Thane is supposed to be the man to talk to if we wanna go 'round Lee's boys. We'll head toward his headquarters, some town called Kiln. Shouldn't be too far, no more'n a few days of hard riding. We can make a few more stops along the way, lay the ground work as we travel."

Lucy shook her head. They had been away from BELLE JE for too long. Her report, such as it was, would have been in the hands of people who knew what to do with it for at least a week. Somehow, however, she could not bring herself to care. Watching Jesse gather people around himself during these past weeks had been astounding. Listening to him make his case for equality among the people of the south had stirred something deep inside her.

Similar feelings had driven her into the bosom of the Union all those years ago. Back then, she truly believed that the Union was fighting for freedom and honor. As the battles dragged on, she had realized that only a small group of men and women still carried that particular flag. As more and more enemies rose out of the shadows, there was less and less time for the crusades of the past. Now, with Grant lashing out in all directions, and even the noblest of the Union's defenders fixated so strongly on the new enemies, it seemed as if those ideals had stopped mattering entirely.

Except to some, it appeared, among her old enemies. Jesse James was the most stalwart enemy of the Union that had ever existed. He had his reasons, of course, but his unrelieved hatred was irrefutable. And yet here he was, making the cases she herself had made when she was young, before she had been caught up in the new fights like everyone else. Watching Jesse convince these hidebound old rednecks to come around to this new, radical way of thinking had opened her eyes to how far she had fallen from her own ideals, and it hurt at the same time that it gave her hope.

"You think it's really goin' to be that much tougher here on out?" Robert's voice was soft as he whittled at a stick.

Frank nodded. "The folks we knew, out this way . . . a lot of 'em are gonna be deaf to yer words, Jesse."

The outlaw chief shrugged. "Well, that'd be true, years ago. But these folks are the ones who've seen what the Union is capable of. They've seen the meanness an' the violence up close, many of 'em. I'm countin' on that; they're farther from New Orleans, but they're closer to the Union." He shifted his back against his Iron Horse. "Way I figure it, should just about even the balance."

Frank spit a stream of tobacco juice into the fire where it sizzled and danced. "You gotta keep in mind, Jesse, old hates, they run deep on both sides."

Jesse nodded. "I know, Frank. But thanks for the lecture." He turned to Lucy. "Hey, Lucy, you're from the old south. We got a chance?"

She forced herself to smile at the men as they all looked at her with curious eyes. "Jesse, if anyone can do it, you can."

Robert laughed at that, and Will's teeth flashed in the dark. Frank's face was serious as he leaned toward her, resting on one splayed hand. "Seriously, Miss Lucy. They gonna listen? Or 'r they gonna run us out o' town on a rail?"

She looked at Frank for a long moment. There was real concern in his eyes, and it was not for himself. Frank, as always, was worried for his little brother. The ravages of Camp Lincoln were still evident in the gaunt lines of his face and the shadows of his eyes, and yet his first thoughts were still for Jesse. She realized in a flash that Frank would never admit to such emotions, despite the fact that his entire life, as far as she could see, was focused solely on keeping his brother alive. She owed him an honest answer.

"I don't know, Frank." She could not help a slight smile from twisting her lips. "But if anyone can do it, it's Jesse."

Chapter 13

The Drowsy Magnolia on old Delisle Road was once a proud tavern. Like most things in the battered town of Kiln, however, it had seen better days. Kiln was named after the massive charcoal kilns put in to accommodate much of the region's logging in the days before RJ-1027. It had fallen on hard times after the technology began to spread across the countryside, however. The nation was dotted with such places. Towns that had depended on logging, coal, or whale oil; natural resources that had fallen out of use with the power and versatility of Doctor Carpathian's miracle elixir, had withered away. In most of the country, folks had taken to calling the substance RJ. In places like Kiln they called it Devil's Blood; or death.

Tinker Thane, self-styled commander of the Greater-Southern Militias, met them in a small private room over the common area of the Drowsy Magnolia. The wallpaper was faded, the furniture worn, but the beer was good, or so Thane promised as Jesse and Will Shaft were ushered into his presence. Frank, Robert, and Lucy had stayed down in the common area, taking a table in full view of the stairs and as far from the obnoxious RJ-powered piano as they could.

None of them had been happy about being left behind. Lucy and Frank usually took turns accompanying Jesse on his visits, while Robert stayed behind to watch their vehicles and for any sudden change in the local temperament. Will, of course, was always with him, more to make a point than for anything else. This time around, Jesse had gotten an immediate sense that he needed to go this one alone, with just Will beside him. It had been a tense exchange, but at last Frank and Lucy, accompanied by a slightly more resigned Robert Ford, had settled down to taste the local brew and wince through the plinking musical accompaniment, while Jesse, Will, and the militia chief disappeared upstairs.

Thane was smiling warmly on the other side of the table. He had given Will Shaft a curious glance at first and then seemed to ignore him. With a casual wave of his hand, he gestured for Jesse to speak.

The outlaw chief cleared his throat, unsure of how to begin. He was used to having a chance to warm up to his subject, but everything had happened so quickly as they pulled up before the Drowsy Magnolia, his head was spinning.

"Well," Jesse muttered, marshaling his thoughts. "I'm here because—"

Thane's smile widened and he nodded. "I know why you're here, Mr. James." Jesse was getting used to hearing these easterners refer to him as 'mister', truth be told. However, sometimes he wondered if it might not be quite as sincere as he could hope. "You want those of us who are dissatisfied with President Lee's policies to join you in some act of defiance, to prove the vulnerability of our eternal foe in the north, as well as to establish that we of the Confederacy are capable of looking after our own interests." He tipped his head slightly toward Will, standing by the door, without actually looking at him. "And lest we forget, you are also in favor of arming the colored population in furtherance of your military goals. Is that about the size of it, Mr. James?"

Jesse swallowed the plug of acid that had risen from his belly while the smaller man was talking. The smile had not wavered, the eyes still glowed warmly, and yet, Jesse felt as if the past year of his life had just been summed up and dismissed.

"Well, sir, that is about the size of it. And yet—"

Thane nodded. "And yet it sounds so crass and unrealistic when I say it. Right?"

Jesse swallowed again. Even the man's accent seemed foreign; flatter and devoid of some essential element he could not name. "Well, sir, if you're goin' to be the one who says it." He shrugged.

Thane's smile widened. "Well, good. So you can take criticism. I was wondering, what with some of the stories that have been going around."

Jesse was feeling more and more out of his depth. "Do you wanna hear 'bout the plan?"

Thane flipped the question away with one casual hand. "Not necessary. You wish to raise the beleaguered forces of the old Confederacy, in spite of the entrenched passivity of our current leaders. You wish to do this, in part, by arming the most downtrodden and dispossessed among us. And you wish to use these forces to strike a blow for freedom and security for the independent Confederate States of America, long may the Stars and Bars wave."

Jesse sat back, his eyes flat. "I'm startin' to wonder why I'm here at all."

Thane leaned forward. "Why, you're here so I can look you in the eyes, Mr. James, and judge the depth of your conviction."

Jesse decided not to respond. The silence stretched on, however, and soon he gave in with a sigh. "And?"

Teeth gleamed behind a predatory smile. "I find you wanting, Mr. James."

Jesse was brought up short, his head cocked to one side. "Pardon?"

"I have looked into your eyes, into the windows to your soul, and I have found the depth of your conviction in this matter to be . . . wanting." The smile faded until only the flat eyes, gleaming with mild, suppressed mirth, remained.

Jesse was unsure what to do next. He was partly of a mind to draw iron on the croaking little pie eater, but he had come so far, and he had tried so hard not to resort to his pistols in a pinch. Besides, what did this little pissant really hold over him? With a deep breath, he shrugged.

"My faith's my own business, Thane. But I assure you, it's there."

The man laughed at him. Actually LAUGHED, out loud, at him! "I have no doubt, Mr. James. What does remain in doubt, however, is . . . in what do you hold that faith?"

His anger was building. He could feel his right arm, inner workings spinning and whirring, shaking with the desire to draw. He had a moment's fear that he would once again lose control of the arm, but with the thought, the limb immediately stilled. He looked back up at the militia commander with a dangerous glint in his eye. "Thane, we better come to a point mighty quick, 'r your little corner of the South's gonna be lookin' fer a new commander."

The man held up both hands as if to fend off an attack, but his smirk never wavered. "My apologies, Mr. James. Honestly, it's just been so long, stuck out here amongst the civilized as I am, that I have felt such primal surges of emotion. It is . . . invigorating, I must say." Jesse frowned, confused. Thane calmed himself, raising a hand. "I know wherein you hold your faith, Mr. James. Like most strong men, you hold faith in yourself. And so, as you push the world toward this mighty undertaking, you have faith in yourself if in no other part of it."

Jesse opened his mouth to disagree, but the raised hand, shaken once, stopped him. The anger, however, burned even brighter.

"I know you wish to disagree with me, but I implore you, do not. The truth of the matter is, you care no more for the plight of the coloreds, in the silence of your heart, than I do myself."

Jesse felt tension rising along his back and into his shoulders. His pistols were going to leap into his hands any moment. He could feel Will Shaft's presence at his back like the heat of a furnace. "They are, as most human beings are, a means to an end. However, I do happen to agree with your assessment of the Union. In fact, I support wholeheartedly your aims and designs upon the foe."

Jesse eased back into the chair. His vision was still hazed with anger, but now there was confusion in his eyes as well. "But—"

"But nothing, sir." Thane tapped his fingers on the table. "The Union will eventually turn south, and we must defend ourselves. There is little chance of our doing that unless we stand together. And by all, I mean the desirable and the . . ." His eyes flicked to Will. "I abhor that history has brought us to this pass, but I see no way to argue our way out of it without the piercing report of gunfire."

Jesse shook his head. "Then . . ."

"You have western C.R. Georgia, God bless its chimerical name, standing with you. In fact, I have been empowered to pledge to you the strength of all of C.R. Georgia, as well as the more strident militia units of C.R. Alabama. The Midlands, of course, is still rather firmly under the yoke of Robert the Meek and his tame general Mosby."

Jesse was shocked. "You're tellin' me . . ."

Thane nodded, but this time there was no sign of humor. "I am telling you that you will have the support you need to conduct your attack. Your move eastward, and your stops along the way, have impressed those of us with our hands on the levers of power, Mr. James. We would like nothing better than to prove to the world the supremacy of the white man . . . But history, and the thrice damned Doctor Carpathian, has taken that moment away from us." Again his eyes flicked to Will. "We will embrace the distasteful, that we shall live to taste another day."

Jesse stood up, the rising anger warring now with a sudden surge of wary victory. And yet at what cost? To ally himself with men such as Thane . . .

"Mr. James, let us know where we shall meet you, and we shall be there." Thane nodded a dismissal, but then raised his hand yet again to stall Jesse's departure. "But wait . . .You did not mention a target . ...?"

Jesse stood by his chair, unsure whether to leave or stay. And fairly certain he should not mention Warley's suggested target for their endeavor. "Well, Mr. Thane, sir, we have not yet—"

"You mean to attack the Union fort being built in old Tennessee, correct?" Jesse refused to squirm beneath those piercing eyes.

"I wouldn't know as of yet. And besides, I wouldn't—"

Thane threw one arm over the back of his chair, relaxing easily into a friendly pose. "Nonsense. Where else would you attack, raising such a force?" The eyes turned speculative. "And so we come to the crux of the matter, yes? What does Jesse James have faith in? What is in this fortress the hated enemy builds within a stone's throw of our own power?" Jesse leaned over the table, his metal fingers digging furrows in the wood. "Look, chiseler. You best leave off—"

"It's the treasure you want, isn't it, Jesse?" Thane's entire body had stiffened, straightening out, arms outstretched to match Jesse's own. "A treasure being delivered to the fortress from the unassailable strength of Washington is what you truly hunger for."

Jesse leaned in even closer. "I don't know what you're talkin' about. My belly's rumblin' fer one thing, friend, an' that's takin' down the Union. Whatever's left after they fall and burn? Well, I figure we can all fight over that when the deed's done."

"Then you truly do not know about the riches?" The disbelief in Thane's face washed away all of the previous emotion.

Jesse ground his teeth together in an audible rasp. "I swear, I'm about done—"

Again the hand rose, and again Jesse found himself silent. The shaking was marked, now, and he knew that Thane was living on borrowed time. "Our sources tell us that treasures of incalculable value are being brought to that place. That, in fact, this was the purpose of its construction all along. There are those who believe, in fact, that controlling this treasure would be worth more than all the gold the Union has poured into the Contested Territories."

Jesse rolled back on his heels. The intensity of the man's speech was almost enough to make him forget his anger. "Bosh. That don't make no sense. If it's worth so much, why bring it so far south? Why not keep it up in the north? Ah, you don't know manure from a mint julep." He hooked his thumbs behind his gun belt, sure now that he was dealing with a madman.

Thane's intensity only deepened. He leaned over the table, his eyes boring into Jesse's. "You have heard no tales of powerful artifacts or relics, Jesse James? Never heard stories of ancient forces strong enough to tip the balance of power in the modern world? Such relics once decided the fates of nations, I assure you. Should the Union have one, or more than one? Not even your plan will save the Confederacy from annihilation."

Jesse sat back down at the table, Thane easing back into his own seat. Images slashed through the outlaw's mind: the underground chamber out past Diablo Canyon; Carpathian's interest in whatever had been kept there, and a mysterious wooden crate in a jouncing, fleeing Doomsday wagon. Then he got to thinking of the gold the Union poured into the western territories. An image flashed in his mind, crates of gold on a half-sunk war boat. Without that gold they would have lost control over the region decades ago. What could be more powerful than all that coin?

Thane allowed Jesse to mull his words over for a moment longer and then leaned forward to speak in low, conspiratorial tones. "Should you succeed in this quest, Mr. James, you could become the most powerful man on the continent."

Jesse's eyes flicked up to meet the stranger's. He looked closely at the man for the first time. The eyes were hazel, with flecks of light and dark swirling together. In the RJ lamps of the room, they seemed almost to mingle within their margins of green and brown, into a rosy blur.

"I'm not sure what you—" Jesse was lost in those swirling colors.

"Mr. James. I represent some very powerful people, people who wish to see these relics contained or controlled, if possible. They will pay handsomely, should you find them in the fortress and bring them to me."

Jesse shook his head, cocking it to one side and regarding Thane with a distrust growing to match his anger. "I ain't doin' this fer no treasure, and I sure as hell ain't doin' it fer you 'r anyone like you."

Thane sniffed and sat back. "Very well, Mr. James. It was only a thought. There will be plenty of time to speak further."

Jesse stood and stepped backward around the chair. He glanced out of the corner of his eye at Will and saw the man watching Thane with distaste. "We'll fight beside you, Thane. And we'll bring down the Union. After that, we'll see."

Thane nodded as if in satisfaction. "Excellent. And remember, please, Mr. James, that the folks of the true Confederacy do not embrace our darker brothers lightly. You should keep that in mind."

Jesse stopped at the door. His hand had slipped to the butt of his Hyper-velocity pistol. This man was his connection to the rest of the Confederacy. If he was going to take down the Union, it had to start here. He sneered, shook his head slightly, and then gestured for Will to proceed him. As he was leaving, however, he leaned back into the room, his own eyes glowing. "You ever show my friend, or any of his people, such open disrespect again, I will end you where you stand."

Thane's wide smile returned. "We understand each other thoroughly, Mr. James!"

Jesse slammed the door and stalked down the stairs. Will was waiting for him at the bottom, and he gestured for his brother and the others to join him as they headed toward the door.

"I'm real sorry you had to listen to that, Will. Thane's a mean-spirited blowhard, and no mistake." Jesse's frustrated anger was still at a high boil.

The dark man in the faded Confederate grays shook his head. "Ain't nothin' I ain't heard worse of, Jesse. 'S all right."

"Listen to what?" Frank's concern was plain on his face.

"Where we goin', boss?" Robert was hurrying to catch up.

"We got what we came for." Jesse grunted as he threw the door open. "The militias, for what they're worth, are behind us."

"Then what's got you so upset?" Lucy followed, but her voice sounded preoccupied.

"Nothin'," grunted Jesse. "We gotta get back to New Orleans. The militia commanders knew we were comin'. Thane spoke fer all of 'em. We need to go back and plan this thing fer real now."

"Not until you tell us what's got you so fired up." Frank reached out and grabbed Jesse's shoulder.

"Hey!" A rough voice called from across the street. "What ya'll doin' with one o' his kind in the middle o' the street like this?"

Jesse froze. Everyone else stopped also, offended or annoyed, looking to the tall man walking toward them, a scowl on his unshaven face. But Jesse, half way to his 'Horse, was as still as a statue.

"I said hey!" The man was closer now, pointing right at Will. The tall black man's hand tightened on the grip of a blaster, but he said nothing.

"What you thinkin', bringing that n–"

Jesse's metal fist lashed out as he passed the local, catching the man with a back-handed blow across the cheek. The crunching of broken bones underscored the slurred cry from pulped lips as the man spun heavily into the dirt. He lay there, moaning, as the outlaw chief stormed passed.

Jesse flexed the metal fingers of his imminently obedient hand and continued moving toward their Iron Horses.

With an extra spring in his step, he leapt into the saddle. Lighting up the engine, he looked over at Will with a wide grin. "Feelin' better already!"

*****

Lucinda walked slowly down Decatur Street and watched as a small ferry boat labored across the churning waters of the Mississippi. Light from the ornate street lamps reflected in red pools on the shifting river. There had been none of the coded signals she had feared when she returned to New Orleans. The flags were in no special order. The Union's guidons, although far more numerous, were all in standard positions. Regardless of her current fears, it appeared no further orders would be demanding her attention. The pressure was still there, of course – those orders would come – but for now, she felt more at ease than she had in weeks.

She had walked along the waterfront for over an hour. After borrowing a blackhoof from Belle Je, she had ridden into the city on her own. The outlaws and the rebels all had too much on their minds as they tried to train and arm every would-be soldier that flooded onto the plantation. She did not envy them their task, but she had concerns enough for her own mind.

Her stylish boots clicked along the cobbles. It was nice to be out of her trail gear and into something considerably more fashionable. The boots moved almost as if they had a mind of their own, bringing her, once again, to the Café du Monde. She smiled. There was no problem so dire that a beignet and a cup of café au lait could not stave it off, at least. She was thinking of Jesse again, as she often did.

Jesse had grown a great deal since their first meeting. There was a depth to him now, a vision of something larger than himself. The fact that this vision encompassed the destruction of the nation she had called her own for most of her life was something she usually forced from her mind. But in times of quiet reflection, she could see the crossroads coming.

It was at moments like this when visions of that horrible laboratory in Camp Lincoln would rear up in her mind. The madman, sanctioned and supported by the very government she had pledged her life to, leaning over her, leering down upon her helplessness, and describing in vivid detail his plans for her. The empty jars lined along the counters and shelves, waiting to be filled.

She did not know how long she could walk this fine line. Jesse was happier than she had ever known him to be, and her part in that happiness, however small, brought her more peace than she had known in a lifetime of service to the Union. Just being near him these past weeks and months had provided something she had never even known she was missing. She smiled again.

Lucinda shook her head and nodded as the waitress placed a linen napkin on her table beside the plate of pastries. The delicate china cup went down next, and the girl moved gracefully away. The agent looked down at the treats. Whenever her thoughts wandered down these paths, she found it best to focus on something else entirely. The future reared up before her like a monster, and she knew she could only ignore it for so long. Even though no orders had awaited her, there would come a day when they called, and she would have to decide whether to answer or not.

By the time Lucinda finished the beignets, she had calmed down enough to continue her walk with a placid mind. She swung around the slumping back wall of the café and up onto the river walk, looking out over the mighty Mississippi. She allowed her mind to drift along on its own course, free, for now, of those terrible choices.

"Lovely evening, isn't it?" The voice was amused, its tone light. She recognized it immediately.

She pivoted on one high heel and nodded as he came up even with her, as if they had intended to meet all along. "Henry. It's always charming to see you."

His smile widened. He was not looking at her, however, but out over the street to their right. "Really." He did not sound convinced. "Well, that sure is nice to hear."

Her mind was racing once again. Did they know how deeply she was entrenched with Jesse's forces? Did they know about the army or his contacts with the Confederates? She and Henry Courtright had been partners for years, but he could easily have been sent to eliminate her if Pinkerton deemed her a threat to the nation.

She kept the slight smile firmly in place and tilted her head dramatically to look at him out of the corner of her eye. She wore the mask of a coquette, but her eyes searched for any sign of violent intent. She was fairly sure she could best him as long as she kept her mind sharp and her eyes open. But she would rather not test the theory. He was nearly as good as she was, and when he meant to kill someone, they usually ended up cold.

"There are folks eager to hear from you." His tone was still even, but the humor was gone. She sensed no imminent threat, but there was only a thin veneer of the friendly banter that had been the foundation of their partnership. Learning what that veneer covered, she realized, could well mean the difference between life and death.

"I filed a report weeks ago. And before that, there was the report from Camp Lincoln." Her own tone was even. She was not defending herself; not yet, anyway. She was explaining her position. "It's been hard to get away. They're a tight-knit bunch."

He did look at her, then. His sardonic smile did not reassure her. "Yes, they certainly are, at that. I saw those reports. They were excellent examples of your usual . . . concise, work?"

She shrugged. The humidity of the river hung about them like a pall. She was almost certain the chill down her back was entirely in her mind.

"Conversation with you always grows tedious when you believe you're getting clever." The words would have made him laugh a year ago. Today, he had no response at all. Her patience reached its end. "Why did they send you?"

He grunted, and at least that sound was slightly amused. "Why do they send anyone anywhere? They want to know what's going on."

"With me?" She forced a light smile. "I'm doing wonderfully, thanks for asking. Have a safe trip north."

He stopped abruptly and grabbed her by one shoulder. He gently but firmly spun her around to face him. "They want to know what you're doing, Luce. You've been gone too long, with too little to show for it. And we've been wasting our time with Carpathian, so patience is wearing thin."

She looked into his eyes and was relieved to see no promise of violence there. So, there was still hope that she could escape this moment without making that last, definitive step one way or the other. She slouched slightly, throwing one hip out, and shrugged again. "You know what I'm doing. I'm close to James and his gang. They trust me now, they bring me with them when they go out on the trail. I've been watching every step they've made."

"And they have no idea you're an agent?" There was precious little faith in his eyes.

She looked over his shoulder, out over the roiling water. "I've convinced them I've left that all behind me."

He let her shoulder go and stepped back a pace. "Convinced them, or convinced yourself?" Now she could see the genuine concern in his eyes, and her heart hurt to think that she might disappoint Henry. Her choice was not between Jesse James and the heartless, violent Union. She would be leaving behind far more than that if she turned her back on it all now.

Lucinda forced the lines of her face into a disciplined frown, revealing nothing. "I am as loyal as you ever were, Henry." Her voice was clipped, although she kept it low. Despite the presence of the Union troops, or maybe even because of them, New Orleans was not a friendly city to the forces of the Republic. "Jesse James is possibly the greatest threat to the Union we have faced since the war ended. I'm the closest agent to him, and I will keep an eye on him and his friends and allies, for as long as I can. And when I have something concrete to report," she stepped into him, her eyes burning. "I will damn well report it."

He watched her silently for a moment. "He's a greater threat than Sitting Bull and his savages, or the European?"

She looked away before nodding. "He could very well be, yes." She was skirting the line again; flirting with the crossroads. She could feel herself balancing on a knife's edge.

Courtright's eyes were flat. "How could he be such a threat? When we ran into him in Kansas City, he was nothing but a washed up desperado playing to the gallery. Now, he's a threat to the nation?"

The heat in her chest was rising again, and Lucinda knew that she was going to have to give something away to justify her continued work with Jesse. If Courtright passed along an order to return with him, there would be no turning back. There was no way to know what his orders were, concerning her, if she refused.

"He's made contact with some Confederate rebels. He's developing a following down here and along the coast."

That made Courtright smile. "So? Lee's so damned concerned for his precious personal honor, he dances to Grant's tune with every note and trill. James could gather up every last rebel and the most he'd manage to get Lee to agree to would be a parade."

She did not want to give anything else up, but if she wanted to step away from this encounter alive, she was going to have to cleave to the middle of the road for a while longer.

"He's got his posse, and a large crew from the territories, as well as the men that he liberated from Camp Lincoln. They've got several Rolling Thunder wagons, and some civilian Ironhides." She wrapped her arms around herself against the chill in her heart. She was watching Courtright's face, trying to gauge when she had given him enough. Not yet. "There are elements among the rebellion that don't care much for Lee's methods. If there are enough of them, they could cause some serious trouble if he gets them all pointed in the same direction."

She could not give him more than that. It would have to be enough, or she was going to have to look for an escape route. Would she be able to swim the river, with that current? Her elaborate dress could well be the death of her, if she had to jump.

Henry watched her eyes for a moment, and Lucinda started to wonder what he was learning there. She knew he was almost as good as she was. She schooled her face to impassivity and smiled mildly once again.

Courtright shrugged and shook his head. "Don't matter. They'd need a lot more men than they'll ever raise to be a threat, no matter what they had with them or whose riding in front." He looked away, over the streets and the skyline of New Orleans. "I guess you can stay here a bit longer. Check it out, see if there really is a threat. But the president himself wants you to come back in. He wants you to report to this new fort Grant is putting in, up in old Tennessee, as soon as you can."

She kept her face completely blank. "A fort, in Tennessee? Isn't that a bit close to the Confederacy?"

He grinned. "On their doorstep, in their parlor, makes little difference when they can't really fight back." The grin slipped. "There's something big going down, Luce; bigger than any of us. They're calling everyone in. They've even put out a contract, bringing in renegades they haven't worked with in years." His eyes flicked back to her. "They're bringing in Tanner and the Wraith."

That stopped her. "Both of them? What could they possibly want with those butchers?" There was both fear and contempt in her voice.

He shrugged. "No one knows. Everyone's rendezvousing at this fort." He looked away. "You need to be there."

She nodded. "Big enough, I'll be able to find it, I assume?"

His smile widened. "They say it's huge, actually. More like a castle than anything else. So yeah, I think a gal with your skills shouldn't have trouble finding it."

"And the president is ordering me there? Not Pinkerton?" She dreaded clarifying this last bit of information, but knew it was important.

His smile vanished. "The president orders and requires you to report to Fort Knox in no less than one month's time. Failure to report will be seen as proof of high treason."

She nodded, looking out over the water. She tried one last ploy. "Which president?"

His smile returned, but this time it was cruel. "There's more than one?"

Chapter 14

The courtyard of Fort Frederick was a frozen mess, filled with a deafening cacophony of roars, grumbles, clashes of kit, and shouting troopers as the 7th Cavalry Regiment of the Union Army prepared to take the field, many bundled in wool cloaks and fur-lined hoods. Captains rallied their squadrons, sergeants exhorted their charges to greater efforts, and the command staff stood with their colonel on the wall above the main gate, looking down into the swirling chaos.

Colonel Custer stood with his arms folded over his chest and surveyed the scene. Nothing was being done to his satisfaction, but that was what he had come to expect since his exile into the middle of nowhere. His lip curled as the word occurred to him. He slowly pushed it through his mind and relished the aptness of its taste. Exile. He had been exiled to this northern outpost, slave to a madman, where his genius would be thwarted and he would find no outlet for his warlike spirit.

But the Powers That Be had not factored in Custer's gumption and his drive. Where there was a will, there was a way. He had always thought as much, and these last months had solidified the belief. The constant Warrior Nation attacks had grown steadily worse since his arrival. They taunted the sentries on the walls every night and fell upon isolated patrols out in the hills in attacks that followed no rhyme or reason. Morale in the fort had been plummeting, and his reports back to Washington and General Grant had barely received even cursory responses.

Custer snarled and turned to spit over the parapet into the churned mud below. He had been played for a fool, but the time for sitting back and accepting his lot was over. His men would not stand for this any longer, and he was not the commander to order them to do so. The entire 7th Cavalry was preparing to ride out and end this frontier menace once and for all. He would prove the error of his detractors and decriers upon the bodies of countless savage dead.

Reports had indicated that there was some sort of schism among the savages on the plains, with various bands clashing against each other despite the desperate fighting back east. Such childish actions could only weaken their hold on the hills, and had offered the perfect opportunity for a strike into their scattered holdings.

His patrols had carefully noted the patterns of movement among the Warrior Nation bands. There was only one possible explanation for everything they had found. A settlement had been established right under his nose, supplying warriors, weapons, and sanctuary to the war leaders who had harassed him since his arrival. Now, his scouts ranged across the plains seeking this new village, and the day of his revenge had arrived. His mouth twisted into a familiar sneer. Not a single one of the flannel-mouthed pikers back east would be able to find fault with his actions when he had soured the region of every last savage threat.

"Sir," Lieutenant Shaw coughed into her gloved hand and stepped close enough to speak behind the gesture. "Here they come."

Custer closed his eyes in frustration. The worst aspect of this entire nightmare assignment had been his forced interactions with the two men now approaching across the parapet. He could not remember the last time they had exchanged a civil word to each other, so the fact that they were both coming at him now, their faces matching visions of righteous indignation, did not bode well.

"Gentlemen," The colonel turned to meet them, seizing the initiative and hopefully pushing them onto their back feet. "What a pleasant surprise to see you both out and about on such a fine day!"

The day was not fine. Early winter snows had come swirling in over a week ago, the corners of the courtyard still sheltering glittering banks. It was brutally cold, and had been for weeks. Many of the troopers were bundled up in their winter gear, those that had it. Requisitions for enough of the equipment for the rest of his soldiers had seen no hope of immediate fulfillment, which was just another fly in his jelly.

Tumblety and Tesla were well-situated for winter gear, though. Tesla was now standing on the parapet in a sensible black wool coat that draped down to his knees, a fur hat crammed over his ears. But Tumblety was a vision in an elaborate crimson uniform long coat that would have done Napoleon's Chief Cook and Bottle Washer proud. The ridiculous mustachios swung out to either side of his bloated face, probably stiff with ice. Custer's casual glance at the self-proclaimed doctor's chest told him that today the man claimed to have been wounded in battle three times, shown conspicuous bravery in the face of the Mexicans, and served with honor at the Battle of Bunker Hill. It would have been more impressive if Custer had not known that the 'doctor' had never once suffered so much as a hang nail even near a battle, had never been to Mexico, and the Battle of Bunker Hill had not happened the better part of one hundred years ago.

"Colonel, this will not stand!" It was Tumblety, of course, who began the attack. Tesla was more even-tempered, although he could be quite violent when provoked. In situations like this, he was more likely to hang back and let his tempestuous colleague lead the charge, and coincidentally take the brunt of the resultant grapeshot. Tumblety was breathing heavily from his hurried climb to the parapet, his face beet red behind the wildly waving facial hair. “You must not embark upon this lunacy, sir!”

Custer took a deep breath, looked down at his boots for a moment, and then looked up again, a pleasantly-bland expression firmly affixed to his features. “What will not stand, doctor?”

The man’s beady eyes flared. “Do not play the fool with ME, sir! We know full well what you intend! Riding off into the hinterlands with your full power, leaving our experiments and personnel without so much as a corporal’s guard!” He was heaving, now, trying to stand upright while his anger conspired to keep him short of breath. “For shame, colonel! With a duty as clear as your own, to spend not a moment’s thought or preparation for your primary charges! This is not why I had you put in charge here, as you well know!”

The colonel felt his gorge rise at that last accusation. Unfortunately, it held enough truth that he let it go for now. Custer’s eyes flickered back to where Tesla stood hiding behind his chief rival. At the moment, however, he was nodding vigorously in support of Tumblety’s case. The colonel shook his head and turned back to the primary target.

“Doctor, I assure you, I have nothing of the sort in mind for you or this installation while I am away.” The words were as mild as he could make them, but his nerves were wearing thin. He was not sure how much longer he could maintain the facade of propriety.

Apparently, Nikola Tesla had had enough of playing second fiddle and so stepped forward to add his own grist to the mill. “Colonel Custer, we know you are mobilizing the entire 7th Regiment. The cream of our best efforts were wrenched away and thrown back east nearly a month ago. Our newest creations are not nearly ready to shoulder the burden of defending the fort. So with what forces do you propose to keep us safe from the savages while you are away?”

Custer was at the end of his rope. Explaining himself to uninitiated laymen had never been a skill at which he excelled. “Mr. Tesla, I assure you that I will not be leaving Fort Frederick undefended in my absence.” He raised one gloved finger to forestall the coming objections from both men. “I am taking the 7th with me, that is true. And elements of the garrisoning units as well, riding along as mounted infantry in support. However, there will still be more than three quarters of the garrison soldiers left behind. More than enough to watch over the fort until we return.”

Tumblety was not comforted, his head still pivoting back and forth in vicious denial. “No, no, no! You are taking the best of the soldiery with you, sir! You are leaving the dregs behind, and you know it!”

Custer was stepping toward the ‘doctor’ before he realized it, his hand rising as if to strike the man. He stopped himself, but did not drop his arm. They were very close, their noses almost touching, and the colonel sneered as he muttered, “If I ever hear you denigrate men under my command again, DOCTOR, we will see how well you fare beyond the walls without them.”

Tesla stepped forward, his dapper face struggling to conjure up a smile. “Gentlemen, no need for a confrontation among friends!” He clapped both men on their shoulders, far more comfortable in the role of reconciler. “I’m sure we can come to some sort of agreement, colonel? A few squadrons to be left behind, just in case, maybe?”

Custer shook his head and stepped back himself, looking out over the courtyard as if dismissing the two men of science. “Firstly, two squadrons would be nearly half my force. And secondly, no, I can’t. Our strategy has been very carefully planned out, and I intend to implement it without amendment or adjustment.” He glared back at the two men. “I will be bringing with me enough force that the savages will be crushed in a single engagement. I’m going to split the regiment into three prongs, and we will be coming at their new settlement from entirely different vectors of attack. There will be no way they can defend against our numbers, our technology, and our spirit.”

Tumblety shook his head, even more forcefully. “Colonel Custer, you cannot leave us without adequate defenses! Do you not understand that I am engendering the future of the nation here? Tomorrow's world is being born today, right here in this fort, and you threaten to abandon it to ignorant savages and barbarians!"

Custer grimaced as the words registered with the smaller scientist.

"YOU are engendering the future?" Tesla's anger boiled back to full burn in the blink of an eye. "You engender nothing but waste and fodder for circus side shows! The future of the Union is in metal hands, you charlatan!"

"Charlatan?" Tumblety's eyes were bulging from his head as he shook within the enormous confines of his uniform coat. "Who, pray tell, are you referring to as a charlatan, you quacksalver? You should superintend your words more closely, or I shall demand satisfaction!"

Custer watched the two men turn on each other, their arguments with him forgotten. Of their own accord, his eyes rolled. He looked over to his command staff. With barely-concealed contempt, they were being careful to look anywhere but at the two scientists whose shrill cries were rising higher and higher, bouncing off the tall tower and the surrounding cliffs.

To one side, Lieutenant Shaw was having words with a young runner, and the look on her face sent an alarming chill down Custer's back, despite the cold. She nodded to the young man, snapped off some quick orders of her own that sent him running back down the stairs, and turned to look at her commander. Her brown hair, kept in a tight bun beneath her uniform cap, had sent several escaping tendrils questing out into the cold air. They whipped against the side of her pale face as she approached.

"Sir, there's been a development." Her voice was pitched low.

Custer nodded, not taking his eyes off the howling spectacle before him. He knew he was not going to like what she had to say, and could probably guess where it was coming from as well.

"It's the general, sir." The title, said with heavy infliction, could only mean one man. Custer turned to stare at his adjutant. He could feel dismay settling over his face, but he gestured for her to continue.

"His eastern fortress is almost complete." She looked away, as if she could not bear to see his reaction. "Apparently, the actions against the savages back east are not going well, however. He cannot spare any of his own forces to man the fort. He orders you to take the 7th, depart without delay, and report to Fort Knox before the month is out."

He felt numb and knew it was more than the cold. "Within a month." He mumbled. There would be no time for his grand assault. "They would take even this away from me."

Shaw leaned closer, her eyes betraying her own anger. "Sir, they can't do this to you. There has got to be another way."

Custer turned his gaze back to the two grumbling men. Apparently, their energy was not equal to a sustained assault. He grunted at his adjutant and then moved toward the scientists. Tesla saw him first and cringed from his expression. The reaction warned Tumblety, who spun around as if he expected to find Sitting Bull himself had leapt atop the wall.

"Gentlemen." The colonel's eyes were intense as he regarded the two men. "How close to deployment are your respective projects?"

Tumblety and Tesla exchanged a wary glance, suddenly less than enthusiastic to compare the preparedness of their work. Tesla was the first to turn back to the colonel, straightening his shoulders and schooling his features to some semblance of calm confidence.

"Well, the shipment east that Washington demanded took all of my active units, including even my most experimental items. But I will be able to deploy a small, elite unit of combat automatons within the next few weeks." He shrugged. "I would have to retrofit weapons from existing stock, which will not be ideal. I would have liked a chance to field test my displacer gauntlets, but they took those as well. But I am confident that new combat units would be able to take the field within a few weeks' time."

Custer turned his gaze upon Tumblety. Pride wrestled with caution and fear across his face, and threw them down. "I am confident that I will be able to field at least a company of new Reconstructed in half the time!" As he continued to speak, his voice strengthened, his posture stiffened. Reality, in his own mind, changed before his eyes to conform to his growing conviction.

"I, too, was required to send subjects east, as you know. However, the Reconstructed that I can put into the field will be stronger, faster, and more resilient than the metal automata of my colleague, and more effective in battle as well." Tumblety finished his little speech with a flourish of his hands and then placed them firmly on his hips, mimicking a statue of a war hero he had once seen while vacationing in England.

Custer was still and silent for a moment while he measured his own reaction to their reports. He smiled for a moment, looked down at his boots again, and then over at Lieutenant Shaw. She was staring at the men with her mouth hanging partly open in naked horror.

"Sir," Shaw muttered, turning her back on the scientists. "You cannot leave the defense of the fortress to these men's creations. Since Washington stripped them of their active units, neither of them have anything remotely ready for the task. The Warrior Nation has been ramping up its attacks for months. With winter coming on, there will be almost no resupply for the foreseeable future. The chiefs have a burning hatred for us. If we leave things in the hands of those two . . . men . . . there will be nothing at all left when we return."

The colonel nodded slowly. He pivoted on his heel and moved to the outer wall, his gloved hands resting lightly on the cold stone. The rolling terrain of the Black Hills stretched out beneath the walls of the fort and into the distance. The jagged gray bones of the Earth were visible where the soil had been worn away by centuries of wind and rain. It was harsh country, and he had come to respect the land. He knew that even at that moment, the land concealed countless enemy scouts, watching his fortress with dark, hostile eyes.

There was no denying the truth of Shaw's words. Something about this complex had enraged the savages. Whether it was the experiments and technologies developed here, the placement of the fortress upon some sacred site, or perhaps even the mere presence of white folks within the ancient hills, they would stop at nothing until Fort Frederick was destroyed.

Custer turned back to his command staff and the two scientists. He began to walk down the parapet, jerking his head slightly as he passed Shaw, indicating that she should follow him. He knew from her expression that she did not like the glimmer in his eye. There had been a lot of quiet, respectful dissent from his command staff over his proposed attack into Warrior Nation territory. Shaw, although never one to question him before the rest of the troops, had expressed her own questions when they were alone. Everyone had lined up behind him when he'd put his boot down, and he knew they would do so again.

"Lieutenant, I would like to leave three companies behind." He tilted his head toward the scientists. "When these gentlemen are ready with their own forces, I think such a joint force will be sufficient to teach the savages a lesson they won't forget before we return." He stopped and turned to face her. "If I leave any of my commanders behind, however, they would most likely countermand my orders as soon as I was out of sight." He looked sourly back at the men and women of his command staff before turning back to her. "You're the only officer here with any real loyalty to me, personally. However, there is no way I could ever ask the seasoned captains beneath me to follow a lieutenant, even if I gave you a field promotion. They would all outrank you in seniority."

Shaw's face set in lines of dissent. Beneath them in the courtyard, the men and women of the 7th continued to prepare, unaware of their twisting fates. "However, if I give you a field promotion to captain, and then split off a small portion of each company's troopers, taking one lieutenant from each group for command –"

"Sir," Shaw's voice was low and sharp, but he silenced her with a gesture. "I would be able to string together an ad-hoc squadron for you, I think. I could leave you the entire garrison, as well. None of this will look unusual, even in Washington." He looked back at his commanders and the two scientists. Both men strove for his attention. He ignored them. "It would be left to your judgment if the abominations of either gentlemen were worthy of inclusion. But you are correct: if someone does not go out and push back against the savages, there will be no stopping them."

Shaw looked at him for a long moment, then back to the rest of the command group. She lowered her head in resignation. "I understand, sir."

The colonel put his hand on her shoulder and squeezed once with a grimace of sympathy before moving back to the group huddled around the stairs. "Gentlemen, there has been a drastic change of plans."

The officers all stood taller. They were hoping, he knew, to hear that his proposed attack on the elusive village was being postponed. The scientists, however, looked as if they were balanced between hope and indignation. It was a natural state for men of science, if these two were an average representation of the breed.

"General Grant is ordering the 7th back east. Apparently, there's trouble with the Rebellion. The general has it in mind that we're the ones to teach them a sharp lesson." He ignored the slumping shoulders and looks of relief that passed among his officers. "I will be brevetting Shaw to Acting Captain and placing her in command of this fortress in my absence." He raised a gloved hand to stop the growing protests among the senior officers. "The general wishes the 7th to arrive on the border intact at the command level."

As the words sunk in, both Tesla and Tumblety were again fidgeting with agitation. "Colonel, once again I must protest." Tumblety, of course. "Leaving our safety in the hands of a feckless girl! It hardly bears thinking upon!"

Tesla's agreement was so emphatic he nearly nodded his head clear off. "With the future of the Union at stake, you cannot—"

"I agree." Custer's simple words brought both men stumbling to a halt.

"You . . . agree . . . ?" Tumblety could hardly believe his ears, clearly.

"I do. But gentlemen, the future of the Union is not only at stake here. It is at stake to the east, where General Grant contends with Sitting Bull and the united chiefs. It is at stake in Washington, where useless politicians daily debate the minutia of bureaucracy while around them the Republic burns. It is at stake in the contested territories, where madmen and bandits flout the law, strutting in their flagrant destruction of civilized convention." He looked gravely at the scientists, happy to see they were lapping his words up like kittens with cream. "Here and now, the future is at stake as well, I agree. But my men and I are called away. And so today, defending the future falls to you, gentlemen. It is you who must hold the line."

Custer could see his regimental commanders, beyond the grinning madmen, looking at each other in confusion. He almost smiled. Instead, he maintained his grave expression and continued. "Captain Shaw will have a solid force with her, as well as the entire Army garrison. And when your creations are ready . . . weeks, I believe you said?" Both men nodded, but there was a sheepish cast to their faces that did not bode well for the prediction. "Excellent, then. Let us say in four weeks' time, Captain Shaw will form an assault force of the most prudently spared forces. They will push the savages back from Fort Frederick with a lesson that will hold them over until my return."

The scientists watched him for a moment, their minds struggling with the dual impressions of abandonment and empowerment. Their egos won the day, as he knew they would, and both men swelled with pride, visions of victory rising in their heads. Perhaps Tumblety was even imagining a few new medals he could add to his collection.

It took several days to shave the numbers off each company and form them into temporary commands. When the 7th Cavalry Regiment prepared to ride east, Shaw, her lieutenants, and the two scientists were there to see them off. The roar of hundreds of Iron Horses and Locust support vehicles was nearly deafening, and the scorching, faintly-chemical smell of RJ-1027 filled the air.

Shaw had already said her goodbyes, and Custer had passed along all the wisdom and advice he could in the short time they had had. Tesla stood, tall and dark in his long coat, face grim with the reality of their situation. But Tumblety, as always, had one more thing to say as the Colonel gunned his engine and began to drift toward the gate.

"Good hunting, Colonel!" The 'doctor' shouted to be heard. Custer knew that was not all he would have to say, however. "I pray you are doing the right thing! History will not be kind to you if the Warrior Nation proves stronger in resolve than you believe, and our efforts here are lost."

Custer grinned despite himself. He was leaving all of this behind and taking the first steps to free himself from the chains Tumblety had forged at Camp Lincoln. And even though he felt bad for Shaw, the idea of commanding in the field once again, far from the puling demands of the scientists, had lifted his spirits amazingly. He tipped his hat to the 'doctor', and shouted in response, "Well and good, doctor. But I do not answer to history. I answer to General Grant. And of the two, he is by far the less forgiving!"

*****

The small balcony shot out from the hostel, leaning over the canyon that gave the town its name. He had paid extra, both for the view and for access to the canyon, in case he needed to lose something in a hurry. The fact that the Lonely Rose was also about as far from the center of town as you could get was a bonus. There had been a lot of law moving through Diablo Canyon recently, and he was not interested in tangling with them so soon after the . . . unpleasantness that had cost him most of his posse out in the desert the last time.

William Bonney tossed back the cheap firewater and with a convulsive heave launched the cloudy glass out into the air. It tumbled erratically, catching the thin winter sun as it twirled, sending dazzling glimmers shooting off in all directions. It sank slowly, as if defying gravity, over the edge and into the jagged rocks below. He watched the glass drop out of sight and then settled against the makeshift railing, his hands tight on the rough wood.

Nothing had gone right for him since Jesse James had landed in the middle of his camp that day. Well, if he was going to be honest with himself, nothing had gone right for him since he had first broken into that damned chamber of horrors beneath the desert. Filled with Carpathian's castoff corpse-slaves and stinking to high heaven, standing in that room, staring at that empty stand, and then his meeting with Jesse afterward, had been the lowest point in his life. Not even losing the rest of his posse down in old Texas at the hands of Pat Garret and those Pinkerton agents had put him lower.

After that, he had had a tough row to hoe. Most of the hired hands were dead. Ringo and Smiley had gone their separate ways. Billy had had a small stash in Diablo Canyon, so he had returned, laid low, and brooded over lost opportunities. The Apache Kid was staying in a room down the hall, having refused to abandon his boss. But the renegade warrior was naturally silent and little help in lifting Billy out of his low spirits.

When those Union agents had come through about a month ago, he thought they were after him and he had hidden in the Lonely Rose for almost a week. He had ventured out finally, bored out of his skull, and convinced he would rather die than spend another day in the miserable little garret. He had run right into an agent, of course. He had been recognized, and prepared to go down fighting. The agent had not cared at all.

That was the second lowest point. There was a time, not so long ago, that Billy the Kid had been one of the most wanted men in the western territories. But there was so much going on right now, he had not rated a second glance even from the agents who had once chased him the length and breadth of the west. He spat out over the railing, but the bitter taste remained.

On the heels of the Washington muscle men, some new-fangled lawman, calling himself Mick Ironhide, had shown up in town, waving a government writ and declaring Diablo Canyon once more under federal protection. This guy claimed to be working independently of the Earps' Federal Bureau of Marshals, and he did not have any of the heavy firepower the Earps generally brought to bear. Turned out, though, that he had more than enough to make the town too hot for Billy's liking.

And now, local gossip-mongers were talking about a large cavalry force, maybe a whole regiment, roaring out of the north west; Warrior Nation territory. They had torn through the territories on their way back east. Hundreds of men and machines, riding hell-bent for leather. It was that thought which had really started to get his blood moving again.

Billy had been hearing the stories about Jesse, of course. How he had found his brother in a prisoner camp out east and pulled him out through some ridiculous heroics. He had been glad to hear that. Frank James was a gentleman of the first water, and Billy would not have wanted to hear that he had been lost. But the stories of Jesse coming out at the head of an army, riding up into Warrior Nation territory and disappearing? Those were stories he could have well done without.

Billy remembered talking to Jesse back in Kansas City about the damned artifact that had ended up in Carpathian's liver-spotted hands. They had talked about leading armies and raising the south against the Union. He could not have honestly said if he had been serious back then, but it seemed like Jesse had. There was even some talk that James had been seen heading back south, maybe even down the great river.

Whatever was going on, though, it was not happening in Diablo Canyon. The place had been a rip for a while, totally lawless without its old UR-30 to keep the peace, except when the big lawmen or their Union masters came through, of course. And now, with Mick Ironclad, the place had died right down again.

Billy turned on a boot heel and sank into a creaking chair, contemplating the canyon through slit eyes. Why would Jesse James be heading down the Mississippi? It skirted the border with the Confederacy. What had happened to the army he had apparently led out of Union territory? The young-looking outlaw could feel the stirring of ambition again. He wanted very much to be out of Diablo Canyon and back into the thick of things. Spending the entire winter here on the margins, away from all the excitement, did not sit well. Carpathian's agents were moving into all the local towns, offering cheap power, generators, and other tech in exchange for a simple promise of allegiance and support in the future. He did not want to be around when they came to Diablo Canyon and met Sheriff Mick.

If James was headed back into the Confederacy, why? How did he think he was going to convince them to listen? In Kansas City, Jesse and Billy had talked up big plans, but back then they were imagining themselves in possession of the mysterious artifact. They had no idea what it might be, but they had imagined it to be some talisman that could convey power and prestige before the cowering remnants of the old south.

Could Jesse have—

A harsh, raucous sound smashed into his thoughts as a heavy object crashed onto the railing beside him. With a muttered curse, Billy's battered pistol was in his hand. Two quick shots snapped off, the second bolt soaring out over the canyon and into the distance. The first bolt had done the trick.

Billy sidled toward the pile of meat, metal, and feathers that had flopped onto the balcony with a wet slap after his shot had done its work. With a little effort he located what must have been the head. A bird skull gave it shape, but most of the actual head had been reconstructed out of crude black metal. A slight red glow was fading fast from its eyes. It had been a large bird of some kind, probably a vulture, but heavily modified with bits of metal, rubber, and wires. The lower jaw was rattling, opening and closing spastically as if laughing at him. Judging by the smell, it had been dead for some time.

Billy nudged the corpse with his boot, moving aside a wing and spreading the pieces out along the floor of the balcony. A small ivory tube, covered in black, oily liquid, poked out from beneath a metal claw. He reached down and plucked it out of the stinking pile. It was a message tube. He wiped it against his pant leg and popped it open. Several small rolls of paper slid into his palm.

The first thing Billy noticed as he unrolled the note that was wrapped around the rest, was the intricate 'C' drawn across the bottom in an elegant hand. The short note was equally graceful, but the contents froze his heart.

"An artifact of your own?"

Billy shuffled through the other two papers. Each was a map; one of the Old States with several locations noted in red ink, the other some sort of underground complex. He stared at the sheaf of papers, at the dead, twitching bird, and then out over the shattered landscape of the canyon. His hand tightened into a fist without his conscious will, crushing the note.

"James." He spat.

Chapter 15

Frank James rested his forearms against the hatch cowling atop the Rolling Thunder wagon. Although his raider's spirit had at first balked at the thought of being trapped in a giant target, the firepower of the Rolling Thunder had brought him around. He had been riding in Ole Bessie the entire trip south, ever since Jesse had left for New Orleans. Frank did not much care for water or boats, and had had no interest in taking to the river himself.

The army of independent Confederate groups had gathered around a quiet little river town called Maycomb. By the time Jesse, Colonel Warley, and the New Orleans contingent had arrived, Tinker Thane and the other militia commanders were already ensconced in town. The commanders had taken the majestic courthouse, easily the largest and most impressive building in town, as their headquarters.

Jesse was still ill-at-ease with the big bugs of the rebellion, but he hid it well. Warley treated him with a great deal of respect, and that lent him a certain amount of implied respectability in the minds of the others. He knew the battle-hardened survivors of Camp Lincoln, the outlaws from Robbers Roost, and Ingram's Rangers, as well as their small contingent of Rolling Thunder wagons did not hurt, either.

The Army of New Orleans, marching with a swinging gait behind the impressive might of their stolen heavy armor, had crossed the border into the Confederacy without hindrance. Sure, there had been some hard looks at the number of dark-skinned soldiers marching with them, but he had been heartened when he saw the soldiers' reaction to these looks. After the first few days, the entire army began marching to the unmistakable cadences of melancholy spirituals. All of the soldiers sang together, loud as could be, with smiles that only got wider as the locals turned red. It was a start, but it was enough to reassure Frank that there was hope to their cause after all.

When they had arrived in Maycomb, Frank was a little saddened to see that most of the militia units were not nearly as integrated as their own. Each group did have its share of black folks, however. They might not have been sharing fires with the white folks often, but they were there all the same. They wore similar uniforms, those that had a uniform, and all were armed with similar weapons. Jesse had managed to save nearly all the weapons when they fled the Warrior Nation in the north, throwing them into the surviving wagons for the long, hungry trek south. Those weapons had first gone to arm the New Orleans forces. The rest were distributed as evenly as possible among the other militias. Frank noticed a funny thing, though: not many seemed to get to Thane's group.

They had not stayed in Maycomb long. Most of the army was already assembled when they arrived. They were only waiting for those few stragglers coming in late, mostly from the deep swamps of what had once been Florida, now part of C.S. Alabama. Frank was still not sure why all the old state names had been changed, or erased altogether, and the old lines redrawn. That was just another thing he could ask President Lee, if everything worked according to plan. There would be some changes when they finally confronted the old coward as the conquerors of Grant's mighty citadel.

If everything they had been able to find out about this Fort Knox was true, they were bringing more than enough men to bury the place several times over. Most reports said the fort was desperately undermanned. Riding in Ole Bessie, visions of swift victory were easy to come by.

The thought brought Frank back to the present. Maycomb was many days behind them now. He cast his eye over the men and women he had come to think of as his own. Most of Jesse's group, outlaws, freed prisoners, and militia, now had Iron Horses of their own, with only a small contingent riding in Ironhide wagons or marching alongside. Many of the best had been seconded to militia units from the towns around New Orleans as advisors.

Their other surviving Rolling Thunders crunched along on the narrow trail just behind Ole Bessie. Considering that the full strength of the independent rebels stretched out as far as he could see in nearly all directions, it was hard to imagine the pile of bricks at the end of their march posing too much of a problem.

The deep-throated roar of a band of Iron Horses rolled over the armored wagon. Frank looked down to see Jesse ride up with Robert and Charlie Ford, Marcus Cunningham under his customary hood, and the beautiful Lucinda. Frank's smile widened and he waved down. Damn, that was a fine looking woman. He knew she had run into a little difficulty the first night the Army of New Orleans had made camp. A couple of the men from an outlying town had taken an unhealthy interest, despite Jesse standing nearby. But Jesse had just smiled, stepped back, and let Lucy speak for herself. The many variations on the story he had heard differed only in the details of how long each man had been unconscious.

Jesse grinned up at Frank and then gestured straight ahead. He followed up with several other gestures they had shared since their time in the war. Jesse was bringing his command group forward to scout ahead. Several mounted squads were already out there, Frank knew, but Jesse always liked to be in the thick of things. He nodded and waved, watching as the five of them thundered away down the trail on columns of thickened air.

Frank looked around for the Ironhide carrying Quantrill, Warley, Captain Carney, and the other commanders of the New Orleans group. He stared hard at Quantrill, his mind returning to the mysterious Allen Henderson. Frank shook his head. The man had vanished months ago, and no apparent harm had come from his strange game. Cole, currently riding herd on the far right flank, had been urging him to forget the specter and focus on the work at hand. None of the big bugs seemed to think twice about it. He had tried to put it aside, but every now and then he was haunted by memories of the man's strange eyes . . .

A dilapidated old Ironhide rumbled up next to Ole Bessie. Frank looked over and grinned widely when he recognized Buford Nash standing in the rusty machine's flatbed. His son, Deacon, crouched next to him, polishing a Union blaster and staring daggers at the outlaw rifleman. Frank could not have given two squats over a full latrine. Buford, however, had become something very close to a friend during the journey north. It was good to know the St. Tammany militia was nearby. Frank did not have many friends among the Confederate fighters, but he knew Jesse trusted the New Orleans folks, and he had gotten to know many of the St. Tammany men himself. He would trust a mud-stained swamp trotter long before he trusted some flannel-mouthed city croaker from Atlanta or Charlotte.

Frank was about to shout a crude joke over to Nash's truck when a low rumbling echoed up somewhere off to the left. A column of smoke rose into the sky from their distant flank. Frank ducked down into the armored heat of the Rolling Thunder and shouted for his driver to pull up. The wagon rolled to a halt, and by the time he emerged, three more columns of smoke rose into the pale winter sky. The rumbling was nearly continuous, now.

"Something not too good goin' on over dere, I t'ink!" Buford shouted.

Frank hoisted Sophie out through the hatch and swung the long rifle around, pointing toward the disturbance. He sighted through the powered scope, searching through the colorful swirl of shifting images for the cause of the commotion. He found one of the churning smoke columns in the sky and followed it down to the base. A raging fire, erupting from the twisted wreckage of an overturned Ironhide, writhed at the bottom of the smoky pillar. The fighters around the vehicle were fleeing toward the main army, many throwing down their weapons as they ran. The entire scene was eerie in its silence.

Frank brought Sophie's gun sight back to the smoke and tried to see through to the other side. There was a hint of surging motion, but nothing more. Some of the militia, braver than most, had settled into cover around fences, tree stumps, or boulders. They were aiming off to the west where a fallow field and clumps of trees hid their targets. The weeds and small trees thrashed violently as Frank watched. It appeared as if something massive was moving toward the army's flank.

"Whatch'ou see?" Buford Nash shouted again. Whatever was happening, they could hear nothing but the distant thunder.

Frank lowered Sophie and looked over at the militia leader. "We're bein' hit!" He pointed toward the smoke. "Somethin' took out three or four wagons. Most folks'r runnin', though some are standin' their ground!"

Buford craned his head off to the left. Around him on the flatbed, his men were all clutching weapons. Aside from ambushing an occasional hapless Union soldier, none of them had seen the elephant up close before. They had felt unassailable in the center of the huge army. The fact that someone was attacking them now was nearly unthinkable.

"We gonna head over, see what there is to see?" Buford was holding a massive blunderbuss that he called his gator stick.

Frank stared back toward the commotion in the distance. There were several wide fields separating them. He looked down at Buford's beat-up old wagon. He shook his head. "I don't think you're gonna make it, old man!" He smiled. "I'll let you know how it stands, though!"

Frank lowered himself back into Ole Bessie's rumbling hull and tapped the driver on the shoulder. The kid nodded. There really was no hope of being heard when the enormous engine filled the compartment with its thunder. The driver turned back to his vision slit, hands grasping the controls.

Ole Bessie lurched around, spinning on its enormous drive wheels, and started to push behind Buford's wagon, off into the field to their left. Two other Rolling Thunders followed suit, pivoting on the packed trail and bursting through a low stone wall. They churned over the turned earth, shaking themselves out into an arrowhead formation. Many of the small militia bands, lacking any real military doctrine to fall back on, ran to follow. They shouted with excitement and waved their new weapons in the air.

"I hope Jesse's turning back 'round." Frank muttered, knowing that his crew would never hear him. Aside from the driver, the small space was filled with three gunners who shared the duties of switching out exhausted power cells, aiming, and firing. The largest weapon, of course, was the enormous blaster cannon on the forward turret. The Gatling cannons that covered the front and sides were nothing to dismiss lightly. Frank was pretty sure that, no matter what had snuck up on their left verge, Ole Bessie and her sisters would be able to take care of it.

Frank was settling down in front of the commander's vision slit when he felt someone tap him on the back of the head. He turned, and one of the gunners pointed back toward the rear of the compartment, where a small vision slit provided a view of the vehicle's back trail. Frank maneuvered his way through men and machinery. He pressed his forehead against the leather brace pad above the viewport.

In the narrow field of vision, he could just make out Nash's old rust bucket lurching over the tumbled stones left behind by the Rolling Thunders. The old wagon was bucking and swaying wildly as it negotiated the rutted, uneven field, but it ground forward nevertheless.

Frank sat back, smirking, and shook his head at the gunner. The man returned the grin. There really was no telling with these swamp folks. Frank returned to the commander's position, but quickly changed his mind and pushed back up through the hatch. He turned and waved at the old Ironhide churning along in his wake. He saw a big arm wave in reply and knew that Buford had been watching for his reaction. Frank's grin widened and he turned back around.

There were men and women running past him now, folks that had been the first to flee from whatever had hit them. Their eyes were wide with panic, their faces pale. Their legs drove them forward, despite obvious exhaustion. They were muddy, battered, and bruised from their headlong flight through the fields. There was no sign that they planned on stopping any time soon, running right past the big wagons crawling across the fields toward the trouble.

Frank watched as one group of militia, moving with the wagons toward the fighting, tried to stop some of their fleeing comrades. The retreating men fought with insane strength to break away, pushing, punching, kicking, and shrieking, until they were released. The attempt took a lot of the excitement out of the fighters moving west. No one else tried to stop the bolting troops.

The Rolling Thunders had crossed about half the distance to the shindig, and Frank brought Sophie up again to look through her scope. There were now seven wagons burning, and an unbroken wave of return fire flashed like sleeting crimson rain off to the west. The weeds and grasses all along that line were burning, sending a pall of smoke in all directions. Within the smoke, Frank could see things moving. The distance, the swirl of smoke, and the play of light and shadow made it impossible to know exactly what he was seeing.

The Rolling Thunder wagons churned to a stop at another low, tumbled wall. Only one field lay between them and what now appeared to be a full-blown battle. The field was strewn with bodies, most of them smoldering or blasted into long streaks of tattered cloth and meat. The group of militia fighters holding the line was much thinner than it had been, with large holes blown into their defensive position. The smoke rising beyond their crouching forms was even thicker, obscuring everything on the other side in a thick haze.

Frank watched as red bolts came tearing out of the smoke. Lines of explosions stuttered in their wake and fighters were sent spinning away into still, crumpled heaps. He looked to either side. The militia who had followed the Rolling Thunders stood gaping, staring at the death and destruction before them. There were times when Frank felt that his brother's ambitions had taken them out of their depth. This quickly became one of them. All of his military training and experience, aside from being decades out of date, revolved around leading small bands of lightly-armed men in attacks against heavy, clumsy, ignorant enemies. He did not enjoy having the situation reversed.

"Get behind the wall!" He shouted at the men on either side of Ole Bessie. He repeated the order again, accompanying his cry with frantic gestures. A few of the quicker fighters caught on and dropped, dragging their slower fellows after them. They assumed defensive positions behind larger stones or old, overgrown tree stumps. Most continued to stand and gape, however, and Frank was ready to turn his guns on them out of frustration when Buford Nash's wagon rumbled up. The Tammany man leapt off the flatbed and began to harangue the men and women standing like tobacco shop Injuns in the mud.

Frank nodded to Buford and then looked back at the faltering line. Shapes swayed back and forth within the smoke, like giant figures emerging from the mists of ancient myth. There were only a few survivors of the initial defense, and while he watched, they all began to scramble backward. First, only one or two moved, but soon they were all clambering out of their cover. He could hear them shouting, thin across the wide field, but it was meaningless sound; carrying no sense.

The first large shape breached the smoke and a low moan passed over Frank's secondary line. The thing was taller than a man. It was hard to make out any detail, but it seemed to move with an unnatural, stiff gait, a single crimson eye peering balefully through the fog. Both of its arms ended in massive Gatling cannons, and it fired directly into the fleeing defenders, cutting them down in showers of red mud.

The militia fighters stood still and silent as several more of the giant shapes strode out of the smoke, their bolts slapping the last of the fleeing figures into the dirt. When the last man collapsed, only a hundred feet or so from Frank's position, the monsters paused. Under the rumble of his wagons, an eerie silence descended upon the battlefield.

He looked to either side. All of the fighters were staring at those enormous shapes. He shook his head and shouted down into his own wagon. "Get a bead on one o' them big galoots!"

A gunner shouted up, asking which one, and he rolled his eyes before yelling, "Any one!"

Buford was still moving among the men, pointing frantically toward the towering shapes. Ole Bessie's turret cranked around. When it fired, the lick of crimson flame reached almost twenty feet into the field. The blast took one of the tall shapes in its broad chest, and in a shower of sparks and deflected energy, tossed its shattered form back into the smoke.

That was enough to break the spell. Suddenly, the entire line erupted as the fighters unleashed their rage and fear on the distant targets. The Rolling Thunders to either side of Ole Bessie added their own cannons to the mix, and soon the line was on fire from end to end. Most of the giant shapes were down, the survivors moving forward with awkward, shambling steps.

Frank did not know what else he could do. He had his troops in good cover, they were firing in the right direction, and they seemed to be hitting their targets at least often enough to get them to think twice. Except they were not. The remaining brutes were firing again, and although their automatic fire was sleeting off the armor of the heavy wagons, they would eventually get lucky. Every few moments, one or two fighters from the line would leap into the air away from their cover, trailing arcs of blood.

More figures were emerging from the smoke, moving forward through the giant armored forms. These new attackers were about the height of a man, but far heavier than the average soldier. They slid forward in a loping run, moving much more smoothly than the larger enemies, long arms hitting the ground every few paces to propel them along.

The Gatling cannons of the three Rolling Thunders responded to the new threats. Streams of ruby destruction sprayed into the smoke, cutting the new targets down as they approached. But there were many of them, and the smoke made them nearly impossible to target. More and more were appearing, running past their towering partners and closing the distance on the secondary Confederate line.

Frank was struggling with an array of bad options when another wagon came rumbling up behind Ole Bessie. He looked back, relief washing over him as he saw Colonel Warley disembarking from the Ironhide. Quantrill, Captain Carney, and a few of the other commanders hopped down into the mud after the dapper colonel. They spread out through the line, stiffening resolve wherever they went. Warley nodded at Frank as he passed. The outlaw nodded back, choosing to take the signal as a sign of approval.

Carney had an enormous weapon attached to his arm, a frame of ornate metal and leather straps holding it in place. He braced himself visibly and leaned into the cannon, letting forth with a radiant burst of crimson fire that sleeted across the field and into the oncoming mob. Around him, heartened by the devastation the dark-skinned officer wrought, the soldiers renewed their own attacks, standing firm and firing into the enemy.

The redoubled power of the rebel fusillade staggered their attackers' charge. For a moment, Frank thought they had turned the tide. Then a ridiculously thick beam of coherent crimson force lashed out of the smoke, striking the Rolling Thunder to the right, full on its front armor. The vehicle flashed like a paper lantern. Illuminated from within, it disappeared in a shattering blast. Infantry all around were scythed down with screaming shrapnel which rattled off the nearby wagons. Frank grunted as he took a jagged bit of metal in the shoulder. With a gasp, he fell back into Ole Bessie's guts. He could tell at once it was only a superficial wound, but it was more than enough to prove to his mother's smartest son that he needed to keep his head down.

By the time Frank got to his vision slit, however, the battle had changed completely. Whatever was firing the heavy beams from the smoke had claimed another victim, this time one of the wagons behind the line. The low, running shapes were emerging from the fog. As he saw them clearly for the first time, all rational thought fled his mind.

In a moment he was catapulted back to that laboratory within Camp Lincoln. There was no doubt in his mind: he was looking at Reconstructed. They were only roughly shaped like men, having been surgically altered to be bigger and stronger. They were also faster. The hide of each creature was varicolored, a patchwork of black and white and tan, but mostly the unmistakable burnished gold of the Warrior Nation. Thick black stitching held the various pieces together. Their faces looked truly alien, as if animal skulls or artificial implants had been combined with their human features to provide enormous biting mouths, wild eyes, and other unnatural features. Hands ended in vicious claws, with the stitching to show where they had been added to the nightmarish whole. Each wore tattered rags, in some cases sewn right into the flesh itself, providing only the barest argument against indecency.

The Reconsctructed made short work of the men and women on the defensive line. Bodies were tossed into the sky, others struck down with sweeping claws slashing through flesh and bone. In at least two cases that Frank could see, rebel fighters were being eaten. The monsters were among them now, and he had no idea what he could do to help from inside the heavy wagon.

Frank tapped one of the gunners. They were all paralyzed, staring in disbelief through their own vision slits. "Keep firing on the big ones in back!" He shouted, and the gunner, shaken out of his daze, nodded. The men began to move with a purpose again, and soon the Rolling Thunder's main gun was lashing out into the smoke once more.

A shape, larger than the others, could now be seen approaching through the haze. It crawled forward on four legs, an enormous cannon on its heaving back. The thing stopped while Frank watched, the legs adjusting themselves as if seeking a comfortable position, and the barrel of its cannon began to swing toward Ole Bessie. Frank's eyes went wide as he realized what was about to happen. He fell down to the floor plate next to the gunners. "Take it down! Take it DOWN!" His voice was hoarse with sudden desperation. There was no way Ole Bessie's main gun turret was going to come around in time.

Chapter 16

Frank was disappointed as his life failed to flash before his eyes. A sudden blast from another Rolling Thunder struck the central body of the figure in the smoke, splitting armor and igniting crimson power cells. A titanic ball of red-tinged flame flashed out, catching some of the smaller shapes in its convulsive destruction and knocking them into the mud.

Frank pressed his head painfully against the leather pad of the vision slit, trying to slow his breathing. A corner of his brain wondered at fear that could cause a man to break out in a cold sweat within the oven of a heavy wagon. He glanced up at the hatch and decided that he needed to see more than he could from inside Ole Bessie's belly.

Working against the primordial fear rising in his throat, he emerged into a swirling confusion of bodies. The commanders had fallen back to their wagon, an elite group of veterans forming a ring of blaster pistols and rifles blazing to keep the nightmare creatures at bay. Captain Carney held the left flank alone, fans of ruby bolts churning up the ground before him. A group of swampers fought from the back of Nash's wagon as a violent melee swirled around it. The vehicle rocked alarmingly as the men on the back shifted from one side to another. Long gaff poles pushed away any beast-man Reconstructed that came too close.

Buford Nash and his son stood back to back on the flatbed, firing calm bursts into the churning mess. Frank felt the tightness in his chest ease to see the old mud-farmer still standing. Before he could turn away, a blurred form leapt from the confusion and sailed toward the pair. He followed the thing's flight in disbelief. It arced over the surrounding combat, unnatural claws slashing downward as it fell. landed on Buford's back, pushing him down into the truck and knocking his son into the surrounding chaos. Frank struggled to bring Sophie to bear, but as he watched, his eyes wide with horror, the thing dug repeatedly into Buford's back, tossing heavy gobbets of flesh in all directions. The old man had stopped struggling at once, but the monster kept tearing at him until one of the Tammany men, turning at the sound, blasted it in the head from point blank range.

Frank roared his anger, Sophie swinging over the armored top of the Rolling Thunder, looking for victims. This was fighting as Frank understood it, and his lip lifted in a cruel sneer as he sighted on his first target.

The thing's musculature was massive, like boulders shifting clumsily beneath the patchwork quilt of its skin. It was drenched in blood and its face, more human than many of the others, was twisted in a madness that would have been terrifying if Frank had not been staring through Sophie's sights. His eye lost its focus for a moment, a vision of John Younger flashing before him. Then he shook his head and leaned in to his shot.

The custom long rifle bucked against Frank's shoulder. The thing's enormous head folded in upon itself, showering the field behind with beads of red and gray. He was sweeping around for his next victim when a high-pitched roaring erupted from his right. Five Iron Horses, followed by countless more, swung in from the army's direction of advance.

Jesse was in the lead, hunched over the controls of his machine and pouring Gatling fire into the monsters all around. Lucinda rode beside him, followed by the Fords and Marcus Cunningham. One of the 'Horses screaming up behind them bucked as twin contrails of rocket exhaust lifted off and spiraled into one of the hulking shapes still holding back in the smoke. It was blown off its wide feet by the twinned detonations.

The Iron Horses roared closer to the attacking monsters. The beasts turned to meet them, many charging past more vulnerable fighters, as if eager for the new challenge. Jesse swerved to miss the tumbling corpse of one construct only to side-swipe the next. His 'Horse tumbled over the screaming beast, crushing it into the mud. Jesse was thrown high into the air.

The outlaw chief rolled to his feet, duster flaring wide and metal hands full of gun. He sent a steady stream of crimson bolts into the approaching monsters. Soon, however, the Iron Horses were surrounded. Robert Ford abandoned his steed to stand beside Jesse, massive hand cannon in one hand and his ridiculously long knife in the other. The rest of them were struggling to join the pair, and the smoke soon swirled up and around the mess, blotting it from view.

Frank realized what was happening as Jesse disappeared behind the scudding curtain. They had been after his brother all along.

Frank dropped back into his wagon and started to shout before he hit bottom. "Go, go, go! Straight at my brother!"

The machine was moving before Frank stopped shouting. As he rose again into the cold air, he saw that the other Rolling Thunder was following. A surge of fighters was also breaking in that direction, released from the pressure of the assault when the flesh-constructs had turned to attack Jesse's group.

Bessie's Gatling guns chattered away, scattering bolts up and down the mob that surged over Jesse's position. Beasts were blown into the dirt all around. None of them showed the slightest interest in self-preservation. Instead, they tore at each other to get at their target; they were all trying to kill his brother.

Sophie barked, blasting one after another, shattering skulls and blowing holes in torsos. There was no need to aim, the press was so tight. Even firing from the pitching deck of the wagon, every shot killed at least one target. As they pulled up, however, it looked like Jesse had everything under control.

The outlaw chief was standing, legs wide, in the center of a circle of blasted, malformed bodies. His Hyper-velocity pistols smoked in his metal hands. Behind him, Robert Ford had taken a knee in exhaustion, but they were both alive. A little further away were the three tumbled 'Horses of his other companions.

Frank scrambled out of the wagon and leapt down into the mud, but as he scanned the area to make sure everyone was okay, he came up short. There were only four figures standing there. Marcus, his hammer clenched cross-wise and dripping black blood, was casting around as if looking for someone. Charlie Ford, crouched beside the wreckage of his vehicle and holding a shotgun in both hands, was also frantically looking all around.

There was no sign of Lucinda.

*****

"She's gone, Jesse." Frank crouched down beside his brother, wrists resting on his knees. "We've combed every inch of the field. She's not there. That has to be good news, right?"

Jesse's back rested against the cold steel of his brother's wagon. He shook his head weakly. "Not many of those things ran, Frank. They weren't thinkin' like that. They didn't take no prisoners."

Frank stood up and looked out over the field. "I don't know, Jesse. I'm just sayin' she ain't here. There's bodies everywhere, but hers ain't one of 'em."

Jesse stared back down at the churned mud between his boots. "I don't get it, Frank. What the hell were those things? What did they want?"

"They wanted you, Jesse." The new voice brought them both around. It was Quantrill, natural arm in a sling and resting on a splintered length of stick instead of his fancy cane. "As for what they were? I don't think any of us know."

"The ones out in the field were metal, like the robot marshals, only bigger." Frank gestured out across the churned mud with one hand. The smoke from the original clash still hung in the air as a haze that burned the eyes and caught in the throat. Salvage parties were moving within the murk, gathering around each downed metal brute. There were not many of them, but they had been more than enough to cover for the approach of the true nightmares.

The man-beast constructs had, indeed, been Reconstructed. They had been living, breathing creations sewn together from the parts of countless men and beasts, with metal enhancements to add to their horror. They had required no RJ-1027 to function. There was no way, Jesse knew, that the drastic surgeries and modifications that the poor souls had undergone would have been possible without the foul Devil's Blood somewhere in the mix. There had been no engines, batteries, or other powered elements in their design; just the twisted energy of life. Doctor Tumblety's perverse creations, rather than Carpathian's.

Jesse pushed himself up and away from the Rolling Thunder and looked at Quantrill. "Why'd they want me? Why'm I so important?"

Quantrill's smile was cutting. "Didn't you want to be? Isn't that what all this is about?" He gestured with his makeshift cane at the enormous force of rebels and militia fighters that surrounded them.

Jesse frowned, his eyes hard. "I just want to kick the Union where they'll feel it for the next hun'erd years, colonel. I ain't got nothin' in my head past that." He turned and moved off into the field.

Robert Ford was crouched down by his brother, disconsolate beside his overturned 'Horse. Runnels of clean, pink flesh had been carved in the dirt and grime that caked Charlie's face. He had been crying.

"What the hell's his problem?" Jesse moved up, his frustration, grief, and guilt settling on a target at last.

Robert stood up, trying to smile as he stepped in front of his brother. "He's worked up over Loveless, is all." Robert's words were quick and thin. "Blamin' himself, as usual."

Jesse sidestepped him and stared down at Charlie. The man refused to meet his eyes. "What's your beef, Ford?"

Charlie cringed at his name. He looked off over the blasted field, not seeing anything. "Told you I wasn't brave."

"What the hell's he talkin' about?" Jesse looked around. Marcus was nearby, elbow-deep in the guts of his own 'Horse. Frank and Quantrill, who had followed Jesse out into the field, shook their heads. Robert chewed on his lower lip but said nothing. Jesse looked down at Charlie again. "What the hell are you talkin' about, Charlie?"

The man was shaking. He looked away. "When they came at us, I froze." His head darted up with the speed of a rabbit, staring at Robert, then Marcus, then the other men. "You saw 'em! They were straight out of a nightmare! I froze!"

Jesse reached down with one metal hand and cupped Charlie's jaw, forcing him to look up. When their eyes met, Jesse leaned in and whispered. "What is it yer sayin', Ford?"

Charlie collapsed in on himself, sobbing. "She was watchin' my back, Jesse! I froze, and Lucy was watchin' my back. I din't see what took her, but all of a sudden-like, she was just gone!"

Jesse stared down, dumbfounded. Then, faster than any of the men watching could see, he hauled off and cracked Ford across the face with the back of his metal hand. Charlie was thrown into the mud. The outlaw chief followed almost as fast, his duster billowing out behind him, and came to rest crouching down beside the sobbing man. Jesse leaned in close and whispered into the dirt-filled ear.

"You are now livin' on borrowed time, Ford." Each word was ground out between gnashing teeth. "There's gonna come a day when I'm feelin' tetchy, and I'm gonna end you. 'Till that day comes, you man up, you little worm, and you walk tall, or that day'll come all the quicker." He stood, spitting into the mud beside Charlie's head. "Now you know. If you're gonna be scared o' somethin' on this earth, Charlie Ford, you be scared o' me."

Jesse shook his head and stalked off, leaving the Fords behind to deal with their own mess. Quantrill followed after as quickly as his new cane would allow. Frank took a couple quick steps to catch up. "Jesse, we got a lot we gotta consider, an' not a lot o' time for considerin'."

Jesse stopped and turned around. "What, Frank? What is there to consider?"

"You got an army you have to deal with, James. This is no time for you to retreat into that brooding head of yours." Quantrill's face was stern.

Jesse just looked at him. "Now what the hell are YOU talkin' about?"

"The joint commanders were in the thick of this, Jesse." Quantrill gestured over his wounded shoulder. "There have been casualties at the very top of the chain. They want to talk to you."

Jesse looked to Frank, who shrugged. The outlaw chief cursed under his breath, kicking at an offending clod of dirt. His head came back up and he looked around them. "Where the Youngers at, Frank? I ain't seen 'em since before this started."

Frank looked awkward, his eyes shifting to the distant trees off to the east. "They were on the right flank as we marched, Jesse. Them and the California Rangers. I ain't seen any of them, neither."

Jesse shook his head again, with even more conviction. "Well, who'd we lose, colonel?"

Quantrill turned and gestured for him to follow. "Warley's down. He might be okay, but he's done for the season. Carney's okay, but you know we lost Buford." His eyes would not meet Jesse's as he muttered. "And Tinker Thane's in a bad way. Several of the other commanders from out east are goners. Thane, though, he's holdin' on. Wants to talk to you, he said."

Jesse snorted and started to move toward the battered command Ironhide. A makeshift infirmary had been established in the bed of the wagon, with several of the commanders lying on low pallets. Warley was laid out toward the rear. Carney, standing nearby, nodded to the outlaw chief as he passed. Jesse started as he recognized the figure standing over the colonel: Marie Laveau. The woman looked at Jesse with the regal bearing he had come to expect and nodded a fraction of an inch in recognition.

Jesse tipped his hat to her. "Ma'am, I didn't know you were with us."

"Thank God Almighty she came, Jesse." Warley's voice was soft. Jesse saw that a bandage covered most of his chest. "None of these old army sawbones would have been able to drag me back, that's for sure."

The woman's full lips curved in a slight smile."I have enough gad palè for now, colonel. No need for more."

He smiled wanly and then turned back to Jesse. The outlaw had to lean in close to hear his words. "Jesse, you have to lead the Army of New Orleans, now. And you listen to Captain Carney. He won't steer you wrong." Jesse started to protest, but a sharp shake of the colonel's head stopped him. "The men know you. Black and white, you brought many of them together. We lost too many in this foolish skirmish. The army has to go on, and you have to lead them."

Jesse stood up, looking to Frank with raised eyebrows. Frank gave a grave nod. "He's right, Jesse. We come this far. Ain't nothin' that brought us out in the first place been changed by what happened here today."

Jesse looked between his brother and the wounded colonel. "But, I'm not a—"

"It's worse than that." The voice that spoke now came from farther down the wagon bed. Jesse searched the wounded until he found the man speaking. His face was swathed in bandages black with blood. One hand was gone at the wrist, and more bandages covered him from the waist to the neck. A garden of red blossoms spread across the snowy white. Jesse had to look hard before he realized it was Tinker Thane leaking out his last moments on the dirty pallet. The outlaw's lip curled just a little.

"What d'you mean, worse?" Jesse spat the words across the wagon's bed.

It was impossible to tell beneath the bandages, but it sounded as if Thane was smiling. "Too many of us are gone, James . . . Too many of the regional commanders are dead, or dying, or too wounded to continue . . . You're the man with the vision, James. You're the man who brought all this together . . . You have to finish it."

Jesse shook his head. "No way, Thane. Did they tell you how hard we got hit? We lost nearly a quarter of our fighters to those things. And more'n that went runnin' so fast, they ain't gonna stop 'till they hit the Gulf."

Warley grabbed Jesse's metal arm. The feedback pads told him the wounded man was applying considerable pressure. "Jesse, everything that drove us this far is still true. The Union can't keep that fort where it is. And whatever they built it to hold? If we can take that, then the South may yet have a role to play in the future of this continent."

Jesse looked down at the man in pity. "Colonel, I'm right touched you think I can do this, but—"

"It's not a question of can, James." Thane spat from where he lay. "It's a question of must . . . You can't leave this where it stands or you'll rob the Confederacy of the . . . last reserves of bravery it possesses. This army is scared now . . . You don't walk away from a battering like this without scars that last a lifetime."

"We won, din't we?" Jesse's voice was sour as he spoke the words. His mouth worked with an intense desire to spit.

Warley stretched his pale, thin lips into a smile. "A win like this is almost worse than a drubbing, Jesse. You know that."

"He knows." Quantrill muttered.

Jesse stood where he was, his head tilted back and his eyes focused on the scudding clouds overhead. He looked down at his boots, his eyes haunted. "This ain't what I wanted."

Thane's voice rose again, sharp as one of Bob Younger's knives. "You gotta go through this valley before you . . . get what you want."

Jesse's head snapped up, his eyes now hard again. He jumped up onto the bed of the wagon and stalked across the wounded men until he was crouching down beside Thane. A single eye watched him from within the entombing bandages. The eye was very calm.

"I'll do it." Jesse muttered, then he whispered. "But there's something I want you to know, Thane. I walked the line of casualties after the battle. More than half the boys lying there? They were darker than you 'n me. The colored folks held, Thane. And the rest of the boys know it. You take that down with you into Hell when you go."

The wounded man's head slid back and forth, his chest heaving. Jesse thought for a moment he was coughing out his last, but then realized that Thane was convulsing in laughter.

"What's so funny, you squirrelly bastard?" Jesse spat.

"You really think that matters to us, James?" The man's eye was cruel. While Jesse watched, the blood from a broken vessel invaded the yellowed white, turning the orb a gruesome burgundy. "You're all animals, you fool. The death of any of you makes this world a better place." The chest convulsed again.

"You filthy, fen-sucking maggot," Jesse reached down and grabbed the man by his stained lapels. As he stared down into the man's eye, however, he felt as if his mind suddenly opened up. Light crashed in around him. An impression of vast distances, enormous spaces, and immense stretches of time washed over him. He saw a blur of faces snap by; some he knew, most he had never seen before. He recognized Ty, the young kid from Kansas City, among them. Then he saw Allen Henderson's smiling face, clear as day, and he fell back against the wagon's sidewall.

"Why you—" Jesse did not know what he had just witnessed, but the feeling of heavy evil it had left in his mind rattled him. His metal hand fell to his holster, pulling at a pistol of its own volition. Even as one orderly tried to stop him, another leaned quickly over Thane's quivering body. The shaking stopped, the tension eased from the limbs, and Jesse did not need to be told that the commander had escaped his wrath for good.

*****

Jesse stood with his brother near the wreckage of Lucy's 'Horse. The earth was a churned, muddy mess, dark with blood and swarming with flies.

"What the hell we doin' here, Frank?" Jesse's voice was pleading. He stood in the mud, his feet wide and his mechanical thumbs hooked behind his gun belt. He stared down at his boots, head shaking back and forth. "How the hell'd we get so far from home?"

Frank watched his brother, not sure how to help. "We're fightin' the battles neither of us wanted to give up on all those years ago, Jesse. We're gonna hand the Union their heads with this, an' the old Confederacy, she's gonna come back stronger than before because of it. That's gotta mean somethin'."

Jesse nodded and then looked up at his brother from beneath the broad brim of his hat. "Don't you miss bein' back in the territories, takin' down banks and holdin' up trains? Back where Billy was the closest thing to competition we had to worry about?"

Frank smiled. "Part o' me does, sure. I was always happier closer to home. But you, you've always been driven faster, farther, an' I just got in the habit o' followin' you."

Jesse nodded again, back to staring at his boots. "There's somethin' goin' on here that don't even start to make sense, Frank. Thane – there was somethin' in him. Somethin' evil."

Frank snorted. "You hated that polecat the moment you first laid eyes on him. There don't need to be no deeper thinkin' on it than that."

Jesse shook his head. "It wasn't just what he said. When I looked into his eye there at the end, it was like I was seein' for the first time." He put one metal hand to his head. "I can't really put words to it, Frank, but it was mighty queer." He looked up from beneath his hat brim. "And it felt . . . heavy . . . somehow."

Frank watched his brother and then shook his head. "I don't know from heavy, Jesse. An' I don't know from evil. Seems to me, every man or woman makes their own way in the world, and those that get jealous, they get to shoutin' words like 'evil'. All I know is what we got here an' now. An' what we got here an' now is a machine you helped to build, runnin' headlong into disaster without no one sittin' at the controls."

Jesse gave him a sour look and turned away. For a long moment there was only silence and then he muttered, softly. "She's gone, Frank."

Frank looked at his brother with concern in his eyes. There was no comfort he could offer. "The Fords have gone over every body, Jesse. She ain't here."

Jesse barked a bitter laugh. "So she got taken by those things? That's supposed to make me feel better? You remember that cracked Union doctor even better than I do, Frank. Her bein' taken ain't a better scenario."

Frank sighed, looking off at the surrounding fields. The dead had been buried in mass graves, all except the most prominent men and women who had fallen. Buford Nash, for instance, got his own plot. Frank's chest tightened at the thought. Small bonfires smoldered some ways away where other fighters had piled up the abominations and set them ablaze. The destroyed wagons had been scoured for anything that might be salvaged and now stood empty like stripped carcasses.

"Jesse, she's a tough woman. If anyone'd be okay, it'll be her." He searched for anything else he could say. His brother's practical nature made such comfort hard to find. "They'd have taken her for a reason. And that reason'll keep her alive. She'll find a way to escape, and she'll be back."

His breath gusted again, this time even harder. "Thing is, little brother, that it don't even matter."

Jesse gave his brother a sharp look, and Frank forced himself to meet the glare with a hard face of his own. "You gotta lead this circus north, and you gotta take that fort, and it wouldn't matter if Lucy was dead in front of you or draped all over you, kissin' yer ugly mug. You gotta lead."

Jesse's shoulders slumped. He looked one last time at the devastation around them and then turned away with a nod.

"Well, then, best start leadin'." They walked back toward the band of suspicious commanders together. Behind them, the shattered wreckage of Lucy's Iron Horse leaked smoke into a grey, leaden sky.

Chapter 17

They said nothing, staring at her in a silence that stretched far beyond mere social discomfort. She sat, spine straight, with hands resting lightly on her thighs. The fabric of the utilitarian dress they had provided to replace her worn riding gear was rough beneath her hands. The desire to avert her eyes, to look down at the dusty floor or at the scattered papers on the table before her, was nearly overwhelming. It took every trick she had ever learned to keep those eyes steady, to keep her hands firm. The only visible sign of discomfort, whether fear, frustration, or anger, was a slight tightening of her jaw. Unfortunately, the men staring at her were among the few in the world that she could not fool.

"And they're coming here." Robert Pinkerton sat loosely in front of her. His legs were crossed, his hands clasped in his lap, and his eyes mild. But she knew him. He had been her mentor for the entirety of her career. He was angry, suspicious, and very, very tired. She knew, no matter how relaxed and calm he seemed, her freedom, and perhaps her very life, hung in the balance.

"They are." She kept her face cool, but beneath the facade her soul was boiling. Slipping away in the middle of a battle was not her way, and a part of her could still not believe she had left that poor boy, Charlie Ford, quailing beside his Iron Horse. She thought she had timed her departure well, while there was still enough chaos to hide her leaving, but late enough that the rebels' victory was a foregone conclusion. Still, leaving a fight before it was finished – she could not remember ever having done that.

Henry Courtright stood behind Pinkerton, one elbow resting against the sill of a long window. His face was cold and empty as he stared at her and then turned slightly to gaze out. She had been unable to gauge his position on her return since she arrived the night before. She did not know if the anger she sensed radiating from his enigmatic mask was real or if it was in her imagination. She did know that if she had lost his trust, there was no hope of her leaving this fortress alive.

"I'm not sure why we're taking care of this up here, and not down in a dungeon somewhere." Levenson Wade was a young agent. He had joined the Pinkerton Secret Service after she had left Washington for her first assignment in the western territories. She had heard of his recent exploits, of course. He was one of the most successful agents Pinkerton had put into the field in recent years. He also had a ruthless reputation. From his voice, she knew he was serious.

Pinkerton's mouth quirked into a slight smile and he looked down, shaking his head. "Well, Lev, that'd be great if this pile of rock even had a dungeon."

Henry grunted and spat on the floor. "This is crazy. If she was a traitor, why'd she come back?"

Wade's lip curled in contempt and he shifted his eyes to the other agent. "If she wasn't a traitor, why'd it take this long?"

Pinkerton stood up with a huff and swept his hands apart in a separating gesture. "Gentleman, if Agent Loveless had not stayed with James and his mob of ruffians for as long as she did, we would still be guessing at his true target. The military would be forced to spread its assets all across the border. When they struck, we would be in a much weaker position. Let's not forget that."

Wade snorted and looked at his chief in disbelief. "I think you're not giving any of us much credit if you honestly think there was a doubt in anyone's mind that they were heading straight here, sir."

Courtright took a step toward the other agent and only stopped when Pinkerton's rigid hand shifted to point a warning at him. Her old partner nodded to the chief, but then glared back at Wade. "When you can give me one good reason why she would have come back here, if she's a traitor, I'll start to listen."

"One reason?" Wade did not move, but his body was stiff, ready for a fight. "Maybe she's going to open the gates in the heat of battle. Maybe she's going to note our dispositions within the walls and then scamper off to her boyfriend." His eyes flicked to Pinkerton and then back to Courtright. "Maybe she's here to assassinate some of our top-level commanders, decapitate our forces, and then open the gates."

"You Copperhead bastard—" Henry started toward Wade despite Pinkerton's outstretched arms. The commander jumped in front of him, grabbing the lapels of his coat to get his attention.

"Courtright, stand down!" Pinkerton was shouting, flecks of spit striking the agent in the face. "This gets us nowhere, and only helps that flea-ridden mob riding hell-bent for leather right at us!" He pushed the younger man back. Courtright nodded curtly, his face tight.

"Now, Wade, you don't know Agent Loveless, and your head's in the right place." He looked over his shoulder at Lucy, still sitting in her chair. "But you've gotta stand down too. I have trusted her, implicitly. If she says Jesse James is headed this way, then we damn well better get ready to greet him."

Lucinda felt a distant rush of heat behind her cheeks. It was almost as if she were watching the humiliation of a stranger as her mentor defended the indefensible.

Wade looked at her for a moment, then back up at the chief, then across to where Henry was glaring at him. He nodded, but there was still heat in his eyes. "Okay, you're right. I don't know Agent Loveless. If you trust her, sir, I'll give her the benefit of the doubt."

Pinkerton watched him for a moment, looking for any sign of dissent or insincerity. There was none, but then, these were the best liars the country had ever produced. He shrugged and nodded.

"Alright, then. We move forward, and we bring this information to Colonel Campbell and his merry band of shovel pushers." He held up one warning finger. "And we do not air our dirty laundry in public. Agency problems are handled entirely within the Agency, and this one's been dealt with. Is that clear?"

Pinkerton looked to each of his agents in turn, not moving to the next until each had nodded in assent. When they had all agreed, he nodded himself and gestured toward the low, narrow door.

"Now, shall we go see the colonel and let him know his day is about to get worse?" The old agent's face was sour.

"Sir, if you don't mind, I'd like to bring Agent Loveless up to speed on our situation here." Henry did not look at her as he spoke.

Pinkerton looked from Henry to Lucinda and back again, then nodded, his face blank. "Of course. Wade?"

Wade was staring at her as he moved to the door. He went through with only a slight hesitation. The chief nodded once more and then closed the door softly behind him.

Henry stood by the window for a few moments, looking out over the scoured plain. When he spoke, he did not turn around. "So, you decided to come back after all."

Lucinda did not know what to make of the flat voice, the rigid back. She looked down at her hands, clasped on the table before her. Her mind began to scan the papers there out of habit. They were technical drawings, and the surest proof, if she had needed any, that Pinkerton had trusted her all along. She wondered what Wade would have made of it, if he had noticed them laying there.

She forced herself to look back up and was surprised to see that Henry had turned back to face her. His expression was bland, and she was frustrated, once again, that she could read nothing there.

"I was always coming back, Henry." She thought she did a pretty good job of keeping her voice level.

He nodded, sighed, and slouched into a chair opposite her. "Yeah, I know. I just wish you hadn't been so dramatic about it, is all."

His trust in her should have been reassuring, but instead it just added weight to her guilt. "I left them as soon as I could sneak away without suspicion."

He smiled, but it was a tired, thin expression. "Well, that won't matter much if you run into him at the little party we'll be having here shortly. Or at any time in the future, either, I guess." He sat back, tilting his head to stare unseeing at the ceiling. "But I've got a choice here, and I'd rather live in a world where I still trust you, no matter how loony you're acting, than in a world where you're every bit as guilty of treason as you sometimes appear."

She stared at him for a long moment, then shook her head and looked back down at the papers. "What's all this, now?"

Henry looked back down and pulled a paper toward him. He glanced at it for a moment and then flipped it back onto the pile. "The inventory and specifications on the cargo sent back from Fort Frederick. Tesla and –" He shot a look at her deepening frown. "Well, you know."

Lucinda had tried not to think of Tumblety and his madness since she had escaped with Jesse from Camp Lincoln. Whenever she did, it made reconciling her loyalty to the Union that much harder. She shook her head and lifted up a sheet of flimsy paper.

A heavy, ancient-looking glove was sketched there. It seemed to be attached to an ungainly-looking pack by cords and wires, paragraphs of cramped writing filling most of the blank space.

"What's this?" She asked as she scanned the writing.

Henry craned his neck to look at the paper and then sniffed. "That's Tesla's latest. He claims it can open a hole in the fabric of the world or some-such nonsense." His voice was flat, and he shook his head. "It's supposed to be able to transport objects through thin air. Might prove very useful in a battle, or even in our line of work, if it operates as he claims." He shrugged. "I haven't heard anyone mention it, so I doubt it does. I know it didn't go south with his heavy automatons and the other – things." He trailed off.

Lucinda continued to work through the close writing.

"Well, shall we head up?" Henry stood, adjusting his heavy pistol. "I thought you could use a moment to settle down. We wouldn't want you to be prying the young Master Wade's head off in front of the brass, now."

She marshaled a smile she did not feel, let the paper drop to the table, and stood. "I would have waited until they were looking elsewhere."

Together they left the room and made their way up toward the battlements.

*****

Jesse moved forward on his belly, his elbows and knees driving him through the cold mud. The difference in sensation, as the mud soaked through his trousers and registered against the feedback pads of his arms, was enough to trigger one of those rare moments when his world seemed to spin, as if in a dream. The weight of his metal limbs bore more heavily upon him. He shook the sensation off and pushed himself slowly to the crest of the hill.

On either side, Frank and Cole Younger scrambled through the undergrowth, coming up even with him as he stopped. Jesse pulled his monocular from its pouch on his belt. He flipped a switch and the crimson telltales of RJ power cells began to glow. The fading stain of sunset was little more than a memory. He would need the tricks of the new tech to see his target.

Cole was holding a similar device to his face, his grin peeking out from beneath its boxy structure. Frank sighted down Sophie's length, her enormous scope providing even more amplification, if not quite as much of the light-enhancement as the monoculars.

"Anything?" Frank muttered to his brother as he settled the long gun into a firing crouch.

Jesse shook his head. "Nah. See some sentries along the top of the wall, maybe. And looks like some gun emplacements. Heavy stuff." He looked over at his brother. "But nothin' that'd make me think they know we're comin'."

"They'd have to be pretty damned dumb not to know we're out here somewhere." Cole's voice was light, his grin unfazed. Even though the Youngers had been on the far flank during the attack, away from the action, he had seemed like his old self since the battle. For some reason, though, Jesse was still uncomfortable around Bob and Jim. And he was not entirely sure he could trust any of them. Sadly, he still trusted them more than he trusted the rusty old pie-eaters that he was serving with.

Jesse nodded, despite his misgivings. "Yeah, we're not goin' to be surprisin' anyone, and it's best we not fool ourselves into thinkin' we can."

Frank's head rose up from behind his scope. "There's some serious firepower up there, brother." He shrugged his shoulder toward the fort brooding on the horizon. "And no cover for those heavy wagons. My poor Ole Besse'll be nothin' but target practice for those blue-bellies, we come straight at 'em."

Jesse looked again through his monocular. The image was hazy and gritty, as if seen through a piece of heavy red burlap. Figures skulked along the ramparts of the double walls, manning watch posts and weapon stations. Each time they swept their own monoculars in his direction, he felt a crawling between his shoulder blades, despite knowing that the tech could never differentiate three prone men among all the foliage of the forest's edge.

He could identify several heavy cannon emplacements along the wall, the massive barrels thrusting out into the night. At one corner, a guard tower rose away from the rest of the squat structure. Figures huddled in the compartment on top, peering from behind large Gatling cannons that could tear a squadron of 'Horses to shreds. Far below, the gate was a uniform cold gray, metal or stone. It was massive.

Jesse shook his head and then gestured for the others to follow him. He shrugged his way backward, down the back slope of the hill. When they had cleared the crest, they stood and moved back into the tall trees. Jim and Bob Younger came forward to meet them, with Marcus and the Ford brothers not far behind. Farther back in the woods, their faces hidden by the shadows of their caps and hats, stood the other commanders of the allied Confederate army. Postures stiff, these were the men who had relinquished, some under protest, command of their own units to this outlaw from the western territories.

Jesse nodded a quick greeting to his friends and allies while raising a metal hand to the others, holding up one finger to forestall any questions. He turned to address Frank and Cole as they came out of the trees.

"So, what d'you boys think? Ain't much tougher than some o' the banks we taken down over the years." His grin was wide, and the only people in the world who would have recognized it as forced, were the men he was speaking with at that moment.

Cole grunted, his own grin still firmly in place. "Even if they're crammed in there cheek-to-jowl, we got 'em outnumbered. An' you KNOW they ain't packed in there nearly so tight."

Frank watched Jesse and Cole, then shook his head. "We ain't got nothin' near so big as the heavies they're packin' on top of those walls, Jesse. Even the Rolling Thunders ain't close."

Jesse nodded again, acknowledging the point. "Yeah, I know. How many hits you think a Thunder could take from somethin' that big, afore it's knocked to flinders?"

Frank shrugged, looking off into the dark woods as he tried to imagine Bessie getting knocked about by the enormous weapons. "Not more'n two or three hits, I'm thinkin'."

Jesse rubbed his jaw with one metal hand, the bristles of his unshaven cheeks rough against the feedback pads. "An' how many times you reckon they can fire, afore a Thunder would reach the wall, startin' far enough, they can't hit us?"

Bob Younger barked a harsh laugh, shaking his head at Jesse. "That's a fort, you corn cracker. They got as much power as they want. They'll be blastin' us the minute they see us, an' they won't stop 'till they run outta targets."

His brother Jim nodded while grimacing slightly at the insult. "There ain't nowhere to hide up there. We go in, we go in with all the world seein' us swingin'."

Jesse lowered his hand and hooked his thumbs behind his belt. "Yeah, there's that." He looked around at the forest, only starting to dampen from the winter rains. When the idea struck, he felt his eyes light up. He knew Frank had noticed when his older brother's face tightened in suspicion.

"What?" Frank snapped, distrust heavy in his voice.

Jesse's grin widened, not forced at all now, and he slapped his brother on the back as he moved past him toward the waiting Confederate commanders. "Come on, Frank. We gotta talk to these boys who keep callin' me 'mister.'"

"You like that too much, Jesse." Cole's tone was light, but his gaze was flat. The outlaw chief's steps faltered slightly as their eyes met. The force of Jesse's grin did not waver, and he nodded to Cole as if nothing had passed between them.

"Gentlemen," Jesse's voice was robust as he moved into the center of the ring of officers and commanders. "I'm going to need you to divide your forces into three equal groups. My riders will assemble up front, forming a spearhead. Once we have everyone reshuffled and we've loaded the deck, our real work begins." He rubbed his mechanical hands together in a gesture of unmistakable excitement.

"It's goin' to be a long, hot night!" His grin, even in the dark, was bright enough for all of the men around him to see.

*****

They stood atop the wall above the massive gate, looking out over the blasted, rolling plains that surrounded Fort Knox. For nearly a mile in any direction, there was nothing but tangles of trampled grass, torn down trees, and rutted mud. Colonel Campbell panned his monocular along the distant horizon, unable to distinguish any threats among the tangled life-aura of the far-off forest. Major Dalton stood nearby, his attention evenly divided between his commander and the strange contingent of Washington agents conversing nearby.

Dalton moved up beside the commander's adjutant, Blogdett, and leaned in close. "William, what do you make of the tall one in the old hat?"

William Blogdett lowered his massive sniper rifle. He had made a point of keeping in practice ever since leaving the marksmen during the war, and was looking forward to putting the old girl back into action. He glanced over his shoulder at the agents. "The one who always keeps to the shadows? The one with the hood under his topper?" The old sniper shrugged. "They're agents from the president, sir. I don't make anything of them at all. Way above my pay-grade." The man turned back to the parapet and braced his long rifle against the stone surface of one raised merlon. "I'll tell you what, though, sir. I'm thinkin' it's a bad night comin' our way."

Dalton nodded, shifting his eyes slowly from the agents to the blackness out beyond the wall.

"What are the two of you muttering about?" Campbell's voice shook slightly, and Dalton knew he was holding himself together more through fear of losing face before the men from Washington than through any form of natural courage. As the fort had taken shape on its low hill, Campbell had really started to come into his own, and the soldiers had responded.

When the UR-10s had been sent back to Washington, however, things started to get strange again. And then, when the special deliveries began, and first the nightmare strike force from Fort Frederick had arrived, and then the UR-30 Enforcers with their secret cargo, the old, awkward Campbell had started to show through. The sense of impending attack, coupled with the arrival of the mysterious agents, had nearly undone him.

"Just our guests, sir." Dalton jerked his head back at the small group huddled around the tall stranger. "Since they sent those abominations of Tumblety's and Tesla's down south, and the Enforcers disappeared into the vaults, they're the only decent topic of conversation we've got left."

A shiver gripped the colonel and Dalton cursed himself. His superior had come a long way, but the man was still a bundle of nerves where any of the current intrigue was concerned.

"Colonel, if I might have a word?" Agent Pinkerton, the director of the president's Secret Service, beckoned Campbell to him. "I believe your lookouts should be seeing some movement on the road soon."

Colonel Campbell gave a quick start and turned a little faster than Dalton would have liked. "Yes?"

The old agent jerked a thumb up at the main tower. "Your boys up there should see two men approaching. I need you to let them come forward."

Major Dalton watched conflicting reactions twist his commander's face before resignation barely won out over fear and indignation. He nodded. "Just two?" Dalton was proud of the hint of sarcasm, anyway.

Pinkerton nodded, resting his hands upon the stone of the battlement. "Yes. We're bringing in a couple of contractors."

A bubble of resentment rose in Dalton's throat. "Contractors?" He had not spoken more than a few words to any of the agents, but he could not stop himself.

The old man nodded. "Yes. They've worked with us in the past. I was hoping they would arrive earlier, to be more fully-integrated into your defenses, but I only got word this evening that they were near. Thankfully, before the Rebs attack, but too late to get the best use out of them, I'm afraid."

As if the mention of the two men had conjured them out of the night, a sentry far above called out. Dalton looked up to see the soldier point out onto the plain. All along the battlements, monoculars were raised. Dalton quickly jerked his up as well.

Two men approached the fortress, walking calmly as if without a care in the world. One bore an enormous sniper rifle casually slung over his shoulder. The shadows beneath his hat brim were impenetrable, even to the advanced tech of the monocular. There was something subtly but fundamentally wrong with the figure that walked beside the first. The arms were too long, jointed in the wrong places and in the wrong directions. But as Dalton watched, he saw that the man's arms were perfectly proportioned. He bore two massive blades affixed to his forearms, their serrated edges arcing out past his clenched fists.

A cold sweat curled down Dalton's spine. He recognized those weapons. And if the killer with the blades was who he appeared to be, then the sniper strolling along beside him could only be one man.

"Not Tanner and the Wraith!" The major muttered the words under his breath, but the colonel heard him. His head snapped around at the note of disbelief.

"You know these gentlemen, major?" Campbell's voice was tense.

Dalton almost laughed, but he knew it would come out as a sick croak, so held it in. "Mercenaries, of no good reputation. Certainly not gentlemen, sir."

The colonel turned to the older agent. "You vouch for these men, sir? My second in command seems to have some reservations."

"He ain't the only one." William Blodgett nodded toward the two figures now emerging from the darkness, visible to the naked eye. "The Wraith, he's got a mean name even amongst sharpshooters."

"I will admit to a growing alarm, sir." The colonel's voice was firm, but Dalton could hear the ever-present shaking just beneath the surface. "It appears these two contractors of yours are known to my men, and—"

"You will allow them into the fortress, colonel." The tall man, his face still shrouded in darkness, said in a voice higher-pitched than Campbell would have expected. "We will see that they behave."

Colonel Campbell stared at the gaunt, mysterious figure. Something moved deep in his eyes before he gave a slight, jerky nod. He muttered an order that the gate be opened and watched as the group of Washington men, each nodding their thanks, moved past him and through a door on the inner wall.

"This just got uglier." Blodgett's voice was bleak as he turned to watch Tanner and The Wraith disappear beneath the wall, the clanking of the opening gate echoing into the night.

*****

The construction of Fort Knox was far less conventional within than without. The fort consisted of a squat main building with a second, slightly smaller structure above, and presented only these two-leveled walls to the outside world. The parapet, rising thick and crenelated before the fighting platforms of each level, gave the fortress the appearance of an ancient castle, its tall outer wall guarding a keep within.

However, the true keep of Fort Knox was not the second-story defenses, but an independent structure built within the fortress itself. The main gate opened out into a large open chamber featuring several defensible redoubts that led, like a maze, inward toward the center. A low stone keep crouched there, dwarfed by the massive, cathedral-like space around it. Another heavy gate, iron studded with RJ-1027-enriched bolts that glowed a sullen red, was sunk into the smooth surface of the keep; the entrance to the vaults below.

Lucinda rested against the keep, the cold stone leaching the warmth of her body through her clothing and the heavy cloak draped over her shoulders. Henry was with the others on the main wall, surveying the defenses and making whatever contingency plans they deemed necessary. They had left her here, guarding the entrance to the keep like a common soldier. At least Pinkerton had had the decency to look embarrassed when he had given her the orders.

The design of the entire fortress confused her. Despite the formidable appearance of Fort Knox from the outside, the high inner walls contained even more fighting positions, directed into the massive chamber at the heart of the structure. Perhaps the intention of the architect was for the defenders to hold the outer wall as long as possible, and then to fall back to the redoubts, and rain fire down upon the attackers as they fought their way through the main gate. The tall walls of the central chamber were riddled with firing ports and fighting positions that would serve that purpose well. Anyone who had forced their way through the main gate was in for a very hot time.

She knew her understanding of defensive architecture was rudimentary at best, but she could not shake the feeling that the entire building seemed more like a trap than a fortress. Lure someone here, allow them to break through the main gates, and then destroy them, inside, in detail. Having watched the garrison prepare, she had seen no sign that this was their plan. They meant to conduct a standard defensive action, with no intention of allowing Jesse and his forces to gain entrance. She knew, also, that Pinkerton and his crew were thinking along the same lines.

They did not know the true size of the army Jesse was bringing down upon them. She had downplayed their strength, and exaggerated their losses at the hands of the horrors that had struck at them from the twisted minds of Tesla and Tumblety. Her mind was being painfully dragged in too many directions, with no escape in sight, and she knew, with a chill that was worse than the piled betrayals themselves, that her mind was fracturing under the tension.

But it kept coming back to one nerve-jarring thought: if Fort Knox truly was the trap that it seemed, who was it intended for, and who had set it?

A commotion around the enormous gate caught the agent's attention and she pushed herself away from the wall. One gate swung open, its thickness surprising, given how smooth it seemed to move. Soldiers rose from their positions on either side, blaster rifles raised, as two men walked through the narrow gap. Behind them, the gate reversed its motion and quickly sank back into place with a dull, heavy sound.

A large door to one of the primary stairways was pushed open and the men who had been her comrades for years came out, moving toward the gate. Courtright was the only one who looked her way, one eyebrow raised in a sardonic question. The impulse to join them was nearly overwhelming, but she knew that the ice beneath her feet was too thin for even the appearance of disobedience. She held her ground, hands on hips, and kept her distance, waiting to be brought into whatever was happening.

The agents moved to greet the two newcomers. There were hands shaken and heads nodding as one would expect, but there was little warmth in any of the faces as they turned and approached the keep. The two new arrivals wore no uniforms, but had the look of hard-bitten men of violence. She had never met them in person, but knew them by reputation. One man was just removing a pair of massive blades that had been strapped to his forearms. The other cradled a truly impressive sniper rifle in the crook of one arm.

Courtright and Levenson Wade moved toward Lucinda while Pinkerton and the two men held back, their heads bent together as the chief agent spoke to them with an earnest, somber expression. The two men, their own faces impassive, nodded. Their eyes flicked toward her for a moment and then back to Pinkerton. It happened so quickly she wondered if she had imagined it.

"So, I'd say that means we're in it up to our necks, Luce." Courtright stopped beside her and tilted his head toward their chief. "If Robert's called in their marker, I don't much like our odds."

Wade, standing beside her old partner, looked back at the two strangers, shook his head, and looked away. "Tanner and the damned Wraith. They've each themselves done nearly as much damage as Jesse James ever did."

Lucinda's eyes narrowed. "How could Pinkerton have possibly gotten them to agree to come here? Never mind fight for the Union, for God's sake! I'm chained to this stone relic," she slapped the keep. "But he brings them in?"

Wade looked away, his eyes scanning the interior defensive positions. "He wouldn't tell any of us why they're here or how he got them to come. They must owe him for something, at some time. One thing's for sure: as long as they're here, I'll be watching my back."

Henry nodded. "And you better, too, Luce. I don't like the feel of this."

They quieted down as Pinkerton approached, gesturing toward the two mercenaries with one hand. "Lucy, you've heard of Sasha Tanner and the Wraith?"

She nodded, first to him and then to the two strangers. They each gave a single, shallow nod in return.

"They're going to be keeping an eye on the keep with you. A little extra insurance outside the chain of command, if you will." Pinkerton's face was grave, but there were things going on behind his eyes that she could not decipher.

"What would General Grant think, sir?" She kept her tone even. She had never much liked the general, and lately those feelings had deepened. Whether it was Jesse's opinions rubbing off on her, or a rising awareness of the world at large, she had not examined too closely.

Pinkerton's face was sour. "From what I've been able to gather, Lucy, Grant's been pulling the strings on this from the beginning. But I'm sure the general wouldn't mind my having brought in a little extra muscle."

"You think you're going to need them?" She kept her voice calm despite the frustration and guilt roiling in her gut. "Those doors look pretty thick, and the walls are high. If the Rebels can overcome all that, two more men probably won't make a difference."

Pinkerton turned to look at the main gates and shrugged. "We have our orders, Lucinda. The general has something in the works, and he knows that we're all here. I'd like to have a little ace up my sleeve, just in case. I'd suggest you get acquainted with your new compatriots. You've got a little time. The grey-backs aren't at the door yet."

"Of course, sir." She stood straighter, her eyes fixed on a blank space of wall across the inner chamber.

Pinkerton nodded again and then jerked his head toward the side of the keep. He moved off in that direction and after a confused moment, she followed him. When they were around the corner, he turned to stare into her eyes. "Lucinda, General Grant's got a little secret somewhere within the vaults beneath our feet, along with whatever Tesla sent east that didn't get chewed up by the rebels. I get the feeling he thinks the stakes are very high indeed. I can't trust those grasping mercenaries near the entrance to the vaults alone. If this whole action gets knocked into a cocked hat, I'm going to need someone I trust watching that door."

She nodded, but could not meet his eye. "Sir, if there's something down there that powerful, why can't you just go down there, drag it up onto the wall, and point it at Jesse James? For that matter, why not go through whatever Tesla sent? See if it might help?"

Pinkerton chewed on his bottom lip and shook his head. "Lucinda, for all I know, it's a ton of used dynamite and a pansy patch." He snorted. "And from everything I've seen, it's more than a man's worth to go poking around in Tesla's wardrobe without him standing beside you." He patted his gun. "We'll stick to what we know and, God help us, trust that the general's not too far gone."

The chief agent moved back toward the others and they made their way to the stairway door. She watched them disappear, Henry's quirked eyebrow the last thing she saw.

"So." The man was strapping long blades to his arms and gave what he probably thought was a charming smile. "What did you do to deserve being left in the basement with the hired help?"

She looked at him wordlessly for a moment. There was nothing she wanted less than to spend any time with these two animals.

The Wraith, lights glinting off various skulls secreted among his clothes, chuckled a low, evil laugh. "I'm not sure how I feel, not being the least-trusted wolf in the henhouse."

She sniffed and turned away, eyes fixed on the heavy door. Somewhere below them were the last items Tesla had sent east. Anything that had not been deployed against Jesse and the rebels . . .

"Fire!" The cry echoed across the massive space of the inner chamber. Lucinda's head whipped from side to side as she tried to see where it was coming from. Concern and confusion rippled through the defenders.

"The plains are burning!" Something about the echoing sound of the voice made her look up. She saw, from a concealed firing position high on the wall, a soldier standing, shouting down to the soldiers below.

"They've set the plains on fire! The fields are burning!"

Chapter 18

Jesse crouched low behind the control console of his Iron Horse, his cheek pressed to the cool metal. Against the inferno swirling all around, the temperature was soothing. Directly in front of him, one of their big Ironhide wagons had logs, rags, and bags of sawdust jammed into every possible nook and cranny. It raced straight for the big fort, burning like the fires of Hell. An elaborate rig of chains, leather straps, and metal struts kept the thing barreling forward at its top speed without a driver.

Jesse gritted his teeth as a curl of bright yellow flame flashed past over his head. He gave out a Rebel yell as he felt the burn, despite his hat. He heard several answering calls through the roaring fires, the RJ engines, and the blood in his ears. He knew that Frank, the Youngers, the Fords, and many of his other men were hugging their own machines around him, tucked in behind the racing furnace. He squinted, even behind his thick goggles, and could only hope the drivers had been on target when they'd bailed out of their vehicles a few moments before.

There were nearly twenty wagons tearing across the fields toward the fort. Most of them were the ragtag rattle boxes that passed for command transport. Hidden among them, however, were their four surviving Rolling Thunder wagons. Jesse cringed to think of what the crews of those wagons were going through at the moment. The wood and fabric bonfires attached to all the wagons obscured their outlines and would hopefully hide the heavies in a shell-game any huckster would be proud of. But in order for his surprise to work, those heavies needed to stay hidden until their weapons were in range.

Each Rolling Thunder was filled with casks of water and sodden sheets and blankets. The crews had been doused just before igniting their vehicles. So far, they had covered over a hundred yards, and there had been no fire from the fort. He grinned, his dry lips cracking. If there was no cover to be had, you made cover or you died. So he had made some serious cover.

The burning wagons bore down on the fort at considerable speed, despite the terrain. The flames confused the sentries' tech, blinding their vision enhancement and hiding the number of infantry rushing along behind. Three walls of flame were tearing across the dry fields, from the south, east, and west; each aligned with a tall, forbidding wall. His two Rolling Thunders were nearby, aimed directly at the main gate. Each of the flanking forces had one of the beasts, prepared to take advantage of targets of opportunity or weak points that might become clear during the fighting.

Jesse slid his 'Horse to the side, peeking past the burning flank of the wagon. He caught a glimpse of the massive fort in silhouette just as a terrible rending crash erupted off to his right. He cringed, ducking back behind cover. He surged past the wreckage of a burning Ironhide canted into a smoking crater. Fiery debris was scattered all around the ruin, the grass beginning to smolder in a widening ring.

He shook his head at the luck. He knew he should be happy it took this long, considering how many unmanned vehicles were dashing across the broken ground. He knew he should also be happy that the fort still seemed too confused to—

A wall of horrendous noise crashed down upon the racing Confederate line. The massive guns all fired in disciplined unison with the sound of an avalanche. Between the difficulties of hitting moving targets in the dark, the dazzle of the blazing light, and the interference of the boiling flames on targeting tech, no more of the initial shots struck their targets. Most fell short, blasting huge holes in the fields and sending blooms of crimson fire high into the night sky. Two shots went long, however, and blasted matching holes in the charging infantry. More than a hundred men went down, torn to shreds, pounded into the mud by the pressure wave, or burned beyond recognition by the rising fireballs. Jesse crouched lower, silently urging the wagons to greater speed.

The cannons began to put down a steady, rolling pattern of fire. The crews were adapting to the situation quickly, and first one wagon, then several more, were reduced to twisted shards of metal and billowing flame, cutting down the infantry around them. One chassis, the body of the wagon ripped entirely off, continued to roll forward with the inertia of its mad drive. A second bolt from the wall threw it onto its side where it rolled once and then rocked to a gentle stop.

There was no way to pass orders now. Jesse and the other commanders had known that once they crested the low rise, they were going to be committed to the assault. Thousands of men and women were charging across the field, the bulk hidden by large wagons and roaring flames. As the wagons were torn apart, the flames were slowly spreading into the high grass as the infantry ran past. Soon, their retreat could be cut off by a wall of fire rising in their wake.

Jesse swerved aside for another look ahead and was heartened to see that the fort was only a few hundred yards away. More than half the wagons had been hit now, most of them torn apart to scatter their flames into the grass and surrounding troopers. Through a minor miracle, neither of the Rolling Thunders in the frontal assault had been destroyed. He had seen one take a direct hit, blasting the wood and fabric away from its armored hide, but having little further effect. They were approaching their own maximum range, so their charmed existence would not last much longer.

As the Rolling Thunders crossed the invisible line that freed their weapons, both vehicles staggered in their forward progress by the bellowing roar of their own main armament. One crew had opted to fire directly at the strong main gate, barely visible through the swirling smoke and flame. The shot scored a glowing line of molten rock and metal that cut into the door and then dragged along the main wall. The gate, however, was still standing. The other wagon, struck by the earlier enemy blast, had opted for a more personal target. Their shot blasted home into one of the armored turrets along the wall. The shot was either lucky or masterful, as the turret peeled open like a prairie flower, sending several men arcing to the ground far below and lighting up that entire section with ruby-tinged flames.

As the Rolling Thunders began their fire, rebels armed with heavy weapons decided their time had come as well. Jesse cursed them. He had known, however, that despite the repeated warnings of the experienced fighters in the group, there would be no stopping men and women with so little training from wanting to strike back in the savage chaos of battle. Fighters dropped to their knees, hoisting rocket pods, missile launchers, and even heavy blaster cannons to their shoulders. Streaks of crimson flame lashed out from the infantry all along the line. Most of the shots struck the impervious stone of the main wall, but several arced over to explode upon the parapet or against the secondary wall behind. More blue-bellies tumbled to a fiery death.

Jesse knew something most of these new fish had never been given the chance to learn: if you can shoot them, they can shoot at you. Heavy Gatling blasters, snipers' long rifles, and medium cannons lit up all along the wall. They were not aimed at the still-charging vehicles, but at the dark, crawling mass of infantry behind; the tightly-packed mass that had illuminated itself with the premature fire from its leading elements.

The heavy fire from the fort was devastating as it fell among the ill-equipped and under-trained militia. Men and women were cut down where they stood. Bodies were torn apart by heavy Gatling rounds. Heads fountained gore all around as snipers took their toll. All across the line, the rebel fighters were blasted back into the dirt. Any shot fired into the mob could not help but hit. Most shots were blasting through several victims before their fury was spent. Under the withering punishment, the entire contingent of infantry working toward the gates began to falter.

Jesse pulled his Iron Horse up short, riding in a sharp turn back toward the infantry. He pulled one of his Hyper-velocity pistols and fired it into the air, trying to get their attention. He saw his entire plan crumbling before his eyes as the militia fighters began to shrink away from the incoming fire, some turning toward the blazing flames rising up behind them.

Jesse was about to throttle for the back of the mob, expecting to get a Union round through the spine at any moment. A shape flashed past, first on his left, then another on his right. He recognized Bob and Jim Younger, waving their hats at him to return to the attack. Looking back, Jesse saw Frank, the Fords, and Cole had pulled up, waiting for him.

Jesse nodded, waved to Cole's brothers, and then tore back around again, throttling hard to regain his position behind the massive wagon. He roared through his posse as they leaned into their own machines to keep up, when the wagon that had sheltered them disappeared in a blinding flash of red and white light. Jesse raised a hand to shield his eyes from the blast, despite his goggles. Even as he swerved to avoid the wreckage, he grinned, however. By the strobing light of the Ironhide's destruction, he saw that the rebel fire had taken a toll on the fort. Several of the heavy turrets had been reduced to burning wreckage, and the gates, although still standing, had been pounded and lashed into slag.

Jesse swerved past the burning hulk of the wagon and lined up on the gate. He passed the torn hulk of one of his Rolling Thunders, smoke pouring from the vision slits and a massive hole blasted into the driver's station. As he looked for the hull markings of Frank's Ole Bessie, he was distracted by a flash of movement ahead. His head came up just in time to see a disciplined line of Iron Horse cavalry rounding the corner of the fortress and aligning for a vicious charge. The riders wore the blue and yellow of the Union army, and the guidons that flapped in the hurricane wind of their charge bore crossed sabers beneath a bold '7'.

Jesse's flanking forces erupted in chaos as the Union cavalry tore past them. The enemy could have devastated both detachments if the cavalry had crashed into their unprotected flanks. But the cavalry commander knew his business. The roaring Union vanguard dashed down the walls on either side, ignoring the flanking rebel forces and driving straight for the main assault on the front gates. Behind these lead elements, following companies wheeled to face the flanking units, confronting the Rebel assault all along their line of advance.

Twice in as many minutes, Jesse saw his entire plan crumbling. Who the hell was the 7th, and where had they come from? It soon became clear that there were not enough of the cavalry to stop a determined push on the gates. Even with the presence of several Union Locusts, those heavily-armored bastards he had first seen outside of Diablo Canyon, the cavalry were too late. The sheer volume of fire the untrained militia poured into the newly-arrived enemy shattered their counterattack. Jesse shook his head and gunned his own machine forward to meet the charge. He crouched low once again, and the Gatling cannons beneath the faring of his 'Horse spat ruby bolts into the oncoming 'Horses.

The lines crashed against each other, and the disciplined formations of the Union cavalry were shattered, devolving into ugly individual fights for survival beneath the towering walls of Fort Knox. Jesse watched as Cole whipped out his stubby shotgun, leveling it at a junior officer in a blue shell coat, and blasting his face back through his head. Another trooper rose high from his saddle, energized saber raised high for a killing blow against the back of Charlie Ford's neck, when his brother brought his own 'Horse crashing down on the tail of the trooper's machine, putting four bolts into the man's back as he tumbled from the saddle.

The Union commander came straight for Jesse, face wild behind sweeping blonde mustaches. With a grimace, the outlaw chief drew one of his pistols. At this range, it would be impossible to aim the 'Horse's own weaponry. Jesse sent a stream of bolts at the man's torso, but they tore into his mount instead. A blast of sparks and crimson flames flared up, obscuring him, and when the 'Horse canted off to one side, dragging itself to a stop, the Union officer was gone.

Jesse took advantage of a lull in the fighting to bring his Iron Horse around to face the steaming, slumping gate. A rising tide of militia fighters was pressing the Union cavalry back to either side. Rebel yells echoed off the cold Republican stone, and Jesse smiled grimly before adding his own voice to the chorus. He could tell the enemy cavalry were not beaten. They were retreating back along the side walls, still keeping those flanking columns back long enough to make a decent retreat. They would return, he knew. The rebels would need to secure the fort before that happened or they would be crushed between the defenders and the cavalry coming back with blood in their eye.

Jesse stood before the massive front gates of Fort Knox and regarded their daunting, metallic solidity. Frank pulled up beside him and jumped down into the dirt. They were soon joined by the three Younger brothers, and Robert and Charlie Ford, both grinning far more than was seemly. Jesse looked around at the surging Confederate infantry pressing toward the walls, firing up into the blue-bellies on the parapet. Above them, the fighting positions and mounted weapons above the front gates had all been reduced to crimson smoke belching wreckage and slumped, still bodies.

Jesse searched the mob for Marcus and Quantrill, uneasy at their apparent absence, when he saw them moving together through the press.

Colonel Quantrill had been with the bayou fighters, accompanying the surviving New Orleans commanders. Marcus had decided to stand with the bayou fighters as well. The big black man was impassive as always as he strode across the bloody and burning field of death. Quantrill, however, was much the worse for wear. He clutched a new ornate cane in his crude metal hand, but it sank too deeply into the mud to offer much support. Jesse had begged him to stay in the rear, but the old man was determined to be in on the kill. Captain Carney stalked along beside the two men, his enormous cannon seeking further targets. Behind the captain stood Will Shaft and his Exodusters, their white teeth flashing in cruel grins.

"Well, I don't know who they were, but they don't seem to have put a damper on your little shindig, James!" Quantrill's smile was wide as he moved up beside the outlaw chief. "This is not really our sort of battle, son, but it seems to be goin' okay."

Frank barked a dark, disbelieving laugh. "We've lost thousands of men, sir! We're not even inside yet! How can you—"

"Well, the greater allied army has lost thousands," Captain Carney smiled. "But by far the most casualties have been sustained by the groups from the eastern states. So WE have not lost nearly so much." The smile was predatory, his teeth flashing in the dancing flames.

Frank looked away, shaking his head. Quantrill turned to Jesse. "Nevertheless, we do need to secure entrance, or all of this vigorous activity will have been for naught."

Jesse nodded and looked back up at the massive slabs of melted steel. He cocked his head to one side, and then, without a word, gestured for his men to move away. Those who knew him moved quickly, pulling any laggards with them as the outlaw chief drew both of his pistols and regarded the slumping metal slabs.

Jesse brought the two pistols up, his metal arms at full extension. The guns came together and arcs of intense red light reached out, linking the two weapons with a blazing energy bridge. Both pistols began to hum violently, their RJ cells flared like tiny red suns, and with a rushing roar, a wave of furnace heat blasted out before him. The concussion struck the gates with a deafening clang. The thick metal slabs withstood the pressure, sloughing off sheets of melted armor that scorched the ground where they struck. Even through the thick, rippling, tortured air, the men could see that the doors remained closed.

Jesse leaned forward, his shoulders hunched as they drove his metal arms at the gates like spears. The humming rose to a painful level and the heat shimmer emerging from the guns rippled out in visible waves of destruction. The gates groaned, showers of metal pouring down their canted faces, and then with a deep, visceral concussion, they shattered, metal fragments and droplets of molten armor blasting back into the fortress.

Jesse grinned at his friends over his shoulder. "We're in."

*****

"Damn, Jesse, what've you gone and done now?" Through the monocular, the scene across the plain looked to Billy like something out of some Gospel-sharp's Sunday morning harangue. The fields all around were burning, sending curls of flame high into the air. Above, columns of thick, churning smoke drifted over the spectacle, under-lit by the flames. The fires illuminated a squat fortress surrounded by an enormous, surging mob.

Crimson bolts rose out of the rising tide of attackers to splash against the high outer wall. Occasionally, something heavier would fire, momentarily revealing a section of the scene in lurid red highlights. There were still defenders on the walls, firing down into the surging crowd, but they seemed almost halfhearted as a response to the enormous wash of fire coming up at them.

"Looks like we got a bunch of blue-belly cav forming up behind there, Billy." Johnny Ringo pointed with one gloved hand off to where a large group of men on Iron Horses was gathering together. The outlaws riding with The Kid were all exhausted and covered in trail dust after riding hell-bent for leather for over a week. Billy had been hounded by a sharp sense of urgency ever since reading Carpathian's note.

Down on the fields behind the fortress, flags and pennons flapped in the fitful winds coming off the prairie fires. William Bonney slid his monocular off to his right until he saw them. They looked like they had been battered; some rode pillion, obviously having lost their mounts.

Billy grunted. "They got kicked in the fork, but they're goin' to be goin' back fer more. Hope Jesse's ready for 'em."

Billy was not entirely sure if he really did hope that. As he watched the surging attackers flood toward the front gate, he knew that he was watching Jesse realize the dream they had shared in the Arcadia Saloon back in Kansas City. Somewhere over there, Jesse James was leading a damned army against the Union . . . The army that should have been his.

"What do we do?" The Apache Kid looked across at the battle, the flames reflecting in his flat black eyes.

Billy eased back in his saddle, one hand resting on his knee, and twisted his face into a parody of deep thought. "Well, boys, it looks like this to me." He pointed to the forces flooding through the front gate. "We got a nice chance to kick up a little row against those blue-shirted chiselers over there. Kick 'em when they're down, maybe grab us some plunder as we run through." He cocked his head over to the side to address the savage renegade. "But this ain't our fight. We copper our bets. We look for the main chance, but we keep our eyes clear in case we gotta skedaddle fast."

The outlaws gathered around their boss nodded, eager to get in on what looked like a clean Union kill. "Now, boys, if we get in there, you keep together. I don't wanna lose anyone cuz they went off on their own. If the opportunity arises, I've got the doctor's little map. If I make my guess, what I'm lookin' fer'll be in the basement. I'll try to go down there, a couple of you can follow, if you want. If we do, we'll be leavin' by the doc's back door, though, so don't wait fer us. We've got a few more 'Horses laid in at the exit in case we need to head out that way."

Again, the men nodded. They loosened their weapons and stared across the plains with eyes glowing with greed.

Billy's smile turned sharp. "An' if any of ya'll see James, you leave 'im to me. That boy got me in the neck but good last time, an' I'm keen to get a little o' my own back."

*****

Jesse's throat was raw from the smoke and continuous shouting. His Rebel yell echoed constantly off the high walls as the militia fighters streamed past him, rushing through the broken gates and into Fort Knox. There would be no stopping them now. There was fighting within the fort, of course. No one ever accused the bastard Union troopers of being bad at their jobs. But there was just no way they could stop the flood of Confederate militia with what they had left.

As the rising tide of rebel soldiers pressed through, Jesse watched them pass with a growing smile on his face. The uniforms were patchwork and haphazard, the weapons mismatched. The faces, though, were what struck Jesse at that moment. Black faces and white faces, sharing expressions of triumph. Every face was grinning with the fierce rush of victory. Success here was going to redefine the world, not just the Confederacy. And no one would ever forget that he was at the head of this army as it charged to triumph.

He had been nervous when the Union cavalry made their appearance, but the weight of fire seemed to have seen them off. His brain was flying high with the heady rush of victory within his grasp. All around him were the people he trusted the most, and they would walk into the most formidable Union stronghold south of Washington beside him.

His grin slipped a tick at the thought. There was one person he had come to trust nearly as much who was not with him. The grueling march and furious preparations for the assault had not left him much time to brood over Lucy's disappearance. His heart refused to believe she was dead, but his head knew how easily it was for a man to fool himself in a situation like this.

"Jesse, did ya see Charlie?" Robert Ford thumped his brother on the back, his smile stretching his black-smudged face. "Did ya see him, when those Billy Yank bastards came ridin' 'round the corner? He got right in there, Jesse! Right in there!" His eyes glowed like a child who had potted his first tin can with daddy's rifle.

Jesse leaned toward the weasel-faced young men, trying to suppress his own smile. "Stay focused, boys! We got a long way to go afore we're hoistin' a whiskey in Charlie's honor!"

Despite his sour response, he did not know if he had ever seen a man as happy as Charlie Ford at that moment. With the burning thrill of victory rushing through his veins, he had a hard time stifling his own grin.

"Let's go, boys, before they string up all the blue-bellies and there ain't no more for us!" Jesse's metal arm rose up to urge his posse through the press of men at the gates and into the fortress.

Chapter 19

As Jesse pushed through the roaring crowd of fighters and into Fort Knox, he was brought up short by the immensity of the inner chamber. The room was huge, clearly taking up most of the fortress within the high walls. Across the hall were carefully positioned defensive emplacements that his people had paid dearly to silence. There were bodies strewn everywhere around the bunkers and barricades, in both the blue uniforms of the defenders and the motley array of clothing worn by his own folks.

The walls above them were broken up by firing positions and balconies clearly designed to give the defenders on the walls easy access to the giant chamber within. Brilliant slashes of crimson fire were snapping all around as rebel forces fired upon the soldiers overhead and were fired upon in return. There were several unprotected stairways up the thick walls leading to the upper levels. Many doors along the ground floor clearly gave access to larger stairways within. His people had pushed out toward them, and fierce battles were raging across the floor.

In the center of the huge room, looking strangely out of place beneath the high ceiling overhead, was another, smaller structure. A thin haze of smoke hung in the air, but it looked to Jesse as if another castle, with another armored door, had been built within the bulk of Fort Knox. A shoal of sprawled bodies was stretched out in front of the smaller fort, a testament to how far his men had pushed into the hall before they turned back toward the high walls. They were now attacking the doors and stairways, leaving the small fortress alone.

"Damn, it's hot in here!" Charlie Ford's grin was still huge. "Come on, boys, afore there ain't none left fer us!"

Jesse could not help but smile at the young man. There was still an edge of anxiety in his eyes, and his words shook just enough to hint at the bluster that was meant to hide it. He was on the shoot, a curly wolf in his own mind, and Jesse was glad the kid had come around. He nodded to the boy, turning to wave the rest of his posse through the press of fighters. Charlie pushed in front of Jesse and then jerked backward slightly, the fear and boasting draining from his eyes, replaced with confusion and pain.

Jesse watched Charlie fall. The gaping hole in the young man's chest, shirt slick with blood, barely registered. Robert Ford lunged down to catch his brother. The younger man's face was twisted with horror and rage, his pistol forgotten on the stone beside him. Charlie, blood bubbling from his mouth and nose, looked up into his brother's eyes. He looked like a frightened little boy, eyes wide with shocked confusion. Robert was shaking, trying to hold the dying man steady.

The sharp report of a heavy rifle sounded in the distance, loud enough to be heard over the general clangor of battle. Jesse looked up, tracking the course the killing bolt had to have followed. He saw a man in dark clothing ratcheting the recharge lever of a heavy sniper rifle just around the corner of the strange little castle. He wore ornate personalized armor beneath his duster, a leering metal skull flashing on his chest as he raised his rifle to fire again. At Jesse's feet, Robert howled as the light left his brother's eyes.

Jesse roared with his own anger and frustration as he brought both of his pistols up. He sent a torrent of fire flashing at the little fort. The sniper ducked behind the stone as the bolts shattered the corner in a detonation of powdered rock. The outlaw chief lowered his weapons, breathing heavily with grief and anger, and saw another man, decked out in fancy but nondescript black, running toward him.

The new assailant wore long glittering blades strapped to his forearms. They would be vicious in both attack and defense, and Jesse decided that he would rather not find out. He raised his pistols again to end the man. His shot was spoiled, however, as Marcus Cunningham, his usually impassive face knotted in rage, rushed past, heavy hammer held high over his head.

Jesse lowered his pistols as he watched the enormous black man bring his hammer down toward their attacker. The man raised one bladed forearm and dodged to the side, guiding the hammer past his head and leaping across to slash at Marcus's side. The big man threw himself away, the haft of his hammer coming up to block the cut. The strange attacker's other arm came up in a swift jab that punched the tip of his serrated blade up into the big man's side. The blade slid out his back, dark with blood, and Marcus staggered backward, the blade pulling free. He shook himself, gripped his hammer tighter, and hunched his broad shoulders. The blade-wielder's eyes widened in mild surprise.

The two men circled each other warily as the battle raged on around them. Jesse felt the near-overwhelming urge to blast the bladed man where he stood, but the stranger and Marcus were once again engaged, swirling around with weapons flashing in the dim red light. A shout from above caught his attention and he turned to look up the high wall behind him.

A broad balcony stretched across the length of the fortress's front wall, above the shattered gates, where the defense of the fortress could best be coordinated. A knot of men and women in blue uniforms heavy with gold braid were gathered at one end of the balcony with a smaller group of men in dark civilian clothing. Jesse felt his eyes tighten: Pinkertons. And where those agents were, the commanders of this damned blue-belly shindig would undoubtedly be as well. That had to be the command group for the entire fortress, cornered up on that balcony like rats.

Even as Jesse glared up, Frank grabbed him by one shoulder and shouted into his ear. "Jesse! Those riders are goin' to come back soon! If we take out the commanders, these boys'll drop their weapons, an' we'll be able to get ready for the next dance!"

Jesse looked at his brother, uncomprehending, torn between grief and rage. Then his eyes widened as he remembered the cavalry. Frank thought the troopers would be returning for another hand. Jesse started to shake his head and then stopped himself. If Frank was right, then he was also right about decapitating the defense of the fort. Even if Frank was wrong, they would still have to take out the officers. He nodded.

"Okay, boys!" Anger and sadness clashed within him as Jesse looked one last time at Charlie's collapsed body, his brother crumpled beside him. He pointed with one of his pistols at a doorway that had been cleared by militia fighters. "Up those stairs and at the big bugs! Let's show these folks who are in charge, and then we'll see what's what!"

Carney stepped away from the posse, hoisting up the massive Gatling blaster. With a gleaming grin, he engaged the enormous weapon and sprayed a fan of ruby death toward a knot of Union troopers holding out by a shattered defensive position. The soldiers were caught in the flashing red light, many blasted from their feet or diving for cover as the stone of the bunker detonated in a cloud of gray dust. Under the cover of that howling torrent, Jesse and his followers ran toward the stairway, their faces set in a mask of grim determination.

Robert Ford, tears still streaming down his dirty face, gently dragged his brother's body forward and rested it in a sitting position against a barricade. He reached down with one gloved hand and slowly pressed the eyelids down over the flat, glassy orbs. Wiping his face with an angry gesture, he trotted toward the doorway after Jesse James.

*****

Lucy paused on the stair landing to catch her breath. The box was heavier than it had first seemed when she'd dragged it from the vault. She hoped she had grabbed the right one. As her world came crashing down around her, and every pathway crumbled beneath her feet, she had given in to desperation and ran for the vaults and the treasures she thought she might find there. If this was, in fact, a trap, then there was only one possibility that might let her take a hand. The chest, she felt, would be her best hope.

But it was so damned heavy. It would probably have been easier to empty the chest and carry the contents loose, but there was no telling if anyone she encountered would have recognized it for what it was and stopped her with awkward questions.

She took a deep breath and hefted the thing up in both hands just as a commotion broke out around a bend in the stairs above her. Running footsteps could just be heard over the shouting. It was not the disciplined advanced of trained soldiers moving down to clear the vaults, however, but the sounds of a riotous mob. She had not met a single soul since abandoning her position by the small keep's door. With a cold, distant curiosity, she drew one of her powerful derringer holdouts. She wondered how this would play itself out.

Had Tanner and The Wraith been killed? From what she knew of them, that was not likely. Far more likely, they had abandoned their assigned posts, the filthy mercenaries . . . Her full lips quirked into a sad grin as the irony of the thought struck her.

The men who came trotting down the stairs were dressed in a mismatched array of clothing and armor that owed nothing to the Union Army Uniform Code. They bore a hodgepodge of various weapons ranging from old RJ hunting rifles to the latest military-issue blasters. As they saw her, their weapons all came up as one. Her pitiful pistol rose slowly in response, but then the lead man's cruel face split into a surprised smile.

"It's Jesse's girl! Boys, put yer shootin' irons up! it's Lucy! She's alive!"

The crew of outlaws all lowered their weapons, grinning foolishly at her. With open, honest faces they asked how she got into the fortress, if she was alright, and if she needed help.

Lucinda's hand was rigid, but the men did not seem to notice the gun still bearing on them. She tried to formulate some rational response when the shattering stutter of blaster fire echoed down the stairs. She cringed back, pressing against the cold stone of the wall, but no one was firing on her. A group of soldiers must have entered the keep and taken the small mob of rebels from the rear.

The militia fighters cried out, spinning around and firing their weapons blindly back up the stairway. One of the older weapons fired an ear-splitting spray of red light up around the corner, and a scream rose above the shouts and gunshots.

The rebels began to press their way up the stairs, return fire snapping all around them and crashing into the stone. "Come on, Lucy!" One of the men waved her forward. "Let's light a shuck!"

Lucinda looked around her, realizing that she might well be committed for good. She noticed a side door just a few steps down. With one last look at the rebels, now hard pressed by the invisible Union forces above, she hefted the box into her arms and shouldered the door open. The last thing she saw was one of the rebels looking back at her, a strange smile playing about his lips as his eyes caught the red light from an overhead bulb.

Lucy followed the small hallway through a series of storage rooms and chambers until she found another flight of stairs leading up. Much narrower than the main course, the crate was nearly impossible to muscle through in the confined space, but she managed, step by step. She could just hear the sounds of battle continuing to rage in the stairway behind her.

At the top of the stairs, a door opened out into the little keep, the main stairway off to her left. Distant sounds of battle could still be heard down there, but obviously the Union boys had pushed the rebels deeper into the vaults. She hoped none of them returned any time soon.

She put the crate down just inside the small keep's door and spun around to push her back against the opposite wall. She glanced carefully outside, her derringer once more in hand. There was no sign of Tanner or The Wraith, but that was no surprise. The bodies scattered all across the hall of the main chamber were a surprise, however. The battle had been fierce, and she could see that, although the rebels had obviously pushed on into the fort itself, they had paid a terrible price.

She took another glance, trying to gauge the flow of the battle. The fighting had moved into the upper regions of the fortress, with streaks of crimson flame crisscrossing through the air overhead as Union and rebel soldiers traded fire from the defensive positions scattered across all four walls. Many of the balconies and firing emplacements were blasted and scorched; rockets and missiles screeched across the vast space to detonate with deafening explosions against the walls.

It was hard to discern who had the upper hand with most of the combat going on in the walls and out of sight, but it seemed like most of the men she saw fighting were in the mismatched clothing of the rebels. The conflicting emotions that sank into her belly at the thought were enough to force her to one knee. She was in a nightmare born into the real world, as her conflicted loyalties played out all around her.

Lucinda sat within the keep, back pressed again against the hard cold stone. A new sound began to rumble beneath the general chaos of the battle. A sound she would never forget from her time with Jesse after Camp Lincoln. A large number of Iron Horses were approaching. Her head came up. The 7th Cavalry was returning.

Lucy peered around the corner again, twisting to get a good look at the command balcony over the twisted remains of the gates. She could see the command group, their blue and yellow uniforms indistinct in the scudding haze of battle. With them were the dark forms of her fellow agents, an unmistakably tall figure rising above them all. They were defending against a haphazard push by some rebels, but seemed to be focusing primarily on rallying troops on the fighting parapet for the main wall, behind their current position.

As she watched, however, fear threatened to choke her as her throat tightened. A new force of rebels burst from a stairway on the far right end of the balcony and pressed toward the Union commanders. She recognized the men even as they pushed into the press of soldiers.

Cole and one of his brothers were firing their pistols into the defenders from the back of the mob, while another Younger, it had to be Bob, was thrashing at nearby Union soldiers with a knife glittering in either hand. Robert Ford seemed to be using his blaster to bludgeon anyone who rushed at them rather than firing it, a knife sparkling in his other hand. Frank James was near the back, his massive rifle raised as he kept watch on the main chamber, as if fearing a sniper's bolt might hit them from the flank; the Wraith, most likely. There was no sign of Charlie Ford, Bill Carney, or Marcus Cunningham.

At the head of the small formation, both pistols blazing away, strode Jesse James.

Lucinda watched with a growing sense of dread as the man she was terribly afraid she loved rushed toward the man who had saved her from her own past. Like a scene from a nightmare, she watched as they rushed toward each other. Her heart began to hammer at her ribs. There was no way this could end but in heartbreak.

The trap had sprung.

*****

Jesse forced his way onto the balcony over the body of the doorway's last defender. He saw a sea of blue before him. The caps of the officers and the array of civilian hats worn by the agents were clearly visible at the other end. He knew this would boil down to time. Without waiting for the rest of his posse, he waded into the press of bodies. His Hyper-velocity pistols blazed away, their muzzle flashes charring the flesh of his targets; he was so close. Shattered bodies were tossed into their friends, onto the stone floor, and over the parapet to the left.

At first, the blue-bellies could not have known what was happening. The stairway had been a secure flank only a moment before, all of their attention on the doors to the outer wall and over the parapet into the cavernous inner chamber. They adapted quickly, though. These were the elite soldiers of the garrison unit, the best the Union had to offer. They had been sent to guard their most precious outpost in enemy territory. Soon, return fire was snapping past his head and charged saber blades flashed on all sides. He raised his pistols and pumped bolt after bolt into the seething mass of enemy soldiers, ducking and weaving to avoid their attempts to cut him down. The customary grin swept across his grimy face as the old sense of invincibility rose up within him. Crimson bolts flew past close enough to warm his flesh. Blades whistled by and he could feel the wind of their passage. He wove through it all without a scratch.

A sword blade caught him on the wrist with a blow that would have sheared his natural hand away. It clanged off the metal but scraped along his mechanical thumb, stripping the pistol from his grasp and sending it tumbling to the paving stones. Jesse growled as he realized he had lost one of his precious weapons, bringing the other around to punch two bolts through the offending swordsman's face. He relished the look of disgust and horror on the men behind as they were showered in droplets of their friend's head. If they thought taking a pistol away from him would stop his rampage, they had not paid close enough attention to his legend. He would just as easily kill them with his bare metal hands as with his storied weapons.

As he moved across the balcony, Jesse was aware of his friends fighting alongside him, finally removing some of the pressure of the Union men's growing desperation. Bob and Jim Younger were to either side, Jim's pistol barking defiance while Bob's long knives flashed in the dim light, sending arcs of crimson fluid into the air with every slash.

Robert Ford's eyes were wild as he leapt over the slumped bodies at the doorway. He was not even firing his pistol, but using it like a club in his crazed rage, a knife slick with blood in his off hand. He knocked two Union soldiers back into their companions. A third jumped at him with a flashing knife and he fell to the floor in a tangle of limbs.

Frank and Cole were the last out of the stairwell. Frank caught sight of something off in the main chamber, but Jesse had neither the time nor inclination to scrutinize the blaster-torn walls. His brother moved toward the parapet, dashing one blue-clad soldier into the ground with the butt of his sniper rifle. He took up a position at the railing, scanning the chamber for threats, his eyes tight. Cole's shotgun would have been murder in the confined space on friend and coot alike. He held it across his body, looking for a clear shot at the commanders gathered on the far side.

Jesse focused back on the fighting ahead and saw that a tall man in a strange hat seemed to be the center of the Union effort. Even the other commanders were defending the man from the fresh rebel assault. He wielded a long-handled axe with a broad, ornate head, brandishing the weapon in the air as his eyes searched for a likely target. They settled on Jesse with the weight of a coffin lid.

Before the tall man in the hat could move toward Jesse, Jim Younger rushed past with a howl of crazed, animal rage. The outlaw chief had no idea what had so enraged Cole's brother, but he knew the boy would probably follow their brother John's fate if he was left to his own devices. Jesse charged in after him.

Jim obscured the tall man as he charged, blocking any clear view Jesse might have had. He saw the axe swing up and then spin, as if the man was going to meet Jim's charge with the butt of the handle. There was a sharp report, a flash of crimson, and Jim was flying back toward Jesse, his body spinning as he came.

Jesse dodged to one side and watched as Jim Younger, his eyes wide with confusion and pain, landed on the ground beside him. The boy's face was shattered, nothing but glistening meat and shards of bone from the nose down. Blood poured from the wound to pool around his head, his eyes glazing over while Jesse watched.

As he saw the light fade from Jim's eyes, John Younger's face flashed before him again. Outrage rose up in Jesse's chest, made even more powerful by the surge of guilt. Of the three remaining Younger brothers, Jim had been the most even-tempered, the most willing to forgive him for what had happened to John. Jesse howled at the boy's killer standing before him, and raised his remaining pistol as his vision darkened. Soldiers tried to shield the tall man with their bodies and he cut them down as he charged, his only thought fixated upon blowing the bearded stranger's head into the far wall.

Cole and Bob Younger, shouting their own horrified cries for vengeance, rushed forward at his side. Bob began to match blows with a man that Jesse thought he remembered from Kansas City. The man was fighting with a pistol and a knife, an enormous Gatling rifling slung over his back. He matched Bob's speed with brutal strength. Cole blew four soldiers crouched by the parapet away with a single shot that took most of the low wall with it. Even as the stone and dust cascaded down into the chamber below, he turned back to square off against a tall, dashing-looking agent and an older man in a bowler hat. A glancing blow with the butt of the shotgun took the old man in the face, and he was going down as Jesse rushed past them.

Jesse paid no further attention to the combat around him, the tall man filling his vision. The man's axe was back in a cross-body guard position, ready to receive his charge. Jesse's pistol came up to fire into the man's gut, but the axe spun around fast as lightning, knocking the weapon aside. Jesse lashed out with his empty metal fist, crashing off a concealed chest plate. They settled down into a rhythm of attempted destruction, each trying to find a way past the other's guard.

As Jesse slowed his own combat to take stock of his enemy's abilities, he saw Robert Ford take a sword strike across the abdomen, just below his battered chest armor. His self-professed bodyguard hollowed out his attacker's head with a return shot, having finally remembered the primary utility of his pistol, but sank to his knees right after, lost in the surging melee.

Frank was still at the parapet trading shots with another sniper across the hall. With a cold certainty, Jesse realized it must be that damned Wraith again. He hoped Frank was as good as he always claimed.

The axe-man reversed his grip without warning, and Jesse lurched to the side as the broad head swept past, close enough for him to hear the whistle. He caught the return stroke on his metal forearm and then, with the long weapon bound away, brought his remaining pistol up toward the man's face. There was something about the face, seen from barely a foot away now, that nagged at his mind despite the desperation of the situation. He shook off the distracting fancy. Plenty of time to study what was left of the face after he had killed the bastard. Even as he thought it, the man's eyes widened as he realized his danger. The tall, familiar-seeming stranger fell backward, surrendering his solid stance in favor of getting his head out of the line of fire.

Jesse growled. This old man was harder to kill than he should have been. Nearly blind with frustration and finally-released rage, the outlaw chief began to rain blows down on the old man's head, lashing in from either side with metal fist or pistol butt. The pistol, rebounding from a solid block with the axe, snapped up and crushed the man's tall, peculiar-looking hat. The hood fell away with the topper, revealing the man's face to the dim light.

Jesse froze.

The face was completely familiar to him: the object of his hatred for over two decades. The jaw-framing beard, the beady eyes, the sharp nose; they had been etched into his mind with the force of ultimate, eternal hatred. That face that always robbed him of any reservation or control. Even on a mourning pin, that face was enough to drive him to acts of madness.

Abraham Lincoln.

Jesse staggered back, his mouth hanging wide. He stuttered, a sense of deep betrayal washing away much of his anger and guilt. This man, the man he had blamed for nearly every bad thing that had happened to him since he was a boy, was supposed to be nearly twenty years in his grave.

"You . . . You're dead!" Jesse stammered out, his mind desperately grasping for a certainty that eluded him.

The man's cold eyes tightened at the confusion and the disordered hatred he saw in Jesse's face.

"Son, I don't know you." The voice was completely devoid of emotion. With a grunt, the axe rose into the air.

Jesse's mind was still struggling with a reality that could not be, when he realized the axe was hurtling toward him, driven with all the strength his enemy's tall frame could muster.

The outlaw chief tried to launch himself to the side, bringing up his pistol in a desperate attempt to blast the revenant before the axe could land. He knew, even as he threw himself down, that he was too late. The invulnerability that had seen him through countless shootouts and battles had deserted him in the face of his most hated enemy, seemingly risen from the grave.

The heavy blade came crashing down into his shoulder, just where the metal of his artificial arm merged with the flesh of his body. The blade bit deep, tearing at metallic components and gouging through vulnerable flesh. A grunting whimper sounded in his ears and he was horrified to realize that it had come from him.

Jesse was dashed to the ground with the force of the blow, spinning as he fell. He landed on his remaining arm, the damaged limb falling free, dragging pieces of bone, wire, and tubing with it. Blood, glowing RJ-1027, and a viscous black fluid began to spread. His vision started to dim as his heart pumped furiously, widening the pool beneath him.

Chapter 20

A large chunk of the balcony's parapet detonated, sending a shower of crimson sparks and gray dust out into the chamber and over the struggling forces below. Lucy cringed from the blast, trying to follow what was happening through the haze and the smoke. She thought she had seen Robert Pinkerton fall, Henry pressed back against the forward wall beneath a vicious onslaught. Her killer's instinct faltered as she watched the two halves of her life collide before her eyes. As the parapet blasted away, the balcony opened up. Her heart froze.

Jesse and President Lincoln were locked in vicious combat. The president's axe, William's Wrath, spun and whirled, coming at the shorter outlaw from too many directions at once. But Jesse's arms were flashing with incredible speed, his iron forearms clashing against the axe handle, stopping the head inches from his flesh at every blow.

Even from this distance, through the swirling grit and smoke, she could tell that Jesse was faltering. His shoulders were slumped, his arms slower with each shattering fall of the axe. Most of the world had thought Abraham Lincoln dead these past two decades and more. Even within the Union government and military, only a tiny fraction had been privy to the layered deception of the faked assassination. Cries of disbelief, horror, and jubilation rang through the hall as realization of his identity swept through the fighting. The presidents eyes were impassive, his face calm, as the axe blurred around him, cutting away at the outlaw's last reserves of strength.

Lucinda spun around and dragged the heavy crate toward her. With desperate fingers she pried the top off and stared in growing frustration at the contents. Grabbing a nest of belts and webbing, she pulled a heavy pack out and slung the tangle over one shoulder. Forehead wrinkled in concentration, she then began to assemble the primary components. Although designed by the mad genius, Tesla, it had been built with battlefield utility in mind. The pieces fit together cleanly and quickly.

As her hands worked to tighten the connections on the power lead, she peeked around the corner again to check on the progress of the battle. She froze.

Jesse was off balance. Something had gone wrong, and he was falling. Whether he was purposely dodging or collapsing in defeat, she could not tell. The axe arced through the air, falling toward the fallen outlaw. Jesse's gun was rising to meet the blow, but somehow, she knew he would be too late.

Even from across the cavernous chamber, she saw the axe land. The President's shoulders shook with the impact, Jesse's body collapsed beneath the blow. When he rolled away, he left a piece of himself behind.

Lucinda shrieked a single syllable, slumping against the keep's doorway, her eyes wide with shock and horror. Tesla's creation lay forgotten in her lap.

The President stood over Jesse, the axe held loosely in both hands, and he said something to the prostrate outlaw. The axe came up again, swung with a workman's skill, no anger or hostility behind it: just a job needing to be done.

But Jesse was not finished yet. As the axe rose, so did the legendary outlaw. Pushing off the floor of the balcony with his remaining arm, Jesse stood like some ancient god rising from the underworld. He was off-balance, one mechanical arm lying at his feet; but his other arm snapped up, still gripping his custom pistol, and the barrel rose like a serpent ready to strike.

The gauntlet was on her hand, although she had no memory of how it had gotten there. She wanted nothing more in the world than to separate the two men rushing toward their final confrontation. She reached out, as if grasping for Jesse's distant form.

The power pack surged, flaring with bright light and flooding the inner keep with ruby illumination. Her back, where the pack rested against it, burned with a seething, gut-wrenching pain. Lucy felt as if her arm was being ripped off. There was a thunderous crack, her nose filled with a heavy metallic scent, and something heavy crashed into her at high speed. She was knocked back against the wall of the keep, the breath dashed from her burning lungs. She collapsed to the cold flagstone floor. A heavy weight draped atop her. Something warm began to wash over her arm and side.

*****

Frank screamed, reaching out with one hand as the axe fell toward his brother's head. There was no way Jesse would survive, even if his pistol came up in time to destroy his killer. Already suffering from the brutal injury, all of the infamous speed and artistry was gone. The old nightmare had finally come to pass: his brother was going to die in front of him, and there was nothing he could do to stop it.

When Jesse disappeared in a blinding flash of ruby light, Frank fell back against the parapet, his hand rising to shield his eyes. His brother's attacker, face eerily familiar now that the hat and hood were gone, cast about in stunned confusion. The agents and officers around him were dazed as well, blinking away purple afterimages that plagued their vision.

There was a sudden lull in the combat. Faintly, through the passages out to the main parapet, Frank heard a sound he had been dreading since entering the fortress. Massed Iron Horses were approaching, and that could only mean one thing. He had known the cavalry had not been routed, that they would return before the battle was finished. He had hoped to secure the fort before their arrival. Safe behind the high walls, Jesse would have had more than enough men to hold the fortress against a single regiment of cavalry.

But they were nowhere near securing the fort, and now Jesse had disappeared, literally. If they did not make a push for the gate soon, they were going to be trapped inside and slaughtered like cattle.

Frank turned to look out over the vast chamber, looking for someone to marshal the rebels and organize a fighting retreat for the door. As he scanned the floor of the central chamber, however, his eyes fell upon two figures slumped against the door of the small inner keep. One of them, lying on top of the other, had only one arm. The other, struggling to rise from beneath the first, was the last person he had expected to see.

Lucinda Loveless looked up at him, her beautiful face a mask of fear and concern. Frank looked around, the two were alone. He began to wave her toward the front gate when the parapet in front of him exploded, chips of rock stabbing into his face as he ducked beneath the stone.

That damned Wraith again. Frank swore he was going to execute that dark bastard before the day was done.

*****

Lucinda gave a sharp gasp as Frank James fell, a cloud of powder and crimson sparks erupting from his position. She watched for a moment, hoping to see him rise again, but there was nothing more than swirling smoke and glittering dust. She realized she could not wait for Frank, and looked around for anyone who could take Jesse to safety.

Jesse barely clung to consciousness. Blood continued to pour from the horrible wound at his shoulder, mingling with a black, foul-smelling liquid, and dribbles of RJ-1027. His eyes rolled in his head and his mouth worked desperately, but the sounds carried no meaning.

There were no rebels nearby. Most were fighting on the walls or running for the entrance. Lucinda gathered herself to lift Jesse up, planning to move him toward the gate, when a new flood of men came rushing into the fortress. The redoubts and barricades obscured the newcomers as they scrambled for cover against the desperately retreating rebels, but their insignia was clear. The 7th had recovered from whatever debacle they had suffered outside the fort and were back for revenge.

Lucinda looked around, but there was nowhere to hide. Only the keep, rising behind her, offered any sort of shelter. Her heart sank. Running now would be futile, she knew. She refused to lay there for Custer to find, with Jesse at her feet. With a grunt, she shoved the door wide and dragged the outlaw chief's limp body after her.

She pushed the heavy gate closed with her gauntleted hand and slid down against it, her breath coming in ragged gasps. Jesse's chest rose and fell with a fluttering motion that reminded her of an old hunting dog breathing his last. Blood was seeping from the corner of the outlaw's mouth, staining the short beard a deep black in the gloomy half-light. His eyes were heavy-lidded, pupils darting feverishly as if following a will-o-the-wisp that only he could see.

Lucinda scrambled to Jesse's side and hauled him back up so that he was resting against her leg, rocking him gently. For the first time in her life, she did not know what to do.

Jesse's mouth moved slowly, as if in a dream, and the shallow breaths came in a pattern barely recognizable as speech. She urged him to rest as she took off his hat, leather thongs clutching the scorched remnant of an owl feather. She brushed the hair away from his sallow face. As a single coherent word forced its way through his muttering, Lucinda felt her throat tighten painfully.

". . . home . . ."

Her resolve stiffened beneath the ringing of the single word. She hoisted him roughly to his feet.

"Come on, Jesse. On your feet, bastard! We can't go out, and we can't go up, so we're going to go down." Her voice was hoarse as she whispered the words, draping his remaining arm over her shoulders and bracing him as best she could. She flexed the fingers within the gauntlet, hoping the little machine would be able to produce another miracle down in the vaults.

The stairs were brutal as she maneuvered downward, the heavy power pack hanging from its tangled straps over her other shoulder. Every few steps she had to stop to catch her breath, resting Jesse against the cool stone of the wall for a moment before gathering him up once again with a grunt and dragging him a few more steps deeper down.

Lucinda's memory was betraying her, she knew, but she thought they were only a few steps from the bottom when the sound of a single pair of running feet broke into her concentration. Someone was running up, from the vaults, straight at them.

The agent settled Jesse into a sitting position against the wall and then drew one of her derringers. At this point, there was no telling who they were going to run into, but she would be damned if they were going to take him away from her.

She had never met the man who came stumping around the corner, but she recognized his face from a hundred wanted posters and a thousand fireside conversations with

Jesse James and his posse. William Bonney had a distinctive face, and even without his signature arrogant smirk, she knew him.

The derringer came up just as Billy the Kid's own battered pistols drew a bead on her. His eyes widened as he saw that she was a woman.

Billy's arms froze, slowly drifting wide. The weapons' barrels pointed at the high ceiling in a show of peaceful intent. A ghost of the smirk emerged from the mask of dirt, grime, and disappointment.

"Well, I'll be damned." He nodded politely. "You must be Jesse's new girl, eh?" His face quirked slightly, his head cocking to one side. "What the hell you wearin', sweet thing?"

Lucinda lowered her own pistol but kept her arm stiff, ready to bring it up in a moment. She nodded back, despite her annoyance with the label. "William Bonney."

The smirk widened. "Call me Billy, please." His eyes glittered with amusement, and for a moment she wondered what he thought was so funny. Then, his eyes darted down and past her, to where Jesse lay, all but unconscious, against the stone. "Oh, damn –"

The derringer rose again as Lucinda stepped in front of Jesse. "You might want to step back a pace or two, Mr. Bonney." She kept her voice calm, but there was an edge that could not be missed.

Billy's pistols rose a bit higher and he bowed his head to show he understood. He gestured with his guns, then looked down at his holsters and up again with a single quirked eyebrow. She nodded, but kept her derringer on him until his own were secured.

"Can I look at him?" Billy gestured vaguely at his fallen rival. She nodded reluctantly and stepped aside, lowering her pistol.

"I was trying to get him out of the fort, but—" She did everything she could to control her voice, but she could hear an edge slipping in. Any moment now, and she was either going to break down into inconsolable sobs or tear back up the stairs and kill everything in sight.

Billy nodded even as he cursed. "Those Billy Yank trotters're back, eh?" He was kneeling beside Jesse's broken body, shaking his head at the other outlaw chief's condition.

Lucinda went to one knee beside him, also looking into Jesse's pain-twisted face. "I don't know what else to do." She made a gesture with the gauntleted hand. "I think this could be used to dig a tunnel, but I'm not sure how to make it do that." Her face tightened with frustration and concern. "And I'm not sure about Jesse. His arm . . ."

The outlaw gave her a grin she supposed was meant to be comforting. "Nah, miss. He's a tough ol' road agent. This ain't the first time this has happened to him, remember."

Her eyes did not move. "There's no way out, Billy. Once the cavalry have secured the fort, they'll come down here."

His smirk returned with full force. "Well, that ain't entirely so, miss. What would you say if I told you someone had . . . passed along a little consideration to some of the workers here, to build in a little tunnel, a little hidden back door, in anticipation of future need?"

Her eyes snapped up to Billy's grinning face. He nodded before she could speak, and continued. "I got a map. If we can't go up, like you say, we can always go down."

Her eyes narrowed. "You're offering to take Jesse away from here? After what he did to you out in the desert?"

The smirk faded, and the outlaw shrugged. "Well, yeah, that stung, a bit. But . . ." He nodded down at Jesse. "This ain't the way I wanna take the gold ring, miss. I don't want the story of the greatest rivalry of the Wild West to be settled by some blue-belly chiselers hundreds of miles from anyone who cares." The smirk returned. "Asides, I know a man who'll pay good money for the tech, if Jesse comes a cropper."

Lucinda rose to her feet, the pistol once again coming up, and Billy scrambled away a bit, his smirk still in place despite his raised hands. "Just havin' a bit o' fun, miss. I'll see him back to the doc, get him all fixed up. I swear it by my sainted father." A gleam arose in his eyes to match the smirk, but she let it pass.

She looked down at Jesse and then back up at Billy, her resolve once again wavering. When she moved, however, it was with the quick, sure motion of a striking rattler. Before he was even aware he was in danger, a derringer was pressed against his forehead.

"You're going to take him, and you're going to get him to safety." Her words were cold, her eyes flat. "And if anything happens to him before he is fully restored, and I mean ANYTHING at all, there is nowhere on earth you will be able to hide from me."

Billy nodded quickly, his hands held just a little higher. "I promise, miss. He'll get back to Payson safe."

She nodded in return, her pistol lowering slowly, and then she gestured with it, back down the stairway. "I hope you don't mind, but I think maybe I'll accompany you to the back door?"

Billy's frown deepened. "You ain't comin' with us, miss? I was thinkin', him in the shape he's in, you wouldn't be wantin' to stick around with those that nearly done for him."

Lucinda shook her head, looking back up the stairway. "I've got unfinished business up there, but I'll see you two safe away," she nodded toward Jesse. "I'll make sure you've gotten him out, but then I have to go back up." Her face turned grim. "There are a couple people who owe me some answers."

Billy looked at her for a moment and then nodded. "Well, suit yourself, lil' lady." He reached down, hoisted Jesse's body up with a grunt, and began to drag him back down the steps. He looked over his shoulder to pick his way down the stairs and then turned back to her with a smirk. "You think you wanna take the lead here, sweetheart?"

*****

Abraham Lincoln stood upon the broken wall of Fort Knox and looked out over the still-burning plain and the columns of smoke disappearing into the unrelieved darkness of the night sky. The last of the rebels had been ridden down by the cavalry or escaped into the broken land beyond, but the shattered walls and the scorched earth was a stark reminder of the battle. The massive holes in their ranks would be a harsher reminder still.

Robert Pinkerton was in the fortress's infirmary along with a score of other officers. Major Dalton had fallen protecting Colonel Campbell from the worst of the rebel's final assault, but even the Colonel had waded into the battle at the end, picking up several wounds of his own. Courtright had been cut savagely across his abdomen and arms, but had returned to duty as soon as the bandages had been applied. Despite the direst warnings of the infirmary's doctors, he would not be pulled from the president's side, and haunted the parapet like a silent shadow.

"Sir," the voice was hesitant. The rank and file within the fortress were all struggling with the problem of how to address him. Some, he knew, whispered that he was some vile replacement cooked up in a lab in Washington. Others were firmly convinced he was some sort of ghost, or a tool of Carpathian. Even those who believed he was who he said he was did not really understand. And every one of them would have to be sworn to secrecy, if there was to be any hope of rebuilding his anonymity.

He turned slowly to look at the young soldier addressing him. "Yes, son?"

The boy swallowed and nodded with a jerk. "Sir, Colonel Custer wishes to return to Fort Frederick. We've just received a report regarding some sort of attack his forces back west were conducting. It seems something's gone wrong up there. He's afraid for the security of the base."

The tall man bowed his head. Below the wall in front of him, and within the fortress itself, his dead and wounded were still being dug from the wreckage. Was this not tragedy enough for one night?

He nodded without looking up. "Certainly. Give him our thanks, and make sure he takes sufficient resupply for the return journey." The tall man's lip twisted slightly, "General Grant's reinforcements should be here before the sun rises." He looked up at the distant, dark horizon. "I doubt the rebels will have even stopped running by then."

The boy gave a sharp salute and pivoted on his heel. "Sir, yes sir."

The old man looked back out over the smoldering plain. After a moment, he tilted his head to speak to the shadow behind him. "Any word on prisoners, Henry?"

The agent shook his head. "No, sir." His voice was a whispered ruin. "The fighting was fierce around the gate, but a lot of the dogs escaped. We've got prisoners, of course, too many to count, really. Wade's begun interrogations, but he hasn't discovered anything of account yet."

There was a moment's silence, and then the agent continued. "Sir, that was a close-run thing." He looked out over the smoking plains, refusing to meet the president's eyes. "That damned outlaw almost had you. When he recognized you, I thought you were lost for sure. There isn't anyone on the continent that bears a hatred that hot for anyone."

The president nodded and continued his silent vigil. Behind him, in the shadows of the secondary wall, Henry Courtright's eyes were fixed on the hellish prairie fires. Lucy was still missing, and he hoped she would turn up soon. It was going to be a long night.

*****

Billy dragged the unconscious weight of his rival down the echoing hall, sweat stinging his eyes and weakening his grip. The clicking of the woman's heels echoed off the cold stone all around them, working its way into his head and making his brain itch. He had not really bargained on carrying Jesse James, all but a corpse and incapable of standing on his own, all the way back to the Contested Territories.

"We need to be careful moving through here." Her voice, a voice he would have loved to listen to under other circumstances, was just another annoyance as his back burned and sweat beaded down his forehead.

"Why?" He grunted out.

"The UR-30 Enforcers that were sent here were never deployed up in the fortress." She was probing ahead of them with a small hand light, a derringer in her other fist. "I'm thinking they were probably put down here. I know there are at least ten of them, and I haven't seen them since I arrived last night."

With a shrug, he continued on.

The tattered map he had crammed into his pocket was barely legible at this point. He was already deeper into the vaults than he had been during his brief search for treasure. All he had found in his initial exploration had been empty vaults, solid metal doors swinging loosely on their hinges. The last several doors they had passed had been closed tight. He was fairly sure he had stumbled upon the part of the place Carpathian had meant him to find all along.

Billy was brought up short as he realized that the woman agent had stopped at the next corner. She was making a patting gesture with her gauntleted hand as she peered around in the gloomy red half-light on the other side. The outlaw dropped his burden beside the wall, just a little less gentle than he could have been, and moved up beside the woman, his own pistol drawn again.

The hall continued on for about thirty feet before it reached an intersection, branching off to the right and left. In the center of the wall straight ahead was another vault door, this one closed tight. At the intersection, standing as still as statues, were four

UR-30 Enforcers, their weapons holstered and their eyes burning a dull crimson.

Billy ducked back behind the corner, his spine to the wall, and smiled. The agent stooped beside him, her face dark. "What's so funny?" Her harsh whisper was not quite enough to overcome the appeal of her soft lips, and his smile widened.

"I'm just thinkin'," he shrugged. "I come a long way, miss. I'd like to have a little somethin' to show for the journey afore I hightail it back to the territories." He nodded his head toward the guarded passage. "I'm thinkin', they got so many metal marshals standing guard just there, might be that's a door I'd want to open on my way out."

She snarled at him. "We're trying to get the two of you out, not indulge in petty thievery."

He shrugged. "The size of that door? I'm not sure 'petty' would be the right word for it." His eyes hardened slightly. "Either way, not sure I was givin' you a choice in the matter."

She looked down at him with a sneer and then closed her eyes, huffing in exasperation. "What are you thinking?"

The grin brightened even more, and he scrambled around to gesture to the gauntlet and its power pack. "You said that thing can put a hole in anything, right?"

She nodded with a frown. "I was thinking maybe I'd try to dig out, before we met up with you. But yes, that's what I read."

He smiled. "Well, then, fancy givin' a lad a chance?" He held out his hands, and after a moment she stripped the gauntlet off and shrugged out of the power pack's nest of straps and harness clamps.

Billy untangled the harness and then hoisted the pack into position, putting both arms through the straps and tightening it over his chest. He looked up at the woman with eager eyes. "You reckon you can help me make a hole, say, about this big?" He held his hands about a foot apart.

"I think so." Her brow furrowed as she tried to remember the papers she had seen. With hesitant fingers, she fiddled with some knobs and sliders on the gauntlet's wrist. When she was done, some numbers in a little window, glowing red with RJ-1027, seemed to have changed. "That should to do it."

Billy nodded again and then gave her a questioning look, raising the gauntlet in a shrug. "And so I . . . ?"

The lovely mouth quirked in a smile that he thought showed some promise, then the agent reached out and turned the gauntlet palm up. "You reach toward whatever you want to open up, and you just grab at it, with a twist." She tapped on the thumb. "There's a button in there, against the nail?" He nodded when he felt the button. "As you reach out, flick that. It'll do the trick."

He felt a rush of excitement. He had always wanted to get a leg up on Jesse and his damned arms. This was the first time he had gotten the chance to play with some of this new tech himself. If his idea worked, this was going to be a legend he could put up against anything Jesse had ever done.

"Ready?" Without waiting for a response, he wheeled around the corner, racing for the intersection. He heard the agent swear under her breath as she charged out after him.

Billy laid down a solid stream of fire with his off-hand, the crimson bolts zapping down the corridor, illuminating everything in shifting, tottering highlights. The bolts slapped into the wall all around the metal men, some sleeting off their armored hides. The figures were still while he took his first full strides down the hall, then suddenly leapt into motion, as if triggered by some unseen puppeteer. All four drew their massive pistols, and the air filled with their humming, vibrating shots. Answering bolts flashed down the hall toward him, and he knew the time had come.

Billy dodged to the side and reached up with the heavy gauntlet. He made as if to snatch at the head of the robot on the far left of the line and flicked the button with a backward nudge of his thumb closing the hand and bringing it quickly back toward his shoulder.

There was a red flash from the pack on his back, his arm wrenched painfully, and an awful, mechanical smell filled his nostrils. Something flashed into the air by his head and he threw himself down onto the stone floor. He was just able to make out the head and shoulders of a robot sailing over him, trailing wires, tubes, chunks of glowing metal, and crimson sparks.

Billy howled in uncontrolled glee as he rolled over onto his back to watch the bits of metal marshal bounce down the corridor. A massive detonation caused him to spin around again, and he whooped even louder. Glowing red traced where the head and chest sections had once been attached. The robot flailed wildly, its enormous pistol firing shots into the walls and ceiling. One of the shots, at point blank range, took the next Enforcer in line in the chest, blowing metallic components out its back and down the side passage. In a blinding flash of ruby light, both robots collapsed into a loose jumble of twitching metal scrap.

A cloud of dust and smoke, lit from within by flickering crimson lightning, spread out from the downed figures, obscuring their partners. The agent's bolts snapped into the cloud as she ran past Billy, dropping to slide across the stone floor beneath the erratic spray of fire, her skirts flaring in a very intriguing way. For a moment, there was only stunned silence as Billy lay on his back, staring at the spreading cloud, while Loveless crouched by the far wall, her derringers at the ready. The shooting within the churning dust had stopped.

With more dignity than they probably deserved, the two remaining UR-30s toppled out of the arid fog, a glowing hole in each of their burnished chests.

Billy sprang up with a whoop and snatched his hat off his head, slapping his knee. Rock dust puffed into the air. The agent rose more slowly, her guns trained on the thinning mist. It took a moment for either of them to realize that the cloud seemed to be glowing a rich golden color, getting brighter by the moment.

Billy slid the gauntlet off his hand, shrugged out of the straps, and let the power pack drop to the floor. He pulled his second pistol, finding comfort in the familiar grips of his regular weapons, and stalked toward the crumpled shapes of the metal men. As the dust and smoke continued to drift away, he approached the warm glow, one hand outstretched. The glow was shining out of the open vault door. Somehow, as the gauntlet had pulled the robot's head off, it had also grabbed a chunk out of the door behind. And as unlikely as it seemed, it appeared that he had pulled out parts of the locking mechanism.

He heard the agent step up beside him, and looked over with his customary smirk. "Pretty good for a first shot, if I do say so myself."

She looked at him with an arched eyebrow, her gaze flickering up over his head. "Yes, well, you did. You're also very lucky you're so short."

He had always been sensitive about his height, but this comment was so brutally random, coming at him from out of nowhere, that he forgot to get ornery. "What?"

She nodded to his hat. He took it off and looked at it. Two neat holes, their edges still smoldering, had been punched through the felt. He did not know whether to laugh or curse. He finally decided on a sarcastic little chuckle and then turned back toward the open door.

The chamber beyond was an exact duplicate of the room buried in the desert sands beyond Diablo Canyon. It lacked the piled dust of centuries, of course, and the horrid stink of Carpathian's abandoned creations, but other than that, he could very well have been back again. Except for one alarming difference; the pedestal in the center of the chamber beneath Fort Knox was not empty.

A fragment of stone, one surface polished and intricately-carved, hung suspended in the air above the column. It was longer than his forearm, thick and heavy. Swirled engravings swept along its full length, a silvery sheath curling around a portion of the stone. The radiance, however, was shining out from the buttery-golden rock itself. It was as if he were looking at a chunk of heaven fallen to earth, and its light flooded through him, overwhelming him with a sense of safety and warmth such as he had not known since before his mother had coughed her last breath.

"Holy mother of God . . ." A hoarse voice spooked Billy and he jumped, turning with one hand on a pistol, to see Jesse holding himself up by the door frame. "What the hell—"

Billy smiled widely. "This, I think, is what we been fightin' over for more'n a year, James."

The older outlaw chief could not take his bruised and hollow eyes off the floating piece of stone. "What is. . ." His words drifted off, his eyes rolled up into his skull, and he slumped back to the stone floor.

Billy's smile widened. "It's mine, is what it is." He turned to approach the object as the reverberating sound of metal feet echoed off the walls.

"The other Enforcers." The woman was beside Jesse, looking up at Billy. "You have to get him out of here. Is your tunnel nearby?"

Billy took a moment to recall what she was talking about and then nodded. "Yeah. We're almost there."

The beautiful woman nodded, her eyes cold. "Alright, then. You both go that way. I'll lead the rest of the robots off, then make my way back up to the fortress."

Billy's smile slipped a bit. He looked around her at the smoking robots in the hall. "You're still not comin' with us? Even after all that?"

The dark eyes hardened even further. "Especially after all that. These units wouldn't answer to any of the commanders upstairs. This whole thing has been a trap, designed to bring two implacable enemies face to face, and I'm not sure who was bait and who was prey. There's a deeper game going on here, and I'm going to dig up some answers before I move on."

Billy's smile disappeared for good. His head snapped from the artifact, to Jesse, to the agent, and back. With a snarl he lurched toward the stone, reaching out with both gloved hands.

"You idiot!" The Union woman lashed out with one hand to stop him, but missed.

The heat radiating off the stone became more uncomfortable with each step. The glow seemed to grow more and more intense, and he had to shield his eyes with one raised forearm.

"You don't even know what that thing is, you moron!" She was calling out to him, still standing at the door. "Trust me, it takes more than you've got here to make off with something like that! We need to get out of here now!"

Billy stopped beside the pedestal, looking up at the hovering chunk of ancient stone. With a tentative hand he reached up, thinking to topple it off its stand. The stone would not budge. He grunted and put both hands on the warm, smooth rock, pushing with all his might. It did not move.

With a roar of frustration, Billy backed away from the object, again shielding his eyes. When he stood once more beside the woman, he glanced at her through his pained squint. With a vicious twist he turned around, grabbed Jesse none-too-gently beneath his shoulders, and dragged him down the hall, away from the approaching metal footsteps.

"Don't matter none." He spat over his shoulder. "Someday, one of those rocks is gonna be mine."

Her smile, out of the corner of his eyes, held no amusement. "Whatever you say, you curly wolf, you." Before he could summon up a response, she was gone, running in the direction of the pounding metal feet.

The two outlaw bosses were far down the corridor by the time they heard the high, sharp reports of the derringers. The clang of falling metal bodies was followed soon after by the quick tapping of the agent's high-heeled boots moving off into the distance. No sounds of further pursuit spurred them to greater speed. Billy dropped Jesse in exhaustion and disgust, shaking his head and gasping for breath.

The rest of the way to the secret tunnel was quiet and dark as they moved through rough and unfinished corridors. The door itself was concealed behind a pile of wood and canvas tarps. Billy pushed his way through and then dragged Jesse out behind him. The tunnel was long, dark, and narrow. By the time they emerged, the young outlaw chief was panting again from the exertion.

The cold night air welcomed them to the surface, jerking Jesse awake with a painful snort. His eyes rolled wildly as he tried to fix his position, but his face was slack and confused. Billy squatted down beside him, looking into those wild, uncomprehending eyes, and thought seriously about leaving Jesse there in the abandoned gully to die.

But there had been the heat of truth in the lady agent's threats. Billy knew he would do everything he could to get Jesse back to Carpathian. They would both owe him, then, and that suited William Bonney just fine.

Although, thinking of debts, something occurred to Billy as he crouched there beside his dazed old foe.

The young outlaw chief took out his pistol slowly, feeling the heavy weight of the blaster, the heat of the RJ power packs glowing from the vents and indicators. Then, with a savage lurch of his shoulder, he brought the butt of the pistol across Jesse' jaw. With a grunt, the older man slumped into the wet grass, his breath releasing in a long, heavy sigh.

"Now I reckon we're startin' from even, Jesse me boy." The smirk was back as Billy stood, looking around for the Iron Horses they had hidden away earlier that day.

Epilogue

"Have no fear. You will be compensated for your losses and for your good service here today."

Something about the voice was familiar. There was an echo of a foreign accent. No name immediately came to mind, only a vague sense of pain, loss, confusion, and danger.

"Damn straight I will!" That was a voice more easily recognized, with the curves and burrs of the western territories. "Your pretty boy here'd be dead if it weren't fer me! An' if I hadn't been draggin' his sorry ass all over God's creation, I coulda walked away with a shiny little prize, too: a nice shiny rock just the match of your'n over there."

The voice's petulance was jarring, discomforting. It made his cheek throb with phantom pain. Something in the voice was uncomfortable and irritating, even through the cool shadows.

"So you said." The first voice spoke again. "And believe me, we will discuss that more at a later time. For now, I have work to do."

The phrase sent a shock of cold through the darkness, jerking him toward consciousness. A sudden, deep-seated fear stabbed through him.

"Yeah, I guess you do." The harshness of the second voice was colored with amusement now. The tone instantly shifted the fear to anger. "You gonna make 'im a new one, 'r leave 'im as is?"

Jesse James was catapulted back to full awareness with these final words ringing in his ears. Bloodshot eyes snapped open and his neck surged from side to side as he tried to take stock of his situation. His entire body ached as if he had been dropped off a cliff. His left arm burned, and a particularly deep ache throbbed throughout the left side of his face. His vision was blurry, as if he had just emerged from deep water. He peered through the pulsing distortion, and could just make out a figure leaning over him. A shock of white hair hovered over the half-formed features of a blurred face.

"Ah, James! Welcome back to the land of the living!" The voice clicked into place in his memory, and Jesse lurched forward again.

He was on a hard bed, rough sheets draped over his body. He surged upward, reached back to push himself off the bed, and pitched to the left as his arm failed to support him. He nearly fell, flailing wildly with the right arm and barely catching the edge of the bed-frame before he slid onto the floor.

Carpathian was hovering over him, but as Jesse burst upward, the doctor backed quickly away. The outlaw chief steadied himself on the bed and sat up straighter, raising his left arm to inspect it. He did not have a left arm. The twisted metal wreckage that had remained jutting from his wound had been removed, and the insertion points covered over in rough bandages spotted with old, brown blood.

"Wha—" Jesse's head whipped around. His vision was clearing, and his frantic motion settled upon Carpathian. A self-satisfied smirk twisted behind the doctor's beard. Jesse snarled, his brows drawing down heavily over his eyes. "You bastard . . ."

Carpathian's smile widened and he put one hand out in a calming gesture. "Now, James, no need for base mockery."

Jesse's scowl deepened. He gestured with the shattered, cloth-wrapped stump of his left arm. "Then you best be callin' me Mister James, then, yeah? You left me out in that desert to die, you scrofulous dust gnat! You turned 'em off, dumped me into the sand, an' left me to die!"

Carpathian's face took on a calm, fatherly cast and he shook his head. "No, James. I left you there to continue your education." The doctor moved around the table, his eyes taking in the ruin of the outlaw's arm. The smile returned, although a little more subdued. "And it looks to me as if you're off to a fine start!"

Jesse looked down at the throbbing stump and then back up at the old man. "What happened at the fort . . . Where's Frank?"

Carpathian's eyes turned sad for a moment. "Oh, I'm afraid the assault on Fort Knox was unsuccessful, James. I'm not certain of the disposition of your compatriots, however—"

Jesse tensed, trying to sit up. "I failed, then. I lost everything that mattered in that damned fort." His eyes hardened. "But if you think that's broken me down, you go ahead and shut off the other arm, doc. I'll jump off this bed and kick you to death, and tear your heart out with my teeth!"

He lurched forward, planning on lunging at the doctor, trying to catch him unprepared, but he was brought up short by a leather strap around his waist. The outlaw chief was thrown back against the bed. Jesse growled low in his throat. It was a dangerous, cornered-animal sound, and it deepened as Carpathian's smile widened in response.

"Now, James. What makes you think you failed?" The man's eyes were almost kindly as he looked down on the wounded outlaw. If Jesse had been less familiar with the man, he would have almost believed him. "You have accomplished great things, my boy. Great things!"

The words scratched like tiny claws across tender flesh, and Jesse fell back against the bed with a heavy, desolate sigh. "I doomed the Confederacy. I sold them a hope, then got it burned away. I shamed 'em into standin' up, an' they got slapped down. Those folks won't be lookin' up from their yokes again."

Carpathian eyes now burned with sincerity as he firmly shook his head. Jesse felt a twist in his gut, shocked with the direct, honest power of the European's gaze. "No, James. You proved to them that they can stand up! You showed them the way, and they know they can do it now. You placed the sons and daughters of slaves on an even footing with the children of the old masters, and there won't be any closing that Pandora's box! The army you led against the Union was barely a fraction of the fighting strength of the new generation,

James. And now they have martyrs to worship, and they know they can fight. They will rise again when the time is right." His smile was now almost predatory, and Jesse looked quickly away, a feeling of wrongness skittering down his spine.

"Well, they ain't gonna be fightin' any time soon." The voice behind his head spoke again, and for some reason, the pain in his left cheek gave a sickening lurch. "Leastways, not the ones I saw runnin'."

Jesse turned awkwardly around to stare at Billy the Kid with hard, cold eyes. The younger outlaw chief smirked at him and waved a jaunty hand. "Howdy, Jesse!"

"What the hell're you doin' here?" Jesse's voice was dangerous beneath its hoarse roughness.

Billy gave a pained expression with all the sincerity of a five cent whore. "Why, Jesse, who d'you think dragged you outta that mess? Why, without me, you woulda bled out on that floor!"

Fragmented impressions of his flight through the dungeons beneath Fort Knox came back to him in a rush. One image rose above the others, his heart racing with equal parts fear and hope. "Lucy?"

Billy looked at him with a blank face for a moment, and Jesse could see that he was weighing options in his mind. When the Kid shrugged, he knew he was going to get the truth. "Yeah, she was okay. Last time I saw her, anyway. She was headin' back into the fort. You reckon she's Union through an' through, Jesse?" The jab cut deep.

Jesse ignored the question and posed his own. "You know what happened to Frank? The Youngers?"

Billy nodded. "Yeah, most of 'em got out. Jimmy Younger came up a cropper, I heard, an' that Ford galoot, Charlie, was it?" He shrugged. "The rest of 'em made it out, much as I can tell. They's scattered all over hell's half acre, though, makin' their way back to the territories by a dozen different trails."

Jesse nodded, relief at his brother's survival outweighing his current distaste for the source of the news. His face turned bleak. "What about Lincoln?"

Billy's face paled slightly. "You heard that, eh? No one seems to know fer sure. Lots o' rumors, but that's it. He weren't seen after the battle by any o' my boys, so who knows?" He shrugged. "Maybe you can ask Frank when you see 'im next."

"And you will have plenty of time and opportunity to gather the old gang back together." Carpathian turned and began to work on something lying on a table behind him. "We need to get you back in fighting trim, James." The doctor tapped on his remaining metal arm. "I'm sure you will wish to have a working complement when you gather your friends again. And I'm sure William has someplace he needs to be."

Billy's smirk widened, the cruel light in his eyes flaring high. "Sure do. There ain't but room for one curly wolf in the woods." He nodded down at Jesse's mangled shoulder. "And it sure ain't gonna be no old Algerine down a paw, neither."

"Keep talkin', Billy." Jesse sneered at The Kid. "When I get outta this bed—"

The doctor waved a free hand at Billy. "Now, Mr. Bonney. If you could see your way out?"

Billy sneered for a moment, then straightened to his full height, tugged his vest down, and nodded once to them. "Well, I'll see you boys out on the trail, no doubt." He tipped his hat to the doctor and then Jesse. "And I trust we'll all remember today."

A door behind Jesse's head closed with a dull thud. He shook his head and muttered. "I ain't likely to forget that soaplock, no matter how far he carried me."

"You will have plenty to occupy your mind, James." Carpathian spoke over his shoulder, still working on the table. "I did not let you loose into the great wide world so you could damage my costly gifts, boy. The world has big plans for you, but it will all be for naught if you go and get yourself killed with carelessness."

Jesse turned back to look at the doctor. "I don't carry your water, doc."

Carpathian paused for a moment in his work, his shoulders tensing. Jesse would never have admitted to the sudden concern he felt as the seconds ticked away, nor the relief that came over him as the old man shrugged, obviously deciding to ignore the slight, and went back to his work.

"James, there are wheels within wheels churning just beneath the surface of our world. There are forces at work that none of us can even begin to comprehend." He turned slowly, placing his tools gently back on the table behind him. "There will come a day when we must all band together or we will all die alone." His eyes grew more intense as he leaned toward the bed. "It is not a question of carrying water, James, but of survival."

Jesse shook his head. "I ain't followin' you, doc." It felt good to push his luck further. "An' we ain't so situated that I'm takin' a lot on faith just now."

Carpathian ignored the belittling title completely, reaching back to pull a stool closer to the bedside. "You have noticed them moving through our lives, James. I know you have. The fiery-eyed avatars of a power that we are only beginning to perceive?"

Jesse's eyes tightened. "Fiery-eyed? You mean . . . folks with red eyes . . ."

The doctor shook his head. "Sometimes, James, but not always. Often there is no way to detect their presence until after their infernal work is done, or they are ready to move on." His eyes lost their focus as he shifted on the stool, his head lowering, voice growing distant. "They may appear as normal men for days, weeks, even years. But when their job is done, when they are ready to depart, you will realize that their advice has been poison." The doctor's eyes were bleak. "Everything they have offered you has turned to ash."

Jesse sank back against the rough sack beneath his head. In his mind he was seeing young Ty, who had died so strangely outside of Diablo Canyon, and Henderson, the false emissary of Captain Quantrill. He remembered the croaking last words of Tinker Thane as blood flooded the whites of his eye in the back of an Ironhide wagon.

"Who . . . what are they . . . ?" Jesse's voice was a whisper. He could not forget the eerie smile on Ty's face just before he was obliterated by Union fire.

Carpathian shook his head, looking back down at the outlaw chief. "Who are they? What are they? I don't know, James. And they have plagued my life longer than anyone else I have ever encountered." He gestured with a wave of his hand at the apparatus that surrounded them. "I have them to thank for all of this, ironically. They have haunted my every step since I was a young man, whispering dark words into my egomaniacal ears."

Jesse knew the confusion bubbling up in his mind was clear on his face.
"You have them to thank for all of this?"

The doctor sighed, his shoulders sagging as he slouched down on the stool. "I believe so, yes. At several points in my career, when the world seemed ready to reject me or my discoveries, they would find me. They would assist me, point me in the right direction, offer me inspiration or insight." His eyes were unfocused again. "I never considered the cost until it was too late."

Jesse struggled back up, resting on his one metal elbow. "Wait a minute, doc. Does this mean you ain't fixin' to end Grant no more?"

Carpathian's eyes hardened. "Oh, no, James. The existence of this dark cabal of mysterious strangers has no bearing upon the debts I owe that butcher. There will be a reckoning before long, never fear."

He stood up and began to pace beside the bed, Jesse watching him with confusion. "Throughout history, I believe, these dark strangers have plagued mankind. I do not know who or what they are. Yet. They seem to exist outside the normal order of nature's laws. I do not know what their motives might be." He turned to look directly into Jesse's eyes, and the wounded man knew he was hearing the truth. "But I am close, James. I am so close. And when I understand it fully, I will wrestle with that power, and I will bend it to my will."

The doctor stood up tall again, looking down his regal nose at Jesse's wasted body. "When that time comes, I will need allies, and I will not stand with a man like Grant.

I will need those who understand the enemy, and the stakes. I will need allies like you, James."

Jesse shook his head. "I still don't cotton to your meanin', doc. I ain't gonna march to your tune any more than I was woulda marched to Lee's or Grant's, or anyone else's."

Carpathian sat back down, a slight smile now playing around his mouth. "Of course not, James. But when these dark days finally dawn, we will all be fighting for our lives, our friends, and perhaps even our very souls. In a battle such as that, one has no chance of winning without wealth. We will need gold to arm and equip our friends. We will need the strength of men and women willing to fight for a cause they believe in. And we will need experience to show us the way."

Jesse sat up straighter, looking at the doctor in disbelief. "You wanted this all to happen. You set this all up." His voice sounded flat, even in his own ears. When the doctor nodded, he felt a sour surge rise to the back of his throat.

"Yes, James. Yes, I did. Well, most of it. The trap itself was devised by others, meant, I believe, to provide both you and your resurrected arch nemesis an irresistible lure that would bring you together. I assume the intent was for you to kill each other, or at the very least, for one of you to die. That's all speculation, you understand. But I was more than happy to utilize the trap, insofar as I could assure your survival and extraction, when the time was right."

Jesse stared up at the doctor with leery eyes. "How could you o' known there'd be those who coulda gotten me out? You couldn't a'—"

Carpathian smiled kindly and shook his head. "Please, James. Don't think our enemies are the only ones capable of manipulation. I needed you there, and then I needed you taken away." He gestured around them. "And now here you are. It was a gamble, of course. You are not the only horse I laid money on. You were just the favorite to win."

Jesse shook his head, but could not marshal a more coherent denial.

"You needed experience, you see. And I needed to know that the Confederacy was still capable of rising from the ashes." The lecturing tone nearly drove Jesse out of the bed despite the restraining belt. "The men who rule there now are pale shadows of their former selves, and, I believe, completely in thrall to our real enemies. I have not even begun to disentangle the purposes of this Dark Council. They seem to instigate violence more often than anything else, but they have counseled caution and docility as well, when it suits them. I have been able to come to only one conclusion as to their deeper motives."

The doctor leaned down to look directly into Jesse's eyes. "They seek to weaken us all."

"Why?" Jesse struggled with the complex web of possibilities the doctor wove. "They ain't workin' fer Grant?"

Carpathian waved that away. "No, no more than he is working for them. Each of us retains our free will, James. Each of us makes our own choices. That is why I will hound Grant to the ends of the Earth for his crimes. But no, these beings do not work for him, or any other power I have been able to discover. They work for themselves, undermining our every effort."

Jesse thought about it for a second. "They're going to attack us."

Carpathian nodded, his eyes dark. "Weaken us, play us against each other, and then strike when we are at our most vulnerable."

Jesse eased back on the bed again. A thought occurred to him that made something in his conscience itch. "What about the Warrior Nation?"

The doctor shrugged. "One would think they would be ideal allies. They seem impervious to the influence of this Dark Council. But they reserve a very special hatred for the advances these beings have made possible." His eyes turned cold. "I do not intend to surrender my technologies to join the savages in their tents in the forest, James. I will defeat these creatures, seize from them their knowledge and their power, and then . . . Well, then we shall see who rules this continent."

Carpathian stood once again, stared at Jesse for a moment, and then turned back to his table of instruments. "I do not expect you to carry water for me, Jesse. You will do no man's bidding, I know. And yet, now, with the abundant riches of experience earned in the bitter crucible of a lost cause, you will serve my purposes, and the purposes of mankind, quite well." He looked over his shoulder, his eyes carrying a heavy weight. "And you will do it with joy in your heart Mister . . . President?"

Jesse was caught off guard, confused, and his frustration was mounting. "What're you shovin', doc?"

Carpathian turned back to a bright replacement arm on the table behind him, shrugging. "When the Confederacy rises again, it will be fighting these new enemies and a depleted Union. The continent will need a new leader. A position I do not covet, despite what you may think of me." He held up a syringe and flicked its thick needle with a graceful finger. "The possibility bears thinking on, I believe?"

Carpathian turned while Jesse was still trying to make sense of the words. The quick sting of the needle sinking into his neck was a nasty surprise, and he squawked out a curse as he tried to shy away. Almost immediately, the light in the room grew hazy and the bed began to sway gently beneath him. His suspicions and convictions began to melt away.

"Wha—" Jesse tried to form words, but the effort seemed too much in the pleasant haze descending upon him.

A door opened behind the outlaw chief and a massive man in dark leathers, strange metal serpents swaying behind his broad shoulders, loomed up into his vision. Jesse felt a welcoming smile wash over his face.

"Kyle . . ." Jesse could not remember what he wanted to tell Carpathian's surgical assistant.

"Rest now, Mister James." Carpathian leaned down over Jesse, his face cold. "We all have a lot of work to do, and time is growing short."

The words made no sense at all as he felt himself sinking deeper into a foggy world of warm thoughts and soft edges.

"Lucy—" He tried to say as he felt a vague but persistent tugging on his left shoulder.

The End

The Outlaw's Wrap-up

By

Craig Gallant

Johnny Ringo gunned his Iron Horse, trying to draw ahead of the men following up behind. He did not try to hide the sneer on his face, nor the look of contempt he shot them from time to time. None of them were companions of his own choosing, but rather cannon fodder sent down by Billy to get a little seasoning in the wilder border regions. As far as Ringo was concerned, they were nothing but worm food, the whole lot of them. Especially the creepy Injun fella. That tall tombstone was the strangest of the lot.

"Why ain't we going back up to Billy's?" The Injun had brought his own 'Horse back up in line with Ringo's. "We done the job they asked us, didn't we? Why ain't we headed back?"

Ringo gripped the steering handles of his vehicles tighter, ground his teeth, and did his even-handed best not to spit in the Injun's face.

"Billy asked me to swing through here, see everythin' was alright, and see how this lot reacted to a little more lively environment before we swing back around to his place." He spit a plug of tobacco juice off to the side of the road in the other direction. "We'll be back with the rest of the gang before the week's out, never you fear, skeetzee."

The Injun was silent for a moment before looking at Johnny again. "We are not friends, and your pronunciation was terrible." He looked ahead again, a smile breaking across his broad face. "Still, thank you for making the effort."

Ringo's teeth were close to splintering under the pressure, but he shook his head and held his tongue.

"Hey, Johnny, where we headed, anyhow?!" It was one of the younger hands, farther back in the column, and so he shouted to be heard above the rumbling of the Iron Horses.

Ringo pitched his voice louder and shouted over his shoulder. "Little burg called Diablo Canyon."

One of the older men brought his machine growling up beside Ringo, opposite the Injun. "Diablo Canyon? That place is a rat's nest!"

"Comin' from a rat as big as you, Rusty, that ain't sayin' much." Ringo arched another wad of chaw into the dust. "Diablo Canyon ain't got no law, and never had none. Folks there, they do as they please, and ain't no one gonna stop 'em lessen they're tougher, stronger, 'r faster'n they are."

"And why we headin' there?" The man's face was suspicious.

Ringo gave the man a long cold stare before shaking his head again and turning to face down the long, dusty road. "You're goin' there because I told you you're goin' there. I'm goin' there because Billy told me to drag your sorry asses there and see if we can't recruit some talent, or at the very least, let 'em see there's a new order o' businesses, and those that fall in line might find life a little easier than those that try to buck the system."

"They even got a bank in Diablo Canyon?" Another of the men shouted from the back. Ringo could sense that his boys were losing their edge, questioning this next move.

"Not that I heard tell. They got a passel o' saloons, gaming parlors, and cat houses, though. And no sheriffs nor marshals within nearly four days' ride." He twisted around in his saddle to scan the group riding sullenly behind him. "We're goin' in, checkin' the lay of the land, and maybe doin' a little business. We're gonna see who's callin' the shots, who's holding the chains, and see if they wanna play. Then, either way, we're leavin' the place without a doubt that you wanna be on Billy the Kid's good side, no matter what."

Several of the men shouted further questions but Ringo was done. He turned his back on them, pulling his bolero jacket tighter across his shoulders, and goosed the Iron Horse into a speed that left the rest of the men trying to keep up, the less-experienced men too busy trying to control their vehicles to talk.

He kept up the pace for several miles. When the dusty trail joined the old, weed-covered railroad bed that emerged from the scrub-pine off to their right, he slowed down enough to talk with the young Injun again. He nodded to the tracks.

"Dumbasses were layin' track years ago, not payin' attention to where they was headed." He jerked his chin down the road in front of them. "Laid the track right to the edge of a damned canyon, with no way to cross it. Plans for buildin' a bridge'r still in the works, they say, but the town that built up around the railhead? That ain't no safe place for a lady, I'll tell you that. Not even Big Nose Kate from up Tombstone would have anything to do with that dirt hole. God knows if she don't want to run a whorehouse there, the people doin' it must be a roughed up bunch." He grinned wickedly.

The young warrior in the tattered leathers nodded. "And so you will bring us there to test their mettle. It makes sense. They must earn their way into the brotherhood."

Ringo snorted. "Brotherhood . . . you ain't been around long, have you, Kid?"

"Long enough that you should know I'm not Apache." There was no anger in the voice, and his dark eyes sparkled with amusement.

"Billy calls you the Apache Kid." Ringo sounded a little defensive.

"Billy saved me when my people left me for dead, he had his people heal me, and accepted me as a friend. I am not Billy's slave, and I ride with whoever I please. But he can call me whatever he wishes, and so, most know me as the Apache Kid." He looked back over at Ringo. "Which is more than most know about you. Didn't you die?"

Ringo grunted and rode along for a few moments before turning to the Kid. "What's your real name?"

The young warrior grinned wider. "Here and now?" He shrugged. "The Apache Kid."

Ringo shook his head and goosed his machine back to the head of the column. The band rode for another hour before the path rose and came up over a lip. Below them, the road and its companion tracks traced a gentle slope down to a distant canyon far below. A small town of forty or fifty buildings huddled along the edge of the canyon, absorbing both the road and the railroad tracks into its dusty streets.

Ringo and his men pulled up along the ridge to look down at the town of Diablo Canyon. Nothing seemed to be wrong; they could see folks walking the streets, moving about in the normal patterns of any of the frontier towns any of them had ever seen. Still, Ringo's brows came down with confusion and concern.

The Apache Kid regarded Ringo and asked, "Something is wrong?"

Ringo nodded. "Place has never been this quiet. I haven't heard a gunshot yet, and there ain't no movement over on Boot Hill." He pointed to a rather large cemetery set a little ways along the canyon's edge, away from the town. "On a normal day, they got at least one funeral goin', usually two. And they shoot guns down there usually more'n a fifty cent whore turns Johns."

"It doesn't look like anything's wrong." The Kid shaded his eyes from the sun, peering intently down into the town.

"That's what's wrong, you dumb savage." Ringo grunted and gunned his mount forward. The rest of the men followed.

As the party came down Hell Street into the town center, many of the folks looked nervously at them and then began to quickly move away. Many of the younger outlaws were used to this behavior now. Anyone seen riding an Iron Horse was running with either Jesse James or Billy the Kid, or one of the lesser outlaw gangs that was sworn to them. And folks generally knew to give anyone attached to those famous names a wide berth. Even the tough independent gangs, known simply as cowboys, looked the other way when these boys made their presence known. But Ringo saw something in the townsfolks' eyes that did not sit right with him.

Ringo called a timid-looking man over to him and launched himself off the Iron Horse. "Hey, come here, ya granger. We wanna talk to ya."

The man tried to get away, but Ringo got him by the collar and hauled him up. "Now, now, son, no need to show your petticoats. We just got a couple questions."

The man stuttered, trying to reply, but could not take a deep enough breath to speak.

"Just calm down, boy. We just wanna know who's the big bug in town?"

The man gulped several times, trying to speak, but could not calm his breathing down.

"Oh, for God's sake." Ringo turned to his men. "Gimme a canteen."

After the man had half a day's supply of water poured down his throat, he sputtered and coughed, waving his hands frantically as he begged the big outlaw to stop. Ringo knew the man was well aware of the crew's RJ-1027 weapons and their tell-tale illumination. Their crimson glow was a dead giveaway that these men had a major advantage when it came to gun play.

"The mayor! Mayor McPeake! He runs the Canyon now!" The stammering man paused, seeming unsure of himself, but did not continue.

"Runs the Canyon?" Ringo sounded disbelieving. "Nobody runs the Canyon. There ain't never been a mayor here before."

The man shrugged. "He got a lot of the workers to side with him, then he sent a letter up to Tombstone, asking for help. We had four or five flushers, tried to sheriff . . . but they was all cut down."

Ringo looked thoughtful. "And Tombstone?"

The man hesitated again, looking around the now deserted street. The furtive glances gave Ringo a bad feeling, and he gestured for his men to fan out and get ready for trouble. "Tombstone sent someone?" he asked the cowering man.

The man shook his head. "A box. They sent a box. With . . . with . . . something in it."

There was no denying the man's fear now, and Ringo saw his men starting to catch it as well, listening to the man's tone and the look on his face. "Something? Unless that something is Doc Holliday, I ain't impressed. Hell knows Tombstone has nothin' worth frettin' about outside of that lunger bastard."

The man looked puzzled and then hurried on. "They got the box about a month ago. Pried it open, and pulled out all the straw. There was a shape inside, like a man. We were all there, because the mayor said what was inside was going to keep everyone safe. But we couldn't lift it out of the box. It was heavier than a ten foot boulder. The mayor fished out a bunch of papers, read through them, and then reached in and flipped a switch somewhere. The thing stood up, looked at each of us with one unblinking eye, and then stalked off."

"He hit a switch and it came to life?" The cold feeling on Ringo's back was getting stronger. "Like . . . a dead body coming to life?" He was beholden to no man, and ran with whatever crews he liked, but a little of Billy's deep and abiding hatred for the European and his unnatural monsters had rubbed off on him. He did not like the thought of one of Carpathian's creations getting here first.

"No, God no!" The man shook his head, looking at Ringo with horrified confusion. "It was a man made of metal. Had clothes on and everything, including a hat and a sheriff's badge. But all made of metal."

Ringo calmed down a bit at that. "So, this metal man is somehow the law in this town. Boys, what has this world come to? Just when you thought this technology had its limits we get this; a fake lawman patrolling the streets of a dirt ball town like Diablo Canyon. Hot damn, I love the wild west!"

He stood up and scanned the empty street. "And so, now this metal lawman is where, exactly?"

The townsman shook his head. "You can't hardly ever tell! He's walking around all day long! There's no jail or nothin' here, and so, when he arrests someone, he takes them to the edge of the canyon and tosses them off! He's arrested a whole bunch of folks, most of 'em never even doin' much of anythin' wrong!"

Ringo shook his head. "So, you got a metal lawman on the loose, tossin' folks into the canyon for nothin', and you ain't taken care of him yet? This just gets better every minute. Where's this mayor of yours?"

The man pointed down Hell Street. "He's been locked in his house since the day they opened the crate. He won't come out for nothin'."

"Well, maybe he'll come out for us, right boys?" Ringo grinned at his men and moved toward his rumbling mount. "You go hide now, friend, and we'll see if we can't clear this up in a jiff."

Ringo was leaping into his saddle when they heard a deep vibrating thrum and one of his men turned into a fountain of gore that sprayed twenty feet across the street, dousing the rest and splashing the side of Ringo's own Iron Horse with blood and entrails. A strange, buzzing, inhuman voice echoed through the street. "Possession of contraband military hardware and weaponry excessive to personal protection. Summary provisional sentencing."

Every man in the street whipped their heads around trying to follow that empty voice. A single figure had emerged from an alley not far away, silhouetted by the lowering sun. It raised one of its arms, and again they heard the voice.

"Consorting with distinctly outlaw elements. Summary provisional sentencing."

The man Ringo had been squeezing for information gave out a terrified squawk and turned to run. A muzzle flash longer than a man's arm lanced out from the figure in the alley and the townsman's cry ended abruptly as the flesh and blood of his body washed across the storefront he had been running for.

"God damn!" One of Ringo's younger men screamed, then hunched low over the controls of his Iron Horse. The machine spun in place, digging a deep trench in the road and throwing up a choking cloud of dust. "Come on, you freak a'—"

The front of the Iron Horse disappeared in a ball of crimson flame that devoured the metal and the arms of the driver alike. The man was thrown as the remnants of his vehicle plowed into the street, screaming as the stumps of his upper arms, flailing wildly, sprayed deep red blood into the dust. Another thrumming blast disintegrated the man's upper body and silenced his screams.

"Run!" Ringo screamed and spun his Iron Horse around, away from the figure emerging from the alley. The rest of the outlaws, terrified into silence, followed after him. "He didn't even ask us to surrender!" One of the younger men in the back of the pack was screaming. "He didn't even ask—"

The rear half of the unfortunate boy's vehicle exploded, sending his body, back stripped of leather, cotton, and flesh, pin wheeling down the street.

The inhuman voice carried clearly over the revving engines and screaming men. "Possession of contraband military hardware, weaponry excessive to personal protection, and fleeing the scene of a crime. Summary provisional sentencing."

Ringo and his men fled down Hell Street, but soon were brought up short by the crumbling edge of the canyon. Around them were stacks of construction equipment covered in ancient dirty tarps, the tracks of the defunct railroad ending a few feet out in midair nearby. He stopped his vehicle and looked down into the valley far below as his men joined him. Whipping his head to either side, Ringo discovered that the massive piles of old equipment would not allow the Iron Horses to escape through the construction zone. It did not matter much anyway, as the terrifying voice behind them all began to speak.

"Multiple counts of suspicious assembly, multiple counts of possession of contraband military hardware, multiple counts of weaponry excessive to personal protection, and multiple counts of fleeing the scene of a crime. Summary provisional sentencing."

The demonic weapon lashed out time and time again, blasting Iron Horses into the canyon, their riders' screams fading into the distance. Ringo tried to bring his machine back around, but was blasted from the seat as another of his men detonated beside him. He pulled his guns and started to fire blindly in the direction of the thing with the inhuman voice. He could not believe this was going to happen to him again.

One of his shots connected with the metal man's eye socket and flung its head back. Another round slapped into the thing's chest. Still the automaton kept coming, repeating its message of justice and death.

Ringo was sure he was taking his last breath when an arrow wreathed in blue flame sank into the monster's arm. One of its massive pistols fell to the ground.
Spirit arrows, he thought in a daze.

As the automaton gathered itself again and aimed with the other hand, several more crimson bolts crisscrossed the dirt filled road.

Ringo was struck in the side and expected to go down into the dust or fly back off the cliff, but instead he felt a strong arm sweep him up and back, and soon he was draped across the back of an Iron Horse, speeding through the dust and smoke of the massacre. Looking as far to the side as he could, he saw a familiar stream of black hair waving out behind him.

"Kid . . ." he could barely breathe, let alone talk.

"No talking now. Running now. Talking later." The Apache Kid bent low behind the faring of his Iron Horse and sent it roaring down the street, the sounds of the greenhorns' dying fading into the distance.

* * * * *

"Jesus, Kid, the whole gang?" The man's smooth face was twisted with frustration as he shook his head in disbelief.

The Apache Kid nodded. "The whole gang, Billy. One of those machines wiped them all out. I was lucky I got me and Ringo out."

Billy the Kid, leaning against the dull metal body of his Iron Horse, nodded glumly. "And I guess that proves you can't do none of that fancy changin' into animals, neither, or you woulda then, eh?"

The black haired warrior nodded. "I told you I never achieved that level of discipline. My connection with the Great Spirit is . . . not strong."

Billy punched him in the shoulder. "Oh, don't sweat it, Kid. Those bolts of lightning you shoot out of that bow of yours are impressive enough. I'm still glad I dragged you out of that barn."

The Apache Kid bowed his head but said nothing.

"But . . . a whole gang . . . damn. And it was only one of those things?"

"Only one, Billy. It cut us up somethin' fierce." The Apache Kid raised his head, refusing to appear defeated.

"Damn. We're going to have to step up our game if we're goin' to stay afloat out here. The damned lawmen sending fire-breathing metal men after us, we got the whole damned army breathin' down our backs, we got the damned savages—no offense," he looked a little sheepishly at the Kid for a moment but went on at a slight nod. "And of course, that thrice-damned Carpathian and his unholy creations." The Kid's face twisted in irrational hatred. "I'll tell you what. If I found him, I'd put one between his eyes, ram one of those damned batteries into the back of his damned fool head to bring him back so I could spit on him and kill him again!"

The Apache Kid just nodded and remained silent.

Billy spit into the dirt, possibly imagining Carpathian's face, and then snarled. "Oh, to hell with it. None of them guys was practiced hands, anyway."

A group of Billy's most trusted men were scattered around the clearing waiting for orders, lounging by a small fire or tinkering with their Iron Horses. None of them knew why they were away from civilizations, squatting in the wilderness like this, but if Billy wanted them out here, there was a reason and it would heat up presently.

"What time is it?" Billy rolled to one side, enough to shout at one of the men standing by the fire.

The man fished out a stopwatch, popped it open, and shouted back. "Nearing on noon, Billy."

The outlaw leader nodded as he turned back around. "We better get into position. We got a Union convoy comin' through here in an hour or so, should set us up nice with some of the heavy stuff Jesse's been keeping for his own pretty self lately."

"Trouble with James?" The Apache Kid tensed a little. He held no hatred for Jesse James, but the outlaw was notorious for his dislike of the Warrior Nation, and his intense personality had often led to conflicts between the Apache Kid and the younger James. Not to mention, any trouble between the major outlaw bands would mean trouble for all the men and women that ran with them.

"Nothin' more than usual." Billy spit into the dirt again. "He's Carpathian's grinder monkey, of course, and getting' all the pretty baubles from that old snake oil salesman. That, and those damned arms he flaunts in everyone's face every chance he gets." The young man shrugged. "But other than that, no, nothin' much."

"But you said he was holding out—"

"Oh, he is." Billy straightened up. "He always is. But that ain't nothin'. We got plenty o' blasters, and with this score, we'll have plenty of heavy guns, and the fuel to use 'em."

"So, we're here to hit a Union convoy?" The Kid nodded toward the dusty trail behind them. "Now it makes more sense, the number of men you dragged out here with us. But still, those army boys don't travel light. You think we'll have enough firepower to take 'em?"

"Oh, don't worry." An evil grin crept over Billy's face. "This is an emergency convoy. Some of Grant's boys were hit last night by some of your folks, and they're desperate for help. These boys playing fetch and carry? They ain't half as bad as the usual lot."

"But—" The Apache Kid started, but then stopped suddenly, his head tilting as if hearing something no one else in the clearing could.

"What?" Billy had only known the Apache Kid for little over a year, but he knew to trust the man's instincts without question.

"Something on the wind." The Apache Kid's eyes were distant and unfocused, his body tense and his face blank. "Something is approaching . . . from the opposite side of the road. Something . . ." his eyes snapped back into focus and darted to Billy's face. "Something dead."

A wave of fury washed over Billy the Kid's face as his own eyes tore away from the warrior's and over his shoulder to the road in the distance. "Carpathian," he spat.

"Boys, I think you might want to get up now." The Apache Kid addressed the rest of Billy's posse, and the men rose without question or sound, moving to their vehicles and loosening their weapons.

Billy stalked from the clearing and into the trees that bordered the road. Crouching down in the ferns and scrub he peered out, casting around for any sign of Carpathian's creatures. The Apache Kid slid silently up beside him and joined in the search.

"They are not very far away now." The native whispered. "But they barely move at all."

"Damn." Billy swore under his breath. "They must be after the convoy too."

The two men stood still for several minutes, but no further signs emerged from the other side of the road.

The Apache Kid shifted slightly. "What do you want us to do?"

Billy gestured for them both to move back into the trees, and maintained a brooding silence until he had his men gathered around him at the far side of the clearing.

"Okay, boys, our hand looks like this: we want what that convoy is carrying . . . but we need to destroy that rat bastard's toys. If we take out Carpathian's stench-ridden hangers on, we won't be in any shape to take on the convoy."

"But boss," a young outlaw gripping the butt of his pistol tightly stammered. "You said we needed what was in those carts."

"No," Billy's smile was vicious and humorless. "I said I wanted what was in those cards. I need to kill Carpathian's fiends. Send him a message. One that James will get too, if we play our cards right."

Most of the men looked eager for any kind of action, and Billy never would have taken cowards with him out on the road, so he knew he was going to be well-served whichever way he jumped.

"Okay, boys, so this is the plan." Billy knelt down and grabbed a stick. He drew a line in the dirt, and then began to sketch out details on either side. "We're dealing with men whose brains ain't worked for God knows how long. This ain't g oin' to be all that hard."

A few minutes later, Dirty Sam Collier revved the massive engine of his Iron Horse, sending sooty, red-tinged exhaust billowing out behind him. Collier always seemed to get the worst jobs when Billy was planning a heist, so he had been prepared for this one. He revved the engine again, just to feel the rumbling vibration and the power. He might be bait, but he was bait with bite.

Billy's plan was simple. The entire posse was lined up in the woods just beyond their encampment, ready to spring on the living dead across the road when they made their move. Sam and a couple other guys had muscled the vehicle through the woods back up the trail, then doubled back on the road making as much noise as they could. He was not sure they sounded like an entire Union convoy, but he knew they sounded a hell of a lot louder than they normally did.

He revved the engine yet again, just for the effect.

The trees were dense on either side of the road, and Sam could not help but turn his head to the right repeatedly, trying to peer into the shadows of the forest for any sign of the looming attack. He did not envy his two companions walking beside him, when he wasn't ripping ahead a bit. Both had their blaster rifles out, trying not to look right too often, just like him. None of the three of them were doing a very good job of it.

Sam came around a sharp turn in the road and thought he recognized the patch of woods off to the left that hid Billy and the rest of the posse. That meant that the monsters were close by . . . and Sam did not want to screw this up. On a sudden impulse, he turned to the outlaw pacing beside him on his right and said the first thing that came into his mind.

"God bless General Grant, eh?"

The man looked at him as if all sense had left him. "What? What the f—"

"I say, God bless General Grant!" Sam all but yelled the words into the man's face, trying with only his eyebrows to indicate the stretch of trees where Billy's tame Injun claimed the freaks were hiding. Sadly, his eyebrows were not equal to the task.

"Look, Sam, I don't know what game you're playin', but—" The words died in a spray of blood as a massive metal blade erupted from the man's chest and then quickly pulled him back into the trees.

"It's on!" Sam stood in his saddle and waved his hat in the direction of Billy and the gang. The trees beside him whipped wildly as if some hidden beast were devouring the screaming man who had disappeared. A smattering of red-tailed bullets slashed out of the trees, slapping against the armored hull of the 'Horse and catching Sam's other partner in the knee. The man spun screaming into the dirt.

Billy and the rest of his posse erupted from their hiding places and tore across the road, sweeping up and around and taking the ambushers in their right flank. As they roared over the dusty path and into the trees on the other side, their sun-blind eyes could make out little but hazy movement in the shadows. When Billy broke into a clearing and saw the main force of the attackers for the first time, his face paled and twisted into a disgusted snarl.

"Oh, hell no!" The anger in his eyes exploded into a red-hot fury and he jammed his fingers down on the firing studs of his Iron Horse as he glared over the cowling at these newest refugees of nightmare.

Blaster bolts ripped out from multiple muzzles set into the nose of the machine. The crimson missiles streaked through the clearing and detonated amid the crowd of nightmare shapes that were still moving toward the road. There were still dead, decaying bodies present, as most of the desperados were expecting. But what none of them had anticipated was the next step in Doctor Carpathian's mad scheme: each desiccated body ended at the waist where it was melded somehow into a mechanical metal chassis.

Some of the gawping monsters were slowly rolling over the irregular ground of the forest floor on single, improbable-looking wheels that reminded Billy of circus or dancehall performers. They would have been laughable if they weren't gibbering, flailing dead bodies tacked to rolling wheels. But these were somehow the least offensive of the creatures in the clearing. Others were carried along on fully-articulated metal legs designed much like those of some nightmarish spider. Each leg ended in a nasty-looking bladed foot that sank deep into the loam of the forest.

Billy's bolts stitched across the clearing, blasting steaming holes in the ground, shattering trees, and knocking the grotesque corpse/machine hybrids onto their backs. Some of the corpses were still where they lay, huge chunks of their bodies gone. Head wounds put them down for good, as all the outlaws knew. Or enough damage to their bodies would often shock them back into death as well. But many, those with their heads intact or who had suffered only superficial damage, immediately began to drag themselves upright once more, moaning hopelessly as they did so.

The Apache Kid, kneeling beside the trunk of a gnarled old tree, had his bow grasped easily in his right hand and was launching bolt after bolt of blue energy into the writhing crowd. Each shot sank through metal constructs and bolted armor as if it wasn't there, detonating deep within his targets and sending them lurching back down into the dirt. As Billy watched, The Kid whipped around, his black hair flying out in a flat spray, and launched a bolt that sizzled through the trees, weaving through the melee in the clearing, and potted a huge brute on pistoning insect legs that had reared up behind Sam. The thing convulsed around the arrow, its blood-soaked forelegs quivering, and sank gracelessly into the underbrush.

"Billy, watch it!" The voice from the road called out, and a hail of ruby bolts slashed from the sunlight of the trail into the green shadows of the forest, cutting down two spider-like monsters that had been approaching the bandit leader from behind. Billy waved his hat and then gunned his machine around and back out toward the road.

All around Billy the forest was thrashing as if it was alive. Red bolts of energy from the weapons of both sides lashed out. Somewhere nearby, a man was dying a loud, seemingly painful death, but the core group of Billy's posse stuck close with him, watching his back and taking aimed shots at each dead target that presented itself. As they road through the forest, most of the ambushing force was soon lying still on the ground, twisted bits of metal and machinery lying amid gelid clumps of quivering flesh.

As things began to settle down, Billy jumped off his 'Horse and pulled his blaster pistol. Most of his men were putting single bolts through the heads of anything that even looked like it was thinking of moving, and he stalked deeper into the woods. The tracks of the shambling mob were not difficult to follow, between the crushed wheel prints of the unicycle monstrosities and the enormous divots tilled up by the spider-legged horrors.

Occasionally, Billy or one of his posse would run into a breathless body standing stock-still in the shadows, and put paid to its ticket with a point blank shot to the forehead.

Billy's face was twisted in furious loathing the entire time, only the hint of a smirking leer curling the edges of his lips at each shot. The creatures were no longer moving toward the road, but sitting still in the gathering gloom, only lunging out when one of the outlaws ventured close. But with each shot, the men were deeper and deeper into the forest, and the shadows were growing thicker with each step.

"Billy, you think maybe we should head back to the road?" Sam was standing beside him, gesturing over his shoulder. "We put down more'n enough of these dogs to send any message you wanted."

The Apache Kid nodded. "Doctor Carpathian will know he has an enemy in the man who arranged this carnage."

Billy cast around the nearby forest looking for further targets, but nothing moved. The wild look cleared slightly from his eyes and he shook his head. "Yeah. Yeah, I guess you fellers is right." He slipped his blasters back into their holsters. "Round 'em up, and let's head back to town before the Union drops by."

The outlaws began to withdraw down their back trail, still throwing dark glances over their shoulders, further back into the woods. They had not gone far when the Apache Kid held up one hand, sending totemic feathers fluttering, and pivoted on one heel to face back the way they had come.

"Something is coming." His voice was low and ominous.

Billy sent his men fanning out into the woods to either side of their path, all holding tightly to weapons that had been holstered or shouldered a moment before. There was no doubting the Apache Kid's instincts now, and most of the men had had their fill of fighting the dead already. Only Billy looked fresh as a daisy, eager to tear more of the abominations into the mud.

The sound was a low growl, and at first Billy thought they were going to be facing other 'Horses, or some other vehicle that Carpathian's fevered, diseased mind had conjured up. But as the tall shapes swept toward them out of the shadows, even Billy was taken aback for a moment, caught without a word in his head.

The things were similar to the unicycle troops they had been putting down all afternoon, but much larger, bulkier, and taller. And hunched atop them, wobbling slightly with the erratic movements of the machines, were armored human torsos with helmeted heads lolling loosely on unseen necks. Billy's eyes widened in horror, his hatred and cynicism momentarily washed away by the sheer revulsion of what he was seeing.

Three of the things ground out of the shadows, each piloted by an undead wretch whose arms had been completely removed. Only armored shoulder guards remained to mark where the arms of a human would be. Shaking the horror from his eyes, Billy tried to see what the threat of the things would be, given their near-blind appearance and lack of arms. He was still staring when The Apache Kid slammed into him, tossing him into the dirt. The two men rolled through the ferns and underbrush, Billy getting a mouthful of dirt as he tried to scream for the Injun to get off of him. He was in the process of choking on the rich loam when he heard a stuttering series of explosions rip through the woods. His head came around to look up and he saw streaks of crimson force flying through the gathering shadows, lighting the trees from below with a hellish red glow. Each of the three things seemed to be spitting unending streams of bolts at his remaining men, most of them having dived for cover, but several were sprawling still in the dirt, or squirming and screaming in pain.

"Get up!" Billy screamed, forcing the fallen Warrior Nation man off him. "Don't let them gun us down like dogs!"

Billy skinned both of his pistols with one smooth motion and began to beat the closest metal horror with lashes of ruby energy. Most of the blasts ricocheted right off the thick armor, but several sank home into the thing's chest and neck, and suddenly the tall, ungainly vehicle began to spin wildly. Red-tinged smoke was billowing from the massive engine on its back before it sailed off into the trees and crashed into a huge pine with shattering force. Bits and pieces of machine and corpse came raining down on the outlaws.

"They can be killed – destroyed – ended!" Billy was at a loss for the right words, but he knew his men would understand him easily enough. "Get 'em!"

Soon, hails of red bolts were slamming repeatedly into the two remaining machines, counterpointed by the azure streaks of The Apache Kid's spirit arrows. The two unnatural things were pounded backward, shuddering with each successive impact. The armor was deforming under the steady hail of shots, and bits and pieces of their pilots were being chewed away as if by the sands of a century in the Mojave Desert in a single moment.

After one last volley of shots, the two towering constructs toppled backward into smoking heaps. One of them continued to twitch, its large, studded wheel spinning wildly backward and forward until Sam walked warily up to it and put a bolt through its armored head. The thing shook violently for a moment and then lay as still as its two brothers.

"Who's got paper?" Billy dusted himself off and looked around at his men. They stared at him with blank faces. "Seriously? Not a single one o' you illiterates has so much as a scrap of paper to wipe your rear ends with?"

"Here," The Apache Kid pulled a small bound journal from a pocket of his vest and held it out to the outlaw leader.

Billy's eyes narrowed in amusement. "You a poet, Kid? You holdin' out on us?" He took the notebook and ripped a piece of blank paper from it as he shook his head. The Apache Kid accepted the notebook back and slid it into the pocket. "Not a poet, no. But I have thoughts, and sometimes I like to write them down."

Billy looked at the big warrior fondly, still shaking his head. "Okay, so who's got a pencil?"

Billy scribbled a quick note on the paper and then stalked over to the nearest demon machine. He took a quick glance at the ruined head, snarled a moment at Sam, then moved on to the next smoking form. He tried to pry the helmet away, but even with all his strength he could barely make the armored bucket move. He spit on his hands, got a solid grip, tested his footing on the thing's armored chassis, and then gave a mighty heave.

The helmet came away with most of the corpse's head still inside, strings of rotten flesh, tendons, and veins swaying between the ruin of a human face and the helmet held high over Billy's head.

"Damnit, you've gotta be kiddin' me." The creature's lower jaw had been removed to make room for a series of cables and wires that ran up its torso, inside the armor, and into its head. "How am I supposed to ram a note into its mouth if it don't have a damn mouth to ram a note into!"

"Maybe you could –" One of the men began to suggest something, but whatever it was, was drowned out by the report of Billy's pistol blowing a hole straight through where the thing's mouth would have been.

"There," he said with some satisfaction. "That ought to do the trick."

The men of Billy's posse moved back through the woods toward the trail, eager to be away from the stink of blood and death, and from the unnatural things that lived on to fight the battles of a mad man long after their souls had passed from this earth. No one was eager to tangle with the Union convoy in their present shape. They were nearly out of power, with several men down. Not an ideal time to take on an armed and armored convoy. But well worth it, to Billy the Kid, for the satisfaction it had offered him.

"So, Billy . . ." The Apache Kid was hesitant. "What did the note say?"

Billy's smile was as the sky. He chuckled and then said, "Just said 'Carpathian, you're next'."

The men walked on for a few moments in silence, thinking this over. Most thought it was a fitting sentiment, but Sam could not understand one thing.

"That's a damned fine letter, Billy, but why's it funny?"

Billy smiled wider, his laughter nearly choking him as it echoed off the surrounding trees.
"Cuz I signed it 'JJ', that's why!"

About the Authors

Craig Gallant spends his hours teaching, gaming, podasting, being a family man and father. In his spare time he writes outlandish fiction to entertain and amaze people .

In addition to his position as co-host of the internationally not too shabby podcast – The D6 Generation, he has written for several gaming companies including Fantasy Flight, Spartan Games and of course Outlaw Minatures.
You can follow Craig's writing experience and other fun things at:

www.Mcnerdiganspub.com

C. L. Werner was a diseased servant of the Horned Rat long before his first story in Inferno! magazine. His Black Library credits include the Warhammer Hero books Wulfrik and The Red Duke, Mathias Thulmann: Witch Hunter, the ongoing saga of Grey Seer Thanquol and the Brunner the Bounty Hunter trilogy. His first full-fledged foray into the gothic sci-fi universe of Warhammer 40k occurred in 2012 with The Siege of Castellax. He is the author of Moving Targets, a novella set in Privateer Press' Iron Kingdoms featuring the iconic heroes Taryn and Rutger. He has also written several fantasy stories about the wandering samurai Shintaro Oba for Rogue Blades Enterprises. Currently he is labouring upon further instalments of the Black Plague series for Warhammer's Time of Legends line, as well as more adventures of mercenaries Taryn and Rutger in the Iron Kingdoms. An inveterate bibliophile, he squanders the proceeds from his writing on hoary old volumes – or at least reasonably affordable reprints of same – to further his library of fantasy fiction, horror stories and occult tomes.

https://clwerner.wordpress.com/

EXPERIENCE THESE TALES
ON THE TABLE TOP
WITH THE OFFICIAL
35MM MINIATURE
SKIRMISH GAME!
OUTLAW
PURCHASE MODELS, RULE BOOKS, TEMPLATES, DICE AND MORE AT:
WWW.WILDWESTEXODUS.COM

CPSIA information can be obtained at www.ICGtesting.com
Printed in the USA
BVOW07s0848220115

384447BV00001B/1/P

9 780989 692670